Books by Arthur Walworth

SCHOOL HISTORIES AT WAR

BLACK SHIPS OFF JAPAN

CAPE BRETON: *Isle of Romance*

WOODROW WILSON: *American Prophet*
(awarded the 1958 Pulitzer Prize in biography)

WOODROW WILSON: *World Prophet*

AMERICA'S MOMENT: 1918

WILSON AND HIS PEACEMAKERS

TERRITORIAL CHANGES AS
A RESULT OF WORLD WAR I

──── Line of Treaty of Brest–Litovsk

TERRITORIES LOST:

By Russia

By Austria–Hungary

By Germany

By Bulgaria

Plebiscite areas

─·─·─ 1914 boundaries

WILSON
and His
PEACEMAKERS
American Diplomacy at the
Paris Peace Conference, 1919

ARTHUR WALWORTH

NEW YORK *W. W. Norton & Company* LONDON

Copyright © 1986 by W. W. Norton & Company, Inc.
All rights reserved.
Published simultaneously in Canada by Penguin Books Canada Ltd, 2801 John Street, Markham, Ontario
L3R 1B4.
Printed in the United States of America.

The text of this book is composed in Times Roman, with display type set in Bembo. Composition and
manufacturing by The Maple-Vail Book Manufacturing Group.
Book design by Nancy Dale Muldoon.

First Edition

Library of Congress Cataloging in Publication Data
Walworth, Arthur, 1903–
    Wilson and his peacemakers.
    Bibliography: p.
    Includes index.
    1. Paris Peace Conference (1919–1920) 2. World
War, 1914–1918—Peace. 3. World War, 1914–1918—
Diplomatic history. 4. United States—Foreign
relations—Europe. 5. Europe—Foreign relations—
United States. 6. United States—Foreign relations—
1913–1921. 7. Wilson, Woodrow, 1856–1924. I. Title.
D645.W34 1984   940.3'141   83–19491

ISBN 0-393-01867-9

W. W. Norton & Company, Inc., 500 Fifth Avenue, New York, N.Y. 10110
W. W. Norton & Company Ltd., 37 Great Russell Street, London WC1B 3NU

1 2 3 4 5 6 7 8 9 0

Contents

Part Five: *The Fading of the Vision* 435

Foreword

THE word *diplomacy* can be a will-o'-the-wisp and may mislead those who would study the work of diplomats. The word in common usage may connote nothing more than tact or *savoir faire,* with perhaps an implication of guile. Often it is applied with imprecision to the relations of governments of states. It should not be used as a synonym for foreign policy, which gives direction and purpose to intercourse among governments. Nor should it be identified with international law, which supplies a common understanding of rights and precedents. Properly, according to *The Oxford English Dictionary,* diplomacy is "the management of international relations by negotiations."

The present work has to do with the performance of those Americans who took part in the essential task of negotiating peace treaties that would bring World War I to an end. My study was undertaken in response to a suggestion made twenty-five years ago by Charles Seymour, who was himself an American delegate at the Paris Peace Conference of 1919 and the author of *American Diplomacy during the World War.* He was most generous of advice, as was Frank Lord Warrin, who was the personal assistant to David Hunter Miller, the legal counselor of Wilson. These men and many others have contributed much during the years of waiting for the opening of the last of the essential documentary sources in the United States and abroad. Most fortunately, the quarter century of my research has been a period during which many of the eyewitnesses have still been alive to testify, and also a time when the last of the essential files of state and personal documents have been opened.

Several years after the release of the official American and British minutes of the sessions of the inner councils of the Paris conference, two volumes were published that made available the notes of Paul Mantoux, Clemenceau's translator, who faithfully recorded in French the words of the conferees as they were spoken in the meetings of the Supreme Council. For access to these and other important notes of Professor Mantoux, I am deeply indebted to Mme. Mathilde Mantoux, whose encouragement and assistance have been constant and indispensable. I have been aided also at Paris by Professors Pierre Renouvin, Jean-Baptiste Duroselle, and André Kaspi.

Cary T. Grayson Jr., Ambassador Philip Bonsal, and Professor Agnes Headlam-Morley of Oxford have generously facilitated the use of the intimate records of their fathers. Katherine E. Brand, who years ago reviewed my notes from the Wilson Collection at the Library of Congress, has remained a faithful counselor. Colonel James B. Rothnie has transcribed notes written in shorthand by Wilson. Professor Arthur S. Link and David W. Hirst have been most accommodating in sharing the rich lore of the Wilson Papers at Princeton. Professors George W. Pierson and Gaddis Smith of Yale, Professor Elizabeth Monroe of the Middle East Centre, Oxford, and Professor Arnold W. Mayer of Princeton have read and criticized certain parts of the manuscript. Of all of these contributions I am sincerely appreciative.

The Sterling Memorial Library of Yale University has provided an essential and secure base, and the staff of the Manuscript and Archives Room has been unfailingly and cheerfully cooperative; the Rockefeller Foundation and the American Philosophical Society have supplied subsidies for wide-ranging research; and the MacDowell Colony, the Virginia Center for the Creative Arts, and the Rhode Island Center for the Creative Arts have permitted me to enjoy havens in which I could lift my eyes to pleasing horizons. Without such support this work could not have been completed.

INTRODUCTION
A World to Be Saved
by Democracy

AT the end of World War I four great empires had fallen. Traditions of government had been shaken to the breaking point. Complex industries, dependent on a flow of raw materials and fabricated goods over an intricate system of rails and waterways, were dislocated; and there was human misery from the Rhine to Vladivostok. In Russia a militant party had displaced the czar as absolute ruler, while among insurgent groups in the West there was agitation that might destroy the very freedoms that made it possible for them to agitate.

During the long ordeal cries had arisen for a peace that would prevent a repetition of the holocaust that had killed and crippled millions of men, devastated many hundred of villages, brought on famine, and saddled posterity with a huge burden of debt. It was now to be seen whether the war that Woodrow Wilson had tried to justify as a means of making the world "safe for democracy" had indeed achieved that goal. For the first time in the long history of Europe, democratic governments were to bear the responsibility of re-establishing the Continent's international structure and of ordering its affairs. Democracy, now at its high watermark in the world's history, bore full responsibility for constructing a durable peace. It made embarrassing demands on diplomacy.

The peacemakers would find little guidance in history for arranging relations among industrialized nations in a rapidly changing world society. In the comparatively well-ordered diplomacy of nineteenth-century Europe the peace had been kept by statesmen who viewed international problems from the light of their own nation's interest and who undertook to maintain a balance of power. The native aspirations of small populations were used often by the great and imperial powers as justification for "protection." The concert of Europe, recognizing no legal right of "self-determination," had considered this to be merely a formula that depended on political circumstances in each case in which it was invoked. The word, long current in the vocabulary of German philosophers, was conjured up by Wilson in February 1918 as propaganda appealing to German leftists. "An imperative principle of action," he called it, "which statesmen will ignore at their peril." In the course of the failure of the balance of power that had existed in 1914, the latent forces of small nationalities were at liberty to establish native governments. They were to enjoy not only freedom of action, but substantial encouragement from the great democracies of the West.

Through all the dark days of the fighting the people of the democracies had clung to a conviction that a complete victory would bring redemption of personal and national losses, and assurance of lasting peace as well; and the political leaders exploited this popular belief in order to stimulate efforts toward the coveted victory. With the passage of the last desperate sacrifices of war, it was necessary to take account of a surge of impatience in human hearts. In the flush of victory it seemed that the old Europe had all but passed away. There was little tolerance of the past while much was demanded of the future. Nationalism, which had gone to lengths beyond all reason, was to be curbed; and yet all distinct peoples were to have a sovereign right to self-government. Idealists asserted that the peace to be made must be different; it must be moderate, just, and compassionate; and the whole world must be brought together and organized to prevent war between nations and to serve the common interests of all mankind. Popular movements toward these goals had begun before the war and were given fresh impetus by the shock of the catastrophe and by speeches of Woodrow Wilson.

At the same time there were those who insisted that human nature changes but slowly, and that a resort to physical force in a physical world could not be prescribed by any concept purely mental, such as the sacred compulsion of an agreement. Still others examined the origins of the war with a predilection for some specific element in the complex chain of causation, and demanded that this element be eliminated. Among the delegates of the victorious nations who met at Paris in 1919 there was no unanimity in the prescriptions for enduring peace.

In attempting to revive the old European ways of life that had gone on for a century in relative security, the peacemakers would have to consider national traditions and sentiments that were so rooted in history that they seemed ineradicable; and at the same time they would have to reckon with malign passions that had flared during the fighting. The total war, more horrible than any in the past, left smoldering embers. Moreover, there was continuing warfare among peoples who were emerging from imperial rule and forming native governments; and these new governments were wooed by propaganda from the great powers.

With the signing of the Armistice of Rethondes in November of 1918 there came a slackening of the cohesive force that had been exerted by the common danger. The governments of the Western alliance and their responsible officials were released from the extreme tension that existed while war menaced the survival of their nations. When immediate danger gave way to a remote possibility of another holocaust, the victors became less responsive to the cause of peace. Indeed a belligerent spirit of nationalism, fortified by the patriotic sacrifices that war had called forth, ran strong and limited the freedom of the peacemakers to pursue the distant goals of idealists. The prevailing hatred toward the defeated enemy made it difficult for diplomats to make a rational peace without being denounced as "pro-German." The wisest of the statesmen realized, after the cessation of the fighting, that unless they were able to reverse the baneful psychology of wartime quickly, no enduring peace could be signed, much less dictated.

Furthermore, the European democracies during the war had set up obstacles that would embarrass the diplomats in the making of peace. Under the necessity of survival the governments of the Allied powers had made secret commitments to the satisfaction of national aspirations. The 1915 Treaty of London, concluded in order to bring Italy into the conflict on the side of the Allies, had promised that nation a frontier that would place hundreds of thousands of Austrians and Slavs under Italian rule. To persuade the Japanese to step up their naval activity, Japan had been offered concessions in China and a share of Germany's islands in the Pacific. Although agreements to which Russia was a party became invalid when the Soviet government made peace with Germany, nevertheless the interests of France, Great Britain, and Italy in the lands of the Ottoman Empire remained as they had been defined in understandings reached in 1916 and 1917. These secret understandings gained force from popular indignation against the violations of treaty obligations at the time of the outbreak of war in 1914.

The settlement at the war's end could not disregard the commitments and the national aspirations that existed in 1919 and that no one could expect to alter quickly. Compromises were inevitable. For one thing, there had to be an accommodation among various prescriptions for dealing with the German enemy. At the end of the war the European diplomats were of two minds about a policy to preserve the peace. One, the more appealing to the English-speaking authorities, would avoid peace terms that might incite violent reactions among the vanquished and also would provide for a continuing process of adjustment. The other, advocated by the French, would create alliances with a preponderance of military power that could put down any opposition. During the long war of attrition France's deficiency in manpower had worsened; it was clear that the French nation, fighting alone, could not hope to withstand another onset of German might.

The peacemakers were forced in practice to follow the forms and procedures in international intercourse that usage had confirmed through a long period of history. These forms and procedures had all the force of custom, that creation of slow growth and even slower decline which constitutes the supreme reality in the domain of politics, and from which all conventional human relations derive their legitimacy. Peace treaties must be signed, of world-wide range, and affecting an unprecedented number of nations. Before the terms could be determined in detail, the victorious powers would have to reach a general understanding among themselves; before they could do so, secret negotiation among the great powers would have to run its course. In the meantime the peoples of the democracies would have to wait. The strain on their patience and on their faith in their leaders would be very great.

WILSON
and His
PEACEMAKERS
*American Diplomacy at the
Paris Peace Conference, 1919*

PART ONE

A New Order for a New Era

THE American peacemakers of 1919 viewed the postwar chaos from the perspective of a nation that was remote and self-sufficient. The United States, entering the war late, had the good fortune to escape the exhaustion that had overtaken the European Allies. Its surplus resources put it in a position to exert a stabilizing influence in vacuums that had been created.

The American people were shocked by the breakdown of European diplomacy in 1914 and were in revolt against what they vaguely denounced as "the old system." Distrustful of precedent, they saw no adequate basis for a lasting peace in what one of them called "a re-weaving of the Penelope's web" that had been unraveled by every peace congress of the past two centuries.[1] Many Americans advocated a league of all the nations, and some looked to such a league as an influence for social justice as well as for peace. They foresaw a conflict of their ideals with the purpose of European peacemakers who hoped to safeguard peace by a policy of strategic security and by accommodation of national interests through traditional diplomacy.[2]

Actually Georges Clemenceau, president of the French Council of Ministers and also minister of war, was convinced that the peace terms would have to be enforced upon Germany. His people demanded above all some assurance that France could exist next to its potentially powerful neighbor without danger of becoming a satellite. Determined to avoid any concession to the enemy that might weaken the resilience of his own people after the ordeal of war, he could be expected to advocate measures that would guarantee strategic security for France.

Prime Minister David Lloyd George, representing an empire at the height of its sway and probably not yet fully aware of the gap that had widened during the war between British power and British responsibilities, saw less need to be concerned about national security. The two essentials of his policy in the peacemaking were to produce a treaty that would dispose Germany to keep the peace, and to bring the United States into the European settlement in a permanent and practical way.[3] Lloyd George's task was complicated by demands of the Dominions for the annexation of

---

1. Tasker H. Bliss to Secretary of State, December 15, 1918, *Papers Relating to the Foreign Relations of the United States, 1919, Paris Peace Conference* (hereinafter designated as *F.R., P.P.C.*), vol. 1, p. 296.
   Complete bibliographic information, when not given in the footnotes, may be found in the List of Abbreviations (p. 571) and in the Bibliography (pp. 572–585).
2. See Arthur Walworth, *America's Moment: 1918*, pp. 2, 3, 6.
3. D. R. Watson, "The Making of the Treaty of Versailles."

German colonies and by "blue sea" Englishmen for domination of the oceans, as well as by public clamor for compensation for the costs of the war and for the trial of German militarists accused of war crimes.

The American peacemakers would have to take account of special national interests, many of which had been recognized in the secret treaties concluded among the Allied powers under the stress of war. Although not fully briefed as to the particulars of these treaties, Wilson was aware of many of the war aims of the Allied powers. Thinking some of them provocative of future conflicts, he had undertaken during the period of America's neutrality to make eloquent speeches in behalf of a decent and rational peace, "a peace without victory." After his address of December 4, 1917, he said with tears running down his cheeks: "I hate this war! I hate all war, and the only thing I care about on earth is the peace I am going to make at the end of it."[4] At the beginning of 1918 he had enunciated certain liberal principles and "fourteen points" that he thought essential to the enduring peace that all men yearned for. The society that he envisioned for the world was that which his own nation had developed in its fortuitous isolation. When the German government turned to him in October of 1918 to negotiate an armistice, he had seized the moment and insisted on the American principles.[5] In prearmistice negotiations Edward M. House, his intimate friend and confidential agent, secured from the European premiers an unwritten commitment, with certain reservations, to an interpretation of the program that Wilson tentatively approved.[6] Thus, the president was placed in the position of moral arbiter. He had to be propitiated because he represented the richest and most powerful nation, which wanted little for itself and therefore could not easily be bargained with.[7]

The leader who brought the war to an end on high moral grounds took upon himself the responsibility of negotiating in person at a peace table with adroit politicians whose concepts of the common good had grown out of the crises of the moment and the practical necessities of their peoples. Swayed by evangelical overconfidence—some critics have written "arrogance"[8]—Wilson had misread the "common thought" that he aspired to "clarify." Actually any Europeans—and there were many—who sincerely believed in his doctrine and shared his highly cultivated sense of justice were outnumbered by those with other ideas. During the war, as Walter Lippmann pointed out, the American prophet had "embodied . . . all the different kinds of salvation for which men yearned. . . . He could both win the war and end the war, rebuild Europe and feed the hungry, and politically, he was an excellent stick with which to beat" opponents. At the war's end, however, the boons that Wilson offered gradually became less irresistible.[9] Would the true believers be able to bring pressure on their governments to make them follow the prophet?

4. William C. Bullitt and Sigmund Freud, *Thomas Woodrow Wilson*, pp. 200–201.
5. See Walworth, pp. 18–31. The Fourteen Points and supplementary principles may be found on pp. 275–284.
6. *Ibid.*, pp. 72–73.
7. James Bryce to J. F. Rhodes, March 29, 1919, Bryce papers, vol. 23, p. 146, Bodleian Library.
8. See H. G. Nicholas, in *Wilson's Diplomacy: An International Symposium*, ed. J. Joseph Huthmacher and Warren I. Susman, p. 89.
9. Walter Lippmann, "The Peace Conference," 719.

In the negotiations to come Wilson could not expect, and indeed would not welcome, expert assistance from a diplomatic service that he had not taken into his confidence in his intuitive guidance of foreign relations during the war. Most of the men whom he appointed to serve with him at Paris were as inexperienced as he in the give-and-take of international conferences and in the ways of the foreign offices of Europe. Beginning with the first session of the Peace Conference on January 12, 1919, and continuing through the year, they would have to negotiate as best they could with the skilled practitioners of diplomacy of the Old World. As we shall see, they were to respond to the circumstances of each day with improvisations and sometimes with more zeal than tact. Comparative amateurs in a society of professionals, the Americans were to find their capacity taxed to the utmost.

The president of the United States, afloat on a tide of history that endowed him with preponderant economic and military power, arrived at Paris in December 1918 with the most dynamic political platform for the world, but with a national mandate that was of dubious validity.[10] His party had just lost control of both houses of the American Congress. Nevertheless, as Lloyd George explained to the British Empire delegates, the European premiers would not remind Wilson of this embarrassing circumstance. They could ill afford to damage the prestige of the prophet from whom they hoped for a sanctification of the war aims of their governments.

As a political leader who would not have to account to his constituency at the polls for almost two years, Wilson stood in a privileged position among European premiers who, restricted by the necessity of retaining the support of parliaments from day to day, were restrained from subordinating immediate needs to ultimate ideals. He was thus granted time to educate his people and to bring them to accept the price that would have to be paid for participation in an international organization to keep the peace of the world. In his drive toward the military victory that would give the opportunity for peacemaking that he coveted, he had felt compelled to refrain from any proposal of specific provisions for a league-of-nations constitution. To have raised such a controversial question during the war would have been at the risk of slackening the prosecution of the fighting.

The president ventured on a course teeming with hazards. When he insisted that only in ideals does a wise man find the ultimate reality, he relieved his own conscience at some cost. For the claims of practical necessity have always demanded a hearing, both in domestic and international affairs, from those who govern mankind. Vital immediate issues are sometimes blurred by the introduction of ethical conflicts.

Actually, Wilson's imprecise moral formulas, presented with evangelical eloquence, encouraged unrealistic popular expectations that presaged disillusion and at the same time led to confusion in the deliberations of the peacemakers. Indeed, his urgent but vague call for a new political organism was frightening to some thinkers who were inclined to build the future upon past experience and present realities.[11] Sir Halford Mackinder, for example, pointed out that two "going concerns" were at hand that might serve as nuclei for international organization: the

10. To some Europeans Wilson did not seem "a representative American." John Buchan, *History of the Great War* (Boston, 1922), IV, p. 36.

11. See Walworth, pp. 10–11.

Supreme War Council and other interallied bodies of wartime cooperation,[12] and the British Empire. He was unwilling to risk the empire "for any paper scheme of a Universal League." Other British thinkers would make use of the experience and prestige of the World Court that had been set up at The Hague; and, moreover, they would promote technical cooperation among the nations in many spheres in which the common interest could be served.

French officials insisted on logical analysis of Wilson's proposals. The Foreign Ministry asked, in December 1918, whether it was wise to attempt to fix all frontiers. Any guarantee of territorial integrity seemed a weighty responsibility; for national sentiment did not speak with indisputable authority, and, moreover, economic changes and the migrations of peoples that resulted would come to modify the population of many regions in a way that would raise new problems of government.[13] Moreover, French logic required that a league of nations should have a military establishment under a unified command such as had served the Allies during the last year of the war. The diplomats of Europe, examining Wilson's Fourteenth Point in the light of the interests of the various nations, were inclined to regard it as "the harmless Utopia of a puritanical mind."[14]

In his eagerness to apply his principles to the European polity Wilson appeared ready to lift the ban of the Monroe Doctrine against American intervention in the Old World. The overseas expansion of the United States that had followed the war with Spain suggested that American participation in a world polity might spring from the circumstances that existed in 1919. This was the hope of the European peacemakers. Beset with the domestic problems that were raised by the transition from war to peace, some of them saw the possibility that Wilson's program might provide a practical way to deal with the challenge of bolshevism as well as with the restlessness of colonial peoples. Furthermore, they sought cooperation in correcting the economic maladjustment between Europe and the United States that had grown out of war conditions. American resources were needed to feed the peoples of Europe, and American credits and raw materials were essential to the restoration of its industry. Yet at the end of 1918 the Allies were formally notified by the United States Treasury of a disinclination to add to its extraordinary credits extended in the war emergency, now that the fighting was over.[15]

Europeans who took pains to read the interpretation of Wilson's Fourteen Points that House had presented to the prearmistice meetings noted that some of the vital interests of the Allies were in jeopardy.[16] The British were being asked to give up their right to blockade the seas in time of war, and the doctrine of self-determination

12. H. J. Mackinder, *Democratic Ideals and Reality,* p. 195. "The creation of numerous inter-Allied organizations during and after the first world war was one of the phenomena of the period. Not for a hundred years had anything like it been seen . . . the great powers found it difficult to operate through the usual diplomatic channels. . . . Sir Maurice Hankey . . . surely . . . had some warrant for writing: 'diplomacy by conference has come to stay'" (Carl L. Lokke, "A Sketch of the Interallied Organizations of the First World War Period and Their Records," *American Archivist* [October 1944]:225–235).

13. Pierre Renouvin, *Les Crises du XXe siècle:* vol. 1, *De 1914 à 1929,* p. 187.

14. Pierre Miquel, *La Paix de Versailles et l'opinion publique française,* p. 40.

15. See Walworth, p. 247.

16. *Ibid.,* pp. 269–272.

seemed to encourage revolt in their domain. Wilson was skeptical about French plans for a secure eastern frontier and for the annexation of the valley of the Saar River. Italy was denied the Adriatic cities of Fiume and Trieste, which were to become free ports. Claims for reimbursement of the Allies for the costs of the war were to be satisfied by compensation only to the extent of direct damage.

Until mid-February 1919, when he was obliged to return temporarily to the United States, the president would keep the initiative that he took in the last months of 1918. Putting off the solution of awkward questions, he would use his privileged position, his eloquence, and his moral and material power to get the approval of all the conferring states, great and small, for priority in drafting a constitution for a league of nations. He envisioned this new body as a guarantor of the treaty to be made as well as a bulwark of enduring peace. In the early months of the Peace Conference this was the "single track" on which Wilson's mind would run persistently.

1

The Battle of the Peace Begins

In Paris, after the end of the last year of France's epic struggle for survival, the Seine was in flood and a damp chill clung to the earth. The venerable city, long accustomed to high affairs of state, looked to the future with hope but also with many fears. In the first week of 1919 the process of peacemaking seemed to be retrogressing. President Wilson was wooing the Italian people; Prime Minister Lloyd George was in London, meeting political challenges; and Georges Clemenceau complained to President Poincaré that the peace conference was becoming more of a myth each day.[1]

The French government had placed the Murat Palace, which had been the residence of Napoleon's marshal, at the disposal of the president of the United States. There, enjoying privacy behind high garden walls with sentry boxes at an entrance guarded by French soldiers, Woodrow Wilson was remote from the masses of people to whom he wished to bring peace. In a bedroom decorated in green, spotted with the golden bees of the First French Empire, the American democrat sat at a Napoleonic writing table to work out the charter of a new world.

Living with the Wilsons in this relic of imperial grandeur was Dr. Cary T. Grayson. This Navy physician would be constantly at the side of the president and, dressed in his admiral's uniform, would on occasion act as an aide. He vigilantly guarded Wilson against fatigue and vetoed every plan for him to work amidst the hubbub at the Hôtel Crillon, where the American Commission to Negotiate Peace had its headquarters. Two days of complete rest were ordered at the beginning of January so that the president might recuperate after strenuous journeys to England and to Italy.[2] *envoy having full power*

The four American plenipotentiaries who with the president made up the American Commission to Negotiate Peace (ACTNP) took up residence in the Crillon. Three of the men—Secretary of State Robert Lansing, General Tasker H. Bliss, and Henry White—were lodged on the floor immediately above the entresol, in rooms ornate with tapestry, mirrors, and gilding. On the story above, where Admiral William S. Benson, the military attachés, and the advisers on economic matters had their quarters, Navy yeomen stood guard before a door that led to the inner sanctum of Colonel Edward M. House. This seat of authority became known as "upstairs."[3]

The president gave House few explicit instructions. The Texan "colonel," an intimate friend and counselor for eight years past, could be useful only so long as

---

1. Raymond Poincaré, *Au Service de la France,* vol. 11, p. 47.
2. Charles Swem and Charles C. Wagner to the author. Walworth, *America's Moment: 1918,* pp. 146–153, 166–170. Charles T. Thompson, *The Peace Conference Day by Day,* p. 83.
3. House's staff numbered thirty-two, more than twice the size of that of any other American commissioner. It served the entire delegation, House diary, January 7, 1919. On the personnel of the American Commission, see Walworth, pp. 121–124.

he held the confidence that Wilson placed in him as in no other man. Shrewdly evaluating the reliability and importance of sources of information, and sometimes filtering out tidings that would be most distasteful to Wilson, he managed to broaden the president's view of European affairs. When strong wills were frustrated, House was at hand to speak a cheering word, in a husky voice with a soft drawl. "He sees everything, understands everything," Clemenceau said of him, "[and] *'n' agissant qu'à son idée'* knows how to command a respectful hearing everywhere."[4] Advocates for sundry causes and the spokesmen of nations large and small, born and reborn, passed through the colonel's door with messages for the president, who remained at a distance from petitioners. Well briefed as to these men and their causes, House was able to give counsel both sympathetic and wise.

Long and intimate association had given House a clear understanding of the strengths and weaknesses of the president's character. The colonel feared to give any impression that he might appear to be usurping power when he spoke for a prophet who was jealous of his pulpit. He thought he detected an ambition in Mrs. Wilson to cut a fine figure on the summit of world society, dressed royally in her favorite color, purple. And so House had not taken the risk of advising Wilson to stay away from Paris, although he had felt that a Wilsonian peace could be negotiated more swiftly and effectively if the president remained at Washington as a "god on the mountain" and did not go abroad to contend with clever Europeans.[5]

Unfortunately, however, House practiced nepotism in a way that offended both the president and scholars of the Inquiry, the group of specialists who served at Paris in a department of political intelligence. Gordon Auchincloss, House's son-in-law and secretary, had incurred the dislike of the president when he accompanied Wilson to London at the end of 1918. Moreover, Dr. Sidney Mezes, House's wife's brother-in-law and the nominal head of the Inquiry, failed to command the respect of the scholars, and Dr. Isaiah Bowman assumed the direction and coordination of their studies.[6]

Pourparlers that House carried on were of vital importance to the success of the talks at the "summit" that were impending. At the prearmistice conference and afterward he had taken pains to assure Clemenceau that Wilson was both approachable and reasonable. He had elicited from the French premier a promise to bring up no matter at the peace table that was not discussed first with the Americans.[7]

Lansing, Bliss, and White depended on House for contact with the fifth plenipotentiary, Woodrow Wilson. The president seldom attended the daily meetings of the American Commission. In these, Lansing frequently elicited sympathy from White and Bliss for legalistic opinions that were distasteful to Wilson. Although the

4. Pierre Renouvin, *Le Traité de Versailles*, p. 50. On House's services to Wilson, see Walworth, *Woodrow Wilson: World Prophet*, vol. 2, pp. 238–239n.

5. George S. Viereck, "Behind the House-Wilson Break," p. 152.

6. See Seymour, *Letters from the Paris Peace Conference*, pp. xxvi–xxx. Also see Walworth, *America's Moment: 1918*, pp. 82, 148, 258, 262. One of the scholars, Professor Clive Day, wrote in his diary: "Mezes uses his opportunity, as head of the organization, to indulge his personal curiosity and vanity, and rarely to help along in the public interest the men who are under him," entry of December 21, 1918, Y.H.C.

7. See Walworth, *America's Moment: 1918*, pp. 41–42, 99.

discussions among these commissioners sometimes led to greater administrative efficiency of the delegation, they had very little effect upon policy or its fulfillment.

Henry White, the only career diplomat among the five, played the role of a benign elder statesman, always ready to foster good will—a master of protocol, courteous, and disciplined. He commanded respect as the ranking American diplomat and a veteran of the Conference of Algeciras. The president had appointed him because he thought him more trustworthy than more prominent Republicans. Mrs. Wilson soon discovered his value as an adviser on social affairs.[8]

In contrast with White, General Bliss was not versed in the ways of polished diplomats and tended to view them with a provincial suspicion. An authority on American military history, he craved peace and swore beautifully. He was, in the view of one of the scholars of the Inquiry, "honest-to-God American."[9] Yet in Wilson's opinion Bliss had a more statesmanlike mind than any other peace commissioner.[10] Save for House he was the only one of the five plenipotentiaries who had been directly in touch with the affairs of Europe during the war. As the military representative of the United States, he had enjoyed more independence in political action than the European generals had, and he had endeavored to use this freedom to touch upon questions of state policy.[11] Nevertheless he was thought by some of his fellow Americans to be slow of understanding and of action in political matters.[12]

Confusion and uncertainty prevailed within the ACTNP.[13] In order that the commission might operate effectively, much expert assistance was required. Never before had so many American civilians been abroad on a diplomatic mission. The delegation was made up of distinct groups that tended to maintain their identities.[14] The career men of the State Department and their associates at the American embassy found themselves on the sidelines when the negotiating began. In contrast with the other delegations, which were staffed almost entirely by civilians, the American roster was made up largely of military and naval personnel. The men of the Inquiry took responsibility for political intelligence; and Bowman effected some consoli-

8. *Ibid.*, pp. 123–124. The fact that his son-in-law was an officer in the German army made White a valuable purveyor of information from Berlin, but this association somewhat limited his usefulness in negotiations with the French, Paul Cambon, *Correspondance,* vol. 3, p. 315. "The French do not like Mr. White for a number of reasons," Harrison to Polk, February 9, 1919, Y.H.C. However, Jules Cambon, one of the French plenipotentiaries, was heard to speak appreciatively of White's "great charm and experience," Bonsal note, March [12], 1919, Bonsal papers, box 25.

9. Westermann diary, January 16, 1919, Columbia University Library.

10. Grayson diary, January 8, 1919, Wilson papers, Princeton University Library.

11. Bliss diary, January 1, 1919. See Walworth, *America's Moment: 1918,* p. 23, n. 19.

12. Benham diary letter, December 5, 1918. House diary, December 16, 1918. Grew diary, October 8, 1919, Grew papers, Houghton Library, Harvard University.

13. See Jordan A. Schwartz, *The Speculator,* p. 116. "We putter around in an aimless sort of way and get nowhere," the secretary of state wrote, Lansing's confidential notes, January 16, 1919. Bliss diary, box 65, L.C. Actually, brief minutes of the meetings were kept by the secretariat of the American Commission to Negotiate Peace (hereinafter designated as ACTNP) and may be found in part in the Leland Harrison papers, L.C., in part in the Grew papers, Houghton Library, Harvard University, and for January 31, 1919, *et seq.*, in *F.R., P.P.C.*, vol. 11, pp. 1–339. Shotwell, *At the Paris Peace Conference,* p. 168.

14. Clive Day to Mrs. Day, January 11, 1919, Y.H.C. See Walworth, *America's Moment: 1918,* p. 257.

dation in the interest of efficiency. Nevertheless, a sense of futility grew among the scholars.[15] Advisers on economic affairs from the president's war cabinet, the Treasury, and the Central Bureau of Statistics formed another distinct group.

The relationships and lines of communication within the American delegation took shape adventitiously and without benefit of experience in peacemaking or of careful supervision by Wilson or by House, who hesitated to assume executive authority that belonged to the president. In the first weeks at Paris the American delegation grew to a size that seemed to the commissioners to be excessive. On February 1 Secretary Lansing told Bliss and White that he was appalled. He objected particularly to the large number of men in the office of House and in the military and communications sections.[16]

Another difficulty defied permanent solution. The president did not look with favor upon the presence of the wives of members of the American peace delegation. Yet Mrs. Wilson was at his side, and House and his relatives were accompanied by their consorts at their expense. This seemed to delegates who were lonely to set a precedent.[17] To the embarrassment of the State Department the commission ruled that certain of the "temporary gentlemen" might have their wives come at their own expense.[18] Three months afterward the question was still a source of annoyance

15. See Walworth, *America's Moment: 1918*, pp. 42n and 258. At the end of January the Inquiry made a formal complaint, stating that in seven weeks since they reached Paris they had had only one conference with the president and this lasted only five minutes, Stephen Bonsal, *Suitors and Suppliants*, pp. 219–220. "I can only insist," House explained to Bonsal, "that the overburdened president would like to do this but has not the time for these meetings in 'common council' of which he speaks so often but so rarely indulges in. But barring these conferences, everything possible has been done for the members of The Inquiry. . . . Their reports when they do arrive, not I think as promptly as we could wish, are carefully considered."

16. A committee including Bliss and White was appointed to investigate and reduce personnel to a minimum. Minutes of the ACTNP, February 1.

Mezes wrote to House on February 3, 1919: "No one is a competent administrator . . . when a difficulty arises they call for *more servants* instead of planning *better service*. This is a delightful winter resort for servants' servants. Remedy: Appoint a competent administrator," handwritten note in Y.H.C.

Charles Seymour wrote on February 15: "The incapacity, the pettiness, and the red tape of our government instutitions, whether military or civil, combined with favoritism, simply passes comprehension," *Letters from the Paris Peace Conference*, p. 161.

Joseph C. Grew, the secretary of the ACTNP, recorded in his diary that his first days at the Crillon were "a nightmare of confusion," and later, that there was "continual electricity in the air." *Turbulent Era*, vol. 1, pp. 365–376. Grew reported to the State Department on February 10 that the new organization charts were in preparation and that the committee had concluded that the commission was not overstaffed, N.A., R.G. 59, doc. 763.72119 / 4071. Yet House characterized the organization as "wretched" and thought Grew's responsibility "far beyond his capacity," House diary, February 23, 1919.

One of the economic experts left this record: "One could scarcely step out of his room without falling over a group of privates, who were there to act as orderlies. Many of the officers, in order to justify their retention there, spent their time issuing bulletins and orders, to be countermanded later." Conditions of work were "minus zero." In rooms that were partly above Maxim's restaurant, they "worked in an overpowering atmosphere of cooking and stale wine. Stenographic assistance was almost non-existent. The various expedients of the Commission to cut expenses were almost ridiculous in view of the importance of the work. Attempts to cut down the force were entrusted to the State Department and to Army officers and in each case results were small and much hard feeling developed," C. K. Leith, "Notes on the Paris Peace Conference," Edwin Francis Gay collection, Hoover Institution Archives, box 1.

17. "Most of the regular State Department employees want to go home," Auchincloss wrote to Polk on January 5, 1919, letter in Y.H.C.

18. Seymour, p. 91 and footnote.

to the president, who then asked the secretary of state to rescind any special arrangement that had been made.[19]

At the beginning of January Wilson wished to continue the informal conferences that he had had with Clemenceau and Lloyd George in December.[20] He thought these might be enlarged from time to time by calling in spokesmen for lesser states. When House reported the president's wish to the other American commissioners, they expressed the opinion that a preliminary conference of the larger Allies was essential.[21] The failure to define what was meant by the term "preliminary peace," and the resulting lack of precision, caused infinite confusion.[22]

At a meeting of the ACTNP at House's office on January 7, Wilson learned that the French government was willing to begin discussions immediately. Clemenceau, just back from a vacation, came in while the Americans were in session. House excused himself and went into another room to greet the Tiger of France.[23] Heretofore he had been able to do no more than win Clemenceau's friendly indulgence of the president's aims. A week earlier he had talked intimately with the old man about his future in French politics, offering sympathetic advice in the manner he had found effective in dealing with American politicians. Clemenceau, thanking House warmly, had said frankly that he did not hold the old diplomacy of balanced power responsible for the outbreak of war in 1914. Nevertheless, he would accept a league of nations, but only as a "supplementary guaranty" while demanding something more practical, something tested by experience.[24]

Actually Clemenceau did not agree with Ferdinand Foch, the commander in chief of the victorious armies, in putting a high value on the Rhine as a barrier against another incursion by the enemy that had invaded France twice in the past half century. "In the future," he prophesied, "the bandits will travel in the air, not on the ground." He had no enthusiasm for the annexation of Germans, who "would need watching." Although he agreed with Foch that France should maintain a good posture of defense and prevent the Germans from arming, he felt that the only way to prevent German aggression was by a firm understanding, a military pact if possible, with Britain and America. When House agreed that the air fleets would fly over Foch's bridgeheads, unseen, the Tiger, according to the record of an eyewitness, put his arms on House's shoulders and, looking him straight in the eye, said: "My dear friend! I believe you are right. . . . I am henceforward for the league as you

19. Auchincloss, diary, December 10, 1918. Polk to Lansing, January 4, February 17, 1919, N.A., R.G. 59, 763.72119P43 / 207a. Wilson to Lansing, March 24, 1919, Wilson papers. Swem to the author, February 7, 1949. Minutes, ACTNP, December 31, 1918.

20. See Walworth, *America's Moment: 1918,* pp. 144–150.

21. Minutes, ACTNP, December 31, 1918, Grew papers, Auchincloss diary, December 30, 1918, Y.H.C. T. H. Bliss to N. D. Baker, January 4, 1918, N. D. Baker papers, L.C. See F. S. Marston, *The Peace Conference of 1919: Organization and Procedure,* pp. 48–50.

22. See below, p. 202.

23. House confessed years later that the sudden appearance of Clemenceau in House's room, unannounced, upset Wilson, and that he, the colonel, did everything he could to "smooth out" the situation, Viereck, p. 152. "I told Gordon [Auchincloss] not to announce to the papers that Pichon, Foch, Clemenceau, the president and Lord Robert Cecil had been my visitors during the day. I am afraid of hurt sensibilities," House diary, January 7, 1919.

24. House diary, December 28, 1918. Bonsal, *Suitors and Suppliants,* p. 212.

see it. I will work with you and between us we ought to be able to take care of Foch" and—pausing—"of Wilson." He gave what House took to be an unconditional pledge to work for the league as House had it in mind. The colonel's apprehension of a clash between Wilson and Clemenceau relieved, House appeared, when he came away from the tête-à-tête, to be "walking on air." In mentioning the possibility of "a military pact" between the United States and France, however, he seemed to be challenging isolationist sentiment in the American Senate.[25]

Three days later House, having perfected arrangements with André Tardieu, an able journalist who was one of the five French plenipotentiaries, was able to tell the American commissioners that the president would meet with the Allied premiers on January 12 and 13.[26] He spoke of the proposed gatherings as "a glorified war council meeting," after which more formal discussions would take shape.[27]

The political leaders of France and Great Britain were men of extraordinary self-confidence, trusting themselves to deal with complex and controversial matters without consultation with their foreign ministers. Like Wilson, they used the powers that came from the voters to rule the diplomatic and military establishments. Clemenceau, whose prestige as father of the victory had led the French Chamber of Deputies to vote overwhelmingly in support of his leadership in the peacemaking, ignored Foreign Minister Pichon with as little compunction as Wilson felt in disregarding Secretary of State Lansing.[28]

Lloyd George gave less attention to the long experience and reasoned opinions of Foreign Secretary Balfour and to the well-founded advice of the Foreign Office than to politicians and to his able executive staff. Indeed, there were only eighteen Foreign Office men in the British delegation of about four hundred.[29] A large majority of the British voters had confirmed the position that the prime minister had won by effective leadership in the war; and on January 10 he had formed a coalition cabinet. The "hard-faced men" of the new body could not be expected to carry out the ideals that had inspired the Liberal party. Liberal opinion, looking for leadership outside Parliament and even outside Great Britain, responded to the challenges of Woodrow Wilson.[30] This political consideration reinforced the compulsion exerted by Europe's economic dependence on America. It would be imprudent, given the circumstances, to question the strength of the president's mandate or to fail in respect for the person and ideas of this president who had broken all precedent by coming to Europe to make its peace according to the American concept of justice.[31]

Lloyd George lived with his secretary-mistress in a flat in the rue Nitot, below one occupied by Balfour. In contrast with Wilson's remoteness from the American

25. House diary, January 7, 1919. "It is to be hoped," House's aide wrote, "that none of the words by which House won over Clemenceau will reach the ears of isolationist senators." Unprinted script in Bonsal's diary, January 8, 1919, Bonsal papers, box 17.

26. House diary, January 8. Minutes, ACTNP, January 7 and 10, 1919, Harrison papers, L.C.

27. Arthur Willert's record of a talk with House, January 9, 1919, Willert papers, Y.H.C.

28. See Renouvin, p. 51. "Nice fellows, "Clemenceau said of his ministers. "They had only one fault. They were too decent, not made for war," Jean Martel, Le Tigre (Paris, 1929), p. 33.

29. Lord Hardinge, The Old Diplomacy, p. 230.

30. See Martin Gilbert, The European Powers, 1900–1945 (London, 1965), p. 169.

31. See Winston Churchill, The Aftermath, pp. 148–149.

delegates, the prime minister met almost every morning with the representatives of the British Empire. Both policy and tactics were discussed, as well as matters that were to come before the Supreme War Council on that day. Lloyd George usually followed a policy that was approved by his British colleagues.[32] Early in January he explained to them, in confidence, the predicament in which he found himself. There were strong indications that the American Congress would not accept commitments that their president might make in the interest of the general peace.[33]

When the president came together with the European prime ministers in the Supreme War Council to take up the task that brought them all to the peace table with a large entourage of advisers and secretaries, the political leaders fell naturally into the established practice of diplomats. Nothing could be more serviceable than a series of informal meetings in which each of the chiefs participated and, speaking "off the record," enjoyed entire freedom of expression as well as complete control of the protocol that reported his own part. The official summaries of the discussions and conclusions, recorded and agreed upon by their secretaries, must have unanimous approval in order to be valid.

Major Maurice Hankey, the secretary of the British cabinet, profiting by his experience in recording and printing the proceedings of the Supreme War Council, was the guiding genius of the daily routine of the secretaries. The efficient bureau that Hankey had set up during the war at Versailles became the nerve center of the secretariat of the Peace Conference, although the official head of this body was a French functionary at the Quai d'Orsay. Hankey worked to keep the diplomatic atmosphere both clear and courteous. He took responsibility not only for records, but for the preparation of purposeful agenda. Wilson's confidence in the honesty of this "recording angel" eventually became so complete that he was willing to entrust to Hankey the keeping of minutes of intimate sessions with Lloyd George and Clemenceau in which no American secretary was present. The French secretariat, not well organized, also depended upon Hankey.[34]

The first meeting of the Supreme Council of Ten, on January 12, was actually an enlarged session of the Supreme War Council of the Allied and Associated powers. Protected from the glare of publicity, the statesmen sat in the hot, stuffy reception

32. Sir Clement Jones, secretary of the Empire delegation, to the author, October 8, 1959. Jones ms., "The Dominions and the Peace Conference," P.R.O., Cab. 21 / 217. Crown copyright records in the P.R.O. have been used in this work by permission of the controller of H. M. Stationery Office.

33. See Nicolson, *Peacemaking, 1919,* p. 205. Nicolson wrote of "our incessant suspicion that the Americans would not be able to deliver the goods" (p. 219).

34. General Maxime Weygand, *Mémoires,* vol. 2, p. 29. Mantoux, *Proceedings,* p. xv. Hankey to the author, October 14, 1959. Hankey, *The Supreme Control,* p. 25. Sir Charles Webster to the author October 20, 1959. Captain André Portier to the author, November 18, 1959. U. S. Grant III to the author, March 21, 1961. Réné Massigli to the author, November 9, 1959. See Hankey, *The Supreme Command,* vol. 2, pp. 846–847, and *The Supreme Control,* pp. 192–193. For Hankey's philosophy of diplomatic negotiation, see *Diplomacy by Conference.* For his account of the organization of a secretariat, see *The Supreme Control,* pp. 23–25. See also L. S. Amery, *My Political Life* (London, 1953), vol. 2, pp. 172, 178.

Edith Benham's diary letter of May 21, 1919, records that Wilson considered Hankey "an invaluable person" and "a fine and honorable gentleman."

The work and difficulties of the secretaries are explained in detail in a paper written by Frank L. Warrin, Jr., Miller's legal assistant, and filed in the Walworth papers, Y.H.C.

room of the French foreign minister in the old Palais Bourbon. Above the old rose and gray carpets, brocaded chairs, and Rubens tapestries, lively frescoes depicted the life of Marie de Médicis. Wide French windows looked out upon a formal garden. Clemenceau, the downright humanist with his eyes wide open to every frailty of man, presided at a plain Empire table, a simian body in repose, clad in a black jacket and skull cap, holding in a gray-gloved hand a large pencil that he used to tap upon a Louis XV writing table, and sometimes to point over his shoulder at Professor Paul Mantoux to give emphasis as he said through his drooping white mustache: "Traduisez!"[35]

The French premier, with Lloyd George and Wilson, formed a triumvirate with far-reaching power, "an old man of the world, a *femme fatale,* and a non-conformist clergyman," Keynes called them.[36] They were now to establish *de facto* supremacy. It was essential to the exercise of their power that they maintain unity of action and decision. They were to sit in the Supreme Council with their foreign ministers, the premier and foreign minister of Italy, and two Japanese diplomats.[37] Initial discussions made it clear that several practical matters had to be settled before the convoking of an assembly of all delegates. Such a plenary session was postponed for five days.

Sitting in the Supreme Council in a special chair decorated with gold, Wilson proved himself a good listener. He attempted to consider all aspects of each issue under discussion. Leaning forward and resting on the arms of his chair, he spoke like a professor. The singularity of his manner commanded attention. But British secretaries, who were accustomed to colorful performances by Clemenceau and Lloyd George, found him tiresome. He was thought a "quaint bird" when he telephoned for his old typewriter and, taking it from the tray on which a messenger delivered it, placed it on a table in a corner and tapped out a memorandum.[38] He did not try to exploit his rank as the only chief of state sitting in the Supreme Council,[39] but it seemed clear to European diplomats that his peculiar position was a factor in his predominance. He appeared to lack the agility and precision of thought of a skillful diplomat and, when in agreement, to be too enthusiastic and pleasant, and, when in opposition, too dour. Superb in appeals to morality, he showed only a limited awareness of the thoughts of his European associates and little deftness for timing or aiming sallies at their mental defenses.[40] The president disturbed House by a tendency to deal intimately with questions that he did not fully understand and by allowing delicate matters to be discussed without adequate briefing.[41]

Despite the absence of a constructive response from London or Washington to

35. Esme Howard, *Theatre of Life,* vol. 2, p. 301; "Everything reminded me of a faculty committee meeting, rather than a gathering of statesmen," Seymour wrote of a later session of the council, p. 134.
36. Keynes, *Collected Writings,* vol. 10, p. 22.
37. Italy and Japan were represented in most of the meetings of the Supreme Council during the first two months of the Peace Conference, the former as a major Allied power and the latter as a matter of practical politics rather than as a reward for war sacrifice. The spokesmen for these nations seldom took a spirited part in discussion of questions that did not bear on the particular interests of their nations.
38. Lord Riddell, *Intimate Diary of the Peace Conference and After,* entry of January 22, 1919.
39. A. H. Frazier ms., Y.H.C., p. 9.
40. See Walworth, *Woodrow Wilson,* vol. 2, pp. 242–243.
41. H. Wickham Steed, *Through Thirty Years,* vol. 2, p. 271.

the tentative plans that had been circulated earlier by the Foreign Ministry of France,[42] the Quai d'Orsay persisted in efforts to give system and logic to the proceedings. Revision and refinement of the early French plans had been carried on under the direction of André Tardieu, a plenipotentiary on whom Clemenceau depended much and who often talked informally with House. The French would give priority to consideration of territorial and economic matters. Their plan[43] stated that "once these . . . types of problems have been solved . . . the principal foundations of the league of nations will be laid." Such an order of procedure, which would facilitate the satisfaction of the immediate needs of the Allies, challenged Wilson's commitment to a new order. Noting that the Russian question was at the bottom of the French agenda, he said to the council that this called for immediate decision. Anxious about the political instability that existed east of the Rhine, he remarked that the peacemakers must "remove quicksand before they could begin to walk." The American legal advisers studied the French document and gave their opinion of it to Secretary Lansing on January 12. They considered the Tardieu plan "a great improvement" over the earlier French papers; yet they observed that definite conclusions could not be reached on other matters until there was agreement on the nature and scope of a league of nations. Lansing appeared to be "very dissatisfied with what had happened" in the first meeting of the Supreme Council and "very much up in the air about the whole proceedings."[44]

At this juncture Colonel House was incapacitated. On January 9 he had become so ill that there were rumors of his death.[45] Although Wilson went to his bedside after meetings of the Supreme Council, there was apparently no one to brief the president on the French plan. When Pichon brought it before the council on January 13, Wilson introduced an agenda of five topics: a league of nations, reparations, new states, territorial adjustments, and colonial possessions. He proposed that when the recommendations of the various national delegations were in hand, these subjects could be discussed "by the present Conference in the order given." He had asked the day before whether the question of procedure could not be reserved for a plenary session of the Peace Conference, where the small states would be represented. Probably feeling that they would be more active than the large powers in behalf of the common interest and the creation of a league of nations, he had reminded his colleagues that everything that affected the world's peace was the world's business.[46] Now, on January 13, Clemenceau proposed a meeting of all the

42. See Walworth, *America's Moment: 1918,* pp. 94–98. House pointed to the lack of a plan as the "great fault" of the peace conference, Nicolson, p. 103. According to Nicolson, both Wilson and Lloyd George "rejected, and indeed resented, any written formulation of what, or how, or when, they were supposed to discuss."

43. "Plan des premières conversations entre les ministres alliés," dated January 5, 1919. A translation of this plan, as submitted to the American embassy at Paris by the Quai d'Orsay, is in *F.R., P.P.C.,* vol. 1, pp. 386–396.

44. Auchincloss diary, January 12, 1919, Y.H.C. Harold Nicolson, a very young British delegate who was later to write a classic book on the peacemaking, noted "the absence of a central focus," Nicolson, p. 131.

45. See below, p. 29.

46. This remark by Wilson was recorded in the American, but not in the British, minutes of the council's meeting on January 12, *F.R., P.P.C.,* vol. 3, pp. 485, 502, 536.

delegates, after which the great powers could meet to examine solutions of such questions as that of policy toward Russia.

On the question of representation and voting power of the nations at the Peace Conference the political leaders were forced to enter into specific discussion and to risk controversy. It was obvious that there could be no progress toward the negotiation of a treaty of peace until it was decided who was to negotiate. The fall of the great empires left a scattering of governments of dubious status in all of eastern Europe.[47] As for Russia, there appeared to be no government in that vast land that seemed qualified to speak for all its people.

Wilson acquiesced in this decision although he had feared then that any convocation of the triumphant powers would make any subsequent parley with the Germans a mere sham. Now, however, when German revolutionaries wondered why their nation was being denied that right to discuss peace which Wilson had been willing to give to the German empire during the war, Wilson justified his position by his apprehension that communists might appear at the Peace Conference.[48]

It was not easy to reach an understanding as to representation of even the victorious powers. Vital considerations of national might and prestige were involved, and the arrangements made at Paris would affect the internal politics of certain states. It had been agreed among Allied statesmen conferring at London on December 3, 1918, that each of the five great powers should send five delegates. Each of the small Allied states and the British dominions were to be represented only at discussions of questions of special interest to them; but the number of delegates to be allotted to them was not then fixed.

At its first session the Supreme Council of Ten took up this essential and difficult question. Lloyd George suggested that there be two delegates from each small power. Wilson, however, probably noted that the British government had just pleased the Brazilians by raising the status of its envoy from that of minister to that of ambassador[49] and that Brazil's envoy at Washington was disturbed by the prospect that his nation would have only two representatives. Indeed, four men already had been named. Though Brazil had a very large German population, it protested its loyalty to the Latin American policy of the United States and recalled that it was the only state in South America that had declared war promptly and cooperated actively by sending ships.

The Pan-American Union at Washington had reminded the president that Latin Americans rejoiced that he was going to Paris and regarded him as their spokesman.[50] Moreover, the State Department had received several queries from its representatives in Latin America, asking what place the nations of that region would

47. For example, the Austrians and Hungarians claimed that their revolutions had rendered them neutrals and taken them out of the war without a treaty of peace; and the Poles and Czechs held that their revolutions had made them belligerents without a declaration of war. The Serbian government denied its own existence and claimed recognition as the government of Yugoslavia, of which Serbia became a part. The Italian government, however, denied the existence of Yugoslavia. The Ukraine, juridically neutral, was actually an enemy at Lemberg, an ally at Odessa. See R. C. Binkley, "New Light on the Paris Peace Conference," *Political Science Quarterly* 46, no. 3 (1931):352–353.

48. See Klaus Schwabe, *Woodrow Wilson, Revolutionary Germany, and Peacemaking*, pp. 163, 174.

49. Headlam-Morley diary, January 19, 1919.

50. John Barrett, director general of the Pan-American Union, to Tumulty, December 3, 1918, Wilson papers.

have at the Peace Conference. Lansing spoke to the American commission of the advantage that would accrue from the presence of Latin American delegates who would vote with the United States; and early in January the commissioners decided that governments that had broken diplomatic relations as well as those that were at war with Germany should have representation.[51] In pleading for special treatment for Brazil, Wilson cited the fact that it was a country larger than Belgium or Greece and warned of the danger of a revival of the strong German influence that had existed before the war. The Supreme Council, however, felt that Brazil should have but two seats, since it seemed unjust to give this South American people preferment over Europeans who had fought and suffered.

When Lloyd George, speaking for the British Empire, suggested that two seats be awarded to India and to each of the dominions, Wilson complained that such an arrangement would lead the small powers to think that the great powers were managing the peace conference. Lloyd George, however, was not easily persuaded. He was wont to plead with overwhelming vigor. Entering the council chamber a moment late, with a step that seemed to swagger and with greetings bluff and genial, he would plant his short, thickset body in a chair, clasp a knee in his hands, and lean back as he questioned his secretary about the agenda. Then he would rest on his right arm and wait confidently for the rough and tumble to begin, his eyes twinkling under a high brow, ready to wrinkle at the corners when he smiled, his silver hair brushed back from a clear, pink forehead, and a short white mustache curving over his lips. His talk flowed like a cascade in his Welsh mountains—leaping from point to point, changing course, splashing down ideas that sparkled in the rays of his wit He gushed approval or spouted anger. When under attack by men whose knowledge was greater than his, he often fell back on the devices of truculence and indifference.

To Wilson's argument that the great powers might seem to dictate the peace, Lloyd George replied that it was these powers that had managed the war. Wilson, speaking respectfully of the dominions and their war effort, then remarked that the effect of their representation would be to give Great Britain the power to make its views prevail on questions of interest to the dominions. He went so far, however, as to concede that the dominions might have one representative each and also, as a group, one among the five British delegates. When Lloyd George asked for time to discuss the matter with the Imperial War Cabinet, Wilson begged him not to give that body the impression that jealousy inspired the American argument. Nevertheless, the very first session of the Supreme Council of the conference closed on a note of discord, and the peril of "summit diplomacy" became apparent.

On the morning of the next day, January 13, Sir William Wiseman, the British diplomat who worked closely with House as liaison between Lloyd George and Wilson, made an effort to repair the damage that had been done by inadequate preparation.[52] A telephone call over the private wire that linked British headquarters

---

51. Minutes, ACTNP, December 27, 1919, Grew papers. Polk to the secretary of state, January 10, 1918, *F.R., P.P.C.*, vol. 1, pp. 223–235. Argentina, a neutral, sought membership in the League of Nations but not in the peace conference, Polk to Ammission, January 28, 1919, N.A., R.G. 59, 763, 72119 / 3518.

52. On the House-Wiseman understanding see Walworth, *America's Moment: 1918*, pp. 33–34 and *passim*.

at the Astoria with the Crillon informed House's secretary, Gordon Auchincloss, that the situation had become acute.[53]

Auchincloss and Wiseman had discussed Anglo-American relations with the utmost frankness the day before. Wiseman remarked that Lloyd George's appointments to his new cabinet had not been well received in England and that Wilson was stronger there than the prime minister on all matters involved in the peacemaking except the question of freedom of the seas. Consequently, Wiseman said, Lloyd George was afraid to oppose the president on major issues. At the same time Wiseman made it clear that the British government was fully aware that the political position of the president in the United States was precarious. He said that Clemenceau, while in London in December, had proposed an alliance of the nations of western Europe against Germany without regard to the United States, and that Balfour had rejected this proposal.[54] Wiseman asked Auchincloss to urge upon the president that the dominions be represented at the conference separately from Great Britain and equally with the most favored small nations.

Conveying Wiseman's plea to Wilson, Auchincloss found the president eager for advice and curious to know whether the private wire to the Crillon went to House's bedside. Auchincloss explained that British conservatives desired that the mother country speak for the whole Empire; but liberals looked to Wilson for aid in getting adequate representation for the dominions and were very much upset because he did not support them fully in this.

To this the president responded sympathetically, explaining that there had been a misunderstanding and he would not oppose separate representation for the dominions provided that their delegates would not be under the control of the British government. He asked Auchincloss to straighten out the matter.[55] That afternoon, when Lloyd George reported to the Supreme Council that the president's remarks of the day before had disappointed the Imperial War Cabinet, Wilson's response was conciliatory. He agreed that the dominions[56] and India should have two delegates each, to sit in the council only when questions affecting their governments came under discussion.

Having made this concession, Wilson reopened his argument for preferment for Brazil. He dwelt on the danger that Germany, whose people had great influence in many of the states of Brazil, might regain its prewar position in that country if the

53. The ministers of the dominions met on January 13 at 10:15 A.M. and decided to insist on two delegates each, thinking this "a real test of their status as autonomous nations of the Commonwealth." At eleven o'clock Premier Borden of Canada put the case before the Imperial War Cabinet. It was agreed that the dominions have only one representative each, subject to arrangements for a panel from which five British Empire delegates would be chosen, General memorandum no. 2. "The difficulty had really arisen," Borden commented, "from anomalous conditions within the British Empire in regard to international relations," General memorandum no. 2, Borden papers, OCA 198,81565, National Archives of Canada, Ottawa.

54. See Walworth, *America's Moment: 1918,* pp. 100 and n. 32.

55. Auchincloss diary, January 13 and 14, 1919.

56. Except New Zealand, which was to have only one delegate, and Newfoundland, whose representative was to be included in the British delegation and thus, like the delegates of India and the dominions, could be included in the representation of the British Empire by use of the panel system, *F.R., P.P.C.,* vol. 3, p. 548. This was a provision of great constitutional significance within the empire.

present government weakened. The president carried his case, and after the council agreed to allow Brazil three delegates it decided to award the same number to Belgium and Serbia. A Brazilian delegation arrived at Paris early in January, and in April its head, Pessôa, was elected president of Brazil.

In the case of another government that had American sympathy, that of China, Wilson spoke of "its delicate situation in respect of Japan"[57] and asked for two seats for its delegates.[58] In the end thirty-two states or dominions were approved as members of the Peace Conference, only fourteen of which were active belligerents. The question of the representation of Russia, left open on January 13, was one that the conference was never able to solve.

It seemed to the leaders of the Allies that the five large nations that had altogether some 12 million men under arms should take political responsibility commensurate with their power. They desired to give the small countries a sense of participation; and at the same time the members of the Supreme Council refused to submit matters that touched vital interests of their own nations to the scrutiny of delegates of lesser states. Wilson, remarking that he did not see how one could tell in advance what questions would interest small powers, suggested that the nonbelligerent nations be represented in the proceedings only when they were called in.[59] Obviously an executive council that included delegates of all the states represented in the conference would be a farce. Wilson concurred in the decision of the Supreme Council to control the proceedings of the plenary sessions of the Peace Conference, of which the first convened on January 18. Colonel House, assured of Clemenceau's collaboration in matters of the first importance, was content that illness made it unwise for him to attend this dramatic but perfunctory event.[60]

The question of a second extension of the German armistice, which was to expire on January 17, claimed the attention of the Supreme Council of Ten in its first sessions. In the meeting on the twelfth the president asked that the original terms of the armistice be read. He then suggested that they should agree among themselves precisely what was prescribed and that such precision, so arrived at, would suffice. At this point the generals and admirals withdrew from this initial conference, and with their withdrawal the Supreme War Council became the Supreme Council of the Peace Conference—at first composed of ten members. The next day it was decided that financial counselors, including Americans, would be present at the meeting to be held with Germans at Trier on January 16 to renew the armistice.[61]

---

57. See below, pp. 73 ff.

58. French procès-verbal of the meeting of the Supreme Council on January 12, entry following the last remark by Pinchon that is recorded in *F.R., P.P.C.*, vol. 3, p. 502.

59. French procès-verbal record of the discussion that is reported in *F.R., P.P.C.*, vol. 3, p. 535. See Marston, pp. 71–74.

60. *I.P.*, VI, p. 273. House said to his doctor: "Even if I hadn't been ill I would have welcomed any excuse to have escaped. This is not where I do my work and, of course, the meeting today is nothing but bunk," Dr. Lamb's notes, Princeton University Library.

61. Pershing wrote to House and also to Foch on January 13 in protest against French efforts to control the action of the Permanent Inter-Allied Armistice Commission through subcommittees having French chairmen, Pershing to House, January 13, enclosing telegram from General Barnum of January 11, 1919, Y.H.C.

Other technical experts were to consider and advise upon the use of German ships for feeding the enemy.[62]

In the meeting on January 13 Louis Klotz, the French minister of finance, argued that the enemy's failure to honor the conditions of the armistice required the imposition of new financial exactions.[63] During the reading Wilson appeared to be irritated, and rose and stood behind the chair of Clemenceau's interpreter.[64] He had been warned by House that the French government had asserted that Marshal Foch had a right to make future changes in the terms of the armistice without the assent of the United States.[65] Now the president suggested that they must not act in haste, but instead might grant an extension of the armistice for eight days while at the same time issuing a solemn warning. As to the degree to which they were all bound by the prearmistice agreement that House had concluded, there was no discussion.[66]

After the meeting on the thirteenth Bernard M. Baruch, the American economic adviser who acted as go-between in place of the ailing Colonel House, sought out Louis Loucheur, the French minister of munitions. Baruch told him that the president had been hurt by Klotz's speech because it seemed to suggest that Wilson was thought to favor the Germans too much when actually he intended only to be just. Loucheur replied that one must understand the point of view of the French, who also stood for justice but were not on that account simpletons. Baruch then undertook to soothe the president, and Loucheur was to talk with Clemenceau.[67] According to Baruch's biographer, he, like House, often stayed away from meetings and depended on other men to relieve himself of tedious drudgery while volunteering advice and services that brought him close to the president.[68]

It was not until December 18 that the president had acted upon a proposal, made by House two months earlier, for the inclusion of a small body of economic counselors in the peace delegation. Those who were already at Paris addressed a memorandum to Wilson on December 31, asking for a ruling as to their "exact status" in relation to the American commission.[69] Early in January, at Wilson's request,

The desire of American advisers to take the negotiations for renewal of the armistice out of the hands of Marshal Foch and to entrust this matter to civilians experienced in economic affairs was expressed in an undated memorandum entitled "Proposals to be Submitted to the Supreme War Council by the President of the U.S.A." and a "Memorandum for the President," January 14, 1919, N.A., R.G. 256, 185,001 / 6.

62. See below, p. 88.

63. See below, p. 87.

64. Louis Loucheur's handwritten notes, Loucheur Papers, Hoover Institution, Palo Alto.

65. See below, p. 49 and Walworth, *America's Moment: 1918,* p. 107. House was informed of the Klotz proposals in a memo of January 10, 1919, from Norman H. Davis, N.A., R.G., 256, 185.001 / 6. Auchincloss diary, January 11, 1919.

66. See Walworth, *America's Moment: 1918,* p. 73. Temperley has pointed out that the Allies did not admit the binding character of the prearmistice agreement until they replied on June 16 to German protests against the proposed peace terms. According to this English historian, the Allies were puzzled by the "infraction" of the agreement by Wilson's principles and by the "new-fangled diplomacy." Temperley pointed out certain inconsistencies in Wilson's Fourteen Points. See *A History of the Peace Conference at Paris,* vol. 1, pp. 275–277; vol. 2, pp. 366–367, 381–384, 388–393; vol. 6, pp. 539–540.

67. Loucheur, *Carnets Secrets 1908–1932,* p. 70.

68. Jordan A. Schwartz, *The Speculator,* pp. 118 ff., 121.

69. Memo in Wilson papers; Auchincloss diary, January 3, 1919. When Bernard M. Baruch and Vance McCormick arrived in January to join Herbert C. Hoover and Edward N. Hurley in the group, Wilson had four members of his war cabinet at his side.

Baruch had come over from Washington, where his War Industries Board closed its doors, and with him came Vance McCormick, chairman of the Democratic National Committee and of the War Trade Board. They lodged away from the Crillon, at the Ritz; and Baruch, who before leaving Washington had regaled newsmen at a sumptuous champagne party, entertained at Paris on a scale that enhanced his influence. According to his biographer, his "experience, loyalty and judgment" were of value to the president, who was glad to use Baruch's purse to meet extraordinary expenses that were imposed upon the Wilsons by official duties.[70]

The advisers, desiring better information about the day-to-day negotiations and the tactics of their chief, and noting that the entire British delegation met almost daily with the prime minister, decided to ask House whether they could not confer frequently with the entire American delegation. This was not arranged, however, although their own group met more or less regularly, with Wilson usually absent and House presiding. Auchincloss, feeling that House was out of touch with the men of affairs, complained about the "great embarrassment" caused when the Treasury and the war boards at Washington sent messages to their representatives through the embassy at Paris instead of directly to the American commission.[71]

Wilson's vagueness in delegating responsibility for economic intelligence, and a resulting conflict of authorities,[72] was overcome to some degree when John Foster Dulles, the nephew of Mrs. Lansing, asserted himself. Sent to Paris to represent Edwin F. Gay, chief of the Central Bureau of Research and Statistics, he quickly reached an uneasy accommodation with Professor Allyn Young of the Inquiry despite what he described as "a very distinct atmosphere of hostility" on the part of Young.

Dulles was appalled by the waste of time in discursive talk and the failure to deal systematically with proposals that the European delegates were putting forward for the control of trade after the war. On January 29 he reported to Gay that he had taken upon himself executive responsibility for promoting liaison between the advisers and those making decisions, and that relations between his group and the Inquiry were satisfactory.[73]

70. Schwartz, pp. 110–113, 119. James Grant, *Bernard M. Baruch,* pp. 182–183, 188–189.

71. Polk from Auchincloss, January 8, 1919, Auchincloss diary.

72. See Walworth, *America's Moment: 1918,* pp. 251–252.

73. Dulles thought that "Uncle Bert" Lansing should become aggressive and should employ someone like Auchincloss "to hustle around and pick up gossip" and extend Lansing's "sphere of influence," Dulles to Gay, January 24 and 29, 1919, J. F. Dulles papers II, correspondence, 1919, Princeton University Library.

Wilson, upon request, signed an executive order defining the status of the Central Bureau of Statistics, S. Phenix to Dulles, January 4 and 20, 1919, Gay papers, box 1, Hoover Institution Archives. Dulles put Gay's men at the service of the ACTNP on condition that he serve informally in liaison between Young's office and the president's economic advisers. Dulles reported to Washington that Young had agreed that with a few exceptions all cables to America would be sent through Dulles, Dulles to Phenix, January 29, 1919, J. F. Dulles papers.

"Dulles quite consciously sought to create a position of potential for himself while negotiating a settlement of the interagency rivalries." (*Cf.* below, p. 172.) As the recognized channel of communication with Gay, he became valuable to the American representatives on the Commission of the Reparation of Damages of the Peace Conference, and he served as these men's legal adviser, Ronald W. Pruessen, *John Foster Dulles,* pp. 30–31. In February Gay was warned by others of his men that too much dependence should not be placed upon Dulles, who was said to be "playing his own game," James A. Field to Gay, February 17, 1919, Dr. Walter S. Tower to Gay, February 21, 1919; Gay papers, box 1, Hoover Institution Archives.

The Peace Conference of 1919 was confronted by a vast quantity of executive work that was not present at the Congress of Vienna a century earlier. Because of the urgency of preserving civil order in the society that had grown out of the industrial revolution, economic provisions and settlements could not be separated from the traditional concerns of diplomacy.[74] Among the American delegates were strong and resourceful men with little or no experience in diplomacy who during the war had been accustomed to grapple with unprecedented crises that demanded intelligent consultation, quick decisions, and precise direction. Under the chief whom they had learned to trust and to respect at Washington, they expected to play, in coping with the new dimensions of peacemaking at Paris, the influential role into which they were thrust by the economic position of their nation. Yet, by the end of January, Wilson was so preoccupied by the meetings of the Peace Conference that Dulles wrote that it was "practically impossible for anyone to get to see him or for him to give time to purely American conferences."[75]

While the American delegation of more than a thousand men, moved here by impulses to serve and there by personal ambitions,[76] attempted to work out a *modus vivendi* in the Crillon, the political chiefs who had led the great powers to victory, meeting for the first time on a "summit," came to agreement on essential matters of organization and procedure for the Peace Conference. They followed the pattern that prevailed in the national democracies. There was an executive council, a secretariat, expert commissions, and a body of delegates who met in plenary sessions. In the Supreme Council of Ten—two months later to be reduced at times to five, to four, and to three—the leaders were to assume direct responsibility for many of the terms of the peace, and even to oversee the drafting of certain articles of the treaties. As a result of faulty liaison with the diplomats and the various technical advisers, the chiefs who negotiated at the top level were to be forced at times into the role of diplomats, and even into that of technicians. For such functions they were not well qualified, and it was not surprising that confusion and delay resulted. Their experience as political practitioners in democracies, however, gave them a unique capacity to keep their footing in the political battles that were to be fought in the course of producing a treaty of peace that their several national legislatures might be expected to accept.

C. K. Leith, professor of geology at the University of Wisconsin, who served several of the war bureaus at Washington and who accompanied Dulles to France, recorded that work routed through the State Department and its "pulchritudinous youths" sometimes suffered the same paralysis that had been noted in Washington. Paying tribute to the broad vision and good judgment of Young and deploring the lack of any systematic assignment of men to duties, Leith wrote: "Each man was left to work out his own salvation," "Notes on the Paris Peace Conference," Gay papers, box 1.

74. Arno J. Mayer, *Politics and Diplomacy of Peacemaking*, p. 11.

75. Dulles to Gay, January 29, 1919, Gay papers, box 5.

76. Baruch's biographer writes of "Americans with axes to grind" and "parasites and grafters" trying to attach themselves to the peace delegation, Schwartz, p. 112.

2

The Voices of the People

The leaders of the major powers, meeting in closed sessions and improvising procedures for the essential business of negotiating a treaty of peace, soon found themselves importuned by advocates of social causes. Voices that heretofore had not been heard in meetings of diplomats were being raised. The champions of laborers spoke out for provisions for protection against inhumane conditions of work; organizations of women presented petitions; spokesmen for the black and yellow races sought recognition of equality with the white. Moreover, journalists, many of whom sympathized with some of the various causes, were not content to serve merely as publicizers of official bulletins. United in protest against the inhumanity of war and in insistence on respect for human rights, partisans of the new movements brought their pleas to the doors of the Peace Conference. They challenged the professional diplomats by serving notice that they would not be satisfied with a mere reconstruction of an old social fabric that they thought beyond mending.

The response of some of the American peacemakers to the rising voices of unrest was sympathetic. American liberals, who were not revolutionaries, believed that the exercise of human reason might mitigate the curses of poverty, disease, and war.[1] Woodrow Wilson had been responsive to the new social forces. It was to be expected, then, that the Americans at Paris would give attention to the spokesmen of labor who aspired to have a share in the shaping of an ideal peace. They were disposed, too, to listen carefully to pleaders for the rights of women and for recognition of equality of the races; and they sympathized with the yearning of the common man for reliable news of the proceedings of the Peace Conference.

The promise of full publicity was reassuring to those who remembered that the people of England and France had been kept in ignorance of diplomatic commitments that had brought them into the war in 1914. Actually there were many who believed that the fatal confrontation of alliances would not have occurred if the peoples had not been committed secretly to international obligations which, had they been made public, might have been rejected by the parliaments, or at least might have forestalled acts of aggression. Newsmen advocated a literal application of the first of Wilson's Fourteen Points—"open covenants of peace, openly arrived at"—not only as a preventive of new secret treaties, but as a guarantee of their right to be present during all negotiations and to tell the people what was happening from day to day. Believing that they had a champion in the president of the United States, they were disappointed when he forbade them to enter Germany or Russia, the regions that most excited their curiosity.[2]

However, censorship of mail and cables could no longer be justified by the war

---

1. See Christopher Lasch, *The American Liberals and the Russian Revolution*, pp. vi–xvi.
2. William Allen White, *Autobiography*, p. 550. Oswald Garrison Villard, *The Fighting Years*, p. 397.

emergency. House, acting for the president, had taken up the question with the British and French governments immediately after the armistice of November 1918, and they had agreed to stop the practice, although commercial communications were still to be subject to control by the authorities that enforced the blockade of the enemy. When the postmaster general, who had controlled American communications as a war measure, found that the needs of the State and War Departments required that he operate the transatlantic cables, he assured the news associations that they would be given facilities in transmitting dispatches during the peace conference. Nevertheless, the press and the congressional opposition attacked the administration vehemently.

Senators imagined a conspiracy to muzzle the press, and they sought the scalp of George Creel, chief of the Committee on Public Information (CPI).[3] However, the president, assuring Creel that the criticism of the senators was too contemptible to be worthy of notice, agreed to take him overseas provided he kept the CPI out of the peace negotiations. Its Paris office was closed on February 7.[4]

When Creel announced that the Peace Conference would be wide open to the press and any accredited correspondent could obtain a passport to Paris, some three score American newsmen took him at his word. Sailing December 1 from New York in an old transport provided by the government, they found little to do and much to complain about: lice-infested quarters, lack of transport ashore, and clogged cables. They formed an association, choosing Herbert Bayard Swope of the *New York World* as the president.[5] Considering themselves "ambassadors of public opinion," they demanded that the people be fully informed of the work of the American Commission to Negotiate Peace.

Swarming about the periphery of the Peace Conference and hungry for news that would satisfy their employers and their readers, more than a hundred American correspondents functioned in Paris, capable of exerting a powerful influence on the public opinion on which the peace commissioners depended for their political mandate. Young men who were at the beginning of distinguished careers, unawed by the tradition that had held an earlier generation at arm's length from public policy in the making, were asserting a quasi-professional prerogative to enter into the confidence of the peace delegates.

Wilson, looking forward to a peace conference that would make public as much of its work as possible, had explained to the secretary of state as early as June 1918 that in championing open diplomacy he meant "not that there should be no private discussions of delicate matters, but that no secret agreements should be entered into,

3. Creel, who had little knowledge and less appreciation of the traditions of European diplomacy, was at loggerheads with the Department of State as a result of activities of CPI propagandists abroad that were beyond the control of the department. See Inga Floto, *Colonel House in Paris*, p. 291, nn. 79 and 81. The committee drew strength from Wilson's appreciation of Creel's services during the war and from the president's determination to keep the conduct of propaganda in his own hands.

4. On the *George Washington* Creel antagonized the scholars of the Inquiry, boasting loudly that he was the president's "confidential man." Seymour to the author. Shotwell interview, Columbia O.H.R.O., p. 73. Seymour, *Letters from the Paris Peace Conference*, p. 16. E. L. Bernays, *Biography of an Idea* (New York, 1965), pp. 161–167.

5. Ralph Hayes to N. D. Baker, December 24, 1918, N. D. Baker papers, L.C. E. J. Kahn, Jr., *The World of Swope*, pp. 213–214. Ray Stannard Baker, *Woodrow Wilson and World Settlement*, vol. 1, pp. 120, 144 (hereinafter designated as "Baker").

and that all international relations, when fixed, should be open, above board, and explicit.''[6] The president was devoted to the principle of freedom of the press. ''It implies the difference between the darkness of Russia and the light of England and America,''[7] he had written to a college friend at the age of twenty-four. In his political campaigns he had taken pains to entertain the newsmen, and he was the first president to hold press conferences in the White House. In 1915, however, after war broke out in Europe, he had given them up.

Before leaving for Paris, the president was told by Sir William Wiseman that a full reporting of the deliberations of the peace conference from day to day would prove to be impossible; and Wilson replied: ''We should make it as public as possible. . . . I am deeply committed to the policy of open diplomacy.''[8] Aboard ship he said: ''I favor a small council composed of the premiers of England, France, Italy and myself, which would examine and collate the details of the proposed treaty . . . and later submit these propositions to a conference of all the belligerent powers. . . . This would involve secret conferences, exactly as questions are discussed by the foreign relations committee [of the Senate]. If we announced partial results, or one decision at a time, it might easily result in bloodshed. . . . When we reach real decisions everything must be made known to the world.''[9] He conceived of the Supreme Council as a kind of world cabinet in which the members would merely exchange views. Unfortunately the president did not make this explanation to the public.

After Wilson reached Paris, Colonel House spoke to him about the attitude of the American press, and instructions went to Joseph P. Tumulty, the vigilant secretary who had remained at Washington: ''It will be the policy of the [peace] commissioners to be very frank with the newspapermen and to give them as much information as is practicable, trusting to their discretion in not publishing any information that would be indiscreet in any way.'' Tumulty was asked to keep a close lookout on the press, to send a precise report of its behavior, and to make any suggestions that might be helpful in dealing with the newsmen at the Peace Conference.[10] There was grave danger of distorted reporting of the processes of negotiation not only by American journalists who were personally disgruntled, but by those who represented newspapers in sympathy with political opponents of the president.[11]

Efforts were made by friends of Wilson as well as by his political enemies to

6. Wilson to Lansing, June 12, 1918, quoted in Baker, vol. 1, p. 46.

7. Wilson to Bridges, August 22, 1881, Meyer Collection, L.C.

8. Wilton B. Fowler, *British-American Relations, 1917–1918,* p. 290. Walworth, *America's Moment: 1918,* p. 58.

9. Swem ms., Princeton University Library.

10. Polk for Tumulty from Auchincloss, December 19, 1918, Tumulty papers, box 4. *F.R., P.P.C.,* vol. 1, pp. 214–215.

11. *F.R., P.P.C.,* vol. 1, pp. 215–216. Letters, Wade Chance to Balfour, December 4 and 22, 1918, Balfour to Chance, December 17, 1918. A Foreign Office minute of December 25, initialed by Balfour, said the latter would try to see Chance on December 28, while Wilson was at London, P.R.O., FO/ 800/211. Cable, Murray to Wiseman, December 13, 1918, Wiseman papers. ''Confidential Memorandum,'' December 17, 1918, Wiseman papers, Y.H.C. Ambassador Thomas Nelson Page recorded that articles from the anti-Wilson press in the United States ''were reproduced again and again in the Italian press and, indeed, in the press of Paris and to some extent in London also,'' *Italy and the World War,* p. 398. McCormick described the Paris edition of the *New York Herald* as ''a rotten anti-Wilson sheet,'' intent upon embarrassing the president, diary, April 21, 1919.

influence the picture given to the American people by the press.[12] The president himself, however, continued to depend on his eloquence in appealing to the public and to those who shaped its thinking. In addition to addresses made during visits to England and Italy, he spoke in Paris at the city hall, at the Sorbonne, and in the Senate. When he consented to go to a French hospital and comfort the wounded poilus, he compensated in some degree, in French opinion, for his refusal to visit the battlefields and see the devastation wrought by the German invasion.

Wilson and House decided that the members of the American peace commission, except the president, would meet the newsmen daily for confidential talks.[13] They were relieved of much annoyance when they put responsibility for contacts with the press on the shoulders of Ray Stannard Baker, who was well known as an essayist and liberal journalist. Acting as a political intelligence agent in Europe during the closing months of the war, Baker had urged that the president "often blow upon the embers of liberalism and democracy."[14] After he was assured by the president that he would be admitted completely into the confidence of the American peace commission, he agreed to undertake what he considered a "terrific task."[15] Aware of the insatiability of good newsmen, he insisted that he be thoroughly briefed on everything that happened. He explained to the American correspondents that he would be absolutely open with them, give them untinted facts, and, when there was information that he could not pass along, tell them so frankly.[16] He won their confidence and cooperation.

In a building only a few steps from the Hôtel Crillon, Baker opened a bureau to serve the press. The newsmen, however, continued to agitate against exclusion from the sessions of the Peace Conference. Since news was scarce, and very few journalists had enough knowledge of Europe to attempt an analysis or to speculate on a solution of matters awaiting consideration,[17] experts of the Inquiry undertook to prepare bulletins on matters of general interest without any commitment in respect of national policy. These releases were welcomed and used. Secretary Lansing strongly opposed this procedure, fearing that it might complicate negotiations at the peace table; but the president gave his approval.[18]

Wilson could not be persuaded to talk regularly with the American newsmen. His confidence was betrayed in respect of a trivial matter, and he gave few inter-

12. Tumulty to Grayson, three cables of December 16, 1918; Grayson to Tumulty, December 21, 1918, Wilson papers.

13. House diary, December 18, 1918. Bliss diary, December 18, 1918, Bliss papers, box 65, L.C.

14. R. S. Baker (London) to Polk, May 28, 1918, Y.H.C.

15. Robert C. Bannister, Jr., *Ray Stannard Baker* (New Haven, 1966), pp. 177–183.

16. White, p. 550. Baker, vol. 1, pp. 127–129. Steed, *Through Thirty Years,* vol. 2, p. 167. It seemed to Steed of the *Times,* in retrospect, that "the American press was best treated."

17. Arthur Willert to his wife, January 18, 1919, Willert papers, Y.H.C. It seemed to the historian of the British Foreign Office that the American newsmen were "incredibly ignorant," James Headlam-Morley diary, January 19, 1919, in the possession of Agnes Headlam-Morley.

18. Baker, *American Chronicle,* pp. 374–377. Mezes felt that it was hazardous to give information bulletins to newsmen. "In cabling this news," he wrote to Grew, "the pressmen will inevitably interlard it with discussions and statements of policy which some of them will at times attribute to the plenipotentiaries, entailing embarrassment and calling for denials or more serious action. It is evidently not for this section to decide whether that risk is to be assumed," memo, Mezes to Grew, January 17, 1919, Y.H.C. *F.R., P.P.C.,* vol. 1, pp. 219–220.

views to journalists.[19] Baker urged him to make common cause with them and to enlist them in his crusade. When he demurred, Baker found it exceedingly difficult to satisfy the persistent demands of the correspondents for items about the president's personal activities.[20]

The hunger for news was not appeased when the Supreme War Council came together on January 12 for preliminary discussions. No representatives of the press were admitted. At the end of the session Wilson raised the question of a press release, and it was decided to issue only a five-line communiqué. However, the next day a bundle of the minutes of the meeting lay on the reception desk of the Majestic Hotel, where the British delegation lodged and where any passing journalist might pick them up.[21] Apparently the American correspondents did not get wind of this. Thoroughly exasperated, bewildered by false rumors, and indignant when French newspapers told the inside story,. which had been denied to them, they met in the Press Bureau and drew up a formal protest to the president, citing the first of his Fourteen Points. Baker transmitted the protest to Wilson with the explanation that British newsmen were taking a similar step, and that as for the French, their delegates had friends to whom they passed on news of the conference no matter what the rules were.[22]

Some five hundred reporters from many nations were at work in Paris. "The newspaper correspondents," Lippmann wrote, "struggling with the elusive and all-pervading chaos, were squeezed between the appetite of their readers for news and the desire of the men with whom the decisions rested not to throw unconcluded negotiations 'into the cyclone of distortion' that whirled about the conferees."[23] A kind of informal international congress of the press developed, and French hospitality provided a club in a hotel on the Champs Élysées. The journalists were entertained with dinners, shows, and receptions for prominent men. Able to send stories overnight to the far side of the globe, they formed a nerve center of opinion such as had been unknown to the international conferences of the nineteenth century. The press was in a position to make its power felt.

Discussion of press relations by the Supreme Council led to a middle course. In the closed sessions of this body the publicity policies of the various governments were explained with a frankness and precision that would not have been possible in a public meeting. French officials feared that the enemy would make capital of any indiscretion, and they, like the British and Wilson, foresaw time-consuming oratory for political effect at home if the meetings were open to the public.[24]

Almost immediately leakages from the proceedings appeared in the French press.

19. White, p. 566.

20. Baker, vol. 1, p. 151.

21. Twenty-five-page paper on the Paris Peace Conference of 1919 by Sir Charles Webster, p. 16, Webster papers, British Library of Political and Economic Science, London School of Economics and Political Science.

22. Baker to Grayson, January 14, 1919, Wilson papers. In a talk with the writer on November 11, 1959, André Géraud ("Pertinax") confirmed Baker's description of French practice. G. Bernard Noble, *Policies and Opinions at Paris, 1919*, pp. 304–360.

23. Walter Lippmann, "The Peace Conference," *Yale Review* 8, no. 4 (July 1919):711.

24. Benham diary letter, January 29, 1919. Tardieu, *The Truth about the Treaty*, pp. 110–111. *F.R., P.P.C.*, vol. 3, pp. 551, 569. Baker, vol. 1, p. 143.

Lloyd George protested vigorously, and on January 15 the Supreme Council decided that the press should receive only bulletins given out by the official secretariat of the Peace Conference. The next day the formal protest of the American journalists against secrecy was introduced in the council by the president. He remarked that he doubted whether anything less than complete publicity would satisfy his people; for when the public learned that the delegates had reached agreement, it would want to know by what processes. Wilson inquired whether the plenary sessions were to be public. Informed that the first one, on January 18, would not be, he suggested in a quiet, tentative way, that full publicity be permitted. He felt that nothing of an embarrassing nature would be discussed, and he preferred open and accurate reporting by eyewitnesses to "leakages" that might lead to false interpretations. At first several of the Europeans objected; but they yielded when Lloyd George accepted the president's view. It was decided to admit newsmen to the first general gathering, and this set a precedent that prevailed for the most part thereafter, insofar as the plenary sessions were concerned.

Wilson, wishing to give the newsmen a sense of participation in the decisions of the conference, departed radically from diplomatic tradition. He suggested that the correspondents be told of the predicament of the Supreme Council and of its desire to keep the public as fully informed as possible, and that they be asked for suggestions. When the council agreed to this, hundreds of newsmen from many nations were brought together at the Inter-Allied Press Club. The Americans still held out for complete publicity for everything; but the British, more experienced and more conservative, were not sure that this was either wise or possible. Ray Stannard Baker was confident that veteran American journalists could be trusted to act responsibly if they knew they were being treated frankly. Feeling that he was not free to promise them "real frankness" because of what he conceived to be a wicked conspiracy of Allied leaders to divide the spoils of war, Baker reported to his chief that the results of the meeting at the Press Club were not satisfactory. The American newsmen seemed unappreciative both of the compelling necessities of the situation and of the president's concern for their interests. They joined with the press of the Allied nations in demanding a complete communiqué and full summaries of each day's proceedings of the Supreme Council. They also sought free access to the delegates.[25]

In response to resolutions presented by a "special committee" of Allied and American newsmen, Clemenceau moved that the Supreme Council supplement its oral appeal to the press by a general communiqué. Lloyd George brought in a draft that compared the conversations of the council, acting as a cabinet for the world, with the secret deliberations of national cabinets. Wilson then added lines that made it clear that except "upon necessary occasions," the press would be admitted to the plenary sessions.[26] Accordingly, newsmen attended the formal meeting that opened the Peace Conference on January 18, with the result that the proceedings were relatively colorless and, therefore, disappointing to them. On January 21 Wilson

25. Baker, vol. 1, pp 145–152; vol. 3, pp. 50–52.
26. *F.R., P.P.C.,* vol. 3, pp. 543–545, 550–553, 568, 576, 578–580, 585–588, 595–599, 609–611. The statement on publicity released on January 17 is in Baker, vol. 3, pp. 47–49. A draft corrected by Wilson is in the Wilson papers, microfilm, p. 7084.

cabled to Tumulty: "The issue of publicity is being obscured, not cleared, by the newspaper men and we have won for the press all that is possible or wise to win, i.e., complete publicity for the real conference. Publicity for the conversations I am holding with the small group of the great powers would invariably break up the whole thing, whereas the prospects for agreement are now, I should say, very good indeed."[27]

House, acutely aware of the importance of favorable publicity, worked to turn the power of the press to the advantage of the president.[28] For news the American correspondents looked to House more than to the other commissioners.[29] They knew that he was a mainspring of action, and closest to the president. Although seldom saying much in the news conferences of the commissioners, he would speak persuasively when alone with journalists. He exhausted his energy in politely fending off friends and enemies of the president and importunate pleaders of national and other causes. He said that he was accustomed to doing this sort of thing, that he had no nerves and nothing ruffled him. "They can't tire me out, that's sure," he declared. But on January 11 a kidney stone forced him to bed.[30] The private telephone wire from Wilson's residence was extended at once into the colonel's bedroom, and the president came almost daily to consult with him. Wiseman found him, on January 17, "lying in bed unshaven," weak in voice, looking bad, but very cheerful and "as usual perfectly delightful." "Criticism of the president on the usual lines, and of the commission generally," Wiseman recorded after luncheon with George W. Wickersham of the *New York Tribune,* "but I notice all seem to have a good word for House."[31] When House was too ill to see them, the newsmen had to depend on the other commissioners. The resulting conferences were, in the words of one journalist, "rather dismal affairs."[32] The correspondents soon found that they could get more information from the British delegates than from the Americans, and espe-

27. Cable in Tumulty papers.
28. In his diary House had written on July 26, 1917: "The thought that I am trying to convey to publicists is that we can build up throughout the world a public opinion which will influence nations just as individuals are now influenced by their respective communities. When this is done, we will have the road toward international peace." House went driving with Walter Lippmann, who was no longer attached to the American commission. (See Walworth, p. 259.) He lunched with Melville Stone, the head of the Associated Press, and arranged for him to be received by Wilson against the president's personal inclination, House diary, December 26, 1918. Also a statement by W. S. Rogers to R. H. Nolte, January 2, 1962, given by John M. Blum to the author. House welcomed Senator Owen and tried to brief him so that the senator could tell his colleagues at Washington what mischief they had wrought. He kept in touch with British and French journalists as well as with the Americans, and learned that certain French officials were spreading anti-Wilson propaganda, Auchincloss diary, January 23, 25, and 31, 1919. "My days recently," House wrote in his diary on January 4, "have been largely taken up in trying to formulate and direct public opinion in England, France, Italy, and the United States. I praise, condemn, and threaten in turn as seems best."
29. White, p. 415. Baker found the colonel's faith in American purposes "contagious and compelling" and recorded in his journal that House was "the small knot-hole through which must pass many great events, incomparably the most influential of the American commissionioners," and "the big center," Baker, journal, December 16, 18, and 23, 1918.
30. Thompson, *The Peace Conference Day by Day,* p. 29. Baker, *American Chronicle,* p. 379. "House became ill with what turned out to be a stone in the kidney. . . . He was really quite miserable after the pain let up. Couldn't take much to eat and had nausea," notes, Dr. Albert Lamb, Princeton University Library.
31. Wiseman diary, January 17, 1919; Auchincloss diary, January 11, 13, and 14, 1919, Y.H.C.
32. White, p. 566.

cially from Lord Robert Cecil, whose intelligence and veracity they learned to respect.

All through the Peace Conference some of the American newsmen were restive, even rebellious. They got no sensational stories from the bulletins that reported agreements. For their purposes a conference would be most newsworthy when it broke down or its participants quarreled. Aware of the privileges that the American Constitution conferred, they sometimes abused them. Their manners did not always conform with the usage of professional diplomats. Few of their number had any real understanding of the responsibility of the plenipotentiaries. The behavior of the press sometimes complicated the task of those at Paris who were charged with the formulation and carrying out of American policy.[33]

Later, when the meetings of the leaders of the democracies became even more shielded from the public, criticism of their secrecy became more widespread, not only among journalists but among the delegates of small powers and even those of the great powers. The excessive expectations aroused in undiscerning minds by the Wilsonian promise of "open convenants . . . openly arrived at" were to prove illusive.

In maintaining the liaison with public opinion that had become so important in the diplomacy of the democracies, the peacemakers of 1919 found it necessary not only to cope with the aggressive assertions of the rights of the press, but at the same time to deal with the aspirations of laborers and the politics of their leaders.

One of the humane causes that a league of nations was expected to further was the improvement of conditions under which men worked. The parties of the Left, aware that Wilson had championed American legislation to tax large incomes and to protect labor, thought of him as a useful ally in their own striving for political power. In the eyes of French and Italian workers and of their oracles, Wilsonism was a religion and its founder crowned by a mystic halo.[34] As the middle class allowed their concern for their own interests to exceed their wartime devotion to Wilson's ideals, he became the more dependent on the fervent support that came, according to Lippmann, from "a section of the working class somewhere about the left centre."[35]

The power of labor had contributed much to the latent political force that had made it possible for Colonel House to impose the American program upon the prearmistice negotiators.[36] He, therefore, thought it very important to keep in touch with responsible labor leaders. At the same time he perceived that Wilson, in deal-

33. "This madadjustment of the American newspaper men at the Paris Conference . . . raises a point which has not been sufficiently considered in the history of democratic diplomacy," Shotwell, *At the Paris Peace Conference,* p. 46. Auchincloss wrote his opinion of each of the most important journalists, American and English, in his diary, April 16, 1919. "I knew at the start that the press would be the most dangerous element which we should have to handle," Joseph C. Grew, *Turbulent Era,* vol. 1, p. 366.

34. Page, p. 387. Pierre Miquel, *La Paix de Versailles et l' opinion publique française,* pp. 44, 62 ff., 89 ff. See Walworth, p. 138.

35. Lippmann, 720.

36. Wiseman to Murray, August 30, 1918, Murray to Wiseman, September 9 and October 1, 1918, Wiseman papers, Y.H.C.

ing with the Allied governments, might be embarrassed by demonstrations of foreign workers in behalf of his program.[37]

The president felt pressure at Washington from organized labor for special representation at Paris. The secretary of the American Federation of Labor (AFL) which was unaccustomed to taking a responsible part in government, sought a place of prominence in the councils of the world. In response to a letter from him Wilson wrote on November 22, 1918:

Many special bodies and interests of our complex nation have felt, and felt very naturally, a desire to have special spokesmen among the peace delegates. I must say, however, that my own feeling is that the peace delegates should represent no portion of our people in particular, but the country as a whole, and that it was unwise to make any selection on the ground that the men selected represented a particular group of interest, for after all . . . no proper representative of the country could fail to have in mind the great and all-pervasive interest of labor or of any other great body of humanity.[38]

After reaching Paris the president discussed the matter with House. "He and I realize," House recorded, "how necessary for the future conduct of all governments a liberal program is," Wilson wanted to do something at the Peace Conference—though he confessed that it would be irrelevant to the peacemaking—to limit the hours of labor throughout the world to eight a day. In his preliminary draft of a constitution for a league of nations covenant he included a supplementary clause binding members to seek to establish and maintain humane conditions of work.[39]

At the same time labor parties in the European democracies were seeking a place at the Peace Conference. Agitation in England had come to a climax at the end of November when the Labour party issued a manifesto demanding an international labor charter and economic cooperation. Meetings at Albert Hall resulted in turbulent demonstrations in favor of a league of nations, and there was talk of a general strike.

Labor leaders in Allied nations wished to convene independently of the peace conference and discuss matters on which they wanted the responsible statesmen of Europe to act. They planned to meet with leftists of the neutral countries of Europe in an attempt to revive the Second International, which before 1914 had striven to prevent war. Torn apart when national components responded to patriotic pressures during the war, its remnants now sought a part in making a Wilsonian peace.[40]

37. Receiving confidential reports on the views of British labor from W. H. Buckler, who was attached to the American embassy in London, House suggested that Ida Tarbell, a distinguished journalist who was *persona grata* to French intellectuals, come to France and keep in touch with the Left. Wilson persuaded Miss Tarbell to do this, House to Wilson, November 18, 1918, Wilson to House, November 20, 1918, Y.H.C. Arthur Henderson suggested Labour demonstrations in England in support of Wilson's doctrine, but Buckler told him this would embarrass Wilson in dealing with European governments, Buckler report, December 18, 1918, Y.H.C.

38. Wilson to Secretary Morrison, of the AFL, November 22, 1918, *F.R., P.P.C.*, vol. 1, p. 168.

39. House diary, December 16, 1918. "I thought that it could be done," House wrote. "I do not know just how. . . . It can be done by resolution, but that would not be binding." See Wilson's draft covenant of January 10, 1919, in Robert Lansing, *The Peace Negotiations*, pp. 293–294.

40. Arno J. Mayer, *Politics and Diplomacy of Peacemaking*, pp. 375 ff. Henry R. Winkler "The British Labour Party and the Paris Settlement," in *Some Pathways in Twentieth-Century History*, ed. Daniel R. Beaver (Detroit, 1969), pp. 118–120.

This delicate question had been discussed by the Allied statesmen at their meeting in London on December 3. They were not eager to admit political opponents to the peace table. To treat with the International would raise the question of its relation to the national authorities that were represented at Paris; and to invite leftists who might be in sympathy with Soviet Russia was to risk embarrassment when the Peace Conference came to discuss anti-Bolshevik measures and to deal with the unrest of labor in Germany. In the end it was decided only to put no obstacle in the way of labor, religious, or other conferences, provided they met in a neutral country.[41]

The British and French governments, favoring the creation of a new world organization to deal with labor relations and conditions of work, had formulated proposals to be put before the peace conference for the establishment of an international labor conference and for its composition and functions.[42] The British delegation at the Peace Conference included experts on labor, and one of the five peace commissioners was George N. Barnes, a conservative union man. Clemenceau, however, determined not to allow any labor conference to meet at Paris, refused to appoint a representative of labor to the French delegation.[43] The only Continental labor leader to serve as a plenipotentiary was Émile Vandervelde, a Belgian socialist.

Unlike the British, the Americans went to Paris with little preparation for dealing with labor as a factor in international relations. On the day after the armistice, however, the American Federation of Labor, apprehensive that European workers might be captured by communist doctrine, appointed five delegates to go to an international labor conference. One of them, Samuel Gompers, president of the AFL and of Dutch parentage and London birth, had traveled in the Allied countries during the last months of the war. His presence at labor meetings had helped the governments to combat pacifism and bolshevism,[44] and his return to Europe was being sought by the French government and by many in Great Britain who felt that he would give stability to the European labor movement.[45] Gompers was disposed to issue a call for a conference at Paris, where it could not be dominated by sympathizers with Germany or Soviet Russia. He wished to put the burden on the Allied governments for refusing to let it meet.

The president, though unwilling that Gompers be one of the five American peace commissioners, nevertheless informed him that his presence would be "of real service."[46] Wilson informed Lansing that the only wise, prudent, and expedient course

41. Notes of an Allied conversation in the cabinet room, December 3, 1918, P.R.O., Cab / 23 / 17. *I.P.*, vol. 4, p. 24. Miller to House, December 3, 1918, Y.H.C. Laughlin to the acting secretary of state, December 4, 1918, *F.R., P.P.C.*, vol. 2, pp. 409–412.

42. James T. Shotwell, ed., *The Origins of the International Labor Organization*, vol. 1, pp. 86–91.

43. In France "the socialist party became more revolutionary. Its members increased from 72,000 in 1914 to 133,000 in 1919. The Conféderation Générale du Travail had probably more than two million members. There were more than two thousand strikes in France in 1919," Jean-Baptiste Duroselle, *La Politique extérieure de la France de 1914 à 1945* (Paris: Les Cours de Sorbonne, n.d.), p. 143.

44. See Walworth, p. 16.

45. Samuel Gompers, *Seventy Years of Life and Labor*, vol. 2, pp. 475, 479–480. Lansing to Wilson, November 29, 1918, Wilson papers. Polk to Lansing, December 2, 1918, Y.H.C.

46. Wilson to Gompers, December 2, 1918, Wilson papers. Gompers hesitated to go abroad without assurance that the labor conference would be held at Paris and he would have a position of dignity, Gompers, vol. 2, p. 477. Polk diary, December 6, 1918, Y.H.C. Polk to Ammission, December 16, 1918, N.A., R.G. 59, 763.72119 / 3086a. Polk to Ammission, December 21, 1918; Wilson to Lansing,

was "to let these people hold their sessions when and where they will." He feared that in a neutral country their discussions would "certainly be dominated by dangerous radical elements."[47]

Gompers and the other men who were appointed by the American Federation of Labor sailed for England on January 8 and met at London with a committee of the Trades Union Congress. At Paris, Gompers engaged in talks with executives of the Confédération Générale du Travail and with Belgian representatives.

The president, who sympathized with moderate demands of laborers everywhere, welcomed the support that European workers gave to his peace program. At the same time he was frightened by the extravagant hopes that had been kindled in their hearts by his fervent advocacy of a new order in the postwar world.[48] He learned that the American labor leaders at Paris were "very irritated because they thought themselves ignored," and that Baruch had promised them an interview with the president.[49]

At length, on January 28, Gompers was received. He got the impression that his inclination to keep away from a revival of the Second International at Bern had the approval of Wilson. Despite urging to the contrary by liberals in the American delegation, he let it be known that he would not talk with Germans, or with socialists of any nationality. Fearful that the conference at Bern would "play the German game," he proposed instead an immediate inter-Allied gathering of trade-unionists at Paris.[50] Clemenceau vetoed this idea; but French labor men went to the Bern conference, vented their nation's hatred of Germany on the enemy's delegates there, and found in Wilsonism a convenient cause in which various factions could unite.

The possibility of using the Bern conference in promoting Wilson's work at Paris was perceived by William C. Bullitt. A liberal journalist who had joined the State Department and served as an export on bolshevism and European socialism, Bullitt was denounced by Gompers as a "faddist parlor socialist." Nevertheless, he apparently convinced House, by a memorandum submitted on January 27, that it was possible "to steer the conference at Bern" so that it would be "an enormous support to the president." Two days later he was appointed to act as an observer; and

December 24, 1918, Wilson papers. Lippmann noted that the Gompers's pride was easily wounded and that he had to be treated with "proper deference," Lippmann record, Columbia O.H.R.O. p. 94.

47. Wilson to Lansing, December 24, 1918, Wilson papers. *F.R., P.P.C.,* vol. 1, pp. 341–343, 539–541. The circumspection of American officials in dealing with this novel aspect of foreign relations resulted in an aura of secrecy, Lansing to Polk, December 18, 1918, N.A., R.G. 59, 033.1140 / 44. Gompers, vol. 2, p. 487.

According to a record of Sir William Wiseman, the State Department refused for a time to give passports to the AFL delegates because of "certain indiscretions by Gompers when last in Europe," "Confidential Memorandum," n.d., Wiseman papers.

48. Bullitt diary, January 10, 1919, Y.H.C. Shotwell ms., Columbia O.H.R.O.

After reading a bundle of labor and radical papers from England, Ray Stannard Baker wrote in his journal on December 27: "It is amazing to see what heartiness there is in the support of Wilson among all these groups." "The leaders of these movements are working in perfect accord and all of them regard Mr. Gompers without sympathy," memorandum, Bullitt to House, January 27, 1919.

49. Baruch to Wilson, January 20, 1919, Wilson papers.

50. Gompers, vol. 2, p. 474. Grayson diary, January 28, 1919. Hugh Wilson, *Diplomat between Wars* (New York, 1941), p. 73. A. Van der Slice, *International Labor Diplomacy and Peace, 1914–1919,* p. 332.

when he returned to Paris he reported that "the entire conference showed an almost pathetic confidence in President Wilson." He warned that unless a league of nations constitution made some provision for their representation, the leftist leaders would oppose the covenant.[51]

Actually, the Permanent Commission of the International, though without official contact with the sessions of the Peace Conference, exerted moral suasion through the press and by lobbying at Paris. Occasional parades and strikes gave emphasis to its representations. Later the commission criticized the economic terms of the Treaty of Versailles as well as territorial settlements deemed to savor of imperialism.

At British initiative it was announced in the first plenary session of the Peace Conference, on January 18, that international labor legislation would be third on the agenda. Thus, it suddenly became necessary for the American delegation to act quickly to arrive at a policy in respect of this matter.[52] They were ill prepared, however, to enter into discussions of the question. No plan had been developed that was comparable to a proposal on which the British representatives were united.[53] American newsmen were so unfamiliar with the international labor movement that they needed help in covering this subject. Baker, therefore, sought the aid of Professor Shotwell, who had at heart the interests of the working people of the world.[54]

Consideration of labor legislation came to a head in the Supreme Council on January 23. A proposal by Lloyd George that they appoint a commission elicited from Wilson a suggestion that it be made clear that the proposed labor organization would be brought under the aegis of a league of nations. Finally the council adopted a resolution that provided for a commission to "recommend the form of a permanent agency to continue such inquiry in cooperation with and under the direction of the League."

In accord with this provision, which was approved by the plenary session of the conference on January 25, a commission was created that included two representatives of each of the great powers and of Belgium, and three to be elected by the other powers attending the Peace Conference. During February and March this body held thirty-five meetings. Gompers was made chairman in order to satisfy his *amour-propre* and to strengthen the cause of nonpolitical unionism.[55] He found himself in the anomalous position of presiding over a body that was proposing to do the very thing that he refused to countenance—that is, to frame legislation to be brought before national parliaments.[56]

The aspirations of labor received support at Paris from lobbyists representing emancipated womanhood, who in addition pleaded special causes of their own.

51. Dispatch, Bullitt to House, February 5, 1919, Y.H.C. Mayer, pp. 405–406. Floto, pp. 106–107 and notes.

52. James T. Shotwell, *The Long Way to Freedom* (Indianapolis, 1960), pp. 432–437.

53. F. S. Marston, *The Peace Conference of 1919*, pp. 74, 89. Van der Slice, p. 351. George N. Barnes, *From Workshop to Cabinet*, pp. 248–249.

54. Shotwell, *At the Paris Peace Conference*, pp. 127, 215, 389–392, and *Origins*, vol. 1, pp. 97–105.

55. Mayer, p. 382.

56. Shotwell ms. O.H.R.O., pp. 121–122. See below, p. 316.

French working women asked Wilson to go to the Trocadero on January 25 to attend a mass meeting and to be saluted as the "incarnation of the hope of the future." The president received the invitation cordially but referred the women to their own government for permission to stage a demonstration. When Clemenceau required that the occasion be a musical fête for society ladies at which no allusion would be made to Wilson's political program or that of the working women, sixty delegates went instead to Wilson's residence and presented gifts and exchanged speeches.[57]

Delegations of English-speaking women waited upon Wilson to promote the cause of woman's suffrage. One came from England, where in the recent election women had voted in great numbers, and another from the United States, where the question of woman's suffrage was before the Congress. They sought confirmation of their aspirations by the Peace Conference. Representatives of the Conference of Allied Woman Suffragists, including two from the United States, presented certain proposals that had to do mainly with the conditions of women in industry.

Wilson, who disliked aggressiveness in women, nevertheless accepted the inevitability of their enfranchisement. He received an American pleader and convinced her of his concern for the rights of womankind.[58] Sounding his colleagues in the Supreme Council on February 13 as to what they might do to recognize feminist aims, he asked whether they would agree to invite the national suffrage associations to send delegates to Paris as consultants; and he asked also whether they would agree to the appointment of a commission to inquire into and report upon the question and to determine whether any international regulations were in order. To a pioneer English suffragist he reported: "I found practically all of the conferees entirely sympathetic with the cause of woman suffrage, but if I may say so confidentially, very much embarrassed by the objections raised by representatives of India and Japan to a world-wide investigation, which would raise questions most unacceptable to them. It was evident that to press the matter would lead to some unpleasant controversies."[59] The feminists, however, took part in achieving eventual recognition in Point Nine of a labor charter which provided that they should share in inspecting working conditions.[60]

Thus the American peace delegates, responding politically to impulses that were current in the American democracy but not entirely trustworthy as factors in state policy and good diplomacy, gave sympathetic attention not only to the champions of the press and those of labor, but to those of women's rights as well.

The Americans were less responsive, however, to racial minorities in the United States that sought sympathy for their kin in Africa and in Asia. Prominent American

57. Edith Benham, diary letter of January 27, 1919. R. S. Baker, *American Chronicle*, pp. 272–273. Creel, *Rebel at Large*, p. 214. Bullitt to House, January 23, 1919, Y.H.C. "Memorandum for the President," January 22, 1919, letter, Bullitt to Close, January 23, 1919, designated in Wilson's hand for "private file," Wilson papers.

58. Mary Anderson, *Woman at Work* (Westport, Conn., 1913), pp. 117, 121. According to Bonsal, Wilson, "at last" agreeing to receive a delegation of American women, found them "very intelligent, knowing exactly what they want to say and agreeing to say it all in twenty minutes," *Unfinished Business*, p. 164.

59. Wilson to Mrs. Fawcett, February 14, 1919, Wilson papers.

60. Shotwell, *At the Paris Peace Conference*, p. 179.

blacks looked forward to the eventual withdrawal of European powers from political responsibility in Africa. As an immediate goal they advocated the creation in Germany's lost colonies of native governments that would be under the guidance of an international commission and would realize the concept of Africa for the Africans. They pledged support to the ideal of a league of nations.

The United States was here concerned not only because of its large Negro population. American blacks had migrated to Liberia; and shortly after the Armistice of 1918 Negroes in the United States petitioned their government to assume a policy of increasing assistance to Liberia, where an already unstable economy had been disrupted by the effect of the war.

Wilson's early years in the Deep South had left him cool to any sudden change in the status of Negroes;[61] and the State Department was disinclined to discuss this question at the Peace Conference. Nevertheless, it acted upon the opinion of legal advisers to the effect that Liberia, which was in effect under American guardianship, was entitled as a belligerent to representation at the peace conference.[62] Two delegates, appointed by its president, arrived at Paris in January. The State Department advised the American commission that these men be cautioned against "introducing any local questions" that might provoke a general discussion of Liberian arrangements with France and Great Britain.[63] To George Louis Beer, the American expert on colonial questions, it seemed that one of the representatives of Liberia wished, contrary to the policy of the State Department, to open a controversy with France and Great Britain regarding boundaries.[64]

Certain blacks in the United States took a long and general view of African affairs. Immediately after the armistice W. E. B. Du Bois, editor of the *Crisis,* was authorized by the NAACP to promote a pan-African congress, which he advocated as a means of focusing attention on the aspirations of blacks everywhere. Arriving in France with the other newsmen on the *Orizaba,* and disappointed because he had no response to a letter to Wilson in which he had hinted that he would like an official position at the Peace Conference, Du Bois undertook to organize a conference of blacks to promote his ideas for their advancement.[65] He did not publicly proclaim his political purpose, for he feared that the great powers might frustrate him the moment they heard of his intent. Informed by American delegates that no gathering of blacks would be permitted in Paris, he sought the aid of a Senegalese, Diagne, who sat in the French Chamber and had assisted the French government in the recruiting of African troops.[66]

When the British and French governments learned what was afoot, they informed

61. See Paul Gordon Lauren, "Human Rights in History: Diplomacy and Racial Equality at the Paris Peace Conference," *Diplomatic History* 2, no. 3 (Summer 1978):263.

62. Miller, *My Diary,* vol. 2, p. 313.

63. Polk to Ammission, January 23, 1919, N.A., R.G. 59, 763.72119 / 3516b. See below, p. 67.

64. "Evidently he wants our money and advice," Beer wrote, "while preserving intact Liberian independence," Beer diary. Minutes, ACTNP, February 5, 1919.

65. See Clarence G. Contee, "Du Bois, the NAACP, and the Pan-African Congress of 1919."

66. W. E. B. Du Bois, *The World and Africa* (New York, 1947), pp. 8–9. Du Bois, "My Mission," *The Crisis* 18 (May 1919):7–9. Colin Legum, *Pan-Africanism* (London, 1962), pp. 24–25. Donald L. Wiedner, *History of Africa South of the Sahara* (New York, 1962), p. 327.

American diplomats that they were not favorably disposed. However, after a long delay, Diagne persuaded Clemenceau to permit a congress of carefully selected black delegates to meet in Paris. It was stipulated that there should be no publicity.

The Pan-African Congress met very unostentatiously at the Grand Hotel, on February 19, 20, and 21. There had been difficulty in securing passports from the colonial governments as well as from the United States.[67] The fifty-seven delegates—sixteen from the United States, twenty from the West Indies, twelve from nine African countries, and a few officials representing Belgium, France, and Portugal—were for the most part blacks who happened to be in Paris. The assemblage resolved formally that the powers should set up a code of law for an international protection of native populations similar to that proposed for labor, and that a league of nations should maintain a permanent bureau to oversee application of the statutes. It was asserted, too, that blacks should be governed according to certain principles as to land and resources, conservation of capital and taxing of profits for social and material benefits, labor regulation, education, and gradual political freedom and responsibility, until Africa came to be ruled by the consent of the Africans and a league of nations publicized infractions.[68] In voicing their aspirations for self-government, the blacks went beyond the thinking of white statesmen at that time, but they did not assert a right to complete independence.

The NAACP was disappointed by the limitation upon publicity that Clemenceau imposed. Yet there were some reports in the press; and Du Bois told his sponsors that he distributed a thousand copies of the resolutions of the congress to delegates and newsmen. Du Bois was kept under surveillance by American intelligence officers, some of whom attended the meetings of the Congress.[69]

Colonel House was not entirely taken by surprise when his aide telephoned to say that the blacks were meeting at the Grand Hotel. House had warned his fellow commissioners that the African question was sure to demand attention at the Peace Conference. He conferred with Du Bois, who in a talk with Beer gave the impression that he would like to send American blacks to rehabilitate Liberia. The American peace commission took no action on a suggestion by House that Robert R. Moton, an eminent educator of blacks who was at Paris to strengthen the morale of American soldiers, be made an adviser to the commission.[70]

Another ethnic group appealed to American sympathies. Orientals, often dramatized as the source of a sinister "yellow peril" to the United States, had champions at Paris who pleaded for explicit recognition of the equality of races. Their most

67. Cables, Polk to the embassy, January 17, 1919. R. W. Bliss to the secretary of state, Wilson papers. Sharp to the secretary of state, February 18, 1919, Polk to the embassy, February 19, 1919, N.A., R.G., 59, 763.72119 / 3806. *The Crisis* 17 (March 1919):224–225. W. Phillips, journal, January 16, 1919.

68. Du Bois, *Autobiography,* p. 27; *Dusk of Dawn,* pp. 260–262; *The World and Africa,* pp. 10–12; "The Pan-African Congress," *The Crisis* 17 (March 1919):271–274. Legum, p. 28. Two of the black governments represented—those of Haiti and Liberia—had representatives at the Peace Conference.

69. Contee, *op. cit.* Report of Lt. Col. Ward, forwarded to the secretary of state with dispatch, Sharp to the secretary of state, March 3, 1919, N.A., R.G. 59, 763.72119 / 4352.

70. Note penciled by Bonsal, who reported the Pan-African meeting to House, Bonsal papers, box 15. Minutes, ACTNP, January 4, 1919. House diary, March 10, 1919. Beer diary, March 1, 1919. R. S. Baker, journal, December 21, 1918.

influential spokesmen were the delegates of the Japanese empire—the first nonwhite nation to gain admission to an international congress as a power of the first rank. The press in Japan demanded, the public petitioned, and the government at Tokyo gave instructions that a guarantee be secured at Paris against any disadvantages resulting from discrimination on grounds of race. Wilson was challenged to redeem his wartime pledge to make "a peace between equals."[71]

Japan had played only a limited and isolated part in the war, and its government had not been active in the preparation for peacemaking. Its territorial aspirations centered upon the Pacific islands and China. However, the Japanese delegates were charged with the mission of protesting against the racial discrimination that seemed to menace the peace of the world. The *Tokyo Asahi* asserted that "fairness and equality must be secured for the colored races who form 62% of the whole of mankind."

To grant Japan's plea would enable Asiatics to demand the repeal of laws of the United States that excluded them, and this would outrage public opinion on the Pacific coast of the United States. Nevertheless, the Americans listened sympathetically to Japan's spokesmen. When they suggested to House that the Peace Conference proclaim the principle of race equality in a league of nations covenant, the colonel drafted a resolution that he conceived would satisfy American idealists. Wilson approved it with minor alterations. The Japanese, however, found the American formula practically without meaning. Moreover, Prime Minister William Hughes, who was committed to a "white Australia," would tolerate no concession to the Japanese demand. Furthermore, Foreign Secretary Balfour did not accept a statement in the American draft that "all men are created equal." He thought that such a statement would have the triple disadvantage of stirring hopes in Japan that would not be fulfilled, exciting fears among English-speaking peoples that they might be, and burdening a league of nations with perpetual controversy.[72]

When the Japanese brought a counterproposal to House and gave him to understand that they would not join a league of nations unless satisfied in this matter, the colonel perceived that their proposition was entirely unacceptable to Hughes and to Balfour. Nevertheless, with persistent optimism he wrote in his diary: "I have a feeling that it can be worked out by a satisfactory compromise which will in no way weaken the American or British Dominions' position and yet will satisfy the *amour-propre* of the Japanese." However, when the Japanese came to him three days later, after he had been unable to move Balfour and Hughes toward an accommodation, he gave up for the moment and, as he put it, placed the Japanese "on the backs of the British."[73] The question of race equality was to pose one of the major difficulties to be overcome in bringing Japan within an association of nations.[74]

It seemed apparent to some of the American delegates, and particularly to Colonel House, that the voices of pleaders of popular causes were speaking with a polit-

71. Miller, vol. 17, pp. 345–346. See Lauren, 258–262.
72. Miller, vol. 1, p. 116, and vol. 5, p. 214. Notes dictated by Balfour, February 10, 1918, FO / 608 / 240, doc. 642 / 2 / 4. House diary, February 4 and 6, 1919.
73. House diary, February 6, 9, and 12, 1919.
74. See below, pp. 309–311.

ical authority that required sympathetic recognition. The president, however, was hesitant to venture further on uncharted waters than to give sympathetic hearings to the new voices of the age. Indeed, when the aims of the various social and racial groups conflicted with the national policies of the great powers at the peace table, Wilson found himself with no recourse except faith in the future efficacy of a league of nations and his ability to educate the peoples of the democracies in the essentials of keeping the peace of the world.

3

Wilson's Vision and Europe's Interests

While the delegates in Paris toiled over facts and figures and some strove for position and prestige, and while the voices of the people demanded a new order that would prevent war and would bring "social justice," the American prophet kept his eyes upon his envisioned horizon. During the first weeks of the Peace Conference he pursued his main purpose, his Fourteenth Point: the creation of an association of nations. In each of his positions of responsible leadership—at Princeton, in the governor's chair in New Jersey, and in the presidency—Wilson had acted promptly to champion great causes of the day that served the common interest. It was preordained that now, when the world looked to him for political leadership, he should honor his wartime commitment to the development of an international organism to prevent war. A league of nations, moreover, became in Wilson's mind a practical necessity for coping with the circumstances that followed the end of the fighting.

When the American prophet first embraced his great-hearted vision, which had long been the subject of idealistic speculation in Europe, it brought new hope to the exhausted peoples of the Old World. It shone like Utopia before survivors of the carnage, who longed for security and stability. It appealed to those who felt burdened by social injustice. The pressing business of the world at large, the aspirations of its races, the adjustment of its international boundaries, the effective governance of its undeveloped regions, the revival of its economy, and the welfare of its laborers—all these concerns were calling for the ministration of a permanent international authority. And the revolutionary turmoil that loomed in the east gave urgency to the popular clamor for immediate and drastic action to protect the values of society in the democracies.[1] These practical considerations called for bold political leadership.

Wilson and House perceived the opportunity that was opened for conspicuous service to mankind. They could hope to make their names, as well as that of their nation, illustrious in history. Moreover, the League of Nations could serve in the next presidential election as a great cause that would strengthen Wilson's popular mandate as well as the declining fortunes of the Democratic party.

When the president had visited England in December, he had talked with Lloyd George about building a league of nations. The prime minister was relieved to learn that Wilson's thought was, in general, in harmony with that of English advocates and that he did not wish to attribute executive powers to a world body. Lloyd George had hoped that by agreeing with the American program it might be possible to avoid tension over such explosive issues as the freedom of the seas and the disposal of the German colonies.

1. On the menace of bolshevism, see Arno J. Mayer, *Politics and Diplomacy of Peacemaking*, Prologue.

Wilson found divers opinions, however, among British leaders. Prime Minister Hughes of Australia went so far as to say that the American prophet, who was not qualified to dictate by his nation's relatively small contribution to the military victory, actually had no practical proposal for an enduring league, which like the British Empire must be "framed in accordance with historical associations and practical needs." Hughes warned that they might find themselves "dragged quite unnecessarily behind Wilson's chariot."[2] Conservative diplomats looked upon Wilson's advocacy of a league as largely a political ploy that was vital to his re-election. On the other hand, Lord Grey, who had been British foreign secretary and now was president of the League of Nations Union, advised House that the undercurrent of opposition in England would be "completely snowed under by an overwhelming mass of public opinion." Grey wrote that without the United States, a league of nations would be as susceptible to internal intrigue as the Concert of Europe had been in the nineteenth century. At the same time he warned against the inclusion of a league constitution in a peace treaty that might be rejected by the American Senate.[3] Yet just a few days before this, while crossing the Atlantic, Wilson had said: "I am going to insist that the League be brought out as part and parcel of the treaty itself."[4]

Opinion in many quarters favored immediate agreement on the practical settlement of urgent matters and the postponement of discussion of those principles of enduring peace and world order that Wilson thought fundamental. For example, the permanent undersecretary of the British Foreign Office thought it "eminently desirable . . . that, until the questions arising out of the war were settled, no attempt . . . be made to handle so difficult a question as that of the machinery for maintaining peace afterward."[5] It was pointed out that Wilson himself had said, in a note addressed to the belligerents at the end of 1916 with reference to the creation of a league of nations by international treaty: "Before that final step can be taken . . . each [party] deems it necessary first to settle the issues of the present war upon terms which will certainly safeguard the independence, the territorial integrity, and the political and commercial freedom of the nations involved."

The French authorities, for their part, proposed that the procedure of the Peace Conference give priority to the consideration of territorial, financial, and economic matters. "Once these three types of problems have been solved," it was stated, ". . . the principle foundations of the league of nations will be laid."[6]

In addition to the apathy of officials of the British and French governments, Wilson, in his determination to get priority for the creation of a league of nations,[7] had to overcome a general sentiment that favored a quick termination of the state of war[8] as well as philosophical dissent founded upon the imperfect nature of the law

2. Minutes, I.W.C., November 28 and December 30, 1918.
3. Grey to House, December 30, 1918. Pamphlet, "The Peace Conference and After," Y.H.C.
4. Swem, book ms., ch. 21.
5. Memorandum, Hardinge to Balfour, October 10, 1918, Conf. F.O. document, Borden papers, National Archives of Canada.
6. Tardieu, *The Truth about the Treaty,* p. 89.
7. See above, p. 5.
8. Noble, *Policies and Opinions at Paris, 1919,* pp. 105–106.

of nations.[9] Unfortunately for his cause, the president met with obstruction from an American official on whose assistance he was entitled to rely. Secretary of State Lansing, convinced that America was "entirely unselfish in its political policies," thought that the president should say to "these selfish politicians": "The United States signs peace with Germany by March 1, alone if necessary, and then our armies come home." It seemed to Lansing that Wilson, unversed in the diplomacy and power politics of Europe, was risking too much in attempting to speak upon many of the issues that would be presented at Paris.[10]

Early in January there was still no agreement as to the place of the creation of a league constitution in the agenda of the conference. It had been a full month since House's legal adviser, David Hunter Miller, after conferring with officials of the Foreign Office, had reported from London that no program for peace talks could be agreed on in advance, that President Wilson would have to make up his own program of topics to be discussed and arrange the order of priority.[11]

A league of nations was the first of five topics of the agenda that Wilson presented to the Supreme Council on January 13.[12] On the seventeenth, when the council resumed discussion of the question of procedure, Foreign Minister Pichon suggested that the president put his program before the first plenary session of the conference on the next day. And so in the inaugural gathering of all the delegates on January 18, forty-eight years to the day since the German Empire was proclaimed at Versailles, Wilson spoke for his cause. The seventy-two plenipotentiaries met in the Salle d'Horloge of the Ministry of Foreign Affairs. No crowns and few titles distinguished those who took their places on the gilded, damask-covered chairs. Most of the men present were eager to plead the special interests of their several nations, believing that the common good lay in the adjustment of their claims in the tried ways of diplomacy rather than in any experiment in international organization.

A very heavy cold had made it doubtful that the president would be able to attend this meeting.[13] However, Wilson, a trim figure in black, stepped forward after an address of welcome by President Poincaré. He spoke of the war suffering of France and the historic importance of its capital in the making of peace. Then, acting on a suggestion by House, he nominated Georges Clemenceau as permanent chairman of the conference. The old Tiger, saluted by Lloyd George as "the grand young man of France," presided with vigor and dispatch. There was no vote, only an opportunity for "observations" and quick rulings from the chair: "Adopté." Thus Wilson's program was tacitly accepted.

However, the doubts of Lansing, which were shared by Bliss and White, persisted. They asked Wilson to confer with them on January 20. The secretary of state was in despair because the Peace Conference, like the American commission, seemed

9. See Walworth, *America's Moment: 1918,* pp. 9–11.
10. Lansing, private memoranda, December 17, 1918, January 22, 1919, Ac. 3518, Add. 2, box 2, L.C. John W. Davis diary, January 25, 1919.
11. Miller, *My Diary,* vol. 1, December 6 and 9, 1918.
12. See above, p. 15.
13. Dr. Grayson's diary, January 18, 1919.

to be drifting without any plan, Wilson to be floundering, and the French "doing about as they please." Lansing spoke of his desire to present a resolution in regard to the league that would clear the way for a quick preliminary treaty. But he was rebuffed by the president in a manner that led him to write in his diary: "He apparently resents my making any suggestions and seeks to belittle their value by flatly turning them down. It is humiliating, and makes it hard for me to keep my temper."[14]

In a meeting of the Supreme Council of Ten on the next day, Lansing, encouraged by support from some of the European delegates, presented his ideas informally to the council. Wilson asked him, *sotto voce*, whether he had prepared a resolution embodying his views and, getting a negative reply, said that he would be obliged if the secretary of state would prepare one.[15] Thus the president established control over Lansing. As he had once said of William Jennings Bryan, it was better to have the secretary of state in his bosom than on his back. Lansing, after discussing a preliminary draft with Bliss and White, sent the president a resolution on January 31 that was more to Wilson's liking.[16]

Meanwhile House, now convalescing, summoned enough strength to put a definite plan of action before the president.[17] Arranging for Lord Robert Cecil, the Christian statesman who was devoted to the cause of peace, to confer with Wilson, House advised that they collaborate on a resolution to be adopted by the Peace Conference, calling for the appointment of a commission to prepare a constitution for a league of nations. House proposed that the resolution should firmly and publicly commit the conference to the creation of a league as "essential to the maintenance of the world peace." Accompanying a letter to Wilson in which House gave this counsel was a text for a covenant.[18] This was supplied by Cecil, who also prepared such a resolution as House desired. It was presented to the Supreme Council by Lloyd George on January 22, and was approved.[19] Thus by the open advocacy of Wilson and the efforts of House, and Cecil behind the scenes, the stage was set for a major British-American achievement.[20]

At the second plenary session of the Peace Conference, on January 25, the pres-

---

14. Lansing, *The Peace Negotiations,* pp. 113–114, 201; supplementary diary, January 19 and 20, 1919. On Lansing's dissent in the drafting of a league covenant, see below, pp. 110 ff.

15. Lansing, *The Peace Negotiations,* pp. 115–117; supplementary diary, January 31 and February 2, 1919; private memoranda, January 22, 1919.

16. Lansing, *The Peace Negotiations,* p. 120. Minutes, ACTNP, January 31, 1919.

17. On January 21 McCormick noted in his diary that House was "getting about for the first time in ten days—very weak."

18. Auchincloss diary, January 19, 1919. *I.P.,* vol. 4, pp. 287, 289–290, 291. House's letter of January 19 to Wilson was drafted by Wiseman, Miller, and Auchinloss.

19. *F.R., P.P.C.,* vol. 3, p. 678.

20. On January 23 Wiseman found André Tardieu, Clemenceau's spokesman, eager for the quick completion of a covenant. According to Louis Aubert, Tardieu's assistant, they saw the implications of Wilson's plan for the future. "The important thing was to tie the claims of France to it. Wilson was a remote man. . . . We were in constant touch with Colonel House and his experts." Aubert, *Tardieu, Haut-Commissionaire en Amérique,* pp. 62–63. At House's suggestion Wiseman enlisted General Smuts of South Africa to canvass the Italian and Japanese delegates in behalf of Wilson's program, Wiseman diary, January 23, 1919. According to Stephen Bonsal *(Unfinished Business,* pp. 34–36), Smuts excelled in "missionary work with recalcitrant delegates."

ident, speaking extemporaneously, presented the resolution that had been approved by the council. He dramatized the issue that in his eyes transcended all others. This was the question of human survival. Describing the league as "a vital thing" with "a vital continuity," he said: "It should be the eye of the nations to keep watch upon the common interest, an eye that does not slumber, an eye that is everywhere watchful and attentive." By vigilant, continuous cooperation it was to keep science as well as military might within the bounds of civilization. "We can set up permanent processes," he said. "We may not be able to set up permanent decisions." At the end he held up his hands, seized a wrist, and shouted: "The very pulse of the world seems to beat to the surface in this enterprise."

Tears streamed down the face of Léon Bourgeois, France's constant advocate of peace. "Light and leading has come to us at last," he exclaimed, "and it has come from the West."[21] House was ecstatic. He penciled a note and passed it to Wilson: "I believe that what you have said today will hearten the world as nothing you have said before. It was complete and satisfying." And the president replied: "We have got them all very solemnly and satisfactorily committed."[22]

There was skepticism among the Europeans, however. Indeed the secretaries omitted from the minutes an assertion by Wilson that a league of nations would do better than Christianity in keeping peace in the world.[23] Nevertheless Clemenceau, who listened to the prophet's speech with eyes closed and face immobile, declared that the resolution as adopted[24] would take effect and that a commission on a league of nations should meet forthwith to draft a constitution.

It remained to decide upon the representation of the nations on the commission. Eager as Wilson was for the participation of little states in the operations of the league that was to act for their protection, he thought it impractical to include many of their spokesmen in the body that drafted its charter. He feared that their presence would so enlarge the commission that it would be inefficient and inelastic, and he was in favor of consulting only the wisest of the delegates of small nations.[25] Neutral states, who had no voice at the Peace Conference, could not take part in drafting a covenant because of Wilson's determination to include it in the treaty of peace.

Lloyd George, for his part, insisted that the committee include representatives of small powers that had contributed to the victory. He observed that these men were

21. Bonsal, p. 18.
22. *I.P.*, vol. 4, facing p. 290.
23. Frances Stevenson, *Lloyd George*, p. 175.
24. Bonsal, p. 18. The resolution, as presented to the plenary session on January 25, was "1. It is essential to the maintenance of the world settlement, which the Associated Nations are now met to establish, that a League of Nations be created to promote international cooperation, to ensure the fulfillment of accepted international obligations, and to provide safeguards against war. 2. This league should be created as an integral part of the general Treaty of Peace, and should be open to every civilized nation which can be relied upon to promote its objects. 3. The members of the league should periodically meet in international conference, and should have a permanent organization and secretariat to carry out the business of the League in the interval between the conferences. The conference therefore appoints a committee representative of the Associated Governments to work out details of the constitution and functions of the League."
25. Baker, *Woodrow Wilson and World Settlement*, vol. 1, pp. 241–242. The discussion in the council on January 22 of small-power representation on the League of Nations Commission is recorded in the French minutes with some detail not found in *F.R., P.P.C.*, vol. 3, pp. 679–682.

complaining that they had no part in the peacemaking. Clemenceau remarked that the great powers held effective supremacy and, confident that the small powers would follow the lead of the large, he thought it wise to give them a sense of participation.[26] Therefore in the second plenary session, on January 25, the small powers were asked to convene and choose five men to sit with two from each of the five great powers on a commission on a league of nations. Three other committees of fifteen similarly constituted were formed to consider labor legislation, war guilt, and arrangements for ports, waterways, and railways.[27] For a fifth commission, to deal with reparations, the council itself chose three men to represent each of the five great powers, and two each from Belgium, Greece, Poland, Romania, and Serbia. Delegates from Czechoslovakia and Portugal were added in February.

Murmurings of dissatisfaction arose from the delegates of lesser states. Their new governments—in some cases headed by leaders who had been exiles during the war—had sent them to Paris to confirm their independent existence and to support their claims during the peacemaking. These men were busy in advancing the various national interests by concerting their efforts and by soliciting the aid of sympathetic major powers. When they learned how greatly they would be outnumbered in the commissions by the great powers, they were in a rebellious mood. In the meeting of January 25 one of their number asked from the floor that they be allowed to vote on the resolutions proposed by the council.

Clemenceau, realizing that the small states held a majority that would enable them to outvote the great powers, spoke out with a frankness that at least one American delegate thought "brutal."[28] Explaining that the great powers had contributed most to the martial victory and now offered to permit their allies to share in the settlement, he urged the delegates to get on with choosing their representatives on the commissions. He invited them to send their "observations" to the Bureau of the Conference. Before anyone could rise to prolong the discussion, he snapped out an "Adopté!" Thus the statesmen of Europe came to accept the creed of the New World by an application of political power that was familiar to the Old. Despite juridical assumptions of equality among sovereign states, the small nations, faced in their postwar weakness with the alternative of carrying on alone, yielded to obvious *force majeure*.[29] House, feeling that the wound to their pride could have been avoided by proper canvassing, arranged for better liaison in the future.[30] The American experts were instructed to drop other work in order to get the confidence of their particular foreign protégés and to entertain them at government expense.[31]

26. See F. S. Marston, *The Peace Conference of 1919*, pp. 66–67.

27. *Ibid.*, pp. 71–79. *F.R.*, *P.P.C.*, vol. 3, pp. 678–683, 686–690, 699–701.

28. G. L. Beer diary, January 25, 1919.

29. Mackinder, *Democratic Ideals and Reality*, pp. 268–269.

30. Steed memorandum to Northcliffe, January 27, 1919. *F.R.*, *P.P.C.*, vol. 3, pp. 177–201, 700. Beer diary, January 26, 1919. Shotwell, *At the Paris Peace Conference*, pp. 147–148. Dispatch, Polk to Auchincloss, January 29, 1919.

31. Diary letter, Clive Day to Mrs. Day, January 28, 1919, Y.H.C. Seymour, *Letters from the Paris Peace Conference*, pp. 130–131. Auchincloss recorded in his diary on January 29 that he had arranged that the American specialists would "entertain" delegates of small nations and report on their "personalities" so that House would have "something particular and important" to say when he talked with them. "This will make them much more ready to support our programme," he wrote.

On January 27 the delegates of the small states met to choose the five that were to be represented on each of the four commissions authorized by the plenary session. Jules Cambon, one of the French plenipotentiaries, was in the chair.[32] It was decided that Belgium, Brazil, China, Portugal, and Serbia would have seats on the Commission on the League of Nations. In response to a formal request of the small states for more representation the Supreme Council agreed, despite the objection of Wilson, to give to the League commission the right to add members. As a result the Commission on the League of Nations was enlarged early in February to include representatives of Czechoslovakia, Greece, Poland and Romania. When American members were chosen as chairmen by all commissions except that on reparations, it was largely in recognition of their impartial position. By the end of January the Americans had won recognition as trusted arbiters, as well as priority for the main concern of their president, the creation of a league of nations.

Wilson insisted not only on realization of his vision of collective security. At the same time he pursued a policy of moderation that would allow the enemy, once purged of its militants, to win an honorable and prosperous position among the nations. Having lived in the South in the aftermath of the Civil War, he could fully understand the necessity of making a compassionate and constructive peace. Wilson had made it clear many times that he would oppose anything of the nature of a Carthaginian vengeance. By calling for the unseating of the "military masters," the election of a constituent national assembly, and the preservation of civil order, he had thrown his influence on the side of moderate and liberal Germans who wished to set up a democratic government rather than be ruled by councils of workers. Since the American program, recognized by the Allies as the basis of peace, seemed to promise relatively lenient terms, the new political leaders of Germany found it expedient to adjust their foreign policy to Wilson's doctrine. "When the German government began to work out its peace program . . . ," historian Klaus Schwabe writes, "it oriented its thinking to Wilson's Fourteen Points and never lost sight of them afterward."[33] Yet, Germany's conception of the peace differed from Wilson's in that it was not willing to accept Germany's military defeat as a basis for peace.

The first and most immediate concern of the peacemakers was the treatment to be given to the enemy. This was considered along with the related question of a westward thrust of arms and ideology from Soviet Russia. Prudence seemed to require that the German state be kept strong enough to resist revolution but at the same time weak enough to remain at peace.

Following the abdication of the kaiser and the forming of two ministries, one of social democrats under the presidency of Friedrich Ebert at Berlin and the other

32. Jules Cambon, "La Paix (notes inédites, 1919)." Cambon wrote of the delegates of the small nations (p. 9): "They meet less to do something than to make believe that they have done something, and I fear that the explosion of opinion against the incapacity of the Allies to make decisions may only be delayed." The representation of small nations on the eight commissions that were eventually in action is discussed in Marston, pp. 75–83.

33. Schwabe, *Woodrow Wilson, Revolutionary Germany, and Peacemaking*, p. 299.

under Kurt Eisner in a soviet republic at Munich, the possibility of political chaos continued to appear as a potent threat that could be exploited by German politicians.[34] The American government refrained from commitment to any party, and refused to correspond with German authorities without consulting with its associated powers; but Herbert Hoover undertook to revictual the German people.[35] There were differing opinions among the American delegates as to the likely outcome of the German revolution and as to the measures that Wilson might take in order to assure that there would be a stable regime with which he could negotiate. Actually, the danger of anarchy in enemy lands seemed to many of the American delegates at Paris to be less imminent than was suggested by various journals and by alarming memoranda written by William C. Bullitt.[36] The Americans had reliable information on which to base an evaluation of the menace of bolshevism in Germany: reports from American and Allied agencies, regular and special; confidential intelligence from the British Foreign Office; and a number of reports of the Inquiry.[37] The scholars were not dismayed by the possibility of a bolshevist state in Germany.[38] They were skeptical of the ability of capitalistic Germans to make political conquests over Russians who had a religious love for their country.[39]

The relentless passion of the French people for protection from domination by Germany challenged the American concept of a moderate settlement. The wartime losses of France had far exceeded those of the United States and in proportion to its resources had been greater than those of most of the Allied peoples. More than 2 million French soldiers had been killed or crippled. Mines in the north and the east had been flooded, and industrial plants ravaged. Even the promised reacquisition of Alsace and Lorraine could not bring adequate compensation in manpower or in economic strength. French leaders were convinced that the more numerous Germans, goaded by the shame of defeat, would try again one day to dominate Europe and undertake another invasion of France. They wished to disarm Germany, set up

34. On the German revolution see Hajo Holborn, *A History of Modern Germany*, vol. 3, pp. 509 ff.

35. See below, p. 84.

36. See Mayer, pp. 61–68, 258–259.

William Bullitt, the State Department's adviser on current conditions in Germany, advocated American support for non-bolshevist politicians in both Berlin and Munich. He conceived that Wilson should become the champion of the moderate Left in Europe as against bolshevism. Secretary Lansing had informed Wilson on November 28, 1918, that both governments were in the hands of good and moderate men who should be strengthened.

37. *Ibid.*, pp. 254, 281–282. J. W. Davis to Lansing, January 6, 1919, N.A., R.G. 59, 763.72 / 12726. See Schwabe, pp. 118–138, 192.

38. The Inquiry and its expert, Wallace Notestein, had found Germany "an impossible field for effective research" in the chaotic conditions of the moment, Shotwell, diary entry of January 21, 1919, p. 139. See Lawrence E. Gelfand, *The Inquiry*, pp. 198–199, 213–215; Ludwig F. Schaefer, "German Peace Strategy in 1918–1919," pp. 46–48, 64; Mayer, pp. 65 ff.; *F.R., P.P.C.*, vol. 2, pp. 125–129.

Miller and Scott, in sending a skeleton draft for a treaty to Lansing on December 30, 1918, advised that the separate independent societ republic formed in Bavaria should be included among the signatories of the treaty of peace.

39. Actually, Mayer has written, it was the consistent policy of the postwar German foreign ministry "to pursue the decentralization of Russia with the aid of the nationality principle," *op. cit.*, pp. 233, 252.

uffer state on the Rhine, and compel the enemy to pay in full for the damages it had inflicted. They were in no mood to make moral distinctions, to weigh the words *security* and *revenge*. Any farseeing vision that seemed to temporize with the essential, persisting peril was in the French view blind stupidity.[40]

In French opinion the German appeals to Wilson's principles were efforts to soften the peace terms. The suspicion prevailing at Paris of any dealings with the enemy discouraged any independent exchange of views on the part of Wilson with men in Germany who professed to share his ideals. In the opinion of Charles Seymour the failure of the Americans to keep in touch with those Germans supporting Wilson's ideas was "one of the tragedies of modern times."[41]

Just as the peacemakers at Paris held their first meeting, battles broke out in the streets of Berlin and two radical leaders were assassinated. On January 19, however, a national election chose members of a constitutional assembly that was to meet at Weimar to form a social-democratic government. The regime at Munich lacked such an electoral mandate. It seemed to the Americans that the Weimar government was the more worthy of trust.

The severity of French demands upon the enemy was revealed in the first session of the Peace Conference, during which the Supreme War Council was transformed into a Supreme Council of Ten. On January 12 Foreign Minister Pichon called on Marshal Foch and the French minister of marine for a report on German compliance with the terms of the November armistice, and certain infractions were alleged. In three meetings of the Supreme War Council during the preceding weeks the members had shown uneasiness about the possibility of a renewal of resistance.[42] It was now proposed that when the armistice was next renewed, new conditions be imposed with respect of the pacification of Germany's eastern frontiers, where in a sort of no man's land between great powers—a region inviting invasion by both Germans and Russians—native armies collided. French generals were actively planning to build up some of these armies, and the chief of the British general staff advocated a *cordon sanitaire* between Germany and Russia.[43]

The Americans were eager to assure the stability of the buffer states that were developing and to prescribe frontiers that would give promise of permanence. Concern for Wilson's principles as well as for the sentiment of millions of American citizens who were kin of the peoples in the border lands[44] gave the plenipotentiaries a lively interest in the decisions of the Peace Conference affecting fragments of the broken empires.

General Bliss, noting that the British and French peoples were war-weary and that their armed forces were dwindling,[45] feared the creation of a situation in which

40. Étienne Mantoux, *The Carthaginian Peace*, pp. 20–21, 28. Martin Gilbert, *The European Powers 1900–1945*, pp. 91–92.

41. Seymour to Schwabe, December 7, 1962, Seymour papers, box 12, folder 730. Later, during the spring months, German financial advisers conferred with those of Great Britain and the United States at Château Villette. See below, p. 384.

42. Loucheur, *Carnets Secrets*, diary entries of January 7, 8, and 10, 1919.

43. Document of War Office, General Staff, "Appreciation of the Internal Situation in Russia," January 12, 1919, preface by Sir Henry Wilson, P.R.O., Cab / 29 / 98.

44. See Joseph P. O'Grady, *The Immigrants' Influence on Wilson's Peace Policies*.

45. In mid-January, as the second armistice agreement was about to expire, the French people were pressing for a return of the poilus to civil life, and in England a similar feeling expressed itself in

Americans would feel compelled to assume an enormous policing burden in order to save what was left of European civilization. Already friction had developed between French and American soldiers. An American army had crossed the Rhine in December and was thought by the French to be too friendly with the enemy. Moreover, there was a rumor of bad relations between American and French troops, and even in Paris there was ill feeling.[46] Bliss was vigilant to detect French military propaganda and to warn the president.

The vital issue of France's security was entangled with the question of demobilization. Marshal Foch, who spoke with authority by virtue of his effective command of the victorious armies, placed more emphasis upon the policing of Germany's western frontier than on disarmament of the enemy. He conducted the second renewal of the armistice on January 16 with only a grudging regard for American opinion.[47] The marshal took it for granted that the Rhine would be the frontier and that French troops would hold the bridgeheads for many years.[48] "Who can say," he asked newsmen, "that Germany—where their democratic ideas are so recent and perhaps so superficial—will not quickly recover from her defeat and will then in a very few years attempt for a second time to crush us? Russia is *hors de combat* for a long while. England has the channel to cross. America is far away. France must always be ready to safeguard the general interests of mankind." The marshal inquired of an American observer whether Wilson fully comprehended European military geography and the necessity for maintaining neutral barriers as frontiers. He was assured that the president was a scholar of repute. Foch then paid an eloquent public tribute to the "enormous material aid" that France had received from the United States during the war and to the virility of Pershing's men, to whom he attributed "the devil's own punch." Nevertheless, two days afterward Wilson told his family at luncheon that he thought the marshal, though very able, was narrow and given to prejudices.[49]

During the first week of the formal sessions of the Supreme Council of Ten and while Colonel House was ill, Wilson was determined to oppose the will of Italy as well as that of France when his doctrine was violated. He undertook to talk with Premier Vittorio Orlando about the extravagant territorial claims that Italy brought to the peace table. These claims were sanctioned, for the most part, by the secret

demonstrations by restive soldiers and laborers. Lloyd George was being criticized by his French allies for demobilizing too rapidly, and by his own press for not demobilizing swiftly enough, Nicholson, *Peacemaking, 1919*, p. 261. Demobilization of the British and American fleets was making it more difficult to continue to enforce the blockade of Germany, Marston, p. 126.

46. On February 10 Joseph C. Grew wrote to William Phillips: "The honeymoon between America and France is over. . . . There is friction between Pershing and Foch and this is carried all the way down to the ranks." Grew cited "well-substantiated fact," *Turbulent Era*, vol. 1, pp. 372–374. "There was a good deal of brawling in the streets and conflicts with the French police, and to these causes undoubtedly the unpopularity of America and Americans in Paris was largely due," Hardinge, *The Old Diplomacy*, p. 231.

47. See below, p. 88. K. L. Nelson, *Victors Divided*, pp. 52, 56, 285.

48. Bonsal ms., Bonsal papers, box 17.

49. Memorandum, General Preston Brown, Trèves, January 16, 1919, Pershing papers, box 97, L.C. Benham diary letter, January 18, 1919, Helm papers, box 1, L.C.

Treaty of London,[50] signed in 1915 by France and Great Britain as the price of winning Italy to their side in the desperate conflict with Germany. The provisions of this pact would place alien peoples under Italian rule. This would violate Wilson's Point Nine: "A readjustment of the frontiers of Italy should be effected along clearly recognizable lines of nationality." In his wartime speeches the American prophet had committed himself so ardently to the principle of self-determination that he could not now, without grave risk to his political leadership, accept the terms of the treaties concluded by the Allies under the stress of war and kept secret. "Here was an opportunity," Harold Nicolson wrote, "for the prophet of the New World to enforce his message upon the old. The Italian problem thus became, for them that knew, the test case of the whole Conference."[51]

Actually, the Italians had invited a crisis by hastening to occupy not only the lands promised by the Treaty of London, but also the city of Fiume (now Rijeka). There the Italian residents—a majority in the city proper but not in the surrounding region—had proclaimed annexation to Italy and had invoked the support of the United States, "the mother of liberty and universal democracy." The occupation, represented by the Italians as a measure for the preservation of order, had gone beyond that function. The participation of an American regiment and American warships with Allied units in operations in the Adriatic had been permitted by House at the urging of British and Italian as well as Yugoslav spokesmen and with Wilson's cabled assent. Almost immediately the American naval commander in the region reported that Fiume "had every appearance of being occupied by the Italians and not by the Allies."[52]

When Wilson visited Rome at the beginning of 1919, he was aware of propaganda advocating the expansion of Italy east of the Adriatic; yet he thought that he perceived an impulse among the "common people" to make sacrifices in the interest of enduring peace.[53] After the president's departure Ambassador Thomas Nelson Page conferred with Foreign Minister Sidney Sonnino, who stood securely in control of his government's foreign policy, a man respected for his proven devotion to Italy's interests.[54] Page, reporting that Italian leaders were much impressed by the sympathy of Italian socialists with the American program, informed Wilson that Sonnino was ready "to concede much more than ever before."[55]

When the Italian diplomats reached Paris, there was some prospect that the threatening impasse might yield to professional diplomatic treatment. Almost immediately upon Orlando's arrival he went to the Crillon.[56] There House expressed a personal desire to give Italy everything that it was good for it to have, and nothing

50. The text of the Treaty of London is in René Albrecht-Carrié, *Italy at the Paris Peace Conference*, pp. 334–339.

51. Nicolson wrote: "Nothing could disguise the central fact, that the fulfillment of the pledges of the Secret Treaty [of London] would violate the principle of self-determination to the extent of placing under Italian rule some two million unwilling and very self-determined people," pp. 161–177.

52. See Walworth, pp. 163–166, and Dragan R. Zinojinović, *America, Italy and the Birth of Yugoslavia*, chs. 7, 8, 10, 11.

53. Grayson diary, January 6, 1919.

54. Thomas Nelson Page, *Italy and the World War*, p. 394.

55. T. N. Page to Wilson, telegram, January 7, 1919, *F.R.*, *P.P.C.*, vol. 1, p. 472.

56. Auchincloss diary, January 9, 1919, telegram for Polk from Auchincloss.

that might sow seeds of future war. If Italy insisted upon Dalmatia and the Treaty of London line, House said, it would certainly mean discord and conflict. Afterward House spent the evening with the president.[57]

Wilson was deeply concerned and puzzled by the Adriatic crisis. Two days before landing in France he had told the Italian ambassador, Viscount Machi di Cellere, that he had received a copy of the Treaty of London; and, according to the ambassador's record, Wilson was "extremely sympathetic with Italy" and "disposed to favor it in every way in return for some slight sacrifices in the Adriatic."[58] But he had learned when in Rome that Italian army officers were using American troops as a shield against Yugoslav animosity and Italians were rioting when they occupied territory east of the Adriatic.[59] Early in January, moreover, he read a dispatch from the American chargé at Belgrade that aroused his protective feeling toward the Slavs. To Lansing, who sought his views on the dispatch, Wilson replied: "This communication concerns matters unhappily accumulating with which I confess I do not know how to deal." He suggested that the secretary of state confer with Sonnino.[60] He himself talked for two hours with Orlando, who wished that Sonnino, with whom Orlando's relations were strained, should know nothing of this conversation. Wilson debated "in his own mind," he said, to what extent he could disappoint the Italians and at the same time reach an amicable settlement.[61] Meeting with the American commissioners on January 10, he shared their indignation at Italian efforts to influence the judgments of the Peace Conference by using unauthorized force to establish themselves in territory they desired.

At this juncture House was trying to use the pen of Henry Wickham Steed to influence Wilson's thinking. Steed was urged to continue to use editorial pressure to stir the American delegates to haste in making peace. Asking House to point out the "most sensitive spots" to be "punched,"[62] he published an article in London that professed to give Wilson's views on the Adriatic question. Thereupon the president, probably not suspecting House's part in this, protested to his European colleagues in the Supreme Council against the newspaper article and what seemed to him its presumptuous revelation of his mind. As a result Balfour found it necessary to send a letter to Wilson giving assurance that the British plenipotentiaries had not been indiscreet and that Steed's article grew out of "common gossip" in the Foreign Office.[63]

57. Telegram, Polk from Auchincloss, Auchincloss diary, January 9, 1919. House diary, January 8, 1919. Frazier's notes on House-Orlando talk, January 9, 1919, Y.H.C. At this time House advised Vesnić of Yugoslavia not to press his government's claims at the moment, House diary, January 8, 1919.

58. G. Andruilli, "How We Alienated Wilson," *Living Age* 8th Series, 21 (1921):266–270.

59. Grayson diary, January 9, 1919.

60. The dispatch protested against invasion of Montenegro by Italy and against Italian intrigue in Albania and the Banat of Temesvár. Letters, Lansing to Wilson, January 6, Wilson to Lansing, January 9, 1919, filed with the minutes of the ACTNP, Grew papers.

61. Grayson diary, January 9, 1919.

62. Steed's reports to Northcliffe, January 14, 17, and 22, 1919, Steed papers, Archives of the *London Times*.

63. Balfour to Wilson, January 17, 1919. Lloyd George approved this letter and asserted that he and Law had not mentioned the substance of their talks with the president to anyone, letter, Kerr to Drummond, January 19, 1919, Balfour papers 49692.

Wilson resolved to deal directly with Orlando and to solicit the support of Clemenceau and Lloyd George for his policy. Drafting a letter to the Italian premier, he sent it to House with a request that the colonel get the French and British leaders to acquiesce in its content. Although House became too ill to perform this service, he was able to seek legal counsel from David Hunter Miller, who advised him that the Treaty of London had been in effect abrogated by the prearmistice agreement, which based the peace on Wilson's program.[64]

Doubtless Miller's opinion reached Wilson and confirmed his own wish. Very much disturbed by House's illness, the president told Auchincloss that he would attend to the matter himself.[65] On January 9 he handed to Orlando a brief "memorandum of suggestions," the text of which has disappeared.

On January 14, a day on which the Supreme Council did not meet, Wilson spent the afternoon with Lloyd George, Balfour, and Bonar Law. Balfour made it clear that the British delegates had no love for the Treaty of London but were bound by it.[66] Actually Wilson was already aware that the British and French were looking to him "to haul their chestnuts out of the fire" and he had confided to Dr. Grayson that he would not do this.[67] Wishing to give them a share of responsibility in denying Italian claims, he drafted a letter to Orlando indicating agreement on the part of Clemenceau and Lloyd George; but they objected to this.

The next day, January 15, Wilson wrote a two-page letter to the Italian premier, who had returned to Italy to face a cabinet crisis. A paragraph to which the British took exception was omitted.[68] The letter, which was never delivered, provides our best evidence as to what the president proposed to Orlando.[69] This letter of January 15 mentioned the benefits already assured to Italy as a result of the martial victory, benefits "so great that they could not possibly have been anticipated at the time when Italy joined the Allies." "Definite guarantees can be and should be secured," the president wrote. To that end he proposed that, in addition to a requirement that the "new States . . . accept from the League of Nations a limitation of their armaments,"

64. Miller, vol. 1, p. 73; vol. 3, pp. 237–238.

65. Auchincloss diary, January 11, 1919.

66. Nicolson, p. 241. English liberals were ashamed of the concessions made in the secret treaties, Nicolson, pp. 161, 177, 241. In a meeting of the Imperial War Cabinet on December 18, 1918, it was suggested by Balfour, who recognized that the outcome of the war had changed the situation to which the Treaty of London applied, that it might be wise to let the Italian plenipotentiaries be dealt with by those of the United States, since Italy was very dependent upon America for funds and raw materials. Bonar Law thought that Wilson would be able to use financial power to challenge the Treaty of London. But Lloyd George insisted that Italy would know that its claims would be honored if the British government pressed them. Under the bond they owed Italy their wholehearted support, and it seemed to the prime minister wrong to use President Wilson to get them out of the bargain. If any persuasion was to be exerted, he thought, it should come from the British in the form of advice from a friend, minutes, I.W.C., December 18, 23, and 30, 1918.

67. Grayson diary, January 6, 1919.

68. According to Auchincloss, the president agreed with the British leaders on the fourteenth to revise the text of his draft so that he would indicate merely that he had consulted with his British and French colleagues and felt sure that their views coincided with his, Auchincloss diary, January 14, 1919.

69. Letter, Wilson to Orlando, January 15, 1919, found with a large map in a sealed envelope addressed to Orlando, Wilson papers, docs. 6808–9.

(a) the Yugoslavic State be erected on the understanding that it maintain no navy except the few small craft necessary to maintain a coast police,[70]

(b) the Austrian fortifications on the islands and eastern coast of the Adriatic be destroyed and the arming of those coasts and islands be forbidden by international mandate, and

(c) it be one of the fundamental covenants of the Peace that all new States should enter into solemn obligations, under responsibility to the whole body of nations, to accord to all racial and national minorities within their jurisdictions exactly the same status and treatment, alike in law and in fact, that are accorded to the majority of the people.

I think that it ought also to be seriously considered whether Fiume should be erected into a free city and constituted a permanently free port. . . .

The "Pact of London," I respectfully submit, cannot wisely be regarded as applying to existing circumstances or carried out consistently with the agreements upon which the present peace conferences are based.

The prophet went on to an overconfident assertion of his higher purposes:

I am seeking, in short, at one and the same time to make the Italian population on the eastern islands and coasts of the Adriatic safe and secure by international guarantees and to assure Italy of neighbors who will henceforth not suspect and jealously watch her but deal with her in every way that is likely to produce mutual trust and confidence. The League of Nations now seems assured; the United States will be a party to that great association—the United States which is made up of and is the friend of all nations—and the forces of the world are united for the maintenance of all guarantees of right.

A map that was enclosed with the undelivered letter showed the Italian border east of the Tyrol as defined by the Treaty of London and as revised by the American specialists in such a way as to give the Dalmatian coast to Yugoslavia. The boundary drawn became known as the "Wilson Line." It denied to Italy much of the territory promised by the Treaty of London,[71] as well as the city of Fiume.

It is not known what moved Wilson to withhold this letter and map after they were placed in an envelope and addressed to Orlando. Possibly he followed advice from House. Perhaps he was restrained by the objections of his British and French colleagues or by a threat of Italian withdrawal from the Peace Conference. According to testimony given by Orlando three months later, the president showed him in January a map with a boundary line that was unacceptable, and Orlando made it very clear that Italy, confronted by such a settlement, would have no choice but to leave the Peace Conference.[72] The question of the Adriatic frontier faded in the ensuing weeks from the recorded discussions at the top level.

At this juncture the finance minister at Rome resigned in protest against Sonnino's policy.[73] It seemed to Ambassador Page that the life of what he called "the present patched-up Cabinet" depended primarily on the benefits that Italy could draw from the Peace Conference. Page talked with Orlando and found him greatly

70. Wilson asked Dr. Grayson to tell newmen not to put too much confidence in Yugoslavia, "a turbulent people who ought not to have a navy to run amuck," Helm diary letter, January 18, 1919.

71. See below, p. 337.

72. Extract from Aldrovandi's diary, April 19, 1919, in Albrecht-Carrié, p. 480.

73. Page advised the American commission at Paris that Nitti's resignation appeared to be "a move to make himself premier in the near future," dispatch, Pope to Ammission, January 16, 1919, Wilson papers, 6947–8.

troubled by Wilson's view, which in his opinion could not possibly be accepted by the Italian people, excited as they were by their press and by the aggressiveness of the Yugoslavs.[74] Commending Wilson to Orlando as a good friend with whom it would be well to reach accord, Page reported all this to the American commission at Paris.[75]

The president dined at the Italian embassy on January 17.[76] On the thirtieth he received Orlando after a trying day in the Supreme Council. Wilson agreed with him on many points, and proposed that a league of nations assume responsibility for all former territories of Austria-Hungary. Unfortunately, on this occassion the question of Italy's northern frontier with Austria was settled in a manner that the president was to regret.

Italy's purpose in the North was, primarily, to repatriate some 400,000 Italians in the Tyrol and, secondarily, to gain security by setting the frontier along the crest of the highest ridges and across the Brenner Pass, as the Treaty of London provided. Such a boundary would be strategically as strong as possible, but it would offend the principle of self-determination and invite political agitation in the future by including within Italy about a quarter of a million German-speaking people as well as places famous in Teutonic folklore. In the commentary on Wilson's Point Nine that House had presented in the prearmistice meetings, it was suggested that some deviation from self-determination might be justifiable in the Tyrol. The scholars of the Inquiry, however, held differing opinions. The interweaving of ethnic, strategic, and economic factors made a complex knot for the territorial specialists to unravel. Their "Black Book" of January 21 defined a frontier well south of the Brenner Pass.

In the conversation of January 30 Orlando refused to consider Italian control of the Tyrol under an international mandate. Wilson then said: "I cannot consent for Fiume to go to Italy, but you may count upon me for the Brenner line." This was enough to move Orlando to show enthusiasm for a league of nations; and Wilson came out of the conference in high good humor, calling Orlando a fine fellow and a most remarkable man.[77]

Thus, at the very beginning of the Peace Conference, the settlement of Italian claims drifted from the hands of the specialists into the vortex of the council, where political sensibilities had to be considered as well as concepts of "justice." Nicolson has written of the disillusion of young British liberals: "The spectacle of Woodrow Wilson billing and cooing with Orlando filled us with a blank despair. . . . It was his early shambling over the Italian question that convinced us that Woodrow Wilson was not a great or potent man. That conviction was a profound disappointment; on its heels demoralization spread through Paris like a disease."[78]

74. The Yugoslavs claimed "the whole Istrian peninsula . . . the counties of Gorizia and Gradisca, Fiume and the Quarnero islands, and Dalmatia with its archipelago," Ivo J. Lederer, *Yugoslavia at the Paris Peace Conference*, p. 103.

75. T. N. Page to Ammission, January 16, 1919, H. White papers, Ac. 3976, box 7.

76. Benham diary letter, January 18, 1919.

77. *I.P.*, vol. 4, p. 435. Helm letter, January 30, 1919. Seymour, "Woodrow Wilson and Self-Determination in the Tyrol," 582–585.

78. Nicolson, pp. 161, 164, 177, 184.

A few weeks later the government of the Tyrol and its German and Ladinian citizens, lacking representation at Paris, protested vigorously to Wilson that their "right of self-determination" was being violated.[79] Moreover, the American specialists were aggrieved when they heard of Wilson's disregard for their recommendation. However, they were told to transfer their attention from the Tyrol to the Adriatic coast. On April 14, when Wilson drafted a memorandum to Orlando accepting the Tyrol boundary that he had agreed upon, the matter was closed.

In May Wilson confessed to Seymour that he had made an unfortunate mistake that was based on insufficient study, and to Baker also he pleaded ignorance.[80] The validity of this confession has been questioned recently, however.[81] It seems possible that Wilson was well aware of his offense to the principle of self-determination at the time it was committed. Not only the American experts, but Nicolson in a casual briefing, had indicated the presence of hundreds of thousands of Germans in the northern Tyrol, with sympathies that, if not pro-German and pro-Austrian, were for the most part "pro-Tyrol."[82]

When Wilson made his concession to Orlando, he took the occasion to say that Fiume could not be awarded to Italy. It may be that the president felt that the yielding of the Tyrol was not too high a price to pay for a prospective Italian yielding of Fiume as well as for Orlando's allegiance to the cause of the League of Nations. Unfortunately Wilson did not insist on Orlando's explicit assent with respect to Fiume. The absence of any precise understanding on this point reveals a lack of professional diplomacy in the handling of this most controversial aspect of the peacemaking.

During the first weeks of the Peace Conference the Americans found themselves drawn into efforts to cope with Italian aspirations in the Adriatic region. Yugoslav spokesmen were no less ardent than the Italians in seeking American support for their territorial claims. Disappointed because their new state had been given no vote in the Peace Conference,[83] the Yugoslavs thought that Wilson would be a most favorable arbiter.[84]

79. Protest of February 26, 1919, Wilson papers.

80. *I.P.*, vol. 4, p. 434n. Baker's journal, May 28, 1919. This explanation is supported by Shotwell's record in the O.H.R.O. (p. 135). According to Shotwell, Wilson's eye "missed" a line that the experts drew—"the only case in the whole complicated negotiations where Wilson slipped in a fundamental point," Shotwell, O.H.R.O., p. 135.

Professor Lunt of the Inquiry had submitted in December a full report on Italy's northern boundary and a map showing three lines. The most northerly, following the central chain of the Alps, was offered to Italy in the Treaty of London and was the line set by the Armistice of Villa Giusti. Lunt thought that this, though "the best strategic frontier," was not justified historically or linguistically. The southernmost, "linguistic," line would not be easy to defend. The middle line was deemed "reasonably good" for defense but brought some 70,000 Germans within Italy, letter, Lunt to Young, December 12, 1918, clipped to handwritten note, Young to Wilson, December 13, 1918, with a sketch map, Wilson papers. The map is clipped to a copy of the full report in the D. H. Miller papers, L.C.

81. See Sterling J. Kernek, "Woodrow Wilson and National Self-Determination along Italy's Frontier," 255–264.

82. Nicolson, p. 236. Quite possibly Wilson found it more convenient to confess ignorance than to admit any deviation from principle.

83. Serbia was given two votes, and Montenegro one. See Seymour, *Letters,* p. 112.

84. See Lederer, pp. 82–84, 94–107, 135–136.

The Yugoslav cause, effectively argued before the governments of the Allies and supported by influential English publicists, was represented in the United States by sympathizers who raised volunteers for the Serbian army and funds for the Yugoslav National Committee that functioned in London. The South Slavs found in Wilson's doctrine both justification and support for their national existence. They were less confident, however, that Wilsonian principles could give effect to the various boundary settlements desired by Serbs, Croats, and Slovenes, who were uniting to form the new state. The ambiguous status of Yugoslavia, as well as Italy's mistrust of it and the existence of political strife among its national elements,[85] had led Wilson to temporize when during the closing months of the war he received Yugoslav pleas for a favorable definition of the American policy.[86]

Ante Trumbić, the foreign minister of the new state, had talked with Wilson on February 6. The meeting was arranged by Steed, whom House asked to discover the final terms of the Yugoslavs, so that if those terms seemed just, the president might insist upon Italian acceptance of them. Trumbić, finding Wilson cordial and very kind, placed before him a map on which extreme demands of both Slavs and Italians were shown and also four other suggested boundaries. According to Steed, Trumbić told the president that the drawing of the frontier in Istria would be left to his judgment. Wilson remarked that he could arbitrate only if asked by both sides to do so. He suggested that the Yugoslavs make a formal proposal through Clemenceau, the president of the Peace Conference.[87] Trumbić agreed to do this. The next day Lansing released a declaration that had been prepared by the American advisers on southeast Europe.[88] It welcomed the union of the Serbs, Croats, and Slovenes, and was regarded by both Yugoslav delegates and the American State Department as equivalent to recognition.[89]

On the same day Trumbić wrote thus to the cabinet at Belgrade: "A serious American source suggested to me the idea of Wilson's arbitration. I was told that Wilson will soon be off to the United States. Whether he returns will depend on various circumstances. It is better for you if your problems are settled while he is here."[90] The Yugoslav cabinet then voted to accept Wilson's arbitration of the whole dispute with Italy. Informed of this, the president sent word to the Yugoslavs that he was "deeply moved" by their confidence in him.

85. On August 19, 1918, the secretary of state had reminded the president that the Austrian Yugoslavs could not claim recognition as cobelligerents, although the Serbs were. Lansing warned that "the jealousy of Italy and the desire of Serbia to absorb the Yugo-Slavs rather than to become federated with them makes it necessary to be cautious in deciding on a policy," *F.R.*, Lansing papers, vol. 2, p. 140.
86. Victor S. Mamatey, *The U.S. and East Central Europe, 1914–1918*, pp. 358–359. Walworth, pp. 180–182. *F.R., P.P.C.*, vol. 2, pp. 287, 892. Wilson to William Phillips, November 20, 1918, N.A., R.G. 59, 763.72/12413.
87. Steed, *Through Thirty Years, 1892–1922*, vol. 2, p. 278. Memorandum, Steed to Northcliffe, February 3, 1919, Steed papers. Lederer, pp. 145–147.
88. Memorandum, Seymour to A. W. Dulles, January 22, 1919, Y.H.C.
89. The State Department later recognized that the declaration of February 7 did not technically effect formal recognition, Phillips to Lansing, March 28, 1919, Wilson papers. It included a proviso that the final frontiers would be determined by the Peace Conference "in accordance with the wishes of the peoples concerned," Mamatey, pp. 374–375. Lederer, p. 148. *F.R.*, vol. 2, p. 346. Ammission to Polk, February 6, 1919, *F.R., 1919*, vol. 2, pp. 892–899.
90. Lederer, pp. 147, 159, 163–171. Steed, vol. 2, p. 278.

This maneuver, instigated by House and furthered by Steed and Trumbić, placed the Italian delegates in an embarrassing position. They could not accept the challenge to arbitration without risking the loss of much that the Treaty of London promised them east of the Adriatic. A refusal, on the other hand, would imply a lack of confidence in the justness of their own claims. Moreover, it would suggest that they, unlike the Yugoslavs, lacked faith in the American president.

At that very time, the Italian delegation dimmed any prospect of settlement by presenting to the Peace Conference a formal statement of claims that went beyond the Treaty of London.[91] Yet Orlando went to see Wilson and promised to respond to the Yugoslav challenge as soon as he could consult with the cabinet and the king of Italy. On February 17 Clemenceau told the Supreme Council of the Yugoslav proposal. Thereupon Sonnino, in the absence of Orlando, declared that his government found arbitration unacceptable. He refused, moreover, to engage in open debate with Yugoslavs before the council and declined to permit any international committee of experts to study the question. Thus Yugoslavia was denied an equal status with Italy in the consideration of matters vital to both.[92]

This was an extraordinary departure from the regular procedure of the Peace Conference in territorial matters. It angered the Yugoslav cabinet, which was sorely beset by both domestic and external pressures. The integrity of the new state was menaced by separatist tendencies that were encouraged by Italian propaganda, as well as by sporadic border skirmishes that the inter-Allied commission at Fiume ascribed largely to Italian provocation. The Yugoslav government and its representatives at Paris got no satisfying response to their frequent protests.

The dangerous controversy dragged on, while popular feeling rose and made accommodation the more difficult. During the month of February the American peacemakers reacted adversely to Italian interference at Trieste with shipments of food that were intended to relieve the distress of civilians in central Europe. After the inter-Allied Blockade Committee had refused to relax its restrictions, Herbert Hoover had acted independently to send agents to distribute food; and on his request Admiral William S. Benson, confident that no one would venture to stop any American ship bent on a mission of relief, ordered the naval commander in the Adriatic to cooperate completely. Hoover, overcoming objections by Foch and by Italian delegates, received from the Supreme Economic Council a mandate over all railways in the Hapsburg lands provided that he work through this council. Notifying Wilson of attempts to cripple rail and port facilities, and asserting that the blockade in the southeast was "being used . . . for purely economic goals," he suggested that the Treasury of the United States be instructed to withhold any further credits to the Italian government until this matter was settled to his satisfaction.[93] On the same day, Norman Davis of the Treasury reported to the president that Italian officials were asking that, now the British Exchequer had discontinued advances to

91. Lederer, p. 153.

92. *Ibid.*, pp. 153–155. Steed, vol. 2, pp. 278–281. *F.R., P.P.C.*, vol. 4, pp. 27–28. Nicolson p. 164. Auchincloss diary, February 8 and 10, 1919. Gino Speranza, on whom Ambassador Page relied for a sympathetic interpretation of Italian opinion, recorded in his diary (entry of March 9, 1919) that Italians almost unanimously supported the refusal of their delegates at Paris to agree to arbitration.

93. Hoover, *Ordeal of Woodrow Wilson*, pp. 161–162. Letter, Hoover to Wilson, February 12, 1919,

Italy, the American Treasury, which heretofore had been making loans to finance purchases within the United States, should supply a credit of $25 million for Italian use in neutral countries. Davis, stating that the Treasury was reluctant to grant this request, pointed out that a loan might easily be made contingent upon a cessation of the obstruction of which Hoover complained.[94]

After considering the matter for a few days the president sent this message to the Treasury: "I sympathize with your reluctance, but I consider it of public interest and necessity that the situation in Italy be not allowed to grow worse and if you can see your way to do so, I would approve of your advancing to Italy, upon such conditions as you may determine, up to twenty-five millions toward meeting her current neutral purchases which may appear to be otherwise unobtainable."[95] By cutting off credits for Italy the president would risk the development of conditions that bred ill will and revolution. He was not yet ready to go to this extreme. Indeed, it appeared that such a drastic step might be counterproductive, when Silvio Crespi, an Italian plenipotentiary, shocked the Supreme Economic Council by a threat of blackmail.[96]

South of Dalmatia another Italian-Slav controversy raged in the tiny mountainous land of Montenegro. There King Nicholas, father of the queen of Italy, had been deposed by a people's assembly that voted to unite with Serbia. Living in Paris, he had called on House three days before the armistice of November 11 and had expressed hope that the United States would take the place of Russia as his friend and protector.[97]

The issue was not clear cut. The peacemakers at Paris did not know exactly to what extent the movement for union of Montenegro with Serbia resulted from Serb pressure, and to what extent from sentiment that was genuinely indigenous. The question was important as an example of the strain put upon diplomacy by Wilson's principles. The president had proclaimed in Point Eleven that Montenegro should be evacuated and its occupied territory restored, and that its relations with other Balkan states should be "determined by friendly counsel along historically established lines of allegiance and nationality." It was not easy, however, to apply this formula to the existing situation. The Italian government kept the issue alive by appeals to both Great Britain and the United States for aid in combatting Serbian influence in Montenegro.[98]

Wilson papers *F.R., P.P.C.,* vol. 4, p. 262. See Zinojinović, pp. 225–235.

94. Letter, Davis to Wilson, February 12, 1919, forwarding a cable of January 21, 191, from Secretary Glass, Wilson papers. As early as December 1918 Davis had discussed with Bliss, Crosby, and Hurley the possibility of withholding American loans to Italy until the Italian army was demobilized, Bliss diary, December 23, 1918, Also see Bliss to Lansing, January 9, 1919, Bliss papers, enclosing a report from General di Robillant.

95. Wilson to the secretary of the treasury, February 19, 1919, Wilson papers.

96. McCormick diary, February 17, 1919, On Wilson's economic power over Italy and his reluctance to exploit it, see John Wells Gould, "Italy and the U.S., 1914–1918," pp. 409–415.

97. House diary, November 8, 1919.

98. Lederer, pp. 114–115. Bonsal, pp. 88, 93. It was the opinion of Bonsal that some Italians wanted Montenegro included in Yugoslavia in order to weaken the new state.

When the government of Serbia announced that it had absorbed the little country, King Nicholas appealed to Wilson. In response the president drafted a sympathetic note on January 9, sent it to Lansing, and asked that it be delivered unless the secretary of state saw "some diplomatic complication in it." Expressing his admiration for "the sturdy independence of the little kingdom" into which Serbia was sending troops, he requested Lansing to have a "frank talk" with Milenko Vesnić, the Serbian minister at Paris, keeping in mind the fact that the sympathies of Americans were as much with Montenegro as with Serbia. Lansing put the president's note before the American commission, and it was decided to forward it to the king and to send an American agent to Montenegro to investigate and report. When Nicholas sought an interview with the president on January 11, Wilson asked Lansing for "a tip" as to whether it would be wise or serviceable for him to receive the monarch; and the secretary of state replied that in view of the attitude of the Allied governments toward Nicholas, this would be unwise at the present time.[99]

On January 12, when the council discussed Montenegro's representation at the Peace Conference, Wilson insisted that no new state had a right to decide the fate of another without its consent. He resented the presence of Serbian troops in Montenegro and doubted that its "national assembly" was legally convoked. Nor did he accept the government-in-exile that the chief adviser of Nicholas set up. He doubted that a qualified man could be found to represent Montenegro at the Peace Conference.[100] In the end Nicholas failed to gain independent representation at Paris.[101]

Conditions in Montenegro were disturbing American intelligence officers,[102] and the question of military action became critical. To counter the presence of Serb troops in the capital of Montenegro the Italian government sent a force into the port of Cattaro, with orders not to move inland. The contingent consisted of three battalions: American, French, and Italian. On January 16 Sonnino reported the maneuver to Lansing as a *fait accompli*.[103] Thus the Peace Conference was confronted with an act of intervention in which American troops were involved.

When General Bliss put before the president a French proposal that an American company at Cattaro go inland to the capital to participate with British forces in supervising an election, Wilson forbade the use of American troops in this or any similar way without his specific approval. Such approval was not forthcoming.[104]

99. *F.R., P.P.C.*, vol. 2, pp. 362–368, 370. Minutes, ACTNP, January 6 and 11, 1919, Grew papers, Houghton Library, Harvard University.

100. *F.R., P.P.C.*, vol. 3, p. 489. Official French procès-verbal for the meeting of the Supreme Council of January 12, 1919.

101. Lederer, p. 116.

102. The assistant military attaché at Rome, a nephew of Ambassador Page, reported to the president after six weeks in Montenegro that withdrawal of all foreign intervention would result in anarchy, that a decided majority of the people wished to join the Yugoslav state provided that they could maintain autonomy, and that they were opposed to occupation by an international force, A. W. Dulles, "Report on Current Events in the Balkans," January 13–20, 1919, copy in Y.H.C. Reports by Captain Bruce and letter, Bruce to T. N. Page, February 3, 1919, enclosed with letter of T. N. Page, February 2, 1919, Y.H.C.

103. Sonnino to Lansing, January 16, 1919, Y.H.C.

104. The French proposals were made to Bliss, and through Bonsal to House, Bliss diary, January 20, 1919, box 65. Copy of message of January 20, 1919, telephoned by Bliss to Pershing, box 7, file

The British Foreign Office endeavored in February to shake the American position. It supported an Italian desire that the United States undertake to intervene alone, and pressed this proposal as the only way to arrive at the "true wishes" of the Montenegrin people. The United States, it was pointed out, was the only power to which all European nations would gladly give a mandate. But this idea was firmly rejected.[105] Consequently Balfour wrote to House at some length on March 28 to say that all Allied forces were to be withdrawn. Balfour proposed an Anglo-American commission to ascertain "the real wishes of the Montenegrin people."[106]

Within a week Wilson accepted Balfour's proposal. The American representative on the investigating commission reported at Paris on May 19. Forwarding his statement to the president on the thirtieth, Lansing wrote: "His conclusions confirm reports from many other sources that the solution of the Montenegrin question which would best meet the wishes of the people concerned, is the incorporation of this country into Yugoslavia under guarantees of autonomy and the protection of local rights."[107] This was the settlement finally accepted by the powers. The Americans could feel that the principle of self-determination had been applied in this confusing situation in accord with the best advice that was available.

National dreams of expansion challenged self-determination in yet another region east of the Adriatic. Italy's concerns brought it into conflict with Greece, an allied country where a "National Government" had upset the monarchy of Constantine. Eleutherios Venizelos, the premier of a revolutionary democracy, wished to recapture a measure of the glory of ancient Hellas. He hoped to liberate some 2 million kinsmen who were under foreign rule and thus to bring at least three of every four Greeks within the borders of the nation. One object was redemption of the Greeks in Thrace—a land of statistical chaos and ethnographic mixtures—claimed on grounds of strategy, ethnography, and commercial advantage. Greece likewise desired the islands of the eastern Mediterranean and coastal regions in Asia Minor,[108] as well as the southern part of Albania, in which the Greek population was rebellious.[109]

no 5/0, no. 88, Bliss papers, L.C. Memorandum for the president, January 17, 1919, Wilson papers, box 15. Derby to Curzon, February 23, 1919, Curzon papers 22:F/6/2.

105. *F.R., P.P.C.,* vol. 2, pp. 370–372. J. W. Davis to Ammission, February 5, 1919, Y.H.C. Barclay to State Department, February 19, 1919, Polk to Barclay, February 28, 1919, N.A., R.G. 59, 763.72/12859. T. N. Page to the secretary of state, January 8, 1919, *ibid.,* 763.72/12647.

106. Balfour's letter, with an endorsement by House, is in the Wilson papers. Balfour's recommendation was similar to one made to the American commission on March 10 by the Division of Current Diplomatic and Political Correspondence, memorandum in Y.H.C.

107. *F.R., P.P.C.,* vol. 12, pp. 736–744; Ammission to Coolidge (Vienna), April 4, 1919, Wilson papers. Professor Clive Day, reporting to Lansing that King Nicholas, who had again sought Wilson's aid in a letter promising to respect the will of a parliament, was thoroughly discredited in the Balkans, advised that the union with Yugoslavia was inevitable, Day to Lansing, May 5, 1919; Day to Wilson May 6, 1919, Wilson papers.

108. Haskins and Lord, *Some Problems of the Paris Conference,* p. 281. Seymour and House (eds.), *What Really Happened at Paris,* p. 173. *F.R., P.P.C.,* vol. 3, pp. 859–875. F. O. Handbook no. 15, pp. 46, 50. Memorandum by Venizelos, December 30, 1918, in his *Greece before the Peace Congress.* See Dimitri Kitsikis, *Propagande et pressions en politique internationale.*

109. None of the armistices had made provision for the occupation of any front in Albania; and the American peace commission thought that country, which had seemed about to fall apart until a national assembly convened on December 25, 1918, and elected a president, was not qualified as a nation for

There was conflict at many points with the aspirations of Italy as well as with those of native populations.

Venizelos, emerging from the war as the all-powerful ruler of Greece, was confident of support at the Peace Conference from Great Britain and to a lesser extent from France. He had arrived at Paris before the signing of the armistice and established an office that poured out propaganda. A pleader with great perspicacity and charm, and a former university professor who had led students in revolt in the cause of a greater Greece, he quickly won Wilson's sympathy when he called on the president in December. He professed enthusiasm for a league of nations and was chosen as a representative of the small powers on the commission that was to frame the constitution.

It was the opinion of Secretary Lansing, writing two years after the event, that the views of this mild-mannered and professorial revolutionary, who had once lived as an outlaw in caves in the mountains of Crete, weighed more heavily in the Supreme Council than those of any other single delegate. Yet the secretary of state did not fall entirely under the spell of the smile and the voice that seemed to diffuse nothing but virtue.[110] The Greek premier's insatiable appetite for territory made Lansing wonder whether a man with so wide an experience in Balkan diplomacy could believe sincerely that the future peace and prosperity of Greece would be served by an expansion that seemed sure to provoke future reprisals by neighboring states. The Inquiry shared these doubts.[111]

Venizelos, whom Bonsal thought "so charming that everybody was afraid of him,"[112] wooed House and the American specialists ardently.[113] Pleading before

---

admittance to the Peace Conference. See Robert L. Woodall's dissertation, "The Albanian Problem during the Peacemaking."

The Treaty of London had allotted northern Albania to neighboring Serbia and the central region to a protectorate under Italy, which already had occupied the port of Valona; and the Italians were eager to extend their sway southward. However, many Greeks lived in southern Albania. The American experts, who in their "Black Book" made recommendations that in many respects challenged Greek claims, thought that the disputed territory in southern Albania should go to Greece because of "ethnic affinity and economic advantage." They later proposed a compromise under which Albania would retain the region around Koritza [Korcë], a center of nationalism, and Greece would be denied about two-thirds of the area it claimed. See N. Petsalis-Diomidis, *Greece at the Paris Peace Conference*, pp. 140, 145. This recommendation brought them into conflict with the British specialists, who yielded to a French desire that Greece have Koritza. Gelfand, pp. 220–221. Haskins and Lord, pp. 278 ff. Miller, vol. 10, pp. 286–287, 302. Edith P. Stickney, *South Albania and North Epirus in European International Affairs 1912–1923* (Stanford, Calif., 1926) p. 111. Professor Day did not share the desire of Sir Eyre Crowe, the veteran British diplomat, to settle the question "on a cold bargaining basis." Day wrote, "The Albanians come constantly to protest. I am sorry for the poor devils."

110. Venizelos was so wise in tactics that, recognizing the power of his personality, he feared that too forceful an exertion of it might cause his friends in the Supreme Council to lean backward in an effort to make fair judgments, Wilson to Lansing, December 10, 1918, Wilson papers. House diary, October 27, 1918. Joseph C. Grew, vol. 1, p. 343. Nicolson, pp. 33, 251.

111. Lansing, *The Big Four and Others at the Peace Conference*, pp. 142–160. Venizelos used the American delegates as a "sounding board" for most of the ideas that he presented in a memorandum of Greek claims dated December 30, Nicholas Rizopoulos, "Greece at the Paris, 1919." Of Venizelos, Clemenceau said: "Ulysses n'était qu'un petit garçon à côté de lui," Gooch, *Recent Revelations of European Diplomacy* (London, 1930), p. 323.

112. *Unfinished Business*, p. 308.

113. "The Greeks certainly are running us hard," Clive Day, Chief of the Balkan Division of the Inquiry, wrote in his diary. "I have been assured so often that Greece wants nothing that does not

the Supreme Council on February 3 he took up almost two sessions with a presentation of claims that were shrewdly calculated. He was seeking help from the treasuries of France, Great Britain, and the United States.[114] When he attributed the quality of the native schools in the main centers of Albania to the fact that they had American teachers, Wilson beamed and brought his palms together gently, saying, "Hear! Hear!"

Lloyd George proposed the appointment of a committee of specialists to consider Greek claims. Clemenceau asked for "objections," then abruptly said "Adopté". The Italians gasped. They did not want an objective inquiry that touched upon national territorial claims, for it would set a precedent that might embarrass them when they presented their own.[115] Nevertheless, the proposed commission was set up, and in meetings in February and March it was unable to reach agreement on the question of the Greek-Albanian boundary. Professor Day, one of the American members, wrote: "We cannot hope for a reasonably clean peace without a downright fight with the Italians; and Wilson is the only man who can possibly make it and win it. We hope and pray he'll do it."[116] The prayer of the scholars was soon to be answered.[117]

During the first weeks of the Peace Conference Wilson succeeded in giving some effect to the policies that he had proclaimed with moral fervor. He had won prior consideration of his fourteenth and last point (the one that he thought most vital): the creation of an association of nations to keep the peace. At the same time he had checked the ardor of French nationalists for a settlement that would in the long run prove damaging to Europe's economic life and might goad the German people to seek vengeance. Moreover, although he had offended against the principle of self-determination in the Tyrol, he had stood fast against a like violation on the Adriatic coast. Though Wilson's language and manner were more nearly those of a schoolmaster or preacher than those of a diplomat, and he sometimes irritated and exasperated his colleagues and at times the temper he held barely in leash escaped his control, the president of the "associated power," the legitimacy of whose participation in the governance of Europe was in question, was listened to with a degree of respect.

The prophet of a new order, comprehending the complexity of his task, confessed his bewilderment after a few days of give-and-take with the European premiers. There was some truth in a jocose remark that he made when a Princeton pupil, now a soldier on leave in Paris, was brought up to him by Allen Dulles, a fellow pupil,

---

rightfully belong to her, that I am almost inclined to doubt it," Day diary, January 5 and 6, 1919. To Day it seemed that the statistics of population adduced by the Greeks were "not trustworthy," that some obviously were "manufactured," diary, January 8, 1919, Y.H.C. Day's control of facts was "matched by the judicial care with which he weighed them. At Paris there was no American to whom the European delegates listened more readily," Seymour, *Letters,* p. xxvii.

114. O. T. Crosby to Wilson, January 14, 1919, Wilson papers.

115. Nicolson, pp. 255–256. Westermann diary, February 4, 1919. See Petsalis-Diomidis, pp. 146–147 and map.

116. Day diary, March 20, 1919.

117. See below, ch. 18.

and blurted out blithely: "Well, what are you doing over here, Mr. Wilson?" The burdened peacemaker, startled by this effusion of campus breeziness, replied very frankly: "I'm really not sure that I know."[118]

118. William M. Whitney, Princeton 1912, to A.W. "I dare say that you know as much about what is going on over here as we do who are on the ground," Wilson wrote to Newton D. Baker, the secretary of war. "The difficulty of weaving all the threads into a single pattern sometimes bewilders me," Wilson to Newton D. Baker, January 23, Wilson to Senator John Sharp Williams, January 13, 1919, Wilson papers.

4

"Possessions" or "Mandates"?

In January the Supreme Council discussed the disposal of the seized German colonies—the Pacific islands, East Africa, South West Africa, the Cameroons, and Togo. Consideration of this question, following only a few days after the controversy with the British dominions over the matter of representation,[1] precipitated a conflict between President Wilson and the spokesmen for the Allied governments. This encounter raised the question of future relations among the English-speaking peoples, as well as difficulties posed by a secret wartime understanding among the Allies.

It was vital, in Wilson's opinion, that any arrangements made for the government of colonial peoples should come within the purview of a league of nations and should serve to solidify the position of the new international body. Obviously the league must be created before it could be entrusted with authority to supervise the rule of the less advanced peoples of the world. Immediate introduction into the proceedings at Paris of the question of the governance of the ex-German colonies was a threat to the American program. In placing the league of nations first among the five topics that the Peace Conference accepted on January 18, Wilson hoped to ensure that the new regime would not be, as the French foreign ministry had proposed, merely a source of moral sanction for the acquisition of German territories. George Louis Beer of the Inquiry recognized the import of the challenge and wrote in his diary: "Whole question a test case and vital to league of nations. It is absolutely fundamental."[2]

European colonization in Asia and Africa had a long history, going back more than three centuries, and the life of each colony down through the years had responded to the manners, thought, and ethics of its foreign ruler. Native aspirations to self-government, which reflected the general trend in the world toward democratic polities, were sometimes repressed, sometimes guided by the ruling power.

Opinion in the United States was far from well informed as to the policies of the chief imperial powers. Many idealists tended to assume that colonial government was always oppressive. Americans, proud and sentimental about their own revolt of 1776, sympathized with restless colonial peoples. There was a wish that undeveloped countries might be guided to become independent, self-respecting members of the family of nations. Leftists in the Western democracies were not unsympathetic to Lenin's denunciation of "imperialism."

Wilson recognized this sentiment. In his view the colonial system offended the principle of self-determination by exerting a right to hand peoples about from sovereignty to sovereignty as if they were property. In the fifth of his Fourteen Points

1. See above, pp. 17–18.
2. Beer diary, January 28, February 1 and 5, 1919, Special Collections, Columbia University Library.

he had demanded "a free, open-minded, and absolutely impartial adjustment of all colonial claims, based upon a strict observance of the principle that in determining all such questions of sovereignty the interests of the populations concerned must have equal weight with the equitable claims of the government whose title is to be determined."

When Wilson put "colonial possessions" at the end of his agenda and required that a league of nations be formed at once to deal with this question and to protect the welfare of the native peoples, spokesmen for the empires felt that their vital prerogatives were slighted. The losses of the war had been so high that some of the British dominions conceived that they could secure adequate reparation only by adding to their territory certain German possessions that had been a potential menace to their communications and even to their national integrity. It was generally understood that, following the precedent set by America's obliteration of Spain's empire in 1898, Germany would be stripped of all its colonies.

Even though two of the dominions—Australia and South Africa—hoped to take over certain German territories, the rulers of Great Britain had no desire to add to the burden of governance that they had long borne with faith that their task was God-given and man-nurturing. Although the bonds of empire had gained strength during the war, it now seemed too great a task for Great Britain, a nation of some 45 million which had lost a million of its best men, to govern nearly ten times as many people overseas.[3] British statesmen hoped for American collaboration in ordering the affairs of the world after the pattern of the empire. The government of colonies under an international trusteeship seemed to offer an expedient solution of problems facing British administrators.[4]

Advanced by British Labour during the war, the ideal of trusteeship had been propagated by a forum that was known as the Round Table. Under the leadership of Lord Milner, who was an authority on the affairs of the empire and a champion of its administrative ideals, and who insisted on the prime importance of Anglo-American collaboration,[5] conspicuous young men who scorned connections with political parties made the most of their abilities and social position to advance well-considered policies. They had presented a liberal philosophy of colonial rule in the *Round Table,* a journal of small circulation but wide political influence. Philip Kerr was its editor until the end of 1916, when he undertook to serve Lloyd George, first in the administrative reorganization of the war cabinet and then at the Peace Conference as personal secretary.[6] Kerr advocated "a larger, more constructive and more generous conception of international reconstruction based upon the idea of responsibility." It seemed to him that Woodrow Wilson, a "Gladstonian liberal"

3. Eustace Percy, *Some Memories.* D. H. Miller, "Origins of the Mandates System," *Foreign Affairs* 6, no. 2 (January 1928):281.

4. William Roger Louis, "The U.S. and the African Peace Settlement of 1919," *Journal of African History* 4, no. 3 (1965):413–415, q.v. for a bibliography of works on the origin and development of the concept of trusteeship.

5. Cobb to House, November 9, 1918, Y.H.C.,

6. Kerr, desiring a close understanding between Great Britain and the United States, was thought by Professor Shotwell to be "idealistic but practical at the same time," *At the Paris Peace Conference,* p. 151. As Lord Lothian, Kerr was later ambassador to Washington.

whose views were admirable as far as they went, was proposing a settlement so lacking in precise definition of responsibility that it appeared to be "negative" and to contain within itself "the seeds of disaster."[7]

In the *Round Table* in December 1918, it was pointed out that the British Empire, in which matters that could not be settled in correspondence were considered in an occasional conference of ministers, was a genuine league of nations and a good deal more, that the world would be wise to consider the road by which the empire had achieved unity. It was proposed that the Peace Conference become, in effect, a permanent annual gathering of ministers that would serve as a symbol of the human conscience and would share Britain's burdens. Liberia was cited as an example of an application of American good will without adequate assumption of responsibility.[8]

Actually, current allegations of corruption in the oligarchy that ruled Liberia cast a shadow on its American sponsors. The model colonial government in Nigeria was cited in contrast. The British and French governments were annoyed by a threat that was posed by anarchy in the hinterland of Liberia to the maintenance of order in their adjacent colonies. They wished to participate equally with the United States in the financing of the native Liberian government.[9] The American government, arguing that international control had proved to be inefficient, had provided credit for maintenance of an effective constabulary under American officers.[10] London and Paris were informed that the American loan was for good government and equal commercial opportunity for all.[11] American officials protested the disinterestedness of their nation, using the phrase "next friend" to give moral sanction to their venture in Africa much as the British had employed "the white man's burden."[12]

There was much force in the contention that if European colonizers were to be responsible to an international league under trusteeships, the United States also should be answerable for its befriending of Liberia, where an American citizen was acting as financial adviser. Indeed the British officials adopted the very policy that Wilson had used in dealing with those aims of the Allies that seemed to him imperialistic; they suggested that the question of Liberia's future be considered at the Peace Conference.

The idea of colonial trusteeship was not foreign to Americans.[13] Nevertheless

7. Butler, *Lothian,* pp. 68–70.

8. *Round Table* 9, no. 33 (December 1918):20–35; also no. 34 (March 1919):249–260.

9. Notes exchanged between the State Department and its London embassy, December 8–21, 1918, enclosed with letter, Bell to Harrison, December 31, 1918. Letter, Bell to Harrison, February 6, 1919, Harrison papers, box 103. Westermann diary, December 11, 1918, Special Collections, Columbia University Library. Minutes, I.W.C., December 20, 1918.

Ambassador Jusserand alleged that the United States government had established "practically a protectorate" over Liberia without any formal treaty that would require the Senate's approval, Beer diary, December 11, 1918.

10. *F.R., 1918,* pp. 537–537, 545. *F.R., 1919,* vol. 2, p. 494. See Louis R. Harlan, "Booker T. Washington," *American Historical Review* 71, no. 2 (January 1966).

11. N.A., R.G. 59, 763. 72119/319a and 3243. The State Department proposed to create an American receivership of customs and internal revenues and to improve the Liberian economy.

12. *F.R., P.P.C.,* vol. 1, pp. 534–539. *F.R., 1919,* vol. 2, p. 465.

13. President Theodore Roosevelt had suggested before the Algeciras conference that in Morocco, France and Spain be "the mandatory of all the Powers," and the United States government conceived

there was opposition in the United States, particularly on the part of leaders of the Republican party, against the assumption by the American government of a trustee's responsibility[14] even in this region in which the nation's economic interest was substantial; and the American government did not wish to discuss this question at Paris.

George Louis Beer of the Inquiry, a man of affairs and an authority on British colonial policy who had kept in touch with members of the Round Table and served as its American correspondent, undertook to deal with the Liberian situation.[15] Finding it "absurdly complex," he negotiated an agreement under which France and Great Britain would forgo participation in the financing of Liberia and the United States would guarantee an "open door" and the protection of native rights. A draft of a treaty was sent to Washington with Lansing's endorsement on April 17; but it was not until the end of 1919 that a necessary understanding with the Treasury was reached.[16]

Lloyd George, approaching the peacemaking with all the canny respect for public opinion that had made him conspicuously successful in British politics, perceived that the dominions, having contributed vitally to the common victory, chafed at the limitations of imperial rule and sought a measure of autonomy. Wishing to hold them loyal to the crown, he was disinclined to deny their claims to possession of territories that were to be taken from Germany. Indeed, the peacemaking was a test of the capacity of an emerging commonwealth to recognize the interests of the several dominions.

Having strengthened his popular mandate in the United Kingdom by winning the December election, Lloyd George sought to ascertain the thinking of the Imperial War Cabinet. They were caught between demands of the dominions for outright annexation and the clamor of Liberals and Labour for trusteeships that would uphold the standards that the Colonial Office was already striving to maintain. The prime minister, wishing to discuss no question with Wilson without knowing in what respect he would have to "put his foot down" in particular instances, wanted

---

that in building the Panama Canal it acted as "the mandatory of civilization," Quincy Wright, *Mandates under the League of Nations,* p. 20.

14. Roosevelt to J. Murray Clark, December 15, 1918, forwarded with a letter, Clark to Balfour, January 9, 1919, Balfour papers, 49749. Letter, Murray to Wiseman, July 22, 1918, "very confidential," and enclosures, Wiseman papers, Y.H.C. Laughlin to Lansing, October 29, 1918, *F.R.,* Lansing papers, vol. 2, pp. 413–415.

Senator Lodge informed Lord Bryce that he was averse to the idea of creating mandatories that would be "subject to continual interference by a league of nations." Lodge wrote to Bryce on February 3, 1919, thus: "I rather shrink from committing the U. S. to continually meddling, "letter in Bryce papers, 7, p. 166, Bodleian Library.

15. Beer diary, December 22, 1918. Shotwell, p. 90, no. 2. When members of the Round Table had visited New York during the war, a confidential relationship had developed with the Inquiry. "Nothing was held back," Shotwell wrote, "and we had the feeling that we were dealing with men who were of the utmost integrity," Shotwell, O.H.R.O. Record.

Of Beer's work at Paris, Seymour wrote: "It was he who picked up the ideas of General Smuts on colonial mandates and adjusted them to fit the mental processes of Woodrow Wilson. In this respect Beer made one of the most vital contributions," *Letters from the Paris Peace Conference,* xxix.

16. Beer diary, January 11, 1919, and *passim.* Beer, *African Questions at the Paris Peace Confer-*

instructions that would leave him free for maneuvering, especially in situations in which delegates of nations other than the United States might undertake "log-rolling."[17]

Balfour thought that the first question to be put to Wilson should be directed to ascertain the policy of the United States in regard to sharing the burden of preparing inexperienced peoples for self-government; and at the same time he made it clear that he felt that the president would be unable to give an answer that would bind the Senate at Washington. Lloyd George concluded that there was general approval of the principle of trusteeship and that he should sound out Wilson as to the acceptance of responsibility by the United States.[18] The British desire for American cooperation in the governance of undeveloped regions was widespread.

However, when the imperial ministers fell into discussion of specific territories that might be mandated to the United States and the relative risks to British interests, Lloyd George expressed an earnest hope that the American republic would not be let into Europe and, above all, not into so dominant a position as Constantinople. He warned, moreover, against entrusting Palestine, amid the complicated interests of Great Britain in the Near East, to an absolutely untried power like the United States.[19] He foresaw that everyone with complaints against British administration would run with them to Washington, which would not be able to resist the temptation to meddle, and this might lead to a serious quarrel. Actually, the principle of self-determination was posing a threat to political stability in Egypt, where, on December 10, 1918, the National party had appealed to the United States for support.[20]

As to conquered territories in South-West Africa and in the Pacific ocean south of the equator, the British leaders felt compelled to support the demand for annexation that was put forward by the dominions whose troops occupied them. London could neither control the policies of the dominions nor dissociate itself from their decisions.[21]

In the prearmistice meetings House had tried to allay the fears of European imperialists. Although his interpretation of Point Five held that the conduct of colonial administrations was to be "a matter of international concern and may legitimately be the subject of international inquiry," he gave assurance that there would be no interference with the sovereign rights of overseas domains. Moreover, he made it

---

ence, pp. 424–425, 431. *F.R., 1919,* vol. 2, pp. 471–473. See Emily S. Rosenberg, "The Invisible Protectorate . . . ," *Diplomatic History* 9, no. 3, 198–199.

17. Minutes, I.W.C., December 18, 1918. The opinions of the various members of the cabinet on the question of colonialism between August and December 1918 are summarized by Gaddis Smith in "The British Government and the Disposition of the German Colonies in Africa, 1914–1918," in *Britain and Germany in Africa,* ed. Prosser Gifford and W. R. Louis (New Haven, 1967), p. 296.

to give Constantinople and the Dardanelles to the United States, and that he had not suggested to Wilson an American mandate for Palestine, Mesopotamia, or East Africa. This paragraph is omitted from the long quotation of the minutes that Lloyd George printed in *The Truth about the Peace Treaties,* pp. 135–201. Some members of the cabinet thought that a mandate for Armenia might safely be offered to the United States. Lloyd George was to speak in May in favor of American control of Anatolia. See below, p. 494.

20. See below, p. 509.

21. G. P. de T. Glazebrook, *Canada at the Paris Peace Conference* p. 90.

clear that it was intended not to open old questions of colonial rule, but only to adjust claims that grew out of the war. Accepting the present system as one that could benefit both the mother countries and their dependencies, House was ready to come to an understanding with the British statesmen as to a proper policy.[22] He sought to work closely with Balfour, and in this he used the good offices of Wiseman.

Even before Wilson received House's report of the prearmistice meetings, however, the president, who himself understood that England sought no new lands to govern, had shown awareness of anti-imperialist feelings among the American people. He confided to Wiseman that he would be content to see the German colonies administered by Great Britain, whose empire he considered a model for the world in many respects; but at the same time he warned of the great jealousy of non-British peoples including, he confessed with regret, a large number of Americans. Fearing that international ill will would result from the establishment of British sovereignty over the German colonies, Wilson suggested to Wiseman that they be administered by single states in trust for a league of nations.[23] At one time before he left Washington he thought that some of the small noncolonial nations of Europe might act as trustees, and aboard the *George Washington* he spoke of this possibility. The vagueness of his ideas alarmed George Louis Beer.[24] This adviser did not believe that governments such as the Scandinavian, having scant resources and little experience in colonial administration, could hope to serve as well as the great powers. Beer's misgivings as to the inadequacy of the president's thinking grew.[25]

During Wilson's visit to London at the end of 1918 he exchanged views with Lloyd George and Balfour. According to Lloyd George's report of the conversation,[26] Wilson pointed out that the United States was very proud of its disinterested position. Yet he went so far as to say that once a league of nations was constituted to supervise trusteeships, his country might be less reluctant to consider the acceptance of a mandate. Lloyd George showed a willingness to permit a league of nations to dispose of German East Africa, with provisions that would guarantee the security of India and that of imperial communications. Arguing for different treatment of lands adjacent to British dominions and conquered by them, he spoke of the impossibility of separating South-West Africa from the Union of South Africa. Then, drawing Germany's Pacific islands into the discussion, he alluded to the commitment that had been made secretly to Japan in 1917. This promised to support the Japanese claim to islands north of the equator in exchange for Japan's support of

22. See Walworth, *America's Moment: 1918*, p. 69.

23. Wiseman's interview with Wilson, October 16, 1918, Y.H.C. It was Wiseman's opinion that Wilson, although never willing to admit it, actually conceived of a league of nations as an Anglo-American instrument, Wiseman to Arthur Willert, in Willert, *The Road to Safety* (London, 1952), p. 59. Cf. below, p. 313.

24. Bowman's notes on Wilson's conference with the *Inquiry* on the *George Washington*, December 10, 1918, Bowman papers, *I.P.*, vol. 4, p. 281. Beer diary, December 10, 1918. See Walworth, pp. 132, 150.

25. On April 5, 1919, Beer wrote in his diary: "Wilson is strong on principles, but is absurdly weak on their application."

26. Minutes, I.W.C., December 30, 1918. Lloyd George, p. 192.

the empire's claims in the southern islands.[27] Lloyd George argued that in view of this, Australia could not fairly be denied the German islands south of the equator, which it thought essential to its security. But Wilson said that he was by no means prepared to accept the secret convention with Japan, which perhaps he now became aware of for the first time.[28] He could not with consistency approve the annexation of islands either by Japan or by Australia. Indeed, he was doubtful if the Japanese could be admitted, even in a mandatory capacity, to the Pacific islands that they had conquered in 1914, closed to foreign trade and perhaps fortified.[29] The president hesitated to deliver to them a chain of isles that were potential naval bases.

American naval advisers, willing to permit Japanese expansion in Siberia, joined with scholars of the Inquiry in opposing the annexation of German islands by Japan.[30] Warning of the peril that was to become very real in World War II, they insisted that the United States should increase its navy and should not miss the opportunity the better to secure its strategic position in the Pacific. In acknowledging a navy report to this effect, Wilson wrote: "I am mighty glad to get it."[31]

At the end of 1918 Lloyd George reported to the Imperial War Cabinet that the attitude of the president was not entirely irreconcilable. The prime minister said he had made it clear that the question of colonies would have to be fought out at the Peace Conference, where the ministers of the dominions would present their own cases. He explained to the cabinet the tactics that he himself planned to use at Paris. If Wilson proved obstinate, the British delegates could, as a last resort, claim the final verdict to which they thought their war sacrifices entitled them.

Other governments than the British had a vital interest in conquered territories. France, for example, had suffered grievous losses in trade during the war, and some of its citizens now hoped to recover its foreign markets and to increase commerce.[32] The French government thought it right to retain all territories that were under

27. Prince Konoye had just published an article complaining that Anglo-Saxon economic imperialism prevented the free development of Japan, which had limited territory and slender resources. He predicted that Japan, like Germany, might feel obliged to destroy the status quo, dispatch, Polk to Ammission, January 8, 1919, Wilson papers, 5632.

28. "It was doubtful whether he [Wilson] knew of the treaty with Japan until he reached Paris. I cannot recall having such knowledge myself and my papers do not indicate that either of us knew," letter, House to Seymour, April 9, 1982, quoted in *I.P.*, vol. 3, p. 62. See *ibid.*, vol. 3, pp. 46–51, 61–63; vol. 4, pp. 364–365. Details of the secret agreement with Japan were revealed to Secretary Lansing in 1917, Lansing desk diary, August 12, 1917.

29. Roy W. Curry, *Woodrow Wilson and Far Eastern Policy*, pp. 257–258.

30. Dr. Mezes was well aware of the navy's interest in Pacific lands where coal and other supplies might be procured, and he advised that the scholars take this into account, James Brown Scott's diary, January 5, 1919, Georgetown University Library.

31. Wilson to J. Daniels, December 7, 1918, Wilson papers. Gelfand, *The Inquiry*, pp. 269–270. Miller, *My Diary*, vol. 1, January 30; vol. 2, doc. 17. The naval advisers recommended that the United States "acquire" the Marianas for submarine bases and also take the Carolines and the Marshalls or insist on their internationalization, memorandum, Planning Committee to Chief of Naval Operations, SECRET, December 2, 1918, with attached report signed by Admirals Evans, Hart, and Yarnell. Admiral Benson, however, recommended that the islands in question not be assigned by the Peace Conference to the United States but be given an international guarantee of free trade, protection of the natives, and freedom from fortification, one-page statement, signed by Benson, n.d., filed under December 17, 1918, Wilson papers. Lloyd George described Wilson's "whole attitude" at the end of December as "strongly anti-Japanese," Lloyd George, p. 188. Documents bearing upon the disposal of the Pacific islands may be found in Breckinridge Long's papers, "P.C." folders, box 186, L.C.

32. Pierre Renouvin, *War and Aftermath*, pp. 130–131.

occupation. Moreover, Ambassador Paul Cambon, at London, had been seeking an enclave for France near the mouth of the Congo and had suggested that Portugal, the owner, should be compensated by concessions in east Africa. European colonizers asked themselves a question that was justified by subsequent history: whether international interference, at first limited to the former German colonies, would not spread to all the rest of their own overseas possessions.[33]

On January 23, when Clemenceau introduced this controversial subject in the meeting of the Supreme Council, Wilson suggested that the state of affairs in Europe was the prime cause of unrest and should have immediate attention, and that the colonial settlement could be discussed in intervals. But he did not contest Lloyd George's practical suggestion that they deal with the question while the pleaders for Continental nations were preparing their cases.[34] The dominions had long been ready to present their claims.

As was to be expected, the most outspoken opposition to international authority came from the southern dominions. Australia dreaded the presence of a foreign and perhaps unfriendly power in the southern Pacific islands that it was occupying and expected to govern. Nor did South Africans welcome the prospect of the development in South-West Africa of a separate government with its own control of finance, commerce, and labor. General Smuts had privately professed a willingness to make concessions to Wilson in respect of a league of nations in order to overcome the president's objection to annexation of "a little German colony here or there."[35] However, on January 19 Smuts learned in a talk with Wilson that the president was set against the annexation of any German colony by any dominion. House had perceived the danger of conflict and had warned Wilson and Lloyd George that it would be best to postpone formal consideration of the matter until he recovered from his illness and was able to mediate.[36]

On the afternoon of the twenty-fourth Lloyd George proposed that none of the colonies seized from Germany be returned. To this Wilson agreed readily. The prime minister then lost no time in responding to an invitation from Clemenceau to bring in his "cannibals" from the antipodes. In introducing his imperial colleagues Lloyd George cited practical considerations that appeared to make annexation more desirable than mandates that might not prove to be permanent.

Prime Minister William Hughes spoke for Australia. This fiery little man, who called himself "a Welsh tribesman," scoffed at Wilson's ideals.[37] The Pacific islands

33. Minutes, I.W.C., December 20, 1918. Louis Aubert, *Tardieu*, p. 63.

34. According to Ray Stannard Baker, Wilson thought that his mild suggestion was enough to effect a postponement of discussion of the colonies until the league of nations was created, Baker, vol. pp. 252–254. On the question of the bearing of the general concern about bolshevism upon the decision to take up the colonial question, see Arno J. Mayer, *Politics and Diplomacy of Peacemaking*, p. 366 and n.

35. Smuts to W. Long, November 28, 1918, cited in Louis, "Australia and the German Colonies," *Journal of Modern History* 38, no. 4 (December 1966):416–417, 419. Hancock, *Smuts, the Sanguine Years*, pp. 498–499.

36. Smuts to Lloyd George, January 17 and 20, 1919, Lloyd George papers, F/65/9/27. Drummond to Kerr, January 16, 1919, Balfour papers, FO/800/215.

37. *Times*, November 8, 1918. Consul General at London to Lansing, November 9, 1918, *F.R.*, Lansing papers, vol. 2, p. 490. Wiseman reported to Murray of the Foreign Office on August 30, 1918,

south of the equator, Hughes said, were "at the very door of Australia" and were as necessary to her as water to a city. His government had seized them from Germany and proposed to continue to hold them for national security.[38] Control by a league of nations, in his opinion, would lead to a confusion of authority. "When you internationalize New Guinea," he said, "you internationalize Australia."[39]

Smuts then expounded the claim of the Union of South Africa to the southwest territory. Unless this region's economy could be integrated with that of South Africa, he warned, the South African government would be overthrown and its policy of union jeopardized.

Thus it became apparent very early in the Peace Conference that in disposing of parts of the German empire the delegates were at the mercy of conflicting purposes that at first seemed irreconcilable. The southern dominions demanded annexation; but at the same time there was a strong current of opinion among the English-speaking peoples in favor of international control. There was general agreement, however, that the native populations in question lacked capacity for immediate self-government.

In the next discussion of this perplexing question in the Supreme Council, on January 27, Wilson asked whether the Japanese should not be heard before any decision was made as to any part of the Pacific region. The president's initiative at this point was perhaps stimulated by Beer, who had agreed two weeks before that "the easiest way out" was first to give mandates to Japan for islands north of the equator and then, after there was general agreement upon limitations to be placed upon Japan, to insist that it was impossible without offense to Japan to allow the dominions to govern islands south of the equator without similar restrictions.[40]

At the meeting on the twenty-seventh Wilson argued that interested nations should be represented at deliberations that affected them. He had at heart the interest of the Chinese people, to whom his missionary cousins were preaching the Gospel. There was an inclination in certain circles in the United States to regard the Chinese as wards under American political and religious tutelage. In mid-January the American commission at Paris received a message from the legation at Peking, asking that the question of foreign infringements on Chinese sovereignty be settled permanently at the Peace Conference; and moreover, Polk of the State Department urged that for-

---

that Hughes, visiting the United States in June en route to London, "did quite a lot of harm." The president wished to instruct the London embassy to refuse to give Hughes a passport visa, but was dissuaded by Lansing, cables, Wiseman to Reading, August 31, 1918, Reading to Wiseman, September 6 and 12, 1918, Wiseman papers, Y.H.C. Hughes told the Imperial War Cabinet on December 20 that the president was "the most self-centered of men" and "as unresponsive as the Sphinx," Hughes, *Policies and Potentates,* p. 229. Hughes recorded that when he asked House to intercede in behalf of the annexation of New Guinea, House said: "If I ventured to offer my advice to him [Wilson] on a matter on which he has definite views I should lose all my influence with him." Hughes approached Secretary Lansing with no success.

38. Australians feared that under a mandate it might be necessary to open New Guinea to immigration of Orientals and that the mandate might later be transferred to another member of the league of nations, perhaps even Japan, Ernest Scott, *Australia during the War* (Sydney, 1939), p. 772.

39. Smuts then expounded the claim of the Union of South Africa. S. Sonnino, *Diario,* vol. 3, p. 332.

40. Beer diary, January 12 and 24, 1919.

eign investment in China be controlled by the formation of an international consortium.[41]

The sympathy of Americans for the Chinese people was in contrast with their distrust of the Japanese. The war had strengthened Japan's position among the nations. It had been promised not only Pacific islands, but also the special rights that the Germans had enjoyed in the Chinese province of Shantung; and it could be expected that the Japanese would violate the principle of the "open door" there, as they had already in Manchuria. At the same time, the American plenipotentiaries at Paris were not unaware of a psychosis of suspicion in the attitude of the Japanese people toward the United States. Before the end of 1918 word had come from the embassy at Tokyo of a general fear of America's growing power and distrust of its motives.[42]

Japan was represented at Paris by Baron Makino, a former minister of foreign affairs, and Viscount Chinda, the ambassador at London. The other Japanese plenipotentiaries were en route to France by ship and did not arrive until March. The two delegates present sat through the earlier meetings of the Supreme Council silent and rigid. On January 27, however, Makino demanded full possession by Japan of those Pacific islands north of the equator that its forces had seized from Germany. In response to this Wilson eloquently expounded the principle of trusteeship under a league of nations. He gave assurance that the league would not interfere so long as the mandatory power did its duty.

The delegates sat in stodgy boredom. Three appeared to be sleeping soundly. The president told a story to give point to his argument, and Lloyd George smiled. A loud laugh from an American expert provoked frowns from foreign plenipotentiaries who could not understand the story in translation and were perhaps shocked by the intrusion of levity into a discussion so weighty.[43]

The creation of an effective league of nations, unanimously approved by a plenary session of the Peace Conference two days before, was always in the forefront of the president's thought. He hoped that the sharing of the responsibility of trusteeship might steady and strengthen a league, much as a joint interest in the Mississippi Valley territory had helped to bind the American states together in 1787. He warned his colleagues that rumors were rife that the Peace Conference met for the purpose of dividing up the spoils of war, that annexations would feed such gossip and destroy public confidence in the ideal of a league of nations. A league must succeed, he said; and if all in the room decided that it must, it would. The anxiety of the Australians about their security seemed to him to show a fundamental lack of faith.

The ministers of the dominions, however, raised practical questions. They argued that annexation was not bad in itself, but only when power was irresponsibly used; and they professed virtuous motives on the part of their governments. Massey of New Zealand argued that the difference between a mandate and annexation was that between a leasehold and freehold tenure, and observed that "no individual would

---

41. Grew to Close, January 15, 1919; Polk to Ammission, January 17, 1919, Wilson papers. See below, p. 362.

42. Morris to the secretary of state, November 27, 1918, *F.R.*, *P.P.C.*, vol. 1, pp. 490–492.

43. E. T. Williams "Japan's Mandate in the Pacific," 431–432.

put the same energy into a leasehold as into a freehold'' and ''it would be the same with governments.'' To give point to his argument Massey asked what Washington and Hamilton would have said if the Northwest Territory had been offered to them under an international mandate.

Finally, when the discussion tended toward bitterness, Lloyd George expressed a desire to consult his experts with particular reference to matters of finance. He posed a fundamental query. Would it be possible, he asked, for the league of nations to levy payments from its members ''to enable, say, France to develop the Cameroons?'' To this Wilson replied that he thought it not inconceivable that a league of nations might make an assessment upon its members to defer a part of the expenses of trusteeship. It appeared to Beer that the president's concept of a mandate was ''very loose.''[44]

Lloyd George and Balfour were willing to accept a system based on the practical experience of their Colonial Office. They would have powers held responsible as trustees for good government, with particular attention to control of traffic in arms, liquor, and slaves and to the preservation of an open door to trade; and they would expect criticism in meetings of the league of nations for any derelictions of duty. British delegates, however, continued to question the incurring of financial responsibility.[45]

Secretary Lansing further alienated himself from his chief by a sincere effort to raise questions about the validity of the new system from the point of view of international law. He was perplexed particularly by the question of the residence of ''sovereignty.'' It seemed clear that the system, as a means of avoiding the appearance of dividing the spoils of war, was ''a subterfuge which deceived no one.'' It was obvious to him that the right of the council of a league of nations to supervise would be without force if the trustee was one of the great powers with a seat in the league council and veto power there. He perceived that it was to the advantage of the colonial powers to take the German possessions under mandates and thus avoid the deduction of the value of these possessions from their claims for indemnification by Germany for the costs of the war. Dramatizing virtue and vice, Lansing gave way to moralistic ardor and wrote in his diary of ''greedy statesmen,'' and of ''the re-establishment of the old order of things which caused the war.'' But after learning from House that Wilson's mind was set, he gave up hope of influencing the

44. Beer diary, January 29, 1919.
45. Clement Jones, ''The Dominions and the Peace Conference: A New Page in Constitutional History,'' typescript, F.O., Cab/21/21/7. Jones to the author, October 8, 1959. Letter, Kerr to Milner, January 31, 1919, Lothian papers. Kerr stated the shortcomings that British leaders perceived in Wilson's thinking and that they were too polite to dwell upon in sessions of the Supreme Council. It was clear to Kerr that if you were to give to the inhabitants of these territories the right of continuous appeal to the league against the mandatory power, there would be no hope of steady political development because the budding political life of these countries would tend to develop factious agitation for the purpose of playing off the mandatory power against a league of nations. Again, it became obvious that if a league were really to undertake financial responsibility, it would have to maintain an army of inspectors who would probably make the position of the mandatory power intolerable, while at the same time the liability of being assessed to pay for the mistakes of the mandatory power would act to prevent nations from joining the league at all. In preference to mandates Kerr would have the several great powers temporarily exercise protectorates over nations in embryo, note, Kerr to Lloyd George, January 27, 1919, Lloyd George papers, F/89/2/2.

president's thinking. Indeed, Wilson characterized his objections as "mere technicalities."[46]

The give-and-take went on in the Supreme Council on January 28, morning and afternoon. The Chinese plenipotentiaries, who were divided in opinion and embarrassed by factional strife within China, were inclined to focus their efforts on the restoration directly to China of the particular rights that Germany had held in parts of Shantung province that Japanese forces had seized, rather than on the termination of all extraterritorial rights that were exercised in China by foreign powers. Wellington Koo pleaded his nation's case with an eloquence that did credit to the education that he had received in the United States. The Japanese were so disturbed that they sent a spokesman to the Crillon the next day to warn the Americans that Japanese opinion on this question was very intense and that the United States would be held responsible if the German holdings in Shantung were handed directly back to China.[47] Not for three months did the Supreme Council come to grips with this delicate question.[48]

After the Chinese case was heard Lloyd George brought the discussion back to the main track. He said that in most respects Wilson's concept would not appreciably alter the colonial practices of Great Britain; but he asked that the case of the southern dominions be regarded as "special." He warned that the European powers would not sign a peace treaty that left it to a league of nations to assign the trusteeships.[49]

In the afternoon of the twenty-eighth the views of France and Italy were presented. France had a strong interest in the African settlement only in the equatorial region and in Morocco, where it wished to be free of all international control.[50] The colonial minister told the council that he saw no difference in effect between trusteeships and good colonial rule. He presented France's claim to full sovereignty in central Africa with the same argument that the dominions had put forth for annexation, and with assurance of his country's colonizing ability and good intentions.

Wilson, discouraged by the rebuffs received from the dominions, the Japanese, and the French, remarked that it appeared that his road diverged from theirs, that it would be wise to discontinue the discussion—perhaps for a day—for fear that otherwise they might come to an impasse. He said that they must agree upon the principle and leave its application to the league. Nothing could shake his insistence that the immediate assignment of trusteeships would impress the peoples of the world as a reprehensible division of spoils.

The European premiers, however, lacked confidence in a league of nations. Orlando of Italy suggested that to leave everything to a league would be to confess impotence and thus to invite the world's reproach as a do-nothing peace congress. Clemenceau, who had been presiding in skeptical silence, made it clear that though he

46. Lansing, *The Peace Negotiations,* pp. 149–161; private memoranda, February 3, 1919; supplementary diary, January 27, 1919.
47. Lansing, p. 253.
48. See below, ch. 19.
49. Minutes, British Empire Delegation, January 28, 1919, P.R.O., Cab/29/28/1.
50. Beer diary, December 24 and 30, 1918. Cable, Auchincloss to Polk, March 19, 1919, Auchincloss diary, March 19, 1919. See below, p. 509.

would not stand in the way of any international arrangements on which the others insisted, he had enthusiasm for a league only in so far as it would guarantee the security of France. Lloyd George continued to urge prompt selection of trustees before the establishment of a league.

The question of priority still shadowed the whole American program for the ordering of human affairs by a league of nations. There was snow now on the ground and on the roofs of Paris, and the atmosphere in the council chamber was as chilly as that outdoors.

In the evening Wilson telephoned to House and, expressing anxiety about the turn taken by the discussion, suggested that he might break the deadlock by giving both sides of the case to the public. House told him that the sessions smacked of "star chamber methods" and that this was arousing criticism as well as preventing control over Lloyd George and Clemenceau by publicity.[51] Two days later the president told the council that he might be forced to appeal to the public.

As the impasse developed at the top level, it became clear that compromise was essential. It was more than a year since Beer had proposed that "mandatory powers" for African territories be appointed by a league of nations.[52] Now, behind the scenes, British and American negotiators were trying to work out the details of a system that would be acceptable to all parties. They drew upon the proposals of Lord Robert Cecil and General Smuts.[53] Lloyd George, under the necessity of maintaining good relations with both the United States and the dominions, turned naturally to Smuts for aid in resolving the crisis. It could hardly have escaped the prime minister that the South African statesman, who had promoted the union of disparate peoples in his own land, enjoyed the esteem of Woodrow Wilson.[54] Lloyd George approved a modified draft of Smuts's proposals as a basis of compromise; and on the morning of January 29 Smuts visited House to ask whether this would be agreeable to the President.

Accepting the Wilsonian principle that the lands severed from the German and Turkish empires should be "entrusted to advanced nations" that would act as mandatories in behalf of a league, the British resolution introduced the theory that "the character of the mandate must differ according to the stage of development of the people, the geographical situation of the territory, its economic conditions, and other similar circumstances." Mandates of three classes were defined: (A) "those for parts of the Turkish empire which had reached a stage of development where their existence as independent nations can be provisionally recognized" and where

51. House diary, January 28, 1919, Auchincloss diary, January 29, 1919.

52. Beer, "The Colonial Question," Inquiry papers, Yale Library Mss. and Archives, box 10, f. 127, p. 1.

53. "Draft Convention Regarding Mandatories," January 20, 1919, handed to Miller by Cecil on January 25, Miller, *My Diary,* vol. 1, entry of January 25, and vol. 4, pp. 43–47. Cecil diary, January 27, 1919. After talking with House, Cecil took a strong stand against annexation in a meeting with his imperial colleagues, Wiseman memorandum, January 27, 1919. Cecil found House "as much disillusioned about the British as he was a week or two ago about the French," Cecil to Balfour, January 27, 1919, Cecil papers, 51131. House diary, January 29, 1919. *I.P.,* vol. 4, pp. 294–298. Miller, *My Diary,* vol. 1, entry of January 29, 1919. Borden, *Robert Land Borden: His Memoirs,* p. 906.

54. Wilson's personal esteem for Smuts persisted after the Peace Conference, Bliss Perry to the author.

the wishes of the inhabitants must be a prime consideration in the selection of a mandatory power; (B) those of "other peoples, especially those of Central Africa," whose administration would be supervised by mandatories under conditions that would prevent abuses and would also "secure equal opportunities for the trade and commerce of other members of the league of nations," and (C) those for "territories such as South-West Africa and certain of the islands of the South Pacific," which because of special circumstances could "be best administered under the laws of the mandatory state as integral portions thereof, subject to the safeguards above-mentioned in the interests of the indigenous population." The C mandates would not require a guarantee of equal opportunities for trade; in fact the American specialist on the Far East thought that they practically granted the plea of the southern dominions for annexation.[55] It was generally understood that independence was not contemplated for peoples placed under B and C mandates.

When House read the compromise resolution brought to him by Smuts on January 29, he approved it with a few changes in wording. It seemed to him that the British leaders had come far toward the American position. Receiving the British draft at 10:30, House, hoping that Wilson would accept it, sent it to him at the Quai d'Orsay, where he was to meet with the Supreme Council at eleven. On the document House wrote: "Lloyd George and the Colonials are meeting at 11:30 and this is a draft of a resolution that Smuts hopes to get passed. He wants to know whether it is satisfactory to you. It seems to me a fair compromise. E.M.H."[56]

Wilson replied "I could agree to this if the interpretation in practice were to come from General Smuts. . . . My difficulty is with the demands of men like Hughes and the certain difficulties with Japan. The latter loom large. A line of islands in her possession would be very dangerous to the United States."

It is doubtful, however, that any answer from Wilson reached the Crillon before House gave America's consent to Smuts, for delivery by the latter to the British Empire conference by 11:30.[57] Lloyd George, who was absent from the eleven o'clock session of the Supreme Council in order to meet with the dominion delegates, put House's acceptance of the British proposal before them when they convened at 11:30. Hit by a foaming cataract of protest from Hughes, the prime minister gave voice to a fear that Great Britain's disagreement with the United States might become chronic after Wilson's return to Washington. He gave assurance that under the C mandates, the laws of Australia could be imposed. It was agreed that the compromise resolution be presented formally to the Supreme Council.[58] When this was done, Clemenceau ruled that it was accepted.

The die-hard advocates of annexation, however, were not content to let the matter rest there, and they used the press to attack Wilson's policy. The French were becoming impatient with Americans in general and with the president in particular,

---

55. Williams, p. 433.
56. Document in Wilson papers. Miller, *My Diary,* vol. 1, p. 96.
57. In "Origins of the Mandates System" (286) Miller wrote: "Wilson . . . had not agreed to the compromise proposal in advance," Miller, *My Diary,* vol. 1, entry of January 29, 1919.
58. Minutes, B.E.D., January 29, 1919, P.R.O., Cab/29/28/1. General Memorandum No. 5, Borden papers. Borden, pp. 904 ff.

despite a belated visit by him to French battlefields on January 26.[59] Yet Wilson had been treated by the Quai d'Orsay with decorous deference. Not one, but both of the double doors were flung open when the president arrived for meetings of the council.[60] Foreign Secretary Pichon himself escorted the American guest into the conference chamber and to his gilded chair. But now the controlled French press began to persecute the prophet, whom some papers had hailed at first as a savior.[61]

French journals, informed by friends in the Foreign Ministry about what had transpired behind the doors at the Quai, appealed to history to prove the mandate system fallacious. Radical editors interpreted "mandates" as but a euphemism for acquisition of territories by the great powers.[62] Conservatives pointed to threats to French interests that would result from international interference in colonial affairs. The president was lampooned as an irritating busybody. Moreover, critics perceived that in spite of his eloquent appeals to spiritual truth, his zeal was not entirely disinterested. It appeared that Wilson's persistent pleading, like that of Hughes, was not unrelated to concern for his position as a political leader in his own nation.[63]

Wilson was peculiarly vulnerable to such innuendos as bounced lightly from the well-weathered skins of European politicians. He confided to a journalist[64] that he would like to kill the man who invented the myth that he could not smile and was "a Puritan thinking machine." When Swope of the *World* asked him for an interview, his reply was: "I am surrounded by intrigue here, and the only way I can succeed is by working silently."[65] He was resentful because he thought French troops were restrained from cheering him when he visited the battlefields on January 26.[66] And he was profoundly shocked when the Continental *Daily Mail* printed an article, inspired by Hughes,[67] suggesting that Lloyd George and Balfour had been

59. Of a luncheon given by the French press at the Maison Dufayel on January 27, 1919, Harold Nicolson wrote in his diary: "I gathered a vivid impression of the growing hate of the French for the Americans. The latter have without doubt annoyed the Parisians. There have been some rough incidents. The United States authorities are beginning to get uneasy and are importing their own military police. Wilson shares this growing unpopularity. Lafayette is becoming a hazy bond of union." Two days later Nicolson observed that the French press was beginning to sneer at President Wilson and the Americans, *Peacemaking, 1919*, pp. 250, 252. Hardinge, *Old Diplomacy*, p. 231. The behavior of American civilians in Paris led Clemenceau to observe years later that exhibitionism, "one of the most hideous maladies of the age," was "a foreign and especially an American importation," Adam de Villiers, *Clemenceau parle* (Paris, 1931), pp. 41 ff.

60. Mme. Paul Mantoux to the author, November 1959.

61. Nicolson, p. 249

62. Noble, *Policies and Opinions*, pp. 108–109, 112–113.

63. Curzon wrote from the Foreign Office to the British ambassador at Paris on January 23: "The French Ambassador [Paul Cambon] concurred with me in recognizing that the object of President Wilson, in pushing forward his scheme for the League of Nations at the present stage, was probably to a large extent political, and sprang from the desire to have something in his hand when he returned, as he would presently have to do, to his own country," dispatch No. 165, Curzon papers, box 72, Mss. Eu., F112/302. Cf. below, p. 183.

64. A. G. Gardiner, Benham diary letter of January 22, 1919.

65. Wilson to Swope, February 1 and 7, 1919, Wilson papers.

66. E. B. Wilson, *My Memoir*, p. 235; Benham diary letter, January 26, 1919.

67. L. F. Fitzhardinge to the author, January 7, 1964. Actually Hughes made changes in the proof that somewhat tempered the story that a *Daily Mail* reporter based on remarks made by Hughes at lunch, Kerr to Milner, January 31, 1919, p. 7; Keith A. Murdock to Lloyd George, February 2, 1919, Lothian papers, GD40/17/216. On January 31 the *London Times*, doubtless at the government's behest, denounced "the account which appeared in certain papers yesterday," and the *Daily Mail* printed a moderating editorial, Steed to Northcliffe, January 31, 1919, Steed papers.

kowtowing to Wilson and had disappointed the dominions, and that there was serious danger of a breaking up of the empire in consequence. Having refrained from using the threat of publicity as a political weapon, the president was indignant at what he regarded as a breach of confidence on the part of colleagues.[68]

When the council resumed its discussion of mandates on January 30 after a day of back-stage diplomacy, Wilson warned his colleagues that if repetition of this offense could not be prevented, he might be compelled to make a full public disclosure of his own views.[69] Thoroughly aroused, he launched into a long series of remarks that raised more questions than they settled. Like Hughes, he spoke as a political leader rather than a diplomat.[70]

Lloyd George, who had been put under an intense strain, professed despair. He explained to the council that it was with the greatest difficulty that he had prevailed upon the dominions to accept the proposed compromise, that they had acceded only in order to avert the catastrophy of a break in negotiations. The delegates of the Allies then spoke of reservations. Orlando wanted assurance that Italy would get its share of mandates or of territories to be militarily occupied;[71] Hughes, objecting that they were declaring a principle without indicating to what extent it should apply, or to whom, or when, so irritated the president that Wilson later referred to him as "a pestiferous varmint."[72] At the close of the morning session on the thirtieth the president proposed a resumption of discussion in the afternoon, although Clemenceau already had given the verdict that Lloyd George's compromise resolution was accepted.

During the break at noon Wiseman, finding Lloyd George annoyed by protracted remarks of Wilson that had provoked a reopening of the whole question that appeared to have been settled in the morning, telephoned House's office and urged that the president refrain from pressing his case in the afternoon session. The colonel being at lunch, Auchincloss sent a note to Wilson transmitting this advice.[73] The president, however, was in no mood to heed any advice from House's secretary. At

---

68. A few days later Wilson was not averse to making use of the foreign press, but he despaired of doing so effectively. On February 3 he wrote to Herbert Hoover: "I dare say it would be serviceable to discuss these matters with the press as you suggest, but how can you when the French press is so carefully censored by the Government that everything is excluded which they do not wish to have published?" Wilson papers.

69. According to Arthur Sweetser, assistant to Ray Stannard Baker, the president took a stenographer into the council to emphasize his threat to give his views to the public, Sweetser to Newton D. Baker, February 4, 1919, N. D. Baker papers, L.C.

70. According to Riddell's diary (entry of February 2), Wilson asked to have his speech deleted from the official procès-verbal.

71. Miller, *My Diary*, vol. 1, entry of January 30, 1919.

72. Bonsal, *Suitors and Suppliants*, p. 229.

73. House, who spent the noon hour with Lord Robert Cecil in friendly consideration of a covenant for a league, recorded in his diary that there had been "a first class row" that might teach all participants a lesson and so do some good. "It is the first time the president has shown any temper in his dealings with them and it was a mistake I think to show it at this time. The British had come a long way, and if I had been in his place I should have congratulated them over their willingness to meet us more than halfway," House diary, January 30, 1919.

"He [Lloyd George] was very anxious that House should attend the conference," Wiseman wrote in his diary. "I went to see House and explained the situation, and he, as usual, is intensely helpful," entries of January 29 and 30, 1919, Y.H.C.,

luncheon with his family, appearing very tired and depressed, he condemned his adversaries as unacceptable reactionaries.[74]

The first speech in the afternoon session provoked him to require a precise definition of the position of the dissenting dominions. Massey of New Zealand declared his belief that annexation would be the best solution for both Europeans and the native races. Nevertheless he agreed to accept the compromise that defined C mandates. If President Wilson would accept it, said Massey, he thought this would clear the ground sufficiently to enable them to proceed.

This brought an unnecessary and provocative response from Wilson. Disregarding Massey's conciliatory proposal, Wilson challenged Hughes, who was speaking with his face turned away, apparently unaware he was being addressed. "Am I to understand that Australia and New Zealand have presented an ultimatum to the Conference?" the president asked. Someone nudged Hughes and he replied: "That's about the size of it, Mr. President."[75] However, when pressed further by Wilson, Hughes accepted the special provision for C mandates. After the meeting Wilson explained that he bore down hard in order to clarify the situation and to prevent representatives of 6 million people from holding up a decision in behalf of 1.2 billion.[76]

The tension was eased by an eloquent, conciliatory speech by General Botha of South Africa that won the respect of Wilson. A few minor amendments were approved, and France was assured that there was nothing in the compromise resolution that would prevent the recruiting of volunteer colonial troops in the way that had become customary.

At the end of this session the president summed up the achievement of the turbulent day. They had arrived at a satisfactory provisional arrangement, subject to reconsideration when plans for League control were fully developed.[77] Though no mention was made of the ultimate solution that native populations envisioned—freedom from control by Europeans—nevertheless hope was kept alive for the governance of undeveloped countries under a system of international responsibility; and a long step was taken toward the long and gradual process of accommodating the colonial practices of Europe with the aspirations of native peoples. The compromise with the British Empire on the question of mandates left freedom of the seas, punishment of war criminals, war debt and reparations as the only issues on which there were major differences between Great Britain and the United States.

74. Benham diary letter, January 30, 1919.

75. L. F. Fitzhardinge, "W. M. Hughes and the Treaty of Versailles, 1919," *Journal of Commonwealth Political Studies* 5, no. 2 (July 1967):137. Wilson's grim question was recorded by Miller, who was present, Miller, papers, box 61, L.C. Lloyd George, p. 542. E. T. Williams, diary quoted in Williams, "Japan's Mandate in the Pacific," 432.

One of the Australian secretaries explained afterward that Hughes did not respond quickly because his electrical hearing aid failed, Bonsal, *Unfinished Business,* p. 42. It is probable, however, that this was one of the occasions on which Hughes turned off his device in order to avoid hearing something distasteful.

76. Miller, *My Diary,* vol. 1, entry of January 30, 1919. Lloyd George described Wilson's maneuver as "a heated allocution rather than an appeal," *Truth about the Peace Treaties,* p. 542. On the Wilson-Hughes confrontation, see W.J. Hudson, *The Birth of Australian Diplomacy,* pp. 23–26.

77. See below, ch. 25.

Afterward Miller, congratulating the president on a victory that though not complete was still substantial, found the prophet's zeal unsatisfied. Wilson said that the solution fell short of his hopes. Speaking of the northern Pacific islands, which had not been specifically mentioned in the adopted text, he pointed out that they lay athwart the route from Hawaii to the Philippine Islands, that they were nearer than California to Hawaii, that they could be fortified and made into naval bases by Japan, that indeed they were of little use for anything else, and that the United States had no naval base in the region except at Guam. However, when Japan was given responsibility for the governance of the islands under a mandate of the B type that forbade fortifications, the League of Nations appeared to be of practical value as a guarantor of the security of the United States, which could fortify its Pacific islands. Rejecting a French proposal for on-site inspections to enforce the ban on armament, Wilson suggested that mandatory powers could be trusted to honor their commitments. In the absence of restraining measures, Japan was able to develop the military values of the mandated islands.[78]

On February 8 Smuts proposed that mandates be defined and supervised by the council of the League of Nations with the advice of a permanent commission. With this addition and a few changes the resolution adopted on January 30 became Article 22 of the League Covenant. On May 7 the Supreme Council assigned mandates for the ex-German territories in Africa and the Pacific.[79] A loophole was left for an assertion of a right to close the "open door" in mandated territories of the C class, in order to provide for protection against unregulated Japanese immigration.[80]

The controversy in the Supreme Council at the end of January severely strained the improvised organization of the Peace Conference. The leaders of the great powers were challenged to exert their political talent in order to preserve their essential unity of action. By forcing the concept of League mandates upon unenthusiastic and dissenting Asiatics and Europeans, Wilson came close to breaking the bonds of "the possible" under which effective diplomacy must operate. His prophetic zeal and his lack of assurance as to assumption of responsibility by the United States left serious doubts in the minds of both American and foreign officials.

---

78. D. H. Miller, "Origins of the Mandates System," 287. Russell H. Fifield, "Disposal of the Carolines, Marshalls, and Marianas at the Paris Peace Conference," 472–473. Richard D. Burns, "Inspection of the Mandates, 1919–1941," *Pacific Historical Review* 37, no. 4 (November 1968):457.

79. See below, pp. 485–486, and Wright, pp. 32, 41–42.

80. "Nothing less like a legal instrument can be imagined," a British scholar wrote in 1922 of Article 22, Baty, "Protectorates and Mandates," in *British Year Book of International Law (1921–1922)*, pp. 109–121.

5

Men of Affairs and Scholars as Diplomats

While the president contended with some success against French proposals of excessive exactions upon the enemy, against Italian aggression, and against the misrule of colonies by imperial powers, the American delegates took initiatives in other directions. They brought their influence directly to bear on the very subsistence of European peoples as well as upon the adjudication of their territorial claims that were pressed day after day by ardent spokesmen.

The Americans pursued the plan they had developed at the end of 1918 for the use of food to alleviate conditions that invited political instability. The people of the United States were accustomed to responding generously to elemental human needs. Through missionary channels and the Red Cross they had acted to relieve suffering abroad. An organization of volunteers under Herbert C. Hoover had taken shape during the war to supply the peoples of occupied Belgium with essential foodstuffs; and when the fighting ceased, Wilson had given his blessing to a plan developed by Hoover for the distribution of food and clothing to relieve hardship in central and eastern Europe.

Hoover foresaw the frustration that would result from active military intervention in nations in which he detected a danger of "large military crusades" on the part of the Russian Soviet government. "We should probably be involved in years of police duty," he said privately to the president in 1919, "and our first act would probably, in the nature of things, make us a party to establishing the reactionary classes in their economic domination over the lower classes. This is against our fundamental national spirit and I doubt whether our soldiers under these circumstances could resist infection with Bolshevik ideas."[1] Instead of guns, Hoover put his faith in a sharing of American surpluses with needy people in Europe. During the month before the peace conference opened, he had pressed, with the president's support and with an independence that British officials thought presumptuous, for immediate measures of relief that he was prepared to put in operation. Proposals made by an inter-Allied conference were unacceptable to him because they might result in the control of the markets of the world, including those in America, by an inter-Allied board. He conceived that the United States—the power that had the resources that were in demand—should independently direct their use. This attitude did not endear him to European officials who thought it important that their governments should not appear to stand aloof from the work of relieving distress in Europe. Moreover, Hoover's prewar operations in London as an aggressive mining engineer and financier, conducted under limitations that discriminated against foreigners, had involved competition with English interests. Ill will was aroused in financial circles,

1. Joan Hoff Wilson, *Herbert Hoover, Forgotten Progressive*, pp. 54–55.

and an enterprise in China in which Hoover played a key role had evoked the disapproval of officials of the Foreign Office.[2]

Wilson, convinced that famine existed in many parts of Europe, had notified the Allied governments that the United States would act immediately to organize relief. At the same time he encouraged the appointment of Allied officials to cooperate in missions of succor in the distressed regions. In some instances British and French representatives worked with American army officers who were sent to investigate actual conditions of life in Austria, Czechoslvakia, Poland, Romania, Yugoslavia, and other countries. However, Hoover's ardent efforts to develop a relief organization under American leadership had provoked friction with the Allies in the last months of 1918,[3] and controversy continued at Paris. A relief council that was set up by the great powers before the Peace Conference began was scorned by Hoover as "a futile chatterbox"; and in the emergency that he perceived to threaten civil order in Germany he had taken it upon himself to find supplies, ships, docks, and rails in order to carry out his mission. He was thwarted, however, by actions of the Allied Blockade Council.

Three days after the armistice was signed, Hoover had written to the president to suggest the creation of a "revolving fund" to finance the feeding of liberated and neutral peoples. Although not expecting that all of the loans granted to the new nations could be repaid by their governments, he nevertheless thought it best that they be required to assume a degree of responsibility. "Collective political morals are so constituted," he wrote in explanation of his policy, "that candidates for elective office will not refrain from obtaining public acclaim by squirming out of debts to other governments. Nevertheless, by requiring governments to sign such obligations, we secured a certain moderation of demands that would not have been observed had it been a gift. And we secured more economy and efficiency in distribution than would have been possible on a gift basis. Also it 'saved the face' of these governments to be treated as sound debtors wanting no charity. . . . Each of these governments sold supplies to those of its people who could pay. The government thus received their local currency. And with this currency they could conduct the government with that much less taxation. We required them to pay the incidental expenses of our staff and offices within their countries from this currency."[4]

Actually, however, credit had to be provided to finance Hoover's program in some instances. Despite the hostility of American opinion to any possibility of having to pay for nourishment for the enemy, Wilson asked Congress for a special appropriation of $100 million. On January 10 he cabled urgently from Paris to the administration's spokesman in each house.[5] In a message to Secretary of the Treas-

2. George H. Nash, *The Life of Herbert Hoover* (New York, 1983), vol. 1, pp. 202, 218, 379, 402, 453–462, 473, 489, 656. Historians differ as to the relative weight given to the idealistic, the commercial, and the political motives of Hoover at the Peace Conference. See Lawrence E. Gelfand (ed.), *Herbert Hoover: The Great War and Its Aftermath*, pp. 87–89, 148–149, 153 ff., and Schwabe, *Woodrow Wilson, Revolutionary Germany, and Peacemaking*, pp. 139–145, 152. Schwartz writes (in *The Speculator*, p. 134): "Wilsonians blended their economic self-interest with their humanitarianism."

3. See Walworth: *America's Moment: 1918*, ch. 13.

4. Hoover, *Memoirs*, vol. 1, p. 304.

5. Wilson to Tumulty for Senator Martin and Congressman Sherley, January 10, 1919. Tumulty

ury Glass he revealed the extent of his concern about "the tide of anarchism." "The peril to Western Europe is very real," he said. "It can only be met by aid from outside in relieving the food and economic situation. It is now exclusively a practical question of reestablishing sane governments capable of resisting the advance of bolshevism."[6]

However, the bill put before the Congress met resistance. The Democratic leaders repeatedly asked the State Department for facts and arguments, and Polk cabled to Paris for help. Replying at the request of the president, Hoover warned of the temporary and inadequate character of relief in progress. Estimating that the United States had realized "a considerable profit" on its food surplus, he said that the Congress was being asked to use only a part of the profit for "this humanitarian and expedient undertaking." He cabled: "We cannot be niggardly in the world's greatest problem today, that is, how to get food."[7]

The House passed the food bill promptly, but in the Senate the Republican opposition added a crippling restriction. Although Henry White cabled from Paris to his friend Senator Lodge that it was "of the utmost importance" that the president's request be granted unconditionally, the Senate in passing the measure added an amendment that prohibited the use of the fund to feed the peoples of enemy countries. This restriction put in question the policy that Wilson had stated in his Armistice Day address to Congress and in a message to the new provisional government of Germany, a policy of supplying food provided that the Germans preserved order.[8] The new legislation, releasing American credit for humanitarian enterprises for which the Allied governments lacked resources, sanctioned an innovation in American foreign policy that was to have far-reaching consequences to the diplomacy of the century. It set a precedent for the appropriation of many billions of dollars in foreign aid by the United States government.

The fund of $100 million covered only about 5 percent of all relief operations in 1919, the balance coming from the Food Administration, cash sales, and various credits.[9] Hoover contrived to finance relief to Austria by drawing on the president's funds and on loans made to the Allies by the United States; but he could not carry out a decision made on November 8 to include Germany in his program.[10] Actually, his agents had been talking confidentially with responsible Germans about Germany's need for food and about provisional plans for meeting it by American shipments.[11] However, German hopes for a lifting of the blockade and for a resumption

hesitated to make Wilson's message public for fear of the effect upon the country of its recognition of "the rising tide of bolshevism," Tumulty to Wilson, January 11, 1919, Wilson papers.

6. Dispatch, Wilson to the secretary of the treasury, January 3, 1919, N.A., R.G. 59, 033.1140/122.

7. Hoover to Rickard, acting food administrator, January 5, 1919; Hoover to the secretary of state, January 7, 1919, Wilson papers.

8. H. White to Lodge, January 8, 1919, *F.R., P.P.C.*, vol. 2, p. 711. Polk to Ammission, January 24, 1919, N.A., R.G. 59, 763.72119/3516a. Minutes, ACTNP, January 8, 1919. On January 28 Wilson asked the secretary of the Treasury to tell the congressional conferees how important it was to avoid any amendment of the bill. But the two houses adopted a conference report that made little change in the limitation imposed by the Senate, Hoover to Wilson, January 27, 1919 Wilson to Glass, January 28, 1919, Wilson papers.

9. Arno J. Mayer, *Politics and Diplomacy of Peacemaking*, p. 272.

10. Hoover, vol. 1, p. 305.

11. Schwabe, p. 192. On German misgivings with respect to the financing and supervision of a relief program by foreigners, see *ibid.*, pp. 145 ff. This scholar points out that although the German negotiators

of trade with the United States had been blighted when Foch ruled at the end of 1918 that arrangements for shipping food to Germany must be made through the armistice commission with an Allied authority in London.

To make it possible for Hoover to revictual Germany it was necessary to reach understandings on three matters that involved national feelings of extreme delicacy. Arrangements had to be made to finance the purchase of supplies, to provide ships to carry them, and to allow them to enter areas that had been blockaded during the war. The negotiation of agreements on these matters raised perplexing issues.

It became clear that international financial negotiations could not easily be isolated from the functioning of relief. The necessary German credits and a means of transfer were difficult to arrange. It was impossible to discuss the matter without impinging upon the expectations of the Allied powers that any credit for food supplied to the enemy would be added to the other claims of the victors against the vanquished. To any such arrangement, which would require the United States to take its chances on recovery of its war loans rateably with the Allies' prospects of receiving reparation, the American peacemakers were not legally empowered to agree.[12]

A committee of the Armistice Commission, meeting at Trier in mid-December and renewing the truce for a month with the addition of new Allied claims, had made the German government agree not to dispose of, and to place an embargo upon, its gold, securities, and all negotiable goods or property. These liquid assets were considered to be a pledge over which the Allies held a lien for purposes of reparation. To combat French demands upon German assets Norman Davis, the Treasury's representative at Paris, immediately undertook talks with the French officials. He made common cause with John Maynard Keynes, whom he considered the only member of the British delegation who had "any marked ability."[13]

On January 10 Finance Minister Klotz sent for Davis, explained the French position and delivered a statement of new conditions that the French wished to insert in the armistice agreement when it was next renewed. Complaining that the Germans had not yet returned French bank notes and securities that were seized and taken into Germany during the war, and had not placed an effective embargo on the export of German securities and credit,[14] Klotz feared that Bolshevists might seize control

---

"may have exaggerated" the food shortage at the end of 1918, their fears of a famine in February of 1919 were "altogether realistic." *Ibid.*, p. 148.

12. Louis L. Klotz, *De la Guerre à la paix* (Paris, 1924), pp. 99–102. Davis to Wilson, February 6, 1919, copy in N. H. Davis papers, box 43. Helde, "The Blockade of Germany," pp. 124–127, 129–132. On the war debts see below, pp. 164–168.

13. Whiteman, "Norman H. Davis and the Search for International Peace and Security," pp. 82–83. Davis to R. S. Baker, July 26, 1922, Davis papers, L.C.,

Keynes wrote (in *Two Memoirs*, pp. 13–14) that the Americans were "very suspicious as usual lest they should not be in the front rank of the stalls." Memorandum from General Barnum to Pershing, enclosed by the latter in a letter of January 11, 1919, to the president, Wilson papers.

14. Secretary Lansing gave American support to the Allied policy of embargoing exports of German assets when he directed the heads of American diplomatic missions in neutral countries to inform the governments in those countries of the armistice provisions forbidding the export of German property and to ask assistance in enforcing this ban. Not sure that transfers could be legally prevented, the secretary of state felt that he could discourage them by publishing the armistice terms and by warning transferees that their titles might not be good, Lansing to the acting secretary of state, January 26, 1919, N.A., R.G. 59, 763.72119/3525.

of the government's gold and mint in Berlin. Davis, however, put forth the Ameran view that food relief was the most effective preventive of Bolshevism. It seemed to him that the second renewal of the armistice, in mid-January, offered a good opportunity to insist that the Allies agree definitely that Germany should receive food and pay for it with liquid assets.

The approach of the January renewal provided an opportunity for constructive negotiations on the shipping as well as the financing of cargoes for relief. The obvious way to alleviate the shortage of tonnage was to employ German vessels that lay idle in home and foreign ports. These ships could serve to earn exchange to finance the purchase of supplies.[15] When the armistice had been renewed in December, however, the Germans, complaining bitterly against a tightening of the blockade, had asked under whose control and with what crews the cargo vessels would operate. The meeting broke up without any definite understanding as to which should have priority: a German pledge to provide ships or a promise by their adversaries to supply food. This question defied solution for three months.[16] British military authorities insisted that the intricate machinery of the blockade could not safely be dispensed with, for it could not be reassembled easily in case the Germans refused to come to terms; and French officials thought the blockade "the potent arm that remains."

The Americans objected to the French view that there should be no bargaining with the defeated enemy and that Foch should be empowered to insist on enforcing new and more onerous provisions in the January renewal. Wilson was urged by his advisers[17] to make it clear to the Supreme Council of the peace conference that Foch was not authorized to change the armistice terms without the permission of the United States.[18]

The president had an opportunity to do so on January 13, when the question of revictualing Germany came before the highest authority. The views of American and French officials as to both financing and shipping were in lively conflict. Wilson asked what terms were to be introduced into the armistice, and stated that in his opinion the control of Germany's hard assets was not a military question to be decided by Foch but rather one that should be settled by agreement with German authorities. The president observed that in view of the threat of bolshevism, it was imperative to act immediately not only in Germany but in all lands where stable government was in jeopardy. "As long as hunger gnaws the foundations of government crumble," he said. If the Germans were not fed, he observed, they would not be able to pay any indemnity at all. After listening patiently to French arguments

15. Auchincloss diary, December 12, 1918. Telegram, Pershing to Foch, December 12, 1918, Pershing papers, box 75, L.C. Suda L. Bane and Ralph H. Lutz (eds.), *The Organization of American Relief*, p. 19.

16. See below, pp. 158–161. Louis Loucheur's Notes, January 7, 8, and 10, 1919, Loucheur papers, Hoover Institution archives. Some of the British officials were willing to consent to relaxation if and when the problems of shipping and finance were solved, William Arnold-Forster, *The Blockade, 1914–1919*, No. 17 in Oxford Pamphlets on World Affairs (Oxford, 1939), p. 33. Bane and Lutz, *The Blockade of Germany after the Armistice*, pp. 32–36.

17. Auchincloss diary, January 9 and 13, 1919, Y.H.C.,

18. See above, p. 49.

he expressed hope that the French Ministry of Finance would withdraw its objections. But Klotz, while willing to grant a measure of priority to the debt that Germany might incur in purchasing food, would not agree that payment be made with German assets that he regarded as already owed for reparations. Finally, with strong support from British delegates, the Supreme Council was persuaded to charge its financial advisers to discuss methods of payment with German representatives, to arrange if possible to use German credit abroad, and, failing that, to make recommendations to the council. Wilson cut to the heart of the impasse when he declared that because the armistice commissioners had failed in December to reply adequately to the German request for assurances as to the fate of the crews of their vessels, they bore some responsibility for the delay. He proposed that, in the forthcoming renewal of the armistice, an effort be made by nonmilitary negotiators to persuade German civilians to assent to the use of their ships as specified by the Allied Naval Council and that if this effort was unsuccessful, Foch should insist. The Supreme Council gave assent to this in general, though the question was later re-examined.

When on January 15 Foch left Paris for Trier to arrange a second renewal of the armistice, Norman Davis and Keynes stepped aboard his train, to the obvious disgust of the marshal. He paid as little attention to them as possible. In the railway carriage in which they resided the two men and civilian colleagues conferred with six Germans.[19] Dr. Carl Melchior, a banker who managed to preserve an intellectual dignity in defeat, spoke for the Germans. Although hopeful that the peace talks might go on until the common front of the enemy was weakened by differences among them, he was moved by the necessity of obtaining food. When he made ingenious suggestions for the financing of shipments by American credit, he had to be told that this was politically and legally impossible, that Germany might better use some of its assets to buy food rather than give them outright to the Allies by way of reparations. The conferees succeeded only in reaching a provisional agreement on a small scale, whereby Germany would give up credits in neutral countries as well as 100 million marks in gold in exchange for a supply of grain, fats, and condensed milk, on condition that German merchant ships be placed at the disposal of the relief authorities. As Melchior pointed out, the German government had the dismal alternatives of dipping into its hard assets or else forfeiting food that it must have before the next harvest and thus risking serious political unrest. From his talks with the Americans, however, he drew some hope that the Germans could get private loans and make use of property confiscated in the United States in order to finance imports of food; and he learned that Americans wished to do business with Germans without the political provisos that Hoover's men had required.[20]

The negotiations of the shipping delegates, conducted later in the week and separately, were even less fruitful than those of the financiers. The Germans felt that their merchant marine was one of the few bargaining levers left to them, and they were exceedingly tenacious of it. The Allies did not wish to use force to seize the

19. Keynes, pp. 14, 31. Keynes to his mother, January 25, 1919, King's College, Cambridge.
20. Bane and Lutz, *The Blockade of Germany,* p. 42. Miller, *My Diary,* vol. 1, p. 82. Keynes, pp. 33–34. Schwabe, p. 195.

ships—it would be an awkward undertaking, the British Admiralty reported; nor could a seizure be legally justified; nor was it likely that their people would stand for the reopening of hostilities over this issue. It became a question, therefore, of persuading the Germans, in diplomatic negotiations that required the use of the carrot and the stick and a certain amount of bluff, that it was worthwhile for them to trade vessels for food. But the German delegates—"bewildered, cowed, nerve-shattered and even hungry," according to Keynes—demanded a definite *quid pro quo*.[21] They were unable to put trust in the intention of the enemy to supply food; and the Americans and British could not assert the honesty of their intent convincingly because of their differences with the French.

The German shipping men came to Trier with Erzberger; and being too numerous for accommodation in a railway carriage, they joined their adversaries in the back parlor of a public house. They surprised the Americans by showing a copy of a letter that they claimed to have been written by General Pershing, offering the United States an opportunity to charter German passenger ships—a letter that according to them had elicited no response. They immediately repeated the demand that had been made at the renewal of the armistice a month earlier: that German crews be allowed to man the ships at least in part, in order to relieve very serious unemployment in Germany.

Edward N. Hurley, the American chairman of the delegation from Paris, listened sympathetically and explained that he and his associates were "humane negotiators" and not "exacting representatives of the military authorities."[22]

He was brought up sharply, however, by a summons from Foch, who stated that in another hour the armistice would be renewed without a clause providing for the taking of the German ships. The marshal was deaf to pleas for a delay of one hour. With no time for full discussion, the civilian delegation could do no more than ask Foch to insert in the text of the new armistice certain clauses regarding German vessels that the council of the Peace Conference had presented.

A squabble ensued between Foch and the civilians. Each party considered that it had a mandate from the Supreme Council. The marshal argued that the Germans had not approved the dictated clauses and that he had no authority to include them. However, to Hurley's surprise he did include them. The Allies promised that German crews could man the ships but only until the vessels were delivered. They pledged, as compensation for use of the vessels, the lowest rates currently paid by Great Britain or its allies to their shipowners.

German owners urged their government not to ratify the agreement and protested against what they termed a "violent subversion of Germany's economic development."[23] But their protest was entirely futile. Concluding that Foch was not bluffing, their delegates signed the agreement as dictated. One of the articles provided that "all questions of details" were to be settled by a special agreement to be concluded immediately. But no significant action was taken under this understand-

21. Keynes, pp. 27–29.
22. Hurley's conduct led Keynes to regard him as "a vain and almost imbecile American," *ibid.*, p. 35.
23. Helde, pp. 132–144. Hurley, *The Bridge to France*, pp. 266–285.

ing for some time. And so the January conferences at Trier, though they established conditions under which Germany would pay cash for food and would supply ships to carry it, actually did not result in any significant flow of relief supplies.

The Americans learned at Trier, however, that the Germans, actually having no assets and only obligations in neutral countries, were much worse off than had been supposed.[24] Afterward American efforts to break the blockade were protracted and bitter. The French suspected that the dominant motive of the United States was to sell surplus food products and get payments in cash. They resented the intrusion of foreigners in the discussion of a matter that they wished to settle according to their own standard of justice. It seemed to Hoover that every day for the next two months the American delegates "were given the run-around from one authority to another on some pretext." On February 4 he addressed an urgent letter to the president, pointing out that no solution seemed possible except by mandatory action at the highest level. At the same time, the American advisers insisted that if Germany were not allowed a measure of industrial recovery, it would have no resources to pay any bill of damage. They presented a grim alternative: either destroy the German race, or try to strengthen democratic elements in order to encourage formation of a state that would take an honorable place among the nations. Finding the Allies reluctant to give up a weapon that might have to be used at any time until the enemy signed a treaty of peace, Wilson was unwilling to exert economic pressure on them in order to force compliance with the American views. Buttressed by Hoover's letter and by the advice of House, Bliss, Benson, and the economic advisers, Wilson induced the council to consent, in principle, to relaxation of the blockade; but still food did not move in large volume.[25]

At the end of January Davis suffered an attack of pneumonia and McCormick was not well. But they persisted in their negotiations. They persuaded the French minister of blockade to recognize the Superior Blockade Conference. At its meeting on February 4 that body, subject to regulation by the Supreme Council and the governments concerned, provided for the abolishment of restrictions on commerce with Czechoslovakia, Turkey, Asia Minor, Black Sea ports, and three Balkan countries under conditions designed to prevent re-export to the enemy. The Americans were not able to prevail, however, in a hot discussion of the freeing of exports to the northern neutral nations, which Hoover had recommended in December.[26] Moreover, further discussions with German delegates at Spa were unproductive.[27]

Hoover, acting with an independence and vigor that offended officials of the Allied governments as well as some of his American associates,[28] was managing a

24. Schwabe, pp. 197–198.

25. Hoover to Wilson, letter of February 4, 1919, and resolution drafted by Hoover and McCormick, Wilson papers. Hoover, vol. 1, pp. 225–230. Hoover's arguments for feeding Germany are given in detail on pp. 347–348.

26. See Frank M. Surface, *American Pork Production in the World War* (Chicago and New York, 1926), pp. 84–85.

27. *F.R.*, 1919, vol. 2, p. 813. McCormick diary, January 14, 20, 31, February 2, 6, 11, 1919.

28. It seemed to Auchincloss that Hoover was trying "to get control of the entire blockade policy of the United States. . . . McCormick told him that he simply would not stand for it and Hoover backed down," Auchincloss diary, January 14, 1919, Auchincloss to Polk, January 5, 1919, Y.H.C. McCormick

large and efficient relief organization that extended far beyond Germany into eastern and southern Europe. His men supplied valuable political information to the American peace commission at Paris, and tried to use the economic strength of the United States to encourage and support those new governments that accepted American concepts of democracy. American administrators of relief were particularly active in regions in central Europe where local hostilities erupted and where the peacemakers at Paris hoped to sanction new states that would serve as potential buffers between Germany and Russia and essential elements in a balancing of power. Obstructed by the Allied blockade of enemy ports, they encountered difficulties of transport and finance that often taxed the patience of the economic advisers at Paris and on some occasions required action by the Supreme Council itself. Yet the faith of Americans in relief as a sedative for revolutionary ferment was to persist through the Peace Conference; and they continued to press for relaxation of the blockade.[29]

It soon became apparent at Paris that the ministration of relief in Europe would not immediately put an end to the fighting among national armies. The nascent peoples were exhibiting the sort of belligerence that had raged in the Balkans before the world war. All wished to seize new territory up to the limit of their grossest claims, hoping that in the final settlement possession would prove to be nine points of the law.

In east central Europe new frontiers were being contended for by peoples whose national aspirations had long been controlled by imperial regimes. There were past injuries to avenge and urgent needs to fulfill. Trade was interrupted, communications almost cut off. In the confusion of conflicting claims there was violence on the spot, and debate and intrigue at Paris. The quick rise of chaos, which has been called "the second major surprise of the war," drew from Balfour a remark that was much quoted by the Americans at the Crillon: "Five years ago we entered upon this war in order to end war, and now we are entering upon this peace in order to end peace."[30]

The extravagant expectations that Wilson had encouraged in his wartime propaganda were raising issues that were embarrassing. He feared a revulsion of sentiment when the nascent peoples found that he could not procure for them all that they wanted.[31] In a meeting of the Supreme Council on January 22 he expressed a fear that arms shipped from the West might pass into irresponsible hands and suggested that all the warring nationalities be told that they prejudiced their cases by using force to seize land that they coveted. Actually such a pronouncement had been in the minds of British and American policy makers for several weeks;[32] and the American commission had approved a tentative declaration for the president's

---

diary, January 13, 1919. "Hoover seems to be getting into a dreadful pickle and the whole relief business is in chaos," Keynes wrote to Davis on January 30, 1919, N.A., R.G. 256, 185.001/6.

29. See below, pp. 157–161.

30. Mayer, p. 371.

31. Benham diary letter, February 2, 1919, Creel, *Rebel at Large*, p. 214.

32. *F.R., P.P.C.,* vol. 1, p. 415. House diary, January 2, 1919. See Kay Lundgreen-Nielsen, *The Polish Problem at the Paris Peace Conference,* pp. 165–166.

consideration.[33] On January 24 he presented to the Supreme Council a revised version of the proposed declaration. It gave "a solemn warning" against the seizure by armed force of territory that the Peace Conference reserved the right to dispose of. Those who disregarded this injunction would "thus put a cloud upon every evidence of title they may afterward allege and indicate their distrust of the Conference itself."

This pronouncement was adopted by the council and immediately published to the world. It proved to be ineffective, however. A similar edict, released a fortnight later, was equally so. The great powers, having supplied arms to the nascent peoples, failed to provide a control strong enough to give legitimacy to their use. The brush fires were not extinguished, and indeed more broke out.

As the parleys at Paris went on into the winter, the fervent pleading of national causes and bitter conflicts of interest indicated that the fundamental loyalty of Europeans was to a nation rather than to a social class or any international organization.

It was upon the stability of the governments of the democratic nations and upon understanding among them that the world's polity had to depend for the preservation of peace. In assuming responsibility for a new world order the American government would have to take upon itself the primary task of adjusting through diplomacy those controversies that might lead to conflict. This was a duty of far less glamor, and of greater immediate importance, than that of writing a new constitution for mankind and leading public opinion to accept it.

According to the commentary on the Fourteen Points that House had presented in the prearmistice conference, the United States was "clearly committed to the programme of national unity and independence. The delegates were, therefore, bound to heed the pleas of nation builders who lobbied energetically at Paris with sage counsel and active help from the British editors of the *New Europe*, Steed and Dr. Seton-Watson. House asked Steed to keep him informed of dissatisfaction among the spokesmen for the new nations and to arrange for him to talk with those who were disgruntled.[34]

It had been arranged in December for American scholars of the political intelligence section to talk with the leaders of the nascent nations and to listen, cordially but without commitment, to their pleadings.[35] Thus at the very beginning of the Peace Conference scholars were thrust into the role of diplomats. They were instructed to disclaim any information about politics, and to pay no attention to secret treaties.[36] Acting in the capacity of specialists, they undertook the delicate task of defining new states. They analyzed the peoples concerned: their history, current situation, and ideals for the future; their character, institutions, motivations, and

33. Minutes, ACTNP, January 3, 4, and 9, 1919, Harrison papers, L.C.; letter, Grew to Bliss, January 10, 1919, Bliss papers, box 69, "Grew" folder.

34. Steed, *Through Thirty Years*, vol. 2, p. 274. "Steed is being of enormous assistance to the president," Auchincloss wrote in his diary on February 14, 1919.

35. Bowman to Mezes, December 20, 1918, Inquiry papers, Mezes papers, box 1, Y.H.C.,

36. Seymour to the publication committee of the Yale University Press, December 4, 1957, Seymour papers, box 9, f. 553.

political experience and tradition. Several thousand miles of boundaries would have to be drawn to establish frontiers that would be just and lasting. However, these boundaries would be at the mercy of conflicting local hopes and fears that defied any guarantee of permanence. In spite of the reliable information at hand, each decision was at times and in some measure controlled by political considerations, and was then often opportunistic and hurried, tentative and incomplete.[37] The American contributions to the final settlement were influenced often by the personal characteristics and abilities of the spokesmen for the new nations. Changes in the American representation on various committees, and consequent shifts in attitude, disconcerted European diplomats who looked for an American position that they could count as fixed.[38]

A practice of referring difficult questions of boundaries to committees of experts developed gradually in January. It arose out of the need of the Supreme Council for advice on issues that became controversial and urgent and on which they were obliged to render a well-founded and just decision. No action had been taken on a suggestion by the French Foreign Ministry that questions pertaining to the new states be referred to special commissions;[39] and the Supreme Council had allowed its sessions to become a forum for political oratory on the part of the pleaders for the small nations. Though there had been some collaboration by the American specialists with those of the British Foreign Office, and somewhat less with French scholars, no official system of liaison had developed. Finally a way was improvised.

The imprecision that begat confusion yielded bit by bit to exigencies that grew out of the confusion. The American and British specialists soon established contacts that, facilitated by a common language and by private wires connecting their offices, resulted in a sense of partnership.[40] On January 22—the day of a decision of the council to send a commission of specialists to Warsaw to deal with Poland's bound-

37. Memorandum, Bowman to Mezes, December 20, 1918. Isaiah Bowman, "The Strategy of Territorial Decisions." Marston, *The Peace Conference of 1919*, pp. 111–112. The Inquiry had about 2,000 scholarly documents ready for use; and although many treated matters that never entered into the deliberations at Paris, others were of real value. For an analysis of the studies made by the Inquiry, see Gelfand, *The Inquiry*, pp. 181–312.

Thirteen "immediately pressing territorial questions" were set down in a list that Lippmann prepared on December 5, 1918, *F.R., P.P.C.*, vol. 1, pp. 287–288.

38. One of those disconcerted by changes in American policy was Jules LaRoche, a French member of territorial commissions, LaRoche, *Au Quai d'Orsay avec Briand et Poincaré*, p. 100. LaRoche to the author, November 13, 1959. It seemed to Bowman however, that LaRoche, the polished diplomat, was evasive and "slick," Bowman to Day, November 4, 1919, Day papers, box 5. Nicolson, *Peacemaking, 1919*, p. 311. Coolidge and Lord, *Archibald Cary Coolidge*, p. 229.

39. Perman, *The Shaping of the Czechoslovak State*, p. 121.

40. "If we are going to accomplish anything here," Day wrote in his diary, "I feel confident that we shall do it by working with the English, who are far less selfish and particularist in their aims than any of the other powers except ourselves," entry of January 8, 1919, Y.H.C. Seymour wrote: "We very soon found that it was not only possible but very pleasant to work with the British." He noted an admirable pride among the permanent officials of the Foreign Office in its tradition of honesty, *Letters from the Paris Peace Conference*, p. 153. "The meetings with the American delegates were very secret," James Headlam-Morley, *A Memoir of the Paris Peace Conference*, p. 33. Shotwell received from the British headquarters a complete list of its printed documents that had been prepared with a view to the peace conference and postwar foreign policy, Shotwell, *At the Paris Peace Conference*, pp. 157, 161, 167.

aries—[41] Wiseman suggested that inter-Allied committees be constituted to examine specific questions of frontiers and to report within a fortnight. House, who was already lamenting the lack of a well-ordered procedure, agreed that some such system was absolutely necessary. He told the president this when Wilson called at his office at noon.[42]

Although the scholars had been asked by House early in January for reports and recommendations on the various territorial questions, and they had presented a "Black Book" on the twenty-first containing an "Outline of Tentative Recommendations," their influence had been narrowly limited in practice. However, Wilson, coming out of a tedious session of the Supreme Council on January 29, spoke to Beer and Seymour of the lack of progress and suggested that they act with British experts in preparing joint reports with a view to expediting matters. Beer returned to the Crillon very much excited by Wilson's proposal.[43]

Because of their geographical position between Germany and Russia, whose potential as great powers was of prime concern to the statesmen at Paris, the nascent states of Poland and Czechoslovakia had a strong claim upon the attention of the Peace Conference. French policy called for new nations strong enough to serve as a counter to German power and a check against Russian expansion, and the spokesmen for the governments in the borderlands found it effective in presenting their claims to say: "This, or else bolshevism!"

Aggressive Polish patriots asserted their nation's woes with a vigor that forced repeated and protracted hearings and deliberations at the Peace Conference. Assured by Clemenceau that he regarded their country as the France of eastern Europe, the Polish spokesmen looked to French influence to consolidate the military advances already made into neighboring Prussian lands, where bands of volunteers were offering resistance. Aspiring also to occupy parts of Galicia and Silesia, and to a large extent realizing this aspiration by military action early in 1919, the Poles argued that their nation must have a large population if it was to give effective resistance to both Russian and German aggression.[44]

A Republic of Poland had been formed at Warsaw, with General Pilsudski as its president. The premier and foreign minister, Jan Paderewski, had won House's admiration, and Wilson had listened with sympathy when this great concert pianist visited the White House in November 1919. Moreover, Roman Dmowski, chairman

41. See below, p. 95.
42. Memorandum dated January 22, "To E.M.H., 23/1/19" penciled at top by Wiseman, Wiseman papers Wiseman diary, January 22, 1919. Auchincloss diary, January 22, 1919, Y.H.C.
43. Beer diary, January 29, 1919. Seymour, p. 136. Day recorded on January 30 that Wilson said to Seymour: "This sort of thing must not go on. Can't you men get together with the British experts and agree upon some conclusions that we can put through the conference?" If two or three specialists could agree in advance, Day observed, this would "give a great initial advantage to the plan that they favored." Moreover it would keep the plenipotentiaries "out of the melee" until questions and solutions had taken shape and thus "help to uphold their prestige, as well as to save their time," Day diary, Y.H.C.

The president communicated his wish to House; and the colonel put Tyrrell of the Foreign Office in touch with Mezes and asked them to facilitate cooperative study of territorial questions, House diary, January 30, 1919. See below, p. 100.
44. Bliss to N. D. Baker, January 12, 1920, Bliss papers, box 75. Lundgreen-Nielsen, pp. 206 and 491, n. 67.

of a Polish National Committee at Paris, had pleaded Poland's cause at Washington. He had applauded the principle of international organization; but before he left America he hinted at the possibility that Polish voters in the United States would turn against Wilson if they were not satisfied by the peace settlement.[45] A conservative aristocrat, he was at odds with fellow delegates at Paris who were loyal to the socialistic president, Pilsudski. It was in the moderation of Paderewski that the American peacemakers saw the best prospect for constructive negotiations,[46] and it was with American support that he was made premier. Hoover sent a staff of men to direct food distribution and railway administration, and his good friend, Hugh Gibson, became the first American minister at Warsaw.[47]

The chaos that was developing called for judicious dealing with the spokesmen for the various political movements in east central Europe. The peacemakers had power to steady shaky governments by an application of economic aid as well as by political recognition and diplomatic concessions.[48] Two delegates each from Czechoslovakia, Poland, and Romania were given seats at the Peace Conference. Their claims were weighed in the light of the knowledge supplied by the scholarly specialists, by reports from an intelligence network that had been improvised by House and Hoover,[49] and by observers in missions dispatched by the Supreme Council. In addition, Wilson had to consider the political sentiment of American voters whose blood ties made them partial to one or another of the contending new nations in Europe.[50] And the issues were further confused by the dread of bolshevism both at Paris and in the United States.

At the beginning of January Russian Soviet forces were not much more than a hundred miles from Warsaw, which was under martial law. Dmowski, representing Poland at the Peace Conference,[51] approached Bliss to ask for American troops. Foch also explored this possibility and proposed to House that the United States supply a division.[52] In one of the marshal's military conferences it was taken for granted that the United States would contribute units to an Allied force that would have access to Poland through Danzig and Thorn.[53] Foch pointed out that Polish

45. Roman Dmowski, *Politya Polska* (Hanover, 1947), pp. 389–392, 400–402, cited in Louis L. Gerson, *Woodrow Wilson and the Rebirth of Poland*, pp. 95–96, 98–99. Dmowski recorded that he found Wilson to be "a man of great culture, pleasant manners" but that "he did not know much about Polish affairs, . . . and did not understand European politics, . . . simplified too much their most complex aspects."

46. On the Polish factions and their struggle for power, and on the American attitude toward Polish peace aims before the peace conference, see Lundgreen-Nielsen, pp. 79–124; Watt, *Bitter Poland*, pp. 43, 52–54, 65–68; Ian F. D. Morrow, *The Peace Settlement in the German-Polish Borderlands*, pp. 8–10.

47. Murray N. Rothbard in Gelfand (ed.), *Herbert Hoover*, pp. 101–102.

48. See Mayer, pp. 366–367.

49. See Walworth, pp. 189–194.

50. See Joseph P. O'Grady (ed.), *The Immigrants' Influence on Wilson's Peace Policies*.

51. See Walworth, pp. 176–180.

52. In a handwritten note that he left with House on January 7, Foch advocated "indirect opposition" to bolshevism by the organization of Poland's army and the use of a British regiment, a French regiment, and an American division under an American commander, note in Y.H.C.

53. Bliss diary, January 2, 13, and 15, 1919, L.C. "Note sur la situation en Pologne," January 11, 1919, and "Projet de clause pour le renouvellement de l'armistice," January 11, 1919, Archives du M.A.É., À paix, A1018.1, f. 57.

forces were fighting not only the Bolsheviks, who might be attacking them, but also the Ukrainians, whom they chose to attack, and the Germans, from whom they wished to wrest territory. The marshal advocated prompt action to supply arms and military advice and to arrange for the return to their native land of Polish regiments which had fought on the side of the Allies in France under General Josef Haller.[54] Article 16 of the armistice agreement permitted the victorious powers to supervise the provisioning of Poland, which Hoover undertook through Danzig. Haller's units would travel through that port under the protection of troops to be supplied principally by the United States. This project was turned down by Wilson and Lloyd George. The question of using Haller's army persisted, however, and plans were made in April for its transport.

Foch unfolded his plans before the Supreme Council on January 22, the day on which the United States became the first nation to recognize the regime at Warsaw as the *de facto* government of Poland, the only new state specifically called for by the Fourteen Points.[55] The American commission had discussed the matter. It concluded not only that the American people were not disposed to send troops to Poland, but that it would be well not to do so in view of the existence of political factions in that country.[56] Dismayed by Foch's proposal, Wilson thought it unwise to resort to military action before the Supreme Council agreed on a policy for checking the advance of bolshevism westward. He expressed doubt that this social and political danger could be averted by force of arms. Warned by Secretary of War Baker against any military involvement of Americans in Poland, the president had ruled against an extension of the wartime arrangement whereby American Poles not subject to the draft had been permitted to join Haller's Polish troops in France.

When Lloyd George agreed with Wilson that the defining of a general policy was the first necessity, the Supreme Council decided to appoint an investigating commission to be made up of a civilian and an army officer from each of the great powers. On January 29, the day on which Dmowski pleaded Poland's case, the council gave instructions to the commission. It was to warn the government at Warsaw against aggression toward its neighbors, to assess its capacity to maintain civil order and an adequate defense, and to cooperate with administrators of relief who were about to set out from Paris. General Kernan, who would represent the United States, called on House for final directions, and the commission departed

54. Haller, the commander of a brigade of the Polish legion that fought for the Central Powers, had gone over to the Allies in 1918. Brought from Murmansk to France, he commanded a well-equipped army of 50,000 men. President Pilsudski feared at first that Haller, a supporter of Dmowski, might not be loyal. On views of the British and French governments and of the Polish factions on the repatriation of Haller's army, see Lundgreen-Nielsen, pp. 136–161. Also see Watt, pp. 73–74. See below, pp. 227 and 260.

55. *F.R.*, 1919, vol. 2, pp. 741–745. *P.P.C.*, vol. 3, pp. 670–674. The American commentary prepared at the prearmistic meetings gave this interpretation of Point Thirteen: the chief problems were to determine whether Poland should have a corridor to the sea, the Vistula should be internationalized, and Danzig made a free port; Poland should get no territory in which Lithuanians and Ukrainians (who showed a strong national consciousness) predominated; minorities of Germans and Jews should have rigid protection; to draw frontiers justly, "the taking of an impartial census" might be required in certain districts.

56. Minutes ACTNP, January 11, 1919. Bliss wrote in his diary: "Everyone talks about sending troops, but always someone else's."

for Warsaw early in February.[57] Professor Robert Lord, who regarded the emancipation of the Poles as "a decisive victory for the cause of human liberty," was the American civilian member of this five-power mission. He and his colleagues, faced by the complex task of defining frontiers that had been fluctuating back and forth for centuries, made territorial recommendations that largely supported the Polish claims.[58]

In the new state of Czechoslovakia, the independence of which had been recognized by the powers meeting at Paris, the Americans found leaders who were both able and reasonable. It was required only to define frontiers. The Czechs, like the Poles, were seeking land from the Hapsburg domain. Thomas G. Masaryk, president of the parliamentary republic that had been proclaimed at Prague, found a place in Wilson's heart as a fellow professor with a liberal philosophy. He and Eduard Beneš, the foreign minister, had pleasing personalities as well as a reputation for moderation and reliability. They advocated the preservation of peace in *Mittel Europa* by a collaboration of small nations. Wilson was thrilled when the Czechoslovakian declaration of independence, in the course of translation into English by American scholars, was revised to conform with American tradition. Masaryk, leaving Washington in mid-November 1918 with Wilson's blessing and a loan of $10 million, had called on House at Paris and had made sure of American sympathy at the peace table. His departure for home was hastened by reports of Bolshevik propagandizing in his country.[59] If Masaryk counted on building a power bloc at the Peace Conference upon the organization of "oppressed nationalities" that he had promoted in the United States and that Wilson had recognized, he was to be disappointed. There was to be constant controversy between Czech and Polish statesmen, and solicitation of American support by both parties.[60]

Late in January military action on the Czech-Polish border challenged the peacemakers at Paris. The little duchy of Teschen, an industrial region just below

57. House diary, February 7, 1919. See Mayer, p. 371. On the organization of the commission and of a committee at Paris to which it was to report, see Lundgreen-Nielson, pp. 170–178. For the view of a Polish historian on the question of the Polish-German frontier, see Titus Komarnicki, *Rebirth of the Polish Republic*, pp. 313 ff.

58. Haskins and Lord, *Some Problems of the Peace Conference*, pp. 153–156. Dmowski, envisioning a Polish state in which almost half of the residents would be of foreign blood, demanded eastern Poznań, Upper Silesia, and much of Prussia, including the city of Danzig, Headlam-Morley, "The Eastern Frontiers of Germany," F.O. doc. N2267/43/55. *F.R., P.P.C.,* vol. 3, pp. 778–782. According to Gelfand, "forty-two reports were actually completed by members of The Inquiry on the subject of Poland and its fate at the peace settlement." This scholar notes that two Poles serving the Inquiry gave information to Dmowski and Paderewski that aided them in directing propaganda in the United States, *The Inquiry,* pp. 205–208. Lord and his British colleague, Howard, wanted to re-establish Poland's old ethnographic frontiers. See Komarnicki, pp. 326–327. After the peace conference Lord defended his position in *Some Problems of the Peace Conference,* pp. 172 ff., and in Seymour and House, *What Really Happened at Paris,* p. 71. See Piotr Wandyce, *The United States and Poland,* p. 133.

59. Bonsal, *Unfinished Business,* p. 83.

60. See Walworth, pp. 174–177. Perman, pp. 33–37 and *passim;* Victor S. Mamatey, *The U.S. and East Central Europe,* pp. 316–317; Thomas G. Masaryk, *The Making of a State,* pp. 235–236; O. Jaszi, "The Significance of Thomas G. Masaryk," *Journal of Central European Affairs* 10, no. 1 (April 1950):2–4; Arthur J. May, *The Passing of the Hapsburg Monarchy, 1914–1918* vol. 2, pp. 753–755, 820–821; Herbert A. Miller, "What Woodrow Wilson and America Meant to Czechoslovakia," in *Czechoslovakia, Twenty Years of Independence,* ed. Robert J. Kerner; and Zbynek Zemen, *The Masaryks* (London, 1976).

the southern tip of Silesia, was rich in coal that was of vital importance to Prague as well as to Vienna and Budapest. It was inhabited by a mixture of peoples. The Polish National Council had made an arrangement with the Czech National Council for a division of the territory, whose five districts were predominantly of Polish blood.

When troops of the two parties disarmed the Austrian garrison in November 1918 they agreed provisionally to a division on ethnic lines.[61] However, Czechoslovak leaders became dissatisfied when they realized that the Poles would hold all the railway lines and a large part of the coal mines. Proposing to give the eastern part of Teschen to Poland and to make the Vistula the frontier, Beneš argued that Czech possession of a coal supply was essential as a lever of control over Austria and Hungary.[62] Alluding to the menace of bolshevism, he informed the French foreign ministry that the Poles could not maintain order in Teschen. At the same time he notified his own government that it should not intervene without French aid. Nevertheless, when the Poles attempted to consolidate their position by planning to hold elections of delegates to their National Assembly, the Czech authorities, in disregard of the counsel of Beneš, on January 23 sent troops across the line that had been agreed upon in November and advanced until they were checked in a battle with a Polish garrison. They persuaded an American lieutenant of Czech extraction and army officers of the chief Allied powers to demand, ostensibly in the name of the Peace Conference, that the Poles quit the district; and they thought that the coup would be accepted at Paris as a *fait accompli*. When the Polish government decided that violence must be met with violence, war seemed imminent.[63]

The Supreme Council considered the unauthorized Czech coup the more heinous because of the stern warning against the seizure of territory that the council had published only three days before. On January 29 Beneš and Dmowski were brought in to discuss the crisis. The Czech minister explained that his government had tried in vain to reach agreement with that of Poland; and in reply Dmowski, who delivered a long speech calculated to appeal to Wilson's sympathies, denied that his people had invaded Teschen and warned that if the offending Czechs did not withdraw, "bloodshed must follow."[64] Wilson discouraged the dispatch of troops by the Peace Conference, although both parties to the dispute desired them.[65] The opinion of his advisers as well as his own inclined toward Poland's side of the case.[66]

The council concluded that a commission of control must be sent to Teschen

---

61. See Komarnicki, pp. 355–358.

62. Watt, pp. 162–163.

63. Coolidge and Lord, p. 209. Emanuel V. Voska, *Spy and Counterspy* (London, 1941), p. 299. Perman, pp. 97–109. Komarnicki, pp. 358–359.

64. *F.R., P.P.C.*, vol. 3, pp. 773–782, Gerson, p. 126 and source cited. On Dmowski's speech, which he extended with Clemenceau's help to include the Polish question in general, see Lundgreen-Nielsen, pp. 168–169, and Watt, p. 19.

65. French official procès-verbal for the meeting of the Supreme Council on January 31, 1919, 3 P.M. *F.R., P.P.C.*, vol. 3, pp. 818–822.

66. The Black Book proposed a division of Teschen that would give Czechoslovakia only a small area in the western part. "Division was the only solution. But a division acceptable to both sides was almost impossible," Robert J. Kerner, *Czechoslovakia*, p. 67. Perman, pp. 112–114.

immediately in order to avoid conflict, assure equitable distribution of coal, and find a basis for a permanent solution. Beneš was persuaded to join with Paderewski in signing an agreement that the council approved on February 1. This provided that mines that the Czechs held to be essential to their resistance to bolshevism would remain temporarily in their hands, as well as a strategic railway line.[67] The conditions of the Czech-Polish pact of November 1918 were to continue in force, and no measure implying annexation on the part of either party would be binding. This dictated agreement undercut the authority of the commission, whose recommendation to Paris was rejected. The altercation over the rule of this district plagued the Peace Conference to its end.[68] It became evident that commissions that were intended to supply reliable information to the peacemakers and to help in arriving and enforcing a unified policy were capable of confusing chaos.[69]

Other claims of Czechoslovakia with respect to its boundaries were difficult to adjudicate. This new democracy sought the defensible frontier that the historic boundary of Bohemia offered and that would bring many Germans under its rule. However, Wilson had already received, from Germans residing in Bohemia and from the new Austrian government at Vienna, assertions of the right of self-determination and appeals for a plebiscite. The Germans in Bohemia complained of Czech military rule, and Austria held the Czech government responsible for the withholding of essential supplies of coal.[70] In reply Beneš alleged that propaganda emanating from Vienna, as well as bands of Bolshevists crossing into Bohemia from Germany, were making it difficult for the Czech authorities to control a frontier population that was disposed to accept Czech rule quietly despite its German blood. Political agitation from outside, he claimed, was preventing the mining and transport of the very coal that Vienna reproached the Czechoslovak state for not supplying. Reminding the victorious powers of Czech loyalty to their cause, he suggested that the Allies now give to Czechoslovakia the boundaries that he outlined. He promised that all inhabitants of the new state would enjoy equal civic rights under a democratic government.[71]

Beneš arranged with the French government for Czech troops, operating under the orders of Foch and thus exercising a right to enforce the armistice with Austria-

67. *F.R., P.P.C.,* vol. 3, p. 836. Of the agreement the British expert on Poland, Sir Esme Howard, wrote: "We had to force it down their throats," *Theatre of Life,* vol. 2, p. 305. Beneš insisted that the settlement be imposed by the Supreme Council in order to spare him political embarrassment, Steed, vol. 2, pp. 264–265, 278–279. Perman, pp. 114–120.

68. See below, pp. 423–424.

69. See Lundgreen-Nielsen, pp. 180–183. According to Seymour, the practice of delaying decisions by sending out investigating commissions, and thus prolonging the confusion and violence that fed upon uncertainty, was "generally regarded as extremely dangerous," memoranda and letter, Seymour to Auchincloss, January 30, 1919, Y.H.C. Seymour was at first designated to go to Teschen as a member of the commission. He demurred, however. Lansing thought it a mistake to send technical experts away from Paris, especially when their services were greatly needed there, Seymour, p. 164. Minutes, ACTNP, February 5, 1919. See Kerner, p. 67, and Eugene Kusielewicz, "The Teschen Question at the Paris Peace Conference."

70. Coolidge reported from Vienna that "no question concerning the future of German Austria weighs more on the minds of public men here than does that of the German-speaking portions of Bohemia, Moravia, and Silesia." In the eyes of the German Austrains, Coolidge wrote: "The issue is a clear one between the new doctrine of self-determination from which much is hoped and naked imperialism of the old discredited type," *F.R., P.P.C.,* vol. 2, pp. 122–126, 233–235, 376–377.

71. See Perman, pp. 56, 75–76, 85–87.

Hungary, to take control of territories in which Germans and Magyars were numerous. Calling attention to the potential of Czechoslovakia as a bulwark against the spread of bolshevism, and insistent upon the protection that a fringe of hills would provide, Beneš would not give up any of the territory in Bohemia that was inhabited by some 3 million Germans. At the same time he sought a southern boundary that would include in his nation a minority of about 750,000 Hungarians. He demanded a frontier on the Danube and Ipel rivers, a "natural" boundary that could be defended easily. And Beneš would preserve a historic line that would protect Slovakia against Polish encroachment.[72] House was persuaded, according to the record of Beneš, to acquiesce informally and orally in a historic frontier that would place millions of Germans under Czech rule.[73] Moreover, the Black Book of the Inquiry approved the inclusion of the Sudeten Germans in Czechoslovakia on the grounds that they "seem rather to prefer union with the new . . . state."

Beneš presented the formal claims of his government to the Supreme Council on February 5. He explained that his efforts to temper immoderate demands that were made by some of his countrymen exposed him to the violent opposition of influential Czechs. Lunching with American specialists,[74] Beneš declared that he had met resentment on the part of his nation's press against his policy of moderation, but that he intended, after presenting his case fully and frankly, to abide loyally by decisions made by the great powers, to whom the Czechs were deeply indebted. He adduced ingenious arguments to reinforce his position.[75] He had the support of a few spokesmen for Germans in Bohemia who testified that the industries of the country would be disrupted by a political division and that many of the German-Austrian manufacturers would be content to operate under Czech rule, with suitable guarantees of minority rights.[76]

The Americans were impressed by the moderate tone of the Czech pleader and by his cogent economic arguments and his concern for the rights of minorities. When the Supreme Council, perceiving that technical advice was needed, appointed a committee of specialists to deal with this difficult territorial question, the American members were Seymour and Allen W. Dulles, who was only twenty-five years old and who had served at Vienna and as secretary of the legation at Bern. These men, who had carefully studied the smaller administrative divisions of the Hapsburg empire,[77] depended on language as the surest guide to national loyalty and had a large store of maps and statistics and a mastery of their significance.

---

72. Victor S. Mamatey and Radomir Luza (eds.), *A History of the Czechoslovak Republic, 1918–1948*, pp. 35–36.

73. Perman, pp. 90–91. The record of Beneš, a very persuasive diplomat, should be evaluated with consideration of House's custom of listening to pleaders so sympathetically that they often overestimated the extent of his commitment to their causes.

74. Day, Johnson, and Seymour. Report from Johnson to House, February 7, 1919, Y.H.C.

75. Bonsal, *Suitors and Suppliants*, pp. 146–151.

76. Kerner wrote later that the separation of the German districts from Czechoslovakia would have meant "virtual economic disaster," *Czechoslovakia*, p. 63.

77. Bowman to Phillips, November 7, 1918, N.A., R.G. 59, 763.72119/2735. Seymour thought Dulles "absolutely first-class" and received valuable assistance from him and from Christian A. Herter, who also had served at Bern and was secretary to Henry White at the Peace Conference. Of such career diplomats Seymour wrote: "When they find that we are not 'professorish' and don't want to decide the future regardless of practical exigencies, they are very cordial," *Letters*, pp. 62, 130, 170.

Another controversy that required adjudication came before the Supreme Council on January 30. When Clemenceau suggested that the Romanian and Serbian spokesmen be allowed to present their conflicting claims, Wilson politely[78] proposed that the council ask the specialists to confer and find out what conclusions they could agree upon. These conclusions could then be submitted to the interested states for their opinions, and there would be no waste of time in the council. The president offered to adduce the recommendations already submitted by the American scholars, with the understanding that the recommendations should serve only as a basis for discussion and not as specific American proposals.

Lloyd George, jogged by the press and by his own delegation, was well aware of the general impatience with the halting procedure of the Supreme Council.[79] He did not wish, however, to deny the political leaders of the small states the satisfaction of pleading before the council. Moreover, it was thought that the specialists would benefit by hearing the pleas. It became customary, therefore, for scholars equipped with briefs and maps to sit behind their chiefs in meetings of the Supreme Council that considered territorial questions. Often they were invited to whisper advice.

On the last day of January the American experts, meeting with the Supreme Council, felt the full force of the nationalistic fervor of the premier of Romania. That nation was bursting its legitimate boundaries in all directions: in Bukovina, Transylvania, and Dobruja, as well as in the Banat of Temesvár. No official spokesman for the Ukrainians, Hungarians, or Bulgarians was at Paris to protest; but Serbian delegates took up the cause of their nationals in the Banat.[80]

Premier Ian Bratianu held that Romania was entitled to much of the land that its armies were seizing and that was awarded by the terms of the secret treaty that had brought the nation into the war on the Allied side in 1916.[81] The American minister at Bucharest warned the State Department, however, that Bratianu was claiming not only everything promised by the 1916 treaty but a great deal more.[82] Bratianu repeatedly waved the magic wand that all leaders in eastern Europe found effective

78. "Mr. Wilson . . . was very genial in his general manner. He conceals excellently his vexation at the slow way in which things are going" Seymour, p. 143. See above, p. 93.

79. Auchincloss inspired an editorial on "The Dangers of Delay," by Steed, published in the *Daily Mail* on January 23, 1919. Letters, Borden to Lloyd George, January 21, 1919, Borden papers, CC A 198, 81570 ff. Memorandum initialed "A.J.B.," January 31, 1919, and covering note from Ian Malcolm, n.d., Y.H.C.

80. See below, pp. 462–463.

81. By the "Treaty of Bucharest," signed for Romania by Bratianu on August 17, 1916, Romania was promised not only Transylvania, Bukovina, and all the Banat of Temesvár, but a wide strip of Hungary to which Romania had no valid claim on ethnic or strategic grounds, Mamatey, p. 861. The American Department of State had no copy on February 10, 1919, Polk to Ammission, February 10, 1919, N.A., R.G. 59, 763.72/127100. The British government had notified the American peace commission at Paris that it considered the pact of 1916 to have been abrogated when Romania made a separate peace with Germany in May 1918. Bratianu, however, argued that the Allies had not fulfilled obligations undertaken in a military convention that was a part of the treaty of 1916, also that the treaty of 1918 with Germany was never signed by the Romanian king, memorandum of conversation with M. Bratianu, Y.H.C. "Several flaws affected the legality of the ratification of the Treaty of 1918," Sherman Spector, *Rumania at the Paris Peace Conference,* p. 55. Johnson to House, February 6, 1919, copy in Day papers, Y.H.C.

82. *F.R., P.P.C.,* vol. 2, pp. 404–405.

in dealing with officials of Western governments. He talked of famine and economic distress, and the consequent vulnerability of his people to bolshevism. Calling together the envoys of the United States and the Allies at Bucharest, he asked whether their governments intended to honor the treaty of 1916.[83]

The American peacemakers shared the general desire of western Europe for protection against bolshevism. Moreover, they were aware of a substantial material interest in Romania on the part of influential entrepreneurs in the United States. Romania had great wealth in oil deposits that awaited development. The stake of a subsidiary of the Standard Oil Company of New Jersey was estimated to amount to $100 million. It was feared that American interests would suffer at the hands of a national oil monopoly that seemed to have been taken over by the party in power and to be in charge of Bratianu's brother. Bratianu was well aware of the trading power that he held in dealing with foreign governments.[84] Early in 1919 this delicate situation was brought to the attention of the secretary of state and Colonel House by the Standard Oil Company of New Jersey. The chairman of the board stated that a local monopoly of Romania's oil would result in higher prices, "and the driving away of American and Allied capital would have a most detrimental effect upon the industry and commerce of the country." The American oil men, in keeping with their policy of developments abroad, did not ask for special privileges but only "positive guarantees" from the Romanian government that their operation would be secure and that the advantages that Romania gained from foreign economic aid would not be turned against citizens of the nations that provided it.[85]

A report to House on a discussion among the American economic advisers stated that there was danger of exclusion of Americans from the oil fields in Romania and also in Mesopotamia. "Our practice," it said, "is to permit the citizens of other countries to acquire holdings of oil and other raw materials in the U.S. This is not the practice of other countries." This report emphasized the importance of oil to the operation of American naval and merchant ships.[86] Baruch, told that an Anglo-French group was being formed to take over "all sequestered oil properties in Romania," cabled to Washington, asking whether the American "oil people" were interested, and promising to "insist on equal rights."[87]

Wilson, with some misgivings, approved a loan for which the government at Bucharest applied; and the State Department recognized that Romania was entitled to credits as a cobelligerent. At the same time Lansing agreed to American partici-

83. The ministers of the Allied powers at Bucharest advised their governments to meet Bratianu's demands with respect to the Banat and Dobruja, *F.R., P.P.C.*, vol. 2, pp. 404–405. The American minister reported on January 10 that he had advised Bratianu to go to Paris, Spector, p. 72.

84. "The question of petroleum concessions and other natural resources was of primary interest to these powers [France and Great Britain], and Bratianu knew it. He juggled their offers and bid up the price quite skillfully, always tying concessions to a softening of their attitudes," Spector, p. 305.

85. C. V. Swain to E. M. House, March 18, 1919, enclosing a copy of a letter, A. C. Bedford, chairman of the board of the Standard Oil Company of New Jersey, to the secretary of state, February 27, 1919, and a memorandum, "Rumanian Oil Monopoly," Y.H.C. Protesting against discrimination in favor of British oil interests, Bedford wrote: "All that petroleum industry of the United States desires is an equal opportunity in an open field," A. C. Bedford to Baruch, May 9, 1919.

86. H. M. Robinson to House, April 14, 1919, Lamont papers, Baker Library, Harvard University.

87. Baruch to Peck, April 7, 1919, Baruch papers.

pation in a joint *démarche,* proposed by France, opposing certain annexations decreed by Romania.[88]

Bratianu reached Paris on January 13. He sought out the American specialists and invited three to dinner on the evening of the last day of the month, between two sessions of the Supreme Council in which he presented his nation's claims. He complained that the council was a sleeping judge putting Romania on trial. He described a talk the day before with House, who had received him with enforced courtesy, as his most cheering experience at Paris. However, his immoderate claims, reflecting promises made by the Allies in 1916, did not evoke any encouragement from the specialists.[89] Wilson was already prejudiced against Bratianu's case by military aggression on the part of Romanians. Moreover, when Bratianu came before the council on the last day of January, the president took a strong dislike to him.[90]

Returning to the attack the next day, the Romanian premier gratuitously insulted the members of the council, and claimed everything promised to Romania by the treaty of 1916, and Bessarabia, too. He indicated that he was not averse to using force, if necessary, to rule the Hungarians in Transylvania. At the same time he played upon his favorite theme: he promised, if given a free hand, to wipe out the "serious and contagious disease" of bolshevism. A protracted and warm debate with Yugoslav spokesmen ensued.[91]

The president reserved judgment; and the Supreme Council sidestepped the responsibility of dealing with an issue that in earlier days would have been resolved by professional diplomats. Wilson avoided any conference with Bratianu, and it fell to House to receive him in March after putting him off for weeks. Arranging to have Bonsal present to record all that was said, the colonel listened patiently to a tirade against the conduct of the Allies in 1916.[92] Bratianu, turning his ire upon Hoover, charged that the American administrator would not provide loans or food except in return for concessions of oil fields. Giving no credence to this, House

88. *F.R., P.P.C.,* vol. 2, pp. 722–724. Spector, p. 75 and n. *F.R., P.P.C.,* vol. 1, p. 266, and vol. 2, pp. 404, 407n, 722–724. Polk to Ammission, January 18, 1919, Wilson papers, 7104. As a result of the *démarche,* to which Italy also subscribed, the French general staff interposed a line of separation between Serbian and Romanian troops. Spector, p. 74 and n.

89. The Americans preferred to talk with Bratianu's political rival, Take Jonesçu. House diary, December 23, 1918. Seymour to the author. Walworth, p. 186n.

Memorandum, Lord to Mezes, January 28, 1919, forwarded to Lansing, memorandum, Seymour to Auchincloss, January 30, 1919. Memoranda, Johnson to House, January 30 and 31, 1919. Memorandum of a talk of Johnson, Day, and Seymour with Bratianu, January 31, 1919. Memorandum, Seymour to Auchincloss, reporting on "a number of interviews, some of which were of extremely intimate character," February 14, 1919, Y.H.C.

Johnson and Seymour recommended that the Romanians be told that the Allies would trust statistics provided by their own experts rather than those presented by Bratianu. Seymour advised that a temporary boundary be traced in the Banat, memorandum, Johnson to House, January 30, 1919, Y.H.C. Seymour, pp. 156, 173, 268.

90. When Wilson later asked Queen Marie for an opinion of her prime minister, she described him as "a tiresome, sticky and tedious individual," but withal "a man of much ability," Grayson diary, April 10, 1919.

91. The debate is described in some detail in Seymour, pp. 142 ff.

92. Thinking Bratianu "undoubtedly the most unpopular of the prime ministers" assembled at Paris, Bonsal recognized that he had a "nuisance value" so high that he sometimes seemed able to exact more from the Supreme Council than Paderewski and Venizelos could win by their charm, *Suitors and Suppliants,* pp. 170–171. Nicolson's description of Bratianu was "a bearded woman, a forceful humbug, a Bucharest intellectual, a most unpleasing man," p. 248.

asked that the charges against Hoover, Lloyd George, "American Jews," and others who were excoriated be put in writing. Bratianu promised to do this, according to Bonsal's record, but there is no evidence that he did.[93]

Informed the next day of the allegation against him, Hoover remarked: "Bratianu is a liar and a horse thief." He told his American associates that Romanians had informed him that they were offered a loan by France in return for an exclusive concession to operate the state-owned oil wells and to collect a royalty on exports.[94] Perceiving that lubricants were needed to keep the railways of central Europe running, Hoover's men tried to arrange for the exchange of food for the needed oil. They found, however, the Romanian officials were little concerned as to whether food reached their people, of the opinion that they were doing a favor to the Americans in accepting their aid, and in at least one case skillful in marketing shipments of food to line their own pockets.[95]

The Serb-Romanian debate in the Supreme Council on February 1, which was both acrimonious and protracted, further brought home the necessity for positive steps. All but Orlando were inclined to refer the question at issue to a body of experts who would hear the litigants and recommend a verdict that they thought just. Finally, the Italian premier, assured that the invalidation of the 1916 Treaty of Bucharest should not be considered a precedent that would deprive Italy of the benefits of the 1915 Treaty of London, accepted the council's decision to create a Commission on Rumanian Affairs. This body was asked on February 18 to extend its study to the frontiers of Yugoslavia, but only those in which Italy had no interest. Its American members ware Professors Day and Seymour.

On February 12 the Supreme Council, having no advisory body on Polish affairs at Paris, appointed still another committee to deal with all reports and requests that came from the commission that had just departed for Warsaw. In the absence of precise instructions the Paris committee considered itself empowered to take up any matters affecting Poland, and its authority to work on Polish boundaries was confirmed by the council.[96]

Before the end of February committees of specialists were considering the boundaries of all the succession states. Sometimes they went beyond their instructions and consulted with representatives of the interested parties, who also continued to appear occasionally before the Supreme Council in sessions that entailed "a wastage of time and a falsification of proportion."[97] On February 26, when the territorial commissions were hard at work but without adequate intercommunica-

---

93. Bonsal recorded that Bratianu, who had received bad news from Romania, was nervous and said: "I have been advised that no assistance of any kind will be forthcoming unless special privileges are granted our Jewish minority. And the American Jews, bankers and big businessmen, seem to think that our country is to be turned over to them for exploitation," Bonsal, *Suitors and Suppliants*, pp. 170–171.

94. Baker, vol. 2, pp. 422–423. Minutes of meeting of American economic group, March 15, 1919, N. H. Davis papers, box 46. Davis to Rathbone, March 18, 1919, "Peace Mission" file, Treasury Department.

House wrote in his diary: "[Bratianu] tries to link up both Baruch and Hoover with the Standard Oil Co. I do not believe for a moment that their action has had anything to do with the interests of that company in Rumania," House diary, April 26, 1919.

95. Hoover, *Memoirs*, vol. 1, pp. 407–410.

96. *F.R., P.P.C.*, vol. 4, pp. 139–141. See Jules Cambon, "La Paix," 16.

97. Nicolson, pp. 115, 127–131.

tion, the Supreme Council set up a coordinatng committee, with Mezes representing the United States and Tardieu as chairman. The choice of Tardieu as chairman of this important committee added to the prestige and power that had accrued to France through its control of the chairs of three commissions considering the claims of the states of east central Europe.

Confusion persisted within the American delegation because Bowman was the active head of the section of political intelligence and he and Mezes, the nominal chief, did not always coordinate their activities.[98] In several cases scholars were drafted to deal with regions upon which their training and experience did not qualify them as expert.[99] Although the American specialists found that their ideas as to territorial settlements coincided closely with those of the British, the English-speaking delegates encountered obstacles to general accord in what Nicolson, a British member of two of the committees, called "French and Italian susceptibilities." The adventitious origin of the committees left them without precise guidelines. No provision was made for interchange of thought with the economic advisers of the conference despite French insistence that the main duty of the territorial specialists was to provide the new states with the essentials of economic self-sufficiency. The Commission on Rumanian Affairs, for example, was instructed merely to "reduce the questions for decision within the narrowest possible limits and to make recommendations for a just settlement." Discouraged from expressing any views on principles or politics, the specialists[100] did their work at first under the delusion that they were preparing only preliminary recommendations for the consideration of a final conference at which the enemy would be represented.[101] They were surprised when they found themselves drawn into the shaping of policy. When the tentative and often uncorrelated territorial reports went into the final treaty,[102] inadequacies and contradictions resulted. In the end the settlements of boundaries were to be largely the result of the response of the delegates of the great powers to immediate political pressures in the nations concerned, without benefit of an integrating intelligence at the top or of the broader perspective that the presence of enemy delegates would have given. The total effect of the territorial decisions upon the enemy powers was not adequately considered.

"It is in an analysis of this elusive page of the history of procedure," Shotwell wrote, "that the future historian will find the clues . . . to the reason for the difference between the Fourteen Points and the Treaty of Versailles." The work of the territorial committees gave intellectual sanction to a weakening of commitment to the prearmistice understanding—a tendency that grew naturally out of an accentua-

---

98. Shotwell, pp. 154–155, 201–202.

99. Statement of Charles Seymour, cited in Gelfand, *The Inquiry,* pp. 314–315. "The discouraging part of the Conference is that it seems so difficult to get an orderly program," Seymour, p. 137.

100. Marston, pp. 116–119. Nicolson, pp. 127–130, 257–262.

101. On March 6 the council asked each commission to recommend a draft of clauses to be inserted in a "preliminary treaty."

102. "With the sole exception of the Polish report, all unanimous reports of the committees were adopted [by the Supreme Council] without further discussion, and in cases where the reports were not unanimous the committees were asked to discuss the matter further with the hope of reaching unanimity," Nicolson, p. 129.

tion of the common interests of the powers that sat in the Supreme Council, as well as from their awakening to the dangerous consequences of a literal and general application of Wilson's Points.[103]

Nevertheless a significant step in twentieth-century diplomacy was taken when House and Wiseman encouraged cooperation of the specialists of the great powers. When Wilson proposed in the Supreme Council that, instead of confining themselves to advising the American plenipotentiaries, the scholars should confer directly with their opposite numbers in foreign delegations, he facilitated what Shotwell called "the diplomacy of fact-finding." In contrast with the precise chief negotiator of the British Foreign Office, Sir Eyre Crowe, the American scholar-diplomats, assuming the role of fair and disinterested arbiters and prolific of facts and theories, appeared to some Europeans to lack an appreciation of political realities.[104]

Nevertheless, despite its shortcomings, by the middle of February the American delegation at Paris had projected its influence far into the affairs of Europe. The Supreme Council, preoccupied by issues that were of immediate concern to one or more of the great powers, came to make use of the specialists not only for technical advice, but for negotiation and settlement of boundary claims as well.

In the process of dealing with immediate realities it became clear that Wilson's vision of "easily recognizable frontiers of nationality" was actually a delusion. Once begun, nevertheless, the concert of intellect spread, both as to subject matter and as to the nations concerned. Indeed, the labor of the territorial committees and of various others[105] was a precursor of joint intellectual efforts in the interest of peace that were to develop under the League of Nations and the United Nations.

103. Shotwell, pp. 33–40.
104. LaRoche, p. 72.
105. At the Paris Peace Conference fifty-eight international commissions and committees held more than 1,500 meetings, Tardieu, *The Truth about the Treaty,* p. 93.

6

The Triumph of Wilson's Great Cause

Having won the vote of the Peace Conference for the immediate drafting of a constitution for a league of nations, Wilson took the leading part in the construction of what he liked to call a "covenant." In ten meetings in February he sat with the committee that the Peace Conference had appointed and gave it the prestige of his presence, serving as its chairman. Lacking confidence in Secretary Lansing, Wilson asked House to sit on the league commission. The colonel, continuing to make what he called "moves . . . on the board," suggested to Orlando, who was solicitous of Wilson's good will, that the way to "get closer" to the president was to serve on the commission; and the Italian premier agreed to do so.[1] Lloyd George and Clemenceau stood aside. The British and French members were advocates of a league of nations: Lord Robert Cecil, General Smuts, Léon Bourgeois, and Professor Larnaude, dean of the law faculty of the University of Paris. Japan was represented by Makino and Chinda, and the small powers by their most able delegates.

The Americans had yet to get the consent of the Allies to the sort of league that they envisioned. There was little public interest in France.[2] However, a committee headed by Bourgeois had prepared recommendations that supplied what seemed to Lloyd George to be "far and away the most detailed, precise, and far-reaching definition of the constitution and powers of the projected League which had yet been presented to any belligerent government."[3] French thinking centered upon the value of a league as a guarantee of French security by Great Britain and the United States.[4]

Wilson had been wary of any specification. It seemed to him that a project so delicate required protection from the pressures of politicians and publicists.[5] Wilson perceived that an extention to the international level of practices that were routine in municipal law would not be immediately acceptable to many nations, and perhaps least of all to his own. He recognized the force of the aversion to "entangling alliances" that his people had long felt. Six weeks before the armistice he had taken the precaution of explaining publicly that in this "new day" he sought "a general alliance which will avoid entanglements and clear the air of the world for common understandings and the maintenance of common rights." He talked much of the power of moral suasion; yet mere precept in the presence of the undeniable right of states to go to war was to him fatuous. He alluded to the work of the Hague Con-

---

1. *I.P.*, vol. 4, pp. 303–304. House diary, January 23, 1919.
2. Shotwell, *At the Paris Peace Conference,* p. 100.
3. Lloyd George, *The Truth about the Peace Treaties,* p. 610.
4. Miller, *My Diary,* vol. 1, p. 26, entry of December 3, 1918.
5. "His enemies here and abroad hope that he will particularize so that they can attack him," Tumulty cabled. "People of the world are with him on general principles. They care little for details." Tumulty to Grayson, December 21, 1918, Tumulty papers.

ventions as a "wishy-washy" business,[6] and from first to last he felt that a league of nations should depend upon the body of usage that would grow out of its own executive and legislative acts. In March of 1918 he had written to House: "Any attempt to begin by putting executive authority in the hands of any particular group of powers would be to sow a harvest of jealousy and distrust which would spring up at once and choke the whole thing. To take one thing, and only one, but quite sufficient in itself: the United States Senate would never ratify any treaty which put the force of the United States at the disposal of any such group or body. Why begin at the impossible end when there is a possible end and it is feasible to plant a system which will ripen into fruition?"

When Wilson visited London in December, he had received proposals for a league constitution that were put forward by two British proponents: General Smuts and Lord Robert Cecil. He respected Smuts as a fellow prophet in the cause of lasting peace. The general's experience as one of the founding fathers of the Union of South Africa, as well as his work in behalf of the British Empire, gave wisdom and prestige to his ideas. Like Wilson, he took a farsighted view of the future of Germany. (In a meeting of the British War Cabinet on October 26, 1918, he said: "If we were to beat Germany to nothingness, then we must beat Europe to nothingness too.")[7] Fearing that America might become as great a rival of the British Empire as Germany had been, Smuts had suggested making the United States the "chairman of the board" in a joint enterprise. He was disposed to support Wilson's ideas, which seemed to him nebulous, with the hope that the president might be persuaded to drop some of his contentious points.[8] In the preface of his pamphlet "The League of Nations: A Practical Suggestion," Smuts wrote: "To my mind the world is ripe for the greatest steps forward ever made in the government of men. . . . If that advance is not made, this war will, from the most essential point of view, have been fought in vain, and great calamities will follow." Wilson studied the proposals of Smuts, marked certain sentences, and drew upon the language as well as the ideas. It would be good politics, he remarked to Dr. Grayson, to play the British game more or less in order to get support that otherwise might be witheld from a program that might seem to be exclusively his own.[9]

6. Bonsal, *Unfinished Business*, p. 152.
7. Minutes, B.W.C., Curzon papers, box 72, F/12/132.
8. "Our Policy at the Peace Conference," December 3, 1918, P.R.O., Cab/29/49.
9. Grayson diary, January 6, 1919.
See George Curry, "Woodrow Wilson, Jan Smuts, and the Versailles Settlement." Passages in the pamphlet of Smuts that are underlined in the copy in Wilson's papers are:

"The League should be put in the very forefront of the programme of the Peace Conference, and be made the point of departure for the solution of many of the grave problems with which it will be confronted.

". . . The Conference should look upon itself as the first or preliminary meeting of the League, intended to work out its organisation, functions, and programme.

"In all the above and similar cases where the assistance and control of an external authority is necessary to supplement the local autonomy of the territories in question, the external authority should be the League of Nations.

"Three proposals for general disarmament . . . are: (a) abolition of conscription; (b) limitation of armaments; (c) nationalization of munitions production. All bristle with difficulties."

Also marked is a recommendation for the delegation of the league's authority to a mandatory power.

Lord Robert Cecil, a devout Christian, hoped that the formation of a league might compensate to some degree for the war's wickedness. Unwilling to prescribe compulsory arbitration, he recognized the moral power of public opinion as the chief instrument for keeping the peace. "What is wanted is a great idea," he wrote to Wiseman on August 19, 1918, "and that must be found in the old Hebrew—and let me add, Christian—conception of the reign of peace. I believe that a great formless sentiment of this kind exists. If it does not, I can do nothing. . . . If we try to impose on all the nations of the world a form of government which has been indeed admirably successful in America and this country, but is not necessarily suited for all others, I am convinced we shall plant the seeds of very serious international trouble." He appealed for allegiance to what he regarded as "a noble cause—the cause of Christianity itself."[10] Distrusting schemes involving large invasions of national sovereignty, and questioning whether territorial integrity should be singled out for guarantee apart from other treaty obligations, Cecil emphasized delay and consultation as preventives of war. Proposing that the league make use of an international court, he recommended strong "sanctions" and advocated frank recognition of the obvious necessity for control by the great powers. Membership should be open to every nation that could be trusted by its fellows to accept "ex animo" the principles and basis of such a society. Cecil put his ideas into a draft of a covenant that House sent to Wilson on January 19.[11]

With the proposals of Smuts and Lord Robert Cecil before him, Wilson sat down at Paris at the beginning of 1919 to revise the Covenant that he and House had tentatively drafted in the preceding summer and that they held in confidence.[12] The president included Smuts's plan for trusteeship for territories to be taken from Germany and Turkey. He also provided for a permanent council that would act as the league's executive and would report on the adjustment of disputes. He conceived of a league executive body as "a solution of the main difficulty of his earlier plans which left in a perpetual minority the great powers, upon whom the responsibility for maintaining the League would fall."[13] Furthermore, he included a proposal of an international bureau of labor.[14] Two other provisions would require new states to give equal treatment to all racial and religious minorities, and would affirm the "friendly right" of each of the signatory nations to direct the attention of the Body of Delegates to any circumstances anywhere which threaten to disturb international

Smuts's biographer has described his pamphlet as "an impressive achievement in intellectual engineering in which three theories were firmly interlocked: a theory of Imperialism, a theory of the Commonwealth, and a theory of the League of Nations," Hancock, *Smuts,* vol. 1, pp. 500–502.

Smuts was not surprised that his ideas were taken over without acknowledgment. Realizing that his paper was written hurriedly and in need of amendment, he regretted that even his mistakes had been appropriated by Wilson, Smuts to M. C. Gillett, January 20, 1919, W. K. Hancock and Jean Van der Poel (eds.), *Selections from the Smuts Papers,* vol. 4, p. 43.

10. Lord Robert Cecil to J. H. Thomas, December 23, 1918, Cecil papers, 51162. See Peter Raffo, "The League of Nations Philosophy of Lord Robert Cecil," 186–192.

11. See above, p. 43.

12. See Walworth, *America's Moment: 1918,* pp. 13, 132.

13. *I.P.,* vol. 4, p. 285.

14. For an analysis of Wilson's three Paris drafts of a covenant see Miller, *The Drafting of the Covenant,* vol. 1, ch. 7.

peace or the good understanding between nations upon which peace depends.[15]

The draft of the president did not have the approval of Secretary Lansing or that of his legal advisers.[16] Lansing's legalistic view tended to exalt the unrestricted sovereignty of nations that it was the purpose of Wilson to curtail.[17] The secretary of state insisted that "pure" nationalism was the essential basis of the political structure of the world and as such must be preserved as a bulwark against class rule. While defending the legitimacy of nations, however, he perceived the confusions that could arise from devotion to the general principle of self-determination. To what political unit should it be applied, he queried: to a race, to a region, or to a community?[18] Lansing's views were, in brief, these: democracy was enough; no international sanctions or legislative power was necessary; expansion of the powers was legitimate in the lands of half-civilized peoples; and rival claims on colonial territories could be settled by diplomacy or court action.[19] He thought that three doctrines should be incorporated in the peace treaty: "hands off," "the Open Door," and publicity for international agreements.[20]

Filled with dread that the appalling conditions in enemy lands would lead to chaos by the time a treaty of peace could be concluded, Lansing made a proposal that he thought quickly negotiable and consonant with the Constitution of the United States. He suggested to the president that each sovereign nation undertake a negative "self-denying" guarantee that it would not violate the territory or independence of others, instead of the positive pledge to oppose aggression upon which Wilson insisted. The president's desire for a positive guarantee, enforced by united military and economic power, seemed to Lansing "dangerous" if there were to be majority rule in a league council, and without significance if each member nation could exercise a veto. Lansing advised that a positive guarantee would invite a divergence of opinion among the powers that opponents of a league would use to promote discord.[21] The secretary of state pointed out that, without the approval of the Congress, participation by the American government in commercial or military sanctions under the direction of a league council would be unconstitutional. Frightened by the possibility of widespread class conflict, Lansing had no sympathy with the wish of the president to make provision for the welfare of labor. Regarding the policies of France and Great Britain as sinister, and sharing Wilson's fear that Cle-

15. The first of these provisions was to be rejected by the Commission on the League of Nations. The second became Article XI of the Covenant, which Wilson later spoke of as his "favorite article," *I.P.*, vol. 4, pp. 284–286.

16. Lansing, *The Peace Negotiations*, p. 79. Ambassador John W. Davis, a lawyer, thought Wilson's draft "crude and needing considerable condensation," diary, January 22, 1919, Y.H.C.

17. A. D. Lindsay, *The Modern Democratic State* (New York, 1947), ch. 60, sec. 6, esp. p. 217. Commenting on twenty-four questions that Lansing drafted, Lindsay wrote: "Mr. Lansing's theory of sovereignty will not fit simple facts. . . . Sovereignty is treated as a material thing like the guns and tanks which pass from conquered to conqueror without difficulty."

18. Private memoranda, December 20, 1918, Lansing papers, L.C.

19. "Woodrow Wilson, la Suisse, et Genève," in William E. Rappard, *Centenaire Woodrow Wilson* (Geneva, 1956), p. 43.

20. Private memoranda, January 4, 1919.

21. Lansing to Wilson, December 23, 1918, enclosing "Suggested Draft of Articles for Discussion," December 20, 1918, Wilson papers. Lansing, pp. 123–124; private memoranda, entries of December 8 and 17, 1918.

menceau's program might lead to a repressive alliance like that formed at Vienna a hundred years before, the secretary of state wrote in his diary: "As I see it, the dominant spirit in the Peace Conference is selfish materialism tinctured with a cynical disregard of manifest rights . . . Will American idealism [which Lansing thought his nation's "greatest heritage"] have to succumb to this evil spirit of a past era?"[22] This attitude did not augur well for the usefulness of Lansing as a diplomat.

On January 6 he talked twice with House and understood that the colonel accepted his plan of a negative guarantee in the constitution of a league of nations. House gave him the tentative draft of a covenant that Wilson had brought to Paris, and Lansing was asked to suggest amendments that would bring the paper into harmony with his own views. But to Lansing this appeared impossible. He said to House that the two plans, being founded on contradictory principles, could not be reconciled. In his opinion Wilson's draft indicated a lack of knowledge of the Hague conventions and indeed was "one of the crudest and most inartistic documents of the sort" that the secretary of state had ever read. Concerned by Wilson's deficiency as an international lawyer, Lansing thought that the president was lured from the path of reason by an inordinate desire to cut a great figure in history.[23]

House, convinced that Lansing's cast of mind disqualified him as an effective negotiator, had encouraged the drafting of a skeleton treaty in order to give the secretary of state employment and a sense of participation in the peacemaking.[24] The resulting draft proposed the negative guarantee that Lansing advocated, and it provided for a court of arbitration based on that at The Hague. In these respects it ran counter to Wilson's ideas.[25]

The inevitable confrontation of views occurred in a meeting of the American peace commission on January 7. Lansing mentioned the draft that had been prepared at his direction and with House's encouragement. Wilson then said sharply: "Who authorized them to do this? I don't want lawyers drafting this treaty." Afterward the secretary of state wrote in his diary: "I was deeply incensed . . . as he knew I was a lawyer." Although House tried to soothe him by suggesting that the president must be unwell, Lansing, frustrated by Wilson's resistance to every form of suggestion, had an impulse to resign. But he told himself that on the morrow he might feel differently.[26]

Lansing set down House's tactful approaches to the president as evidence of

22. Lansing's private memoranda, February 3, 1919.

23. Lansing, pp. 78–79, 124; private memoranda, December 31, 1918, January 6, 1919. Auchincloss diary, January 10, 1919.

24. Miller, *My Diary*, vol. 1, entry of December 27, 1918. Minutes, ACTNP, December 27, 1918. Lansing, private memoranda, January 3, 6, and 7, 1919. Bliss diary, January 10, 1919. House diary, January 8, 1919.

25. Minutes, ACTNP, December 27, 1918. *F.R., P.P.C.*, vol. 1, pp. 298–333. Miller, *My Diary*, vol. 1, entries of January 1, 2, 3, and 11, 1919. House diary, December 14, 1918. Lansing, private memoranda, Appendix, December 21 and 17, 1918, January 3, 1919. Lansing, *passim*.

26. Lansing, pp. 106–108, 200; desk diary, January 7, 1919; private memoranda, January 10, 1919; Bliss diary, January 10, 1919; Bliss to N. D. Baker, January 11, 1919, N. D. Baker papers, L.C. House, chagrined because his effort to indulge Lansing had miscarried, wrote in his diary on January 7: "I was at fault more than anyone. I did not know that Bliss and Lansing were to spring it on the president today. Otherwise I should have prepared him."

weakness. He wrote in his diary of January 1: "House does not openly oppose him but endeavors to change him by putting his own interpretation on the president's words. The method seems to work, but I could not follow it. I must either keep quiet or else speak frankly my views." Yet Lansing himself had written a letter to Wilson on December 23 in which he modified his own opinions in deference to expediency; and for a time he withheld from Wilson his own dissent as to the wisdom of the positive guarantee of national integrity that was so dear to the president.[27]

Henry White told Edith Wilson of Lansing's distress, and the president sent a copy of his own draft to the commissioners and to some extent heeded their suggestions.[28] But the manifest breach was too wide and too deep for healing.[29] Lansing declared to Bliss and White that he would take no part in writing the sort of league constitution that Wilson had in mind. The position of the secretary from day to day became more difficult, his dissent from the president's policies more profound.[30] His personal convictions demanded that he resign, but his sense of public duty required him to spare the president the embarrassment that would result from the resignation of the secretary of state at this critical juncture.

On the evening of January 8, after listening to Lansing's denunciation of Wilson's ideas, House conferred with the president. Apparently he did not risk Wilson's displeasure by mentioning the views of the secretary of state. That afternoon House had invited Lord Robert Cecil to his room and talked more freely than at a previous conference at which Lansing was present. House showed confidence, as usual, that agreement could be reached, and advocated a meeting of the American and British experts to draft a text. Emphasizing the provisional nature of Wilson's paper, he swore Cecil to absolute secrecy, contrary to the British desire that Wilson's draft be published.[31]

Of all the delicate tasks that Colonel House undertook, the reconciliation of the views of Wilson and those of the British statesmen as to the provisions of the Covenant was perhaps the most precarious. Each of these idealists felt competent to speak. The president had a proprietary interest in the language as well as in some of the ideas of his own draft; and Lord Robert Cecil was less interested in reconciling the ideas of various nations than in gaining acceptance of British legal con-

27. Lansing to Wilson, December 23, 1918. Lansing's private memoranda, appendix, entries of December 17, 1918, and January 1, 1919. *The Peace Negotiations,* p. 50.

28. E. B. Wilson, *My Memoir,* p. 226. Bliss diary, January 11, 1919; Lansing desk diary, January 11, 1919. Minutes, ACTNP, January 11, 1919.

29. The breach remained, Lansing wrote in *The Peace Negotiations* (p. 108), "until my association with President Wilson came to an end in February, 1920. I never forgot his words and always felt that in his mind my opinions, even when he sought them, were tainted with legalism."

30. According to entries in the diary of Lord Robert Cecil, Lloyd George regarded Lansing as insolent and not overfriendly. Cecil thought him stupid, but noted that Lansing's jeers against the president ceased in mid-January, diary entries of January 13 and 15, 1919.

31. Lord Robert Cecil's diary, January 8, 1919, Cecil papers, British Museum, 51131; "Record of an Interview with Col. House at Paris, Thursday, Jan. 9, 1919," *loc. cit.,* 51094.

House wrote in his diary on January 8: "We got along because I opened up my mind to him and told the whole story of the League of Nations Covenant as the president and I had written it. It was something I could not explain to him before Lansing."

cepts.[32] In the opinion of at least one of his colleagues, he had "an amiable touch of vanity."[33]

It was at this critical juncture that House became ill.[34] When Cecil, finding it difficult to get the ear of the president,[35] sent word to House that he would welcome a discussion that might enable American and British representatives to reach a preliminary understanding, Auchincloss replied that House was not able to enter into *pourparlers* and the president was revising his plan and not quite ready to discuss the matter in detail.[36] Actually, when Wilson completed his revision, he asked Dr. Grayson to put it in the hands of Smuts, not into those of Lord Robert Cecil.[37]

To A. G. Gardiner the president explained that he feared to seem dictatorial and realized that any plan drafted in the United States would have to be changed when European views and issues were studied firsthand. Wilson sent a copy of a draft to this favorite journalist and received suggestions.[38] The president also invited criticism from General Bliss[39] and Miller in preparing his second Paris draft. Miller, who had at hand a large collection of pertinent studies to which the president gave no attention, was disappointed.[40] Thinking Wilson's document "very poor," he perceived that it included various features that were "clearly unconstitutional." Miller noted that the Monroe Doctrine was being abandoned and that power to arbitrate disputes between nations was to be vested in a political council rather than in courts. He thought, too, that Wilson, "unconsciously no doubt," was adopting the point of view of British imperialists who looked to the United States for protection against the future. It seemed to Miller, as to House, that nothing needed to be surrendered in order to carry through the program on which the German armistice was based, that a mere hint of American withdrawal from Paris would presage the fall of every government n Europe.[41] Miller's thinking was perhaps influenced by a statement made by Wiseman to the effect that Lloyd George's new cabinet was not being well received in England and Wilson, except for his views on naval matters,

32. Hugh Cecil, "Lord Robert Cecil: A Nineteenth Century Upbringing," *History Today* 25, no. 2 (February 1975):124.

33. House diary, January 8, 1919; Riddell, *Intimate Diary,* p. 25. Lord Robert Cecil confessed in a letter to Lloyd George that he regretted a little that they had "let that eloquent pedagogue [Wilson] 'patent' this question," letter of December 19, 1918, Lloyd George papers, F / 6 / 5 / 53.

34. See above, p. 29.

35. Lord Robert Cecil and Lionel Curtis dined on January 8 with Beer, Shotwell, and Young of the Inquiry. Shotwell, p. 110. Beer diary, January 10, 1919.

36. Cecil to House, January 12, 1919, Auchincloss to Cecil, January 13, 1919, Auchincloss diary, January 13, 1919. Cecil to Auchincloss, January 13, 1919, Auchincloss diary, January 16, 1919, Y.H.C.

37. Benham diary letter, January 18, 1919.

38. Benham diary letter, January 21, 1919. A. G. Gardiner to Wilson, February 1, 1919, Wilson papers.

39. Bliss submitted many suggestions in detail in a letter dated January 14, 1919, which is printed in Baker, vol. 3, pp. 111–116. On January 17 Wilson wrote to Bliss: "Thanks. I have gone over the draft with your suggestions by me and they have been of great service. I think all the points are covered," letter in Wilson papers.

40. See Gelfand, *The Inquiry,* pp. 300 ff. A fifty-eight-page brief on points of international law had been prepared by Scott, Miller, and Woolsey of the State Department, D. H. Miller papers, box 83, folder I-7. A long report was prepared for General Bliss by Captain H. C. Bell of Military Intelligence. This was based upon a huge bibliography of historical and contemporary sources, Miller papers, box 84, folder II, 21, a, b, c; N.A., R.G. 256, 185. 111 / 101-1 / 2. The navy also had a paper on the subject.

41. Miller, *My Diary,* January 6 and 11, 1919, and doc. 162. Auchincloss diary, January 14, 1919.

had a better following in England than the prime minister.[42]

Lord Robert Cecil was not satisfied with a tentative British draft that he had received from the Foreign Office. This paper included a positive pledge like that advocated by Wilson.[43] To Cecil this undertaking, which in the opinion of the president was demanded by the people of the United States, was not one that most of the world's governments were prepared to honor and carry out. He therefore thought it unsound and eliminated it. He sent a copy of his own draft to House on January 18, and it was passed along to Wilson the next day.[44]

In the evening of January 19 Lord Robert Cecil came to the president for their first talk and stayed until midnight.[45] Obliged to listen while the president went through his second draft, Cecil thought the author vain and dogmatic and his draft verbose and at times obscure or irrelevant. The American prophet seemed to want the Covenant to appear nominally as his work, although actually it was largely the production of others.[46]

During the week following there was little discussion at the top level of the particulars of a league constitution, except in the course of the controversy regarding mandates that has already been described.[47] House instructed Miller to meet with Cecil and to go as far as possible toward an agreement with the British. Accordingly, these men composed a text that Cecil described as "mainly American" and "deplorable," yet in substance nearly the same as his own. Seeking authorization to negotiate on the basis of this draft, Cecil sent to Lloyd George a formula that the Americans proposed on the question of freedom of the seas, which had to be understood to Lloyd George's satisfaction if he were to accept a league of nations.[48]

42. Auchincloss diary, January 11, 1919.

43. Eustace Percy, *Some Memories*, pp. 67–69.

44. On January 18 Cecil read his draft, just completed, to George Louis Beer and asked for suggestions. Beer emphasized the importance of developing a real international public opinion. When the American specialist proposed that the League of Nations hold periodic conferences on such questions as Africa and Labour, Sir Eyre Crowe of the Foreign Office obected that this would give an opportunity to "faddists," Beer diary, January 18, 1919.

Cecil asked Wiseman whether it was true that he was disliked by Wilson. Wiseman denied this, Wiseman diary, January 18 and 19, 1919, Y.H.C. *I.P.*, vol. 4, p. 288. The Cecil draft is in the Wilson papers microfilm, pp. 7301 ff.

45. Benham diary letter, January 21, 1919. Lord Robert Cecil, *A Great Experiment*, p. 68. Wiseman's diary records: "House thinks the president has the idea that Smuts is working more on his lines than Cecil and he particularly asked that Smuts should go there with Cecil," entry of January 19, 1919, Y.H.C.

46. Observing that Wilson was a vain man, "a trifle of a bully," and always mindful of the American polls, Lord Robert Cecil recorded that he tried to deal with him "firmly, though with the utmost courtesy and respect." The president seemed eager to work with the British and French delegates in a committee, hoping thus to arrive at a final text in a fortnight, Cecil diary, January 19, 1919. Edith Benham, in a diary letter of February 6, recorded that Cecil was a man "for whom I don't think he [Wilson] cares very much."

The president did not like the new British draft, and the British did not like the American draft. Wiseman told House that his people thought that the Americans were "grabbing the whole shooting match and there was trouble ahead," Bonsal, p. 21. Cecil recorded that Lloyd George took "no real interest" in a league of nations and insisted the project must be sponsored not by Wilson but rather by the Commission on a League of Nations, diary, January 20, 1919.

47. In ch. 4, above.

48. Lord Robert Cecil to the prime minister, January 29, 1919, Lothian papers, Gd40 / 17 / 51.

Apparently the prime minister, hoping to exploit Wilson's commitment to the League of Nations in such a way as to get concessions and to bring the United States into a partnership that would advance British interests,[49] responded favorably. For on the next day, when Wilson was engaged in hot controversy with Lloyd George and the southern dominions, House wrote in his diary: "Lord Robert Cecil was my most important visitor. We went over the Covenant for the League of Nations and there was but little disagreement between us. He agrees with our views more than he dares admit, because he sees that his people will not follow him. I am to get Orlando in line and he is to get the French, and when this is done we will have a general meeting." That evening House and Wilson met with Orlando to compare their draft with the Italian recommendations. With assurance of Orlando's support for the league of nations, Wilson became so exuberant that he made a concession of territory to Italy that was most unfortunate.[50]

The proceedings took a long step forward on the last day of January, when the president and House met at the Crillon with both Lord Robert Cecil and General Smuts. "We discussed our difficulties regarding the League and brought them nearly to a vanishing point," House recorded. "We decided that Miller, representing us, and [Sir Cecil] Hurst, repesenting the British, should draft a new form of Covenant based upon the one which the president and I jointly prepared."[51] This was done promptly, and House sent Miller to Wilson with the Hurst-Miller draft to explain the changes and the reasons for making them.

The president, however, was disappointed by the product. It seemed to him to have no warmth or color. Telling House of his dissatisfaction, he asked that his own draft be rewritten so that it would include certain clauses of the Hurst-Miller paper.[52] He planned to put the revised document before the Commission on the League of Nations at its first meeting, as a basis for discussion.

Miller worked all night to meet the president's wish. The next morning—that of the day on which the commission was to meet for the first time—Sir William Wiseman got wind of what was transpiring. He reported to House that Lord Robert Cecil was greatly perturbed[53] by the prospect of a reopening of this matter he thought settled. Wiseman warned that Cecil should not be allowed to enter the first meeting of the commission feeling as he did.

House then acted immediately and effectively. He arranged for the president and Cecil to meet in his study fifteen minutes before the commission was to convene

49. Anthony Adamthwaite, review in the *English Historical Review* (October 1981):935–937.

50. See above, p. 54. "We came near to agreement and without much difficulty," House recorded. "The exceptions that Orlando made to our draft were rather pertinent and some of them we agreed to accept," *I.P.*, vol. 4, pp. 298–299.

51. *I.P.*, vol. 4, p. 300. See Miller, *Drafting*, vol. 1, pp. 65–71.

52. The clauses concerning religious equality, the publication of future treaties, and the prevention of commercial discrimination among members of the League. Wilson's third Paris draft and the Hurst-Miller draft are in Miller, *Drafting*, vol. 2, pp. 131–154.

53. "Cecil, when I told him, was furious," Wiseman diary, February 3, 1919. "I was much agitated," Cecil later wrote in his autobiography (*A Great Experiment*, p. 69), "partly because there were things in the President's draft which would have been very difficult for the British to accept, and partly because I feared—quite groundlessly, as it turned out—that the President regarded himself as a kind of dictator."

there. To prepare Wilson for an accommodation of views, he explained to him over the telephone that they could not afford to alienate the man in the British delegation who had the league of nations most at heart. "The three of us met promptly at 2:15 in my study," House recorded. "The meeting bade fair to be stormy for the first seven or eight minutes. After that things went better and the president finally decided . . . to take the joint draft of Miller and Hurst and use it as a basis for discussion. After that, everything went smoothly. The full committee of fifteen met in one of my salons and all during the discussion Lord Robert was on our side. I think the president was quite content that he had yielded the point."[54]

Wilson held the attention of the members of the commission with a little speech while Miller hastened to fetch copies of the Hurst-Miller draft.[55] While expressing gratitude for the ideas of the French and Italian delegations, the president said he assumed that all would agree that the Anglo-American draft would serve as a basis for discussion. Though this assumption was less than agreeable to the Frenh delegates, they acquiesced.

Working with a secrecy and a precise definition of purpose that were in the tradition of Old World diplomacy, the Commission on the League of Nations created a charter for a new world. The nineteen members met ten times within eleven days. The Hurst-Miller draft, consisting of twenty-two articles, presented the main features and much of the wording of the Covenant that was finally adopted. It was considered by the commission, article by article, and agreement was reached in principle by a first-reading debate. A drafting committee, on which Miller represented the United States, made the changes required, and the revised text underwent a second reading.

The British and American members pressed for a quick acceptance. From the chair Wilson, permitting discussion when it was needed, checked it when it ran too far afield or sank too deeply in technicalities. He said at the outset that the proceedings should be informal and unrecorded so that he would be able to change his mind without hindrance. He expressed the hope that they might work in secrecy until their task was done, like the men who drew up the Constitution of the United States. The French delegates, however, wished to have a record of the proceedings, and the others agreed. Wilson was eventually persuaded to accept a secretariat; and yet he persisted in opposing the circulation of any record, fearing that this might lead to unwelcome publicity. His critics continued to talk of the revival of secret proceedings by one who promised "open covenants . . . openly arrived at".[56]

Rejoicing in the ability of Wilson to conduct the discussions, House wrote in his diary: "The President excels in such work. He seems to like it and his short talks

54. *I.P.,* vol. 4, 300–303. Miller, *My Diary,* vol. 1, January 31, February 2, 1919.
Cecil recorded that when he met with Wilson and House, he did not conceal his "severe disappointment." He noted that Wilson seemed "mildly surprised" and "a little apologetic," agreed to accept the Hurst-Miller draft as a skeleton, reserving a right to add flesh and blood. Because the president responded so nobly, Lord Robert wrote, "I supported all his most tyrannical proposals" in the League of Nations Commission, diary, February 3, 1919.
55. Wiseman diary, February 3, 1919.
56. Bonsal, pp. 27, 61. When secretaries were chosen at the third meeting, it was suggested that they record decisions only, but this restriction was not maintained. The minutes of the February meetings were not circulated until about March 22, F. S. Marston, *The Peace Conference of 1919,* p. 90.

in explanation of his views are admirable. I have never known anyone to do such work as well."[57] Wilson was content to let Cecil share the burden of exposition and bring his parliamentary skill to bear upon the debate. "Practically everything originates from our end of the table," House recorded, "that is, with Lord Robert Cecil and the President."[58]

House, whose initiative and tact had played a large part in setting the stage, spoke at none of the February meetings until the last. "My province is to keep things running smoothly," he wrote in his diary after the second session of the commission. "I try to find in advance where trouble lies and to smooth it out before it goes too far. In this way we have gotten over some pretty bad hurdles. Cecil and I do nearly all the difficult work between the meetings . . . and try to have as little friction at the meetings as possible. The president often tells me that under no circumstances will he do a certain thing and, a few minutes later, consents."[59]

The text agreed upon followed the Hurst-Miller draft in most respects. The positive guarantee on which the president set his heart became Article X, which flatly guaranteed "as against external aggression the territorial integrity and existing political independence of all Members of the league." Article XI, which Wilson had drafted, declared that "any war or threat of war" was a matter for concern and action on the part of the whole league of nations. The draft did not go so far as to provide specifically for enforcing arbitration, as House and many of the minor powers wished. Cecil, apologizing for being "a stumbling block to the realization of a dream," said that although England would accept "very drastic restrictions" on its right to make war, including arrangements for delay, his country must have in the end, if civilized methods failed, "the right to seek the arbitrament of arms." "I cannot assume," he said, "at least not just at present, responsibility for discarding war as an instrument for the maintenance of the peace of the world."[60]

Article X was Woodrow Wilson's and his alone. It gave satisfaction to European politicians even though they knew it would not be effective.[61] The president said that it represented, more than all other provisions of the Covenant, the will of "the plain people of the United States." Cecil, however, said to the commission: "But do any of us really mean it?" Unable to persuade Wilson to give it up, he set him down as no idealist but rather a man of "a certain hardness coupled with vanity and an eye for effect."[62] By this time he had concluded that although Wilson listened courteously to his arguments and usually agreed with him, he did not like the American prophet. But he wrote in his diary on February 6: "I still like House very much."[63]

57. Of Wilson's work at this time Leland Harrison, assistant secretary of the American commission, wrote: "The president is superb. Keen, alert, ready, tactful, smiling, insistent yet ready to concede when a good point is made," letter to Polk, February 9, 1919, Y.H.C.

58. *I.P.*, vol. 4, p. 312. Hankey remarked that Wilson had begun to dominate the Peace Conference, having learned "the dodge of preparing resolutions beforehand"—an act of which Hankey himself was a master, memorandum, Kerr to Lloyd George, February 11, 1919, Lloyd George papers, F / 89 / 2 / 6.

59. House diary, February 4, 6, and 7, 1919.

60. Bonsal, p. 30.

61. Lord Robert Cecil's diary, February 6, 1919.

62. *Ibid.*, February 6, 1910.

63. Years later Cecil wrote of House: "He was a high-minded and clear-sighted American, devoted to the president and profoundly convinced that a good understanding between the British Empire and

The Commission on the League of Nations approved the preamble of the covenant almost as Wilson had presented it. It accepted also the president's recommendations for publicity of treaties and armament programs. Important changes were made, however, in the clauses defining the league's executive and judicial functioning. The commission dropped Wilson's idea that members of the league might be represented at the meetings of the assembly by their ambassadors and ministers at the city that would serve as the league's capital.[64]

Discussing the question of the legality of treaties to be concluded in the future, the president was content to let the verdicts be passed by public opinion. "Every public declaration constitutes a moral obligation," he asserted, "and the decision of the court of public opinion will be much more effective than that of any tribunal in the world, since it is more powerful and is able to register its effect in the face of technicalities. Frequantly the law decides one way and public opinion gives judgment in a manner that is broad and more equitable." At this Professor Larnaude, who as dean of the law faculty at the University of Paris had little respect for the court of public opinion, is said to have asked his colleague Bourgeois in an undertone: "Am I at a Peace Conference or in a madhouse?" Larnaude asked aloud whether the United States and England would give to public opinion the power to rule upon technical questions of law.[65]

A profound difference of opinion arose over the Covenant's provisions for adjudication of disputes. Wilson's early drafts had provided only for noncompulsory arbitration according to prewar standards and for no judiciary. But the president's aversion from the creation of a court of justice was overcome. The Hurst-Miller recommendation of a permanent court of arbitration, to be established by the league council, went into the approved draft without any provision for compulsion in resorting to this court.

Attention was given to the defining of standards for membership in the league and to voting power. It was Wilson's idea from the beginning that eventually all nations should come in, but he was willing to yield to France's desire that Germany be excluded for at least a period of years. The delegates of the small powers demanded seats in the executive council and had the support of Wilson and the French, who argued for "abstract justice." The British, however, pointed out the practical inconvenience of a large executive body. They persuaded House that only two seats, at most, should be granted to little states.[66] In the end they were given four. The

America was vital for the peace and prosperity of the world. If men may be divided into those whose ambition is to do something, and those who want to be something, he emphatically belonged to the first class. He cared nothing for position. But he cared immensely for what he believed to be in his country's interest. He was consequently a delightful person to work with. In discussion he always put forth his real opinion, supported by his real reasons. There was never any danger that agreement reached on that basis would be upset for personal and private considerations," *A Great Experiment*, p. 64.

64. When Wilson reached Paris, he envisioned the transaction of a league's business by a council of ambassadors meeting in the capital of a small power. In order to avoid the jealousy and contention that he had observed when two representatives of a nation functioned in one place, he thought it might be best to appoint no special envoys to the league's council, *I.P.*, vol. 4, pp. 280–283. Miller, *Drafting*, vol. 1, p. 42.

65. Bonsal, p. 49. Minutes of the Commission on a League of Nations, 7th session, Miller, *My Diary*, vol. 5, p. 414.

66. Lord Robert Cecil's diary, February 4, 1919. Until the league assembly made a choice, the four small states to be represented on the league council were Belgium, Brazil, Spain, and Greece.

five great powers were to have one seat each. It was decided that certain neutral states would be invited to join; and the admission of other "self-governing countries" was to depend upon the consent of two-thirds of the body of delegates.[67]

The representation of the British dominions, which had been the subject of controversy in the allocation of seats at the Peace Conference,[68] was not discussed. It was taken for granted that each would have one vote in the League's assembly. Wilson objected to the representation of India on an equal basis because that country's policy was controlled by the British parliament; but he was persuaded to agree by an ingenious argument advanced by Smuts.[69] In an annex to the final text of the Covenant the four dominions and India were listed among the "original members," indented under "British Empire"; "Great Britain" was not listed separately.[70]

The question of a military establishment for the league flared up persistently. Prior to the armistice Wilson had favored the creation of an international police force.[71] Before he reached Paris, however, his opinion changed. Neither his drafts of a covenant nor those of the British made provision for an international army. Wilson had explained that though armed force was in the background of his program, it was to be used only as a "last resort."[72]

The French delegates, desiring some supplement to the guarantee given by Article X, argued for an international military staff with such pertinacity that Wilson felt that they were filibustering. Doubting that Clemenceau was adhering to his promise to House to accept the league as the Americans planned it,[73] the president gave credence to rumors that Bourgeois was under instructions from the premier to delay and obstruct proceedings as much as possible.[74] In a session of the commission that lasted all day on February 11, Bourgeois, observing that under Wilson's Covenant the League's council could merely recommend economic and military action by member states against an aggressor, argued for a strong sanction that would give authority to the league's constitution. But Wilson and Cecil said repeatedly that this proposal never would be accepted by their peoples. The president explained that the creation of a unified military machine in time of peace would merely substitute international militarism for national, that in any event the Constitution of the United States would not permit foreign control of its army and navy. At the same time Wilson tried to reassure the French by an expression of his own

67. The minutes of the meetings of the Commission on the League of Nations are in Miller, *Drafting*, vol. 2, pp. 229 ff.

68. See above, pp. 17–18.

69. Smuts offered the suggestion that India, being one of the signatory powers, would have automatically a right to a delegate. "The president accepted this and, I think, rather gladly," House diary, February 6, 1919.

70. This arrangement, adopted by Shotwell in drafting the final text, was characterized by him as "revolutionary" in its consequences for the empire, *At the Paris Peace Conference*, p. 174 and Appendix V.

71. Wilson to Charles Eliot, November 25, 1918, Wilson papers. Wilson foresaw the possibility of a fatal impasse over the question of the command of such a force, Rappard diary, November 20, 1918, quoted in *Centenaire Woodrow Wilson*, p. 53.

72. David F. Trask, "Woodrow Wilson and the Coordination of Force and Diplomacy," 14–15.

73. See above, pp. 11–12.

74. Benham diary letter, February 4, 1919. Wilson was perhaps influenced by a note received from Lansing, Lansing to Wilson, January 31, 1919, Wilson papers.

feeling of solidarity with them. "When the danger comes," he said, "we too will come, but you must trust us."[75] Bourgeois, however, was unreconciled. He accepted the inevitable, but only after repeated protests.[76]

On February 13 the commission gave the amended Covenant a second reading. In the morning the president, eager to depart the next day for the United States, exerted pressure to hasten decisions. In the afternoon he had to attend a meeting of the Supreme Council, and House arranged that the chair be taken by Lord Robert Cecil, who was quicker than Wilson to put questions to a vote in order to cut off discussion.

When the Japanese submitted a resolution against racial discrimination,[77] Cecil, recognizing "the nobility of thought," remarked that the question of racial equality had raised extremely serious problems within the British Empire and that it was better, for the present, that the commission not allude to race or religion. House agreed, subject to the president's approval, to withdraw an American proposal of a clause guaranteeing "the free exercise of religion."[78] Though the issues raised by the Japanese and by the French were temporarily put aside, they were by no means settled. The French proposal of a military force and the Japanese advocacy of racial equality remained before the commission until the final draft of the Covenant was approved in April.[79]

In the Supreme Council, Wilson asserted the right of the Commission on the League of Nations to report directly to a plenary session of the Peace Conference. When Clemenceau suggested that the report should come first before the council, the president's view prevailed, as did his opinion that after he presented the Covenant the delegates in attendance should be allowed to make comments if they so wished.

Accordingly, at a general session on February 14 the American president, with a hand on a copy the Bible that he had asked for, read the Covenant aloud and commended it to the world in a speech that was ardent and prophetic. He read in even tones, without gestures, and then, reporting unanimity on the part of the league Commission, he became the eloquent advocate. "This document . . . is not a strait-jacket, but a vehicle of life," he declared. "And yet, while it is elastic, while it is general in its terms, it is definite in the one thing that we were called upon to make

75. Miller, *Drafting,* vol. 2, pp. 295–297. In an address to the Chamber of Deputies the president reaffirmed his concern for French security. "Whenever France or any other free people is threatened," he said, "the whole world will be ready to vindicate its liberty."

76. Bourgeois suffered because it fell to his lot to protest the shock that French prestige sustained when, contrary to the tradition of European diplomacy, the French language was not used in drafting the Covenant. The nature of the drafting process made it impractical to work in two languages, and Wilson's lack of familiarity with French made it inappropriate to use that language. The French delegates felt that sufficient pains were not taken at first to keep them *au courant.* According to Miller, the Covenant lacked a French translation "in any proper sense of the word" even after the eighth meeting of the commission, Noble, *Policies and Opinions at Paris, 1919,* pp. 113–114. Miller, *Drafting,* vol. 1, pp. 131–132; letter, Frank L. Warrin, Jr. to author, March 3, 1965.

77. Cf. above, p. 38.

78. House diary, February 13, 1919. "In a sense it was a religious-racial deal," Bonsal, p. 33n.

79. See below, pp. 118, 310–311.

definite. It is a definite guaranty by word against aggression.'' Citing the provision made for labor, he declared the league to be one that could ''be used for cooperation in any international matter.'' He commended the Covenant as a document that was ''practical, and yet . . . intended to purify, to rectify, to elevate.'' At the same time he warned that, as a last resort, ''if the moral force of the world will not suffice, the physical force of the world shall.''

The voice that House had counted upon to carve out a niche in history had not failed. He scribbled a chit that he passed to Wilson: ''Your speech was as great as the occasion.'' House was now convinced that he had erred in advising the president not to sit at the Peace Conference. But for the pressure that Wilson exerted in person, House thought, the Conference perhaps never would have convened, certainly never would have buckled down to work on a general plan for peace; and the powers would have split into groups and made contradictory treaties that would have been worthless.[80]

Among those who heard Wilson's speech there was loud applause, but some blank faces, too. Lord Robert Cecil said: ''You have raised a standard to which all men of good will should repair.'' For the moment the prophet had overcome both the caveats of men learned in the law and the importunities of those who feared anarchy and pressed for a prompt imposition of severe terms upon the enemy and an immediate division of the spoils of war. The Europeans had yielded to the president's determination that the League Covenant be intertwined with the treaty of peace, and they had bowed to his insistence upon an unqualified and positive guarantee of territorial integrity and political independence. This was enough to convince Wilson that he could in good conscience sign the peace treaty even though it should contain some provisions of which he could not approve. With the league a reality, there would be hope for later improvements by common consent as experience might require.[81]

But the triumph was not to be long enjoyed. As soon as the president finished his address to the plenary session, Bourgeois arose and presented the dissent that grew out of French interest and French logic. And a Japanese spokesman made a plea for recognition of racial equality. However, Clemenceau brought the session to a close by declaring that the commission's report was to be filed with the secretariat for examination by the interested powers and for discussion at a later session of the Peace Conference. Woodrow Wilson could feel that he had successfully met the great challenge to his political leadership and that he might now return home to assure American support for his program and to address the Congress. That night he took a train for Brest, where he boarded the *George Washington.*

---

80. Bonsal, pp. 282, 284. *I.P.,* vol. 4, facing p. 318. House wrote in his diary on February 14: ''The president . . . talks entirely too much, but he does it so much better than anyone else that he always interests me. . . . It amounts to genius, and as far as I know, he is in a class unto himself.''

It was the judgment of Smuts, in retrospect, that although Wilson made a mistake in coming to Europe with an inadequate staff, and a worse mistake by coming unaccompanied by any of his political adversaries, only Wilson could have put through the League, J. C. Smuts, *Jan Christiaan Smuts,* p. 204. Smuts denounced Keynes's ridicule of Wilson in *The Economic Consequences of the Peace* as an old Presbyterian so ''bamboozled'' that he could not be ''debamboozled.''

81. Bonsal, pp. 47, 57.

The triumph of Wilson's great cause was not won without cost to the immediate work of peacemaking. The delay that had been caused by the tardy arrival of the political chiefs at Paris had been extended by their protracted speechmaking in the Supreme Council. Because of Wilson's diversion of energy into the work of the Commission on the League of Nations, the impatient French press attributed to him rather more than his share of responsibility for deferring the benefits that were most craved by those who had borne the brunt of war: security, demobilization, and compensation for losses. Now, three months after the armistices, French partisans felt that every day of indecision not only diminished their chance of working their will upon Germany, but at the same time added to the danger of a revival of German power. Public morale in Paris was sunk in a depression that was known as *la malaise*. Labour agitation in Great Britain appeared to be a manifestation of bolshevism; and the prime minister, expecting it to increase, departed for London.[82]

When Wilson was shown an order said to have been issued by a bureau of the French government, instructing journals to emphasize American obstruction, he lost patience. Particularly annoyed by stories in the French press that reported political opposition in the United States, he asked Dr. Grayson[83] to drop a hint to the American newsmen to write a story to the effect that if the French authorities continued their propaganda, the Peace Conference probably would move to a neutral city.[84] Actually, three American peace commissioners already had expressed a wish that, because of the atmosphere of intrigue at Paris, the Conference meet elsewhere.[85] However, the press release authorized by Wilson surprised and distressed House. He asked Grayson to see the president at once and advise him to prevent the cabling of the story to the United States. He persuaded Steed to suppress it in the Northcliffe papers, and it was cut from the Paris edition of the *New York Herald;* but it was circulated in America by the Associated Press.[86]

Soon reporters were plying House with questions. He was told by Grayson that the president refused to retract the press release and even went so far as to assert that Lloyd George and Orlando concurred in it.[87] "To my mind," House wrote in his diary on February 11, "it was a stupid blunder. What the president and the two prime ministers should have done was to have gone directly to Clemenceau and read the riot act to him. In the first place the threat was childish. The Conference

82. General memorandum no. 8, February 13, 1919, Borden papers, OCA 198, 81596-8, National Archives of Canada.

83. Grayson diary, February 12, 1919. The order, issued by La Maison de la Presse, asked also that journals stress disorder and anarchy in Russia as a means of provoking Allied intervention, and publish articles demonstrating Germany's ability to pay a large indemnity, Baker, *American Chronicle*, p. 387. Wilson read the order to Professor Rappard and said that France's press was not free, and her government was as bureaucratic as Russia's, Rappard, in *Centenaire Woodrow Wilson*, p. 56.

84. Benham diary letter, February 10, 1919.

85. Minutes, ACTNP, February 10, 1919, *F.R., P.P.C,* vol. 11, pp. 24–25, 28.

86. Steed's memorandum to Northcliffe, February 11, 1919, Steed papers, *Times* Archives.

87. Lloyd George wrote to Kerr: "I do not think President Wilson's official message to the press was the right way of doing it. I thought he was going to unofficially intimate to the American correspondents his dissatisfaction. . . . His notice was a blunt intimation and, what was still worse, it was official," letter of February 12, 1919, Lloyd George papers, F / 89 / 218.

could not be moved until at least a preliminary peace has been signed. So why make the threat?''[88]

Clemenceau was in a fury, and sent Louis Aubert to discuss the matter with House.[89] According to his own record, House was true to the compact of complete frankness that he had made with the French premier. He told Aubert practically everything the president said, but in a way calculated to avoid giving offense; and he asked that their conversation be repeated to Clemenceau. House took this opportunity to talk frankly with Aubert about the short-sightedness of French aims and, according to his diary, he "obtained a personal promise from him."

"The fact that there are two Germans to one Frenchman," House wrote, "and the further fact that Russia now feels more kindly toward Germany than she does toward France, makes the situation dangerous. . . . If the conditions we impose upon her are too unjust, it will simply mean the breeding of another war. Aubert admitted this. Our only chance for peace, I thought, was to create a league of nations, treat Germany fairly and see that she did not have an opportunity to again equip and maintain an army that would be formidable." House left no indication that he suspected that the French were deliberately delaying proceedings so that they could get concessions from him after Wilson left Paris.[90]

A perspicacious view of the delicate situation of the moment was taken by Philip Kerr, who in a message to Lloyd George, now at London, reported: "The French . . . fill the Agenda paper with small points and more or less openly admit that they want to postpone discussion of all important questions until President Wilson has gone. Hankey thinks they will then raise a row in the Press and the Chamber about delays . . . with a view to forcing decisions on all questions before the president returns, it being much more difficult for us to resist them than for the U.S.A. It is evident that the president has begun to realize this and that his explosion in the Press . . . was partly due to it."[91]

Diplomats of the Old World were puzzled by the American statesman who was willing to give them an unqualified guarantee of protection but unwilling to make practical arrangements for its execution. Jules Cambon, a French plenipotentiary, jotted down his misgivings: "France would have time to be swallowed up before it was even decided whether the league of nations would act, if action is not automatic and the question is submitted to parliaments. Cambon perceived that the keeping of the peace would still depend, league or no league, upon the genius of diplomats. Their task yet remained to be done, and it was complicated by the fact that Wilson had stirred human passion along with compassion. Cambon doubted that under a regime of "open diplomacy" the public would be able to perceive and to judge the

88. On February 12 Acting Secretary of State Polk cabled from Washington that the publication in America of Wilson's threat created great excitement. He asked what House could do about this. Auchincloss replied that the French press had been "acting outrageously," that the news report had been "permitted to leak out," and that "the matter was handled by the president exclusively," Auchincloss diary, February 13, 1919, Y.H.C.

89. Kerr to Lloyd George, February 11, 1919.

90. House diary, February 11, 1919.

91. Kerr to Lloyd George, February 11, 1919, Lloyd George papers, F / 89 / 2 / 7. Quotations from the papers of Philip Henry Kerr are printed with the gracious permission of the present marquess of Lothian.

motives behind the decisions of a league of nations any more than it comprehended the patient efforts of diplomacy to adjust conflicting interests.

"Man is not as changed as one thinks," the veteran diplomat philosophized. "He always obeys the same instincts, and the league will crash if it pretends to obstruct movements that are the essential manifestation of the growth of peoples. The difficulty always will be in distinguishing whether these ferments that from time to time disturb the surface of the world are a useless and sterile disorder or, quite the contrary, the first symptoms of an awakening life. Who is to be the judge of all that?"[92]

Ambassador Paul Cambon, observing the Peace Conference from his post at London and greatly disappointed at the slow progress of its essential business, lamented that Clemenceau had abandoned France to the "caprices" of Wilson. Cambon admired Wilson's ability to dominate as much as he deplored the president's policy.[93] On February 10 he wrote: "Wilson shows himself ignorant of the very crux of the situation [regarding the dismemberment of Germany]. . . . He continues to play a disintegrating role. His society of nations which doesn't even exist seems to him to be equal to everything."[94] It seemed to this master diplomat that the American president, infatuated and intoxicated by his triumphal promenade in Europe, would be disillusioned in his belief that he could disarm opposition to his league of nations during a brief sojourn in the United States. Commenting on the restraint of the British press with respect to the political climate at Washington, Paul Cambon advised that French papers would do well also to ignore the plight of the American prophet. "The less we concern ourselves with President Wilson," he wrote on February 19, "the more the opposition that he arouses at home will avail. . . . It is of the highest importance to let the position of Wilson break up of itself."[95]

Wilson had disappointed British statesmen also and had given offence by his failure to ascribe credit to English contributions to the Covenant. He proposed no practical role for the League in promoting the economic welfare of all nations in a world that would be largely dependent on American resources. American policy seemed to some to be neither consistent nor precise.[96] The president, who at Washington approved a huge naval-building program, advocated at Paris "adequate guarantees . . . that national armaments will be reduced to the lowest point consistent with domestic safety." He refused to make a definite commitment of American military force to give sanction to the Covenant of the League of Nations. Moreover, he was unable to pledge his own nation's participation in a system of mandates that

92. Jules Cambon, "La Paix," 12–14. "The League of Nations," Cambon foresaw, "will not be able to follow fixed ideas or dogmatic principles. As it assumes a political task, it will conduct itself according to the rules of politics. It will take account of imperious reality; it will realize that the primary need of nations is assurance of security; by the very force of circumstances, it will have to reconcile the new concept that has presided over its own founding with the necessity for special agreements that the nations can be led to make among themselves."

93. Dispatch, Curzon to Derby, January 23, 1919, Curzon papers. Mss. EUR, F112 / 302.

94. Cambon, *Correspondance*, vol. 3, pp. 307–308.

95. *Ibid.*, p. 310.

96. Sir Robert Borden's memorandum no. 9, February 22, 1919, National Archives, Ottawa. Sir James Headlam-Morley of the Foreign Office was of the opinion that the plan for a league of nations derived all its merit from British thinking. He felt that Wilson's speeches had created distrust and opposition, letter of February 15, 1919, to John Bailey, in the possession of Professor Agnes Headlam-Morley.

he prescribed for others. The duality in American foreign policy that had long perplexed the diplomats of Europe was now more palpable than ever.

Wilson's adversaries in the United States quickly exposed the vital flaws. A week
before the Covenant was published in the newspapers on February 15, *Harvey's
Weekly* pointed out that the League of Nations "must be either a strenuous body so
transcending nationality as to be impossible of American approval, or a futile thing
of pious aspirations and impotent achievement." In the isolationist sentiment among
American voters, the Republican leaders had a resource that challenged the impulse
of those who coveted for their nation a leading part in the economic and political
life of the twentieth-century world.

7

The Russian Question

Woodrow Wilson left Paris in mid-February in the midst of a controversy about one of the most persistently vexing of the issues of the peacemaking.

For the nations opposing Germany in the war there had been two paths to peace. One was by unrelenting pursuit of victory in the hope that once it was attained the terms for an enduring peace might be dictated. The other way—the easy one—was to get an immediate surcease of fighting by surrendering. The Russian Soviet government, overthrowing a revolutionary regime that had maintained some resistance to Germany, had chosen the path of capitulation at Brest-Litovsk, and in so doing had aroused enduring resentment on the part of the Allies in the West.

When the Allies sent arms and troops to strengthen the forces of "white" anti-Bolshevist generals and pressed the American government to share the burden, Wilson had reluctantly given his consent in the summer of 1918.[1] This concession became acutely embarrassing. Friction developed among the armies of the powers that had been sent to north Russia and to Siberia.[2] The morale of the troops was not good, and the White Russians were doing little to advance their own cause.[3] The presence of foreign forces in Russia served to create cynicism among the Russian people and to stimulate recruiting for the Red army. House, who had joined with British agents[4] in urging American participation in the intervention, thought it nec-

1. See Walworth, *America's Moment: 1918*, pp. 198 ff. The question of American policy toward the Russian revolution and that of Wilson's motives have evoked differing interpretations from historians. See the summary by Eugene P. Trani, in "Woodrow Wilson and the Decision to Intervene in Russia," *Journal of Modern History* 48 (September 1976):440–461, and also Betty Miller Unterberger's chapter, "Woodrow Wilson and the Russian Revolution," in *Woodrow Wilson and a Revolutionary World*, ed. Arthur S. Link. Also see John Bradley, *Allied Intervention in Russia*, and John W. Long, "American Intervention in Russia: The North Russian Expedition, 1918–1919," *Diplomatic History* 6, no. 1 (Winter 1982), in which an excellent footnote on p. 45 summarizes earlier studies.

2. Sir Charles Eliot to Curzon, February 22, 1919, Curzon papers, box 65, F112 / 210. Polk to John W. Davis, February 1, 1919, Davis papers, Y.H.C.

3. "Memorandum on the Russian Situation," February 15, 1919, Balfour papers, 4975. Notes of conversation with C. T. Williams, deputy commissioner of the Red Cross, February 22, 1919, Bliss papers, box 248. On conditions in Siberia see Unterberger, *America's Siberian Expedition, 1918–1920*, ch. 7, and Unterberger (ed.), *American Intervention in the Russian Civil War* (Lexington, Mass., 1969), esp. "Suggestions for Additional Reading." The Japanese, whose aggressiveness Wilson had hoped to curb by ordering General Graves to Siberia with a few thousand men, had sent many more soldiers than had been specified, but had indicated at the end of 1918 that the number would be reduced to the minimum needed to keep order, Polk to Ammission, December 30, 1918, transmitting dispatch, Morris to the secretary of state, December 29, 1918, Wilson papers. After protracted negotiations at Tokyo, Ambassador Morris was able to conclude with Japan a compromise agreement that confirmed the control of the trans-Siberian railway by American engineers; and the arrangement was accepted by France and Great Britain in February 1919, memoranda, Lord to Bullitt, January 17 and 19, 1919, Y.H.C.; *F.R., 1918, Russia*, vol. 3, pp. 269, 278–280, 301–303, 307. See Mayer, *Politics and Diplomacy of Peacemaking*, pp. 337–339.

4. Memorandum dated February 11, 1919, in Wilson papers, with endorsement by House commending this paper to Wilson, who already understood that the intervention was exploited by Bolshevik propaganda.

essary to say to the press at the end of 1918 that it was "inconceivable" that the
United States would ever take part in a war against Russia.[5]

During January the question that was to infect international relations of the twentieth century raised its virulent head at the Peace Conference. Because of the revolutionary propaganda of the new Soviet regime, all contact with it would be a venture
not only in peacemaking, but in preserving the essential stability of Western society
as well. With Russia as well as Germany unrepresented at Paris, Woodrow Wilson
could hardly hope to create a peace of the world-wide dimension that he envisaged.
He came to Paris, therefore, eager to bring men to the Peace Conference who could
speak with authority for the Russian people.

The Soviet government, for its part, had given indications that it was not unwilling to treat with the West. Its own survival required that it avoid the failure of the
provisional government that preceded it to satisfy the bitter resentment of a people
who saw no reason in the terrible war into which they had been led by the czar and
the Western powers.[6] The statesmen at Moscow thought it important to free Russia
from economic blockade and from military intervention by foreigners who kept
alive the resistance of counterrevolutionary armies. The Soviet leaders were ready
to temporize with the Western enemy against whom ideological war had been declared.
Secretary Lansing was notified indirectly just before the armistice of November 11
that the Soviet government would be willing to negotiate anywhere on the question
of liquidating hostilities.[7] The Sixth All-Russian Congress of Soviets publicly endorsed
this offer, with the proviso that the great powers cease to intervene. Moreover,
Maxim Litvinov, an experienced diplomat who had been deported from England
and became assistant commissar for Soviet foreign affairs, addressed a persuasive
appeal to Wilson and the Allies on Christmas Eve. He asked for an impartial investigation of the charges brought by Western critics and for a chance for his government to present its case to the world. The Allied response to these overtures was to
send an expeditionary force in December to Odessa under French command, to aid
"White" opponents of the "Reds" at Moscow.[8]

Wilson, however, was moved by Litvinov's appeal.[9] When the Allies made no
response, he encouraged an independent effort to make contact with Litvinov. The
utmost secrecy was essential in view of the righteous revulsion of many Americans
to the excesses of Bolshevik terror.[10] Diplomatic relations with the United States

5. Walworth, pp. 208–209.
6. George F. Kennan, *Russia and the West under Lenin and Stalin,* p. 149. According to Kennan,
the "great and pervasive conceptual error" of the Allied statesmen at the Peace Conference was "an
inability to assess correctly the significance and consequences of the war in which Europe had just been
engaged," *ibid.*
7. The minister to Norway to Lansing, November 8, 1918, Lansing to the minister to Norway, November
9, 1918, *F.R., Lansing papers,* vol. 2, p. 484.
8. Renouvin, *Les Crises du XXe siècle: I, De 1914 à 1929,* p. 169.
9. Just before the Peace Conference opened, the president, still hoping to develop a policy jointly
with the Allies, had tentatively checked a movement at Washington to recall the American troops in
Siberia, Walworth, p. 207.
10. Senator Lodge expressed the opinion of many American citizens when he declared in the Senate
on December 21 that the weak Bolshevik government was "no more fit to be dealt with than a band of

had been broken, and its ambassador fled from Moscow.

At the urgent behest of Wilson,[11] William H. Buckler[12] went to Sweden to meet Litvinov, who had arrived at Stockholm on the last day of November and made contact with American and British agents. They engaged in three informal talks that both agreed to hold in confidence, and Buckler reported at Paris with notes of the conversations, initialed by Litvinov.[13]

The Soviet spokesman asked whether the real aim of the Western powers was to make peace or to destroy the Soviet government and thus create anarchy. Explaining that the military interventions had called forth revolutionary propaganda, violence, and terror, he said these were to cease when hostilities stopped. Amnesty would be granted to domestic opponents. Russia's need for technical help from foreigners was so great that the Soviet government was ready to compromise on the repudiation of debts contracted under the czar. The Russians invited a statement of Allied terms and demanded only that the West lift its blockade, end its military operations, and cease to support anti-Bolsheviks in Russia. These conciliatory proposals were commended to the American commission by Buckler, who said that the Bolsheviks would prove to be malleable negotiators provided their government was respected. Buckler described Litvinov as, "with Lenin and Chicherin, one of the conservative ring"—a very intelligent man who was convinced that his government would prove to be responsible.[14] Food relief, which in Wilson's opinion was "the real thing with which to stop bolshevism," seemed to Litvinov futile so long as millions starved as a result of the Allied intervention and blockade.[15]

Wilson read Litvinov's proposals to the Supreme Council on January 21, the day on which the Inquiry in its Black Book proposed that prewar Russia be divided into a number of independent national states. The council already had discussed this most baffling question at great length. It rejected a French proposal that the Russian Political Conference at Paris, composed of anti-Bolshevik émigrés, be called on for advice.[16] However, with Wilson's consent, a hearing was given to the French and

anthropoid apes." At the same time he said: "Some proper settlement of the Russian Question is absolutely vital to the modern civilization of which we are a part. We can not stand by as idle spectators . . . without making an effort to aid Russia to rid herself of the poison which is now eating out her life," *Congressional Record*, 65th Congr. 3d sess., 1918, pp. 723–728.

11. When on January 3 the American commission delayed Buckler's departure, Wilson wrote on January 10 to Lansing to urge that he get Buckler started to the interview, which the president thought "of capital importance," letter in Wilson papers. Minutes, ACTNP, January 3 and 7, 1919, Harrison papers, L.C.

12. Buckler, brother-in-law of Henry White, was a "special assistant" in the American embassy at London and was acquainted with Litvinov.

13. W. H. Buckler to G. G. Buckler, January 31, 1919, Buckler papers, Y.H.C. Buckler's notes of his talks with Litvinov are in the Y.H.C. His report is in the Wilson papers. Litvinov's proposition was confirmed by a recapitulation telegraphed by his chief, Chicherin, to Stockholm on January 13. This reached Wilson on January 20, *F.R., 1919, Russia*, pp. 8–9.

14. Minutes, ACTNP, January 30, 1919. Buckler (Copenhagen) to Lansing (Ammission), January 18, 1919, Wilson papers. Buckler reported that Litvinov explained as a mistake a note of October 24, in which Chicherin had classed Wilson with the "imperialist robbers."

15. Wilson to Lansing, January 10, 1919, Wilson papers. Litvinov to Buckler, January 22, 1919, *F.R., 1919, Russia*, pp. 33–34.

16. *F.R., P.P.C.*, vol. 3, pp. 490, 593. Wilson and Lloyd George feared that by listening to the émigrés, the Peace Conference would appear to recognize them as representing Russia.

Danish ambassadors who had left Russia. It was on this occasion that Wilson, pressed by the British to give labor legislation a prominent place in the agenda of the Peace Conference, remarked that distrust between employers and workers provided fertile soil for the seed that the Bolsheviks were sowing. He was constantly in dread of what he called "the curious poison" of the revolutionaries. "We are running a race with bolshevism and the world is on fire," he would say when his doctor begged him to slacken the pace of his work.[17] Wilson probably would have recognized the Soviet regime as a *de facto* government had this been politically possible, and Lloyd George would have done so also.[18] On January 21, the day on which Wilson read Litvinov's proposals to the Supreme Council, Lloyd George, who clearly saw the folly of military intervention in the civil war in Russia, proposed a plan on which his British associates had agreed: to bring leaders of all the Russian factions to Paris, much as the Romans had summoned barbarians to the Eternal City, and there to admonish them to reconcile their differences.[19]

This proposal already had been made through diplomatic channels to the American and Allied governments. The French Foreign Ministry reacted negatively, declaring that the Bolshevik regime, lacking food, transportation, and credit, would not be able to endure if it were refused recognition and treated "as an enemy." It was the hope of French officials that the revolutionary regime might be destroyed, or at least quarantined by a *cordon sanitaire* of new nations in east central Europe, and that the Russian market might be opened to French trade.[20]

The American economic advisers shared the French antipathy to the British proposal. When it became known in Washington, Polk expressed the opinion that it would have no effect on the Bolsheviks and would discourage their opponents. Tumulty cabled anxiously to the president: "Proposal of Lloyd George . . . produced very unfavorable impression everywhere. It is denounced as amazing." Lansing thought that nothing would come of the venture.

Nevertheless, Wilson persisted in his rational argument. He explained to the Supreme Council that since military intervention served to strengthen the political power of the revolutionary leaders, and since it was clear to all that no troops were available for an invasion of Russia on the scale that would be effective, the only practical course was that proposed by Lloyd George.

In view of the resolute French opposition to the presence of Bolshevik negotiators

---

17. Grayson, *Woodrow Wilson: An Intimate Memoir*, p. 85.

18. Lloyd George, *The Truth about the Peace Treaties*, p. 331.

19. Minutes, British Empire delegation, January 13 and 20, 1919, P.R.O., Cab / 29 / 28 / 1. Lloyd George, pp. 327–330. Lloyd George, urged by the dominions to stop the intervention and to attempt to bring Russian factions together, did not fear the Bolsheviks as did his Continental associates, nor detest them as did Wilson. He thought their aspirations not entirely unworthy and their political prospects not wholly unpromising, John M. Thompson, *Russia, Bolshevism, and the Versailles Peace*, p. 78; Wiseman diary, January 19, 1919, Y.H.C.; Sir Clement Jones, "The Dominions and the Peace Conference," P.R.O., Cab. 21 / 217; Borden, general memorandum no. 4, January 22, 1919, Borden papers.

20. Dispatch, Pichon to French ambassadors, January 5, 1919, Archives du M.A.É., Europe 1918–1929, Great Britain, f. 60. Barrère, at Rome, objected that the British proposal seemed almost a recognition of the Soviet government and would encourage bolshevism in all the Allied nations, Barrère memorandum, January 26, 1919, M.A.É., Europe 1918–1929, f. 96, p. 12. Étienne Clémentel, *La France et la politique économique interallié*, pp. 337–338.

at Paris (Clemenceau threatened to resign if they came), Lloyd George suggested that another meeting place be chosen.[21] Clemenceau then accepted the plan of his colleagues in the interest of harmony. At the same time he took the opportunity to flatter Wilson by asking him to draft a paper that would explain the position of the Supreme Council.

The president had a text ready the next day. A preamble stated that ''Europe and the world cannot be at peace if Russia is not.'' In keeping with his purpose of helping the Russian people, as stated in his Point VI, and recognizing their right to ''direct their own affairs without dictation or direction of any kind from outside,'' Wilson invited ''every organized group'' in Russia to cease fighting and, having done this, to send representatives before February 15 to a meeting in the Princes Islands, in the Sea of Marmara. They were invited to confer there with agents of the Associated powers with a view to bringing about ''some understanding and agreement by which Russia may work out her own purposes and happy cooperative relations be established between her people and the other peoples of the world.'' The statement did not recognize any faction, and allotted three representatives to each regardless of its importance. The message was broadcast to Russia on January 23 by short-wave radio.[22]

Thus the president took a step that proved to be of more value as an assurance to Americans impatient for action against what they thought to be evil than as a tranquilizer for warring Russians. Liberals in the United States applauded the selection of the journalist William Allen White as one of two American delegates to go to the proposed meeting.[23]

However, Wilson's advisers hoped for very little. Actually the regime at Moscow, the three Baltic countries, and the Soviet Ukrainian government were the only factions that made a favorable response to the project, which was known as ''Prinkipo.'' By this time it was clear that the Bolsheviks had failed in efforts to under

21. Balfour to Lloyd George, January 19, 1919, Lloyd George papers, F / 3 / 4 / 7. Clemenceau suspected that the Soviets were laying a propaganda trap. He thought that the commissars would like to be able to say to their people, scornfully: ''We offered them great principles of justice, and the Allies would have nothing to do with us. Now we offer money, and they are ready to make peace,'' Lloyd George, p. 357.

22. *F.R., P.P.C.*, vol. 3, p. 677. On January 24 the Soviet radio invited all genuine revolutionaries to form a new International at a conference that did not convene at Moscow until March 2, Mayer, p. 408. See *ibid.*, p. 431.

23. Memorandum, Lord to Bullitt, January 29, 1919, Bullitt papers. This collection was, but is no longer, in the Y.H.C.

The American asked to accompany White was George D. Herron, who was a foe of bolshevism and was in touch with Russian reactionaries, Palmer, *Bliss*, p. 367; W. A. Williams, *American-Russian Relations, 1781–1947*, p. 167. A socialist Congregational minister who was defrocked when his wife divorced him and who had declared that ''the coercive family will pass away with the coercive economic system'' (Polk to Ammission, February 3, 1919, N.A., R.G. 59, 763.72119 / 3862c), he had performed peaceseeking missions for the American government during the war and European diplomats had come to consider him as almost a spokesman for Wilson, Leo Valiani, *The End of Austria-Hungary*, p. 276. Herron won Wilson's confidence by writing a book sympathetic to the president's purposes as well as by his contacts with European intellectuals, E. W. McAdoo to the author. He had Wilson's ear during January, and for four months no one dared to bring the shortcomings of this man to the attention of the president, Bullitt to Grew, January 3, 1919, Bullitt papers, Y.H.C.; Wilson to Herron, January 23, 1919, Wilson papers. See Mitchell P. Briggs, *George D. Herron and the European Settlement* (New York, 1971).

mine or to treat with the new government of Germany, and the need for economic contacts with the West was pressing.[24] Desiring a lull in hostilities during which he could consolidate his power, Lenin called for an advance of the Soviet armies, perhaps to strengthen his hand in bargaining. Kiev was occupied on February 4. At the same time Chicherin wondered whether the invitation from Paris was indeed authentic; and he notified Wilson by radio that there would be no response until a direct invitation was received.[25] However, Wilson remarked in the Supreme Council on February 1 that to send an official bid to Moscow would be tantamount to recognition, and none was sent.

On February 4, nevertheless, the Soviet government did make a full reply. Published in *Le Matin* on the seventh, it professed eagerness to make "important sacrifices" in order to end hostilities,[26] and even to purchase an understanding by meeting the demands of the Western powers in respect of loans and by granting mining, timber, and other concessions "in accordance with strictly regulated conditions." The possibilities of loss of territory on the border of Russia and of the maintenance of foreign armed forces in Poland and Finland were not excluded. The Soviet government, although unable to curb the freedom of the revolutionary press, was ready to agree not to intervene in the internal affairs of the Associated powers.

The message failed, however, to meet the essential condition that the Peace Conference had prescribed. There was no undertaking to stop the westward advance of the Soviet armies, which the statesmen at Paris had hoped to check until Poland and the Baltic provinces could be protected against invasion. Moreover, the reaction of the White factions to the Prinkipo proposal was entirely negative. The Russian Political Conference at Paris protested indignantly, thinking the Prinkipo project both immoral and presumptuous and one about which their opinion should have been asked.[27] Encouraged in their opposition by conservative French officials, the émigrés elicited sympathy from anti-Bolsheviks everywhere.[28] On February 12 the "unified government of Siberia, Archangel, and Southern Russia" formally rejected the proposal of the Peace Conference, declaring that no reconciliation with the Bolsheviks was possible. It was now clear that the animosity between Reds and Whites was too deep-rooted to yield to any sort of parley.

Recognizing that no anti-Soviet movement in Russia had "real popular support," the American consul at Archangel nevertheless favored a policy of "avowed and active hostility to the Moscow Government" as "the more courageous, honest, and

---

24. "In mid-January 1919 German-Soviet relations were at a complete impasse," Mayer, p. 251.

25. Ullman, *Intervention and the War,* p. 111. For an account of other inquiries by Chicherin, see Mayer, pp. 436–437.

26. *F.R., 1919, Russia,* pp. 41–42. Thompson, pp. 112–115. Mayer, pp. 535–540.

27. Headlam-Morley diary, January 25, 1919, in *A Memoir of the Paris Peace Conference, 1919,* p. 15.

28. Mayer, pp. 289–291, 433. Boris A. Bakhemeteff, the envoy at Washington who had represented the defunct provisional government of Russia, had gone to Paris. He petitioned Lansing for a proper representation of Russia at the Peace Conference as an entity that might later be subject to a test of self-determination. He acted as spokesman for the Russian Political Conference and as their liaison with the American peace commission. See Linda Killen, "The Search for a Democratic Russia: Bakhmetev [*sic*] and the U.S."

therefore in the long run best."[29] Furthermore David Francis, the American ambassador who had fled from Moscow, came to Paris to warn that if the Bolsheviks were permitted to dominate, Russia would be exploited by Germany "completely and effectively." Francis asked for more troops and suggested that the American and British governments had a weakness toward bolshevism. General Bliss, however, thinking that the White government at Archangel was a "personal pet" of the fugitive ambassador, pointed out that there were different views of ways to combat bolshevism, but some people were so childish that they thought their way was the only possible one and unjustly accused dissenters of being Bolsheviks.[30]

Just at this time distrust of the Bolsheviks and despair of dealing with them was becoming more manifest in the United States. On February 4, the day after a general strike was called in Seattle, the Senate's Committee on Judicial Affairs was given full power to investigate Bolshevik propaganda in the nation. A subcommittee pursued a hunt for "Reds" in a spirit far from judicious.

As he prepared to leave for Washington, the president, resenting the mundane tone of the response from Moscow to his exalted plea to the Russian factions, and regarding the Soviet reply as "studiously insulting," was finding it more difficult to tolerate the Bolsheviks. While ashamed of conservative associates at Paris to whom the payment of Russia's foreign debt appeared to be the prime consideration, Wilson was exasperated by the revolutionaries. "The Bolsheviks," he asserted, "so far as we could get any taste of their flavor, are the most consummate sneaks in the world. I suppose because they have no high motive themselves, they do not believe that anybody else has."[31]

Wilson had no heart to pursue the Prinkipo project further, and came to regret his choice of George D. Herron to represent the United States.[32] This political venture into the deep waters of "open diplomacy" met the fate that Lansing and the experienced diplomats of Europe had forecast. The suspicions and jealousies in

29. D. W. Poole (Archangel) to Ammission, January 22, 23, and 30, 1919. Dispatch, Poole to the secretary of state, *F.R., 1919, Russia,* pp. 35–38, 42–43, 47, 51–54.

30. Palmer, pp. 368–369. Minutes, ACTNP, January 30, 1919, Bliss diary, February 3, 1919.

31. Tumulty, *Woodrow Wilson As I Know Him,* p. 374. Swem ms., Princeton University Library.

32. Herron came to Paris from Geneva. He and White, with the aid of Samuel Gompers, entertained Russian conservatives. The two sons of the American Midwest, as inexperienced in diplomacy as they were zealous to do good, wined and dined their guests on the best fare that Paris offered, while Herron talked persuasively.

Herron had few friends. An editorial in the *New York Times* identified his views with those of Lenin and Trotsky. The American press continued to condemn his appointment and said that he could not with propriety represent his country at any time or for any purpose, memorandum, February 11, 1919, Y.H.C. Articles in American journals exposed the man's marital infidelity. Senator Lodge read one "with delight," he confessed to a cousin, Lodge to John T. Morse, Jr., February 20, 1919, Morse papers, Massachusetts Historical Society. When the scandal was made known to Wilson by Lansing, the president replied: "No doubt some of the particulars are true, but the fact remains that Herron is much the best man we could use in the circumstances and it would be most unfair now to cancel his appointment. I think we shall just have to let the comment pass," Wilson to Lansing, February 13, 1919, copy in Wilson papers.

After the president's departure from Paris in February the American commission agreed that Herron and White could no longer remain attached to the commission, *F.R., P.P.C.,* vol. 11, p. 87. On May 12 House, who until then had refrained from expressing himself frankly to Wilson because he perceived the difficulty of shaking the president's loyalty to this admirer, wrote in his diary: "I took occasion to tell him [Wilson] of his friend Professor George D. Herron. He looked somewhat embarrassed and said with some asperity, 'I am through with him,' " entry of May 12.

which Russian politics was enshrouded poisoned the atmosphere in which the men at Paris groped toward peace. Despite Litvinov's scorn of food relief, the president fell back again upon economic aid as the only way in which he might possibly help the Russian people. Early in February he told Vance McCormick, the head of the War Trade Board, that relief was more important than ever and that the funds of the Russian Bureau of the board, which had been operating on a small scale in Siberia, should be used to send supplies to Murmansk and also to south Russia. He wished this to be done despite criticism that might arise in the Congress, and left to the discretion of Polk the question of keeping the legislators apprised.[33]

The question of Russia—an unexorcised demon that the peacemakers preferred not to mention publicly—reappeared in the discussions of the Supreme Council on February 14, the day of Wilson's departure from Paris. Lloyd George had gone home to respond to questions in the House of Commons.[34] Learning that Clemenceau wished to drop the Prinkipo plan until Wilson departed and thus kill it, the prime minister had discussed the matter in the war cabinet. The British people were growing restless about casualties incurred in Russia, and the anti-Bolshevik forces that the Allies supported were deteriorating.[35] Winston Churchill, then secretary of state for war, spoke to the cabinet of the menace of a German-Russian combination and said that, "assuming Prinkipo was at an end," they should settle on a definite policy toward the anti-Bolshevik Russians. He would raise a British army of a few thousand volunteers and would take up a Japanese offer to send a large force to aid the Omsk Whites in crushing the Reds in return for parts of Sakhalin Island and Kamchatka and control of the Manchurian railway. He wanted a decision before Wilson left Paris. In this Lloyd George concurred, thinking that Wilson should be present to share the responsibility for any course adopted. Churchill considered that he was authorized by the cabinet to go to Paris and try to get action from the Supreme Council.[36]

Churchill appeared before the Supreme Council at Paris on February 14, late in the day, when the delegates were impatient to go to dinner and Wilson, to depart for America. He challenged the Prinkipo plan. This moved Wilson to defend it as an effort to get reliable information rather than as a bid for a *rapprochement* with the Bolsheviks. He observed that the Soviet reply, insulting though it was, offered

33. Lansing to the secretary of state, January 11, 1919, N.A., R.G. 59, 033.1140 / 177. Ammission to the secretary of state, February 3, 1919, Y.H.C. On the congressional opposition and the difficulty of finding funds for the Russian Bureau and the Siberian railway, see Williams, pp. 164–166.

34. Mayer, pp. 443–444.

35. See below, p. 135. Balfour stated early in January that no more British troops would be sent to Russia, and British warships were withdrawn from the Baltic, Lord to Bullitt, January 14, 1919, Y.H.C. Kerr told Buckler on January 30 that the British were very eager to withdraw troops from Archangel as soon as possible, and by May 1 anyway, minutes, ACTNP, January 31, 1919.

36. Minutes, B.W.C., Curzon papers, mss. EUR, F112 / 132. Churchill "would make a plain proposition to the United States that if they were not prepared to come in and do their share they would have no right to stop the Omsk [white] Government from coming to terms with the Japanese," copy of letter, Lloyd George to Kerr, February 12, 1919, Lloyd George papers, F / 89 / 2 / 7 and 8. According to his secretary, Lloyd George thought that Churchill was "planning a great war in Russia," Stevenson, *Lloyd George*, p. 179.

a number of considerations that had not been sought, such as concessions of resources and repayment of debts. He suggested that perhaps an effort should be made to get in touch with the Soviet leaders through unofficial representatives. As for the foreign troops in Russia, Wilson now denounced their operations with a fervor that had been building up for several weeks under the stimulus of reports from Washington and from General Bliss.[37] These troops, he said, were doing no sort of good, knew not for whom or for what they were fighting, and ought to be withdrawn. Obviously the existing forces could not stop the Bolsheviks; not one of the Allied powers was ready to increase its commitment; and the Whites to whom arms had been sent appeared to be making very little use of them. When Churchill pressed a proposal for sending volunteers and technical experts and supplies, and remarked that withdrawal would doom the non-Bolshevik armies of half a million men and pull "the linch-pin from the whole machine," Wilson declared that if this was true, the Whites would not succeed even with foreign support. Some might prove to be reactionaries. Sooner or later the foreign troops would have to leave Russia, and when they did, many Russians might lose their lives. A cruel dilemma, he said. At one point he made a confession that was extraordinary in view of his condemnation of military intervention. He acknowledged a feeling of guilt because the United States had contributed insufficient forces in Russia, explaining that this could not be helped because conscripts could not legally be raised now and volunteers probably could not be enlisted.

When Churchill asked whether the Supreme Council would approve the arming of anti-Bolshevik forces, the president returned no definite answer and said that he would cast his lot with the Allies. Churchill wrote later that, contrary to his expectations, Wilson was actually "affable."[38] Churchill took his imprecision to mean that if the Prinkipo plan failed to produce a settlement, the United States would support a policy of active aid to the anti-Bolshevik Russians.[39] Unfortunately, Wilson left Paris without any adequate top-level analysis or decision as to the next step in a joint policy toward Russia. As Kennan has pointed out, this critical issue was the victim of inadequate "summit statesmanship."[40]

During the president's absence in February House groped for a constructive plan. Previously he had questioned the wisdom of efforts to unify the factions in Russia and thus create a country that in his opinion would be "too big and homogeneous for the safety of the world." He envisioned a separate Siberia and a division of European Russia into three parts.[41] He had told newsmen that he asked only two things of the Bolsheviks: that they confine their propaganda to their own country;

---

37. See Unterberger, "Woodrow Wilson and the Russian Revolution," pp. 75–84.

38. *F.R., P.P.C.,* vol. 3, pp. 1041–1044. Martin Gilbert, *Winston S. Churchill,* vol. 4, pp. 244 ff. Churchill, *The Aftermath,* pp. 173–174.

39. Churchill was led to report to Lloyd George: "I conceive that we are entitled to count on American participation in any joint measures which we may entertain," dispatch, Churchill to the prime minister, [February 15, 1919], Lloyd George papers, F / 8 / 3 / 16. Kerr to Lloyd George, [February 14, 1919], Lloyd George papers, F / 89 / 2 / 16. In reporting to Lloyd George the Churchill interpretation of Wilson's remark, Kerr wrote: "The minutes are not so definite."

40. George Kennan, *Russia and the West,* p. 134.

41. House diary, September 18, 1918.

and that they establish peace and cease to disturb the rest of the world.[42] He hoped to "finesse the situation" against them, and actually he was less apprehensive about "the Russian peril" than he seemed when he conjured up this ogre to play upon the fears of the peacemakers and thus expedite the work of the Peace Conference.[43]

House was present on February 15, when the Supreme Council continued the discussion in which Wilson had taken part before he left. The French chief of staff described the situation on all fronts and explained that although the Red Army was advancing everywhere except in Estonia, it could be defeated easily at very slight cost by a relatively small number of well-armed Allied troops. Churchill then insisted that the council act to avoid endangering the Allied units already operating as well as their Russian friends. Proposing a ten-day ultimatum that would demand an end to Soviet military action, he recommended the creation of an Allied council for Russian affairs and the organization of a military section at once, to draw up a definite scheme for war and thus prepare for a Soviet defiance of the ultimatum. He called Russia "the key to the whole situation" and predicted that unless Russia— "the counterpoise of Europe"—became an associate in the League of Nations and a friend of the Allies there would be neither peace nor victory.[44]

When the discussion was adjourned for two days House used the interval to talk with Balfour and then with the American commissioners in an effort to establish a common position. Meeting again with the Supreme Council, on the seventeenth, he had in hand a paper by General Bliss, asserting that to the American people bolshevism was but "one of the many confused blotches which disfigure the map of Europe," and that they would not willingly take action in Russia while the uncertainty in central Europe complicated the situation.[45] House had also a memorandum reiterating the desire of the United States to help in relieving the distress of the Russians by supplying food and raw materials if hostilities ceased.[46]

42. W. A. White to Mrs. White, February 9, 1919, in *Selected Letters*, p. 197.

43. House diary, January 8, 1919. See below, p. 147. In this diary entry House expressed the opinion that military intervention could be successful "if gone about properly, with a voluntary and mercenary army of very small proportions, equipped with artillery and tanks."

44. *F.R., P.P.C.*, vol. 4, pp. 13–21. Churchill, pp. 173–176.

45. *F.R., P.P.C.*, vol. 11, pp. 42–46. House diary, February 16–17, 1919.

46. Auchincloss diary, February 17, 1919. A paper prepared by House's advisers made the following recommendations:

1. Don't say negotiations are broken off.
2. Issue statement saying Bolsheviks have not complied with conditions for meeting and have misinterpreted the Allies' note.
3. Allies will now make another statement to clear the issues.
4. What we will do if they come [to Prinkipo]:
   a. don't want to interfere in Russia.
   b. foreign loans, concessions, etc., are not our only interests in Russia.
   c. in favor of peasants having land.
   d. want to be of service in Russia.
5. What we will do if they do not come:
   a. conclude Russia does not want to join world peace.
   b. will protect neighboring states from their terroristic armies
      i. by sending forces to these states.
      ii. by drawing an economic cordon around Russia.

Lansing substituted "by every means in our Power" for "by sending forces to these states." House added a statement of willingness to help the Bolsheviks with food and raw materials if they ceased hostilities. *F.R., P.P.C.*, vol. 11, pp. 43–45. Drafts of this memorandum are in the Wiseman papers, Y.H.C.

The Imperial War Cabinet agreed in the morning of February 17 that in the afternoon "the British Representatives should press . . . for the institution of the Military Commission proposed by Mr. Churchill." However, House, in talks with British Labour leaders, learned of the strength of political opposition in England to any military action that might result.[47] Churchill's record as sponsor of the military disaster in Gallipoli did not encourage confidence in his judgment.

Actually Lloyd George, at London, had become so perturbed by dispatches[48] from Churchill at Paris that he telegraphed to warn him that an expensive war of agression against Russia would be "positively mischievous," that commitment to "a war against a continent like Russia" was "the direct road to bankruptcy and bolshevism" in the British Isles.[49] The prime minister asked that a copy of this telegram be shown to House, and Kerr did so a half hour before the meeting of the Supreme Council began. Churchill was told of this extraordinary sharing of confidence with a foreign diplomat, whereupon he became very indignant and took an attitude toward House that, according to the latter, was "not amiable."[50]

Much of the debate in the Supreme Council was too acrimonious to be recorded in the minutes.[51] When Churchill proposed that they direct the military advisers to report soon on the feasibility of military assistance to the anti-Bolshevik armies and on measures that might protect the states on Russia's western border, House opposed this with some vehemence, joining with Balfour in favoring informal secret conferences. It was finally agreed that the Prinkipo proposal no longer stood and that each delegation should consult its military advisers, who would then exchange views in confidence and report to their respective delegations. After that, there was to be another discussion in the council.[52] "It was literally Balfour and myself against Churchill, the French, and the Italians," House wrote in his diary on February 17.

47. Minutes, British Empire delegation, February 17, 1919. House diary, February 17, 1919. Gilbert, p. 255.

48. Churchill, recommending after reconsideration that no ultimatum be sent at present in respect of the Prinkipo plan, proposed "to set up a Military Commission at once to take stock of the whole situation, to prepare out of the resources which are available a plan of war against the Bolsheviks, to submit that plan when completed to the Supreme War Council together with an expression of authoritative military opinion, as to whether it has reasonable chances of succeeding or not." "What would be utterly indefensible," Churchill wrote, "would be to come to this truly awful decision without accurate, comprehensive and authoritative military advice," Gilbert, p. 254.

49. Lloyd George, p. 372. "There is only one justification for interfering in Russia," Lloyd George telegraphed to Kerr, "that Russia wants it," telegram in Lloyd George papers, F / 89 / 2 / 19. See Hankey, *The Supreme Control*, pp. 71–72, and Henry Pelling, *Winston Churchill* (London, 1977), p. 255.

50. House diary, February 16 and 17, 1919, House to Wilson, February 19, 1919. Telegram cited, Kerr to the prime minister, February 17, 1919, Lloyd George papers, F / 89 / 2 / 21. Lloyd George, p. 374.

51. Auchincloss recorded that Balfour was "mad clean through" when Clemenceau "made a disagreeable speech," Auchincloss diary, House diary, February 17, 1919.

52. Cable, House to the president (February 19, 1919), telegram, Lansing to the president (February 17, 1919), Wilson papers. Hankey, p. 70. Auchincloss diary, February 17, 18, and 19, 1919. Gilbert, p. 255. Churchill, pp. 177–178. According to Kerr, House was opposed to the appointment of a commission of inquiry "because it would certainly be boomed by the French as the beginning of an anti-Bolshevik war which in turn would produce anxiety among the working classes in England and America, which would force both the British and American governments immediately to declare their Russian policy. . . . He was in favor of keeping in touch with the Bolsheviks with the object of gradually bringing them to terms, restoring Allied influence in Russia and so composing a peace," Kerr to the prime minister, Lloyd George papers, F / 89 / 2 / 21.

Actually, however, Balfour was less firmly committed to the American position than House liked to think.[53]

The stormy proceedings of the seventeenth were reported immediately to the president.[54] When Wilson reached Washington, where Secretary Baker had just announced that American troops in Russia would be withdrawn at the earliest moment possible, he cabled at once to House: "Hope you will be very plain and decided to the effect that we are not at war with Russia and will in no circumstances that we can foresee take part in military operations there against the Russians. I do not at all understand why Churchill was allowed to come to Paris on such an errand after what Lloyd George had said with regard to the British sending troops to Russia." Two days later the American commission notified the president that the proposal of Churchill was "dead."[55]

At this time Wilson went still further toward disengagement in north Russia. Informed by Bliss that the British were requesting two companies of American railroad troops to guard the line from Murmansk to Archangel, the president demanded as a condition of compliance "the prompt withdrawal of American and Allied troops in North Russia at the earliest possible moment that weather conditions will permit in the spring."[56] Authority to make this decision public was given to Secretary Baker, who had reported to the president on February 12 that American opinion, fearing that the number of soldiers sent to Russia was insufficient for their safety and that they might find themselves "opposed to popular governments and in alliance with reactionaries," wanted all of them brought home.[57] At Paris, General Bliss told his Allied associates that they could expect no more military support from the United States in north Russia.

53. Replying to a letter of February 16 from Churchill saying that if the Foreign Office gave up the Prinkipo plan, use might be made in Russia of "many forces on the chess board" (such as those of General Alby, Czechoslovakia, Romania, Bulgaria, and Japan), Balfour wrote: "You have no choice but to take the lead," copy of letter in P.R.O., FO / 800 / 215. Agreeing that "Churchill's line" was "the right one," Kerr informed Lloyd George that in reality Churchill was "bent on forcing a campaign against Bolshevik Russia, . . . financed and equipped by the Allies," "Memo for the Prime Minister, Prinkipo," February 14 [?], 1919.

54. Telegram, Lansing to the president [February 17, 1919]. Cf. cable, House to Wilson [February 19, 1919], Wilson papers.

55. Telegram, Wilson to Ammission, February 19, 1919; cable, Wilson to House [February 20, 1919], Wilson papers.

56. *F.R., 1919, Russia*, pp. 617–618. Bliss to Wilson, February 12, 1919, Wilson papers.

57. At Archangel the Americans found themselves drawn into local politics and fighting battles under orders from the ranking British commander, Long, 65 and n., 66. This scholar found "no evidence to support the contention that Wilson was motivated by an ideological desire to crush bolshevism," *ibid.*, p. 67. Memorandum for the president, February 12, 1919, Bliss papers, box 70. Bliss to N. D. Baker, February 14, 1919, N. D. Baker papers, L.C.

In the view of the British War Office, the Americans in north Russia "who arrived totally untrained" and who included "a large proportion of Russians and Poles," were "still unreliable under fire," and "also somewhat doubtful in their attitude toward the enemy," secret document, "Appreciation of the Situation on the Archangel Front," February 4, 1919, Foster papers, file 135, National Archives of Canada. Also see dispatch, Consul D. G. Poole to Ammission, January 24, 1919, Y.H.C.

General Wilds P. Richardson, who took the American command at Archangel in April after being briefed personally by the president, stated in a report of July 23 to General March, the American chief of staff, that there had been during the occupation as many as five mutinies of British soldiers, five among Russians, a serious one of the French (in November 1918), and one incident, not very serious, in the U.S. 339th Infantry, Company T, document in Y.H.C.

The American and British officials at Paris continued to consider the possibilities of reviving and modifying the Prinkipo plan. Foch, however, submitted a grand plan to the Quai d'Orsay for combating bolshevism all along Russia's western borders. He conceived that pro-Allied Russian armies should be reinforced by interned prisoners, matériel, and a unified command.[58] On February 25 he unfolded to the Supreme Council a scheme for the conquest of Russia by armies of Japanese and eastern Europeans and proposed an occupation of indefinite length, with financing from the United States.[59]

To this Balfour responded indignantly, saying that Foch was building a very great edifice on the small foundation of moving Haller's army to Poland, and that it was futile to talk of such an expensive project until Wilson returned.[60] Foch submitted no estimate of costs. On March 7 Kerr revealed figures supplied by the British military that, according to his record, "staggered" Clemenceau. At this time Kerr intimated that it was the intention of his government to evacuate north Russia as well as Omsk and Vladivostok, and to supply General Denikin and Admiral Kolchak with whatever material could be spared so that the "Whites" might defend themselves against Soviet attacks. House and Clemenceau agreed with this policy and were opposed to any plan for the invasion of Russia.[61]

Just before leaving Washington, in a talk to members of the Democratic National Committee, Wilson explained his policy of noninterference in Russia: "I read the Virginia Bill of Rights very literally but very elegantly to mean that any people is entitled to any kind of government it pleases and that it is none of our business to suggest or to influence the kind that it is going to have. Sometimes it will have a very riotous form of government, but that is none of our business."[62]

Even before Churchill's proposal was scotched and the Prinkipo plan finally abandoned, a *démarche* had been initiated in secret by House and Lansing. Told by their advisers of a deplorable deficiency in information about affairs in Russia,[63] they had set in motion a venture that followed up a remark that Wilson made in the Supreme Council on the day of his departure. The president had said that he would be content if American representatives should talk informally with Soviet delegates. He was not seeking a rapprochement, he said, and he was not disposed to grant recognition in any form to the Soviet government. What he wanted was information.[64]

Colonel House had been thinking for some weeks of a constructive venture in

58. See Mayer, p. 459, and Kerr's memorandum for chief of Imperial General Staff, Lothian papers, 9040 / 1171.

59. When Foch spoke to Bliss on February 25 of his plan to "settle bolshevism" by armed invasion, Bliss warned the American commission against such a project, Bliss to N. D. Baker, March 4, 1919. Palmer, p. 378.

60. Bliss to N. D. Baker, April 3, 1919. Bliss papers, box 75. See above, p. 95.

61. "Notes of an Interview between M. Clemenceau, Col. House and Myself [Kerr]," March 7, 1919, Lothian papers, Scottish Record Office.

62. Swem book ms., Princeton University Library.

63. Script in R. S. Baker papers, box 18, folder 2, Princeton University Library.

64. See Norman G. Levin, Jr., *Woodrow Wilson and World Politics*, p. 212.

diplomacy. American liberals had been encouraged in their optimistic view of the Soviet regime by the publication of its constitution in the *Nation* on January 4; and several of the young men in the peace delegation at Paris dared to hope that time would temper the excesses of the revolution.[65] William C. Bullitt, who had supplied the American commission with daily bulletins of political intelligence, had been impressed by Litvinov's proposal to Buckler. On January 19 he had communicated with House about the possibility of missions from France, Great Britain, and the United States "to examine conditions in Russia, with a view to recommending definite action."[66] No socialist himself, Bullitt thought socialism a means of averting bolshevism. Believing that the new Russia "represented brotherhood, a spiritual conversion, indeed a state of peace,"[67] he advocated the immediate offer of an armistice to the Soviet government and the prompt withdrawal of foreign troops from Russia.[68]

On February 16, two days after Wilson spoke of informal talks with Soviet delegates to elicit information, House conferred with Lansing and found him inclined to send Bullitt to Moscow to "cure him of bolshevism." The secretary of state instructed Bullitt that he was "to proceed to Russia for the purpose of studying conditions, political and economic, therein, for the benefit of the American commissioners." Lansing took precautions to maintain secrecy.[69]

Bullitt and House found a strong supporter for the enterprise in the person of Philip Kerr, with whom they consulted before the mission departed.[70] In a letter of February 18 Kerr reported the American project to Lloyd George,[71] asking for a

65. See Christopher Lasch, *The American Liberals and the Russian Revolution,* pp. 141–156.

66. Memorandum, Bullitt to House, January 19, 1919, Bullitt papers. See Mayer, p. 465. Bullitt informed House that Lloyd George inclined toward this action and probably would appoint Smuts to represent Great Britain.

67. Beatrice Farnsworth, *William C. Bullitt and the Soviet Union,* pp. 12–13, 35–39. Mayer, p. 468.

68. Bullitt's postscript on copy of dispatch, Poole to Ammission, January 31, 1919; memos for Colonel House, February 11, 1919, Bullitt papers.

69. Lansing to Bullitt, February 18, 1919, Lansing to the secretary of state, February 24, *F.R., 1919, Russia,* p. 74. Lansing to State Department, dispatch of February 23, 1919, N.A., R.G. 256, 184.022 / 5. Lansing cautioned the American legation at Stochholm to "scrupulously avoid showing any connection with Bullitt's mission, lest the Soviet government make valuable propaganda of it," dispatches, February 26, March 1, 1919, N.A., R.G. 256, 184.022 / 5 and 184.02202 / 1. According to Bullitt, Minister Ira Morris, at Stockholm, "arranged things admirably," dispatch, Bullitt to Ammission, March 4, 1919, N.A., R.G. 256, 02202 / 1. According to the diary of Arthur Sweetser, who was Ray Stannard Baker's assistant and in charge of the American press bureau while Baker was with Wilson in the United States, Bullitt threatened to resign and join the British Labour party in protest against the failure of the League of Nations Covenant to provide for an international parliament. Sweetser recorded that House acceded to Bullitt's desire to go to Moscow in order to avert his resignation, undated diary entry. On May 5, 1919, when Bullitt finally resigned, Sweetser wrote: "Months ago Bullitt's attitude was such that resignation seemed the only right thing for him to do."

70. Mayer, p. 434. Orville H. Bullitt (ed.), *For the President: Personal and Secret,* pp. 4, 5. Bullitt notebook. W. C. Bullitt, *The Bullitt Mission to Moscow,* p. 4. House diary, February 18, 1919. Grew, *Turbulent Era,* vol. 1, p. 383n.

71. Memo by Kerr, n.d., Lloyd George papers, F / 89 / 2 / 17; letters, Kerr to the prime minister, February 13 and 18, 1919, *loc. cit.,* F / 89 / 2 / 16 and 23; Lloyd George to Kerr, February 19, 1919, *loc. cit.,* F / 89 / 2 / 25. Lloyd George suggested that House ask the French military the cost of their schemes for intervention. It would be necessary, he said, to give full military support to Poland, Finland, and other states that came under the protection of the League of Nations. He had not decided whether the Baltic states should be in the same category. Russia must be saved by itself, he thought, not by outside powers that would confer a "parasitic liberty."

reply by telephone, and it is possible that the prime minister gave oral consent. In any event Kerr drafted for House a statement of terms for a settlement with the Soviet government. Thanking Kerr, House assured him that there was no need for further discussion until Lloyd George returned to Paris. The colonel forwarded the British views to Wilson, remarking "[they] apparently coincide with ours."[72]

Bullitt set out bearing a proposition that was based on an understanding he had reached with House as well as on Kerr's statement. The proposals differed little from terms derived from Litvinov's talk with Buckler and from the Soviet reply to the Prinkipo invitation. Therefore, there was reason to think the conditions might be accepted by the Soviet government. Bullitt was accompanied by Lincoln Steffens, a liberal journalist who was acquainted with certain of the officials of the Soviet regime,[73] and by Captain Walter W. Pettit of Military Intelligence, who had lived in Russia, had been a social worker, and was at Paris as acting chief of the Russian section of the American commission. The three men arrived in London on February 23, and after talking with British officials they traveled secretly through Stockholm to Petrograd and Moscow. On March 9 they began *pourparlers* with the highest Soviet officials.[74]

Meanwhile other young American liberals, at Paris, sought to encourage the responsible leaders to face up to the great challenge to the diplomacy of the century despite the revulsion that was apparent in their political constituencies. Adolph Berle, astonished at the age of twenty-four to find himself acting as chief of the Russian section, lunched with Marcel Cachin, the French radical editor. Berle was assured that French radicals would support a policy of nonintervention and conference with the Soviet, who were said to be willing to stop propaganda abroad, end the terror, and withdraw from the Baltic lands.[75]

Would the political chiefs of the victorious nations of Europe, whose mandate of leadership had rested during the war on their ability to marshal the resources of their peoples for the defeat of the common enemy, be equal to the task of reaching a *modus vivendi* with a new regime that the Western peoples hesitated to recognize as inevitable and permanent? Foreign military intervention, tentative and limited, did violence to the national spirit of Russians and to their desire for peace. The Prinkipo plan, a naïve venture in diplomacy, was equally futile. The conventional channels were inadequate; the professionals in the foreign offices, lacking mutual trust, had no rapport. The wave of violent social revolution, riding upon a groundswell of pacifist sentiment among the Russian people, threatened to inundate the border lands and even to strain the ancient moorings of the American ship of state.

72. *I.P.*, vol. 4, p. 348. House to Kerr, February 22, 1919, Y.H.C. According to his subsequent testimony, Kerr took pains to make it clear to Bullitt, with whom he talked several times "in a perfectly unofficial manner," that any opinions that he expressed were solely his own, Kerr to Sir R. Graham, July 11, 1919, *Docs. on Brit. For. Policy 1919–1939, First Series, 3, 1919*, p. 426. Kerr to Balfour, February 21, 1919, cited in Farnsworth, pp. 38, 192. Bullitt's testimony before the Committee on Foreign Relations, *Congressional Record*, 66th Cong. 1st sess.

73. Bullitt to the author, April 2, 1951.

74. See below, p. 235.

75. Office memorandum, March 5, 1919, Berle papers, box 1, F. D. Roosevelt Library.

PART TWO

The Prophet on the Summit

WHEN Woodrow Wilson left Paris on February 14, his star was at a zenith. True to the concept of leadership that guided him as president of Princeton, governor of New Jersey, and president of the United States, he had pledged himself to further the common interest of his constituency. He now conceived his constituency to be all humanity. He was responding to the elemental desire that was more universal than the aspirations of any race, religion, or nation: mankind's yearning for lasting peace.

He had made his purposes clear in public utterances of prophetic tenor; and for a month he had entered with vigor and dignity into the deliberations of statesmen of the Old World. Supported by European liberal opinion, he had insisted on a covenant to control sudden aggressions and other causes of war. He had set scholars of good conscience to work in cooperation with those of the Allies to provide facts that bore upon critical issues. And all the while he had shown a canny regard for certain special interests of his own nation: quick demobilization; the financial obligations of European governments to the Treasury of the United States; protection from the menace of Japanese expansion in the islands of the Pacific; prestige in Latin America; and beyond these immediate considerations, the immense stature to which the United States might grow as leader of the world in a league of nations.

Little progress had been made in the first month of the Peace Conference, however, toward defining the precise terms of the treaty to be offered to the defeated enemy. Dealings with the spokesmen for the new rulers of Germany were in the hands of military men who were intent on curbing the enemy's power. No policy had been established that would bring reliable Germans into the discussions of the conditions of peace.

Meanwhile, as the horrors of war receded in men's memories, the mystic halo with which the war-weary masses had glorified the prophet of peace and justice was beginning to lose its radiance. Workers in Europe were disappointed in their hope of using this foreign voice to further their interests. Wilson had taken no part in their effort to make common cause at Bern. He was proving unable to help the masses of Russia to attain political tranquillity. His colleagues in the Supreme Council of Ten were disappointed by his inability—restricted as he was by the power of the American Congress—to give specific pledges of an assumption of responsibility by his nation for the execution of arrangements that he advocated. The Europeans had accepted the part of Wilson's program that seemed relatively harmless. Their pride smarted, however, under the admonition of a prophet who suggested that their concern for human welfare was less than his because their proposals for serving it fell into channels that grievous experience had molded. Sometimes Wilson aroused the antipathy that meets the evangelist who ventures to reform the marketplace and take part in the affairs of Caesar. By the time he took ship for America in mid-February, his spiritual sway had begun to weaken.

As the statesmen of Western Europe contemplated the lessons of the past and the probabilities of the future, they realized that the font of their own power had run almost dry. They were under pressure to get on with measures to protect their people against the menaces that loomed out of the experience of the past and the uncertain prospect of the future. No citizen of France could fail to remember that twice in the past half century German armies had invaded his land; and the fundamental French demand upon the peace was that it provide every possible guarantee against domination of any kind by Germany. Moreover, British opinion, maintaining its traditional abhorrence of the possibility of the seizure of the ports across the Channel by German armies, was determined that the German threat to British naval superiority should be forever at an end.

At the same time the major Allied nations looked with foreboding toward Russia. They could no longer count on the power of the czar as a check upon German aggression. Indeed there was apprehension, nourished by the lingering of enemy armies in the Baltic states, of an alliance between Berlin and Moscow. Many observers agreed with Winston Churchill's prediction that it was from the East that the political weather was coming.

To meet the two great perils to the perpetuation of their democracies—the menace of military attack and that of social disintegration—the western Allies needed support from America. Aware that Wilson would have to return to the United States in mid-February, they had thus far made no decisive effort to compel him to subordinate the drafting of a covenant to the discharge of the obligation of the Peace Conference to make an immediate peace. They were reluctant to run the risk of coming to loggerheads with the American prophet; and some shared his hope that if they waited, a democratic federation might one day emerge from the chaos in Russia and the turmoil in central and eastern Europe might settle down.

Meanwhile the threat of economic collapse within the fallen empires persisted. Millions of Europeans faced winter without adequate food or clothing, and existing deficiencies often were aggravated by hoarding. The Americans had been moved to take humanitarian measures. At the beginning of 1919 Herbert Hoover, acting with an independence and lack of tact that offended officials of the Allied governments, was managing a large relief operation that extended far beyond Germany into eastern and southern Europe. The faith of Americans in relief as a sedative for revolutionary ferment was to persist through the Peace Conference and after. The administrators were particularly active in regions where local hostilities erupted and where they hoped to sanction new states that would serve as buffers and as essential elements in a balancing of power. Unfortunately, some Europeans tended to notice and resent the benefits that American trade might derive from Hoover's operations.

The American peace delegates had found ways, other than through the relief program, of adding to the contribution to civilization that they conceived their people had made in fighting German militarism. Their specialists were working with committees created by the Peace Conference to set equitable and tenable boundaries between the states that replaced the empires. Americans sat also on the commissions that considered other matters: a league of nations; reparations; war guilt; conditions of labor; and regulations for ports, waterways, and railways. In serving with these bodies they often dealt with questions that were of concern to their nation only insofar as they affected the common welfare and were susceptible to the application of Wilson's principles.

In mid-February, however, the essential work of the Peace Conference was only beginning. The ending of the state of war and the drafting of a treaty of peace that all parties would ratify would require not only skillful negotiation at Paris, but also adroit dealing with political opponents who were coming into power in Washington. In accepting subservience to his great cause on the part of spokesmen for aggressive European nations, Wilson had incurred a risk of embarrassment when these men sought his support for special national interests. At the same time he would have to remember that the Constitution of the United States, written by men suspicious of foreign "entanglements," required the votes of two-thirds of the senators for the ratification of any treaty that the president might make. It was not at all certain, in view of the growing power of the opposition, that the needed votes would be forthcoming.

8

A Month of Diplomacy

The president spent all of the morning of his last day at Paris, February 14, at the Crillon. He gave the American commission the draft of the Covenant, about which they had been told little. Wilson stipulated that the entire Covenant must be included in the peace treaty with not one word revised. However, Secretary Lansing, eager to negotiate a preliminary treaty that would end the state of war, was certain that the Covenant would have to be amended[1] and that no American at Paris would dare to undertake this task in Wilson's absence. The secretary of state had surmised, three weeks before, that the French and Italian statesmen were hoping to avert American opposition to their claims by falling in with the plan for a league of nations. While the president was away, they could be expected to press their national causes.[2] Wilson, however, suspecting that the French had been deliberately delaying the work of various commissions in anticipation of his departure, said to his family: "I'll fool them, for I am going to come back here."[3] It seemed clear that the final drafting of a treaty would have to await Wilson's return.

On the eve of his departure the president told the Supreme Council that he did not want the essential and urgent work of the peacemaking, including such questions as those of territorial boundaries and reparations, to stop while he was away. He expressed confidence in his military advisers, and said that he had asked House to join Lansing in the Council of Ten. In Wilson's view the colonel had proved to be of inestimable value in reporting on both public opinion and the actual ideas of important men. However, the president was less appreciative of House's ability as a negotiator of necessary compromises and of his role in contacts with the press.[4]

Wilson talked with House alone for half an hour before they parted. When the colonel outlined a vigorous program of negotiations that he wished to follow during his chief's absence, the president took alarm. House, watching Wilson's face intently, realized that he had presumed too far. He was quick to explain that he did not contemplate final action, but merely discussions that would make it possible for the president to bring matters to a conclusion when he returned to Paris.

1. Lansing supplementary diary, entry of February 14, 1919. Lansing to Edward N. Smith, February 19, 1919, Lansing papers, box 111, f. VII, Princeton University Library.
2. Lansing to Polk, January 25, 1919, Y.H.C. Lansing, *The Peace Negotiations*, pp. 136–137.
3. Alden Hatch, *Edith Bolling Wilson*, p. 154. E. B. Wilson, *My Memoir*, pp. 236–237.
4. *F.R., P.P.C.*, vol. 3, p. 104. "At one point Mr. Wilson considered asking Mr. Lansing to resign. . . . Colonel House had worked staunchly for the League, and Mr. Lansing had not," E. B. Wilson, p. 237.

An instance of House's influence on the president's public relations is recorded in his diary under February 14: "The newspaper men sent in a request for a five-minute interview with the president. He wished to put them off . . . but I suggested that he see them at once and get it off his mind. . . . He consented reluctantly and then, to my astonishment, went into the other room and talked to fifteen or twenty American correspondents for nearly an hour—all of them standing. He spoke in the pleasantest and frankest way to them . . . he did not want to see them, and yet when he got to talking, he was so enthused with what he had to say that it looked as if he would never stop."

The time had come for specific applications of Wilson's policy for dealing with the defeated enemy, a policy that called for punishment for wartime offenses and, at the same time, a tempering of the punishment enough to avert collapse and revolution in Germany. As Wilson expressed it, he would put the Germans in a position in which they could be punished.[5] In his last meeting with the American commission, however, he said that he had no instructions for them and decisions could await his return, but hearings and reports could proceed during his absence.[6]

At this juncture good diplomacy required precision. Colonel House, recognizing the responsibility of the Americans to make a peace in the common interest as well as in their own, ventured to suggest that in order to arrange a preliminary peace four things were necessary:

1. a reduction of the German army and navy to a peace footing
2. a delineation of the boundaries of Germany, this to include the cession of colonies
3. decision on the amount of reparation to be paid and the length of time in which to pay it
4. an agreement as to the economic treatment of Germany

Asked whether he wished to add any topic, the president gave House to understand that these were sufficient. The colonel, wishing to prevent any expectation of the impossible, then said that compromises as to detail might be necessary, though none of principle would be permitted. He was himself willing, as he expressed it, "to yield the things of today in order to obtain the things of tomorrow," and he realized that the president must play his cards well in order to carry the treaty through the Senate. He was disturbed when Wilson received his counsel of conciliation with a resolve to "fight" his adversaries.[7]

After his chief's departure House felt the full weight of the greatest responsibility that he had ever undertaken. In his zeal for the great game that he and his friend were playing he had assumed the charge without instructions that any practicing attorney would consider adequate. House understood that he was not authorized to settle anything definitely, but only to arrange matters so that Wilson could make final judgments on his return.[8] His position as a member of the Supreme Council would be the more difficult because, although he had the official minutes of its previous meetings, he had been absent and was not entirely posted on everything that had been said nor was he aware of the meanings that had been conveyed by tone and expression. Moreover, neither he nor the president was in rapport with Lansing, who in Wilson's absence became the nominal chief of the American commission and continued to sit in the Supreme Council. House was apprehensive of

5. For an analysis of Wilson's policy toward Germany, see Levin, *Woodrow Wilson and World Politics*, pp. 123–139.
6. Lansing, private memoranda, February 14, 1919.
7. Bonsal, *Unfinished Business*, pp. 59–60. House diary, February 14, 1919. House to David F. Houston, January 24, 1919, Y.H.C.
8. F. L. Warrin, Jr., to the author. Bonsal, *Unfinished Business*, pp. 49–50.

"trouble" with his fellow commissioners when Wilson asked that the cables that he and House would exchange in their private code be shown to no one. Despite the danger of friction, however, he ventured to take positive steps toward tentative arrangements, on no authorization except the president's tacit acquiescence in the four-point program. He wished that he might have precise instructions in writing, and was glad he did not have *carte blanche* to settle anything definitely.[9]

In pursuing Wilson's purpose of giving prompt attention to military and naval matters, House would have to contend not only with designs of Marshal Foch but also with a feeling, expressed by British General Haig, that American indulgence of Germany reflected a desire on the part of the president to win the votes of German-Americans and to promote American trade.[10]

On February 19 House transmitted to the president a paper by the British chief of staff that reported an interview with Foch. In this the marshal, asserting that the German government would accept any terms prescribed, declared that it should be left no territory west of the Rhine and should be required to pay an indemnity no less than that claimed by the French treasury. Warning that delay might jeopardize the strong position that the victors now held, Foch recommended that he be sent in a week's time to present final terms to the German delegates. He felt that he could guarantee that they would accept on the day following. Once such a settlement was arrived at, Foch said, the vital question of Russia could be given the careful and protracted attention it demanded. All this House reported to Wilson immediately. The next day the president sent a reply.[11]

At the moment when House sent his cable, lawlessness menaced the door of the peacemakers. On February 19—the day set aside for informal consideration of the question of Russia—Clemenceau was shot as he was driving to a meeting of the Supreme Council. The assassin's bullet barely missed his spine and lodged behind his shoulder blade. For two days it was not known whether, or when, he might be able to continue the negotiations. This act of violence was taken to be a symptom of general unrest.[12] "I have been trying very hard," House wrote in his diary on February 19, "to frighten the Allies and to make them feel that if peace is not made soon, trouble may some day come overnight and make it imperative that a hasty and ill-considered peace be signed. . . . There are so many disorganized minds and the world is in such a ferment that any of us are likely to be killed at any time."

As the peacemakers held their breaths while they awaited a report on the condition of the old man who could speak with authority for France and who was determined to maintain the wartime alliance, House wrote in his diary: "Outside the personal side of it, it is a great misfortune that Clemenceau should have been shot at this time. He had come to our way of thinking that it was best to make a quick and early peace with Germany." However this "accident"—as Clemenceau insisted

9. House diary, February 14, 1919. Bonsal, pp. 49–50.
10. Robert Blake (ed.), *The Private Papers of Douglas Haig* (London, 1952), p. 356.
11. Memorandum of Feb. 18, 1919, House-Hankey correspondence, Y.H.C. House to Wilson, February 19, 1919, Wilson to House, February 20, 1919. *I.P.*, vol. 4, pp. 332–336. For Wilson's reply see below, p. 150.
12. Dispatch, H. White to H. C. Lodge, February 20, 1919, N.A., R.G. 59, 763.72119 / 3820.

on calling it—made it easier for House to scare the Supreme Council into acting promptly.[13]

On the morning of February 22, three days after Clemenceau was shot and while House was awaiting a reply to the message he had sent to Wilson three days before, House and Balfour talked *à deux* with the convalescing premier.[14] Clemenceau spoke to House of his eagerness to expedite the entire process of peacemaking. He feared that a preliminary military settlement might be followed by petty controversies and a long delay in arriving at a final treaty. This was a reversal of his earlier desire to impose military terms first. "He was brought to this," House wrote in his diary, "not only by a realization that Germany was, as Foch had said, 'flattened out,' but because there are grave signs of unrest in the French army."[15] It is possible that Clemenceau saw an opportunity to get a territorial settlement favorable to France while Wilson was away.[16]

Balfour, however, the cool diplomat who "made the whole of Paris seem vulgar"[17] and whom Clemenceau in a moment of pique called "cette vieille fille,"[18] doubted whether final agreement was possible in Wilson's absence on such difficult questions as those of Danzig and the left bank of the Rhine. Nevertheless Balfour and House agreed[19] on a plan of action. Balfour was to canvass the Japanese delegates and House, the Italians. They would then talk with Clemenceau in the hope that he would accept their program and they would not have to override him. In the meeting of the Supreme Council on the twenty-second Balfour presented a resolution that provided for the consideration but not the final determination of "preliminary peace terms" other than military. It was proposed that the various advisory commissions that had been set up before the president's departure be directed to submit reports by March 8 so that they would be ready to be reviewed by Wilson when he returned. Since the Balfour resolution provided only for a tentative consideration of preliminary terms rather than any decision, House supported the proposal. At the same

13. The journalist Wythe Williams wrote of the personal regard and understanding between House and Clemenceau. "I really have a great affection for him [House]," Clemenceau said to Williams. "We are almost like brothers who disagree on everything. But I'll tell you why I like him. I can talk to him frankly, and he talks that way with me, and then we don't go behind each other's backs. He is a straight-shooter in this, just as with a pistol. . . . He doesn't always see eye to eye with the Great Mogul, Wilson, but he is intensely loyal," *Dusk of Empire* (London, 1937), p. 185. The same witness also quotes House: "Clemenceau and I get along like brothers, even though we disagree about almost everything. I not only admire but I really love that old man," Williams, *The Tiger of France*, p. 188. For Clemenceau's appreciation of House, see Clemenceau's *Grandeur and Misery of Victory*, p. 148, and Bonsal, p. 67.

14. House reported to Wilson on his talk with Clemenceau in a dispatch of February 23, 1919. House gave his opinion that Clemenceau was "by no means out of danger."

15. House diary, February 16, 1919.

16. Lloyd George wrote to Kerr on February 12: "The old Tiger wants the grizzly bear back in the Rocky Mountains before he begins tearing up the German hog," letter in Lloyd George papers, F / 89 / 218. Balfour suggested this possibility to House two weeks later, Balfour to House, February 25, 1919, Y.H.C. See McDougall, *France's Rhineland Diplomacy*, p. 41.

17. Nicolson, *Peacemaking, 1919*, pp. 330, 340.

18. Sidney H. Zebel, *Balfour: A Political Biography*, p. 258. When Balfour, in House's office, heard of the shooting of Clemenceau, his remark was "Dear, dear, I wonder what that portends?" Bonsal, p. 64, *q.v.* on "the lackadaisical Arthur Balfour."

19. The appointment of Wiseman as Balfour's "special adviser" on Anglo-American affairs facilitated House's efforts to maintain a close understanding with the foreign secretary, Balfour to Wiseman, February 24, 1919, copy in Balfour papers 49741.

time he expressed the opinion that the Germans would be the more inclined to accept the rigid military terms if at the same time they could know the whole reckoning. In this meeting he was embarrassed by remarks of Lansing, who seemed to House to have little comprehension of the situation.[20]

Approval of the Balfour resolution was held up while the members of the council discussed a question raised by Sonnino. The Italian was apprehensive lest, in concentrating on the settlement with Germany, they neglect to prescribe for Austria-Hungary and thus require Italy to keep its citizens mobilized longer than those of the other Allied nations, and perhaps provoke them to revolution. A long discussion ensued. Finally House, perceiving that the terms for Germany might become entangled with those for Austria in a way that would cause interminable delay, proposed a compromise plan that was accepted by Balfour and, reluctantly, by Sonnino. This called for four resolutions almost identical in form, one to apply to each of the enemy states.[21] House reserved a place for consideration of the League covenant by arranging the insertion of the words *"inter alia."* The Balfour resolution finally read, in respect of each of the enemy states:

> The Preliminary Peace Terms, other than the Naval, Military, and Air conditions, should cover *inter alia* the following points.
> (a) the approximate future frontiers of _____[for Germany only: "and the ren unciation of colonial territories and treaty rights outside Europe."]
> (b) the financial conditions to be imposed on _____
> (c) the economic conditions to be accorded to _____
> (d) the responsibility for breaches of the laws of war.

"I did not want to bring this [the Covenant] up at this time," House wrote in his diary, "and I explained to Lansing that if we did, it would cause an interminable discussion with the French, and that we had better merely leave room for this and any other subjects [by the phrase *'inter alia'*] without mentioning them by name.[22]

When the amended draft of Balfour's resolution was accepted as a basis for discussion, House told a few trusted news correspondents that this was what the American peace delegates most wanted and more than they had hoped for, and that it now appeared that peace would come earlier than had been expected.[23] Soon House was receiving credit in the press for a quickening of the proceedings. Auchincloss continued to extol the prowess of his father-in-law as a diplomat; and House himself was so indiscreet as to confide to a few journalists that Wilson was inclined to do things in the most difficult way, that proceedings were going more smoothly in the

20. Hankey reported to Lloyd George that Lansing "rather queered his [House's] pitch," letter, Hankey to Lloyd George, Lloyd George papers, F / 23 / 4 / 22.

21. See *I.P.,* vol. 4, pp. 339–340. House diary, Auchincloss diary, February 22, 1919.

Hankey explained to Lloyd George that House's proposal would give to the Italians the impression that negotiations with Austria were on a par with those with Germany—"a rather cumbrous solution, but not lacking in ingenuity," Hankey to Lloyd George, February 23, 1919, Lloyd George papers, F / 23 / 4 / 22. House intended that all the resolutions except that concerning Germany would be "sidetracked," Auchincloss diary, February 22, 1919.

22. House diary, February 22, 1919. As Floto has observed, to defer discussion of the Covenant raised possibilities for misunderstanding, *Colonel House in Paris,* pp. 363–376.

23. House to newsmen, February 22, 1919, notes of Arthur Sweetser.

absence of the President and Lloyd George.[24] Nevertheless he asked Steed, who had succeeded Geoffrey Dawson as editor of the *Times,* to help bring Lloyd George back. House thought, as he had at the time of the armistice, that it would be best for the president to give direction from behind the curtain in Washington.[25]

House was of the opinion that, instead of conferring with Balfour and Tardieu in an informal steering committee, he could accomplish more and with greater harmony by talking intimately with one and then the other. He sent Bonsal to call on Clemenceau almost every evening to discuss the developments of the day and to convey messages.[26] Aware that he had lost the thread of affairs when ill in January, House was for a time not sure that he had "ever gotten fully back." Laboring under such responsibility as he had never borne before, he did not see how he could find strength to carry on. His confidence was buoyed, however, when Wiseman told him that Hankey thought he had contributed to an acceleration of the proceedings.[27]

On February 24 House informed Wilson[28] that the Balfour resolution had been adopted. The message reported also that Bliss was working on the military terms and the territorial experts were "in substantial agreement with the British and French in respect of the boundaries of Germany." "At the present time," House told the president, "the plan we are pursuing is as follows: The giving of priority to the work of committees involving matters essential in the preparation of [the] peace treaty with Germany. Reports from these committees should be available by March eighth and should, upon your arrival, be in shape so that you can consider them without delay." Negotiating tentatively and avoiding final commitments, House hoped to get the approval of all the powers at a plenary session in time to adjourn the Peace Conference in April.

However, on the day on which he reported the adoption of the Balfour resolution, House received the reply to the message that he had sent to Wilson on the nineteenth.[29] Its tone was ominous. Commenting on the statement of Foch's plans that the colonel had forwarded, the president acknowledged it with "warm thanks." Wilson said: "The memorandum . . . seems to me like an attempt to use the good offices of the French to hurry us into an acquiescence in their plans with regard to western bank of Rhine. . . . I know I can trust you and our colleagues to withstand such a programme immovably, except of course I am willing to have the strictly military and naval terms promptly decided and presented to the Germans. I am not willing to have anything beyond the military and naval terms decided and believe that the conference of ten [the Supreme Council] would be going very much beyond

24. *I.P.,* vol. 4, p. 361. Sweetser notes. House diary, February 27, 1919. Cf. below, p. 162.

25. Bonsal, pp. 60–61. Steed to Northcliffe, March 5, Steed papers, Printing House Square papers, *Times* archives.

Auchincloss recorded in his diary on March 6 that Lloyd George, returning to the conference on that day, had "a distinctly good effect" on the deliberations. "He hurries things up," Auchincloss wrote. Miller, *My Diary,* vol. 1, p. 141.

26. Bonsal, pp. 68, 71.

27. House diary, February 16, 26, March 3, 1919.

28. *I.P.,* vol. 4, pp. 339, 348–350. Cable, House to Wilson, February 25, 1919, Wilson papers.

29. See above, p. 147.

its powers to attempt anything of this sort. The determination of the geographic boundaries of Germany involves the fortunes and interests of the other peoples, and we should not risk being hurried into a solution arrived at solely from the French official viewpoint.''[30] Actually, Wilson harbored dark suspicions of Clemenceau's tactics. Before leaving Paris he had confessed to Dr. Grayson that he perceived in the French premier a trickiness that he thought House failed to detect.[31] If House did suspect that the French were trying to take advantage of the fact that he was less resistant than Wilson, as Balfour suggested, he left no record of such a suspicion.

It was clear now that it was going to be most difficult to persuade the Americans to satisfy the legitimate concern of the French people for security from future attack. Their demand for a defensible frontier was persistent and hard to resist. They wished to set the western boundary of Germany at the Rhine and to occupy the principal bridgeheads on the east bank of the river. In the French view the inhabitants of the west bank had been the unwilling subjects of the Prussian crown for more than a century. When House visited Clemenceau on February 22, the wounded premier insisted on the creation of an independent republic as an alternative to annexation of the west bank by France.[32] He had not been convinced by Wilson's argument in the Supreme Council on January 15 to the effect that to carry out French plans for the Rhineland would eventually turn the sentiment of the world against France.[33]

Returning to his seat in the Supreme Council on March 1, Clemenceau met opposition. In the prearmistice meetings, when House went along with Lloyd George in accepting Foch's plans as satisfactory in general, they had received a pledge from Clemenceau that France would end occupation of the left bank of the Rhine as soon as Germany fulfilled the conditions of peace.[34] Thinking that it would be unwise to separate about 4 million Germans on the west bank from their fatherland, House had written in his diary on February 9: ''The French . . . do not seem to know that to establish a Rhenish Republic against the will of the people would be contrary to the principle of self-determination, and that if we should establish it, the people could at any time become federated with the other German states. If we did such a thing, we would be treating Germany in one way and the balance of the world in another. We would run the danger of having everything from the Rhine to the Pacific, perhaps including Japan, against the Western Powers. The Germans would at once begin to intrigue to bring about such a combination against England, France, and the United States. Their propaganda would be that England, France, and the United States were undertaking to form an Anglo-Saxon supremacy of the world, and that we were using France as a pawn for the accomplishment of our purpose. I told Balfour this and he agreed to everything I said; yet we both have a profound sympathy for France and for the unhappy situation in which she finds herself. . . .

30. Copy in Wilson papers. In the transcription at Paris of Wilson's coded message, the word ''decided'' was omitted, Auchincloss diary, February 24, 1919. Seymour supplied ''settled'' in *I.P.*, vol. 4, p. 336.
31. Grayson diary, February 8, 1919.
32. House diary, February 22, 1919. Auchincloss diary, February 23, 1919. Bonsal, *Suitors and Suppliants*, p. 214.
33. Grayson diary, January 15, 1919.
34. Walworth, *America's Moment: 1918*, p. 50.

The only hope France has for the future is the League of Nations and the spirit we hope to bring about through it. If after establishing the League, we are so stupid as to let Germany train and arm a large army and again become a menace to the world, we would deserve the fate which such folly would bring upon us.''

However, House did not strictly follow the instructions of the president to ''withstand . . . immovably'' the French pleas. He realized that the unanimity and force of French opinion required that Germany be confined in a military sense at the Rhine. In order to assure French cooperation in the League of Nations, as well as to expedite proceedings, House undertook, on his own responsibility, the task of accommodating the conflicting views. The president had forbidden any attempt to decide ''anything beyond the military and naval terms''; but the arrangements for the Rhineland seemed to be, at least in French opinion, essentially a matter of military security.

In order to keep negotiations open House did not inform the French of Wilson's instruction that he stand ''immovably.'' Instead, he elicited terms for compromise from the French spokesmen and presented them to Wilson accurately, reminding the president that they would safeguard his principle of self-determination.[35]

On February 23 Clemenceau proposed to House that the envisioned Rhenish Republic should be exempt from the payment of any indemnity and should have no armed force. He suggested, moreover, that everything should be done to make the citizens prosperous and contented so that they would not want to join the German federation. If they had any such desire, they were to be restrained. House dutifully reported this proposition to Wilson, being convinced himself that it was a denial of the right of self-determination and, therefore, entirely unacceptable to the president.[36] He was able to reassure Wilson in respect of self-determination, however, by reporting a talk that he had with Tardieu, who spoke for Clemenceau. ''Tardieu . . . said to me yesterday,'' House cabled,[37] ''that France would be willing to have the Rhenish Republic set up only for a limited period of years, at the end of which the population would be permitted to decide for themselves what their future should be. He said that in this way a breathing space would be given us all and France would secure protection until she recovered from the present war. The principle of self-determination would in this way be safeguarded.''[38]

The president's reception of this proposal was probably tainted by personal feelings. Wilson disliked and distrusted Tardieu, whom he suspected of being in sym-

---

35. In regard to the reception given to the French arguments by the Americans, Tardieu wrote that House ''appreciated their importance'' and that Wilson ''seemed to acknowledge their weight'' and ''at the beginning of March had not yet, according to his most intimate collaborators, any definite objection to them,'' *The Truth about the Treaty*, pp. 170–171.

The commentary on the Fourteen Points that House had presented to the Allies at the prearmistice meetings and that approved the complete restoration of Alsace and Lorraine to France did not mention the Rhineland.

36. House to Wilson, February 23, 1919 (received February 25), Wilson papers. Bonsal, *Unfinished Business*, p. 53. The strength of Wilson's indignation at any possibility of French annexation is attested by Professor Rappard's record of an interview on February 12: ''Sur Rhin: Ignorait intentions française. Mais indigne. Toujours les mêmes, toujours egotistes. . . . Sur annexions Wilson sera inexhorable. 'Rather be stoned in the streets than give in,'' *Centenaire Woodrow Wilson*, p. 56.

37. House to Wilson, February 24, 1919 (received February 25), Wilson papers.

38. *I.P.*, vol. 4, pp. 346, 349.

pathy with the political adversaries at Washington.[39] In the opinion of House, however, "no man worked with more tireless energy [than Tardieu] and none had a better grasp of the delicate and complex problems. . . . He was not only invaluable to France, but to his associates from other countries as well. He was in all truth the one nearly indispensable man at the Conference."[40]

On February 25, at the behest of Clemenceau, Tardieu put on paper a long and persuasive argument that served as a basis for discussions. Arguing that to prevent Germany from repeating its attacks of 1870 and 1914 it was essential to set the frontier at the Rhine and to occupy the bridges with an international force, he said there was "no question of annexing an inch of German soil; only of depriving Germany of her weapons of offense."[41] At the same time Tardieu let it be known through Lord Robert Cecil that, once the question of the Rhine was settled satisfactorily, the French would be less persistent in demanding military power for the League of Nations.[42]

House was inclined to accept Tardieu's views. He cabled immediately to inform the president that Tardieu had defined the French position, and House promised to report fully after studying the document.[43] He received no guidance from his chief, however. He had only a message of February 27, saying that because of a new code that was extremely complicated and imperfectly transmitted, the president felt "out of touch and unable to advise."[44] Actually, however, the parts of these dispatches that dealt with the question of the Rhine frontier were clear enough. Yet the president gave no evidence of understanding the concessions made by Tardieu and no encouragement to House's effort at compromise.

House felt there was no alternative but to carry on the exploratory conversations in the tradition of good diplomacy and to exercise his own judgment. His position was strengthened by the fact that he had just saved the French government from a financial debacle.[45] On March 2 he had a long talk with Tardieu, and they came

39. House diary, May 6, 1919. Benham diary letters, January 9, March 19 and 28, 1919.

40. *I.P.*, vol. 4, p. 393. Auchincloss thought Tardieu "without doubt the smartest man in the French government," and exerting a control over French newspapers that was "very complete." "We have been giving him some attention lately," he wrote to Polk on February 27, 1919, Y.H.C.

Seymour testified that in the Central Co-ordinating Committee of the Peace Conference, Tardieu, its chairman, "did the work amost single-handed" and that "the value of his contribution lay in his personality and his relations with Clemenceau and House," Seymour to the author.

41. Tardieu, pp. 147–170. On French thinking on the Rhenish question, see McDougall, pp. 17, 38–39, 58–61.

42. Memorandum, Kerr to Lloyd George, February 28, 1919, Lloyd George papers, F / 89 / 2 / 35. Cecil diary, February 28, 1919.

43. House to Wilson, February 27, 1919.

44. Two cables that Wilson received were in a naval code on which House's office had insisted because the code of the State Department was not considered safe from British intelligence; and the adoption of the naval code late in February was causing difficulties that embarrassed those who had resorted to it, Floto, pp. 125 and 194n. House explained to Wilson that he had used "the regular code" in order to spare Wilson the labor of deciphering it in their private code, House to Wilson, February 19, 1919, Y.H.C. Auchincloss confessed in his diary that his office was "partly responsible for the trouble," entry of February 28, 1919.

See W. Stull Holt, "What Wilson Sent and What House Received," *American Historical Review* 65 (April 1960):569–571.

45. See below, p. 177.

close to an understanding. The diary of Vance McCormick, in whose room the conference took place, gives this account:

> At 5:00 Colonel House and Tardieu came for tea, also Aubert with Tardieu. They agreed on plan for Rhenish Republic and discussed method of getting Lloyd George's approval, also on Saar Coal Basin. Agreed Poland should have Danzig and Belgium, Luxemburg, all of these, of course, with proper reservations. Agreed to push to conclusion work of committees so that reports would be ready for president upon his arrival.

House wrote in his diary: "We got nearer together on the question of the Rhenish Republic and Luxemburg."

In a talk with Clemenceau the next day, however, the Tiger seemed less tractable than Tardieu. The left bank of the Rhine was discussed, but no understanding was reached, and House complained to Wilson about Clemenceau's "very unreasonable attitude."[46] A prompt reply came from Wilson: "Am made a little uneasy," it said, "by what you say of the left bank of the Rhine. I hope you will not even provisionally consent to the separation of the Rhenish Provinces from Germany under any arrangement but will reserve the whole matter until my arrival."[47]

On March 10—the day before Wilson's caveat was received—it was agreed to refer the responsibility of drawing boundaries to a secret committee consisting of Mezes, Kerr, and Tardieu.[48] When these men met, the conversation was largely a friendly dialogue between Kerr and Tardieu, who stressed the fact that Clemenceau was the only man able to persuade the French people to accept a moderate peace. Tardieu asserted that the inhabitants of the left bank would consent to separation from Germany if given economic privileges and relieved of their share of the war debt. Kerr, for his part, agreeing that the military frontier of Germany must be set east of the Rhine, said that English opinion would accept neither the maintenance of British occupying forces east or west of the Rhine, nor the separation of the Rhenish provinces from the rest of Germany against the will of their inhabitants. Kerr stressed the importance of arriving at a settlement that would command such public approval in the British Empire and the United States that they, or the League of Nations, would act to enforce the provisions made.

Mezes, for his part, explained that he had no instructions, that he had talked about the matter only briefly with House, who wished to await the return of the president before reaching any conclusion. At this Tardieu showed surprise, for he had understood that they were to arrive at a provisional agreement. Kerr was enjoined from any conclusive commitment by Lloyd George, who was determined to bargain with France.[49] Therefore, the Committee of Three was able to come to agreement only on the proposition that they could not agree as to the extent or the duration of the existing military occupation, and that this thorny question would require a deci-

---

46. "He [Clemenceau] said that he did not believe in the principle of self-determination, which allowed a man to clutch at your throat the first time it was convenient to him," Kerr's notes of an interview between M. Clemenceau, House, and Lloyd George, March 7, 1919, Lothian papers, GD40/17/1173.

47. House to Wilson, March 7, 1919; Wilson to House, March 10, 1919, received by House March 11, 1919, Auchincloss diary, Y.H.C.

48. House and Auchincloss diaries, March 11, 1919.

49. F. Stevenson, *Lloyd George: A Diary*, p. 171.

sion by their political chiefs.[50] House had to abandon his hope of tentatively framing a compromise plan for the Rhineland before Wilson came back.

Tardieu, meeting with what he called "a psychological barrier," sent to House a letter for Wilson with an explanatory memorandum from the commander of French troops on the Rhine. At the same time he wrote: "It seems to me very bad to start with German frontiers before the president is here, and before the agreement is complete between the prime ministers and President Wilson. . . . I suggest to postpone all the matter until Monday [March 17]."[51] (It was expected that by that date Wilson would be present.) At this juncture House, perceiving in Tardieu a negotiator more tractable than any French official who might succeed him if he failed, made a special effort to be agreeable. When Clemenceau told House that he had chosen Tardieu as his successor, House accommodatingly advised Clemenceau to send Tardieu to the Crillon when he wanted to ask favors, so that Tardieu would get the credit when House was able to grant them.[52]

In assuming responsibility for independently exploring a compromise, House exposed himself to indictment in the court of history for disloyalty to his chief. Actually, whether House went further than was necessary to prevent such a disaster as Clemenceau's resignation and his replacement by a less tractable nationalist is a question for speculation." Any judgment that may be rendered, however, must take into account not only the casualness of Wilson and faulty communications, but also the historic exigency of the time. It should be remembered that the lack of "common agreement" among the American peacemakers not only was attributable in part to the president,[54] but was a consequence of a crisis in history in which the United States was confronted with the alternatives of isolation and commitment, with strong forces pulling in each direction.[55]

50. Kerr's notes of discussions with Tardieu and Mezes, March 1–11, 1919, Lloyd George papers, F / 89 / 2 / 40. Memorandum, Kerr to Hankey, March 13, 1919, Lothian papers, GD40 / 17 / 117 / 4 / 1. Notes on conversations of March 11 and 12, 1919, Fonds Clemenceau, 6N72-73-78. Tardieu, pp. 145–176. Tardieu drafted seven articles for the Supreme Council to consider. See Floto, pp. 161–162.

51. Tardieu, pp. 172–176. Letter and memorandum, Tardieu to House, March 12, 1919, copy of letter, Frazier to Tardieu, March 13, 1919, Y.H.C.

52. House diary, March 10, 1919. Auchincloss diary, March 12, 1919.

53. See Floto, pp. 123, 129, 154, 237, 239. Floto quoted a statement from House's diary to the effect that he agreed with Clemenceau and Lloyd George that they would "thresh everything out before the president came and arrive at decisions" as a means of greatly expediting matters. She wrote: "With this, House had shown his readiness definitely to exceed his instructions. He was now ready for *decisions,* which, although they could not be binding on the president, were still of a nature to ruin his bargaining position in the event of his taking a different standpoint," *ibid.,* p. 154. Of House's conference of March 2 with Tardieu Floto wrote: "It is quite clear that House here acted if not against the letter then against the spirit of Wilson's instructions," *ibid.,* p. 129.

54. "To leave the delegation without directives," Floto has written, "in blind trust to absolute communion of minds with his [Wilson's] closest adviser, was irresponsible, to say the very least," *ibid.,* p. 126.

55. Floto explains House's seeming "weakness as a negotiator" by writing that he "underestimated the political consequences of the negotiations" and "was acting under double pressure, partly from the Allies . . . and partly from the president . . . , and . . . no doubt . . . was very uncertain as to the president's intentions. He simply did not know what Wilson wanted," Floto, p. 239. This explanation does not seem to the writer to justify the charge of disloyalty. Nor is it possible to accept Floto's assertion that after March 13 "it was no longer the American policy that interested House, but his own role as leader and manipulator of the whole Conference," Floto, p. 123. In his mind the success of American

One must consider also the unsettling effect exerted just at this time by news from Germany that made a second revolution there seem imminent.[56] Doubts held by some of the Americans about the permanence of the Ebert-Scheidemann government gave way to a realization that this regime held out the best hope for the negotiation of a piece treaty and that, therefore, it would be well to sustain it by shipments of food. Two agents returned from Germany in mid-February with a report that the populations of large German cities would be without foodstuffs in about two months. The arrangements that had been made in respect of finance and shipping had not been carried out,[57] and each party was suspicious of the good faith of the other. Hoover's relief work in enemy lands was still being interrupted by a continuation of the blockade.

While the president was away, progress was made by way of arranging for the use of German ships to carry food. The same arguments were bandied interminably at Paris. At the same time, differences of public opinion persisted in Great Britain. British traders both sought trade with Germany and feared a revival of German competition. The blockade, which had contributed much to the victory, was a shibboleth dear to the British people[58] and a valued instrument for assuring German compliance with the terms of the armistice.

American and British observers in Germany made dire predictions of economic and political disaster; and their apprehension was stimulated by German politicians who exploited the fear of anarchy that was rife among the peacemakers. McCormick recorded in his diary that Americans were being attacked in Germany and the peacemakers were "living on the top of a volcano."[59]

The supplying of food was involved with so many questions of finance and transportation, and also so many military and political consequences, that it was deemed necessary to form a Supreme Economic Council to provide overall direction. Holding its first meeting on February 17, the new body voted to establish under its

policy depended to a large degree upon his services as a diplomat, so that the two considerations were inextricably intertwined. In view of the effectiveness of his work in the past in catalyzing the relations of Wilson with the European statesmen, House conceived, not without some justification, that it was important for Wilson's success that he remain in a position of influence.

It was the considered opinion of one of the most reliable of the Inquiry's scholars, James T. Shotwell, that though perhaps House went too far in exploiting his relationship with Wilson, "at heart and in reality he was *never* a betrayer of Wilson, but from the outside it did look that way," Shotwell record, O.H.R.O. Another respected scholar, Professor Allyn A. Young, while questioning House's wisdom, wrote: "He was loyal to the president, I am sure," Young to R. S. Baker, December 24, 1919, R. S. Baker papers. Ray Stannard Baker wrote that House "never intended for a moment to be disloyal to the president," Baker, vol 1, 304–307. Cf. Bonsal's statement in *Unfinished Business*, p. 303, and Frazier to Bonsal, February 3, 1939, Bonsal papers, box 2.

56. "At the end of February," Schwabe writes, ". . . one disaster followed on another. Eisner was murdered. Political strikes . . . broke out in Berlin. . . . reports from Berlin and other industrial cities painted a picture of near civil war. . . . The last semiofficial observer for the United States was ordered to leave Berlin," *Woodrow Wilson, Revolutionary Germany, and Peacemaking*, pp. 192–193.

57. See above, pp. 89 ff. and Arnold-Forster, *The Blockade, 1914–1919*, pp. 34–35.

58. See Walworth, p. 58 and n. On February 12 Curzon stated that the British cabinet was opposed to relaxation of the blockade, dispatch, Curzon to Derby, Curzon papers, mss. Eur., F 112 / 302, box 72. Later, however, the departments of the British government were almost equally divided on this issue, seven-page government memo, undated, written after February 20, Foster papers, file 82, Canadian National Archives.

59. Entries of March 1 and 5, 1919. See Mayer, pp. 493–509.

authority subsections on blockade, communications, finance, food, maritime transport, and raw materials. These sections took over the powers and organization of
the inter-Allied agencies that had operated in the various fields during the war.[60]
The first session of the new council made little progress toward the relaxation of the
blockade. The American members, indignant at what they regarded as attempts at
financial extortion by the Allies whenever the subject was mentioned and unwilling
that the Allied governments dominate American food markets by controlling the
purchasing of northern neutrals as well as that of their own peoples, threatened
independent American action if the restrictions were not relaxed.

Action at the highest level was required. There was evidence that food shortages
in Germany would become serious in May; and surpluses were still deranging the
market in America. To get French assent to his plans, Hoover made some concessions in respect of allotting food to the Rhineland. He even made it possible for
France to receive German gold in order to purchase food that France would import
from the United States and pay for in francs. Believing that the present German
government was the best possible, Hoover thought it necessary to open the door at
least halfway in order to enable Germany to carry on trade. In view of the current
disorder, he came to give more emphasis to political stability and less to benefits
for German trade. But the French remained determined to retain the blockade as a
weapon in the negotiations with the enemy.[61]

Progress in this critical matter was made before Wilson's return in mid-March.
On the third of this month the Supreme Economic Council sent delegates to Spa to
negotiate with German civilians on the matter of shipping.[62] The enemy was willing
to compromise by delivering some ships in return for a limited supply of food, and
additional vessels in proportion to further supplies. But the Germans adhered to the
position that before giving up their vessels they must have definite assurances as to
food deliveries.[63] The delegates of the Peace Conference decided to slip away to
Paris late at night to report the impasse to their chiefs.[64]

The battle of the blockade finally came to a climax on the afternoon of March 8,
when a compromise plan worked out the day before by the Supreme Economic
Council was considered in a four-hour meeting of the Supreme Council of Ten. The

60. See Marston, *The Peace Conference of 1919*, pp. 105–106. Wilson advocated the creation of the
Supreme Economic Council at the suggestion of his economic advisers, forwarded by House. Davis was
chairman of the Finance Section, Hoover of the Food Section, *I.P.*, vol. 4, pp. 276–277. The constitution of the council was drafted by Hoover, and it was composed of not more than five representatives of
each interested power. The United States was represented by Baruch, Davis, Hoover, McCormick, and
Robinson.

61. See Schwabe, pp. 192–193, and also n. 112, citing Hoover to Barnes, March 19, 1919, N.A.,
R.G. 256, 103.97/1232A. Cf. Robert Skidelsky, *John Maynard Keynes*, vol. 1, pp. 360–361.

62. Included in the delegation were two of the American financial advisers, Thomas W. Lamont and
Albert Strauss, French minutes, Supreme Economic Council, Fonds Clemenceau, 6N65.

63. Note du Maréchal Foch, February 18, 1919; report of meetings at Spa, March 4 and 5, 1919,
Archives Nationales, F12:8103. Dispatch, Ammission to State Department, March 9, 1919, N.A., R. G.
59, 763 72119 / 4078. Thomas W. Lamont, *Across World Frontiers*, pp. 146–149.

64. Keynes, *Two Memoirs*, pp. 42–52. T. T. Helde, "The Blockade of Germany," pp. 192–196.
Frank M. Surface, *American Food in the World War and Reconstruction Period* (Stanford, 1931), p.
135. A dispatch, Davis to Rathbone, March 8, 1919, explained the complicated situation and suggested
ways to cope with it, Davis papers, box 43. On Germany policy in respect of relief see Schwabe, pp.
193–197.

ministers of the British dominions had just discussed "the very serious conditions in Germany."[65] British military men had been moved by the distress that they found in occupied territory.[66] Charles Webster, an officer on the General Staff and stationed at Paris, drafted a telegram that General Plumer, commander of the British army of occupation, was directed to send from Cologne as his own.[67] This message dramatized the plight of the German civilians and reported that the menace of death by starvation resulted in "great activity by subversive and disorderly elements." Lloyd George felt that conditions inside Germany had reached a state of emergency. Calling in Hoover, he asked why the Germans were not getting food.

The nerves of both men were frayed. The American administrator had been chafing for weeks under obstruction by both British and French officials. His manner had become very brusque.[68] Lloyd George, noting Hoover's "surliness of mien and a preemptoriness of speech that provoked a negative answer to any request," thought that the American "ruffled French susceptibilities by his manner of extracting German money" in payment for American food—money that the French thought rightfully theirs by way of compensation for war damages.[69]

The Americans, noting that Clemenceau attributed the undernourishment of Germany to the failure of the United States Treasury to finance supplies, had no desire to withhold hard German assets from American producers of food so that these assets might be seized by a French government that refused to impose an income tax.[70] Hoover welcomed a chance to release his pent-up feelings in the presence of the prime minister; and Lloyd George, impressed by the facts of the American if not by his manner, asked Hoover to deliver parts of his speech to the Supreme Council.[71]

Hoover did so on March 8, and on that day Lord Robert Cecil presented a plan upon which he and Hoover agreed.[72] To promote this proposal Lloyd George staged a drama before the council. A secretary bustled in with a sealed envelope. Lloyd George opened it and drew out the telegram that General Plumer had been instructed to send from Cologne. Reading the message, he then launched into a torrent of oratory that overrode objections by French spokesmen. He insisted that not only was the honor of the Allies involved, but their security against bolshevism also.

65. Lord Robert Cecil's diary, March 7 and 8, 1919. General Memorandum, no. 11, March 8, 1919, Borden papers, folder OCA 198, P. C. (M. G. 26H, 1b), vol. 152.

66. Sir Henry Wilson to Lloyd George, March 5, 1919, Lloyd George papers, F / 47 / 8 / 6. Headlam-Morley to Kerr, March 5, 1919, Lothian papers, GD 40 / 17 / 72.

67. Webster to the author, October 20, 1959. *F.R., P.P.C.,* vol. 4, p. 286. Webster to the editor of the *Times Literary Supplement,* January 24, 1948.

68. McCormick diary, March 1, 1919.

69. Lloyd George, *The Truth about the Peace Treaties,* pp. 305–306.

70. Minutes, ACTNP, March 7, 1919. Steed memorandum to Northcliffe, March 3, 1919.

71. Hoover wrote (in *The Ordeal of Woodrow Wilson,* p. 164): "Lloyd George demanded to know why I did not send food. . . . Not often do I lose my temper. But this was too much. . . . I immediately regretted this outbreak, apologized for it."

72. "The plan," according to Hoover (*ibid.,* p. 164), "included German payment for food with hire of their ships, acceptable commodities or gold; the immediate transfer of their merchant ships and an undertaking that if they kept the Armistice agreements they would be assured a stipulated monthly quota of food, as far as supplies permitted, until the following August."

Turning in a righteous fury upon Finance Minister Klotz, who seemed to personify the demand of the French treasury for German gold, he excoriated him as a Shylock, and one who would rank with Lenin and Trotsky among those who spread bolshevism in Europe. With a gesture he suggested the image of a miser clutching sacks of gold. Keynes, who thought the performance superb, heard the prime minister threaten half aloud, as he sat down, that if this sort of thing went on, he would order the British troops out of Europe the next day.

House spoke briefly in support of Lloyd George; but Clemenceau persisted in resistance, asking merely for time to bring the French public to a realization of the importance of this matter. When everyone was standing and talking and the session was on the verge of a break-up, Loucheur suggested to House a proposal that the colonel found acceptable and commended to Clemenceau. Rapping for order, the Tiger announced: "Colonel House and the French have come to an agreement so the matter is settled." At the suggestion of House a committee was appointed and soon came back with a text of an understanding. The Germans were now to have official assurance that, on condition that their government acknowledge and undertake to execute their obligation to supply ships under the armistice agreement of January 16, the Associated governments would proceed with revictualing in accord with the plan of the Supreme Economic Council.[73]

The next day it was decided at House's office that Hoover and two other American delegates would go to Brussels to represent the United States in the negotiation of an understanding with Germany. With some thirty delegates of the Allies they met with eight or ten Germans in the Belgian capital on March 13 and 14. It was agreed that Germany was to get a monthly quota of cereals and fats if the world supply permitted, and could export certain commodities in limited amounts. "Every effort will be made," the American financial advisers cabled to the Treasury, "to have Germany pay for food out of proceeds from hire of her merchant ships, from neutral credits, from sale of German cargoes in neutral ports, and from export of commodities from Germany. But none of these resources can be turned into a considerable amount of dollars. Therefore we must make use of German-owned foreign securities and gold."[74] Both the American and the German negotiators came away from Brussels relatively satisfied. According to Schwabe, the results of the Brussels talks encouraged the Germans to offer strong resistance to the presumably harsh terms of the treaty.[75]

While the Brussels agreement was being negotiated, the Americans worked in meetings of the Blockade Council at Paris to lift restrictions on shipments to the territory of Austria-Hungary and also to Poland and to the Baltic states, where the threat of Bolshevism seemed particularly lively.[76] They were successful with respect to German Austria, which the statesmen at Paris were attempting to woo both from

73. *F.R., P.P.C.,* vol. 4, pp. 274–293. Keynes, pp. 54–62. Hoover, pp. 165–170; *Memoirs,* vol. 1, pp. 341–344. House diary, March 8, 1919. Auchincloss diary, March 8 and 10, 1919. Helde, pp. 208–220. Mayer, pp. 509–514.

74. Davis, Strauss, and Lamont to the secretary of state for Rathbone, March 17, 1919, N. Davis papers, box 43. See Samuel G. Shartle, *Spa, Versailles, Munich,* pp. 71–77.

75. Schwabe, p. 209.

76. See below, p. 250.

bolshevism and from political union with Germany.[77] Efforts at relaxations in behalf of the other countries evoked objections which, although they were attributed to military considerations, the Americans thought to be motivated by a desire for an advantage in trading. However, the Americans succeeded on March 20 in freeing Poland from blockade.[78]

During the five subsequent weeks arrangements were made to take over almost the entire fleet of Austria-Hungary and nearly a million tons of German shipping. The vessels were divided among the victors, the United States receiving eleven large passenger vessels on condition that it supply tonnage for relief shipments. After the delay of four months the American relief administration at last had enough vessels so that within ten days it was able to move into Germany some 200,000 tons of victuals that had accumulated in ports of the United States and Europe. When Wilson returned to Paris in March, Hoover persuaded him that half a million tons of additional American ships were required; and the president cabled to Washington to say that it was essential that this tonnage be found, even at the expense of the War Department and "commercial routes which may promise large profits."[79] Eventually more than a million tons of food and medical supplies were delivered.[80]

But still the larger question of Germany's place in the postwar economy of the world was unsolved. The victors hesitated to sheathe their sharpest economic weapon until the enemy signed a treaty of peace. Europeans who had felt the full force of German militarism did not easily accept the American argument that it would always be possible to reimpose the blockade, that indeed if it were relaxed for a time the possibility of its revival would be a greater deterrent to German recalcitrance than was its present enforcement.[81]

Wilson brought up the question on April 23 and again on May 1; but Lloyd George and Clemenceau insisted that the complete raising of the blockade must await the ratification of the treaty. The best course, he thought, was to make the Germans certain that they would get the raw materials needed to put their people to

77. Early in March, Hoover again complained, as he had to Wilson a month earlier, that the Italians were obstructing shipments for the relief of Austria, and he asked Lansing to threaten Sonnino with a cessation of American aid to Italy, Minutes, ACTNP, March 5, 6, and 7, 1919. However, in the Supreme Council, Sonnino continued to resist Hoover's control of the railways to Austria. Afterward, House was "almost uncivil" to Crespi (according to Lord Robert Cecil, who was present at their talk in House's room) in threatening to stop food shipments to Italy if those to Czechoslovakia and Yugoslavia continued to be held up. Cecil thought that the Italians should be coerced into behaving reasonably, and the British joined with the Americans in the Supreme Economic Council in declining to grant favors to Italy, Cecil diary, March 3 and 5, 1919. See Zinojinović, *America, Italy and the Birth of Yugoslavia*, pp. 233–238.

Relief shipments did not become entirely free of obstruction by the Allies. When Hoover informed the president that trainloads of food purchased by Hungarians were being held up at Zagreb by order of a French general, Wilson obtained assurance from Clemenceau that the latter immediately sent a telegram directing the release of the shipment, Hoover to Wilson, March 31, 1919, Wilson to Hoover, April 2, 1919, Wilson papers.

78. McCormick diary, March 12, 15, 17, 19, 20, and 21, 1919. See James A. Huston, "The Allied Blockade of Germany, 1918–1919," 154 ff., 162–163 and footnotes.

79. Wilson to the secretary of state for N. D. Baker and Hurley, March 22, 1919; Hoover to Wilson, April 25, 1919; Wilson to H. M. Robinson, April 28, 1919, Wilson papers.

80. "By the end of August, when deliveries under the Brussels Agreement ended, the total, including 110,000 tons of clothing, was 1,215,000 tons," Arnold-Forster, p. 35. On April 7 the Supreme Economic Council abolished the AMTC and itself assumed direct control of the Transport Executive, J. Arthur Salter, *Allied Shipping Control*, pp. 223–230.

81. Hoover, in Seymour and House (eds.), *What Really Happened at Paris*, p. 344.

work after the conclusion of peace. The break in the blockade, Holborn has written, "was late and not dramatic enough to impress the German people. Thus the poisonous assertion that the Allies had starved innumerable Germans to death by continuing the blockade until after the signing of the peace treaty could go unchallenged in Germany."[82]

Actually, despite repeated efforts by American and British negotiators, the blockade did not end officially until Germany ratified the treaty of peace on July 12.[83]

As the chief American negotiator during Wilson's absence, House had moved far toward finding a basis for a settlement of the four questions that he had proposed to Wilson in mid-February and that the president had appeared to be willing to have tentatively considered.[84] There was substantial agreement on the military and naval terms to be presented to the enemy. In the matter of the boundaries of Germany, those on the east seemed to House to be virtually settled, with Danzig to go to Poland; and it was tentatively proposed that the Rhenish Republic on which French leaders insisted would exist only for a limited time and subject to a plebiscite, while the final delineation of Germany's western frontier was reserved for the judgment of the Supreme Council. Although a formula for relaxing the blockade had been developed, little progress had been made in respect of economic and financial dispositions.[85]

In the course of his conversations with the European leaders House had felt the full force of the national feelings by which they were controlled. Recognizing that Wilsonian principles must make concessions to European political necessity he thought it was best to begin at once in specific instances. To spur the Europeans to immediate action, he dwelt persistently upon the danger of anarchy and bolshevism in central Europe.[86] Facing realities, and preferring to continue to deal with his present associates in the council rather than with intractable men who might succeed them if the nationalistic ardor of the European parliaments was not satisfied in some measure, House used the tactics of good diplomacy. Resourceful and unruffled, he talked in private with the principal negotiators, with an understanding of their real interest and of the welfare of their peoples. He made use of these personal contacts to explore solutions and to recommend them. He spoke little in the formal meetings, indeed continued to be casual in attendance, aware that his work could best be done in reconciling contrary views in private before they clashed in a semipublic forum and took a rigid form. House was, as Shotwell testified, "absolutely invaluable as an aid" in the negotiations in the early days of the Peace Conference.[87]

82. Hajo Holborn, *A History of Modern Germany, 1840–1945,* vol. 3, p. 559.

83. "The American attack on the blockade as a whole did not let up for a moment until the Peace Treaty was signed," Hoover wrote in *The Ordeal of Woodrow Wilson,* p. 178. "All through these efforts we were obliged to seek President Wilson's advice and authority constantly. . . . His concern over the blockade was profound, his prediction of its ugly results accurate. He never spared himself in his efforts to lift it."

84. See above, p. 146.

85. *I.P.,* vol. 4, pp. 356–361. Lloyd George, pp. 284–292.

86. House diary, March 4, 5, 6, and 14, 1919. *I.P.,* vol. 4, pp. 377–380.

87. Shotwell ms., Columbia OHRO. Sir William Wiseman came early every morning to the Crillon to maintain liaison with Balfour and Lloyd George. "I would leave tomorrow but for House," Wiseman cabled to Reading on April 6, Wiseman papers, Y.H.C. House talked frequently with Tardieu.

Unfortunately, at the suggestion of Auchincloss, the colonel gave interviews to newsmen in which he talked so frankly and freely as to endanger his understanding with the president. He gave an account of his activities that played up his initiative and skill in negotiation. Indeed, he went so far as to assert that he had unsuccessfully urged his chief to make greater use of the newsmen at Paris, that Wilson had rendered the peacemaking more difficult by failing to do so, and that the president had a unique faculty for doing the right thing in the hardest way and thus made trouble for himself.[88]

Rumors began to circulate to the effect that the colonel's head had swollen and that he had made concessions in respect of principles that were dear to Wilson. House's criticisms of the president, made in a friendly spirit and heretofore confined to his diary, now circulated among the American journalists and reached men who were critical or possibly envious of the colonel's influence. The intimate relationship that had long bound the two friends and that had been strained even before the opening of the Peace Conference was now in grave jeopardy of breaking.[89]

A humane cause to which House applied his talent was the organization of an International Red Cross. He urged Henry P. Davison of the Morgan firm, chairman of the American Red Cross, to give executive direction to an international conference at Geneva. After bringing Wilson and Davison together at the Crillon, House with Wilson's approval wrote a letter to the Allied premiers in support of Davison's work. He secured a promise from Wiseman to take up the matter with Lloyd George, and used his influence with Clemenceau to elicit enthusiastic support, Auchincloss diary, January 10, 15, 24, February 4, 6, 16, and 17, 1919; *I.P.*, vol. 4, pp. 257–260; House diary, January 4 and 26, 1919; Lloyd George to House, January 21, 1919, Y.H.C.

88. Sweetser's notes on news conferences of February 26, 27, March 5, 1919, Sweetser papers, L.C. While Wilson was away, House conducted some twenty-three briefings of selected American newsmen, J. B. Donnelly, "Promoting the Idea of the League: Arthur Sweetser and American Journalism at the Paris Peace Conference of 1919," a paper read at the AHA meeting on December 28, 1979, p. 7.

89. See Walworth, pp. 262–264.

9

War Debts, Reparations, and Financial Crisis

In his parting talk with Wilson on February 14 House had set down as one of the four essentials to the making of a preliminary peace "a decision on the amount of reparation to be paid and the length of time in which to pay it." This matter, according to one of the Americans who dealt with it, "caused more trouble, contention, hard feeling, and delay . . . than any other point of the Treaty of Versailles."[1]

The question of reparation by Germany for damages inflicted during the war had a vital bearing on the financial stability of all the powers. It affected the capacity of the Allied governments to redeem the loans made to them during the war by the Treasury of the United States.[2] The reparation settlement, moreover, would affect the ability of the defeated nations to pay for food and to revive their trade. The negotiators had for their guidance the principle accepted by Germany and the Allies at the time of the armistice. It had been agreed then that compensation would "be made by Germany for all damage done to the civilian population of the Allies and their property by the aggression of Germany by land, by sea, and from the air."

The vital question was not that of the total bill for damage, which obviously was far beyond the possibility of payment by any of the methods recognized by civilized states, but rather that of what sum could be collected. The answer involved the whole question of the economic treatment of the enemy.

Before 1914 Germany had been both the best customer and the best supplier of most of its neighbors.[3] A failure to provide for the revival of German industry would put the economic life of all Europe in jeopardy. If the German goose were to be plucked and bled ruthlessly as well, the prospect for reparation payments would be dim indeed. The delegates of the Allied powers at Paris would have to weigh contradictory considerations in dealing with this difficult question. They felt that they must build up Germany sufficiently so that she would be capable of producing revenues for her own support and also for the payment of adequate reparations; and on the other hand they feared to permit the Germans to become so strong as to pose a threat of war or of dominance in trade.[4]

---

1. Thomas W. Lamont, "Reparations," in Seymour and House (eds.), *What Really Happened at Paris,* p. 259. Wiseman, at Paris, cabled to Reading, at Washington, on February 2, 1919: "Reparation discussion has caused more friction between us and the Americans than any other question at issue," Wiseman papers, Y.H.C.

2. The amounts of the debts of European governments to the United States is recorded in Walworth, *America's Moment: 1918,* Appendix B. On the debt of France, see Lucien Petit, *Le Règlement des dettes interalliés (1919–1929),* pp. 3–24, 207–215.

3. See Pierre Renouvin, *Les Crises du XXe siècle:* I, *De 1914 à 1929,* p. 199.

4. Thomas W. Lamont, *Across World Frontiers,* p. 109.

With the matter of reparations were entangled fundamental questions of current financing. In some countries lively inflation was already well under way. For the most part the governments of the Continental Allies needed large accessions from the enemy in order to balance their budgets and avert national bankruptcy. The finance ministries, responsible to parliaments that feared to impose larger taxes, made their positions tenable only by refraining from challenging popular expectations for indemnification on a scale that went beyond economic realities. The bitterness of war hatred moved the victorious peoples to demand reparation not only for destruction that in their view was wanton, but even for all the costs that they had borne in waging a war in which they thought themselves put upon. They claimed compensation enough to cover damages to civilians as well as external loans.[5]

Until European industries and commerce could function, the governments could not collect taxes to meet their obligations; and to finance production and marketing, long-term credits were needed. However, the depreciation of currencies made it difficult for manufacturers to buy what was required to put their factories in operation. American bankers regarded most European assets as "frozen," and after the armistice a Federal Reserve restriction prevented the financing of American exporters by long-term notes.[6] The "oil of credit" was gone, and Europeans looked to the United States Treasury for lubrication. The Treasury was able to do little, however. It was limited by accountability to a Congress that was responsive, in turn, to an electorate that desired primarily to have done with foreign loans of doubtful security and to get back to the customary pursuit of trade and profit.

While the nation was at war, four acts of Congress had authorized credits totaling $10 billion to the governments of the Allies for martial purposes. This sum, enough to pay all the expenses of the federal government for the eight years before the war, appeared to be as high as outer space.[7] Less than $2 billion of the $10 billion remained unspent, and it seemed unlikely that Congress would appropriate more. In order to pay for supplies desperately needed, it would be necessary to consider the possibility of postwar loans from the balance of the sum authorized.

There were thoughtful men in Europe who envisioned a common international control of not only the finances but the economic life of the new industrial society that had developed in the years before the war. France's men of affairs were no less resourceful in planning for security against German economic domination than her generals were in insisting on military security. They were not lacking in constructive proposals of great historical significance. Clémentel, the minister of commerce, was convinced that the transition to a peacetime economy required a continuation of the councils by which common burdens and resources had been apportioned during the war.[8] He advocated that the economic affairs of the world be ordered by

5. For a list of economic claims on the part of the Allies, see Margaret Coit, *Mr. Baruch*, p. 260.

6. Albert Demangeon, *Le Déclin de l'Europe*, pp. 40–47. Louis B. Wehle, *Hidden Threads of History*, pp. 70–76. On March 3, 1919, a law was enacted that gave the War Finance Corporation power to make loans to finance exports with adequate security. Extending credits that rested partly on the unknown recuperative power of European industry, this corporation, according to Wehle, its counsel, "lost nothing on all its transactions."

7. Glass to Wilson, December 19, 1918, *F.R.*, *P.P.C.*, vol. 2, p. 544. See Walworth, pp. 245–246.

8. "Intrigues by American exporters," Jean Monnet wrote, "induced the United States government to rob all these [wartime] agreements of their substance; lists of exceptions made the whole organization useless," *Memoirs*, p. 73.

the League of Nations in the common interest and that all nations have equality of opportunity under basic principles. He would remove barriers to trade, while at the same time taking precautions against economic domination.[9] One of the men who had a voice in developing this farsighted proposal was Jean Monnet, then very young, but to be prominent forty years later in the forming of the European Economic Community. He already perceived the importance of looking at the economic problems of the world "as a whole and in the light of the general interests," rather than from the viewpoints of several nations.[10]

At a luncheon in Paris on January 20 the president of the French Senate, Antonin Dubost, applauding Wilson's professed desire for "a new world harmony," suggested that the United States pay a third of the expenses of the war since its beginning in 1914. He conceived that a consortium of powers, neutrals included, should act together to cope with the deficit that weighed upon all of Europe. It seemed to him that the society of nations might be strengthened by its having financial responsibility and a sort of international bank to assess and cash the world's taxes and issue a standard currency for the world.[11]

On the day after Dubost presented his ideas, McCormick found Wilson "considerably exercised"; and the president warned his advisers not to participate in any financial discussions except those having to do with the settlement with the enemy.[12] When the French proposal came to him in writing, he responded with decorous caution.[13] Preoccupied with his prime concern for a viable league of nations, he held himself aloof from the controversial economic aspects of international relations. He was not unaware, however, of the financial leverage that he could use in applying pressure to realize his political goals.[14]

9. Clémentel, *La France et la politique économique interalliés*, pp. 311, 337–348. Doc. handed by Clémentel to McCormick, Jan. 17, 1919, containing a translation of a memorandum for Clemenceau, D. H. Miller papers, L.C., box 89, IV, 21. The plan of the American advisers was for the memorandum to be presented to Lloyd George by Reading, and to Wilson by McCormick, J. F. Dulles pocket diary, January 16 and 17, 1919, Dulles papers, I.F. 1919 folder, Princeton University Library.

For a discussion of Clémentel's plan for a permanent economic bloc and Clemenceau's reaction to it, see Marc Trachtenberg, "Reparations at the Paris Peace Conference," Walter A. McDougall, "Political Economy versus National Sovereignty: French Structures for German Economic Integration after Versailles," and "Comment" by Gordon Wright and Klaus Schwabe. After a study of French and German sources and taking a new perspective, McDougall, viewing Clémentel's plan as an effort to solve France's basic problem—how to live next to a powerful Germany without being reduced to the status of a satellite—points out that the French had no choice but to try for Franco-German economic integration "based on coercive restriction of Germany's political and economic sovereignty."

10. Monnet, p. 83.

11. Memorandum by Dubost, November 15, 1918, enclosed on January 30 with a brief note to Wilson, calling attention to the "capital importance" of the question and expressing a wish that Wilson would have it studied by competent men, Wilson papers.

12. McCormick diary, January 21, 1919.

After listening to Wilson's comment on Dubost's proposal, Edith Benham, Mrs. Wilson's secretary, wrote in a diary letter: "These people seem to regard America and the Americans as legitimate prey to be exploited."

13. Wilson to Dubost, February 5, 1919, Wilson papers. The Americans were equally cool to a formal proposal by Klotz, the French minister of finance, for the creation of a financial section of the League of Nations. Klotz's proposal of January 27 is in the Wilson papers. A copy, with English comments, is in P.R.O., FO/608/242. The economic and financial policy of the French treasury was stated in a letter of January 20 from Klotz to Oscar T. Crosby, Crosby papers, box 5, folder "1919," L.C.

14. Edith Benham, foreseeing "a final test" of the president's political strength and his ability to

Early in January the president asked House to handle this matter as he thought best.[15] On the seventh House had a long talk with Clemenceau. He sympathized with the financial plight of the French government and conceded that an increase of taxes would create almost a state of rebellion in France. But at the same time he deplored what he thought to be foolish suggestions that might prejudice the Americans against the French.[16]

Immediately after the November armistices Oscar T. Crosby, who had represented the United States at London on the Inter-Allied Council on War Purchases and Finance, had pointed out that the continuation of liberal loans by the United States would strengthen the hands of those in political office in Allied capitals, men who advocated a central control of economic life that was foreign to American practice and who in some instances sought credits as protection against labor agitation that might unseat them.[17] At the same time he warned that American acquiescence in a program of loans for general commercial uses would subject the United States to the necessity of developing an opportunistic policy as well as to the risk of inviting invidious comparisons by recipients of the loans. Crosby thought that by using available private assets, purchasers in Allied countries could find means to buy almost all of the materials needed.[18]

Paul Cravath, a Treasury expert who had advised Crosby during the war and had conferred with Keynes and David Hunter Miller during the Allied conference at London on December 2 and 3,[19] wrote a memorandum that was highly regarded by the American delegates at Paris as well as by the government bureaus in Washington. Pointing out that the United States led all other nations in exports to Germany and that it did not make sense to destroy German purchasing power, Cravath urged moderation.

During the war William G. McAdoo, the secretary of the treasury, had guarded against the use of American funds by the Allies for the advancement of their foreign trade.[20] Although he was determined that government loans abroad decrease greatly, he was responsive to pressure from American exporters, and he proposed credits for purchases of goods produced in the United States that could not be financed otherwise. The Treasury had no power to consider or discuss cancellation of foreign loans but would discuss at Washington, with the governments concerned, the conversion of demand obligations to long-term credits. The American delegates were not to deal with loans at the Peace Conference, where the Treasury would not be

force his ideals on the Allies, wrote in a diary letter on January 5, 1919: "They may be too poor to dare to refuse."

15. Auchincloss diary, January 10, 1919. "I telephoned Close [Wilson's secretary]," Auchincloss wrote, "to get him to send all telegrams on economic matters drafted by the president through me and he agreed to do this."

16. *I.P.*, vol. 4, p. 269. "I want to treat the matter sympathetically and generously, but I do not want to see the United States forced into an impossible and unsatisfactory position," House wrote.

17. See Burton I. Kaufman, *Efficiency and Expansion*, p. 23.

18. McAdoo from Crosby, November 13, 1918, *F.R., P.P.C.*, vol. 2, pp. 533–535. Crosby resigned from the government at the beginning of 1919 and published a book that some of his colleagues thought indiscreet: *International War: Its Causes and Its Cure.* "Memorandum, Dec. 21, 1918," Wilson papers. N. H. Davis to Leffingwell, December 2, 1918, "Peace Commission" file, Treasury Department.

19. See Walworth, p. 105.

20. See Kaufman, pp. 195, 197, 236–239. House would have liked to have McAdoo at Paris, but the president, wary of nepotism, did not take advantage of the obvious availability of his son-in-law.

officially represented. McAdoo stated his opposition to the use of American credit "to conciliate rival claims for indemnities and other advantages." He had assured the Congress that the nation's foreign loans "were good and would be collected in due season," and that he was certain that cancellation would not have the approval of the American people, who would thereby incur additional taxation.[21]

Carter Glass, succeeding McAdoo in December 1918, had served in the House on the Banking and Currency Committee and was thoroughly familiar with the one-dimensional thinking of legislators on financial matters. Cabling immediately to the president to express "grave concern" about foreign loans, he received Wilson's assurance that there was "no proper basis" for a discussion of loans at the Peace Conference. Secretary Glass hesitated at first to send an assistant secretary of the Treasury to Paris for fear that this would encourage the Europeans to raise the question of the debt. Instead it was determined that Norman H. Davis, who was already serving as an armistice commissioner, would represent the Treasury. Davis was instructed to avoid discussion of the war loans at Paris.[22] As the weeks passed, the position of the Treasury was stiffened by its current transactions.[23] Davis, strictly bound by the Treasury's policy, warned Wilson against any kind of consortium that might have the effect of giving foreign governments a blank check upon that of the United States.[24] On February 16 Davis sent assurance to Washington that the financial fort was unbreached and the interests of the United States were well protected. He reported success in insisting on the Treasury's position and "warding off numerous requests for advances."[25] Nevertheless, the matter of intergovernment debt cast

---

21 House from McAdoo, *F.R., P.P.C., 1919*, vol. 2, pp. 538–540.

22. See Walworth, pp. 244–247. Dispatch to President from Glass, January 2, 1919, N. H. Davis papers.

Believing that the Food Administration was going too far in regard to credits, the Treasury began to use the benefits of American food relief to assure itself of an equal footing with foreign exchequers, cable, for Davis from Rathbone, January 18, 1918; two cables for Davis from Glass, January 19, Wilson papers; cable for the president from Glass, January 15, *F.R., P.P.C.*, vol. 2, p. 720. For specific instances with respect to Belgium, see Davis from Rathbone, January 18, Wilson papers, and cable for Davis from Rathbone, February 21, 1919, Miller, *My Diary*, Doc. 403.

23. Letter forwarded to Wilson with letter, Davis to Wilson, February 12, 1919, Wilson papers.

24. Baruch was also vigilant, Baruch to Wilson, February 4, 1919, Davis to Wilson, February 2, Wilson to Davis, February 5, 1919, Wilson papers.

In the negotiations on relief Davis had shown ability to get on with the English officials, notably the Chancellor of the Exchequer. In Baruch's opinion he was "a veritable find, faithful and loyal to the president," Baruch to McAdoo, February 13, 1919, McAdoo papers. Cables, Glass to the secretary of state, January 2, 1919, N.A., R.G. 59, 184 / 73A, Glass to Wilson, January 15, 1919, two cables, *loc. cit.*, 763.72119 / P43, 48 and 033.1140 / 170. Cable, the president from Glass, January 6, 1919, Lamont papers, 85–12, Baker Library, Harvard University. Dispatches in *F.R., P.P.C.*, vol. 2, pp. 558–559, 563. J. F. Dulles to E. F. Gay, January 2, 1919, J. F. Dulles papers, II, correspondence, 1919.

Albert Strauss, an assistant secretary of the Treasury, arrived at Paris in January but returned to Washington in March. Seeking another man whose professional standing and patriotism inspired confidence, Glass enlisted the services of Thomas W. Lamont of the house of Morgan, who trusteed his ownership of the *New York Evening Post* in order to avoid suspicion of a conflict of interest and acted as a financial adviser at Paris from February through June, Glass to McAdoo, January 29, 1919, Glass papers, 1, Alderman Library, University of Virginia. Wilson said to Dr. Grayson: "I chose [Lamont] because I wanted him to see at first hand exactly the plans and purposes and manner of the administration's way of doing business. I wanted him to be a partner for reform," Grayson diary, May 24, 1919.

25. Dispatch in "Peace Commission" file, Treasury Department Archives. The negative response of the American Treasury to various British and French proposals for a readjustment of war debts is detailed on pp. 208–210 of Petit. The Treasury even went so far as to inform France that it would not consider

a shadow over the economic negotiations all through the Peace Conference. Failing to get any American concession in respect of war debts or the creation of a *Societé Financière des Nations* to continue the wartime cooperation in economic matters, officials of the Allies were to become the more inclined to make unwise demands upon Germany. In March the French government went so far as to begin talks at Berlin looking toward Franco-German negotiations that might lead to substantial revision of the economic terms of the treaty after it was signed.[26]

On January 21 Wilson agreed to begin to hold conferences with economic counselors at Paris. House presided when the president was too busy to attend, and Secretary Lansing was not one of the group.[27] The advisers' interpretation of Wilson's Point Three, which declared that world trade was to be free "so far as possible" from barriers and inequalities, reflected the interest of their own nation's commerce. Bernard M. Baruch put his faith in natural economic law and believed that the prime objective of every nation must be full employment and prosperous trade. He worked frankly for the commercial interests of his own country.[28] As disdainful of the blockade as Hoover, Baruch arranged for the sale of nitrate to neutrals who would resell to Germany; and his concern for German potash provoked a French protest.[29] He challenged the efforts of a French group to entrench itself in the Romanian oil fields,[30] and it was to him that American distillers, cotton growers, and manufacturers of chemicals looked to discover markets abroad. "The greatest problem of all is coal," he wrote. "The Supreme Economic Council has passed this up [*sic*] to me."[31]

Baruch was fretful in his first weeks at Paris because he found little work of importance.[32] He aroused the distrust of other Americans. His relations with Lamont and Davis became strained; and House gave little attention to him.[33] Baruch made

---

any future advances to any government that was favorable to a repartition of debts. See Étienne Weill-Raynal, *Les Réparations allemandes et la France,* vol. 1, pp. 52–59.

26. See below, p. 304, n. 38.

27. McCormick diary, January 21 and 29, 1919.

28. "We should get busy and build up our export trade," Baruch wrote to McAdoo on February 13, 1919, letter in McAdoo papers, L.C. Coit, pp. 228, 230–235. Watchful to see that the United States did not get any "raw deal," Baruch advocated, when American business became slack in February, that the Commerce Department "spend a lot of money . . . for the establishment in every country in the world of a body of experts who will see that our goods are constantly put before the people." Government agents abroad, he thought, "should pay less attention to afternoon tea parties and more to seeing that our commerce is sold." Every financial assistance should be given to exporters, and American shipping should be brought to the same efficiency as that of competitors. Baruch made recommendations to the president for the stimulation of American commerce, Baruch to Senator Charles S. Thomas, February 13, 1919, Baruch papers, Princeton University Library. See Jordan A. Schwartz, *The Speculator,* pp. 107, 135–136.

29. Tardieu to House, March 25, 1919, Y.H.C.

30. See above, p. 103.

31. Baruch to Garfield, March 18, 1919, Baruch papers, XV, pt. 2. See Schwartz, pp. 136–137.

32. Baruch, *The Making of the Reparations and Economic Sections of the Treaty,* p. 89. In February the president provided funds for a staff for Baruch, who brought over eight or ten of the "boys" of the War Industries Board, including Frank W. Taussig, chairman of the U.S. Tariff Commission, Coit, p. 228. "It looks to me as though Baruch was setting up a separate organization," cable, Polk to Auchincloss, March 20, 1919, Y.H.C.

33. See Schwartz, p. 120. Auchincloss diary, January 27, February 27, March 20, 1919. Miller, vol.

it clear in meetings of the Supreme War Council that the wartime controls of raw materials that the Allies wished to perpetuate could not have American approval without specific action by the Congress. He believed that American business opinion "very properly" opposed extension of joint controls beyond the end of the war, and he advocated a prompt restoration of private initiative. "We have been pounding pretty hard all along the line," he wrote to Senator Charles S. Thomas on February 13, "trying to open up the commerce of the world, excepting that which will benefit Germany."[34] Unfortunately, Baruch's fervid pleas for an ideal world for trade appeared to some Europeans, as his biographer has written, as "an exercise of economic supremacy."[35]

The State Department received from the president, on the last day of February, notice that in Washington a committee had been formed, consisting of one representative from each of certain bureaus of the government, to consider matters of foreign trade.[36] The department was instructed by Secretary Lansing on March 17 to facilitate trade that had been developed in central Europe, and especially in states that had been recognized. Consulates were to be opened and passports issued to responsible businessmen.[37] Although wartime controls over commercial financial dealings had not been entirely abandoned, Wilson wrote to Senator Robert Owen on January 27: "It is the policy of the secretary of the Treasury to withdraw all control over private transactions just as rapidly as conditions seem to warrant and the restrictions of foreign exchange and banking are being relaxed accordingly. They cannot, I should judge, with safety be discontinued altogether nor can our control of the export of gold and silver be abandoned so long as we are supplying foodstuffs to devasted European countries on credit."[38]

It was advantageous not only to the commerce of the United States, but also to the security of its war loans, that the exactions of the peace treaty should not be

---

1, February 17, 1919. Polk diary, March 12, 1919, Beer diary, February 7, 1919. Beer wrote: "Baruch is suspicious and asks for reservations on all points."

In retrospect Lamont wrote charitably about Baruch, describing him as "a roving ambassador" who "made himself useful in almost every direction and showed . . . capacity for handling problems and persons . . . , a great favorite of the president," who "commanded his complete confidence," *Across World Frontiers,* p. 174.

As Wilson's confidant Baruch inevitably came into conflict with Colonel House. See below, p. 300, and Baruch, *The Public Years,* p. 95. When Baruch became disgruntled and talked of going home, Dulles explained in a letter to his wife that this was "because he can't stand anything less than being at the top." letter of February 1, 1919, J. F. Dulles papers, Box 503. On Baruch's dictatorial manner and undiplomatic bearing, see Grant, *Bernard M. Baruch,* pp. 185–187.

34. Baruch to Charles S. Thomas, February 13, 1919, Baruch papers, Princeton University Library.

35. Schwartz, p. 131.

36. Wilson to State Department, February 28, 1919, N.A., R.G. 59, 110.7/ 112.

Lamont advised against the sending of delegates from the U.S. Chamber of Commerce to Paris, but cabled in February: "If Bedford [of the Standard Oil Co. of N.J.] and two or three others like him having sagacity and international repute were to come . . . in about a month as individuals I think they would find the trip of advantage to American and International interests." Lamont recommended contact with the British and promised to cooperate, cable, Lamont to Stettinius, February 14, 1919, Lamont papers, 165–29. See R. H. Tawney, "The Abolition of Economic Controls, 1918–1921," 1–30.

37. Dispatch, Lansing to the secretary of state, March 17, 1919, Wilson papers.

38. Wilson to Senator Owen, January 27, 1919, Wilson papers.

crippling to the German economy. Although the American government did not claim any indemnity to be paid to it directly by Germany, the huge debt due to its Treasury from the Allied governments gave to the American peacemakers an indirect interest in keeping the German economy healthy enough to permit payments to America's debtors that would enhance their solvency.

The men who spoke for the Allies, however, had a more immediate interest. Lloyd George and Clemenceau could not hope to hold their political mandates if they did not insist that Germany pay the costs of the war to whatever extent was possible. On the one hand Lloyd George was advised by John Maynard Keynes that the enemy's capacity to pay was $10 billion at the most, while on the other hand a committee of conservatives set a far larger amount. The prime minister cannily refrained from commitment to either view and had an exponent of each at hand to advise him at the Peace Conference. He was accountable to a House of Commons of which a majority had promised the electorate more compensation than it was prudent, or indeed possible, to extract.[39] On December 24 the Imperial War Cabinet decided that the national policy at the Peace Conference would be "to endeavor to secure from Germany the greatest possible indemnity she can pay consistently with the economic well-being of the British Empire and the peace of the world, and without involving an army of occupation to collect."[40] Lloyd George warned the cabinet that the question of indemnities was the only one on which they would meet hard resistance from Wilson; and actually the president, reading in the ship's newspaper on his voyage to Europe that the prime minister had said that Britain would demand an enormous indemnity, exclaimed bitterly: "Not if I can prevent it!" He explained that he would oppose the levying of compensation beyond the amount of actual damage, which he thought should be determined scientifically.[41]

Optimistic statements of British electioneers were in sympathy with false hopes across the Channel. The citizens of France had not forgotten that in 1871 a victorious Germany had exacted an indemnity that then seemed huge. Publicists were shouting for as large a payment as possible, with little effort to distinguish between restitution for damages and indemnity for all costs of war.[42] During the five years ending in 1918 the debt of the French government had increased from 31.5 billion francs to 170 billion francs. Ribot had suggested in the French Senate on December 17 that the situation could not be met by taxation. He argued that since France had suffered greater losses in men and productive capacity than the other Allies in western Europe, it would be strict justice, and not generosity, to give France priority in

    39. Philip M. Burnett, *Reparation at the Paris Peace Conference from the Standpoint of the American Delegation*, vol. 1, pp. 10–13. Keynes, *The Economic Consequences of the Peace*, pp. 139–147. Tillman, *Anglo-American Relations*, pp. 230–232. Minutes, I.W.C., December 24, 1918. *The Collected Writings of John Maynard Keynes*, ed. Elizabeth Johnson, vol. 16, pp. 336–383. Robert E. Bunselmeyer, *The Cost of the War 1914–1919: British Economic War Aims and the Origins of Reparation*, pp. 171–178. Skidelsky, *John Maynard Keynes*, vol. 1, pp. 355–357.
    40. Minutes, I.W.C., December 24 and 31, 1919.
    41. Bullitt diary, January 9, 1919, Benham diary letter, December 8, 1918.
    42. Noble, *Policies and Opinions at Paris, 1919*, pp. 191–192, Tardieu, *The Truth about the Treaty*, pp. 281–284. "Finance Minister Klotz, addressing the French Chamber on December 3, 1918, referred to Clemenceau's earlier statement that 'the most terrible of accounts between peoples' had been opened," Noble, p. 192.

indemnification, and to pool the expenses of the war if Germany's resources could not cover them.[43] However, Davis told the American commission that in his opinion French taxes could be increased threefold, since the country was more prosperous than before the war and a large volume of payments was flowing to the French people in support of the American troops in France.[44]

To satisfy the electorate, French politicians advocated policies that would impair Germany's capacity for large ultimate payments.[45] Arguing that the enemy must assume the cost of occupation of the Rhineland, they proposed measures that would restrict the industrial productivity upon which Germany's ability to pay depended. French officials sought to use the early renewals of the armistice to strip the enemy of hard assets that were needed to support the German currency, set factories in motion, and pay for the food and raw materials required to combat unemployment and prevent a desperate resort to bolshevism. Moreover, they advocated policies that would impair Germany's capacity for large ultimate payments.[46] Wilson was warned by Pershing that Foch was using the American occupying army to further French purposes that were political and economic rather than military.[47]

The American delegates were certain that the proposals of immoderate French officials for extracting wealth immediately from the enemy were born of desperation and were not to the ultimate advantage either of France or of all Europe. It was their opinion that to demand more than restoration for actual damages resulting from the war would result in an assessment that Germany could not possibly bear, and moreover such a demand would be inconsistent with the terms under which the enemy had signed an armistice and, therefore, without warrant. They were aware that Germany was already paying in several ways: by maintaining armed forces of the victors on German soil; by making transfers of wealth of various kinds to the Allies under the armistice; and by surrendering colonies, shipping, and overseas markets. The American experts agreed in denying the legitimacy of a principle that theretofore had been accepted by the states of the world but had been invalidated by the development of an industrial complex in western Europe: the unlimited right of the victor to impose a punitive indemnity upon the vanquished.

In January discussions on the question of reparation went on among the experts and at a distance from the president. On the sixth House, perceiving the gulf between American thinking and the demands of the Allied peoples, told his fellow members of the American peace commission that they were going to encounter financial

---

43. *Journal Officiel*, pp. 829 ff. See N. H. Davis, "Peace Conference Notes," R. S. Baker papers, and Petit, pp. 20–24.

44. Minutes, ACTNP, January 6, 1919.

45. France had a budget of about 22 billion francs against about 8 billion from taxation. "It was difficult for a government to remain in power which failed to meet the issue by increasing taxes to cover the budget, and on the other hand it was difficult to remain in power by doing so," Davis, "Peace Conference Notes," July 5, 1919.

46. For example, the French demanded that Germany be required to deliver amounts of coal and potash that would far exceed France's present needs. "France would become an exporter of coal, which did not arouse any enthusiasm on the part of the British. The French subsequently came down," notes by C. K. Leith, March 1919.

47. "Extract from report re [Inter-Allied Armistice] Committee on Finance, Economics, and Industry," enclosed with letter of January 25, 1919, Pershing to Wilson, Wilson papers.

controversies at every turn of the peace negotiations, and therefore "might as well
. . . have a show-down" with the delegates of the Allies. He thought it wise to
ascertain how much the enemy could pay within a reasonable time, and then let the
Allies settle among themselves what part of the proceeds each would receive. House
was disappointed that Germany's liability had not been set at a sum that the bankers
of the world would underwrite.[48]

On January 25, after a brief discussion in which Wilson suggested that this complex question could not be brought under a general rule or separated from territorial
settlements, the Supreme Council set up a Commission on the Reparation of Damages (CRD) to deal with the issue.[49] It appointed three subcommittees to consider
how much the enemy should pay; how much they could pay; and by what method,
in what form, at what time, and under what guarantees payment should be made.[50]

In the meetings of the first of the three subcommittees the Americans filed a
statement asserting that under the terms of the armistice there should be compensation only for "direct physical damage to property of non-military character and
direct physical injury to civilians."[51] They argued that to include war costs in the
bill would not only violate the prearmistice agreement, but would inflict upon Germany a liability that it could not possibly discharge. When the full CRD met for the
first time in the salon of the French Ministry of Finance and the European majority
proceeded to work its will, the Americans protested and obtained some concessions
to their views.[52] However, the basic division of opinion persisted. At a conference
of the American economic advisers with their peace commissioners on February 11,
they affirmed the national policy that indirect war costs should not be included in
the claim for reparation, and a definite sum should be set that would be within
Germany's capacity to pay within a limited period of years. All looked to the president, who was not present at this meeting, for the definitive interpretation of the
word "reparation."[53]

48. House diary, January 6, February 6, 1919.

49. *F.R., P.P.C.*, vol. 3, p. 701.

50. Three delegates from each large power sat upon the Commission on the Reparation of Damages
(CRD) with two delegates from each of seven small states. The representatives of the United States were
Baruch, Davis, and McCormick. Thomas W. Lamont was alternate, and John Foster Dulles legal coun-
sel. (Dulles—ambitious, industrious, and competent—had succeeded in establishing himself in a pivotol
position, in liaison with both the independent economic advisers and the specialists of the Inquiry,
Dulles, letters to his wife, box 503, Dulles papers, Princeton University Library. See above, p. 21n.)
The Supreme Council rejected a proposal by Secretary Lansing that Brazil be given a seat on the CRD,
F.R., P.P.C., vol. 4, p. 84. Finance Minister Klotz was elected chairman—a post that Baruch and
McCormick did not want for an American because they feared that the chairman would be blamed for
the disappointing settlement that was inevitable, McCormick diary, January 30, 1919, Y.H.C. The
Americans wanted a fourth subcommittee, on "principles," but their colleagues on the CRD would
agree only to submit this suggestion to the full peace conference (*ibid.*, February 4, 1919), and nothing
came of it.

51. On the question of reparations see Baruch, *The Public Years*, pp. 99–109.

52. Miller, *My Diary*, vol. 1, February 3, 1919. "We blocked them on the secretariat as well as the
sub-committee. . . . We put over two English-speaking secretaries and one French and one Italian so
the minutes could not be misinterpreted. They are all playing for big stakes—billions—and want to
control the machinery of the commission," McCormick diary, February 3 and 4, 1919.

53. At the meeting of February 11 consideration was given to the question of using the assets of
German citizens in the United States toward reparation, minutes, ACTNP, February 11, 1919.

When Wilson departed from Paris in mid-February and there had been no ruling on this question, the conflict of opinion between America and French delegates approached a crisis. It seemed to McCormick that the opposition was "playing politics for home consumption and claiming the earth." On February 15 Klotz made what McCormick thought a "vicious speech," ignoring the prearmistice agreement and appealing to the reservation stated in the armistice convention: "any subsequent concessions and claims by the Allies and the United States remain unaffected."[54] The French minister argued that this clause permitted the victors to demand indemnification for the full cost of the war. Rebuffed in their efforts to get American assent to the plan of Clémentel for economic integration in Europe, French negotiators wanted Germany to sign an agreement that would be of the nature of a blank check. The Americans, however, foresaw that unless at least maximum and minimum amounts were set, Germany would not know how to make arrangements to pay and would never address itself vigorously to its responsibility. Some French nationalists jumped to the conclusion that any American objection to severe terms indicated prejudice in favor of Germany at the expense of France.

The American delegates now resorted to the recourses of diplomacy. After Wilson had gone, House joined with Balfour in a plan to detour the impasse. On February 16 the foreign secretary undertook to advise conservative Lord Sumner of the British financial delegation to adjourn discussion of principles by the commission on reparation.[55] On the next day House similarly instructed Lamont; and the American economic advisers persuaded their Italian colleagues as well as the Belgians, whom they had invited twice to luncheon, to agree to refer the whole matter of principles back to the Supreme Council. They managed to avoid a formal vote, which their bitterest opponent, Hughes of Australia, tried to force because it would show the Americans to be in a minority.[56] On February 19, after an exposition of the American position by John Foster Dulles that in spite of its eloquence failed to change any minds, and after the commission resolved in a "first reading" that the victors were entitled to *reparation intégrale,* the Americans persuaded their colleagues to agree that the question be placed once again before the chiefs of the great powers.[57]

The American experts prepared a message to Wilson, giving a full report of the divergent views and seeking instruction as to whether they should persist in their contentions. They showed a draft of their dispatch first to Lansing, and then to House, who, feeling that he and Balfour had the matter well in hand, gave approval without enthusiasm.[58] The message asked for a statement from Wilson that would help to defend the American position.

54. See Walworth, p. 68.

55. House diary, February 16, 1919; Auchincloss diary, February 17, 1919. "The reparation commission," Auchincloss recorded, "are having a terrible struggle over the adoption of these principles."

56. Lloyd George, at London, gave his support by telephone to the demand of Hughes for reimbursement for the cost of the war, letter, Kerr to Hankey, February 16, 1919, Lloyd George papers, F / 89 / 2 / 18.

57. McCormick diary, February 14, 15, 17, 18, and 19, 1919. Lamont, "Reparations," p. 263. Baruch, p. 25.

58. Baruch, *Making,* pp. 25–26. McCormick diary, February 19, 1919. Dispatch for the president from Lansing, House, Baruch, Davis, McCormick, n.d., Wilson papers. The arguments of the American

The president's reply upheld his men emphatically. "I feel," he said, "that we are in honor bound to decline to agree to the inclusion of war costs in the reparation demanded. The time to think of this was before the conditions of peace were communicated to the enemy originally. We should dissent and dissent publicly if necessary not on the ground of the intrinsic injustice of it but on the ground that it is clearly inconsistent with what we deliberately led the enemy to expect and can not now honorably alter simply because we have the power."[59] This statement, Keynes wrote later, was "the authentic voice of the president in the plenitude of his power."[60]

On the day on which this dispatch reached Paris, House asked Miller whether the United States, in signing the peace treaty, would become responsible for the collection of whatever indemnity it stipulated. Advised that a moral but not a legal responsibility would devolve upon the American government, House cabled again to Wilson: "It now seems possible that we shall arrive at a solution of the reparation matter which we can accept without abandoning the principle accepted by Germany and the Allies at the time of the Armistice. In the event, however, that this principle is seriously threatened with repudiation by the Allies, it may be wise for us to intimate that, as we do not wish to impair in any respect the agreement between the Associated Governments and Germany at the time of the Armistice, we would prefer to withdraw from any participation in any recovery from Germany except to the extent of our own claims for reparation which we can satisfy out of the funds in the hands of the Alien Property Custodian. If this intimation is given it may be that the Allies will reconsider their position."[61]

No reply came from Wilson, and House continued to negotiate. He advised that the settlement be hedged with safeguards so that in no event would the United States be bound, either morally or legally, to take part in enforcing payment. "The talks I have been giving Tardieu and to the English and the French have caused them to pause," House recorded. "I do this in the gentlest and friendliest way possible, but . . . from past experience they know that I will not hesitate to act if the occasion demands it. . . . I thought the British were as crazy as the French but they seem only half crazy, which still leaves them a good heavy margin of lunacy." The Americans serving on the joint committee after a long discussion agreed on a total assessment of $30 billion.[62] The British were not in agreement among themselves

and British delegates, as summarized in this dispatch and in a paper addressed to Balfour by Sumner on February 20 (Balfour papers, 49749) were: the Americans contended that damage can be legally claimed only for breaches of established law or of contract; the Germans had broken only certain rules of war in individual cases, and since making war was not in itself an illegal act, it could not be a cause of action for damages; the acceptance of the Fourteen Points by Germany was a contract which, not mentioning the costs of war, excluded any right to claim them. The British answered that the victor had a right to impose "just" terms, and that it was just to make the vanquished pay costs that had been inflicted by an aggressive war taken as a whole; and that the armistice contract, preliminary and not exclusive of what it did not include, was supplementary to the "general right" of the victors. They argued that general principles of justice enunciated by Wilson justified the claim of the associated powers for restoration as nearly as possible to the condition that existed before the war.

59. Wireless from the *George Washington* to Ammission, February 24, 1919, Y.H.C.

60. "America at the Peace Conference."

61. Miller, vol. 1, p. 135. Cable, House to Wilson, February 24, 1919, *I.P.*, vol. 4, p. 349. At least one of the British delegates, Lord Sumner, was aware of an American threat to withdraw and thought it "a bluff," Sumner to Balfour, February 20, 1919, cited above.

62. McCormick diary, February 23, 25, and 26, 1919. McCormick discussed with his American colleagues the possibility of making concessions.

and seemed to be seeking a compromise with the position of the United States.

It was the desire of House that, before the president's return to Paris, the financial experts arrive at a comprehensive understanding that would deal with the vexing question of intergovernment debt. Apparently he communicated his desire to Wiseman in a way that suggested a possibility of American concessions; for Lloyd George was informed through Kerr that America would agree to cancel the debt if the matter was handled properly, though it would never agree to it if the British attempted "any kind of hold-up."[63] Kerr advised Lloyd George that they should not agree on a total of reparation until they knew Britain's share and until the United States indicated what it would do about war debts. It seemed to him unfair to expect the British to let off the Germans and the Continental Allies unless Great Britain was equally liberated from its obligations to the United States. Actually there was pressure upon the Americans not only to ease the burden on the debtor nations, but to make new loans to meet current needs.[64]

In spite of the awkward entanglement of the question of reparation for damages with the settlement of war debts and the lifting of the blockade, House succeeded in guiding proceedings so as to avoid any break in the essential negotiations. At one point he optimistically told himself that the postponement that had been effected by referral of the matter to the Supreme Council might be extended until the question of reparation "would die a natural death."[65] Vigilant to prevent the hardening of the American and British positions into irreconcilable forms, he instructed the American delegates not to press for a conclusion. But actually the day of decision could not be averted much longer.[66]

Lunching with Lloyd George on March 6, House reached what he described as "a fairly complete understanding." Afterward he wrote in his diary: "Lloyd George was especially interested in the question of reparations and said if I would help him out in this direction, he would be extremely grateful. He wanted the amount named to be large, even if Germany would never pay it, or even if it had to be reduced later. He said he did not want to let the Conservatives 'throw him' on a question of such popular concern. . . . It always amuses me to have George say in his naïve way that he has done this or that or the other for political effect, but that he really knew better."[67] Actually, House's own tactics in dealing with the prime minister

C. K. Leith, recording that Lamont used the figure of 30 billion as a basis for trading, stated in a report that it was twice the amount specified by his experts and too much to be collectible. According to Leith, the amount to be specified depended on a judgment as to what pressure could be put upon Germany, especially in regard to export trade—"the great resource for payment." "Until Mr. Lamont came in," Leith wrote, "the meetings of the general reparation committee were of the most casual nature," Leith's notes, pp. 4–5.

63. Memoranda, Kerr to Lloyd George, February 28, March 2, 1919, Lloyd George papers, F / 89 / 2 / 35 and 37.

64. On March 5 Italy was granted an American credit of $25 million, France one of $100 million, dispatch for Davis from Rathbone, March 10, 1919, N.A., R.G. 59, 102.1 / 1849j. In approving these and other credits to Continental countries Wilson counseled secrecy; and Glass, agreeing, expressed eagerness that such advances be made dependent upon the fulfillment of certain international agreements, Glass to Wilson, March 1, 1919, Wilson papers.

65. Burnett, vol. 1, pp. 27–28, 34, 36, 51, 53. House diary, March 1, 1919.

66. Kerr to prime minister, March 1, 1919, Lothian papers, GD40 / 1236.

67. On March 4 House wrote: "He [Lloyd George] does not seem to have any ingrown sense of right

were not entirely ingenuous. "I always lead him on," the colonel wrote in his diary, "and let him feel that I am innocent of his motives and that he apparently succeeds in accomplishing his purposes with me."[68]

The next day House proposed to Lloyd George and Clemenceau that financial experts of their countries join in seeking a fundamental understanding in respect of debt.[69] When Davis, reporting House's proposal to the Treasury, asked consideration of a credit to the British Exchequer of perhaps half of an amount to be loaned by it to France, he received an immediate reply. Secretary Glass showed deep concern in respect of loans to governments which, in his view, were endeavoring to escape repayment of advances already made to them. Apparently without consultation with the American negotiators at Paris, Glass sent a stiff note to the governments of France and Italy:

"I have . . . to state most emphatically that the Treasury, which, as you are aware, is clothed by the Congress with full authority to deal with foreign loans which it has made, will not assent to any discussion at the peace conference, or elsewhere, of any plan . . . for release, consolidation, or reapportionment of the obligations of foreign governments held by the United States. . . . The Treasury cannot contemplate continuance of advances to any allied government which is lending its support to any plan which would create uncertainty as to its due repayment of advances made to it by the U.S. Treasury.[70]

In a conference of House with Clemenceau and Lloyd George on March 10 it was decided to limit consideration of reparations to a very few minds meeting in strictest confidence. (Secrecy seemed to be necessary, House recorded in his diary, for fear that "Clemenceau would get in trouble with Klotz . . . and Lloyd George with his financial advisers.") They appointed an informal committee of three men known for their moderation and asked them to report in three days after reviewing Germany's capacity to pay.[71]

According to the record of Davis, the American member, the committee found itself "practically in accord." His British and French associates, however, recognizing the political difficulty that existed, demurred at giving so low an estimate to the premiers. Therefore, on March 14, the day of Wilson's return to Paris, it was Davis who gave the committee's report to the three chiefs in Mrs. House's sitting room. When Davis left the meeting, he thought that there was a "tacit understanding" that they "would proceed to work out a solution on a sane, constructive basis along the line proposed by the experts." It seemed that Clemenceau and Lloyd George were convinced that it was best to face up to the facts and agree upon reasonable figures.[72]

or wrong, but only looks at things from the standpoint of expediency . . . with all his faults, he is by birth, instinct, and upbringing, a liberal," House diary, March 4 and 6, 1919, Y.H.C.

68. *Ibid.*, May 29, 1919. Bonsal, *Suitors and Suppliants*, pp. 255–256. Cf. below, pp. 327–328.

69. *I.P.*, vol. 4, pp. 357–359. House, with Clemenceau's aid, explained that "it was useless to skim the surface and patch up bad situations from time to time."

70. Petit, pp. 539–540, Rathbone to de Billy, March 8, 1919, Davis from Rathbone, March 3, 1919, Davis to Glass, March 6, 1919, "Peace Commission" file. Davis from Rathbone, March 4, 1919, Glass to Davis, March 8, 1919, "Cables—sent Treasury Representatives (Treasury Series)," Treasury Department files. Davis from Glass, March 4, 1919, N.A., R.G. 59, 102.1/ 1780.

71. House diary, March 10, 1919. Burnett, vol. 1, pp. 52–54.

72. Burnett, vol. 1, pp. 53–55.

House, perceiving that more pressure must be put upon Lloyd George to commit him to a solution that would be politically unpalatable, suggested to Balfour that "the wise thing to do would be to tell the British public that Germany was bankrupt" and that it would be well to take what it could actually pay or what was in sight.[73] To this proposal Lloyd George was not unresponsive. Lunching with Davis on March 22, he seemed to accept a proposal by Keynes of a total payment of nearly $25 billion. He said, however, that agreement on this reduced sum would be of no avail unless his conservative counselors could be persuaded to agree.[74] He expressed a hope that the American advisers would help to persuade them.

While the question of reparations was being considered, a currency crisis had arisen. On February 24 Klotz came with Pichon to the Crillon in distress. They said that unless the British government provided France with some sterling exchange almost immediately there would be a serious break in the franc. The next day Klotz came again with Tardieu and others and asked House to intervene at once in order to get a few million pounds of exchange to avert disaster until the Chancellor of the Exchequer could come to Paris for a conference. Promising to do what he could, the colonel sent an urgent message to Lloyd George and obtained a promise of £2 million to tide over the French treasury for a week. House reported his action to Wilson immediately and received the president's approval of what he had done.[75]

The crisis exposed the fragility of national credits and the importance of American participation in measures to strengthen them. In coming to the relief of the French government when its balance at London approached zero, the Chancellor of the Exchequer explained that he could not make a durable arrangement with France without at the same time getting support for the British pound from the American Treasury. The Treasury could not help without action by the Congress. The British cabinet, however, sanctioned the emergency loan to France without consulting Parliament, and in so doing decided that the chancellor should press the United States for support for the pound. The chancellor went to Paris to present the British case, and Lloyd George wrote to House to ask why dollars would not be as helpful to

73. "I thought it wise to inform him [Balfour] so that he might advise Lloyd George in the direction I think he should go." House gave the same advice to Wiseman. House diary, March 16 and 17, 1919.

74. "Lloyd George appointed these men [Cunliffe and Sumner] when he had great flights in regard to this matter and now he cannot control them. Montagu and Keynes agree with our people, but George believes he will be crucified at home if his original experts are not also brought down to reasonable figures," House diary, March 24, 1919.

75. Cables, House to Wilson, February 26, 1919, Wilson to House, February 28, 1919, Y.H.C. Auchincloss's diary gives a detailed account of the day of crisis, February 25. He reported to Polk that the French were "terribly grateful" to House, diary February 25 and 27, 1919, Y.H.C.

The crisis had developed after Keynes had insisted on the suspension of Great Britain's wartime monthly subsidies to France, Curzon to Derby, February 21, 1919, Curzon papers, mss. Eur. F 112 / 302. Keynes advised the French government to allow its currency to go to its natural level. French officials admitted that a revision of their system of taxation and a reduction of the volume of their currency would be beneficial, but considered these measures beyond their province, dispatch, Davis for Rathbone, February 22, 1919, N.A., R.G. 59, 851.51 / 118.

In order to remain in office Klotz thought it necessary in mid-March to tell the French Chamber that resort would not be had to the heavy taxation that he had threatened a few weeks before until everything possible was taken from Germany by way of indemnity. The Chamber supported the finance minister with 240 yeas, 108 nays, and 146 abstentions, Sharp to the secretary of state, March 17, 1919, N.A., R.G. 256, doc. 851.00 / 69.

France as pounds sterling.[76] But early in March, Secretary Glass notified the French government that there would be no more advances from Washington if the French transfer of dollars to London was not stopped or at least greatly reduced.[77]

The attitude of the Treasury brought a prompt and protesting response from the British foreign secretary. On March 12 Balfour notified Reading, who had returned to the British embassy at Washington for a limited time,[78] that unless the United States Treasury continued the present system of "dollar reimbursement" until it could be conveniently ended, the transactions already entered into for the benefit of France must be closed, with a resulting stoppage of food shipments that would be "disastrous." Balfour informed Reading that he had told Davis of "the very painful impression" that had been made by an apparent attempt of the Treasury to force the Exchequer to make further loans to France and Italy by threats of withholding dollars due to Great Britain under previous arrangements. The tone of a letter that the Treasury had written to Reading in respect of dollar reimbursements to France was characterized by Balfour as "inadmissible."[79]

This altercation was not conductive to successful negotiation of the question of reparation. Davis explained the position of the Treasury as best he could. He told Klotz that it was unwise to press for more American advances and at the same time for reapportionment of the war debts. He reported to the Treasury that at a conference with House, Klotz, and the British Chancellor of the Exchequer, there was tentative acceptance of the general principle that French difficulties could not be solved until France helped itself by freeing trade and using private resources.[80]

At the same time Davis joined with his American colleagues in dispatching a long message of protest to the Treasury. Reporting that the chancellor had been irritated greatly by the communication that Balfour thought "inadmissible," they gave the opinion that negotiations would go smoothly at Paris if those conducting them had advance notice of offensive effusions on the part of officials at Washington. Moreover, they expressed an earnest desire to maintain the closest of relations with the British officials, whom they found "most satisfactorily cooperative," and they wished to prevent any serious financial crisis in France. Having been informed by Keynes that Great Britain's financial difficulty was wholly a matter of avoiding an increase in its unfavorable balance of trade, and that about $125 million were needed to pull it through irrespective of any additional help that it might give to

76. Minutes, B.W.C. "Message from the prime minister to Col. House," February 25, 1919, enclosed with a letter from Kerr, Y.H.C.

77. Petit, p. 533.

78. Wiseman was asked by the American peacemakers at Paris, who did not enjoy negotiating with Reading, not to encourage his return to Washington. Great Britain was to be left without an ambassador at Washington. See Walworth, p. 223, n. 48. Auchincloss diary, January 5, 12, 13, and 23, 1919. Wiseman diary, January 19 and 21, 1919.

79. "Am perfectly willing to enter discussion of whole situation," Balfour stated. "We cannot possibly make more concessions regarding loans to Allies, which necessitates additional loans from United States to us. We have already done more than can possibly be required of us. . . . I am not prepared to continue . . . to interpose British credits between United States advances and real ultimate recipient," telegrams, Balfour to Reading, March 11 and 12, 1919, Wiseman papers, Y.H.C.

80. Davis to Rathbone, March 10, 1919, "Peace Commission" file, Treasury Department. The "financial embarrassment" of the French government was explained by Davis in "Peace Conference Notes, July 5, 1919," Davis papers.

France, they recommended a credit of $150 million for Great Britain. They explained that they had repeatedly told Italian and French officials that the Congress had given no one power to discuss war debts and that any proposals should be presented at Washington rather than at Paris. This, however, had not prevented French newspapers from creating the impression that negotiations at Paris were possible, and the matter was mentioned in a debate in the French Chamber. The American financial experts reported that they were fighting off French efforts to induce the United States Treasury to finance food shipments to Germany and to stabilize exchange by making indefinite and uncontrolled advances.[81]

The Treasury replied with instructions for the maintenance of its position, particularly with respect to the controversy over German payments for food, which was at its height at this time. The resources that Germany possessed should be used for American food rather than for indemnities. To attempt to get a huge indemnity from Germany and then take measures to make payments impossible would create an awkward situation. It was important to have an understanding with the British as to the use of indemnities to pay war debts. The officials at Washington advised a clear and direct statement of American policy, regardless of foreign "susceptibilities."

From the beginning the Treasury's representatives at Paris had been warning of the danger of fixing a reparation charge so high that the enemy would give up and challenge the Allies to come in and collect what they could. The Germans were allowing the mark to depreciate; the French, thinking this a deliberate attempt to avoid payments, were now urging the seizure of all of Germany's silver and gold; the British were opposing so radical a step; and the Americans were divided in opinion.[82]

French partisans thought it unfair for Americans to demand Germany's hard assets in payment for shipments that would relieve the United States of an embarrassing surplus of products. Moreover, the British found it difficult to suggest a solution until they knew what the United States would do by way of participating in a general financial settlement that might stabilize conditions. Constricted as they were by the national outlook of their Congress and Treasury, and with little understanding of the actual problems of the Weimar government, the Americans were able to offer no adequate proposals to revive the economy of Germany.[83]

81. Digest of cable, Davis, Lamont, and Strauss to Rathbone; cable, Davis, Lamont, and Strauss to Glass, March 12, 1919, "Peace Commission" file, Treasury Department. A cable to Davis from Rathbone dated March 26 gave information that the Treasury had been authorized, as a military measure until peace was proclaimed, to establish credits for cobelligerents, but only for purchase of American goods, and up to the limit of the unexpended $1.5 billion left over from the wartime appropriation of $10 billion.
Rathbone approved a suggestion by Davis that it be arranged with Czechoslovakia, Romania, and Serbia that all advances made to these countries to purchase food in the United States should have a first claim on reparations received by them, with advances to them by the Allied governments to rank *pari passu*, cables, Davis to Rathbone, March 18, 1919, Davis from Rathbone, March 26, 1919, "Peace Commission" file, Treasury Department.
82. Arthur Salter, *Memoirs of a Public Servant*, pp. 155–156, Lamont, Davis, and Strauss to Rathbone, March 13, 1919, "Peace Commission" file, Treasury Department.
83. Schwabe, *Woodrow Wilson, Revolutionary Germany, and Peacemaking*, p. 247. Lamont to Leffingwell, March 29, 1919, Lamont papers, 165–168, Baker Library, Harvard University. The constriction that Lamont noted was not relieved when the Ways and Means Committee of the House of Representatives refused a request by the Treasury to extend credit, during the year after peace was

In all of the give-and-take on financial matters during the president's absence, the American delegates had little guidance from their chief other than his enunciation of principle. When he returned to Paris, his men were asking whether the imposition of terms too severe might not impel the enemy to refuse them and thus command the sympathy of world opinion. Perhaps they might even be driven into the arms of the Bolshevists. Wilson suggested in the Supreme Council that the Weimar government, not necessarily better than the Imperial regime that preceded it, was weaker and lacking in credit and might be replaced by a government with which it would be impossible to negotiate. He understood the political pressure brought upon his European colleagues by the wartime psychosis of their peoples, and at the same time he must be responsive to manifestations of economic nationalism at Washington.[84] Thus the domestic politics of the democratic nations complicated the task of international diplomacy.

signed, to cover the interest due on obligations of the Allies, dispatch, Davis from Rathbone, April 7, 1919, Wilson papers.

"A magnanimous financial policy was essential," Keynes wrote. "The financial position of France and Italy was so bad that it was impossible to make them listen to reason on the subject of the German Indemnity, unless one could at the same time point out some alternative mode of escape from their troubles," *Economic Consequences of the Peace,* p. 150 and n.

84. Davis wrote to Newton D. Baker on September 8, 1926, as follows: "You can imagine what would have happened in this country if he had come back with the Peace Treaty and an announcement that, in order to get it, he had agreed to recommend a cancellation of debts. . . . President Wilson was opposed to mixing the debts with German reparations, and I felt as he did about that," letter in N. H. Davis papers, box 2.

10

Defense of the Covenant

During Wilson's absence from Europe and while the mood of the people he had wooed there turned from optimism to bewilderment and impatience, Charles Seymour viewed the situation in historical perspective. "Unless the United States undertakes the burden of helping to keep peace over here," he wrote, "another war is inevitable, and the past three years prove that we are vitally concerned in any European war. . . . What people at home seem to fail to realize is that the war has brought Europe, and with her the world, to the very brink of complete demoralization; you can't realize it until you come here and read the telegrams from Central Europe. It is far worse than after any war of recent or even medieval history because of the interdependence of nations at the beginning of the twentieth century."[1]

When Wilson returned to America, however, he found that he had to contend with more than general ignorance of the extremity of Europe's plight. The president was obliged under the Constitution to be in Washington to pass upon legislation enacted during the final days of the old Congress before it adjourned on March 4. There was danger of a fatal clash between Wilson and his Republican adversaries, and in particular with Henry Cabot Lodge, who would be chairman of the Foreign Relations Committee of the incoming Congress.[2]

In a discussion of domestic politics on the first day of 1919 Wilson and House had agreed that their cause would be hurt if the president acceded to the Republican desire that he call an extra session of the new Congress.[3] But they differed upon an aspect of strategy that was vital. Wilson showed a belligerent determination to veto any legislation that his adversaries might propose. House, on the contrary, advised that the president say in a magnanimous way that he would leave the Republicans free to carry out the mandate that they had received from the voters in the congressional election of 1918. Thus, the colonel reasoned, the opposition would receive a large share of the blame that was, in his opinion, sure to be heaped upon men in a position of responsibility. Observing that Wilson found it hard to give up the extraordinary power that had come to him out of the necessity of winning the war, House doubted that he would act on the advice given. Actually, the president was not eager to hold out olive branches to those who questioned the practical validity of the doctrine upon which he based his leadership and power. It was hard, he wrote

---

1. Seymour, *Letters from the Paris Peace Conference*, pp. 179–180. Reprinted with the permission of the Yale University Press.

2. "Events had long since precluded even the possibility of Lodge and Wilson listening to one another," W. C. Widenor, *Henry Cabot Lodge and the Search for an American Foreign Policy*, p. 299.

3. House diary, January 1, 1919. "The Republicans, of course, want an extra session for two reasons: first, in order to get the offices when they reorganize the House and Senate; and secondly, to be in session so they can embarrass the president. Since Roosevelt died, every Republican senator thinks he is a presidential possibility, and therefore arises to give his views on every subject. On the Democratic side, we have no organization," letter, Polk to Lansing, March 3, 1919, Y.H.C.

to Secretary Josephus Daniels from Paris, to tell from a distance "how far the malicious partisan attacks that are constantly being made reflect any considerable body of public opinion."[4] From his pulpit in the White House he hoped to test the sentiment of his national constituency.

House undertook from Paris to placate Wilson's political adversaries as well as to build confidence in his peace program among Americans. He gave a summary of the tentative draft of the League Covenant to two officials of the League to Enforce Peace, so that these men and the League might help.[5] On the last day of January, House asked Polk, at Washington, to make liaison with the committees of the Congress that were concerned with foreign affairs, to tell them what was happening at Paris and, after ascertaining what perplexed them, to report to the peace commission; but in reply Polk gave the opinion that only a statement from the president in person would satisfy the legislators.[6] House was particularly solicitous of the good will of ex-President William Howard Taft, who declared publicly that Wilson was justified in going to Paris and that the Senate should not retaliate because it was ignored.[7]

The president's return to Washington had been planned before the Peace Conference opened.[8] Tumulty, the faithful secretary who was guarding Wilson's political fences, had urged a triumphant homecoming celebration. Pointing out that the president had not been in Boston for six years, he suggested that he now carry the impending battle into the land of the archenemy, Senator Lodge of Massachusetts.[9] Wilson demurred; but House suggested that an enthusiastic popular reception at Boston would make a good impression in Europe.[10] The president reluctantly agreed to go there. House drafted a message for Lodge that he persuaded Henry White to sign and send, explaining that Wilson was landing at Boston because the mayor had been begging him for more than a year to come to that city. Lodge was assured that Wilson had no intention, when leaving Paris, of making a speech at Boston or elsewhere before meeting members of the Congress. While Wilson was at sea, however, he accepted an invitation to speak at Mechanics Hall, at the same time explaining to Tumulty that he was thinking "of the impression on the hill" and that

---

4. Baker, *American Chronicle,* p. 384. Letter, Wilson to Daniels, January 31, 1919, transcribed from Swem's notebook, Princeton University Library.

5. Auchincloss diary, January 31, February 8 and 10, 1919. Miller, *My Diary,* vol. 1, p. 124, entry of February 16, 1919.

6. Auchincloss diary, January 31, February 8 and 10, 1919.

7. On February 8 House took pains to send Taft "heartiest congratulations" on the "admirable work" being done by the League to Enforce Peace, Auchincloss diary, February 8, 1919. There were 3,500 delegates present at a meeting at Atlantic City of the league, over which Taft presided. Wilson was informed that they would uphold him, W. H. Short to Wilson, February 9, 1919. On Taft's contributions to the cause of the League of Nations see George and George, *Woodrow Wilson and Colonel House,* pp. 233–234.

8. "Confidentially . . . plan here is to leave for home about the 15th Feb.," cable, Grayson to Tumulty, January 7, 1919, Wilson papers.

9. Tumulty to Wilson, January 1, 1919. Wilson papers. Cable, Grayson to Tumulty, January 23, 1919, Tumulty papers.

10. House diary, February 14, 1919. House advised that Wilson's remarks in Boston should be confined to generalities and a full report should be reserved for the legislators at Washington who were responsible for foreign affairs, House to Wilson, February 20, 1919.

he wished to make the whole country realize that he knew his immediate duty was to get to Washington.[11]

Actually, on February 24 in Boston, the president spoke at greater length than he had intended. He responded to a rousing display of patriotic fervor. Exuding evangelical optimism, he glorified the role of the United States in the world and exulted in its interest in dispensing justice for all men. He even went so far as to suggest that any questioning of his grand vision would be regarded by him as selfish and provincial and would stir his fighting blood in a way that would give him pleasure. In the seats the audience found copies of the new international Convenant, which had not yet been formally presented to the senators who would have to act upon it.

This performance in the bailiwick of Lodge and in his absence—a performance that was the outcome of Wilson's reluctant acceptance of advice from House and Tumulty did not warm the heart of the senator from Massachusetts. Lodge agreed with the diplomats of Europe in thinking that peace should be established before a league of nations was considered.[12] Having respected a request from Paris that the Covenant be not discussed until the president could explain it to members of the Congress, Lodge felt that Wilson had not played fairly, that his head had been turned by the adulation of European crowds, and that he was championing the Covenant in order to advance his own political interest.[13] Some political observers among the journalists also questioned the disinterestedness of the prophet. Frank H. Simonds, for example, a respected correspondent of the *New York Times*, denounced Wilson as "a repudiated but extraordinarily astute politician" who hoped to make political capital by presenting the League to the American people as a triumph for their ideals without committing their government to anything in particular and without mentioning military and financial costs.[14]

With his critics circulating such interpretations of his position, Wilson went on to Washington with his zeal for his great cause unabated. Finding there the same panicky dread of bolshevism that had haunted the sessions at Paris, he told his cabinet that if a league of nations was not established, Europe would be swallowed up by revolutionaries. He asserted that scarcely a nation on the Continent trusted its government and that the people of all countries had confidence in the United States. He explained that in the drafting of the Covenant he had required that its terms be not in violation of the American Constitution.[15] He learned at his first meeting with the cabinet, however, that it would be difficult to get further appropriations to sup-

11. Wilson to Tumulty, two dispatches, February 22, 1919; Wilson to Tumulty, February 23, 1919; Tumulty papers, box 6. Auchincloss diary, February 19, 1919.

12. On Lodge's internationalism and his priorities, see Widenor, pp. 296–298.

13. Garraty, *Henry Cabot Lodge*, p. 351; Cobb to House, January 9, 1919, Y.H.C. Lodge thought Wilson's draft of the Covenant "not only loose, ill-drawn, full of questions about which the signatories will be disputing within a twelfth-month, but . . . a breeder of misunderstandings if not of wars," letters, Lodge to his cousin John T. Morse, Jr., December 25, 1918, and February 20, 1919, Massachusetts Historical Society.

14. Lloyd George was apprised of this criticism, draft report, Kerr to Lloyd George, February 21, 1919, Lothian muniments, GD40 / 1227 and 1228.

15. Diary of Charles S. Hamlin, February 26, 1919, L.C. Letter, Polk to Lansing, March 3, 1919, Y.H.C.

port the American peace mission at Paris after July 1.[16]

Public opinion in the United States, as it appeared to the British embassy at Washington, was not greatly concerned by the prospect of the entry of the country into an international order. Though inclined to support the ideal of a league of nations and to welcome it as a safeguard against war, the people felt no necessity for an international guarantee of their safety. Some looked upon the Covenant as subversive of the time-honored Monroe Doctrine and a potential cause of entanglement in future wars that otherwise might pass the nation by. While Taft, rising above a personal dislike of Wilson, toured the country to champion a league of nations, other Republicans were reluctant to support a program that might enhance their enemy's stature in the eyes of the electorate. The Democrats, despite the defection of Irish and German elements, were content to follow their chief but unable to provide effective leadership in the Congress. Nevertheless, in the opinion of British observers, no popular opposition had yet developed that the president would be unable to overcome.[17]

During the fortnight that Wilson passed in the United States, in the course of which he had to deal with many urgent domestic issues, he made three particular efforts to win Americans to his cause.

Before leaving Paris, though doubtful that he could influence the vote of dissenting legislators by meeting with them, he had been persuaded by House to invite members of the congressional committees on foreign affairs to dine with him in order that he might go over the league Covenant, article by article, before it became the subject of debate in the Congress.[18] Accordingly, thirty-four men came to the White House on the evening of February 26; and after a dinner that certain senators found unsatisfying to their tastes in liquor and cigars,[19] the president sat down with them in the East Room, reported on his work at Paris, and answered questions. No official statement was issued afterward, and legislators interviewed by the press failed to agree on what happened.[20] Salt was rubbed into the wound of Lodge's pride when Edith Wilson, sitting next to him at dinner, expressed enthusiasm for the warm reception that had been given to her husband in the home city of the senator.

Wilson made a second effort at conciliation at a luncheon with members of the Democratic National Committee on February 28. Only a few hours earlier Lodge,

16. "Cabinet: President discussed League of Nations and Peace Conference. Told him no money for Peace Mission after July 1. Told me to apply to Congress for $5 million dollars, as Secretary Lansing had indicated. I did so, but Senators Martin and Sherley both said it was hopeless to try," Polk diary, February 25, 1919, Y.H.C.

17. Cable, Reading to Wiseman, February 21, 1919. Also see cable "from a reliable source in New York," March 10, 1919, and comments on it, Wiseman papers, Y.H.C.

18. Telegram for Tumulty from the president, February 14, 1919, Auchincloss diary, Y.H.C.

19. Chandler Anderson's diary, March 10, 1919, L.C.

20. Republican Senator Brandegee told a friend that the president had no copy of the Covenant at hand and showed dense ignorance, Anderson diary, March 13, 1919.

To Republican congressman John J. Rogers it seemed that Wilson, though determined that the Covenant should remain "unchanged in the slightest degree," had never appeared "so human and so attractive," memorandum by Rogers, n.d., Henry White papers, Special Collections, Columbia University Library.

who conceived his prime duty to be "to keep the Republican Party in the Senate together,"[21] had addressed that body in criticism of the Covenant. He warned that one should give deep thought to all the implications of so sharp a change of foreign policy. Were the American people really prepared to undertake the obligation implicit in Article Ten, to guarantee the political integrity and independence of all member states? Did they actually intend, by agreeing to submit international disputes to decisions by an international league, to forfeit their right to control immigration into the United States? Suggesting amendments that would safeguard national prerogatives, he took up the Covenant article by article, praising some and questioning others. He had, he said, "no intention of opposing a blank negative to propositions which concern the peace of the world." His reasoned argument challenged proponents of the league to justify many of its aspects.

Lodge's remarks were not wholly free from touches of sarcasm;[22] and these doubtless served to fan the ire that was rising in Wilson against all who threatened the international structure that was being erected with great travail at Paris. In any event the president talked to the Democratic committeemen not in the language of academic reason, but as a chief of tribal warriors. The League of Nations, he asserted, was "the heart of the treaty . . . the only machinery . . . the only solid basis of masonry" in it. He had declared himself, he said, "perfectly willing . . . to stump the country" to see whether the people would respond; but he could not truthfully say that they would, because he did not know. He asked the men of the national committee to get in touch with the state committees, secure their endorsement for the League, and persuade them to make contact with local Republican organizations and urge them to follow the leadership of Taft.[23]

The full extent of congressional dissent became apparent on the night of March 2, when Lodge managed adroitly to introduce on the floor of the Senate a declaration signed by thirty-seven Republicans. This number was more than enough to vote down ratification of a peace treaty. They declared that American negotiations should "be directed to the utmost expedition of the urgent business of negotiating terms of peace with Germany . . . and that the proposal for a league of nations . . . should be then taken up for careful consideration." The Senate adjourned *sine die*, failing to approve vital appropriations and thus making it necessary that it be convened again before July 1, despite an announcement by the president that it would not be called into an extra session.

Having taken pains to discuss the peace treaty with political leaders—first with members of the Congress who held key positions and then with Democratic

21. Lodge to Beveridge, March 21, 1919, quoted in Garraty, p. 356.
22. Garraty, p. 353. "I do not believe," Lodge wrote to Bryce on March 4, 1919, "that the president thought out in the least all that the proposed League of Nations involves, judging by the conversation [at the White House]," letter in Bryce papers, V. 7, p. 170, Bodleian Library. For Lodge's views in respect of a league of nations, see Widenor, pp. 315–320.
23. Democratic National Committee, February 28, 1919, Swem transcription, Princeton University Library. Polk diary, February 28, 1919, Y.H.C.
Breckinridge Long of the State Department was asked to confer with Tumulty to see what he could work out as desirable "in the way of systematic discussion, and instruction of public opinion as to the real facts and the real purpose and character of the proposed league," Wilson to B. Long, February 26, 1919, Long papers, box 62.

politicians[24]—Wilson made a third effort in behalf of his cause. He decided that he must again go to the people, as he had in the greatest triumphs of his career, in order to whip their representatives into line.

The opportunity to make a beginning was at hand. He was to speak at the Metropolitan Opera House in New York on the eve of sailing for France. Tumulty advised that Taft also address this meeting, and the president jotted on the proposal: "All right, if Taft can be got."[25] When the ex-president accepted the invitation, Wilson telegraphed to him to express pleasure.[26]

Taft, returning from an arduous speaking tour in behalf of the League, walked out on the platform at New York arm in arm with Wilson on the evening of March 3. In an introductory speech he refuted many of the objections to the Covenant. "If the president insists, as we hope he will," Taft said, "that the League be incorporated in the Peace Treaty and brings it back, then the responsibility for postponing the peace is with the body that refuses to ratify it."[27]

Wilson then flung down the gauntlet before his adversaries. His face turned angry and his voice hardened as he said:

When that treaty comes back gentlemen on this side will find the Covenant not only in it, but so many threads of the treaty tied to the Covenant that you cannot dissect the Covenant from the treaty without destroying the whole vital structure. The structure of peace will not be vital without the League of Nations, and no man is going to bring back a cadaver with him.

This was not the posture of conciliation and instruction that House had urged. Opponents in the Senate interpreted the president's remarks as a threat to cram the Covenant down their throats by giving them, as an alternative to compliance, only the prospect of rejecting the entire treaty of peace. Thus, in the view of at least one senator, the president appeared to supply his opponents with a weapon more formidable than any of their own fashioning.[28]

Actually, although he dreaded any renegotiation of the Covenant at Paris and rebelled against any appearance of surrendering authority to political adversaries,[29] Wilson was not insensitive to the damage to his cause that could result from action on his part that might seem precipitate. He responded with some circumspection to a proposal from House that the League should be organized at once. The colonel reported that he had the approval of Balfour and Lord Robert Cecil for a plan under

24. In addition to meeting with the National Committee, Wilson made himself accessible to suggestions from other influential Democrats, Wilson to T. J. Walsh, February 26, 1919, Wilson papers.

25. Tumulty to Wilson, February 26, 1919, Tumulty papers, box 6. Wilson had gone so far as to write to Taft to acknowledge his great service to the cause of the League of Nations, Wilson to Taft, February 26, 1919, Wilson papers. "Taft . . . appears more prominently and vigorously every day as President Wilson's champion," *Springfield Republican*, January 6, 1919.

26. Wilson to Tumulty, February 28, 1919, Wilson papers.

27. E. B. Wilson, *My Memoir*, p. 242. *New York Times*, March 4, 1919, L.C.

28. Thomas, *Silhouettes of Charles S. Thomas* (Caldwell, Idaho, 1959), p. 200.

29. R. S. Baker recorded on March 8: "The president is a good hater, and how he hates those obstructing senators at Washington. He is inclined now to stand by the Covenant word for word as drawn, accepting no amendments, so that the 37 of the round robin will have no chance of saying afterward: 'Well, we forced the amendments, didn't we?' " ms. for *American Chronicle*, R. S. Baker papers, II, box 167.

which the members of the League of Nations Commission would act provisionally as the executive body of the League and make recommendations to the Supreme Council on such matters as were referred to them. House wished to explain the Covenant to delegates of neutral nations and to promise them invitations to membership in the League. But just before leaving Washington, the president sent to House this cautious reply, in which he cast doubt upon the very tactics that he affirmed publicly at New York the next day:

Your plan about starting the League of Nations to functioning at once disturbs me a little because I fear that some advantage would be given to the critics on this side of the water if they thought we were trying in that way to forestall action by the Senate and commit the country in some practical way from which it would be impossible to withdraw. If the plans you have in mind can be carried out with the explicit and public understanding that we are merely using this machinery provisionally and with no purpose of forfeiting any subsequent action, perhaps this danger would disappear. The people of the United States are undoubtedly in favor of the League of Nations by an overwhelming majority. I can say this with perfect confidence, but there are many forces, particularly those prejudiced against Great Britain, which are exercising a considerable influence against it, and you ought to have that constantly in mind in everything you do.[30]

Even before the cautioning message came from Wilson, talks with Miller and Wiseman had convinced House that nothing could be done before the president's return. He notified Wilson to this effect and promised to work meanwhile to "shepherd the neutrals into the fold."[31]

It was now apparent that the entire peace settlement would be in danger of rejection by the Senate unless the Covenant could be so amended that its threats to American sovereignty could be mitigated. In his speech at New York, Taft favored a specific reservation in respect of the Monroe Doctrine and remarked that construc tive proposals of other amendments could be found in Lodge's address in the Senate. Senator Gilbert Hitchcock, chairman of the Committee on Foreign Relations, discussed the question with Republican Senator Knox and gave guidance to the president in the form of definite recommendations, one of them for safeguarding the Monroe Doctrine.[32] Hitchcock encouraged Wilson to believe that some of the thirty-seven dissenting senators actually would vote for the Covenant if it became a part of the peace treaty, and that still more would support it if the changes specified were made. At this time most of the large newspapers, Republican and independent

30. Cable, House to Wilson, February 27, 1919; telegram, Wilson for House, March 3, 1919, 3:00 P.M., Y.H.C.

31. Miller, vol. 1, pp. 143–144, entry of February 28, 1919. Auchincloss diary, February 28, 1919.

32. Hitchcock to Wilson, March 4, 1919, Tumulty papers, box 5. The amendments suggested were: "First, a reservation to each high contracting party of its exclusive control over domestic subjects. Second, a reservation of the Monroe Doctrine. Third, some provision by which a member of the League can, on proper notice, withdraw from membership. Fourth, the settlement of the ambiguity in Article 15. Fifth, the insertion on the next to the last line of first paragraph of Article 8, after the word 'adopted,' of the words, 'by the several governments.' Sixth, the definite assurance that it is optional with a nation to accept or reject the burdens of a mandatory."

Even before receiving the advice of Taft and Senator Hitchcock, Wilson was inclined to raise the question of the Monroe Doctrine when he returned to Paris, letter, Wilson to Samuel McCall, February 28, 1919, in the possession of Margaretta Miller MacDonald.

as well as Democratic, were not in opposition; nor were the governors of the states.[33]

The adversaries in the Congress, however, had been neither placated by the White House dinner nor cowed by Wilson's public lashing. Lord Reading, surveying the scene from the British embassy and perceiving that Republican senators were playing politics, was distressed by the angry anti-British sentiment of Americans of Irish blood. He lamented that Wilson had added fuel to the fire by stating that American drafts of the Covenant were set aside in favor of a British version. It seemed that the opposition to the League had "to some extent taken an anti-British aspect," that in particular there were objections to the fact that the Covenant as it stood gave several votes in the League's assembly to the British Empire and only one to the United States. Although Reading cabled that the bitterness at Washington was still intense, he reported on the day of Wilson's return to Paris, that serious objection to the peace treaty was improbable.[34]

Wilson returned to Europe fully aware of the difficulty of commanding support on both sides of the Atlantic for his program of peace. Ready now to respond to popular sentiment in Europe, he volunteered to visit the war-ravaged areas to which he had gone belatedly and unwillingly during his first sojourn in France. In order to make a demonstration of his sympathy, he informed House that he would disembark at Antwerp, go thence to Brussels, and so "through the devastated regions" to Paris,[35] unless such a schedule would cause a conflict with the plans of Lloyd George. To this House replied that the British prime minister thought it essential for the president to reach Paris as soon as possible, since Lloyd George would have to return to England within a fortnight to face a Labour crisis. "If you arrive in Paris by the 13th or 14th," House cabled on March 1, "we both believe it may be possible to settle preliminary terms with Germany by the 23rd and name a day [House had April 2 in mind] for the assembling of the Congress [of peace]."

The president therefore decided to land at Brest, and House went there on March 13 to meet the *George Washington* and to give an account of his exercise of the authority Wilson had conferred upon him. The president's mind was filled with suspicion that the Europeans had "put over" something on House. Quite possibly he recalled that House's advice that he land at Boston had served only to irritate Lodge; and he frankly complained that the White House dinner suggested by House had failed as a measure of conciliation.[36] Moreover, it seemed that House, in his impatience with the delay that invited chaos, had impaired the president's position in negotiating with the Europeans.[37]

33. Cables, Reading to Wiseman, March 2, 7, and 10, 1919, Y.H.C.

34. Cables, Reading to Wiseman, March 7, 11, and 16, 1919, Wiseman papers, Y.H.C.

35. Wilson to House, February 28, 1919. A suggestion that Wilson follow this route was cabled to the president by McCormick with House's approval on February 26, 1919. The State Department inquired whether the Netherlands would object if the president sailed up the Scheldt without stopping, and the reply was that the queen would not be pleased unless Wilson stopped for at least twenty-four hours, N.A., R.G. 59, 033.1140 / 226 and 226a.

The president made a second trip to the devastated region of France on March 23. See E. B. Wilson, p. 252, and Cary T. Grayson, "Memories of Woodrow Wilson," pp. 66–76.

36. House diary, February 14, 1919.

37. The writings of Lansing and Baruch reveal a lack of appreciation of House. See Lansing, *The Peace Negotiations*, pp. 73, 154, 160–161, 210–211, private memoranda, January 1, 1919. Baruch wrote that during Wilson's absence the colonel "gradually became intoxicated by power," Baruch, *The*

Conferring with the president on the overnight trip to Paris, in the evening and again after breakfast,[38] House appraised his chief of the most important developments of the past month. According to the records of Mrs. Wilson and Baker, the president spoke acrimoniously about a lack of emphasis on the League of Nations in recent sessions of the Peace Conference. Later Wilson told his wife with bitterness, according to her record, that he would have to work to restore the League to the prominence that House's weakness had caused it to lose.[39] Apparently he had forgotten that House, who had reserved a place for the League, *"inter alia,"* in the final settlement,[40] and who had told newsmen that he favored placing a live issue like the Italian-Yugoslav dispute before the international body immediately in order to give it prestige,[41] had in fact recommended to the president that the League begin to function at once.[42] It was Wilson who had advised that they go slowly in view of the political opposition at Washington.[43]

Neither House nor Auchincloss made a diary record of any censure by the president. The bond of long and successful association, already strained by House's nepotism and by his indiscreet remarks to newsmen, was worn thinner but not yet entirely broken.

Public Years, pp. 95, 141–144. See also C. T. Grayson, "The Colonel's Folly and the President's Distress," 99–100.

Dr. Grayson accepted the view of his good friend Baruch and informed McAdoo that House was physically unequal to his task, letter of March 4, 1919, McAdoo papers.

Herbert Bayard Swope, whom Baruch described as his "most intimate friend and most trusted confidant" *(The Public Years,* p. 80) and who was president of the association of American journalists at Paris, took a walk at Brest with House and Auchincloss while they awaited the landing of Wilson. Shortly thereafter Swope joined the presidential party when it boarded the train for Paris. He is reported by one who was present to have said that in the peace negotiations of the past month Admiral Benson had shown a stiffness of backbone that was lacking in other delegates of the United States, Bonham diary letter, March 14, 1919. The allusion appears to have been unmistakable, and may well have been confirmed by specific criticism by Swope of Colonel House similar to that uttered by Frank I. Cobb, Swope's colleague on the *New York World.* See Walworth, *America's Moment: 1918,* p. 263. Cf. E. J. Kahn, *Swope,* p. 226. Swope's assertiveness moved Polk to comment to Auchincloss: "He will not be happy until you make him a delegate," dispatch, Auchincloss diary, January 19, 1919.

House's defense against criticism that he thought maliciously circulated by Baruch and others may be found in an article by Charles Seymour, "End of a Friendship," pp. 5 ff.

38. Grayson diary, March 13 and 14, 1919. House diary, March 14, 1919.

39. E. B. Wilson, p. 246. Baker, *American Chronicle,* p. 392. See Walworth, *Woodrow Wilson,* vol. 2, p. 281.

40. See above, p. 149.

41. Sweetser's notes, February 27, 1919.

42. "The president was misled by someone and was obviously disturbed. . . . somebody fed him with further accounts of the 'conspiracy' to separate the Covenant from the German Treaty, along with accusations against Colonel House," Hoover, *The Ordeal of Woodrow Wilson,* p. 189.

According to Steed, House "wished to conclude the main points of a general treaty as quickly as possible, to set up a working league of nations in some form and to let it cooperate in making the final peace," Steed, *Through Thirty Years,* vol. 2, p. 289.

House denied the existence of a plot against the league in a letter to Seymour of July 3, 1922, Y.H.C. Hankey made what he called "a very careful investigation of facts" and reported to Balfour: "You and Colonel House were moved solely by a desire to accelerate the making of the Treaty. It is equally true that at every stage you kept in closest touch with Colonel House and that it never entered your mind to circumvent President Wilson, or to undo any of the work that had been done, while he was at Paris," Hankey to Balfour, July 10, 1922, Balfour papers, 49704. On the question of House's "disloyalty," see George and George, p. 242, and Bonsal, *Unfinished Business,* pp. 302–304.

43. See above, p. 187.

Despite House's enthusiasm for an active League of Nations, a strong tide of European opinion was rapidly carrying the ark of the Covenant toward oblivion. Politicians and publicists had fixed the attention of the Allied peoples on the necessity for quick demobilization, huge indemnification, secure frontiers, and order in eastern Europe. Meanwhile, the vision of an ideal association of nations inevitably grew dim. Only the leader of the country that was now the world's most powerful and was relatively disinterested might have enough force to arrest the drift of opinion.

In contrast with Wilson's triumphal arrival three months earlier, however, his second entry into Paris in mid-March evoked little response from the people when he was driven to the "hôtel" of Prince Roland Bonaparte in the Place des États-Unis. Less commodious and less comfortable than the Murat Palace, the new residence was supplied gratuitously at the insistence of Clemenceau and was staffed with French servants who were to become suspect as spies.[44] The president could look out upon the park where a statue of Washington and Lafayette symbolized the debt of the American colonies to France. The apartments of Lloyd George and Balfour were across a narrow street.

Wilson no longer had the warm support of journals of the Left.[45] The French were alarmed by the prospect that the United States in the twentieth century would not be bound by ancient ties. The possibility of rejection of the treaty at Washington became the "ghost at all the feasts."[46] Indeed Foreign Minister Pichon had warnings from Washington of this dire possibility.[47] Expressing the prevailing French opinion to American newsmen, Pichon said that the principle of a league, but not the entire constitution, might be included in the preliminaries of peace.[48] This remark was reported in Paris editions of American newspapers and stirred excitement in Washington.[49]

At first Wilson was inclined to issue a denial; but he was persuaded by Baker to assert affirmatively, so that the press reception would be better, that he stood upon the Peace Conference resolution of January 26, making the Covenant an integral part of the general treaty of peace. The resulting news release, quoting that resolu-

44. Grayson diary, March 14, 1919. See below, p. 292, n. 73.

45. See Miquel, *La Paix de Versailles et l'opinion publique française,* pp. 62–214.

46. Nicolson, *Peacemaking,* p. 108. Max Weygand, *Memoires,* p. 28. On French awareness of the opposition to Wilson in the United States, see Miquel, pp. 45n and 204. American citizens appeared at Paris to speak for the Republican party, avowing its eagerness to defeat the league and accede to the desires of the Allied nations, Miller, vol. 1, March 11, 1919, Steed's memorandum to Northcliffe, March 5, 1919.

47. Renouvin, *Les Crises du XXE siècle:* I, *De 1914 à 1929,* p. 207. According to Renouvin, three warnings received from the French embassy at Washington in February and March 1919 were not put before the French Chamber.

Lloyd George received, through an intermediary, three American letters critical of Wilson's ideas as to the League. Two of these were from Senator Lodge and one from Democratic Senator Thomas. The letters were written to Moreton Frewen, uncle of Winston Churchill, who forwarded them to Lloyd George on March 7, 1919, with an explanation that Lodge was not opposed to a league of nations as such, Frewen papers, box 52, L.C.

48. Noble, *Policies and Opinions at Paris, 1919,* pp. 128–129. Ms. of *American Chronicle,* Baker papers, L.C., II, box 167.

49. Cable, Reading to Wiseman, March 19, 1919, Y.H.C.

tion, asserted that it was "of final force."[50] Very soon a telephone call came from Pichon, giving assurance that the remarks to newsmen had been entirely misunderstood and misinterpreted and that, as a matter of fact, he had never desired to be recorded as believing that the League of Nations constitution could be deferred.[51]

The necessity of making the Covenant acceptable to the Senate, which was understood not only by the American delegates at Paris but by those of other nations as well, required Wilson to seek concessions from the European negotiators with whom he had covenanted. Before reconvening the commission by which the Covenant of February 14 had been drafted, Wilson and House considered suggestions for amendment from many Americans, including the six of Senator Hitchcock.[52] Lodge debated the question publicly at Boston with President Lowell of Harvard, and the next day the State Department forwarded to Paris, at Lowell's request, a suggestion of three amendments. These would safeguard the Monroe Doctrine, provide for withdrawal of a member nation after ten years, and except domestic issues. Lowell thought that such amendments would enable Lodge to "back down." Polk, forwarding a report of the Boston debate to Paris, expressed agreement with a statement by Lowell to the effect that if such amendments were not provided at the Peace Conference, public opinion would probably support the making of reservations by the Senate, and this would put the president in a humiliating position.[53]

Taft cabled that if certain specified reservations were made, "the ground would be completely cut out from under the opponents of the League in the Senate"; and Wilson sent an appreciative acknowledgement of this advice.[54] He had to be persuaded, however, to give attention to the counsel of Elihu Root, whose influence upon the Republicans in the Senate was greater than that of Taft, and who thought the latter was tolerant of folly. Root accepted biased reports of the White House dinner of February 27, and in a letter to Lowell wrote of Wilson's "arrogant denial of anybody's right to criticize."[55] Root's ideas were published by George Harvey,

50. Baker, vol. 2, p. 311. R. S. Baker to Wilson, March 15, 1919, Baker papers, II, L.C. Miller, vol. 1, March 14, 1919.

51. Grayson diary, March 18, 1919.

52. See above, p. 187. Among the suggestions that came to the president were messages from Senator McCumber, a Republican member of the Committee on Foreign Relations, from Democratic senator Robert L. Owen, and from Premier Borden of Canada. They suggested specific amendments. Hamilton Holt and Oscar Straus, officers of the Paris committee of the League to Enforce Peace, worked behind the scenes to eliminate misunderstandings between American and European delegates. Warren F. Kuehl, *Hamilton Holt*. Straus, *Under Four Administrations*, pp. 396–426. Miller, vol. 1, April 11, 1919. W. G. Sharp, *War Memoirs*, vol. 1, p. 407.

53. Polk to Ammission, March 21, 1919, N.A., R.G. 59, 763.72119 / 429 a and d. In the Boston debate Lodge said that he disapproved of the Covenant as drafted and that he would support a league that really promoted peace and worked no injustice on the United States. See Widenor, p. 318. Lowell, on the other hand, said that the Covenant, though defective in drafting and easily misunderstood, should be accepted and improved, Polk to Ammission, March 20, 1919, N.A., R.G. 59, 763.72119 / 4294 b.

54. Baker, vol. 3, p. 328. Cables, Tumulty to Wilson, March 16, 1919, Wilson to Tumulty, c. March 17, 1919, Wilson papers. Auchincloss diary, March 22, 1919.

Taft called on Reading at Washington on March 17 and seemed confident that with a little management all difficulties still might be surmounted, dispatch, Reading to Prime Minister and Balfour, March 17, 1919, P.R.O., FO / 608 / 244. doc. 165 / 2 / 1.

55. Jessup, *Root*, vol. 2, p. 394.

whom Wilson despised. They stressed the development of international law by periodic conferences, and called for obligatory arbitration of "justiciable questions."
Root like the statesmen of the Allies emphasized "a continuance of the present
alliance . . . for the purpose of reconstruction which must necessarily follow the
war."[56] On March 19 Lamont forwarded to the president a cable from his partner,
J. P. Morgan, commending Root's attitude as constructive and transmitting his
views on the Covenant. Two days later Wilson replied that there was "a very good
prospect" that some of the chief difficulties that were apparently in Root's mind
might be removed by clarification or amendment of the Covenant.[57]

Unfortunately, however, Wilson's public defiance of senatorial opposition had
widened the breach between him and the Foreign Relations Committee. He had not
acknowledged the deference to the Senate that was required by law, and members
of that body took offense. House, wishing to disarm Wilson's adversaries by giving
attention to amendments that they advocated, cabled to Polk to ask him to send over
privately any specific suggestions that the senators might have. Moreover, House
persuaded Henry White both to write to and to cable his friend Lodge for the exact
phraseology of amendments of the Covenant that the Senate considered important.
Urging haste, White asserted a desire on the part of the peace commission to meet
the ideas of the Senate as closely as possible, with due consideration of the prospect
that special American pleas would stimulate other nations to advocate revisions in
the interest of their own particular concerns.[58] However Lodge, after consulting
Root, replied with a tart message that Root drafted.[59]

Polk had no better success in securing recommendations from senators. "No one
here seems to have the authority to . . . answer criticisms of Republican senators,"
Polk cabled to Paris. "The opponents are carrying on a very active campaign and
something must be done."[60]

Unable to get any helpful response from Lodge and his friends, Wilson and House
proceeded to consider the suggestions that had come from many quarters, American
and foreign, friendly and hostile. It was to be expected that any attempt to alter the
text of the Covenant would encounter objections from the French members of the
Commission on the League of Nations, whose views had received scant sympathy
from their English-speaking colleagues. Obviously any reopening of discussion would
enable the French to present again their arguments for an organization to direct the

56. Root to Hays, March 29, 1919, Root papers, L.C.
57. Cables in Wilson papers. Lamont, *Across World Frontiers*, pp. 191 ff. Root's views were given
by Lamont to Miller, who wrote a commentary on them, Miller, *Drafting*, vol. 1, pp. 298–301. Also
see *ibid.*, pp. 368–377, 382–389, and below, p. 306.
58. Cable, White to Lodge, March 9, 1919, Nevins, *White*, p. 399. Bonsal, p. 290.
59. "I am now sending Henry White a cable precisely as you drafted it," Lodge wrote to Root on
March 14, 1919. "I had the same feeling about it that you have. I saw the net spread and was determined
not to get into it. . . . Wilson's whole performance is intolerable. If he were thinking of anything but
himself—a feat he never performs—he would have submitted the draft to the Senate at once and asked
their advice. . . . The other nations, I know directly from the best authority, are quite ready to make
concessions and accept our amendment because they are so anxious to have us in the League," letter in
Root papers, L.C. See Jessup, pp. 385–387, and Lodge, *The Senate and the League of Nations*, pp.
123–124. Cable, White from Lodge, March 19, 1919, N.A., R.G. 256, 185.111 / 145.
60. Dispatch, Polk to Lansing, March 20, 1919, Wilson papers.

military operations of the League. Moreover, Finance Minister Klotz was proclaiming in the French Chamber that the League could not endure without powers in the domain of international finance, and the French press was promoting this idea.

It was Miller's opinion that changes in the draft of February 14 should be kept at a minimum since the Covenant provided for its own amendment.[61] House, however, was ready to arrange such compromises with the Europeans as were necessary to secure alterations that would satisfy the American Senate.[62] With this in view the colonel got help from Lord Robert Cecil, who understood the political embarrassment of the Americans and the importance of their participation in the work of the League. House brought Wilson into conference with Cecil on March 16. The English statesman recorded that Wilson was "in a very truculent mood, fiercely refusing to make any concessions to Republican senators," and that he and House "had to be quite careful to avoid making any allusion to the fact that any change in the Covenant . . . was one recommended by these worthless beings." Nevertheless, as they drove away from the meeting House calmly assured Cecil that actually the president would make concessions. Thinking it "nearly impossible" to meet the wishes of the Senate, House nevertheless persuaded the English statesman to draft proposals for amendments.[63]

Two days later House conferred with Cecil and went over the British draft; and in the evening they dined with the president.[64] He could not find the letter in which Senator Hitchcock made suggestions, but did his best to recall the contents. He seemed ready to accept most of the ideas of Cecil, of whom he appeared to be very fond.[65] A sentence had been added to Article Ten that mitigated the rigidity that had seemed unwise to Cecil as well as to French officials: "In case of aggression or . . . any threat or danger of . . . aggression the Executive Council shall advise upon the means by which this obligation shall be fulfilled."[66]

After dinner they discussed the revisions that prominent Americans had proposed. Wilson and House feared that if an amendment barring interference in domestic affairs was sought in order to please senators opposed to Japanese immigration, it would displease those who sympathized with Ireland's wish to be free to plead before the League. Wilson thought any such reservation unnecessary, since the League was in his view essentially an advisory body, and, moreover, Americans familiar with their own constitution would understand that powers not explicitly delegated to a federation would be reserved to the members. The Americans also apprehended that a special reservation in respect of the Monroe Doctrine might provoke a Japanese claim for a sphere of influence in Asia. The result of the discussion with Cecil was that he agreed to try to draft an amendment covering this difficult matter.[67]

61. Miller, *Drafting*, vol. 1, p. 302.

62. *I.P.*, vol. 4, p. 410.

63. House diary, March 16, 1919. Cecil diary, March 16, 1919, Cecil papers, 51131. Cables, Wiseman to Reading, March 16 and 17, 1919, Y.H.C.

64. Miller, *Drafting*, vol. 1, pp. 279–283.

65. Edith Benham's diary letter, House diary, Cecil diary, March 18, 1919.

66. Miller, *Drafting*, vol. 2, p. 584.

67. Cecil diary, March 18, 1919. Miller, *My Diary*, vol. 1, March 18, 1919.

One decision of great consequence was taken at the afterdinner conference on March 18. It was agreed to require a unanimous vote to validate action by the council or the assembly of the League. This fundamental principle was presented by Cecil at the next session of the League commission and accepted without discussion. Thus, by this affirmation of the right of veto, a single dissenting nation would be able to block forceful action by the League. The United States would be protected from compulsion to act against its will,[68] and at the same time it accepted the right of any other power to negate any majority vote that it might regard as contrary to its own interests. The influence of this decision on the history of the century was to be far-reaching and at times critical.

It was tentatively agreed that, in the interest of neutrality, the seat of the League should be at Geneva or Lausanne and not at Brussels, as French and Belgian delegates wished.[69] Provision was made for additions to the executive council by approval of a majority of the League's assembly in order to provide for the future participation of Germany and Russia.

On March 20 House gave an interview to the Paris *Daily Mail* in which, to allay fears and raise morale, he ventured to predict that the treaty would be ready in a fortnight.[70] On the same day and the next he canvassed an assemblage of representatives of neutral states and gave a sympathetic hearing to their suggestions. Cecil answered their questions patiently and lucidly. They were encouraged to propose changes in the Covenant and did so.[71]

It was one thing, however, to consider amendments in discussions with sympathetic colleagues and cooperative neutrals, and quite another matter to get the approval of the League commission. Wilson called its members together to get on with the task of altering the text upon which all had agreed in February. In three sessions, on March 22, 24, and 26, the Covenant was given a first reading; and at two others, on April 10 and 11, a second reading.[72] On the agenda were certain amendments suggested by neutral nations that had the support of at least one of the members of the commission.[73]

At the session on the afternoon of March 22 Cecil continued to play the moder-

68. Miller, *Drafting,* vol. 1, pp. 296, 301; vol. 2, p. 339. House diary, March 15 and 18, 1919.

69. In a meeting of the League of Nations Commission on March 22, Wilson read a letter from the Swiss government offering hospitality to the League. After a reminder by Hymans of the interest of Belgium, he accepted a suggestion by Bourgeois that the matter be referred to a committee. To sit on it he appointed House, Smuts, Orlando, and Makino. After negotiations conducted through Professor Rappard (See W. E. Rappard, in *Centenaire Woodrow Wilson,* pp. 54 ff.), the committee reported in favor of Geneva, the seat of the International Red Cross. Giving consideration to the special problem posed by Swiss neutrality, the commission adopted the report. "This is a more significant choice than perhaps we are aware of," said Wilson, Miller, *My Diary,* docs. 719, 721, 745.

70. Noble, p. 132. On April 2 House rued his earlier optimism. Upon rereading eighty-four pages of his diary, he wrote: "It reminds me of how very inconsistent a large part of the diary will appear and also what a false prophet I shall have made of myself in many instances," *I.P.,* vol. 4, p. 391.

71. House did not take part in the discussion, but left it to Cecil to conduct the meeting, Miller, *My Diary,* vol. 7, docs. 561, 562, 576. House wrote in his diary on March 21: "The neutrals seem happy to have had a hearing and we have given them all the time they desired. . . . There are no 'long-distance' talkers among them. They had their papers well prepared and everything has gone expeditiously. Some of the *prima donnas* from the great powers might well take lessons from them." See Bonsal, p. 147.

72. See below, p. 307.

73. Miller, *Drafting,* vol. 1, pp. 303–309; vol. 2, pp. 592–645.

ating role that had served so well in the conference with neutrals. When he suggested that a protocol in respect of the League be signed after the treaty, Miller, taking alarm, wrote a chit to House which the colonel handed to the president. "The matter of procedure is one of great difficulty for us," it said. "It is getting to the point where the Senate will ratify the treaty and not the Protocol and then there will be no League."[74]

Two amendments typed out by Wilson in order to meet the suggestions of Taft and the first three of Senator Hitchcock's[75] were submitted through House to Cecil, who had already agreed to them. One of the amendments, that of Article Fifteen, reserved domestic questions from the jurisdiction of the League. This was accepted at a meeting of the Commission on the League of Nations on March 24 in spite of the president's warning of an unfavorable reaction from partisans of an Irish Free State.

Another amendment, that of Article Fourteen, defining the conditions under which League members might withdraw, became the subject of protracted discussion and of some alteration. Making use of language that had been suggested by Lowell, Wilson's draft proposed that states after ten year of membership have a legal right to withdraw on a year's notice. (Taft had suggested that the period of notice be two years, and Lowell, two months.) The president explained to the commission that he sponsored this amendment with reluctance, having always been an "anti-secessionist." Asserting that actually only moral force could hold the League together,[76] he said that sovereignty was "a sort of fetish" of public men, especially those in the United States, and that the commission must make concessions to existing ideas. He spoke of the essential contradiction between the interests of "national sovereignty" and those of "humanity," and prophesied that the latter would ultimately prevail.

As was foreseen, the French vigorously opposed the American amendment permitting withdrawal.[77] They feared that such a change might endanger the League's permanence and its guarantee of their security. They were unmoved by Wilson's assurance that no nation had a *moral* right to leave the League and that it would be impossible for any state to do so without becoming "an outlaw"; nor did they accept the president's prophecy that the day was near when Americans, who now demanded concessions to their desire for independence of will and action, would become as eager champions of the sovereignty of mankind as they then were of that of their own nation. Despite the French opposition, however, the commission agreed on March 26 that members of the League in good standing would have a right to

74. The text of this note, written from memory by Miller after the meeting, is in the Miller papers, L.C. Miller, *My Diary*, vol. 1, March 22, 1919, p. 196. See below, p. 575. Cecil later wrote that he was "quite ready to go almost any distance to secure the two-thirds majority in the Senate needed for ratification," *A Great Experiment*, pp. 82–83.

75. Miller, *My Diary*, vol. 1, entry of March 24, 1919. On the Monroe Doctrine reservation, see below, pp. 305–309.

76. After remarking that a state had a right to denounce any treaty, Wilson accepted the argument of Cecil, supported by Miller, that though states had that *power*, and in practice often used the doctrine of changed conditions *(rebus sic stantibus)* as justification, they had no *legal* right to denounce a treaty, Miller, *My Diary*, vol. 1, March 18, 1919; Miller, *Drafting*, vol. 1, p. 293.

77. Miller, *Drafting*, vol. 1, p. 293.

withdraw on two years' notice. A provision to this effect became a part of Article One of the final Covenant.

The acceptance by the commission of the two American amendments was not achieved without a revival of French pleas that had been rejected in February. The very fact that the Americans were now proposing changes in a document that had been exalted by their president to a sacred status encouraged the French spokesmen to press once more for additional guarantees of security.[78] Clemenceau, aware that the president would not concede what the French advisers demanded in the Rhineland, nor all that they claimed by way of indemnification, nor the institution of an economic section of the League, did not discourage the renewed obstruction by Bourgeois and Larnaude. They argued at great length for amendments providing for the inspection of armaments and for their control permanently by an international military organization, in order that the obligations imposed by the treaty would be fulfilled and would be effective in moments of emergency. When the French proposed an addition to Article Eight that would require the council of the League to formulate plans for the reduction of armaments, Wilson, despite his commitment to the principle of disarmament, said that such a provision would offend the susceptibilities of sovereign states. Aware that any specific submission of American military power to international direction might seal the fate of the Covenant in the Senate, he insisted on leaving the nations free to improvise means to meet emergencies.

The president ignored a suggestion by House that they assuage the wound to the French by giving Bourgeois "a pat on the back." Wilson, irritated by the repetitive argument,[79] refused to console the old French champion of peace by supporting a suggested amendment to the Covenant to the effect that the League take up and complete the work commenced at The Hague, with which Bourgeois had been closely identified. The president vigorously denounced the whole "wishy-washy" business of the "talkfest" at The Hague while explaining that of course he disliked to hurt the feelings or the brains that conceived them. It fell to House to try to console the French delegate, who lamented that his life's work had gone for naught.[80]

While the president occupied himself with the fine points of constitution making, Europe seemed closer than ever to revolutionary chaos. As idealism ebbed and the Peace Conference gave the public no evidence of substantial progress toward a settlement of immediate and pressing questions, rumblings of popular protest assailed the delays, the secrecy, the lack of decisive action. Wilson's insistence on priority for the League Covenant appeared as the chief obstacle. Some of his zealous adherents felt that he was losing ground to the Europeans, as they traded their national claims against the ideals he put forward in the name of humanity.[81]

Wilson felt that the French were responsible for the delays that were attributed to him. The American delegates who were actively engaged in negotiations reported

78. Bonsal, p. 209.
79. Grayson diary, March 24, 1919.
80. Bonsal, pp. 151–152.
81. "There is great danger to you in present situation," Tumulty cabled to Wilson on March 25. "I can see signs that our enemies here and abroad would try to make it appear that you are responsible for delay in peace settlement and that delay has increased momentum of bolshevism in Hungary and Russia. Can responsibility for delay be fixed by you in some way?" Wilson papers.

that the French were holding them back and engaging in endless debate. In the secret talks with Lloyd George and Wilson, Clemenceau, subject to fits of coughing brought on by the assassin's bullet lodged in his chest, was a tenacious advocate for France. Wilson likened him to a trout whom one had to play for a while.[82]

On March 27 Wilson, acting on the advice of Baker, asked that a declaration be drawn up for the press. He edited a rough draft so that it became a dignified statement that absolved the League commission of all blame for delaying the proceedings of the Peace Conference.[83] He explained that the group had met in the morning at hours which did not interfere with other business; and he announced that the revised Covenant, "practically finished," was in the hands of a drafting committee and would "almost immediately" be given to the public.[84]

House was able to report to Polk that thirteen important changes had been effected in the Covenant. "You will notice," his dispatch of April 4 concluded, "that we have tried to meet the objections which have been raised in America".[85] Actually, in the first three sessions of the League commission, Wilson, with the aid of House and Cecil, had progressed far in a difficult diplomatic mission that was repugnant to him. He told the Council of Four on March 27, however, that he was still determined to defy the Senate by combining the Covenant with the peace treaty. "Otherwise," he warned, there would be "prolonged debate and possible difficulties."

82. Grayson diary, March 18, 1919. Also see John W. Davis diary, May 14, 1919, Y.H.C.

83. Baker, *American Chronicle,* p. 395. "The drafting of the Covenant did not, in fact, materially interfere with the main work of the Conference. . . . The emphasis thrown by some historians upon the responsibility of President Wilson is apt to disguise another, and to my mind, more important cause of delay. That cause was the absence of any agreed or unified purpose," Nicolson, p. 56.

84. *P.P.,* vol. 5, p. 459. Auchincloss diary, March 27, 1919.

85. Auchincloss diary, April 3, 1919.

PART THREE

Attrition and Compromise

W HEN Wilson came back to Paris in March, he was still ostensibly a political leader, offering peace and freedom to the people of the world. However, forced as he was to attempt to reconcile the demands of American politics with the requirements of the world's diplomacy, he encountered tensions that threatened to destroy him. He would be vulnerable when Europeans demanded concessions to their purposes as a condition of their acceptance of American amendments to the Covenant. He had much to learn about the work of diplomats and was in danger of failing in their essential task: that of negotiating precise agreements that can be ratified.

Three days after Wilson's return to Paris, a question was raised that revealed the seriousness of his predicament. In the meeting of the Supreme Council on March 17 the chairman of the drafting committee of the Peace Conference sought a precise ruling as to the character of the document that was being framed. Were the military terms that had been drafted by Foch's committee to be considered final conditions of the peace? It was a question that challenged the American prophet to clarify his strategy.

Before his departure from Paris, Wilson had told the council that he wished the preparation of a preliminary peace to go forward during his absence provided that the League Covenant was given due regard. Although he did not want the consideration of territorial adjustments and reparations to be held up, what he had in mind particularly was a military convention that would be in the nature of an exalted armistice, the terms of which would be included eventually in a formal treaty.

The president was not sure that a separate and prior military treaty could be concluded without submission of it to the Senate. In the meeting of March 17 he asked for time to obtain technical counsel. Although he was told by his legal advisers that it was within his power as commander in chief to conclude any kind of armistice convention without reference to the Senate, and though a revised draft of military terms recognized a relationship of the treaty to the Armistice of Rethondes, even a tentative state of peace could not be attained legally without ratification by the Senate. According to Lansing's record, Wilson leaned toward him in a meeting of the Supreme Council and said in a low voice: "You do not mean to say that all these preliminaries have to be ratified by our Senate?" When the secretary of state replied: "Why, of course they have to be, Mr. President," Wilson showed surprise and remarked that this created difficulty.[1] The president's advisers hoped that news of what he had in mind would not reach Washington, where, as Bonsal put it, this would have been regarded as "another, if futile, attempt to kick over the senatorial traces."[2] A statement by Wilson's advisers was put in his hands, and he accepted its verdict.[3]

In sober reality, it was not only the so-called "preliminaries," but the whole treaty of peace that was in danger of rejection by the Senate. The American pleni-potentiaries and their legal advisers were painfully aware of this danger. They were in peril of placing their nation beyond the pale of civilized diplomacy. David Hunter Miller, perceiving the danger, wrote to House on March 6 that it would be a "reproach to the honor of the United States" to make it possible for the Senate to accept a treaty that included provisions to which the Allies agreed because they depended upon a league of nations, and at the same time to reject the League Covenant on which the Allies relied.[4]

The peril of a failure to meet the immediate requirements of peacemaking was no less threatening than the hazard of a rejection by the Senate. There was danger of specifying terms for Germany that would give extreme provocation toward future wars; and yet the fundamental and ineradicable insistence of France on strategic security persisted. French nationalists, hoping to rule the Rhineland; the Italians, to whom the president had made an unwise concession in respect of the Tyrol; and the nation builders of east central Europe, where fighting went on despite the ban issued by the Peace Conference—these and others expected more territorial dispensations than could be justified under the doctrine of self-determination. The Japanese dele-gates would demand their due under arrangements made with the Allies and with China during the war, and they would seek a *quid pro quo* for their compliant withdrawal of their demand for a statement of racial equality in the Covenant of the League of Nations.

House, having advised Wilson to endeavor to conciliate his adversaries in Wash-ington, had worked toward accommodations in those matters that aroused the strongest passions in both victors and vanquished. Trying to smooth the jagged edges of morality that Wilson and Lansing often projected, House made it clear both to his chief and to the Europeans that the United States should participate in a common search for such measures of compromise as might be essential to unity among the victors. He was willing to dodge—to "finesse," as he put it—questions that seemed insoluble at the moment and that might cause crises if pursued immediately.

From his place in the center of the melee during the absence of the president House had observed the situation with remarkable detachment. "It is now evident," he wrote in his diary on March 3, "that the peace will not be such a peace as I had

1. Lansing, private memoranda, March 19, 1919, and *The Peace Negotiations*, p. 206.
2. Bonsal, *Suitors and Suppliants*, p. 257.
3. Miller, *My Diary*, vol. 1, March 17, 18, and 19, 1919.
4. D. H. Miller, memorandum for Mr. Auchincloss, March 6, 1919, Y.H.C. In Miller's view the Covenant of the League of Nations was "an integral part of the Treaty of Peace in reality, whatever it may be in form"; and if the Senate rejected this treaty, another could be made on the basis of American isolation. "But," the opinion concluded, " . . . to make a peace which had been agreed to upon the belief that our policy of isolation was ended but which came into effect with the knowledge that our policy of isolation was not ended, would be so unjust as to be difficult of characterization"

hoped, or one which this terrible upheaval should have brought about. There are many reasons why it will not be one: . . . the elections of last November in the United States, . . . the British elections and the vote of confidence Clemenceau received in the French Chamber of Deputies. . . . If the president should exert his influence among the liberals and laboring classes, he might possibly overthrow the Governments of Great Britain, France, and Italy; but if he did, he would still have to reckon with our own people and he might bring the whole world into chaos. The overthrow of governments might not end there, and it would be a grave responsibility for any man to take at this time. I dislike to sit and have forced upon us such a peace as we are facing. We will get something out of it in the way of a League of Nations, but even that is an imperfect instrument. . . . All our commissioners, experts, and economists tell of the same *impasse* and come almost hourly for consultation. . . . The situations are many in number and both varied and complex in character."[5]

Applying himself to the essential business of diplomacy, House, despite the precautions that he took, aroused jealousies and criticism among American associates who wished to make a peace in accord with their own convictions and who found themselves frustrated and dependent on him for access to the president. Several of them formed the opinion, not without justification, that the colonel talked too freely to newsmen and, by sympathizing unduly with European pleaders, awakened unwarranted expectations of American concessions and support. Actually, under the pressure of responsibility far greater than he had ever borne, House lost the veil of modesty and tact with which he had been careful to protect himself. Indeed, the veil was shredded when his secretary asserted that actually House controlled the president's actions. (Auchincloss was indiscreet enough to speak of Wilson as "little Woody," dependent for success on House.)

Bringing the Three together in his suite in the Crillon on March 18, House wrote afterward: "They got nowhere. They still skirt around trouble and I am becoming discouraged." From that time until April 4 he did not sit again in the top-level council, but he continued to try to guide it.

By the end of March the spread of bolshevism into central Europe was no longer merely a threat. It had become a fact. On the twenty-first the weak government of Károlyi resigned at Budapest. Béla Kun, an imprisoned revolutionary leader, came into power. Certain of the Americans at Paris gave way to black despair and fear that this was but the first step in a general social disintegration. Lansing wrote that the volcano was beginning to erupt; Hoover advised against recognizing the "murderous tyranny" of Hungary; American observers at Budapest, seconded by specialists at Paris, suggested a friendly military intervention but this was opposed by Bliss and by Hoover, who continued to put faith in economic relief. As for House, he exploited the fear that was awakened by news of the Hungarian revolution. Continuing his campaign for haste, he implored the president to spur the Allies to agreement on the issues that he had been considering tentatively with the Europeans and that must be resolved before peace could be restored.

By this time the work of the committees charged with preparation of the eco-

5. *I.P.*, vol. 4, p. 362.

nomic and territorial terms was progressing so rapidly that it seemed probable that the entire treaty might be made ready for the Germans before the end of March. In view of these considerations, and informed by his legal counselors that any mere executive agreement, unratified by the Senate, could not end the war, Wilson confessed that he had been misled by the term "preliminary treaty of peace." He now said there would be only one treaty, though after its signing many questions would remain to be worked out by commissions.

On March 24 the Four—Wilson, Clemenceau, Lloyd George, and Orlando—met in secret session. In the afternoon the president spoke of a "veritable race between peace and anarchy" and the impatience of the public.[6] He proposed that The Four discuss among themselves the most difficult and urgent questions, and Lloyd George and Clemenceau accepted this proposal readily. A "preliminary peace" was not considered further, though the term appears in the minutes as late as April 25.[7] It connoted to the Germans merely the drafting of terms that would be presented to them without any prior consultation.[8]

The president fell into the pattern of secret negotiations that House found productive of solutions; but when Wilson fully came to understand the extent of the concessions that must be made in order to save the League and his ambition for the role of *arbiter mundi* was challenged, he tended to accept much of the criticism of House that was circulated by members of the president's household and their friends. The old counselor seemed—as Wilson said later to his daughter Eleanor[9]—to "wear a different face," that of a deserter from a sacred cause.

In the first week of April illness confined the president to his bed. In this emergency House took his place in the Supreme Council and urged compromises that Wilson accepted reluctantly. When his strength returned, the president seized the reins and held them firmly in his own hands. As April wore on and House's independent ventures in conciliation and facilitation became embarrassing, the president continued to withdraw the confidence that he had extended to the colonel through many years. Attempting to function as diplomat as well as political leader, he plunged into intricate negotiations that he had at first avoided. When his principles were challenged, he threated to go home and to deprive Europe of the American support upon which the Europeans depended for reconstruction and a guaranteed peace. Up to this point, wishing to avoid the image of a dictator, Wilson had avoided such an assertion of the power that was in his hands.[10]

6. Memorandum of interview of Wellington Koo with Wilson, March 24, 1919, Koo papers, 001, Columbia University Library.

7. The confusion attending the matter of a "preliminary peace" is explained at some length in Marston, *The Peace Conference of 1919*, pp. 131–158. An illuminating paper on the subject, written by Webster for the Foreign Office and dated March 24, 1943, is in the Charles Webster papers, British Library of Political and Economic Science, London School of Economics.

House thought, in retrospect, that a quick conclusion of a preliminary peace "would have saved an infinite amount of suffering and would have brought the world sooner to normal," House to W. A. White, December 8, 1924, Y.H.C. Cf. Haskins and Lord, *Some Problems of the Peace Conference*, p. 8.

8. Schwabe, *Woodrow Wilson, Revolutionary Germany, and Peacemaking*, p. 217.

9. E. W. McAdoo to the author, October 1950.

10. Grayson diary, January 21, 1919.

11

The Control of Germany

In March and April, while the Americans were pressing for a revision of the League Covenant, it became apparent that an ordered sequence of talks was impossible. The political chiefs were loath to settle any question on its own merits. Sometimes they insisted on relating an issue to others in which their governments had stakes that they regarded as vital. The time had come for the "rough-and-tumble" that Balfour had foreseen.

"The prime ministers have skirted around the difficult questions long enough," House wrote in his diary on March 14, "and I am determined that they shall get at them, troublesome as they are, and settle them this week if it is possible. The president is willing, but first Lloyd George, and then Clemenceau shies. The reason I wanted them to meet in my rooms was to keep my hand on the situation. If they go to the Quai d'Orsay or the Ministry of War or to the president's house, matters get out of hand. . . . My main drive now is for peace with Germany at the earliest possible moment, and I am determined that it shall come soon if it is within my power to force action. I have the Northcliffe press at my disposal in this effort, and every day editorials and articles appear which have a tendency to frighten, persuade or coerce." House, convinced of the ineptness of Lansing as a diplomat, thought it important to the speedy realization of Wilson's program that he maintain the contacts that he had fostered with Lloyd George, Balfour, and Clemenceau. Otherwise, he feared, serious difficulties might befall the president, who had confessed his bewilderment at the ways of the Europeans and who sometimes tended to confuse diplomatic negotiatons by the crusading zeal that he expressed so effectively in his political speeches.

By House's arrangement Lloyd George was waiting for conferences when Wilson arrived at his new domicile in Paris at noon on March 14. Boasting of the support that his people had given to him in the "khaki election," the prime minister had asked House more than once whether America was behind Wilson.[1]

Deeming France's demand for security against German domination to be of the first importance, Wilson and Lloyd George met this challenge with a momentous proposal. They agreed to offer Clemenceau formal defensive alliances in return for renunciation of any plan for permanent occupation of the left bank of the Rhine.

They talked for more than an hour about the major problems facing the Peace Conference. The prime minister said he could not afford to remain at Paris for much more than another week because of Labour agitation in England. Afterward Wilson went to the Crillon to confer with the American commissioners.[2] According to the record of Dr. Grayson, who, attired in his admiral's uniform, accompanied his

---

1. Bonsal, *Suitors and Suppliants,* p. 246.
2. Grayson diary, March 14, 1919.

patient everywhere, each of the commissioners gave an account of the matters that had been left to him; and the president criticized their failure to insist upon priority for the League Covenant and to stand immovably against French plans for the Rhineland. Wilson complained that the French had officially announced that the terms of peace would provide for the creation of a Rhenish republic.[3]

On the morning of the next day the president went to the Crillon for the first of a series of private conferences with Clemenceau and Lloyd George.[4] When the question of a preliminary military treaty came up, Wilson made it clear that he was opposed to such a program and that he still insisted on priority for the League Covenant. Rebelling against the pressure to which House seemed to be subjecting him, he sent word that he would not be present at the afternoon session of the Supreme council. It was to take up the terms recommended by the military advisers. He had not received the text of these, nor had he a complete report of the proceedings of the Council during his absence. Unwilling to discuss a matter that he had not had an opportunity to study, he remained at home and gave his attention to the essential papers when they were hurriedly brought to him.[5] House sat in the meeting that he had arranged, very embarrassed by his chief's absence. Little was accomplished, and Lloyd George was annoyed by the waste of time.[6] British newsmen released stories that gave no explanation of the president's absence from the Supreme Council, and it seemed to Wilson that they were unfairly suggesting that he was determined to "rule or ruin."[7]

The first of the questions on which House had undertaken tentative negotiations during Wilson's absence was a reduction of the German army and navy to a peace footing. Lloyd George and Balfour had discussed this matter with Wilson at London; and when the president had asked for a definite understanding, they were willing to agree only that armaments must be limited and conscription forbidden in the vanquished nations.[8] In the discussions of the question by the Supreme Council in January and February, the military advisers had presented a plan that provided for the availability of fifteen American divisions in Europe at the end of March. General Pershing gave the opinion that if adequate shipping was available, the American force could be reduced to ten divisions by May.[9] Pershing thought that Germany was too disorganized to reopen hostilities, and he had the support of the

---

3. *Ibid.* There were no minutes of this meeting. House mentioned it in his diary as "uninteresting."

4. Auchincloss diary, March 10, 1919. From March 17 to 24 The Three continued to attend the six meetings of the Supreme Council of Ten as well as holding several private conferences. At one of these conferences, on the twentieth, Clemenceau and Lloyd George almost came to blows over the question of Syria, and Wilson felt compelled to intervene as conciliator, House diary, March 20, 1919. See Baker, vol. 2, pp. 26–72; vol. 3, pp. 1–22; and below, p. 501.

5. Grayson diary, March 15, 1919.

6. House diary, March 15, 1919, Marston, *The Peace Conference of 1919*, p. 152. In the evening House telephoned to Wilson and expressed fear that the French would blame the president for delaying proceedings. Auchincloss diary, March 15, 1919. Frances Stevenson wrote in her diary on March 15 that Lloyd George was "furious at the delay" and "Wilson insists on re-opening questions that have been settled so it looks as though there will be a row." And on March 14: "Clemenceau cannot tolerate him at any price," Stevenson, *Lloyd George,* pp. 172–173.

7. Grayson diary, March 15, 1919.

8. Minutes, I.W.C., December 30, 1918. Auchincloss diary, December 27 and 30, 1918.

9. James J. Harbord, *The American Army in France,* p. 548.

president, whom he found not only "accessible" but "very much alive on military questions."[10]

The approach of the date on which the armistice must be renewed for the third time required that the Supreme Council act upon the report of an *ad hoc* committee that it set up on February 10 to produce recommendations in two days.[11] Those submitted by Foch and Bliss were in conflict. As a check upon German chauvinism Bliss depended less upon a reduction of personnel than upon prohibition of the production of munitions; yet he protested against a French inclination to seize German territory beyond the Rhine if the enemy did not surrender surplus war matériel. In a memorandum to Wilson he advised that Foch's thinking was political rather than military.[12] "The one thing that all the American advisers of President Wilson are especially concerned in," Bliss wrote to Lansing, "is that nothing be done, at their suggestion or by lack of their suggestion, that at any time could with any justice be alleged to impugn his good faith."[13] He noted a tendency of Foch to effect *faits accomplis* at the armistice renewals that it would be difficult to counter in the treaty of peace.

Actually Bliss, too, was not unmoved by political considerations. Willing to accept the new German republic and its democratic philosophy, he feared that any treatment of the German people that might be regarded as dishonorable or unjust might lead to a coup from the Left or the Right, or possibly to a renewal of hostilities—a development that he suspected some French militarists desired. Such a turn of events might destroy America's legal position under the Fourteen Points. In the opinion of Bliss disarmament should not be dictated, but rather worked out in a way that would not force the new government of Germany to lose the respect of its people and would not weaken its resistance to extremists on both the Left and the Right. While Foch proposed that military terms be imposed immediately, Bliss thought it best to curb German power by provisions of the peace treaty rather than by irritating renewals of the armistice.[14]

During the days of controversy in early February some assurance of stability within Germany came from Weimar, where an elected assembly met on the sixth to frame a constitution for a democratic state. The controlling coalition represented the hope of the bourgeoisie for a peace that would neither crush the nation's economy nor greatly reduce German territory in Europe or overseas.

10. Pershing to N. D. Baker, February 1, 1919. Wilson thanked Pershing heartily for a letter of January 25 in which statistics were presented that indicated that a report of Foch to the S.W.C. on January 24 exaggerated German strength on the western front, letters in Pershing papers, box 373, L.C.

11. Wilson had acquiesced in the decision of the council that the military leaders should arrange a program for the demobilization of Germany and that a special committee should be appointed to make recommendations as to the strength of the armies to be maintained on the German front and the guarantees to be exacted from Germany. General Bliss and Norman Davis were the American members of the special committee. The chairman was Louis Loucheur, French minister of munitions. For its report see Baker, vol. 3, pp. 189–194. On the work of the committee and another body of three who considered the question of German surrender of war matériel and on which Lansing sat, see Marston, pp. 127–130.

12. "Memo. for the President," February 6, 1919, Wilson papers. Bliss diary, February 5, 1919, Bliss papers, box 65. *I.P.*, vol. 4, p. 325. House diary, February 5, 1919.

13. Palmer, *Bliss, Peacemaker*, p. 371. Bliss diary, January 23 and 24, 1919. Memorandum to Lansing, February 6, 1919, Bliss papers, box 69. F.R., P.P.C., vol. 3, pp. 920–921.

14. Bliss diary, February 11, 1919.

Before the appointment of the special committee on February 10, with instructions to report in two days, the Supreme Council engaged in warm debates. Briefed by Bliss, Wilson spoke strongly on February 7 against the French recommendations. His concept of disarmament—reduction of armies "to the lowest point consistent with domestic safety"—had been challenged the day before in a meeting of the Commission on the League of Nations by French spokesmen.

Advised by Foch that the enemy could be forced to accept new requirements, Wilson suggested that it was unsportsmanlike to attempt now to correct the oversights of the original armistice, that moreover it would be very risky to make a threat that they would not want to be challenged to follow up. He cautioned against a degree of demobilization that would increase unemployment in Germany, add to unrest, or reduce the eventual capacity of Germany to pay reparations.

The president's own proposal was that a commission of civilians negotiate with a similar body of Germans and offer, as compensation for the demobilization and disarmament of Germany, a reduction in the Allied army of occupation and also a relaxation of the blockade to allow the passage of nonmilitary supplies. This proposition met with a measure of support from Lloyd George, although the prime minister did not recognize the existence of any obligation of honor or of sportsmanship and thought the practical question before them to be one not of morality but rather of tactics. The president, however, spoke again of the great moral advantage in approaching the German delegates through a commission of civilians who would not threaten them. He hoped that negotiations might begin immediately and before the next expiration of the armistice on February 17.

At this point the old Tiger of France showed his claws. Much of the time he had sat passively in the presiding chair, eyes on the ceiling. But now, when Wilson suggested negotiating with the enemy, he sprang from his crouch, his voice vibrating. In his determination to prevent a third German attack upon France, he insisted that the prime essential to control the enemy was a military reckoning. "You do not know the Germans!" he exclaimed. "We are at a decisive moment. It is very unfortunate that we should be obliged to act thus, but it is necessary."

To Clemenceau the question before them was psychological. Though he did not object to the eventual granting of economic advantages to the German people, he would not consent to negotiate when the Allies had a right to make demands. He thought it a *sine qua non* that these demands should be presented as a matter of right and not as a subject for parley. The German spokesmen already had become insolent, he said. If they detected a disposition to yield on the part of the Allies, they would grow arrogant and even ferocious. Though he protested a disinclination to starve the Germans, he advocated the use of the blockade to enforce disarmament. Once the demands of the victors were granted, they might then, if necessary, state that as an act of grace they would consider the question of relaxing the blockade. But if he so far forgot the interests of his country and of Europe as to consent to the proposal of President Wilson, the French Chamber undoubtedly would dismiss him, and rightly so.

The president, respecting the strong feeling with which Clemenceau spoke, admitted that the assertion that the Germans could be moved only by force might be correct.

But he still preferred to try to negotiate, letting it be known that a threat might follow. If they began with a threat and then offered concessions, in his opinion the force of the threat would be reduced. The discussion had led, finally, to agreement on February 8 that American civilians would be included in the Armistice Commission, although it was not until February 24 that two Americans were formally appointed to serve.[15]

When on February 12 the Supreme Council met to consider the report of the special committee, Clemenceau urged haste. At this point Wilson once more protested against the delay occasioned by the imposition of demands upon the Germans that he thought petty. At the same time he expressed willingness to renew the war in the event of German refusal of the whole peace settlement that was to be prepared. In the afternoon Clemenceau showed uneasiness as to the effect of Wilson's forthcoming departure for Washington upon discussions of final military terms. But when assured by the president that these matters would be left in the hands of his technical advisers and House, Clemenceau approved in substance a proposal by Wilson that the armistice be renewed *sine die*, without change, and that final military terms be imposed as soon as they could be prepared. There was agreement on a resolution proposed by Balfour.[16]

It was agreed that the substance of this resolution be communicated by Foch to the German armistice commission at the time of the mid-February renewal. At Wilson's suggestion, however, it was decided not to inform the enemy of two clauses that concluded the Balfour resolution. These provided that, after the German acceptance of the final military terms and with the advice of the Economic Council of the Peace Conference, controlled quantities of food and raw materials were to be allotted to Germany with due regard to prior claims of Allied countries, particularly those whose industries the enemy had deliberately damaged. The decision to withhold this from the enemy allayed Clemenceau's fear that the victors might seem to be bargaining for acceptance of terms that they claimed the right to impose.

Acting under the instructions of the Supreme Council, Foch was able by a threat of force to compel the Germans to sign an agreement at Trier on February 16, extending the truce and giving to the Allies a right to terminate it on three days' notice, and also requiring the enemy to stop fighting in Poznań on a line that would bring a large part of that province into Poland. In this third parley at Trier the civilians from Paris were unable to overcome the obstacles to the relaxation of the blockade that had developed at the second renewal of the armistice. The problems of shipping and financing remained unsolved.[17] The Germans who signed the agree-

---

15. Grew to Lamont, February 24, 1919, N.A., R.G. 256, 185.001 / 5. Lamont and George McFadden were the two.

16. Balfour's resolution provided that (1) Marshal Foch stipulate that the Germans desist from all offensive operations against the Poles; (2) the armistice with Germany be renewed for a short period terminable by the victors at three days' notice; (3) final naval, military, and air conditions be drawn up by a committee presided over by Foch and, when approved by the Supreme Council, be presented to the Germans for signature. The Germans were not required to withdraw from the Baltic countries. See memorandum in N.A., R.G. 59, 763.72119 / 4323.

17. See above, pp. 13 ff., and Keynes, *Two Memoirs*, pp. 36–52. On the German reaction to the February proceedings at Trier, and on the influence of Colonel Conger on Germany's acceptance of the

ment protested Germany's good faith in carrying out the armistice terms and in establishing a democratic, parliamentary regime; and they insisted that the conditions dictated by the Allies not only made peace precarious, but prepared the way for bolshevism. It was asserted that each renewal of the armistice was a "new source of distrust, hatred, even of despair."[18] The Germans pleaded for the repatriation of prisoners of war[19] and objected to Allied seizures of industrial properties in the occupied areas of Germany and to the delays of the Peace Conference. Their chief objections, Foch reported, were to the Allied demand for a cessation of hostilities against the Poles and to Allied accusations that the Germans had failed to carry out provisions of the armistice.[20]

Immediately after the agreement of February 16 was signed, Foch proposed a summary settlement. Thinking that the Germans would accept any terms for a quick peace, he wished to make the Allies free to concentrate on the difficult Russian question, perhaps with German cooperation. He submitted a grand plan to the Quai d'Orsay for combating bolshevism all along Russia's western border.[21] In the ensuing military deliberations Bliss, with the hearty support of his American colleagues, repeatedly resisted French plans for policing ventures in eastern Europe that would require substantial support from the United States.[22]

Bliss was equally determined in his resistance to any American participation in the supervision of Germany's military establishment in the future. Fully conscious of the will of his nation's Senate and of the fact that America's status as an "associate power" would end with the signing of a peace treaty, he debated doggedly with Foch on February 26 and secured agreement to limit the authority of a planned joint commission of control to a period of three months, after which the European powers would be responsible for enforcement, leaving America's option open.[23] The Americans were aware of the dreams of German generals—Groener in particular—that the United States might share in an anti-Bolshevik crusade.[24]

On March 7 House, acting under the impetus given by prevailing political unrest, managed to come to an agreement with Clemenceau and Kerr, who spoke for Lloyd George, on the size of the German army and its method of recruiting. House con-

---

new agreement, see Klaus Schwabe, *Woodrow Wilson, Revolutionary Germany, and Peacemaking*, p. 218, n. 56.

18. Statement handed by the German Armistice Commission to Marshal Foch, February 17, 1919, N.A., R.G. 59, 763.72119 / 4152. Grew diary, February 17, 1919.

19. In the January renewal of the armistice the victors had reserved "the right to arrange for the repatriation of Russian prisoners of war to any region which they may consider most suitable." There was apprehension that Foch would try to use these men to strengthen Polish resistance to Soviet attack. Hoover feared that they might join the Soviet forces if repatriated. After some delay they were fed from American and French stocks of food. It was not until 1922 that an exchange of German and Russian prisoners was completed, Gelfand (ed.), *Herbert Hoover*, pp. 132–133.

20. On the territorial claims of the Poles and Foch's treatment of them in the renewal of the armistice, see Lundgreen-Nielsen, *The Polish Problem at the Paris Peace Conference* pp. 178–180.

21. Foch conceived that pro-Allied Russian armies should be reinforced by interned prisoners and matériel, and should have a unified command, Projet de l'État-Major, February 17, 1919.

22. Bliss to N. D. Baker, October 16, 1919, Bliss papers, box 75. Palmer, pp. 372, 376. Grew, *Turbulent Era*, vol. 1, p. 378.

23. Bliss to Mrs. Bliss, February 26, 1919, Bliss papers.

24. Schwabe, p. 222.

firmed what Wilson had said before his departure—that the only real guarantee of German disarmament was the public opinion of Europe, but the principal members of the League of Nations would have to maintain sufficient arms to enforce its will and the treaty of peace.[25] He concurred in the decision that for a minimum period of twelve years the German armed forces should be raised only by voluntary enlistment. Unfortunately, he agreed that the army and air force could have as many as 100,000 men and thus, as Hoover has pointed out, "a fatal mistake was made." "The old warrior caste was allowed to organize and command the 100,000," Hoover wrote.[26]

On March 6 the advisory commission of admirals[27] presented a draft of naval terms, calling for destruction of the enemy's ships. A French reservation, however, would partition them among the Allies. The British statesmen were about to give support to this when House, at the suggestion of Admiral Benson, undertook to persuade Lloyd George to agree to destroy the vessels, contrary to the president's earlier policy.[28] Lunching with the prime minister, House argued that the addition of German ships to the British navy would stimulate naval building in the United States and possibly bring on a rivalry like that between England and Germany before 1914.[29] (In a subsequent talk Lloyd George said that an agreement must be reached to prevent rivalry in naval building.)[30] The next day, in a talk with Clemenceau and Kerr, it was agreed that the German vessels would be distributed among the Allies and that then Great Britain, Japan, and the United States—the three great naval powers—would sink their shares. The naval advisers were directed to consider an allotment to France of ships of a type that it lacked, in compensation for its loss of naval production during the war. Like all agreements made during Wilson's absence, however, this one was dependent on his approval when he returned.

Tentative drafts of the military and naval terms, which Wilson wished to have settled promptly, had reached the president before he left Washington on March 4;[31] and at Paris on March 15, staying away from a meeting of the Supreme Council

25. Kerr to prime minister, February 18, 1919, Lothian papers, GD40 / 17 / 1222.
26. Herbert C. Hoover and Hugh Gibson, *The Problems of a Lasting Peace*, p. 119. Kerr's "Notes of an interview between M. Clemenceau, Col. House and Myself," March 7, 1919, Lothian papers, GD40 / 17 / 1178. Hankey, *The Supreme Control*, pp. 90–91. Palmer, pp. 374–375.
27. See Marston, pp. 128–129.
28. Seth Tillman, *Anglo-American Relations at the Paris Peace Conference*, pp. 166–167. House diary, March 8, 1919, Auchincloss diary, March 7, 1919. Admiral Benson had advised Wilson in February that American naval interest demanded that no one of the vessels taken from Germany would remain in existence, although Wilson had earlier characterized a proposal to destroy them as "a silly extreme" to which he was opposed, memo for the president from Benson, February 7, 1919, N.A., R.G. 59, 763.722119 / 3724 1 / 2. Wilson to Tumulty, December 22, 1918, Wilson papers. Benson, lacking both instructions and adequate staff studies, had been questioning most of the clauses that his European naval colleagues suggested, discussion, "Approaching the Versailles Settlement," at the American Historical Association meeting, December 1966, reported in a letter, George F. Howe to the author, December 30, 1966.
29. The records of House and Lloyd George as to the talk on March 7 are not entirely in agreement, Lloyd George, *The Truth about the Peace Treaties*, pp. 284 ff. House to Wilson, March 7, 1919.
30. *I.P.*, vol. 4, pp. 356–360.
31. Bliss to adjutant general and secretary of war, March 3, 1919. Admiral Benson sent to the Navy Department a draft of the tentative naval terms with his comment, and this went to Wilson on March 4 with a handwritten note from Secretary Daniels, docs. in Wilson papers.

that House had arranged, he studied this question.[32] Advice from Admiral Benson and General Bliss now led him to question some of the tentative arrangements.

Apprehensive that the United States might become a party to a perpetual treaty of alliance against Germany, Benson suggested that certain detailed exactions would provoke annoyance and "a perpetual series of incidents of such a character as to be dangerous to the continuance of Peace." Benson objected both to any limitation of the German navy after its strength was once reduced, unless by action of the League of Nations, and to any continuing curb of Germany's right to defend its coasts. Furthermore, he cautioned that no action be taken in respect of the Kiel Canal that might set a precedent adverse to the interests of the United States in the Panama Canal or any other strictly American waterway.[33]

Bliss counseled in a similar vein. He thought the terms recommended would "do more to create, than to prevent war." In his opinion the enforcement of petty details by a continuing military supervision would give to revolutionaries in Germany "every temptation to make trouble." Rather than the indefinite period of control that the military advisers suggested, he preferred to trust in the League of Nations and a growth of democratic sentiment in Germany. He thought that these political forces would give France better protection than continuing harassment by French officers acting in the spirit that they had shown in enforcing the armistice.[34]

So advised, Wilson set forth the American position in a session of the Supreme Council on March 17, the day for the fourth and last renewal of the Armistice of Rethondes. The president upheld the assertion of his advisers that the United States would never assent to any permanent military domination of Europe by Germany. Assured by Foch that a German army of 100,000 would suffice to protect the eastern border, and worried that a larger force (as proposed by Bliss) might attack the new small states, Wilson agreed to the limit that Foch set, and this was stipulated in the Treaty of Versailles. He suggested that supervision by a commission of control might be ended not in three months, as Bliss had proposed, but as soon as the requirements for disarmament were met. (Later, in mid-April, he agreed that the League of Nations might act to control the German military potential.) In the treaty a date (March 31, 1920) was set for effective compliance by the German government with the military and naval terms; but no time was specified for the termination of commissions of control. The fate of Germany's warships, which was the subject of inconclusive talk in the Supreme Council on April 25, was not settled until June 21, when the German crews of vessels that were interned at Scapa Flow scuttled most of them.[35]

32. See above, p. 204.

33. Benson to Wilson, March 14, 1919, and notes by Admiral Benson regarding naval terms, March 14, 1919, Wilson papers.

34. Bliss to Wilson, March 14, 1919, and attached "Brief Analysis" of military terms; Bliss memorandum on "Proposed Military terms," March 17, 1919, Wilson papers. Five days later Bliss had a report from General Nolan to the effect that the German army could not renew hostilities, that neither it nor the German government had any intention of doing so, and that the Germans would sign peace terms with Great Britain and the United States that they would not sign with France because of bitter hatred of the latter, memorandum, Nolan to Bliss, March 24, 1919, Bliss papers, L.C.

35. See below, p. 430.

During the following weeks the drafting committee of the Peace Conference pre-pared a final text of military terms that would be not "preliminary," but part of the treaty of peace. Wilson's advisers were vigilant to detect clauses that seemed con-trary to American purposes.[36]

At the urging of his three colleagues in the Supreme Council, Lloyd George agreed in mid-March to remain at Paris for another two weeks[37] while the main questions might be settled and the treaty put into an initial form. His indignation at leakages in the French press aggravated the differences between his policy toward Germany and that demanded by French opinion. When the ensuing week brought little progress, Lloyd George retired on March 22 to the forest of Fontainebleau to confer with advisers who were warning him that the accumulaton of exactions upon Germany threatened to put that nation in an impossible position. From their unblinking analysis of public opinion in England, France, and Germany resulted a memoran-dum that was, in the opinion of at least one American delegate, the most statesman-like of all the utterances of the chiefs at the Peace Conference.[38]

The Fontainebleau memorandum, sent to Clemenceau and Wilson on March 25, dealt with the most vital questions of the peacemaking and treated them from a long perspective. It was comparatively easy, the prime minister wrote, to "patch up a peace" that would last for thirty years. "What is difficult, however, is to draw up a peace which will not provoke a fresh struggle when those who have had practical experience of what war means have passed away. . . . The maintenance of peace will then depend upon there being no causes of exasperation constantly stirring up the spirit of patriotism, of justice, of fair play. To achieve redress our terms may be severe, they may be stern and even ruthless, but at the same time they can be so just that the country on which they are imposed will feel in its heart that it has no right to complain. But injustice, arrogance, displayed in the hour of triumph, will never be forgotten or forgiven." Lloyd George opposed the encouragement of irre-dentism by the transfer of lands inhabited by Germans to the rule of other nations. He professed a desire to avoid stirring up a passion for vengeance such as that which had possessed France after the German exactions of 1871.

In this paper Lloyd George reaffirmed his conviction that there would be no secure peace until the statesmen dealt effectively with bolshevism. Unlike the French

36. For example, see Lansing to Wilson, April 23, 1919, Bliss papers, box 69. "Lansing" folder, and Bliss to Wilson, April 24, 1919, Wilson papers.

37. Wilson to Lloyd George, March 17, 1919, copy in Fonds Clemenceau, 6M72-75. House diary, March 17, 1919. Telephone message, March 19, 1919, Lloyd George papers, F / 30 / 3 / 31.

38. Lloyd George "was apparently the only statesman of importance there who took the precaution at that early stage to try to add up the whole treaty into one and see if it came to more than Germany could take," Shotwell record, Columbia O.H.R.O. The purpose of the Fontainebleau memorandum was to give the whole peace settlement a more inspiring appearance and one more in sympathy with the progressive forces making themselves felt all over the world, dispatch, Wiseman to Reading, March 23, 1919, Y.H.C. Hankey, pp. 98–101.

British observers were not uncritical. Lloyd George was called "the snipe" because of zigzags in his maneuvering, Bryce to J. F. Rhodes, March 29, 1919, Bryce papers, Bodleian Library. However Nicol-son wrote in retrospect: "Lloyd George taught me that apparent opportunism was not always irreconcil-able with vision, that volatility of method is not always indicative of volatility of intention. In his memorandum of March 25 . . . he showed that a politician is better, when it comes to reasonableness, than a theorist," *Peacemaking, 1919*, p. 109.

revolution at the end of the Napoleonic wars, the social revolt of the twentieth century was "still in its infancy" and in France, Great Britain, and Italy was expressing itself in strikes, a general disinclination to settle down to work, and revolt against prewar conditions. Germany, therefore, should be offered peace terms that a reasonable government might expect to be able to carry out and that would be "preferable for all sensible men to the alternative of bolshevism." It would be "safer," he thought, for Germany to be inside the League rather than outside; and it was idle to impose a limitation upon the armament of Germany unless the founding members arrived at an understanding among themselves in this matter.

There was little in the Fontainebleau memorandum with which Wilson could not concur. When it reached him on March 25, the spread of bolshevism into central Europe was no longer a mere threat but had become a fact. The weak Hungarian government of Károlyi collapsed and Béla Kun, an imprisoned revolutionary leader, came into power.[39] Certain of the Americans at Paris gave way to fear that this was but the first step in a general disintegration of society. House, exploiting the fear, continued his campaign for haste. He implored the president to spur the Europeans to agreement on the issues that he had been considering tentatively with them and that must be resolved before peace could be restored.

As the colonel was losing intimate contact with the president, he kept in touch with the proceedings in the inner council through Clemenceau, who called him in to ask his aid in moderating the views of Lloyd George in respect of the Rhineland. House had recognized from the beginning the importance of satisfying Clemenceau's comparatively modest demands, else it might become necessary to deal with less reasonable French nationalists, and it might be impossible to revise the League Covenant. Comprehension of this reality seemed for a time to be beyond Wilson's capacity as a diplomat, and when he finally granted its compelling force, he did so bitterly, as a jousting political leader.[40]

It was at the same momentous time—the twenty-fourth of March—that Wilson, Clemenceau, Lloyd George, and Orlando met in secret session with Wilson at his house, after seven unproductive sessions at the Quai d'Orsay. The president, speaking of a "veritable race between peace and anarchy" and the impatience of the public, proposed formally that they discuss among themselves the most difficult and urgent questions. Lloyd George and Clemenceau accepted this proposal readily. Thereupon the large formal sessions of the Supreme Council of Ten ceased and were followed by meetings of a council composed of three, four, or five chiefs of the delegations of the major powers. In accepting the new arrangement, Wilson gave the impression that he did not like it but was acceding to Lloyd George's plea for security against "leaks."[41]

39. See below, p. 223.

40. Baker, vol. 2, p. 39. House wrote in his diary on March 22 that he had undertaken to champion the security of France. See Floto, *Colonel House in Paris,* pp. 180–182. This scholar, in her relentless pursuit of details, appears to have overlooked the necessities of good diplomacy when she wrote: "House was thus willing to become Clemenceau's tool." Actually, it was fortunate for each man and for their nations that, though often disagreeing, they could talk frankly and with mutual respect.

41. H. White to Lodge, April 22, 1919, White papers, Special Collections, Columbia University Library, correspondence, box 1. Letters, Hankey to the author, May 5, 1951, February 22, 1954.

Immediately there were protests against this secrecy from the press, which had chosen to give Wilson's Point One the liberal interpretation that was in keeping with its own interest. House felt compelled to explain the matter to journalists who complained. "With four men sitting alone," he said, "there is no incentive for a speech; and they must talk intimately and get down to business. We are going to see results out of this, and while at the outset the meeting of The Four is private, yet everything will be known immediately upon reaching a conclusion."[42] An unfortunate effect of such an effusion was to make it appear to at least one French delegate, Jules Cambon, that House was publicly promising a quick peace in order to permit the United States to impute responsibility for the delay to the diplomats of Europe. Cambon thought that the old diplomacy would have settled everything already, and he perceived that the domestic politics of the democracies were at fault.[43]

In settling upon the terms for the Germans, it was not possible wholly to ignore the responsibility of those who were deemed to have first drawn the sword and therefore might be held accountable for the horror that ensued. Nor could the violation of Belgian neutrality in 1914 by a power that had guaranteed it be overlooked. And the peacemakers were faced also by the facts of the enemy's resort to submarine atrocities and to other forms of frightfulness, all in disregard of the restraint theretofore imposed by custom upon the conduct of hostilities by civilized nations. The law officers of the British crown recommended to the Imperial War Cabinet that the ex-emperor of Germany, Wilhelm II, be brought from his asylum in Holland and arraigned before an inter-Allied tribunal. Accepting this legal opinion unanimously, the cabinet resolved that "so far as the British government have the power, the ex-kaiser should be held personally responsible for his crimes against international law."[44]

Clemenceau and Orlando had approved this resolution when they met with Lloyd George in London on December 2, 1918; and Wilson, asked for his opinion, agreed to co-operate. But the diplomats of Europe raised fundamental questions.[45] Would the government of the Netherlands give up the accused? If the Allied governments

---

The Council of Four—occasionally lacking an Italian member or with a Japanese delegate added—met 206 times in 101 days. In six sessions before April 19, and regularly thereafter, Hankey kept formal minutes. Clemenceau's translator, Paul Mantoux, kept notes of what was said in the meetings from March 24 to June 28, and these were published in *Lés Délibérations du Conseil du Quatre (24 mars–28 juin 1919), Notes de l'Officier Interprète*. This work is referred to hereinafter as *Délibérations*. The notes bearing on the early meetings were translated into English by John Boardman Whitton and published under the title *Paris Peace Conference 1919: Proceedings of the Council of Four (March 24–April 18)*. This work is hereinafter referred to as *Proceedings*.

The foreign ministers continued to meet in a council of four (or five or three), and on five occasions they came together with the top-level Council of Four, as they had earlier, in a Supreme Council of Ten. See Marston, pp. 161–176; Hankey, pp. 97–106; and Pamphlet No. 1, Proceedings of the British Institute of International Affairs of the Royal Society of Arts, November 2, 1920.

42. Charles T. Thompson, *The Peace Conference Day by Day*, p. 267.

43. Cambon, "La Paix," p. 21.

44. Lloyd George, pp. 54–56. See David Albert Foltz, "The War Crimes Issue at the Paris Peace Conference 1919–1920," ch. III.

45. Foltz, pp. 49 ff. Hankey, p. 13.

set up a tribunal, would the world at large accept the jurisdiction of such a court to try and to punish an ex post facto felony? Would not lawlessness on the part of the enemy find an excuse in the lawlessness of the victors?

The provisional government of Germany, representing a people told by their rulers that war had been forced on them in 1914 by conspiring enemies, persistently urged the creation of a neutral commission to inquire impartially into the origins of the conflict. The German foreign minister, addressing the foreign offices of the major Allies, conjured up the ideals of lasting peace and international confidence. From London and Paris, however, he received blunt rebuffs, asserting that the responsibility of Germany for the war had long ago been incontestably proved. The American State Department, after communicating with the peace mission at Paris, replied in the same tenor.[46]

At Paris, Wilson suggested that the question of national and individual crimes against decency be settled in the comparative privacy of the Supreme Council; but when Lloyd George brought up the matter in that body for a second time, it was decided to place the subject on the agenda of a plenary session. As a result the Peace Conference decided on January 25 to create a commission to study the question.[47] Secretary Lansing and Dr. James Brown Scott became the American members. Representing a nation that had suffered less than the Allies from the misconduct of Germans during the war, they were not so ready as their European colleagues to cloak the exercise of power in dubious legal form. They pointed out that "international law," as it was understood in 1914, had no provision under which heads of states who caused war could be held personally accountable.[48]

Notwithstanding this American opinion, however, a large majority of the commission agreed that at the next renewal of the armistice the Germans should be required to deliver certain war criminals and also relevant documents; furthermore, Allied commanders in occupied territory should be ordered to secure such wanted persons as lived in regions under their control. However, Lansing, who was chairman of the commission, refused to transmit these suggestions to the Supreme Council, arguing that as appointees of a plenary session the commission could report only to the full Peace Conference. The secretary of state preferred that the conference, instead of trying Germans, issue a severe indictment. He proposed that a committee of inquiry be appointed to consider the question in the light of documents in the archives of the enemy, and to report to the participating governments.

46. Ludwig F. Schaefer, "German Peace Strategy in 1918–1919," p. 31. *F.R., P.P.C.*, vol. 2, pp. 71–72. Dispatch, Solf to State Department, forwarded to House, December 11, 1918, Y.H.C.

47. The Commission on Responsibility of Authors of the War and the Enforcement of Penalties, composed of delegates of the five great powers and five small states—Belgium, Greece, Poland, Romania, and Serbia—was instructed to consider "the responsibility of the authors of the war"; "the fact as to breaches of the laws and customs of war committed by the forces of the German Empire and their allies"; "the degree of responsibility for these offenses attaching to particular members of the enemy forces"; and "the constitution and procedure of a tribunal appropriate to the trial of these offences," *F.R., P.P.C.*, vol. 3, p. 699.

48. To create a penal responsibility for such past acts "would be extralegal from the viewpoint of international law, . . . contrary to the spirit both of international law and of the municipal law of civilized states and . . . would, in reality, be a political and not a legal creation," memorandum by Miller and Scott, c. January 18, 1919, Miller, *My Diary*, vol. 3, pp. 456–457.

Lansing's ideas were rejected by the commission over which he presided.[49] When its report came to the Supreme Council on March 29, however, the American members attached a statement to the effect that the views of the majority contravened American principles. The secretary of state thought that the British knew the practical impossibility of the action that they were forced by public opinion to advocate and were depending on the United States to block it. Lansing found the president even more strongly opposed to trying the kaiser than he was himself. Both feared that physical punishment of Wilhelm II would make him a martyr and would lead to the restoration of the dynasty.[50]

On April 8 The Four discussed the question at great length. "I am afraid," Wilson said, "it would be difficult to reach the real culprits. I fear that the evidence would be lacking."[51] The president thought that in the violation of Belgium's neutrality a crime had been committed for which eventually the League of Nations would find a remedy. He warned against dignifying a culprit by citing him before a high tribunal, and against stooping to his level by flouting the principles of law that were already accepted. When Lloyd George told the Council of Four that he wanted "the man responsible for the greatest crime in history to receive the punishment for it," the president replied: "He will be judged by the contempt of the whole world; isn't that the worst punishment for such a man?" He thought the German militarists doomed to "the execration of history."[52] The president agreed that the Allied peoples might not understand if the kaiser were allowed to go free; but he said: "I can do only what I consider to be just, whether public sentiment be for or against the verdict of my conscience." He received support from Orlando, who spoke as a jurist.

At this Clemenceau burst into an impassioned appeal that was shrewdly aimed at the president. "For me," he said, "one law dominates all others, that of responsibility. Civilization is the organization of human responsibilities. Mr. Orlando says: 'Yes, within the nation.' I say: 'In the international domain.' I say this with President Wilson who, when he laid the foundations of the League of Nations, had the honor to carry over into international law the essential principles of national law. . . . We have today a glorious opportunity to bring about the transfer to international law of the principle of responsibility which is at the basis of national law." Wilson still demurred, however. He pointed out that there was no legal or other means of forcing Holland to give up the kaiser.

At this point Lloyd George declared that this question, like that of reparations, interested English opinion "to the highest degree," and his people could not accept a treaty that left it unsolved. He suggested that they could bring Holland to deliver

49. James B. Scott, "The Trial of the Kaiser," in Seymour and House (eds.), *What Really Happened at Paris*, p. 241. Lapradelle (ed.), *La Paix de Versailles*, vol. 3, pp. 26–28, 457–482. See Foltz, ch. V.

50. *F.R., P.P.C.*, vol. 11, pp. 93–94. Lansing, "Memorandum of Reservations," April 4, 1919; Lansing to Wilson, April 8, 1919, Wilson papers. Foltz, pp. 135–174. Letter, Lansing to Polk, March 14–15, 1919, Y.H.C. Geneviève Tabouis, *The Life of Jules Cambon*, pp. 319–320.

51. Wilson had said on the *George Washington* in December that probably the kaiser had been "coerced to an extent" by the general staff. Swem book ms., ch. 21, p. 9, Princeton University Library.

52. Mantoux, *Proceedings*, p. 83.

Wilhelm II by threatening exclusion of that nation from the League of Nations.

Under this well-directed attack Wilson, who at this very time was about to go into the final meetings of the Commission on the League of Nations to seek approval of an amendment in respect of the Monroe Doctrine, yielded.[53] The next morning he read to the Supreme Council a draft that he had prepared. It satisfied Clemenceau and Lloyd George, and provided the substance for Articles 227 and 229 of the Treaty of Versailles. The Four accepted the compromise formula, and Wilson said that he would try to get the signature of Makino of Japan.[54]

In withdrawing from his opposition to the war-crime clauses, Wilson recognized that they were too ineffectual to warrant any determined resistance to them. When he was asked by Ambassador Davis whether he expected to "catch his rabbit," he said no, "it was all damned foolishness anyway."[55] Lloyd George's enthusiasm waned after he had a stong protest from Botha and when the vindictive feeling of the British people subsided somewhat.[56] Wilson brought up the matter on June 25, and Lansing drafted a note that was sent to the Dutch government requesting compliance with Article 227 of the Treaty of Versailles, under which the five great victorious powers were to try Wilhelm II before a "special tribunal" on the charge of "a supreme offense against international morality and the sanctity of treaties." However, Jules Cambon and others advised the Dutch government to refuse the request and thus to get the Allied statesmen out of a disagreeable scrape.[57] A reply from the government of the Netherlands gave the expected refusal, arguing that the usage of political asylum should be respected. No further action was taken, but the British and French leaders could appease their constituencies with evidence that they had tried to satisfy the prevailing demand for retributive "justice."[58] Nevertheless, the assertion by the Peace Conference of a right to punish war criminals was a novel departure from tradition, one that set a precedent for action at the end of the next world war.

While the generals and admirals drew up specifications to meet the immediate necessity of curbing German power, and while the political chiefs spent precious

53. See below, p. 307.

54. Wilson to Lansing, April 9, 1919. Wilson's text with minor changes became Part VII of the Treaty of Versailles, Foltz, pp. 201–202. A diary letter of Edith Benham of April 9 records that it was at the suggestion of Mrs. Wilson that the president prepared his compromise formula and secured the signature of his colleagues.

55. John W. Davis's diary, June 5, 1919, Y.H.C.

56. On the anniversary of the Treaty of Vereeniging, Botha pointedly reminded the British delegation of the incendiary effect upon the Boers of an English proposal that he and Smuts be tried for the crime of causing the Boer War, Grayson diary, April 23, 1919. Stevenson, p. 307. Ambassador Davis noticed "a marked cooling in the eagerness to try the kaiser and a growing disinclination to have the trial staged in London," J. W. Davis to Lansing, July 30, 1919.

57. Curzon to Robertson, July 17, 1919, Curzon papers, box 22, f 112 / 302.

58. The paragraphs above are based on Hankey, pp. 13, 114, 116, 184, and on Mantoux, *Proceedings*, pp. 144–151, and *Délibérations*, vol. 2, pp. 524–525.

Eventually Germany was allowed to try its war criminals, using lists of names and evidence submitted by the Allies, who reserved the right to pass upon the decisions of the German court. The United States and Japan presented no names for indictments, Scott, p. 253. Only twelve cases came to judgment, and those who were convicted received mild sentences, Erich Eyck, *A History of the Weimar Republic*, 2 vols. (Cambridge, Mass., 1962), vol. 1, pp. 187–188.

time in a fruitless effort to cater to the public hatred of "war criminals," the peacemakers failed to produce a grand political design for all the German-speaking peoples that would both satisfy their national aspirations and perhaps reduce the likelihood of military aggression.

Unlike the Hohenzollerns in Germany, the Hapsburg dynasty escaped punitive measures on the part of the Peace Conference. The Supreme Council decided that arrangements should be made whereby the Swiss government would give asylum to the imperial family of Austria-Hungary.[59]

The Hapsburg domain having split into fragments, national councils were petitioning the United Sates for food and for policing. The Foreign Office of rump Austria had addressed Wilson directly with a plea for recognition "in accordance with the principles so often proclaimed"; and the president replied on November 30, 1918, that he would take the matter "under the most serious consideration" when he reached Paris. The scholars of the Inquiry, who were eager to maintain the economic cohesion that existed under the empire and had taken it upon themselves before the armistice to consider what form of confederation might be developed, had come to realize that dismemberment must be accepted and boundaries drawn for new states.[60] They recommended the formation of an independent German Austria that would include only the Crownlands of Upper and Lower Austria, Carinthia, the German Tyrol, Salzburg, Styria, and the Viralberg.[61]

In their isolation and weakness the Germans of Austria turned naturally toward their kin to the north. On November 12 the National Assembly at Vienna, repudiating allegiance to the Hapsburg crown and invoking the principle of self-determination, had proclaimed a new democratic republic of German-Austria and had declared it a constituent part of the German Republic. Nevertheless Coolidge, the American observer at Vienna, thought the assembly's vote for union was inconclusive, and public opinion fluid and unpredictable.[62]

After the election on February 16 of an Austrian constituent assembly in which socialists won a majority, it was anticipated that the Peace Conference would soon be presented with an *Anschluss* as a *fait accompli*. Scheidemann, Germany's chancellor, insisted on the right of the new German state to join with Austria. Moreover, a secret agreement was signed at Weimar on March 2, providing for union. The German and Austrian governments maintained a close liaison but feared to offend French opinion by pressing their case publicly.[63]

France looked on the question of Germany's future as a matter of life and death. French statesmen had stressed the prime importance of undoing the unifying work

59. *F.R., P.P.C.,* vol. 4, pp. 332–334.

60. "In 1919 each of the victorious nationalities was bent on going its own way. Economic principles, however wise theoretically, had to be and were sacrificed," Coolidge, *Ten Years of War and Peace,* pp. 261, 266–267. Dispatch, Coolidge to Ammission, January 7, 1919, Y.H.C.

61. See Gelfand, pp. 199–205.

62. Coolidge to Ammission, January 30, 1919, N.A., R.G. 256, 184.01102 / 12. Coolidge had talked with Dr. Bauer, minister for foreign affairs, and found him of the opinion that Austria lacked economic resources to stand alone and therefore should be united with Germany. S. W. Gould, "Austrian Attitudes toward Anschluss," *Journal of Modern History* 22 (March–December, 1950):220–231.

63. Schaefer, p. 67. Stanley Suval, *The Anschluss Question in the Weimar Era* (Baltimore, 1974), p. 11.

of Bismarck and of avoiding any strengthening of Berlin's hold upon the nation.[64] Some thought it inevitable that the Austrian Germans sooner or later would join with Germany. Indeed, they saw certain advantages in such a movement and thought that it should be guided into a confederation similar to that under the Diet of Frankfurt in 1848.[65] Public opinion in France, however, was not greatly influenced by the analysis of wise statesmen. The wartime hatred of the Germans did not permit the political chiefs to accept any policy that seemed to run counter to the passion of the people to emasculate their enemy. Pichon had made it clear to the Chamber on December 28, 1918, that the French government was as determined as the people to oppose an *Anschluss,* although there were assertions by the Left that under Wilson's doctrine the Austrians should be left free to determine their own future. In the spring of 1919 French diplomacy was developing plans for a neutralized Danubian confederacy and for extensive and permanent economic assistance to Austria.[66]

On February 23 Clemenceau spoke to Colonel House of his concern about the union of Austria with Germany. Believing that this would not happen if the Allies made it plain to the Austrian government that they were opposed, Clemenceau insisted that a warning be given to Vienna. His position found support among career men in the State Department. However, the Cobb-Lippman interpretation of the Fourteen Points had stated that Austria "should of right be permitted to join Germany," and Secretary Lansing felt that because of the president's principle of self-determination he could not oppose *Anschluss.* Lansing expressed interest in the possibility of a union of Austria with Bavaria as a means of splitting Germany on regional and religious lines.[67] The question, important though it was to the future peace of Europe, had a low priority in Wilson's thinking. No response came from him when he received Clemenceau's plea through House.[68]

Wilson and Lloyd George did not feel sure enough of any policy, or of their ability to dictate to Austria, to issue the strong warning that Clemenceau sought. The Americans preferred to relax the blockade and to provide credits for food for the Austrians as a means of dissuading them from union with Germany.[69]

At the end of March the question of *Anschluss* was becoming more acute each day.[70] A resolution of March 14 of the Austrian assembly called for the inclusion of the nation in the German Reich. On April 1, Clemenceau informed House that the French agent at Vienna, who was under instructions to remind Chancellor Karl Renner that France expected Austria to remain independent, was having difficulty

64. "Clemenceau said that the more separate and independent republics were established in Germany the better he would be pleased." "Notes of an interview between M. Clemenceau, Col. House and myself [Lloyd George] . . . at 10:30 A.M., 7th March 1919," Lloyd George papers, F / 197 / 1.

65. See the brief by Gabriel Hanotaux, a former minister of foreign affairs, entitled "Après la signature de l'Armistice . . . ," Klotz papers, 18 / 2.

66. On French opinion and policy in respect of an *Anschluss,* see Alfred D. Low, *The Anschluss Movement, 1918–1919, and the Paris Peace Conference,* pp. 259 ff. On the German view, see Duane Paul Myers, "Germany and the Question of the Austrian Anschluss, 1918–1922."

67. Reports by Dolbeare, Dresel, and Allen W. Dulles, February 12, 1919, N.A., R.G. 256, 185 / 1136 / 1. Minutes, ACTNP, March 1 and 3, 1919. Low, pp. 322–323.

68. *I.P.,* vol. 4, p. 335.

69. Low, p. 323.

70. Bonsal, *Unfinished Business,* p. 169.

in making an impression.[71] Good diplomacy required that any pressure must be exerted in a way that would neither provoke an increase in the popular demand for *Anschluss* nor shake the stability of the government at Vienna.[72] When Clemenceau asked for unofficial American aid, House agreed, having no strong views on the matter and being particularly eager at this juncture to give Clemenceau a *quid pro quo*. House hoped that a word of caution spoken in advance in a friendly and private way might prevent precipitate action by Austria. He therefore attached his deputy, Stephen Bonsal, to a mission under General Smuts that was going to Budapest to deal with revolutionaries there.[73] Bonsal was instructed to inform Renner that the treaty of peace would formally forbid a union with the German Reich, and therefore it might be well for Austria to avoid any commitment that it might later have to give up.

When the American agent hastened to carry out his orders, Renner confessed that he had within the hour been persuaded by a German envoy that he should submit a German proposition to the Austrian council the next morning. Protesting that he looked upon a union with the Weimar Republic only as a *pis aller*, the chancellor said that the American advice would carry great weight in the national council. Pleading that his little country could not stand alone on the checkerboard of Europe, he asked what assistance might be expected from the United States. Bonsal, unable to offer anything specific, spoke of "a reservoir of great good will" that had made Americans reluctant to declare war on Austria-Hungary; and he cited the relief program. Before the interview was over Bonsal was authorized to report to House that "somehow and in some way yet unexplored" the Austrian government would follow the American counsel, despite the indignation that it felt because the Allies were permitting Slavs to make inroads in territory that it regarded as properly Austrian.[74]

On April 22 Clemenceau got the assent of Wilson and Lloyd George to a resolution on which House and Tardieu had agreed and on which Article 80 of the Treaty of Versailles was to be based: "Germany acknowledges and will respect strictly the independence of Austria." The president accepted this departure from

---

71. The French agent, Allizé, was urging the Austrians to combine with Bavaria, Nicholas Roosevelt, *A Front Row Seat*, p. 114. "Few of our people are enthusiastic about union with Germany," Renner told Bonsal, who, after talking with old acquaintances in Vienna who were well informed, accepted Renner's opinion. At the same time Bonsal was aware of a desire among Austrians for union with Bavaria and the Catholic Rhinelands, Bonsal, *Unfinished Business*, pp. 88, 95, 136–137, 142–143. On Austrian opinion on the question, see F. L. Casten, *Revolution in Central Europe 1918–1919* (Berkeley and Los Angeles, 1972), pp. 294–298.

A report submitted on March 20 by Wallace Notestein of the Inquiry stated that an immediate plebiscite in Austria probably would favor union with Germany. He alluded to "rapid manipulation by people with very provisional authority who were determined to attain their ends before better constituted authorities could interfere." Opposition to union seemed to be growing, and separatist tendencies were becoming evident in mountain districts. Report in Notestein papers, Yale Library, mss. and archives, box 11.

72. Dispatch, H. H. Field to the ACTNP, March 19, 1919, N.A., R.G. 256, 184.01402 / 19.

73. When General Smuts asked that an American accompany him on this mission (see below, p. 225), House designated Bonsal. Secrecy was observed so that the French and Italians would not be offended because they were not represented, House diary, April 1, 1919. According to Bonsal, House acted after getting Wilson's approval, *Unfinished Business*, pp. 75–90. Roosevelt, p. 117.

74. Bonsal, *Unfinished Business*, pp. 87–89, 94, 103, 132.

self-determination as a necessary political expedient. However, in the course of a final review of the article by The Four on May 2 Wilson objected to the wording. While desiring to prevent immediate *Anschluss,* he was unwilling to impose a permanent ban. He therefore proposed a modifying formula. Under this Germany was required to respect the independence of Austria as "inalienable" except by consent of the Council of the League of Nations. France, as long as it held a permanent seat in the council, would be in a position to veto an *Anschluss.*

By the failure at Paris in 1919 to work constructively toward integration of Austria in a peace-oriented German polity, the way was left open for Corporal Hitler, at that time an Austrian citizen, later to exploit the natural and frustrated impulse of peoples of German blood to unite.[75] The essential "German problem" was to persist in the history of the century. Thoughtful men were asking how the great resources of the German people and of their country might play a constructive part in the life of the postwar world. Should the victors grant to the vanquished the opportunity which German liberals sought, that of membership in the new League of Nations? And, if the answer was affirmative, when should their participation begin? These questions were not answered until a few days before the signing of the treaty with Germany.[76]

75. A. J. P. Taylor, *The Origins of the Second World War,* p. 26. "Perhaps the worst crime of the treaty against the right of self-determination is the barrier which it has set up between Austria and Germany," H. K. U. Kessler, *Germany and Europe,* p. 35.

76. See below, pp. 425–427.

12

Revolution in Southeastern Europe

The question of the future of the Hapsburg lands was complicated by an ideological challenge from Moscow. A manifesto issued by the Soviet government on November 3, 1918, had saluted the "liberation" of minorities from "oppression."

Wilson had immediately matched the Russian *démarche* with a counterappeal to those who had "achieved liberation from the yoke," urging them "to restrain every force that may threaten either to delay or to discredit the noble processes of liberty." He was hopeful that the revolutionary movements would result in the emergence of constitutional regimes.[1]

Near the end of March, however, the government of rump Austria, which was committed to social democracy, was menaced by a turn toward bolshevism in neighboring Hungary, the other remnant of the Hapsburg empire that was treated as an enemy by the peacemakers. Hungary was regarded by Lenin as a land ripe for a proletarian revolution. The military establishment of Austria-Hungary had melted away, and French and Serb commanders at Belgrade had signed a military convention with Hungary on November 13 under which Allied armies penetrated Hungarian lands. The American State Department, acting in harmony with the French government, had rebuffed a Hungarian attempt at rapprochement through the old Austro-Hungarian legation in Switzerland.[2]

Count Michael Károlyi, becoming president of Hungary in January, had endeavored to conciliate the victors and salvage something from the debacle. He had visited the United States in 1914 to raise a fund for an independent and democratic Hungary. With the support of moderate Social Democrats, he now asked America for economic aid and for recognition in accord with the principles it proclaimed. Complaining that Hungary had been reduced in population from 20 million to 8 million, and admitting that the social revolution had gone further than he wished, Károlyi said to one of Hoover's men who talked with him, "Why do you go on pretending that you are fighting for the rights of small peoples? Why not . . . say frankly: 'We have won and shall now do with you exactly as we please?' Hungary would then know definitely where she stood."[3] One American observer regarded Károlyi's policy as conciliatory, independent, and reasonable; and another, "tremendously impressed" by him, reported to Wilson that the Allies had broken the armistice agreement and the only way to save Károlyi's government was by inviting

1. See Walworth, *America's Moment: 1918*, p. 174. On the propaganda of the United States and Soviet Russia at the end of 1918, see Peter Pastor, *Hungary between Wilson and Lenin*, pp. 52–59.

2. Dispatches of November 19, December 19, 1918, *F.R., P.P.C.*, vol. 2, pp. 193–195, 204–205. A. Coolidge to ACTNP, January 16, 1919, Wilson papers. See Mayer, *Politics and Diplomacy of Peacemaking*, pp. 527–528.

3. Hugh Gibson to "Dearest," January 9 and 11, 1919, Gibson papers, boxes 9 and 10, Hoover Institution Archives.

him to send a delegation to the Peace Conference.[4] The French government, however, would not permit this.

Károlyi was distressed by military aggression committed by Hungary's neighbors with French sanction, as well as by the delay and indecision at Paris. Early in January his entire cabinet resigned. A month later he petitioned the Peace Conference for representation before it, and he asked that the United States give a hint as to the delegates that would be acceptable. In forwarding this message to Paris, Coolidge reported that the Hungarians felt they had "a great and legitimate grievance." Elections in Hungary were postponed indefinitely because of uncertainty as to boundaries; Károlyi would be forced to armed resistance to invasion lest he be unseated; and there was "a great danger of Bolshevist revolution" against a government that had no armed force with which to meet it. Immediate action by the Allies would save the situation. The Hungarians placed their only hope in the sense of justice of the United States and its leader. Coolidge reported "emphatically" that it was in American interest that Károlyi should remain in power.[5]

The Supreme Council was slow to grapple with its complex task. Boundaries must be drawn for Hungary that would encourage stability and at the same time satisfy the neighboring states that had been wartime allies. Finally, on February 26, the council approved the creation of a neutral zone in Transylvania between Hungary and Romania, but it disregarded a proposal by General Bliss that the western boundary of this zone be moved some twenty-five kilometers to the east, as recommended by the American observer in Budapest.[6] The head of the French military mission, Colonel Vyx, notified the Károlyi government of the council's decision just as the last days of winter were intensifying the distress that resulted from shortages of food and fuel. He demanded an answer the next day.[7] Nicholas Roosevelt joined the Allied representatives at Budapest in accompanying Vyx. Exactly what was said in the talk with Károlyi has not been ascertained. According to the *Memoirs* of Károlyi, however, his first question was "whether the boundary was just a temporary military one, or whether it was political as well. The answer came [from Vyx] that it was a political one."[8] Roosevelt suggested that Károlyi might have

4. C. M. Storey, an American observer at Budapest, to Coolidge, January 21, 1919, N.A., R.G. 256, 184.01102 / 30. Creel to Wilson, February 3, 1919, Wilson papers. Perman, *The Shaping of the Czechoslovak State,* pp. 84–89. Károlyi alleged that the armistice terms had been violated by Czechs, Serbs, Rumanians, and Ukrainians, and that he had been told by a French colonel, Vyx, that the United States as well as France approved the Czech occupation, A. Coolidge to ACTNP, January 16, 1919. Gibson letter cited. According to Bonsal, Károlyi, impoverished by gambling, had made "a rabble rousing trip" to America during the war and was interned in France, *Unfinished Business,* p. 26n.

5. Coolidge to ACTNP, January 16, 1919, Y.H.C. *Ibid.,* January 20, 1919, Bliss papers, box 72, "Hungary, misc." folder. Coolidge to A. W. Dulles, January 24, 1919, A. W. Dulles corres., box 6, Mudd Library, Princeton University.

H. J. Coolidge and R. H. Lord, *Archibald Cary Coolidge,* p. 202. "The choice may lie between treating with a Károlyi Government or dealing with a Bolshevik Hungary," memorandum, "Hungary," by Allen W. Dulles, January 1, 1919, Y.H.C.

6. Memoranda, Bliss to Lansing, March 8, 1919, Bliss papers, box 72, "Hungary, misc." folder; Bliss to White, April 5, 1919, Bliss papers, box 69, "White" correspondence. Bliss to Wilson, March 28, 1919, Wilson papers. Dispatch cited, C. M. Storey to Coolidge, January 21, 1919. On the question of the boundary in Transylvania, see C. A. Macartney, *Hungary and Her Successors, 1919–1937* (London, 1937), pp. 275–279.

7. Francis Deák, *Hungary at the Paris Peace Conference,* p. 57.

8. Károlyi, *The Memoirs of Michael Károlyi* (New York, 1957), p. 153. According to Alfred D.

"twisted Vyx's oral communication" for his own purposes.[9] Károlyi was said to have declared that no government could survive at Budapest that accepted boundaries that took away much of Hungary's food and most of its coal, and that the Allies might as well occupy the entire country.[10] When a British naval order required that he turn over the Danubian fleet of Hungary to Czechoslovakia,[11] Károlyi's political position became impossible. On March 21 he was removed from office by socialists to whom he turned for support.[12]

The nationalist regime of Béla Kun filled the vacuum. A war prisoner who returned from Russia to Hungary in November 1918, Béla Kun had been close to Lenin and had embraced bolshevism and returned as a propagandist to Budapest, where he was jailed in February 1919.[13] He now sought to align himself with Moscow. A telegram addressed to Lenin by "Comrade Bélakun" was intercepted in Germany and delivered to General Bliss. The message requested "instructions" and "protection" and proposed affiliation with the Soviet government. "We turn with arms in our hands against all enemies of the proletariat," it said.[14] There was a general mobilization, and the population was cowed by a reign of terror.[15]

This turn of events, foreseen by Bliss, forcefully suggested to the Peace Conference that any measures short of military intervention might be insufficient to preserve peace in southeast Europe. Yet the peacemakers hesitated to bear down upon the regime of Béla Kun to an extent that would make Hungarian patriots desperate. Fearing that the disorder might spread to neighboring states, The Four hoped that Kun might serve in liaison with Lenin. But this hope was blighted by the emotional revulsion toward bolshevism that swayed even responsible men in the Western democracies.[16]

News of the coup at Budapest reached Paris on the same week-end on which Lloyd George retired to Fontainebleau to reappraise the policy of the peacemakers.[17] The crisis in Hungary illuminated a statement by him to the effect that the greatest present danger was that all eastern Europe would be "swept into the orbit of the Bolshevik revolution." The most immediate peril lay in Austria. The Vienna

Low, Vyx denied Károlyi's allegation, *The Soviet Hungarian Republic and the Paris Peace Conference,* pp. 30–31.

9. N. Roosevelt, *A Front Row Seat,* pp. 101 ff. Temperley wrote that Károlyi distorted Vyx's communication, *A History of the Peace Conference at Paris,* vol. 1, p. 353. Also see Mayer, p. 548. Deák, p. 58n. Nicolson, *Peacemaking, 1919,* pp. 297–298. Minutes, ACTNP, March 27, 1919. Ammission to the secretary of state, March 28, 1919, Wilson papers. N. Roosevelt, pp. 101 ff.

10. Dispatches, Ammission to the secretary of state, March 27, 1919, N.A., R.G. 59, 763.72119 / 4334, March 24, 1919, N.A., R.G. 59, 763.72 / 12944.

11. Memorandum, A. W. Dulles to Bowman, March 24, 1919, A. W. Dulles papers, correspondence.

12. For a full discussion of the March revolution see Mayer, ch. 16, and Peter Pastor, pp. 136–147.

13. Memorandum for the president from Lansing, March 22, 1919. The new Hungarian cabinet was "probably not all extreme revolutionaries," Dodge (Belgrade) to Ammission, March 28, 1919, Wilson papers. See Károlyi, pp. 144, 152.

14. Pershing to Bliss, March 27, 1919, Bliss papers, box 202.

15. Nicolson, pp. 301–303. Bonsal, pp. 120–127.

16. Nicolson, p. 293. The anti-Bolshevist hysteria of the day appeared, for example, in a letter to House from a former Georgia schoolmate of Wilson who was now minister to Switzerland. It would be better for civilization to "go down fighting this most insidious evil," Pleasant Stovall wrote, rather than try to "bridge over differences" with Moscow with the aid of Béla Kun, letter, April 9, 1919, Y.H.C.

17. See above, p. 211.

press expressed sympathy with Béla Kun's coup, and Coolidge was warned by the Austrian government that its position was precarious and the only salvation was the sending of Allied troops.[18]

American specialists at Paris suggested a friendly military intervention, but Bliss and Hoover continued to put faith in economic relief.[19] Coolidge, who had been summoned to Paris three days before the fall of Károlyi, was instructed to notify the Austrian government of the establishment at Vienna of an inter-Allied trade commission and of the restoration of commerce, with the prohibition of re-export to Germany, Hungary, or Soviet Russia. The flour ration was doubled. Rioting was suppressed by the Volkswehr and by timely rainfall. Early in May, when Austrian delegates came to Paris to receive the terms of a treaty of peace, it seemed that Austria would be spared the pains of violent revolution.[20]

The stabilization of government in Hungary, however, was a trying and protracted task. In the meeting of The Four on March 29, Orlando introduced a report from the Italian ambassador at Belgrade, who had just gone to Budapest and who found the rebel movement to be "socialist, not bolshevist." Its leaders were said to be desirous of establishing relations with the Allies.[21] The ambassador transmitted, at the request of the members of Béla Kun's government, an indication that they still recognized the armistice agreement.

Wilson found this report convincing. He felt that the demarcation of the boundary in Transylvania by the Supreme Council was not exactly what it should have been and that the council was not without responsibility for Károlyi's downfall.[22] In the course of a discussion in the Supreme Council on March 31 in which the foreign ministers participated, the president said: "The Budapest government is not burdened with the crimes with which we charge the Bolsheviks of Russia. It is probably nationalistic. It is a government of Soviets because that is the form of revolution now in fashion, and there may be many aspects of soviets." "I am prepared," he confessed, "to begin talks with any rascal so long as his proposal is acceptable and my honor remains intact." Nevertheless, he was unwilling to enter into diplomatic relations with Béla Kun. He went only so far as to advocate sending qualified observers who would open an opportunity for the new regime to communicate with the Peace Conference. Clemenceau, however, asked his colleagues to bear in mind that Kun's governments had made an offer of alliance to Moscow and had imprisoned Colonel

18. Another report informed Wilson that Chancellor Renner advised that military occupation of Austria would create a grave crisis, dispatch, N. Roosevelt to Ammission, April 1, 1919, Wilson papers.

19. Dispatches quoted in Mayer, pp. 716, 720–721. Ammission to the secretary of state, March 24, 1919, N.A., R.G. 59, 763.72 / 12951.

Military occupation was discussed by the Allied representatives at Vienna and was desired by Austrian conservatives, and also by the Italian government and by the French military representative, Italian ambassador to French minister of foreign affairs, April 7, 1919, Fonds Clemenceau, 6N 75; Lansing to the secretary of state, March 26, 1919, N.A., R.G. 59, 864.00 / 3.

20. Mayer, pp. 722–724.

21. Lansing informed Wilson that Italian friendliness toward Hungary reflected a desire to strengthen that country as a check upon Yugoslavia, Italy's enemy, Lansing to Wilson, March 27, 1919, Wilson papers.

22. American experts thought mistakes had been made and deemed it "vital" to act to prevent their repetition, memorandum, A. W. Dulles to Bowman, March 24, 1919, with comment by Bowman, A. W. Dulles papers, correspondence.

Vyx. Lloyd George, apprehensive that they might repeat the mistake of intervening in Russia, acceded with enthusiasm when Wilson proposed that they send to Budapest a trustworthy man of experience and authority who would elicit information from the provisional government. "It might be desirable," Wilson suggested, "in order to avoid every appearance of a diplomatic negotiation, to send a high-ranking soldier who has personally the qualities of a diplomat." Lloyd George proposed the name of General Smuts, "as much a statesman as a soldier,"[23] and a man who entertained hope of negotiating constructively with the Russian Soviets through Budapest.[24]

On March 24 the American peace commission notified Coolidge at Vienna that it would be undesirable to break off all connections with the new government at Budapest for fear of throwing it into the arms of Moscow. The next day Professor Philip Marshall Brown of the Coolidge mission, acting as an American observer at Budapest, reported that the Béla Kun regime was an expression of protest against measures taken by the Allies, against whom the Hungarians were now openly defiant. He thought that a "friendly understanding" could be reached with the new government on a basis of economic relief and self-determination, and if that failed, military intervention, "with conciliatory assurances," might be necessary. This would be easy to effect, in his opinion, but of doubtful value in eliminating communism permanently. Brown reported that Béla Kun had called on him and talked in a moderate way, that he was treating the American mission very well and better than other foreigners, and that, indeed, the new government had decreed that all foreigners should retain their rights and privileges. Others of the American specialists made recommendations that included military measures.[25]

Smuts set out from Paris on April 1. During two days at Budapest he made a proposition to Béla Kun that had no provision for the withdrawal of the Romanian invaders and that therefore was deemed unacceptable. Appealing to Wilson's principles and asking for a settlement of Hungary's frontiers and consideration of economic necessities by a conference with neighboring states under Smuts's chairmanship, Béla Kun replied that food was of the first importance and that if his government fell, the Allies would have to assume responsibility for the government of Hungary.[26]

At the request of House, Bonsal, going to Budapest with the Smuts party after performing a secret mission for House at Vienna,[27] investigated conditions in the Hungarian capital. Finding that the banks and stores had been looted and at least a thousand landlords and thirty citizens killed by soldiers who in many instances had criminal records, he contrived in the role of journalist to interview Béla Kun and to attend a session of the Workers' and Soldiers' Council of the Revolution. Thankful to escape unharmed, he assured House that the reports of Brown were "very clear,

23. Mantoux, *Proceedings,* pp. 55–56, 69–74.

24. Smuts to Lloyd George, March 26, 29, and 31, 1919, Lloyd George papers, F / 45 / 9 / 29, 31.

25. For analyses of American opinion, see Mayer, pp. 575 ff., and James Smallwood, "Banquo's Ghost," 293–294.

26. Memorandum, Smuts to Balfour, April 4, 1919, Fonds Clemenceau, 6N75, "Austria-Hungary" folder.

27. See above, p. 219.

extremely fair, and always illuminating.''[28]

Advised by neutral consuls that a pall of terror hung over the city and that the new regime was a passing phenomenon that was incapable of giving effect to a treaty, Smuts made no protracted effort to come to a formal understanding. To avoid giving any hint of recognition, he remained in his train and made Béla Kun come to him there. Returning to Paris, he recommended that the Peace Conference take no immediate action except to send a military force to occupy a neutral zone in Transylvania and then lift the blockade. Advocating prompt consideration of the economic and financial needs of the former Hapsburg lands by a subconference at Paris, he worked out a scheme to reactivate the Danubian economy. This proposition never reached the Supreme Council. Wilson, despite his respect for Smuts, did not act upon Lansing's urging that he bring it up there.[29] Nor was there any response to a suggestion of Smuts that Hungarian delegates be invited to Paris. Allen Dulles tried in vain to save the recommendations of Smuts, with which he entirely agreed, from the ''burial'' that the British authorities gave them.[30]

Almost everyone of importance at Paris was too busy with the German treaty to give close attention to the affairs of Austria and Hungary. For some weeks there was no authority to give effect to the rulings of the Peace Conference in respect of Hungary.[31] The *ad hoc* procedure of the conference was entirely inadequate to deal with this comparatively remote matter in a month of more immediate crises. The Italians, with whom relations were coming to a breach,[32] were opposed to any subconference on Austria-Hungary that might weaken their territorial claims. Premier Bratianu of Romania also protested.[33]

Béla Kun's seizure of power at Budapest gave impetus to revolutionary movements in neighboring states other than Austria. Accepting advice by radio from Lenin, he sent agitators to Bulgaria, Romania, and even to Munich, where unemployment, severe weather, and a bankrupt city treasury had set the stage for violent revolt. There was talk of forming a new Soviet that would include Bavaria and Austria with Hungary.[34]

Marshal Foch now thought it more imperative to close the gap between Polish and Romanian forces at Lemberg (Lwów), through which Budapest and Moscow might move to make contact. In a session of the Supreme Council on March 17 he had presented a comprehensive plan similar to that already introduced by him at the

28. Bonsal, *Suitors and Suppliants,* pp. 118–128. According to Nicolson, who accompanied Smuts, they found Brown ''idealistic but bewildered.'' Brown talked of ''a natural social revolution'' and said that Béla Kun, despite ''a few foolish excesses,'' was maintaining order with a Red army of only about 7,000 men, *Peacemaking, 1919,* pp. 297–307.

29. Bliss to Wilson, April 11, 1919, Lansing to Wilson, April 17, 1919, Wilson papers. The Smuts report is in the Wilson papers and the Lloyd George papers, F / 197 / 2. Archibald Coolidge thought that actual conditions raised practical difficulties to economic union that seemed insurmountable.

30. A. W. Dulles to Seymour, April 11, 1919, Dulles to Frazier, April 18, 1919, Dulles to Wilson, April 17, 1919, A. W. Dulles papers, correspondence. Dulles, memorandum to the American commission, ''The Present Situation in Austria and Hungary,'' April 1, 1919, A. W. Dulles papers.

31. A. W. Dulles to Brown, April 15, 1919, A. W. Dulles papers.

32. See below, pp. 336 ff.

33. Memoranda by H. White, April 8, 1919, Bliss papers, box 69, ''White'' correspondence.

34. Richard M. Watt, *The Kings Depart,* pp. 322, 325, 331.

end of February. He told the council that the loss of Lemberg, a city of Polish population that was surrounded by besieging Ukrainians, would bring about the fall of the Pilsudski-Paderewski government and throw the reborn Poland into anarchy. Foch, advocating the transport to Lemberg of Polish troops then at Odessa and also a regiment from Haller's army in France, would add to this aggregation some ten or twelve divisions of Romanians under the command of a French general, and he would send supplies to them.[35]

The coup in Hungary created a favorable atmosphere at Paris for a renewal of Romanian pressure upon the Supreme Council. The Allied ministers at Bucharest had just reported that the situation there was "extremely grave," the morale of the army bad, a Bolshevik force to the north ready for action in a season that was favorable, and Hungarians attacking on the western border. They pictured Romania as "the sole barrier against the overflowing tide of bolshevism," and asked that it be given credits and supplies.[36] Intelligence reports from French generals, brought before the Council of Four on March 25, told of a need of clothing to supply the Romanian army and of food to prevent the fall of the city of Odessa to Bolsheviks. At this juncture Wilson asked why one should try to hold Odessa, a small island surrounded—almost submerged—by Bolsheviks. Thinking that the Peace Conference should restrict itself to preventing bolshevism from invading other parts of Europe, he said: "They will stew in their own juice until circumstances make the Russians wiser." It was decided that Odessa should be evacuated.[37]

General Bliss was not present at the session of March 25. He was told the next day that General Weygand, Foch's deputy, expected to be informed immediately of the extent of the American contribution to the French project. Alarmed, Bliss wrote to the president:

If my advice were asked, I would suggest to the prime ministers that the United States is doing, apparently, some eight times more for the checking of bolshevism by general relief work in Europe than the other Powers combined; that, inasmuch as we can continue this relief work without the embarrassment that would probably result from having to ask Congress for authority to engage directly or indirectly in operations of war in Eastern Europe, it would be better if they were to agree that we should continue to furnish assistance in this way and let them charge themselves with the equipment and maintenance of armies. . . . The assistance which we are asked to give . . . brings us face to face with the final and positive determination of our future policy in European affairs. . . . If we take the first step, . . . that will commit us to what may be perhaps a long series of wars for the purpose of throttling the revolutionary movement in Europe. . . . I cannot convince myself that it is wise, from any point of view, for the United States to engage in the work of combatting these new forces of revolution.[38]

On March 27 Foch, appearing before the Supreme Council, said it was "absolutely necessary" to secure the lines of communication through Vienna, which he

35. Bonsal, *Suitors and Suppliants*, pp. 135–144. Telegram, Lord from Mezes, March 12, 1919, Gibson papers, box 6, folder 1.

36. Dispatch, Sharp to the secretary of state, March 18, 1919, forwarding telegram of March 13 from the Allied ministers at Bucharest, Wilson papers.

37. Mantoux, *Proceedings*, p. 8. Mayer, p. 598.

38. Bliss to Wilson, March 26, 1919, Wilson papers. Bliss to Newton D. Baker, April 3, 1919, Baker papers.

wanted American troops to occupy. Moreover, it seemed to him important to "clean up places in the rear which, like Hungary, may be infected." His entire plan, he said, contemplated "not an offensive action, but a defensive barrier, behind which we can proceed to clean up the region."[39]

Bliss, however, was still unhappy. He informed Wilson that Foch's present plan for a *cordon sanitaire* was unknown to him thirty minutes before it was presented and that he was told it was intended to serve to execute decisions made by the council.[40] Bliss alone among the military advisers had opposed the French proposal. It seemed to him that it would mean "the resumption of general war and the probable dissolution of the Peace Conference," and that this was "the deliberate intention of those who . . . proposed it." Various facts and inferences from facts had come to his knowledge that he hesitated to commit to writing. A fortnight later Bliss came to view French militarism as "the greatest menace to present and future peace." He advocated that the Romanians be brought in line by a threat of a loss of all aid from the Allies.[41]

Through House, reassurance was given to Bliss that under no circumstances would the president send a man to southeast Europe, although it might be necessary to give some military supplies to the Romanians. Of Foch's proposal of joining together the Polish and Romanian forces and making them face toward the east, Wilson said in the council's session of March 27: "This would be the prelude to a march toward the east and raises the question of military intervention in Russia. We have examined the question more than once. Each time we reached the conclusion that military intervention must not be contemplated."[42]

Wilson had not lost the conviction that he had expressed on the first voyage to Europe when he remarked that bolshevism was accepted because it was "a protest against the way in which the world has worked." According to the record of Dr. Grayson, the president now said to his European colleagues that although some aspects of the behavior of the Bolshevists merited the utmost condemnation, there were many things in their program that he could almost agree with. Some of their doctrines, Wilson said, had been developed entirely from the pressure of capitalists, who had disregarded the rights of workers everywhere; and he warned that if the Bolshevists ever should adopt a sane policy of law and order, they would soon spread all over Europe, overturning existing governments.[43] After Foch had left the meeting on the twenty-seventh, Wilson said:

The word "Bolshevist" means many different things. In my view, any attempt to check a revolutionary movement by means of deployed armies is merely trying to use a broom to

39. Mantoux, *Proceedings,* p. 35.

40. Bliss to Wilson, March 28, 1919, Bliss papers. House diary, March 28, 1919. Bliss to Mrs. Bliss, April 7, 1919, Bliss papers.

41. Bliss to Wilson, April 11, 1919, Wilson papers. On April 8 Foch told the supreme military council that a turn toward bolshevism in Germany and Austria would afford a favorable opportunity to occupy those countries and to wring from them all their wealth in payment for the wrongs they had committed. On that day Bliss wrote to Wilson to urge that Foch be permitted to give no orders involving the use of American troops or money or matériel, except on the German front, without the specific permission of the president, Bliss to Wilson, April 8, 1919, Wilson papers.

42. Mantoux, *Délibérations,* vol. 1, p. 52.

43. Grayson diary, March 25, 1919. These remarks by Wilson are not in Mantoux's record.

sweep back a high tide. Besides, armies may become impregnated with the very bolshevism they are sent to combat. . . . The only way to act against bolshevism is to eliminate its causes. This is a formidable task; what its exact causes are, we do not even know. In any case, one cause is that the peoples are uncertain as to their future frontiers, the governments they must obey, and at the same time, are in desperate need of food, transport, and opportunities for work. There is but one way to wipe out bolshevism: determine the frontiers and open every door to commercial intercourse.

To "clean up Hungary" meant to him to contain bolshevism. "If this bolshevism remains within its own frontiers," Wilson said, "this is no business of ours."[44]

Nevertheless, the petty warfare on the borders of Hungary and the economic distress of the peoples of the region challenged the Peace Conference to take action. The Americans shared in the common effort to drawn boundaries that the contending armies would respect. Moreover, they participated in attempts to arrange financial settlements that would be equitable and would not crush economic life.[45] Most of them were less troubled than their European associates by the possibility of a recrudescence of German influence in this region.

The Americans continued to put emphasis on the power of their relief program, rather than that of arms, to stabilize the societies of the successor states. Although on March 28 the Supreme Economic Council had denied Hungary the relaxation of the blockade that had been contemplated two weeks before, certain exceptions were made. A trainload of American food, paid for by the Károlyi government and held up by French forces after the coup at Budapest, was allowed to go through by order of Clemenceau, whose intercession Hoover and Wilson got. The relief administration managed to continue the distribution of children's food despite arrests and executions of some of its Hungarian associates. However, the council announced on May 27 that the blockade would be ended only when Béla Kun's government ceased to exist. This eventuality did not seem remote in view of his difficulty in reconciling the factions among the revolutionaries, to say nothing of military pressures from the Romanians and the Slovaks.[46]

Hoover was determined to break the government of Béla Kun, which by interrupting shipments on railroads and on the Danube was making economic recovery difficult. He resolved to control the dispensing of supplies so that they would not be used to support the present regime, which he denounced for its violations of civil rights. The American administrator intended thus to give warning to other countries that might consider straying from the pattern of government that the Western peoples approved.[47] He did not despair of the recovery of Hungary to a position of self-support if raw materials were available and the currency and financial institutions were reorganized.[48]

On April 28 the American commissioners looked upon the situation in Hungary

44. Mantoux, *Proceedings,* pp. 33–35.

45. See below, pp. 450 ff.

46. Hoover, *Memoirs,* vol. 1, p. 398. Mayer, pp. 745–746. British, French, and Serbian authorities at Belgrade deplored the prestige accruing to Kun's regime from the contact with Smuts and the food shipments. These men regarded the revolutionaries in Budapest as an enemy to be extirpated, dispatches, Dodge (Belgrade) to Ammission, April 8 and 17, 1919, Wilson papers.

47. Hoover, *The Ordeal of Woodrow Wilson,* p. 136.

48. Hoover to Lamont, May 24, 1919, Lamont papers, 169-9.

as complex but not "hopeless," provided the country was not abandoned to the armies of neighboring states and to the French military. They suggested that delegates from Budapest be asked to come to the Peace Conference as soon as a representative government existed there. Two days later Wilson asked in the Council of Four whether it would be wise to open negotiations with these allies of the Bolsheviks. But Lloyd George thought The Four could not refuse to make peace with the Hungarians merely because they did not like the present government.[49] The president accepted this argument, and the next day remarked that if they established communication with Budapest they could the better avoid a series of upheavals if and when Béla Kun's weak government fell. Letters were drafted inviting Austrian and Hungarian delegates to come to Paris; but that addressed to Budapest was withheld by British and French officials at Vienna who were in contact with counterrevolutionaries in Hungary and opposed the delivery of any invitation that might strengthen Béla Kun's tottering regime.[50]

On May 19 Wilson brought up the question of Hungary in the Council of Four. He had just received a report from Brown at Budapest.[51] Accepting the analysis of this moderate observer, the president said to the Europeans that it would be unjustifiable to invite Béla Kun's unrepresentative government to make peace in the name of the Hungarian people. Referring to reports that the Italians (whose delegate was not present at this meeting) were intriguing in Hungary, Wilson went on: "The conclusion of my representative is that the only means for settling the Hungarian question is a military intervention. There would be no resistance. Béla Kun himself is ready to obey the orders of the Entente if they are imposed on him. The French troops in Belgrade will be able to carry out the occupation if they are asked. Once this has been done, we are advised to send a political mission to Budapest with a man like General Smuts at its head, to assure the establishment of a stable government." Now that a prospect appeared for successful military action, Wilson, despite his earlier aversion to it, perhaps regarded the Hungarian revolution as a challenge to law and order that might be met as effectively as those in the Caribbean that the United States had dealt with by sending the marines.

Clemenceau immediately took issue with an assumption that the policing burden would be undertaken by France. In any event it could not take this difficult task alone, he said. Some Romanian troops would have to be used, for it appeared that neither the British nor the American army would be able to help. Wilson, thus reminded of the weakness of his position, had little to say. He warned, however,

49. Mantoux, *Delibérations,* vol. 1, p. 429. A month earlier Lloyd George had remarked in the Supreme Council that few countries needed a revolution so badly as Hungary, Mantoux, *Proceedings,* p. 36.

50. Roosevelt, pp. 113 ff. Marston, *The Peace Conference of 1919,* p. 203. According to Nicolson there was a row about this, *Peacemaking, 1919,* p. 327.

51. Memorandum on "The Hungarian Situation" by Philip M. Brown, on his return to Paris after three months at Budapest, forwarded to House by Frazier with a letter of May 17. Brown's opinions were largely confirmed by dispatches, Coolidge to Ammission, April 16, 25, and 28, 1919, Wilson papers.

R. S. Baker recorded in his journal on May 21 that when he took Brown's report to Wilson, the president read it carefully and said: "Like most of the reports we get: good enough in presenting the facts; but they do not tell us what to do. They all ask us to make more war."

that the use of Romanian forces would stir hostility among the Hungarians.[52]

While the victors abstained from policing Hungary, its infantry, confined to six divisions by the armistice of November 13, grew beyond this limit. An army entered Czechoslovak territory in defiance of the edicts of the Peace Conference. The Czechs, as well as the Romanians, had been advancing into territory that had been a part of Hungary; and Hungarian defenders, in a successful counterattack, entered Slovakia early in June. Moreover, Hoover's agent at Budapest reported that Béla Kun had seized the gold of the national bank and subsidized a communist conspiracy in Vienna. The food administrator reluctantly advised that the only way to prevent the fall of the governments at Prague and at Vienna was to send French troops to Budapest without delay.[53] But still no military action was taken by the Peace Conference. Although some Americans would engage in humanitarian enterprises that gave a measure of control over the politics of the new states, Wilson was willing to take no military measures that might offend nationalist sentiment in Hungary.

Wilson's Point Four, limiting armament to that required for domestic safety, was being flouted by the successor states. Cynical observers noted that fourteen small wars were going on in Europe at one time and remarked that there was one for each of the president's Points. General Bliss was thoroughly disgusted by the rapacity of these new states that many Americans idealized. Nevertheless, he supported a proposal of the military representatives that would grant the new states armaments that were said to be not large enough for purposes of aggression, but sufficient for policing. On May 23 Wilson joined with Lloyd George in proposing quotas for the small nations that would be proportionally larger than that contemplated for the army of Germany; and Clemenceau and Orlando gave their assent.[54]

It became apparent, however, that it was difficult for The Four to impose any effective limit on the armies of the new states. By the end of May some of their delegates were in a mood of rebellion against the benevolent tutelage of the great powers. The chronic restiveness of the spokesmen for Poland and Romania was aggravated by treaties proposed for the protection of racial minorities.[55] Nevertheless, the Council of Four persisted in efforts to use its prestige to stop the most disruptive of the wars that were going on. While warning Béla Kun to refrain from aggression, they enjoined Romania not to occupy Budapest.

In response, Bratianu asserted bluntly that the great powers could not be counted on always to enforce the high principles of the peace. He pointed out that Romania was not a party to the Armistice of 1918 with Hungary and therefore was compelled to provide its own troops for the defense not only of its frontiers, but also of a cause—antibolshevism. Béla Kun, for his part, replied that he would restrain his

52. Wilson's reply to Clemenceau, as recorded by Mantoux, was imprecise: "Nous aurions peut-être du prendre ce parti," *Délibérations*, vol. 2, pp. 109–110. The American opposition to the use of their troops to restore order was made clear in his remarks in the Council of Four on June 17, 1919, *F.R., P.P.C.*, vol. 11, p. 122, vol. 6, p. 534.

53. Hoover, *The Ordeal of Woodrow Wilson*, pp. 135–142; *Memoirs*, vol. 1, p. 298; Hoover to Wilson, June 9, 1919, Wilson to Hoover, June 10, 1919, Wilson papers.

54. Mantoux, *Délibérations*, vol. 2, pp. 184–186.

55. See below, pp. 472 ff.

troops if those of Hungary were held back.[56]

On June 10 the spokesmen for Czechoslovakia and Romania were brought before The Four. Wilson opened the meeting with a summary of his understanding of the present situation and the events that had led up to it. "Béla Kun," he asserted, "came to power in consequence of the Rumanian offensive, and has been strengthened by the Czechoslovak offensive. Nothing could be more fatal to our policy. We are trying to arrive at a just partition of territory and a durable understanding among the peoples: hence our great desire to dispel all causes of irritation and mutual aggression." He was confident that bolshevism would subside if the Hungarians were convinced that the boundary lines, once fixed, would not be violated.

The Four came to a decision that Wilson announced to the delegates of Czechoslovakia and Romania. "The armistice lines and all the temporary arrangements have not given satisfaction," he said. "We are going to ask our ministers of foreign affairs to . . . reach a final decision on the frontiers. . . . Immediately afterward we shall say to Hungary: 'There are your frontiers! if you break them, we refuse to negotiate with you.' We expect that you will respect these frontiers. . . . On your doing so will depend the aid that the Allied and Associated Powers will give to you."

Beneš and Bratianu acquiesced in this, and Wilson pressed for prompt action. "As it stands now," Bliss wrote to the president on June 10, "the United States is giving millions of dollars worth of food supplies to these nations which take the money thus saved and expend it on military operations." Bliss advocated that unless this ceased, and the offending states concentrated on blocking Bolshevik expansion, they would get no more assistance from the West. On the sixteenth Wilson answered: "I think that my colleagues are coming more and more to the view that we must put the utmost pressure upon the Middle European States, and I need not tell you with what sympathy of judgment I have read your suggestion."[57]

At the suggestion of Wilson, Balfour drafted telegrams to the three governments concerned. These messages defined the boundaries ordained by the Council of Foreign Ministers after consultation with the committees of specialists who had been working on this matter for months. Clemenceau signed and sent off the telegrams on June 13.[58]

Béla Kun's answer complained of the frontiers that were contemplated for Hungary and suggested that representatives of the successor states meet at Vienna to consider the questions raised by the break-up of the Hapsburg empire. This recalled to Wilson Smuts's proposal of a conference.[59] He remarked now that he doubted that such a conference would be possible without direction by an outside authority.

The reply from Kun announced that he had ordered an end to hostilities against

---

56. *F.R., P.P.C.,* vol. 3, p. 409, vol. 6, pp. 133, 255–261. Sherman D. Spector, *Rumania at the Paris Peace Conference,* pp. 140, 144. Telegram, Béla Kun to Clemenceau, June 6, 1919, forwarded to Wilson with Clemenceau's card, Wilson papers. Bliss to Wilson, June 7, 1919, Wilson papers. Deák, pp. 79, 461.

57. Letters in Wilson papers.

58. Mantoux, *Délibérations,* vol. 2, pp. 368–375, 387–391, 415–416. Miller, *My Diary,* vol. 16, pp. 399–412.

59. See above, p. 226.

Czechoslovakia, and at the same time he asked the powers to make the Czechoslovaks stop a threatening advance. The Four then authorized Bliss to confer with Czech delegates at Paris and to attempt to arrange a withdrawal of troops behind the lines proposed. He talked immediately with Beneš, who said that he would be politically embarrassed if he took any action that might appear to open negotiations with Hungary. Therefore, as a face-saving measure, Bliss proposed that Foch should give the necessary restraining orders through the French commander of the Czechoslovak forces. The Four approved this plan, and on June 26 Beneš informed Wilson that hostilities had ceased.[60]

Romanian operations against Hungary continued unchecked, and after the final departure of Wilson from Paris in June the possibility of military action in Hungary by the powers became even dimmer.[61] Their statesmen, possessing the greatest military force in the world, confessed themselves impotent to impose their will upon fractious small states.

60. Mantoux, *Délibérations*, vol. 2, pp. 465, 525.
61. See below, pp. 458–461.

13

Failure in the "Acid Test"

During the month of March the impulse of the peacemakers to build stability in central Europe was strengthened by the continuing revolution in Russia. The Soviet government was proving to be less evanescent than ill-wishers had predicted it would be. In existence now for more than a year, it had maintained itself in central Russia—in an area comprising hardly a fourth of the czarist empire—against military forces of the old regime. Meanwhile, those forces, operating on the borders of European Russia, were receiving material support from the West.

The Soviet government met the military threat with a novel political weapon. With the formation of the Comintern in March of 1919 a nucleus took shape for proselyting abroad; and this branch of the Soviet system undertook to undermine governments with which the foreign office endeavored to negotiate.[1] It was at this time that Lenin issued his implacable challenge: "The existence of the Soviet Republic together with the imperialist states is in the long run unthinkable." More and more the Soviet regime appeared to Western statesmen as an enemy.[2]

The Western governments had made no perceptible progress in carrying out their intention to remove the troops that they had sent into Russia.[3] Dispatches from General Graves at Vladivostok reported profiteering, wastage of supplies sent by the United States, and worsening of railway operations. Each native faction was asserting that those who were not its friends were its enemies; and Graves, still lacking specific instructions as to political matters, was holding aloof from conflicts among the factions. He declined to join with British and Japanese commanders in using policing measures against elements of the population whose radicalism he thought perhaps less dangerous than the vindictiveness of reactionaries.[4]

1. See Theodore H. von Laue, "Soviet Diplomacy, 1918–1930," in Gordon Craig and Felix Gilbert, *The Diplomats.*

Lenin justified the subversive work of the Comintern in other nations by saying: "Just as during the war you tried to make revolution in Germany . . . so we, while we are at war with you adopt the measures that are open to us," Arthur Ransome, *Russia in 1919* (New York, 1919), p. 224.

2. Adam B. Ulam, *Expansion and Coexistence* (New York, 1971), pp. 96, 98. Kennan, *Russia and the West,* pp. 158–161, 166.

3. "Russia does seem to be in a hopeless way," Polk wrote to Auchincloss on March 20, 1919. "We have committed ourselves to assist in the railroad in Siberia, and having just jammed that through, I do not see how we can turn right around and get out," Y.H.C.

In view of the political situation at Washington, the State Department was instructed to take temporary measures, and on March 3 Wilson authorized the expenditure of $117,000 from his Fund for National Security and Defense for "actual maintenance" of the American railway corps in Siberia. He expressed concern about securing funds in the future, Lansing to Polk, January 31, February 9, 1919. Wilson to Polk, March 3, 1919, Wilson papers. The War Trade Board supplied $1 million in March, N.A., docs in R.G. 59, 861. 77 / 62a, 675, 690, 735d, 835; Polk to Ammission, February 10, 1919, Wilson papers.

4. The awkward position of Graves is explained in George Stewart's *The White Armies of Russia* (New York, 1933), pp. 250–252. Also see Robert J. Maddox, *The Unknown War in Russia* (San Rafael, Calif., 1977), pp. 62, 70, 73, 97–100, 103, and William S. Graves, *America's Siberian Adventure 1918–1920* (New York, 1931).

During the weeks of Wilson's absence from Paris, House and Lloyd George entertained some hope of making contact with the Soviet government as a result of William Bullitt's secret mission to Moscow—a venture that Bullitt himself had promoted, House had furthered, Lloyd George had acquiesced in, and Lansing had authorized. Bullitt approached Russia early in March determined to establish liaison between the Soviet statesmen and the Peace Conference. From Stockholm on March 4 he sent a message to House: "The hardest part will be in Paris, but you have got to put it across."[5]

Leon Trotsky, commissar of war, was suspicious of the Western powers and their emissaries.[6] It seemed to Russians no mere coincidence that armed forces of Poland were concentrating near the Russian border just as a mission from Paris arrived at Warsaw. Nevertheless, economic disorganization inclined some of the Soviet leaders toward an accommodation with the West.[7] Bullitt, arriving in Russia two days after important sessions of the Comintern ended, was met at Leningrad by Chicherin, the foreign minister, and was invited to Moscow.[8] Lenin, Litvinov, and Chicherin appeared to Bullitt to be resentful of the world's low opinion of their honor, but confident that President Wilson, whose Fourteen Points they praised, would understand that inexperienced people were trying conscientiously, and at the cost of great suffering, to find a better way to live for the common interest. Bullitt found the ruling party strong, politically and morally. People were blaming their shortages, which he ascribed to a lack of railroad transport, on the blockade that had been imposed by the West. A message that he dispatched to Paris stated that earlier reports of civil disorder were ridiculously exaggerated.[9] Bullitt was told by Lenin that by exerting his will against that of Trotsky and the generals he had been able to persuade the Central Executive Committee to agree to listen to a reasonable proposal from Paris. The initiative could not be taken by the Soviet government because they would have to fill any proposal they made with bombastic denunciations of capitalistic states in order to satisfy the Bolsheviks.[10]

The rosy picture painted by Bullitt's hosts, which was unsupported by any extensive exhibit of the conditions of life of the Russian people, affirmed his sympathetic

---

5. Telegram, Bullitt to House, Y.H.C. See above, pp. 138 ff.

6. Trotsky telegraphed Lenin on March 17, 1919: "A unified command has been set up by all our enemies. . . . A general offensive, combined with internal uprisings, was in preparation for March. . . . Against this moment America sent off its eavesdroppers to assess whether we should hold firm or not and to determine our policy," Jan M. Meijer (ed.), *The Trotsky Papers, 1917–1922* (The Hague, 1964), p. 305.

7. "The month of March saw a steep increase in the number of strikes and peasant risings," Meijer, p. 305n. See Alfred M. P. Dennis, *The Foreign Policies of Soviet Russia* (New York, 1924), pp. 73–74. Bulletin No. 47, addressed to the five great powers by the Soviet government, N.A., R.G. 59, 763.72119 / 4153. Memorandum, Lord to Bullitt, February 17, 1919, Y.H.C.

8. Farnsworth, *William C. Bullitt and the Soviet Union*, pp. 39–42.

9. Dispatch, Bullitt for Lansing and House, March 10, 1919, Y.H.C. This dispatch, forwarded by Pettit from Helsingfors, reported that Chicherin and Litvinov had expressed themselves as very favorably disposed to a truce but feared difficulty in controlling their Russian opponents while peace talks went on.

10. Bullitt to the author, April 2, 1951. Whitney Sheppardson to H. Gilchrist, September 9, 1919, and enclosure, Gilchrist papers, L.C. box 8A, folder 5. P. H. Kerr to Sir R. Graham, July 11, 1919, Documents of British Foreign Policy 1919–1939, First Series, 3, 1919, p. 426.

view. He relayed to Paris a formal proposal from Chicherin, stating that the Soviet government would entertain a proposition from the Western powers if the latter would agree to cease to support anti-Soviet forces in Russia and to open channels of communication.[11] A two-week truce was proposed, to be followed by an armistice and a conference in a neutral country. A resumption of trade was suggested; also free movement of persons provided they did not interfere in domestic politics; a general amnesty of political offenders within and outside of Russia; the withdrawal of foreign troops; the recognition by the Soviet and other Russian governments of responsibility for Russian financial obligations, the details to be agreed on; and the raising of the blockade and the furnishing of supplies on equal terms for all, under the observation of inspectors from the West.[12]

Unfortunately, the essential cloak of secrecy was already shredded, and imprecise stories circulated.[13] Lincoln Steffens, the liberal journalist who was a member of the Bullitt party, described the regime at Moscow, which he thought to be firmly seated in power as "the most autocratic government" he had ever seen, and he stated that Lenin was "farther removed from the people than the Tsar." Nevertheless Steffens warned that if the Peace Conference did not act on the proposition, the Bolsheviks would "listen to Kautzky," who spoke for revolutionary Europe.[14]

On March 25, the day after revolution broke out in Hungary and when the negotiations in the Council of Four were approaching a crisis, Bullitt reported in the evening at Paris to House. Excited by the possibility of bringing order out of chaos in eastern Europe, House telephoned at once to the president. But Wilson, who was to become violently ill a week later, complained of a headache. He did not receive Bullitt that night. House advised the young man not to express his sympathy with the Soviet regime in the presence of others at Paris who might have little capacity for diplomacy and a marked propensity toward fear.[15]

Bullitt went immediately to Philip Kerr, secretary to Lloyd George, who had given unofficial encouragement to his venture. The prime minister had just asserted in his Fontainebleau memorandum that "if the Peace Conference is really to secure peace . . . it must deal with the Russian situation." At breakfast, with Balfour, Kerr, and Smuts present, Lloyd George questioned Bullitt about conditions in Rus-

---

11. Bullitt (Helsingfors) to Ammission, March 16, 1919, Wilson papers. A "complete file of telegrams from Bullitt" may be found in the Bliss papers, box 174, "Russia, Soviet," January–November 1919 folder.

12. Penciled "Notes on a Conversation with Chicherin and Litvinov," Bullitt papers. These "Notes" and also certain dispatches, most secret for the president, Lansing, and House only, sent from Helsingfors March 16 and 18, 1919, were, but are no longer, in the Y.H.C. Papers pertaining to the Bullitt expedition are in *F.R., 1919, Russia*, pp. 74–96.

13. On March 15 Lansing handed to Foreign Minister Pichon a statement explaining that the Americans had gone to Russia with his permission but "in a purely unofficial capacity" in the hope of eliciting valuable information, and that publicity was undesirable, lest it exaggerate the significance of the affair. The *New York World* printed a brief report of Bullitt's "secret" mission as early as March 20, and the whole story was told in *Le journal du peuple* on March 29, 1919.

Letters from Edward Bell of the London embassy to Leland Harrison, assistant secretary of the American commission at Paris, reveal the distaste of these career men for the amateurs who had rushed in where professionals feared to function, letters, March 24 *et seq.*, 1919, Harrison papers, L.C., boxes 102, 103.

14. Letter, Steffens to Bullitt, April 2, 1919, with a report, Bullitt papers.

15. Bullitt to the author. House diary, March 25, 1919.

sia and about the Bolshevik leaders and their attitude. According to Bullitt, the prime minister said that if Wilson would take the lead he would follow.[16] Any enthusiasm that Lloyd George may have felt, however, was dampened by an editorial in that morning's *Daily Mail*. Steed, to whom Auchincloss leaked the news that talks with the Soviet government were going on, published an alarmist leader entitled "The Intrigue That May Be Revived."[17]

Wilson, at the moment concerned primarily with issues raised by the necessity of making peace with Germany, left the vexing question of relations with Russia to House. The only remaining hope for the contact with Moscow on which House had set his heart lay in the influence of Lloyd George. Therefore, the colonel lunched with the prime minister on March 28 and argued that a settlement with Russia would make it possible to treat with Germany "in a much more positive and satisfactory way." He asked that action be deferred until he could "get up a plan."[18] House, however, was straining the bounds of the possible. The question was politically too hot to be touched. Wilson was well aware of this; and when Baker, at House's suggestion, sought permission to release Bullitt's report, it was denied.[19]

Bullitt did not easily accept the lack of response on the part of the political chiefs. In private talks he gave peace delegates a lively and hopeful account of life under the Soviet regime.[20] He thought that a general strike in protest against the inertia of the Peace Conference might be called in England, where a new Labour newspaper challenged the government to publish Bullitt's report.[21] On April 2 he reminded House that the project would come to nothing in eight days if no constructive action were taken.

Although House did not give up his conviction that some arrangement might be made with the Bolsheviks, the Americans were unwilling to trust the new government at Moscow that had not yet proven the good faith that it professed.[22] News-

16. Bullitt to the author.

Of his breakfast meeting with the British statesmen, Bullitt wrote to Pettit on April 18, 1919: "They all seemed a good deal impressed with the necessity for making peace with the Soviet government, particularly Balfour and Smuts. Lloyd George showed himself very much afraid of the attitude of the Northcliffe press and the conservative press in general. Colonel House was very keen for the proposition," copy of letter in Bullitt papers.

17. Steed entertained an unverified suspicion that "the prime movers were . . . international financiers who wished . . . to secure a field for German and Jewish exploitation of Russia," Steed, *Through Thirty Years*, vol. 2, pp. 301–305, House diary, March 26, 27, and 28, 1919. House and Auchincloss took Steed for a drive and chided him for violating their confidential understanding by the indiscreet editorial, which stimulated an avalanche of criticism in the French press, Auchincloss diary, March 27, 28, and 30, 1919. According to House's record, Steed was told that he ought not to have written about so important a matter without first consulting House, House diary, March 28, 1919. From this talk Steed concluded, possibly correctly, that his editorial "got under the president's hide," Steed, vol. 2, p. 304.

18. House diary, March 26 and 28, 1919.

19. Baker's journal, March 29, 1919.

20. Bullitt gave to McCormick the impression that he was quite "pro-Bolshevik" and characterized Lenin as a "big man and able," McCormick diary, April 6, 1919. Henry White was now of the opinion that "before long" it would be "necessary to recognize the Bolshevik Government, or rather the conservative wing thereof, under Lenin," who appeared to be "a man of great ability," White to Mrs. J. A. Burden, April 8, 1919, White papers, Columbia University Library, notes and correspondence, box 1.

21. Editorial by George Lansbury in the *Herald*, March 31, 1919. Bullitt to the author.

22. "No one has the courage to go forward in the matter," House wrote in his diary on April 5.

men, getting wind of Bullitt's mission, sent stories to the United States that fanned the "anti-Red" fervor that had been whipped up by hearings before a committee of the Senate.[23] Tumulty cabled the president on April 2: "The proposed recognition of Lenin has caused consternation over here."

Dispatches from the State Department had brought word to Paris that the Soviet government, instead of assuming responsibility for Russian debt in the United States, had sent a representative to New York who revealed a Soviet "constitution" and proposed to deposit $200 million in American gold in European banks to cover initial purchases of commodities of many kinds. This agent, a German citizen named Martens, claimed to be empowered to negotiate for the speedy opening of trade relations for the mutual benefit of America and Russia. Reporting this *démarche* to Paris, Polk pointed out that the Soviet constitution advocated the abolition of private property, the repudiation of foreign obligations, and the elimination of entire classes of people from any share in the government. Polk reported that it was being said in commercial circles in New York that it was hoped in Moscow that a favorable report by Bullitt at Paris would facilitate the negotiations of Martens.[24]

Actually the State Department had been taking steps to induce economic stability in Russia. Consideration was given to a plan for new currency that was developed by Ambassador Bakhmeteff, but no agreement could be reached with the governments of the other powers that had intervened in Russia.[25] Private investors had been put off by the chaos that followed the Bolshevik revolution. By the end of March, Russian assets in the United States had shrunk alarmingly.[26] The State Department was instructed from Paris to refrain from collecting both interest and principal due on loans by the Treasury, and to use their influence to prevent legal action by private creditors to redeem bonds that matured on May 1.[27] The Americans at Paris were considering what they called a "constructive plan" for using the Russian funds.

In mid-April, in pursuance of Wilson's desire to protect and use Russian assets

23. The hearings of the Overman committee were held from February 11 to March 10, 1919. Cf. above, p. 131. On the "Great Red Scare" of 1919, which Thomas A. Bailey has called "primarily a domestic disease," see Bailey, *America Faces Russia* (Ithaca, 1950), pp. 249–250.

24. Dispatches, Phillips to the secretary of state, March 25, 1919; Phillips to Ammission, March 29, 1919, Wilson papers.

On April 17 Lansing notified the State Department that no credence should be given to claims by the Soviet Bureau in New York to Russian funds in the National City Bank, since the Kerensky government's ambassador, Bakhmeteff, was still the only recognized envoy of Russia to the United States, dispatch, Ammission to the acting secretary of state, April 17, 1919, *F.R., Russia, 1919*, pp. 133–148; letter, Polk to Lansing, March 18, 1918, Y.H.C. For an account of the operations of the Soviet financial agent, Martens, in New York and of American opinion of his propaganda, see Leonid I. Strakhovsky, *American Opinion about Russia, 1917–1920*, ch. 8. Breckenridge Long, an assistant secretary of state, wrote in his diary on December 29, 1919: "Martens will be deported shortly."

25. See Linda Killen, "The Search for a Democratic Russia: Bakhmetev and the U.S.," 243 and sources cited.

26. The outstanding loans to Kerensky's provisional government by the American Treasury at the end of 1918 amounted to $325 million in credits and $188 million in cash, O. T. Crosby to Wilson, December 1918, Wilson papers. In the spring of 1919 the Russian assets in the United States had a value of about $33 million, *F.R., 1919, Russia*, pp. 3, 56.

27. Dispatches, Polk to Lansing and McCormick, April 11 1919; Ammission to the secretary of state, May 5, 1919, Wilson papers. Polk diary, April 23, May 29, June 4, 1919, Y.H.C. Killen, 244–245.

of various sorts for the benefit of Russia provided that there was a "definite constructive plan" and no recognition or "obvious assistance" to any Russian government, Lansing discussed with Bakhmeteff certain measures that the ambassador seemed "disposed to accept." It was deemed that if the redemption of the maturing bonds could be postponed, legal proceedings might be avoided and there would be cash to pay the interest for the next twelve months and also to meet expenses of "essential" Russian officials in the United States. There would even be a remnant for loans to the Siberian railway.[28] During May, the prospect of recognition of Admiral Kolchak's White regime at Omsk improved so greatly[29] that Wilson thought it more important to avoid a collapse of Russian finance in the United States. In order to maintain a prospect of American financing of Russian development when a hoped-for political stabilization might transpire, it seemed wise to have interest paid on private loans made to earlier Russian governments. On May 26 Wilson went so far as to approve the use of Russian assets in the United States to make interest payments on debt to private creditors.[30]

When they learned of Bullitt's venture, the men of the State Department could not conceive of any useful parley with a government that seemed irresponsible, despite the willingness professed by Lenin and Litvinov to negotiate on the question of debts. Polk read Bullitt's report and cabled: "I do not think I would be prepared to act on any report framed by Bullitt and Steffens after a three days' stay in Russia."[31] The conservative view of the question was presented by the counselor of the American embassy at London: "To admit the Bolsheviks as contracting parties in international agreements is simply to abandon the reins of government. Agreements . . . cannot be binding . . . because Lenin and his associates do not recognize the obligations of international morality. Their sole object in proposing such arrangements to Bullitt is to secure a respite from attack and enlarged opportunities for propaganda. To treat with them . . . involves the final abandonment of the idea of a league of nations and an abject confession of moral and material defeat."[32]

In England the attacks of the Northcliffe press upon Lloyd George now included Wilson. Parliament questioned the prime minister so insistently about Bullitt's expedition that Lloyd George felt that he must deny any intimate knowledge of the affair.[33] On April 10 he was informed by Winston Churchill, who deemed Lenin's

28. Dispatch, secretary of state from Lansing and McCormick, April 16, 1919, Wilson papers.

29. See below, p. 244.

30. Dispatch, Lansing and McCormick to State Department, May 26, 1919, N.A., R.G. 59, 861.51 / 587. See Maddox, pp. 92–93.

31. Polk to Auchincloss, April 5, 1919, Y.H.C. Polk diary, April 10, 1919, Y.H.C.

32. J. Butler Wright to L. Harrison, April 14, 1919, enclosing a clipping from *The Observer* of April 13, Harrison papers, L.C.

33. Dispatch, Wiseman to Reading, April 8, 1919, Y.H.C. Dispatch, J. W. Davis to Ammission, March 31, 1919, Wilson papers. Letters, Bell to Harrison, March 25, Harrison papers, box 104, April 3, 1919, box 102. It seemed to Auchincloss that Steed, catering to the prejudice of his employer, Northcliffe, was "writing some pretty rough stuff now in the London *Times*," Auchincloss diary, April 3, 1919.

Bullitt addressed a letter to Wilson dated April 18, pasting on it a clipping of a news story which quoted from Lloyd George's denial in a speech to the Parliament in which he said: "If the President of the United States had attached any value to them [the suggestions of 'some young Americans who had come back from Moscow'] he would have brought them before the conference, and he certainly did

proposals to be "in themselves fraudulent," that parliamentary debate had shown "a practical unanimity against any negotiations with the Bolsheviks." "I do trust President Wilson will not be allowed to weaken our policy against them in any way," Churchill wrote. "His negotiations have become widely known and are much resented."[34]

Wilson's advisers did not lose sight of the far-reaching nature of the challenge to American policy. Noting that newspapers were associating the Bullitt mission with alleged American concessions in Soviet Russia, the American experts in the Russian section at Paris proposed that the United States government repudiate insinuations that it wished to buy peace by accepting concessions.[35] It was recommended that the president issue a declaration in respect of Russia such as that which had led to the armistice with Germany. The advisers, making specific suggestions for such a statement, wrote: "Failure to isolate the Russian revolution may involve us in the disastrous policy of having to fight the European Revolution (a thing we neither can nor should do) through inability to dissociate the German and Hungarian revolutions, of whose sincerity there is doubt, from the terribly genuine radical movement in Russia."[36]

House, however, perceived that it would be futile to press Wilson for action. It is doubtful that the president thought the Soviet government could be depended on to honor agreements. In any event he could not believe that the proposal of Lenin, which parliamentary protest had forced Lloyd George to disregard and which left to the Allied governments "no latitude of negotiation,"[37] would be acceptable to public opinion in the West.

At this most critical stage of the peacemaking, Wilson's health was failing.[38] He did not submit his political position, already severely shaken both by the call from America for revision of the League Covenant and by the national demands of the Allied governments, to the torrent of criticism that negotiation with the Soviet regime would surely provoke. For sound political reasons Wilson as well as Lloyd George, rejecting the risk of constructive diplomacy, turned away from what George F.

---

not." Bullitt challenged the president: "I should greatly appreciate it if you would inform me whether . . . this statement of Mr. Lloyd George is true or untrue," letter in Wilson papers, with Wilson's shorthand indication that he read it. To this letter there was no reply. Almost a year later Bullitt wrote in a letter to Lippmann that they had both been "bamboozled" by "little Eddie [House]," who had convinced them of the wisdom of Wilson, letter of January 21, 1920, Lippman papers, Series I, box 5. On Bullitt's resignation in May, see below, p. 395.

Bullitt's own account of his mission, as given to the Senate, is in U.S., Congress, Senate, *Congressional Record,* serial 7605, 66th Cong., 1st sess., Sen. Doc. 106, pp. 1161–1292. See also *The Nation* 109, pp. 428–434, 475–482; *Current History* 9, pt. 1, p. 121; and the *New York Times,* March 22, April, and September *passim, 1919.*

34. Martin Gilbert, *Winston S. Churchill,* vol. 4, p. 276.

35. See Noble, *Policies and Opinions at Paris, 1919,* pp. 290–291. A "Statement concerning the Bullitt mission," dated April 16, recorded that the only concession known to have been granted by the Soviet government was to a Norwegian bank (Hannevig & Co.), which had its head office in London and in which Americans were perhaps interested, document in N.A., R.G. 256, 184.022 / 25.

36. Asserting that the Soviet government sincerely desired an armistice, the American advisers outlined a five-point program in a "Memorandum from the Russian Section: The Russian Policy," Berle papers, box 1, ACTNP, Berle memoranda, 1918–1919, F. D. Roosevelt Library.

37. Kennan, p. 131.

38. See below, p. 285.

Kennan has called "the most favorable opportunity yet extended . . . to the Western powers . . . for the creation of an acceptable relationship to the Soviet regime."[39]

The Prinkipo plan and the Bullitt venture having failed, little prospect remained either for an end of civil war in Russia or for a rapprochement of the West with any stable government there. The Americans at Paris fell back upon their favorite remedy for social distempers, one that they were applying with some effect in countries smaller and less chaotic than Russia. They began to conceive an enterprise that would relieve grievous shortages among the Russian people and that might one day lead to economic arrangements that would be of mutual benefit. The communications with the Soviet leaders had given evidence that they were aware of the advantage that could accrue from Western aid in developing the economic resources of their country.

Wilson, who as a young student of Manchester economics had been taught that trade was a "nurse of liberal ideas," was not unsympathetic to such a venture. On March 27 he asked House to inquire whether they could get ships and food to Russia if they wished to do so. Doubtless apprehensive that any sort of economic activity by citizens of the West on Russian territory would awaken fears of "exploitation," they thought it wise to use a neutral agency as an intermediary. House, raising the ogre of Russian hordes "sweeping over all of Europe," insisted that something must be done, and said that a relief program would have the advantage of not requiring the cooperation of the French, who had no enthusiasm for feeding Russians.[40]

The day before, the president had asked Hoover for advice. He found Hoover convinced that European civilization, in its present debilitation, could ill afford to experiment with an economic system that he thought utterly foolish. Of the opinion that the use of force would only aggravate the current crisis, he hoped that Russia's turn to bolshevism was merely a step in a painful transition from despotism to democracy. He proposed the establishment of a neutral relief commission to be headed by Fridtjof Nansen, an Arctic explorer who was respected as a leader in humanitarian enterprises. After enlisting the aid of the Norwegian prime minister in overcoming Nansen's reluctance to serve,[41] Hoover drafted a letter addressed to the members of the Supreme Council. It stressed the nonpolitical nature of the contemplated commission and its devotion to the "humanitarian purpose of saving life."[42]

An American reply to the Hoover-Nansen letter was prepared by Auchincloss and Miller. In the opinion of Bullitt, however, their text was neither straightforward nor acceptable to the Soviets. He thought it would make fools of House and Hoo-

---

39. See Kennan, pp. 130–135.

40. House diary, March 27, 1919.

41. Murray N. Rothbard, "Hoover's Food Diplomacy in Retrospect," in Gelfand (ed.), *Herbert Hoover: The Great War and Its Aftermath*, pp. 106–107.

In turning to Nansen as a figurehead for his contemplated venture in Russia, Hoover was perhaps not uninfluenced by the fact that his own very profitable operations in the Urals and Siberia some ten years earlier exposed him to communist suspicions of "exploitation." See George H. Nash, *The Life of Herbert Hoover: The Engineer, 1874–1914* (New York, 1983), ch. 21.

See Mayer, *Politics and Diplomacy of Peacemaking*, p. 473, and Thompson, *Russia, Bolshevism, and the Versailles Peace*, pp. 231–233.

42. Mayer, pp. 474–479.

ver.[43] He foresaw that the Russian leaders would not agree to surrender control of their country's railways or to cease resisting White generals whom they could not trust to reciprocate. Bullitt thought that his associates at Paris, in their ignorance, were asking the Soviet government "to put its head in the lion's mouth." He knew that Lenin would have to answer Trotsky's allegation that any armistice would be used by the Allied powers to supply equipment to the White forces. After protesting emphatically to House, Bullitt was allowed to redraft the document.

On April 6 Wilson, recovering from a severe illness, reviewed the question in a bedside conference with the other American commissioners. The president accepted the text as modified by Bullitt.[44] On April 9 Wilson brought it before the Supreme Council after authorizing the addition of a clause to the effect that the Soviet government would have to bear the cost of relief operations. It was not until April 16, however, after France's demands with respect to its eastern border were satisfied, that House secured Clemenceau's signature.[45] The arguments that the colonel used were not only humanitarian, but very material.[46]

Having at last won unanimity on the policy of relief, House was dismayed when Hoover, who had been most cooperative, suddenly proposed to denounce publicly "the tyranny, cruelty, and incapacity of the Soviet regime . . . men whose fingers even today are dripping with the blood of hundreds of innocent people of Odessa." Perceiving that such a denunciation would "absolutely destroy" any chance of success for Nansen's program,[47] House tried at first to reason with Hoover. Then, when the food administrator persisted in his intention, House brought the matter before his fellow commissioners and, fortified by their opinion that Hoover was acting childishly, conveyed to him the president's wish that he desist.[48] However, on April 21 Hoover did make a public pronouncement in his own name. It included paragraphs from his intemperate draft. It was perhaps this breach of discipline more than anything else that turned Wilson against him.[49]

When Nansen at length received the American-drafted text for a note, he had difficulty in transmitting it to Moscow. Spectacular advances by White armies were persuading the wavering statesmen at Paris that collapse of the Soviet regime might be imminent. French distaste for relief had hardened into active opposition, and the government refused to send Nansen's telegram. Moreover, Lloyd George ruled that to transmit the message through British channels would be to strip it of its neutral gloss. It finally went to Lenin through neutral channels. On May 4 its receipt was acknowledged.[50]

43. Berle's memorandum of "conversation between Bullitt, Morison, and myself," April 19, 1919, Berle papers, box 1, "ACTNP. Berle: Memos. 1918–19," F. D. Roosevelt Library, Hyde Park.
44. See Mayer, pp. 479–481.
45. See below, p. 326.
46. "When I told him [Clemenceau] about Russia and the good it would do the French and the rest of us to open it up, he saw it at once and was willing," House diary, April 14, 1919.
47. "It is the most foolish thing I have known Hoover to do yet," House wrote in his diary on April 19. "Whether his [Hoover's] action is because of his inordinate desire for publicity I do not know."
48. Hoover to House, April 19, 1919; House diary, April 19, 1919; Sweetser diary, April 18, 1919.
49. *New York Times*, April 25, 1919. Hoover to Wilson, April 21, 1919, Wilson papers Mayer, pp. 482–483. Thompson, pp. 257–259. See below, p. 560.
50. Thompson, pp. 259–260. Mayer, p. 485.

The reply was long and prolix, teeming with the sort of fervent propaganda that the Soviet radio had been addressing to the workers of the world.[51] The West was denounced for causing by its blockade the misery that Nansen now proposed to relieve. The Soviet government asserted that it would make no concessions on matters that seemed essential to its existence, such as a cessation of its hostilities against its White enemies and the transfer of troops and materials within Russia. However, there were two conciliatory proposals. Separating the humanitarian aspect of Nansen's proposition from its political undertones, Chicherin offered to pay for supplies and to confer on the details of carrying out the plan. At the same time he expressed eagerness to discuss with the Allies the general question of ending the intervention and the civil war.[52]

On May 15 the Soviet reply to Nansen came to Paris. It perhaps derived strength from an awareness at Moscow that a White offensive had just been checked.[53] The peacemakers, however, seemed unaware of the adverse turn of the military tide. Deluded, they were jubilant about the prospects of Admiral Kolchak's regime at Omsk and were developing a policy of more energetic support for him. The Americans, discouraged by the tone of the Soviet reply to Nansen's proposal, fell back upon the prospect that had been raised by the White military advance.[54] They inclined toward acceptance of the continuing effort of the Allies to support the White armies and thus, hopefully, to promote the unification of Russia under a reliable government. Although Hoover thought that the Soviet reply to Nansen was largely "for internal consumption" and "left a crack open," he decided after conferring with various members of the Peace Conference to advise Nansen that it was "extremely inadvisable to arrange any meeting with the Bolsheviks until the entire matter" was given further consideration by the Western governments.[55]

After almost a year of uncertainty, Wilson now found himself again in the quandary of the summer of 1918, when he had aquiesced reluctantly in the policy of intervention that the Allies pressed upon him and that seemed to serve American interest in Siberia. He had made it clear on February 14 that he was fundamentally opposed to any sort of recognition of a regime that offended his moral sense as did that of Lenin. His Point Six had not prescribed democracy for Russia, but only "an unhampered and unembarrassed opportunity for the independent determination of her own political development and national policy . . . under institutions of her own choosing." However, it would be damaging to his political image as a champion of liberalism to express faith in a military chief with a record so reactionary as that of Kolchak, who had gained nominal supremacy over Siberia and was unable to control Cossack freebooters.[56] Yet Kolchak might be depended on to counter

51. Thompson, pp. 262–263.

52. Mayer, pp. 483–487. Thompson, pp. 263–264. Ullman, *Intervention and the War*, p. 160.

53. Mayer, p. 814.

54. Late in April, Polk had suggested from Washington that Kolchak's government be recognized, McCormick diary, April 21 and 24, 1919. Mayer, pp. 484, 818. Thompson, p. 264.

55. Hoover, *Memoirs*, vol. 1, p. 418; *The Ordeal of Woodrow Wilson*, p. 123. Gelfand (ed.), *Hoover*, p. 129.

56. Unterberger, "Woodrow Wilson and the Russian Revolution," in *Woodrow Wilson and a Revolutionary World*, ed. Arthur S. Link, p. 86.

Japanese influence, and he might rid Russia of bolshevism. Visiting the United States in 1917, he had made a favorable impression on members of the State Department.[57]

The question of recognition of Kolchak was debated by The Four in a meeting of May 9, six days before the Soviet reply to Nansen reached Paris. When Wilson was urged by Lloyd George to share in a common policy, he said that he did not "believe in" Kolchak. On that day the president received a message from General Graves, reporting that Kolchak's men were circulating "malicious propaganda" and threatening to obstruct the Americans who protected the Siberian railway if they did not become wholeheartedly anti-Bolshevist.[58] Wilson shared an opinion of Lloyd George that a revival of imperial Russia was more to be feared than bolshevism. Actually, the American government had acted informally in various ways to support anti-Bolshevists in Siberia. Indeed, the State Department had been advised by its consuls at Vladivostok and Archangel, as well as by John F. Stevens of the railway administration, that Kolchak should be recognized if he provided adequate assurance of liberal purposes.[59]

Facing up to the alternatives of supporting Kolchak or withdrawing the Americans from Siberia and giving Japan a free hand, the president showed reluctance to accept the second choice. Wilson, however, was not satisfied by testimony about Kolchak's purposes that he received from military men. He determined to send Ambassador Roland Morris from Tokyo to Omsk to make an independent appraisal.[60] However, when Polk reported that Morris was occupied in May "by serious questions pending" at Tokyo, Wilson regretfully instructed Lansing to "call the whole thing off" for the time being.[61]

On May 20 The Four, brushing aside the Soviet reply to Nansen that had been received five days before, came to agreement on a course of action. Wilson, unwill-

57. Charles J. Weeks, Jr., and Joseph O. Baylen, "Admiral Kolchak's Mission to the U.S., 10 Sept.–9 Nov. 1917," *Military Affairs* 40, no. 2 (April 1976):63–67.

58. Dispatch, Graves to Morris, May 7, 1919, Roland Morris papers, box 1, L.C. Graves reported that he was squarely up against the proposition of using force or getting out, dispatch N. D. Baker to Bliss, May 8, 1919, forwarded to Wilson by Bliss, May 9, 1919, Wilson papers. Polk diary, May 10, 1919. See Thompson, pp. 291–294. Polk complained that Graves showed a lack of tact and large experience, indeed was "a useless old woman and puts everything here to be decided . . . and so the result is that our men are not as effective as park policemen," letter, Polk to Lansing, April 17, 1919, Y.H.C. Polk to Ammission, April 15, 1919, Hornbeck papers. Early in May it was learned at Paris that Kolchak regarded the American troops in Siberia as "the dregs of the army" and "only a factor of decay and disorder," Thompson, p. 287. See "Note on Attitude of American Forces in Siberia to Kolchak," P.R.O., F0 / 800 / 216.

In a telegram sent to Paris on May 21 Secretary of War Baker defended Graves and reported that he and Polk had agreed that there should be no change in policy until a decision was made at Paris. Two days later Wilson replied that he concurred, documents in Wilson papers. When Lloyd George criticized Graves in a meeting of "The Four" on May 14, Wilson defended the general as a man of most unprovocative character, *F.R., P.P.C.*, vol. 5, p. 608.

The first of the three aims that Wilson had stated in July 1918 had not been achieved: the rescue of Czechs who had been prisoners of war. See Unterberger, pp. 67–80.

59. Thompson, p. 291 and n.

60. Wilson to Tumulty, May 14, 16, and 19, 1919, Tumulty papers, box 6. Wilson asked that Secretary Baker request Morris to "confidentially advise" as to whether "it would relieve unnecessary friction at Vladivostok if someone else should take the place of General Graves."

61. See below, p. 246.

ing to go so far as to consider recognition of Kolchak's government, said that "at least pledges could be exacted" to justify continuing support for the Whites in Russia. He proposed a formal challenge to them to declare their purposes. In the session the day before he had read aloud from a letter from Alexander Kerensky, the exiled leader of the Russian provisional government of 1917. Kerensky advised the Peace Conference to proclaim a democratic program for the governance of Russia and to support any group that accepted it.[62] This, Wilson remarked, "seemed to provide the rudiments of a policy." Kerr was instructed to draft a declaration in this vein. However, when Lamont was deputed to consult the spirited Russian, they spent a long night together in a Paris restaurant and Kerensky was found to be better endowed with enthusiasm than with any capacity to "get down to earth."[63]

A note was prepared to go to Kolchak, whom the anti-Bolshevik regimes of Generals Denikin and Miller appeared to be prepared to accept as provisional ruler of all Russia. This communication was signed on May 26 by the five great powers after the Japanese plenipotentiaries had been brought in belatedly.[64] The note, alluding to the "cardinal axiom of the Allied and Associated Powers to avoid interference in the internal affairs of Russia," then explained, to justify the obvious Western interference that was now to be continued, that military intervention had resulted from a desire to assist Russians who wished to carry on the fight against Germany and to bring freed Czech prisoners of war home from Siberia. The powers declared themselves ready "to assist the Government of Admiral Kolchak and his Associates with munitions, supplies, food, and the help of such as may volunteer for their service, to establish themselves as the government of all Russia"—but only if the White leaders would first accept certain liberal principles.[65]

Kolchak's reply, received at Paris on June 11, acknowledged Russia's debts and pledged not to restore the czarist regime and to hold popular elections to a constitutent assembly "at the moment when the Bolsheviks were definitely crushed." It agreed to accept the good offices of the League of Nations in altercations between Russia and its people of other nationalities, to whom he promised autonomy. The independence of Poland and the *de facto* independence of Finland were recognized.[66] Kolchak claimed to "speak in the name of all National Russia."[67]

---

62. Thompson, p. 291 and n.

63. Lamont, *Across World Frontiers*, p. 155.

64. Thompson, pp. 301–302. Ullman, p. 167.

65. Kolchak was asked to promise, if and when he assumed power in Moscow, to call a freely elected assembly, or at least to summon the Constituent Assembly of 1917 to sit on an interim basis; "to permit" in the areas under his control free elections for local assemblies; to preserve the civil and religious liberties of all Russians, leaving the settlement of questions such as land tenure to the assembly; to recognize the independence of Finland and that of Poland and to submit boundary disputes to the League of Nations; to settle relations with the Baltic and Caucasian countries under League auspices, if necessary; to abide by his own declaration in 1918 recognizing Russia's debts, and to join the League and agree to limit armament and military organization. The last clause was suggested by Wilson. Clemenceau objected to any pledge to "abolish conscription," apparently wishing to maintain Russian manpower as a curb on Germany, Thompson, p. 300; *F.R., 1919, Russia,* pp. 367–70.

66. See below, p. 250.

67. *F.R., 1919, Russia,* pp. 375–378. Ambassador Bakhmeteff, who had introduced Kolchak to Wilson on October 17, 1917, joined with other Russians at Paris to draft Kolchak's reply. Bakhmeteff ms., Columbia O.H.R.O., pp. 422, 428–429. A revised copy of the French text of Kolchak's reply, forwarded with a note, Grew to Close, June 12, 1919, is in the Wilson papers.

By the time Kolchak's reply was received, The Four were becoming aware of the weakness of his armies, although Denikin and Miller still gave some hope of effective resistance to the Soviets.[68] Nevertheless, Wilson acquiesced in a suggestion by Lloyd George on June 12 that the correspondence with Omsk be published and that they notify Kolchak that they were now ready to send assistance. Accordingly, Kolchak was informed that aid to him and to his associates would continue because the "tone of his reply" contained satisfactory assurances for the freedom, self-government, and peace of the Russian people and their neighbors.[69]

The correspondence with Kolchak shocked the young liberals in the American delegation. Samuel Eliot Morison was moved to resign from the Russian section, directing a vigorous protest to the president.[70] It asserted that the "mass of Russians," however much they disliked the Bolshevists, had "no faith in Kolchak and would not supply the manpower on which the Allies counted, that eventually the United States would be called upon for men and money, and moreover, that even if American financing and the blockade should put Kolchak in power, the Russian people would not be satisfied and at peace." Morison predicted that under Kolchak there would be "a general massacre of Jews" and a forcible reintegration of the border states with Russia.[71]

At the same time there was a widespread delusion in the United States, fed by White propaganda, that the Soviet government would collapse.[72] Moreover, the White Russians at Paris pressed the Americans for recognition of the Omsk regime.

When McCormick put the question to Wilson in June, the president, embarrassed by a Senate resolution calling upon him to justify the intervention in Siberia, responded negatively to proposals of recognition of Kolchak. He again directed that Ambassador Morris go from Tokyo to Omsk.[73] Explaining that the question of recognition was still open as well as that of the extent and nature of the support to be given to Kolchak, Wilson instructed Morris to be guided by the spirit of the Peace Conference's note to Kolchak. The envoy was to impress upon the Japanese government America's great interest in the Siberian situation and its intention to adopt a definite policy that would include "the 'open door' to Russia, free from Japanese domination." Morris should find out whether Kolchak was strong enough to control the men around him. There was to be "no present recognition," but "a sympathetic

68. Among General Denikin's advisers were some Americans. See Albert P. Nanarokov, *Russia in the Twentieth Century* (New York, 1968), pp. 133–148. British General Ironside was given a free hand to continue his campaign in the north, with the purpose of facilitating the withdrawal from Murmansk; but Ironside decided that it would be unwise to attack, minutes, B.W.C., June 18, 27, July 4, and 9, 1919, Curzon papers, mss. Eur., F 112 / 132. On the British withdrawal from north Russia, see Richard H. Ullman, *Britain and the Russian Civil War* (Princeton, 1968), pp. 181, 199.

69. *F.R., 1919, Russia,* pp. 378, 379.

70. N.A., R.G. 59, 861.00 / 721.

71. Memorandum from S. E. Morison to the president: "Kolchak: conclusions from information received in the Russian Division," June 10, 1919, Berle papers, box 1, ACTNP General Memos, 1918–1919.

72. During the two years following November 1917, the *New York Times* alluded to the probable fall of the Bolsheviks no fewer than ninety-one times, according to a study by Lippmann and Merz cited in Betty M. Unterberger (ed.), *American Intervention in the Russian Civil War* (Lexington, Mass., 1969), p. 5.

73. President to Polk, June 24, 1919, *F.R., Russia, 1919,* p. 380.

interest in Kolchak's organization and activities.''

McCormick and Hoover spoke to the president of the importance of economic aid to eventual political stability in Russia, and McCormick pointed out the difficulty of finding funds to finance assistance to an unrecognized government. Answering specific questions from Ambassador Bakhmeteff, Wilson said that no financial credits to the Whites were contemplated on the part of the United States.[74]

Wilson reverted to the long-range view of the Russian revolution that grew out of his understanding of political history and that had made him question foreign intervention from the beginning. It seemed to him that European powers had made a great mistake in trying to interfere in the French Revolution. The Russian people must solve their own problems without interference, he said to McCormick on June 23. Any economic aid given at this time would have to be channeled through an inter-Allied organization, and inevitably it would become entangled with the interests of the powers.[75] Since Kolchak had not been recognized, it seemed impossible to extend credit, although anything could be supplied that could be paid for. Wilson intended to take up at Washington the question of a great constructive program for aiding Russia through the Siberian Railway. He suggested that the only way to finance assistance to Kolchak was to tell the Congress the whole story and appeal for funds for the railway, to which McCormick had been directing money from the Russian Bureau of the War Trade Board.[76]

Actually, the State Department and Bakhmeteff drew upon Russian assets in the United States at their discretion. Ten million dollars went to the operations of the Russian bureau in Siberia and certain sums to the railway and to the purchase of arms for Czech and White Russian forces. On June 4 American bankers were informed that nothing could be done to prevent default when Russian bonds matured, while the press was told that the assumption of financial responsibility would be a prerequisite for recognition of any Russian government.[77]

At length, in July, Ambassador Morris went to Omsk and conferred there for several weeks with English, French, Japanese, and Chinese envoys. He reported that the Japanese were pursuing the same tactics that had led to "tragic results" in

---

74. McCormick diary, June 21, 1919, Y.H.C. *F.R., 1919, Russia,* pp. 384–385. Hoover, confident that the Soviet government would "fall of its own weight" or "be absorbed in a properly representative government," suggested to Wilson on June 21 that a mandate be given to a single Western state to set up an economic commission under one strong and responsible man with the purpose of commanding the resources in Russia and reorganizing the currency and the transportation, *F.R., 1919, Russia,* pp. 117–119.

75. McCormick diary, June 23, 1919. Wilson's colleagues on the American commission had urged him on May 26 to get from the members of the Council of Four "assurances that no special concessions enuring to the benefit of the countries which they represent have been given or offered by the Kolchak government and that there is no intention to accept such concessions in the future." Assured by Lansing that there was no specific basis for concern, Wilson wrote: "It is a very difficult matter to handle, and I shall have to await a favorable opportunity," Thompson, pp. 303, 307.

76. Dispatches, Polk to Lansing and McCormick, April 16, June 26, 1919, Wilson papers. McCormick diary, May 2, June 11, 1919. Wilson had proposed to Polk in January that the Congress should be asked for funds to repair and improve the trans-Siberian railway; but the cabinet had advised that such a request would be fruitless, *F.R., 1919, Russia,* pp. 243–251. On the termination of the Russian Bureau on June 5 and the use of its funds thereafter, see Killen, *The Russian Bureau,* pp. 121–124.

77. Killen, "The Search," 244–245.

China, and that in order to impress the "military clique" in Japan and the reactionaries in Siberia with whom it intrigued, one must speak in the only language that they understood—policing by an adequate American force. At Omsk, Morris found an "extremely critical situation," the "complete demoralization of Kolchak's army," and morale and equipment inferior to that of the Bolsheviks. Kolchak seemed to be lacking in military knowledge and experience in public affairs, and unable to command the confidence of anyone but discredited reactionaries. Convinced that the White leaders could not survive without more foreign aid,[78] Morris advised that in keeping with the pledge made by the Peace Conference in June the United States send arms on credit or by using the Russian funds in the United States. The council of foreign envoys at Omsk suggested a credit of $75 million to begin the movement of goods, strengthen the ruble, and open the way for private transactions.[79] Actually, in the desperate hope of establishing a regime that would validate the Russian debt, good money was thrown after bad. Russian funds in the United States that might have been used to meet in part the obligations to the American government and its citizens were diverted to the lost cause of Kolchak and Denikin. With Wilson's consent, "surplus" materials were sold to Kolchak at long discounts.[80]

For some weeks after his return from Paris the president could bring himself to no decisive action with respect to the question of further intervention in Russia, a question that was to loom malignantly in the history of the century and that he had described a year earlier as mercurial. Polk, citing the material sent to Kolchak by France and Great Britain, strongly urged that American assistance not be limited to military supplies; and Norman Hapgood, the liberal minister to Denmark, expressed faith in the "healing effects" of trade and sent information about commercial ventures in Russia on the part of Danes, Englishmen, and Germans. At the same time, Lansing and Tumulty were asking Wilson for a public denunciation of Bolshevist doctrines which were "extending far beyond the confines of Russia" and seemed to menace the social order.[81]

Finally in September, as the president's health failed (Dr. Grayson's diary recorded

78. See Graves, pp. 228–237.

79. Dispatches, Morris to State Department, July 22–August 22, 1919, B. Long papers, box 80, July 24, 31; *ibid.*, August 5, 6, and 10, 1919, H. White papers, box 44, L.C. See Maddox, pp. 120–122.

80. Polk to Wilson, July 12, 1919, Wilson papers. Strakhovsky, pp. 100–104. Maddox, pp. 119–120. George A. Brinkley, *The Volunteer Army and Allied Intervention in South Russia, 1917–1921* (Notre Dame, 1966), p. 221 and nn.

When the State Department learned informally from Bakhmeteff that American and British bankers were preparing to lend £10 million to Kolchak, no objection was raised. At the same time, Lansing informed Morris that the government could give no American credits without action by the Congress, and no action could be urged until the question of ratification of the Treaty of Versailles had been settled. However, bank notes were to be provided, to be paid for out of the bankers' loan. Shipments of rifles (presumably purchased with Russian funds) would continue, and the secretary of war was prepared to increase contracts with Russian operatives from $15 million to $25 million, dispatches in *F.R., 1919, Russia*, p. 420. See Maddox, pp. 122–123.

On July 19 Secretary of War Baker assured the vice-president of the American Defense Society that both arms and ammunition were being supplied to Kolchak "in considerable quantities" by the United States government, Strakhovsky, pp. 103, 106. According to Killen, however, the supplies sent were never in sufficient quantity to have measurable impact ("The Search," 251).

81. Polk to Wilson, July 12, 1919, Lansing to Wilson, August 7, 1919, N. Hapgood to Wilson, August 8, 1919, Wilson papers.

that Wilson "was not feeling very well" on September 13), his resistance to rec-ognition of Kolchak weakened. Confronted and shaken by the Boston police strike and a demonstration in Seattle by militant members of the Industrial Workers of the World, he continued to clutch at the remote prospect of constitutional rule in Russia under Kolchak and the protection of an "open door" in Siberia. He no longer held to his ban on credit to the unrecognized government at Omsk. "I fully approve," he replied to the State Department, ". . . with regard to furnishing such supplies as are available." It was the opinion of Polk that the enfeebled president would have eventually consented to the recognition of Kolchak had he not been entirely disabled a few days later.[82]

In the end Omsk fell to the Red Army in November, and France and Great Britain ceased to send assistance to Kolchak.[83] He was captured, and executed on February 7, 1920. Denikin was driven back during the last days of 1919. Yudenich, receiving British support, advanced in October to within a few miles of Petrograd, only to be thrown back.[84]

The British evacuated Murmansk on October 12 (the Americans having departed in July), and Bolshevists took over north Russia. On December 4 Lansing officially notified Ambassador Davis that he might tell the British government, if he thought it wise, that evolution toward a responsible rule had not progressed far enough in Russia to make it either desirable or possible to endeavor to reach an understanding with the Soviet rulers.[85] On September 23 the secretary of state reported to the stricken president that if the troops in Siberia did not leave, they would have to wage war against the Bolshevists. By the following April their withdrawal was completed. Japan's troops did not leave until November 1922.[86]

Wilson had been deluded by the ideals of the revolution of March 1917 and by his hope for effective resistance on the part of the White generals. Actually, all the undertakings to intervene had availed naught against the inexorable tide of the most potent revolution of modern times.

In the Baltic lands on Russia's western border the Americans found native roots for democratic government, and they cultivated these with a program of relief. In the states of Estonia, Latvia, and Lithuania, which had been provinces of czarist Russia and from which many emigrants had gone to the United States, liberal and agrarian parties were seizing the present opportunity to realize long-cherished hopes for independence. They were contending against Soviet forces and also against

82. Phillips to Wilson, September 19, 1919, Wilson to Phillips, September 21, 1919, Polk diary, October 1, 1919, Phillips to Polk, October 1, 1919, *F.R., 1919, Russia,* p. 436.

83. Dispatch, Polk to the secretary of state, November 28, 1919, N.A., R.G. 256, 861.00 / 1175A. Churchill to Loucheur, November 21, 1919, in Loucheur, *Carnets Secrets,* pp. 78–80.

84. Ullman, *Britain and the Russian Civil War,* pp. 254, 265–266, 273, 284. Hoover did not trust Yudenich's army and refused to supply food to it. His misgivings were justified when the troops looted provisions that American agents had assembled for the relief of Petrograd, Hoover, *Memoirs,* vol. 1, pp. 418–419.

85. Dispatch, Lansing to embassy, London, December 4, 1919, J. W. Davis papers, Yale Library.

86. Dispatch in N.A., R.G. 59, 861.00 / 6107, cited in Maddox, p. 126. Arrangements were made by the State and War Departments for the repatriation through Suez of the Czech and German prisoners of war in Siberia.

large landowners of German blood, known as "Balts." Such order as existed was due largely to the presence of German troops that had been permitted under the Armistice of Rethondes to remain in the region as a barrier against bolshevism. The political turmoil was aggravated by shortages of food.

Uncertain as they were of the outcome of the Russian revolution and hopeful that governments might emerge that would represent the will of the peoples, the American peace commisioners were not inclined toward military intervention.[87] Hoover's determination to check bolshevism by administering relief became the moving influence. He developed a program for Finland, which had become an independent "republic" under the strong rule of General Mannerheim, and he found that relief work could be facilitated by recognition of the military government. On April 26 he wrote urgently to the president about the matter; and a week later the Council of Foreign Ministers decided that the American and British governments would grant recognition, which the French had already given. Wilson wrote to Lansing that he was "very keen" for it and, contrary to the view of protesting White Russians at Paris, he did not regard Finland as "an integral part of Russia."[88]

Wilson was receptive also to another proposal by Hoover, who said that starvation and anarchy were "simply terrible" in large Baltic areas held by Bolshevists. Hoover proposed a collaboration with British and American naval authorities to preserve order and distribute foodstuffs. A few weeks after the Armistice of Rethondes, acting with characteristic independence, he had set up a relief mission of thirty-six American officers in order to respond, as he has written, to "prayers . . . for food, medical supplies, clothing, and raw materials." On March 23 another party of Americans—military observers—went out from Paris. Lieutenant-Colonel Warwick Greene, their leader, found conditions most chaotic in Latvia, where political intrigue was intense among the Balts, the bourgeoisie, Bolshevists, Jews, and Lett socialists. He thought that the native government was too weak to be recognized and yet entitled to consideration in respect of all questions concerning finances and the importation of food.[89] Very soon the German army seized Libau, and General von der Goltz made himself military governor; and on April 22 Greene reported to

87. The Russian section of the American delegation recommended that the independence of Estonia, Latvia, and Lithuania be recognized, that their governments be supported so long as their struggle with bolshevism continued, and that recognition be limited by a reservation that questions of frontiers, free ports, and transit to Russia must be regulated by the Peace Conference or by the League of Nations at such time as Russia was able to present its case, "Memorandum from the Russia Section: The Russian Policy," March 30, 1919. Berle papers, box ACTNP. Many resolutions and petitions in favor of independence had been addressed to Wilson and the American Congress by Lithuanian-American organizations. See Albert N. Tarulis, *American-Baltic Relations, 1918–1922: The Struggle over Recognition* (Washington, 1965).

For a discussion of the complex situation in the Baltic states, see Mayer, pp. 315–318.

88. Hoover, *Memoirs,* vol. 1, pp. 363–366; *The Ordeal of Woodrow Wilson,* pp. 124–126. *F.R., P.P.C.,* vol. 4, pp. 662–668. Thompson, pp. 331–332. Miller, *My Diary,* vol. 1, pp. 239, 241, 245–246.

89. The provisional government of Latvia was headed by Karlis Ulmanis, who had emigrated the United States at the age of ten and was educated there, and who had Hoover's admiration. Driven out of Riga by radicals, he had overturned a Communist government at Libau and, fortified by American food, seized control there in March for a few days, and later headed a provisional government, Hoover, *The Ordeal of Woodrow Wilson,* p. 131; *Memoirs,* vol. 1, pp. 368–370. Gelfand (ed.), *Herbert Hoover,* pp. 103–105.

Paris that an immediate departure of German troops would deliver the country to bolshevism unless they were replaced by other forces.[90]

The American specialists, perhaps sharing the general fear of a projection of German power into Russia,[91] were shocked by the violence done to the principle of self-determination. Professor Lord proposed that a commission be appointed to study the question of the governance and future boundaries of the three turbulent little countries; and when Wilson received this recommendation, he put it before The Four on April 16 and got their approval of sending a mission "to investigate on the spot."[92]

The confusing struggle for power that went on in the Baltic countries and the uncertainty of its issue made the Europeans at Paris reluctant to ship supplies without a precise understanding of their destination and their effect upon the governance of the region. On April 19, in agreeing to allow a continuance of shipments of food, the Council of Foreign Ministers stipulated that the recipients be neither Bolsheviks nor Balts. With Hoover and McCormick, Lansing continued to press vigorously for economic assistance. "Even if the Germans were devils in Hell," he said, "the people must be fed."[93] On May 9 The Four approved a clause for the treaty of peace requiring all German troops in the Baltic states to withdraw as soon as the powers at Paris should think the moment suitable, having regard for the internal situation of these territories. And on the same day, Lansing made it clear to the Council of Foreign Ministers that American policy, committed to the territorial integrity of Russia, called for carefully avoiding dissection of former czarist territory except in the cases of Finland and Poland.[94]

Lloyd George endeavored to cool the ardor of Americans to make use of their surplus of food in a way that might exert political leverage on starving peoples. When on May 20 Wilson brought up Hoover's proposal that a relief program be carried out in cooperation with British naval authorities, The Four went only so far as to agree that Hoover should discuss the question of relief with the admirals of Great Britain and the United States.[95] Acting on this decision and learning that

90. *F.R., P.P.C.*, vol. 12, pp. 136–227. Lord to Bonsal, May 8, 1919, Bonsal papers, box 7. Hoover, *Memoirs*, vol. 1, pp. 372–373. On the operations of von der Goltz, "Chief of all the Free Corps" in the Baltic provinces, see Mayer, p. 318, and Stanley W. Page, *The Formation of the Baltic States*, pp. 145 ff.

91. *F.R., P.P.C.*, vol. 11, pp. 198–200. After examining the papers of the German Foreign Office, Ludwig Schaefer concluded that there was some basis for apprehension that Germany would exploit the riches of Russia, "German Peace Strategy in 1918–1919," pp. 216 ff. Bonsal, *Suitors and Suppliants*, p. 249. Foch said to The Four on March 31: "We do not know what resources the Germans may find in Russia," Mantoux, *Proceedings*, p. 65.

92. Memorandum to ACTNP from Lord, April 8, 1919, Lansing to Wilson, April 10, 1919. Wilson to Lansing, (April 16), 1919, Bliss papers. Mantoux, *Proceedings*, p. 203. *F.R., P.P.C.*, vol. 5, p. 315.

93. Very precise minutes of this meeting, kept by Berle, show Lansing, in his blunt advocacy of making food relief the prime objective, to have been "arrogant, self-righteous, and tactless," in contrast with the suave Balfour, "The Council of Five Mentions the Baltic," typescript in Berle papers. Cf. *F.R., P.P.C.*, vol. 4, pp. 589–593.

94. See Linda Killen, "Self-Determination vs. Territorial Integrity: Conflict within the American Delegation at Paris over Wilson's Policy toward the Russian Borderlands," *Nationalities Papers* (Spring 1982).

95. Mantoux, *Délibérations*, vol. 2, p. 129. *F.R., P.P.C.*, vol. 5, p. 737. Hoover, *Ordeal*, pp. 127–130.

weeks would be needed to organize a program, Hoover acted in a way that countered the efforts of the Supreme Council to expel German troops from the region. He asked von der Goltz, who had established a precarious control at Libau, to seize Riga. At the same time he ordered his own men to arrange to distribute food to the hungry populace. His operations were supported by an American naval vessel. The immediate result, according to Hoover, was that "a White Terror replaced a Red Terror with its round of executions."[96] The American "compact with the devil" was turning out bad. The German troops remained in the Baltic lands until the end of 1919, despite repeated orders from Paris that they withdraw.[97] On September 15 Polk agreed that the German government be notified that further defiance would be met by a blockade and, as a last resort, action by the Polish army. But on further consideration Polk vetoed the possibility of using Polish forces.[98]

Early in June the Commission on Baltic Affairs recommended from Libau that the Peace Conference provide for loans to the provincial governments "for civil purposes" and subsidize native armies to be directed by a military commission "for the protection of the Baltic provinces against bolshevism." However, American loans to the three weak governments already amounted to a total of $25 million.[99] When the commission's recommendation was discussed by The Four on June 25, Wilson said: "We haven't any money to send to them."[100]

On July 4 the British cabinet decided that a state of war with the Soviet government existed and British ships should enforce a blockade;[101] and on the twenty-fourth Balfour urged Wilson to reconsider, in view of the existence of a situation in which British and White Russian men were being killed. The president, however, insisted that he could not officially sanction an act of war without legislative approval. Nevertheless, the United States government did join in refusing to clear ships for Soviet ports, the Americans at Paris proposed that the Allies continue the blockade, Wilson suggested that neutrals be asked to cooperate,[102] and British warships turned back cargo vessels that tried to go through the Gulf of Finland.[103]

In the summer and autumn of 1919 Polk, after he took charge at Paris, decided that the State Department should deal with Baltic questions through regular channels.[104] Finding it difficult to agree with his colleagues in the top-level council upon

96. Memorandum by A.J.B., June 10, 1919, Balfour papers, 49750. Hoover, *The Ordeal of Woodrow Wilson*, pp. 131–133; *Memoirs*, vol. 1, pp. 374–375. Thompson, p. 337. "What is called justice is largely reprisals and vengeance," dispatch from Greene to Ammission, June 4, 1919, copy in Wilson papers.

97. Three times (on June 18, August 1, and September 24) Foch transmitted an order that the Germans must evacuate the Baltic lands. See Page, pp. 154–159.

98. Miller, vol. 16, pp. 523–524. Polk to Clemenceau, September 16, 1919, Y.H.C. Thompson, pp. 338–340, 344–345. Komarnicki, *The Rebirth of the Polish Republic*, pp. 460–464.

99. Hoover, *Memoirs*, vol. 1, pp. 371–378.

100. Mantoux, *Délibérations*, vol. 2, p. 514.

101. It was the opinion of American economic advisers that the British wished to maintain a blockade of Poland and Baltic countries in order to facilitate an "ultimate commercial invasion," minutes, Economic Group, March 19, 1919, N. H. Davis papers, box 46.

102. B. Long's diary, August 2, 1919.

103. Ullman, *Britain and the Russian Civil War*, pp. 287–293. The Supreme Economic Council took the position that after the conclusion of a peace the blockade could not be legally maintained but that it was undesirable to indicate in any way that the powers favored a resumption of trade, note from S.E.C. for Council of Heads of States, British papers, M249, Wilson papers. *F.R., 1919, Russia*, pp. 149–151.

104. See Grew, *Turbulent Era*, vol. 1, p. 399.

policies, he suggested on November 11 that this matter be referred to the foreign offices.[105] Advised by the cautious secretary of state, who was out of touch with the disabled president, Polk made it plain that his government "could not do otherwise than advise against any attempt at a compromise with the Bolsheviki." "The experience of this government," Lansing stated, "has convinced it that it is not practicable for non-Bolshevik governments to deal with the Bolsheviks. The ultimate purpose of the latter is to overturn all non-Bolshevik governments and seeming compromises which they may make with these are presumably but temporary and tactical experiments."[106] The eventual inclusion of the Baltic states as "constituent republics" in the Soviet Union bore out a dissenting opinion that was expressed by Professor Sidney B. Fay of the Inquiry, but rejected.[107]

Thus in the end the Americans and their allies had indeed failed in the "acid test" of the peacemaking. Alarmed during the war by German power over Russia, revolted by Bolshevik terror, sympathizing with the plight of the Czech troops in Siberia and suspicious of Japanese intentions, hopeful that limited intervention might effect a constitutional government, forced to seek an arrangement with Kolchak in order to protect the American position in Siberia, and concerned about loans to earlier Russian governments, the thinking of Americans was tossed on waves of revolution, while they waited in vain for a constitutional regime to emerge from the depths. Western idealists who would encourage a democratic Russian government despite the long tradition of despotism were to be given a frustrating lesson. Although the expansion of Soviet power was checked, it was at the cost of accepting such undemocratic regimes as those of Admiral Horthy in Hungary and General Mannerheim in Finland.

Worst of all, the abortive efforts to enter into relations with Russian factions under conditions prescribed at Paris, the presence of foreign troops on the soil of Russia, and the persistence of Soviet propaganda in Western nations created irritations that deepened the gulf between the Russian people and those of the West. The inconsistency of the policy of the West and its half-hearted bets on White generals who proved to be dying horses, evoked allegations of hypocrisy and provoked distrust. The two brief articles dealing with Russia that were put into the Treaty of Versailles had to do not with the nature of its government but with the nation's territorial integrity, its independence of all ties with Germany, and its right to "restitution and reparation" for war damage.[108]

It was proving to be more difficult than it had been in the comparatively tranquil society of the late nineteenth century for diplomats to function with precision and responsibility. And in the absence of reliable negotiations by professional diplomats, propaganda played upon fear and ignorance. The relation of Russia with the West had deteriorated into a long truce that grew so uneasy that it was to be known

---

105. Heads of Delegations meetings of October 28 and November 11, 1919, *F.R., P.P.C.,* vol. 11.

106. Lansing to Ammission, November 21, 1919, H. White papers, box 45.

107. Fay, according to his testimony to Gelfand, argued that Latvia and Estonia "be joined with Russia in a federal union of some kind with large autonomy; that from every point of view—political, economic, historic—they were a part of Russia; that if given complete independence they would certainly come into conflict with Russia because they formed Russia's natural outlet to the Baltic, and that in such a conflict they were too small and weak to maintain their independence," Gelfand, *The Inquiry,* p. 332.

108. Articles 116 and 117.

as a "cold war." The United States government had become so deeply involved that its people came to be associated in Russian propaganda with the "imperialist robbers" of Europe.[109]

109. See André Fontaine, *Histoire de la guerre froide* (Paris, 1965), p. 49.

The failure of the Peace Conference to deal effectively with the Russian question has been cited by Kennan as an example of the defects of the "summit diplomacy" of twentieth-century democracies, *Russia and the West under Lenin and Stalin,* pp. 129, 134–135.

14

Boundaries for Germany

In March, when The Four formed the habit of meeting for secret talks, questions of national boundaries were considered not only by them, but by the territorial commissions and by the council of foreign ministers.

Neither the speeches of Wilson nor House's commentary on the Fourteen Points drew precise lines for the frontiers of postwar Germany. According to the commentary, occupied areas were to be "restored," and Alsace-Lorraine was to be "restored completely to French sovereignty" in order "to right the wrong done to France by Prussia in 1871." No definite plan had been advanced for the future of many borderlands. Yet the studies that the Inquiry had carried out for the past year made it possible for the Americans to take part intelligently in the work of the territorial commissions not only with respect to Germany's eastern and western frontiers, but also with respect to questions that affected its boundaries on the north with neutral Denmark and the Netherlands. Nevertheless, when the time came to apply academic wisdom to the drafting of articles for a peace treaty, no one could say with authority how much German territory could be conceded to claimants on several fronts without causing the fall of the new Weimar Republic. Territorial specialists such as Haskins and Lord tended to sympathize with the national claims that they had studied; and their prime concern was for a satisfied France and a strong Poland rather than for a sound government in Germany.[1]

The English-speaking political chiefs, however, had profound respect for the opinion of the German people. Lloyd George, fearing there would be an explosion in Germany if they took too much of its territory and wealth, dismissed Foch's fervent pleas by declaring that Foch, a great general, was "just a child" in his thinking on political questions. Wilson, supporting Lloyd George, said in a session of The Four on March 27; "We do not want to destroy Germany and we could not do so. Our greatest mistake would be to furnish her with powerful reasons for seeking revenge at some future time. Excessive demands would be sure to sow the seeds of war." In modifying frontiers and changing national sovereignties, he said, they must not give their enemies "even an impression of injustice."[2]

The demand for the creation of strong and friendly states to stand between Germany and Russia increased as the prospect of rapprochement with the Soviet regime grew dimmer. Foch included Poland with Czechoslovakia and Romania in a projected *cordon sanitaire*. However, the "liberated" peoples could not be expected to form an effective barrier so long as they themselves engaged in petty wars in defiance of the edict that the Peace Conference had issued. Hostilities became chronic,

1. Schwabe, *Woodrow Wilson, Revolutionary Germany, and Peacemaking,* pp. 161–171.
2. Mantoux, *Proceedings,* pp. 24–29.

0
50
100
150
MILES
DENMARK
SCHLESWIG
1920
NORTH SEA
KIEL
CANAL
Kiel
HELIGOLAND
Hamburg
ELBE
WESER
NETHERLANDS
Rotterdam
Antwerp
Brussels
BELGIUM
Düsseldorf
Cologne
RHINELAND
RHINE
EUPEN
1920
MALMEDY
Koblenz
Frankfurt
Mainz
MEUSE
LUX.
SAAR
BASIN
1935
UNDER
LEAGUE OF
NATIONS
TO 1935
SAAR
PALATINATE
RHINE
Metz
LORRAINE
BAVARIA
Strasbourg
ALSACE
Munich
FRANCE
SWITZERLAND
AUSTRIA

Western Boundaries of Germany

BOUNDARY OF
GERMANY
1923

BALTIC SEA

LITHUANIA
(LITVA)

FREE
CITY OF
DANZIG
(GDAŃSK)

EAST
PRUSSIA

Marien-
werder
(Kwidzyn)

•Allenstein
(Olsztyn)

WEST
PRU SSIA

ALLENSTEIN &
MARIENWERDER
1920

VISTULA

Poznań•

•Warsaw

POLAND

ODER

UPPER
SILESIA
1922

VISTULA

•Teschen (Cieszyn)

Territory lost without plebiscite

Territory lost after plebiscite

Territory retained after plebiscite

Demilitarized zone

CHAZAUD

Eastern Boundaries of Germany

and the Supreme Council, finding that it had little control over military and political developments in areas to the south and east of Poland, left in abeyance the fixing of frontiers there.

It would obviously be difficult to reconcile the principle of self-determination with Wilson's promise to Poland of "free and secure access" to the Baltic Sea.[3] The Poles, desiring a good harbor and access to it by rail, demanded both banks of the Vistula and the port of Danzig, once a great medieval city under the protection of Polish kings. After the partition it was a part of Prussia, developed industrially by a population in which German blood predominated overwhelmingly. The Danzigers made it known by violent demonstrations that they wished to retain their German nationality.

During the president's absence from Paris the French had pressed measures to further their policy of strengthening Poland. Their purpose was supported when in February, Bowman and Lord reached accord with their British associates. The Black Book of the Inquiry strongly supported the claims of Polish nationalists.[4]

The question of Poland's western and northern frontiers was taken up in March by the Paris Committee on Polish affairs, and Bowman was appointed to serve on a subcommittee that was to prepare recommendations. In the subcommittee, of which French general Le Rond was chairman, the German-Polish frontier from Czechoslovakia to the Baltic was discussed. A most competent scholar, Bowman did not appear to negotiate effectively in defense of the American principle of self-determination, and in some instances he conceded priority to considerations of economics and administration rather than to that of ethnography. While opposing limitations upon the sovereignty of Germans in East Prussia, Bowman fully supported the contention that Poland should have Danzig. In this he had the approval of House and therefore, Bowman doubtless supposed, that of Wilson.[5]

Actually, however, the president had not committed himself specifically on the question of Danzig. Pressed by Dmowski at Washington, Wilson had asked whether Poland's purposes would not be served if the lower Vistula was neutralized and Danzig made a free port; and the Pole had replied that this arrangement would give his people full liberty to breathe, but with a German hand on their throat. When on February 23 House reported to his chief that the British experts, though not their government, had joined with the American specialists in accepting most of the Polish claims, there was no response from the White House. Therefore, House had allowed Clemenceau and Lloyd George to understand that the American delegates thought that Danzig should become a part of Poland.[6]

3. See Ian F. P. Morrow, *The Peace Settlement in the German-Polish Borderlands*, pp. 48–50.

4. House to Wilson, February 22, 1919, H. I. Nelson, *Land and Power*, pp. 147–151. Gelfand, *The Inquiry*, pp. 206–207.

5. See Nelson, pp. 151–166; Lundgreen-Nielsen, *The Polish Problem at the Paris Peace Conference*, pp. 194–201. Nelson points out that "Shotwell and Young were not convinced that the Danzig corridor was wise or in Poland's best interests, but key figures like Bowman thought otherwise."

According to Lundgreen-Nielsen, Bowman's activity left an impression of lack of diplomatic experience and negotiating ability. Bowman was not, however, unaware of the part that commercial interest played in determining British policy, Bowman in Seymour and House (eds.), *What Really Happened at Paris*, pp. 160–161.

6. "Notes of an Interview between M. Clemenceau, Col. House and myself," March 7, 1919, Lloyd George papers, F / 197 / 1. House recorded that many of the decisions reached in the tripartite conver-

In its report to the full commission on March 6 the subcommittee proposed the inclusion of Danzig in Poland, a plebiscite for Allenstein, and a definite line for the German-Polish frontier elsewhere except in western East Prussia. The next day an alteration placed more Germans in Poland than Bowman desired.[7] Thus violence was done to the principle of self-determination to an extent that alarmed Lloyd George and disturbed Wilson. It could be expected that Germany would object strenuously to the isolation of East Prussia as well as to the loss of Danzig.[8] The report of the commission provided for a corridor to the Baltic that would result in Polish rule over many people of German blood in the city of Danzig and in the land along the Vistula.

In the session of the Supreme Council on March 19 Jules Cambon, the chairman of the Polish commission at Paris, explained that its report gave more weight to economic and strategic necessities than to ethnography and that it had been found impractical to adhere everywhere to the ideal of self-determination. He asked that the council hear comment by French general Le Rond, who for the most part supported Poland's claims while tempering the most extravagant of them. However, Wilson very politely objected that Poland's western frontier was "a political matter and not a military one." When he suggested that the discussion should proceed without military men, the generals left the room.[9]

Lloyd George objected particularly to the transfer of Marienwerder, a district on the right bank of the Vistula in which the population was largely German. Such an arrangement, he warned, might sow "the seed of future war." He suggested that they ask the commission to reconsider, with a view to the exclusion from Poland of territory that was historically and ethnically Prussian. He asked a disturbing question: If, as was proposed, more than 2 million Germans were to be included in Poland, and if they rebelled against their rulers and were supported by a future government of Germany, would the great Western powers go to war to maintain Polish rule over them?[10]

Wilson, caught in the conflict between the promise of free access to the sea and that of self-determination, called for a balancing of the antithetical considerations. Alluding to the difficulty experienced by the Poles in the past in governing themselves, and prophesying that religious differences would create factions in the future, he said that the state they were creating in Poland inevitably would be weak. He tried to palliate violence to self-determination by suggesting that there would be compensating instances in which areas historically Polish would be left within Germany. The inconclusive discussion resulted only in agreement to instruct the commission to reconsider in the light of what was said. The next day, however, the advisory body voted to stand by its original recommendations in every respect, and

---

sation were not communicated to the president "because much explanation would have been needed," diary, March 7, 1919. Possibly a full explanation was given on the train from Brest to Paris on March 13, *I.P.*, vol. 4, p. 434. See above, p. 189.

7. Nelson, pp. 151–165.

8. See Haskins and Lord, *Some Problems of the Peace Conference*, pp. 173–188.

9. French official minutes, March 19, 1919.

10. Kaltenbach has observed that Lloyd George was moved more by expediency than by any firm commitment to self-determination as a general principle that might be applied embarrassingly in Ireland, Egypt, or India, *Self-Determination, 1919*, p. 58.

it stated the reasons for assigning to Poland the region through which the Warsaw-Mława-Danzig railway passed.

When the subject came up again in the Supreme Council of Ten, Lloyd George gave voice to his growing fear that Germany would not sign a treaty that included the settlement recommended. A formula proposed by Wilson was adopted, reserving the question "for final examination in connection with subsequent boundary determinations affecting Germany."[11] Actually, the Germans were infuriated by the possibility of losing Danzig,[12] and it seemed possible that they would be driven to overthrow their new government, just as the Hungarians had revolted in protest when the Peace Conference gave a slice of their territory to Romania.

Linked with the question of the disposal of Danzig was the problem of repatriating Haller's Polish army, which was in France and which Foch wished to use in his grand plan for resisting Soviet aggression. There was an immediate need for assurance from Germany that these troops, as well as American foodstuffs, could move safely through Danzig to Poland. Foch had advocated the transport of Haller's army, and House had supported the marshal. At the time of the January renewal of the armistice, Wilson and Lloyd George had turned down Foch's proposal.[13] However, both Foch and Noulens, the French chairman of the commission sent to Warsaw by the Peace Conference, pressed for the shipment of Haller's troops and the end of German rule in Danzig, where an American destroyer was anchored and stood ready to supply marines to aid the German military authorities in preserving order.[14] The Warsaw commission, asked by the Supreme Council at Paris during Wilson's absence to study the question of loading Haller's troops on trains in a German-controlled Danzig, demanded of German negotiators that they guarantee the security of Haller's troops, and it was hinted that the city probably would be occupied by Polish forces or by those of the Associated powers. To this demand the Germans did not respond, having been directed from Berlin to profess a lack of instructions. Remembering riots that were precipitated by Paderewski's appearance in Poznań,[15] they feared a similar uprising on the part of the Polish minority in Danzig if Haller entered the city. They wished to bring the matter before the Armistice Commission at Spa, where they counted upon the sympathy of American and British military men to check French designs.

When Noulens turned to Foch for action, and the tense situation at Danzig threatened to bring the armistice to a violent end, Foch put the question before the Supreme Council of the Peace Conference on March 17. Actually, the credibility of the German government's peace policy was at stake. Nationalistic demonstrations within Germany impelled the officials toward violation of the armistice; but realizing the futility of outright resistance, Erzberger, who spoke for Germany in the armistice talks, suggested an ingenious way out of the dilemma. He proposed that Haller's troops travel by rail across Germany from one of the Rhine bridgeheads that were under occupation. To transmit this proposal to Wilson he used the military channel

11. The deliberations of The Four and the Supreme Council of Ten are summarized in Eugene Kusielewicz, "Wilson and the Polish Cause at Paris," 67–68.

12. Lloyd George to Bonar Law, March 30, 1919, Law papers, 97 / 1 / 17.

13. See above, p. 95.

14. Schwabe, p. 260.

15. See below, p. 329, n. 45.

that had been established by Colonel Conger at Spa with a German at Berlin, Major Loeb.[16] Erzberger's message, which included a temperate statement of Germany's position on issues of the peacemaking, was in the hands of the American peace commission on March 31.

The American military men realized fully that the German goverment was under pressure from Right and Left and was, as General Bliss put it, "fighting for its life," and might be overwhelmed if it consented to the transport of Haller's army through Danzig. "It seems a pity," Bliss wrote to the president, "that she [Germany] cannot in any way be heard while the peace terms are being discussed." He recommended that the idea of moving the Polish troops across Germany by rail should be taken up by Foch with the Germans immediately. Hoover, who had been directing shipments of food through Danzig since mid-February with German cooperation, warmly supported the plan for keeping Haller's army out of Danzig and thus averting a risk of violence. He opposed ceding the city to Poland.

After Foch brought the matter before the Supreme Council on March 17, Wilson and Lloyd George persistently questioned the arbitrary actions of French diplomats and military men, who had committed the peacemakers to a position in respect of Danzig that would be difficult to disavow without loss of prestige. Finally, on the morning of April 1 Wilson, warned by his advisers that the Berlin government might give way to one that would be either reactionary or Bolshevist and that might not sign a treaty of peace, put Erzberger's proposal before Clemenceau and Lloyd George. It appeared to offer not only a means of countering the French and Polish intention to take Danzig from Germany; it was also a practical answer to the difficulty raised by a lack of ships.[17] Therefore, Wilson was willing to accept the German suggestion that the troops be moved by rail from the Rhine, provided that a contingent should be allowed to pass through Danzig as a symbol of their right to do so. The Supreme Council instructed Foch to go personally to discuss the possibility of rail transport with the German armistice commissioners at Spa. Wilson warned that no guarantee was to be given as to the future status of Danzig, and he urged the marshal to adopt the tone of a diplomat rather than that of a soldier. Accordingly, Foch negoitated an understanding that both maintained the right of the Allies, acting under Article 16 of the armistice, to route Haller's troops through Danzig, and also took advantage of the German proposal to move them by rail. It was agreed that the United States would provide its share of the supervisory officers that would be needed. The problem was finally solved in part by the transport of the army across Germany in three hundred trains provided by the Allies. Thus the German government won the acclaim of its nation's press for a diplomatic success.[18] The use made of Haller's repatriated troops, however, was the subject of further controversy at Paris.[19]

The question of the future of Danzig, which the long negotiations over the trans-

16. See Schwabe, pp. 155–160, 218, 221, 263.

17. According to Grayson's record, Wilson was "very stern" in insisting on the transport of Haller's army by rail in order to conserve shipping, Grayson diary, April 2, 1919.

18. Much of the above is based on Schwabe, pp. 258–266. Wilson to Bliss, April 9, 1919, Bliss papers, box 50. Mantoux, *Proceedings,* pp. 32, 51–54, 75–77, 86–87, 130. Watt, *Bitter Poland,* p. 74. Shartle, *Spa, Versailles, Munich,* p. 67. Lundgreen-Nielsen, pp. 193–197.

19. See below, p. 247, n. 59.

port of Haller's army had kept urgent, was discussed at great length near April 1 by the Supreme Council. For support of his proposal that Danzig be a free port and the Poles have transit rights, Lloyd George read a memorandum from General Smuts, whose opinion he could count on to influence Wilson. "The fact is," Smuts wrote, "the Germans are and have been, and will continue to be the *dominant factor* on the Continent of Europe, and no permanent peace is possible which is not based on that fact."[20] At the same time, on the other hand, Wilson was pressed by Clemenceau to give due regard to the lessons of history and to the unquenchable national spirit of the Poles. The old veteran of Europe's wars urged Wilson to accept the fact that Europeans were "a tough bunch" and had to be handled with gauntlets of steel. He despaired of bringing the American prophet to see what he regarded as inescapable realities, but he hoped that Colonel House was right in saying that their differences could be "ironed out."[21]

Wilson, perhaps influenced by his desire to endow the league of nations with responsibilities, inclined toward Lloyd George's position. It seemed to him that France was intent upon weakening Germany by giving Poland territory to which it had no right.[22] He was impressed by the similarity of the situation to that at Fiume, where, he told Bowman, the real struggle between high principles and national demands would come. He feared that consistency would require him to give Fiume to Italy if he gave Danzig to Poland. On April 1 he told Mezes that he was willing to make Danzig and the surrounding German-speaking territory "free or international or independent," with transportation and customs in the hands of the Poles.[23] The administration was to be under a local body, supervised by a high commission of the League of Nations. The Poles were to have a corridor along the Vistula, but Marienwerder was to be disposed of by a plebiscite—an arrangement that House's advisers saw to be equivalent to turning it over to Germany.

After he received these instructions from the president Mezes conferred immediately[24] with Lloyd George's adviser, James Headlam-Morley. Without consulting any representative of France, they prepared a paper for the afternoon session of the Supreme Council providing for the cession of Danzig and certain areas along the Vistula to the League of Nations, which would determine the exact boundaries and deliver the territory to Poland on condition that relative autonomy was assured.[25]

Wilson presented this new project to his European colleagues together with other possible solutions, and he commented on their advantages and disadvantages. Lloyd George then spoke in favor of the "free cities idea" for Danzig under the League. This would give British merchants and shippers an opportunity to develop profitable

20. Hancock, *Smuts*, vol. 1, pp. 510–511.

21. Bonsal, *Suitors and Suppliants*, pp. 132–133.

22. Baker, vol. 2, pp. 59–60.

23. Bowman's record of a talk with Arthur Sweetser, February 26, 1919, Bowman papers. Bowman, in *Seymour and House* (eds.), p. 162. Shotwell, *At the Paris Peace Conference*, p. 305.

24. Miller, *My Diary*, vol. 1, p. 209.

25. Mantoux, *Proceedings*, pp. 79–80. It was agreed that because of the difficulty of communicating with Danzig and procuring reliable information, it would be wise to exclude "all matters of detail" from the clauses drafted, Headlam-Morley, "The Eastern Frontiers of Germany," p. 11, paper in the possession of Agnes Headlam-Morley.

trade.[26] When he urged that Marienwerder be left in East Prussia, Wilson, who preferred a plebiscite, said that he would like to refer the question for further study by experts.

The next day the president conferred with Mezes and Headlam-Morley, and on April 3 he presented to the Council of Four a proposal that was agreed upon.[27] The conditions were those that he had proposed to Mezes two days before. Clemenceau assented reluctantly, remarking that he did not want to break with the Poles and they were "not always easy to handle." Lloyd George came away from the meeting boasting that he had won Wilson over by persuading him that the desired plan was in reality his own,[28] a stratagem that House had often found effective. The matter was not finally settled, however, until April 18, after Paderewski came to Paris to plead the Polish case.[29]

The president of the United States, acting in the role of arbiter without prejudice, could hardly expect that Polish patriots who had worshiped him as a liberator, or indeed their kin in the United States, would receive his Jovian dispensations with glee. Wilson found it difficult to regard the Poles as less chauvinistic than the Germans in view of reports to the effect that the troops of General Haller, which were now to be transported to Poland by rail, would be sent to fight the Ukrainians at Lemberg.[30]

The drawing of a frontier between Germany and Czechoslovakia brought up the same questions of principle that proved vexing in arranging the boundaries of Poland. The American Black Book called for a border that would follow "the historical frontiers of the Bohemian crownlands," and took the position that the resulting inclusion of 2.5 million Germans in Czechoslovakia would be justified by economic advantages that they would share with the racial majority in the new state. Wilson did not repudiate this position.[31]

Although House had let Foreign Minister Beneš understand that Wilson would acquiesce in a historic frontier, the American members of the Commission on Czechoslovak Affairs, to whom the question was referred on February 5, were by no means willing to concede all that the Czechs asked. They stated in the first meeting, and kept constantly before the commission, a principle that went into its final report: i.e., "the incorporation within Czechoslovakia of so large a number of Germans involved certain disadvantages to the future of the new State." While recognizing the importance of defensible frontiers and economic unity, they argued

26. See below, p. 329.
27. Headlam-Morley, a fellow historian, found Wilson "very agreeable and quite intelligent . . . , quiet," unhurried, and willing to listen patiently to frank criticism of his ideas by his advisers, Sir James Headlam-Morley, *A Memoir of the Paris Peace Conference*, pp. 62, 66.
28. Frances Stevenson, *Lloyd George*, p. 177.
29. See below, p. 328.
30. See below, p. 331.
31. See above, p. 98. In a statement to Professor Young, Wilson had said that "it would be too complicated to draw any new boundary in Bohemia, even though there is a clear line which could and should be drawn eliminating two million Germans from Czechoslovakia," Bullitt's diary on board S.S. *George Washington*, entry of December 12, 1918, quoted in *The Shaping of the Czechoslovak State* (p. 139), by D. Perman.

that the restlessness of alien minorities within Czechoslovakia would imperil its constitutional processes and indeed its national existence.[32] The delegates of the United States, however, were isolated and outvoted by Europeans.[33]

The commission, accepting the historic frontiers between Bohemia and Germany and between Slovakia and Poland, rejected Czechoslovak claims to Lusatia and to a corridor to Yugoslavia. It drew a Slovak-Hungarian boundary closely following the request of Beneš, and approved a provision, promoted by Ruthenian immigrants in the United States, for the inclusion of Ruthenia in Czechoslovakia and for its autonomy. The recommendations of the commission were approved by the central territorial committee on March 25 and were taken up by the Council of Foreign Ministers on April 1.

In the sessions of the territorial committee and in those of its subcommittee the American delegates advocated the award to Germany of the salients of Rumburg and Eger (Cheb), where the population was almost entirely of German blood. The Europeans, however, did not accept this opinion; but they did report the American dissent to the Council of Foreign Ministers.[34]

In the meeting of the Council of Foreign Ministers on April 1 the American secretary of state conducted himself in a way that served only to antagonize the Europeans and to discourage concessions on their part. Instead of working informally with Balfour, who hoped for a clarification of policy,[35] Lansing made an ill-calculated effort to champion Wilsonian principles.[36] The delegates of the United States, he said, objected to the whole method of drawing frontier lines on strategic principles, and any delineations made with a view to military strength and in contemplation of war were directly contrary to the whole spirit of the League of Nations. Jules Cambon, presiding over the commission, was wearied by what he later called the *Pharasaïsme* of the American, but he refrained from embittering the debate by

---

32. Seymour, "Czechoslovak Frontiers," 279–280, 282–284. Seymour's concern for racial minorities is expressed in his letters to Coolidge and to W. G. Davis, February 14, 1919, and to Dulles, May 2, 1919, Y.H.C.

33. Perman, pp. 146–147.

34. The deliberations of the committees are related in Nelson, pp. 293–301, and in Perman, pp. 125–175 *passim*.

On the French view of the question of Rumburg and Eger see memorandum, Seymour to the secretary of state, April 2, 1919, Y.H.C. Professor Seymour asserted that without these regions the Czech state would still have excellent natural frontiers, suffer no serious economic inconvenience, and "be freed of 330,000 persons of German blood whose influence on the Czechoslovak state might lead to grave political difficulties," Seymour to Czechoslovak commission, March 14, 1919, minutes of meeting no. 7, Y.H.C.

"There have been some doubts as to Professor Seymour's qualifications for diplomatic work," Perman, p. 142n. Seymour was not brought into service as a diplomat but as a scholar. When called upon to function as a diplomat, he wrote of his task: "It is far more important than any work I expected to be called upon to do over here," *Letters from the Paris Peace Conference*, pp. 168, 173.

35. "Note on the Report of the Czechoslovak Commission," April 1, 1919, Balfour papers, 49750.

36. *F.R., P.P.C.*, vol. 4, pp. 543–547. Seymour was "irritated as well as amused" when he talked with Lansing about Czech boundaries and found him "perfectly genial but rather testy at having to be told the meaning of things." Seymour observed that in the meetings of the Council of Foreign Ministers, Lansing "never knew when he was on strong or on weak ground, . . . argued with great vehemence," but failed "to catch the important nuances in the different questions and always confused the debate." Seymour tried to put him right with whispers in his ear, to the amusement of Tardieu, who sat on Lansing's right, *Letters from the Paris Peace Conference*, p. 207.

any reference to the policy of the United States in respect of racial minorities in California and Puerto Rico.[37] Balfour, lacking precise instructions from Lloyd George, stood aside. The meeting ended in a deadlock. The American experts were not consulted by Wilson, and their dissents fared no better in a session of The Four on April 4 in which House took Wilson's place.[38]

The question of the western frontiers to be imposed on Germany was a matter of life or death to the people of France and Belgium, who demanded assurance that the German invasions of the past not be repeated. They found no adequate satisfaction in the Covenant of the League of Nations, which lacked adequate sanctions and might not be ratified by the American Senate. Neither the Covenant's provision against aggression nor the treaties of guarantee that were offered by Wilson and Lloyd George to Clemenceau and upon which the French premier put his primary reliance reassured French militarists.[39]

Wilson's Point Eight provided that the wrong done to France in 1871 should be righted, and House had interpreted this in the prearmistice meetings to mean that the seized provinces of Alsace and Lorraine were to be "restored completely to French sovereignty." Thus it was clear that the Rhine would be the frontier as far north as the River Lauter. However, the future of the left bank, from the Lauter up to the Dutch border, raised complications that became embarrassing to the peacemakers.

North of the Lauter, the area occupied by the victorious armies included about 7 million inhabitants and stretched from the western boundary of Germany to the Rhine, with bridgeheads across the river at Cologne (Köln), Koblenz, and Mainz. It was composed of several districts that had a long history of divisions and reunions and had been united under France only for a score of years before 1814. Its people had a distaste for government from without and a leaning toward self-rule. In considering French plans for this area the American specialists found it "not always possible to distinguish what was imperialistic by nature from what was necessary to the restoration and protection of France."[40]

French troops had taken over the southern region bordering France and were thus in a strategic position to control traffic across the frontier to the advantage of their nationals. The American Third Army, constituting less than a third of the occupying forces, was stationed in the central area and at the bridgehead at Koblenz. Its objective was stated in a directive of the Fourth Division: "We are to help build a new government to take the place of the one we have destroyed; we must feed those whom we have overcome; and we must do all this with infinite tact and patience, and a keen appreciation of the smart that still lies in the open wound of their pride."[41]

---

37. Cambon, "La Paix," 25–26. Perman, p. 141 and n.
38. See below, pp. 286–287.
39. McDougall, *France's Rhineland Diplomacy*, p. 59.
40. See Charles H. Haskins, "The Rhine and the Saar," in Haskins and Lord, pp. 123–132, and "The New Boundaries of Germany," in Seymour and House, pp. 49, 52. For a bibliography of French propaganda see McDougall, pp. 390–393. On "the myth of Franco-Rhenish affinity" see *ibid.,* p. 17.
41. Keith Nelson, *Victors Divided,* p. 31.

It was the purpose of the American military authorities to conform with Foch's policy of preserving normal civil life.

Early in 1919, however, rifts had developed in the common front. General Pershing, who had lost French confidence to such an extent that just before the armistice his removal from his command had been requested by Clemenceau, was deeply offended when Foch arbitrarily reduced the area of the American zone. Moreover, controversy between these commanders over the rate of repatriation of American troops became so heated that it was carried to the Supreme Council for adjudication.[42] There was discord also over responsibility for occupation of the Duchy of Luxembourg.[43]

Concern for the economic welfare of German citizens in the Rhineland was stirred by certain commercial operations that were carried on under French military protection. Under the authority of a commission that was set up in Luxembourg to license commerce, the trade of the Rhineland was being reoriented toward France. French businessmen, eager to make up for the lean years of the war at the expense of the enemy, were able under the protection of Foch's high command to disregard German import tariffs and to get licenses at Mainz that were valid in all occupied zones. Although the influx of French goods provided immediate comfort for those who could pay for them, the prospect for protecting any local production that could support an enduring economy was darkening. The German populace, which at first had welcomed the American army as the least unfriendly of the victors, was disappointed by its failure to check French designs.

In the American zone the commanding officer announced that the offensive licenses were merely "advisory." However, complaints were made to the Supreme Economic Council, which was created to deal with such matters; and Pershing protested to House.[44] Wilson was aware of the situation before he left Paris in February and doubtless recalled the behavior of Yankee carpetbaggers after the Civil War, which he had witnessed as a boy. He had warned House by cable that Foch was acting "under exterior guidance of the most unsafe kind."[45]

On March 6 the office of the War Trade Board at Paris, following an example set by the British Foreign Office, sent a civilian to replace American army officers on the supervising commission. This representative was able to make little progress against the prevailing French policy. Nevertheless, a prospect of relief from exploitation appeared when on March 17 the Supreme Council decided that an inter-Allied commission of control should supplant the High Command. It was not until late in April, however, just before German delegates were given the terms of peace at Versailles, that an effective American protest took shape. Controversy continued into May and June.

42. *Ibid.*, pp. 40–43.

43. See below, pp. 270–271.

44. K. Nelson, pp. 52–53, 99–101. Pershing to House, January 25, 1919, Y.H.C.

45. The Americans came to suspect that some of the "exterior guidance" came from French cabinet ministers who wanted to play "a lone game in German commerce," McCormick diary, May 19, 1919. On the French interests involved in the Rhineland see McDougall, p. 53, K. Nelson, pp. 33 and 104, and Miguel, *La Paix de Versailles,* pp. 504–525.

As a substitute for the permanent separation of the left bank from Germany, the president, immediately after his return to Paris, had joined Lloyd George in offering to France a binding promise of immediate military aid in the event of an unprovoked attack. (The prime minister had suggested earlier to House that France should be given this guarantee until the League of Nations proved its worth.)[46] On March 17, however, Wilson received a French note that, while acknowledging the value of the guarantee proposed, nevertheless insisted on the necessity for something more; for it was "really not possible for France to give up a certain safeguard for the sake of expectations." If attacked, the nation would have to defend itself alone until its allies from overseas could bring their strength to bear. Past experience had made it clear that the French armies must control the Rhine in order to be able to resist invasion immediately and effectively. Clemenceau now conceded, however—as Tardieu had earlier[47]—that the peace treaty might set a time limit to the occupation of German territory. He sent a copy of the note of March 17 to House, hopeful that the colonel might persuade Wilson to modify his views.[48]

However, the president was irritated by the French refusal to accept the proffered treaty of guarantee as sufficient. "I know the bitter feeling which the president had against England and the British government," Edith Benham wrote on the day the note was delivered, "and now that is all gone and the bitterness is transferred to the French government, but not the French people."[49] For a month after the president's return to Paris, the future of the Rhineland remained undecided.[50]

A further division of opinion arose in respect of the Saar valley, where there were rich deposits of noncoking coal. The political status and the supervision of the region, as well as the question of the place of its resources in the industry of Europe, were the subject of controversy.[51] In 1917 the Quai d'Orsay had informed the British Foreign Office that France would insist on the return of Alsace and Lorraine with the boundary that had existed prior to the European settlement of 1815.[52] Actually, however, the French coveted an area that included rich mines beyond the boundary of 1814.[53] Clemenceau, wary of a German monopoly of Saar coal and pressed by his people to seek compensation for the wrecking and flooding of the

46. Bonsal, pp. 215–216.

47. See above, p. 153.

48. Clemenceau's covering letter to House read: "I send you confidentially and for your personal use a copy of the note I am addressing this morning to Messrs. Wilson and Lloyd George. Very affectionately yours." The note was in three parts: I. Resumé de la Proposition Française (3 parts); II. Examen de la Suggestion Présentée (3 parts); III. Causes Possibles d'Accord (6 parts), Y.H.C. At this time House suggested to Wiseman that a temporary buffer state be created on the left bank of the Rhine, House diary, March 17, 1919.

49. Benham diary letter, March 17, 1919.

50. See below, pp. 325–327.

51. See the notes of C. K. Leith, "Discussion of the New German Boundaries." This geologist, in discussions with the historians and geographers of the Inquiry, argued that the taking over of the Saar basin by France would run counter to the economic needs of the iron and coal industries of Europe. On French and German interests in the Saar coal and efforts to reach an accommodation, see McDougall, pp. 88, 110–111.

52. Briand to P. Cambon, January 12, 1917, Cmd. pa., 1924, No. 2169, nos. 2, 3. James Headlam-Morley, "A History of the Peace Conference," May 28, 1923, H.M.G. ptd. doc. conf. c / 9743 / 493 / 18, Headlam-Morley papers.

53. Hajo Holborn, *A History of Modern Germany,* vol. 3, p. 560.

mines in occupied France, had discussed the matter frankly with House prior to the Armistice of Rethondes.[54]

The Germans, whose empire was said to have been "built more truly on coal and iron than on blood and iron," argued that the Saar valley was inhabited mostly by Germans and had been theirs for a millennium, except for a few years prior to 1815 when it was part of France. Nevertheless, Professor Haskins, the chief American expert on the question, giving less attention to historic than to economic and strategic considerations, early came to the conclusion that the French claim was valid.[55] But Wilson, upon his return to Paris in March, was troubled by the palpable threat to his cherished principle of self-determination. It was becoming apparent that some ingenious form of political administration must be invented that would prevent German interference with French operation of the mines and would at the same time protect the population, predominantly German, from alien rule.

When the matter was taken up by The Four on March 28, Lloyd George, who in his Fontainbleau memorandum had just proposed that France be granted the frontier of 1814, shifted his position. He now would go only so far as to give the Saar an autonomous government, with French ownership of the mines. But to this Wilson would not agree. As the president saw it, "To grant a people independence they do not request is as much a violation of the principle of self-determination as forcibly handing them over from one sovereignty to another." He recognized no principle but the consent of the governed, and would not consider French ownership of the mines, but only an arrangement for the delivery of coal by Germany to France.[56]

Feeling ran high in this meeting on March 28. In an interchange not recorded in the minutes, Clemenceau complained that Wilson was pro-German; the president, obviously hurt, asked whether he should not return to the United States. Whereupon Clemenceau walked out of the room without a further word.[57] At noon Wilson said to his advisers: "I do not know whether I shall see M. Clemenceau again. I do not know whether he will return to the meeting this afternoon. In fact, I do not know whether the Peace Conference will continue."[58] However the president, urged by House to yield a little so that his position would be supported by the British, asked his scholarly advisers to work with their British colleagues[59] toward some settlement that would not require any annexation by France.

After a ride in the Bois with Dr. Grayson, during which Wilson confessed that he had been "insulted grossly" and feared he could not control his temper when he returned to the fray that afternoon, he addressed the three premiers in an impas-

54. House diary, November 9, 1918, Y.H.C. Clemenceau was under pressure from the army, the steel industry, French labor, and Briand, letter, J. B. Duroselle to the author, June 28, 1974.

55. Haskins and Lord, p. 139. Gelfand, *The Inquiry,* pp. 194–195.

56. Headlam-Morley, "A History of the Peace Conference." Mantoux, *Proceedings,* pp. 46–49.

57. Cary T. Grayson, *Woodrow Wilson: An Intimate Memoir,* pp. 75–76. House diary, March 28, 1919. Auchincloss diary, March 28, 1919.

58. Bowman, in Seymour and House, p. 464.

59. House diary, March 28, 1919. Wilson said privately that he might join with Lloyd George in defining peace terms and, if the French dissented, publish that fact and the terms and go home. This threat was ascribed by Miss Benham to the fact that Wilson was "getting so outdone," diary letter, March 27, 1919.

sioned plea that Grayson thought the most eloquent that Wilson had ever made. The president said that he had come to Europe with the conviction that if the work performed at this conference was well performed, all the future generations would honor their names as world benefactors; that this task in which they were engaged was the most solemn task that could enlist the thought and energy and patience of men; that it would be easy enough merely to punish Germany, merely to wreak vengeance for wrongs done; that he himself had no illusions as to what Germany had done—she had in the fury of her war madness put herself outside the pale of civilization; he was not doubting that; but he believed they had a greater mission than the mere punishment of Germany; Germany should be made to pay for what she had done and pay to the last farthing; they were arranging for all that in the terms which they were drawing up and had been drawing up in this room for weeks and months past; but if they should crush Germany, wreck her economically, they would assuredly turn the ultimate sympathies of the world toward Germany; the terms laid upon Germany should be stern—justice is stern—but they should be terms which the unenraged generations of the future could read and say: "This is justice, not vengeance." "This is no time to see red," said the president. He insisted that they in that room, charged with responsibility for the future as well as the present, must rid themselves of the passions and the rancors of the moment and look to the future, to the children and to the generations unborn, in whose name and for whose sake they were striving to establish a peace which could outlast all men's hot anger, recriminations, bloodthirstiness, and cries of vengeance.

The prophet stood as he delivered this exhortation. At one point Clemenceau moved as if to rise from his chair, and with a backward sweep of his hand Wilson said fiercely: "Sit down. I didn't interrupt you this morning when you were speaking." The Tiger slunk back, but later, when the speech ended, he got to his feet, his dark eyes burning under the white brows. When he stretched out his arms toward the president, no one knew what might happen; but the tension ended when he took Wilson's hand in his, softly patted it, and said: "You are a good man, and a great one."[60]

Haskins thought the president too severe, and impervious to his French environment.[61] Fearing a complete rupture, he worked with Headlam-Morley to draft a basis for compromise. The Council of Four, accepting their work, entrusted the task of devising practical political arrangements to Haskins, Headlam-Morley, and Tardieu. These men already had met unofficially and had gone far toward an understanding. During the month of April they gave advice that helped Wilson and Lloyd George to agree upon a compromise with Clemenceau.[62]

60. What was said on the afternoon of March 28 was not recorded in the minutes, but Dr. Grayson's account is in the Axson memoir, section 49, Wilson papers, Princeton University Library.

61. Haskins to R. S. Baker, January 10, 1920, Baker papers, box 30.

62. See below, p. 324; and the "docket" on the Saar negotiations in the N.A., R.G. 256, 185 1134 / 16 and 34. On the negotiation of the compromise see Schwabe's detailed account in *op. cit.*, pp. 270–272.

Haskins wrote two letters to Wilson, dated March 31 and April 1, proposing a compromise, Wilson papers. "From the point of view of general interests," he wrote, "I see more possibility of friction in French exploitation of the mines under Prussian administration than in temporary administration by

The specialists who dealt with the question of the Saar were not unaware of its close association in French minds with that of the future of the principality of Luxembourg. There was agitation for a change in the economic and political orientation of this little state, which had been toward Germany. British experts hoped that its future affiliation would be with Belgium. However, France had economic ties with Luxembourg; soon after the armistice Marshal Foch established his headquarters there.[63]

Foreign Minister Hymans complained of French propaganda and its effect on Belgium's interests. Fearful that French expansionists might force a plebiscite that would be unfavorable to Belgium, he kept House fully informed of notes that were passing between the Belgian and French governments. Repudiating any policy of annexation but desiring closer relations with Luxembourg, he urged the colonel to "take a sharp stick to the French," and he appealed often and angrily to the British delegates.[64]

House and Balfour agreed to ask Clemenceau to keep hands off Luxembourg, and on March 4 they found him willing to withdraw the small French force that was there. Nevertheless, House was convinced that the French intended "to take a selfish and rather ugly attitude." He wrote: "Clemenceau talked fairly but I have my doubts."[65] Clemenceau, however, denied any intention of annexation and insisted only that he should do nothing that would put him in the position of offending his people by appearing to give Luxembourg to Belgium.

The German grand duchess of Luxembourg was the victim of a coup on January 9 and abdicated in favor of her sister. Early in March a new government of the duchy, not yet officially recognized, asked for a hearing at the Peace Conference.

In the American Department of State there was apprehension that the autonomous duchy, with which official contact had ceased during the war, would be left unarmed

---

France under a definite mandate with ample guarantee of all local liberties, especially in view of the obvious French interest to conciliate the population in view of the ultimate plebiscite."

The proposal of Haskins was (1) France to have permanent ownership of the mines with full facilities for their exploitation; (2) the mining area to be held for a period of fifteen years by the League of Nations, which will hold a plebiscite at the end of this period, either *en bloc* or by communes, and will thereupon hand over the area, or the respective parts, to Germany or France, according as the vote shall determine; (3) during this interval France to administer the territory under a mandate from the League of Nations.

By the terms of the mandate France should be charged with the maintenance of order, including the appointment of such officers as were now named by the Prussian or Bavarian governments. There were to be no fortifications or military establishments within the territory.

The inhabitants should retain their German citizenship (except that any individuals so desiring may be free to acquire French citizenship), their local representative assemblies, religious arrangements, law, language, and schools, and should be exempt from military services. They should not be entitled to vote for representatives in either the German Reichstag or the French chambers. Any who desire to leave the district were to have full opportunity to dispose of their property on equitable terms.

63. Howard Elcock, *Portrait of a Decision*, pp. 59, 109.

64. *I.P.*, vol. 4, pp. 353, 355. British Empire Delegation paper, "Brief Notes on Present Conference Situation," by Balfour, February 25, 1919, Balfour papers, 49750, pp. 110 ff. Memo, Kerr to Lloyd George, February 12, 1919, Lloyd George papers, F/28/2/9. Belgians resented the loss in 1839 of the German-speaking part of Luxembourg, which for a time had sent representatives to the Belgian Parliament, Miller, vol. 5, p. 6.

65. House diary, February 27 and 28, March 1, 2, 3, 4, and 6, 1919. Cable, House to Wilson, March 4, 1919. On March 2 Tardieu agreed with House that Belgium should have Luxembourg. See above, p. 154.

in the midst of powers that might seize it. Thus it could become a menace to the peace of Europe. When a Belgian delegate at Paris invoked "the great spirit of President Wilson and of the American government" to protect Luxembourg against any imposition of a foreign will, Lansing apprised the president of the "slightly baffling" situation. Wilson replied that it seemed unwise to receive a delegation from the duchy and that the matter should rest with the proper committee of the Peace Conference.[66] The State Department then gave to Luxembourg the status of "a friendly neutral."[67]

During the month of April, after Hymans offended the Supreme Council by importunate pleading and King Albert of Belgium asked the council to permit union of his nation with Luxembourg, the question was discussed in several sessions without advice from experts. Balfour took up the Belgian cause with Wilson, and the president suggested that they defer any decision until a plebiscite could be held. On May 15 the constitution was liberalized, and a referendum on September 28 resulted in a 4-to-1 vote for a continuation of the country's independent status under the limited monarchy, and a 3-to-1 vote in favor of economic union with France rather than with Belgium.[68] In the peace treaty the German government renounced all rights in respect of the duchy and accepted in advance all international arrangements that might be concluded by the Allied and Associated powers.

The Belgian delegates, who were in an anomalous position as representatives of a government that for four years had been separated from the people to whom they were responsible, became aggressive in promoting national purposes other than the annexation of Luxembourg. Under the German occupation Belgium's land and industries had suffered beyond the possibility of reparation in full. Now its government was demanding a large measure of compensation. Moreover, it saw a prospect of liberation from servitude to treaties that had been imposed in the 1830s and that had guaranteed Belgium's neutrality. These old treaties now appeared to be both ineffective and obstacles to the nation's exercise of sovereignty. In September of 1918 the Belgium government had notified both France and Great Britain, whose own security depended to a large degree upon that of Belgium, that it thought a policy of neutrality no longer possible and desired complete independence. On November 20 the French government had accepted the Belgian position.[69]

Wilson had stated in Point Seven that "Belgium . . . must be evacuated and restored, without any attempt to limit the sovereignty which she enjoys in common with all other free nations." Moreover, the prearmistice commentary had promised full compensation for all damage consequent to the "illegitimate" German inva-

66. Lansing to Wilson, January 25, Wilson to Lansing, January 29, 1919, N.A., R.G. 59, 850A.001 / 6, 7, 9, 9A, 10, R.G. 256, 185.1132 / 7.
67. McAndrew to T. H. Bliss, March 7, 1919, Bliss papers, box 202.
68. Sally Marks, *Innocents Abroad,* p. 250. See pp. 224–254 for a detailed account of the unsuccessful effort of the Belgians to get effective support for their policy from Great Britain.
69. Frank Lord Warrin, Jr., "The Neutrality of Belgium," pamphlet, Washington, 1918. Paul Hymans, "Belgium's Position in Europe," *Foreign Affairs* 9, no. 1 (1930):54–64. Haskins and Lord, pp. 66–67. Dispatch, Sharp (Paris) to the secretary of state, November 20, 1918. N.A., R.G. 59, 185.3411 / 12, filed after 185.1131 / 12.

sion. Germany's violation of Belgian neutrality in 1914 had stirred righteous anger in American hearts, and Wilson listened to the Belgians with sympathy.[70] Nevertheless, he was wary of commitments. He refused their invitation, as he had at first declined that of the French, to visit devastated regions.[71]

The Belgian government persistently sought American advice and support.[72] Early in February its delegates pressed territorial claims in disregard of self-determination, the very principle that they themselves had invoked in protesting against French aggression in Luxembourg. In order to augment the commerce of Antwerp by improving the channel in the lower Scheldt, the Belgians went so far as to seek territory bordering the river. This land had been in full possession of the Dutch crown for more than a century,[73] and the inhabitants of that part of Zeeland that lay south of the Scheldt opposed transfer to Belgian sovereignty. Nevertheless, the Belgians announced that they would present to the Supreme Council a claim to territory in Zeeland and also in Limburg, a province that had been divided between Belgium and the Netherlands in 1831[74] and in which the Belgians sought economic facilities as well as protection against Germany. The secretary-general of the Belgian delegation turned to House for aid and suggested that German territory might be transferred to Holland in compensation for land that Belgium desired. He found House sympathetic.[75] Haskins, however, was of the opinion that, although there were good strategic reasons for a readjustment, the absence of evidence of any desire on the part of the German inhabitants for a transfer to Belgium was an obstacle.[76]

On February 11 Hoover, who was particularly close to the hearts of the Belgians because of his ministrations to them during the war, returned to Paris from conferences at Brussels and reported to Wilson that the situation was very serious. From Haskins the president received an opinion that Belgium's demands raised a question of procedure and that the United States should favor full consideration of the Belgian claims but "could appear directly only if requested to act as *amicus curiae*."[77] In the afternoon of the same day Hymans presented to the Supreme Council the claims that had been discussed already with the American technical advisers.

The next day the Supreme Council set up a Commission on Belgian Affairs. Haskins, one of the two American members, presented to it the conclusion of the Inquiry: that the treaties of 1839, the basis of which had been in part destroyed by

70. The official State Department study, noting that the neutrality treaties of 1831 and 1839 had been faithfully respected by Belgium, denied the use of the principle of *rebus sic stantibus* to exculpate Germany, Warrin, *op. cit.*

71. Charles T. Thompson, *The Peace Conference Day by Day,* pp. 50–51.

72. Miller, vol. 1, docs. 202, 301–302.

73. *Ibid.*, vol. 10, pp. 176 ff. The Belgians complained that the Dutch had failed to dredge silt from the channel in the river Scheldt and to maintain the canal connecting Antwerp and the Rhine because of a desire to divert traffic through Rotterdam, memorandum, Kerr to Lloyd George, February 12, 1919, Lloyd George papers, F / 89 / 2 / 9. See Robert H. George, "The Scheldt Dispute."

74. Miller, vol. 1, docs. 301–302, 202. On Belgium's claims, see Hymans, *op. cit.*, and Haskins and Lord, pp. 66–67.

75. Miller, vol. 1, p. 111.

76. *Ibid.*, vol. 5, pp. 3–6.

77. Hoover to Wilson, Haskins to Wilson, February 11, 1919, Wilson papers.

the war, should be brought before the Peace Conference for revision, with Holland joining in the talks with Belgium and "the five Powers which have general interests in the Conference." The Americans looked forward to new safeguards for Belgium that would derive from the Covenant of the League of Nations rather than to any renewal of the guarantee of neutrality.[78] The commission, of the opinion that the old guarantee of neutrality was established "as much against Belgium's interest as in her behalf,"[79] reported on March 8 that the pacts of 1839 should be revised in their entirety, with Holland participating so that the resulting treaty would come under the guarantees contemplated by the League of Nations.

On March 31, when Hymans presented the Belgian demands to The Four, he did so with a lack of restraint that irritated his auditors. Wilson reminded him that he was offending Dutch sensibilities by bringing up Belgium's plea for Dutch territory without first discussing the navigation of the Scheldt directly with Holland. When Hymans asserted a right to participate in discussions affecting his nation's interests, Wilson explained that The Four had felt obliged to go into executive session "for the sake of greater speed and to avoid possible leaks."[80]

The Belgians continued to press their case in sessions of the Commission on Belgian Affairs. This body proposed that Germany be compelled to accept the loss of territory on the Ems River as compensation to Holland for cessions to Belgium if the population so voted in a plebiscite. However, Wilson, who had twice before spoken of the impracticality of the idea, remarked that he did not see how German territory could be given to a state that took no part in the war.[81] Actually, there was no prospect that the Dutch government could or would agree to the cession of any territory or would compromise its neutral status by accepting any taken from Germany by force.[82] The question went to the Council of Foreign Ministers, which, after a long discussion on June 5, entrusted the task of studying the matter to a seven-power commission, on which both interested parties were represented. This commission and its successor, a body of fourteen, met from July 1919, to March 23, 1920, and decided that the Netherlands would retain sovereignty over the lower Meuse and the lower Scheldt. Moreover, the persistent efforts of Hymans to replace the old neutrality treaties with new guarantees by America, France, and Great Britain came to naught.[83]

A minor Belgian claim, set forth by Hymans in the Council of Four in April,

---

78. Miller, vol. 1, p. 108, and docs. 298–309. A legal opinion written by Warrin held that "an adequate consideration of a juridical system derivable from the neutralization of a State is impossible in the present state of the development of international law, and loses itself in a maze of doubtful questions, for the solution of which neither precedent nor rationale exists," *ibid.,* doc. 309.

79. *Ibid.,* vol. 10, p. 182.

80. Mantoux, *Proceedings,* p. 67. Auchincloss wrote in his diary on February 6 that Hymans seemed "somewhat malicious and considered himself spokesman for small nations." According to Bonsal, Hymans asserted that the great powers were bullying the small nations, *Unfinished Business,* p. 162.

81. Mantoux, *Proceedings,* pp. 204, 206–208. Wilson had the support of Belgian Socialists, Emile Vandervelde, *Souvenirs d'un militant socialiste,* pp. 286–288.

82. F. L. Warrin, Jr., to the author, April 12, 1963.

83. See Marks, pp. 255–297. The Belgians were unsuccessful in efforts carried on through the year to have their nation included in the treaty of guarantee that Wilson offered to France, *ibid.,* pp. 334–337.

evoked from Wilson a defense of the principle of self-determination. Belgium hoped to strengthen its frontier by acquiring the tiny Prussian administrative districts of Eupen and Malmédy and the railroad connecting these cities. When Hymans admitted that the inclusion of the railway would bring some 4,000 Germans under Belgian rule, Wilson rose to defend the principle that he was conscious of having broken in giving the Upper Adige to Italy.[84] In the present instance, in which he had British support and only a minor interest of a small city was involved, the president could afford to speak boldly. "Ought we not to have as many scruples," he asked, "whether it is a question of 4,000 Germans, or of four million?" As a result the settlement called for the protection of the Germans along the rail line by a provision of the peace treaty whereby dissidents might make their opinion known to the League of Nations six months after Belgium annexed the districts. Actually, this recourse proved to be, as one historian has described it, a "travesty upon the exercise of the right of self-determination." However, it served to humor Wilson.[85]

The principle of self-determination gave the United States an interest in the fixing of a frontier between Germany and Denmark. Prussia had seized Danish territory in 1864 and two years later promised that a part of it would be returned if the population so voted. However, subsequent demands on the part of the inhabitants had been ignored. Now the Danish government, which subscribed to the League of Nations and its ideals, looked to the Peace Conference to restore at least a share of the lost territory.[86] This case attracted the lively sympathy of the governments of Great Britain and France. They expressed to the State Department a desire that Denmark, though a neutral, be encouraged to bring the matter before the Peace Conference; and the department itself thought that a new boundary in Schleswig should be drawn in accord with the wishes of the inhabitants.[87]

The Commission on Belgian Affairs, which studied the question of a Danish-German frontier and on which Professor Haskins sat, recommended that German forces in the area concerned should be required to withdraw within ten days, and that a plebiscite be held in a northern, a central, and a southern zone. The specific provisions that were drafted served as a model for other plebiscites.[88]

In accord with the expressed wish of Denmark, as reported to Wilson by his new

84. See above, p. 55.

85. H. I. Nelson, pp. 312–318. See also Haskins, "New Boundaries of Germany," p. 44. Miller, vol. 10, p. 171. Elcock, pp. 183–184. See Marks, pp. 167–168 and *passim,* and Miller, "New Boundaries of Germany," in Seymour and House (eds.), p. 44.

86. The other Scandinavian neutrals also brought claims to the Peace Conference. Norway wished to acquire sovereignty over Spitzbergen—a sort of no-man's land—and Sweden over the Aaland Islands, which were then a part of Finland and, though not fortified, had a strategic position in the Baltic Sea. King Gustaf of Sweden asked the American minister at Stockholm to bring before President Wilson, at the proper time, the desire of the inhabitants of the Aaland Islands for union with Sweden, *F.R., P.P.C.,* vol. 1, p. 300; vol. 2, p. 447. The Black Book recommended this, but in 1921 they were assigned by the League of Nations Council to Finland. See James Barros, *The Aaland Islands* (New Haven, 1968).

87. *F.R., P.P.C.,* vol. 1, pp. 236–240, 288, 272, 302; vol. 2, pp. 450–461.

88. Clauses in respect of Schleswig were drafted by Miller and Warrin with British, French, and Italian legal advisers, and were put before the Commission on Belgian Affairs on March 10, 1919, Miller, vol. 1, p. 161.

minister at Copenhagen[89]—a wish that was disregarded by Haskins and the commission because it seemed to grow out of a long-standing dread of German might[90]—it was finally decided that inhabitants of the proposed southern zone should not vote and should remain German.[91] The result of the plebiscite in the other zones, conducted in the spring of 1920 under the supervision of an international commission, was the assignment of the northern zone to Denmark and the central to Germany. Haskins was well satisfied by the outcome, and later called the settlement "one of the distinct triumphs of the Peace Conference."[92]

In the meeting of the Council of Foreign Ministers on May 14, Admiral de Bon stated that Admiral Benson had said that the United States could contribute 1,000 to 1,500 marines to the international force that was to supervise the plebiscite. On June 12, however, Lansing wrote to the president, in response to a request for advice, that he was firmly of the opinion that the United States could not contribute troops to the policing of the plebiscite in Schleswig before the peace treaty was ratified by the Senate.[93]

The fixing of definite boundaries of Germany was essential both to the stabilization of the governments of Europe and to the keeping of peace among them. Moreover, it had a bearing on the will and the ability of the Germans to make reparation for the damages of the war.

The procedures that the English-speaking delegates had improvised and that for a time had seemed to delay definite conclusions were beginning, at the end of March, to shape a territorial settlement that could be presented to the enemy with some confidence that it would be accepted. In certain cases, however, final arrangements would have to await the outcome of plebiscites under the supervision of the League of Nations.

The Americans at Paris often found themselves called upon to compose conflicts of policies of the Allied powers that reflected immediate national interests that in many cases grew out of deep historical roots and that sometimes conjured up prospects of future wars. The delegates of the United States, heeding scholarly advice, weighed the arguments of the various interested parties, giving due regard to strategic, economic, and political consequences. They found it not always practical to adhere to the principle of self-determination.

---

89. Norman Hapgood, who passed through Paris en route to Copenhagen and called on House on May 22, House diary, May 22, 1919.

90. Report of Commission on Belgian and Danish Affairs, with note transmitting same, Haskins to Wilson, March 23, 1919, and map and two-page "confidential note," Wilson papers. See Miller, vol. 1, pp. 166–167; vol. 10, pp. 3–175, 211–240. For the German view of the plebiscite see Kaltenbach, pp. 96 ff. Mantoux, *Délibérations*, vol. 1, pp. 255–256. *F.R., P.P.C.*, vol. 4, pp. 529 ff.

91. Mantoux, *Délibérations*, vol. 2, p. 424. *F.R., P.P.C.*, vol. 6, p. 454. See brief, "Political Clauses, Schleswig," Pt. III, Sec. 12, by P. W. Slosson, Y.H.C.

92. Haskins, "New Boundaries of Germany," p. 42.

93. Wilson to Lansing, June 7, 1919, Lansing to Wilson, June 12, 1919, N.A., R.G. 256, 185.1143 / 156. A contingent of American soldiers, held at Brest to be used in Schleswig, was brought back to the United States in December 1919. Letter to the author from the director of Marine Corps History, August 19, 1919. Letter, General Bliss to General H. T. Allen, October 26, 1919, Bliss papers, box 202.

The immediate necessity of controlling the power of the enemy, complicated as it was by the menace of general anarchy and a possible alliance of the vanquished peoples with Moscow, as well as by nationalistic chauvinism, led the plenipotentiaries of the United States, in pursuit of their commitment to peace and justice for all peoples, to take part in the peacemaking in regions of Europe in respect of which their own people had little interest and only superficial knowledge. The involvement in the affairs of remote lands, which had begun before the opening of the Peace Conference as a result of *ad hoc* missions of relief and intelligence, now extended to negotiations at the highest level. It seemed likely that the American government would be brought into the politics of Europe to a degree that the American people and their Congress might not accept.

15

Week of Crisis

As the Peace Conference entered its most critical period, those who bore the burden of reaching agreement were more than ever obsessed by a desire for haste. There was an accumulation of fears and alarms. The popular demand for settlements increased after revolution flared in Hungary and violence in parts of Germany. The inexorable pressures of national politics made themselves felt, and a period of intense negotiation and efforts at compromise began.

Early in April the secretariat was taking account of progress made and found much still to be accomplished. The reports of only three commissions were ready, three "nearly ready," seven "not ready."[1] Moreover, matters of the first importance had not yet been entrusted to any committee. Consideration of them was thought by The Four to be too hazardous to be undertaken by any but themselves.

On the return of Wilson and Lloyd George from their national capitals, the heads of the delegations had undertaken to consider certain issues that were very controversial. For two weeks at the end of March their talks seemed only to intensify the deadlock. Clemenceau would not abate French demands for security and reparation; Lloyd George would not give way with respect to categories of war damage that Germany was to make good; Orlando persisted in his demand for the lands promised by the Treaty of London and for sovereignty over Fiume, too; and Japan adhered to its claim in China.

Wilson still insisted on imposing his concept of justice; and he was not permitted to forget what was expected of him by his idealistic friends. Ray Stannard Baker, who regarded the Peace Conference as a moral battle of the New World against the Old and who came to the president late in each day to gather news for the journalists, spoke of the frustration that he and fellow liberals felt. Moreover, a cable from Tumulty informed the president that his political enemies were holding him responsible for the delay. Wilson perhaps was reminded of this criticism by twelve congressmen whom he received when they were in Paris for a day.[2]

The negotiations that had progressed secretly under the wise ministration of House, Balfour, Kerr, and Tardieu, and from which there could be no escape if the terms of a treaty of peace were to be acceptable to the European democracies, came to a number of crises in the month of April.

The several committees to which matters relatively free from controversy had been referred had shown a capacity to function well. The diplomats and scholars sitting in these advisory bodies, appointed to deal with national demands as they

1. Four-page brief, undated, summarizing progress on all topics under negotiation; Harrison to Close, April 7, 1919, enclosing a compendium of reports from the secretaries of the Americans sitting on various commissions; Hankey's mimeographed report on "State of Reports of Commissions," April 4, 1919, Wilson papers.
2. Tumulty to Wilson, March 25, 1919, Tumulty papers, box 6. Grayson diary, March 30, 1919.

were presented and with situations as they arose, worked on their difficult assign-
ments with little direction from the plenipotentiaries. The American members, without authority to develop national policies, found themselves in the position of arbiters
whose judgments sometimes proved to be definitive.

The liaison of the American delegates with the president was tenuous. In contrast
with the Europeans, who for the most part functioned under a discipline imposed
by tradition, the Americans at the Crillon, many of whom were uncertain as to their
powers and duties, hesitated to approach the chief who had bidden them to come to
him with their perplexities but who often was too busy to grant a hearing. Even his
personal staff were fearful of crossing him. They did not dare to assume authority
to catch up loose ends and protect him from irrelevant interruption by special pleaders. "Such a picture as I could draw of this household!" Baker jotted in his journal
on March 31. "No one there with any authority and all afraid of the President." As
the president placed less dependence upon House's efficient secretariat, the inadequacy of Wilson's immediate staff of only four men—a stenographer, two secretaries, and Dr. Grayson—became obvious.

In a conference of American specialists with the president on March 29 the lack
of rapport was painfully clear. Wilson remarked that Lloyd George could quote the
opinions of American experts of which he was not aware while he, himself, did not
know what his advisers thought. This led Beer, when he heard the president's remark,
to comment: "In view of his inaccessibility, this is delightful."[3] Wilson, urged to
state publicly his understanding of the reason for the delay in reaching decisions,[4]
was not yet ready to proclaim that the French were to blame, nor was he prepared
to make relentless use of the financial power that was in his hands.[5] He still must
solicit the assent of Clemenceau, as well as that of Lloyd George, to an amendment
to the Covenant of the League that would explicitly protect the Monroe Doctrine.

When The Four held the first of their long series of secret sessions at Wilson's
house on March 24, the president had remarked upon the "race between peace and
anarchy" and the impatience that the public was manifesting. "It is my view," he
said to Clemenceau and Lloyd George, "that we should take in hand the most
difficult and the most urgent problems." First among these he mentioned the war
damages, which Lloyd George called "the most difficult of all" questions.

Just before Wilson left Paris in February, he had been advised that indirect war
costs should not be included in the claim for damages, and his counselors had
advocated the fixing of a definite total of liability that would be within Germany's
capacity to pay over a limited period of years.[6] While Wilson was away, House,
after reaching what he called "a "fairly complete understanding with Lloyd George,"
had proposed to Clemenceau and Lloyd George that the financial experts join in
seeking a fundamental basis for agreement.[7] America, as a creditor, was unlikely

3. Beer diary, March 30, 1919. George and George, *Woodrow Wilson and Colonel House*, p. 249.
4. R. S. Baker, *American Chronicle*, pp. 394–395, 397–398.
5. The Allied governments were gently reminded of the financial power of the United States. Westermann diary, March 30, 1919. N. H. Davis to Wilson, April 22, 1919, Wilson papers.
6. See above, pp. 172 ff.
7. See above, p. 176.

to dissociate itself from a financial reckoning that would affect the solvency of its debtors.

On March 25 The Three found that they could agree neither upon the total bill to be presented to Germany nor on a rough apportionment among the Allies. Wilson then put forward a plan of his advisers for an ongoing commission on reparations that would determine annually the sum to be paid, between a maximum of $35 billion and a minimum of $25 billion, and also the proportion payable in marks.[8] It appeared to be understood that there would be no reparation for war costs other than losses inflicted on civilians by the death or mutilation of close relatives.[9] The president was not yet convinced that definite sums could not be set. He was willing to discuss the matter with the Germans.

At this point the Council of Four shifted its emphasis to the question of evaluation of damages to persons and property, and the experts were busily defining categories of damage and proposing methods of appraisal. On March 28 a subcommittee of the reparation commission accepted pensions as a category of damage.[10] The British negotiators did not fail to perceive that the inclusion of pensions and allowances to families of servicemen would bring to Great Britain, and more particularly to the dominions, a larger share of reparation; for in relation to the losses of its Allies, those of the British Empire had been larger in respect of violence to persons than in direct damages to property.

Again, as in the controversy over mandates,[11] the prime minister took advantage of the esteem that General Smuts enjoyed in the eyes of Wilson. On the last day of March, Smuts, who had supported the American desire for the naming of a fixed sum, wrote a memorandum giving his own interpretation of the key phrase in the prearmistice agreement[12]—"all damage done to the civilian population." Wishing to get a larger share of reparations for the British Empire, he argued that disablement pensions or separation allowances were all items representing compensation to members of the civilian population for damages sustained by them, for which the German government were liable.[13]

8. Mantoux, *Proceedings*, pp. 3–5. Wilson's suggestion reflected expert advice in reports dated March 25, 1919, Wilson papers. The British and American experts had compiled a paper—begun on March 19—that was known as the "Third Revise." This included, as an actual base of negotiations, tentative formulas that had been drafted by John Foster Dulles. See Philip M. Burnett, *Reparation at the Paris Peace Conference* vol. 1, pp. 57–58. "The idea of setting up a reparations commission came from Dulles," Seymour to the author.

9. Burnett, vol. 1, p. 28.

10. *Ibid.*, 1, pp. 40–46. After six weeks of negotiation the subcommittee concerned with categories of damage adopted a report on March 31 that was approved by the full commission on reparations on April 7, when the experts became directly involved in discussions of the subject in the Council of Four.

11. See above, ch. 4.

12. A copy of the three-page memorandum "Note on Reparation" is in the Wilson papers. See George Curry, "Woodrow Wilson, Jan Smuts, and the Versailles Settlement."

13. Burnett, vol. 1, pp. 773–775. "Put briefly, General Smuts's argument maintained that, whereas we were not entitled to claim for damage done to a soldier, but only for damage done to civilians, a soldier may at some later date, after the war, revert to being a civilian, and that any damage suffered by him as a soldier which persists up to the date when he becomes a civilian again can properly be classified as damage to a civilian," Keynes, "America at the Peace Conference," 91.

Of the Smuts memorandum his biographer wrote: "He wrote it in a hurry on the eve of his departure for Hungary. He made a bad mistake. After his return from Hungary he did his utmost to retrieve the

Although the French delegates fell in with the British proposal,[14] the American specialists were not ready to accept it. They continued to argue that the only legal basis for exacting payments from the enemy was to be found in the conditions of peace stated in the American note of November 5, 1918, to the German government, and that pensions were popularly and legally recognized as governmental costs of conducting a war, no more subject to reimbursement than other expenses of military operations. Moreover, the president had stated that they were "in honor bound" to decline to include war costs in the reparation demanded.[15] Apart from the legal technicalities, it had seemed to Wilson not honorable to raise the reckoning against a prostrate debtor.[16]

At this time Wilson's advisers were warning against any strictures upon the German economy that would discourage productivity and profitable trade between victors and vanquished. On the last day of March the president read to the Council of Four a letter from Baruch that alluded to the interest of the United States that had been created by its war loans and to its moral obligation to help Allied and new governments in Europe with additional advances. Some questions of economics and finance might be referred to the League of Nations, Baruch suggested. However, Baruch was notorious as a promoter of American commerce. Suspicious Europeans were inclined to discount his practical idealism.[17] They were not moved to relax their demands for the inclusion of pensions in the bill to be presented to Germany.

On April 1 the American negotiators, hard pressed by their European colleagues, went to the president to seek his continuing support for a scheme, developed the day before with Keynes and Montagu, that would bring the disputed question of pensions to an arbitral decision. They explained that not a single lawyer in the American delegation would accept the argument of Smuts.

---

mistake," Hancock, *Smuts,* vol. 1, pp. 540–542. Smuts later described his paper as "merely a legal opinion."

Keynes wrote a few months after the event: "If words have any meaning, or engagements any force, we had no more right to claim for those war expenses of the state, which arose out of pensions and separation allowances, than for any other of the general costs of the war. And who is prepared to argue in detail that we were entitled to demand the latter?" *The Economic Consequences of the Peace,* p. 156.

14. Étienne Weill-Raynal has written of the French government's action: "By the support given to the British government for the inclusion of pensions in the damages, the French government seemingly increased the levy upon Germany, but in reality reduced the share of its own country in the payments to come, extended the term of the German debt, made the payment of it more uncertain, and, finally, altered the character of the reparation for damages by substituting a financial problem for an economic project," *Les Réparations allemandes et la France,* vol. 1, p. 128.

"The inclusion of pensions and separation allowances promised to raise the British portion of German payments from about seventeen to near twenty-five per cent," Robert E. Bunselmeyer, *The Cost of the War, 1914–1919,* p. 180.

15. See above, p. 174.

16. Wilson approved four "principles of reparations" that Dulles submitted to the commission on reparations. These, interpreting what was claimed within the framework of the prearmistice agreement, plainly denied the right to claim reparation for war costs. See Burnett, vol. 1, pp. 17–28, and Tardieu, *The Truth about the Treaty,* pp. 285–289.

17. Beer, who kept in close touch with the English delegates, was perhaps influenced by their opinion when he wrote after dining with five of the American economic advisers: "In all these commercial men there is markedly developed an American group spirit and a competitive attitude. They are extremely nationalistic and all that is American is right and must be defended, while what is foreign is wrong," Beer diary, March 20, 1919.

Nevertheless, Wilson yielded to political necessity. He was at this time seeking British aid in revising the Covenant of the League; and Lloyd George had warned that he, as prime minister, would have no authority to sign a treaty that did not include pensions, and therefore he might as well return to London if Wilson insisted on their exclusion.[18] Although Dulles explained that if pensions were included the logic of international usage would require the inclusion of other undesirable categories, the president said: "I don't give a damn for logic, if you will excuse my French. I am going to include pensions."

That afternoon Wilson stated his decision to the Council of Four.[19] The American advisers were grievously disappointed, but they took comfort in the thought that because of the inexorable limit that economic law placed upon Germany's capacity to pay, the inclusion of pensions could not in effect increase the burden on the enemy. Moreover, it would provide a more equitable basis for division among the Allies.[20]

Under an agreement reached by the American and British financial advisers at the end of two days of almost continuous sessions, in only the first of which the French and Italian delegates took part, Germany was to be held responsible for all damages done to civilians and their property, and for the cost of pensions and separation allowances. A commission would be appointed to decide (a) the value of claims under certain specified categories and (b) the total amount that Germany could pay to satisfy these claims. This commission on reparations was to report by the end of 1921 and was given power to modify the time and mode of payments thereafter. An initial sum was to be paid, and annual installments over a period of not more than thirty years.[21] This settlement was a compromise between the ill-founded expectations of the voters to whom the statesmen were responsible and the counsels of reason that came from the more far-seeing of the peacemakers.

"The prime minister could claim," Keynes wrote a few months after the event, "that although he had not secured the entire costs of the war, he had nevertheless secured an important contribution toward them, that he had always qualified his promises by the limiting condition of Germany's capacity to pay, and that the bill as now presented more than exhausted this capacity as estimated by the more sober authorities. The president, on the other hand, had secured a formula which was not too obvious a breach of faith, and had avoided a quarrel with his [European] asso-

---

18. Handwritten letter, Lloyd George to B. Law, March 30, 1919, Law papers 97 / 1 / 17. Law to Lloyd George, March 31, 1919, Lloyd George papers, F / 30 / 3 / 39. Mantoux, *Proceedings,* p. 116.

19. Burnett, vol. 1, pp. 775–776. McCormick diary, April 1, 1919. McCormick's memorandum of a conference at Wilson's house on April 1, 1919, R. S. Baker papers, IB, L. C. Mantoux, *Proceedings,* p. 79. Lamont, notes on meeting of April 1, 1919, Lamont papers, 168-4.

20. N. H. Davis, Peace Conference notes and letter to Baruch, June 21, 1928, Davis papers. Burnett, vol. 1, p. 64. Keynes, *Economic Consequences,* p. 161. Lamont to Burnett, June 25, 1934, Lamont papers, 85-11, Baker Library, Harvard University.

Wilson explained to McCormick that it was particularly important to include pensions because otherwise England would not get the share that it was entitled to, McCormick diary, April 1, 1919.

Sidelsky has observed (in *John Maynard Keynes,* vol. 1, p. 366) that the exoneration adduced by the American experts was invalidated by Lloyd George's agreement on April 5 that, if necessary, the period for payments might be extended beyond thirty years.

21. Copy of two-page memorandum dated April 1, 1919, with two annexes, Wilson papers.

ciates on an issue where the appeals to sentiment and passion would all have been against him, in the event of its being made a matter of open popular controversy.''[22] The secrecy of the Council of Four appeared to be yielding progress in arriving at terms of peace. At the beginning of April, however, the Europeans were still not entirely reassured.

Wilson bade his advisers to consider with the experts of the Allies the difficulties that might ensue; and during the days following they attempted to arrive at a formula that would be acceptable to all. The main lines of the settlement of the question of reparation were in view. The constitution of a supervisory commission remained to be agreed upon, as well as many details having to do with the duration, limitation, method, and guarantee of payments, and with the apportionment of proceeds among the victorious powers.

Negotiations continued among the experts, and the Americans were embarrassed when Keynes asked whether the thirty-year limitation that Wilson insisted upon imposing on German payments would apply also to European war debts to the United States. They conceded that there should be no time limit upon Germany's obligation to pay the total sum that the reparations commission would decide to be possible; but to this concession was attached a demand for a degree of flexibility in the commission's operations that the Europeans would not agree to. The impasse continued even after Wilson consented on April 1 to the inclusion of pensions; and the break came only after Wilson's health failed and he was replaced in talks with Clemenceau by House.[23]

Since the president's return from Washington in mid-March the breach between him and the French nationalists had widened. While Wilson was opposing French demands for a frontier with Germany based on that of 1914, he was advised by General Bliss, on March 28, that the plans of Marshal Foch for containing bolshevism were inspired by an intention to break off the general armistices. Such a policy, Bliss feared, might lead to the disruption of the Peace Conference and a resumption of the war.[24]

When the French militarists encountered American resistance, the nation's press blamed Wilson for delaying the peacemaking by his insistence on the creation of a league of nations. Clemenceau, however, whose prime object from beginning to end was France's security, lacked enthusiasm for Foch's projects. Nevertheless, his own political position did not permit him to speak against them, and he could not have been unappreciative of their value in his negotiations in pursuit of his essential goal of security. It was convenient to trade upon the fear that Wilson confessed helplessly to Baker—that if Clemenceau were to resign, they would probably ''get some man like Poincaré in his place.''[25] Ever since Wilson's return to Paris had put in jeopardy the tentative arrangements made in early March between House and Tardieu, Clemenceau's irritation had been growing.

22. Keynes, *Economic Consequences,* p. 157.
23. See below, pp. 287 ff.
24. Baker, vol. 2, pp. 29 ff.; vol. 3, doc. 26.
25. *Ibid.,* vol. 2, p. 39. Clemenceau encouraged apprehension of his replacement by instructing a French secretary to tell the press that he was being beaten down by his colleagues in the inner council. The next morning he would show the newspaper stories to Wilson and Lloyd George and reproach them for embarrassing him so, André Portier, the secretary, to the author November 18, 1959.

In the last week of March Wilson opposed French demands for a frontier with Germany based on that of 1814. On April 1 he boasted to Baker: "We have put Clemenceau down. If we can keep him there, we are all right. It is going to be a difficult job."[26] The next day, when The Four bickered over petty matters,[27] he told his family that the French were intentionally obstructing proceedings, hoping to break him down. Their attitude, he said, was "damnable."[28] Urged to tell the truth to the press, he replied: "If I were to do that it would immediately break up the peace conference—we cannot risk it yet. But we've got to make peace on the principles laid down and accepted, or not make it at all." He might have to make a positive break, he said, if a decision could not be reached by the middle of the next week. He went so far as to tell Baker he would not object if newsmen wrote stories about the lack of progress toward peace.[29]

House's patience, like that of his chief, was ebbing fast. Determined to close the rift between Wilson and Clemenceau, the colonel had just turned to Steed, the London editor, asking him to use his power of persuasion. Steed found Clemenceau despairing of negotiating with a man like Wilson, whom he spoke of as "a fellow who thought himself the first man for two thousand years who has known anything about peace on earth." Steed insisted, however, that Wilson's intentions toward France were good, that the president's political position required that his general principles be respected, and that Wilson would in fact agree to an acceptable solution of the differences that had arisen as to the left bank of the Rhine and the valley of the Saar. Clemenceau then responded constructively. At his suggestion Steed prepared a paper that in general ran parallel to proposals that Haskins sent to the president at this time.[30]

House sent Steed's paper to Wilson. According to Steed's record, Wilson did not read far before he burst into a long denunciation and threatened to go back to the United States unless his principles were accepted in their entirety. It seemed to Steed that a man who, on his return to Paris, found it necessary to ask for concessions by the Europeans that would permit amendment of the Covenant of the League of Nations, should take a more conciliatory position and talk more with leading French journalists. "He is sitting in his villa like a sort of Dalai Lama," Steed wrote. "He will presently find himself in a very difficult position." Steed was told by House's assistants that it was not easy to speak frankly to the president, that even House could not always talk to him, and that "nobody dared to tell him the truth." Steed proposed to tell him the truth in public as soon as possible.[31]

House, troubled by the delay in arriving at terms for Germany and Russia, did

26. Sweetser diary, April 1, 1919. See above, p. 268.

27. For example, Wilson insisted that, in keeping with diplomatic protocol, German economic negotiators who were at a chateau under French guard should have their own couriers to Berlin and not be required to use a French gendarme, as the British and French authorities wished, Grayson diary, April 2, 1919.

28. Letter, Gilbert Close to his family, March 22, 1919, Princeton University Library. According to Stockton Axson, Wilson was well aware that his adversaries at Washington were in touch with aggressive French partisans who desired harsh terms for the Germans, Axson memoir, section 49.

29. Sweetser diary, March 28, 1919.

30. See above, p. 269.

31. Memoranda, Steed to Northcliffe, April 1 and 2, 1919, Archives of the *Times*. Steed, *Through Thirty Years*, vol. 2, pp. 310–315. Auchincloss diary, April 1, 1919. House diary, April 2, 1919.

not act directly himself to force counsel on the president. He knew from long experience that he could be more effective if he waited for Wilson to invite his aid, as he thought the president must. "I saw things coming to an impasse," he wrote in his diary on April 2. "The more I let them alone, the quicker the impasse would come." Meanwhile he talked with Balfour to consider ways in which they might re-establish the co-ordination that they had effected in February. Secretary Lansing, belligerently advocating a "show-down" in which Wilson would subdue the Tiger of France, remarked to House that it had been a mistake for the president to come back to Europe. House agreed but at the same time showed a determination to make the best of the situation that had existed since Wilson's confidence in him had waned. He refused to join with the other commissioners, whom he now seldom saw, in signing a letter to the president advocating the acceptance of the greater part of the French and of the British demands if this would quickly produce a treaty that Germany would sign.[32]

The indispensability of House was recognized by Ray Stannard Baker, the only American official who talked with the president almost daily. "Without Colonel House," Baker wrote in his journal on March 23, "this peace commission work could not go on. He is the universal conciliator, smootherover, corrector! He is a kind of super-secretary. . . . He is the only man who keeps closely in touch with the president, constantly informing and advising him, getting people together, helping along publicity by seeing the correspondents—a busy, kindly, useful little man . . . indefatigable in his service—and so far as I can see is without personal ambition."

On April 2 at eight in the evening the call came that House had been expecting. In a telephone conversation that lasted for three-quarters of an hour, Wilson, saying that he feared that no one liked him, complained of the stubbornness of Clemenceau. It seemed to House that his chief, not at his best when compelled to negotiate, was losing his judgment as well as his temper. "What he really means," the colonel wrote in his diary, "is that he cannot get Clemenceau to come to his way of thinking." Asked to go to Tardieu for aid in bring Clemenceau around to the American view, the colonel complied immediately. He was now willing to deliver, in private, the ultimatum that the president had been urged to utter publicly. House said that he would tell Tardieu that if no conclusion were reached within ten days, Wilson would have to return to the United States to take care of urgent business there. The next morning, House recorded, he did just as he had promised and reported to Wilson afterward by telephone.[33]

32. House diary, April 3, 1919. "I have stopped trying to keep in touch with my fellow-commissioners. I have not seen Lansing for days. This conference has been run so far by the president, Lloyd George, Balfour, Tardieu, and I [*sic*]. I do not approve of the lack of organization that has brought this about," *ibid.*, April 5, 1919.

33. *Ibid.*, April 1 and 2, 1919. Henry White made intimations of the same substance to his French friends and encouraged Wilson to be firm with the French, letters, W. H. Buckler to his wife, March 31, April 4 and 6, 1919; White to J. W. Davis, April 2, 1919, Y.H.C. In a letter of April 9 to Congressman Rogers, White said that Lloyd George made mischief by telling the French he was ready to support their claims and Wilson was not, whereas he often talked with the Americans with a sympathy for their policy that he said the French did not share, letter in White papers, notes and correspondence, box 1, Columbia University Library.

In the afternoon of April 3—the day on which House delivered the ultimatum—the president came to the end of his physical resources, on which he had been drawing recklessly for three weeks.[34] In taking upon himself the responsibilities that European heads of state had habitually given over to their diplomats, Wilson had put himself in a lonely position.

In October 1918, when the Germans, acknowledging defeat, had turned to the president of the United States to ask for an armistice, Wilson had insisted that if they were to have it they must accept the principles he had formulated and announced as the basis of a lasting peace. He recalled this now and reminded his advisors of it.[35] The prospect of losing control of the application of his principles was appalling. His confusion of the affairs of God with those of Caesar led to a depressing sense of frustration which, Dr. Grayson thought, may have been aggravated by his disappointment in the behavior of Colonel House.[36]

Early in the morning of April 3 the economic advisers called on the president to give him a list of categories of damage they had worked out during the night. He approved them and in so doing remarked that Lloyd George had almost "put something over on him."[37] When the advisers came again at six to protest against the attitude of their British associates, they found the president ill, disgusted, and threatening to go back to the United States. He had been taken violently sick in the Supreme Council, while the Yugoslavs were protesting against Italian claims on the Adriatic coast. In the evening[38] Mrs. Wilson telephoned to House to inquire whether her husband, who was in distress and had retired, should try to go on with the discussions the next day. "I advised remaining in bed," House wrote in his diary, "since, as far as I can see, it would be just as effective as any meeting which they might have."[39]

After a night that Dr. Grayson described as "one of the worst" through which he had ever passed and during which Wilson's heart may have been affected,[40] the

---

34. "No one of the great leaders at Paris," House recorded later, "worked so hard as the president and no one carried so heavy a load of responsibility," House diary, October 10, 1919. Charles Swem, Wilson's stenographer, wrote in retrospect: "It was his [Wilson's] tendency to overburden himself that broke his health," ms. for unpublished book, Swem papers, Princeton University Library. See Baker, *American Chronicle*, pp. 397–398.

35. I. Bowman to R. S. Baker, June 4, 1921, Bowman papers, Johns Hopkins University Library.

36. Grayson, "The Colonel's Folly and the President's Distress."

37. McCormick diary, April 3, 1919.

38. Despite his illness, Wilson received McCormick and Davis in the evening, *ibid.*, April 3, 1919. Grayson diary, April 3, 1919.

39. House diary, April 3, 1919.

40. Grayson to Tumulty, April 10, 1919, Tumulty papers. Dr. Edwin A. Weinstein, Professor Emeritus of Neurology at the Mount Sinai Medical School, has described the illness and analyzed its effect on Wilson's subsequent behavior in a work entitled *Woodrow Wilson: A Medical and Psychological Biography* (Princeton, 1981). He writes: "Wilson's history of cerebral vascular disease and severe behavioral sequelae of his illness has suggested that he may have had another stroke. However, the evidence of the Grayson diary shows his acute symptoms to have been typical of influenza" (p. 338). Dr. Michael F. Marmor, associate professor of ophthalmology at the Veterans Administration Medical Center at Palo Alto, while agreeing that Wilson had "vascular disease" and that it was doubtful that he had a stroke at Paris, writes that "Wilson clearly did not have a severe encephalopathy," Marmor to Alexander L. and George and Juliette L. George, *Political Science Quarterly* (Winter 1982):657–659, 663–665; Marmor, "Woodrow Wilson, Strokes, and Zebras," *New England Journal of Medicine* 307, no. 9 (August 26,

patient's condition the next morning was "distinctly serious," according to his physician's record. Wilson asked that the public be told the truth, saying that he did not want anyone to think he was quitting and that only the fact that he could not sit up prevented him from continuing his work. Dr. Grayson therefore informed the newsmen immediately that the president was suffering from a severe cold and it was absolutely imperative that he remain in bed. Then, at Wilson's request, the doctor went across the street to tell Lloyd George of the illness and to convey the president's wish that his colleagues go on with the business, especially as he had invited the king of Belgium to be present that morning. Lloyd George suggested that House sit in Wilson's place. "If you have Secretary Lansing there," he said, "every other secretary of state will deem it his duty to be present and it will be equal to a council of ten."[41]

Actually, there was no one but House to whom Wilson felt that he could leave the dangerous and difficult negotiations that had overwhelmed him. House now stepped into a situation where he could negotiate with all the latitude enjoyed by a man who was not hampered by bearing the ultimate responsibility. His chief, although ill, was close at hand. Communications would not be limited, as they had been in February, by distance and by garbled messages in code. House would no longer have to take such risks as he had assumed earlier in interpreting imprecise instructions from the president. He could now take initiative in diplomatic negotiation with Clemenceau, who, when he heard of Wilson's illness, rubbed his hands together as if to say: "Now we can get down to business."[42]

The colonel's first meeting with the premiers, on the morning of April 4, was held in the apartment of Lloyd George. King Albert of Belgium appeared and explained the needs of his people. His dignity was in contrast to the earlier importunities of his minister, Hymans. The king spoke of Belgium's neutrality, of the Scheldt, of Limburg, and of Luxembourg; he specified what was essential to the "restoration" that Wilson had promised to Belgium in his Fourteen Points; and he sought priority in respect of reparation payments. The last appeal was supported by House.[43]

In the afternoon session on April 4 consideration was given to a plea of the American specialists in behalf of the Germans in Bohemia. House came early to this meeting. Before it opened he agreed to accept what Clemenceau presented as "the simplest solution," leaving the historic frontier of Bohemia unaffected by alterations that the American specialists had urged.[44] Thus Czechoslovakia inherited

---

1982), pp. 528 ff. See the observations of Weinstein and Marmor and those of other physicians in *New England Journal of Medicine* 308, no. 3 (January 20, 1983):164–165.

Doctors have observed that Wilson's coughing and shortness of breath during his Paris illness, which Dr. Grayson attributed to asthma, may indicate that his heart was affected, Weinstein, p. 338 and n.; Wilbur Cross and John B. Moses, *Presidential Courage* (New York, 1980), p. 138.

41. Grayson diary, April 3 and 4, 1919.

42. Nicolson, who was present when Lloyd George told Clemenceau of Wilson's illness, to the author, October 25, 1959.

43. See below, p. 305.

44. House diary, April 4, 1919. Perman, *The Shaping of the Czechoslovak State*, pp. 169–176. See above, pp. 264–265. It was not until a few days later that House had a firsthand report of the views of Masaryk and of those of the German minority in Czechoslovakia. Stephen Bonsal, visiting Prague with Smuts early in April, found Masaryk strong enough to counter Bolshevik propagandists, who, encour-

a large share of the industrial districts of the Hapsburg empire, the coal and lignite fields and also fertile land, and therefore it appeared to be economically independent.[45] However, so little weight was given to the factor of native blood that more than a third of the polyglot population of the new state were Germans, Magyars, or Ruthenians. Nevertheless, even had the conscientious efforts of the American specialists been entirely successful, the irredentist sentiment that Hitler was to exploit twenty years later would not have been reduced by a decisive extent.[46]

The strong, consistent policy of the French delegates carried the day, though Clemenceau was careful to reserve "the opinion of President Wilson."[47] House, having satisfied Clemenceau in this matter that he considered to be of secondary importance and to which he gave no detailed study, thought the "general situation" and the prospect of a speedy settlement to be "greatly improved."[48]

One question that all seemed willing to discuss was that of reparations. On the afternoon of April 4 House brought the session to a close by stating that the time had come to arrive at a decision on this matter. Lloyd George, fearing that a reasonable settlement would hurt his political fortunes, wished to await the recovery of the president, who had just yielded in the matter of pensions. But House was determined to force decisions and to make the most of the relationship that he had cultivated with Clemenceau.[49] He told Clemenceau that he disliked to evade difficulties that must be met; and when the Tiger replied that he was no "dodger," they agreed to come to grips with this major question. House informed the American experts that it was necessary to let the French know "in a clear, impersonal way" where the real trouble was.[50]

In the morning session of April 5, which was held at Wilson's residence so that House would be immediately in touch with his chief, the colonel went back and forth through a secret door in a bookcase between the salon and the bedchamber in which the president lay. House cautioned against any reparation settlement that

aged by the coup in Hungary, were gaining adherents in certain districts. Masaryk felt it necessary to the success of his government that the Sudeten hills and their German population be included within his nation. The Germans of Bohemia asserted to Bonsal that Masaryk never would permit a plebiscite among them and they would not be averse to one under international control. They asked for representation at the Peace Conference, Bonsal, *Unfinished Business*, pp. 79–83, 85, 96–97.

45. Seymour, in Seymour and House (eds.), *What Really Happened at Paris*, pp. 105, 109–110.

46. Seymour, "Czechoslovak Frontiers," 283.

47. Mantoux, *Proceedings*, p. 114.

48. C. T. Thompson, *The Peace Conference Day by Day*, p. 285. Of House's acquiescence in French policy, Seymour wrote: "They [The Four] are evidently going in for settlements on large general lines, and some of the labored hours we have spent in working out details may go for nothing. But we don't object strongly so long as they realize the necessity for speed," *Letters from the Paris Peace Conference*, p. 193.

49. House, noting in his diary on April 4 that Tyrrell of the British Foreign Office had advised Clemenceau to seek agreement with Wilson rather than with Lloyd George, formed the opinion that all the British peacemakers were in revolt against the prime minister except his immediate secretariat.

"The colonel admitted . . . that George was trying to undermine the colonel's position and was fighting him just as hard as he could. . . . George sees that the colonel and Clemenceau can play together and that they can put the steam roller over him, while with the president George has a much better chance of getting away with his side of the argument. It is an exceedingly interesting game that is being played here now," Auchincloss diary, April 4, 1919.

50. House diary, April 4, 1919.

might appear to violate the prearmistice agreement. Lloyd George and Clemenceau, however, insisted that Germany must explicitly recognize the totality of its responsibility and the right of the Allies to full compensation.[51] Then, in an effort to mitigate the severity of the terms and to lighten the financial impact on the German economy, Norman Davis remarked that a clause could be written to the effect that Germany was *morally* responsible for the war and all its consequences and legally responsible for damage to persons and property.[52] Such a solution had been under consideration in the American delegation for several weeks. Dulles had proposed a number of drafts, the first of which circulated on February 21, in which he offered a psychological sop to the Allies by a formula that would recognize Germany's responsibility for reparation of all loss and damage caused by its aggression. At the same time Dulles would state that the actual liability must be limited by Germany's resources for payment.[53] These provisions supplied the substance for Articles 231 and 232 of the Treaty of Versailles. The first of these articles, requiring a confession of Germany's responsibility for "causing" all the loss and damage in a war "imposed" by their "aggression," became notorious in Germany as a "war-guilt lie" used to justify exorbitant claims. Although this confession, dictated under duress, did not increase Germany's financial liability, its immediate psychological effect, probably not appreciated by Dulles and Davis in their effort to conciliate Clemenceau and Lloyd George, was devastating. The Weimar government was given a grievance that it could exploit to unite the nation. The two articles, taken together, provided a basis for the argument that if the Germans could prove their innocence of war guilt, they should be free of responsibility for reparation.[54]

In the critical session on April 5, in which an Anglo-American draft of reparation clauses was considered, Clemenceau and Lloyd George insisted that the prescription by the reparations commission of Germany's capacity to pay should not be limited to a period of thirty years. House and Davis, however, made it clear that Wilson and the American experts understood that the limit should be thirty years and had acted upon this understanding when they yielded on the matter of inclusion of pensions. House remarked that if the sum set by the commission was not paid within thirty years, the payments could be spread out over a longer span. At the end of the session he went so far as to say, in his determination to break the deadlock quickly: "Why . . . not simply say that Germany recognized its obligation to pay for the reparation of damage caused to property and to persons, without enumerating all the categories which have been suggested and without stipulating for a thirty-year limit?" House's inclination to avoid controversy was perhaps strengthened

---

51. See Burnett, vol. 1, pp. 825 ff.
52. Mantoux, *Proceedings*, p. 117.
53. See Pruessen, *John Foster Dulles*, pp. 32–38.
54. *I.P.*, vol. 4, p. 409. Hajo Holborn, *A History of Modern Germany*, vol. 3, pp. 563–565, 571–574. Bunselmeyer, p. 182n. Burnett, vol. 1, pp. 66–70. On "war guilt" see Lentin, *Lloyd George, Woodrow Wilson and the Guilt of Germany*, pp. 66–67 ff.
Whiteman has written: "Davis inspired the words that later gave Hitler such a potent propaganda weapon. . . . Far from wishing to heap humiliation or pass a moral judgment, Davis was seeking a compromise." Hitler "vented his explosive opinions on war guilt" when Davis met him in 1933, Whiteman, "Norman H. Davis and the Search for International Peace and Security," pp. 108–109.

when, on this very day, he received from Wiseman a memorandum analyzing the present status of loans among the Associated powers and urging that Wilson make some concessions to America's debtors and thus put himself "in the position of absolute master of the situation" at Paris.[55] This communication served as a reminder of the possibility that Lloyd George might further complicate the negotiations by introducing the festering issue of indebtedness.[56]

In the afternoon Clemenceau stated the French position very emphatically. Denying the right of any commission to determine Germany's capacity to pay, he would charge the reparations commission with the duty of collecting everything that was owed under the categories of damage that the experts had defined. If it proved to be impossible for Germany to complete payments within thirty years, the commission might prolong the period; but it should be given no authority to reduce the amount due.

Clemenceau observed that his proposal appeared to represent the opinion of the majority of those present; and House, seeing that he was outvoted, was moved to remark that the proposal of his French friend came "close to the American proposal." Davis protested bitterly. In his view such a settlement would negate all the work that the American experts had done for three months to persuade the Europeans that Germany should be held liable only for a fixed sum that would be within its capacity to pay. However, the political necessities of the chiefs of the democracies had overridden the requirements of good diplomacy. Clemenceau's statement became the substance of Articles 233 and 234 of the Treaty of Versailles. In spite of strenuous efforts made in June by Davis and Wilson to get action on German counterproposals and to set a fixed total of indebtedness, Clemenceau and Lloyd George were never persuaded to give up the position that they deemed vital to their political survival.[57]

House instructed the American experts to work with the Europeans to produce a revision of the Anglo-American draft of articles for the treaty; and Clemenceau approved the new version.[58] Taking it up with Wilson, House argued that it would be best to accept the compromise that had been reached after much travail.[59]

During the deliberations on the fifth, while on the one hand he was satisfying Clemenceau, House acted also to give counsel to Wilson that might provide an opportunity for the president to assert his independence. Stepping into his chief's bedchamber, he suggested that if there was no agreement with the premiers by the end of the week, the president should draw up a statement of what the United States was willing to sign, and at the same time he should quietly and firmly announce

55. Wiseman to House, April 5, 1919, with memorandum, Y.H.C.

56. Keynes wrote in retrospect: "If the American delegation had gone too far in pressing the Allies to abate their claims on the enemy, they might have laid themselves open to awkward pressure from the Allies to be allowed corresponding abatements in what they themselves owed to the United States. If Germany could pay so little, could the Allies pay so much?" Keynes, review of Baruch, *The Making of the Reparation and Economic Sections of the Treaty,* in *Living Age* 8th ser., no. 21 (January–March 1921):90–93.

57. Somewhat divergent accounts of the meetings on April 5 are given in Mantoux, *Proceedings,* pp. 116–128, Burnett, vol. 1, pp. 825–836, and *F.R., P.P.C.,* vol. 5, pp. 21–38.

58. Loucheur, *Carnets Secrets,* pp. 74–75.

59. *I.P.,* vol. 4, pp. 400–401.

that unless the Europeans came close to the American position, they would have to make peace without him. By giving this advice he both catered to Wilson's abhorrence of capitulation and guarded against backsliding on the part of Clemenceau.

Going to the president's house on the afternoon of the next day, House found his three fellow commissioners assembled by the bed of Wilson, whose fever had almost subsided. It had required a real crisis to bring the president into touch with the other American plenipotentiaries. He had reached a point at which he was almost ready to take the drastic action that had been urged upon him. The day before, he had gone so far as to instruct Secretary Glass to withhold approval of applications from France or Great Britain for "any kind of financial accommodations."[60]

Just at this time Tumulty sent political advice that reinforced the counsel of House. He cabled from the White House to Dr. Grayson: "The president must in some dramatic way clear the air of doubts and misunderstandings and despair which now pervade the whole world situation . . . or political sabotage and scheming will triumph. Only a bold stroke by the president will save Europe and perhaps the world. . . . This occasion calls for the audacity which has helped him win in every fight."[61]

Although Wilson felt that the very complex situation had improved after House's two days of negotiations with the premiers, he decided to give some satisfaction to anxious Americans as well as to the impatience of his fellow plenipotentiaries.[62] At the two-hour conference on Sunday in the president's bedchamber, which Wilson described as "a council of war," he said that if nothing happened within the next few days, he would say to the prime ministers that unless peace was made according to the Fourteen Points, he would either have to go home or he would insist on having the conferences in the open—in other words, on having plenary sessions with the delegates of the small powers sitting in.[63]

Soon after the commissioners departed from his room, Wilson asked Grayson to cable an order directing the *George Washington* to make ready to come from the United States to Brest. "I hope that I can get things in hand," he said, "and that we can work them out when I get up. But if we don't within a specified time, I am going to tell all of the peace commissioners plainly what I am going to do. And when I make this statement I do not intend it as a bluff. . . . When I decide, doctor, to carry this through, I do not want to say that I am going as soon as I can get a ship."[64]

The next morning Grayson released news of this move to the press. When Clemenceau asked the doctor whether it was merely a gesture, the latter replied: "If he ever starts for Brest to go aboard the *George Washington,* you and the entire French

60. Wilson to Tumulty for Glass, April 5, 1919. Glass replied that he was already committed to certain further concessions to Great Britain and France but expected Great Britain to use private financing after July 1, president from Glass, April 5, 1919, cables in Tumulty papers, box 6.

61. Cable, Tumulty to Grayson, April 5, 1919, Tumulty papers, box 6.

62. Cable, Grayson to Tumulty, April 6, 1919, Wilson papers. Lansing desk diary, April 4, 1919. Bliss to N. D. Baker, April 3, 1919, N. D. Baker papers. L. C. Sweetser recorded in his diary on April 6 that Lansing, Bliss, and White had been "about ready to bubble over for some time."

63. *I.P.,* vol. 4, pp. 401–402.

64. Grayson diary, April 6, 1919.

army cannot turn him back."[65] The effect of the incident was to add to the austerity of the president's public image. Yet it was unthinkable that he could impulsively overthrow the concert of Western nations, upon which depended not only the maintenance of the peace of the world but the realization of his own vision of a league of nations. Tumulty, who had just called for "a bold stroke," now characterized the call for the *George Washington* as an act of "impatience and petulance" and said that withdrawal would appear to be a "desertion." Reporting of the incident in the French press was somewhat restrained by censorship.[66]

In the afternoon of April 7 House went to a meeting in the apartment of Lloyd George with the hope that the arrangements as to reparations that had been made informally would be confirmed by the three Europeans. He had advised American delegates to tell their European colleagues that they could get better terms while he sat as one of the Council of Four than would be possible after the return of Wilson, who was in a belligerent mood.[67] If this remark reached Wilson, it did not please him.

The session of the Supreme Council on the seventh was stormy—"a long windy meeting . . . everyone standing up in the middle of the room and all talking at once in both languages."[68] House spoke only twice, in an assenting way, and at six o'clock he showed his displeasure with the disorganization by walking out. "We wasted the entire afternoon, accomplishing nothing," he wrote afterward, expressing impatience with the whole procedure of the Peace Conference.[69] Lloyd George was heard to mutter that he was tired of all the "quarreling." When House was told that Dr. Grayson thought that Clemenceau might have given Wilson his cold, the colonel answered, "I hope that Clemenceau will pass the germ along to Lloyd George."[70] House went across the street to talk with the president, whom he found "thoroughly discouraged." The colonel, having had enough of front-line negotiation and bearing frustration with less patience than the president, appeared to be white with rage. The making of decisions was by no means so easy as he indicated in boasts to newsmen.[71] He was desirous that Lansing take his place at the next session of The Four, which was to deal with the question of responsibility for the war.[72]

---

65. Grayson, *Woodrow Wilson: An Intimate Memoir*, p. 61. Someone informed Wilson that House told newsmen that it was impossible for the president to go home at this point—a remark that did not endear the colonel to the president, Grayson, "The Colonel's Folly," 99.

66. Tumulty to Grayson, April 9, 1919. Noble, *Policies and Opinions at Paris, 1919*, pp. 323–328.

67. House diary, April 6, 1919.

68. McCormick diary, April 7, 1919. Progress was "very slow because ministers are trying to decide matters without thoroughly familiarizing themselves with the details of the subject at hand," *ibid*. Mantoux, *Proceedings*, pp. 131, 133.

69. House diary, April 7, 1919. Auchincloss, who kept a procès-verbal at this meeting, recorded in his diary on April 7 that when the colonel withdrew in disgust, the effect on the meeting was "quieting." Clemenceau was in a bad humor and was obstructive, and Lloyd George's attitude was constructive. Four days later Lloyd George remarked to an aide that Clemenceau "was failing," *Lord Riddell's Intimate Diary*, entry of April 11, 1919.

70. Baker, *American Chronicle*, p. 400. Clemenceau had been equally caustic when, hearing that Wilson's illness was worse, on April 5, he said to Lloyd George: "Do you know his doctor? Couldn't you get round him and bribe him?" Stevenson, *Lloyd George: A Diary*, p. 178.

71. See below, p. 297.

72. Benham diary letter, April 8, 1919. After a talk with Mrs. Lansing, Miss Benham wrote: "It is humiliating [to the Lansings] to have Colonel House doing all his [Lansing's] work here. . . . I think

At six-thirty Ray Stannard Baker made his daily call on Wilson to glean news. He found the president in his study, "fully dressed, looking still thin and pale," a man who seemed to have his back against a wall. "The time has come to bring this thing to a head," Wilson said. "House was just here and told me that Clemenceau and Klotz had talked away another day. . . . I will not discuss anything with them any more. . . . We agreed among ourselves and we agreed with Germany upon certain general principles. The whole course of the Conference has been made up of a series of attempts, especially by France, to break down this agreement, to get territory, and to impose crushing indemnities." The president's vexation manifested itself in peculiarities of behavior.[73]

On the morning of the next day, April 8, House returned to the labors that had brought him, in three days, to the verge of exhaustion.[74] The session at Lloyd George's apartment reached a new nadir of incoherence as the danger of disorders in Germany and Austria was discussed. House suggested that the German delegates be invited to come to Versailles within a few weeks, and he asked a question that led his colleagues to agree to instruct the military and naval advisers to consider measures to be taken if the Germans refused to sign the treaty of peace. Again House left early. He went across the street to give the president an outline of the arguments that would be presented when Wilson welcomed the premiers to his room that afternoon.

When the president, sitting up in bed, received his European colleagues in his chamber on April 8, he asserted his concept of justice once more. He had something to say about each issue. Auchincloss, partial though he was to House, wrote in his diary: "Certainly things are speeding up."

---

the president heartily dislikes Mr. Lansing and I am sorry to say seems to show it in rather a petty way. . . . Everything Mr. Lansing does seems to irritate him. . . . The fact they go out to dinner so much, accept invitations from people he doesn't like." It seemed to her that the Lansings conducted themselves with great dignity through trying circumstances.

73. Baker, vol. 2, pp. 59–60. Irving H. Hoover, *Forty-two Years in the White House,* p. 98. Gilbert Close, who was Wilson's secretary at Princeton as well as at the Peace Conference, wrote in a letter of April 7, 1919, to his family: "I never knew the president to be in such a difficult frame of mind as he is in now. He has jumped all over [Head Usher Irwin H.] Hoover several times and is sore at Swem [Wilson's stenographer for several years past]," Close papers, Princeton University Library. A letter from Close to the writer (May 7, 1951) gives similar testimony of Wilson's unusual irascibility. Herbert Hoover felt, as he wrote five years later, that Wilson "suddenly gained a stubbornness, tended to rely upon his previous decisions, was less open to conviction, resented opposition of opinion, all of which I am told are pathological symptoms," letter Hoover to W. A. White, June 13, 1924, quoted in Gelfand (ed.), *Herbert Hoover,* p. 82. Hoover to author, November 5, 1953. Dr. Grayson recorded that Wilson showed an abnormal concern about the arrangement of furniture, Grayson diary, May 1, 1919. This is cited by Dr. Weinstein as an indication of damage to Wilson's brain, Weinstein, p. 342. In the opinion of Dr. Marmor, however, "Wilson's activities for the remainder of April 1919 seem quite consistent with a history of severe but uncomplicated influenza," papers cited (see above, p. 285n.).

The records of Wilson's staff have suggested that he was unduly suspicious that the French servants in his Paris residence were spies, Baker, *American Chronicle,* p. 488; Benham diary letters, March 29, April 18 and 19, 1919; Grayson diary, March 29, April 8, 1919. This suspicion, however, was not peculiar to Wilson. As early as December 1918, Charles Seymour had a feeling of being spied upon at the Crillon, *Letters from the Paris Peace Conference,* pp. 58–59. Captain Patterson, chief of the American secretariat in the Crillon, was so wary of spies that he ordered papers no longer needed to be burned, typescript in Bonsal papers.

74. On April 9 Auchincloss recorded in his diary that House had "a bad throat and did not feel like talking."

Wilson himself, possessed by a mood of buoyancy that may have been an after-effect of his illness, boasted to Grayson: "We made progress today, not through the match of wits, but simply through my hammering and forcing them to decisions. It appears to me that the *George Washington* incident has had a very beneficial effect on the French. They wanted to know when I was going back and I told them in very plain language that the results would be the determining factor."[75]

On April 19 and 21 The Four devoted themselves to the touchy question of reparations. Wilson had just received a cable from Tumulty advising him to "throw upon the other nations the burden of exacting indemnities and at the same time win their support of a league of nations."[76] Nevertheless, he confirmed his assent to the participation of the United States, as an arbiter, in the work of a commission to regulate and collect payments from the enemy, provided its constitution proved to be acceptable. He hoped that American participation might serve the interest of the United States and weaker nations and might mitigate the severity of the Europeans. As to the granting of a right of veto in the commission—a matter that House had reserved for the judgment of Wilson when Clemenceau and Lloyd George had agreed on a rule of unanimity—the mind of the president was not yet fully made up.[77] He insisted that the reparations commission limit the amount of bonds that Germany could issue to cover foreign loans, probably counting upon American veto power to require moderation. On April 23, when the Council of Four reviewed the draft to be given to the Germans, the Americans attempted to substitute economic sanctions for the war-provoking measures that the Europeans advocated; but they did not succeed so far as to rule out the possibility of military action by at least one of the contracting powers, and thus the way was left open for France to march into the Ruhr in 1923.[78]

In mid-April the talk of the council drifted in a sea of minor questions in which the United States had no vital interest. They concerned Luxembourg, Lemberg, Schleswig, the Belgian-German boundary, the Baltic, and the Kiel Canal. The lack of an executive focus became critical. There were instances of a failure of coordination among the various delegations. The Peace Conference was becoming a multi-ring circus in which the various acts, though often related, were not coordinated by any authority. Steed wrote in the *Times* on April 7 of "the abandonment of sound methods in favor of 'general improvisations'—or what Mr. Lloyd George once called 'happy thoughts.' " Finally, on April 13 Maurice Hankey, the chief of

75. Grayson diary, April 9, 1919.
76. Tumulty to Wilson, April 9, 1919, Tumulty papers, box 6.
77. When the question of voting was raised on April 10 by Lloyd George, Wilson went so far as to say that he favored decisions by majority vote, with a proviso that there be no remission of debts without unanimity. He insisted on a unanimous vote in the fixing of the amount of a proposed bond issue that in his opinion would be placed, "in large part, in the United States," Mantoux, *Proceedings*, pp. 134, 169–174, 184–185. The Treaty of Versailles finally provided for decisions by a majority vote except on certain specified questions.

The decisions reached by The Four with respect to reparations are summarized in a dispatch of April 16, 1919, Auchincloss to Polk, Auchincloss diary. During the following weeks many technical questions were referred to the economic advisers, with general guidance on the part of the Council of Four. See Mantoux, *Délibérations*, vol. 1, pp. 235–236, 268, 397, 423, 435, 494–495; vol. 2, *passim*.

78. Burnett, vol. 1, pp. 1006–1007.

Lloyd George's secretariat, set forth the difficulties in a memorandum to Balfour.[79]. He proposed that an executive secretary be appointed to guard against a continuation of the disorder. He suggested that he might provide this service in rotation with Auchincloss and a French and an Italian secretary.

As a result of this timely proposal, Hankey was given the task of keeping minutes of the meetings of "The Four" as well as that of preparing agenda and following up the decisions rendered. House was of the opinion that an American secretary should be present at each session in which Wilson took part and recommended Auchincloss; but the president, trusting Hankey and resenting any arrangement that might seem to be one in which Auchincloss could be his monitor, would not hear of it. When Hankey produced daily minutes, Wilson would not permit copies to go to the other American plenipotentiaries, not even to House.[80]

Now that the hour of decisions had come, the advocate of open diplomacy was withdrawing into deepest secrecy and holding himself fully accountable for the result. His was the "self-trust" that as a young scholar he had admired in the great statesmen of the nineteenth century. After the threat of withdrawal that was implicit in the calling of the *George Washington,* his leadership became so effective in the Council of Four that Orlando later wrote that after April 6 "no decision was ever taken by the Conference which was opposed to the determined will of the president."[81]

Wilson was not unaware of the animosity that he provoked by the "hammering" to which he resorted after his illness in order to force decisions that had been delayed for too long. Lord Robert Cecil wrote in his diary on March 25 that the president was "curiously unpopular."[82] He appeared to have overborne his colleagues on moral grounds and to have reproved Europeans, who had suffered far more than his own people from the fury of the enemy. He himself once had written that compromise is "the law of Society in all things,"[83] and at Paris he had compromised with more impulsiveness than wisdom. But when House suggested further concessions to the French that seemed to involve at least a temporary violation of the principle of self-determination, he fell in with family tradition. He had once written of his revered father: "Whate'er he feared, he never feared a foe."[84] Opposition had

79. Memorandum in Balfour papers, P.R.O., FO / 800 / 216.

80. Ms., "Col. Edward House," I. H. Hoover papers, L.C., box 2. On April 19 House called on Wilson to say that Balfour had proposed that notes be taken of the meetings of The Four and that Auchincloss would be available for this duty. Wilson expressed thanks; but when House telephoned later in the day to ask when Auchincloss should report, the president replied that he would let the young man know when he wanted him, and then arranged for one of his own secretaries to take notes that day. Evidence of Wilson's extreme dislike of Auchincloss appears in Grayson's diary, April 5, 6, 10, and 19, 1919. See above, p. 212, n. 41.

81. Orlando in the *Saturday Evening Post,* March 23, 1929. The strength of this statement is somewhat diluted by the fact that Orlando was absent from several of the sessions of the Council of Four after April 6.

82. Wilson was advised to make more use of the traditional arts of diplomacy, and his wife suggested holding a tea salon. But loss of time over refreshments at the Quai was one of his reasons for preferring to do business at home, and moreover he was bored by the kind of people who would come. Notes in I. H. Hoover papers, L.C.; Benham diary letter, April 28, 1919; letter, Sir Cecil Hurst to W. E. Dodd, R. S. Baker papers, IB, L.C.

83. Woodrow Wilson, *Leaders of Men* (Princeton, 1952), p. 48.

84. Walworth, *Woodrow Wilson,* vol. 1, p. 81.

served to stiffen a determination that Woodrow Wilson thought holy. This state of mind, which had almost wrecked a theological school in the South and even Princeton University, boded nothing but ill for his long-standing confidence in Colonel House and for a continuation of their relationship.

Thrown into a dour mood, Wilson undertook to defend his position in the Supreme Council without calling upon House often for further help. The colonel, relieved of the burden of attending formal meetings in which he thought his time wasted, resumed his independent activities and undertook to deal with numerous matters that were brought to him because he was presumed to speak with authority. He wrote in his diary: "I make decisions to relieve the president, who is overburdened and does not organize his work."

As fatigue and illness sapped Wilson's vitality, he had tended to yield to suspicion and distrust.[85] He was more than ever perturbed by derogatory stories that were appearing in the press on both sides of the Atlantic. Almost from the day of Wilson's first arrival at Paris, when he had refused to visit the battlefields, the controlled press of France had irritated him by insinuation and ridicule.

In mid-April the tone of the journals had become so offensive[86] that House made use of an opportunity to persuade Clemenceau to put a stop to mischievous stories. The opportunity came on April 15. When House went to the premier with word of the president's assent to a limited occupation of three zones of German territory west of the Rhine,[87] Clemenceau embraced him. The colonel, seizing the moment to exact a *quid pro quo,* brought up the question of the press. According to his record, "Clemenceau . . . summoned his secretary and told him in French, with much emphasis, that all attacks of every description on President Wilson and the United States must cease." The next day House sent the president quotations from nine French newspapers that were favorable to Wilson, and wrote: "Dear Governor! This is what happened. E. M. H."[88] Unfortunately, however, the sudden change in the tone of the controlled press did not remove the distrust of Wilson that lingered in French minds.[89]

House was less successful in efforts to continue his influence over the press of Great Britain. Auchincloss had a long talk with Lord Northcliffe on March 18, and, at the suggestion of House, Mrs. Wilson invited Lady Northcliffe to luncheon. But this did not overcome a feeling on the part of Northcliffe that Wilson was a political adventurer and a vain man whose power was waning.[90] Auchincloss talked fre-

85. Baker, *American Chronicle,* p. 488. I. H. Hoover, p. 98. See the excerpts from R. S. Baker's journal printed in Mayer, *Politics and Diplomacy of Peacemaking,* pp. 571–575.

86. Noble, pp. 130–132.

87. See below, p. 326.

88. Documents in Wilson papers. Sweetser diary, April 18, 1919. Bonsal, *Suitors and Suppliants,* pp. 259–262. See K. Nelson, *Victors Divided,* p. 298, n. 98.

89. Lord Derby, the British ambassador, wrote to Curzon on April 12, 1919: "It is not too much to say that the president is loathed and despised throughout France, perhaps somewhat unjustly, but the worst offenders in abuse of him are the Americans themselves," letter in Curzon papers, box 22, F / 6 / 2. Arthur Willert of the *Times* wrote to his wife on April 9, 1919: "The president has lost a lot of ground since his return. The French press are openly critical: ours by innuendo," letter in Willert papers, Y.H.C. See below, p. 302, n. 3.

90. *Lord Riddell's Intimate Diary,* p. 47, entry of April 9, 1919.

quently with Steed, whose editorials in London papers gave Lloyd George cause for a protest to House.[91]

The prime minister, fearing the opposition in the House of Commons, was embarrassed when a draft of the reparation settlement found its way into the newspapers and revealed to his electorate that their sanguine expectations were to be disappointed. This leak offended Wilson also, for he feared that it would give the Germans an opportunity for intrigue and delay.[92] It was common knowledge that Herbert Bayard Swope was responsible for an illegitimate "scoop," but to this day it has not been ascertained who was his informant.[93] It was natural that suspicion should center on House, who had the habit of conversing, late in the afternoons, with certain American newsmen whom he trusted. "I talk freely to them," he wrote in his diary, "and they get from me practically all the news of the Conference that they get at all. I am sure the president does not approve of my giving our public as much information as I do, but I shall continue until he protests, and then we will have it out together. He and Lloyd George are the ones that frown on publicity as to what is going on, and yet if they did but know it, it is the best thing for them, particularly for the president, whose purposes are so commendable."[94] Baruch suggested forty-two years later—and quite possibly alleged to Wilson at the time—that House, to requite Swope for some favor, had left the confidential paper exposed in a manner that invited Swope to take it.[95] But Swope has denied that House was his informant,[96] and those who knew the habits of the colonel thought it impossible that he could have been responsible for the leak.[97] They suspected Swope's "most intimate friend" Baruch.[98]

In whatever way the news leaked out, the offense made it the more difficult for Baker to exercise control over the American journalists. "Swope having started to steal honey," Baker wrote in his journal on April 20, "the whole swarm is now trying to rob the hive."

91. Auchincloss wrote in his diary on April 4: "I had a short talk with the colonel and Lloyd George. George referred to Steed's attacks and said that Steed had been using matter that we (looking at me) had no doubt given him in confidence and that he, George, thought that was the worst thing a newspaper man could do. I did not comment but just stared George back. He is playing a slick game and is getting nervous on account of the attacks in the *Daily Mail* and London *Times*. I happen to know that he sees Steed almost daily. Of course, I realize that I am playing with fire also but I may be able to escape getting burned." Also see *ibid.*, March 29, 1919.

92. Benham diary letter, April 15, 1919.

93. E. J. Kahn, *Swope*, pp. 223 ff. This "scoop" resulted in an article in the European edition of the *New York Herald* on April 10. Swope gave the tentative draft of reparation terms to Hills of the *New York Sun*, which published it on April 12. But the dispatch that Swope sent to his own paper, the *World*, was intercepted and held up by the British censor, Kahn, *Swope*, pp. 223–226. At one o'clock on April 12 Wilson asked Baker to stop further publication of the story. Baker tried to do so, but, according to a statement ascribed to Dr. Grayson by Miss Benham, "that rascal Swope just kept on banging the keys, sending out his message, and wouldn't see Baker," Benham diary letter, April 10 and 15, 1919. R. S. Baker's journal, entry of April 12, 1919. Reginald Coggeshall, "Was There Censorship at the Paris Peace Conference?" 125–135.

94. House diary, March 20, 1919.

95. Baruch to the author, May 31, 1961. Baruch, *The Public Years*, pp. 141–144.

96. Letter, Swope to the author, November 27, 1951.

97. F. L. Warrin, Jr., and Charles Seymour to the author.

98. See above, p. 189. Dr. Grayson explained that Swope's "scoop" resulted from his cleverness in asking questions and piecing together what he heard from various people, Benham diary letter, April 15, 1919.

House continued to act on his conviction that the American commission should deal constructively with the representatives of the press despite the risk of irritation on the part of the president.[99] To the journalists both House and Auchincloss made remarks that suggested an unseemly swelling of egos.[100] On April 4, when House took the seat of the president in the Council of Four, he said: "Some of these boundaries troubles could be settled in half an hour if the president sat down to it."[101] He also said that he could get the premiers to do more work than when they met with the president.[102]

House's indiscreet remarks reflected an increase of censorious jottings in his diary.[103] On April 18 the colonel gave the appearance of a man who had overplayed his role. It seemed to Sweetser that House was downcast because the president chose to hold a meeting of the American plenipotentiaries in the office of Lansing. Baker, who eleven days before had recorded a tribute to the colonel's effective work, wrote in his journal on April 3: "House more and more impresses me as the dilettante—the lover of the game—the eager secretary without profound responsibility . . . gaining experiences to put in his diary. . . . House has the vice of his own amiability. . . . He placates only to lay up future trouble." And on the tenth: "The rift between the president and the colonel seems to be increasing."

Edith Wilson had not really trusted House and had never felt the appreciation that the first Mrs. Wilson showed for the services of the colonel.[104] When House had discouraged Wilson's participation in the Paris negotiations, the colonel was told by friends that Edith Wilson found the g' 'mour of the Peace Conference alluring

99. House had been receptive as early as December to a suggestion that Wilson talk frankly with Melville Stone, general manager of the Associated Press, who had been close to the Republican Old Guard in the Senate and wished to cultivate relations with the Democrats as a source of news, "Wilson Notes," Walter S. Rogers to R. H. Nolte, January 12, 1962, copy in Walworth papers, Y.H.C., by the kindness of John M. Blum.

"I suggested [to Mrs. Wilson]," House wrote in his diary, "that she break it to the president gently that I wanted Melville Stone invited to lunch within the next few days since he was leaving for home almost at once. When the president came in she broke the news to him by saying: 'the colonel has invited himself and Mr. Stone for lunch on Monday.' The president gave a whimsical sigh and replied, 'Oh dear, I shall be glad when I am out of office so that I can eat with gentlemen.' " Stone lunched on March 31 with Wilson, House, and Lloyd George, House diary, January 6, March 28 and 31, 1919.

100. According to the testimony of Edith Wilson (Hatch, *Edith Bolling Wilson*, p. 161) the president, walking quietly down the hall of the Crillon, passed the door of House's suite and heard Auchincloss gaily ask his father-in-law: "What shall we make the president say today?" Baruch has reported that Auchincloss said to McCormick, after one of House's brief illnesses, that now that the colonel was better, "Woody's batting average" would improve, *The Public Years*, p. 143. McCormick almost punched Auchincloss for remarking that "Woody's" stock was rising, Baruch to the author, September 28, 1959. House's own sense of importance appears in an entry in his diary on March 25: "I have such a large force and there are so many meetings held in my rooms that it has been necessary to add to them from time to time. I now have the entire tier on the third floor front and one tier back. I have twice as many rooms as all the other commissioners put together."

101. Arthur Sweetser's notes of House's news conferences, April 4, 5, 18, and 19, 1919, Sweetser papers, L.C.

102. Dr. Lamb recorded this remark, made to his colleague, Dr. McLean, on April 5, 1919, Lamb's notes, Princeton University Library. See C. T. Thompson, chs. 24, 25 *passim*.

103. House diary, April 1, May 6 and 31, 1919. See Louis W. Koenig, "Sphinx in a Soft Hat," in *The Invisible Presidency*, pp. 246–247.

104. R. S. Baker's interview with E. B. Wilson, December 7, 1925, Baker papers, I, box J. Cf. E. B. Wilson, *My Memoir*, pp. 155, 237, and Walworth, vol. 1, p. 433.

and felt that House was presuming to pose as the director of American foreign policy.[105]

House's power to expedite the negotiations depended entirely upon his position at Wilson's right hand. His fellow commissioners were deeply resentful of his control of events and tended to attribute to him not only their own isolation from Wilson, but policies that seemed to them unwise. Lansing declared privately that he had never tried "to build up a secret personal organization as Colonel House" had, and that it was from that organization that all the worst compromises had come. Only Henry White found Wilson accessible. He had won the confidence of Mrs. Wilson, whom he found surprisingly perceptive and "a valuable channel for communication with the president."[106]

In view of the antipathy that had developed among the commissioners as well as among certain economic advisers and newsmen,[107] House more than ever needed the full support of the president, which once had been given without reserve. On April 18, however, Mrs. Wilson acted in a way that seemed to confirm the gossip that had reached House to the effect that he was suspected of disloyalty to his chief. According to the undated record of both parties, she confronted him with a newspaper article that praised his work in a way that disparaged that of the president. The piece had appeared in the *Washington Post* of April 8. It read in part:

Insofar as there is a real improvement in the prospects of the conference it is believed to be attributed chiefly to the practical statesmanship of Col. House, who, in view of President Wilson's indisposition, has once again placed his *savoir faire* and conciliatory temperament at the disposal of the chief peacemakers.

Colonel House is one of the few delegates who have "made good" during the conference. It is, indeed, probable that peace would have been made successfully weeks ago but for the unfortunate illness which overtook him at the very outset of the conference. When he recovered, the Council of Ten had already got into bad habits. . . . During their [Wilson's and Lloyd George's] absence Col. House, who has never found difficulty in working with his colleagues, because he is a selfless man with no personal axe to grind, brought matters rapidly forward.

In writing this Steed had overdone a deed that Auchincloss had suggested to him.[108] There was enough truth in his observations to make the offense to the Wil-

105. Seymour, "End of a friendship," 8.

If Mrs. Wilson was indeed jealous of House as well as mistrustful, she had treated the colonel with a show of affection. From the *George Washington* on February 19 she sent this message: "Please take good care of your dear self and let us know if we can do anything for you. Love from us both. Affectionately," Y.H.C. During the president's illness she had given House an invitation to lunch, which he declined, House diary, April 4, 1919.

106. Bullitt's records of talks with Lansing and Bliss. Cf. below, p. 395. On April 7 White wrote to Congressman John J. Rogers: "I have discovered . . . that he [Wilson] is really shy, and, in an atmosphere which he does not feel to be entirely sympathetic, . . . his reserve increases in proportion to the absence of sympathy . . . when I see him alone . . . I have found him a very good listener," Nevins, *White*, pp. 409, 447.

107. See Schwartz, *The Speculator*, p. 123.

108. Auchincloss diary, March 29, 1919.

"Several other men in House's entourage were as indiscreet as Auchincloss in their remarks about the relative importance of House and Wilson. There were also among the Americans in Paris a number of old women of both sexes who collected droppings from the House secretariat and ran to insert the tittle-

sons painful. Five years later House wrote in his diary that the unfortunate piece that his son-in-law had instigated was "one of the real grievances" of the Wilsons. "I knew nothing of the article until it was published," he asserted, "and had as little to do with it as the man in the moon." Mrs. Wilson, however, held House responsible and thought him disloyal. She told her husband of the offensive article, and House became an outcast from the family circle.[109]

The president, when he was ill early in April, had spoken to Grayson of his disappointment in the lack of devotion on the part of House to Wilsonian principles.[110] He did not now counter his wife's charge that House was a "jellyfish" who lacked backbone. Wilson was persuaded that House was guilty of "the gravest error of judgment" in failing to oppose prominent men with whom he wished to be on intimate terms.[111] "The notes he passed to me during the larger meetings" House recalled just before his death, "were intimate and affectionate as ever; I merely had a consciousness of hostility on the part of those around him. He and I had no opportunity for long intimate talks, as in the old days. When he was free he was naturally captured for long automobile rides by Mrs. Wilson. I had a sense that she did not want me in the intimate family atmosphere."[112] He did not risk a complete rupture by asking his old friend to define their new relationship.

It is possible that Wilson, overlooking the damaging concessions that he himself had made in respect of the Tyrol boundary and the inclusion of pensions in the bill of reparations, found it convenient to attribute to House the responsibility for all compromises that his conscience abhorred and that seemed to betray the principles for which he liked to conceive that he was "fighting." It is conceivable also that "increased sensitivity to House as a possible competitor" may have contributed heavily to the waning of the president's affection for his old friend.[113]

---

tattle in Mrs. Wilson's ear. Mrs. Wilson began to believe that House encouraged his subordinates to talk disparagingly about her husband in order to make himself appear the great man of America," Bullitt and Freud, *Thomas Woodrow Wilson*, p. 221.

109. House diary, April 23, 1924. Mrs. Wilson's account of the confrontation with House is in *My Memoir*, pp. 250–253. House's comment on her story was: "Mrs. Wilson . . . had been reading a copy of the Washington *Post* in which the Steed article had been published. What she said was: 'Have you read this article by Wickham Steed? It is very unkind to Woodrow, but complimentary to you.' I told her I had read it in the *Mail* when it came out and that I did not think he meant it unkindly or in criticism of the president. That was all of our conversation on the subject," memorandum, House to Bullitt, October 3, 1930, Y.H.C. Mrs. Wilson, before giving the offensive story to House, quizzed the colonel about Steed and was assured that the latter was one of the finest of the journalists and completely under House's control, Grayson, "The Colonel's Folly and the President's Distress," 99. The understanding between House and Steed is described by the latter in *Through Thirty Years*, vol. 2, pp. 283–284. According to Dr. Grayson, some American newsmen resented House's favoring an English journalist, Grayson diary, April 20, 1919.

110. According to Grayson, Wilson said while he was ill: "When you take a man like House and put him in a place the like of which no other man ever occupied in the world, take him into your innermost confidence, unbosom your very soul to him, and then this man is seduced by the flattery of others and goes back on you in a crisis—what a blow it is! It is harder than death. I am a Christian and but for my faith in God it would be hard for me to bear it," Grayson, "The Colonel's Folly and the President's Distress," 100–101. Apparently Dr. Grayson took these words from his memory or from rough notes. They do not appear in the transcript of his diary at Princeton.

111. E. B. Wilson, p. 252, and draft ms. in Marquis James papers, L.C., box 25.

112. House to Seymour, January 5, 1938.

113. George and George, pp. 246, 248.

Nevertheless, the president, disparaging objectionable news stories as merely "another attempt to misrepresent things at home," acknowledged no break in the American front at Paris that might give comfort to his political enemies. He went on using House as a member of the Commission on the League of Nations and entrusted to him the development of a plan for mandates under the league.[114] Moreover, the colonel continued to be indispensable in contacts with Clemenceau.[115] But for more than a week after the confrontation with Mrs. Wilson, House had no tête-à-tête with the president.[116]

Dr. Grayson, who had introduced Edith Galt to the president in 1915 and on whose ministration Wilson relied increasingly in his overwrought and overworked condition, wrote to Tumulty and McAdoo in disparagement of House.[117] In his friend Baruch the doctor found a sympathetic confidant and a comrade at the race track, and he seized every opportunity to further the intimacy of that ambitious adviser with the president.[118] Baruch complained, not without reason, that the colonel's love of participation in great affairs had inflated his ego to an unseemly extent and expressed itself beyond the bounds of decorum. He felt that House did not sufficiently exert his influence with the press to protect the president from attack.[119]

Baruch rented a dwelling at St. Cloud, quiet and with a charming garden, and told Grayson he might use it any day. On Sundays in April the doctor invited the Wilsons and Miss Benham to go there for luncheon, and Baruch joined the party.[120] Here the harassed president could relax in a social circle that was altogether agreeable. In an atmosphere that recalled the Old South and that enabled him to forget his vexing business with House and the Europeans, these intimates freely vented their intolerance of what seemed to them the "slipperiness" of the European premiers. They talked in the confidential way in which Wilson had been accustomed to converse with House. Baruch, with the support of Grayson and Mrs. Wilson, was now filling to a degree the need that Wilson felt for an intimate male friend, although, according to Baruch's own record, he "never exercised any measure of influence with the president equal to that of Colonel House."[121] The president,

114. See below, p. 486.
115. See below, p. 326.
116. Lansing desk diary, April 25, 1919.
117. Grayson to Tumulty, April 10, 1919, Tumulty papers, box 1. Grayson to McAdoo, April 12, 1919, McAdoo papers, box 219, L.C. Edith Benham recorded that from what Dr. Grayson told her, and others hinted, she thought that House was "rather losing his grip on things" and was "being run entirely by his son-in-law," Benham diary letter, April 13, 1919. Letter, Buckler to his wife, June 10, 1919, Y.H.C. Henry Morgenthau's diary, June 25, 1919, L.C.
118. "Old Doc Grayson and I have quiet little McAdoo talks once in a while in a corner," Baruch to McAdoo, February 13, 1919, McAdoo papers. Baruch later described Grayson as an "intellectually compatible friend who wants nothing, who represents nobody, whom he [Wilson] can trust implicitly. . . . A man of keen intelligence and deep religious feeling, Grayson also had a highly developed sense of humor," Baruch, p. 128.
119. Baruch, pp. 141–144. See McCormick diary, October 14, 1921.
120. Grayson diary, April 20, 1919; Helm diary, April 27, 1919.
121. Baruch, p. 141. Grayson diary, April 4, 5, 27, May 18, 20, June 11, 1919. Baruch's position became sufficiently similar to that of House to expose him to the sort of gossip that grows up around any privy counselor, Coit, *Mr. Baruch,* p. 252, citing Lansing's confidential diary. Baruch prided himself on his determination to avoid annoying the president with matters he could solve himself or that would work themselves out in time, *ibid.,* p. 253. In talks with European negotiators, Baruch sometimes

falling under the influence of these people, whom he saw from day to day, gave credence to their denigration of House, who was usually remote in the Crillon[122] and was giving advice that was distasteful. Edith Wilson, jealous of men who appeared to rival her husband,[123] had finally convinced him that House was what she had called him in 1915: "a weak vessel."[124]

Late in April the service of Edward M. House to Woodrow Wilson was approaching an end. House was the victim of lapses in his own discretion as well as of unfriendly criticism, sometimes but not always ill founded. The ruling elder who had established Wilson's principles as the basis of the armistice and who had overcome many an obstacle to the creation of the League Covenant suffered in the esteem of the president because of indiscreet remarks to the newsmen and the over-zealous devotion of his efficient son-in-law.

---

revealed an ignorance and narrowness that scholars of the Inquiry thought "humiliating to the United States," Beer diary, April 9, 1918, recording a talk with Professor Young.

122. House's diary records once, on May 13, that he lunched at St. Cloud.

123. For example, when Raymond Fosdick, asked whether rumors were circulating to the effect that General Pershing was ambitious for the presidency, replied in the negative, Mrs. Wilson turned to her husband and said: "Oh, but Woodrow, he doesn't know what we know about the general," Fosdick to the author, March 10, 1952.

124. See Walworth, vol. 1, p. 433.

16

"The Primary Essential"

Before House's intimacy with Wilson ended in April the colonel was able to continue his work in satisfying national demands that impeded the revision of the League Covenant. A text had been tentatively adopted in February and supplemented by two American amendments in March. A third, designed to safeguard the Monroe Doctrine, was yet to be approved. This prime concern could not be brought up at Paris without a risk of provoking a demand by Japan for a similar reservation in respect of its influence in Asia.[1] It would be difficult, moreover, to get the assent of the British and French delegates unless Lloyd George was first satisfied with respect to sea power and Clemenceau with respect to security. In the face of these obstacles Wilson was reluctant to seek explicit recognition of the Monroe Doctrine. House, however, was insistent.

When Lloyd George let it be known that a formula that would allay British fear of American naval rivalry was a *sine qua non,* House complained to Lord Robert Cecil of the intransigence of the prime minister, from whom he expected some compensation for concessions that Wilson had made to the British Empire.[2]

Lloyd George's position was based firmly upon public opinion in England and upon the support of the British Empire delegation.[3] He was being pressed by the necessity for a reduction in British naval expenditures, and he would like to bring this about without sacrificing British primacy on the seas.[4] The prospect for any understanding on this question was clouded by contentious nationalism on the part of "blue-sea" Englishmen and "big-Navy" Americans.[5]

House was confident that economic necessity would make both sides see reason before very long.[6] Yet only with difficulty had he succeeded in the prearmistice meetings in devising a compromise formula to overcome British resistance to Point

1. Miller, *My Diary,* vol. 1, March 16, 1919.
2. See above, pp. 187, and 281. House diary, March 27. Miller, vol. 1, March 25 and 26, 1919. Auchincloss diary, March 25 and 26, 1919. Cable, Wiseman to Reading, April 11, 1919, Wiseman papers, Y.H.C. "British Empire Interests," memorandum of the British Empire delegation, Lothian papers, box 141. In his Fontainebleau memorandum Lloyd George wrote that the first condition for the success of the League of Nations was a firm understanding among the five major powers that there would be no competitive building of fleets or armies.
3. "Wilson has lost much of his popularity in England and does not get much support now even from liberal and labour press. . . . American insistence on the Monroe Doctrine in the Covenant has created a very bad impression. It is thought that the American attitude is 'everybody else must abate their sovereignty except America!' Altogether it is felt that America has redeemed her ideals somewhat cheaply. This feeling is widespread in England and France," cable, Wiseman to Reading, April 18, 1919, Y.H.C., Wiseman papers.
   Miller, vol. 1, p. 205. Minutes, ACTNP, March 27, 1919.
4. J. Kenneth McDonald, "Lloyd George and the Search for a Post-War Naval Policy, 1919," in *Lloyd George: Twelve Essays,* ed. A. J. P. Taylor, pp. 193–194.
5. Wiseman to Reading, March 26, 1919, Wiseman papers. Polk to J. W. Davis, February 10, 1919, Y.H.C.
6. Arthur Willert, *Washington and Other Memories,* p. 150.

Two,[7] calling for "freedom of the seas." This formula had by no means settled the question of sea power. It had merely postponed discussion. The delegates at the Peace Conference, aware of the disruptive possibilities of the topic, managed to avoid introducing it in the formal sessions.

On the voyage across the Atlantic in December, Wilson had denounced British infringement of the maritime rights of neutrals during the early years of the war. He intended that the United States have naval strength enough to protect its shipping.[8] Near the end of January, when the controversy with the British dominions over the disposal of German colonies was at its height and when Wilson was troubled by the prospect of Japanese expansion in the Pacific, the president informed Admiral Benson that a building program planned by the navy was necessary for the accomplishment of American purposes at the Peace Conference, although he would be willing to change his policy if agreement on disarmament was reached.[9]

The matter became more critical when the House's Committee on Naval Affairs, following a recommendation made by the secretary of the navy and endorsed by the president, adopted a three-year program authorizing the construction of another sixteen capital ships. The Senate withheld its consent, and Wilson later withdrew support. However, the navy already had authorization to complete a building program that had been approved in 1916.[10] American merchant tonnage had grown rapidly; and the United States, building warships at a rate that would bring it to a naval parity with Great Britain in a space of five or six years, was obviously a challenger to the maritime supremacy of Great Britain.[11] This rapid change seemed to menace the British Empire and to be unwarranted by the national necessities of the United States.[12]

British leaders were alarmed. They did not trust in the reasoning that Wilson expounded at Paris, to the effect that in the universal league that he envisoned there would be no neutrals and therefore no controversies over neutral rights.[13] To the cabinet ministers the maintenance of control of the seas was essential to their political existence. As a matter of practical politics there could be no departure from the old and tried assurance of sea power until the promises of a new order were tested by the passage of time and found valid. The British people, discounting the fact that freedom of the seas would be to their advantage in a war in which they were neutral,

7. See Walworth, *America's Moment: 1918*, pp. 58–65.

8. Stenographic record of Charles Swem, Princeton University Library.

9. Close to Benson, January 27, 1919, Wilson papers.

10. McDonald, p. 193. Harold Sprout, *The Rise of American Naval Power, 1776–1918* (Princeton, 1939), pp. 107–108. George T. Davis, *A Navy Second to None*, pp. 264 ff. Memo by D. H. Miller, April 9, 1919, Y.H.C. Lodge informed Bryce that the reason for the failure of the current naval bill in the Senate was a desire to deprive the president of the power "to threaten anyone with competitive armaments," Lodge to Bryce, March 4, 1919, Bryce papers, Bodleian Library, V. 7, p. 167.

11. Sprout, pp. 51–54. Baker, vol. 1, pp. 383–384.

12. Letter, Walter Long to Lloyd George, March 7, 1919, Lloyd George papers, F / 33 / 2 / 22. Forrest Davis, *The Atlantic System* (New York, 1941), pp. 266–267. Ambassador John W. Davis went so far as to report from London on December 19, 1918, that "freedom of the seas" was the sole source of real anxiety in London in connection with the forthcoming Peace Conference, *F.R., P.P.C.*, vol. 1, pp. 413–414.

13. Benham diary letter, January 21, 1919. Memorandum by Miller, December 13, 1918, in *My Diary*, vol. 2, pp. 262–264, quoted in Tillman, 289.

insisted on the supremacy of their navy[14] and its right to enforce a blockade such as that which had been effective against Germany. Moreover, the question of sea power was complicated by the necessity of disposing of Germany's navy, for which no definite plan had yet been made.

Secretary of the Navy Daniels arrived at Paris at the end of March. He breakfasted with Lloyd George and, at Wilson's suggestion, brought up this urgent question. The British government had been advised by its embassy in Washington that it was doubtful whether the Republican Senate would approve competition in naval building as a level to enforce the peace policy of Wilson; and the prime minister said to Daniels that if the United States continued its naval building, he would not give "a snap of his fingers" for the League.[15] Nevertheless, in reporting this to the president, Daniels advised that any stoppage of the 1916 construction program would weaken the case for acceptance of the League by the Congress. He was instructed by Wilson to say to the British that the United States could make no sort of agreement until it was clear what the outcome of the Peace Conference was to be.[16] Daniels left Paris without breaking the deadlock;[17] and on April 9 Admiral Benson presented to the president a paper in which his concept of American prestige and power was set forth starkly.[18]

On April 2, the day before Wilson became ill, he asked House whether Lloyd George was sincere in his demand for reassurance as to naval building. The colonel warned of trouble ahead with the prime minister ("When one talks of the sea, shipping, etc.," House wrote in his diary, "an Englishman becomes as crazy as a Frenchman when a German is mentioned").

At the request of the president House was engaging in talks with Lord Robert Cecil in an effort to resolve the difficulties. Negotiating in secrecy, these men worked with a frankness and precision that was in keeping with the best traditions of diplomacy; and the mutual confidence that they had developed withstood the greatest strain yet put upon it. The British diplomat whom everyone trusted, believing that concessions to American sentiment could be granted at no cost to Great Britain, undertook to convince the prime minister that he would merely enrage the Americans if he insisted on blocking the amendment of the Covenant that their senators were demanding.[19] Cecil had already written to Balfour to ask his aid in persuading

14. Balfour memorandum on "Freedom of the Seas," P.R.O., FO / 800 / 215.

15. Frances Stevenson wrote in her diary on March 21 that Lloyd George was "very annoyed with the American attempt to . . . double their navy, while preaching the gospel of the League of Nations," *Lloyd George*, p. 175.

16. Daniels to Wilson, April 7, Wilson papers. Letter and memorandum, Long to Lloyd George, April 8, 1919, Lloyd George papers, F / 33 / 2 /31. Before his departure from Paris, speeches that Daniels was to give in England were reviewed by House, who warned against offending British sensibilities, Auchincloss diary, March 27, 1919; House diary, March 28, April 13, 1919.

17. Josephus Daniels, *The Wilson Era*, vol. 2, pp. 367–380. Sprout, pp. 64–66, cited in Tillman, *Anglo-American Relations at the Paris Peace Conference*, pp. 290–291, *q.v.*

18. Memo no. 25, U.S. Naval Advisory Staff, Paris, "U.S. Naval Policy," forwarded to the president with a letter of April 9, 1919, in which Benson wrote: "My own opinion is that the necessity for at least two approximately equal naval powers is absolute in order to stabilize the League of Nations," Wilson papers. Daniels thought that Benson carried his insistence on naval parity too far. At Benson's request, House asked the president to keep Daniels away from Paris; but Wilson refused to do this, House diary, April 1 and 3, 1919.

19. Cecil diary, March 26, April 3, 1919.

the "little man" [Lloyd George] that *beaux gestes* really paid in dealing with the Americans.[20] The prime minister was now warned that if anyone had informed the Americans that Britain would not support the League unless its naval primacy was assured, he had put forward the British case very unwisely and in a way that no American government could accept. At the same time Cecil wrote to Balfour that it was quite clear to him that the prime minister intended to use the League "as a stick to beat the President," and that if an American indiscretion should reveal this to the public the League "would be almost on the rocks." He considered the United States, a disinterested party, to be in a stronger position than the British Empire in matters of territory and finance; and therefore he thought it impossible to impose conditions and necessary to use persuasion upon the Americans, whom he had found "very persuadable."[21]

On April 8 the English conciliator wrote persuasively to House to ask that as a *beau geste* the United States give up its building program when the League Covenant was accepted.[22] The next day House responded with a letter giving assurance that the American government would be ready to "abandon or modify its naval construction that had not yet been authorized by the Congress," and also stating that the United States would be "ready and willing to consult with the British government from year to year regarding the naval programmes of the two Governments." At the end House wrote: "I am sending this letter with the president's approval."[23]

In a talk with Cecil on April 10, the day on which the League commission was to consider an amendment on the Monroe Doctrine, House made it clear that the United States could not modify the program of naval building of 1916, which had been delayed by the wartime necessity of producing quantities of small craft to deal with German submarines. Contracts had been let, and the president now had little to say about it. House said more than once that Wilson had no idea of building a fleet in competition with that of Great Britain. Cecil, however, had to report that the prime minister was not satisfied by the formula that House had written the day before.[24]

House made it clear that any amendment of the Monroe Doctrine was one question and sea power another, and that there was no connection between the two. Nevertheless, his British colleague, much upset by the difficulty the naval impasse presented to the acceptance of the revised Covenant, seemed, according to Auchincloss, "disposed to quit the whole thing." But House insisted that the matter was

20. Letter, Cecil to Balfour, March 27, 1919, P.R.O., FO / 800 / 215.

21. Letters, Lord Robert Cecil to the prime minister, April 4, 1919, Cecil to "Arthur" [Balfour], April 5, 1919, Cecil to House, April 8, 1919, copies in Cecil papers, 51076 and 51094.

22. *I.P.*, vol. 4, pp. 418–420. Cecil diary, April 8, 1919.

23. *I.P.*, vol. 4, pp. 420–421. Auchincloss took House's letter on April 9 to Wilson and Cecil, and understood that both approved it, Auchincloss diary, April 9, 1919.

24. *I.P.*, vol. 4, p. 422. Reporting to Lloyd George on his talk with House on April 10, Cecil wrote that he showed House the admiralty's figures on the strength of the two navies, indicating they would be about equal in 1923 on the basis of present plans. House "was not in a position to go into full detail" but quoted his experts as of the opinion that the American fleet as contemplated would be only about two-thirds the size of the British. "It is possible," Cecil wrote, "our naval advisers—not for the first time—have misled us as to the facts," Lord Robert Cecil to Lloyd George, April 10, 1919, Lloyd George papers, F / 6 / 6 / 33.

too important. In his view Cecil was "one of the few rafts floating in the sea that could be used at all."[25] That afternoon he received a letter from Cecil, stating that Lloyd George thought it would be the duty of America and England to co-operate cordially in exchanging information as to their naval programs. The prime minister wished to remind the president of "Great Britain's special position as to sea power." A memorandum accompanying the letter recorded the House-Cecil conversation of the morning. Thus the incendiary subject of freedom of the seas was kept out of the formal sessions of the Commission on the League of Nations and those of the Supreme Council.[26]

There was still no assurance as to the position the British government might take in respect of the Monroe Doctrine when the Commission on the League met that very evening. Informing Cecil that Wilson would present an amendment, House said: "We would like your support, but of course you can oppose it if you see fit." Cecil, seeming very worried, said he could make no promise.[27]

The Americans had given consideration to recommendations from Washington that reflected the strong national tradition of isolation and a deep distrust of radical change.[28] William Howard Taft, who on March 18 advised that a Monroe Doctrine amendment "alone would probably carry the treaty through the Senate," stated ten days later that without such a reservation the treaty would not be accepted by public opinion in the United States.[29]

Suggestions that Elihu Root had sent were analyzed at Paris by David Hunter Miller and for the most part rejected. A concession already had been made to Root's views by amendment of Article XIII, specifying the disputes that could be submitted to arbitration.[30] The most vital of the criticisms, however, and that to which a public statement made by Root was chiefly devoted, was directed at the clause that was most sacred to Wilson—Article X. Root feared that in the course of time this article might transform the League of Nations into "an independent alliance for the preservation of the status quo."[31]

Actually, Wilson shared Root's dread of erecting any barrier against legitimate

25. Auchincloss diary, Miller, vol. 1, entries of April 10, 1919. House came to regard the English aristocrat as "the strongest of all the British—a great man, yet a bit spoiled by his ecclesiastic bee," House-Seymour conversation, March 17, 1920, Y.H.C. In June 1919 House recorded in his diary that Cecil was "a brilliant fellow," but one had "the feeling that at any time he may go off at a tangent." In the opinion of Cecil, House shared with Wilson the distinction of being "the only two men of real courage among the Americans," Cecil diary, May 9, 1919.

26. Armin Rappaport, "Freedom of the Seas," p. 395.

27. Bonsal, *Unfinished Business,* pp. 202–203.

28. See above, p. 191.

29. Tumulty to Wilson, March 28, 1919, Wilson papers.

30. Specific suggestions from Root were forwarded by Polk to Lansing on March 27, 1919. Cables in N.A., R.G. 256, 185.111 / 197. Miller, *Drafting,* vol. 1, pp. 298–301. Cf. above, pp. 191–192.

To Miller it seemed unnecessary, with so many revisions pending, to seek a formal statement of anything as obvious as the League's right to call for the codification of international law. The international inspection of armaments, proposed by Root, already had been advanced by the French and had been found to be unacceptable to the English-speaking delegates. Miller also rejected an objection on the part of Root to the amendment made to Article XV, reserving domestic matters, which Root criticized because it gave the council of the League power to determine what questions were "domestic," Miller, *My Diary,* vol. 1, entry of April 1, 1919.

31. Jessup, *Root,* vol. 2, pp. 389–396.

political change. The president had attempted to guard against the development of a twentieth-century "Holy Alliance" by inserting Article XIX, which provided for territorial adjustment when all parties were in agreement. He was advised by Miller that the political aspirations of peoples would not be suppressed by Article X so long as the Covenant provided for its own revision and so long as member nations could withdraw as provided by the amendment already adopted.

Wilson was persuaded, however, that it would be well to respond to pleas that the Covenant be amended so that it would specifically acknowledge the force of the Monroe Doctrine—a shibboleth as sacred to Americans as was sea power to Englishmen. When Wilson's advisers met with no success in devising a formula that would satisfy all parties, the president tried his hand at it, using language that Taft had suggested. Immediately he encountered objection from Cecil. Proposing an amendment to Article X that defined the Monroe Doctrine without mentioning it specifically, the president received through House a counterproposal from the British that named it without defining it, and at the same time would perpetuate the force of existing treaties of arbitration.[32]

On the evening of April 10—the day on which Lenin's proposal of peace talks expired—the Commission on the League of Nations met for a second reading of the Covenant. British approval of any sort of Monroe Doctrine amendment was still not assured. Although Wilson had just recovered from his severe illness and was engaged all day in strenuous sessions of The Four, he pleaded his cause eloquently. Since the first reading, the entire text of the Covenant had undergone polishing by a committee on which House and Miller represented the United States. Despite the fact that no one could suggest any hypothetical situation in which a violation of the Monroe Doctrine would not be also a breach of the Covenant, and despite Wilson's own belief that specific mention of the Monroe Doctrine in the Covenant would be "mere repetition,"[33] the president explained carefully on April 10 why it now seemed necessary to specify. He said that to doubters in the United States who asked whether the Covenant would destroy the Monroe Doctrine, he had replied that not only was the doctrine confirmed by the Covenant but that actually it was extended to the whole world. This led many Americans to ask whether, if this was so, there would be any objection to making a statement of this fact in the Covenant. It was in response to this reasonable question that Wilson now asked the commission to make explicit something that was already indicated. To reassure certain conscientious Americans, he said, he merely wished to have it stated in plain language that the Monroe Doctrine was not inconsistent with the Covenant.[34]

32. Baker, vol. 1, pp. 327–331.

33. *Ibid.*, p. 327.

34. When Bourgeois asked "Does the Monroe Doctrine contain anything inconsistent with the Covenant?" Wilson replied, "Not so far as I can see. I tried to explain in America that the amendment was unnecessary. But they wanted it put in," notes handwritten by James Butler at the meeting of April 10 of the Commission on the League, read in his study at Trinity College, Cambridge, October 1959. Butler remembered that at one point in the discussion of Article X, Lord Robert Cecil questioned the wisdom of the unqualified guarantee. "Do we really mean this?" he asked; and an American secretary whispered, "Thank God for this man." Miller, *My Diary*, vol. 1, entry of April 1.

Wilson had proposed before the Senate, early in 1917, "that the nations should with one accord adopt the doctrine of President Monroe as the doctrine of the world . . . that all nations henceforth avoid

Immediately both aspects of the Monroe Doctrine were called in question. A Brazilian delegate asked whether the proposed amendment to the Covenant would prevent the League from acting in the Western Hemisphere. He was assured that it would not; the League would henceforth uphold the principles that heretofore the United States had supported alone. At the same time the French delegates, seeking protection against renewed German aggression, saw in the proposed amendment a loophole through which the United States might escape obligations in Europe. When Professor Larnaude said that such an eventuality would be unfortunate, the president replied that if his nation signed the Covenant, it "would be solemnly obliged to render aid in European affairs, when the territorial integrity of any European State was threatened by external aggression." The minutes do not record that he qualified this statement with any reference to the constitutional powers of the Congress whereby it could nullify Article X by refusing to declare war.[35] The French, aware that the American response to renewed aggression in Europe in the future would be subject to public opinion in the United States, were not satisfied. They sought a precise guarantee. Finally, Wilson asked why the French delegates distrusted America and wished to make it impossible; by opposing the amendment under consideration, for the United States to join the League.

In the give-and-take at the critical meeting of April 10 Cecil, whose position had been in doubt, came to the support of Wilson. Though in agreement with the French contention that it was unfortunate to single out the Monroe Doctrine for mention in a reservation, he sought to answer the French misgivings. He urged them to accept the fact that the American amendment merely lent emphasis to what was already fully provided by the Covenant. It was Lord Robert Cecil who, suggesting a way to compromise, proposed that the American reservation be accepted as an amendment to Article XX. Thus they might avoid the appearance of diluting the guarantee of Article X.

Near midnight, after hours of debate, Wilson made a memorable speech, brimming with persuasive sentiment and playing upon the popular revulsion against despotism. It evoked both surprise and admiration. Recalling that President Monroe had first promulgated his doctrine to check the spread of absolutism, he asked: "Are you now going to debate this issue, are we going to scruple on words when the United States is ready to sign a Covenant which makes her forever a part of the movement for liberty? This is not a little thing, this is a great thing. Gentlemen, you cannot afford to deprive America of the privilege of joining with you in this movement."[36]

---

entangling alliances which would draw them into competitions of power. . . . There is no entangling alliance in a concert of power. When all unite to act in the same sense and with the same purpose, all act in the common interest and are free to live their own lives under a common protection." Again, in September 1918, he had said: "Only special and limited alliances entangle; and we recognize and accept the duty of a new day in which we are permitted to hope for a general alliance which will avoid entanglements."

35. "It could not be argued legally," wrote Frank L. Warrin, Jr., Miller's assistant, "that the Congress would retain a 'right' to fail to honor a national obligation assumed by solemn treaty; but the fact remained that by exercising its constitutional right to declare war, the Congress could in effect nullify the treaty," letter, Warrin to the author, March 28, 1968.

36. Notes of Whitney Sheppardson, American secretary of the commission, quoted in Miller, *Drafting*, vol. 1, p. 448. Bonsal, p. 184.

The meeting of April 10 ended in some confusion. The next morning Miller predicted that the French spokesmen would raise their point again. They did, that very evening.[37] In a session of the commission that was its last, they proposed to amend the American amendment. The sense would then be that understandings such as the Monroe Doctrine are not incompatible with the provisions of the Covenant insofar as they do not prevent members from executing their obligations.

Wilson immediately protested that any amendment in such terms would cast unwarranted suspicion on the Monroe Doctrine. He went on to warn the French that if they were to oppose the American amendment publicly, the effect on opinion in his country would be most unfortunate. He rejected the French redraft. They then presented a diluted version that was so devoid of meaning that it seemed to confirm a rumor that they cared nothing about the amendment on the Monroe Doctrine and regarded it as a good thing to trade on.

Fortunately, House, perceiving the fundamental basis of French obstruction, had been making the most of his rapport with Clemenceau. In a talk on the morning of April 10 House had found Clemenceau disinclined to support the protests of Bourgeois.[38] Accordingly, in the final session of the League commission on the eleventh, when the president seemed momentarily disposed to make some concession to the objections put forward by the French, House whispered that they "could go to Hell seven thousand feet deep."[39] Finally, Wilson declared the ambiguous proposal defeated, and the French spokesmen gave notice that they would be heard from again at the next plenary session of the Peace Conference.

About a half hour after midnight Cecil asked how much longer the meeting would continue. House replied: "Until daylight or until we are finished." Experience had taught the colonel that it was the last quarter hour of such a session that got results. "Everyone practically gave up," he recorded in his diary, "and we passed matters almost as fast as we could read them during the last fifteen minutes. . . . It was an exhibition of Anglo-Saxon tenacity. The president, Cecil, and I were alone with about fifteen of the others against us, and yet in some way we always carried our point."[40] The commission accepted the basis of compromise that Cecil had proposed.[41] An amendment was included in the Covenant as Article XXI, affirming "the validity of international engagements, such as treaties of arbitration or regional understandings like the Monroe Doctrine, for securing the maintenance of peace." Actually, the doctrine was neither an international engagement nor a regional understanding. However, this American manifesto became for the first time a part of an international engagement.

In the meetings of the League commission in which this special concession was made to American sentiment, the Japanese delegates met resistance to their efforts to satisfy their people's feelings on a matter of high principle. In the final meeting of the commission, Japan's spokesmen presented their plea for the explicit recog-

37. Miller, *My Diary,* vol. 1, pp. 238–239; *Drafting,* vol. 1, pp. 442–450.
38. According to Bonsal *(Unfinished Business,* p. 203), Clemenceau said: "Larnaude is getting on my nerves and Bourgeois is sapping my vitality."
39. Miller, *My Diary,* vol. 1, April 11, 1919; *Drafting,* vol. 1, p. 454.
40. House diary, April 11, 1919.
41. See above, p. 306.

nition of racial equality that had been denied in February.[42] This was opposed by the British delegates, who felt obliged to heed the violent objections of Hughes of Australia. He continued to insist that the proposal of Japan would conflict with the "White Australia" policy of his government, and he looked for support from anti-Japanese sentiment on the Pacific coast of the United States.[43]

During March the Japanese had continued to seek the support of the American and British delegates for an amendment to the preamble of the Covenant.[44] Japan's case was presented by Ambassador Ishii in a statement that went to Wilson,[45] and also in an address at a dinner of the Japan Society in New York on March 14. Ishii denied that a recognition of racial equality would be exploited to increase Japanese immigration into the United States. Nevertheless, Western senators were wary of this possibility, and there was a fear that American opposition to an amendment on racial equality might result in abandonment of the restrictions that Japan was imposing on emigration to America.[46]

After Wilson reached Paris in mid-March, reports came from Ambassador Morris at Tokyo of indications that the Japanese government had decided to forgo its contention and to claim compensation for its forebearance when its claims in China were considered.

Japanese opinion of the League of Nations was cynical, suspecting that the English-speaking peoples wished to make the new organization an instrument for dominating the world. Almost all of the Japanese press was anti-American. The policy of the United States with respect to Siberia, Manchuria, and Shantung was thwarting the ambition of the Japanese and hurting their pride.[47] Baron Makino went so far as to announce at a press conference on April 2 that if his petition for an amendment to the Covenant was denied, his government might refuse to join the League of Nations.[48]

Obviously, the peacemakers would have to make some concession to Japan in order to win its adherence to the League; and it appeared that the most effective concession might be in the matter of its territorial claims. The president therefore could safely accept the veto by the delegates of the British Empire of a modified declaration of racial equality that Makino eloquently brought before the Commission on the League at its final meeting on April 11. Wilson and House abstained when late in the evening the Japanese pressed their resolution to a vote. Only six

---

42. See above, p. 119.

43. "Hughes, according to his own story, drafted a cable, which he showed to House, to be sent to every editor on the Pacific coast of the United States if the Japanese amendment was adopted." L. F. Fitzhardinge, "W. M. Hughes and the Treaty of Versailles, 1919," 139.

44. See Lauren, "Human Rights in History," 266–267; and Curry, *Woodrow Wilson and Far Eastern Policy*, pp. 253–257.

45. Dispatch, March 4, 1919, B. Long for the president, enclosing a statement just handed to Long by Ishii, Wilson papers. The *Washington Post* suggested that a refusal of the plea of Ishii might result in alliance by Japan with Germany and Russia. Dispatch from Morris to the secretary of state, January 2, 1919, *F.R., P.P.C.*, vol. 1, p. 493; Polk to Ammission, March 15, 1919, N.A., R.G. 256, 185.111 / 144; Phillips to Ammission, two dispatches, April 4, 1919, 185.111 / 225.

46. Lauren, 268.

47. Dispatches, Polk to Ammission, March 20, 1919, quoting dispatch of March 17 from Morris (Tokyo), Auchincloss diary; Morris to State Department, March 20, 1919, L. Harrison papers, box 106.

48. Lauren, 269 and n. 80.

voices were opposed to the measure, against eleven in favor. At this juncture House scribbled a note for the president: "The trouble is that if this commission should pass it, it would surely raise the race issue throughout the world."

Wilson, who was in the chair, accepted the suggestion that a formal acknowledgment of racial equality could in effect only emphasize the existence of the primordial vicissitude of racial divergence. Members of the American Senate of that day would surely question a covenant that put the yellow man and the black man on a par with the white. The president, protesting "the utmost friendship . . . and . . . a view to the eventual discussion of these articles," offered the opinion that it would not be wise now to risk the incitement of public controversies. He declared that the amendment failed to be adopted because it was not unanimously accepted, a ruling that a French delegate promptly but unsuccessfully challenged. Wilson justified his insistence on unanimity by describing this matter as one of substance rather than procedure. He said that in his opinion no one would ever interpret the result of the evening's discussion as a rejection on America's part of the principle of equality of nations.[49] Thus was vetoed a pronouncement with which many of the English-speaking delegates agreed in principle but that in practice would make it impossible for parts of the British Empire to accept the League of Nations.

The Japanese delegates, understanding the desire of the Americans to avoid public controversy, accepted the verdict calmly. In deference to opinion in Japan and on the advice of House, Makino was permitted to state his case at the next plenary session of the Peace Conference, and he did so with great dignity but to no better effect.[50] National pride was further injured; Japanese journals began to attack Wilson personally; and Japanese policy became the more insistent when a territorial settlement was made with respect to China. House, who understood the force of the obligation that the Japanese delegates felt to their people in the presence of victory, was not unmindful of the discreet withdrawal of Japan's claim for race equality when he later came to consider their demands for territory.[51]

The revised Covenant as polished by the drafting committee came before the plenary session on April 28. At this time the French and Japanese delegates again introduced their reservations. However, Clemenceau, faithful to a promise that he had made to House, summarily ended the discussion by declaring the Covenant adopted. At this plenary session Wilson explained the revisions of the Covenant and introduced a motion that House had prepared, nominating Sir Eric Drummond as secretary-general of the League and naming nations that were to constitute the council and the committee on organization. The passage of the motion had the effect of putting the shaping and agenda of the League to a large degree under the control of Colonel House.[52]

The Covenant, standing at the beginning of the Treaty of Versailles, was built upon concepts that had been made familiar before World War I by jurists meeting

49. Miller, *Drafting*, vol. 3, p. 465.
50. House diary, April 15, 1919.
51. Seymour to the author, June 19, 1963. See Lauren, 269–277. Memorandum to Northcliffe, April 12, 1919, Steed papers, Archives of the *Times*, London.
52. House diary, April 10, 11, and 18, 1919. See below, ch. 27.

at The Hague and by the series of bilateral treaties of arbitration that had been negotiated by the American State Department. Articles XII through XVI provided for noncompulsory reference of disputes either to a Permanent Court of International Justice or to the League's council, and for a "cooling off" period before the exercise of that most ancient attribute of national sovereignty—the right to resort to war. At the same time the new charter for world order recognized the fundamental change in the political thought of the world that Elihu Root had defined in August 1918.[53] Articles X and XI, whereby any aggressive breach of the world's peace took on the aspect of a criminal act, comprised the only part of the Covenant that might be thought to give the League the aspect of a superstate. Article XI opened the way to conciliation, "the oldest of all diplomatic devices."[54] The president described Article XI, inserted by him in an early draft, as his "favorite article." He depended on this provision and upon that in Article XIX to compensate for the absence from the covenant of any specific affirmation of the right of self-determination.[55] Counting primarily on *ad hoc* negotiation of issues as they might arise rather than on judicial interpretation of a code of law, the framers of the Covenant adhered to the English tradition of lawbuilding. By requiring a unanimous vote for decisions by both the council and the assembly, they gave assurance to nations jealous of their sovereignty that the League would not become a superstate.[56]

For the first time, delegates of the nations of the civilized world accepted a covenant governing the conduct of their political relations.

The creation of the Covenant was essentially an Anglo-American achievement. It did not please Lloyd George, who was inclined to curse the League on several grounds and especially because of the sharing of power in the council by four small nations representing 50 million people at most with five great powers who spoke for some 750 million.[57] Nevertheless Wilson, after exerting pressure for more than three months, had brought Europeans to accede to the concept that the Americans considered "the primary essential, the foundation of the whole diplomatic structure of the peace."[58] The sublime faith of Anglo-Saxon liberals in public opinion as a sanction that would render international policing obsolete was now enshrined in a formal code.[59]

The Christian gentlemen who were the chief sponsors of the League exchanged felicitations. "I feel," Wilson wrote to Cecil, " . . . that the laboring oar fell to you and that it is chiefly due to you that the Covenant has come out of the confusion

53. See Walworth, p. 8.

54. James T. Shotwell, *The Long Way to Freedom* (New York, 1960), pp. 431–432. Shotwell called Article XI "the subtlest and most effective instrument of peace in the history of the League."

55. *I.P.*, vol. 4, p. 286.

56. "National claims and interests were not to be written into a fixed international constitution and then interpreted by a Supreme Court; rather they were to be discussed and negotiated until, reduced to tolerable proportions, they could be fitted into a reasonable place in the structure of international relations," Lord Eustace Percy, *Maritime Trade in War* (London, 1930), p. 31. For the text of the Covenant, see the Appendix.

57. Churchill, *Aftermath,* cited in Egerton, *Great Britain and the Creation of the League of Nations,* p. 172.

58. Commentary on Point Fourteen, *I.P.,* vol. 4, p. 200.

59. See E. H. Carr, *The Twenty Years Crisis 1919–1939* (London, 1940), pp. 30–35.

of debate in its original integrity. May I not express my own personal admiration of the work you did and my own sense of obligation?'' To this the towering aristocrat replied that it had been an honor to work with the president in so great a cause. But the Covenant, he wrote, was still a ''skeleton,'' a dead body unless a spirit could be infused into it. ''For that we must look under God to the peoples of the world and especially to those of America and England.''[60]

On May 8 Wilson revealed a vision of an Anglo-Saxon ''manifest destiny'' to an English officer who introduced himself and then ventured to ask why a certain boundary recommended by a committee of experts had been approved despite its offense to the principle of self-determination. In reply Wilson invoked the power of the League of Nations to rectify any mistake. ''We Anglo-Saxons,'' Wilson asserted, ''have our peculiar contribution to make toward the good of humanity in accordance with our special talents.'' Naming those talents, he went on: ''The League of Nations will, I confidently hope, be dominated by us Anglo-Saxons; and it will be for the unquestionable benefit of the world. The discharge of our duties in the maintenance of peace and as a just mediator in international disputes will redound to our lasting prestige. But it is of paramount importance that we Anglo-Saxons succeed in keeping in step with one another.'' The questioner, seeing ''greatness'' in this man who seemed personally unattractive, fell into step with him and said: *''Idealism and realpolitik perfectly blended.''* And Wilson replied: ''That should be the aim of every statesman.''[61]

In one particular the British delegates questioned the text of the Covenant that was adopted on April 11. Article IV provided that the executive council of the League would include, with representatives of the five great powers, those of ''four other States which are members of the League.'' Since this formula would exclude the dominions if they were held not to qualify as ''States,'' they asked for a revision. Although House was of the opinion that the dominions should not have seats in the council, Prime Minister Borden of Canada convinced Wilson on May 1 of the validity of the British case; and on the sixth the president joined with Clemenceau and Lloyd George in signing a memorandum to Borden that granted the plea of the dominions. Thus Wilson, overruling House, provoked criticism by Anglophobes and by labor[62] in the United States and raised an issue that was seized upon by his political opponents.[63]

The French delegates took less satisfaction than the British in the Covenant as

---

60. Wilson to Lord Robert Cecil, May 2, 1919, Lord Robert Cecil to Wilson, May 4, 1919, Wilson papers.

''The completed Covenant consisted of elements both evolutionary and revolutionary,'' Tillman has written, ''of which the former were essentially British in origin and the latter American,'' *Anglo-American Relations,* pp. 299–300.

61. James Strachey Barnes, *Half a Life,* pp. 322–325.

62. A committee of the AFL told Tumulty that acceptance of Borden's proposal would provoke the opposition of American labor to the League of Nations. Cable, Tumulty to Wilson, May 2, 1919, Wilson papers.

63. Bonsal, pp. 204–205; Tillman, pp. 298–299. In a speech delivered at Spokane on September 12, 1919, Wilson defended the rationality of his position on this issue: ''As we can always veto, always offset with one vote the British six votes, I must say that I look with perfect philosophy upon the difference in number,'' *P.P.,* vol. 6, p. 161.

finally adopted. The press of the nation made it clear that the public was not pleased by the refusal of the English-speaking members of the commission to accept proposals for the adoption of French as the League's official language,[64] for the designation of Brussels as the capital of the League,[65] for an international army, and for the exact definition of the effect that recognition of the Monroe Doctrine would have upon the obligations of the United States under the Covenant.[66] The sentimental pleas of Bourgeois and the legalistic contentions of Professor Larnaude represented an aspect of strategy that was less essential to the people of France than reparation for the costs of the war and the establishment of a secure frontier. A major effort to secure these objectives was being made by Clemenceau while the question of revision of the Covenant was at issue. Nevertheless, the projected League, with all its shortcomings, seemed to French commentators, by and large, to offer a sufficient prospect of security so that it would be preferable to no league at all.[67]

The Covenant, as it was finally drawn, offered no satisfaction of France's critical financial needs. Those who knew, Henry White wrote on April 7, predicted bankruptcy within the next few months if several billion dollars were not supplied for the reconstruction and restoration of industries, and only the United States could provide this sum.[68] In the first weeks of April, however, French hopes that the pattern of wartime economic co-operation might be preserved under the aegis of the new League[69] were shattered. In the Supreme Economic Council, Baruch insisted that the controls that had been useful in time of war must give way to freedom of commerce for the private operators of all nations. The comparatively well-financed Americans, instead of extending further credit to a French government that they thought remiss in collecting domestic taxes, appeared to be intent on developing their own economy on the sound base that only they commanded at the war's end. There was no prospect for a co-operative understanding such as that which Jean Monnet was to live to see realized in Europe a half century later.

According to Monnet's record, Clémentel, "a generous man," said: "That's the end of the solidarity we worked so hard for. Without it, and without the altruistic, disinterested cooperation that we tried to achieve among the Allies and should have extended to our former enemies, one day we'll have to begin all over again." Clémentel went so far as to ask himself whether the industries of the Allies needed protection against those of Germany so much as against competition from the unim-

---

64. Wilson ruled a French amendment on this subject out of order on the ground that the matter was within the competence of the Supreme Council of the Peace Conference, rather than that of the Commission on the League, Miller, *Drafting*, vol. 2, p. 363.

65. In the meeting of the Commission on the League of Nations on April 10 Wilson spoke against locating the League's headquarters in the nation that had suffered most from the war and recommended Switzerland as a detached nation, Sir James Butler's notes. According to Bonsal, many of the things that Wilson said in opposition to Brussels leaked out and gave "great offense," *Unfinished Business*, p. 169.

66. "If the February draft Covenant had a preponderantly good press on its first appearance, the April Covenant, at its debut, met with extreme hostility or skeptical reserves throughout the entire press. Only isolated and relatively feeble voices were raised in its favor," Noble, *Policies and Opinions at Paris, 1919*, pp. 141–143.

67. *Ibid.*, p. 144.

68. H. White to Wickersham, April 7, 1919, H. White papers, Columbia, box 2.

69. See above, pp. 164–165.

paired productive power of the United States.[70]

Wilson had been led to believe that the amendments he had persuaded the Europeans to accept would be sufficient to satisfy most critics of the Covenant in the United States. This belief was affirmed by the immediate reaction from Washington to the revision effected. Taft thought the amendment with respect of the Monroe Doctrine "eminently satisfactory," and Senator Hitchcock cabled: "Congratulations on great success."[71] The revision dealt with the points that had been raised by more than one Republican critic.[72] However, on April 29, the day of the release of the text of the Covenant by the State Department, Senator Lodge wrote to Elihu Root: "Certainly the League in its new form is but a slight improvement over the first draft. The Monroe Doctrine paragraph is entirely worthless because it would leave the interpretation of the doctrine . . . to the League" rather than to the United States. "Article X, which is the most dangerous article in the League, they have not changed."[73] Conceiving that his immediate duty was to hold the party together, Lodge sealed the lips of the Republican senators by telegraphing to each to ask that opinion be reserved until the latest draft had been studied and until there was an opportunity for conference. Professing a desire to examine the Covenant carefully, he said ominously: "It is obvious that it will require further amendments if it is to promote peace and not endanger certain rights of the United States which should never be placed in jeopardy."[74] Moreover, on April 13 Wilson had a discouraging message from Taft, who two weeks earlier had stated that an amendment protecting the Monroe Doctrine "would probably carry the treaty through the Senate." Taft now reported that the executive committee of the League to Enforce Peace was unanimous in the opinion that Republican senators would defeat ratification of the Covenant and would be sustained by the public.[75] These portents suggested to Wilson that his political adversaries could not be satisfied by amendments.

The plenary session of the peace conference that met on April 28 and adopted the Covenant of the League of Nations gave final approval also to a charter that placed upon the League the responsibility for upholding decent standards for workers throughout the world.

A Commission on International Labour Legislation had been created by the Conference in January upon the initiative of Lloyd George.[76] This body had been at

70. Jean Monnet, *Memoirs,* pp. 75–79. Etienne Clémentel, *La France et la politique économique interallié,* pp. 313–317. and W. Diamond, *The Economic Thought of Woodrow Wilson,* p. 182.

71. Cable, Taft to O. Straus, April 15, 1919, N.A., R.G. 59, 763.72119 / 4572.

72. "Hamilton Holt noted that in the five instances where two or more prominent Republicans agreed on any particular recommendation, those points were adopted. He thought that of the five suggestions by Taft and Lodge, all were included, that six of Hughes's seven points were accepted, that four of Root's nine were incorporated, with three others partially recognized," Kuehl, *Hamilton Holt,* p. 277, n. 25, citing H. Holt, "Republican Contributions to the Covenant."

73. Lodge to Root, April 29, 1919, Root papers, L.C. Lodge criticized the amended covenant in detail in letters of April 30 and May 27 to Bryce, Bryce papers, vol. 7, p. 170. To a cousin Lodge wrote that he was receiving many requests "to save the situation." It seemed to him that Wilson was "personally rapidly going down hill." Lodge to John T. Morse, Jr., May 2, 1919, Morse papers, Massachusetts Historical Society. Garraty, *Lodge,* p. 350.

74. Denna F. Fleming, *The U.S. and the League of Nations,* pp. 196–198. Garraty, p. 363.

75. Cable, Tumulty to Wilson, April 13, 1919, Wilson papers.

76. See above, p. 34.

work on a constitution for an International Labour Organization (ILO) that would function within the League of Nations. A draft prepared by British delegates served as a basis of discussion. Its main features were accepted by the end of February; but a sharp cleavage of opinion appeared between the American and European delegates. Officials of the Old World, accustomed to dealing with labor questions by means of national legislation, now proposed an international parliament that would make labor laws for the whole world. At the outset they met with difficulties that arose from variations in technological development and in the organic law of the sovereignties concerned.

The position of Samuel Gompers and H. M. Robinson,[77] the American members of the commission, was not free from embarrassment. Although the power to enact labor legislation was reserved to the several states by the Constitution, the American federal government, in international negotiations, was jealous of its sovereignty with respect to labor as well as to economic matters. The idea of making common cause with European labor movements was unpalatable to the American labor leaders at Paris. Gompers lived at the Grand Hotel with a dozen or so heads of the great unions of the AFL, who were determined that he should not be captured in any way by European socialism.[78]

On March 8 House put the matter in the hands of Professor Shotwell and Major Berry, who was the American commission's liaison with the labor leaders. After preliminary discussion the labor commission appointed a subcommittee.[79] Shotwell, serving as technical adviser, worked earnestly to arrive at a formula that would take account of the constitutional limitations peculiar to the United States. In January he had prepared recommendations for a world labor organization that would be a part of the League of Nations. It was necessary to meet the insistence of Gompers that the United States be protected against international legislation that might establish labor standards below those prevailing in any of the forty-eight states. Accordingly, the Americans proposed a clause allowing the United States to consider international labor measures as mere recommendations to which it might refuse to conform.[80] After long and patient pleading by Shotwell—reinforced at one point by a threat to break off talks and a burst of eloquence from Gompers—the labor commission accepted a compromise worked out by the subcommittee. Gompers and

---

77. Gompers was appointed to represent American labor, and Hurley of the Shipping Board to represent American employers. When Hurley went home on February 4, Robinson of the Shipping Board, a California banker, replaced him. European labor delegates were surprised that the American government did not choose representatives who were more familiar with labor law and administration, Shotwell, *Origins of the International Labor Organization,* vol. 1, p. 129. Shotwell, *At the Paris Peace Conference,* pp. 155–156.

78. *F.R., P.P.C.,* vol. 57, pp. 69–71. Shotwell, *At the Paris Peace Conference,* pp. 199–200, 204. Shotwell ms., O.H.R.O., pp. 131–132. It seemed to Shotwell that Wilson's interest in Gompers reflected the president's concern for his own political position in the United States, Shotwell to the author, April 22, 1960.

79. Shotwell, *At the Paris Peace Conference,* pp. 199 ff. Report of Berry to Grew, March 17, 1919, in *F.R., P.P.C.* Vol. 11, pp. 527–529. Gompers was not a member of the subcommittee. Buckler had a long talk with him and found him "somewhat disgruntled" because the American commission paid so little attention to him. W.H. Buckler to G.G. Buckler, March 12. 1919, Y.H.C. Shotwell, *Origins,* vol. 1, pp. 156 ff.

80. Article 205 of the Treaty of Versailles.

Berry departed from Europe on March 26, leaving the interest of American labor in the hands of Shotwell.

George Barnes, whose subordination to Gompers as vice-chairman of the labor commission had seemed inappropriate to his British colleagues inasmuch as he was the only member of that commission with the rank of plenipotentiary, eventually assumed a position of leadership. He pleaded in the Council of Foreign Ministers for a hearing before the entire Peace Conference in plenary session, but he found Lansing opposed.[81]

On April 3, the day before Barnes made his plea, a labor congress was called in England to discuss developments at Paris.[82] Lloyd George was moved to champion the work of the labor commission. He overcame objections from the dominions by reminding them that they would invite the spread of communism by a refusal to recognize labor in the treaty of peace. It was at his instance that the labor commission at a plenary session of the Peace Conference on April 11 presented two documents containing proposals for inclusion in the treaty: a constitution for an International Labour Organization, and a charter for labor. This session was staged in the magnificent banquet hall of the Quai d'Orsay, a setting calculated to impress the world's workers with the seriousness of the concern of the peacemakers for their welfare.[83]

The first recommendation of the commission defined a constitution and rules of procedure for an international labor conference that would hold its first meeting in October 1919 in Washington. A permanent labor organization, to which all members of the League of Nations would belong, was to consist of a General Conference of delegates representing the member governments and an International Labour Office that would function under a governing board of twenty-four.[84] The League was to finance both the General Conference and the International Labour Office; and the League's secretariat and permanent court would render executive, financial, and judicial services.

Early in the plenary session of April 11, House came into the room, leaned over Wilson's chair, and gave him a suggestion by Shotwell. The president, following it, expressed regret at the absence of Gompers,[85] and undertook in his behalf to give assurance of "the entire concurrence" of the working men of America in the "admirable document" drafted by the labor commission. Wilson promised that a labor conference would receive "a most cordial invitation" to meet at Washington. Clemenceau, amused by proceedings that he thought fatuous, declared the report adopted unanimously, and it went into the treaty of peace.[86]

Thus for the first time a general peace conference prescribed in detail a legislative

81. Marston, *The Peace Conference of 1919*, pp. 94, 179. Robinson to Wilson, April 4, 1919, Wilson papers.

82. Vandervelde, pp. 351–352.

83. Shotwell, *At the Paris Peace Conference*, p. 244.

84. Americans took a prominent part in the work of the I.L.O., which their country eventually joined and which built up an international Labour code by getting the ratification of hundreds of conventions, Shotwell ms., O.H.R.O., pp. 125–127.

85. Lloyd George, for one, did not share this regret. He wrote later that Gompers "helped things along by his discovery that urgent business demanded his immediate return to the States," *The Truth about the Peace Treaties*, p. 653.

86. Shotwell, *At the Paris Peace Conference*, pp. 255–260. Shotwell, ms. in the O.H.R.O., pp. 128–129.

and executive program to advance the interests of the working man. International cooperation advanced into a new domain, although full adherence by the United States was restricted by its constitutional limitation. The constitution of the International Labour Organization bound it closely to the League; and conversely, the Covenant of the League committed its members to establish and maintain the ILO.

The second document presented to the plenary session of April 11 by the labor commission proposed the adoption of a charter establishing the special rights of labor. The most comprehensive and practical of the resolutions of the Bern conference called for this,[87] and many of the labor leaders ardently advocated a sort of bill of rights for workers. Gompers time and again urged the commission to endorse certain general principles for which he had fought and which he had put before an Inter-Allied Labour Conference at London in September of 1915. It seemed to the commission, however, that his articles were too numerous and loosely phrased. They were revised, and nine were presented at the plenary session of April 11.

The proposal of a charter met with opposition. While Barnes presented the formal report of the labor commission, the statesmen of the British Empire took alarm. Most thought the charter a fad, and some a nuisance. Wilson thought it unwise to champion the measure against British opposition while the fate of the League Covenant was in doubt.[88] To a young liberal in the American news bureau the proceedings in the stiflingly hot room seemed "utterly insincere, perfunctory, and unreal." Not a big statesman spoke for it; Orlando actually let his head fall on one side, asleep; the press moved in and out of their seats during the barrenness of the speeches and the monotony of the translation. Not a man gave expression to the social upheaval moving through the world. Clemenceau announced the meeting was adjourned before the nine-point charter could be considered. Balfour, his face flushed, was asked immediately afterward what happened to the nine points. "Points, I am tired of Points," he exclaimed. When the question was put to Clemenceau, he began to cough in the manner not unusual since his wounding. "Points, I have one in here," he said, tapping his chest.[89]

Borden of Canada, asked by Lloyd George to confer with Wilson and Clemenceau, pointed out that the eighth of the nine points might lead to disorder, even rebellion, on the Pacific coast of North America, where there were many immigrant laborers. However, Wilson, admitting the danger, feared that failure to approve the whole charter would have bad results in Europe.[90] When Balfour and others had difficulty in revising clause 8 to their satisfaction, the president tried his hand at it. His draft, which went almost without change into the peace treaty, read: "The standards set by law in each country with respect to the conditions of labor shall have due regard to the equitable and humane treatment of all foreign workers lawfully resident there."[91]

87. Mayer, *Woodrow Wilson, Revolutionary Germany, and Peacemaking*, p. 398.

88. Shotwell, *At the Paris Peace Conference*, pp. 255–260. Barnes, *From Workshop to Cabinet*, pp. 228, 240, 242, 251.

89. Sweetser's notes.

90. General memorandum, No. 16, April 16, 1919, Borden papers, folder 00A98. On Wilson's view of the "Magna Charta" for labor as a cure for the world's industrial unrest, see Levin, *Woodrow Wilson and World Politics*, p. 166.

91. Wilson to H. M. Robinson, April 23, 1919, Wilson papers.

The commission persisted in seeking recognition of this charter that was dear to American labor. Efforts by Balfour, Borden, and Shotwell produced a compromise text[92] that was approved by the plenary session on April 28 and went into the treaty of peace. Action at the highest level was still required, however, to satisfy a demand of the dominions that each should be represented on the governing labor council. After a discussion with his imperial colleagues, Borden pressed the matter with success,[93] despite a protest to Wilson by the American Federation of Labor. The president instructed Tumulty to give out a statement at Washington on the importance of the labor program and to tell Gompers that the compromise text was the "the best that could be got out of a maze of contending interests."[94]

In the final weeks of the Peace Conference, Shotwell continued to devote himself to the affairs of labor. Serving on a committee appointed by the conference to consider German criticism, he detected insincerity in the German contention that labor had not been given a genuine international parliament. It seemed to him that this objection, coming as it did from a government that had just used force to suppress agitating workers in the streets of Berlin, was a political appeal to revolutionaries in the Allied nations.[95] The Council of Four discussed the question of German participation in the labor conference that was to meet at Washington. Clemenceau and Lloyd George were inclined to admit German delegates, but Wilson preferred to leave the decision to the Washington conference itself.[96]

The close association of the international labor program with the League of Nations was both asset and liability to Wilson's prestige. It allayed doubts as to his sincerity among certain elements of European labor that had thrown their weight to his side of the political scales. Nevertheless, there was bitter dissatisfaction among socialists and trades unionists in England. Leftists described Wilson as "beaten" and "a broken reed" whose promises had been flagrantly violated.[97]

The effect of the International Labour Convention upon Wilson's position in the United States was equally varied. La Follette, the great liberal senator, assailed the treaty of peace because it failed to do justice to the cause of labor. Nevertheless, Gompers, after receiving reassuring messages from the president,[98] was able to give

92. Shotwell to Wilson, April 20, 1919, Wilson papers.

93. According to Borden, "President Wilson acted extremely well and overrode advice of his advisers on Labor," Borden to Lloyd George, April 18, 1919, Borden papers, OC474, doc. 49372. *Ibid.*, April 29, May 2, 1919, Lloyd George papers, F / 5 / 3 / 42. Borden to prime minister, Ottawa, May 6, 1919, Borden papers, OC582(1). Shotwell, *At the Paris Peace Conference*, pp. 264–269; *Origins*, vol. 1, pp. 212–220.

94. Cables of May 1, 2, and 3, 1919, Tumulty papers, box 8.

95. *F.R., P.P.C.*, vol. 11, p. 174. Shotwell, *At the Paris Peace Conference*, pp. 306, 309, 313–315, 318–319.

96. Mantoux, *Délibérations*, vol. 2, p. 95.

97. Carl F. Brand, "The Attitude of British Labour toward President Wilson during the Peace Conference," 244–255.

98. On June 20 Wilson, learning that Gompers was complaining bitterly that he had been "sold out" at Paris and was urgently requesting exact information about changes in the labor clauses, cabled to give assurance that the provisions, not materially weakened, would constitute a serviceable *magna charta*. Explaining that the alterations would bring the labor convention into harmony with the League Covenant, he told Gompers that he counted on his "support and sponsorship," dispatch in Wilson papers.

Wilson took pains to cable his personal sympathy when he heard that Gompers had been injured in an automobile accident. Gompers, "The Labor Clauses of the Treaty," in *What Really Happened at Paris*, ed. Seymour and House, pp. 319–335. Shotwell, *At the Paris Peace Conference*, p. 379.

his constituents a report that gratified their desire to have a part in great affairs without sacrificing the standards that prevailed in their own nation. He testified, at a convention of the American Federation of Labor, that although he had not come home with all that American labor thought it should have, he had secured all that it was possible to get. Accepting his advice and that of their Executive Council, the delegates voted overwhelmingly to endorse the League of Nations and its labor provisions.

At the same time, the fact that Americans had made common cause with Europeans of socialist tendencies and had associated their nation with international action as to labor, even though only tentatively and permissively, hurt the sensibilities of certain citizens who were devoted to the American way of life and fearful of its subversion. For example, Democratic senator Charles S. Thomas of the Committee on Foreign Relations thought the labor section of the peace treaty unconstitutional and "the last expression of demagoguery in international affairs and . . . made to order for the intrigues of international communism." This was a major factor in his opposition to ratification of the Treaty of Versailles; and he felt that there were other senators who agreed with him but feared to speak out because of the political power of organized labor.[99] The question of the participation of the United States in the organization of labor on an international scale became another of the many political hazards to congressional approval of the treaty of peace.

99. Thomas, *Silhouettes of Charles S. Thomas* (Caldwell, Idaho, 1959), pp. 200–208.

17

Compromises with France

The Four, having weathered several crises without a break, were coming to grips in April with issues on which it seemed possible that the victorious alliance would split. Five months had passed since the conclusion of the armistice. While American and British idealists had forced the Peace Conference to give much of its time to measures designed to secure peace among all nations, serious threats had arisen to that community of nations which had emerged from the wartime entente.

The malaise into which public opinion had fallen seeped into the journal of the assistant chief of the American press bureau. "So far the Peace Conference has failed magnificently," he wrote. "It has not brought the peace and the new world order for which all humanity cries out. . . . People everywhere are becoming impatient, almost belligerent, at the continuation of discussions that seem to lead nowhere. The question that is posing itself, especially in France, is that most tragic of all questions, 'Have we really won the war?' The statesmen . . . are united in promises of results. . . . They have made similar promises before, always unfulfilled and perhaps worse, unfulfilled without explanation. At the moment . . . the obstacles before an agreement are stupendous. . . . Yet failure . . . would bring about a period of chaos and disruption unparalled in history." Some Americans who hoped for the emergence of "a diplomatic commander-in-chief who might save the peace as Foch had saved the war" thought Woodrow Wilson "the one man in the world" who could fill this role.[1]

In the early weeks of April the anxiety of Great Britain about its sea power had been to some extent allayed. However, Wilson's deep commitment to the peace of the entire world required him to deal with other issues that an expedient politician might wish to dodge. The essential claims of France, Italy, and Japan were still unsatisfied. These major powers, proud and willful, had essential purposes that were too provocative of strife to be entrusted by the Council of Four to advisory bodies. Their claims were considered by the inner council, and a series of crises arose.

The question of the security of France's eastern frontier came to a settlement after Wilson's recovery from illness. Clemenceau was weighing two alternatives in talks with his advisers: France acting alone on the left bank, or France brought back to the frontier of 1814 and allied with America and England. Refusing to commit himself to various policies that were espoused by prominent Frenchmen, Clemenceau was tenaciously exerting the leadership of his beloved country that he felt no one else could exercise so well as he, and that it was expected he would lose as soon as a peace was concluded. On March 25 he gave warning in the Council of

---

1. Sweetser notes, April 6, 1919, Sweetser papers, L.C.

Four that if the Covenant of the League did not provide for military sanctions and the control of German armament, France would require some further assurance.[2]

In furtherance of the offer that Clemenceau received from Wilson and Lloyd George two weeks earlier,[3] a brief note of March 28 from the president to the French government explained that France was to get "in a separate treaty with the United States, a pledge by the United States, subject to the approval of the Executive Council of the League of Nations, to come immediately to the assistance of France as soon as any unprovoked movement of aggression against her is made by Germany."[4]

The unqualified commitment of American power that the president proposed, which seemed unnecessary in view of the League Covenant's guarantee against aggression, had raised serious questions in the minds of Wilson's fellow plenipotentiaries. They were eager to tell the president of their opposition to this idea but found no immediate opportunity to do so.[5] House, in his eagerness to come to an understanding with Clemenceau, ignored the possibility that the proposed pact would be rejected by the United States Senate and thus fell short of European standards of precision and reliability in diplomacy.[6] He submitted to Wilson a draft of a guarantee, recording in his diary that the American commissioners had "accepted it without reserve, excepting Bliss who made tentative reservations." However, a memorandum penciled by Bliss gives evidence to the contrary. "This draft," Bliss wrote, "is a modification of one proposed by Mr. House and which he suggested to meet the French threat that they would not accept the League of Nations unless this promise were made by the United States. Neither Mr. Lansing nor Mr. White nor I approve of this draft or anything like it. It will surely kill the League of Nations Covenant."[7]

Before any text of a treaty of guarantee was finally agreed upon, The Four arrived at an understanding in respect of the Saar basin and the Rhine frontier. Discussion of the question of the Saar had brought Wilson and Clemenceau very close to a break on March 28. The president had asked his advisers to work with their British colleagues to devise some solution that would not allow France to annex the Saar region in disregard of the principle of self-determination; and at the end of March a committee of three experts had been appointed by the Supreme Council to study the question. Professor Haskins, the American member, had proposed that France administer the mining area under a mandate from the League of Nations, that the

2. Loucheur, *Carnets Secrets,* pp. 72, 73. Sweetser diary, April 6, 1919.

3. See above, p. 203.

4. Tardieu, *The Truth about the Treaty,* pp. 204–205. The question of the treaty of guarantee is treated in great detail in Louis A. R. Yates, *The U.S. and French Security,* pp. 44–86.

5. Minutes, ACTNP, March 21, 1919.

6. Actually, the treaty of guarantee, submitted to the Senate by Wilson on July 29, never came to a vote. See below, p. 327 n. 37, pp. 531 and 543.

7. Penciled memorandum dated March 20, 1919, Bliss papers, box 69, "House" folder. Auchincloss diary, March 20, 1919.

Actually, House warned Wilson of the risk of making an arrangement that might seem to suggest that the Covenant of the League of Nations gave inadequate protection. White spoke to Wilson on March 20 of this danger, and he found the president unconcerned, Lansing desk diary, March 31, 1919. *I.P.,* Vol. 4, pp. 394–395. Bonsal, *Suitors and Suppliants,* pp. 216–217. House diary, March 20 and 28, 1919. Auchincloss diary, March 27, 1919.

inhabitants retain their German citizenship, and that after fifteen years a plebiscite be held.[8] In his opinion the French could be depended on to preserve local liberties in order to encourage an ultimate vote in the plebiscite that would favor France, which meanwhile would have ownership of the mines.

While Wilson was ill, he considered a report from Haskins which presented articles proposed by Tardieu. In the opinion of the American expert these articles seemed to contain in substance the necessary basis for working the mines, provided that provision was made for "some special political and economic regime."[9] During the negotiations House explained to Mrs. Wilson that he was not far from an acceptable compromise. A little later she telephoned to say that her husband hoped that House would beware of any commitment to Tardieu. "I replied," House wrote in his diary on April 4, "that these questions had come up with Tardieu only and I was not committed any further than that Tardieu knew my views and knowing them, had prepared the memorandum."[10] Wilson was willing now to grant to France not ownership of the Saar mines, but only "absolute control" of the output for the period that would be required to put the despoiled mines of northern France in working order.[11]

On the morning of April 8 Lloyd George, citing the risk of war that would result if France owned the mines and Germany retained sovereignty over the people, proposed independence for the Saar under the League of Nations, and a customs union with France. House communicated this proposal to Wilson, at the same time transmitting the latest recommendations of Haskins.[12] This paper suggested the creation of a permanent commission to arbitrate conflicts arising from a division of rights between France and Germany.[13]

Wilson received the Europeans in his bedchamber on the afternoon of April 8, the day after the summoning of the *George Washington*. He objected to Lloyd George's proposal and advanced the suggestion of Haskins for an arbitral commission and, after fifteen years, a plebiscite under the auspices of the League. Clemenceau and Lloyd George persisted in opposing a continuation of German sovereignty. When the president conceded that all industrial operations might be under a French customs regime, Clemenceau said that he would "look into that," and the prospect of agreement brightened.

That evening, however, Clemenceau met with Tardieu and Loucheur and decided

8. See above, pp. 267–270.

9. "The Saar Basin," a report of April 5 by Haskins, forwarded by Auchincloss to Wilson, April 6, 1919, describing four meetings at which Haskins had discussed the Saar with Tardieu and Headlam-Morley in accord with instructions given by the Council of Four on March 31, 1919, Wilson papers.

10. Auchincloss diary, April 4, 1919. Actually Tardieu wrote three memoranda. The first is printed in *The Truth about the Treaty*, pp. 266–268. On Wilson's dislike of Tardieu, see above, pp. 152–153, and House diary, May 8, 1919.

11. "Suggestions Regarding the Mines of the Saar Basin," c. April 6, 1919, written on Wilson's typewriter, Wilson papers.

12. Mantoux, *Proceedings*, pp. 142–143. Headlam-Morley's diary, typescript, p. 70. Mantoux recorded that in the meeting of The Four, House spoke politely of Lloyd George's plan, saying: "This statement seems very reasonable to me and I wish to inform President Wilson about it immediately." But House wrote in his diary on the same day that Lloyd George's plans for the Saar "had no earthly value."

13. Miller, *My Diary*, vol. 1, April 7 and 8, 1919.

not to yield. Tardieu stated their position in a note that was circulated very early the next morning. It observed that while Wilson accepted, save for certain amendments, economic arrangements that were made by the committee of three experts that had been appointed at the end of March, he had failed to mention the political or administrative settlement that the committee deemed indispensable. The French insisted that the arbitral commission that the Americans suggested would invite "a regime of perpetual lawsuits." They accepted this proposal and that of a plebiscite only as supplementary to the suggestions advanced by themselves and by Lloyd George.[14]

In the afternoon of the next day, the ninth, Wilson said that to give sovereignty to Germany or a mandate to France would prejudge the outcome of any plebiscite. He did not demand immediate self-determination, saying that he had no wish "to hold inflexibly to the letter of the principle, if it is possible to reach a reasonable solution." He proposed that a commission appointed by the League not only arbitrate disputes but actually administer the Saar without changing the existing laws and institutions. "I have gone a long way to meet you," the President said to Clemenceau. "Do not make it impossible for me to help you to the limit of my ability." Clemenceau, after getting Wilson's assurance that what was proposed would suspend German sovereignty and suppress elections to the Reichstag, said that they were approaching agreement; and Lloyd George remarked to Wilson that Tardieu had made "a great concession" in accepting the proposal of a plebiscite. Wilson now accepted the necessity of satisfying Clemenceau, which House had recognized early in the Peace Conference as a means of preventing the replacement of the Tiger by some less amenable negotiator chosen by President Poincaré.[15]

The three experts withdrew to prepare a draft it was hoped would be final. Working until three in the morning, with the assistance of legal and economic advisers, they produced a paper that became the substance of section 4 of Part II of the Treaty of Versailles. With a few changes in the wording and a decision that the frontier of the district should follow the limits of the present coal basin, agreement was reached except for provisions for the Saar coal after the fifteen-year period. When, on the eleventh, Loucheur sought assurance that France could get Saar coal even if the district passed under German rule, Wilson, warning against any compulsion as to prices or deliveries, asked that the experts devise a plan that would function with a minimum risk to peace. "I am not a prophet," he said. "I would hesitate to impose a regime whose functioning can be delicate for an unlimited time." Wilson expressed misgivings both about burdening the League with this difficult matter and also about the availability of competent international civil servants. He did not wait for an alternate proposal that he had asked Baruch to prepare, and the three experts proceeded to complete their work.[16] They submitted a plan for a plebiscite after fifteen

14. Note of March 31, 1919, Wilson to Clemenceau, Wilson papers. Tardieu, pp. 269, 272–276. Clemenceau to Wilson, April 9, 1919, Y.H.C. According to Headlam-Morley, Tardieu on April 8 refused to consider a continuance of German sovereignty and administration and stated a preference for any of three British plans that would give political control to France, Headlam-Morley's "History of the Saar Settlement," a Foreign Office paper in the possession of Professor Agnes Headlam-Morley.

15. Mantoux, *Proceedings*, p. 154.

16. *Ibid.*, pp. 154, 159–162, 164–167, 176–179, 193. "Draft Proposals" for treaty clauses in respect of the Saar, with slight changes penciled by Wilson, Haskins to Wilson, April 16, 1919, Wilson papers.

years and also an article (to be agreed upon by Baruch and Loucheur) to assure France of a supply of coal after the plebiscite. After some discussion of details with the experts, the report was accepted by The Four on April 13.[17] Wilson had made a successful stand for the principle of self-determination. France was not to be allowed to have a mandate for the Saar that might be used to influence the voting in the proposed plebiscite. Moreover, an equitable arrangement had been made for the repurchase of the coal mines; and Wilson had succeeded in having removed from the original drafts of the Saar articles a few passages that would have imposed hardships on the working population.[18]

At the same time, as a result of the practical negotiations and the American concessions, Clemenceau no longer had reason to think that Wilson, while insisting on the revision of the Covenant of the League of Nations, was unwilling to make some concession to French claims. The Saar compromise, disclosed semiofficially in *Le Temps* on April 14 and publicly commended in general terms by Clemenceau, was welcomed by a large majority of the French journals as the best arrangement possible.[19] This encouraged an accommodation on the question of the left bank of the Rhine.

On March 17 Clemenceau, accepting with gratitude the Anglo-American treaties of guarantee, had refused to consider this provision a substitute for more immediate safeguards for France. The demand of his people for a secure frontier was growing more insistent as signs appeared of German recovery, and strong sanctions were not provided in the League Covenant.[20] Therefore, Clemenceau now suggested that the peace treaty specify, as a guarantee for the execution of the reparations clauses, a date and also precise conditions for the ending of the current Allied occupation of the left bank and the bridgeheads on the Rhine. At the same time, in proposing a ban upon all German military activities in an area fifty kilometers wide on the right bank of the Rhine, he sought the right of inspection by a permanent commission and a right of occupation in case of violation of the terms of the peace treaty. Foch went further, demanding that the Allies occupy the left bank and the bridgeheads permanently, and he was supported in this by public demonstrations. For the most part the demand for a frontier on the Rhine had the approval of the French press, not only that of the Right, but that of Leftist journals that had been ardent in support of Wilson's ideals. Clemenceau's position, put forward in a note of March 17, was reaffirmed in ten other notes written during the following month.[21]

Wilson and Lloyd George, however, stood resolutely against any arrangement that might resemble the German seizure of Alsace-Lorraine in 1871. On April 12,

Baruch, *Public Years,* p. 101. Thinking the report of the experts unfair to Germany and insisting that Germany would not be able to pay reparations without access to adequate coal, Baruch argued that German industry would be severely crippled by the award of the Saar mines to France and the French still would not be satisfied, Miller, vol. 1, April 4, 7, and 9, 1919; Baruch to Wilson, April 9, 1919, Wilson papers. Memo from Baruch for the president, April 7, 1919. Headlam-Morley diary, memo re Saar Valley, April 2, 1919. Wilson to Clemenceau, April 8, 1919, Clemenceau to Wilson, April 9, 1919, Y.H.C.

17. Docket in N.A., R.G. 256, 185 / 113 / 34. Mantoux, *Proceedings,* pp. 164–167, 176–179, 193.
18. Schwabe, *Woodrow Wilson, Revolutionary Germany, and Peacemaking,* pp. 273–275.
19. Noble, *Policies and Opinions at Paris,* p. 214.
20. *Ibid.,* p. 245.
21. *Ibid.,* pp. 246–247. Tardieu, pp. 177–186.

the day after the French assented to the amended Covenant of the League, the president responded to the torrent of French notes. He sent through House to Tardieu what he called "a very solemn warning." This stated that it was necessary to induce Clemenceau to accept the terms that Wilson and Lloyd George had proposed for a treaty of guarantee and for the exclusion of all troops, both German and French, from the left bank except by direction of the League of Nations. Delivering this message to Tardieu, House, according to his record, read "the riot act."[22]

This subject was too critical to be discussed in the conversations of The Four. However, while Lloyd George was in England to address Parliament in mid-April, House and Clemenceau worked out terms. Clemenceau recognized the danger of an independent Rhenish state as a source of future war.[23] He was willing, in view of the proposed treaty of guarantee, to settle for a *temporary* occupation of three strata of German territory on the left bank, with bridgeheads. Having won this concession from the Tiger, who would have to defend it against the opposition of Foch and that of President Poincaré as well,[24] House, exercising his persuasive powers, induced Wilson to agree.[25] (House seized the moment to enlist the aid of Clemenceau in stopping anti-Wilson propaganda in the French press and to get his signature on the letter proposing a program of food relief for the Russian people.)[26] On April 22 Lloyd George acquiesced in the compromise plan.[27] It called for a military occupation of three zones west of the Rhine and three bridgeheads, and the evacuation of a zone and bridgehead at the end of each five years for a fifteen-year period.

When Wilson suggested at this time that there should be two separate pacts of guarantee rather than a tripartite treaty, Clemenceau accepted this arrangement. The treaties were to have effect only if recognized by the League of Nations as consistent with the Covenant, and they could be terminated when its council ruled that the League gave protection enough. In the course of the discussion of the treaties Clemenceau asked an exceedingly embarrassing question. He had received a letter from Senator Lodge, giving notice that neither the Senate nor the people of the United States would consent to any permanent alliance with any nation in the world.[28] Asked about this, Wilson confessed that he could not be sure of the consent of the Senate.[29] Therefore, Clemenceau raised the question of France's position in the

---

22. Wilson to House, April 12, 1919, Y.H.C., with a memorandum giving Wilson's objections, in detail, to amendments proposed by France, copy in Wilson papers. House diary, April 12, 1919.

23. F. L. Warrin, Jr., to the author, December 16, 1965.

24. "Clemenceau's retreat from a strict Rhineland solution produced a crisis that damaged his prestige and embittered his colleagues and constituents," McDougall, *France's Rhineland Diplomacy, 1914–1924*, p. 59.

25. Bonsal, *Unfinished Business*, p. 215. House recorded in his diary on April 15 that Wilson gave in "with a wry face." Five years later House recalled: "Clemenceau and I worked the matter out together and took it to Wilson who reluctantly approved . . . no writing . . . merely a word of mouth agreement," House diary, February 9, 1924.

26. See above, p. 242. Auchincloss diary, April 15, 1919. House diary, February 9, 1924. House to Wilson, April 16, 1919.

27. A statement by Miller, replying to a charge by Lloyd George that he was not consulted sufficiently about the Rhineland agreement, is in the Miller papers, box 7. Also see the statement by Miller in the *New York Times*, February 7, 1924.

28. J. Cambon, "La Paix," 28.

29. Bonsal, *Suitors and Suppliants*, p. 134. Bonsal testified that Clemenceau flatly denied that France was "hoodwinked" and stated that he was told more than once by Wilson that the consent of the Senate could not be counted on, *ibid.*, pp. 216–217.

event that the treaties of guarantee were not ratified by the legislatures at London and Washington. Thus challenged, Wilson went so far as to agree that if at the end of fifteen years the guarantees against unprovoked aggression by Germany were not considered sufficient by the Allied governments, the military occupation might continue to the extent that seemed necessary.[30] Clemenceau, reassured, explained to Poincaré: "We will have the right [under Article 430 of the Treaty of Versailles] to reoccupy or prolong the occupation if we are not paid. . . . Germany will go bankrupt and we will stay where we are, with the Anglo-American alliance." To General Mordacq he said: "I am no longer anxious. I have obtained almost everything I wanted." His "retreat" was indeed, as a French scholar has written, *"plus tactique que fondamentale"*; and he was able to leave the French high commissioner in the Rhineland in a position to continue to control trade in the interest of French commerce.[31]

The Rhineland agreement of April 22 was announced formally to a plenary session of the Peace Conference on the afternoon of May 6 in a formula that Wilson had drafted that morning.[32] Afterward, the president and Lloyd George handed statements to Clemenceau that made their understanding explicit.[33] The prime minister stipulated that the Anglo-French treaty would "come into force" when the Franco-American pact was ratified. At the same time, the American guarantee was made contingent on ratification by Parliament of France's treaty with Great Britain.[34] Thus one of the most difficult of the negotiations having to do with French security was concluded.

Before the outcome of the negotiations with France was announced, there were disquieting rumors from Washington. Wilson had a cable from Tumulty in respect of a headline in the *New York Sun* to the effect that the president had committed the nation to an alliance with France and Great Britain. "This is bound to cause a great deal of dissatisfaction," the message said. "Now is the time to kill these vicious stories."[35]

Wilson and House were feeling the constraint that political pressure exerts upon diplomats who represent democracies. House, fully conscious of the difficulties that the Senate could be expected to raise,[36] nevertheless wrote in his diary: "It [the treaty of guarantee] satisfies Clemenceau and we can get on with the real business of the Conference." The enormity of this offense to sound diplomacy apparently

---

30. Tardieu, p. 211. Mantoux, *Délibérations,* vol. 1, pp. 318–391. *F.R., P.P.C.,* vol. 5, pp. 113, 118, 244, 247–248, 357.

31. Jacques Bariéty, *Les Rélations franco-allemandes après la Première Guerre Mondiale* (Paris, 1977), pp. 62–63.

32. Mantoux, *Délibérations,* vol. 1, p. 493. *F.R., P.P.C.,* vol. 3, p. 334.

33. Wilson asked Miller to draft a note stating the American guarantee to France, to be similar to a note already given to the French by the British. When Miller did so, the president asked whether he would have to do more than merely agree to submit the matter to the Senate, and was told that he would be bound "to do everything except exchange ratifications," Miller, vol. 1, May 6, 1919. A very brief announcement on May 8 stated that the president intended to bring the matter before the Congress.

34. Copy of memo of May 6 to Clemenceau signed by Wilson and Lansing with penciled note by House saying: "This is a copy of the letter which was finally agreed upon," Y.H.C.

35. Tumulty to Wilson, May 9, 1919, Tumulty papers, box 49. The terms of the treaty of guarantee were not published until June 7, 1919, Noble, p. 259. On June 27 the treaty was amended so that it could be validated by a majority vote of the League council, Yates, p. 71.

36. Bonsal, *Suitors and Suppliants,* pp. 248, 254, 264.

did not impress him. He appeared to be undisturbed by this deviation from his pledge to be completely frank with Clemenceau.[37]

Whatever misgivings Wilson may have had about his ability to get his nation's assent to the treaty of guarantee, and indeed to the League of Nations Covenant, were countered to a degree by the adoption of the Monroe Doctrine amendment by the League commission on April 11. Moreover, on the seventeenth, Secretary of War Newton D. Baker came to lunch and reported that in a tour of the American West he had found popular sentiment to be in support of the League about 10 to 1.[38] Encouraged by these omens and by Clemenceau's support for the League, Wilson could now turn his attention to the national demands of other prospective members of the new international community, in particular, to the claims of Poland, Italy, and Japan.

While the question of French security was under consideration in the Council of Four, the problem of stabilizing the frontiers of Poland haunted the peacemakers. Poland was the most essential link in the chain of states upon which French generals depended to form a *cordon sanitaire,* and Clemenceau had at heart the interests of this revived nation.

Paderewski met with The Four at their request on the first day after Wilson's recovery from his illness in April. He said that the Polish Diet desired "a complete alliance" with the Western powers, and that the inclusion of the port of Danzig in Poland was "a question of life and death." He demanded also Upper Silesia and "the reintegration of Lemberg." The ardent pianist-premier shed tears as he spoke. Paderewski seemed to bridge a schism between Dmowski and Pilsudski's men at Paris, and his value as a stabilizing mediator lent force to his repeated threats to resign. Hugh Gibson, just appointed American minister to Poland, wrote from Warsaw that "Paderewski must bring back something tangible." Gibson suggested a loan from the United States to be used to re-establish industries; and to this House replied that the American Treasury had no authority to make loans of this sort at this time but that the Treasury's men at Paris would try to get private credit.[39]

Wilson explained that the essential purpose of the peacemakers was to establish a Polish state on a basis that would give it as few enemies as possible. On April 18 he read to the Council of Four a text based upon the suggestion he had made on April 1.[40] This was accepted as the basis of a territorial settlement in Prussia. Danzig and its environs would be a free city under the protection of the League of Nations, which would be represented by a high commissioner and would serve as adjudicator of an agreement that Germany and Poland were to make within a year. The new free state would be included in the Polish customs system. Poland would

37. House apparently failed to perceive that his excess of optimism exposed him to criticism of his reliability. Such criticism was not lacking among the British delegates, Sir Charles Webster to the author, October 1958. Cf. above, p. 175.

Bonsal recorded that when Clemenceau mentioned the possibility that the Senate would reject Wilson's work at Paris, House "pooh-poohed the possibility," *Unfinished Business,* p. 216.

38. Grayson diary, April 17, 1919.

39. Gibson to House, April 29, 1919, House to Gibson, May 3, 1919, Gibson to Lord, April 29, 1919, Gibson papers, box 8, f. 4, Hoover Institution Archives.

40. See above, p. 262.

have responsibility for the foreign relations and complete control of the railways, posts, telegraph lines, waterways, and port facilities. Special rights of east-west communication were to be guaranteed to Germany, and similar rights to Poland for railways and telegraph lines running north and south. Districts in Prussia in which the preference of the inhabitants was in doubt were to be awarded to Germany or Poland in accord with the results of plebiscites that were to be held under the supervision of an international commission. Prussia's eastern boundary was drawn along an ethnographical line between Germans and Lithuanians, and a strip on the Baltic including the port of Memel was given to Lithuania. A brief discussion led to only a few changes in the drafting of final terms for the Germans.[41]

The compromise settlement satisfied none of the interested parties. More than a year later a plebiscite in Allenstein and Marienwerder went in favor of Germany overwhelmingly; and at Danzig, Sir Reginald Tower, appointed as the League's high commissioner despite American protests, was placed in a position to look out for British interests,[42] In the end, Jean Monnet has written, the situation at Danzig—"frivously entrusted by the Peace Conference to the care of a League yet unborn—touched off the war in 1939."[43]

When they came to consider other sections of Poland's frontier with Germany, The Four found themselves divided in opinion. The Armistice of November 1918 had allowed Germany to leave troops in the eastern territory it held in 1914; and as a result there had been clashes of arms in regions that Poland expected to acquire in the peace settlement.[44] In order to move toward pacification of the regions in question, the Supreme Council took up on March 19 a report of its advisers. The council demanded reconsideration of recommendations that would place some 2 million Germans under Polish rule. There appeared to be no need for haste in deciding upon a line in Poznania, where hostilities were in fact halted despite the inability of a committee representing the Peace Conference to negotiate successfully there.[45]

41. Mantoux, *Proceedings*, p. 217.

Through House, Wilson gave instructions to the experts to revise the draft treaty in accord with the understanding of the Council of Four. Returning the text to the president on April 21, Mezes wrote that the revision omitted a clause providing for the dissolution of councils of soldiers and workers in Danzig, and made the provisions for a plebiscite more general and thus increased the discretionary power of the international commission of control. The East Prussians were assured of equitable access to and use of the Vistula. Mezes reported that these changes, which Lloyd George had desired, were made in conference with Headlam-Morley. Also there were three minor alterations, memorandum, Mezes to Wilson, April 21, 1919, Wilson papers. See Lord, "Poland," in *What Really Happened at Paris*, ed. Seymour and House, pp. 80–81, and Haskins and Lord, *Some Problems of the Peace Conference*, pp. 184–185.

42. See Ian F. P. Morrow, *The Peace Settlement in the German-Polish Borderlands*, pp. 51–52; Komarnicki, *The Rebirth of the Polish Republic*, p. 336; and Seymour and House, pp. 162–163.

43. Monnet, *Memoirs*, p. 86.

44. On various Polish plans for the future of the Baltic states, and the views of American experts, see Lundgreen-Nielsen, *The Polish Problem at the Paris Peace Conference*, pp. 87–88, 257–258, 399–400.

45. Soon after Paderewski visited Poznań in November 1918, the Poles asserted authority in that province, which had belonged to them until 1793 and where they constituted a large majority of the population. A clause in the armistice extension of February 16 provided for the ending of hostilities in this region along a line that recognized the control by Poles of much of the province. See Lundgreen-Nielsen, pp. 178–180. An armistice took effect on March 5; but a detailed agreement negotiated in Poznań by a committee appointed by the Supreme Council (Noulens of France, Howard of Great Britain,

Efforts made at Paris to bring about a truce in eastern Galicia proved ineffective. On March 19 the Supreme Council sent word to the contending Polish and Ukrainian generals that, as a precondition to obtaining a hearing before the Peace Conference, they must cease violating a truce that had been defined under the mediation of a commission on which Professor Lord sat.[46] Wilson, having received a Ukrainian protest against the supplying of munitions by the French to the Polish forces at Lemberg,[47] did not trust the French authorities to carry out the will of the Supreme Council. Accordingly, General Kernan, a member of the commission that the Peace Conference had sent to Warsaw, was ordered to have the council's message delivered by a trustworthy officer to the opposing commanders. A fortnight later Kernan reported that he had himself performed the mission and the commanders had telegraphed their acceptance,[48] in principle, of an immediate suspension of hostilities. The American envoy, however, found it impossible to persuade the Polish officers to accept a proposal of the Ukrainians to make an unconditional truce and to refer the question of a formal armistice to the Peace Conference. The "West Ukrainian People's Republic" was alleged by the Poles to be a Bolshevik Government; and Paderewski argued that military occupation of eastern Galicia, with French assistance, was necessary in order to prevent revolution.[49] At the same time, a Ukrainian spokesman[50] who sought recognition and a place at the Peace Conference asserted at Paris that the Poles were as aggressive as the Soviet armies against which his people had been fighting for several months.[51]

General Kernan returned to Paris from Warsaw on April 10 after a second unsuccessful effort to put an end to the fighting. On the next day he reported to the American commission. In talking with many people, Kernan had formed the opinion that the Poles and the men in French uniform who were "everywhere in evidence" were merely camouflaging their own military designs when they spoke volubly of the threat of bolshevism. He had a "distinct impression" that the Ukrainians

and Kernan of the United States) failed to become effective when the German military authorities refused to accept the conditions, dispatch, Atter to Bass to Ammission, March 19, 1919, Wilson papers. General Kernan's report on the negotiations, stating that the negotiators were "practically put under arrest by the Polish military authorities," is in the Bliss papers, box 70, "corres. with W. W." folder. Bliss forwarded the report to Wilson on March 26. Kernan did not accept the assertion of his French associates that the Germans were scheming to reopen the war in the regions of Poznań and Danzig.

46. The Polish and Ukrainian commanders signed an armistice on February 22, terminable on twelve hours' notice. According to Lord, the Ukrainian general was forced by his troops to give notice that the truce was broken when the Allied mission left Lemberg on March 2, memoranda, Lord to Bullitt, March 4 and 9, 1919, Bliss papers, box 127.

47. Haskins and Lord, pp. 189–195. Dispatch from Bern from Dr. Paneyko, the Ukrainian minister of foreign affairs, to the president of the United States, March 15, 1919. Dispatch from Ammission to U.S. legation, Bern, for Dr. Paneyko, March 17, 1919, Wilson papers.

48. The order to Kernan was sent in a telegram of March 20, Wilson papers. U. S. Grant III to Bliss, March 19, 1919; telegram, Bliss to A. C. Coolidge (Vienna), March 20, 1919, Bliss papers, box 173, "Poland" folder.

49. Wilson to Lansing, March 19 and 20, 1919; Bliss to Kernan, March 20, 1919; Kernan to Ammission for Bliss, March 28 and 30, 1919, Wilson papers. Kernan had sent several reports to Bliss on the aggressiveness of French officers, one of whom became commander of the Polish armed forces, Lowry, "The Generals, the Armistice, and the Treaty of Versailles, 1919," pp. 266–267.

50. Gregoire Sydorenko, who claimed to be president of a Ukrainian delegation at Paris, Borden to Lloyd George, March 27, 1919, Lloyd George papers, F / 5 / 3 / 24.

51. Ukrainian appeal to the Peace Conference, April 4, 1919, and later protests, Archives du M.A.É., Europe 1918–29, f. 839.

were most eager for a truce and that their leaders were intelligent men "by no means Bolshevik and sincerely desirous of building up a great Ukrainian Republic." He found no evidence of Bolshevik aggression against Poland. He pointed out that "the military disease," once fastened upon the Polish state, was going to be difficult to eradicate.[52] In Kernan's opinion a formal armistice could be concluded much better in Paris than at the front. Kernan's concluding paragraph was: "I advise strongly against Inter-Allied Missions where information or concrete results are sought. Send Americans alone upon such tasks."

Wilson, receiving Kernan's report on April 11,[53] formed the opinion that the Ukrainians were "playing the game" and the Poles were not.[54] He asked General Bliss to discuss the matter of military aggression "in the most earnest fashion" with Paderewski. Carrying out this charge, Bliss reported that the Polish government accepted in principle the armistice suggested by a commission that the Supreme Council had set up on April 3.[55]

Paderewski, however, continued to play upon the menace of bolshevism. He asserted that a temporary armistice would enable the Ukrainians to undermine the Polish army with Bolshevik propaganda. Moreover, he said that the Ukrainians had three or four governments, no one of which was able to speak for them. After a conversation with Paderewski, Bliss recommended that The Four demand that the Polish government order a suspension of hostilities pending final decisions at Paris. At the same time, Bliss wrote, the Poles should be assured that the matter of fixing a boundary in Galicia would be taken up at once. Bliss described the existing situation as "an affront to the Council" and recommended that if the Poles did not accept unreservedly the proposal of a truce, their supplies from the West ought to be cut off.[56]

The president brought Bliss's report before The Four and went so far as to suggest that if the Poles did not refrain from using General Haller's army to build up their force[57] at Lemberg, the Peace Conference could, if necessary, threaten to stop the American relief program. His colleagues concurred, although Lloyd George was fearful that too great severity toward Poland might stimulate bolshevism there.[58]

On May 5 Paderewski appeared again before The Four. Lloyd George, impatient with the militarism of minor nations, confronted him with the charge that Polish troops were still advancing in Galicia. In reply Paderewski explained that his efforts to restrain his ardent compatriots had almost caused the fall of his ministry. He argued that it was impossible to trace a racial frontier in eastern Galicia, which had

52. Confidential memorandum, Major General F. J. Kernan to the ACTNP, April 11, 1919, Wilson papers.
53. Lansing to Wilson, April 11, 1919, with enclosures, Wilson papers.
54. Balfour's report of the session of the Council of Four on April 15, 1919, P.R.O., FO / 800 / Cf / 19 / 1.
55. Bowman and Colonel Embick were the American members of the commission, General Botha the chairman. Lord recommended the creation of this commission in a memo to the president dated April 1, 1919, copy in the Bliss papers, box 173, "Poland" folder.
56. Bliss to Wilson, April 18, 1919, Wilson papers. Bliss to Close for the president, April 17, 1919, Bliss papers, box 70, "Luxembourg" folder. Also see letter, Bliss to Weygand, April 18, 1919, Wilson papers, and memorandum, W. B. Wallace to Bliss, April 19, 1919, Bliss papers, box 70.
57. See above, p. 260.
58. Mantoux, *Délibérations*, vol. 1, p. 312.

been under German and Austrian influence, and that the region should become a part of Poland, with guarantees of local autonomy. He claimed that the adversaries had broken a truce, and it had then been impossible to prevent retaliation by his people. After he returned to Warsaw he sent word through the American legation there that he had stopped an advance of Haller's army to Lemberg.[59] But although he persuaded the Diet against aggression in Lithuania,[60] he could not induce it to give up military operations at Lemberg; and he asked the Council of Four to relieve him of the incubus under which he labored in Warsaw by virtue of his opposition to warfare in Galicia.[61]

Paderewski continued to bring his persuasive talent to bear upon House. Early in April he urged the colonel to sit for a sculptor and a painter, and told him that the Polish people intended to erect a monument to him.[62] House, flattered and also sincerely convinced that Paderewski was the man most likely to succeed in conducting a responsible government amid the turmoil of Polish politics, suggested that Wilson write a friendly letter in commendation of the work of the Polish statesman. The president, who was persuaded that aid could be extended to Poland only as long as Paderewski was in charge, did as House suggested. Moreover, Hoover gave written assurance that shipments of foodstuffs and raw materials could be financed. With these affirmations of American support in his pocket, Paderewski had "something tangible" to show to his people, although he had not been able to end the feud of Dmowski and his French friends with Pilsudski nor to overcome Anglo-American opposition to Polish expansion.[63]

Wilson felt a responsibility to determine a boundary between Poland and the Ukraine that would be conducive to peace.[64] However, the Commission on Polish Affairs, which on April 21 proposed an eastern frontier for Poland north of the latitude of Kholm, did not extend it southward because of the failure of the contenders in Galicia to cease fighting.[65] Bonsal, asked by House to clarify the situation

59. Two telegrams, Gibson to Ammission, May 14, 1919, *F.R., P.P.C.*, vol. 5, pp. 711–715. Gibson reported that Paderewski promised "to maintain a stiff front and do all he could to fulfill the wishes of the president." President Pilsudski also reported efforts to restrain Haller's army from fighting in Galicia, translation of dispatches from French minister at Warsaw dated May 27, circulated at the request of Clemenceau, Wilson papers. See Lundgreen-Nielsen, pp. 314 ff.

A dispatch from Reginald C. Foster, which Lord forwarded to Wilson, reported that Haller's troops were not used in any way in the Polish advance through eastern Galicia. Foster observed that the backbone of the Ukrainian army was clearly stamped "made in Germany," and the so-called "Ukrainian national movement" seemed to be a scheme of a few ambitious individuals who had German and Austrian help. He found no Ukrainian government with a capacity for preserving order. Wilson wrote Lord that he took great satisfaction in reading Foster's report to his three colleagues, documents in Wilson papers. Mantoux, *Délibérations,* vol. 2, p. 7.

60. On May 24, in the Council of Foreign Ministers, Lansing checked a French move to facilitate the replacement of Germans in Lithuania by Poles. On Polish aggression see Stanley W. Page, *The Formation of the Baltic States,* pp. 169–173.

61. "The Present Crisis in Poland," a paper dated May 19, 1919, by H. J. Paton, an English expert who worked with Bowman on Polish boundaries, P.R.O., FO / 800 / 216.

62. House diary, April 6, 1919. Bonsal, *Suitors and Supplants,* p. 252.

63. See Lundgreen-Nielsen, pp. 307–313, 353–355.

64. Mantoux, *Délibérations,* vol. 2, p. 7.

65. Report No. 2 of the Commission on Polish Affairs, April 22, 1919, with map, Y.H.C. *F.R., P.P.C.,* vol. 4, p. 624.

in Eastern Europe, found it to be a "military crazy-quilt" that no one at the Peace Conference could portray with any confidence.[66] Ukrainian factions at Paris, who clamored for hearings and who were almost equally distrustful of Poles, Russians, and Germans, resisted strenuous efforts by House to bring them together in loyalty to the League of Nations. On May 23 the Council of Foreign Ministers delegated the Polish commission at Paris to hear Polish and Ukrainian spokesmen on the question of Galicia, but no recommendation resulted.[67]

The committee that was at work on the negotiation of an armistice in Galicia reported on May 15 that a convention submitted to the two parties had been rejected by the Poles, who raised questions of general policy that were beyond the competence of the committee.[68] It was recommended that the convention be imposed on Poland by force.

On May 19 Wilson reopened the question by presenting to the Council of Four information received from Warsaw. He said there was a choice of two policies: to yield certain points in order to enable Paderewski to remain in office, or to stand firm on their principles at the risk of his fall. Neither alternative was accepted immediately, however. The council decided only to ask General Botha, chairman of the armistice committee, to give full information as to atrocities that were said to have been committed by Ukrainians. Two days later they heard Botha's report and also the testimony of a delegation of Ukrainians. When Botha said that indifference to this matter on the part of the council would undermine the authority of the League of Nations, Wilson was alarmed. He remarked that since Paderewski was doing everything possible to overcome opposition in the Polish Diet, it would be best to support him and address a complaint to President Pilsudski. It was agreed that a telegram drafted by Wilson, threatening to cut off material aid to Poland, should go to Pilsudski and also to Haller through a French liaison officer. On May 24 The Four had assurance that Haller's troops had been sent not to Lemberg but to the German front.[69]

The status of eastern Galicia was further obscured when it was reported to Wilson on June 5 that Romanians had occupied part of the region.[70] On the sixteenth, Polish and Ukrainian delegates signed an armistice agreement that set a provisional line of partition; but Gibson, who had been appointed American minister to Poland in mid-April, reported that refugees from Ukrainian cruelties were fleeing to Lemberg and

66. Bonsal, *Suitors and Suppliants,* p. 249.

67. *Ibid.,* pp. 140–414. *F.R., P.P.C.,* vol. 4, p. 758.

While The Four considered ways of ending hostilities in Galicia, discussions of the territorial settlement went on in the Polish commission at Paris, of which Jules Cambon was chairman, and also in the Council of Foreign Ministers. Pichon and Sonnino wished to give Poland a League mandate for Galicia. Lansing agreed and pointed out that 60 percent of the Ruthenian population was illiterate and therefore unfit for self-government. But Balfour was opposed, Marston, *The Peace Conference of 1919,* p. 218. Miller, vol. 16, pp. 130–136.

68. Copy of report of May 15 in the Lloyd George papers, F / 147 / 11 / 2. Botha to Lloyd George, May 15, 1919, Lloyd George papers, F / 5 / 5 / 10.

69. *F.R., P.P.C.,* vol. 6, pp. 60–62, 127, 161. Mantoux, *Délibérations,* vol. 2, pp. 90–91, 108, 130–132, 146–148, 234–235, 259. A copy of an undated telegram, Clemenceau to Pilsudski, is in the Wilson papers. The telegram was not delivered promptly, and Clemenceau explained to the Council of Four that the delay was accidental.

70. Paneyko to Wilson, June 5, 1919, Wilson papers. See Lundgreen-Nielsen, p. 333.

the Poles doubted the ability of the Ukrainian leaders to enforce a truce even if they wished to do so.[71]

On June 25 the Council of Foreign Ministers authorized Polish forces, including Haller's troops, to occupy eastern Galicia up to the river Zbrucz as a bulwark against "Bolshevist bands" and without prejudice as to the eventual political settlement for this territory.[72] Poland thereupon established a rule over the disputed territory that it did not relinquish. Despite an American proposal for League of Nations supervision and for an eventual plebiscite, and despite a recommendation of the Polish commission of a twenty-five-year mandate for Poland, the Peace Conference took no effective action to alter the *fait accompli*. Poland gained full title to Galicia by the Treaty of Riga, concluded with Soviet Russia in 1921.[73]

In the sessions of the Council of Four, under the necessity of satisfying the clamor of the peoples for substantial progress toward peace, the political chiefs of the democracies were making some concession to the usage that professional diplomats had long honored. Conversing face to face daily, they attained a degree of secrecy, precision, and responsible decision that had been impossible in the more open meetings of the Council of Ten. If they could continue to keep their talks "in the family" and insulated from distempers of public opinion, they might hope to deal successfully with other crises no less acute than those resulting from the demands of France and its ally, Poland.

71. Dispatches, Gibson to Ammission, June 18, and 19, 1919, Wilson papers.

72. *F.R., P.P.C.,* vol. 6, pp. 677–678, 687–688, 731. James T. Shotwell and Max M. Laserson, *Poland and Russia, 1919–1945,* pp. 6–7, 15–16. Mantoux, *Délibérations,* vol. 2, pp. 307–308.

73. Tillman, *Anglo-American Relations at the Paris Peace Conference* pp. 384–386. Tillman wrote: "The British government took a firm position against Polish annexation of Eastern Galicia . . . while the United States again displayed a curious solicitude for Polish ambitions." "In general," Lord wrote to Gibson on August 7, 1919, "we have insured to the Polish government a very strong hold on the country as long as this provisional regime lasts," letter in Gibson papers, box 8, f. 4. On the pacification of eastern Galicia see Wandycz, *The United States and Poland,* pp. 138–142.

18

Crisis and Deadlock: Italian Expansion

Near the end of April, after the demands of France were satisfied, the pressures of other national spokesmen were still insistent. Three of the Allied Powers could not be depended on to accept the treaty that was taking shape. Before the signatures of Italy and Japan could be counted on, territorial claims that conflicted with the principle of self-determination would have to be considered. Moreover, Belgium was insisting on a prior lien upon the reparation that was to be made by Germany.

Wilson, in his eagerness for Italian support for a League of Nations, had promised the upper Adige to Orlando while denying the Italian claim to Fiume.[1] In April, when the revised Covenant was about to be finally approved by the Peace Conference, the Italian delegates pressed their claims on the Adriatic coast. Although not without justification on grounds of military security, and for the most part sanctioned by provisions of the Treaty of London, these demands flouted the ninth of the president's Fourteen Points: "A readjustment of the frontiers of Italy should be effected along clearly recognizable lines of nationality." The definition of Italy's boundary with Yugoslavia, a matter too critical to be delegated to any committee of experts, became the subject of turbulent discussion in the Council of Four.

The Yugoslav delegates used tactics well calculated to win American sympathy. On February 12, five days after the United States formally recognized the Kingdom of Serbs, Croats, and Slovenes, the cabinet of the new nation had agreed to accept arbitration by Wilson of their whole dispute with Italy.[2] The Italians, however, declined this recourse. Their official statement of demands sought the Brenner frontier (which Wilson had already promised to Orlando), and the parts of Istria and central Dalmatia awarded by the Treaty of London. Furthermore, they claimed Fiume on the ground of self-determination, and also laid claim to Spalato (Split) and its vicinity as well as to the Sexten Valley and the Tarvis basin.[3] Orlando had warned Wilson that if the minimum demands of Italy were not met, he might be forced to walk out of the Peace Conference.

Foreign Minister Sonnino had proposed a compromise to Clemenceau early in March. The timing of this move was perhaps not unrelated to the absence of Wilson and to the atmosphere of accommodation that House was at pains to create. Professing to act in a "spirit of conciliation," Sonnino wrote: "In view of the general disintegration of Austria-Hungary, which had not been contemplated at the time of the Treaty of London of 1915, we cannot now give up the Italian city of Fiume; and, in compensation, the better to facilitate Yugoslavia's outlets and lines of eco-

1. See above, pp. 54–55. Territory in Gorizia promised by the Treaty of London was conceded to Italy, Seymour, *Letters from the Paris Peace Conference*, p. 210.
2. See above, pp. 55–56.
3. See the Italian memorandum of February 7, 1919, in Mario Toscano, *Alto Adige—South Tyrol* (Baltimore, 1975), pp. 8–9. Memorandum, D. Johnson to House, March 17, 1919, Y.H.C.

nomic communication to the sea, we would be ready to concede to Yugoslavia some territory in Dalmatia from that which had been recognized as ours [by the Treaty of London]." Three days later Sonnino addressed a similar letter to House and Lloyd George.[4]

Wilson had been aware of the importance of this question even before the Peace Conference began.[5] For a while he left the matter of boundaries in the Adriatic region largely to House and those who advised him. Immediately upon his return to Paris, however, he protested to Orlando that the Italians had been aroused by propaganda to believe that he would not deal fairly with Italy's claims; and Orlando, assured of Wilson's good will, told Italian newsmen that it would be very embarrassing to Italy and to himself if they continued their anti-American propaganda.[6]

In mid-March, House had learned from Ambassador Page, at Rome, that an ever-growing sentiment in Italy demanded everything promised by the Treaty of London and "whatever else can be got."[7] House and Orlando, foreseeing the impasse to which popular agitation was to bring their diplomacy, were eager that the Adriatic question be settled at once; but they did not induce Clemenceau and Lloyd George to act. By March 21 the opportunity for an effective accommodation had passed, never to return. On that day the Italian delegation announced what they had previously said only in private: they would withdraw from the Peace Conference if the city of Fiume was denied to Italy. The reporting of this in the press focused the incendiary rays of publicity upon the delicate negotiations of the diplomats.[8]

At the beginning of April, Sonnino was no longer willing to barter. He insisted on the line of the Treaty of London, and Fiume too.[9] Moreover, Orlando explained to the Council of Four on the third day of the month, as Wilson was on the brink of illness, that the intense feeling of his people impelled him to claim more than had been promised to Italy in 1915. A crisis of the first magnitude was building up.

The British Foreign Office, which in the years before the war had endeavored to alleviate tensions in the Balkans, was, in the words of Balfour, "hopelessly trammeled by . . . treaty engagements." Balfour was unwilling to deviate by a jot from the terms agreed upon in the Treaty of London. In his dilemma he turned hopefully to the Americans, with whose proclaimed principles the regrettable treaty was at odds. During Wilson's absence in February he wrote to House that only the Americans could explain to the Italians with good grace that Italy had "not done badly in the war," even if it did not get all that it had hoped for on the eastern coast of the Adriatic.[10] Moreover, Clemenceau and Lloyd George, as well as Balfour, gave House to understand that they thought certain provisions of the Treaty of London

4. Sonnino to Clemenceau, March 8, 1919, Fonds Clemenceau, 6N76. Sonnino to House, March 11, 1919, Y.H.C.
5. See Walworth, *America's Moment: 1918,* p. 160.
6. Grayson diary, March 14 and 16, 1919.
7. T. N. Page to House, March 15, 1919. A dispatch from Page said that it was "apparently probable" that the "true source" of increasing criticism of Wilson at Rome was Paris, Page to Ammission, March 18, 1919, Y.H.C.
8. On March 22 a feature story in the *New York Times* revealed the Italian intention.
9. Sweetser diary, April 3, 1919.
10. Memorandum, Balfour to House, February 26, 1919, Y.H.C.

inapplicable and that the United States was in a position to protest.[11] The diplomats of the United States were thus challenged to play the role that British statesmen often had assumed in efforts to keep the peace on the continent of Europe.

Actually, there was a division of opinion among the Americans. Mezes, influenced by advice that took into account the importance of giving to Orlando something that would enable him to persuade his excited people to accept the verdict of the Peace Conference, recommended on March 16 that Italy be given the line of the treaty of London in the north, the Dalmatian islands that it sought, and also the city of Fiume with provision for a free port. At the same time, Miller argued that Serbia, not being a party to the Treaty of London, had no better legal claim to Fiume than Italy. He spoke very frankly to Orlando about his own pro-Italian views, perhaps thus awakening unwarranted hopes, though he explained that territorial matters were outside his purview. According to Major Douglas Johnson, chief of the Division of Boundary Geography, Miller and Mezes "were inclined to make large concessions to Italy" and "sought to secure a solution which . . . could be if necessary imposed upon the Jugo-Slavs without their consent." They felt that too much attention was being given to local question of demography at the expense of large considerations of general policy.[12]

Johnson, an adviser on whose judgment the president was to depend increasingly, was most averse to compromise. He had drawn a boundary that became known as the "Wilson Line" and represented the American concept of justice. This line ran north and south down the watershed of the Istrian peninsula and left some 365,000 Yugoslavs, but not Fiume, under Italian rule. Slight adjustments were made from time to time, sometimes with the president's consent, to the advantage of Italy.[13]

At the same time, other experts who were closely concerned supplied the Amer-

---

11. According to House's record, Clemenceau and Lloyd George were willing to accept the internationalization of Fiume. House diary, March 10, 1919. House to Seymour, May 28, 1928, Y.H.C. Seymour, p. 210.

12. Memorandum, Mezes to House, March 16, 1919, Miller papers, L.C. box 87, IV, Col. House's papers, 9. Miller, *My Diary*, vol. 1, p. 172. Mezes thought that the Italians should give up the Dodecanese islands and their claims in Albania and Asia Minor. See below, p. 352. His views were similar to those of Shotwell, Miller, and Beer. *I.P.*, vol. 4, p. 439. Miller, vol. 6, pp. 411–415, 451–453. Birdsall, *Versailles Twenty Years After*, pp. 271–273. D. Johnson, "Résumé of Negotiations in re: Adriatic Problem," T. H. Bliss papers, box 250.

Mezes explained his position to Johnson thus: "I do not personally see the necessity of standing up so much straighter here than elsewhere in the settlement. Many compromises have been made in various regions in Europe and I think there might well be room for wise compromise in these especially difficult regions. Of course a wise compromise I need hardly say is one which holds to essentials and yields on non-essentials," letter, April 21, 1919, Y.H.C. House once remarked to Miller that Mezes had just reached agreement on a boundary by giving way and was willing to concede another island to the Italians every time he dined at their hotel, Miller, vol. p. 202, entry of March 25, 1919.

13. Christopher Seton-Watson, *Italy from Liberalism to Fascism 1870–1925*, p. 527. Letter, Bowman to Miller, April 27, 1921, Miller papers, box 1, 2d folder, L.C. Johnson to Wilson, December 18, 1918, copy with map showing a suggested boundary, Y.H.C. "The line was badly placed from the first and remained so," Bowman wrote. "It was made without previous knowledge or consent of other territorial experts than Johnson," letter cited above. A dispatch from Lansing to Ammission on November 29, 1919, gave, according to Lansing, "the official definition of the American [Johnson's] line as accurately as it has ever been defined," dispatch in N.A., R.G. 59, 763.72119 / 7943. The recommendations of the American specialists are treated in detail in Albrecht-Carrié, *Italy at the Paris Peace Conference*, pp. 117–131.

ican commissioners with memoranda in support of their conviction that Italian annexation of Fiume would grossly violate Wilson's principles. These American advisers reckoned that the territory promised to Italy by the Treaty of London included 750,000 Yugoslavs, that the present claims of Italy would take in no less than 836,000 in all, and that Italian annexation of northern Dalmatia would involve 14,000 Italians and 293,000 Yugoslavs. American naval experts thought that Italy would be amply protected by the possession of certain islands off the coast.[14]

On the third of April the Council of Four, giving close attention to the question, heard Orlando's arguments in the morning and in the afternoon those of Trumbić. The Italians feared that the new Yugoslav state might come under the influence of Soviet Russia or might perhaps become a firm ally of France, Italy's rival in the Mediterranean.[15] Orlando, insisting that the question was above all a matter of sentiment, now regarded the acquisition of Fiume as more essential than that of parts of the Dalmatian mainland that were allotted to Italy by the Treaty of London. Wilson, whose health was breaking, had little to say.

In the afternoon, Trumbić made it clear[16] that Yugoslavia was not willing to consider a settlement that denied it Fiume. It soon became apparent to the Americans that concern for trade was a prime factor in the controversy. The Yugoslavs did not want their principal port to come under Italian rule; and the Italians dreaded the prospect of competition by Fiume with Trieste, which they were to acquire from Austria. It appeared to Henry White that the British were "dead against" the Italians in regard to Fiume "chiefly for commercial reasons."[17]

Orlando absented himself while Trumbić was pleading. Explaining in a letter to Wilson that he stayed away in order to avoid embarrassing his three colleagues in the council,[18] the Italian premier sought the aid of House. The day before, Wilson had asked the colonel to explain to Orlando the American proposal for a settlement. When House did so with maps in hand, it became clear that the disposition of Fiume presented the main difficulty.[19]

Meanwhile the public clamor in Italy grew. On April 1 Orlando told the Council of Four that on the twenty-fifth, the date suggested for the appearance of German delegates at Paris, he must be at Rome for the opening of Parliament. He resolutely demanded that the Italian claims be settled before the Germans were summoned. He explained that although he was doing everything he could to calm his excited people, the denial of their expectations would lead at the very least to the fall of his

---

14. Seymour, "The Struggle for the Adriatic," 469. *I.P.*, vol. 4, pp. 438–439. Miller, vol. 6, pp. 457–459. The experts enlisted the support of Steed, who was in sympathy with the Yugoslavs, Steed, *Through Thirty Years*, vol. 2, p. 327. Steed's memoranda to Northcliffe, April 23 and 25, 1919, Steed papers.

15. Lederer, *Yugoslavia at the Paris Peace Conference*, p. 142. Lloyd George, *The Truth about the Peace Treaties*, pp. 807–808. Steed to Northcliffe, March 24, 1919.

16. Mantoux, *Proceedings*, pp. 96–98. Albrecht-Carrié, pp. 440–442.

17. House recorded that Italy's purpose was to "strangle" Fiume in the interest of a "greater Trieste," diary, April 9, 1919. H. White to H.C. Lodge, May 1, 1919, Nevins, *White*, pp. 431–432, 446. See Beer diary, March 30, 1919, and Day to Wilson, May, 1919, Y.H.C.

18. Orlando to Wilson, April 3, 1919, in Baker, vol. 3, p. 272.

19. House diary, April 3, 7, 9, 14, and 15, 1919. House regretted that a settlement had not been made just after the armistice, before the Italian desire for Fiume became an unsatisfied national passion.

cabinet.[20] On the thirteenth he notified Wilson that a quick solution of the Adriatic question was essential not only to a rapid conclusion of peace, but to the reassuring of his people. "Reason and feeling do not always coincide," he wrote, "especially in the mind of a people," and there was "the most acute nervous tension" among Italians. Asking for a conference on that day or the next, Orlando pleaded that it was "a case of absolute necessity."[21]

At this time the Covenant of the League of Nations had been accepted by the commission of which Orlando was a member. Wilson's concern for the League no longer impelled him to make concessions to Italy, as he had when he conceded the South Tyrol in January. The moment had now arrived for the prophet to stand upon the position in which he was placed by both his national policy and what he conceived to be his political interest. His academic advisers had deemed the port at Fiume "vitally necessary to the economic life of Yugoslavia," and therefore a proposal to make it a free port, in which Wilson had acquiesced, seemed to them impractical. Brushing aside Italian arguments based on the history of the region and on Italy's demand for security, the experts agreed unanimously that Fiume should be a part of Yugoslavia "without restrictions."[22] This emphasis on economic welfare was in keeping with the American policy of building a strong Yugoslavia that would be able to resist any interference by any great power with the flow of its trade with the world. Wilson expressed in the Council of Four an apprehension that the Yugoslavs might be driven "into the hands of the Bolshevists."[23]

The compulsion of economic interest coincided with the pressure that came from Wilson's liberal adherents for some dramatic manifestation of his loyalty to high purposes, in particular to the principle of self-determination, which had been violated in setting the boundary in the Tyrol. Wilson was sympathetic with Orlando's political predicament. It was not pleasant to contemplate his replacement in the Paris councils by a less reasonable Italian. The president pointed out on April 13 that the essential difficulty in Italy was that of "giving satisfaction to a badly informed and anxious public opinion," and that he himself had to face a similar challenge in the United States without the advantage of being able to meet the Congress directly. He had urged Lloyd George to tell his people the truth about reparations and persuade them to stand for the right, and now he advised Orlando to bring the Italians to reason. He proposed that the Council of Four discuss Italy's claims on the morrow and then announce that they had them "under constant examination" and were "approaching a settlement."[24]

On April 14, in a talk with Orlando, the president proposed that Fiume be an international port, with a large degree of autonomy but within the customs system of Yugoslavia.[25] However, Orlando insisted that this would not satisfy his constit-

20. Mantoux, *Proceedings*, pp. 175, 181, 191.

21. Orlando to Wilson, April 13, 1919, Wilson papers.

22. Baker, vol. 3, pp. 266–271. See Kernak, "Woodrow Wilson and National Self-Determination along Italy's Frontier," 265–269.

23. *F.R., P.P.C.*, vol. 5, pp. 87, 149, 151.

24. Mantoux, *Proceedings*, pp. 190–192.

25. *I.P.*, vol. 4, p. 443. Pašić to Wilson, April 13, 1919, Wilson papers. Wilson put his proposal in a memorandum of April 14 and gave it to the Italian delegation with permission to publish it in Italy,

uency. The premier felt that the words of the American prophet were "heavy with obscure warnings of future evils."[26] He would not permit his advisers to meet even informally with their Yugoslav enemies in the presence of American specialists.

After the interview Wilson confessed to House that only once before had he had such an unhappy experience. He appeared "very tired and worn" to Baker, who perceived that his chief, though forced to compromise much during the preceding days, had "succeeded in forcing enough of his ideas to antagonize everybody" and would be the man blamed for a treaty that would "satisfy nobody."[27] Though Wilson wrote appreciatively to House of his "fine patient work," the president was determined that Italy should not get Fiume. House suggested that they seek a solution that would prevent a break until passions had time to cool. Wilson then adduced—as his own, according to House's record—a suggestion that the colonel had made the day before and the president had then thought not practical: that the League of Nations might assume responsibility for the disputed territory temporarily. House immediately carried this idea to Clemenceau, who said that he would tell Orlando that it was the only way out of the imbroglio.[28]

On April 16 the Yugoslav delegates proposed to each member of the Council of Four that a plebiscite be held in the disputed territory. The next day Wilson received Pašić, the veteran prime minister of Serbia who headed the Yugoslav delegation. Wilson heard his case patiently, and, while making no promises gave the impression that he would help the new nation with its "just claims."[29] Meanwhile, House was in touch with Orlando, pursuing a faint hope that he might at the last moment bring off a compromise as he had done in the case of the French demands for security. Orlando, however, would have no plebiscite. The controversy reached the point that good diplomats take pains to avoid. Only a palpable yielding by one of the parties could prevent a break.

The president was informed by daily dispatches from Page at Rome that Italian public opinion was now utterly implacable. It was apparent that Orlando was not exaggerating when he said that the annexation of Fiume was essential to his tenure in office. Flag-waving patriots were carrying on what Page described as a "tremendous propaganda"; the claims to Adriatic cities—"almost the only topic of conversation"—had "become a religion"; and there was danger that the friendship between the peoples of the United States and Italy would be broken beyond mending. Rumor predicted that if Italy did not get Fiume, a pro-German government might come to power at Rome. Indeed, there was reason to suspect that during the war the door between Italy and Germany had been left a trifle ajar and Sonnino had taken "a little squint" through it from time to time.[30]

Baker, vol. 3, pp. 274–277. On April 15 he read this paper to Balfour, who thought it "most courteous and conciliatory" and noted that the president was "seriously alarmed" by the prospect that Orlando and Sonnino would leave the Peace Conference, memorandum by Balfour, P.R.O., FO / 800 / 216 / Cf. / 19 / 1.

26. Orlando in the *Saturday Evening Post,* March 23, 1929.
27. Baker journal, April 14, 1919. *I.P.,* vol. 4, p. 443.
28. House diary, April 15, 1919.
29. Lederer, p. 194.
30. Dispatches, Page to Ammission, April 16 and 18, 1919, letter, Page to House, April 17, 1919, to be brought to the president's attention, Wilson papers. On the sixteenth, Page reported: "The apparent placing of Italy on the same footing with the Yugoslavs who up to the signing of the armistice with

The effect of these ominous portents was to stiffen the intention that the president had long held[31] to deny Italy's claim to Fiume. Wilson could not bring himself to accept the opposition of the Italian public. He was angered not only by anti-American propaganda, but by interferences with American efforts to ship supplies of food to needy people in the territory that had been a part of Austria-Hungary.[32] His sympathy with the need of Italy for food and fuel[33] was giving way to an inclination to use the economic power of the United States in such a way as to bring the Italians to his way of thinking. This was a recourse that economic advisers had suggested in February, when Wilson approved an advance to Italy of $25 million toward purchases in neutral countries.[34] Now, on April 17, in a letter to the secretary of the Treasury, the president approved the setting up of further credits of $50 million in favor of the Italian government. But two days later he wrote to Davis: "We have come to a rather difficult issue with the Italians and I am going to beg, therefore, that you will cooperate with me in delaying our reply to the Treasury about the fifty million dollar advance to the Italian government for a few days until the air clears— if it does,"[35] In respect of credits to nations other than Italy, Wilson wrote to Davis on April 15: "I think that it is perfectly legitimate that we should ask ourselves before each of these credits is extended, whether our colleagues are cooperating with us in a way that is satisfactory."

The determination of Wilson was not lessened by a letter that he received on the morning of April 18. It was signed by Douglas Johnson and five other specialists.[36]

Austria were among Italy's bitterest foes has been the chief means of arousing the profound feeling which is now undeniable and is spreading."

31. Wilson reminded his family at this time that from the first interview with Orlando and Sonnino he had told them that Italy could not have Fiume, Benham diary letter, April 15, 1919.

32. Rear Admiral Niblack reported from Fiume on April 5 that Italians there had used American resources lavishly to create sentiment in favor of Italy, and also that Italian policy in northern Dalmatia was "repressive, relentless, reactionary and malevolent," memorandum in Wilson papers. See Zinojinović, *America, Italy and the Birth of Yugoslavia*, pp. 238–239.

33. Page wrote of industrial "paralysis which touches the very sources of the nation's [Italy's] life," dispatch, Page to Ammission, April 16, 1919, Wilson papers. *F R., P.P.C.*, vol. 10, pp. 8–12.

34. Wilson to the secretary of the Treasury, February 19, 1919, Wilson papers. This letter was drafted by Davis, who suggested that before consenting to aid Italy the president should "make representations in regard to the demobilization of the Italian army" and also the raising of the blockade in southeastern Europe, Davis to Wilson, February 12, 1919, Wilson papers. See Gould, "Italy and the U.S. 1914–1918," p. 413. House, reporting that Sonnino was "hopeless," wrote to Wilson on February 17: "We could bring them to their senses by cutting off our financial and economic help but that would create bad feeling and might cause a revolution in Italy." Crespi tried to trade his vote on relaxation of the blockade for credits for food shipments to Italy, McCormick diary, February 17, 1919. On February 26 the American economic advisers recommended to the president that Italy be warned against using control of relief projects for political purposes, summary of meeting of February 26, 1919, Norman Davis papers, L.C., box 46, "American Economic Group 1919."

35. Copy of letter, read by Wilson, N. H. Davis to Wilson, April 18, 1919, with draft of note, for Wilson's signature, to Glass, April 17, 1919; copy of letter, Wilson to Davis, April 19, 1919, N. H. Davis papers, box 11. Davis to Wilson, April 19, 1919, Wilson papers.

For a discussion of Wilson's "great economic power over Italy" and his use of it, see Gould, pp. 409–415.

36. The letter was drafted in a three-hour conference on the afternoon of April 15. "We are all of us agreed," Seymour wrote on April 16, "that the Italian claim to Fiume and Northern Dalmatia is in the nature of a hold-up game. The president never had such an opportunity . . . for striking a death blow to the discredited methods of Old World diplomacy . . . any compromise is immoral," *Letters from the Paris Peace Conference*, pp. 178, 203–204. The letter, read by Wilson, is in the Wilson papers.

The five who participated with Johnson were Bowman, Day, Lunt, Seymour, and Young. "Our

Reminding the president that he had covenanted with them to fight for what was right, the scholars recommended that the American position be taken on the high moral ground of Wilson's principles. It concluded with a crusading challenge: "To the president is given the rare privilege of going down in history as the statesman who destroyed, by a clean-cut decision against an infamous arrangement, the last vestige of the old order."[37]

In offering this advice the six specialists departed from the pro-Italian policy of Mezes and Miller.[38] Wilson read their letter "with the deepest feeling," he wrote immediately, "in a matter which . . . I regard as of the most critical importance." Even though Baker advised him that Orlando was not bluffing and was bound by an irresistible popular mandate, the prophet resolved to speak out.[39] Unfortunately, the crisis called for the ministration of diplomats rather than for exacerbation by a spiritual leader; and at this time Wilson was losing confidence in Mezes and even in House, who found himself caught in a conflict of loyalties to Wilsonian principle and to a world power structure in which Italy would be aligned with the Western democracies.

It is probable that the president noted the divergence of the opinion of the six experts from advice that had come to him in a memorandum from Mezes. This memorandum purported to be based on the opinion of "all of the experts on the Adriatic question." However, the president was informed by General Bliss, who repeated what he was told by Bowman, that Mezes and some of the scholars who shared his view were not in fact specialists in the matter under consideration.[40] If, in fact, Wilson did mark the shadow thus cast on the veracity of Mezes, this probably increased his distrust of Colonel House. At the time at which he received conflicting advice from his counselors,[41] Wilson's faith in House was further strained by the Steed editorial, instigated by Auchincloss, that offended Mrs. Wilson deeply.[42]

---

signatures gave him [Johnson] a toehold with the president," Bowman later wrote. "Johnson arrogated to himself the whole Adriatic matter and submitted memo after memo to the president to keep his mood in the narrow Johnsonian groove. This was a great mistake," letter, Bowman to Miller, April 27, 1921, Miller papers, L.C., box 1, 2d folder. Bowman later deprecated Johnson's unbending moral attitude and vanity of opinion, which "froze negotiations." "Our thought was," Bowman wrote, "that we should come to specific solutions and it would be no weakening of the moral position if we made concessions here and there to the Italians," Bowman to R. S. Baker, May 19, 1921, Bowman papers, file 1, drawer 1. Bowman to S. Duggan, November 4, 1941, copy in possession of Geoffrey Martin.

37. The original letter, read by Wilson, is in the Wilson papers.

38. Seymour lacked confidence in the judgment of Mezes, whom he described as "a good-natured old duck" who liked to monopolize the answers to any questions put by persons of high rank and was "generally half wrong," *Letters from the Paris Peace Conference,* pp. 99, 203–207.

39. Wilson to Bowman, April 18, 1919, Wilson papers. See Kernek, 275.

40. The Mezes memorandum provided for the administration of Fiume by the League of Nations and Yugoslav control of the port of Sušak. It was drafted by Miller and Johnson, Miller, doc. 802. Lansing diary, April 17, 1919. Albrecht-Carrié, p. 128. After working on this plan at House's behest Johnson wrote to Mezes and Miller denouncing it as "fundamentally unjust" and impractical.

41. "Account of Interview with General T. H. Bliss," a paper by Bowman dated August 27, 1939, Bowman papers, file 1, drawer 1. Cf. Birdsall, pp. 274–276.

Meeting with Lansing, Bliss, and White on April 18, House, finding them very definitely of the opinion that Fiume should be under Yugoslav rule, went along with them, explained that the Mezes memorandum of the day before was merely a suggestion, and said it would be well to have it out with the Italians as soon as possible, *F.R., P.P.C.,* vol. 11, pp. 156–157.

42. See above, p. 298.

At this same time Wilson received a note from Orlando, reminding him that in their interview four days earlier the president had stated that the Italian question should be settled within a week. The premier now asked him "to consider the absolute necessity" that the meeting of the Council of Four on the next day "be set aside for the final decisions," with Sonnino present.[43]

At the beginning of the session on April 19 the president invited the Italian premier to present his claims. Orlando, demanding the Dalmatian territory allotted by the Treaty of London and also Fiume, acknowledged that he was caught between two extremes of opinion in Italy, and that whether he appeased the passion of the "patriotic Fascist party or that of the Bolshevik party," the danger of a revolution was serious. But he would choose "the side of death with honor." He spoke as a political chieftain, not as a responsible diplomat. He said on the next day: "Italy made clear reservations and made them [in the prearmistice negotiations] in the presence of Colonel House, who offered no objections." Actually, however, the reservations of which Orlando spoke were not explicitly accepted.[44]

The president replied at great length. He took the high ground that it was not possible to make peace with Germany on certain principles and to invoke others for the settlement with Austria. As to the analogy with Danzig, he pointed out that Italian sovereignty had not existed at Fiume, as had German rule in Danzig, and that the Italians at Fiume were not connected with their country by an intervening population of the same blood. Moreover, the free use of the port of Fiume was essential not just to one country but to Czechoslovakia, Hungary, and Romania as well as to Yugoslavia. He insisted that to unite Fiume with Italy would be "an arbitrary act," inconsistent with his principles. Fiume, he said, was only "an island of Italian population,"[45] and to separate such enclaves from surrounding populations would produce blemishes on the map. He then set forth an ideal that, he hoped, would be "one of the great achievements of this Conference: to keep all the great powers away from the Balkan peninsula." The delicate maneuvers by which European diplomats had tried to maintain a balance of power and which had failed to prevent recurrent war were denounced by the American prophet as "intrigues against the peace of the world." He could recall a time when he felt little concern about what happened in Europe. But now he had come to help the Continent to emerge from the old regime that had led to catastrophe. Insisting that he had the best interest of Italy on his conscience, we could not conceive that the Italians would make the tragic mistake of parting from their friends and the rest of the world. With these conciliatory words Wilson issued a warning. If he did not succeed in his exalted purpose, he said, Italy "had nothing to expect from the American people."

At this point Sonnino entered the debate and brought forward the sort of argument for national security that the French had advanced with respect to their eastern border. Reminded by Wilson that the League would provide an American guarantee

43. "Confidential" letter, Orlando to Wilson, April 17, 1919, Wilson papers.
44. Aldrovandi diary, April 19 and 20, 1919, translation in Albrecht-Carrié, pp. 458 ff., 473. See Walworth, p. 158.
45. The Italians in the city of Fiume outnumbered the Slavs about three to two, Walworth, p. 163n.

of Italy's integrity, Sonnino replied that aid would arrive too late and that the Slavs across the Adriatic knew neither good faith nor law.

This formal confrontation in effect put an end to any likelihood that the issue could be resolved by House. But that busy negotiator and his advisers did not give up. They proposed to Wilson a formula for compromise. House hoped to temporize, thinking that the Italian leaders needed time to educate their public to accept what they must know would be the final decision. He was impressed by the fact that if Italy declined to sign the treaty with Germany and Japan also refused, the peace of Europe would be in jeopardy. Moreover, he was concerned about the effect that a breach with Italy would have on German acceptance of a peace treaty.[46]

The next day, Easter Sunday, the president made a suggestion to the Council of Four that was similar to House's formula. There was no response from the Italians, however. It was possible that they were encouraged by the difference of opinion among the American delegates to believe that they could win their case by persistence.[47] Lloyd George reiterated the pledge of loyalty to the Treaty of London that he and Clemenceau had given, and this reaffirmation of British steadfastness moved Orlando to tears. Wilson tried to comfort him by shaking his hand.[48] The session of April 20 concluded with an understanding that the premiers of the three nations bound by the Treaty of London would meet the next morning without the president. When they did so, with their foreign ministers present, the Italians spoke more frankly of the Americans than had been possible in the presence of Wilson. Sonnino presented the view of the Italian public, which saw the United States as a contributor only of loans and not of blood to Italy's fight against Austria.[49]

When the Council of Four met in the afternoon of April 21, Wilson read a manifesto to the Italian people that he had drafted and that had elicited the approval of the American commission. He wished to give the Italians a fair version of facts that had been misrepresented in the press. He spoke of the millions of Italians residing in the United States, their remittances to relatives in Italy, and the contacts that the government of their native land would not want to put in jeopardy. He was not sure whether he should release his paper immediately or wait until a breach occurred. Determined that if there were to be a fight the Italians should not get in the first blow, he was eager to publish the paper the next morning in order to make clear the reasonableness of his position. But Clemenceau asked him to wait for forty-eight hours, and Lloyd George warned that he might provoke an "explosion" in Italy. Wilson therefore held his fire. That night he told Wiseman that the situation was "very grave."[50]

46. Kernek, 280. House diary, April 19, 1919. Tardieu told House that the relations between the French and Italian governments, none too friendly, were endangered by the failure of Wilson to negotiate realistically. He feared that the Italians, unless "sweetened," would become pro-German, Bonsal, *Suitors and Suppliants,* p. 104.

47. Seymour, *Letters from the Paris Peace Conference,* p. 222.

48. Hankey, *The Supreme Control,* pp. 124–125. Stephen Roskill, *Hankey: Man of Secrets,* vol. 2, p. 81.

49. Aldrovandi's diary, April 21, 1919; Albrecht-Carrié, pp. 476–483.

50. Mantoux, *Délibérations,* vol. 1, pp. 292–315. *F.R., P.P.C.,* vol. 5, pp. 106–109. Hankey, pp. 123–128. Letter, Wiseman to Reading, April 22, 1919, Y.H.C. At this time Wiseman still expected a compromise would be reached.

During the next two days Lloyd George, who was persistently seeking a basis for compromise,[51] continued to discourage the publication of Wilson's manifesto. This brought from Wilson an assertion that there was "a fatal antagonism" between Italians and Slavs, and that if the latter felt that they were the victims of injustice, the way would be open to Russian influence and the formation of a Slav block, with the huge population of Asia behind it, that would be hostile to western Europe. Were they to attract the southern Slavs toward the West and the League, he asked, or throw them back toward bolshevism? He suggested that a plan of Lloyd George for a plebiscite could lead to intrigues designed to influence the voting, and he was unwilling to make more proposals to the Italians that might lead them to think that they would have their way if they persisted. The prophet was now emotionally committed to political warfare. He again asked the assent of his colleagues to publishing his appeal to the Italian people, and he claimed moral vindication. He ascribed to himself credit for leading the United States into the war by instructing American opinion, little by little, in well-known principles, whereas Sonnino had brought the Italians into the war "to conquer territory." He asked whether it would not be better to incur the resentment of Italy, which he thought would be temporary, rather than risk turning the southern Slavs toward bolshevism and away from the League of Nations.[52] The president remarked that it would not seem shocking to him if the Allies repudiated a pact that was made in 1915 when conditions were different. But his colleagues would not admit the application of the doctrine of *rebus sic stantibus* to the Treaty of London, though they shared Wilson's determination to deny Fiume to Italy.

Lloyd George then read a persuasive appeal that was addressed to the government rather than to the people of Italy. This paper warned that if Italy separated itself from its allies, "the Conference summoned to give us peace would leave us at war and Germany alone would be the gainer."[53] No decision was taken April 23 as to when the British document should be sent to the Italians. However, Kerr immediately communicated its essence, if not the text. He assured the Italians that Lloyd George, while denying them Fiume, thought an agreement possible on other points.

While the Italian delegation considered the friendly British proposal, Wilson, losing patience, shot from the hip by releasing his manifesto to the newspapers. Orlando, shocked by this breach of the code of diplomats, notified Clemenceau and Lloyd George that it was impossible to remain at the Peace Conference.[54]

The failure of Wilson to act on House's advice that he take an American secretary into the meetings of the Council of Four had led to a tragic misunderstanding.[55] Lloyd George and Clemenceau, in praising the text of Wilson's manifesto, had

51. Aldrovandi's diary, April 22, 1919. Albrecht-Carrié, pp. 483–485. Hankey, p. 128.

52. Mantoux, *Délibérations,* vol. 1, pp. 328–329, 337–340, 343–345. *F.R., P.P.C.,* vol. 5, pp. 135–137, 149–151. Hankey, pp. 128–129.

53. Baker, vol. 3, pp. 291–296. American delegates were alarmed by the possibility that Germany would exploit a break among the Allies, Shotwell, *At the Paris Peace Conference,* p. 293.

54. Kerr to Bonar Law, April 24, 1919, Lothian muniments, 9D40 / 17 / 983 / 1. "Fiume and the Peace Settlement," April 23, 1919, *ibid.,* —— / 978. Orlando to Clemenceau, April 23, 1919, *ibid.,* —— / 979 / 2.

55. Frazier to T. N. Page, April 25, 1919, Page papers, Duke University Library.

warned that immediate publication might make it impossible to come to terms with the Italian government. Lloyd George thought it was agreed that the paper would not be released until at least the next day.[56] Nevertheless, after the meeting of April 23 the president told Dr. Grayson that Clemenceau approved publication and Lloyd George said he would back it up. Wilson also said: "Lloyd George is as slippery as an eel, and I never know when I can count on him."[57]

In giving his manifesto to the press Wilson asserted that he was "standing out" for his rights. His statement repeated arguments that he had presented to Orlando earlier: the collapse of Austria-Hungary and the commitment to the Fourteen Points that had been made in the German armistice gave the peace settlement a new and moral aspect; the Wilson Line was a natural frontier that would assure Italy of strategic security; and the port of Fiume must serve new states as well as Italy. America was portrayed as Italy's friend, linked with the Italian people in blood as well as in affection.[58] In reply Orlando issued a statement that, at the urging of Lloyd George, used moderate language; but it made clear the seriousness of the offense that had been given to his government and people.[59] The criticism of the American president was received with sympathy by the professional diplomats of Europe, whose mistrust of the prophet's ego grew.[60]

It was clear that the yielding of both Wilson and Orlando to the fervor that is generated by political "causes" in democracies was making conciliation impossible. When Orlando and Sonnino acceded to Lloyd George's urging that they attend a meeting of the Council of Four on the afternoon of April 24, the contending chiefs, professing personal good will, clove to the commitments that they found utterly irreconcilable. Insecure in his political position, Orlando did not take up a suggestion by Lloyd George that Italy might have Fiume if it would forgo the acquisitions in Dalmatia that were promised by the Treaty of London.[61]

During the long session Wilson revealed a motive that had impelled him to insist on acting dramatically and without adequate assurance of support from his European colleagues. The press, he asserted, had so often put him in "so false a light, that it had become necessary to let his own people know" the basis of the American attitude, which was not merely negative. It seemed that the American prophet was putting his position of leadership among his own people above any diplomatic concern for the peace of Europe.[62]

56. Bonsal, pp. 110–111.

57. Grayson diary, April 23, 1919. See Walworth, *Woodrow Wilson,* vol. 2, p. 311.

58. *F.R., P.P.C.,* vol. 5, pp. 149–151. Baker, vol. 3, pp. 287–290. House diary, April 23 and 26, 1919.

59. Baker, vol. 3, pp. 201–205. "The Italian ministers regarded the publication of President Wilson's statement as an insult to their dignity and an offense against comradeship," Lloyd George, p. 840.

60. François Charles-Roux, *Une Grande Ambassade à Rome,* pp. 37–38. Lord Robert Cecil, recording in his diary that Wilson's manifesto was "a great mistake," predicted the president would be "more than ever confident" that he could do anything he liked in Europe, entry of May 6, 1919.

The French press of the Right and Center joined with the Italians in denouncing Wilson's coup, and the French embassy at Rome issued friendly propaganda to the Italian press and officially denied that Clemenceau had inspired, or even approved, the president's manifesto. The *London Morning Post* used the phrase "wild-west diplomacy," and Bonar Law wrote to Lloyd George: "I must say I think Wilson did put his foot in it badly," letter of April 26, 1919, Lloyd George papers, F / 30 / 3 / 39.

61. Hankey, pp. 129–130; Aldrovandi's diary, April 24, 1919; Albrecht-Carrié, p. 486.

62. See Kernek, 277–278.

When Wilson expressed a desire that the Italian parliament might know the measures that he was proposing for the security of Italy, Sonnino warned that it would be even more difficult to reach a compromise once the question was presented to the parliament. Orlando brought the meeting to a close by announcing that he must go to catch a train for Rome. He was not quitting the Peace Conference, as his letter of the previous evening to Clemenceau and Lloyd George suggested, but merely performing the duty he had explained to the Council of Four a fortnight earlier— the obligation to appear at the opening of the Italian parliament. He explained that he was leaving a deputy, Crespi, at Paris for consultation on technical questions. From the window of his carriage he called out "À bientôt," hoping to be back before the Germans received the treaty. At Rome he received from the populace an ovation greater than that given to Wilson four months before.[63] At Paris, in spite of sensational anti-American propaganda in the press[64] and feverish gossip in the corridors, it was taken for granted among those who knew that the Italian leaders would return in time to sign the treaty with Germany and to defend their country's economic interest and reaffirm the validity of the Treaty of London.[65]

The manifesto of the American president, though a masterful stroke of political leadership that brought hurrahs from liberals,[66] was worse than futile as an instrument of diplomacy. Instead of aiding Orlando in standing against the frenzy of his people, it made them the more difficult to control. Regretting the offense that he had given to national feeling among the Germans in the Tyrol, Wilson had now irretrievably wounded the national pride of the Italians and goaded them to fury.[67] The voice of the populace at Rome rose in shouts of "abasso Wilson" and "evviva Italia irredenta," and Wilson was denounced as a hostile meddler. The people in the streets were now ready to crucify the prophet they had feted only four months before.[68] Not even Bissolati and the socialists who had been "waiting for the word" from Wilson now spoke in his defense. The press and wall posters went so far as to suggest that international financiers who wished to develop Yugoslavian resources had influenced the American prophet.[69]

Ambassador Page, who protested that he could not have striven harder for cordiality with Italy if she had been his own mother, bade Americans in Rome to stay

63. Dispatch, Page to the secretary of state, May 3, 1919, N.A., R.G. 59, 763.72 5/13053.

64. According to Loucheur, the Italian government spent some 8 million francs for propaganda in French papers. McCormick diary, April 29, 1919. Derby to Curzon, April 24, 1919, *loc. cit.* John W. Davis's diary, May 7, 1919, Y.H.C. DeCaix, a French official, said all the French press was "bought up" by Italy except the *Journal des Débats*. Westermann diary, April 28, 1919. Noble, *Policies and Opinions at Paris, 1919*, pp. 333–344. Seymour, *Letters from the Paris Peace Conference*, p. 212.

65. Mantoux, *Délibérations*, vol. 1, pp. 355–367. F.R., P.P.C., vol. 5, pp. 210–223. Hankey, pp. 130–131. Article by Auguste Gauvain in *Le Journal des Débats*, April 25, 1919.

66. "The American correspondents whom I have talked with are, for the first time, thoroughly enthusiastic over Wilson," Seymour, *Letters from the Paris Peace Conference*, p. 212. Justice Brandeis thought the manifesto "the best thing that has happened since the Armistice," Brandeis to N. Hapgood, June 7, 1919. Lord Reading reported from Washington that Wilson's manifesto was welcomed there, even by isolationist senators, as evidence of a definite stand against secret treaties, Reading to Wiseman, April 26, 1919, Y.H.C.

67. Albrecht-Carrié, pp. 144–149. Charles-Roux, pp. 41–42.

68. See Christopher Seton-Watson, *Italy from Liberalism to Fascism 1870–1925*, p. 529.

69. According to Ambassador Rodd, Sonnino shared in this suspicion, which was nourished by the moving of the Red Cross to the other side of the Adriatic and by a letter written by George D. Herron to the *Corriere*, Sir Rennell Rodd to Lloyd George, Lloyd George papers, F / 56 / 2 / 27.

indoors; and at the same time he did his best to defend the chief whom he had warned in vain. The envoy notified the American commission at Paris that the Italians might try to use force to seize what they claimed, and that there was talk at Rome of making a separate peace with Germany, with which there was no deep quarrel, and of acting alone to settle affairs with Austria.[70] A dispatch of May 3 brought word from Rome that the situation was desperate, that no government could yield Fiume and hope to stand, that anything might happen. Orlando, engulfed in patriotic adulation and upheld by an overwhelming majority of his parliament, remained at Rome, hopeful that concessions would be made at Paris that would permit him to return to the peace table without loss of countenance.[71]

The Three at Paris, however, were not disposed to relieve the embarrassment of Orlando by any overtures that might be regarded as concessions in the vital matter of Fiume. Wilson held to his independent position, thus enhancing his political leadership among his own people while discouraging any effective compromise by diplomats negotiating in secrecy. Doubtless his resolution was not softened by effusions of Lodge and other Republican senators who courted Italian-American voters by denouncing the president's policy.[72] Wilson's economic policy hardened, and he indulged in what Steed called "counter-blackmailing."[73] On May 6 he said to Clemenceau and Lloyd George: "The best way to stop the enterprises of the Italians is the financial way."[74]

For several days after the departure of Orlando the question of Adriatic boundaries was given little attention by The Three. However, discussions of protocol for the forthcoming meeting with the German delegates made it necessary to consider the status that Serbia, and hence Yugoslavia, would have on that occasion. Wilson, whose government had recognized the new Slav state, brought up the matter and it was referred to the ministers of foreign affairs, who were to confer with Vesnić. Great Britain on June 1 and France on June 5 granted formal recognition to Yugoslavia.

In the first week of May, at the end of which the German plenipotentiaries were to receive the terms of the treaty of peace, The Three discussed the Italian crisis at

70. Dispatch, T. N. Page to Ammission, April 26, 1919, Wilson papers. Speranza, *Diary,* April 27, 1919. Dispatches, Page to Ammission, April 24, 25, and 26, 1919, Wilson papers. Page reported that Orlando, asked to stop the Italian press campaign against the president, said to Page that he had given orders to this effect that were not heeded, Page to Wilson, April 28, 1919, Wilson papers.

71. Dispatches, T. N. Page to Wilson, April 26, May 1, 2, and 3, 1919, Wilson papers.

72. Lodge, having publicly promised his Italian constituents in March that he would support Italy's claims, published a letter in April that criticized the president's position, Kernek, 282. On May 2 he wrote to his cousin: "If Fiume is taken from Italy it will probably throw her into the arms of Germany again. But what business had we, with no national interest . . . to step in as arbiter," Lodge to John T. Morse, Jr., Massachusetts Historical Society.

73. Steed to Northcliffe, May 14, 1919.

Wilson sent instructions to the secretary of the Treasury to restrict advances under credits already established to definite commitments and to absolute necessities, dispatches, N. Davis to Glass, May 6 and 10, 1919, Wilson papers. A memorandum from the Italian treasury to Orlando, dated May 7, stated that the American Treasury had given notice that it would grant no further credits after June 1, and explained that recent political events had adversely affected Italian financing in the United States and that this was due to instructions from the president and had created a state of affairs that, if prolonged, might become "very dangerous" for Italy, memorandum in Wilson papers.

74. Mantoux, *Délibérations,* vol. 1, p. 499.

great length. Wilson protested against the isolation in which he was placed and asked Clemenceau and Lloyd George now to isolate Orlando's government by publishing the British memorandum of April 23 urging Italy to reconsider its claims. Pleading with his colleagues to extricate him from his embarrassment, he asserted that he had understood that the British paper was to have been published the day after his own manifesto.[75] Wilson warned that American opinion might go so far as to demand a break with the Europeans, and he asked whether they preferred a rupture with the United States to one with Italy. He wanted the Italian people to know what Clemenceau and Lloyd George had told Orlando in private: that Italy would be isolated if its government did not cooperate with the Peace Conference. Wilson was indignant because the French embassy at Rome denied that Clemenceau knew of the American manifesto before its publication.[76]

Clemenceau, who had not only known of the president's manifesto but praised it while urging delay in publishing it, now supported Wilson's plea for the release of the Balfour memorandum. But Lloyd George took a contrary view. He explained that he had been implored by the Italian ambassador not to publish this document, and that Orlando, fearing that full publicity would compromise future relations with England and France, had read only a résumé to his parliament, and with disagreeable results. The prime minister warned against further exciting of public opinion and against encouraging the replacement of the friendly Orlando by men who, he suggested, might "play the role of spies of Germany." Lloyd George pointed to a dangerous sentiment that existed at London: that Europe was submitting to the coercion of the United States. He warned that this feeling might grow and put an end to the League of Nations. To break with Italy would be very serious, he said, but to break with America would be disastrous for the peace of the world.[77] Lloyd George could not be persuaded, and Wilson was sorely aggrieved.[78]

As the afternoon session closed on May 3, Wilson spoke vaguely of a compromise that was proposed to Ambassador Thomas Nelson Page, envisaging Fiume as a free city. Actually, diplomats at Rome had collaborated in the tradition of their profession in seeking a solution. Ambassador Barrère presented a plan that was approved by Orlando and Sonnino as well as by Page and the British ambassador.[79] This settlement would give Fiume to Italy on condition that a port be built for Yugoslavia. Meanwhile the city would be administered by the League of Nations,

75. The British did not publish their paper but authorized Orlando to do so if he thought it best. He deemed it unwise, although he soon communicated its sense to his parliament, letter, Imperiali to Malcolm (Balfour's secretary), May 1, 1919, quoting a telegram from Orlando, at Rome, Balfour papers, 49751.

76. On Clemenceau's policy see Bonsal, pp. 115, 117.

77. Lloyd George's feelings toward Wilson changed from moment to moment, Lord Riddell's diary, April 23 and 27, 1919, p. 61. He failed to deny false assertions that he had never seen Wilson's manifesto and did not approve it at all. Lord Robert Cecil's diary, May 2, 1919, Cecil papers, box 51131, British Museum.

78. Axson, ms., Wilson papers, Princeton, section 49.

79. *Ibid.*, p. 49. Sir Rennell Rodd, in a report to Lloyd George, attributed the plan of compromise to Sonnino, who did not want his name mentioned in connection with it. Rodd called it a courageous attempt toward a "working solution." He reported that German agents were hard at work to make an alliance with Italy, Rodd to Lloyd George, May 6, 1919, Lloyd George papers, F / 56 / 2 / 27.

with an Italian as president of the municipal council. Dalmatia, except Zara and perhaps Sebenico, would go to Yugoslavia; and the islands would be divided in accord with the Treaty of London. The test of the proposal was sent to the Quai d'Orsay, and Page communicated its substance to Wilson on May 5.[80]

On the evening of that day Orlando and Sonnino set out for Paris, having received from Clemenceau and Lloyd George messages that in their opinion partook less of the nature of the expected invitation than of a notification *("intimation.")* Five days later Barrère left for Paris[81] on the same train with Ambassador Page, with the purpose of advocating the plan of compromise that had been worked out at Rome. However, the Quai rejected the plan as impossible, and Barrère received a curt telegram from Clemenceau ordering him to return to Rome.

Page, when he reached Paris, encountered a chilling coolness in the American commission and found it difficult to get the ear of the president.[82] Wilson did not enjoy the many frank and lengthy reports of this envoy, who like Ambassador Walter Hines Page at London—another man of letters—irritated Wilson by his voluminous expressions of sympathy for the country to which he was accredited. Thomas Nelson Page told Wilson, orally and in writing, that he wished to resign, and he let House understand that his intention had nothing to do with the present crisis. It was finally arranged that Page would return to the United States late in June and would resign after reaching home.[83]

On May 3, when Wilson went to the Crillon to confer with the American commission, House suggested ways to break the impasse with Italy. He found the mind of the president closed, however. Perceiving the seriousness of the situation and the embarrassing isolation into which Wilson had fallen, House persisted in efforts to negotiate. He talked with Fiorello La Guardia, the Italian congressman from New York, and asked him to approach Crespi about a variation of a solution that Wilson had rejected.[84]

80. Dispatch in Wilson papers. Paul Cambon, at London, told Curzon that Barrère's plan was only a provisional solution of an almost insoluble problem, Curzon to Derby, May 8, 1919, Curzon papers, Mss. Eur., F / 112 / 278.

81. Charles-Roux, pp. 46–51.

82. House diary, May 11, 1919. Lansing to Wilson, May 6, 1919. Lansing's letter stated that Page's decision to come to Paris at this time was unfortunate and that his departure from Rome might be misinterpreted in Italy and cause embarrassment. Edith Benham observed that Page's pleading at Paris "enraged the President pretty thoroughly," Benham diary letter, June 4, 1919.

To one letter from Page, on May 6, Wilson replied politely: "I need all the light I can get." But when Page called at the president's house on May 9, he was refused a hearing. "The president, I think, detests him," Baker wrote, journal, May 9, 1919.

83. House diary, May 11, 1919. Dispatch, Auchincloss to Polk, May 16, 1919, Auchincloss diary, May 17, 1919, Y.H.C. Ambassador Rodd recorded that Page's position was "humiliating" and that he suffered acutely from Wilson's lack of appreciation of his efforts toward conciliation. Rodd, *Social and Diplomatic Memories,* 3d series (London, 1925), p. 382. Wilson accepted Page's resignation in a note perfunctorily expressing "deep regret" and genuine admiration of the spirit in which Page served, Wilson to Page, August 29, 1919, Wilson papers.

84. House recorded in his diary that Wilson rejected the idea of leaving the settlement of Italy's territorial claims to the League of Nations, pointing out that the decision of the League council had to be unanimous and Italy had a veto. House had a notion that the Italians might be induced to waive their right of veto. La Guardia talked with Crespi, who telegraphed to Rome on May 4 but had no reply, House diary, May 3 and 4, 1919.

The immediate crisis blew over, as Wilson had forseen that it would,[85] although Sonnino protested in a formal note against the summoning of Austrian plenipotentiaries to the Peace Conference without consultation with Italy. On May 5 the Italian ambassador at Paris was told that the Treaty of London would be considered null and void if his nation's delegates did not return in two days.[86] Accordingly, Orlando was present at the meeting with the German delegates on May 7.[87] When he came to the session of the Council of Four on that day, Wilson said to him very casually: "You will have the same seat as always."[88]

Members of the American delegation, perceiving both the immediate and the long-range danger of leaving this question unsolved, continued to seek formulas acceptable to both parties. La Guardia talked with Orlando upon the latter's return to Paris, and House sent cards to Orlando and Sonnino, who spoke hopefully of finding a way out of the dilemma. The American advisers made a proposal based on the devices of the free city and the plebiscite and enlisting the services of the League of Nations.[89] The president considered the proposal carefully and discussed it inconclusively with Clemenceau and Lloyd George on May 12,[90] but the Italians rejected the plan, which in effect guaranteed that Fiume would go eventually to Yugoslavia. They hinted at a reaffiliation with Germany.[91]

So dear was Fiume to Italian hearts that Orlando gave Lloyd George to understand that if Italy could have Fiume, it eventually would abate its claim in Asia Minor.[92] The Treaty of London awarded to Italy only "a just share" in the region of Adalia (Antalya), in southwest Anatolia. However, in the conference at St.-Jean-de-Maurienne in 1917 France and Great Britain had recognized Italy's claim to some 70,000 square miles in Asia Minor, including Adalia and Smyrna (İzmir) and a vaguely defined zone of influence stretching as far north as Konya. A final settlement was reserved for the Peace Conference.

It happened that Italy was not the only nation that had interests on the coast of Asia Minor. A minority of Greeks at Smyrna lived in fear of Turkish persecution. In Paris, Venizelos, after meeting opposition to Greek objectives on the border of Albania,[93] dwelt upon his nation's claims in Asia Minor. Upon the return of Wilson

85. Mantoux, *Délibérations*, vol. 1, pp. 437, 478, 488.

86. Stevenson, *Lloyd George*, p. 182.

87. See below, pp. 391–392.

88. H. Hoover in *Saturday Evening Post*, July 7, 1934.

89. The plan submitted to the president by Johnson with the "unanimous approval" of "the territorial specialists concerned with the Fiume and Dalmatian problems" (except Seymour, who was absent) is in Baker, vol. 3, pp. 296–302. D. Johnson to Wilson, May 9, 1919, Wilson papers. See Lederer, pp. 205–209.

90. Mantoux, *Délibérations*, vol. 2, pp. 51–56.

91. H. White to Phillips, May 13, 1919, White papers, Columbia, notes and letters, box 1.

92. Lloyd George reported his talk with Orlando, perhaps not with complete accuracy, to the Supreme Council on May 19, 1919, Mantoux, *Délibérations*, vol. 2, p. 110.

93. See above, p. 60, n. 109. There was continuing controversy in the Greek commission over the line between Greece and Albania in northern Epirus, where Italian troops occupied disputed territory and posed as a protector of Albania. The British and French experts opposed the American recommendation and the Italian desire to give Koritsa to Albania, Nicolson, *Peacemaking*, pp. 174–176, 264–268, 270, 277–278, 282. Venizelos said that he would agree that Koritsa be put under a League mandate if the United States and not Italy were to administer it, letter, W. H. Buckler to his wife, April 11, 1919, Y.H.C.

to Paris on March 14, Venizelos had sent a letter to him outlining the territorial claims of Greece, which he called "the oldest of democratic nations." He suggested that his country would be content with a very small enclave at Smyrna and supervision of the surrounding territory by the League of Nations. Thinking that this acquisition was essential to his political leadership, he preferred it to possibilities suggested by British experts for compensation elsewhere, perhaps at Constantinople or in Thrace.[94]

According to Nicolson, Mezes agreed on a territorial boundary that made a concession to Venizelos. This negated the policy of the Inquiry, the protests of its representatives on the Greek committee, and the opinion of many of the American delegates.[95] However, Professor Westermann, the American specialist for western Asia, resisting the persuasion of Venizelos,[96] persisted in attempting to champion the principle of self-determination. Thinking that the Turkish Empire was indeed "the looting ground of the war," unable to get from Mezes a reason for the decision to yield to Greek demands that he thought imperialistic, and regarding Nicolson as an ill-informed messenger boy for Sir Eyre Crowe, whom he thought "a diplomatic juggler second to none," Westermann was of the opinion that Crowe was trying, by awarding Smyrna to Greece, to create a precedent for giving Italy the place in Asia Minor that had been promised by the Treaty of London. He wrote a vigorous protest; but unlike the American advisers on the question of the Adriatic, who had addressed their dissent effectively to the president himself, he sent it to House, whom Westermann thought responsible for yielding to Greek pressure.[97]

During the month of April, Venizelos bided his time while the Italian delegates at Paris behaved in a way that gave support to his argument. On May 3, Lloyd George told the Supreme Council that Venizelos had received a dispatch indicating that Italians were conspiring with Turks in Asia Minor to take up a policy of anti-Greek terrorism. Venizelos asked that the Allies dispatch a warship to Smyrna and

---

On April 17 the Albanian spokesman, Essad Pasha, claiming the support of all Albanians in America, pleaded with Wilson for complete independence; and on May 6 the president said in the Supreme Council that the Albanians dreaded a permanent rule by Italy and should have independence, Mantoux, *Délibérations,* vol. 1, pp. 498–499. Dissension among the chiefs who spoke for Albania suggested that the tribes of that turbulent country were incapable of forming a government. Recommendations of the Greek commission for a compromise were ignored, and because of the irreconcilable views of the European powers the boundary of northern Epirus was not determined at the Peace Conference. Woodall, "The Albanian Problem during the Peacemaking," pp. 66 ff. Petsalis-Diomidis, *Greece at the Paris Peace Conference,* pp. 139 ff. and map.

94. Letter, Venizelos to Wilson, March 14, 1919, Wilson papers. Nicolson, pp. 278, 284. Petsalis-Diomidis, pp. 182–200.

95. Nicolson, pp. 288, 289, 291. On the reversal of American policy after Wilson's return to Paris on March 14, which Westermann attributed to a decision by "higher-ups" (presumably Wilson and House) that was based on "the necessities of the international situation," see Paul C. Helmreich, *From Paris to Sèvres,* pp. 87–93.

96. Inquiry document no. 604, Westermann's notes on a talk with Venizelos. "Map showing Turkish boundaries" as sketched by M. Venizelos, December 18, 1918, Wilson papers.

Miller, who was frankly "pro-Italian" (Miller, vol. 1, p. 157), was "wholly opposed," believing that the Greeks had not been able to govern themselves, much less anyone else, and should not be given territory of which they occupied only a fringe.

97. Westermann for Mezes, March 25, 1919, Y.H.C. Westermann diary, March 27, 1919, Columbia Special Collections.

proposed also that Greece send a vessel to protect its people there. When Lloyd George suggested that the United States join in this, Wilson hesitated.[98] Venizelos, following up the advantage given him by the departure of his Italian adversaries from Paris, asked The Three to sanction the landing of a division of Greek troops at Smyrna to protect his compatriots.

Two days later Lloyd George announced to his two colleagues that the Italians had occupied Marmaris, and were debarking or about to land at three other places on the coast. "We shall discover one of these days," he said, "that they have occupied half of Anatolia." Clemenceau remarked that Italy already had three warships off Smyrna, and he agreed with Lloyd George that it would be well to decide on countermeasures before Orlando's return from Rome.

On the following morning Wilson explained in a tone of regret that he was restrained by the American Constitution from sending troops to Asiatic regions. He promised that he would ask the Congress for legislation that would permit the system of mandates to function under the authority of the League of Nations; but he warned that the decision could not be made at once. Then, giving voice to the prejudice that had been building up against Italian expansion, he said that the presence in Asia Minor of a people as turbulent as the Italians would be a threat to the peace of the region. He hoped to control them by financial pressure.

Lloyd George, citing the record of failure of economic measures to keep Turkey and the Balkan powers from each other's throats in the past, advised that they permit Venizelos to land Greek soldiers at Smyrna, where rumor predicted an Italian coup.[99] The president, who had already gone so far as secretly to order an American battleship to steam to Smyrna to observe proceedings, responded favorably without any consultation with his scholarly counselors. Indeed, he and his military staff took part in discussions of the proposed operations.[100] His firm attitude toward Italy was further stiffened by reports of Italian persecution of Greeks in the Dodecanese, which the Italians had occupied since 1912. He was in a mood to welcome the argument of Venizelos, whom he accepted as "a man of candor."[101] The adroit pleading of the Greek and his humoring of Wilson's devotion

---

98. Mantoux, *Délibérations*, vol. 1, pp. 452, 456. Heck, the American commissioner at Constantinople, after a two-week visit to Smyrna, had reported to Paris that the Greeks in the city were importing arms and organizing to control the region, which they thought assured to them although the Turks, greatly in the majority, were determined to resist, dispatch, March 28, 1919, Wilson papers.

99. Mantoux, *Délibérations*, vol. 1, pp. 485 ff.

100. *Ibid.*, pp. 497–499. Dispatch, Benson to OpNav, Washington, May 2, 1919, Wilson papers. Manley O. Hudson, in *What Really Happened at Paris*, ed. Seymour and House, p. 194.

On May 6 American and British military advisers, including General Bliss, conferred with Venizelos. They presumed that the Italian and Turkish governments would be duly informed of the action contemplated, which seemed not to be definitely sanctioned under the terms of the Armistice of Mudros, "Conclusions of a Conference in the Astoria at 4:30 p.m., May 6," Benson to Wilson, May 9, 1919, Wilson papers. The next day, however, the military advisers of Great Britain, whose Admiral Calthorpe was to have the operation in charge, met with The Three and Venizelos, who thought it important that the Turkish authorities not be notified until the last moment, so that they could not order their people to resist. Wilson fell in with the plan of Venizelos, saying that while it would be "more correct" to give warning, it would raise hazards, Mantoux, *Délibérations*, vol. 1, p. 511.

101. Benham diary letter, May 25, 1919. Miss Benham recorded that Wilson was impressed by the fact that Venizelos presented considerations unfavorable to his plans as well as those favorable.

to the League of Nations were proving effective. The president went along with his European colleagues in sanctioning a landing of forces at Smyrna without consultation with the Italian delegates and contrary to advice received in telegrams from Smyrna from consular, naval, and military officers of France, Great Britain, and the United States. He overcame whatever reservations he may have had as to the right of the native Turks to self-determination.[102]

The Three engaged in prolonged discussion of the commitment to Italy in Asia Minor under the wartime treaties. As the Europeans endeavored to find legal argument for denying Italian ambitions, Wilson asserted that whatever the legality of the case might be, he saw no moral justification for the cession of Smyrna to Italy. Making it clear that he mistrusted the Italians, who in his view had put themselves beyond the pale by their agitation for Fiume, he said that if he published in America all that he knew about Italian intrigue, it would "make their infernal scheme miscarry." Impressed by the fact that Venizelos had not openly sought to occupy Smyrna but merely called attention to the danger of massacre of his people there, the president went so far as to agree that after British and French forces occupied the forts, they would leave the garrisoning of them to the Greeks.

On May 10 The Three decided to apprise Italy and the Turks of their intentions at Smyrna just before the landing took place. They notified the Italians, on the twelfth, that they would be welcome to join with the Greeks, in equal force with small British and French contingents and under the command of British Admiral Calthorpe. When Orlando objected that the Greeks would be in a position of privilege after the withdrawal of the major Allies, Wilson stood with Clemenceau and Lloyd George in opposing a prolonged joint occupation.[103]

The landing on May 15 was not carried out without bloodshed. There were fatalities before Calthorpe was able to restore order. Bristol, whose American ships took no part in the operation, reported that foreign residents thought the Greek occupation impolitic and unjustifiable. Two weeks later looting was still going on, and the atrocities committed by undisciplined Greek troops were appalling.[104] Farther south in Asia Minor, Italy was proceeding to land troops without notice to the Council of Four. When The Three protested to Orlando, they received the plausible answer that this and similar earlier landings had been made because of local disorders.

102. Mantoux, *Délibérations,* vol. 2, pp. 40, 50. Laurence Evans, *U.S. Policy and the Partition of Turkey,* pp. 166, 173. Letter, Arnold Toynbee to the author, August 23, 1968.

103. Mantoux, *Délibérations,* vol. 2, pp. 34, 43–44, 48–52. The Allies and the United States were to land legation guards and Admiral Bristol would hold a landing force in readiness. Calthorpe was to notify the Turkish authorities on May 14 and enjoin them to maintain order. The Allies were to take possession of the city jointly and then turn it over to the Greeks. See James, *Admiral Sir Wm. Fisher* (London, 1948).

104. Corrected text of dispatch, Bristol to Benson, May 15, 1919, Wilson papers. Strong Turkish protests addressed to Wilson were forwarded by Bristol to Benson on May 20, 1919, Bristol papers, box 27, L.C. Evans, p. 180.

A summary of reports from Greek officials at Smyrna, communicated to Wilson by Venizelos on May 29, put the responsibility for violence on the Turks, who were said to have fired from their barracks on Greek troops. Wilson replied on June 3: "I have been interested and reassured," letters in Wilson papers. Westermann diary, June 13, 1919. Receiving a report on Greek atrocities from Westermann, Wilson wrote: "It is certainly of the most serious character. I am not sure that the Conference can retrace its steps . . . , but I of course feel it my duty to bring such evidence to the attention of my colleagues," letter of June 1919, Wilson papers.

Moreover, Orlando alluded to the precedent that had been set by the secret landing at Smyrna.[105]

The events of mid-May served to aggravate rather than heal the feeling of the Italians that they were unjustly treated at Paris. On the nineteenth Sonnino, representing Italy at a meeting of the Council of Four at which Venizelos was present, announced that he would now talk with the chiefs of the principal powers and with no one else. At this, Venizelos immediately retired from the room on his own volition despite Wilson's assertion that the Greek plenipotentiary was as much a member of the Peace Conference as the others. Wilson then joined with Clemenceau and Lloyd George in telling Sonnino bluntly that the Greek landing at Smyrna was authorized, that it was Italy that had first used force in Asia Minor without consulting its allies, and that though there had been provocative disorders in Adalia, the Italian government had failed to justify other landings which prejudged decisions that should have been reserved for the Peace Conference. When Lloyd George suggested that if the Italians were to be excluded from Asia Minor it might be well to retract some of the judgments made in respect of their Adriatic claims, Wilson did not bate a jot in his condemnation of Italian defiance of the Peace Conference.

After the confrontation with Sonnino the president went out of the room to bring back Venizelos, who then reached an agreement with The Three under which Greece could occupy the coast of the sanjak of Smyrna in order to evacuate Greeks menaced by Turk brutality. At the same time Greek forces would be withheld from making any other advances without the consent of British Admiral Calthorpe. At the end of May, when Westermann spoke to Wilson of the injustice being done to the native Turks, the president did not try to upset the decision of the council.[106]

In the ensuing months Greek atrocities led the Peace Conference to set up an investigating commission. The grand vizier of Turkey appealed to Wilson to end the Greek occupation. Admiral Bristol went to Smyrna with the commission, which took a report to Paris that was considered by the Peace Conference on November 8.[107] The Greeks were found to be guilty, but the Peace Conference merely warned Venizelos that the atrocities must end.[108]

During May and June the behavior of the Italians in Asia Minor did not incline Wilson toward any moderation in resisting their claims in the Adriatic. The American experts were discouraged by the president's intransigence, and their recommendations were at odds.[109] House noted that the pride of the Italian delegates had

105. Mantoux, *Délibérations*, vol. 2, pp. 88, 97–98, 115–122. Clemenceau to Orlando, May 17, 1919, Orlando to Clemenceau, May 18, 1919, Wilson papers.

106. Mantoux, *Délibérations*, vol. 2, pp. 115–121. Nicolson, pp. 344, 346. Evans, p. 173.

107. See below, p. 497, n. 65.

108. W. H. Buckler to Mrs. Buckler, November 8 and 10, 1919. Wilson, ill at Washington, took no action. Dispatches, secretary of state from Ravndal, August 25, 1919, Bristol to General Harbord, August 20, Bristol papers, box 27. Bristol to Ammission for Polk, October 15, 1919, *ibid.*, box 36. A. E. Montgomery, "Lloyd George and the Greek Question," in *Lloyd George: Twelve Essays*, ed. Taylor. Memorandum, Curzon to Balfour, June 20, 1919; Curzon, "Memo on Greek Occupation of Smyrna," August 1919, Curzon papers, mss. Eur., P / 112 / 278.

109. On May 14 Seymour wrote: "The President has said definitely that he will not approve any compromise," *Letters from the Paris Peace Conference*, p. 225.

"It is incredible," Shotwell wrote on May 16, "but this world-incident has narrowed down to an

been wounded, and he felt that in their self-pity they would surely fall into the arms of Germany. But when he pleaded with the president for concessions to Italian sentiment, he found Wilson fearful that Orlando would think him ready to yield in principle if House so much as talked with the Italians.[110]

Nevertheless, House persisted in his self-imposed diplomatic mission of holding Italy within the concert of Western democracies. On May 14, finding Orlando willing to enter into direct negotiations with the Yugoslavs on the whole Adriatic question, he elicited from Wilson permission to bring the two parties together under American auspices to seek an agreement that would be "freely reached."[111] When the Yugoslavs sought satisfaction of their claims in Carinthia[112] as a condition of participation in this project, House promised to urge Wilson to accede.

On May 16 the resourceful Texan, believing that true statesmanship entailed a series of wise compromises, pleased at the prospect of serving again in the role in which he was happiest, and unduly optimistic about the outcome, staged a conference at the Crillon in a manner most unorthodox.[113] The principals never came face to face. Orlando was closeted in a salon, Trumbić in a reception room. Between them House, in his study, directed interchanges of views as he and American specialists went back and forth through the two doors. By holding the negotiators in their rooms for six hours, until nine in the evening, without food, the colonel hoped to weaken all resistance to compromise.[114] However, this strategy, which had been applied earlier to get a decision from a room full of Poles,[115] brought no progress, except that each party agreed that Fiume should not go eventually to the other. The crux of the matter was the boundary of Istria. The Italians required a land connection between Italy and Fiume and therefore demanded that the Wilson Line in Istria be moved to the east. The Yugoslavs would not yield an inch. Orlando would not accept economic or colonial compensation for renunciation of Italy's claims. He explained that actually the territory on the Adriatic was not "worth the candle" and yet the mentality of his people was so peculiar that they would not give up even a few barren islands in exchange for the whole world. House reported to the president immediately, was thanked for his efforts, and was told that Miller could continue

internal dispute in the Inquiry. . . . Johnson upholds the honor of the exact sciences by refusing to budge the Yugoslav frontiers one inch from where he traced his own suggested frontier on the map. So, as Beer put it, the world is really waiting for a solution until Johnson can be brought to make some compromise between geography and politics," *At the Paris Peace Conference*, p. 322.

110. Lederer, pp. 208–213. House diary, May 12, 13, 14, 16, and 17, 1919. *I.P.*, vol. 4, pp. 462–468. Miller, vol., May 18 and 19, 1919. Miller, "The Adriatic Negotiations at Paris." "How," House asked Wilson, "could a solution be found if the question was not discussed?" The efforts of Miller are related in detail in John P. Posey, "David Hunter Miller at the Paris Peace Conference," pp. 144–161.

111. Miller, *My Diary*, vol. 1, May 12, 13, and 14, 1919.

112. See below, p. 446.

113. "There has never been a time," House wrote in his diary of May 14, "when I have felt that it [the Adriatic question] could not have been settled if properly and constantly directed." And on May 15: "It would be a great triumph if I could bring about a settlement of this difficult, delicate, and dangerous problem. . . . The Italians are now talking sense for the first time."

114. Recalling this incident, House said: "If you can get a man tired and hungry, very often finally you can weigh him down and he will accept your proposals," House-Seymour conversation, March 17, 1920, Y.H.C.

115. See Walworth, *America's Moment: 1918*, p. 180.

to negotiate with the Italians. However, both then and the next day, when House succeeded in "whittling down" the Italian claims, Wilson was inflexible in his determination to adhere to the Wilson Line.[116]

Tardieu worked out with Orlando an intricate plan of compromise that the latter thought might be acceptable to the Italian people.[117] House and Lloyd George considered it fair and persuaded Wilson to allow the plan to be taken to the Yugoslavs, who responded with what they called a "concession."[118] House thought that they conceded nothing, and the president felt their position was justifiable. Wilson talked privately with Orlando and concluded that the impasse was complete and might result in war.[119]

In the Council of Four on June 6 the president demonstrated that he had mastered the details of the Adriatic controversy. He had received a delegation of Slovenes the day before and was impressed by their bearing and their moderation. However, Lloyd George, warned by Orlando of the future potential of *"Russia incognita,"*[120] spoke of his fear of a Slavic force that could not be controlled and "could become a terrible danger for the world." Wilson agreed that the most serious menace to Italy was the discontent of the Slavs. When Lloyd George declared that Orlando would lose his office if he capitulated, and Clemenceau said that he would like to help their Italian colleague, Wilson went so far as to speak of the possibility of reconsidering the boundary of a free state of Fiume and the distribution of the islands. It was agreed to refer the question to specialists, and the next day in the Council of Four, with Orlando present, Wilson adduced an outline of a frontier in Istria that represented the utmost that he would approve. Orlando replied that it would have been a great strain on his people to accept the Tardieu plan and they could go no further. The impasse was as complete as ever.[121] Italy was out of it from now on, Lloyd George told Wilson, thanks to the impression given by House to the Italians that The Three were wobbling.[122]

116. D. Johnson's "Résumé" pp. 7, 8. Miller, *My Diary,* vol. 1 pp. 317, 322. Documents in Miller papers, L.C., box 84, II, 18 a and b, and box 87, III, 6. Suggested formula for Adriatic settlement, with the president's suggestion and Johnson's comments, May 8, 1919, Albrecht-Carrié, pp. 510–514.

117. *F.R., P.P.C.,* vol. 6, pp. 78–82. Minutes of a meeting at Lloyd George's apartment, May 28, 1919, Lloyd George papers, F / 200 / 1 / 6. The Tardieu plan called for a demilitarized buffer state of Fiume, to be administered by five commissioners: two to be appointed by Italy, one by Yugoslavia, one by Fiume, and one by the League of Nations, which after fifteen years was to supervise a plebiscite that would determine the rule thereafter.

118. Lederer, pp. 213–216. Johnson's "Résumé," p. 10.

119. Baker's journal, June 3, 1919. House diary, May 28, 29, 30, June 2, 3, 8, 9, and 11, 1919. It seemed to Bowman that House came as near to losing his temper at Wilson's intransigence as he had ever known him to come, Lansing's private memoranda, August 21, 1919.

120. Letter, Orlando to Lloyd George, May 25, 1919, Sonnino personal file, microfilm, 50.1, Y.H.C.

121. Mantoux, *Délibérations,* vol. 2, pp. 322–327, 344–346. The text of a proposal by Miller and the Italian reply of June 7 is in Sonnino's personal file, microfilm 50.1 in Y.H.C. See Miller, *My Diary,* vol. 9, 314, 372, and vol. 19, pp. 543–552.

122. Grayson diary, June 9, 1919. Grayson recorded on June 10 that Orlando accepted the idea of a free state and a plebiscite at the end of fifteen years, and that he qualified this by insisting on a vote by districts, which would result in Italy's acquisition of the city proper, where Italians were a majority. Grayson denounced this legitimate bit of bargaining as the "treachery" of a "fine Italian hand" and wrote: "The president was not disposed to fall into any such trap," Grayson diary, June 10, 1919. Any thought of applying the principle of self-determination to the separate city of Fiume continued to be regarded by Wilson as iniquitous.

Orlando, telling his staff that Wilson was a hypocrite though doubtless a sincere one, explained on June 12 that his presence was required at Rome.[123] Ambassador Page telegraphed that the premier's fall was expected. Page had already sent a dire warning: "Italy is being pushed back, drawn back, blown back . . . into the old connection . . . with Germany, and we may end up with all of Europe against us."[124] On the nineteenth Orlando, defeated decisively in a vote of the chamber, resigned. A cabinet was formed by Nitti; and the new foreign minister, Tittoni, was considered to be pro-German.

At the end of June, Wilson sent to Lansing a statement that was to serve as the basis of discussion with the delegates of the new Italian government. In this he insisted that Fiume could "in no circumstances go to Italy,"[125] which could be permitted to have territory east of his line in Istria only by the sanction of a plebiscite under the League of Nations. It should be made plain to the Italians, he wrote, "that the cooperation and assistance of the United States, including material and financial assistance of all kinds, is dependent upon her [Italy's] accepting as completely as the other powers have accepted the principles upon which the settlements of this peace have been made in respect of all other questions than those affecting Italy." This, of course, was not true in the case of "all other questions." The president's capacity for objective thinking had yielded to his moralistic ardor.[126] At this time a memorandum from Johnson made the unsupportable assertion that the American commissioners and experts were "unanimously of the opinion" that the Italians would accept "whatever solution the president insists upon." After his return to Washington the president continued to heed Johnson's advice, and the deadlock was never broken.[127]

123. Aldrovandi-Marescotti, *Nuovi Ricordi*, p. 61.

124. Page to H. White, June 2, 1919, Y.H.C. Grayson wrote in his diary on June 10: "Clemenceau insists that he has practically positive information that the Italians have been secretly negotiating with the Germans for the past month."

125. Lloyd George observed that "the annexation of Fiume raised Wilson's ire to a heat which it had never reached at any time during the Conference," *The Truth about the Peace Treaties*, p. 810.

126. "Memorandum of Additional Suggestions Concerning Conference with Italian Delegation," signed "Woodrow Wilson" and dated June 27, sent to Lansing with a letter dated June 28, 1919, copy in Y.H.C.

127. Letters, Wilson to Lansing, June 25 and 27, 1919, with memoranda, copies in Y.H.C. and Bliss papers, box 159, folder 105. Johnson to Wilson, June 26 and 27, 1919, Wilson papers. See below, p. 552, n. 31.

19

Crisis and Compromise: East Asia

At the very time in April when the controversy of the Italians and the Yugoslavs was rising to a crest, the plenipotentiaries of Japan spoke up for the rewards that their nation had been promised. Under agreements that had been made in 1917 with the Allies, Japan, in addition to receiving title to the German islands that lay in the Pacific north of the equator, also was to take over the rights that Germany had held in China's Shantung Province under a ninety-nine-year lease.[1] The Japanese delegates were disappointed when they learned in January of 1919 that they would receive the Pacific islands not outright, as they had expected, but under the qualifications of a League mandate. Moreover, their forebearance was taxed when their demand for an acknowledgment of racial equality in the League Covenant was rejected.[2] Now, in April, they were still without any recognition of their claim to the preferred status that Germans had enjoyed in territory in Shantung that Japanese armed forces had seized. The Chinese government at Peking had declared war on Germany on August 14, 1917, thus terminating the German rights.

The claims of Japan touched vital interests of the United States: not only the security of its Pacific frontier and the Philippines, but its future relations with China as well. The Department of State was committed to a policy of long-standing that had grown out of American impulses to befriend the Chinese people and to trade with them. The United States had stood apart from the infringement upon China's territorial integrity by colonial powers, while at the same time benefiting from the security that was provided by this infringement. The American government had sought no special concessions of its own, and for two decades it had advocated the preservation of an ''open door'' for the educational and commercial enterprise of all nations. At the same time American citizens had contributed generously to improve the conditions of life in China.

Japan, a late entrant in the quest for outlets overseas, had been asserting political influence in many parts of China so effectively that Americans wondered whether the Chinese people would be able to absorb the Japanese intruders as they had absorbed earlier invaders.[3] In 1915 Japan, following the example of colonial powers of Europe, had given Peking a forty-eight-hour ultimatum presenting twenty-one demands. It required the transfer of all German rights in Shantung to Japan and also asked for special privileges in other provinces of China. The ultimatum had provoked a public warning from the United States government that it could not recog-

---

1. The texts of the secret agreements between Japan and its allies may be found in the D. H. Miller papers, box 89, III, 11, L.C. The texts were sent to the American commissioners after they discovered on February 5 that they lacked definite information, minutes, ACTNP, February 5, 1919. Lansing summarized the pacts for Wilson, Lansing to the secretary of state, February 26, 1919, Wilson papers.
2. See above, p. 310.
3. See Willoughby's report on China, in Miller, *My Diary*, doc. 420.

nize any agreement or undertaking which had been entered into or any which might be entered into between the governments of Japan and China, impairing the treaty rights of the United States and its citizens in China, the political or territorial integrity of the Republic of China, or the international policy relative to China commonly known as the open door policy.

As early as September of 1917, Colonel House had perceived the difficulty of reconciling the immediate pressure of Japanese expansion with the traditional policy of the open door and the friendly impulses of the American people toward China. He warned Wilson that, inasmuch as Japanese immigration to the United States had been restricted, some concession should be made in the Far East to relieve the overpopulation of the island empire.[4] Shortly after this, Secretary Lansing and Viscount Ishii had worked out a formula of understanding. They were able to agree that Japan would respect the open door and the independence and territorial integrity of China. At the same time the United States would recognize that since "territorial propinquity creates special relations between countries," Japan had "special interests in China, particularly in the part to which her possessions are contiguous." The ambiguity of the Lansing-Ishii agreement left it subject to diverse interpretations.[5]

At the end of the war Secretary Lansing abandoned the policy that had failed to produce anything more substantial than this vague accommodation. He told Ishii on November 16, 1918, that Japan's operations in north China were "certainly opposed" to American views. Encouraged by the installation of a moderate ministry in Tokyo, Lansing went to the Peace Conference convinced that resolute opposition to Japanese plans in Shantung would help the moderates in Japan to overcome the militants decisively.[6]

The question of American policy toward the aspirations of the coalition delegation that China sent to Paris came before the State Department very soon after the armistice. V. K. Wellington Koo, third in rank among the five plenipotentiaries[7] and China's minister at Washington since 1914, talked for fifteen minutes with the president on November 26. Charmed by the diction of the young man ("he talks English the way Macaulay wrote it," Wilson said), the president gave general

4. "Japan is barred from all the underdeveloped places of the earth," House wrote, "and if her influence in the East is not recognized as in some degree superior to that of the Western Powers, there will be a reckoning. A policy can be formulated which will leave the Open Door, rehabilitate China, and satisfy Japan," House to Wilson, September 18, 1917, Wilson papers. See *America's Moment: 1918*, p. 197n.

5. "Lansing viewed the agreement as a stopgap measure designed to prevent full recognition of Japan's position in China. But the term 'special interests' was ambiguously translated. According to the United States interpretation, Japan was conceded only economic benefits. The Japanese, on the other hand, construed the agreement as a political concession," Richard B. Morris, *Encyclopedia of American History* (New York, 1953). p. 310. Ishii, *Diplomatic Commentaries* (Baltimore, 1936). Roy Watson Curry, *Woodrow Wilson and Far Eastern Policy*, pp. 177–184.

6. Burton F. Beers, *Vain Endeavor*, pp. 134–140, 152–155.

7. The other four plenipotentiaries were, in order of rank, Lou Tseng-tsiang, minister of foreign affairs, a northerner; Chen-Ting Thomas Wang, a former minister of agriculture and commerce who, with Koo, represented the provisional government at Canton; Sao-Ke Alfred Sze, minister at London; and Suntchou Wei, minister at Brussels, Wensz King, *China at the Paris Peace Conference in 1919*, Asia in the Modern World pamphlet no. 2 (New York, 1961), p. 4. King was Koo's secretary. Notes on the Chinese peace commissioners, Stanley K. Hornbeck papers, Hoover Institution, Stanford University.

assurance that China would have the support of the Americans at the Peace Conference. However, he alluded vaguely to "many secret agreements between the subjects of China and other powers" and said that the Far East was one part of the world where there might be "trouble" in the future. He went so far as to invite Koo to travel to France with him on the *George Washington*. Soon thereafter it was generally understood in China that with the support of Wilson that country could achieve what Koo had envisioned[8]—namely, the vindication of the principles of territorial integrity, preservation of sovereign rights, and economic and fiscal independence.[9]

Officials of the State Department, however, doubted both the wisdom and the propriety of interference in the politics of China. They wondered to what length they might safely go in giving comfort and advice to spokesmen of a people that had no reliable central government. When the question was brought to the president by Lansing, Wilson gave the opinion that it would be unwise, if not improper, for an American to have any official connection with any foreign government during the peace negotiations.[10]

On January 10 the American commission at Paris received a long telegram from Paul S. Reinsch, the American minister at Peking, with an endorsing memorandum by E. T. Williams, chief of the Far Eastern Division of the State Department and an adviser at the Peace Conference. The purport of these papers was that China should be freed from the exercise of foreign political influence within its borders and that the Chinese people wished to have freedom "to follow in the footsteps of America." Reinsch hoped that China might use Western experts to develop an efficient administrative system. Working for the open door for American business and wishing to thwart Japanese competition, he had secured a copy of Japan's secret twenty-one demands of 1915 and had released it to the press. He alleged that huge mining enterprises were being promoted by Japanese with the help of subservient Chinese of the military clique in the north. "The consequence of China's disillusionment at the Peace Conference on her moral and political development would be disastrous," Reinsch warned, "and we, instead of looking across the Pacific toward a Chinese nation sympathetic to our ideals, would be confronted with a vast materialistic military organization under a ruthless control."[11]

8. "Memo of a conversation with the president at the White House, Nov. 26, 1918, "Koo papers, box 001, Special Collections, Columbia University Library. King, p. 3. R. H. Fifield, *Woodrow Wilson and the Far East,* p. 191. Memorandum by B. Long, November 26, 1918, Long papers, L.C.

9. Koo to Lansing, November 25, 1918, Lansing papers, box 2, Princeton University Library.

10. *F.R., P.P.C.,* vol. 1, pp. 241–245. See Walworth, p. 123 n.

Lansing ruled that the American plenipotentiaries might "confer informally" with the Chinese at Paris. Bowman and other Americans advised them unofficially, and supplied them with maps, Fifield, p. 186; Geoffrey J. Martin, *Mark Jefferson: Cartographer* p. 186; Curry, pp. 251–252.

11. Polk diary, December 23 and 28, 1918. Reinsch to State Department for Wilson, January 6, 1919, *F.R., P.P.C.,* vol. 2, pp. 520–525. Dispatch, Polk to Ammission, January 10, 1919, Y.H.C. For an account of Japanese operations in China at this time, see Paul S. Reinsch, *An American Diplomat in China* (New York, 1922), pp. 328–353, and Noel H. Pugach, *Paul S. Reinsch: Open Door Diplomat in Action* (Millwood, N.Y., 1979). On January 10 Reinsch called the attention of the American commission at Paris to "the important necessity of a thoroughgoing and permanent settlement of the Chinese question," dispatch in Wilson papers, E. T. Williams to Wilson, January 16, 1919, Wilson papers. Long's diary, December 13, 16, 23, and 31, 1918.

The disposition of Chinese authorities to seek financial aid from abroad had already placed them in economic servitude to foreign powers.[12] Indeed, as recently as September 24, 1918, the military party of north China concluded an agreement with Japan under which China received pecuniary benefits and in turn affirmed Japanese rights to police railways in Shantung and in Manchuria. Noting the threat posed to China's sovereignty by loans from foreign powers, Wilson had been unsympathetic to a consortium of bankers that had wished to finance the economic development of China. In order to avert a Japanese monopoly, however, the president acceded to plans of the State Department under which the United States government and those of France, Great Britain, and Japan would give active and exclusive support each to its own national group of bankers.[13] All preferences and options in China that were held by member banks would be pooled, and the administrative integrity and independence of China would be respected. "A very necessary step," Polk advised the American commission in mid-January, "is the immediate completion of the international consortium. . . . Mr. J. P. Morgan is going from London to Paris in the near future. He hopes to be able to get the British and French bankers to favor such a proposal. I hope you will take every opportunity to advance this important arrangement and report fully the progress made. We are still urging the matter here [in Washington] with British, French and Japanese embassies with only general encouragement."[14]

The Japanese, perceiving that such an arrangement might undermine the position that they had established in China, demanded that any consortium of the future must respect their vested rights, especially in Manchuria. Efforts to reach a compromise in this matter went on in the background all through the Peace Conference, complicating and embittering the negotiations.[15] The Japanese were not pleased by the assertion on the part of the American government of a right to share, and thus perhaps to control, their financial operations in China as well as their military activities in Siberia.[16]

The delegates of China at Paris had a very insecure footing. They had to keep one eye on the government at Peking from which they had credentials that might be withdrawn at any moment at the insistence of Japan, to which their government was financially beholden. The other eye was watching a domestic peace conference, assembling at Shanghai in February, in which factions would contend for political

12. C. T. Wang alleged to Miller that Japan had loaned 140 million yen and perhaps more to the government at Peking. Miller, vol. 1, p. 133, entry of February 22, 1919.

13. Lansing to Jusserand with enclosure, *F.R., 1918*, pp. 193–196. David F. Trask, "Sino-Japanese-American Relations during the Paris Peace Conference," in *Aspects of Sino-American Relations since 1784*, ed. Thomas H. Etzold, p. 83.

14. Dispatch, Polk to Ammission, January 17, 1919, Y.H.C.

15. See A. Whitney Griswold, *Far Eastern Policy of the United States*, pp. 223–227, Curry, pp. 18–27, 187–204, and below, p. 376.

16. The United States had curbed Japanese authority in Siberia by sending troops to Vladivostok and by negotiating the agreement of January 9, 1918, whereby the trans-Siberian railway was to be operated under an inter-Allied commission, with the advice of a technical board headed by an American engineer, John F. Stevens. Japanese interests enjoyed a privileged position in Manchuria under treaties with China and with European powers, Griswold, pp. 172, 186, 211, 229–230.

control of the country. In spite of their precarious position, however, the Western-educated Chinese plenipotentiaries, energetic and ambitious, committed their delegation to a far-reaching program. Not satisfied merely to attempt at the Peace Conference to free their people from the servitudes to which they had been committed in 1915 and 1918 by Japan, they undertook to revise as many as possible of the agreements under which sovereign rights had been surrendered to other foreign powers.[17]

The Chinese who resisted Japan had the support of American naval and diplomatic opinion,[18] as well as that of their academic friends. Indeed, the Inquiry recommended that steps be taken at the Peace Conference to modify the special arrangements under which foreigners lived in China and which many of them thought both necessary to their security and beneficial to China. The scholars did not recognize the concessions that Japan received in 1915 and that Chinese spokesmen alleged to have been given under duress. They proposed that the question of Shantung should be settled on its merits, that China regain Kiaochow with compensation to Germany for improvements effected, and that the port of Tsingtao should be internationalized and in no circumstance allowed to remain permanently under the control of Japan.[19]

Encouraged by American professors who had taught them and by assurances of sympathy from influential citizens of the United States, the Chinese nationalists at Paris lost little time in revealing their strategy to American delegates and in seeking their assistance, while their propagandists skillfully stimulated anti-Japanese feeling. The receptivity of the Americans, which was lively from the first, did not suffer from their entertainment at Chinese dinner parties. At a luncheon on January 22, C. T. Wang proposed to three American advisers an arrangement that would return to China all the treaty rights held by Germany and Austria.[20] The Chinese hoped later to do away with the extraterritorial rights of other powers.

When in January the Supreme Council had considered the question of Japan's claims in connection with arrangements for Germany's Pacific islands,[21] Japan's chief spokesman, Baron Makino,[22] asked for the unconditional cession to Japan of

---

17. Wellington Koo's record, O.H.R.O., Columbia University Library, p. 151. "While this program embodied the desires of the increasingly vociferous anti-Japanese elements in China—perhaps of a majority of literate Chinese—it did not embody those of the group that remained in power at Peking and continued to do business privately with Tokyo. . . . The Chinese government itself did not give undivided allegiance to Wilson's cause at Paris," Griswold, p. 243. H. White to Lodge, May 2, 1919, White papers, notes and letters, box 2, Columbia University Library.

18. Curry, p. 262.

19. Gelfand, *The Inquiry*, pp. 260–272.

20. Wang presented a draft article to Miller, Shotwell, and Hornbeck. Koo entertained Shotwell, his former teacher at Columbia, and on February 3 Shotwell was asked to dine with most of the Chinese delegation and found them "a very dignified set of young men, . . . and all of them had doctorates from American universities," Shotwell, *At the Paris Peace Conference*, pp. 136–139, 161, 163. Miller, vol. 1, pp. 60, 88, 160–161, and doc. 215. J. F. Dulles to Mrs. Dulles, January 26, 1919, Dulles papers, Princeton University, box 503.

21. See above, pp. 73, 81.

22. Early in the Peace Conference, Baron Makino had professed a sincere desire to cooperate in building a league of nations, but he had to serve the immediate purposes of his own nation. Prince

all German rights in Shantung province. He justified this demand by the fact that Japanese armed forces had destroyed the German base at Kiaochow and were now in possession there.

At this first formal presentation of Japanese claims, Wellington Koo was permitted, at the insistence of the Americans, to speak for China.[23] Notified only an hour before the Supreme Court met on the morning of January 27, Koo hurried to see Lansing, from whom he understood that he could count on the effective support of the United States.[24] He then appeared before the council and asked that it defer action until he could prepare a presentation of China's case.

Immediately afterward Koo called upon Wilson, who showed surprise and distress at the Japanese presentation and suggested that Koo speak plainly to the council about China's desires. The president agreed to endeavor to enlist the support of the British government, although he supposed that its hands were tied by its alliance with Japan. When Koo pressed him to speak in favor of China in the Supreme Council, however, Wilson would go only so far as to say that he had deep sympathy for China and would do his best to help.[25] The crisis in respect of mandates for the Pacific islands precluded involvement in further controversy with Japan at this moment. Wilson did, however, go so far as to ask that the Chinese and Japanese delegates produce copies of the exchanges between their governments in 1915. Here he met with resistance from Makino, who proposed to consult Tokyo.

Koo proved himself fully capable of pleading his country's cause. In a brilliant speech on January 28—his first of many delivered to international congresses—he posed as "spokesman for one-quarter of the human race" and as defender of Shantung, China's "Holy Land, the Home of Confucius." He argued that Germany's occupation of Kiaochow was a transgression against China's integrity, and that to transfer the special rights now to another power would be to repeat the crime. Although grateful to Japan for rooting out the Germans, the Chinese were unwilling to pay their debt of gratitude by selling what they conceived to be "the birthright of their countrymen," and thereby sowing seeds of discord in the future.

In reply Makino insisted that, in accord with the wartime agreements with China, Japan must obtain the German rights directly from Germany before they could be restored to China. The pride of the Japanese was hurt by the imputation that they were not trusted to do justice eventually to China.

Koo gave assurance that he respected Japan's intention not to retain the rights in Shantung for itself. Saying that he did not propose to break unilaterally the agreements of 1915 and 1918 despite the "disconcerting" circumstances under which

---

Saionji Kimmochi, the senior plenipotentiary of Japan, did not arrive at Paris until March and attended only the plenary sessions of the Conference.

23. The American ambassador at Paris had been instructed to discuss the matter with the Quai d'Orsay and to support the Chinese petition for a hearing, "Memorandum, Nov. 18, 1918," Archives du M.A.É., À paix, A1151.1, f. 139.

24. King, p. 5. Memo of interview with Secretary Robert Lansing, January 27, 1919, Koo papers, box 001, Columbia University Library, Special Collections.

25. King, p. 6. According to Koo's record, Wilson approved an argument that Koo outlined for his speech, memorandum, "Interview with W.W. at the Murat mansion," January 27, 1919, Koo papers, box 001.

Chinese officials signed them, he argued that because they dealt with questions that arose out of the war, they were provisional arrangements and subject to final review at the Peace Conference. Moreover, he invoked the principle of *rebus sic stantibus,* explaining that in declaring war against Germany in 1917 his government had nullified all treaties with Germany, and so at that time the rights in Shantung had in fact reverted to China. And even had they not, Germany was restrained from transferring the leases to another power because of a provision in them that forbade it.[26]

On the day after Koo's eloquent speech, a Japanese delegate notified Lansing that the United States would be blamed if Kiaochow was returned directly to China.[27] While Americans advised their Chinese friends that China should put its faith in Wilson, a British counselor of the Chinese expressed the opinion that they were being used by the Americans to wear down the Japanese.[28]

On February 7 Wilson met the situation tentatively by suggesting to Lansing that the Peking government be counseled to stand firm and that Koo to be advised to follow the course that he thought best. At the same time Ambassador Morris, at Tokyo, should be instructed to have a friendly talk with the Japanese minister of foreign affairs, to disclose the extent of the State Department's knowledge of Japanese operations at Peking, and to express its distress at indications that the Japanese government lacked confidence in the justness of the Peace Conference.[29]

Relations between Washington and Tokyo were strained at this time by events in Korea as well as by differences with respect to China. Militant Korean patriots, rebelling against a Japanese military rule that they denounced as "the most oppressive . . . ever known to history," issued a declaration of independence[30] on March 1. Although a majority of the signers of this declaration were of other faiths, thirteen were Christian ministers, and Japanese observers were inclined to blame American missions for inciting the revolt.[31] Lansing, an ardent partisan of the Chinese nationalists, was not willing to give further offense by championing the Korean revolutionaries.[32]

Actually, Japan's reactions to them were giving quite enough cause for concern

26. *F.R., P.P.C.,* vol. 3, pp. 755–757. For a statement on the matter and manner of Koo's address, see King, pp. 6–11. A formal memorandum that was presented to the council after the speech is printed, with annexes, in King, *V. K. Wellington Koo's Foreign Policy: Some Selected Documents* (Shanghai, 1931), pp. 1–17, 57–114.

27. Richard D. Burns and Edward M. Bennett, *Diplomats in Crisis* (Santa Barbara and Oxford, 1974), p. 134.

28. According to Steed, the British adviser Dr. George Ernest Morrison spent his time "hacking great chunks of anti-Japanese stuff out of Chinese official memoranda," memorandum to Northcliffe, March 6, 1919, Steed papers.

29. Copy of letter, Wilson to Lansing, February 7, 1919, copy in Wilson papers.

30. Note to the Peace Conference from the New Korean Young Men's Society, April 5, 1919, Wilson papers, presented with a "Claim of the Korean People for Liberation," Y.H.C.

31. Ambassador Morris reported from Tokyo that the missionaries in Korea, some of whom were arrested, had not "directly inspired or supported" the movement of passive resistance, dispatch, Morris to Polk, April 6, 1919, *F.R., 1919,* vol. 2, pp. 460–461. Memorandum by E. T. Williams, March 17, 1919, Bliss papers, box 69, Grew correspondence.

32. Dispatches, Polk to Ammission, March 1, 1919, Ammission to Polk, March 4, 1919, N.A., R.G. 59, 763.72119 / 3963a and 3990. To a Korean delegate who came to Paris to ask relief from Japan's repressive rule of his country, Bonsal was obliged to say that Korea's problems were beyond the purview

on the part of the United States government. Americans in China made known their distrust and dislike of Japanese purposes and methods, and this irritated Japanese opinion and provoked protests. When the State Department learned from its Tokyo embassy that officials of the Japanese government were "countenancing, if not encouraging" new stories to the effect that American officials in China were inciting the populace against Japan, the American government immediately denied such improper conduct.[33]

Controversy between the United States and Japan was further stirred when American communications across the Pacific were imperiled by a proposal on April 15 by Clemenceau and Lloyd George that Japan keep the three cables that it had taken over from Germany. Wilson remarked that the island of Yap, where the three converged, should be internationalized so that Japan, governing under a mandate, would not be able to cut the lines linking various nations and "notably between the United States and the Philippines."[34] However, the American position was not clearly recognized in the ratification of the C Mandates on December 17, 1920.

For several weeks the Supreme Council let the animosity between the Chinese and the Japanese fester, hesitant to probe into the venomous feud over Shantung or to entrust the matter to a committee of experts. The Chinese commanded the sympathy of those who put faith in the ideals of Wilson. Japan had the advantage of possession as well as the legal support of treaties.

By mid-April the general situation in the Far East seemed to be worsening and Ambassador Ishii was thinking of resigning from his post at Washington.[35] Wilson was informed by Lansing that there was violent conflict between Americans and Japanese at Tientsin and that in less than two months a substantial battle fleet would be in the Pacific or on its way there.[36] Lansing enclosed a dispatch from the commander of the Asiatic squadron recommending prompt execution of naval plans for maintaining a fleet in the Pacific for its "beneficial effect" on the diplomatic situation. The Chinese at Paris were persistently seeking American intercession in their country's behalf. Koo appealed to Wilson through both House and Lansing and also

---

of the Peace Conference but might one day be dealt with by the League of Nations, Bonsal, *Suitors and Suppliants,* pp. 222–225.

33. Dispatches of March 5 and 23, 1919, *F.R., 1918,* vol. 1, pp. 686–690. E. T. Williams, in whom the American commission at Paris expressed complete confidence (minutes, February 4, 1919), noted that Japanese spokesmen at Tokyo had gone so far as to suggest that the United States hoped to supplant Japan in Shantung. He thought that the Japanese Foreign Office could not "escape responsibility" for anti-American statements in the controlled press.

Secretary Lansing remarked in a meeting of the American Commission that it was time to have it out with Japan once and for all. He took note of the fact that Japan's position, economically and financially, was "greatly inferior," minutes, February 6, 1919. Beers, *Vain Endeavor,* p. 149.

34. Mantoux, *Proceedings,* pp. 197, 315. N. H. Davis to the secretary of state, November 17, 1919. Later treaties concluded with Britain, France, and Japan gave American sanction to the Yap mandate, Aaron M. Margolith, *The International Mandates,* pp. 102–103. See Sumitra Rattan, "The Yap Controversy and Its Significance," 124–136, and Timothy P. Mapa, "Prelude to War? The U. S., Japan, and the Yap Crisis, 1918–1922," *Diplomatic History* 9, no. 3 (Summer 1985):221 ff.

35. Ishii resigned in June. In his memoirs he testified of his awareness of a bias on the part of Lansing in favor of China, Ishii, pp. 122–132.

36. Lansing to Wilson, March 22, 1919, Wilson papers.

in a conversation with the president on March 24, in the course of which Wilson remarked that Kiaochow could not be treated like the German colonies.[37] Koo warned House of a feeling on the part of some of the Chinese delegates that they had best negotiate directly with Japan since the Western powers could not be depended upon.[38]

On April 18 Wilson, urged constantly by Lansing and the expert advisers to befriend China, studied the agreements of 1915 and 1918 between China and Japan.[39] Afterward in a meeting of The Four he expressed fear that the friction that existed in the Far East might burst into war at any moment. The president advocated the renunciation of all zones of foreign influence in China; and Lloyd George went so far as to say that in his opinion the English public would give up a privilege that was "purely nominal," if only the door was kept open to the commerce of all nations. Wilson then indulged in prophecy. "In my view," he said, "once the Bolshevik fever has passed, Europe will be preserved from a great war for a long time, but I fear that this will not be the case in the Far East. I would compare the hidden seeds of conflict which are developing there . . . to sparks concealed beneath a thick bed of leaves." He thought the Japanese "rather difficult to deal with" and "very ingenious in interpreting treaties."[40]

On the morning of April 21 Makino and Chinda went to the residence of Wilson, and the three had a long talk. The Japanese were unresponsive to a proposal of a five-power trusteeship for Shantung Province.[41] Nor did they take kindly to a suggestion that all special privileges of foreign powers in China be renounced. Moreover, they insisted very politely that Japan could not sign the peace treaty if all its demands in Shantung were not met. They had chosen their moment shrewdly. Unlike the Italians, they were not yet committed by economic interest to sign the treaty. The general disorganization of the Peace Conference had put the Council of Four under tremendous pressure to act immediately upon some of the most difficult questions of the peacemaking. It was essential to present a united front to the German delegates; and in the background was the persistent menace of revolution and anarchy.

The next morning Makino and Chinda attended the meeting of the council. Wilson, declaring that he respected the sanctity of international treaties and was the only man present who could speak out untrammeled by them, proposed that in the common interest the powers renounce their preferred positions in China. If they did not, he said, there might be consequences that filled him with anxiety, in view of the awakening of China's 400 million people. But the statesmen of the empires were unmoved. Makino expressed confidence that a way could be found to dispel

37. Memorandum of interview with Wilson *et al.*, March 24, 1919, Koo papers, Columbia University Special Collections, box 001. B. Long to Polk, April 17, 1919, Y. H. C. Koo to Wilson, April 17, 1919, Lou Tseng-tsiang to Wilson, April 16, 1919, Wilson papers.
38. "An Interview with Colonel House," April 2, 1919, Koo papers, box 001.
39. Lansing to Wilson, April 21 and 22, 1919. In a paper entitled "Some Practical Considerations with Regard to the Question of Shantung," the American experts denounced the Sino-Japanese Agreement of 1915 as "extorted under pressure with attempt at concealment," but they did not mention the agreement of 1918, under which China received pecuniary consideration for the concessions made, copy of document, n.d., Hornbeck papers.
40. Mantoux, *Proceedings*, pp. 218–219.
41. Trask, pp. 90, 92.

the sense of injustice that existed among Chinese nationalists. He said that he would be very happy to discuss this matter with the great powers. However, when Wilson quizzed him about the nature of the rights that Japan demanded in Shantung, asking just what was meant by "joint administration" of the railroads and by a "training school" for the police force, Makino was evasive. He insisted that his government's plans were in keeping with the system that prevailed in China and that would disappear if the whole question of extraterritorial rights could be settled by agreement among the powers. Lloyd George, for his part, was willing to discuss only the matters that arose out of the war. He was content to leave the larger question of the "protection" of China to the League of Nations, of which it would be a member. Wilson also was forced to fall back upon this recourse.[42]

On April 22 Lou and Koo had their day in court. Koo continued to plead for the immediate return of the German rights to China. He warned of the political agitation that a refusal would provoke. Lloyd George reminded him, however, that China might now be at the mercy of the iron hand of Germany if Japan had not intervened during the war. Wilson, holding out hope for a future reconsideration of the whole system of unequal treaties, explained that there was no escape from the commitments of the Allies to Japan, deplorable though he thought them. He was so deluded by his aversion to this unpleasant subject that he said to Dr. Grayson on April 25: "Yesterday [*sic*] I found that England had a secret treaty with Japan against China." Actually, this discovery had probably been made earlier, and perhaps forgotten.[43]

When Koo had left the room on the twenty-second Wilson explained to his two colleagues that his main purpose was to avoid an abyss between East and West, and that with this in view he was ready to do what was necessary to assure Japanese participation in the League of Nations. He recognized the contradiction between his attitude toward Japan and that toward Italy, and attributed it to the fact that China still existed and Austria-Hungary, against which the Treaty of London was directed, did not. Actually there was another difference: Italy had given its consent to the League Covenant and Japan was holding back.[44]

At the request of the president, Lansing discussed the issue in a talk with Chinda that Lansing deemed "very unsatisfactory."[45] Chinda alleged that the Chinese delegation had been instructed by Peking to work in harmony with Japan and that Lou, when he traveled through Tokyo, had agreed to co-operate. He asserted further that Tokyo had instructed the Japanese delegation to support China "as far as possible" in such matters as the abolition of special foreign rights in China. In view of this, he deplored propaganda of the young Chinese nationalists at Paris that misrepresented Japan. This had stirred up a great deal of resentment in Japan. It was now a

42. Mantoux, *Délibérations,* vol. 1, pp. 315–317, 320–327.

43. Grayson diary, April 25, 1919. See above, p. 359, n. 1.

44. Mantoux, *Délibérations,* vol. 1, pp. 320–327, 329–336. A Chinese proposal of a compromise, stated in a memorandum sent to Wilson with a letter signed by Lou, on April 24, was presented to The Three at their meeting of April 25, memorandum and letter in Wilson papers, Baker, vol. 2, p. 259. A copy of a letter of April 24, Koo to Wilson, setting down four propositions for a settlement, is in the Koo papers, box 001.

45. Lansing desk diary, April 26, 1919. Typescript signed by E. T. Williams, recording "Conversation between Secretary Lansing and Viscount Chinda, 9:15 Apr. 26, 1919," Wilson papers.

matter of national honor to insist on the exact fulfillment of the twenty-one exactions of 1915.

The question of Shantung, urgent though it was, was crowded from the agenda of the Supreme Council during the days when the issue with Italy came to a climax. However, on April 25, when Orlando had left Paris, Wilson keenly felt the necessity of preventing another major defection. With Italy and Japan disaffected and Belgium disgruntled, Germany might refuse to sign a treaty and might attempt to form an alliance with Russia and Japan. Wilson reasoned that if the Japanese withdrew from the Peace Conference and the League, they would not then withdraw from Shantung.[46] The president said that the three experts who were delegated to study the matter had reported that it was better for China to act under the wartime agreements of Japan with the Allies rather than in accord with the terms of the Sino-Japanese understandings of 1915 and 1918.[47]

Lloyd George warned that the Japanese were not bluffing in their threat to leave the Peace Conference. At the same time the prime minister said that Great Britain could not think of giving up its special rights in the Yangtse valley if Japan kept privileges in Shantung and was free to carry out a "plan of conquest" by administering and policing railways. He proposed that they make use of the services of Balfour, who suggested that Japan be given the German rights but be asked at the same time to discuss the conditions under which they were to be restored eventually to China.[48] Wilson, at his wits' end, agreed.

"The difficulties here would have been incredible to me before I got here," Wilson confessed in a cable to Tumulty on April 26. Fearing that the League would be wrecked, he had confided to Dr. Grayson the day before that the Italian imbroglio would be "only a tempest in a tea-pot compared with the coming controversy with Japan." His only hope, he said, was to "find some outlet to permit the Japanese to save their face and let the League adjudicate later."[49] In his distress he turned to the American commissioners for advice. House again took the position of a diplomat. Opposing the strong inclination of Lansing and Bliss to rebuff Japan, he argued that it would be a mistake to take any action that might make the Japanese

46. R. S. Baker's journal, April 30, 1919.

47. On April 24 E. T. Williams, having conferred with English delegates in accord with the president's instruction, sent a long letter to Wilson with a brief they had written. This paper concluded that either of the alternatives offered to China presented "serious disadvantages" for that country and that it would be less disadvantageous to choose to let Japan take over the German arrangements, which did not convey the right to establish any form of civil administration outside the leased territory, to maintain troops in any town, or to police the railway, which was the property of the Chinese state. Williams proposed a third plan that in his opinion Japan might be brought to accept and that would give an appearance of the diplomatic victory that its people expected, and would at the same time give China its properties. Still another alternative suggested by Williams was direct negotiation between China and Japan in the presence of a third party, perhaps Great Britain, letter E. T. Williams to Wilson, April 23, 1919, *ibid.*, April 24, 1919, with brief attached, Wilson papers. Memorandum, S. K. Hornbeck to Williams, April 24, 1919, with brief attached; statement by E. T. Williams on the Shantung decision, n.d., Hornbeck papers.

48. Mantoux, *Délibérations*, vol. 1, pp. 377–378. Lloyd George wrote to Balfour to ask him to discuss the Shantung question with the Japanese as soon as possible, letter, April 26, 1919, Balfour papers, 49692.

49. Grayson diary, April 25, 1919.

withdraw from Paris. Lansing, who thought, mistakenly, that they were bluffing and were making demands in Shantung that would "restore the shell to China and leave the kernel" in their own hands, urged that the German rights be transferred directly to China, or at least be assumed in trust by the five powers.[50]

In the plenary session of the Peace Conference on April 28, the Japanese still cooperated with the other powers by refraining from pressing, beyond the presentation of a dignified reservation, their desire for a race-equality amendment to the League Covenant. They had made it known through the French press, however,[51] that they were being urged by opinion in Japan to follow the example of the Italian delegates and withdraw from the conference. At the same time a dispatch from Washington reported that Japanese newspapers were intensely hostile both to the League and to the United States and that none believed the American position to be sincere.[52]

Meanwhile, Balfour was carrying out the wish of Lloyd George and Wilson that he take the matter in hand. He was informed by Makino on April 27 that the Japanese government could not sustain both a defeat on the question of racial equality and a rejection of its claims in Shantung. Balfour, learning that Wilson was not disposed to talk with the Japanese until the plenary session on April 28 approved the League Covenant, told The Three on the morning of that day that the Japanese might take drastic action if they were not satisfied in respect of Shantung before they agreed to accept the Covenant without an amendment on racial equality.[53] It was Balfour's understanding that, once Japan had the German rights in Shantung, it would keep only economic concessions without any military control and that it would hand back to China the whole of the leased territory. Wilson remarked that such an arrangement would give China a better position than that held under its treaty with Germany, but his advisers doubted that the Japanese would carry out their professed intention. He himself wished to have these intentions set down in black and white. He conveyed to his European colleagues the substance of a message just received from Tumulty. This asserted that the "designs of Japan" were as indefensible as those of Italy and gave the president an opportunity to "cast another die" similar to the public manifesto that had exacerbated the Italian crisis.[54] The president, however, did not repeat the mistake that he had made in dealing with Italy.

Balfour then addressed a note to Makino, informing him that "The Three" were "quite satisfied" with the arrangement he had proposed.[55] Wilson had been brought to a settlement that was most distasteful to him and was contrary to the recommen-

50. Baker, *American Chronicle,* p. 413. Lansing to Wilson April 21 and 22, 1919, Wilson papers House diary, April 26, 1919. The sincerity of the Japanese is attested by a telegram from their ambassador at Paris to Tokyo saying: "I am refusing formally to sign the peace treaty if the solution of the question of Shantung remains that advocated by President Wilson," telegram, dated April 19, 1919. F.C., 6N76, Japan.

51. Memorandum, Steed to Northcliffe, April 29, 1919, Steed papers.

52. Polk to Ammission, April 28, 1919, N.A., R.G. 256, 185.111 / 257.

53. According to Miller (*My Diary,* vol. 19, pp. 195–197), Makino gave Balfour to understand that Japan would withdraw its plea for an amendment on race equality in exchange for support of its position in Shantung.

54. Dispatch, Tumulty to Wilson, April 24, 1919, Wilson papers. Trask, p. 95.

55. Mantoux, *Délibérations,* vol. 1, pp. 396–400. Balfour gave The Three a written report of his talk with the Japanese delegates on April 27. The report and his note to Makino are in Baker, vol. 3, pp. 311–313.

dations of three of the American commissioners and the advising experts.[56] Indeed, Bliss wrote a vigorous letter to Wilson to state the view of the three dissenters.[57] Balfour and Lloyd George were fearful that the president would be unable to overcome the moralistic presumptions of his advisers and the tug of his own emotions. The prime minister took House aside and asked whether the colonel could not bring his chief to reason; and House then wrote to Wilson in support of the British position.[58]

On April 29 the president talked with Makino and Chinda for an hour about the garrisoning of Tsinen and the guarding of the railway. According to the report that he made to Clemenceau and Lloyd George immediately afterward, Wilson told the Japanese that it was his understanding that Japan, once in possession of the German rights, would restore all to China with the exception of a residential concession and some privileges which did not include those of military occupation of the railway and of instruction of the police. He would oppose any terms that went beyond those of the German lease or seemed to impose Japanese control outside of a domain strictly economic.

The Japanese delegates were forced to listen to close questioning on April 29 by Wilson in the session of the Council of Four. Balfour put emphasis upon the validity of the Sino-Japanese Treaty of September 1918, which was in his view "a voluntary transaction between sovereign states . . . which gave important pecuniary benefits to China."[59] The foreign secretary guided the drafting of a compromise formula that satisfied both Japan's dignity and Wilson's scruples. When the president insisted that the agreement be made public and the Japanese feared the effect of this on opinion in Japan, Balfour suggested the expedient of making a statement in the form of an interview and thus avoiding any impression that Japan was being coerced. In this session Wilson bore down upon the Japanese with a moral fervor that seemed to House ungracious.

Balfour forwarded a compromise text to Wilson for his approval, and he received from the president a version only slightly revised. It was given out as the substance of an interview[60] and was not included in the articles approved for insertion in the

56. See Beers, pp. 163–168.

57. Baker, vol. 2, p. 262. Palmer, *Bliss,* pp. 393–395.

58. "He [Lloyd George] thought the president was unfair to Japan and so does Balfour," House wrote in his diary, *I.P.,* vol. 4, pp. 451–452. Although House characterized the situation as "all bad," he thought it "no worse than the things we are doing in many of the settlements in which the Western Powers are interested." It seemed to him best "to clean up a lot of old rubbish with the least friction" and "let the new era do the rest." It was his hope that public opinion would exert enough pressure through the League to force France, Great Britain, and Japan to "get out of China," House to Wilson, April 29, 1919, copy in Y.H.C.

59. Letter, Balfour to Curzon, May 8, 1919, Balfour papers, 49750, pp. 90 f. Fifield, p. 241. When Chinda pointed to the difference between the Twenty-one Demands of 1915 and the railway concessions of September 1918, Wilson replied: "The convention [of 1918] is the consequence of the articles [of 1915], despite the change of circumstances and, I acknowledge, in the intentions of the present Japanese government," Mantoux, *Délibérations,* vol. 1, p. 403.

Balfour confessed later that he was moved by contempt for the Chinese because they tried to maintain that Shantung was theirs as legitimate spoils of a war in which they had not shed blood or spent money, copy of initialed memorandum, Balfour to Curzon, September 20, 1919, Balfour papers, 49734.

60. Mantoux, *Délibérations,* vol. 1, pp. 401–408, 425–427. *F.R., P.P.C.,* vol. 5, pp. 363–364. Balfour to Wilson, April 29, 1919, Wilson to Balfour, April 30, 1919, Balfour papers, 49687. The text returned to Balfour on April 30 is that printed in Baker, vol. 2, p. 263 *viz.:*

treaty with Germany, whereby the German rights in Shantung went directly to Japan. It was released to *Le Temps* on May 5 and endorsed by Japan's foreign minister in a press conference at Tokyo on the seventeenth.[61]

Thus Japan, having been thwarted in its desire for a declaration of race equality and for outright possession of German islands in the Pacific, received in effect all that it demanded in Shantung. But the satisfaction of its people was marred by the suspicious and admonitory tone of the Americans at Paris as well as by the sympathy for the Chinese nationalists that was aggressively asserted by Americans. The Japanese delegates at Paris became even more sensitive to any slights on the part of their Allies, especially in the matter of representation on committees of the Peace Conference. At their request they were given a part in the work of the committees on reparations, new states, and study of the German observations of the peace terms; and in June, Makino was allowed a seat in sessions of the Supreme Council even when the interests of Japan were not being discussed.[62]

In Wilson's opinion the settlement was "the best that could be got out of a dirty past." A defection by Japan might not only break up the Peace Conference but destroy the League of Nations and result in Japanese alliance with Germany and Russia. China must look to the League for protection from encroachments by foreign powers.[63]

At the request of the president, Baker informed the other American plenipotentiaries of the decision and took word of it to the Chinese delegates as they were dining with American friends. According to one of those present, the banquet "became a wake." The Chinese, apprehensive of personal injury when they returned to China, were inconsolable.[64] On May 4 they addressed a protest to The Four, saying that it would be difficult to explain to their people what the Peace Conference really meant by "justice."[65] E. T. Williams, the chief American adviser, confessed that he was

---

The policy of Japan is to hand back the Shangtung peninsula in full sovereignty to China retaining only the economic privileges granted to Germany and the right to establish a settlement under the usual conditions at Tsingtao.

The owners of the railway will use special Police only to ensure security for traffic. They will be used for no other purpose.

The Police Force will be composed of Chinese and such Japanese instructors as the Directors of the Railway may select will be appointed by the Chinese government.

In the meeting of April 30 Makino and Chinda, replying to a direct question from Wilson, gave assurance that Japan would withdraw its troops from Shantung as soon as practicable.

61. *F.R., 1919*, vol. 1, p. 718. Fifield, pp. 305–306. Dispatch, Ammission to the secretary of state, October 29, 1919, N.A., R.G. 59, 851.00 / 39.

62. Fifield, pp. 306–307.

63. Baker, vol. 2, p. 266; *American Chronicle*, pp. 413–414.

Although E. T. Williams was suspicious that "secret intriguing" went on between Japanese and German officials (see Fifield, p. 221n.), the Americans at Paris put little credence in an alleged secret agreement between Japan and Germany that was published in *The Call* in Moscow on December 7, 1918, intelligence reports and correspondence in Harrison papers, box 106, "M-75" folder. Hornbeck to Lansing, July 11, 1919, Lansing papers.

64. Morgenthau, *All in a Life-Time*, p. 325. Baker, *American Chronicle*, pp. 416–417; journal, May 1, 1919.

65. Chinese protest May 4, 1919, copy in Hornbeck papers. When the Chinese repeatedly asked for the minutes of the Council of Four that recorded discussions of the questions affecting their interests, they were given only the records of the sessions in which they took part, Baker, vol. 2, p. 266. They

"ashamed to look a Chinese in the face." Lansing, Bliss, and White, hoping to reverse the decision, persuaded Williams to campaign publicly against it in a way that would not impugn their loyalty to the president. (They said, according to Williams, "We cannot be responsible. You must be the goat.")[66] Criticism of the Shantung verdict was so widespread, in the United States as well as among the friends of China at Paris, that the president was moved to prepare a brief public statement to explain his position. Apparently wishing to avoid any appearance of a defensive posture, he asked that it not be released as a quotation but used "in some other form for public information at the right time."[67] In his statement Wilson specified the assurances that the Japanese had given and called them "very satisfactory in view of the complicated circumstances." Furthermore, reverting to the vision of a free China that he had revealed to Clemenceau and Lloyd George at the end of their discussion on April 28, he detected, hopefully, "a general disposition to look with favor upon the proposal that at an early date through the mediation of the League of Nations all extraordinary foreign rights in China and all spheres of influence should be abrogated by the common consent of all the nations concerned."[68]

One of the American experts, Stanley K. Hornbeck, lost no time in suggesting that the Chinese now bring up the fundamental question of tariff revision and that of withdrawal of foreign post offices from China. However, when the Chinese formally renewed their plea for a general consideration of the position of foreigners in China, they were told by the Council of Four that this question did not arise out of the war, and therefore it could not be discussed appropriately at the Peace Conference.[69] On May 14 Clemenceau informed Lou Tseng-tsiang that the Supreme Council, recognizing the importance of the questions raised, suggested that they be brought before the League of Nations.[70]

When news of the rebuff at Paris reached China, the political turmoil in that land grew. Dispatches from American officials reported that a "May Fourth Movement" was resulting in violent public indignation and anti-Japanese boycotts in many parts of the country, and a general denunciation of foreigners from which Americans and their president were, for the most part, spared.[71] The political conference that was in session at Shanghai, seeking Chinese unity, was disrupted. American residents

complained of the taking of decisions without consultation with them. See Fifield, pp. 310–311, 314–315. Letters from Koo and Lansing to Wilson protested the exclusion of China from the list of "effective belligerents" who were to be present when the treaty terms were to be presented to the Germans, and they asked the president to use his influence in behalf of Chinese representation. This he did with success.

66. Dimitri D. Lazo, "A Question of Loyalty: Robert Lansing and the Treaty of Versailles," 38–42.

67. Baker, authorized to give out the story as soon as the press had it from another quarter, handed it to the American newsmen immediately. Tumulty, however, cabled from Washington that in his judgment the release of this statement would weaken Wilson's position and that he would withhold it unless the president insisted that it be given out, Baker, *American Chronicle*, pp. 415–416; cables, Wilson to Tumulty, April 30, 1919, Tumulty to Wilson, May 5, 1919, Wilson papers.

68. Baker, vol. 3, pp. 315–316; journal, April 30, 1919. McCormick diary, July 5, 1919.

69. Memorandum, Hornbeck to Williams, May 2, 1919, Hornbeck papers.

70. Chinese memorandum with minutes, and letter, Clemenceau to Lou Tseng-tsiang, May 14, 1919, P.R.O., F / 800 / 209. See Fifield, p. 314.

71. King, p., 27. On the significance of the May Fourth Movement, which Sun Yat-sen called "a gigantic ideological revolution unprecedented" in Chinese history, see *ibid.*, p. 34.

in China wired formal protests to their government, and Japanese officials thought them not free from blame for inciting bad feeling. In the Japanese press vituperation against Wilson continued.[72] There was fear among Americans at Peking that a national uprising in China would give Japanese militarists an opportunity to occupy much of the country on the plea of restoring order.[73]

The American delegates at Paris took every opportunity to attempt to mitigate the blow that was dealt to the Chinese nationalists. American officials were asked by the Chinese for counsel as to whether they should put their signatures on the disappointing treaty of peace. House, consulted by Koo, advised that the Chinese sign with a reservation such as they had presented in the plenary session of the Peace Conference on May 6. This was intended to enable their government to ask, at a suitable moment after the signing, for a reconsideration of the decision with respect to Shantung. According to Koo's record, House went so far as to say that Wilson would not object to a Chinese reservation.[74] Lansing told Koo that he could see no legal objection to this course, and that without a reservation the Chinese should not sign.[75]

Emboldened by American advice, the senior Chinese delegate formally notified the Peace Conference on May 26 that, under instructions from his government, China would sign the treaty with a reservation. There was no ruling until June 24, when the secretary general of the conference, speaking for Clemenceau, gave notice that no reservations would be permitted, either in the text of the treaty or outside. The Chinese protested and, notifying the Americans of Clemenceau's verdict, sought their "friendly offices." Wilson, advised by Lansing that any sovereign power could make reservations in signing, put this opinion before the Council of Four. But Clemenceau said that the proposal of China lacked precedent and also awakened fears of establishing one. He was supported by Lloyd George.

Wilson himself was not so indulgent of a Chinese reservation as House had given Koo to believe. The president was chary of setting a precedent that might be used by his adversaries at Washington to justify American reservations. He had informed Tumulty, just two days previously, that it was his "clear conviction" that "the adoption of the treaty by the Senate with reservations would put the United States as clearly out of the concert of nations as a rejection."[76] Despite a personal appeal from Koo on the evening of June 27, the day before the signing of the Treaty of Versailles, the president took no action.

Negotiations continued up to the moment of the signing of the treaty at Versailles

72. *F.R., P.P.C.*, vol. 1, pp. 691–694, 696–714. King, p. 27. State Department to Ammission, May 6, 1919, N.A., R.G. 59, 763.72119 / 4903a.

73. Dispatches, Peking legation to State Department, May 2, July 3, 5, 1919, N.A., R.G. 59, 763.72119 / 4837, 4841, 5517, 5533. Polk to Ammission, May 5, 1919, forwarding telegrams of May 2 and 3, 1919, Y.H.C. *F.R., 1919*, vol. 1, pp. 691 ff. Reinsch, pp. 358–359, 368–374.

74. House suggested that Koo announce this intention to Wilson and say that China thus acted in accord with the desire of the American commissioners in signing the treaty to make a reservation in respect of the Monroe Doctrine, House diary, May 22, 1919. Memorandum of a conversation with House, May 22, 1919, Koo papers, box 001.

75. Koo's memorandum of a conversation with Lansing, May 29, 1919, Koo papers.

76. Mantoux, *Délibérations*, vol. 2, p. 516. Cable, Wilson to Tumulty, June 23, 1919, Tumulty papers, box 7. See below, pp. 529–530.

on the afternoon of June 28.[77] At the last minute the Chinese delegates notified Clemenceau that they did not "consider themselves qualified to sign the Treaty." At the same time they issued a press statement to the effect that they had been denied justice by the Peace Conference and were submitting their case "to the impartial judgment of the world." However, they signed the peace treaty with Austria on September 10 in order to make China a member of the League of Nations; and five days later they proclaimed a peace with Germany. Under a final settlement concluded on May 20, 1921, Germany agreed to abrogate its special rights in China and to accept the obligations imposed by Articles 128 through 134 of the Treaty of Versailles.

Meanwhile, during May and June the American delegates had been attempting to placate the Chinese nationalists by persuading the Japanese to make a definite disclosure of their plans in Shantung and to set a date for the withdrawal of their troops. After the matter was twice raised urgently by Lansing, Wilson asked the secretary of state to talk with Makino very earnestly. Accordingly, Lansing suggested a text to Makino but found him of the opinion that any further statement at this time would antagonize the Japanese people. When the secretary of state told Balfour that the United States would be pleased to have his support, the foreign secretary, although professing eagerness for a declaration by Japan, accepted Makino's position.[78] On June 5 the Chinese were given by Hankey, in strict confidence, a memorandum containing Japanese assurances for the eventual restoration of Kiaochow to China; but the Chinese found these "misleading as well as unsatisfactory."[79] The American government did not press the Japanese publicly. However, with some support from the British Foreign Office, the State Department made repeated but unsuccessful efforts through diplomatic channels to get an assurance of Japan's good faith.[80]

Finally, on August 2, the Japanese minister of foreign affairs issued a statement confirming that given out on May 5,[81] and Wilson stated publicly his own understanding of the commitments that had been made orally by the Japanese at Paris.[82] On August 27 he threatened to repudiate the articles of the Treaty of Versailles whereby Japan obtained the German rights in Shantung unless Japan gave "immediate assurance" of acceptance of the American position. This evoked no satisfactory response. The question of Shantung was not settled until 1922, when Japan honored its promise to return to China the rights that had been acquired from Germany under the Treaty of Versailles.[83]

77. Lansing, desk diary, June 27, 1919.

78. Lansing to Wilson, June 11, 1919, Wilson to Lansing, June 12 and 20, 1919, Lansing to Wilson, June 16, 1919, Wilson papers. Auchincloss to Polk, June 20, 1919, Auchincloss diary.

79. King, p. 27.

80. See memoranda in Hornbeck papers, "Far East, Remaining Questions" folder.

81. See above, p. 372.

82. *New York Times*, August 6 and 7, 1919, Lansing to Wilson, August 4, 1919, Wilson to Lansing, August 6, 1919, *F.R., Lansing pa., 1914–20*, vol. 2, pp. 454–456, *F.R., 1919*, vol. 1, pp. 718–722. B. Long's diary, August 3, 4, 6, and 30, 1919.

83. See Fifield, pp. 345–360.

Although there was little abatement of the special privileges that foreign powers exercised in China, some progress was made at Paris toward freeing Chinese officials from financial servitudes that might close the "open door." The international consortium which Polk had urged the American commission at Paris to further[84] had been the subject of negotiations by bankers while the Peace Conference was in session. A consortium was formed at Paris on May 12 and 13 for the purpose of dealing with financial and industrial matters in China.[85] According to a memorandum by Lamont, dated June 22, 1919, the consortium was "to constitute a frank and fair partnership agreement among the respective financial groups of Great Britain, United States of America, France, and Japan." It was planned, later on, to admit Belgium, and probably Russia when it had a stable government. The respective groups in each country would "for the present have the exclusive recognition and support of the Governments involved." Lamont said that the Treasury had taken no action and the whole project was in danger of extinction on account of a "mere technicality." Urged by the State Department to clear up the matter, Lamont suggested this might be done if he could sit down at a table for fifteen minutes with representatives of the Foreign Office, of the Treasury, and of the British Financial Group. With the support of Lloyd George this was arranged.[86] Japan offered determined resistance to the inclusion of southern Manchuria and eastern Mongolia, in which they claimed "special interests."[87] It was not until October 15, 1920, that the powers could agree with the government at Peking on the terms of a consortium loan.

The issues that were keeping East Asia in constant turmoil were proving to be too complex for settlement at the Peace Conference of 1919. The peacemakers were able to do little more than temporize with the insurgent forces within China that one day would break the restraints of traditional diplomacy. Unfortunately, the sympathetic attitude of the Americans toward the Chinese revolution and Wilson's moralistic lectures aroused Japanese indignation. In seeking the allegiance of both China and Japan to a new order, Wilson, caught in the unhappy role of arbiter, disappointed Chinese patriots and offended Japanese diplomats. The way was open for Japanese imperialism, striving to emulate that of Europeans, to adopt a policy of martial aggression that one day would strike the United States.

84. See above, p. 362.
85. Wilson was willing to leave this question in the hands of Lansing, Wilson to Lansing, May 27, 1919.
86. Lamont to Kerr, June 23, 1919, with memorandum enclosed, Kerr to Lamont, June 24, 1919, Lothian papers, Scottish Record Office. Kerr to Clerk, June 24, 1919, P.R.O., FO / 800 / 152.
87. B. Long diary, August 27, 1919.

PART FOUR

The Treaty of Versailles

AT the end of April the threat of general social revolution put constant pressure upon the peacemakers to hasten their work. On the last day of the month the Soviet Republic of Bavaria was destroyed violently and its leaders shot or imprisoned. In Paris, on May Day, demonstrators marched to the very doors of the Peace Conference. Soldiers of the United States were ordered off the streets, and mounted French troops, which Clemenceau had brought into the city as a precaution, charged a riotous crowd beneath the windows of the Crillon.

The tension made the peacemakers the more intent upon haste in producing a draft treaty to be presented to the Germans. They had made the most of the expedient of referring difficult matters to small *ad hoc* committees, who reported their decisions to the Council of Four, sometimes with dissenting opinions. In this inner council the chiefs spoke with the utmost frankness and with no American secretary present. This all-powerful body, occasionally aided by the Council of Foreign Ministers, considered and acted upon the many reports that came in. The most perplexing of the questions demanding attention were considered only in secrecy. However, delegates were so active in the corridors and at social occasions that Balfour was moved to remark: "All important business is transacted in the intervals of other business."[1]

The machinery that was improvised had wheels within wheels and gears that did not always mesh. As the delegates met in various groups day after day, each man enjoyed freedom to assert his own weight as well as the virtue of his nation's cause. Imprecise thinking and faulty translation often stood in the way of the understanding and reconciliation of conflicting views. Often too much attention was given to small points and not enough to the fundamental issues.

The day-by-day encounters of the American delegates with their European associates were a challenge to ingenuity as well as to patience. One of the financial advisers, Thomas W. Lamont, unschooled in diplomacy and accustomed to the ways of business in New York, described the "Tower of Babel" in which he lived for several months in Paris. He wrote:

We started out on the principle that all the nations should have liberty of action and freedom of expression. . . . Every nation wanted representatives on every commission. . . . To deny

1. Eustace Percy, *Some Memories*, pp. 60–61.

them opportunity to explain their views—especially if they had particular interests at stake—was impossible. Then each delegation had its own particular domestic political differences. . . . There were jealousies and strife. Who should sit on this commission? Who on that? This difference was frequently settled by a delegation sending several representatives of equal authority to the same commission. Then of course, each delegate had to keep up a show equal to that of his associate, had to talk as often, as loudly and as long. On top of all that was the difficulty of language. Everything everybody said had to be interpreted from French to English and from English to French. . . . Very frequently . . . delegates would get into a hot wrangle for hours over a point badly interpreted and after endless fighting would find they had been arguing for precisely the same viewpoint. . . . Of course the situation got on our nerves. . . . But that is the way men are made. And the delegates at Paris were all human beings, very human, not altogether wise, not altogether just—but on the whole striving hard for certain ideals.[2]

When Wilson had dared to insist on the inclusion of the League Covenant in the peace treaty, he had acted in the aggressive way that he had always taken when faced by a new challenge to his powers of leadership. During the months of daily negotiations with the Europeans, however, he had to a large extent come to terms with the necessities that arose from prevailing circumstances. At first he had looked forward with zest to a contest between good and evil. But as he jousted with the Europeans at first hand, he came to understand their inexhorable political limitations. To be sure, he never entirely gave up the illusion that he represented the peoples of the world against their own political leaders. But he had come to see that to re-establish peace effectively, certain vital issues should be settled promptly and to this end compromise was necessary. It appeared to Baker that the peacemakers, laboring under "the crushing forces of conditions and events," were being "dragged along by the remorseless logic of compromise."[3]

In the weeks following his severe illness Wilson had learned another of the lessons that professional diplomats of Europe accepted as fundamental. This was that responsible leadership by the great powers was essential to the maintenance of peace. When, in one of the last sessions of The Three, Clemenceau said "The League of the people is we," Wilson replied, "Oui, l'État c'est nous."[4]

There was a blurring, in the spring months at Paris, of the bold lines that the American prophet had drawn, when he first set out to make an ideal peace, between European decadence and American virtue, between "selfish" nationalism and, service to all humanity. Having accepted the necessity of reaching compromises with the statesmen of Belgium, France, Great Britain, and Japan, he became zealous in defending and perfecting the arrangements that had been made. Although he lost the adoration of masses of people who felt that he had failed them, he had won the esteem and confidence of men and women with whom he worked closely. As time went on, his European associates came to regard him more as collaborator than as obstructionist.[5] The stature that the president had achieved as a moderator served

2. Paper by Thomas W. Lamont, written on the *George Washington*, n.d., Lamont papers, pp. 164–6.

3. R. S. Baker journal, May 22, 1919.

4. Aldrovandi-Mareseotti, *Nuovi Ricordi,* p. 102.

5. Seymour, "Policy and Personality at the Paris Peace Conference," 527–529, and Seymour, "Woodrow Wilson in Perspective," 182–183.

the Peace Conference well. Balfour told Dr. Grayson that Wilson was the greatest statesman ever, and said: "It is always an intellectual treat to be with him."[6]

Although in some instances the march of events and the play of power politics had prevented adherence to the advice of the experts, the president, relatively sequestered though he was, managed to retain his hold upon the minds of the Inquiry. Although he tended to rely heavily on his own intuition and sometimes was forced to yield to political realities, he heeded expert advice more than did Clemenceau and Lloyd George. In the first peace conference to use the services of a large group of scholars, the American specialists had thrown their weight on the side of reason, providing a store of facts and figures that were invaluable in argument with European negotiators. Although in some respects doctrinaire and not entirely unbiased by personal sympathies, they contributed essential and organized information that was reliable. In some cases they had undertaken the work of diplomats. Their respect for the work of the president rose as the weaknesses of the other commissioners became apparent.[7] On May 31 Seymour wrote: "More and more the feeling on the inside of the Conference is that he [Wilson] is the biggest man here."[8]

Wilson now consulted only infrequently with House, who, after managing compromises with France and Japan that were distasteful to Wilson, and after promoting a *démarche* toward an accommodation with Moscow that was politically embarrassing to the president, would persist in trying his chief's patience by ingenious attempts to reach a diplomatic solution of Italy's controversy with Yugoslavia. Worn down by illness and overwork, and influenced through his wife by Henry White, the president took more notice of Secretary Lansing.[9] Aware of the sensitivity of Lansing, who lamented that the United States was now a party to what he regarded as a palpable division of "plunder" and who wished to dictate terms satisfying to

6. Grayson diary, May 25, 1919.

7. For evaluation of the work of the Inquiry by two scholars whose conclusions are not entirely in agreement, see Gelfand, *The Inquiry*, pp. 322–333, and Mayer, "Historical Thought and American Foreign Policy in the Era of the First World War," p. 86. Also see Herbert George Nicholas in Link (ed.), *Wilson's Diplomacy: An International Symposium*, p. 87. Clive Day, confidential memorandum, May 28, 1919, Y.H.C. As for House, Day wrote: "We have grown to distrust his judgment, . . . thinking that he is essentially of the politician type, inclined to opportunism and to the sacrifice of principle for the sake of agreement." And of Lansing: "He has a keen mind and is a forceful speaker. He does not readily grasp, however, the concrete problems that arise in territorial issues, and reminds one always of a lawyer arguing the case from a brief, prepared for him, without a clear perception of all the points involved." Bliss was "a disappointment"—a scholar, to be sure, but narrow in vision and limited in capacity. And Henry White, "a delightful old gentleman," was "without sufficient fire to make him a positive force in the settlement of questions at issue."

8. Seymour thought "no one living in America could have secured what he . . . secured," *Letters from the Paris Peace Conference*, pp. 226–228, 250. "The president stands head and shoulders above them all," Day wrote, "showing extraordinary power of apprehension, tenacity of purpose, and inclination to get a just and lasting peace," Day memorandum, cited. Ambassador Wallace reported to the State Department that Wilson held the "trump card," that if the treaty was signed it would be "entirely thanks to his moderation and sense of justice," dispatch, Wallace to the secretary of state, May 20, 1919, N.A., R.G. 256, 851.00 / 83.

9. Nevins, *White*, p. 447. Henry White wrote to Assistant Secretary William Phillips of the State Department on May 18, 1919: "[The president] depends more on him [Lansing] now than he did during the earlier period . . . as a result of certain quiet action on my part. . . . I have established very friendly relations with Mrs. Wilson and Miss Benham, whom—particularly the former—I find a valuable channel for communication with the president," letter in White papers, Columbia, Notes and Letters, box 2.

his own conscience,[10] Wilson was now careful to soothe his secretary of state as well as to spare the feelings of House. When Lansing returned from a visit to London, the president welcomed him with seven brief notes. One said: "I am heartily glad to hear that you are back and feeling well. We have missed you very much." And when he referred to Lansing a dossier of correspondence that House had sent to him, he took pains to explain to the colonel: "I am writing to Lansing about it now. I'm sure that that is the course you yourself would take, now that Lansing is back, if you were in my place, Affectionately yours."[11]

During the month of May, when the president was compelled by American law to draft a message to an incoming Congress that would be difficult to control, Wilson was increasingly attentive to the thoughts of his constituency in the United States. His political leadership, and the great cause on which he had staked it, were in jeopardy. Although aspiring to make a rational peace, he could not afford to give an impression to the public that he was pro-German.[12] He was not sufficiently free from national politics to negotiate in the manner of a responsible diplomat. Consequently, many of the hopes that he had raised in moderate as well as liberal Germans were destined to die in a "tragedy of disappointment" that Wilson had foreseen even before the Peace Conference opened.

No one in the American peace delegation could foretell with any certainty what the response of the Germans would be when they were confronted with the stiff terms that were prepared for them, denying them immediate admission to the League of Nations, obliging them to make reparation on a large scale and of unspecified amount, providing for the loss, either temporarily or permanently, of much territory that was populated largely by Germans, and making no provision for any conference in which negotiations could be carried on. There were no advisers at hand who could view the settlement expertly from the point of view of the enemy and appraise the total impact of the exactions upon German society. To be sure, reports on German opinion came to Paris during April from a diplomatic mission sent to Berlin, a military liaison man at Spa, and economic advisers who conferred at Château Villette with German bankers of moderate views. There were indications that the present German government might collapse if it capitulated without negotiating better terms. At the same time, assurance came that any turn to the Left that might ensue was unlikely to result in bolshevism in Germany or in its alliance with Russia. In these circumstances Wilson accepted the dictates of sound politics. He was intent upon preserving the united front of the victorious powers, as well as the consent of his American constituency.

The terms were given to Germany's foreign minister on May 7. He bitterly denounced their departure in many respects from the Fourteen Points, on which

10. Lansing, private memoranda, May 5, 1919.
11. Wilson to Lansing, Wilson to House, May 19, 1919, Wilson papers. Edith Benham, "Report of Conversations Concerning the Resignation of Secretary Lansing," memorandum of February 1920, Helm papers.
12. A message from Tumulty informed Wilson that a great many newspapers were worried lest the president be carried away by German pleading for a less arduous peace. "I know you will not be led astray," Tumulty said, cable, Tumulty to Wilson, May 27, 1919, Wilson papers. Lansing desk diary, May 19, 1919. Baker journal, May 23 and 31, 1919.

German officials had built their hopes and their policies during the past months. This oral protest was followed by a series of diplomatic notes, in which the Germans took advantage of the opportunity to put in writing their case for revision of the most objectionable conditions. They raised some of the questions that the Americans already had advanced, unsuccessfully, in the interest of a nonvindictive and enduring peace. Nevertheless, Wilson resisted most of the German pleas for revision, though some were seriously entertained by his counselors.

When The Three considered German counterproposals for a lightening of the onerous treaty, Wilson, cast in the role of an arbiter between Clemenceau and Lloyd George, was for the most part unsuccessful in effecting changes that he favored or in checking those that he opposed. And so the German government, struggling to maintain its position against challenges from the Right and the Left, was forced to remain outside the League of Nations and was subjected to a terrifying financial burden without provision for credit that would make it bearable. The cabinet resigned to avoid the disgrace of accepting the emasculating treaty, and a new government was formed that found minor officials who performed the repugnant duty of signing the Treaty of Versailles on June 28. Thus was planted the seeds of chaos in Germany and the emergence of a rule by worse "military masters."

By the road of compromise the peacemakers had finally arrived at a settlement with Germany. In the process there was an erosion of those Wilsonian principles that diplomats could not apply consistently in the political circumstances that then existed. The treaty that was signed at Versailles on June 28 did not fully realize Wilson's vision or fulfill German hopes.

20

Disappointment and Disillusion

In the middle of April, a month after Wilson's return to Paris and a week after his recovery from severe illness, he was buffeted by political winds from three sides: from his adversaries at Washington, from the spokesmen of the Allied peoples, and from the German politicians who were losing the faith that they had put in the American program for a just and enduring peace.

On April 15 the Council of Four made a survey of the work still before them. Lloyd George had gone to London, where, answering questions in the Parliament, he dramatized the scene at Paris: "stones clattering on the roof and crashing through the windows and sometimes wild men screaming through the keyholes."[1] Balfour, taking the seat of the prime minister in the Council of Four, adduced the matters that must be settled before the arrival of the Germans. He enumerated twelve.[2] Clemenceau then proposed, and the others agreed, that they would reserve a session to hear the delegates of each of the smaller powers that were directly interested in the treaty with Germany.[3]

It was decided also that the foreign ministers, who had met in council three times near the end of March, should be apprised by Balfour of decisions taken by the Council of Four in respect of the secondary powers. Balfour took this occasion to bring about better liaison between the two councils; and on April 16 they met together to consider what they had accomplished and what still remained to be done.[4]

Wilson took upon himself the adjustment of some details that Europeans were

1. Peter Rowland, *David Lloyd George*, p. 490. Rowland records that Lloyd George returned to Paris from London "wreathed in smiles" after a great forensic triumph, *ibid.*, p. 491.

2. The twelve were (1) reconstruction in kind in the devastated regions (under examination and to be reported on by Loucheur); (2) guarantee of the payment of indemnities by temporary occupation of the left bank of the Rhine; (3) the disarmed zone on the right bank of the Rhine; (4) the disarmament on the left bank; (5) the Kiel Canal; (6) report of the commission on ports, waterways, and railways; (7) economic conditions; (8) stipulations concerning commercial aviation; and (9–12) four territorial questions: Heligoland, frontiers of Denmark, frontiers of Belgium, and Danzig and Marienwerder, Mantoux, *Proceedings*, pp. 196–197. To these Sonnino added "several secondary questions" when the foreign ministers met with The Four on April 16—viz., the prohibition of opium; stipulations concerning the Suez Canal; the drafting of a general clause for renunciation of German territory outside of Europe; and the basis for calculating the expense of the army of occupation. On April 19 the drafting committee that had been set up at the beginning of the month to prepare the text of the treaty referred to the Council of Four thirty points that were still unsettled, Sweetser diary, April 23, 1919. An undated memorandum by Hankey explained difficulties caused by experts who wrangled about details and made alterations in clauses that the drafting committee had thought final, penciled memorandum in F.C., 6N79.

3. See below, p. 389.

4. Miller, *My Diary*, vol. 16, p. 42.

"Four more of these joint meetings were held, on 1st, 2nd, and 12th May and on 17th June, these being in fact revivals of the Council of Ten." It was assumed that any resolution was "ad referendum to the Supreme Council," Marston, *The Peace Conference of 1919*, pp. 172–174. As time went on, the foreign ministers dispensed with specific reference to The Four, in the case of economic problems connected with the blockade and its gradual relaxation, and in the handling of the reports of the territorial committees in general.

accustomed to refer to professional diplomats and draftsmen. He was vigilant to note changes in the text of the draft treaty that seemed to reflect a determination on the part of the French secretariat to commit the United States more firmly to responsibilities in Europe,[5] and he instructed Miller to check the entire English and French texts for "jokers."[6]

When the Supreme Council engaged in discussion of the terms to be presented to Germany and the manner in which this was to be done, Wilson found his capacity for diplomatic negotiation seriously challenged. There had been no formal talks with German representatives about the conditions of peace; and the American Peace Commission had no regular source of intelligence that was constantly in touch with the Foreign Office at Berlin. American agents, however, had made at least three contacts with influential Germans.

The American financial advisers had been made aware of the enemy's economic difficulties by responsible German bankers of the house of Warburg with whom they had conferred in confidence once a week at Chateau Villette, near Compiègne.[7] A statement written by one of the Germans, Carl Melchior, came to Wilson.[8] Another banker, Max Warburg, asserted that America must not now withdraw, "neither sulking nor threatening," from the fulfillment of the terms of the Armistice of Rethondes, else the militarism of the victors would elicit a militarist reaction despite the fact that Germany had, for the present, turned away from this "foolish belief."

Furthermore, the American peacemakers had valuable intelligence through the military channel that had been opened by Colonel Arthur Latham Conger in the course of his negotiations for the return of American and Russian prisoners-of-war. Conger was under the jurisdiction of General Pershing and therefore independent of the peace commission. He received on March 31 from his German liaison, Major Walter Loeb, a copy of a memorandum—"Peace Terms Acceptable to Germany"—that reflected in all essentials certain "Guidelines for the German Negotiations." The guidelines had been approved by the cabinet at the urging of one of the ministers, Matthias Erzberger, the leader of the Center party and a political adversary of the foreign minister, Count von Brockdorff-Rantzau. This German statement sought plebiscites in disputed lands on Germany's borders, an upper limit on reparations, full membership in the League of Nations, and the retention of one colony to be administered under a League mandate; and it offered German labor for the repair of damages inflicted in Belgium and northern France, if this could be financed by an American loan. Conger reported that the German government was "absolutely in a mood to be guided by the advice of the United States in matters of

5. Memorandum, Seymour to House, August 15, 1924, Seymour papers, Y.H.C. A copy of the treaty's provisions on reparations, with checks and deletions by Wilson, is filed under April 21 in the Wilson papers. Some last-minute changes in the reparation clauses were not detected, according to a check made by J. F. Dulles. Baruch wrote to the president about this on May 8, letter enclosing a memorandum by Dulles, Wilson papers.

6. Miller, vol. 1, pp. 290–292, and docs. 870 and 924. Baker, *American Chronicle*, pp. 421–422.

7. Keynes, *Two Memoirs*, p. 67.

8. On April 3 Melchior presented a paper saying the situation was "really on the verge of the abyss" and warning that if the Peace Conference bore down too hard, it might have to deal with such men as those met by Germany at Brest Litovsk, pages enclosed with Keynes to Kerr, April 4, 1919, also in Wilson papers and in Miller papers, box 89, IV-6, "Col. House" folder.

difficulty'' but would not give an inch to France. He suggested the establishment of a permanent and confidential American contact with the German government, such as France and Great Britain already maintained. In talks with Loeb at Spa, Conger had gone so far as to offer American military support in maintaining order in Germany, while he was unresponsive to a proposal of General Groener for the deployment of American forces in Russia.

The German memorandum, forwarded by Conger, was read in part by Wilson to the Council of Four at a session on April 1. Conger, who came to Wilson's attention as a negotiator at Spa on April 3 on the question of the transport of Haller's Polish army, continued to be useful to the president in contacts with German officials.[9]

From still another source—a diplomatic mission—information came to the American peacemakers about German opinion. Ellis Dresel of the State Department, who had spent the first weeks of 1919 observing conditions at Berlin as a secret agent (the American government had not acted on Dresel's recommendations to declare its support for Ebert's government and to set up a permanent liaison at Berlin), returned there on April 18 with instructions from the peace commission and a statement by Hoover that was to be released to the German press. The food administrator, who thought the provisioning of Germany the best means of inducing its government to sign the treaty, warned that ''an equitable and untrammeled distribution'' of foodstuffs was possible only ''so long as stabilized and orderly conditions exist.''[10] Dresel's function was not only to observe, but to prepare the Germans to accept the contemplated terms of peace. Talking with the foreign minister and other officials, he assured them that America did not wish to destroy Germany; and at the same time he reminded them that they had lost the war and must face the consequences. Like Conger, he made it plain that Wilson was eager to have the treaty signed quickly and said that if a treaty was not signed an occupation would follow, or at least a strengthening of the blockade. However, the German minister, under the impression that Dresel hoped to soften German resistance to the terms that were being considered, persisted in resistance. ''I left him in no doubt,'' Brockdorff-Rantzau recorded, ''that under no circumstances would I sign the peace treaty. . . . I told Dresel that if the Entente insisted on these conditions, in my opinion Bolshevism would be unavoidable in Germany,'' and the present government would fall.[11]

Encountering strong antagonism, especially from disillusioned adherents of Wilson's program for peace, Dresel received a prophetic warning to the effect that if the victors insisted on impossible terms, the German nationalist movement would

9. See above, p. 261 and below, p. 390; and Schwabe, *Woodrow Wilson, Revolutionary Germany, and Peacemaking*, pp. 155 ff., 220–223, 309–312, 318–320, 336.

10. Schwabe, p. 313. This scholar has noted that in mid-April Wilson and House gave some consideration to a suggestion of Lloyd George for the creation of a stable German government that would sign the treaty. He thought that this might be done by inducing President Ebert to substitute a cabinet of radical Independent Socialists for the incumbent intransigent officials, *ibid.*, pp. 322 ff.

11. Schwabe, pp. 313–318. Brockdorff-Rantzau's record of his talk with Dresel, in *Akten zur Deutschen Auswärtigen Politik 1919–1945*, Serie A, vol. 1, pp. 422–426, and translation in the Walworth papers, Y.H.C.

Brockdorff-Rantzau recorded that he told Dresel that it was being said that his political opponents were content to let the present government bring about its fall by signing the peace treaty.

gain strength and "a leader, as yet undiscovered, would be found to lead a great popular uprising."

Dresel, making the best of the gloomy prospect for peace, reported to the American peace commission that the present German government was eager, above all, to negotiate with the victors and that, though it was entirely unlikely that it would accept the terms now contemplated at Paris, there was among the workers a growing inclination toward acquiescence in the sacrifices that the peace treaty would require. Although pessimistic about the possibility of the emergence of any other new German government that would be both compliant and stable, he was not apprehensive of a turn toward bolshevism. He recommended the face-to-face negotiations for which the Germans were very eager. Departing from Berlin early in May, Dresel left a young attaché there to maintain liaison.[12]

In a session of the Supreme Council of Four on April 24, Wilson presented a summary of the intransigent position of Brockdorff-Rantzau, as Dresel reported it. His own conclusion was that, though bolshevism existed in the cities, there was "a considerable public," especially in the country, that would accept the proposed terms in order to attain peace. He spoke of the importance of informing the German people that their plenipotentiaries would be permitted to negotiate, and he agreed with Clemenceau's opinion that the discussions must be not oral, but in writing. Wilson was endeavoring to mitigate, in small ways, the severity of the peace terms that were being drafted.

The admirals of France and Great Britain insisted that the German naval base on Heligoland be destroyed so that it would pose no threat in the future to shipping in the North Sea and the English Channel. In Balfour's opinion the English people would not now accept anything less than obliteration of the lair from which German submarines had sallied to their kills. Admiral Benson, however, said that the importance of Heligoland was exaggerated and in view of the plan to reduce the German navy destruction would be unjustifiable. Wilson, not unwilling to destroy fortifications on the island, was reluctant to do "wanton damage"; but he finally yielded to Balfour's argument that the naval port was not useful for refuge or for commerce. The Treaty of Versailles provided for destroying the "fortifications, military establishments, and harbors of the islands of Heligoland and Dune."[13]

The president was successful, however, in modifying other demands upon the enemy. In the Supreme Council he effectively reinforced an objection made by Lansing to a military article that would compel Germany to disclose its processes for making poison gas and thereby reveal scientific secrets that had commercial value.[14] Moreover, Wilson insisted that the return of German prisoners-of-war to their fatherland should be unimpeded by any attempt to use them to repair war damage or by any desire to hold them as hostages pending the release of Germans

---

12. Dresel to Ammission, April 20, 1919, Wilson papers. On Dresel's second mission to Berlin and on conditions in Germany in April, see Mayer, *Politics and Diplomacy of Peacemaking*, pp. 757 ff.

13. Reports enclosed with memorandum, Drummond to Sir G. Clark, April 17, P.R.O., FO / 800 / Cf / 19 / 1. Balfour set down his views on Heligoland in "Notes" written on April 14, 1919, Balfour papers, 49751.

14. *F.R., P.P.C.*, vol. 4, p. 561, vol. 5, pp. 310–311. Borden to Lloyd George, April 16, 1919, Lloyd George papers, F / 5 / 3 / 32. Mantoux, *Délibérations*, vol. 1, pp. 392–393. Article 306 of the treaty.

guilty of crime against *le droit des gens*. Questioning the right of the victors to dictate changes in German statutes, Wilson brought about the alteration of an article requiring the enmy to annul their provisions for military service. As a result Germany would undertake only to effect modifications of these provisions.[15] On the last day of April, Wilson said that General Bliss, asked to study an article of the draft treaty that would prolong certain military stipulations of the armistice, denounced this provision as too general and dangerous; and The Four decided provisionally to suppress this article.[16]

The president raised the question of restricting activities of enemy subjects in the countries of the victors, supporting a contention by Baruch that surveillance should be limited to a period of five years. He accepted with some reluctance a compromise proposed by Borden of Canada, fixing a minimum of five years and a maximum of ten and charging the League of Nations to set up a committee to determine the exact length of time.

In the middle of April The Four decided that it was time to arrange a meeting with German representatives even though many questions were still open. Wilson was asked to draft a statement of the reasons for summoning the enemy. Released on the fourteenth, this was the first communiqué to go to the public from the cloistered Council of Four. A French note to Germany set April 25 as the date for the arrival of its delegates at Versailles to receive the text of a peace treaty as drawn up by the Allied and Associated Powers.

The reaction of the German foreign ministry to the note was far from submissive. The minister of foreign affairs, Count Ulrich von Brockdorff-Rantzau, whom a German correspondent of House had described as "the brain of the whole works,"[17] was an experienced diplomat who appeared to believe that the future belonged to democracy and socialism. He was, however, handicapped by his haughty *Junker* manners in dealing with practitioners of Western democracy.[18] Convinced that the victors did not intend to enter into any negotiations, he was not disposed to go to France to receive what seemed to him to be an ultimatum. His answer, offering to send minor German officials to act as messengers, appeared to the victors offensive and even insolent.[19] They replied with a note drafted by Wilson that insisted that Germany send "fully authorized plenipotentiaries." Though only a little less than an ultimatum, this communication was mistaken by Brockdorff-Rantzau for a conciliatory gesture.

While waiting for German delegates to appear, Wilson gave consideration to a

---

15. Mantoux, *Délibérations*, vol. 1, pp. 409–411, 421. *F.R., P.P.C.*, vol. 5, pp. 338, 353, 371.

16. Mantoux, *Délibérations*, vol. 1, p. 430. Bliss had reported to the president on April 24 that the draft treaty made no provision for the termination of controls over Germany by inter-Allied commissions—a matter that had been the subject of an American reservation to the military terms on March 17. (See above, p. 210.) An article to which Bliss objected—no. 46 of the military clauses—would carry into the Treaty of Versailles all the clauses of the armistice that were not inconsistent with the treaty's terms, Bliss to Wilson, May 1, 1919, Wilson papers.

17. Memo from Karl von Wiegand, March 21, 1919, House papers. Von Wiegand stated that the foreign minister felt that to agree to any exactions upon Germany that went far beyond Wilson's proposals would be to lose the consent of the German people.

18. Hajo Holborn, *A History of Modern Germany*, vol. 3, p. 560. Gerhard Schulz, *Revolutions and Peace Treaties, 1917–1920*, p. 177.

19. Alma Maria Luckau, *The German Delegation at the Paris Peace Conference*, pp. 209–210.

suggestion by Lloyd George that they consider ways of bringing about the fall of Scheidemann's government and its replacement by a more tractable regime. A British agent had reported from Berlin that the signing of the peace treaty by Germany could be achieved only if the victor took measures to improve the economic condition of the German people and at the same time supported a new coalition government that would include the Leftist Separatist regime that functioned in Bavaria. Wilson did not object to this possibility as a contingency plan, and he passed along the British recommendation to Hoover. Although apprehensive of the radical doctrine of the Separatists, the food administrator welcomed the idea of improving economic conditions, which he was trying to do by lifting the blockade; and he had spoken of the Independent Socialists as a force that came "nearer representing the yearnings of the German people at the present time."[20] Wilson pleaded again in the Supreme Council, on April 23 and again on May 1, for the termination of the blockade. On April 25, however, when it was clear that the delegates from Berlin would make an appearance, he remarked in the council that there was no longer a need for another government in Germany. The Soviet Republic at Munich fell early in May.

Wilson was still anxious, however, about the reception of the treaty terms both in Germany and in America; and his anxiety about Germany's action grew when Orlando's departure from Paris seemed to give encouragement to German hopes for a rift among the victors.[21] In view of the strong antagonism that was sure to develop if German and French negotiators came face to face, he accepted a suggestion by Clemenceau that any exchanges with the enemy should be put in writing. The most important question in German minds was of an economic nature, Wilson said on April 23. Yet when Brockdorff-Rantzau was reminded by Dresel that economic revival was recognized by the victors as a necessity in the interest of the world, the German minister had been unresponsive.[22] Wilson felt that in Brockdorff-Rantzau they had a stubborn antagonist, but he envisioned a submissive body of opinion in "a eager public" that would accept the terms prescribed "in order to achieve peace and to be able to earn a living again." On April 25 he said in the Council of Four that the German delegates would not dare to sign any treaty that their people could not be induced to accept. He alluded to the possibility that their government might fall and be succeeded by one "very much more dangerous." The Peace Conference must act in a way, he said, that would release as little force as possible against the equilibrium that they sought to establish. Yet, Germany must be placed in a position in which it could be penalized effectively. When The Four discussed the procedure and agenda to be followed in receiving the German delegates, the League of Nations was omitted from the list of topics until Wilson insisted on its inclusion.[23]

On May 5 a committee appointed by the Council of Four met to determine the strength of the army of occupation after the peace treaty was signed. A statement

20. See above, p. 84, and Schwabe, pp. 320–322.
21. Schwabe, pp. 324–328.
22. Mantoux, *Délibérations,* vol. 1, pp. 341, 351. Schwabe, p. 314.
23. Document in Wilson papers under dates of April 23–26, 1919. Mantoux, *Délibérations,* vol. 1, pp. 369–372.

drawn up by Foch provided for an American contribution of four divisions during the three months following the signing and thereafter one or two divisions. Amazed by this, Bliss wrote to remind Wilson that he had informed Clemenceau that one regiment was the maximum permanent contribution of the United States. American law required that all draftees be mustered out within four months of the signing of peace.[24]

Until almost the moment of delivery of the terms to the Germans, Wilson and Lloyd George wished to keep their options open; and because of this they were insistent that their plans be kept secret. Finally, however, the Council of Four considered how it might best cast off the veil of secrecy. A discussion of this question on April 12, in which Lloyd George asserted that the small nations should not see the treaty until Germany had accepted it, ended in the provisional acceptance of a proposal by Balfour that a ''general outline'' should be read to a plenary session.[25] Accordingly, the delegates of all member states met on the afternoon of May 6, with no newsmen present, and were given an opportunity to be heard. A summary of the terms was read, as well as the substance of the guarantee of France's security that Lloyd George and Wilson offered.[26] Reservations were formally registered by Italy and China, and Marshal Foch asserted that the military arrangements for the security of France were inadequate.

The text of the Covenant of the League had been released for publication in the United States on April 28. The question of publicity for the rest of the treaty, however, was one not easily solved. Lloyd George, apprehensive that the Germans would not accept the treaty and that any premature disclosure of its conditions might provoke revolution in Germany, was of the opinion that publication could be prevented in England, in France, and even, by the use of the president's ''influence with the press,'' in the United States. Clemenceau, however, thought publicity inevitable, and he was prepared to accept it. In his opinion the German people, like the French in 1871, would conclude that there was no practical alternative to acceptance of the victor's terms.[27] Convinced that his people would be resentful if they got their first knowledge of the treaty from the German press, where it would certainly appear, Clemenceau thought it well to give out a résumé of the document.

Wilson felt the force of this reasoning. Yet general publicity seemed to him undesirable. The insecurity of his political position and awareness of the criticism that would assail the treaty from all sides as soon as its terms were known had driven the tiring advocate of ''open diplomacy'' into a mood of furtiveness. His distaste for any sort of interview was growing. He feared that if he talked freely, he would be indiscreet and misjudged. The intelligence reports left doubt in his mind as to whether the Weimar government would sign the treaty. In view of this it seemed unwise to let the German people know what was in store for them.

The president was of the opinion that the best solution, under the conditions that were imposed on the peacemakers by the curiosity of the peoples and their news-

24. Bliss to Wilson, May 9 and 19, 1919, Bliss papers, box 433.
25. Mantoux, *Délibérations*, vol. 1, p. 234. Lansing desk diary, April 12, 1919.
26. Mantoux, *Délibérations*, vol. 1, p. 493.
27. *Ibid.*, p. 351. F.R., P.P.C., vol. 5, pp. 204–205.

men, was to prepare a well-conceived summary, couched in general terms. Accordingly, a text was prepared by Arthur Sweetser, working in harmony with a British official. Going to Dr. Scott of the drafting commission to get precise information, Sweetser found confusion and disarray in the large room at the Quai d'Orsay where the momentous document was being drawn together. Two important omissions had been remedied at the last moment, one largely at the initiative of the drafting committee. There obviously had been a lack of cohesion among the various committees of experts. "The drafting commission was working itself to death," Sweetser wrote, "as very little of the material had been assembled when they took charge, most of it was very badly drafted, and much of it was conflicting, as for instance when reparations, ports, finance, and economics kept running across each other's trails." It was evident that no mind had undertaken the essential responsibility of coordinating the details.[28] On May 6 a release was approved. "It was at that time," according to Baker, "the greatest co-operative undertaking in the distribution of news that had ever been attempted."[29]

Learning that the entire text of the treaty was being sent uncoded to Washington, the president stopped the transmission. Deeply disturbed, he informed Lansing on May 3 that a summary was available and that the State Department should give nothing to the press except under explicit instructions from him.[30]

A German delegation came to Versailles on April 29 to receive the draft of the peace terms. On the train that brought them, Colonel Conger, who for some weeks had provided the Germans with intelligence about American intentions that they took most seriously,[31] talked with Brockdorff-Rantzau and warned him that the victors' tolerance of any revision would be limited and a time would come when Germany would be forced to sign a treaty and sign promptly.[32] Wilson reported this conversation to Clemenceau and Lloyd George, and summarized the intelligence that he received about the views of Erzberger and Chancellor Scheidemann, who expressed willingness to sign a reasonable peace but predicted that if the terms were not such as his government could accept, no other government could make peace for Germany.[33]

The question of publicity presented difficulties when the Germans arrived. They

28. Document describing the preparation of the summary with George Mair of Great Britain, Sweetser papers, box 9. Sweetser to the author, November 12, 1965. Baker, *American Chronicle*, p. 420. *F.R., P.P.C.,* vol. 5, pp. 470, 485. A copy of the summary by Sweetser, with a note, Baker to Grayson, saying that it was for the president to look over, is filed under May 3 in the Wilson papers. According to Sweetser, no official of the American commission read it, although Wilson said in the Council of Four that "everything depended" on the nature of the summary, Mantoux, *Délibérations,* vol. 1. p. 352. Cf. Headlam-Morley to Smuts, May 19, 1919, Smuts, *Selections,* vol. 4, p. 169.

29. Baker, *American Chronicle*, p. 420.

30. Wilson to Lansing, May 3, 1919, Wilson papers. Ammission to State Department, May 4, 1919, N.A., R.G. 59, 763.72119 / 4835. Baker's journal, June 9, 1919.

31. Schwabe, pp. 309–312. On March 28 Conger had predicted a peace that would be tolerable to the Ebert-Scheidemann government and on April 14 he indicated that German plenipotentiaries would be allowed to confer with the victors, *ibid.,* pp. 299–300.

32. *Ibid.,* pp. 318–319, 326–328.

33. Mantoux, *Délibérations,* vol. 1, pp. 446–447. *F.R., P.P.C.,* vol. 5, p. 405. Conger to Bliss, April 30, 1919, with "Interviews of a confidential agent," dated April 30, 1919, forwarded with letter, Bliss to Wilson, May 1, 1919, Wilson papers.

waited for more than a week, with no more contact with their adversaries than a formal exchange of credentials, while the text of the treaty was being whipped into final form.[34] The Three decided that they would not talk with the Germans nor permit newsmen to do so, in order that the enemy would have no opportunity to try to break the common front of the victors.

The American journalists protested this decision.[35] However, Clemenceau said that the exposure of the Germans to journalists would be in bad taste, and Lloyd George suggested that the enemy would object strongly to being exhibited "like a menagerie."[36] The newsmen were allowed only to look from a distance upon the sequestered aliens at Versailles; but by exercising ingenuity they managed to make contacts. And so American and British readers were not compelled to get their news of proceedings secondhand through stories in German newspapers.

Wilson successfully advocated the presence of newsmen at the ceremony when the treaty was to be handed formally to the Germans, in the Trianon Palace, the seat of the Supreme War Council in 1918. The Three made a trip to Versailles and reviewed the arrangements for seating five journalists from each major power and ten to represent the small nations.[37]

The president interceded also in behalf of those small powers whom Clemenceau and Lloyd George called "non-effective belligerents." He was reminded by a note from Lansing that the American commission felt that several Latin-American nations should be allowed representation at the first meeting with the Germans. On May 6 he remarked to the Supreme Council that certain states that had declared war on Germany and would have to sign the treaty had not been invited to the ceremony. Favorable action was taken on Wilson's plea that at least the Chinese be invited, and it was agreed that in view of this Siam could not well be left out. At the plenary session that afternoon, when the summary of the terms was read to the small belligerent powers, Lansing again urged Wilson to appeal in behalf of their Latin American friends. The secretary of state also spoke to Clemenceau, who got the assent of Lloyd George. As a result the countries designated officially as "also present" were Cuba, Guatemala, Haiti, Honduras, Liberia, Nicaragua, and Panama. They received no formal invitation and came to the meeting on May 7 only at the oral behest of Lansing, whom they thanked heartily.[38]

When the statesmen of the victorious powers met on May 7 at the Trianon, the

34. Luckau, pp. 59–63. The treatment of the German delegation of 180 men at Versailles has been described by a member of it, Victor Schiff, in *The Germans at Versailles, 1919*, pp. 52–66, 117. On April 29, Conger informed Brockdorff-Rantzau of two channels through which his delegation at Versailles might convey information to the American government, Schwabe, p. 318.

35. Baker's memorandum to the American commission, April 25, 1919; memorandum, Baker to Close, April 28, 1919, Baker papers, box 97.

36. Mantoux, *Délibérations*, vol. 1, p. 424.

37. *Ibid.*, pp. 490, 504. Baker, *American Chronicle*, pp. 425–426. Baker recorded that the president agreed to intercede for the newsmen only after learning that they were threatening to send no more news to America if they were not represented. According to Baker, Swope "sneaked and bluffed his way into the conference room," and Baker, irritated by an accumulation of offenses on the part of this journalist, told him that he was not "playing the game," Baker journal, May 7 and 8, 1919.

38. Lansing's private memoranda, May 8, 1919. R. S. Baker's journal, June 21, 1919. Mantoux, *Délibérations*, vol. 1, p. 496. *F.R., P.P.C.*, vol. 5, p. 481. Miller, *My Diary*, vol. 18, pp. 117–118.

emotions that had raged during the conflict were rekindled. Clemenceau, prepared to confront the enemy with Wilson at his right and Lloyd George at his left, took his place above a double row of tables at which delegates from twenty-seven nations sat. A small and lower table awaited the Germans. The most critical of all questions was soon to be answered. Would the Germans negotiate on the basis of the terms presented to them, or would another resort to force be necessary?

The doors swung open. *"Les plenipotentiaires allemandes"* were announced. The assemblage rose and stood in silence while a dozen Germans walked to their seats and bowed stiffly. They found themselves in what French newspapers called a "banc des accusés," confronting a semicircle of enemies—a situation that Wilson deplored but had been unable to alter.[39]

The implacable hatreds of warfare marred the decorum of the ceremony. Americans remembered that this day marked an anniversary of the sinking of the *Lusitania;*[40] the British called to mind the German offenses against the usages of civilized men and nations; and the French forgot neither the woe that had befallen them since 1914 nor the victor's peace that had been imposed on their country by Germany in 1871. Clemenceau, who vividly remembered the day on which William I was proclaimed emperor at Versailles, looked directly at the crestfallen German civilians. Sentences came from him in volleys: "It is neither the time nor the place for superfluous words. . . . The time has come when we must settle our accounts. You have asked for peace. We are ready to give you peace. . . . You will be given every facility to examine the conditions, and the time necessary for it. Everything will be done with the courtesy that is the privilege of civilized nations. . . . But we must say at the same time that this second Treaty of Versailles has cost us too much not to take on our side all the necessary precautions and guarantees that that peace shall be a lasting one."[41] He spoke for less than two minutes.

Brockdorff-Rantzau, his face chalky white, his chest sunken, stood to receive a white book containing the terms. He sat down to read his reply to the remarks of Clemenceau. Fearful that his government could not survive what he condemned as a betrayal of the American policy in which it had put its faith, he attempted to make the most of his opportunity to confront the enemies of his country face-to-face. But because of his sullen and defiant manner, his aggressive language, and his insistence on remaining seated while replying to the remarks that Clemenceau had risen to his feet to deliver, many eyebrows were raised even among those who shared his doubts as to the justice and wisdom of the proposed settlement.

The exact condition and motives of Brockdorff-Rantzau have been variously interpreted by historians. According to Schwabe, he remained seated "so as not to appear as an accused man but rather to emphasize that he regarded, this initial meeting as having the character of negotiations." He cherished a hope that Germany could be reunited with the West, possibly in the cause of antibolshevism. Just before leaving for Versailles, he had ordered that all overtures from Soviet Russia were to be rejected. He staked everything on a revision of the conditions of peace that would

39. Benham diary letter, May 8, 1919.
40. Grew, *Turbulent Era,* vol. 1, p. 387. House diary, May 7, 1919.
41. Baker, vol. 2, pp. 501–502.

bring them closer to Wilson's Fourteen Points, which he cited as the only legal basis for the treaty.[42]

After admitting the defeat of German armies, and unjust treatment of Belgium and violations of the code of warfare on the part of Germany, Brockdorff-Rantzau alluded to the starvation of "hundreds of thousands of non-combatants" by the blockade. He then launched into a denunciation of the war-guilt allegation that was made against Germany in an effort to justify the victors' demand for reparations. Attributing the outbreak of the war to the enemy's policies of reprisal, expansion, and "disregard for the right of self-determination," he said: "The demand is made that we shall acknowledge that we alone are guilty of having caused the war. Such a confession in my mouth would be a lie."[43] He proposed that verdicts as to guilt should be arrived at by a neutral commission. Warning that his government might not long survive any betrayal of the American policy in which it had put its faith, he pleaded for the "economic and social solidarity" of all nations in a free and all-comprising League of Nations. He envisioned an economic order in which Germany would have an opportunity to become capable of making reasonable reparations.[44]

Clemenceau, barely able to control the rage that was stirred in him by the matter and manner of the German's address, closed the meeting as brusquely as he had opened it.

The Americans, who had been striving for months for a nonvindictive peace and who had helped to bring about a relaxation of the blockade, were offended. Already prejudiced against Brockdorff-Rantzau, Wilson was now incensed by the foreign minister's conduct. "What abominable manners," he said as he left the room. "The blood went to my head more than once during that speech." In the evening he told Baker that the talk was "not frank, peculiarly Prussian, and stupid." It seemed to him incredible that Germany's "war guilt" was denied. Yet the next day, when The Four exchanged views of the German behavior and Clemenceau spoke of an authoritative report that Brockdorff-Rantzau had declared he would not sign the treaty, Wilson said that their annoyance with the German foreign minister ought not to prevent them from recognizing that people had been starved because the peace terms had not been ready earlier. With the exception of Brockdorff-Rantzau, he said, the German delegates seemed to be reasonable men. He told his colleagues that the Germans would be forced to sign the treaty after two weeks. He wanted to give them only enough time to reconcile themselves to the inevitable.[45]

The reluctance of The Three to reveal their decisions was not without reason. Waves of criticism broke both in Paris and in Washington when the terms became known. Attacks upon the proposed settlement came not only from idealists who

42. Schwabe, p. 330. Cf. Holborn, "Diplomacy in the Early Weimar Republic," in *The Diplomats,* ed. Craig and Gilbert, p. 137. Schiff, pp. 69, 73. Also see Luckau, pp. 63–69, 213–220; Lloyd George, *The Truth about the Peace Treaties,* pp. 675–677; Grew, vol. 1, p. 387; House diary, May 7, 1919; dispatch, Ammission to the secretary of state, May 3, 1919, Wilson papers; Borden, general memorandum no. 20, May 10, 1919, Borden papers; Nicolson, *Peacemaking, 1919,* p. 329.

43. On Brockdorff-Rantzau's argument see Schwabe, pp. 331–332.

44. Luckau, pp. 67–69, 119, 220–223. *F.R., P.P.C.,* vol. 3, pp. 413–420.

45. *F.R., P.P.C.,* vol. 5, p. 510. Baker, vol. 2, pp. 500–506; *American Chronicle,* p. 428. Cambon, "La Paix," 34. Grew, vol. 1, pp. 387–388. Borden, *Memoirs,* p. 963. Riddell diary, May 7, 1919.

were disillusioned, but from the political enemies of The Three and from associates at Paris who complained that their advice had not been heeded. Clemenceau, who had received a written protest from President Poincaré and a threat of resignation from Marshal Foch,[46] now was attacked in the Chamber by socialists who thought the conditions too stern as well as by ardent nationalists who thought them too lenient.[47] In England the press on the extreme Right and Left was critical, though for the most part journals commented favorably.[48]

In dramatizing the Peace Conference as a battle between good and evil and in suggesting that European leaders were obtuse to the interests of humanity, Wilson had given gratification to American citizens who conceived that they had made sacrifices in order to save civilization and to make a better world. Now, however, he found himself the victim of the very questioning of authority in which he had indulged. Many men in his own camp who had most applauded his bold manifestoes to the populace of Europe now turned their insurgent zeal upon the American prophet who seemed guilty of apostasy. Some Americans, familiar with only certain aspects, had not realized the extent of inconsistencies in the treaty as a whole until they read the summary. Scarcely one of the experts was without criticism of specific terms; and the American commission experienced what Schwabe has called "a crisis of conscience."[49]

Herbert Hoover saw the complete text for the first time on the day of its presentation to the Germans. He paced the streets early one morning in agitation over terms that in his opinion would degrade all of Europe and bring on another war. Meeting Smuts and Keynes in the course of his walk, he shared their forebodings.[50] The president had to exert his powers of persuasion to hold the loyalty of the wavering Ray Stannard Baker.[51] Baruch was telling Wilson that the economic conditions were impractical. On May 22 it was said to the president that Smuts, House, Lansing, and Bliss were thinking of refusing to sign the treaty. Wilson, unable to believe this, asked McCormick to sound out Lansing, who was bitter and without hope in the League of Nations because he thought that it was "unjust and unprincipled" and that the veto power made change impossible.[52] James Brown Scott, the legal expert, called the treaty "the worst ever drawn . . . a great human tragedy."

46. Jere C. King, *Clemenceau vs. Foch*, pp. 61–72.

47. Dispatch, Wallace to the secretary of state, May 10, 1919, Wilson papers.

48. Dispatch, John W. Davis to the secretary of state, May 26, 1919, N.A., R.G. 59, 841.00 / 159. For criticism by Labour and its press see Winkler, "The British Labour Party and the Paris Settlement," in *Some Pathways of Twentieth Century History*, ed. D. R. Beaver (Detroit, 1969), p. 124; also Arthur Henderson, *The Peace Terms* (London, 1919).

49. Shotwell, *At the Paris Peace Conference*, pp. 45–46. Schwabe, p. 337.

50. Hoover, *The Ordeal of Woodrow Wilson*, pp. 178, 234. See Gelfand (ed.), *Herbert Hoover: The Great War and the Aftermath*, pp. 14, 63 ff., 72, 151, 162.

51. Baker, *American Chronicle*, p. 429.

52. Baker journal, May 19, 1919. Baker, recording Lansing's charge that "the great fault of the Conference from the start had been too little publicity," wrote: "While I heartily agreed with him, . . . I recalled the fact that no one of the commissioners, in practice, had been more hostile to any real publicity than he. He had been too long disciplined in the school of diplomatic timidity," *American Chronicle*, p. 429. McCormick found Lansing ready to sign but "a bit sore at not being consulted more," diary, May 22 and 23, 1919. On the question of Lansing's "loyalty" see Lazo, "A Question of Loyalty: Robert Lansing and the Treaty of Versailles," 42 ff.

He said: "The statesmen have but given their people what they want and cry for . . . and have made a peace that renders another war inevitable."[53]

Bullitt, after long talks with Lansing and Bliss in which they criticized the treaty, vented his frustration in a letter to Wilson that expressed the despair of "those who trusted confidently and explicitly" in his leadership.[54] His hopes for a "great coalition" of American Wilsonians with European liberals and socialists had been extinguished. Resigning on May 17, Bullitt left Paris, he said, to lie in the sun and watch the world go to hell. The *jeunesse radicale* of the American delegation were challenged to follow him in resigning. Four of them wrote to Lansing, offering to leave if the commissioners deemed that they should. The secretary of state, however, thought he could not get along without them.[55]

When Bullitt asked House to bring his letter to Wilson to the notice of the president,[56] House said this would give the impression that he agreed with what it said. Admitting that the terms of peace fell short of justice in many respects, House expressed the conviction that in the future the League of Nations, strengthened by socialist governments that would come to power in Europe, would right the wrongs. He commended the president for refusing to bolt the Peace Conference and thus invite revolutions everywhere on the Continent, and he explained the difficulties that Wilson would have to face at Washington.[57]

When the summary of the treaty was printed in America on May 8, the day after the complete document was handed to the German delegates, Tumulty informed his chief that publication was a great triumph for the administration and the opposition was stunned.[58] Nevertheless, thoughtful liberals in the United States regretted the departures from the Fourteen Points. Moreover, the adversaries in the Senate raised a storm about the withholding of the complete text. Turning against Wilson the political weapon that he had often used to good effect, they talked of a "conspiracy

53. Sweetser diary, May 18, 1919. The treaties with Germany and Austria were "two of the worst international treaties ever framed," in the opinion of Lord Hardinge, the experienced diplomat who had directed the preparation of the Foreign Office for the Peace Conference but had not been influential at Paris, Hardinge, *The Old Diplomacy*, p. 239.

54. A record of the talk with Bliss is in the Y.H.C. Bullitt revealed Lansing's critical remarks when Bullitt testified before the Foreign Relations Committee of the U.S. Senate in September. Bullitt's letter of May 17 to Wilson is printed in Bullitt and Freud, *Thomas Woodrow Wilson*, pp. 271–272. Berle diary, May 8 and 10, 1919, Berle papers, box 1. John M. Thompson, p. 305. Farnworth, *William C. Bullitt and the Soviet Union*, pp. 55–56. Lansing's agreement with Bullitt was more complete than is indicated in his apology in *The Peace Negotiations*, ch. 19. Lansing, private memoranda, May 18, 1919. White expressed sympathy with Bullitt's protest, but reminded the young man of the duty of a diplomat to further the policy of his government rather than air his own convictions, White to Lodge, September 19, 1919, Lodge papers, Massachusetts Historical Society.

55. Lansing desk diary, May 21, 1919, Lansing to J. W. Davis, May 22, 1919, Davis papers, Y.H.C. See Beatrice B. Berle and Travis B. Jacobs (eds.), *Navigating the Rapids, 1918–1971*, pp. 13–15. Berle, a lieutenant in the army, was relieved of his duties at his insistence and was ordered home on June 30, correspondence in Berle papers, box 1.

56. Bullitt to House, May 17, 1919, Y.H.C. The letter appeared in the *Daily Herald* on May 24 with Bullitt's authorization, N.A., R.G. 59, 861.00 / 4674. Wilson called it "insulting," Baker journal, May 19, 1919. Polk cabled to Auchincloss on May 24 from Washington: "How about Bullitt? A spanking seems desirable," Auchincloss diary, May 5 and 26, 1919.

57. "Conversation with Colonel House," May 19, 1919, Bullitt papers.

58. Miller, vol. 1, pp. 293–295, and doc. 930. House diary, May 7, 1919. Dispatch, Tumulty to Wilson, May 8, 1919, Wilson papers.

of secrecy.'' In two weeks Tumulty reported that there was intense feeling in favor of release of the whole treaty, and Baker suggested that it be printed in the United States. It had been published by the Germans the day after they received it, and copies were for sale in Paris.[59] Wilson, however, agreed with Lloyd George that it would be well not to give official confirmation to what was released in Germany. The Four decided to observe the rule of secrecy at least until a formal reply came from Berlin.[60]

On June 10, after the German reply was received, Wilson instructed Lansing that it would not be in the public interest to communicate to the Senate a text that was "provisional and not definitive,'' that there was no precedent for such a procedure and that he was bound to act in concert with the Allies.[61] However, on that day newspapers published the whole document. Copies had reached Elihu Root in May and were shown by him to Henry Cabot Lodge. And so the treaty, as Clemenceau had foreseen, became what one editor called "one of the most public private things in the world.''

In a ridiculous "sideshow,'' Lodge, pointing out that the treaty had become public in Europe while the American Senate was kept in ignorance, insinuated that the administration had deliberately allowed New York financiers to have the text. The Senate passed a resolution, introduced with Wilson's approval, requiring a thorough investigation of Lodge's charge. The storm, which Polk thought "a tempest in a teapot,''[62] subsided quickly when J. P. Morgan and his partner, Henry P. Davison, testified before the Committee on Foreign Relations that it was proper for Davison, as head of the Red Cross, to have a copy of the treaty and to circulate it, since it had been published in Germany and brought to the United States before it had been ruled to be secret.[63]

The president did not have to be told that the peace terms fell far short of the high ideals that he had championed. The essential demands of the Allied peoples, and the necessity of working with their leaders to achieve a concert of power as a basis of peace, had forced him to arrive at negotiated settlements in the time-honored way of European statesmen. He had not attained a treaty that entirely measured up to his public pledges and his personal concept of justice. The Germans had failed to acknowledge those exertions that he had put forth to their advantage, and now some were ready to use him as a scapegoat for the tribulations that came upon the fatherland and seemed to belie their faith in a Wilsonian peace. Yet it was characteristic of Wilson to close his mind to change after he felt he had been "all around the clock.'' He asserted in a letter to Smuts that though the treaty was "very severe indeed,'' he thought it not "on the whole unjust in the circumstances.'' Although agreeing that they should give "real consideration'' to German objections, he thought

59. Baker, *American Chronicle*, pp. 430–431. Cable, Tumulty to Wilson, May 22, 1919; dispatch, Dresel to Ammission, May 22, 1919, Wilson papers. Dresel reported that the Germans were stunned and the stock market was closed for three days.

60. *F.R., P.P.C.*, vol. 5, pp. 557, 673–674.

61. Wilson to Lansing, June 10, 1919, Wilson papers.

62. Polk to Ammission, June 6, 1919, Wilson papers.

63. Telegrams, Morrow to Lamont, June 14, 1919, Davison to Lamont, June 13, 1919; letter, Lamont to Auchincloss, June 16, 1919, Miller papers, box 89, IV, 10.

it necessary to make evident "once and for all" that Germany's "very great offense against civilization" could "lead only to the most severe punishment." He took no notice of an appeal by President Ebert to the American people.[64]

64. Schwabe, p. 342.

21

The Financial Reckoning

The exactions put upon their nation by the terms presented on May 7 surpassed the worst fears of responsible German moderates. The banker Warburg deemed the proposed settlement to be "world piracy . . . under the flag of hypocrisy," and Simons, the general commissioner of the German delegation, thought the terms, insofar as they were dictated by Anglo-Saxons, to be "the work of a capitalist policy of the cleverest and most brutal kind."[1] Yet some retained a measure of faith in the good will of Wilson, and the German delegates at Versailles urged that the government and press at Berlin refrain from direct attacks upon the American president. The disappointment of Germans in Wilson's hardening attitude was as great as their incomprehension of the refusal of the American government to make loans to underwrite the reconstruction of Europe.[2]

Hope for a revision of the economic terms had arisen from constructive thinking by the financial experts on both sides. On May 20 the American financial advisers welcomed a German request for informal conversations, and the next day Wilson proposed in the Supreme Council that certain clauses of the treaty be explained orally by their specialists in talks with the Germans. He asked whether such an exchange would not make it easier for "sensible" men like Melchior, who Wilson hoped would speak for a German policy, to persuade their countrymen to accept the treaty. Clemenceau insisted, however, that contact with the enemy must be limited to diplomatic notes.

Wilson's confidence in Melchior was not misplaced. The German banker and his colleague, Warburg, elaborated on a compromise that they had presented early in April at Château Villette.[3] They now proposed that Germany meet its obligation for reparation by assuming a debt comparable in amount to the highest estimate of the American experts—125 billion gold marks—to be interest-free for the most part and payable in installments over a long period of time, each annual payment to be limited to a certain percentage of the national income. Warburg envisioned "international economic agreements" that would "ultimately reduce ethnic and national borders to matters of relative insignificance and . . . lead to the formation of a 'supreme parliament' to which the individual nations [would] send their delegates by way of the League of Nations" and where "noble minds" could solve the world's financial and economic problems. The immediate task of such a world organization would be to create a clearing procedure that would re-establish credit where it was lacking.[4]

---

1. Schwabe, *Woodrow Wilson, Revolutionary Germany, and Peacemaking*, p. 332.
2. *Ibid.*, pp. 333 ff.
3. See above, p. 384.
4. On the reasons for the proposal of the German bankers and on its influence upon the government's policy, see Schwabe, pp. 358–360.

The plan of the German bankers, by which they hoped to enhance understanding with the victors and to preserve their nation's territorial integrity and its economic potential, provided substance for a counterproposal that the German government made on May 29.[5] This, in Lamont's opinion, went further than the Americans expected to see the Germans go in writing. It did not require the United States government to guarantee bonds, nor did it impinge on the prospect of repayment of war debts to America.

Actually, the war-shattered economy of Europe was dependent on the support of its principal creditor, the United States, which had established credits in favor of the Allied governments that amounted at the end of hostilities to more than \$8 billion.[6] Of all the great powers, the United States was in the best position to establish new credits. It had already provided funds through the War Finance Corporation to finance exports to France and Great Britain. But it was not enough for America to fund only the moving of its own surpluses. It was of the first importance to give fiscal aid where it was most needed and thus to prime the pump of credit.

In considering the bill for reparation that was to be presented to Germany, the American economic advisers had not lost sight of the bearing of German payments upon the capacity of the treasuries of the Allied powers to meet their obligations to the United States. Any further extension of credit seemed financially unwise and politically impossible. The loan market in the United States was oversaturated, and there was inflationary pressure on the currency. The American Treasury had made its position very clear. It had warned the Peace Commission at Paris against any discussion of plans that might dilute the obligations of unprecedented size that had already been assumed by the Allied powers. At the same time the Treasury continued to grant loans from funds already authorized to meet urgent needs for reconstruction in Allied countries.[7]

A month before the treaty was presented to the Germans, Lord Robert Cecil, who commanded confidence on all sides, had challenged the peacemakers to devise a way to use public resources to provide the "oil of credit" everywhere.[8] Cecil pointed out to The Four on May 9 that the most urgent necessity was to revive the "exchange economy." The vast size of the sums needed and the length of the credits required made the risk of loans too great for private capital. Therefore, it seemed necessary that the governments take joint action to provide liquid credit at the earliest possible moment. The distribution of food was, in Cecil's opinion, only an emergency measure that could never cure the general paralysis. He found the American economic advisers divided among themselves, somewhat jealous one of another, and inclined to an impracticality of which all were not entirely aware and for which one or two

5. See below, p. 414.
6. See Walworth, *America's Moment: 1918,* p. 285.
7. See above, p. 175, n. 64.
8. Note on the General Economic Position by Lord Robert Cecil, April 5, 1919, and memorandum by Cecil, April 9, 1919, copies in Foster papers, file 147, 3, C, National Archives of Canada. Letter, Cecil to House, April 5, 1919, Y.H.C. Mantoux, *Délibérations,* vol. 2, p. 12. On April 5 Wiseman had addressed a constructive proposal to House. See above, p. 289.

apologized.[9] They were hampered by a Treasury and a Congress that were responsible to short-sighted voters.

It seemed clear to British advisers that Europe was menaced by a threat of general bankruptcy unless Germany's credit could be restored sufficiently to enable its industry to become productive enough to make reparations payments possible. On April 24 Lloyd George commended to Wilson an ingenious and comprehensive plan that was devised by John Maynard Keynes. This "concrete proposal," he wrote, was his government's "constructive contribution to the solution of the greatest financial problem ever set to the modern world." The British government was ready to commit itself immediately to the plan "subject to the legislative sanction which it will presumably require in all countries." The British Treasury conceived that the Keynes plan, which provided for a resort to the League of Nations in the event of a default, would put an end to advances to Europe and would provide a basis of credit that might serve in lieu of gold.[10]

Wilson was disposed to give serious consideration to this proposal. He was perhaps influenced by a remark of Lloyd George that some program of this nature was, in the opinion of Melchior, necessary to make it possible for Germany to sign the peace treaty. In any event the president was open-minded when Norman Davis discussed the Keynes plan with him. However, House did not act on a plea from Cecil that the plan be commended to Wilson.[11] The American economic advisers noted that Lloyd George's letter to Wilson had indicated that the proposed bonds might be used to pay off Allied debts, and this might leave the United States holding the obligations of a bankrupt government.[12] Informing Keynes that his plan was unsound both economically and politically, Davis notified the Treasury that he was upholding its opinion that financial aid to Europe had best be provided through private channels. "We are all agreed," Davis wrote, "that if there is anything practicable to be done, it must be done in an American way."[13]

9. Cecil diary, March 21, 30, April 29, 30, May 2, 9, 1919, Cecil papers, 51131, British Museum. Cecil was particularly distrustful of Baruch's ego and his imprecise ideas about American economic aid to Europe, his concern for foreign trade and his "intriguing to get control of financial policy" by "laying stress in the commercial aspects of questions that were essentially financial." Sir William Wiseman also thought Baruch incompetent in matters of international finance, Wiseman to the author, September 28, 1959.

10. Keynes called for issues of bonds by the enemy countries in varying amounts, with a joint guarantee of interest payments by Germany, which would have priority over reparation obligations. A further guarantee was to be undertaken by the governments of the Allied and Associated powers and by five European neutrals, in specified proportions. In the event of a failure of any guarantor to meet its obligation, the financial section of the League of Nations was to take appropriate action and the remaining guarantors would make good the failure in proportions agreed upon. One-fifth of the bonds were to be retained by the issuing governments for the purchase of food and raw materials, and the rest were to be used for the payment of reparations and the discharge of existing debts, Baker, vol. 3, pp. 336–343.

11. Cecil diary, April 22, 1919.

12. Hoover, *The Ordeal of Woodrow Wilson*, p. 149.

Miller advised House, in respect of a plan of M. D. Heineman, a Belgian financier, for American financial aid: "I regard all such schemes as impossible in the sense that they would be disastrous to the credit of the United States and that would create to an unknown extent liabilities against the United States, which would vary according to the solvency of other countries," Miller to House, March 16, 1919, Y.H.C.

13. Dispatches, Davis to Rathbone, April 25, 1919; Davis to the secretary of state for Rathbone, May 2, 1919; Polk to Davis from Leffingwell, May 2, 1919; Davis and Lamont to Rathbone, Leffingwell,

In accord with the advice that the president received from counselors at both Paris and Washington, he responded adversely to the proposal of Keynes. He assured the Treasury that none of the Americans at Paris had any idea of consenting to a guarantee by the United States of German bonds.[14] On May 5 he sent to Lloyd George a letter in which he asked how the expert advisers could be expected to work out a new plan to provide the credits that Germany needed when the victorious Allies seemed determined to take away the small capital that the enemy had.[15] "From the American point of view," Schwabe writes, "the Keynes plan . . . seemed to be the ultimate sanction for reparations terms which all the [American] . . . financial experts thought absurd. But that was a misunderstanding, for one of the things which Keynes had wanted to accomplish with his plan was to block exorbitant desires for reparations. But there was a more profound American motive yet," a "strong desire to clear out of European responsibility. . . . By refusing the Keynes plan, the United States government deprived itself of the economic leverage which it could have had as a co-guarantor" of German bonds.[16]

Actually, the possibility of some concession by the United States did not disappear entirely with the rejection of the Keynes plan. At Wilson's suggestion Davis and Lamont, who conferred with German financial experts and understood their plight,[17] presented a proposal calculated to avert the serious business and industrial depression in America that they feared as a result of any slump in its export trade.

Hopeful that their analysis of the situation, with which they had found McCormick, Hoover, and Baruch to be "in substantial accord," would elicit from their "British and French friends . . . certain fresh proposals far more reasonable" than those of Keynes, they wrote on May 15 to put before Wilson certain suggestions that in the view of these American men of affairs would enable the United States to contribute to general stability in Europe. While insisting that long-term credits should be extended "so far as possible . . . through the normal channels of private enterprise," they recommended that a small European committee of bankers and businessmen be formed, with the approval of the British and French governments, to coordinate "the general scheme of credits that are to be extended through banking and commercial channels." At the same time they proposed that in America a "country-wide investment group of banks and bankers," working in unison with commercial and manufacturing interests, should act under the general approval of the American Treasury in co-operation with a special committee in Europe. The Congress should

and Strauss, April 29, 1919; Davis for Rathbone, May 2, 1919, Wilson papers. Cecil diary, May 9 and 13, 1919. Davis, frustrated by the intransigence of the Treasury and of French officials who, "shell-shocked," still were trying to postpone a balancing of their nation's budget, met with some success in persuading the representatives of neutral creditors to renew maturing obligations of Germany, Davis to Rathbone, April 16, 1919, "Peace Mission" file, U.S. Treasury Department.

14. Cable, Wilson to Tumulty, May 6, 1919, Tumulty papers, box 6.

15. Wilson to Lloyd George, May 5, 1919, in Baker, vol. 3, pp. 344–346. A draft in Lamont's hand is in the Lamont papers, 165–12. Skidelsky has observed that though Keynes countered Wilson's argument and denounced him as "the greatest fraud on earth," he admitted to Kerr that there was "substantial truth" in it, Skidelsky, *John Maynard Keynes,* pp. 370–371.

16. Schwabe, pp. 373–374.

17. The minutes of a meeting with the German experts at Versailles on May 2 are in the Norman Davis papers, box 46.

be asked to grant additional short-term credits to needy countries of Europe and to defer payments of interest, for three years or so, on European debts to the United States Treasury. It was recommended also that the War Finance Corporation be given limited power "to assume the risk of practically direct commercial credits against American exports." The advisers believed that such measures would lead to greater activity and confidence on the part of American exporters and at the same time lessen the amount of credits requested from the Treasury.

Taking a broad and long-range view of the economy of their nation and of Europe, the counselors presented the essentials of a policy for reconstruction that was to prevail during the next decade. "Every consideration of humanity, justice and self-interest," they wrote, demanded that in America, where there was "no real conception" of the situation in Europe, sympathy and a desire for co-operation "be cultivated through the establishment of joint interests."[18] Their recommendations went to the president for his "private consideration" without reference to his European colleagues; and on May 19 Lamont, calling with Davis, Baruch, and McCormick, elicited Wilson's views on the whole financial situation. The president seemed eager to know what the United States might do to mitigate the impossible situation for which he held the Europeans responsible. He had read the recommendations and had been persuaded that some action should be taken to build up the credits that were needed for a revival of European industry and commerce. He saw the necessity of extending the powers of the War Finance Corporation and of inducing the Congress to approve the refunding of interest on loans to Europe.[19] When, at the end of May, he went so far as to agree that if his advisers recommended it he would request the Congress to authorize the Treasury to refund the interest accruing during the next three years on obligations of the Allied governments, Davis conveyed this information confidentially, with Wilson's permission, to a financing committee of the Peace Conference.[20]

Wilson did not, however, address himself to the fundamental necessity of constructing a viable economy for Europe in the postwar years. When he proposed in the Council of Four on May 21 that the experts advising The Three confer with

18. Baker, vol. 3, pp. 352–356.

19. Memorandum of a conference "at the President's House, Paris," May 19, 1919, Lamont papers, 163–13.

The recommendations of Lamont and Davis were reported to the Treasury on May 27, and on June 13 they advised the president that the War Finance Corporation be given enlarged powers for a period of five years, memoranda and letters, Lamont to Wilson, Lamont papers, 165–10, 171–28. Cable, from Davis and Lamont for Leffingwell, May 27, 1919, Davis papers, Ac. 11,743, box II, 29, N.2. See below, pp. 513–514.

20. Davis specified certain conditions: (1) that the governments concerned should not only take all necessary measures to help themselves but that they should also, to the extent of their ability, give assistance to the other governments concerned in meeting their requirements, and (2) that there should not be any financial or commercial agreements by or between any of the governments concerned that would discriminate against the other governments or their nationals. Davis further stipulated that in the event of a refund of interest on obligations of the British Treasury, it should give commensurate relief to France and Italy in the form of credits to pay for wool, coal, and freight charges. A week later Davis informed the president that he explained to Lloyd George and Cecil "the difference between refunding and cancelling, which, apparently, had not been understood by either," N. H. Davis to Lord Robert Cecil, June 3, 1919, Davis to Wilson, June 7, 1919, N. H. Davis papers, box 11.

moderate Germans, he indicated no desire to negotiate with the enemy, but rather advocated a meeting as a means of explaining to the German people that no heavier burden had been laid upon them than justice required and that the reparation commission was empowered to consider the condition of Germany and to adjust its exactions accordingly. The object of this treatment of a "purely practical" question, he said, was to demonstrate to Europe that nothing was left undone that might induce the Germans to accept what was meted out.[21] The proposal of a conference of experts was immediately dismissed by Clemenceau as a concession that would be regarded as a sign of weakness. Lloyd George, wobbling between his respect for the implacable demands of his electorate and his apprehension that the Germans might refuse to sign the treaty, advocated delay until the enemy submitted counterproposals to the proposed terms.[22] Although the two Europeans had just given Davis to understand that they agreed upon the necessity of telling their peoples the facts, actually they were unwilling to face the political consequences of such a course.[23] The two Europeans preferred to abide by the understanding reached in April, leaving the matter in the hands of a reparation commission with a definition of "categories of damage" to guide it. Lloyd George's preoccupation with practical politics and his disregard of economic reason continued to irritate the Americans.[24]

Fifteen years later Lamont wrote: "As to Lloyd George's intention, I am convinced he had no fixed intention. . . . I think Lloyd George simply thought it was easiest to sit on the fence."[25]

In a general conference of the American peace delegation on June 3 a British plea for revision of the treaty's terms for reparations[26] was discussed. On this occasion the financial nerves of the delegates were sensitized by a warning from Norman Davis. Urging a speedy restoration of peace, he said: "If Europe does not get together the situation is going to be awful. Our appropriations have run out, practically; in about another month we won't have any money at all."[27] Davis asserted that the Germans had not yet been told with sufficient clarity of the policy to be followed by the Commission on the Reparation of Damages, and hence they feared

21. A suggestion of a meeting of experts with German businessmen came to Wilson from Loucheur, handwritten note signed by Baruch, Davis, and Lamont, n.d., Wilson papers.

22. Mantoux, *Délibérations,* vol. 2, pp. 157–158. *F.R., P.P.C.,* vol. 6, pp. 800–801.

23. Davis, "Peace Conference Notes," July 5, and Annex "B," May 15, 1919, N. H. Davis papers, box 44.

24. Lamont, in *What Really Happened at Paris,* ed. Seymour and House, p. 267. House diary, June 4, 1919.

Wilson's exchanges in June with Lloyd George were described by Baker as "decidedly tart." The president spoke of the Welshman as "a chameleon," R. S. Baker's journal, entries of June 5, 9, and 10, 1919. Mrs. Wilson told Lansing that the president's "bottled-up wrath at Lloyd George" had given him a headache, Lansing desk diary, June 5, 1919. According to Hoover, Wilson "distrusted Lloyd George and considered much of that statesman's action as part gesture and part secretive power politics," Hoover, *Memoirs,* vol. 1, p. 467.

25. Lamont to Burnett, June 25, 1934, Lamont papers. In this letter Lamont recollected that Lord Cunliffe, who at one time professed in private a willingness to compromise, was the "chief . . . obstacle to the American point of view." Lamont wrote: "I think he was a bit mad. Many sober people in England thought the same. To everyone who knew him as intimately as I did . . . his conduct was simply inexplicable and inexcusable."

26. See below, p. 421.

27. Baker, vol. 3, p. 502.

it would be an instrument for oppression. The president then remarked that the proper function of the commission was constructive—that is, to assure Germany of the facilities and working capital that would be needed to make it possible to pay reparations. The president mentioned a concession that he would grant in respect of the draft treaty's provision for the confiscation of German property in the areas to be ceded to Poland.

The experts went back to America's original proposal, which House had put aside in his compromise with Clemenceau on April 5:[28] that a total fixed sum be set for all German reparations. A counterproposal made by Germany on May 29 reactivated this idea. Davis, having learned from Melchior that the plan for a reparation commission was particularly obnoxious to the Germans, argued that this vexation would be removed if a total sum could be fixed. In his view the problem before them was, after all, more psychological than material. "The crux of the whole matter," he wrote, "is really not so much what Germany will be able to pay, as what businessmen . . . think she will be able to pay." Without knowing the amount of liability, the Germans could not re-establish their nation's credit, issue valid bonds, and thus contribute to the stability of their creditors. It seemed to the American financial experts that the enemy's argument was sound and provided a basis for a practical plan that could be carried through expeditiously. Not satisfied by the device of a reparation commission, they advised that, in order to get reparations rather than unduly incite revenge, the German proposals should be weighed carefully. It seemed possible that they might, with some increases, be more advantageous to the victors than anything that might be obtained later. The experts were given authority by Wilson to try to come to an understanding with the Allied counselors on the setting of a total fixed sum.[29]

When the American advisers argued their case in a special committee that was established on June 3 and on which Lloyd George sat, it became immediately clear that their proposals which set figures only slightly less favorable to Germany than those it sought and which limited the functions of the reparation commission, were unacceptable to the experts of the other powers as well as to Lloyd George himself. It was not the setting of a total fixed sum that he wanted but rather a computation of reimbursement due for losses outside Belgium and northern France (as on the high seas) with Germany made directly responsible, as Erzberger had suggested, for the destruction in the areas ravaged by war.[30]

In several sessions of the Supreme Council the arguments of the American experts were presented by Wilson. He played upon the fear of Lloyd George that the Germans would balk at the severity of the treaty. If concessions had to be made, Wilson said, they must be of real substance. Urged by a letter from the advisers to take a strong stand, the president proposed on June 9 a limit of 120 million gold marks on the exactions to be determined by the reparations commission.[31] He warned that

28. See above, pp. 288–289.

29. T. W. Lamont, "The Final Reparations Settlement, *"Foreign Affairs* 8, no. 3 (April 1930):337–338. Temperley, *A History of the Peace Conference at Paris,* vol. 2, p. 449. Letter, W. H. Buckler to Mrs. Buckler, May 16, 1919, Y.H.C.

30. See Schwabe, p. 370.

31. It has been argued that by its membership on the reparations commission the United States could have expected to prevent by veto any issue of German bonds of an unreasonable amount. However,

any reparation plan would break down if Germany were not allowed to keep its assets, such as reserves of foreign currency and its merchant fleet. When Wilson argued that the bonds that the treaty required Germany to issue would be worthless if its government was financially ruined by reparations, his European associates remembered the American refusal to accept measures to guarantee German bonds.

On June 10 Lloyd George definitely rejected the American opinion; and Clemenceau, who had just resisted a proposal by his two colleagues that the issue of reparations be discussed in face-to-face negotiations such as the Germans desired, said that to adopt the American suggestion would invalidate the principles they had already agreed upon.[32] Wilson was not satisfied by the formal reply that the Peace Conference made on June 16 to the economic counterproposals of the Germans. However, the reply did explain the vital interest of the Allies in the resumption of German industry and the duty of the reparation commission "to take into account the true maintenance of the social, economic, and financial structure" of Germany.[33]

Very weary of the complex and protracted negotiations, the president was unwilling to try[34] to dictate to the Allies in this matter that was of more immediate concern to them.[35] He told his European colleagues on June 10 that the reconciliation of the postion of their governments with that of his was impossible and that he had no further suggestions. Germany was not relieved of obstacles to the development of the trade that was essential to its financial welfare.[36]

In the atmosphere of financial constriction that prevailed in the United States, the efforts of the men at Paris came to naught.[37] The great question, that of preventing chaos by supplying enough of the "oil of credit" to put Europe back to work, had to be solved without any further concessions from the American treasury. The finances of the national governments were locked in a vicious circle that Schwabe has defined well: "The Americans were closed to the idea of international clearing procedures as long as the reparations terms they considered absurd remained in the treaty. The Allies, for their part, refused to change those terms unless the United States was ready to take an active part in restoring credit in the world economy." While defending their position as creditors, the Americans at Paris made their greatest concession to the Allies when they consented to economic arrangements that were, as Schwabe has written, "a blatant affront to the principle of the 'open door.' " Very complex

---

there would have been no control over the exaction of excessive reparations in other ways. See Burnett, *Reparation at the Paris Peace Conference,* vol. 1, pp. 84–91.

32. Mantoux, *Délibérations,* vol. 2, pp. 283–285, 351–356. Grayson diary, June 10, 1919. Wilson to Lamont, June 12, 1919, Lamont papers.

33. Luckau, *The German Delegation at the Paris Peace Conference,* pp. 417–418, 443 ff. The note offered Germany an opportunity to make proposals within four months of the signing of the treaty as to the amount of liability. It promised serious and fair consideration of such proposals, *ibid.,* pp. 445–446.

34. Lamont wrote to Burnett on June 25, 1934: "I do believe that Mr. Wilson had a feeling of being fed up with the Germans. He was a bit irritable just then and wanted to kick somebody in the stomach," letter in Lamont papers.

35. Baker, vol. 3, p. 345. Benham diary letter, June 10, 1919. R. S. Baker's journal, June 11, 1919. The Allies reached no formal agreement for the division of reparations among them, only an informal understanding, telegram, Lloyd George to Borden, Aug. 21, 1919, Lloyd George papers, F / 39 / 1 / 35. Document dated May 1, 1919, *Reparations,* Pt. IV, p. 201, Baruch papers, Princeton University Library.

36. Schwabe, p. 364.

37. Baker, vol. 3, pp. 352–362. See below, p. 525.

economic problems had to be dealt with under limitations that were imposed by legislators who responded to the impulses of electorates of limited vision. In none of the many matters before the peacemakers was the interference of democratic politics with sound diplomacy more embarrassing. There was, however, one consoling fact: Wilson had succeeded in imposing a time limit on economic discrimination against Germany, leaving that nation's potential as a major economic power essentially intact.[38]

Any prospect for the face-to-face parleys on economic matters that the Germans persistently sought vanished on June 7. When Lloyd George proposed that someone, but not one of The Three, explain to the Germans that they were unduly upset, Wilson endorsed this suggestion, only to have Clemenceau veto the idea. The enemy understood the situation very well, he said, and in seeking conversations intended to divide the victors.[39]

In the consideration of financial matters during the spring months, the Americans made one conspicuous exception to their demand for the conserving of Germany's hard assets that could be used to purchase food. They strongly supported a claim by Belgium to special consideration. House's commentary on the Fourteen Points stated: "The principle that should be established is that in the case of Belgium there exists no distinction between 'legitimate' and 'illegitimate' destruction. The initial act of invasion was illegitimate and therefore all the consequences of that act are of the same character. Among the consequences may be put the war debt of Belgium."[40]

The Belgian delegates were discouraged by the coolness of the peacemakers to their aspirations for Dutch territory, for union with Luxembourg, and for the designation of Brussels as the seat of the League of Nations.[41] Foreign Minister Hymans had persistently reminded Wilson and House of the keen interest of Belgium in the establishment of the permanent headquarters of the League at Brussels.[42] Moreover, although Belgium had attained better representation on the commissions created by the Peace Conference than that of other smaller states, its delegates protested that important decisions in matters affecting their nation were made by the great powers without consulting—or indeed informing—the Belgians.[43]

The Belgians, under German military occupation for four years, had suffered beyond possibility of complete compensation. Their highly industrialized economy lay in ruins. Their prime concern was for payments that might be exacted immediately from Germany. On February 16 the American experts, dining with Belgian

38. See Schwabe, pp. 293, 373, 402. On the work of Haguenin and Massigli in Berlin in behalf of a Franco-German understanding on economic matters, see Marc Trachtenberg, *Reparation on World Politics*, p. 86 and n. 96, and Trachtenberg's "Reparations at the Paris Peace Conference," 42–43. Also see *Akten zur Deutschen Auswärtigen Politik, 1918–1945*, Serie A: 1918–1925, vol. 1, pp. 345, 407–408, 422–434, 463–465.

39. Mantoux, vol. 2, pp. 336–337.

40. *I.P.*, vol. 4, p. 196.

41. *F.R., P.P.C.*, vol. 3, p. 292. Whitlock to House, November 8, 1919, Y.H.C. Whitlock (Brussels) to Ammission, January 17, 1919, Wilson papers.

42. *I.P.*, vol. 4, p. 424. Brand Whitlock to House, May 2, 1919, Y.H.C. Wilson said on April 28: "I didn't realize the fury of the jealousies the matter of the seat would arouse," *Centenaire Woodrow Wilson*, p. 60.

43. See Marks, *Innocents Abroad*, pp. 105–338.

delegates, assured them that if they would come out boldly in support of America's position on the question of reparations, they could expect that their claims would receive special consideration.[44]

During the absence of the president in February, Hymans had persuaded House to advocate preferred treatment for Belgium. On April 3 House pledged his active support to King Albert; but he was unsuccessful in committing Lloyd George, who was unsympathetic to Belgian pleas in general and vexed in particular by the aggressiveness of Hymans.[45] When the king came to House's room to make a personal plea, the colonel went immediately to see Clemenceau and returned with assurance of his support; this was confirmed two days later in a session of The Four.[46] The American advisers favored the granting of a priority and thought that the other powers had acquiesced, although as of April 23 Lloyd George seemed uncertain.[47]

On April 29, when the Italians had withdrawn from Paris and the Japanese were unhappy, Hymans saw his opportunity to strike. He presented the case of Belgium at great length and threatened to return to Brussels to get instructions from the parliament. This possibility upset The Three. Clemenceau said jocosely that Hymans ought to be "murdered," and Lloyd George declared angrily that he would not yield to blackmail. Wilson was shocked by the possibility of a Belgian defection at the very time when the Germans were waiting to be received. He asked Lamont and Davis to take Hymans aside and try to hold him in line. They teased, cajoled, threatened, and implored, all to no avail. Finally Loucheur presented a compromise that had the approval of Clemenceau and that Lloyd George accepted with ill grace. After Lamont made it clear that he could not bind the American Treasury to relieve the Belgian government of its obligations to the United States and accept German obligations in their stead, there was general agreement on a formula that would require Germany to meet the Belgian war debts when they fell due.[48]

On May 3 The Three accepted, subject to the approval of the American and British treasuries, a text that the American experts worked out with Loucheur.[49] It awarded the Belgians a priority of $500 million but did not entirely meet their expectation as to the proportion of the entire German payment they would receive. Nor did it take account of a plea by Hymans for indemnification for losses due to the depreciation of the German mark.[50]

This settlement did not satisfy Belgian opinion, which as a result of the benefac-

44. Schwartz, *The Speculator,* p. 127.

45. Marks, pp. 100–101, 112–113.

46. House diary, April 4, 1919. *I.P.,* vol. 4, p. 399. Mantoux, *Proceedings,* pp. 105–108, 123–124, 138–139. McCormick diary, April 5, 1919. Lloyd George held that the expenses of Belgium had been met already by loans from France and Great Britain. See J. M. Keynes, *Collected Writings,* vol. 10, pp. 28–31. Keynes wrote: "The Belgian claims, amounting to a sum in excess of the total pre-war wealth of the whole country, are simply irresponsible," *Economic Consequences of the Peace,* p. 123.

47. Lamont to Wilson, April 23, 1919, Wilson papers.

48. Lamont's notes on the negotiations of April 29, 1919, Lamont papers. Mantoux, *Délibérations,* vol. 1, pp. 411–420. Loucheur, *Carnets Secrets,* p. 76.

49. Lamont to Wilson, April 30, 1919, Lamont papers, 168-2. McCormick diary, April 29, 30, May 2, 1919. Mantoux, *Délibérations,* vol. 1, pp. 458–459. R. S. Baker wrote in his journal on April 29 of the "extreme seriousness" of the Belgian crisis.

50. McCormick diary, April 29, 30, May 2, 3, 1919. Mantoux, *Délibérations,* vol. 1, pp. 411–420, 458–459. *I.P.,* vol. 4, p. 455. "Conference at 4 p.m. May 3 at Crillon on Belgian priority," Baruch papers, "Reparation," Pt. IV, p. 211, Princeton University Library.

tion of American friends had come to regard the United States as an unfathomable source of financial aid.[51] Hymans went to Brussels to calm his agitated people, and Wilson accepted advice that he visit the Belgian capital and try to mend relations. He made the trip with Hoover, for whose ministrations the Belgians had reason to be grateful.[52] They responded politely when the president exalted justice under a league of nations. But according to the observation of Ray Stannard Baker, "when he spoke of giving Belgium help in credits, raw material, and new machinery, one could fairly *feel* the electric charge in the atmosphere."[53] On Wilson's return to Paris from Brussels a letter from Hymans reminded him that before his departure for America the demands of Belgium must be met.[54] In the end the treaty of peace obligated Germany, in addition to compensating Belgium for damages, to make reimbursement of all sums that Belgium had borrowed from the Allied and Associated Governments up to November 11, 1918, with interest.[55] Thus did Belgium receive special treatment. But the American experts did not get any significant support from the little nation, as they had hoped, in their controversies with the Allies over the reparation settlement.[56]

51. House and Auchincloss diaries, May 1 and 2, 1919. "Somehow or other," House wrote, "the president is always put in a false light."

Keynes, noting that the disgruntled Belgians thought themselves highly popular with Americans, wrote: "Since the Belgian claims had nothing to do with the United States, here was an opportunity for the Americans to exercise their dashing propensity for altruism at other people's expense," Keynes, *Collected Writings,* vol. 10, p. 28. Of Keynes, the advocate of "magnanimity," Norman Davis wrote in retrospect: "His idealism never went to the point of advocating that Great Britain give up any rights or debts which he thought could be secured or collected," Davis to R. S. Baker, July 26, 1922, Davis papers, box 3.

52. Minister Brand Whitlock, feeling that American-Belgian relations had been damaged by French propaganda, had urged that the president visit Brussels as early as December 1918, Whitlock to House, December 10 and 12, 1918, Y.H.C. On May 27 Tumulty cabled to ask that Wilson go to Brussels. The next morning the president decided to do so, Tumulty to Grayson, May 27, 1919, Grayson to Tumulty, May 28, 1919, Tumulty papers. In Brussels he announced that Whitlock was to become the first American ambassador to Belgium.

53. Baker, *American Chronicle,* p. 448.

54. Hymans to Wilson, June 23, 1919, Wilson papers.

55. Germany was to deliver directly to Belgium bonds in the amount of nearly 5 billion marks, N. H. Davis, "Peace Conference Notes," p. 4, Davis papers, box 44, L.C.: note of June 24, 1919, Hankey to Dutasta, N. H. Davis papers, box 3.

56. Schwartz has observed that McCormick felt that the intercession in favor of Belgium would reassure other small nations that Wilson wished to help and that looked to America to protect their interests. He notes also that the British had been lining up small debtor nations in their campaign to include war costs in the categories for reparation, so that those nations would be better situated to discharge their debts, *The Speculator,* pp. 126–127, 138.

22

The Signing with Germany

President Wilson remained in Paris for almost two months after May 7, when the draft of the peace treaty was given to the Germans. It was necessary to deal with the enemy's criticism of the terms proposed, the desire of Lloyd George to soften them, and the preparation of a treaty text that was delivered to Austrian delegates at St. Germain on June 2.[1]

When Brockdorff-Rantzau divulged the victors' terms to his people at the Hôtel des Reservoirs on May 7, they fell into the blackest despair. They foresaw a complete breakdown of German credit, the desolation of Germany's ports, the utter destruction of its industry, and a permanent famine in the land.[2] In their gloom they gave themselves to an orgy that left both their residence and their persons in a sordid state.[3]

Brockdorff-Rantzau was no Talleyrand and lacked sufficient ability to insinuate his voice effectively into the negotiations at Paris. Seeing no choice but to adopt the course that the Peace Conference had suggested, he wrote a series of public notes that contrasted the treaty draft with the letter and spirit of Wilson's principles. At the same time his government undertook to formulate criticism and counterproposals that would reveal the provisions of the treaty that it thought exploitative.

Within the fifteen days that were allotted, Brockdorff-Rantzau addressed a volley of notes to the Peace Conference. These were intended to point out absurdities in the conditions imposed and to lead the peacemakers back to what he considered to be the legal basis of the treaty—Wilson's principles. The assumption of German war guilt was challenged, and the demands upon Germany were deemed "intolerable for any nation" and impossible to fulfill. The Germans, suggesting alternatives to some of the terms, presented a meticulous draft for a covenant for a league of nations, and they inquired how they might become members of the league that they were asked to accept by signing the treaty of peace.[4]

The protests, weakened by a lack of executive direction and based on the advice of specialists working in isolation, failed to concentrate on the most intolerable of the terms and advanced many suggestions that would be unacceptable to the victors.[5] The tone of the notes tended to be accusatory rather than conciliatory, and

1. See below, p. 443.
2. Schiff, *The Germans at Versailles*, pp. 78–79.
3. Steed, *Through Thirty Years*, vol. 2, pp. 335–336.
4. Luckau, *The German Delegation at the Paris Peace Conference*, pp. 225–233. Christoph M. Kimmich, *Germany and the League of Nations*, pp. 8–21. See below, pp. 81 ff.
5. Schaefer, "German Peace Strategy in 1918–1919," p. 279. Shotwell, *At the Paris Peace Conference*, p. 48. Bernadotte Schmitt in *Proceedings of the American Philosophical Society* (January 1961). The notes covered these topics: the League of Nations Covenant; the international labor office; repatriation of prisoners and interned civilians; reparations and responsibility; economic questions; territorial questions; the Saar; the treatment of German missionaries; and the liquidation of German private property abroad.

departures from Wilson's prearmistic proposals ("ruses of war," these were called) were denounced without appreciation of American efforts at the Peace Conference to hold the Allies in line. Yet there was enough truth in the German allegations to embarrass the peacemakers. They gave the public only a summary of the texts of the notes.[6]

It was not easy for Wilson to accept German criticism that obviously impugned the integrity of his image as a prophet of justice. On May 10 he declared in the Supreme Council that he considered the peace terms just and had no intention of favoring the Germans. Yet he was not blind to the reasonableness of some of the strictures. He at first showed a disposition toward conciliation. When The Four discussed the German notes and the responses to be made to them, the president endeavored to blunt the cutting edge that the French tried to put in the text of the replies. He advocated that the economic experts at Paris should explain to the Germans at Château Villette—"intelligent men . . . who wanted a resumption of business" without disorder—certain functions of the reparations commission that would help to induce the German government to sign the treaty.[7] Nevertheless, he approved the sentence in an Allied reply of May 20 that denied the contention that "the German people" should not be regarded as accomplices of the "former German Government."[8] Wilson called the present German attitude "incredible," and presented evidence that the German people were allowing personnel of the old regime to speak in their name.[9] Fourteen commissions were appointed by the Peace Conference to deal with the German representations. They promptly drafted and sent replies to all the notes.[10] "As far as harshness of tone was concerned," Schwabe has observed, "the American drafts for the various Notes . . . did not differ much from the French ones."[11]

The entire text of the terms given to Brockdorff-Rantzau on May 7 was published immediately in Germany. In its disillusionment the press protested against a prospect of enslavement and reproached Wilson as a betrayer.[12] The German cabinet, while criticizing Brockdorff-Rantzau's tactics, decided that the terms proposed were unacceptable. Before the National Assembly, meeting at Berlin on May 12, Prime Minister Scheidemann denounced the treaty as a means of imprisoning the German people. However, there were already then a few ministers who admitted that in the end Germany would be forced to sign a treaty.[13] Erzberger was making cautious efforts toward acceptance of the treaty with minimum damage to the fortunes of his political party. Unlike the somewhat truculent Brockdorff-Rantzau, this concilia-

6. The purport of the German notes is given in Schwabe, pp. 343 ff.

7. R. S. Baker's journal, entries of May 20 and 21, 1919. Mantoux, *Délibérations,* vol. 2, p. 157.

8. Draft reply to a German note approved by the legal advisers, with changes in Wilson's hand, enclosed with copy of letter, Klotz to Clemenceau, May 16, 1919, Wilson papers.

9. Mantoux, *Délibérations,* vol. 2, pp. 121–122.

10. The German notes and the replies are in Luckau, pp. 225–302. A digest may be found in Temperley, *History of the Peace Conference,* vol. 2, pp. 244–419.

11. Schwabe, p. 347.

12. Dispatch, Dresel to the secretary of state, May 10, 1919, quoted by Hajo Holborn, "Diplomats and Diplomacy in the Early Weimar Republic," in *The Diplomat, 1919–1939,* ed. Craig and Gilbert, p. 145. State Department summary of German press reports, May 16, 1919, Wilson papers.

13. Holborn, *A History of Modern Germany,* vol. 3, p. 573.

tory politician held out a prospect of German compliance as an inducement to the making of concessions at Paris. He suggested revisions in the victors' terms such as the foreign ministry was to put into formal counterproposals made on May 29.[14]

At the urgent request of Erzberger, which had the approval of Scheidemann, Colonel Conger arrived at Berlin on May 17. The American peace commission was not apprised of this secret mission, which Wilson probably instructed.[15] Conger, whom the Germans counted on to carry their message directly to Wilson, entered into talks with Erzberger at which Bernstorff was present. The American emissary insisted that by rejecting the treaty Germany could neither improve its position nor cause a rift between Wilson and the Allies, and he called attention to what the Americans had done already to moderate the terms. Although not entirely convinced by Erzberger, Conger was not sure that conciliation would not be the better part of wisdom in view of military developments that he observed while in Germany.[16]

During the month of May a controversy of American economic advisers with the French military over the treatment of the occupied Rhineland came to a climax. Although the Supreme Council of the Peace Conference had decided on March 17 that an inter-Allied commission of control should supplant the military authority of Foch, French officers continued to interfere with efforts by Hoover, acting for the Supreme Economic Council, to carry out the measures for relief that were agreed upon at Brussels on March 14. Furthermore, permits from Foch's officers allowed the passage of French goods into the interior of Germany while trade of the other Allied nations was restrained by the continuing wartime blockade.[17]

On April 14 the Supreme Economic Council had proposed the replacement of the Foch-dominated commission of control by a strong body of civilians with whom the council could maintain close contact. The Americans on the council stipulated that the new organization be located at Cologne and that its chairman, who was Foch's controller general, should terminate his connection with the marshal. On April 21 the Council of Foreign Ministers endorsed this proposition. An American manufacturer, Pierrepont Noyes, served as the American representative on a new four-member inter-Allied Rhineland commission. This body reported to a subcommittee of the Supreme Economic Council. Noyes then engaged for forty days in what a historian has called "one long series of wrangles." At first the French chairman obstructed every effort made by the Americans toward reform. He argued that the French and Belgian armies should exercise control in the region since their nations were the most interested. In any event, he said flatly, Foch would not submit to civilian direction.[18]

---

14. See below, p. 414, and Richard M. Watt, *The Kings Depart*, pp. 458–459. *F.R., P.P.C.*, vol. 12, pp. 124–127. Erzberger, who had represented Germany at the meetings of the Inter-Allied Armistice Commission at Spa, had acquired there and by contact with French observers in Berlin a sense of the victors' intentions. He warned his colleagues of the futility of resistance to the treaty while calling it a "demonical piece of work," Watt, p. 457.

15. Schwabe, p. 367.

16. Lansing to Wilson, May 21, 1919, forwarding Conger's report on talks with Erzberger, Wilson papers.

17. See above, p. 266. Keith Nelson, *Victors Divided*, pp. 46, 104, and n. 32.

18. Nelson, pp. 103–105.

In May the Peace Conference began to consider ways to implement the agreement that had been reached in April by The Three for a fifteen-year occupation of the Rhineland.[19] In the plenary session on the sixth, Foch asked for a longer term. General Bliss negotiated with the Allied military representatives on the difficult questions of the size of the occupying forces of the four nations and on the cost of maintaining them. Fearful that American troops would become involved in incidents that might arise from French operations, Bliss advised Wilson that any military force posted in the Rhineland should function only to quell disorder and should take no part whatever in civil administration; and the same advice came from the economic advisers, who, according to Baruch, thought the French proposals "monstrous." Accordingly, the president, thinking this "a matter of very great importance," promised to try to obtain a radical modification of Foch's ideas.[20] In the Council of Four on May 19, when Clemenceau ventured to ask Wilson for concessions, the president replied that after repeated consideration of this "highly important matter" he was convinced that it would not be wise to make further demands on the enemy.[21]

Within a week a crisis was precipitated by Germans who claimed to speak for the people of the Left Bank and who were encouraged by French authorities to seek autonomy.[22] Wilson, warned by his generals that a coup was to be consummated the next day in Koblenz, protested on May 23 to Clemenceau, who immediately sent an agent to investigate. The emissary quizzed General Mangin, the French commander at Mainz, and tried to dissuade him; but on June 1 a French military dispatch reported that on that morning "the Rhine Republic was proclaimed." Although President Poincaré urged that the *Putsch* be supported as "an act of self-determination," Clemenceau ordered Mangin to "confine himself to his military duty" and observe complete neutrality in political affairs. Thereupon the movement collapsed.[23]

Nevertheless, Wilson was determined to review measures for governance of the Rhineland that had been drafted by military men.[24] In a letter to the president, Noyes, the American member of the temporary Rhineland commission, had denounced a French scheme that he thought "brutal," and he had outlined a plan that might

19. See above, p. 326.

20. See Schwabe, pp. 278–279, and Nelson, pp. 93–96. Baruch to Wilson, May 17, 1919, J. W. Davis papers. Bliss to Baruch, May 22, 1919, Bliss papers, box 167, "Germany, army of occupation" folder.

21. Wilson to Clemenceau, May 19, 1919, Wilson papers. Wilson quizzed Clemenceau about the occupation of the Rhineland by black troops from Senegal. This appeared to be an unnecessary irritation to a populace that was less tolerant of color than were the French. Clemenceau replied that he intended to withdraw the one black battalion in the region and that it had been a serious mistake to send it there, Mantoux, *Délibérations*, vol. 2, p. 126.

22. See Louis A. R. Yates, *The U.S. and French Security*, p. 69.

23. Wilson to Clemenceau, Wilson to Pershing, May 23, 1919, Clemenceau to Wilson, June 1, 1919, Wilson papers. 492. Mantoux, *Délibérations*, vol. 2, p. 444. Jere C. King, *Clemenceau vs. Foch*, pp. 61–72. Nelson, pp. 110–113, 306–307. Eric Waldman, *The Separatist Uprising of 1919* (Milwaukee, 1958). Arnold J. Toynbee, "The So-called Separatist Movement in the Rhineland," *Survey of International Affairs* (1928). Baker, vol. 2, pp. 83–97.

24. Mantoux, *Délibérations*, vol. 2, p. 253. Foch's plan for commissions of control under Article 203 of the treaty was forwarded to Wilson by Bliss, with comments, on May 24, 1919, documents in Bliss papers, box 233.

serve as a basis for a permanent commission. He would reduce the number of soldiers to a minimum and would forbid billeting them on private property. Moreover, he would guarantee complete freedom for the legitimate German authorities, with a precautionary proviso that would empower the commission to negate German laws that were contrary to the peace treaty or that endangered the security of the occupation. Thus the High Commission would have power to intervene, given due cause, in every aspect of Rhenish life, and to mediate between the German authorities and the occupying armies. Wilson read this proposal to the European premiers in their meeting on May 29.[25]

On this same day—the twenty-ninth—the Germans at Versailles submitted a note presenting more than a hundred pages of counterproposals on which they had come to agreement with the German cabinet. With them came a protest against any occupation of the Rhineland that would "weaken the economic and moral ties" of that region with the fatherland and would in the end "warp the mind of the population." It was argued that there were better ways of guaranteeing the financial terms of the treaty and that Germany's disarmament obviated any need for military precautions by the Allies. When Conger had talked secretly with Erzberger and Bernstorff, he had given them an understanding that the United States favored a civil control in the Rhineland that would allow local German authorities to function and would permit trade with the rest of Germany to flourish. At the same time Erzberger had gone so far as to suggest that if the term of occupation could be reduced to six months, Germany would maintain no military forces within fifty kilometers of the Rhine and would use customs and internal revenues to pay reparations.

Informed of these *pourparlers,* Wilson instructed his intermediaries to stand firmly on the terms of the treaty. The president agreed with Clemenceau upon the creation of a body of four civilian and four military members which was to draft a convention governing the occupation of the Rhineland. Foch and Loucheur were to represent France and Lord Robert Cecil and Sir Henry Wilson, Great Britain. General Bliss and Ambassador John W. Davis were the American members. With support from Loucheur, who advised the irreconcilable Foch that his troops would enjoy better security under the regime contemplated, Davis managed to persuade the committee to accept, with some alterations, the plan of Noyes that Wilson read to his European colleagues on May 29. The military forces in the Rhineland were to be restrained from interference with local government, and martial law was to be lifted, and proclaimed again for the entire region only by the High Commission.[26]

On June 13, the committee's draft of a Rhineland Convention was accepted by the Supreme Council. The decisions of the Rhineland Commission were to be issued

25. *F.R., P.P.C.,* vol. 6, pp. 108–114. P. B. Noyes, *A Goodly Heritage* (New York, 1938), pp. 107, 245–249. Nelson, p. 107.

26. Nelson, p. 118. Cecil's diary, June 3 and 5, 1919. J. W. Davis, diary, May 29, 30, 31, June 3, 4, 5, 9, 10, and 11, 1919. "Finally," Davis recalled many years later, "I myself wrote the words into the agreement that the civilian authorities should be the supreme control. . . . That was just gall and wormword to old Foch. Every day he would come back as if it had never been suggested. He'd pull his mustache, with his pipe in his mouth, say 'bon, bon' and sit back in his chair. The next day he'd come again just as if it had never been discussed—the most persistent old dog," J. W. Davis record, Columbia O.H.R.O.

"in the name of the Supreme Economic Council and by order of the High Command." In accord with a warning by Noyes that German authority should not be challenged in such matters as tariffs and tax collections, it was agreed that the High Commission was not to use its powers in financial or economic matters. During the drafting of the convention Wilson advocated limitations both on the authority of the High Commission to issue regulations and on the powers of the military chiefs. He wrote on his typewriter a clause that became Article V of the convention: *viz.*, "The civil administration of these areas shall continue under German law and under the authority of the central German government except insofar as it may be necessary for the commission by ordinance . . . to accommodate . . . the needs and circumstances of military occupation." "We have to add a few lines," he explained, "to make it clear that we do not want to separate this area from the rest of Germany."

During the month of May the American plenipotentiaries were unable to fathom the depth of German resistance despite reports from Conger and his deputy during May and early June.[27] The analysis of the situation that Dresel had made in April seemed to be still valid, and on June 5 he impressed upon Wilson the importance of avoiding a rejection of the treaty by the Scheidemann government, since its fall probably would result in total anarchy and then a dictatorship. Actually Brockdorff-Rantzau had kept his foes at Paris uncertain as to the length to which his people could be pressed without their becoming desperate and anarchic. Lansing optimistically assured himself that the Germans would be "foolish" enough to sign. Yet there was fear among the American delegates that if they made no concessions, the enemy probably would renew the war. This possibility grew when news came that German troops in the western provinces had been consolidated in the interior. Indeed, Wilson was haunted by a fear that all governmental authority in Germany might collapse and that no responsible signer of a peace treaty would appear.

The lengthy German note of May 29 put before the peacemakers at Paris certain propositions that it was thought they could not resist without offending the sense of justice of their peoples.[28] Through the counterproposals ran the central purposes of leading the victors back to Wilson's ideals. The Allied statesmen were reminded, with citations of chapter and verse, of their pronouncements of ideal war aims and the failure of the proposed terms to measure up to the conditions laid down in Wilson's notes of October 1918 that had led up to the Armistice of Rethondes.

The Germans asserted that the peace contemplated would be one of might, not right, and would not be the "just" settlement that had been promised. Their people, who had renounced the "military masters" excoriated by Wilson and now professed a desire for democratic government, were asked to confess to a crime of which they pleaded innocent—total responsibility for causing the war. Moreover,

27. On June 11 Erzberger stated to Conger's deputy the terms that would make it possible for Germany to accept the treaty. See Schwabe, p. 353, and dispatch from Berlin from C. B. Dyar reporting interviews with Erzberger and Bernstorff, transmitted by Grew to Close with letter of June 14, 1919, Wilson papers.

28. See *ibid.*, pp. 361–362, on the fading of the hopes of Germans for American intercession in their behalf and their derogation of Wilson.

they were sentenced to make reparation in a way that would utterly destroy the position of Germany as a world power to the advantage of its imperial and commerical competitors. "Such stipulations," it was stated, "amount to a complete denial of that idea of international law according to which every people has a claim to life." Furthermore, it was deemed "incompatible with the idea of national self-determination" for 2.5 million Germans to be torn away from their native land against their own will, without any plebiscite and for the material advantage of other nations. Asserting that Germany now enjoyed for the first time "the possibility of living in harmony with its free will based on law," the German officials adopted the language of the Russian revolutionaries. In the proposed treaty, they wrote, "expiring world theories, emanating from imperialistic and capitalistic tendencies, celebrate . . . their last horrible triumph." The Germans made suggestions for revising the Covenant and expressed willingness to disarm in certain respects if Germany entered the league at the conclusion of the peace. The counterproposals were specific with respect to many of the terms, particularly those having to do with reparations, the Saar, the eastern boundaries of Germany, and the future status of Austria.[29]

To these propositions Brockdorff-Rantzau, who resented above all the so-called "war guilt lie" in Article 231,[30] added the demand that, in order to create in Germany a state of mind in keeping with the Covenant of the League, the question of responsibility for the war and its crimes should be examined by neutrals and without prejudice. The German foreign minister, misjudging political opinion in the victorious countries, thought that popular discontent with the policies of the Peace Conference might force an oral negotiation with Germany in which he could explain the permanent nature of the wound that would be inflicted on the self-respect of all Germans.[31] This, however, would be conditional upon acceptance of his proposals for the retention of Germany's colonies under a League mandate and for self-determination on the part of Germans whom the treaty would place under alien rule. Conceding that the wartime exercise of German imperial power at Brest-Litovsk and Bucharest had been "only the germs of future discord," he begged the victors at Versailles to act in a different spirit in order to bring about "harmony in humanity" through "the collaboration of all nations, the common labor of all arms and brains."[32]

When the German counterproposals were received, Wilson was unresponsive to suggestions that changes be made for the purpose of persuading the Germans to sign the treaty. To a proposal by Lansing on June 3 that the experts be asked to suggest expedient concessions, Wilson replied: "The question that lies in my mind is: 'Where have they made good in their points? Where have they shown that the arrangements of the treaty are essentially unjust?' Not 'where have they shown merely that they are hard?' for they are hard—but the Germans earned that. And I think it is profitable that a nation should learn once and for all what an unjust war means in itself.

29. For the text of the counterproposals see Luckau, pp. 302–406. On the genesis of the counterproposals, see Schwabe, pp. 356 ff.
30. Schaefer, p. 279.
31. Holborn, *A History of Modern Germany*, vol. 3, p. 573. Schaefer, p. 280.
32. Luckau, p. 306.

I have no desire to soften the treaty, but I have a very sincere desire to alter those portions of it that are shown to be unjust, or which are shown to be contrary to the principles which we ourselves have laid down."[33]

In the absence of any conclusive evidence that Germany would not come around to meet the necessity of making peace on the terms offered, Wilson proceeded with his program for what he conceived to be a just settlement and one that would give a prospect of an enduring peace. He continued to be sensitive to the imperative need for unity among the victors. To avoid "sharp lines of division" had become in his view "the great problem of the moment." He must somehow overcome the threat to good diplomacy that was posed by national sentiment in the parliaments of the democracies. Although his integrity had been questioned, he could not afford, in the delicate situation that then prevailed, brusquely to reject Germany's counterproposals, particularly in view of the wisdom that he and his advisers perceived in some of them. Therefore, he did not entirely close his mind to the possibility of concessions. As he prayed over the colossal responsibility that weighed on him, a challenge to action came from Lloyd George and General Smuts.[34]

The treaty as it stood appeared to strengthen France unduly at the expense of Germany and thus to counter a traditional goal of British foreign policy: the preservation of a European balance of power. Moreover, Lloyd George, for his part, was alarmed by rumors that Germany would not sign a pact so emasculating. In the days following May 29 he met with cabinet ministers who came from London and with the delegates of the dominions.[35] He had from Smuts two letters of protest, complaining of provisions that Smuts thought unjust and that in his opinion would make it impossible for Germany to sign the treaty.[36] In the first, which went also to Wilson, Smuts deplored the offenses against the president's principles and predicted that under the proposed treaty Europe would know no peace. To this the president replied that the treaty, although very severe indeed, was "not . . . on the whole unjust."[37]

Smuts found support among colleagues who felt that Lloyd George, losing the close rapport with the Imperial War Cabinet that existed in the early days of peacemaking, had grossly mismanaged proceedings. Balfour was most dissatisfied and wondered whether he should not assert himself, but he could not quite bring himself to do so.[38]

---

33. Baker, vol. 3, pp. 498, 502–503.

34. Schwabe, pp. 354–356.

35. See Elcock, *Portrait of a Decision*, pp. 271–272, and S. D. Waley, *Edwin Montagu* (New York, 1964), pp. 211–212.

36. Auchincloss diary, May 5 and 16, 1919. Hancock, *Smuts*, vol. 1, 520–525. On June 23 Smuts wrote to a friend that he would not sign the treaty, but the next day he decided not to embarrass his collegue, General Botha, by withholding his signature, *Selections*, vol. 4, pp. 244–247. He issued a public statement of his criticisms. Twenty years later he said: "The paramount thing was to bring Germany back into the fold," Harrod, *Keynes*, p. 268.

37. Smuts to Wilson, May 14 and 30, 1919, Wilson to Smuts, May 16, 1919, *Selections*, vol. 4, pp. 157, 160, 208. Smuts to Lloyd George, April 11, May 5, 12, 1919, Lloyd George papers, F / 45 / 9 / 35 and F / 4 5 / 9 / 33.

38. Cecil's diary, May 20 and 31, 1919, Cecil papers, 51131. "Balfour is too great," Cecil wrote, "and philosophically too indifferent, to mind it [the slighting of the Foreign Office]; but Hardinge and

In the British conferences Lloyd George sought a unanimous mandate. According to his record he was empowered to negotiate with a certain latitude on four points that to some extent ran parallel with the German protests of May 29. He understood that he was authorized, in the event of a failure to revise the treaty and a consequent renewal of warfare, to go so far as to refuse British participation in a military occupation or a continuing blockade of Germany. The points cited were (1) modification of the clauses dealing with the eastern frontiers, leaving to Germany the districts where the population was predominantly German when there was no reason for transfer to Poland, and providing for plebiscites in doubtful cases; (2) some assurances to Germany that it might join the League of Nations sooner than contemplated in the draft treaty, provided that Germany made a real effort to perform its obligations; (3) a reduction of the army of occupation, "having regard to the reductions made and about to be made in the German forces," and a shortening of the period of occupation; and (4) fixing of the reparation liability of Germany at a definite amount.[39]

Lloyd George, apparently perceiving the increasing influence of Baruch, inquired of him as to what Wilson would say of the shift in the British position. The reply was that the prime minister should put the question directly to the president; and to facilitate this Baruch took Wilson to Lloyd George's residence. There Wilson appeared to be suppressing anger. Actually, he was, as he confessed to the American delegation on June 3, "very sick" over what he called the "unanimous . . . funk" of the British. Afterward he suffered a headache that he ascribed to bottled-up wrath at Lloyd George. Lansing had never seen him "more pugnacious or bellicose." Indeed, everyone's nerves were on edge, and in the president's official household there was a lack of executive direction, homesickness and grumbling, and contention between civil and military members. But despite his irritation, Wilson said to Lloyd George, according to Baruch, that the united front must be preserved and he would accept the British proposals if Clemenceau would agree.[40]

Clemenceau, however, opposed any changes. He was under political fire from both Right and Left, and in no position to yield any of the exactions on Germany that he had won. He told Wilson and Lloyd George on June 2 that he would be overthrown in the Chamber if he conceded anything.[41] Nevertheless, Wilson said in the Supreme Council that the objections raised by Lloyd George were of such

his principal assistants smart under the negligible status to which they have been reduced." Cecil was distressed not only by the mismanagement, but by the breach of Wilson's principles and by the likelihood of more war. He feared that the United States would no longer trust British statesmanship and would not join in the world concert of powers that he envisioned, memorandum, Cecil to the prime minister, May 27, 1919, Cecil papers, 51076. Disappointed by the failure to overcome French resistance to the early admission of Germany to the League, Cecil left Paris on June 9, Egerton, *Great Britain and the Creation of the League of Nations*, p. 173.

39. Clement Jones ms., cab. 21 / 217, pp. 167–180. Lloyd George, *The Truth about the Peace Treaties*, pp. 718–719. Lloyd George informed Wilson and Clemenceau on June 2 that only he, Balfour, and Massey of New Zealand had defended the treaty in the British councils, Mantoux, *Délibérations*, vol. 2, p. 169.

40. Baruch, *The Public Years*, pp. 119–121. Baker, vol. 3, pp. 502–503.

41. Dispatch, Hugh Wallace to the secretary of state, June 2, 1919. Ambassador Wallace thought on May 10 that it was doubtful if Clemenceau's cabinet could stand much longer, dispatches, Wallace to the secretary of state, June 2, May 10, 1919, N.A., R.G. 256, 851.00 / 82, 74.

importance that he must assemble his delegation to discuss them.[42] He was disinclined, however, to reopen questions that already had been the subject of much study and discussion. He felt that he had been all around the clock. Moreover, some advisers were wondering whether further negotiations would not impair the prestige of the victorious powers and perhaps even cause rifts among them. House asked whether there would be any end to revision once it was undertaken in order to satisfy the enemy.[43] However, he was no longer privy to his chief's thinking, although he received reports from the economic advisers of their conferences with Wilson and continued to be besieged by Europeans who wished to reach the president. He was now complaining to Lansing of his inability to "get to the president" and of his difficulty in finding out what was going on.[44] He wrote in his diary on May 30: "Every day someone calls, stating that they do not wish to disturb the president and that it will answer every purpose if they get instructions from me. Just why I do not get into serious trouble, I do not know. Some day I suppose I will, for the president is intolerant of anyone acting for him. He wishes to do everything himself."

Actually, the colonel already was in "serious trouble." Yet he continued to talk freely to newsmen, though fully aware of Wilson's disapproval of this practice, and he recorded[45] his chief's shortcomings in the pages of his diary, describing him as "one of the most difficult and complex characters" he had known. House wrote: "He is so contradictory that it is hard to pass judgment upon him. He has but few friends and the reason is apparent to me. He seems to do his best to offend rather than to please, and yet when one gets access to him, there is no more charming man in the world than Woodrow Wilson. I have never seen anyone who did not leave his presence impressed. He could use this charm to enormous personal and public advantage if he would, but in that he is hopeless. . . . He speaks constantly of 'teamwork' but seldom practices it." House[46] confessed seven years later: "I was so near Wilson and so eager for him to play the greatest part of any man in history that I was perhaps too critical of his human failings."[47]

Usually House talked with Clemenceau secretly, to avoid giving offense to Wilson. On May 5, however, when the president came to House's room at the Crillon, the colonel broke off their conversation and went to an outer room to confer with Clemenceau, with whom he later returned to Wilson. House attached no importance to the incident at the time but later wondered whether it might have some connection with the fact that this was the president's last visit to the colonel's room.[48]

Actually, the Wilson household felt that the prophet's ruling elder had abused the

42. Mantoux, *Délibérations,* vol. 2, pp. 269–272.

43. *I.P.,* vol. 4, pp. 474–478.

44. T. W. Lamont to P. M. Burnett, June 25, 1934, Lamont papers, 85-11, Baker Library, Harvard University. Lansing desk diary, June 5 and 10, 1919. Lansing recorded that Grayson told him that Wilson "came out of it" [House's influence] and was doing his own thinking.

45. House diary, May 23, 24, 30, 31, 1919. In a cable of May 19 to Tumulty, Dr. Grayson said: "Colonel House confers with newspapermen daily and gives out information of which we have no knowledge," Wilson papers.

46. House diary, May 30, June 10, 11, 1919.

47. Letter, House to Seymour, June 6, 1926, Y.H.C.

48. Letter, House to Seymour, December 9, 1927, Y.H.C.

carte blanche that had been given to him at the beginning of the Peace Conference. Dr. Grayson said at luncheon that many of the president's difficulties were caused by "the little man on the third floor of the Crillon . . . the great little agreer."[49] However, in June the two old friends still talked over their private telephone and corresponded in terms of affection. Their last conversation was on June 28, the day of the president's departure from Paris.[50] Afterward, there was no one in the president's entourage to question his prophetic damnation of his adversaries both abroad and at home. Indeed, his wife and his doctor, to whom his health was the first consideration, supported him with a loyalty that permitted no cavil.

During June, House continued to use his influence with European chiefs in the cause of conciliation. The ogre of social revolution still haunted the Crillon. The French generals, alarmed by mutinies, were bringing troops into Paris, where thousands of strikers paraded with red flags. One of the most critical moments of the Peace Conference had come.[51] House felt that the crisis demanded initiative on his part. He at first thought it futile to make a serious effort to modify the terms given to the Germans, although they seemed to him to be "far afield" from the Fourteen Points. He was tempted to let the Tiger, whom he personally liked and admired, have his "bad peace."[52] However, when Clemenceau and Lloyd George tried to win his support for their conflicting positions, and when Clemenceau came to him on June 2, excited and angered by Lloyd George's demand for a softening of the terms, a disposition to accommodate Lloyd George asserted itself. House handed to Clemenceau a paper in which he outlined seven suggestions as a basis for compromise, and Clemenceau said he would use them. House was overcome with nostalgia for the routine of the prearmistice meetings, when he had met with the premiers in the mornings to decide what was to be presented in the formal sessions in the afternoons.[53]

The bickering between Lloyd George and Clemenceau continued. On June 4 the president said to House over their telephone that Lloyd George had been very offensive to him as well as to Clemenceau, and he, Wilson, had taken the occasion to be ugly himself. House then advised Balfour to caution Lloyd George against dealing with Wilson in the way that the prime minister thought effective in "handling" Clemenceau: that is, "hit him pretty hard at first." According to House's record,

49. Lansing desk diary, June 5, 1919.

50. "The third floor front has permanently passed," Henry White's brother-in-law wrote to Ambassador Davis. "[The] atmosphere is much improved in the Crillon," W. H. Buckler to J. W. Davis, June 30, 1919, J. W. Davis papers, Y.H.C.

51. "All the world seems to be going to smash industrially. . . . Half of Paris is striking," R. S. Baker's journal, June 3 and 9, 1919. Lansing's desk diary, June 3, 1919. "We hear of bitter industrial struggles in China," Baker wrote, "widespread bomb outrages in the United States, deep-seated discontent in both England and Italy," *American Chronicle*, p. 443.

52. "Clemenceau was for a bad peace in the beginning and is for a bad peace now. . . . I like him and admire him, little as I sympathize with his views," House diary, June 1, 1919. House recorded Clemenceau's opinion that Wilson, "although 'narrow,' travels in the same direction all the time while Lloyd George travels in every direction," *ibid.*, entry of May 30, 1919.

53. House, "Memorandum regarding the German counter-proposals, which I gave Clemenceau today," Clemenceau to House, June 10, 1919, House diary, May 31, June 2, 3, 1919, Y.H.C. Mantoux, *Délibérations*, vol. 2, pp. 275–283. Baker, vol. 3, p. 477.

Balfour thought that if the conflict among the chiefs grew worse, he and the colonel might have to act to "bring them to their senses."[54]

While House was operating independently in his usual manner, Lansing, Bliss, and White continued to meet regularly. White, still the gentleman of the old school and brimming with gossip, came to tea with the Wilsons and joined with Mrs. Wilson in repeating the plea made by House that the president take the precaution of having an American secretary record the discussions of the Council of Four. White wrote long letters to Senator Lodge and to Congressman John Rogers, explaining and supporting Wilson's work at Paris.[55] Lansing continued to complain of House and to criticize the compromises that had been effected and the secrecy that had made them possible. General Bliss, by whom Wilson had been warned often against American involvement in European chauvinism, regretted that in all the months at Paris he had conferred with the president for less than twenty minutes and that House was "a great trimmer" and interested in little except the League of Nations. The general, lamenting his own inefficacy in matters of general policy, consoled himself by the thought that the commissioners could justify their presence by "hanging on to the coat-tails" of the president.[56]

On May 31, two days after the formal German counterproposals were received, Wilson came unexpectedly to Lansing's office at the Crillon to attend the daily meeting of the American commission, which the day before had asked the experts to submit reports on the counterproposals that had to do with their several specialities. The commissioners had been asked to prepare a statement of what remained to be done after the German and Austrian treaties were signed. The president told them that he would go back to the United States and wanted them to stay and clean up the work remaining.[57]

On June 2, informed over the telephone by Lansing that a meeting of the American delegates was planned for the next morning, Wilson said he would try to be present. His counselors had suggested that it would be well to bring the delegation together for a general discussion of the German observations. House and Hoover were of the opinion that this should be done for the president's protection against disaffection among his advisers.[58]

Accordingly, on June 3, the day after the president drove to St. Germain to give treaty terms to the Austrian delegates assembled there,[59] he went to the office of the secretary of state. There the American delegates held their first general gathering of the entire Peace Conference. The five commissioners were in large armchairs, fac-

---

54. House diary, June 4 and 6, 1919. Baker, who had told House of Wilson's conflict with Lloyd George, noted the colonel's effort and wrote in his journal: "He [House] is forever trying to help to bring people together—to smooth over hard places. I like him very much but cannot decide whether or not he has had a useful role to play while here," entry of June 6, 1919.

55. Benham diary letter, June 4, 1919. Correspondence in the White papers, Columbia University Library.

56. Bullitt's "Conversation with General Bliss," May 19, 1919, Bullitt papers.

57. One page memorandum signed by Grew, May 30, 1919, Y.H.C. Auchincloss diary, May 20, 1919.

58. Four American commissioners to Wilson, House to Wilson, May 27; Wilson to Lansing, May 29, 1919, Wilson papers. McCormick diary, June 24, 1919.

59. See below, p. 444.

ing a semicircle of advisers. Wilson went from one to another, shaking hands genially and saying a few words about the work of each. These men, whom he had publicly praised for a "complete disinterestedness" that made their views usually prevail, were encouraged to continue to keep in touch with the experts of other nations and avoid "the usual roundabout expressions of diplomacy."[60] Their chief held constantly before them the prime necessities of the moment: they must make peace; they must maintain the alliance with France and Great Britain; and they must not sacrifice justice to expediency. They were invited to give their opinions on the justice of the German arguments. When Hoover ventured to suggest that the necessity of getting the signature of Germany on a treaty was of more importance than the difficult task of discerning what was "just," Wilson said that no one could be sure they had made a just treaty, but the argument of expediency ought not to prevail lest they have to fight again for what had been won.[61]

Determined to avoid giving an impression that by making concessions he would bribe the Germans to sign, and eager to prevent any breach in the unity of the victorious powers, Wilson took satisfaction from the fact that the Americans had "got very serious modifications out of the Allies." If they had written the treaty the way the Allies wanted it, he said, "the Germans would have gone home the minute they read it."[62] The president professed "a very sincere desire" to alter any of the peace terms that were unjust or contrary to his proclaimed principles. Speaking of the German objections that had most impressed the British delegates, he invited discussion of "the biggest point," that of reparations. He gave his advisers authority to try to agree with those of Clemenceau and Lloyd George upon the fixing of a total sum, but they found the European premiers adamant against any changes of great significance.[63]

The next of Lloyd George's four questions on which Wilson asked the American delegates for advice on June 3 was that of the disposal of Upper Silesia, where the coal mines and industries were of great value and largely in German hands. Lying at the junction of three of the empires that had fallen, and once included in Poland, this region had been a part of Prussia and Austria for about two hundred years; and Germans in the north and in the lands west of the Oder River operated thriving industries. The German negotiators at Paris objected vigorously to the decision of the Peace Conference to give to Poland a part of Upper Silesia. Their protest seemed to confirm Lloyd George's doubt that Germany would sign a treaty that summarily took this region from it, and he was determined that there be a plebiscite to demonstrate the will of the inhabitants. He had asserted to Clemenceau and Wilson on May 13 that the Germans were angered most by arrangements on their eastern frontier that placed their people under the rule of foreigners whom they thought inferior.[64]

60. Seymour, *Letters from the Paris Peace Conference*, pp. 253 ff.

61. A stenographic report of the meeting of June 3 is printed in Baker, vol. 3, pp. 469–504. Baker's journal, June 3, 1919. It seemed to Hoover that his remarks irritated the president. Hoover, *Memoirs*, vol. 1, pp. 464–468.

62. Baker, vol. 3, p. 504. Baker's journal, June 3, 1919.

63. See above, p. 403.

64. Mantoux, *Délibérations*, vol. 2, pp. 53, 367.

The president, surprised to learn that the terms of the draft treaty permitted the Polish government to seize wealth in Silesia that Germans had created, suggested a conversation with a Polish representative to seek a solution less objectionable to Germany with respect to its supply of raw materials and expropriation of property. This matter was involved with the question of reparations. Actually, the German delegation had concluded its protest by stating: "Only with Upper Silesia can Germany fulfill the obligations arising from the war, but without it never."

On June 3 the Council of Four considered this most vexing matter. At first Wilson would go only so far as to grant that the German protest should be considered. As against the Germans, he said, he was pro-Pole with all his heart. Yet, although he had agreed with Lloyd George on the principle of a plebiscite, it now did not seem to him that a free vote was possible because of the domination of German landlords, entrepreneurs, and priests. He cited support for this view on the part of his territorial advisers, who in general were less inclined than his economic counselors to reconsider the peace terms.[65] This opinion was supported also by Paderewski when he was invited to meet with "the Four" on June 5. Paderewski, claiming all of Galicia as well as Upper Silesia, explained that his political leadership in Poland depended on the fulfillment of promises made to his people.[66]

In the end the persistence of Lloyd George prevailed. Wilson, influenced by an assertion by Henry White that the Polish peasantry was not ill treated by German employers or hostile to them, accepted the proposed plebiscite.[67] He explained to Paderewski that the Council of Four knew the district to be Polish and desired to have a plebiscite that would convince the Germans of this. Repeating a fallacious prediction that Professor Lord had made, Wilson implied, if he did not state, that the outcome of the balloting would favor Poland.

In the American conference of June 3 Lord stated that no fair plebiscite could be conducted without the presence of Allied troops. However, Wilson objected to any use of military force to supervise the balloting. He argued that it would give cause for the Germans to complain of arbitrary intervention. Asked what the great powers would do if districts that feared to vote in favor of Poland in a plebiscite should later rise against the German regime, Wilson replied that one of the chief functions of the League of Nations was to deal with such questions. On June 14, when the Council of Four considered the report of a special committee to which it had referred the question of drawing up terms of a plebiscite and in which Lord made an effort to protect the Poles, the president spoke in favor of a plebiscite under the superintendence of an inter-Allied commission that would call in policing troops if neces-

---

65. On Professor Lord's "Polonophile sentiment" and its influence on Wilson, see Kaltenbach, *Self-Determination, 1919,* pp. 85 ff. Also see Schwabe, p. 366.

66. Mantoux, *Délibérations,* vol. 2, pp. 275–283, 305–312, 382, 430–433. On the disposition of Galicia, see above, p. 334.

67. White to Wilson, June 1, 1919, Wilson papers. White, who had become familiar with the region in visits to a daughter who had married a German officer, had explained that the Germans, far from "grinding the faces of the Polish peasantry" as Wilson suspected, had in fact won the respect of the Poles, who had been independent proprietors since 1848. "But for your father," Wilson said to White's daughter years later, "I should never have known the truth about Upper Silesia. The French and the Poles had entirely misled me." Nevins, *White,* p. 243.

sary. General Bliss, asked by Wilson whether it was possible to send American soldiers to Silesia as Lloyd George desired, advised that no action be taken until funds were appropriated for this specific purpose.[68] The council then decided that the four major powers should share equally in providing 13,000 troops for the plebiscite area. When Washington sent several thousand American abroad for this duty, strong protest arose in the Congress.[69]

In February of 1920, after the treaty took effect without America's signature, Italian and French troops arrived and an inter-Allied commission on which the United States was not represented assumed control of the plebiscite. A vote in March of 1921 gave Germany a majority of almost three to two of the communes. The voting was followed by open warfare between German and Polish armies. Finally, in October, the League of Nations delivered a judgment that pleased neither party and left a particularly bitter grudge among Germans.[70]

The peacemakers attempted to arrange another plebiscite for the district of Teschen, where Czechs and Poles continued to contend for control of the rich mineral resources, and to which the Peace Conference had sent a commission in February to prevent bloodshed. The impartiality of this body was in question, and it enjoyed little respect and was ineffective.[71] It reported that the agreement that Beneš and Paderewski had signed at Paris in February was ''no longer anything more than a scrap of paper,''[72] and that order could not be preserved if the peace conference did not act immediately and decisively. In early April the specialists conferred day and night. Seymour, modifying his original adherence to the plan of the commission on Czechoslovakia to award three-quarters of Teschen to that state, made a compromise proposal that assured Poland of coal and provided for a large degree of local autonomy under Czech rule.[73] The British, French, and Japanese concurred, but the Italians filed a dissent.

In May serious fighting broke out at Teschen. The Polish minister at Washington asked for American intervention, and this was refused by the State Department. On May 16 Beneš talked with Wilson and explained the Czech position with clarity and moderation. The next day in the Council of Four the president repeated the arguments of Beneš—economic, strategic, and historical—and added that Hoover had stated that the current production of coal had suffered from the uncertainty of the population as to its ultimate political fate.[74] Neither efforts made by Hoover's men,[75]

---

68. Bliss to the president, June 17, 1919, Bliss papers, box 233.

69. Pershing to the secretary of war, Polk to the secretary of state, Aug. 13, 1919, Wilson papers. Ammission to the secretary of state, October 20, 1919, H. White papers, Columbia University Library, box 44. Nelson, pp. 126, 129–131, and nn. 27, 36. See below, p. 526.

70. F. Gregory Campbell, ''The Struggle for Upper Silesia, 1919–1922,'' 382–385. Watt, pp. 154–164. Monnet, *Memoirs*, pp. 88–91.

71. Lundgreen-Nielsen, *The Polish Problem at the Paris Peace Conference*, p. 401.

72. See above, p. 98.

73. Perman, *The Shaping of the Czechoslovak State*, pp. 230–233. See Seymour, ''Czechoslovak Frontiers,'' 285–286.

74. Mantoux, *Délibérations*, vol. 2, p. 92.

75. Hoover had put an American executive in charge of the mines and the distribution of coal in Teschen. Hoover suggested that the duchy be ruled ''from a point of view of coal output rather than politics'' and thought that this might be done with a police force of ''at least a couple of hundred of

nor those of the commission at Teschen, nor negotiations of Paderewski with Masa-ryk and Beneš,[76] nor discussion of the question at Krakow by a Czech-Polish group of eighteen men made significant progress toward solving this issue that became more and more one of clashing national egos. The disorders continued into the autumn. Repeated efforts at Paris to get American participation in the work of an international commission of control elicited no response from Washington.[77] At the insistence of Beneš, who was stalling for time, the Peace Conference decided on September eleven that there would be a plebiscite. But nine months later the clever Czech statesman seized a moment of diplomatic advantage to waive the plebiscite and persuade the Poles to accept an arrangement that left them with a long-lingering grudge against Czechoslovakia.[78]

There was difficulty and delay also in drawing the eastern boundaries of Poland. The American experts considered the question of the frontiers with Lithuania and with Russia to be "highly contentious" and "the possibility of reaching satisfactory settlements . . . now or in the near future . . . very problematical."[79]

A third provision of the treaty that Lloyd George wished to soften was that relating to the duration of the occupation of the Rhineland. Alluding to the psychological support that had been given to the Bolsheviks by foreign intervention in Russia, he said that it would be hazardous to undertake an occupation of German territory that would build a resentment that might become dangerous when Germany regained its strength. Clemenceau, however, insisted that just as the German army had occupied France in 1871 until the indemnity was paid, so now it was necessary to occupy part of Germany until reparation was assured. He feared to do anything that might "break the spirit" of his people.

The question of the timing of the withdrawal of the occupying forces had been under consideration for several weeks. Both General Bliss and Hoover had warned against any commitment to a prolonged American involvement in the Rhineland. Under the compromise with Clemenceau that Wilson accepted with a wry face in mid-April, an inter-Allied force was to occupy three zones for periods of five, ten, and fifteen years. And on April 30, further comfort had been given to Clemenceau by a secret agreement with Wilson and Lloyd George that provided that if on any

either American or British soldiers." Hoover to Lansing, April 28, 1919, cited in Perman, p. 237, q.v. Lansing to Wilson, April 30, 1919, Wilson papers. Lansing desk diary, April 25, 1919. In August, after visiting central Europe, Hoover repeated his proposal, dispatch, Polk to the secretary of state, August 23, 1919, H. White papers, box 44, L.C.

76. See above, p. 72.

77. Dispatches, Ammission to State Department, Sept. 23, 27, 29, Oct. 2, 1919, N.A., R.G. 59, 763.72119/905 1/2 and 7119. According to Perman, "The American delegation . . . was chiefly responsible for the diplomatic defeat of Czechoslovakia during the consideration of the Teschen frontier in August and September 1919," The Shaping of the Czechoslovak State, p. 270. Lord's effort in behalf of Poland in this matter is illuminated in his letters to Hugh Gibson, August 7 and 22, 1919, Gibson papers, box 8, f. 4.

78. See Perman, pp. 237–240, and Wandycz, The United States and Poland, p. 137.

79. Four-page brief, "Contentious Questions to be Settled after the German and Austrian Treaties are Disposed of," n.d., Y.H.C. It was not until September 25 that the heads of delegations at the Peace Conference accepted a report of the Commission on Polish Affairs on the eastern boundary of Poland. See Wandycz, pp. 147–148.

date set for withdrawal the associated governments thought the guarantees against German aggression to be insufficient, the occupation might be extended long enough to obtain the required assurance. On the same day, however, Clemenceau had given his assent to a proposal by Wilson that they eliminate an article in the military terms which required that the terms of the armistice remain in force.

During the ensuing weeks efforts were made by the French to get authorization to prolong or renew the occupation as a check upon any manifestation of German aggression or as a penalty for German failure to carry out the provisions of the treaty of peace. However, when the text of the Rhineland Convention was reviewed by The Three on June 13, Wilson managed to effect revisions that would assure Germany that there was no intention of cutting off the Rhineland from the rest of Germany, and that the military authorities would be permitted to move troops from their barracks only in case of *exceptional* necessity. But he abstained from comment during a discussion of a paper defining relations between the military and civil officials, and in the afternoon of that day he was absent when the British and French delegates considered the question of termination of the occupation. In that session Clemenceau declared himself ready to agree to evacuation of the left bank when Germany had given "the necessary guarantees," such as financial pledges, that it was truly disposed to fulfill the conditions stipulated. Three days later Clemenceau was persuaded to join in signing an ambiguous "declaration." This provided that only a moderate annual payment be required by the reparation commission as soon as the Allied and Associated powers were "convinced that the conditions of disarmament" were "being satisfactorily fulfilled."[80] This agreement was not published, did not become a part of the Treaty of Versailles, and was of dubious legal validity. Actually, as Lloyd George pointed out, occupation was futile as a far-reaching check on German power, for it was likely that Germany would have recovered its strength by the time of the final withdrawal of troops.

In the formal counterproposals of May 29 the German spokesmen had persisted in advancing their views with respect to the League of Nations, and one of Lloyd George's four points had advocated the expedition of German membership. In 1918 Erzberger had written a book in which he commended the ideal of "a Christian community of nations," and many fellow Germans believed in this doctrine as a source of salvation for their nation in the future. Before the end of the war Prince Max had spoken in the Reichstag in support of Wilson's ideas for a league, and a favorable resolution had been passed. A draft of a league constitution that had been worked out by German officials and published on April 24 had proposed a democratic world parliament made up of delegates from the national legislatures. The Germans thought this proposal would be a potent weapon of propaganda during the negotiations that they hoped the victors would grant.[81]

80. *F.R., P.P.C.*, vol. 5, p. 352. Mantoux, *Délibérations*, vol. 1, pp. 406–407, 410, 430. Baker, vol. 2, pp. 100–101, 118. Schwabe, p. 283.

81. On the German league of nations project, see Schwabe, p. 307. There was hope in Germany that the powers at Paris would be so confused by this constructive project that their alliance would break up. "As in Wilson's addresses on his war aims," Schwabe writes, "tactical considerations and honest conviction were closely associated here, too," *ibid.*

In their counterproposals, which Erzberger had a hand in drafting, the Germans stated that their government was ready to take part, on a basis of equality of privilege and obligation, in economic and military disarmament as well as in a mandatory system for colonies. They welcomed the provisions for labor that the League of Nations was to sponsor, and they suggested that the force of "international law" be given to the minimum demands of the International at Bern. Brockdorff-Rantzau sought immediate entry into "a true League" that would include all nations. Thus, Germany might play a constructive part in the new organization.[82]

The exclusion of the enemy from the deliberations of the Peace Conference had the effect of preventing their sharing in the drafting of the constitution that they would be forced to accept. Wilson, who aspired to make of the League a truly ecumenical body rather than merely a club of the strongest powers, had advocated German participation. At the same time he had postulated a proviso.[83] In his first Paris draft of the Covenant he had written: "Any power not a party to this Covenant, whose government is based upon the principle of popular self-government, may apply . . . for leave to become a party." Wilson was inhibited by concern as to the ability of the German people to form a government that would send acceptable delegates to international meetings. In a conference with Lord Robert Cecil on March 18, provision had been made in the Covenant for the eventual admission of Germany to a permanent seat on the executive council of the League. Moreover, on March 22, Wilson had tried—in vain—to effect a change in the regulation for voting in nonmembers that would have facilitated Germany's entry.

On June 3, in a session of the Supreme Council, Wilson reasserted the moral stipulation that was vital to his political leadership. He read a proposed reply to the Germans.[84] This statement, drafted by the League commission, provided that the victors would admit Germany to the League as soon as they were convinced that a democratic government was solidly established and the people were pacific in spirit. Hope was expressed that admission would be possible in a few months. One heard on all sides, Wilson said, that this question gave more concern in Germany than any other. They must choose between delivering an ultimatum and making concessions. He argued, moreover, that Germany could be controlled better within the League than without.

82. Luckau, pp. 225–240, 247–248, 255–259, 304, 320–323, 406–408.

American observers at Berlin confirmed the strong desire of officials there for the prompt entry of Germany into the League, C. B. Dyar's report of an interview with Bernstorff and Erzberger, forwarded by Grew to Close; letter, Dresel to Wilson, June 5, 1919, Wilson papers. Dresel, writing to Wilson at the suggestion of Hoover to advocate German membership in the League, advised that this would immensely strengthen the German parties of order and true democracy.

83. See the analysis of Wilson's changing views by Klaus Schwabe in "Woodrow Wilson and Germany's Membership in the League of Nations, 1918–1919," *Central European History* 8, no. 1 (March 1975).

84. Early in June a reply to the Germans, drafted by Cecil, was approved by a committee on which House sat. This enraged French opinion and seemed to Clemenceau to go too far, Mantoux, *Délibérations,* vol. 2, pp. 346–348, 392, 400, 418. For the reply to the Germans, see Luckau, p. 418; Cecil's diary, June 9, 1919; Elcock, pp. 278, 280, 283. It was anticipated by British delegates that one of the first functions of the first assembly of the League, which Wilson was expected to call into session in the autumn, would be to admit Germany, R. S. Baker's journal, June 27, 1919; Headlam-Morley, "History of the Saar Settlement" (Foreign Office paper in the possession of Professor Agnes Headlam-Morley), p. 23.

Clemenceau, however, was adamant. One would never control the Germans by League membership, he insisted. He knew them too well. Realizing that the day would come when Germany would have to be admitted, he prepared an alternative reply to the German counterproposal, and he won the support of Lloyd George. Willing to risk a rejection of the treaty by the enemy rather than a collapse of the united front of the victorious powers, Wilson felt forced by circumstances to give up his dream of bringing about the prompt integration of victorious and vanquished nations in a new world order. He did succeed, however, in persuading Clemenceau to eliminate a French clause in the military articles of the treaty that would have made compliance with the military terms a condition of Germany's admission to the League.

The reply to the Germans went only so far as to mention the possibility of admitting Germany "in a future not distant," at a time to be determined by the acts of the German government in respect of freedom of communications, equitable treatment of commerce, the rights of foreign minorities, and disarmament. The final text of article I of the Covenant provided that any nation applying for membership had "to give effective guarantees of its sincere intention to observe" its international obligations and had to accept the League's regulations in respect of armaments. The various observations that the Germans had sent to Paris during May had resulted in no alteration in the text of the Covenant, although their arguments had been considered in detail by the Peace Conference. The new German government was denied the immediate recognition that it needed in order to consolidate its position as the sort of stable democratic regime that Wilson had long hoped for but now felt almost without power to assist.[85]

The question of Germany's acceptance of the proposed treaty, which Clemenceau thought inevitable, aroused apprehension in Lloyd George. The military and naval advisers had discussed in April and May the question of measures to be taken in case Germany refused to sign. They had made preparations for a march on Berlin, and it was taken for granted that American troops would participate.[86]

Foch adduced reservations when he was asked on June 16 whether he was still prepared to carry out a plan for using force. He argued that the effectiveness of his

---

85. Cf. Schwabe, *Woodrow Wilson, Revolutionary Germany, and Peacemaking,* ch. VII. Dresel to Wilson, June 5, 1919.

"The German foreign minister had declared in February of 1919 that democracy could not be safe in Germany if it were not secured within the League, and that there would be no better proof of the democratic character of the League than the acceptance of the new Germany as one of its original members. . . . To the [German] Democratic Party the insistence on Germany's early admission to the League had become an issue over which they would leave the government," Schwabe, "Woodrow Wilson and Germany's Membership in the League of Nations, 1918–1919," 21. See *ibid,* pp. 4–22. On Wilson's policy toward Germany see N. Gordon Levin, Jr., *Woodrow Wilson and World Politics,* pp. 123 ff., 156–161, 176–177.

86. Luckau, pp. 411–472. Five-page brief on "Naval action to be taken"; note of Foch summarizing a conference with Bliss, H. Wilson, and Diaz on April 9, 1919, Wilson papers. Memorandum of talk of Pershing and Foch, April 28, 1919; Foch's instructions, May 20, "in case the Allied Armies would have to go forward on the right bank of the Rhine," Pershing papers, box 75. When Wilson learned that certain British generals proposed dropping bombs on German cities in the event of further resistance, he was indignant and threatened to send home any American who stood for such tactics, McCormick diary, June 17, 1919.

strategy depended somewhat on the making of arrangements for the pacification of the southern German states separately. General Bliss had resigned himself to the inevitability of such a measure, but The Three conceded no authority to Foch in respect of political matters. Clemenceau remarked that experiments in separation already had failed in the Rhineland. Wilson's comment was that he could bring back troops from the United States, if necessary. On June 20, when it seemed almost certain that Germany would sign the treaty, Wilson went along with a decision that if they did not, Foch should be permitted to advance to the Weser[87] and should have the authority to arrange separate armistices with German states. The leader who in 1917 had called for the use of force "without stint or limit" to win the war was now equally committed to employ whatever force was necessary to impose the treaty of peace. Thus, the Supreme Council of the victorious powers would give to Foch again, as it had during the first days after the Armistice of Rethondes, an opportunity to create political *faits accomplis* by military orders.

Advised by General Bliss that the American occupation army of 150,000 recommended by Foch could be cut greatly,[88] Wilson hoped that this would be possible. He would have liked to limit the contingent to 5,000 infantrymen. When he left final arrangements to Pershing, however, the general agreed with Foch on June 30 that three divisions (75,000 men) would linger until July 15, two units until August 15, and one until three months after the treaty was ratified, when only an enlarged regiment would remain.[89] Uncertainty as to the degree of military strength that would be needed to hold Germany in submission added to the difficulties that stood in the way of general disarmament.

In case of further German resistance to signing the treaty, still another recourse was available. The blockade of the enemy, which had been relaxed in March, might be stiffened. Hoover, however, deplored any such development, and to avert it he was willing that German objections to the peace terms be met with concessions. He feared the interruption of food shipments to Czechoslovakia and Poland, which had reached a peak in mid-May. A stoppage would lead to surpluses in European ports of foodstuffs for which Hoover would be financially accountable.

Wilson sympathized with Hoover's position and also with his humanitarian and moral aversion to a policy that would penalize a whole people for the folly of their leaders. On May 14, in the Supreme Council, the president warned that a stronger blockade might so disrupt Germany that no one could be found to sign the peace treaty. The British delegates were persuaded to renounce the blockade as a means of putting pressure on Germany. Nevertheless, at the suggestion of Clemenceau, Wilson agreed that it be announced in the press that preparations were being made for use of the blockade if Germany did not come to terms.[90] The Supreme Economic Council instructed the Blockade Council to prepare to reimpose the blockade and to

87. Mantoux, *Délibérations*, vol. 2, pp. 430–438, 442–444, 458–465.
88. See above, p. 389.
89. K. Nelson, pp. 119, 125–126.
90. Schwabe, *Woodrow Wilson, Revolutionary Germany, and Peacemaking*, p. 387. McCormick diary, June 13, 1919.

Hoover had made it known that he would withdraw from the Peace Conference rather than assent to a renewal of the blockade of grain shipments in case Germany refused to sign the treaty, Pichon to French ambassadors, June 1, 1919, Archives du M.A.É., "L'Amérique, États-Unis," f. 168.

give the public the impression that such preparations were being made, even to go so far as to display destroyers in the Baltic.[91]

Wilson, however, was still holding back. He wrote to his chief naval adviser: "It is not, I may say confidentially, at present in contemplation to declare a blockade immediately upon the refusal of the Germans to sign. The matter will be held under advisement pending a military advance." Nevertheless, Admiral Knapp attended a meeting of naval representatives at the French Ministry of Marine on June 21 to make plans to renew the full blockade if necessary.[92] Before the end of the month, however, the Supreme Council gave instructions that restrictions would be lifted entirely when word was received that the German Assembly had ratified the treaty. Accordingly, the blockade of Germany ended on July 12. Shipments of supplies for relief continued for years.[93]

By joining with Clemenceau and Lloyd George in supporting Foch's contingency plans and by preparing for the reimposition of a blockade if military measures failed, Wilson closed ranks with the Europeans to do what was possible toward the goal of immediate peace. For the most part, and conspicuously in respect of questions of "war guilt" and war crimes, he had been unresponsive to both British and German proposals for alterations in the draft treaty. Thus the German officials felt justified in the fatalistic mood into which they had fallen in May after receiving the replies to Brockdorff-Rantzau's notes and also Conger's confidential advice with respect to American policy. Even moderate men such as Warburg and Melchior, disappointed by Wilson's seeming coolness toward the progress in Germany of the democratic alternative to imperial or Bolshevist rule, and convinced that the liberal views that they expressed to Keynes and Davis would receive little support at the top level at Paris, agreed that it would be suicidal for Germany to sign the treaty of peace.[94]

The American prophet who had striven to make the treaty's terms fair in the light of his moral standards was not encouraged in his quest for abstract "justice" by the calumny of rebuffed German idealists who competed with him for leadership of the world's social revolution under the delusion that thus they could enter into collaboration with the victors rather than into subjugation. The injection of nationalistic morality and idealism into what should have been the work of diplomacy—an offense shared by Wilson with the most influential intellects in Germany—made it very difficult for the two parties to negotiate a practical understanding. "The result was," Schwabe writes, "that both sides escalated the collision of their interests at Versailles into a conflict of principle which simply could not be resolved."[95]

An ultimatum that went from the Supreme Council to the Germans on June 16

91. Dispatch, Lansing to the secretary of state, June 15, 1919, Wilson papers.
92. Wilson to Knapp, June 14, 1919, "Re-establishment of a blockade of Germany," British paper M299, Wilson papers.
93. Mantoux, *Délibérations,* vol. 2, pp. 513–514. Minutes, Supreme Economic Council, June 30, 1919.
94. Schwabe, *Woodrow Wilson, Revolutionary Germany, and Peacemaking,* p. 384.
"In the end . . . ," this scholar explains, "the German foreign minister's peace strategy proved to be a failure. He had not . . . been counting so much on an immediate change of heart in Wilson alone but rather on a yielding of all the Associated governments together once they had begun to feel the pressure which the Left in their own countries would exert in response to the progressive slogans being advanced by Germany," *ibid.,* p. 393.
95. *Ibid.,* p. 406. Luckau, p. 133.

replied in detail to their counterproposals. The enemy's allegations of injustice were answered by a blunt insistence that "the war . . . was the greatest crime against humanity that any nation calling itself civilized . . . ever consciously committed." The ultimatum gave the German delegates exactly five days within which to declare that they would accept the terms of May 7, with the few changes specified. If they did not, the Allied and Associated Powers would take steps to enforce their will. The Rhineland Convention was given to Germany along with the ultimatum.[96]

On the fifth day after the dispatch of the ultimatum of June 16, no reply had reached Paris. The anxiety of the victors turned to rage when they learned that the enemy caretakers had scuttled the German warships that had been interned at Scapa Flow. Admiral Benson, who late in April had exchanged threats in an acrimonious talk with the First Lord of the British Admiralty,[97] foresaw that the ships might be used in a way contrary to American interests.[98] British spokesmen were now quick to point out that if they had had their way, and if the ships had been surrendered rather than interned, they would not have been lost. The Americans, under censure for opposing surrender, took comfort in the thought that the sinking eliminated a possible quarrel about the eventual distribution of the vessels among the victors.[99] Agreeing that the sinking of the German ships had violated the armistice and that an appropriate sanction was desirable, Wilson insisted that the world must not get the impression that the war was being renewed. This incident highlighted the difficulty of enforcing the treaty even before it was signed.[100]

After receiving the Peace Conference ultimatum, the German delegation left Versailles, making an escape from a violently hostile crowd in the streets.[101] In Germany officers of high rank advocated defiance of the Allies and made plans for military action. President Ebert said that he would favor rejection of the dictated terms if the Supreme Command saw any prospect of successful resistance.[102] More-

96. Although the German delegates felt that the occupation would prove to be actually "a disguised annexation," their representatives on the armistice commission were not unappreciative of the protection that was to be given to the civil authorities in the Rhineland, Nelson, pp. 119–123 and nn.

Noyes remained with the High Commission for the Rhineland until all special representatives of the United States were withdrawn from Europe in June 1920, though he had no vote after France and Great Britain ratified the Treaty of Versailles on January 10, 1920. According to his record, he used unorthodox tactics such as threatening public exposure, in his efforts to curb military power over civil life. Noyes, pp. 250–261. General Henry T. Allen, commanding the American occupying force at Koblenz, undertook responsibility for ruling that area when the failure of the United States to ratify the convention prevented the Rhineland High Commission from exercising authority. See Allen, *The Rhineland Occupation* (Indianapolis, 1927).

97. See Watt, pp. 486–489. McCormick diary, April 27, 1919.

98. Benson to Wilson, April 28, May 5, 1919. Wilson shared Benson's view but found it impossible to get the desired provision into the treaty, Wilson to Benson, May 6, 1919, Wilson papers.

99. *I.P.*, vol. 4, pp. 135, 484–486. McCormick diary, June 23 and 24, 1919. Paul Schubert and Langhorne Gibson, *Death of a Fleet* (New York, 1932).

100. Mantoux, *Délibérations*, vol. 2, p. 508. *F.R., P.P.C.*, vol. 6, pp. 652–660. The ire of Clemenceau was fanned by news of the public burning, in Berlin, of French battle flags that were to be returned to their owners under the terms of the treaty. He thought of sending French soldiers into Essen in retaliation.

101. Schiff, pp. 123–124. Ambassador Wallace reported that the Germans were hissed and stoned by the populace, whose conduct had thus far been exemplary, Wallace to the secretary of state, June 21, August 4, 1919, N.A., R.G. 59, 851.00/90.

102. Gordon A. Craig, *Germany 1866–1945*, pp. 425–427.

over, Brockdorff-Rantzau, renouncing Conger as an aid to negotiations, advised against compliance. He thought that the United States would not insist on the most objectionable provisions. (The Germans had the text of a statement of the Foreign Relations Committee of the American Senate to the effect that the treaty as it stood had no chance of ratification.) Brockdorff-Rantzau and his advisers saw the rejection of the treaty by Germany as the lesser of two evils.[103]

It was gradually recognized in Germany that a rigid foreign occupation and utter economic chaos was the alternative. Erzberger, who had been active in exploring the possibility of making a peace that his people would accept, cast his ballot in favor of signing the treaty. This created a deadlock in the cabinet. Chancellor Scheidemann and Brockdorff-Rantzau resigned, and the next day Gustav Bauer formed a new cabinet, with Bernstorff as foreign minister. On the twenty-second Bauer persuaded the National Assembly to authorize the signing of the treaty but with reservations that denied the responsibility of Germany for starting the conflict and that refused to surrender Germans who were accused of crimes against the usages of war. No recourse was suggested in case the reservations were rejected.[104]

The peacemakers at Paris, aroused by the incendiary incidents of the past days, were in no mood to dally. "After the signature," they answered, "the Allied and Associated Powers must hold Germany responsible for the execution of every stipulation of the treaty." Wilson explained that he would gladly agree to the German reservations but felt that he must join with his European colleagues in an "absolute ultimatum." There was now general agreement that the Germans would yield.[105]

On June 23 a German note informed the victors of "the acceptance even of those provisions in the treaty which, without having any material significance, are designed to deprive the German people of their honor." At the same time the German government "in no wise" abandoned its conviction that the conditions of peace represented "injustice without example."[106]

It was only with difficulty that members of Bauer's Cabinet were persuaded to sign the loathed document. On June 28, exactly five years after the assassination of the Archduke Ferdinand had precipitated the war, two Social Democrats, Foreign Secretary Hermann Müller and Johannes Bell, filed into the Galerie des Glaces at Versailles. They were very erect but very pale. To celebrate France's hour of revenge, its officials staged one of the great pageants of history. Georges Clemenceau, who had not forgotten the German triumph in 1871 in the same hall, was waiting for the enemy, sitting at the center of a long raised table in front of the row of mirrors. Soldiers whose faces had been badly mutilated were placed in plain view of the

103. Schaefer, p. 298. Luckau, pp. 489–495. On Brockdorff-Rantzau's tactics and those of his political adversaries, see Schwabe, *op. cit.*, pp. 380–385.

104. Luckau, pp. 478–481.

105. R. S. Baker's journal, June 22, 1919. On June 20, while the Germans were considering the Allied note of June 16, they pointed out discrepancies between that note and the revised text of the treaty. Wilson was advised by his legal staff that in five of the twelve cases cited the Germans made their point, memorandum for the president June 20, 1919, Wilson papers.

106. Luckau, pp. 109–112, 482. Schiff, pp. 148–163. Alma Luckau, " 'Unconditional Acceptance' of the Treaty of Versailles by the German Government, June 22–28, 1919." "In the end the leading men in the government were motivated by the idea of buying at a high price security both externally and internally," Gerhard Schulz, *Revolutions and Peace Treaties, 1917–1920*, p. 189.

German delegates. It was all as solemn as a church before a service, with subdued chatter and curiosity that put a premium on the aisle seats. Invited officials sat at both ends of the hall, with generals in the last row; in the center was a table on which the treaty lay open for signature.[107] Paul Cambon commented on the revolution in diplomatic usage: "They lack only music and ballet girls, dancing in step, to offer the pen to the plenipotentiaries for signing. Louis XIV liked ballets, but only as a diversion; he signed treaties in his study. Democracy is more theatrical than the great king."[108] The newsmen, however, had not attained complete liberty to record the proceedings for the peoples of the world. The American journalists complained that they were brought in by a back door like servants and hardly saw what went on. Wilson had joined with Clemenceau in protecting the dignity of the occasion by opposing the presence of cinema photographers.[109]

The Germans signed the Treaty of Versailles and a protocol for giving effect to it; and then the delegates of twenty-six nations that sat in judgment signed. The Americans had failed in strenuous efforts to arrange for the presence of the Chinese, who could not accept the terms in respect of Shantung.[110]

The Three went from the Hall of Mirrors out on the terrace and tried to walk toward their automobiles. But the crowd pressed in, pelted them with flowers, and tried to slap their backs. The rejoicing was so boisterous that House feared for the safety of the president.[111] But the statesmen were rescued by gendarmes and were led out through a barrier that had been erected to confine the German delegates.[112]

In their long and arduous collaboration in making a peace for the twentieth-century world, and while Wilson had come to understand that, as Lloyd George put it, "the chronic troubles of Europe could not be settled by hanging round its neck the phylacteries of justice," The Three had developed an *esprit de corps*. The Europeans came to appreciate the good qualities of the prophet who often irritated them.

And yet Wilson, after signing the bipartite treaty on which Clemenceau depended for the security of France, threatened to fail in his duty as a diplomat in a matter of protocol. He distressed his American associates by refusing, for a few hours, to attend a farewell state dinner given by President Poincaré in his honor. Thanks to the influence of Henry White, however, he did attend the function;[113] and in response

107. McCormick diary, June 28, 1919. Guy Hamilton, who was present, to the author, letter of January 1, 1979.

108. P. Cambon, *Correspondance*, vol. 3, p. 340.

109. R. S. Baker's journal, June 24 and 28, 1919. Baker recorded that despite an adverse decision by the Council of Four, the Quai d'Orsay arranged to have certain movie photographers present, including one American and one Englishman. To Frances Stevenson there seemed to be "men with cameras in every direction," vying to get as near as possible to the principals. "The press is destroying all romance," she wrote. "They are as unscrupulous as they are vulgar," *Lloyd George*, p. 87.

110. See above, p. 374.

Vivid eyewitness descriptions of the signing may be found in Jules Cambon, "La Paix," 36–37; Westermann diary, June 28, 1919; and Shotwell, pp. 381–383.

111. Auchincloss diary, June 28, 1919.

112. Robert H. George, an American delegate, to the author.

113. Lansing desk diary, June 28, 1919, *F.R., P.P.C.*, vol. 6, pp. 735–740. Nevins, p. 448. Poincaré called a meeting of the Council of State to consider the affront to France. House, at the urging of Ambassadors Wallace and Jusserand, telephoned to Grayson and found the doctor inclined not to intercede. Finally, the colonel, who by this time had little to lose in admonishing the president once more, reminded

to Poincaré's toasts to the "continued solidarity" of the Allies, he spoke words that responded to the sentiments of all humanity. "We shall continue to be co-workers," he said, "in tasks which, because they are common, will weave out of our sentiments a common conception of duty and a common conception of the rights of men of every race and of every clime. If it be true that that has been accomplished, it is a very great thing." He went so far as to hail the League of Nations as the first "permanent" association of the nations of the world. Privately, he assured Poincaré, who the next day expressed pleasure at Wilson's remarks, that a hard battle was ahead at Washington but that it would be a one-day battle.[114]

Perhaps wishing to make a start in the contemplated campaign to educate his American constituency, Wilson gave a candid talk to newsmen just before his departure, asserting that the Treaty of Versailles came closer to his enduring principles than he had "any right to expect." To Baker it seemed that Wilson had never appeared to better advantage. Nevertheless, when the Council of Four considered whether the minutes of their meetings that had been kept by Hankey should be released, Wilson became very secretive. He was willing only that their decisions, and not their discussions, be communicated to their successors. He would reveal nothing to the foreign ministries. To him the intimate conversations that had taken place in his own home were a very personal matter. If the question of disclosure were discussed publicly, he might be criticized for not having had an American secretary in the sessions, as House had recommended. Nevertheless, he recognized that each of The Four would have to act in accord with the tradition of his own country.[115]

When Wilson took the train for Brest, he found on the platform most of the European officials with whom he had negotiated. Clemenceau, who had been at times exasperated by the American prophet and at times awed, confided to Dr. Grayson: "In saying good-by to the president I feel that I am saying good-by to my best friend." The man who had assumed the difficult and essential task of reconciling these two great men came forward as the whistle blew; and the president looked at him sternly and said coldly: "Good-by, House."[116]

---

him that Poincaré represented the French nation, whose guest the Wilsons had been for six months. According to House's diary: "He said he'd choke if he had to sit at table with Poincaré. I replied that if I were in his place I would go to the dinner and choke. . . . He said Poincaré was 'no good' and had tried to make trouble by sending a message to the Italian people against him," House diary, June 23, 1919. Finally, Mrs. Lansing put in a word at tea with Mrs. Wilson (Alden Hatch, *Edith Bolling Wilson*, pp. 55, 135), and Henry White wrote a letter explaining the enormity of the offense, Lansing desk diary, June 24, 1919, White to Wilson, June 24, 1919. At the dinner, with Poincaré almost at his elbow, Wilson chatted at some length with Joseph C. Grew and said that the occasion was an awful bore, Grew, *Turbulent Era*, vol. 1, pp. 390–391.

114. General Henry T. Allen's diary, June 27, 1919, Allen papers, box 2, L.C. According to an undated statement, printed in a biography of Smuts by his son, Smuts asked Wilson whether the president could carry the treaty through the Senate, and the president replied: "I absolutely can," *Jan Christiaan Smuts*, p. 205.

115. Mantoux, *Délibérations*, vol. 2, pp. 563–566.

116. Grayson, "The Colonel's Folly and the President's Distress," 101.

PART FIVE

The Fading of the Vision

I N signing the Treaty of Versailles the European plenipotentiaries had concluded a pact that could be ratified by the parliaments to which they were accountable. The treaty, though it left the national aspirations of the victors less than satisfied,
nevertheless served the common necessity of ending a state of general exhaustion
and gave hope for the survival of that form of human society that had become
known as "civilization."

Yet civil order had not been restored in many parts of Asia and Europe. Siberia
was in chaos, and the Soviet government was deemed to be beyond the pale. "Freed"
nationalities were not living in peace with their neighbors. The boundaries of Poland
had not been fixed; and German armies still lingered in the Baltic states in defiance
of the orders of the Peace Conference. The treaty had not made conclusive arrangements for vast territories still in turmoil. For one thing, the Conference had not
completed its task of liquidating the great Hapsburg estate; and it would be necessary to conclude a peace with Austria, as well as one with Hungary as soon as a
stable government was in sight there. Moreover, treaties would have to be signed
with Turkey and Bulgaria, nations against which the United States was not at war
but which were among the countries for whose security America might assume
responsibility as a member of the League of Nations.

The settlement that was imposed on Germany on June 28 offered little hope for
a peace that would be enduring. In order to discourage a future burst of German
chauvinism, the victors had forbidden union with Austria, a restriction that supplied
fuel for the explosion that eventually came. Moreover, the German delegates were
forced to accept what they called a "war-guilt lie" as to their nation's responsibility
for the breaking of the peace in 1914. Then, too, Germany's economy would have
to endure exactions that were ill defined and that would cripple production to a
degree that might make it impossible to satisfy the Allied demands for reparations.
The inconclusive reckoning presaged bankruptcy, a collapse of the German currency, and the development of tension that preceded a second world war.

Worst of all, the prospect of Germany's cooperation in the building of a league
of nations, a prospect on which German social democrats had depended to inspire
confidence in their new government, was left clouded; and as a result the German
people appeared condemned, like the bolsheviks of Russia, to ostracism from world
society. Instead of giving the leadership for which German liberals looked to him,
Wilson had provided a moral grievance that could easily be exploited by politicians.

The peace of Versailles, which might otherwise have been regarded as merely the consequence of a military defeat, became in the German view the breach of an undertaking;[1] and the "moderate left," according to Schwabe, "took serious losses from which it would never recover."

Germans were hurt by some of the treaty's provisions, outraged by others. During the latter days of the war Wilson had indicated repeatedly that the German people would be treated with consideration once they had shaken off their military rulers. Yet now, after a revolution had taken place, the Germans had not been represented in oral discussions of the initial formulation of peace terms, which when imposed were humiliating and unnecessarily irritating. Their fatherland had lost its colonies as well as about an eighth of its metropolitan area, which held a tenth of its population. It gave up 10 percent of its industry and more than 15 percent of its arable land. Not everyone remembered that some of the lost territories had been German only as a result of aggression or of enforced partition and therefore could be taken away with justification under Wilson's doctrine.

It seemed that the peacemakers, by and large, had shown scant concern for the recovery of the vanquished nations under democratic governments that might win the respect of the world. Even among the victors there were those who found little hope for an enduring peace in the arrangements made by their political leaders, who had boldly assumed a task that traditionally had been that of professional diplomats. If Germany were to fill the role in Europe's economy that thoughtful men envisioned, it would have to be allowed to regain its own strength; and when it did, it might acquire a position of dominance unless this were prevented by wise diplomacy. It was to become clear, as the years passed, that certain terms of the treaty could not be enforced against a nation so large and so industrially potent as Germany, and many of the provisions were modified or waived.

In giving satisfaction to popular demands the European political chiefs had offended the concept of justice that Wilson had invoked. During his last weeks at Paris the American prophet had continued to proclaim his gospel. In an address to the International Law Society of May 9 he said: "If we can now give to international law the kind of vitality which it can have only if it is a real expression of our moral judgment, we shall have completed in some sense the work which this war was intended to emphasize. . . . In the new League of Nations we are starting out on uncharted seas. . . . In a sense the old enterprise of national law is played out . . . the future of mankind depends more upon the relations of nations to one another, more upon the realization of the common brotherhood of mankind, than upon the separate and selfish development of national systems of law." The next day the Institute of France listened to his eloquent interpretation of "the spirit of the United States." And on Memorial Day, in a memorable oration at the American cemetery at Suresnes, speaking with emotion that was barely controlled, he appealed to the "unspoken mandates of our dead comrades." "The League of Nations," he said, "is the covenant of governments that these men shall not have died in vain." He

---

1. Schwabe, p. 407. Lamont, *Across World Frontiers*, p. 117. On the influence of the Treaty of Versailles on subsequent German history see Raymond A. Sontag, *A Broken World*, pp. 45–60.

looked to the League to settle problems that were still unsolved, but he had a pre-monition that in twenty-five years it would be necessary for the Western powers to go through the same ordeal again, at far greater cost.[2]

Wilson had allowed Europeans to entertain the hope that his nation might share in arranging and defending a practical concert of the great powers. It was by no means certain, however, that he would be able to support the assurance that he had given to his European colleagues in the Supreme Council and that Colonel House, in loyalty and in spite of grave doubts, had affirmed.[3] Possibly he might be unable to convert the unbelievers in America and overcome political opposition to the settlement that a rough-and-ready diplomacy had improvised at Paris. Indeed, Dr. James Brown Scott told his European colleagues on the drafting committee that in his opinion the Senate would not give its consent to American membership in the League.[4] Issues had been raised at Paris that were provoking protests in the United States. Some of these issues were to perplex the American people and embarrass their diplomats during the ensuing years of the century.

In the course of arriving at peace terms, Wilson's moralistic diplomacy had given grievances to associated powers as well as to the enemy. Fissures appeared in rela-tions among the victors that were to grow into rifts such as German diplomats had hoped for. In his stern censure of the expansion which the Italian and Japanese people demanded as a national necessity, the American prophet had made it easier for a resurgent Germany to find sympathetic allies in another bid for domination.

When Wilson left the Peace Conference, many problems of nationality had failed of solutions that presaged peace. The conference had not dealt conclusively with demands of native populations that, often genuinely but sometimes under the manipulation of politicians seeking power, appealed to the principle of self-deter-mination. At Paris various national and minority movements within fallen empires, as well as aspiring Irish and Zionist leaders, had invoked the aid of the major prophet of independence. In some instances Wilson had overstepped the bounds of diplomatic convention in giving comfort to revolutionary elements, despite uncer-tainty as to the willingness of the United States to take responsibility in unstable areas. Allied plans for the governance of the Ottoman lands stood in suspense while there remained a possibility that the United States might be permitted by its Senate to assume mandatory responsibility.

Four days after Wilson's departure from Paris, the heads of the various national delegations held the first of a series of meetings that lasted from July to December. Clemenceau, who lost no time in submitting the Treaty of Versailles to the French chamber, took the lead in a discussion of the future procedure of the Peace Confer-ence. It soon became clear that he wished to maintain under his presidency the five-power council of Heads of Delegations that succeeded the Supreme Council of the war and that of the Peace Conference. At the same time American delegates were

2. Sir William Wiseman to the author, May 1954 and April 22, 1957.
3. Bonsal, *Unfinished Business,* pp. 58–63.
4. Hankey, *The Supreme Control,* pp. 103–104.

inclined to look toward a transfer of responsibility to the League of Nations and to the foreign offices of the various states.[5]

In the month of July the processes of negotiation at Paris came almost to a standstill. On the twelfth, Secretary Lansing went home, convinced that many provisions of the peace treaties were unsound and personally wounded by the president's disdain and by the preferment accorded to Colonel House.[6] However, his efficient nephews remained. On the recommendation of economic advisers who returned with the president, John Foster Dulles became responsible for organizing the reparation commission and for the articles of the various treaties that dealt with finance. His brother Allen served as chairman of the steering committee of the Peace Conference. Officers of the State Department assumed greater responsibility.[7]

General Bliss and Henry White, the only American plenipotentiaries remaining at Paris, met almost daily in the Crillon. Consulting often with Hoover and other advisers, they reviewed the work of the various field commissions and special agents and considered questions of American military and economic involvement in Europe. Several missions were ordered to return. Others remained into the autumn,[8] and American battalions were held in Europe ready to supervise plebiscites that were called for in the peace treaties.

Bliss gave immediate attention to the disposal of war matériel, the repatriation of German and Russian prisoners, and the refusal of requests from the Allies for American troops to share in the occupation of remote territories and for American officers to serve as instructors in foreign armies.[9] He imagined that there would be an opportunity to meet the necessities of the moment in a way that would be practical and effective. "When you negotiate," he explained, "you have to negotiate, that is, to talk, discuss, argue. . . . Now that the president will be in Washington, when we reach a point beyond which discussion will be useless, we can cable to him. His mind will also be made up from our daily telegraphic reports to him and he has had no one to delay the matter by saying that he wants further discussion with him." The general was quickly disillusioned, however. The meetings of the Heads of Delegations produced few propositions for the White House; and, moreover, it became increasingly difficult to get prompt and clear responses from the president.[10]

Meanwhile in July, Frank L. Polk, the undersecretary of state, having received full reports from Lansing on the formal proceedings at Paris, as well as frequent

5. A. W. Dulles to Alexander Kirk, July 22, 1919, A. W. Dulles papers. Dulles wrote: "I feel that the British in general agree with us."

6. Lazo, "A Question of Loyalty: Robert Lansing and the Treaty of Versailles," 40.

7. W. H. Heinrichs, Jr., *American Ambassador,* p. 42.

8. A report of August 9 stated that missions ordered to return were those to the Baltic provinces and to Fiume, as well as the "Ekaterinodar section of the South Russia Mission" and the representative on the inter-Allied subcommission at Poznań. Missions still afield were those at Berlin and Vienna and in Poland, Tiflis, Syria, and the Rhineland, Ammission to State Department, August 9, 1919, N.A., R.G. 763.72119 / 6075.

9. Palmer, *Bliss,* pp. 407–410, 414. Trask, *Bliss,* pp. 63–64, 68.

10. Bliss wrote to Mrs. Bliss on July 17: "Day after day I go to the Quai d'Orsay and hear discussed the same questions that have been discussed time and time again . . . they seem to have a strange reluctance to have a 'show down' . . . time . . . is wasted on subjects that don't in the least concern us," Palmer, p. 408.

messages from House revealing what was going on behind the scenes, engaged in talks at Washington with the president and men who had returned from Paris with him. Dr. Grayson and Baruch explained the difficulties with respect to House, about whom newsmen and others had been circulating derogatory rumors.[11]

John Foster Dulles, the American representative at Paris on the commission for the execution of the treaty, was informed that the president forbade any formal participation by the United States in the work of this body until the Senate ratified the treaty. Subsequent pleas to Lansing for authority to make temporary appointments of Americans to other commissions set up by the Peace Conference brought no constructive response.[12] However, on September 3 the secretary of state went so far as to empower the peace commission at Paris to assent to decisions of the heads of delegations without clearance with Washington.[13]

In July Wilson discussed many issues with Polk, but Wilson seemed disinclined to act on such difficult question as those bearing upon relations with Italy and Japan. Polk was asked to go to France as soon as possible despite the fact that his heart and nerves had been overstrained.[14] He assumed charge of the American delegation on July 28 with little precise guidance from his chiefs. Taking over House's quarters in the Crillon, he met with Bliss and White every Wednesday.[15] He wrote frankly to Ambassador Davis at London: "I had no idea what they were letting me in for when I came over. The full horrors of the situation are being developed day by day. We are short-handed and all the insoluble problems have been apparently left for me to play with and believe me, 'play' is the word."[16] By September 11, the day after a peace treaty with Austria was signed, Polk concluded that the American delegation had fallen into an incurable habit of meddling in many things that were not properly its business and that the sooner they could "shut up shop" and "let Europe paddle its own canoe," the better. He hung on, however, and conducted the business of diplomacy in a way that won the respect of both Americans and Europeans.[17] "Il est tout-à-fait étonnant," said Clemenceau, who had found Lansing impossible as a negotiator.[18]

A few of the scholars remained at Paris to give technical advice, and some continued to be influential in the shaping of policy. House had proposed that most should return to the United States; and Mezes, who left Paris on May 30, recommended that all members of the Intelligence Section be released about May 15, except Professor Haskins and Beer, if he was needed for advice on colonial mat-

11. "Frank [Polk] told me a great deal of irresponsible gossip respecting jealousy of the colonel and his part in the Peace Conference," Auchincloss diary, August 3, 1919, Polk to Lansing, August 12, 1919, Y.H.C. Polk diary, July 3, 9, and 10, 1919.

12. Ammission to the secretary of state, July 19, 1919; H. White papers, L.C., box 43. Ammission to secretary of state, July 20 and 31, 1919, N.A., R.G. 59, 763.72119 / 5712 and 5004. A list of the thirty-five commissions to be set up after the Treaty of Versailles took effect may be found in *F.R., P.P.C.*, vol. 8, pp. 758–759.

13. *F.R., P.P.C.*, vol. 11, p. 640.

14. Auchincloss diary, July 12, 1919, Polk diary, July 10, 11, and 16, 1919, Y.H.C.

15. Bliss diary, July 29 and August 6, 1919.

16. Letters, Polk to John W. Davis, August 6, 20, Sept. 11, 1919, Davis papers, Y.H.C.

17. Joseph C. Grew, *Turbulent Era*, vol. 1, p. 403. Polk admired the tact and judgment of Grew, who continued to serve as secretary of the delegation, Heinrichs, p. 43.

18. Nevins, *White*, p. 460. House diary, June 23, 1919.

ters.[19] The other peace commissioners did not agree with House, however. Lansing, finding that some who were threatened with release were "greatly incensed,"[20] protested to the president that "the whole expert organization" would be "shot to pieces." Wilson upheld this protest. Nevertheless, Bowman went home in May because of family considerations and resumed his work as director of the American Geographical Society. When he returned in October at the request of Wilson, he found the staff of the peace commission depleted daily as men were called off to special tasks in central Europe.[21]

In the course of the complicated business of the Peace Conference, the academic advisers, acting without precedent and with uncertain direction, by and large had justified the president's confidence in them and had furthered the acceptance of his program. Although not always observing an objectivity befitting scholars in an age devoted to "scientific" thinking, and though sometimes unduly impatient with plenipotentiaries who, caught in the swirls of power politics, seemed less than appreciative of their advice, the experts had supplied knowledge that was reliable; and moreover, they had on occasion entered into diplomatic negotiations to good effect. When Bowman and others left Paris in December, their English and French colleagues, whom they had sometimes irritated, came to the railroad station to say farewell and to confess that without the presence of the Americans at the Peace Conference worse settlements would have been made.[22]

The president returned to Washington in July with confidence that when he explained to his people the indispensability of the League of Nations to the peace of the world, the opponents in the Senate would be forced by popular pressure to capitulate. As the snowball of opposition rolled, he did not take advantage of House's genius for conciliation of adversaries. House, perceiving that he could no longer be useful at Paris, remained for a few weeks in England, carrying out a mission that Wilson specifically entrusted to him—the development of plans for the operations of the League of Nations at Geneva. When he returned to New York, he was too ill for a while to go to Washington to make his characteristic "moves on the board" in

19. Report from Mezes to the president, May 5, 1919, Y.H.C. House wrote in his diary on May 5: "I have been busy too arranging to cut down our force so that some of our experts may return to America." Seymour wrote on May 14 that it was proposed that "six of us should go home this week," Seymour, *Letters from the Paris, Peace Conference,* p. 227. A fotonote adds: "The story that the six signers of the letter of April 17 about Fiume [see above, p. 342] were being punished was subsequently denied by both House and Mezes." However, the denial was not convincing to Day, memorandum of May 23, Inquiry correspondence, Y.H.C. Beer, who shared the views of House and Mezes on the question of Fiume, recorded that they were "furious at the letter" signed by the six, Beer diary, April 29, May 9, 1919. Bowman, one of the six, felt that the scholars had a grievance, Birdsall, *Versailles Twenty Years After,* pp. 280–282; Birdsall-Bowman correspondence; letter, Bowman to Buckler, March 10, 1919, Bowman papers, Johns Hopkins University Library.

In a memorandum written later "for the record," Bowman testified that House had spoken to him about the possibility of his becoming secretary-general of the League of Nations. Bowman suggested that House did this in an effort to dissuade him from signing the protest of the six scholars, Geoffrey J. Martin, *The Life and Thought of Isaiah Bowman,* pp. 94–95.

20. Lansing to Polk, July 26, 1919, Y.H.C.

21. Bowman to Buckler, March 10, 1949, Buckler papers, Y.H.C. Bowman to John Greenough, October 16, 1919, G. J. Martin's Bowman papers.

22. Martin, p. 97.

behalf of ratification of the treaty. Nevertheless, he did his utmost to reach an understanding with Senator Lodge, as did Lord Grey, whom House persuaded to undertake a special mission to Washington in the absence of any British ambassador there. The president was not permitted to know of these efforts, however, and without access to the White House they were fruitless. The estrangement of Wilson from the European governments, against which House had guarded at Paris, became irrevocable and beyond the ministration of diplomats.

Noting the loss of influence that House had suffered, Americans who remained at Paris hesitated to act decisively without specific authorization from the White House. The prospect for continuing economic cooperation with the Allies was clouded; American troops were withdrawing rapidly; the Senate was delaying action on the Treaty of Versailles; and the United States Treasury was insisting on business as usual.

Meanwhile the president was unable to rally to his cause a people who were withdrawing from their crusade in Europe into the pursuits of "normalcy." As the new structure of peace crumbled, Wilson, failing to use his limited strength wisely in negotiation with the Senate, indulged in a polemical appeal to the people of the western states. However, he no longer commanded the powers of leadership that he had wielded to good effect in earlier political campaigns. Under the delusion that his waning eloquence could overcome the indifference of his constituency to the danger of remote and future war, the ailing prophet was unable to transmute the pioneer work accomplished at Paris into a effective political force for the keeping of the world's peace. Surrendering to grim fatalism, he gave the *coup de grâce* to any step toward fulfillment of his vision rather than accept a compromise that might seem to savor of surrender to a political foe.

23

Peace for Southeastern Europe: St. Germain, Trianon, and Neuilly

When the Treaty of Versailles was signed at the end of June, no settlement had been made with Austria-Hungary. The Hapsburg monarchy had undergone a fragmentation that had been blessed by Wilson's wartime propaganda, and during the first half of 1919 some of the fragments showed propensities that threatened to make warfare among them chronic. Each was jealous of its national identity and, despite admonitions from the Peace Conference, quick to use such military force as it could muster to support its claims to territory. Moreover, barriers appeared against the flow of trade that had been maintained within the imperial establishment.

Spokesmen of the several emancipated nationalities argued that it would be unjust to impose on them the same penalties that were to be put upon Austria and Hungary, which as the ruling states in the Dual Monarchy might be expected to bear full shares of responsibility for the consequences of the war. At the same time Austrian officials pleaded that German Austria was only one of several fragments of the Hapsburg estate and should be treated just as the others. Austrians were not invited to negotiate at Paris, however, until the case against them had been well prepared by delegates of the successor states that had been admitted to the peacemaking councils.

The United States in effect affirmed the dissolution of the old empire by recognizing the governments of Poland, Czechosolvakia, and Yugoslavia. The American delegates wished to give to each of these successor states a population and an economy that would minimize its inclination to go to war, and a frontier that would make it difficult for its neighbors to make war upon it. Wilson could be expected to encourage the forming of a "regional understanding" under the sanction of the League of Nations. In the critical month of April, however, he did not pursue the recommendation of Smuts for military control of the new states and a convening of their delegates in a conference that might bring economic interchanges of mutual benefit. Actually, the successor states themselves, whose peoples exulted in their emancipation from imperial restraints, had shown little interest in reaching a general understanding. The Americans were disappointed. Hoover warned that unless a customs union was maintained among Austria, Hungary, and Czechoslovakia, the great powers might find that instead of collecting something by way of reparation they would have to assume the expenses of relief for starving people.[1]

On February 22, House and Lansing had suggested that the Peace Conference "proceed without delay to the consideration of preliminary peace terms with Aus-

---

1. Memorandum from Hoover and N. H. Davis for the president, June 14, 1919, Davis papers, box 11. Seymour, *Letters from the Paris Peace Conference*, p. 148.

tria-Hungary."[2] Professor Coolidge had reported from his post of observation at Vienna that the Austrians put faith in Wilson and his doctrine of self-determination and that they were willing to submit to the loss of lands where other nationalities predominated. They were said to ask merely to retain continguous territory where German was spoken, with only such slight adjustments as might be necessary for economic reasons.[3] It was not until late in April, however, a month after Hungary had fallen under the rule of Béla Kun, that it was suggested in the Supreme Council that Austrians should be invited to the Peace Conference to receive terms for what was called, to save face, an "agreed" and not an "imposed" peace.[4] On April 28, a day on which the maintainance of order at Vienna had become so difficult that the police of the city put a ban on public assemblies,[5] the American fellow commissioners of Wilson addressed a letter to him in which they stated that the situation in the Austrian capital was critical. It was recommended that Austrian delegates be allowed to appear at Paris at once to present their case, since this gesture might be expected to stiffen resistance to communism at Vienna.[6]

On May 12 an Austrian delegation departed from Vienna, reaching Paris two days later. During the ensuing three weeks the Peace Conference managed to agree upon only incomplete terms for Austria, omitting military and reparation clauses. The tentative provisions were given to the delegates in the old castle at St. Germain on June 2.

In dealing with the Austrians the Peace Conference fell naturally into the sort of hasty and uncoordinated action that had thrown together terms for the Germans. In this case, however, the enemy was kept waiting longer. The Council of Four, having less knowledge of the details of the complex questions to be settled, was more inclined to seek expert advice. On May 8, when the arrival of the Austrian delegates was imminent, Wilson reminded his colleagues that it would be necessary to assure the compliance of all parties affected; and he proposed that the Austrian and "the other" treaties contain a clause recognizing the frontiers of all states of the old Austro-Hungarian monarchy as approved by the League of Nations. However, he accepted an amendment by Lloyd George, substituting "the allied and associated powers" for the embryonic League. The essential thing was to maintain their own authority. Otherwise, Wilson said, they would not be able to settle the still more difficult question of the frontiers of Russia.[7]

As a first step in the colossal task of drawing boundaries between the new states, Wilson suggested that they ask the Council of Foreign Ministers to bring in recommendations with respect to the boundaries already determined by the territorial committees. Accordingly, the foreign ministers undertook to consider, that very afternoon, questions bearing on the frontiers of Hungary as well as those of Austria,

2. *F.R., P.P.C.*, vol. 4, pp. 96–97.
3. Letter, Coolidge to Ammission, January 8, 1919, Y.H.C.
4. Mantoux, *Délibérations*, vol. 1, pp. 384–385. Almond and Lutz, *The Treaty of St. Germain*, pp. 38, 236.
5. Dispatch, Coolidge to Ammission, April 28, 1919, Wilson papers.
6. Letter in Wilson papers
7. Mantoux, *Délibérations*, vol. 2, p. 7.

in spite of the failure of the Peace Conference to invite Béla Kun's government to send representatives to Paris.

The southern frontier of Austria had become the scene of violent conflict. Serb regulars and Slovene irregulars had moved to occupy parts of Styria and of Carinthia; and although in Styria the French military command managed to impose a line, Allied officers were unsuccessful in attempts to draw a definitive boundary in Carinthia, where hostilities had begun in the basin of Klagenfurt in December and flared up again at the end of April.

Americans had become involved in this altercation in January. Coolidge, eager to put an end to bloodshed and responding to appeals from both parties, sent Colonel Miles from Vienna to investigate. Arranging an armistice, Miles persuaded both sides first to consent to arbitration and then to agree in writing to accept a division of the region pending a decision by the Peace Conference. However, the Yugoslav government protested through the Serbian minister at Paris against this *démarche;* and the American plenipotentiaries at Paris, embarrassed by this action that had been undertaken without their authorization, unanimously refused to give Coolidge the confirmation that he requested. They forbade him to let it be known that Americans had suggested even a temporary settlement.[8]

Actually, the truce arranged by the Americans was soon broken. In mid-March officers of the Allies were in the troubled area, and the French and Italians were acting in accord with the partisan policies of their governments toward the two states concerned.[9] In the Commission on Rumanian and Yugoslav Affairs, which reported to the Supreme Council on April 6, the British and French delegates were at first inclined to award a part of the Klagenfurt basin to Yugoslavia. However, they were urged by their scholarly American colleagues to accept the fact that this district, inhabited by a mixed population whose national aspirations could not be determined with certainty at the moment, was "a geographic entity" whose economic interests were more closely connected with the districts situated to the north than with those to the south.[10]

8. A. W. Dulles to Walter Davis, February 26, 1919, A. W. Dulles papers, box 6. Dispatch, Ammission to State Department, February 26, 1919, N.A. R.G. 59, 72119 / 3900. Minutes, ACTNP, January 30, 1919, L. Harrison papers, L.C. The American military officers sent to Klagenfurt were accompanied by Professor Robert J. Kerner, a scholar familiar with the Slovene language who as a member of the Inquiry studied the prospects of a Yugoslav state. He dissented from the proposal of the military men to divide the disputed basin. Concluding that it was impossible to draw a line that would satisfy both the wishes of the inhabitants and the demands of ethnology, natural geography, and economics, he recommended the assignment of the basin to the Yugoslavs, with a frontier on the Drava River, Gelfand, *The Inquiry*, pp. 218–921. Lederer, *Yugoslavia at the Paris Peace Conference*, pp. 220–221. H. J. Coolidge and R. H. Lord, *Archibald Cary Coolidge*, pp. 205, 207. Albrecht-Carrié, *Italy at the Paris Peace Conference*, pp. 164 ff., 194 ff., 302–303. Copies of the reports to the American commission are in the Y.H.C.

9. Dispatches from Belgrade (Dodge), forwarded in Ammission to the secretary of state, March 3 and 16, 1919, N.A., R.G. 59, 763.72119 / 13052 and 763.72 / 13087. In general, the French wanted to strengthen Yugoslavia, the Italians to weaken it, Frazier to Seymour, October 26, 1939, Seymour papers, Y.H.C. Dispatch, Allizé to Ministre des Affaires Étrangères, May 3, 1919, Archives du M.A.É., À paix, A1056.1.

10. Almond and Lutz, pp. 504–505.
Seymour and Day found that 170,000 people in the Klagenfurt basin spoke German and 70,000,

During May and June the question of the Austrian-Yugoslav boundary became one of political bargaining in which the positions taken by the Yugoslav and Italian delegates were related to their quarrel over the fate of Fiume. Moreover, the demand of Italy for efficient railway service from Trieste to Vienna had to be considered. The main line, passing through Assling, penetrated territory where, in Wilson's opinion, the population was predominantly Slavic. He refused Italy's demand for a boundary that would give it absolutely untrammeled control of this railway and that would prevent its use as a military threat to Italian territory. At the same time, he agreed to an adjustment of the Treaty of London that would award the Sexten Valley and Tarvis to Italy. This made it possible for rail traffic to pass directly from Italian to Austrian soil over a route to the west of the main line, a route that the Italians thought to be of inadequate capacity and too circuitous for economical operation. Clemenceau and Lloyd George concurred in this arrangement.[11]

After making a direct appeal to Clemenceau on May 18, the Yugoslavs at Paris modified their demands with respect to Carinthia.[12] Meanwhile, the fighting in Klagenfurt became chronic. Coolidge reported that Austria was in possession of practically all of the district. Later, sending word that negotiations between the antagonists had been broken off, he urged that they be ordered by the Peace Conference to maintain the status quo or to respect some other division. On May 28 he telegraphed that he had been in Carinthia, incognito, and had found "intense feeling" against Americans.[13] Despite an order on May 31 from the Supreme Council that the fighting must cease and the armies depart from the region, the offending parties continued to defy the Peace Conference; and in mid-June Italian troops entered the fray on the side of the Austrians.

Wilson gave close scrutiny to this issue and heeded the advice of Seymour, who insisted upon the award of Carinthia to Austria as recommended by the Commission on Rumanian and Yugoslav Affairs.[14] With his colleague Day, Seymour undertook to uphold the principles of political science against what they perceived to be political expediency. They first engaged in a spirited argument with Johnson, and having persuaded him (according to Seymour's record) that they should refuse "the worst of the Yugoslav demands," argued in the committee of specialists against the united Europeans. The French and the British delegates, sharing House's hope that by humoring the Yugoslav government they might make it more conciliatory on the question of Fiume, characterized the dissent of the American professors as obstin-

Slovene. The mission sent to Carinthia in January by Coolidge reported that the greater part of the Slovene-speaking population was opposed to incorporation in Yugoslavia, memorandum to the American commissioners, May 22, 1919, Y.H.C.

11. *F.R., P.P.C.*, vol. 4, pp. 503–504. Mantoux, *Délibérations,* vol. 2, p. 342. A map showing the railways in dispute may be found in Albrecht-Carrié, p. 165.

12. Lederer, pp. 222–223.

13. Dispatches, Coolidge to Ammission, May 16 and 28, 1919, Wilson papers.

14. Seymour wrote on May 14, "Wilson looks tired but has not lost his debonair manner or good humor in debate. . . . Wilson was very genial to me, when I explained the various points of importance, and contrary to our fears raised no objections. The president is temperamental. At times, . . . he works regardless of any advice. . . . At other times he accepted absolutely the advice given him by the men who he thinks are capable and objective," *Letters from the Paris Peace Conference,* p. 226.

acy. It seemed to Nicolson that Lansing, arguing "with great virulence," was definitely "rude."[15]

When on May 27 the territorial committee met with the Council of Four, Wilson said that it would be a grave mistake to divide the basin now and thus accept an unnatural arrangement that might build pressure that would invalidate any plebiscite.[16] Two days later he called in the experts and announced what the chiefs had decided. There was to be a plebiscite in the basin of Klagenfurt, for which the experts were now asked to provide specifications. All those present, the great men and their advisers, got down on hands and knees to examine maps while Wilson pointed out the lines.[17]

When the Yugoslavs occupied Klagenfurt and seized war matériel that though in Austrian hands belonged to the Allies, and after the Supreme Council issued its ineffective order that the contending armies withdraw from the basin, Wilson called House away from a dinner party on June 1 to discuss the matter. The colonel, noting the division of opinion among the experts and not sure which view was right, found his chief as unyielding as in respect of the Adriatic settlement. Later in the evening House had a call from a Yugoslav spokesman, who said that unless his government received satisfaction in Carinthia, it would not send representatives to the meeting on the next day at St. Germain at which the terms were to be given to the Austrians.[18] House met the crisis by reminding the Yugoslavs that the Italians had played this game to no avail, and by suggesting that the Yugoslavs would do well to attend the meeting with the Austrians, which would be only tentative, and to submit reservations in writing.[19] The next day this advice was accepted and acted upon.

15. *Ibid.* pp. 240–241, 245. "House . . . cares more about establishing a compromise between Italy and Yugoslavia than he does about a good frontier for Austria," *ibid.*, p. 267. Nicolson, *Peacemaking, 1919*, pp. 330–331.

The three American specialists resolved to write separate memoranda to their chiefs. Memorandum, Johnson to the American commissioners, n.d., Wilson papers. Johnson based his case mainly on political considerations, apprehension of an "advancing German wave" moving southward, and compensation to Yugoslavia for losses of territory to Italy. "Memorandum to the Am. Comm'rs," from Dr. Day, May 21, 1919, with a notation in shorthand; memorandum, Day and Seymour, to "The Commissioners," May 22, 1919, Y.H.C. The three scholars joined in drafting a "statement of facts" in respect of their disagreement, Almond and Lutz, pp. 505–508.

Seymour and Day had the support of Coolidge and also that of Colonel Miles, the leader of the mission to Carinthia in January. Miles wrote a memorandum to the president on May 22 by which, according to Seymour, Wilson was "strongly affected," Seymour, p. 246. The president commended it to the Council of Four on May 26. Miles's four-page paper, submitted "by direction of Colonel House," is in the Wilson papers, with a map.

16. Mantoux, *Délibérations*, vol. 2, pp. 235–236. F.R., P.P.C., vol. 6, pp. 72, 102, 105–106.

17. Seymour, p. 250.

18. After the details of the draft treaty had become known to the Yugoslavs at the plenary session on May 31, they reacted strongly not only against leaving the question of Klagenfurt open, but against an article designed to protect minorities in the states succeeding Austria-Hungary. See below, p. 475. They argued that such a clause encroached on the sovereignty of Serbia, an ally, Lederer, p. 225. The concerted pressure of the Yugoslavs upon the American delegates was exerted in a letter of June 1 from Vesnić to House. White to Wilson, June 1, 1919, Wilson papers.

19. House diary, June 1 and 3, 1919. Lederer, pp. 225–226. Probably the yielding of the Yugoslavs was facilitated by the fact that the British and French governments, which had implied their recognition of the new state of the Serbs, Croats, and Slovenes by accepting their credentials for admission to the meeting with the Germans on May 7, now extended formal recognition to the Yugoslav state—Great

Immediately after the meeting at St. Germain on June 2, Wilson took up the question of a plebiscite with his advisers and then reported to Clemenceau and Lloyd George that the Americans objected to voting by communes because it might result in the splintering of a region that was an economic and geographic unit centering on the railway junction of Klagenfurt. The two Europeans thought they should hear Vesnić on the subject, although Clemenceau had rejected an appeal from Renner of Austria for a hearing.[20] Vesnić presented his case at great length on June 4, raising the fearsome ogre of pan-Germanism and asking that reduced claims of Yugoslavia be granted without a plebiscite that would prolong the uncertainty and retard the consolidation of the new state.[21]

Wilson laughed at the prospect that he would receive blame "for holding things up."[22] In view of the positive stand of Coolidge, Miles, Seymour, and Day, he did not accept a Yugoslav proposal that Johnson brought to him orally on the morning of the fourth and that had British approval.[23] Instead he presented to the Council of Four a plan for dividing the disputed area into two zones substantially as the Yugoslavs suggested, but with provision for a plebiscite in the southern zone and, if the outcome favored Yugoslavia, a plebiscite in the northern zone. He recommended that the first take place in six months, so that there would be little time for intrigue and pressure on the voters; but he was willing, if the Yugoslavs so desired, to extend the time to three years and put the region under an international commission. In his opinion the only way to close the mouths of critics was to say: "Let the peoples judge."[24] Wilson's solution met objections on all sides. The Yugoslavs found it not entirely to their liking; the Austrians protested with vigor; nor were the American specialists fully satisfied.[25]

In the middle of June the Council of Four was at a loss to cope with the military situation in the disputed region. In response to an appeal from the Austrian delegates at Paris,[26] a commission of army officers was sitting at Klagenfurt to consider ways of enforcing a truce. The American member sent word to Paris that definite instructions from the Peace Conference were needed if the troubled area were to be effectively and objectively policed. Article IV of the Armistice of Villa Giusti gave to Italy a right to protect the routes to Vienna; and Orlando went so far as to order the Italian army to occupy the railway line in Carinthia up to St. Viet.[27]

A refined plan, arrived at by the Commission on Rumanian and Yugoslav Affairs,

Britain on June 1, and France on June 5, Mantoux, *Délibérations*, vol. 2, pp. 262, 385, 411. Almond and Lutz, p. 254.

20. Mantoux, *Délibérations*, vol. 2, p. 265. Marston, *The Peace Conference of 1919*, p. 209.
21. Mantoux, *Délibérations*, vol. 2, pp. 296–299.
22. Seymour, p. 257.
23. Johnson to Wilson, June 1 and 4, 1919, and memorandom and map, Wilson papers.
24. *F.R., P.P.C.,* vol. 6, pp. 173–180.
25. Almond and Lutz, pp. 280–285. Seymour, *Letters*, p. 268.
26. *F.R., P.P.C.,* vol. 6, p. 46.
27. Orlando to Wilson, June 10, 1919, Wilson papers. Orlando to Clemenceau, June 10, 1919, F.C., 6N76, "Italie." Pasić to Wilson, June 19, 1919, Wilson papers. Temperley, *A History of the Peace Conference at Paris,* vol. 4, pp. 370–371, 392. Albrecht-Carrié, p. 196. Lederer, p. 224.
  The Four attempted to put the question on the backs of the foreign ministers, *F.R., P.P.C.,* vol. 6, pp. 189, 234, vol. 4, pp. 835–837, 840–841. Seymour, p. 272. Day to Mrs. Day, June 18, 1919, Y.H.C.

called for the assignment of a southern zone (A) in Carinthia to Yugoslavia and for a plebiscite to be held there, and of a northern zone (B) to Austria with another plebiscite. Both zones were to be placed under the control of an international commission.[28] Voting in zone A on October 20, 1920, favored Austria about three to two, even though a large majority of the voters were Slovene-speaking. It was therefore deemed unnecessary to hold a plebiscite in order to justify Austrian rule of zone B.

The fixing of the financial responsibility of the various fragments of the Hapsburg empire was as difficult as the making of territorial provisions. The victors, and particularly Italy, hoped for some compensation for losses. John Foster Dulles observed that although the capacity of the new governments to make any cash payment was "almost nil," their "ability to make deferred payments should be very material in view of their basic economic resources" and the possibility of such payments could be estimated.[29] The principle that the Americans had applied to the financial reckoning with Germany was to apply also to the case of Austria-Hungary: indemnities were to be "essentially compensatory" and not punitive.[30] The reckoning for states such as Yugoslavia, which had been in part allies and in part foes, was particularly perplexing.

The commission on reparations of the Peace Conference received on May 6 a joint declaration from financial advisers of the new states. It demanded direct inheritance by their governments of all property of the old empire and disclaimed any responsibility for its financial obligations. The pleaders for these nations desired a share of the relatively large German reparation payments and therefore advocated the creation of a joint Allied fund to which all of the enemy states would contribute.[31] The Council of Four was confronted by this demand on May 10.

Wilson's opinion was that the successor states (except Poland, which had suffered conspicuously from acts of the Central Powers) should assume part of the responsibility of Austria-Hungary for reparation of damage, though not for its war debt. This view was accepted and communicated to the experts. The commission on reparations was instructed to estimate the amount that could be paid by "the whole group of states comprised in the old Austro-Hungarian Empire" and then "make recommendations as to the shares of the total sum to be paid by the several states, taking into consideration their pre-war liabilities as well as their means of payment."[32]

Meanwhile, the American economic advisers took an independent position. Thomas W. Lamont informed the president of this just before the Council of Four met on

28. "Basin de Klagenfurt," n.d., a five-page report from Tardieu to the Drafting Committee, stating decisions taken by the Commission on Rumanian and Yugoslav Affairs, Y.H.C.

29. Memorandum by J. F. Dulles, January 9, 1919, in Burnett, *Reparation*, vol. 1, p. 502.

30. "A Preliminary Memorandum upon Indemnities," addressed to Miller and Scott by Frank L. Warrin, Jr., Miller, *My Diary*, vol. 3, p. 112.

31. Lederer, p. 229.

32. Letter, Hankey to Cunliffe, May 12, 1919, Wilson papers. *F.R., P.P.C.*, vol. 5, pp. 581–582. Mantoux, *Délibérations*, vol. 2, pp. 37–38. Burnett, vol. 1, pp. 275–276.

May 22. He argued that the sum that could be charged against the new states seemed negligible and yet might reduce credit facilities in these nations to a degree that would jeopardize their economic life and create serious political difficulties. This view was also that of Smuts and of Keynes.[33]

In reporting their dissent to The Four, the Americans remarked that some of the new states, fearing that their difficulties in establishing credit would increase, were talking of refusing to sign the treaty and that therefore they should not be pressed. However, when Lloyd George vigorously insisted that the new states should not escape a reckoning and thus put a heavier burden on the Allies, Wilson conceded that the prime minister was right "in principle." The president said that there was no question of exemption, but only one of making known as soon as possible just what the liability was. The reparation commission was to proceed in the light of this discussion. Lamont insisted that the United States should withhold loans if they were to be applied to payment of reparations, and the president upheld him.

Lamont talked with Beneš, whom he found "very fair-minded," and with other delegates of the new states; and he was encouraged to accept a compromise that Lloyd George devised.[34] On the fourth of June, Lamont presented to The Four a formula that had been accepted by the Czechs. The new states, he explained, were willing to contribute to the costs of the war but refused to pay "reparations" because they did not wish to be included among those who were responsible for the conflict. The difficulty was to fix the amounts. It was important to avoid a general bankruptcy in these states.[35] This consideration became acute when, after the publication of the incomplete conditions of peace that were handed to the Austrians on June 2, business in Vienna was depressed by a prevailing belief that enforcement of these terms would precipitate failures of banks, a consequent crumbling of credit, and a turn to bolshevism.[36]

The exceedingly complex computation of credits and liabilities, and of a final balance for each of the states concerned, occupied the experts for several weeks. Finally, on June 27, the day before Wilson's departure from Paris, Loucheur reported

33. Handwritten letter, Lamont to Wilson, May 22, 1919, covering another letter of that date, Wilson papers. McCormick diary, May 22, 1919. Smuts to Lloyd George, Lloyd George to Smuts, May 26, 1919, Smuts to Lloyd George, May 27, 1919, Lloyd George papers, F / 45 / 9 / 36 and F / 45 / 9 / 38. Harrod, *Keynes,* p. 251.

34. Lamont's "memorandum as to work—May 26 to May 30," Lamont papers, 169—9. Lamont to Burnett, June 25, 1934, Lamont papers, 85—11, in which Lamont wrote: "I went to Mr. Lloyd George personally and told him that I had discovered a great fellow in Beneš and that he had better take him up and use him. I told Lloyd George that Beneš was very liberal minded and very constructive in his ideas. Lloyd George was quick as a cat. He took up Beneš and never dropped him," letter, Lamont to Wilson, May 30, 1919, Wilson papers. McCormick diary, May 27, 28, and 29, 1919. Mantoux, *Délibérations,* vol. 2, pp. 289–290.

35. Mantoux, *Délibérations,* vol. 2, pp. 231–233, 290–295.

36. Dispatch to the State Department from Vienna, June 14, 1919, Wilson papers. McCormick diary, May 27, 28, and 29, 1919. Hancock and Vauder Poel (eds.), *Smuts,* vol. 4, p. 989. Harrod, p. 252. Almond and Lutz, pp. 204–208.

Hoover described the situation in Austria as "almost hopeless." Without any "consequential industry" and with no financial institution "within calling distance of solvency," the country seemed to him "a sort of hot house plant that simply cannot be made self-supporting," Hoover to Lamont, May 24, 1919, Lamont papers, 169—9. See Perman, *The Shaping of the Czechoslovak State,* p. 197.

to the Council of Four that he and John Foster Dulles had agreed on credits that in the aggregate amounted to a maximum of 2 billion francs against damages amounting to 20 billion francs. They recommended, however, that no bills be presented, because the part each of the victorious powers would receive would be relatively insignificant and because of the critical condition of the finances of the various states. Lloyd George and Clemenceau accepted the recommendation. Wilson, speaking for the first time at the end of this session, proposed that the states be told that they must accept this decision or else be treated as enemies under the treaty with Austria.[37] The financial clauses embodied the recommendations of the economic advisers in respect of "the proportion and nature of the financial obligations of the former Austrian Empire" that each state would assume "on account of the territory placed under its sovereignty." This was one of the considerations that made the new successor states slow to sign the Treaty of St. Germain.[38]

The financial and reparation clauses for Austria were discussed with the experts of that nation in accord with a decision of the Supreme Council on May 26 and were not presented to the Austrian delegates until July 20. Under them the new republic was required to make payments over a period of thirty years on terms similar to those imposed on Germany. The fixing of final figures and arrangements for transfer were left to the reparation commission that was to be appointed. Cautioned by Austrian Notes to avoid exactions of such severity as further to disrupt the delicate mechanism of credit that had its center at Vienna and ramified through the economic life of the old empire, the Peace Conference replied that it was aware of the danger of anarchy of which the Austrians warned but thought its terms justifiable. Austria had to pay reparations, make deliveries of goods stolen, and grant tariff concessions; but the economic burdens placed on it were lighter than those imposed on Germany. Nevertheless, runaway inflation ensued and to avoid anarchy the Austrian government had to resort to a beneficent form of receivership under the League of Nations.[39]

During the drafting and reconsideration of the terms for Austria the Americans made disinterested efforts to treat this "residue" state not as an enemy but as a political unit whose independence and prosperity was as vital as the welfare of the new states to the peace of Europe. Their devotion to this purpose was encouraged by the sensible and conciliatory attitude taken by Chancellor Renner when he received the tentative draft of terms on June 2.[40]

37. *F.R., P.P.C.,* vol. 6, p. 718. Mantoux, *Délibérations,* vol. 2, pp. 543. The development of the specific recommendations of the American economic advisers is summarized in Burnett, vol. 1, pp. 310–314.

38. Almond and Lutz, pp. 141–143. Romania and Yugoslavia did not sign the Treaty of St. Germain on September 10, but later signed declarations of adherence, the former on December 9 and the latter on December 5, 1919, *ibid.,* pp. 502, 561n. Hungary became a signatory when it signed the Treaty of Trianon on June 4, 1920.

39. *F.R., P.P.C.,* vol. 6, pp. 636–637. Notes exchanged between the Austrian delegates and the Peace Conference after the incomplete terms were presented on June 2 and before the signing of the Treaty of St. Germain on September 10. Almond and Lutz, pp. 100–101, 204–209, 225–231.

40. R. S. Baker's journal, June 2, 1919.

Lansing characterized Renner's speech at St. Germain as "humble and adroit," and observed the appropriateness of the pictures of prehistoric and extinct animals that decorated the walls of the confer-

Seymour, who among the Americans had taken the major responsibility for the delineation of the boundaries of Austria and who returned to the United States with the president at the end of June, recognized with regret the impossibility of effecting a statesmanlike reconstruction. "Taken in all its provisions," he wrote prophetically, "the Austrian treaty . . . seems to us impossible. . . . Personally I see no way of preventing the union of these people with Germany except the creation of a Danubian confederation, and that is out of the question because of the hostility of the various component parts of the old Austro-Hungarian monarchy."[41]

The Council of Four was overwhelmed in June by details that arose from the necessity of concluding the peace with Germany promptly. On July 1, in the initial meeting of the new Council of Heads of Delegations, Secretary Lansing proposed that additional committees that were contemplated be established at once. Coolidge already had been chosen to represent the United States on the committee on frontiers.[42] During his months at Vienna he had become fully aware of the justness of many of the petitions of the new republic. He was not in sympathy with the concessions that had been made to Yugoslavia in the Klagenfurt basin and hoped that Austria might be compensated by a revision of the boundary that had been drawn for Styria and that deprived Austria of Radkersburg and Maribor. Coolidge succeeded in getting a reversal of the earlier decision to give Radkersburg to Yugoslavia. For a time it seemed that, with the support of his English and Italian colleagues on the committee, a plebiscite might be arranged for Styria, but an Italian *faux pas* upset this plan.[43]

The Heads of Delegations agreed to ask advice from the experts in respect of an Austrian challenge regarding its frontier with Hungary. Coolidge presented evidence that had convinced him of the validity of a claim of Austria to the Burgenland, "the kitchen garden of Vienna," where the population was largely German-speaking. His recommendations were accepted almost in full in July 7, and Austria thus "redeemed" almost as many of its people as were lost in the Tyrol.[44] Nevertheless, the Austrians continued to plead for the redemption of the lands south of the Brenner Pass that Wilson had impulsively conceded to Italy.

Coolidge endeavored to respond to a plea of Austria for a change in its boundary

---

ence room, desk diary, June 2, 1919. Wilson thought the speech in pleasing contrast to that of Brockdorff-Rantzau at Versailles, Sweetser diary, June 2, 1919.

41. Seymour, *Letters from the Paris Peace Conference*, pp. 269–272. Nicolson realized, and recorded, the brutality of the operation that the peacemakers were obliged to perform. He wrote: "The whole economic and transport structure of the Austro-Hungarian Empire had, for instance, been devised to cut across lines of nationality: many economic sinews, some arteries even, had thus to be severed; yet this necessity was unavoidable, and amply realized at the time," *Peacemaking, 1919,* pp. 126–127.

42. Coolidge was now the American member of the Central Territorial Committee and of special territorial committees on which Seymour and Day had served. Coolidge also sat upon the Committee on New States and on June 22 was appointed to a committee of five that was to examine Austrian Notes and formulate replies, Coolidge and Lord, pp. 216–233. Grew to A. C. Coolidge, July 2 and 3, 1919, Coolidge papers, Harvard Archives, HUG1299.5. Coolidge departed from Paris on September 4.

43. Coolidge and Lord, pp. 224–225.

44. Francis Deák, *Hungary at the Paris Peace Conference,* pp. 87–98. Coolidge and Lord, pp. 225–226. Marston, p. 198 and n. 59. The award of the Burgenland to Austria was an obstacle to the creation of a Czech corridor from Pressburg to Trieste, desired by Italy.

with Czechoslovakia, which the Commission on Czechoslovak Affairs had set on the historic line between the old administrative districts of Austria-Hungary, with slight adjustments in favor of Czechoslovakia.[45] Secretary Lansing, irritated by this appeal from what he considered to be the "mass of covetous and quarrelsome nations" into which the Hapsburg empire had disintegrated,[46] asked the president whether he wished to make alterations in the frontier for ethnographic reasons; and Wilson replied: "The greatest caution should be exercised, especially in a certain district in Bohemia, for example, which is undoubtedly predominantly German in population but which lies within the undoubted historic boundaries of Bohemia and constitutes an integral part of her industrial life. In such circumstances ethnographic lines cannot be drawn without the greatest injustice and injury." He agreed to alteration only when it could be "without such injury."[47] He was reluctant to change the decision with respect to the Bohemian border that had been taken after full deliberation by the Commission on Czechoslovak Affairs. Coolidge was instructed to insist upon the historical boundary of Bohemia and to attempt to satisfy Austria. Under a compromise suggested by Tardieu the territory that had been taken from Austria at Gmünd was reduced, leaving the historic frontier only very slightly changed.[48]

Thus, at last, the president confessed the inadequacy of his great weapon of propaganda as a principle on which to found the making of a durable peace. He had learned much about the statescraft of Europe. What he now knew, however, could not be easily explained to those Americans who were kindred and ardent partisans of many European minorities that he had enchanted, in the stress of war, with his undiscriminating advocacy of liberty and self-determination.

The final text of the treaty was given to Chancellor Renner on September 2, and he was allowed seven days in which to respond.[49] When his people were convinced that no further concessions could be won, their National Assembly voted on September 6 in favor of signing. The ceremony was at St. Germain on the tenth.[50] Afterward Renner spoke appreciatively of the fairness of the Americans in contrast with the attitude of the Continental Allies, who were moved by wartime enmity and a vital concern for their national interests. Actually, by the treaty Austria was deprived of its outlet to the sea and lost some 4 million German Austrians; and it was forbidden to enter an *Anschluss* with Germany that might help it to escape the economic strangulation that its people envisioned.[51]

The Treaty of St. Germain was not submitted to the United States Senate, and not

45. Perman, pp. 199–203. The decision of the Commission on Czechoslovak Affairs, approved by the Council of Foreign Ministers on May 8, was confirmed by the Supreme Council of Ten on May 12.

46. Lansing's private memorandum, June 21, 1919.

47. Letter, Wilson to Lansing, June 25, 1919; telegrams, Lansing to Wilson, June 30, 1919, Wilson to Lansing, July 2, 1919, Wilson papers, Perman, pp. 205–207.

48. Perman, pp 207–210. Almond and Lutz, pp. 467–471.

49. Ammission to the State Department, September 7, 1919, N.A., R.G. 59, 763.72119 / 6549.

50. Also signed at St. Germain on September 10 were a convention revising the Acts of Brussels and Berlin, a convention regulating traffic in liquor in Africa, a convention controlling commerce in arms and munitions, and certain treaties for the protection of racial minorities (see below, p. 475, and *F.R.*, *P.P.C.*, vol. 13, pp. 822–830).

51. A summary of terms of the Treaty of St. Germain may be found in Bowman, *The New World*, pp. 312–313.

until July 1920 was it finally ratified by the European powers and an inter-Allied commission of control began to function at Vienna.[52]

The conclusion of a peace with Hungary was delayed by the lack of a stable government at Budapest and by hostilities with Czechoslovakia and Romania.[53] While armies contended on the northern and eastern boundaries of Hungary, the peacemakers had worked to delineate boundary lines that would give some promise of permanence. In general the territorial specialists of the United States suggested boundaries that were more favorable to Hungary than those envisioned by the Allies.[54]

The Commission on Czechoslovak Affairs, in drawing a frontier between Hungary and Czechoslovakia, found the case predetermined to some extent by arrangements that had been made independently by Beneš with the Quai d'Orsay and that adopted a military line drawn by Foch.[55] The commission's wisdom was challenged by the bitterness of the Slovaks toward Magyars who had ruled them. The linguistic line zigzagged. Furthermore, the hilly character of the terrain complicated the separation of the two peoples. East-west railways that connected the extremities of the elongated Czechoslovak state ran over the plains, well within territory inhabited by Magyars. The American specialists, agreeing that uninterrupted communications were essential to the life of Czechoslovakia, nevertheless managed to reduce the Czech claims, which were supported by France. In persuading the commission to leave to Hungary the strategic hills north of Budapest and to place the frontier in the valley of the Ipel' River, Seymour and Dulles brought about the exclusion from Czechoslovakia of about 40 percent of the Hungarians whom the Czech state claimed.[56] To enable the commission to make a unanimous report, Seymour and Dulles found it necessary, after what the former has described as "a bitter battle" with their French colleagues, to concede to Czechoslovakia a long island in the Danube inhabited by Magyars whose economic contacts were mainly with regions to the north and whose political preference was thought to be in some doubt.[57]

The eastern end of Czechoslovakia presented special difficulties. The Czechs claimed a region there that was inhabited by more than a quarter-million Carpatho-Ruthenians. The Black Book of the Inquiry supported this claim, stating that it was desirable to free these people from Magyar rule and to prevent a thrust of Hungarian territory between Czechoslovakia and Romania. The British and French delegates agreed, being eager to close the so-called "Lemberg gap," for it was through this that Hungarian Communists might communicate easily with Soviet Russia.[58] How-

52. See below, p. 533, n. 29.

53. See above, pp. 231–233.

54. Seymour to Lt. Philip L. Goodwin of the Coolidge mission, February 14, 1919, Y.H.C. The new Hungary that the Americans proposed would have little more than half of its prewar area and population, Haskins and Lord, *Some Problems of the Peace Conference*, p. 233; Deák, p. 29.

55. Perman, pp. 92–96.

56. *F.R., P.P.C.*, vol. 4, p. 676. Perman, pp. 144–145. Deák, pp. 45, 69. "My whole line of argument . . . has been that the fewer Germans and Magyars in the Czech state the better for it," Seymour, pp. 162, 175–176.

57. Seymour, "Czechoslovak Frontiers," 287, *F.R., P.P.C.*, vol. 4, pp. 665–667, 676. Perman, pp. 151–152, Deák, pp. 64–66, 68–69, Nicolson, pp. 324–325.

58. Perman, p. 151. Deák, p. 28.

ever, the people who lived in the territory in question wanted a measure of autonomy. When the Council of Four, on June 25, approved a plan permitting Polish troops to enter Eastern Galicia to protect it from Bolshevist invasion, the Ruthenians were notified that they would have "a full opportunity of determining by plebiscite, within limits to be fixed by the League of Nations," what their future status was to be.[59]

By and large, the Czech delegates were remarkably successful in securing frontiers that were defensible, that strengthened their nation's industrial potential, and that maintained the continuity of important lines of communication. The principle of self-determination was waived so far as to give the new state a population of which more than a third was of foreign nationality. This concession may be attributed in part to the skillful pleading of a master diplomat, Eduard Beneš.[60]

In acting upon the necessity for drawing a boundary between Hungary and Romania, the Americans found it difficult to maintain scholarly objectivity in the face of aggressive tactics on the part of Bratianu. The Romanian premier continued to trade upon the monopoly of oil that he controlled. He cleverly used anti-American and anti-Jewish propaganda to reject the representations of American oil men, while at the same time he made the most of the possibility of American competition when he negotiated with British and French interests. Bratianu intimated to Norman Davis that he had received propositions relating to oil concessions.[61] His negotiations were reinforced by charming Queen Marie of Romania, a granddaughter of Queen Victoria. The queen came to the president's house for luncheon, arriving late, and Wilson waited impatiently for nearly a half hour. An eyewitness recorded: "Every moment we waited I could see from the cut of the president's jaw that a slice of Rumania was being lopped off By the time she did arrive he would scarcely go out into the hall to meet her and it required Mrs. Wilson's powers to persuade him."[62]

On May 7 Davis wrote in a "Memorandum for the President":

I explained to him [Bratianu] that we did not ask for any concessions or advantages, but that it would be difficult for the American government to justify giving financial support to the Rumanian Government if advances from other Governments were given preference as to guarantee or otherwise. He told me that he had been able to remain free, but that if we did not continue to assist his government financially he might be compelled to give concessions to other countries in order to get financial assistance. I then told him that it would probably be a protection to Rumania as well as to our government if he would merely undertake not to grant any such concessions as long as his government owes money to the United States. He told me he would think this over and expected to give a favorable reply, but that he feared that certain governments (he did not specify which) might demand, as a condition of sup-

59. *F.R., P.P.C.,* vol. 6, pp. 677, 687–688.

60. Seymour, *Letters,* pp. 154–155, 268

61. Davis to Beneš, May 19, June 25, 1919; Beneš to Davis, June 26, 1919, N. H. Davis papers, box 10, L.C. See above, p. 101, and Spector, *Rumania at the Paris Peace Conference,* pp. 163, 302.

62. Helm, diary letter, April 11, 1919. Axson recorded that the queen argued that bolshevism could not be checked unless the boundaries of states were drawn to the satisfaction of the inhabitants, Axson ms., 48, Wilson papers, Princeton.

porting Rumania's aspirations as to boundaries, certain concessions relative to the control and exploitation of the oil industries.[63]

Wilson learned from Davis that the Treasury, being of the opinion that it would be a violation of law to advance money now to Romania for the purchase of raw materials, requested that the president withdraw approval already given for the establishment of credits of $5,000,000 each for Romania, Czechoslovakia, and Yugoslavia. Davis advised that without these advances sufficient funds were available for the completion of Hoover's programs. Accordingly, after ascertaining that American army supplies could be provided on credit by the United States Liquidation Commission without recourse to the Treasury,[64] Wilson withdrew the credits to Romania and the other two governments. At the same time he insisted that there was to be no encroachment, without the approval of Hoover, on credits applied to the purchase of foodstuffs.[65]

In the defining of the boundaries of Romania, the Americans did not play a decisive part, although their concern for Wilsonian principles moved them to enter into the discussions. They were inclined to accept the will of a general congress in Bukovina which, meeting on November 28, had voted for a union with Romania.[66] Moreover, they did not at first oppose Romania's claim to Bessarabia, which in November of 1918 had declared its independence. On January 24, 1919, the Romanian parliament approved union of the nation with Bessarabia as well as with Bukovina and Romanian-inhabited regions of Hungary.[67]

When the question of a permanent frontier with Hungary came up in the first meeting of the Commission on Rumanian and Yugoslav Affairs, the Americans, influenced by ethnic considerations, suggested a line farther east than that proposed by the delegates of any of the Allies.[68] However, the report of the commission,

63. Memorandum in Wilson papers. Correspondence between Davis and Bratianu in respect of repayment of American loans for relief is in the Y.H.C. Davis to Beneš, May 19, June 25, 1919, Beneš to Davis, June 26, 1919, N. H. Davis papers, box 10, L.C.

64. Wilson to Davis, May 6, 1919, Davis to Wilson, May 7, 1919, Wilson papers.

65. H. C. Breck to Close, May 17, 1919, Close to Davis, May 17, 1919, with enclosures, Wilson papers. Romania had received two credits of $5 million each for purposes of relief, memorandum, Lord to Bullitt, February 16, 1919, Bullitt papers. House diary, June 11, 1919.

66. Henry L. Roberts, *Political Problems of an Agrarian State* (New Haven, 1951), pp. 36–37.

67. Spector, p. 71. The Black Book awarded all of Russian Bessarabia to Romania. American specialists found it "rather embarrassing" to draw an eastern boundary for Romania because of the absence of any other government in that region with which a treaty could be signed, Seymour, *Letters,* pp. 191–193. Late in 1919 the American delegates at Paris opposed the Romanian claim to Bessarabia, *F.R., P.P.C.,* vol. 7, pp. 457–459, vol. 11, p. 664. The question was not settled until the autumn of 1920, when the European Council of Ambassadors recognized the union of Bessarabia with Romania. The United States government refused an invitation to participate in this decision on the ground that it constituted a dismemberment of Russia without the consent of the people of that country, Spector, pp. 222–225, 317. According to Mayer, "The Entente eagerly compensated him [Bratianu] with Bessarabia and northern Bukovina for his contribution to the containment of Lenin," *Politics and Diplomacy of Peacemaking,* p. 852.

The Black Book awarded to Romania that part of Bukovina that was inhabited by Romanians, as well as all of Transylvania, Gelfand, p. 220. The Romanian commission at Paris recommended a boundary in Bukovina that was approved by the Council of Foreign Ministers on May 23, *F.R., P.P.C.,* vol. 4, p. 749. There was no final decision for months, *British Docs. on For. Pol.,* 1st Series, vol. 1, p. 278. *F.R., P.P.C.,* vol. 11, pp. 365, 406–470, 455–456. Deák, maps 2 and 3.

68. The considerations taken into account are summarized in Deák, pp. 49–50. See Spector, pp. 103, 122.

submitted on April 6, was adopted by the Council of Foreign Ministers with little discussion and with no opportunity for Hungarians to protest. The frontier recommended was prescribed in the peace treaty with Hungary. It excluded from Romania much that was claimed but was somewhat more favorable to that country than the boundary proposed by the Americans.[69]

Efforts to draw a southern boundary for Hungary were frustrated for a time by a conflict of the national claims of Hungary, Romania, and Serbia. The Commission on Rumanian and Yugoslav Affairs set a frontier that included within Hungary the city of Szeged, but the boundary in other border regions was the subject of continuing dispute.[70]

In the drawing of its frontiers Hungary suffered from the failure of the Peace Conference to hear its spokesmen, as well as from an inclination of the peacemakers, and especially the French, to reward friends and penalize foes.[71] It was unfortunate for the Hungarians that the Peace Conference, appointing *ad hoc* committees to consider the claims of neighboring states, gave no concerted attention to the total effect of their several recommendations. Hungary found itself stripped of territory on all sides without due thought about the relative smallness of the remainder.

The American specialists serving on the territorial commissions threw their influence against the prejudices that the war had nourished, and they were not unaware of the lack of a responsible overview of the question of Hungarian boundaries. Indeed, Wilson spoke to his colleagues in the Council of Four in protest against a peace that would lack guarantees because questions were considered separately.[72] Nevertheless, the boundaries drawn stood up rather well against the national pressures that had erupted in warfare often before 1914. Diligent American scholars succeeded, by their labors with the territorial committees, in making a contribution to the common cause of peace such as Europeans were unaccustomed to expect from the New World.[73]

Actually, as Béla Kun struggled in the summer months to retain the power that he had seized at Budapest and as Hungarians continued to fight with Slovaks and Romanians, the situation was too chaotic to permit any effective application of decisions made at Paris. Béla Kun had lost any confidence that he might have had in reaching an accommodation with the Western powers.[74] His regime had been

---

69. Deák, p. 28 and maps 2 and 3.

70. The Yugoslav claim to Prekomurje, a little district north of the Mur at the border of Austria, was rejected. However, in May the commission reconsidered this decision in the light of a proposal by the Yugoslavs to divide Prekomurje so that they would have the portion where their people predominated. Clive Day, who preferred the natural and strategic boundary that was provided by the Mur River, yielded to his European colleagues and agreed upon this ethnic solution. See C. A. Macartney, *Hungary and Her Successors* (London, 1937), pp. 378–379. Lederer, pp. 223–224.

On the prolonged dispute over the boundary in the Bačka and in Baranya, see Macartney, pp. 392–394; Lederer, pp. 100–101, 174–177, 182, 223–224; Deák, map 3. See Leslie Charles Tihany, *The Baranya Dispute, 1918–1921* (Boulder, 1978). On the partition of the Banat of Temesvár, see below, p. 463.

71. Nicolson, pp. 117, 122–123, 127–129. *What Really Happened at Paris*, ed. Seymour and House, pp. 87 ff. Deák, p. 53.

72. Mantoux, *Délibérations*, vol. 1, pp. 508–509.

73. Seymour and House, p. 99.

74. In a dispatch of June 21, thanking Lenin for a telegram approving his policy, Béla Kun said: "I think I know the Entente very well. I know that they will fight us to the end. In this war only a state of

isolated and blockaded by the Allies in the hope that it would soon fall.[75]

On June 26, when Clemenceau read a telegram from Béla Kun protesting against Romanian aggression and asking for recognition of his government, Wilson said that the appeal did not seem unreasonable; and Lloyd George suggested that they could not refuse to recognize Béla Kun's government just because it was one of soviets. However defective that form of government might be, he said, it was on the whole more representative than that of the czar had been. Clemenceau, however, alluded to the all-pervading dread that bolshevism would spread to other capitals; and as for Romanian aggression, he remarked that the Romanians would say that the Hungarians were the aggressors.[76]

In July the Romanian army was advancing on Budapest and giving comfort to those who were most afraid of bolshevism. Herbert Hoover, fearful of losing "control of the situation" in states surrounding Hungary, had devised, as an alternative to direct military action, a policy of "offering decent treatment to Hungary if she would throw off the communist yoke." In June, however, Hoover had yielded to a recommendation from his agent at Budapest that a promise of food and coal as a *quid pro quo* should be supplemented by a military advance. Forwarding this advice to Wilson on June 9, Hoover wrote: "As much as I dislike to suggest it, I can see but one solution and that is for the French troops which are now in Yugoslavia to advance on Budapest without delay."[77] Lansing, too, was willing to accept military destruction of Béla Kun's government in order to protect the prestige of the Allies and to check bolshevism. And even Bliss, critical of Allied bungling and of Romanian aggression, did not oppose the "general purpose" of using force to destroy Kun, although he questioned the legality of any action that would appear to be designed to overthrow a foreign government. It seemed to Bliss that the Allies, rather than Béla Kun's government, had broken the armistice of November 13.[78]

On July 10 the Supreme Council asked Marshal Foch to consult with representatives of Romania, Yugoslavia, and Czechoslovakia about measures for military intervention. Assured by the Czechs that they would make all their forces available, and by the other two governments that they would cooperate under certain conditions, Foch, according to Hoover, recommended an occupying army that "included mostly an American contingent."

After a discussion of the question on July 26, the Supreme Council finally took action. It decided that it would not consider a proposal that had come from Hungary's minister of war, advocating Béla Kun's replacement by a dictatorship of the more moderate members of his cabinet, who would repudiate bolshevism.[79] Instead,

---

armistice can occur, but never peace. This is an out and out fight," text of telegram in Lloyd George papers, F / 197 / 4 / 4. Alfred D. Low, *The Soviet Hungarian Republic and the Paris Peace Conference*, p. 70. Mayer, p. 831.

75. See above, p. 229.

76. Mantoux, *Délibérations*, vol. 2, p. 525.

77. Murray N. Rothbard, "Food Diplomacy in Retrospect," in *Herbert Hoover: The Great War and Its Aftermath*, ed. Lawrence E. Gelfand, pp. 97–99.

78. Bliss diary, July 5, 17, and 25, 1919. Levin, *Woodrow Wilson and World Politics*, p. 195. Ammission to the secretary of state, July 15, 1919, N.A., R.G. 59, 763.72119 / 5647, 5655. See Low, pp. 73–82.

79. Vilmos Böhm, a general of the old regime, resigned from Kun's government and became its envoy to Vienna. He informed the Allies that he would be willing to organize a counterrevolution and

it addressed to the Hungarian people a statement that Balfour had drafted after conferring with Hoover. Released on July 27 as an alternative to military action, the statement gave notice that "if the blockade is to be removed, if economic reconstruction is to be attempted, if peace is to be settled it can only be done with a government which represents the Hungarian people and not with one that rests its authority upon terrorism. . . . All foreign occupation of Hungarian territory, as defined by the Peace Conference, will cease as soon as the terms of the armistice have in the opinion of the Allied Commander-in-Chief, been satisfactorily complied with."[80] Thus was invoked the dangerous procedure, which was often to muddle twentieth-century diplomacy, of appealing to a people over the head of their government.

Meanwhile, the Romanian government made the most of the general dread of bolshevism. It submitted to the Peace Conference certain proposals "for the pacification of Hungary" that were designed to extirpate communism and to give the Hungarians an opportunity "to establish a new constitution on freely determined democratic bases" under a temporary occupation that Hungary was to pay for. Polk, however, was not impressed. Thinking that the Romanians were encouraged by French officials,[81] he spoke to the Heads of Delegations of the danger of atrocities on the part of the invaders, whose appetite for vengeance was not yet satisfied. He asked whether it would not be well to intimate to Romania that disregard of the wishes of the Peace Conference would be punished by economic measures.

On the first of August, Béla Kun and his cabinet resigned and fled the country. The effort of a group of trades-union leaders to form a socialist government and to negotiate with the Peace Conference for protection against the invaders failed when Romanian troops entered Budapest three days later. The council at Paris then decided to send the first of many notes of warning and protest to Romania, giving notice in mild terms that the Peace Conference was dispatching a mission of Allied generals to Budapest to see that the democratic intentions of the new government of Hungary were carried out. When news reached Paris of a Romanian ultimatum of August 5 that made ruinous economic demands, another note went off to Bucharest, pointing out that Romania's exactions were in conflict with the promises made by the Peace Conference to the Hungarian people to induce them to change their government.

When the Romanians gave military support to a coup at Budapest that would establish a government under the Archduke Joseph, Hoover, still hoping for the emergence of a constitutional democracy in Hungary and fearful that a reversion to imperial rule might lend force to Soviet propaganda, protested to the Supreme Council.[82] He also gave to the press a public statement for the American people,[83]

head a socialistic and representative government if the blockade against Hungary were raised. Deák, pp. 102–105. Hoover, *Memoirs*, vol. 1, p. 399. See Low, p. 86.

80. Hoover, vol. 1, pp. 399–400. Hoover, *The Ordeal of Woodrow Wilson*, pp. 137–138. Deák, pp. 102–105. Mayer, pp. 844–847.

81. Secretary of state from Polk, August 11, 1919, N.A., R.G. 59, 763.721119 / 6117.

82. The Romanians went so far as to seize American supplies in a children's hospital in Budapest. After observing their behavior during the first days of their occupation, Captain Gregory of the American Relief Administration wired to Hoover: "There is nothing to be done with this situation except to settle whether Rumanians are going to loot this country under one guise or another and if France is going to back them," Hoover, *Memoirs*, vol. 1, pp. 400–401, Deák, p. 115.

83. *New York Times*, August 24, 1919.

criticizing his government for "supineness" and advocating that it take direct diplomatic action "to save the situation." This public effusion embarrassed Polk, who
thought that intervention to depose the archduke might open the door to more bolshevism. He lost confidence in Hoover's political judgment and thought him carried
away by his own eloquence.[84] Clemenceau and Balfour, however, were of the opinion that recognition of this Hapsburg should not be granted, and on August 22 the
council decided that the archduke should be so apprised. An edict drafted by Hoover—"with zest," he said—was delivered by his agent, Captain Gregory, who
reported the next day in the slang of the Food Administration: "Archie on the carpet
7 p.m., Went through the hoop at 7:05 p.m."[85] Moderate adherents of the archduke
tried to carry on under the handicaps raised by both the depredations of the Romanians and the erratic behavior to which fright of bolshevism had driven the Peace
Conference—behavior that was founded upon the sands of hope and divided counsel.[86]

The military mission of the Peace Conference, exerting itself at Budapest to restrain
the Romanians, sent reports to Paris that contradicted protestations of innocence
from the Romanian government.[87] Yet Bratianu, assuring the Peace Conference that
he was acting correctly to serve the cause of peace, increased his immoderate demands.

The Supreme Council, in view of the fact that the unauthorized occupation of
Budapest seemed to be preventing civil war among factions in Hungary as well as
countering bolshevism, was hesitant to go so far as to demand a withdrawal of
Romanian troops. Clemenceau, although furious at Bratianu's defiance, was reluctant to take any extreme step that might shake France's eastern bulwark—the alliance with Romania and its neighbors. While French officials indulged the Romanians,
Polk, well aware that the treatment of the Hungarians would "have great influence
on Russia,"[88] persistently did what was possible to curb Bratianu. He told the
Heads of Delegations on August 13 that he was authorized by President Wilson to
say that if the Romanians continued in their present course, he would not look
favorably on any of their claims. Polk pointed out that by countenancing the Romanian
occupation of Hungary the Peace Conference was giving to Lenin an opportunity to
terrify his people by portraying the danger of foreign intervention in Russia in terms
of the situation at Budapest. Moreover, Polk adduced a document drafted by John
Foster Dulles that reminded his European colleagues that the principle of solidarity
in reparations, which permitted them to collect payments from Hungary, would

84. Susan Balogh, "The Road to Isolation" (Ph.D. diss., Yale University, 1974), pp. 193–202.
Levin, pp. 195–196.

85. Hoover, *Memoirs,* vol. 1, 403–404, Hoover, *The Ordeal of Woodrow Wilson,* pp. 139–140.
Deák, pp. 128–129. Thomas T. C. Gregory, *Overthrowing a Bad Regime,* p. 164; and Gregory, "Bolsheviks and Archdukes," *Sunset* 44 (February 1920):28. General Bandholtz, the American member of
the Peace Conference's military mission at Budapest, told the Hungarians that Gregory was not authorized to speak for the Peace Conference, General Harry Bandholtz, *Undiplomatic Diary* (New York,
1933), p. 8.

86. Dispatch, Austria (Halstead) to State Department, August 19, 1919, N.A., R.G. 59, 763. 72119 /
6588. See Low, pp. 86–89.

87. Deák, pp. 129–134. Bandholtz reported that the attitude of his French and Italian colleagues was
"peculiar and at times erratic," *F.R., P.P.C.,* vol. 12, p. 660. The French envoy at Budapest was
encouraging Bratianu to prolong the occupation, Spector, pp. 176–180.

88. Polk to Wilson, August 5, 1919, Miller, vol. 20, pp. 378–380. Mayer, p. 849.

amount to nothing if Romania stripped the country. Before the end of August Polk told the heads of delegations that his government had cut off delivery of all supplies to Romania, and early in September it was decided that the United States would provide no more credits.[89]

Meanwhile, Balfour's impatience with Bratianu had been mounting.[90] Early in August he joined in pressing for a decision that Romania must submit to the authority of the Peace Conference or else be barred from the alliance.[91] He suggested to Polk that they wind up the Peace Conference as soon as possible. Polk, however, deemed it essential to remain at work on the issue raised by Romania. He was irritated by an attempt on the part of Lloyd George, after Balfour had left Paris under doctor's orders, to dissolve the Peace Conference in mid-September without consulting the Americans.[92] Lloyd George was told that this was impossible until treaties were signed with Hungary and Bulgaria.[93] Wilson supported Polk's insistence on continuation of the conference by telegraphing from San Diego that a break-up would be nearly fatal to the state of mind of the world.[94]

Weeks passed without decisive action. In September, Polk asked Lansing whether the Supreme Council should not meet elsewhere than at the Quai d'Orsay, since French officials "were creating in Rumania the impression that the British and American policies were antagonistic to their own." At the same time, Polk made the barbed suggestion to Clemenceau that any defection from a united front, grave enough in the case of Romania, would be disastrous in respect of American ratification of the Treaty of Versailles.[95]

In November the Americans, exuding moral opprobrium, were still without any effective means of influencing the conduct of Romania for the better. Wilson, then seriously ill, gave his consent to the withdrawal of the American envoy at Bucharest if the Romanian government continued to defy the Peace Conference.[96] However, a diplomat of the British Foreign Office, finding that the most elementary rights of private property were being violated by the Romanians in Transylvania, had under-

---

89. Polk to the secretary of state, August 25 and 28, 1919; Phillips to Ammission, September 12, 1919, H. White papers, L.C. Polk suggested to Balfour that it might be necessary even to go to the extent of blockading Romanian ports, foreign secretary from Polk, September 5, 1919, N.A., R.G. 59, 763.72119 / 6542. Spector, pp. 169, 172.

90. Memorandum dated June 16, 1919, Balfour papers, 49751. The British and French governments signed an agreement with Bratianu on July 29, 1919, for a joint undertaking to develop oil resources, *British Docs. on For. Pol.*, vol. 4, pp. 1100–1104.

91. Memorandum, Kerr to the prime Minister, August 6, 1919, Lloyd George papers, F / 89 / 3 / 23. Kerr reported that the French, and especially Foreign Minister Pichon, were backing the Romanians.

92. Polk diary, September 9 and 15, 1919. Balfour to Curzon, August 16, 1919, Balfour papers, 49734. Sir Eyre Crowe became head of the British delegation on September 18, and the American delegation took responsibility for the preparation and circulation of the texts of minutes and appended documents. Lord Curzon replaced Balfour as foreign minister.

93. Ammission to the president and secretary of state, September 17, 1919, N.A., R.G. 59, 763.72119 / 6787.

94. Dispatch, September 19, N.A., R.G. 59, 763.72119 / 6823.

95. Letter, Polk to Clemenceau, September 24, 1919, Y.H.C. "All the statements on Rumania's behalf which we have yet received from Mr. Bratianu," Polk wrote, "have proved to be empty promises. You will see, by the reports from our generals, a copy of which I enclose, that the actual situation in Budapest has not changed in the slightest degree, and their promises are no nearer to fulfillment than they were before." Polk alleged to Balfour that the flabbiness of the French and Italians was due to their commercial interests in Romania, Polk diary, September 2 and 11, 1919.

96. Confidential dispatches to Polk, November 14, 1919, N.A., R.G. 59, 763.72119 / 7737, 7765. See Mayer, p. 851.

taken in September to negotiate a settlement.[97] Sir George Clerk, private secretary
to Curzon, went to Bucharest bearing a note from the Supreme Council that threatened to deduct from Romania's reparation claims the value of the Hungarian property that its army had seized. After two months of arduous and delicate negotiation
Clerk managed to bring about the withdrawal of Romanian forces from Budapest
on November 14 and the provisional recognition, on the twenth-fifth, of a coalition
as the *de facto* government of Hungary.[98] The Supreme Council then decided to
summon delegates of Hungary to Paris to receive the draft of the treaty that had
been awaiting them.[99]

In January of the new year Admiral Horthy, the former commander of the Austro-
Hungarian Navy, was elected regent of Hungary, and he ruled with a dictorial hand
until 1944.[100] A Hungarian delegation went to Paris and under protest accepted
terms from an Allied commission on which no Americans sat. When the Treaty of
Trianon was signed by the Allies with Hungary on June 4, 1920, the American
signer was Ambassador Hugh C. Wallace.[101]

The pact, containing territorial provisions that American specialists had helped
to frame, took from Hungary more than half of its land and most of the non-Magyar
population as well as millions of Magyars. Other articles of the treaty closely followed those of the peace concluded with Austria, and the text reflected the observations made by Germans and Austrians on their respective treaties. The reparation
terms for Hungary, like those for Austria, differed from those for Germany slightly
in the direction of moderation.[102]

The United States was not at peace with Hungary until the Senate made a unilat-
eral declaration in 1921.

In the summer of 1919 the American peacemakers found themselves involved in
settling the affairs of the Balkans, a region that the great powers of Europe had been
unable to pacify in the years before the war.

Perhaps the most difficult of the territorial questions to be settled was that raised
by the conflicting claims of Romania and Yugoslavia in respect of the banat of
Temesvár, a rich and densely population region southeast of Szeged, where there
was a crazy quilt of races and a network of communications through which no line
could be drawn without injury to economic interest.[103] When Serbian troops entered
the region and interned inhabitants who agitated for union with Romania, the Supreme
Council at Paris left it to the military representatives to devise a way to keep the
peace. The French army defined and occupied a buffer zone.[104]

97. Dispatch, Ammission to State Department, November 21, 1919, N.A., R.G. 59, 763.72119 /
7965.
98. Spector, pp. 182 ff. Deák, pp. 134–166. Tillman, *Anglo-American Relations at the Paris Peace
Conference,* pp. 390–392.
99. A. W. Dulles to A. Coolidge, October 1, December 1, 1919, A. W. Dulles papers, box 6.
100. See Pastor, *Hungary between Wilson and Lenin,* pp. 151–152.
101. Documents in N.A., R.G. 59, 763.72119 / 8316, 9590, 9784, 9829.
102. A. W. Dulles to Alexander C. Kirk, September 5, 1919, A. W. Dulles papers. Temperley, vol.
6, p. 555. Burnett, vol. 1, pp. 349–350.
103. Miller, vol. 4, pp. 324 ff., and pp. 138 ff. See Macartney, p. 394.
104. Memorandum, Day to J. C. Grew, February 28, 1919, Y.H.C.

A battle over the banat had erupted in a meeting of the Supreme Council on January 31, when Bratianu asserted Romania's right to the entire region.[105] The Inquiry's Black Book proposed a partition on an ethnic basis but with due regard to economic and political criteria. In March, Clive Day, "upbraided" on the subject by Vesnić, acceded to a French request that the strong feeling of the Serbs be met by a compromise.[106]

The Commission on Rumanian and Yugoslav Affairs allotted to Hungary a very thin strip of land that lay on its border, southeast of Szeged. It was the opinion of the American specialists that this area, in the southwestern corner of the banat at the confluence of the Maros and the Theiss rivers, "was Magyar in character" and in close economic relation with Szeged and therefore should be left with Hungary.[107] Most of the western part of the remainder of the banat was given to Yugoslavia, and the eastern to Romania. This settlement left some 75,000 Romanians in Yugoslavia and about as many Slavs in Romania. It disrupted communications by rail and river as little as possible. The commission insisted, in view of the complexity of the question and the passions manifested, that the two nations undertake reciprocal engagements for the protection of minorities under the League of Nations.[108]

Neither party was satisfied, however, by this adjudication. In mid-April, Bratianu sought an interview with Wilson and later repeated, in writing, his claim to the whole banat.[109] The president's concern for world peace had involved him in a virulent local controversy that was remote from American interest and responsibility. He felt the full weight of the predicament in which he was ensnared by the principle of self-determination. Resort to a plebiscite seemed futile in this case of a polyglot population.

When the foreign ministers took up the question on May 23, Lansing for a time refused to accept the partition of the banat without a *quid pro quo* from Romania in favor of a Bulgarian claim in the southern Dobruja; but the French were now the ones to oppose any further dealing in territories and at length the Americans yielded.[110] Wilson concurred in the decision of the Council of Four on June 21 to accept the boundary recommended by the commission.[111]

Although the United States had not been formally at war with Bulgaria, the American peacemakers insisted on a voice in the settlement with its government, for the Covenant of the League was to be included in the treaty of peace with that nation and therefore the United States could be put in the position of a guarantor.

105. See above, pp. 100–102. Nicolson, *Peacemaking, 1919,* p. 254. Spector, pp. 85, 124–125. Lederer, 8 pp. 143–145.

106. Day diary, March 5, 1919, Day to White, March 18, 1919, Y.H.C.

107. "Memorandum on the Proposed Division of the Banat," Y.H.C.

108. Lederer, p. 181. Spector, pp 126–127. See below, p. 475.

109. Wilson to Bratianu, April 17, 1919, Bratianu to Wilson, April 22, 1919, Wilson papers.

110. Spector, p. 139.

111. *F.R., P.P.C.,* vol. 6, pp. 587, 592–593, 731. In August the possibility of Romanian military action in the Banat was so lively that the Supreme Council thought it necessary to warn Bratianu that it would not tolerate the use of force. At the urging of General Franchet d'Esperey the Romanians and Serbs agreed provisionally, in October 1919, to accept the line of division. Not until 1923, however, did both states sign a protocol recognizing the prescribed frontier, Spector, p. 221.

The American specialists were instructed to take part in the work of the committee that was preparing reparation terms.[112]

The Americans were inclined to question certain territorial claims on the part of Bulgaria's neighbors. On November 29, 1918, Romania had gone so far as to move troops into the southern Dobruja, which Bulgaria had been obliged to cede to Romania in 1913 and had retaken during the war. An Inquiry paper had recommended that Romania retrocede this region because a majority of its people were Bulgarian. This position, supported by Lansing and House, was in accord with the assertion by American scholars of the right of the victors to correct injustices in prewar boundaries.[113] The British were more or less in sympathy with this view; but the French would give to Romania not only southern Dobruja, but even more land along the Black Sea. Bulgaria had requested that English and French troops occupy the disputed region pending a verdict by the Peace Conference; the French command had permitted Romanian gendarmes to evict Bulgarian administrators; and by the end of 1918 the district was under the control of Romania. Bratianu demanded that it remain so.[114]

On May 28 Wilson insisted that although he recognized the awkwardness of giving territory of a friendly nation to an enemy, there was no necessity for violating the principle of self-determination. Then, on July 25, he sent a warning to Paris that unless Romania retroceded the part of Dobruja inhabited by Bulgarians, there would be continued irritation.[115] It was suspected that his persistence in a matter in which his country had no political interest reflected the concern of American philanthropists for their work in Bulgaria.[116]

Through the autumn the Americans continued their resistance and offered alternate plans. But they succeeded only in putting off the inevitable acceptance of the status quo, under which Romanian merchants secured a vital hold upon that one-fourth of Bulgaria's foreign trade that moved over the Danube.[117] Polk was unsuccessful even in placing in the treaty with Bulgaria a provision for an adjustment through bilateral talks between Romania and Bulgaria; and he failed to persuade his European colleagues to provide specifically, in a minorities treaty with Romania, for the rights of Bulgarians in southern Dobruja.[118]

112. Letter, Davis and Lamont to Wilson, June 26, 1919, Wilson papers.

113. *F.R., P.P.C.,* vol. 11, pp. 575–577. *F.R., Lansing pa.,* vol. 2, p. 157. Haskins and Lord, pp. 264–265, 275–277.

114. American consul (Sofia) to the secretary of state, December 4, 1918, N.A., R.G. 59, 763.72 / 12435. *F.R. P.P.C.,* vol. 2, pp. 241–242, 251–253. Spector, pp. 72, 94, 99–101, 133, 285–286. In the meetings of the Commission on Rumanian and Yugoslav Affairs, Day proposed a frontier in Dobruja that would respect ethnic facts. He and his British colleagues favored a boundary that was defensible from both sides and that protected the economic interest of the Bulgarian majority in the south. White pointed out that in the territory that the French would award to Romania there were 66,000 Bulgarians and only 867 Romanians, *F.R., P.P.C.,* vol. 4, pp. 718–719.

115. Dispatch for H. White from the president, August 6, 1919, N.A., R.G. 59, 763. 72119 / 5740 and 6144 B.

116. *F.R., P.P.C.,* vol. 4, pp. 750–751. Nicolson, *Peacemaking 1919,* p. 347. Spector, pp. 139, 347. Mantoux, *Délibérations,* vol. 2, p. 241. The Americans at Paris learned that American missionaries left Bulgaria for propaganda work in the United States, N.A., R.G. 59, 763.72119 / 6121.

117. Seymour and House, p. 172.

118. Spector, pp. 194–195, 219.

The Americans were unsuccessful also in attempts to apply the principle of self-determination to the boundary between Bulgaria and Yugoslavia. Serbia, as one of the victorious Allies and now a component of Yugoslavia, asked for the inclusion in Yugoslavia of a small strip of territory along its eastern border that was ethnically and historically Bulgarian. This was desired both as a safeguard against a repetition of the attack by Bulgaria that had inflicted a military disaster in 1915 and also to protect a rail line that was vital to the Serbian system of communications. The Inquiry, however, recommended that Yugoslavia's eastern frontier be that of Serbia before the war. But the American protests were weakened by the delay of the United States in acting to ratify the Treaty of Versailles. Yugoslavia was awarded land with a population that was largely Bulgarian.[119]

Another most difficult decision affecting Bulgaria's frontier was that pertaining to its southern boundary. Venizelos sought all of Thrace for Greece, basing his claim on the principle of ethnography as well as those of security and commercial advantage. He had the constant support of Lloyd George, and he addressed pleas directly to Wilson.[120]

The American experts had agreed conditionally in March with their colleagues on the Greek commission that western Thrace should be ceded to Greece. In July, however, Coolidge and Johnson questioned Greece's ethnological claim to this region, where the ethnic and political preferences of the inhabitants were very difficult to ascertain.[121]

The American commission had firm advice on this question from Washington, where Wilson was still trying to keep his hands on the negotiations at Paris. The president was not moved by a message from Venizelos, pleading that the ethnological claim of Greece should outweigh the economic interest of Bulgaria. He urged that, "as a practicable solution" both Eastern and Western Thrace should be included with Constantinople in a mandate and that Bulgaria should have a corridor running to the Aegean Sea.[122] He threatened not to sign the Bulgarian treaty if it did not promise a settlement that in his opinion would be permanent. Polk, reporting that the Allies were negotiating "in a spirit of barter," advised Washington that it was "almost desirable" to inform the European powers that the Americans were seriously thinking of withdrawing from consideration of the treaty with Bulgaria.[123]

On July 25, the day on which Bulgarian delegates arrived at Paris, Balfour wrote in despair to House to ask him to urge Wilson "to maintain the decision which they [the American delegates] accepted last March—a decision which he [Wilson] him-

---

119. Bowman, in Seymour and House, pp. 167–173. Lederer, pp. 97, 128–130, 137–138, 180–181, 223–224, 256–257. The national identities of the mixed population in this region could not easily be ascertained by linguistic studies, Gelfand, pp. 219–202. Haskins and Lord, pp. 263–280.

120. Venizelos to Wilson, June 28, 1919, Wilson papers. Mitchell, "The U.S. and Greek Policy at the Paris Peace Conference," 32 ff.

121. Ammission to Sec. State for Pres., July 20, 1919, N.A., R.G. 59, 763. 72119 / 5719. 5723, 5754. Coolidge and Lord, pp. 229–230.

122. H. White from Pres., July 25, 1919, N.A., R.G. 59, 763.72119 / 5740 and 6144B. Dispatch, Sec. State to Ammission, August 4, 1919, N.A., R.G. 59, 763.72119 / 5920. See Laurence Evans, *U.S. Policy and the Partition of Turkey, 1914–1924*, pp. 198–200.

123. Polk to Sec. State, August 1, 1919, White papers, L.C., box 45, Bliss papers, box 233.

self accepted.'' Nicolson, who protested vigorously against repudiation by some Americans of the recommendation of the Greek committee in which other Americans had conditionally acquiesced, now worked with Major Johnson to produce a compromise that would give to Bulgaria the port of Dede Agach (Alexandroúpolis) and a connecting corridor, and to Greece only the western part of Thrace. But Polk, thinking this the best settlement possible, could not clear it with Washington.[124]

"We have made a compromise on the Thracian situation,'' Polk informed House, "after a hard fight against the whole 'bunch' and were then told by Washington that they would not listen to any compromise whatever, but wanted East and West Thrace in an international state. That of course is out of the question, for as long as it is not known who is to have the mandate for Constantinople, neither the British nor the French would be willing to run the chance of the other getting all the territory along the Aegean. . . . I have telegraphed again to Washington and am waiting to see whether I am going to get 'spanked' or whether we can close up the Bulgarian treaty."[125]

The Europeans were shocked by American partiality to the Bulgarians—a bitter enemy whose conduct during the war had been no less barbarous than that of the Greeks at Smyrna. Moreover, it was suspected that Wilson's proposal for enlarging Constantinople by the addition of Eastern Thrace reflected American greed for fattening a mandate that they thought Wilson hoped to secure. Men who had long been accustomed to think in terms of empire had doubts about America's disinterestedness, especially when the Greek embassy at Washington learned from Wilson's adversaries in the Senate that the president was being influenced by anti-Greek missionaries and tobacco merchants.[126]

In view of these considerations, and after it was agreed between Tittoni and Venizelos on July 29 that Greece, in return for its recognition of Italian claims in Asia Minor and Albania, might receive satisfaction in Thrace, Clemenceau and Balfour ruled out the American ideas for a settlement. They addressed a note to Polk on September 1, giving arguments against a proposal made by Wilson for an international state to be composed of Eastern and most of Western Thrace. Nevertheless, on September 4 they sought Polk's agreement to a compromise plan for an international state, and Polk forwarded this to Wilson; but the president, touring the West and breaking in health, did not respond. During the last week of the month, however, just before a complete breakdown, he replied to a personal plea from Venizelos, protesting that there was no one at the Paris Peace Conference whom he respected more. Yet he could not agree that Greeks were in a majority in Western

124. Ammission to the secretary of state, August 3 and 8, 1919, White papers, L.C., box 44. *Documents on British Foreign Policy,* 1st series, vol. 1, pp. 361–364. *F.R., P.P.C.,* vol. 11, p. 365. Note signed "DWJ," August 7, 1919, Y.H.C. Balfour to Polk, August 6, 1919, Y.H.C., also an initial draft, corrected by hand, P.R.O., FO / 800 / 212.

The British were dismayed by the indecisiveness of the Americans. Kerr reported to the prime minister that they were referring questions of detail to Washington, "really a hopeless system," Kerr to prime minister, August 6, 9, and 14, 1919, Lloyd George papers, F / 89 / 4 / 2 and 7. See Mitchell, pp. 30–44.

125. Polk to House, August 20, 1919, Y.H.C.

126. Petsalis-Diomidis, *Greece at the Paris Peace Conference,* pp. 275, 285n.

Thrace. He insisted that his own proposals would serve the cause of peace better than those of the Greek premier.[127]

Balfour produced a formula for a southern boundary for Bulgaria that approximated that originally recommended by the Greek committee and a plan for ceding Thrace to the great powers, to be disposed of by them. Polk accepted this arrangement at the same time stating that the United States could not participate in occupying territory taken from Bulgaria.[128]

On September 19 the terms of a treaty were presented to the Bulgarian delegates. After strenuous American objections were rejected, the pact was signed at Neuilly on November 27. In the following summer the European powers, without reference to the views of the United States, turned over Western Thrace to Greece; at the same time Greece acquired Eastern Thrace by the Treaty of Sèvres, which concluded a peace between the Allies and Turkey.[129] Bulgaria was left without the seaport that the Americans desired it to have.

The United States withdrew from any part in the enforcement of the Treaty of Neuilly, and Wilson forbade American representation even on the commission that was to collect reparations. Polk signed the pact by direction of the president. By this time the rejection of the League Covenant by the Senate had made the United States no guarantor of the Bulgarian treaty.[130]

The battles that the American scholars had fought in the cause of justice to Hungary and Bulgaria left them with little respect for the diplomats of the foreign offices of the Allied powers. Bowman protested to the heads of delegations "tooth and nail," he said. He warned them on November 1 that the terms of the Treaty of Neuilly "guaranteed a future war." In his disgust, he wrote: "The work of these men makes me pray that the United States Government will never in God's world ratify the Treaty [of Versailles] without adequate reservations." He foresaw that his country was in danger of being "thrown again and again against the wrong nation" because of "purely nationalistic and entirely selfish foreign office groups."[131]

---

127. Venizelos replied in a letter to Wilson that House carried to America on October 5, promising to support the content, which asserted that except for certain Moslem valleys Greeks were in a majority in Western Thrace. *Ibid.,* pp. 273–278. But House could no longer reach Wilson.

128. On the complicated determination of boundaries see *ibid.,* pp. 268–276.

129. On the disposition of Thrace see Tillman, pp. 387–388; Coolidge and Lord, pp. 228–231; Bowman, in Seymour and House, pp. 173–174; Haskins and Lord, pp. 281–285; Petsalis-Diomidis, pp. 256–290 and map; and Paul C. Helmreich, *From Paris to Sèvres,* pp. 153–158.

130. State Department to Ammission, November 25, 1919, N.A., R.G. 59, 763.72119 / 8006a. Dispatch, Ammission to the secretary of state, July 27, 1919, Lamont papers, 172-5. *F.R., P.P.C.,* vol. 6, pp. 498–500.

131. Bowman to Day, November 4, 1919, Day papers, box 5.

24

Self-Determination and Minorities

We have seen the complications that beset the diplomats as a result of appeals to the principle of self-determination, which in the diplomacy of Europe had served less as a moving force than as a formula that was useful in coping with existing circumstances.

American policy in 1919 was subject to particular stress from two minorities that appealed to Wilson's predilection for self-determination. Advocates of Irish independence and those of a Zionist establishment in Palestine, wielding a political influence in the United States that was disproportionate to their numbers, looked eagerly to the delegates at the Peace Conference for sympathy and support.

Irish-Americans, determined to aid their kin who were in revolt against the British government,[1] had tried unsuccessfully to induce McAdoo to represent them at Paris, and both Tumulty and Creel had importuned the president to give heed to their cause.[2] Wilson, however, deemed it unwise to press the matter. On January 26 the president cabled: "I frankly dread the effect on British public opinion . . . of a Home Rule resolution by the House of Representatives. . . . It is not a question of sympathy but of international tactics at a very critical moment."[3] The conflict between responsible diplomacy and political expediency was embarrassing.

Nevertheless, when agitation for Irish independence rose to a crest on St. Patrick's Day, the House of Representatives passed a resolution asking that the Peace Conference "favorably consider the claims of Ireland to self-determination." There was danger that if the American commission at Paris failed to act aggressively to get a hearing for the rebels, the Irish in America would oppose the League of Nations.[4]

While in Washington in February the president gave assurance to Lord Reading that he would do nothing that could commit the British government in any way to bring the Irish question before the Peace Conference. At the same time, Reading

1. Sixty members of the Irish Parliamentary party, which on November 5, 1918, introduced in the House of Commons a resolution that the Irish question should be settled in accord with President Wilson's principles, signed an appeal to Wilson that was transmitted through the American embassy at London, brief no. 490, doc. 841D.00 / 2, Y.H.C. Alan J. Ward, *Ireland and Anglo-American Relations, 1899–1921* (London, 1969), pp. 167–168. Joseph P. O'Grady, "The Irish," in *The Immigrants' Influence on Wilson's Peace Policies,* ed. O'Grady, pp. 59 ff.

2. Tumulty to Wilson, December 29, 1918, Tumulty papers, box 2. Creel to Wilson, March 3, 1919; letter, five senators to Wilson, March 28, 1919, stating that both the future of the Democratic party and early ratification of the treaty required that the Peace Conference do something "to meet the reasonable expectations of the Irish People," Wilson papers. See Tillman, *Anglo-American Relations at the Paris Peace Conference,* pp. 197–198.

3. Tumulty to Wilson, December 31, 1918; Wilson to Tumulty, January 7, 1919. Tumulty replied that to convey Wilson's message to Congressman Flood would be to put the president in the role of an opponent of "deep sentiment" in the House, Tumulty to Wilson, January 28, 1919, Wilson papers.

4. *Weekly Intelligence Review,* March 23, 1919, Bliss papers, box 127. The *New York Times* of March 16 quoted a boast by a representative of the Sinn Fein: "We can stop ratification of this League of Nations in Congress if the Irish question is not settled."

approved the issue of American passports to three Irish-Americans who had been commissioned by a convention of their people to attempt to gain a hearing at Paris for spokesmen of the rebels in Ireland.[5]

The president found no time to receive a delegation of twenty-four Irish delegates who traveled to Washington to see him. But on the eve of sailing from New York he allowed Tumulty to bring Irish-American delegates to the Metropolitan Opera House for an interview backstage, excluding one man who had a record of disloyalty during the war.[6] They pleaded for Wilson's intercession to secure a hearing for Irish revolutionaries at the Peace Conference. But in view of the necessity that Wilson was under to satisfy the demand for a reservation to the League Covenant that would confirm the Monroe Doctrine's ban on foreign interference in American affairs, he thought it wise to state publicly that the Irish question was one to be solved by Great Britain acting alone.[7]

The president did, however, ask Lloyd George what could be done, saying that if the question was avoided at Paris, the Irish might campaign against the League of Nations and raise embarrassing issues of race and religion. In exasperation he suggested to the prime minister that the question be solved by putting it in the hands of the Irish people and reserving the cinema rights.[8]

However, he received the three Irish Americans, and they asked him to obtain a British safe-conduct to Paris for the representatives from Ireland. Afterward, House, recording that the president had "cheerfully unloaded them" on him, tried to arrange for a visit to Ireland by the three Americans and he found the Foreign Office cooperative. At luncheon two days later Lloyd George, who apparently hoped to explore a path toward ending the political ferment that had disturbed Anglo-American relations for many years, said that he would like to see the three Americans when he could find time. While the prime minister kept them waiting, it was arranged to give them British passports to visit Ireland. The three were welcomed convivially by their brethren in Dublin; and while driving down Sackville Street under the patronage of His Majesty's government, they burst into insults to the crown.[9] Bonsal recorded that one of the offenders, having returned to Paris filled with remorse, said he partook immoderately of usquebaugh and did not remember what happened in Dublin but had been told that he called upon all who heard him to join the boys

5. Dispatch, Auchincloss from Polk, May 14, 1919, Y.H.C. Polk explained that Reading took the view that the Irish in America would be irritated if passports were refused, and the three delegates would do no great harm in Paris, Polk diary, March 4, 6, and 8, 1919, Y.H.C.; dispatch, Reading to F.O., March 5, 1919, P.R.O., FO / 608 / 243; copy of letter J. W. Davis to Lansing, May 19, 1919, Davis papers, Y.H.C. The three Irish-Americans, F. P. Walsh, E. F. Dunne, and M. J. Ryan, were to intercede in behalf of Eamon de Valera, Arthur Griffith, and Count Plunkett, in accord with a commission given them at Philadelphia by the Irish Race Convention on February 22, 1919, letter, Walsh, Dunne, and Ryan to Wilson, April 16, 1919, Wilson papers. See Ward, pp. 171–173, 177–178. Walsh had been co-chairman of the War Labor Board.

6. Tumulty to Wilson, March 4, 1919, Wilson papers. At the Opera House, Wilson was exasperated by the vehemence of the Irish spokesman in objecting to the barring of Daniel F. Cohalan, Baker, *American Chronicle*, pp. 385–386. See Ward, p. 174, and C. C. Tansill, *America and the Fight for the Irish Freedom, 1866–1922* (New York, 1957), pp. 302–303. Myles McCahill to the author.

7. Bonsal, *Unfinished Business*, p. 174.

8. Edith Benham diary letter, March 31, 1919.

9. House diary, April 18, 19, 21, and 30, 1919. Bonsal, p. 175–178.

from America and throw George the Fifth into the Shannon.

This affair led to severe attacks on Lloyd George in the British press, and King George V complained to the prime minister about the issue of passports to the Americans.[10] On May 7 Lloyd George explained in the Supreme Council that it was impossible now for him to receive the Irish rebels at Paris.[11]

Nevertheless, the rebels and their American sympathizers persisted in demanding a hearing at the Peace Conference. The three Irish-Americans put their case in a note to the president.[12] House, according to his record, persuaded Wilson against a brusque refusal and in favor of a moralizing response.[13] Accordingly, Lansing was instructed to say that the behavior of the Irish-Americans in Ireland had given the deepest offense to those with whom they sought to deal and made it impossible for the American commission to serve them further. However, a letter that Lansing and House wrote in accord with their chief's instructions did not satisfy F. P. Walsh,[14] the head of the Irish-American delegation.[15]

The American commission then fell back upon a technical explanation that the president had rejected. They notified the Irish-Americans that it was not within their province to ask the Peace Conference to receive certain delegates from a participating nation in respect of a matter that had no relation to the making of peace with the enemy.[16] But Walsh sent a copy of the commission's interview with the president. It was now clear that the bitter feeling of the Irish-Americans was not to be allayed by evasion, admonishment, or reason. "These gentlemen are certainly making it hard for their friends," Wilson complained to Lansing.[17] The American com-

---

10. Lord Stamfordham to the prime minister, May 9, 1919, Lord George papers. This letter, conveying the king's displeasure, observed that the government of the United States would not tolerate such behavior in their country by British citizens.

11. Wilson was distressed by a news report of statements made by the head of the Irish-American delegation that seemed to place responsibility on the United States government for its visit to Dublin. The State Department took the position that the British visa for travel in Ireland had been granted without any American urging, Kerr to Wilson, May 12, 1919, Wilson-House correspondence. J. W. Davis to Lansing, May 19, 1919, Davis papers, Y.H.C. Harrison to Bell, May 9, 1919, Harrison papers, box 103. Auchincloss diary, May 12 and 14, 1919. House and Lloyd George had contrary recollections as to responsibility for the presence of the offending Irish-Americans in Dublin. Each attributed to the other the initiative for an interview of the three with Lloyd George. House to Lloyd George, May 9, 1919; Lloyd George to House, May 10, 1919; House to Wilson, May 9, 1919, Y.H.C. House diary, May 10, 1919. "It was Lloyd George's own idea that he see them," Auchincloss diary, May 9, 1919. Auchincloss took up the matter with Kerr.

12. Letter, Walsh, Dunne, and Ryan to the president, May 20, 1919, draft with corrections in Miller papers, box 89, IV, "Col. House's pa."

13. Auchincloss diary, May 13, 1919. House diary, May 20, 1919.

14. Letters, Lansing to Wilson, May 18, 1919, Wilson to Lansing, May 20, 1919, Lansing to Wilson, May 21, 1919, Wilson to Lansing, May 22, 1919, Wilson papers. House diary, May 21 and 24, 1919. According to House's diary, Wilson thought Lansing's draft too formal and asked House to edit it.

15. Walsh to Wilson, May 27, 1919. Lansing to Wilson, May 26, 1919. With each of these letters was enclosed a copy of a letter, Lansing to Walsh, May 26, 1919, Wilson papers.

16. Grew to Walsh and Dunne, May 31, 1919, Wilson papers.

17. Letters, Walsh to Wilson, June 2, 1919; Wilson to Lansing, May 28, 1919, Wilson papers. Complaining of the "miserable mischief-making" of these men who "see nothing except their own small interest," the president said to Baker: "I have . . . one terrible weapon which I shall not use unless I am driven to it. . . . I have only to warn our people of the attempt of the Roman Catholic hierarchy to dominate our public opinion and there is no doubt about what Americans will do," Baker journal, May 31, 1919.

missioners agreed to talk informally with them, individually and separately.[18]

The bearing of the Irish question upon the attitude of the American Senate toward the peace treaty became still clearer when that body passed, with only one dissenting vote, a resolution that requested the American commission to secure a hearing at the Peace Conference for the Irish rebels. At the same time Walsh and Dunne further pressed their case by reporting to the president on their observations while in Ireland and demanding an investigation of conditions there.[19]

When notified of the Senate's action, which according to a message from Tumulty[20] reflected sentiment not confined to Irish-Americans, Wilson instructed his vigilant secretary to explain that because of the "extraordinary indiscretion" of the Irish-Americans he did not know how to act without creating a breach with the British government. "I made an effort yesterday in this matter," he cabled, "which shows, I am afraid, the utter futility of future efforts." Thanked by Tumulty and urged to persist, in view of the feeling of the Irish-Americans about the League Covenant, the president asked Lansing what he should do or say.[21] His fellow commissioners then recommended that the Senate's resolution be sent to Clemenceau, with a request that he lay it before the Peace Conference.[22] This was done, and Clemenceau replied on June 25 that intervention in the domestic affairs of Allied states was something that the Peace Conference could in no way consider under any circumstances whatever.[23] Grew explained to the Irish pleaders that only Clemenceau, as president of the Peace Conference, could introduce the Irish question into the formal proceedings, and therefore nothing could be done.[24]

Wilson asked Walsh and Dunne to come to talk with him, personally and unofficially,[25] but he was not able to give satisfaction to these zealous promoters of Irish freedom. He explained to them that the Council of Four had agreed that it would hear the case of no small nation if any one of the four objected. Moreover, only nations actually involved in the war had been heard. Reminded of his commitment to "self-determination," Wilson confessed that he was suffering great anxiety because he was learning to what extent the hopes that he had raised were incompatible with the arrangements and commitments by which the Europeans were bound. He was

18. House diary, May 31, 1919.
19. Polk to Ammission, June 6, 1919, Walsh and Dunne to Wilson, June 6, 1919, Wilson papers. According to Dr. Grayson, Reading told Wilson that Republican senators used the threat of a pro-Irish resolution to try to induce Lloyd George to oppose all of Wilson's policies. Wilson described the passing of the Senate resolution as an infringement on the sovereignty of Great Britain and an unfriendly act, Grayson diary, May 22, June 12, 1919. Polk to Auchincloss, May 5, 1919; Polk to Lansing, May 5, 1919; Polk diary, April 26, 1919.
20. Tumulty to Grayson, June 7 and 9, 1919, Tumulty papers, box 3. Lodge's explanation of the Senate's feeling was that it was in reaction to English assertions that any questions in respect of the Monroe Doctrine were to be decided by the League of Nations, Lodge to Bryce, June 10, 1919, Bryce papers, vol. 7, p. 187, Bodleian Library.
21. Wilson to Tumulty, June 8 and 9, 1919, Tumulty papers, box 3. Tumulty to Wilson, June 9 and 25, 1919, Wilson papers.
22. Wilson to Lansing, June 10, 1919, four commissioners to Wilson, June 10, 1919, Wilson papers.
23. Lansing's desk diary, June 14, 1919. Ammission to the secretary of state, June 20, 1919, N.A., R.G. 59, 763.72119 / 5350.
24. Ward, p. 185.
25. Grew to Close, June 9, 1919, Wilson papers. "It is plain that at every point the president is thinking of American public opinion," Baker journal, May 31, 1919.

involved, he said, in a "great metaphysical tragedy." When the president completed his frank and eloquent explanation of the limitations that duty put upon him, one of these men who had come in a hostile mood had tears in his eyes.[26]

When the substance of this interview was published in the United States, even those Irish-Americans who were loyal to Wilson became dismayed. They found it hard to accept Wilson's appeal to the principle of unanimity in the Council of Four as justification for the barring of spokesmen for Ireland. They gave strength to the opposition that was growing ominous at Washington. "You know what the Irish vote is in this country," Senator Lodge wrote to Henry White on July 2. "As far as I can make out, they are bitterly opposed to the League, and the fate of the Democratic Party in the Northern States is in their hands."[27]

The president attempted to turn the incident to the advantage of his great cause by asserting that the League would provide a new forum for bringing the opinion of the world, and that of the United States in particular, to bear on just such causes as that of the Irish.[28] However, House, wishing that the Irish might accept dominion status in the British Empire and like Canada and the others "practically make themselves what they would," saw political strife ahead and wrote to Tumulty: "It is a critical period in the president's career, and I doubt whether he realizes it as much as you and I."[29]

The Irish rebellion was but one of the political movements that in the name of "self-determination" embarrassed the peacemakers at Paris. In southeastern Europe this principle that Wilson had exalted in his political speeches was proving to be an unreliable measure of the legitimacy of native ferment. The mere impulse of a minority group to constitute an independent state was not always a sound basis on which to build viable new governments that would have the practical essentials for a prosperous life.[30] The oppressed, now liberated, were undertaking to oppress others. Actually, Italy, Czechoslovakia, Poland, Romania, and Greece acquired large populations of alien blood that might be expected to agitate for the civil rights of minorities, if not for their independence.

House's commentary on the Fourteen Points had asserted that the United States, while "clearly committed to the programme of national unity and independence, . . . must stipulate . . . for the protection of national minorities." The American policy, as Wilson had stated it in a note to Orlando in January, was that "it be one of the fundamental covenants of the Peace that all new states should enter into solemn obligations, under responsibility to the whole body of nations, to accord to all racial and national authorities within their jurisdictions exactly the same status and treatment, alike in law and in fact, that are accorded to the majority of the

26. Memorandum of an interview between Bliss and Walsh and Dunne, June 13, 1919, Bliss papers, box 248, 836a; Grayson diary, June 11, 1919. See John B. Duff, "The Versailles Treaty and the Irish-Americans," 596.

27. Nevins, *White*, p. 455. Ward, p. 168.

28. Wilson to Tumulty, June 27, 1919, Wilson papers.

29. Letter in Tumulty papers, box 1.

30. See Étienne Mantoux, *The Carthaginian Peace*, pp. 36 ff.

people.'' This concept was not without precedent in the history of the nineteenth century with respect to religious minorities; but Wilson would apply it to political subgroups as well.[31]

The governments of small states, however, resisted the realization of this ideal. New governments, though willing to agree voluntarily to protect the rights of minorities, were as emphatic as the great powers in objecting to interference in their domestic affairs. The new authorities asked why they should submit to supervision any more than the government of Italy, which was required only to make an oral declaration that it would respect the rights of the large German and Slavic minorities in the territories that it acquired.

The Americans met with some success in efforts to protect subgroups. They were eager to apply the democratic concept of civil rights in the nations of eastern Europe, and especially in Poland, whence stories of cruel persecution were coming to Paris. (Many of the tales were verified later by an investigation, and others were not.) The behavior of occupying troops such as the Romanians in Hungary stirred up a wave of popular protest against the treatment given to minorities; and the work of drawing frontiers was complicated by the concern that was felt for the fate of those people whose blood was alien to that of those who ruled. On April 1 the question was brought before Wilson by Coolidge, whose observations at Vienna had convinced him that the Peace Conference should issue a definition of at least the minimum rights of minorities—political, linguistic, and ethnic—that would subsist in the new states of eastern Europe.[32]

When two prominent American Jews asked House in mid-April what they could do to get protection for their people, they received a friendly assurance of assistance and were advised to avoid publicity, to talk with the British and French delegates, and to suggest a definite plan.[33] This they did; and Miller and Professor Manley O. Hudson considered their proposals and, suggesting certain changes, alternatives, and compromises, worked with the Jews to arrive at a draft that Wilson put before Clemenceau and Lloyd George on May 1. The president spoke of ill treatment of Jews in Poland and their loss of civic rights in Romania. He thought it necessary to provide guarantees of the rights of national as well as religious minorities, and he remarked upon the protection that would be given to Germans who were to be subject to Polish rule.

Headlam-Morley, delegated to represent the British, joined with Miller in recommending to the Council of Four that since the restrictions that should be imposed on new states with respect to minority rights were too complicated to be stated in the treaties of peace, this matter should be covered in separate pacts to be signed by the new states and the five great powers. As a result a Committee on New States

31. Manley O. Hudson, ''The Protection of Minorities,'' in *What Really Happened at Paris,* ed. Seymour and House, pp. 209–210.

32. Letter, Lansing to Wilson, April 1, 1919, enclosing a memorandum from Coolidge on ''Rights of National Minorities,'' Wilson papers. Coolidge and Lord, *Archibald Cary Coolidge,* pp. 231–232. See Wandycz, *The United States and Poland,* p. 160.

33. House diary, April 15, 1919; Miller, *My Diary,* vol. 1, April 1919, pp. 19, 20, 22, 23, 29, 30. The two Jewish spokesmen were Julian W. Mack, a federal judge and a Zionist, and Louis Marshall, an advocate of the League of Nations and not a Zionist.

was appointed to draft appropriate articles.[34]

It distressed Headlam-Morley that Miller had leaned heavily upon the recommendations of the American Jews who undertook to advise the Crillon.[35] The American expert, Lord, thought that the Poles would consent neither to the constitution of the Jewish population as a national minority nor to the imposition of a particular form of electoral procedure. Nevertheless, Headlam-Morley, though agreeing with Lord, drafted a single brief clause for the treaty with Germany that would bind Poland and Czechoslovakia to agree to make treaties with the Allied powers that would protect race, language, or religion. The Council of Four accepted this solution of the question.[36] Moreover, on May 22 they approved a recommendation of the Committee on New States for the insertion in the treaty with Austria of a clause requiring the government of Yugoslavia to accept a similar undertaking.

Wilson, under continuing pressure from American Jews, asked Tumulty to give them assurance that the necessity of protecting their people was fully appreciated.[37] He gave careful attention to the text proposed by the Committee on New States for a treaty to be imposed on Poland. In his desire to improve the status of the Jews, he was moved both by good will and by the fact that oppression and outlawry encouraged bolshevism. Yet he wished to avoid any arrangements that would enable a minority to become a state within a state. On May 31, when the terms for the proposed treaty with Austria were read at a plenary session, Wilson, the avowed champion of the political integrity of small powers, strongly supported the position taken by the Council of Four. He asserted the responsibility of the great powers for the world's peace and their consequent right to make provision, under an organization such as the League of Nations, for the protection of religious and political

34. On this committee, which held 64 meetings between May and December, were Miller and Hudson, Berthelot representing France, and Headlam-Morley, who thought that minority treaties under the League of Nations presented to the great powers and the Balkan states an opportunity to escape from provisions of earlier treaties that had become anachronisms, James Headlam-Morley, *Studies in Diplomatic History,* p. 143. Miller, *My Diary,* vol. 1, May 2, and doc. 915. Problems arising in the drafting of a minority treaty with Poland, and the part played by American Jews at Paris, are discussed by Lundgreen-Nielsen, *The Polish Problem at the Paris Peace Conference,* pp. 305–306, 342–343, and Wandycz, p. 162.

35. Miller, *My Diary,* vol. 1, May 5, 12, 13, 26, 1919. Frankfurter, who lobbied at Paris as the eyes, ears, and spokesman of Justice Brandeis, called frequently on House and appealed to Wilson.

It seemed to Headlam-Morley, the British expert, that Hudson, whom he found "obstinate and difficult to deal with," was "very much in the hands of Marshall," Headlam-Morley to Louis Namier, June 30, 1919, Headlam-Morley papers. "I got the feeling," Headlam-Morley wrote, "that what the Americans were thinking of was much more the vote of the New York Jews than the real advantages to be won for the Jews in Poland. I am left with the firm conviction that this political Jewish element may in fact be a very dangerous factor in the League of Nations."

36. *F.R., P.P.C.,* vol. 5, pp. 439–444, 625, 816–817. Mantoux, *Délibérations,* vol. 1, pp. 440, 474, vol. 2, pp. 92–94. Headlam-Morley's diary, May 2, 1919. Articles 86 and 93 of the Treaty of Versailles.

37. On May 27 Wilson asked Tumulty to reassure Rabbi Wise, cables, Tumulty to Wilson, May 6, 1919, Wilson papers. Wilson to Tumulty, May 8, 1919, Wilson papers. Wilson to Tumulty, May 27, 1919, Tumulty papers, box 5.

House suggested that Justice Brandeis be told that the Jews were hurting their cause by propaganda of dubious authenticity. According to House, Frankfurter told Hugh Gibson that the Jews in the United States had almost decided to block Gibson's confirmation by the Senate as minister to Poland because they thought him unsympathetic, House diary, June 23, 25, and 26, 1919.

minorities. At the same time he promised that the council would confer with representatives of the small powers before the treaty with Austria was signed and would meet their views as far as possible.[38]

A separate treaty that was signed by the great powers and by Poland on June 28, simultaneously with the signing of the Treaty of Versailles, confirmed recognition of the Polish state and guaranteed to all inhabitants the rights of citizenship: equality before the law, free use of languages, religious freedom, and the right to private or public education. It provided for a right of appeal to the council of the League, which would have power to enforce and modify the provisions. Disputes as to matters of fact or of law were to be referred to the Permanent Court of International Justice.[39]

The pact with Poland was a model for similar treaties that were concluded later with Czechoslovakia simultaneously with the signing of the Treaty of St. Germain on September 10 and in December with Yugoslavia and Romania, whose delegates protested vigorously against the possibility of interference in their domestic affairs. Protection for minorities was provided also in the settlements with Austria, Hungary, Bulgaria, and Turkey.[40]

The acquiescence of the Polish government was facilitated by the wielding of American economic power and by Wilson's acceptance of a suggestion of his advisers that an American mission go to Poland to investigate the status of the Jews. The concern of the Americans for the Jewish minority was particularly strong with respect to Poland, where Hoover's agents were supporting Paderewski's government by relief work.[41] One of Hoover's friends, Hugh Gibson, the first American minister

---

38. *F.R., P.P.C.*, vol. 3, pp. 398–410. Spector, *Rumania at the Paris Peace Conference*, p. 143. Miller, *Drafting*, vol. 2, pp. 103, 153–154. Hudson, p. 213.

The president was reminded by Balfour that there was good precedent in European history for imposing conditions for the treatment of minorities upon states that were granted increases in territory, memorandum initialed "A. J. B.," May 31, 1919, Balfour papers, 49741. Wilson read this paper and jotted on it: "Lansing's recollection is the same."

Headlam-Morley had been disillusioned by Wilson's gift of the Tyrol to Italy and had come to the conclusion that it was "impossible to place any real reliance" on Americans for support in carrying through Wilsonian principles. He detected no enthusiasm among the French for a formal guarantee of minority rights and wrote: "The Americans are curiously unsatisfactory. Miller has gone and we have only Manley O. Hudson, who is very young and inexperienced and frightened of coming to any decision on his own responsibility," letter, June 2, 1919, to Namier, Headlam-Morley diary. Scott, he noted, "chattered interminably," and Miller seemed "a dull fellow," "Protection of Minority Rights," a paper by Headlam-Morley, undated but probably May 19, 1919, in the possession of Professor Agnes Headlam-Morley.

39. Miller's part in the drafting of the minorities treaties is described in J. F. Posey's "David Hunter Miller at the Paris Peace Conference," pp. 163–177. The texts of the minorities treaties are in Temperley, *A History of the Peace Conference at Paris*, vol. 5, pp. 432 ff. See Nathan Feinburg, *Le Question des minorités à la Conférence de la Paix de 1919–1920 et l'action juive en faveur de la protection internationale des minorités*, Seymour and House, pp. 204–230, and Wandycz, pp. 162–165.

40. Temperley, vol. 4, pp. 138, 236. Pasić and Vesnić protested to Polk that the clause in the Treaty of St. Germain that protected minorities would deprive Yugoslavia of sovereignty over Macedonia and keep dissident propaganda alive there. But when Polk, expressing sympathy, warned them that by aligning their government with the obstructive policy of Romania they would forfeit the financial support of the United States, they decided to sign, Polk diary, September 8, 1919. See Temperley, vol. 4, pp. 408, 434–435, vol. 5, pp. 130–132, 432 ff.

41. Wilson did not accept an invitation from Paderewski to visit Poland but instead asked Hoover to go. When Hoover did so in the summer of 1919, the popular welcome convinced him of Polish accep-

at Warsaw, devoted himself to getting the truth about alleged persecution. He observed that propagandists of all sorts, including those of a big German bureau, were spreading exaggerated stories of instances of alleged injustice.[42] Gibson's reports on the "pogroms," however, satisfied neither the international community of Jews nor the British advisers at Paris.[43] Wilson instructed the investigating mission to "make careful inquiry into all matters affecting the relation between the Jewish and non-Jewish elements in Poland." Differing from the other American plenipotentiaries, the president thought that the investigating committee of three should include one Jew, and he insisted that Henry Morgenthau serve despite Zionist opposition to his appointment.[44] Walter Lippmann, receiving an invitation from House to accompany the mission in an official capacity, declined to serve.[45]

The mission went to Poland on July 10 and in October made a report to the American commission at Paris. It exonerated government officials, civil and military, and told of anti-Semitic prejudice and propaganda as well as of political hostility to the state on the part of Jews. Finding Pilsudski bitterly resentful of outside interference in what he considered to be a domestic matter, and noting that anti-Semitism had its roots partly in indignation against Jewish cooperation with Germany, Morgenthau sought to aid in the quest of the Poles for "self reliant, successful independence" and to help them to establish a sound currency and to secure needed raw materials. He recommended in a letter of August 10 to Paderewski that a corporation be organized that would give the United States no commercial advantage and would be financed by France, Great Britain, Italy, and others, with the American secretary of the interior, Franklin K. Lane, at its head.[46]

Meanwhile, the American commission at Paris was, according to Professor Lord, "overwhelmed" with grievances brought by Jewish spokesmen,[47] some of whom made their way to Poland and greatly embarrassed the diplomacy of Gibson.[48]

---

tance of democracy and of the nation's resistance to bolshevism; and he continued in ensuing months to further American ministration, George J. Lerski, *Herbert Hoover and Poland,* pp. 20 ff.

42. Gibson to "Dearest," May 29, 1919, Gibson papers, Hoover Institution Archives, Palo Alto, box 10. General W. R. Groves reported from Warsaw on January 9, 1919, that there were "daily combats of a very local character" between Jewish merchants and soldiers searching Jewish quarters for hoards of food and arms, and that the soldiers fired shots, presumably to scare people, *F.R., P.P.C.,* vol. 2, p. 427.

According to Dmowski, more than a quarter of the Jews of the world lived in Poland, where they constituted about 10 percent of the population. Bonsal, asked by House to "feel out" Dmowski on this subject, received from the Polish statesman an opinion that the eastern Jews were peculiarly trying to those who lived in daily contact with them, and an admission that in communities in which the Jews seemed too numerous there were "at times small pogroms," *Suitors and Suppliants,* p. 124.

43. Henry Morgenthau, *All in a Life-Time,* p. 356. Lundgreen-Nielsen, pp. 303, 347, 375.

44. Wilson to Lansing, Lansing to Wilson, June 14, 1919, Wilson to Lansing, June 16, 1919. On the origin and development of the Morgenthau mission, see Lundgreen-Nielsen, pp. 371–373, 384–385, and Wandycz, p. 166.

45. Telegram, House to Lippmann, June 26, 1919, Lippmann to House, July 19, 1919, Lippmann papers, series I, box 14, f. 564. A handwritten paragraph filed here says that Lippmann would accept House's invitation only if pressed to do so and if Morgenthau were not a member of the mission.

46. Morgenthau, pp. 352–384, 407–423. *F.R., P.P.C.,* vol. 11, pp. 232–233 and *passim.* Morgenthau to Paderewski, August 10, 1919, Morgenthau to Hoover, August 12, 1919, Gibson papers, 8-5B.

47. Lord to Gibson, August 22, 1919, Gibson papers, 8-4.

48. Gibson recommended that, in order to avoid embarrassment, Frankfurter not be given a passport to Poland and that other private citizens—"Zionists and other trouble-makers"—also be excluded, let-

In western Asia, as well as in Europe, the assertion of minority rights was a hazard to the peace of the future. The peacemakers at Paris were importuned by Zionists to make good upon a pledge that had been made by Balfour in 1917. Like the secret treaties that divided the spoils of war, the Balfour Declaration was born out of the necessity of commanding loyalty to the martial effort. The question that it raised, which proved to be one of the most portentous of the century, was from the beginning one of great delicacy.

The international Zionist movement that had developed late in the nineteenth century had gained strength during the war. As early as 1915 Justice Louis D. Brandeis had assumed the leadership of American Zionists, whom he called "the new Pilgrim Fathers." In his opinion the assimilation of Jews in the nations in which they dwelt was "national suicide."[49] In 1917 Brandeis assured the British Zionists that the American Jews would do all they could to advance the cause though it was not "prudent" for him, as a justice of the Supreme Court, to say anything for publication. He had what he considered a satisfactory talk at Washington with Wilson and Balfour.[50]

A leader of the Zionist movement, Chaim Weizmann, had spent seven months in Palestine with General Allenby and had given valuable help to Lloyd George in the production of munitions.[51] In October of 1917, when the enemy powers seemed about to develop a Zionist program,[52] Weizmann cabled to Justice Brandeis the text

---

ter, Gibson to Harrison, July 8, 1919, Harrison papers, box 107, folder "M-143." Morgenthau wired to Grew that Lansing did not want Frankfurter to go to Poland and thought Frankfurter meant to "make mischief," Morgenthau to Grew, July 14, 1919. After consulting Hoover, Grew telegraphed that arrangements had gone too far for him to stop Frankfurter, Grew to Morgenthau, July 17, 1919. Frankfurter made the trip in July, told Gibson that Morgenthau was "totally unfitted" for his task, and resented Gibson's inclination to leave the matter in Morgenthau's hands, Gibson to Grew, July 31, 1919.

Realizing that an investigating mission was inevitable and that the Poles, for all their splendid qualities, suffered from factional strife and could be very exasperating, Gibson tried to be hospitable to Frankfurter while firm against intervening. Gibson to Grew, July 31, 1919, Gibson papers 7A-4. He explained to Lippmann that the mission's job—"loaded with poison"—was "outside the boundaries of diplomacy." Though he thought it not the business of the United States government to investigate excesses that were "wrapped up in doubt and misrepresentation and exaggeration," he recommended endless forebearance with unreasonableness of all kinds, Gibson to Lippmann, August 9, 1919, Gibson to Laughlin, December 31, 1919, Gibson papers, 8-4. He warned Brandeis, in a conversation at Paris on June 28, against exaggerated statements, Bruce Allen Murphy, *The Brandeis-Frankfurter Connection* (New York, 1982), p. 62.

Gibson reported from Warsaw that the Polish government was very generous to visiting American Jews, a number of whom outrageously abused the privileges granted, letter, Harrison to Winslow, July 24, 1919, Harrison papers, L.C. Gibson to Harrison, July 8, 1919, Gibson papers, 7A-5. "Their publicity is destroying the reputation and financial credit of Poland," Gibson to Harrison, October 16, 1919, Gibson papers, 7A-4.

49. Allen Gal, *Brandeis of Boston* (Cambridge, Mass., 1980), pp. 181, 206. Leonard J. Stein, *The Balfour Declaration*, p. 193.

50. Rothschild to Brandeis, April 21 and 30, 1917, Brandeis to Rothschild, May 9 and 17, 1917, Wiseman papers, Y.H.C.

51. Charles Webster, "Notes on Zionism," Webster papers, 3 / 7 (32), British Library of Political and Economic Science, London School of Economics, pp. 1, 3. Lloyd George, *The Truth about the Peace Treaties*, p. 1117.

52. Laurence Evans, *U.S. Policy and the Partition of Turkey, 1914–1924*, pp. 46–48. Webster, p. 3.

"Weizmann and Sokolow in London and Brandeis in Washington together represented *de facto* the

of a declaration that had the approval of the British Foreign Office and the prime minister. Opposition was expected from assimilationists, the message said, and it "would help greatly if President Wilson and Brandeis would support [the]text."[53] Wilson at first felt that there were "dangers lurking" behind the British proposal,[54] and instructed House to say that he "concurred in the formula suggested" but thought a public commitment by him would be injudicious.[55]

As the Turkish forces in Palestine were withdrawing before the advance of Allenby, and at the outbreak of the Bolshevik revolution in Russia, Balfour had issued on November 2, 1917, a declaration of the intention of His Majesty's government to "use their best endeavor" to facilitate the establishment of a national home in Palestine for the Jewish people, "it being clearly understood that nothing shall be done which may prejudice civil and religious rights of existing non-Jewish communities in Palestine." (The qualification was in respect of pledges that had been made by British agents to Arab nationalists and in response to the caveats of assimilationists who foresaw that the declaration might involve the Jews in the bitterest feuds with their neighbors of other races and religions.)[56]

Early in 1918 the French and Italian governments publicly expressed willingness to cooperate.[57] In England two Zionist periodicals prospered, and the movement won much popular support. Though many American Jews of wealth and influence were devoted to the principle of assimilation, a large majority welcomed a chance to take part in realizing the prospect that was opened. A Zionist Organization of America, dedicated to the defeat of Germany, attained much influence at Washington under the leadership of Brandeis and other intellectuals.[58]

Wilson was not unmoved by pressure from American Zionists. He had a profound respect for Brandeis, whom he had appointed to the Supreme Court in the face of bitter opposition. Moreover, many of the Zionists were ardent advocates of the League of Nations, while most of the anti-Zionists were Republicans and some were pro-German. Although it was pointed out to Wilson that the American government had not been at war with Turkey and could not legitimately champion independence for Palestine,[59] he had advocated in Point Twelve, for nationalities

main directing force of the movement, except so much of it as recognized the jurisdiction of the rising Executive in Berlin," Stein, p. 194.

53. Cables, Weizmann to Brandeis, September 15, October 10, 1917, Wiseman papers, Y.H.C.

54. House to F.O. for Cecil, September 10, 1917, Wiseman papers.

55. Wilson to House, October 13, 1917. Brandeis to Weizmann, September 26, October 19, 1917, Wiseman papers, Y.H.C. See Stein, pp. 405–410, and Morton Tenzer, "The Jews," in O'Grady (ed.), pp. 292–304.

56. Alfred M. Lilienthal, *The Zionist Connection,* p. 14.

According to Lloyd George, "It was contemplated that when the time arrived for according representative institutions to Palestine, if the Jews had meanwhile responded to the opportunity afforded them by the idea of a National Home and had become a definite majority of the inhabitants, then Palestine would thus become a Jewish Commonwealth," *The Truth about the Peace Treaties,* p. 1139.

57. Stein, pp. 587–592.

58. See Tenzer, pp. 292–304.

59. This and other considerations had been cited by Lansing as reasons for refraining from announcing an American policy in respect of Turkish territories, letter, the secretary of state to the president, December 13, 1917, N.A., R.G. 59, 867.01 / 13 i / 2a. The persistent disapproval of Zionist purposes by the State Department is discussed in Stein, pp. 597–601. However, Tenzer writes that "the State Department did many petty favors for the Zionists," who in 1917 had established an office at Washington for liaison with the American government, *op. cit.,* pp. 300–301.

under Turkish rule, "an undoubted security of life and an absolutely unmolested opportunity of autonomous development." On the last day of August 1918 he had gone so far as to write a letter to Rabbi Wise, for release on the eve of the Jewish New Year, asserting his "satisfaction . . . in the progress of the Zionist movement in the United States and in the Allied countries." Thus Wilson had committed himself, probably not without regard for the Jewish vote, to the cause of the Zionists.

In December of 1918 five hundred men who claimed to represent more than 3 million American Jews appealed for a Jewish commonwealth in Palestine under a trusteeship of Great Britain. An American Jewish Congress appointed a Zionist-dominated delegation to go to Paris to lobby for minority rights in Palestine as well as in Europe. The State Department informed the peace commission that a refusal to hear pleas of American racial organizations "would arouse a great deal of ill feeling among the members of these races in the United States."[60]

In January, Weizmann told House of the Zionist approval of Great Britain as a trustee for Palestine;[61] and the colonel, who thought himself "entirely conversant" with every phase of the Jewish question, introduced the Zionist leader to the president. House advised Weizmann not to plead for Zionism but merely to thank Wilson for his sympathy.[62]

In giving heed to Zionist aspirations House was moved by considerations other than sympathy for a persecuted people. He found this to be true also of Balfour, who seemed to present "a very curious theory regarding the Jews." "He is inclined to believe" House wrote in his diary on the last day of 1918, "that nearly all bolshevism and disorder of that sort is directly traceable to Jews. I suggested putting them, or the best of them, in Palestine, and holding them responsible for the orderly behavior of Jews throughout the world. Balfour thought the plan had possibilities." House had a talk with Wilson and shortly afterward discussed the matter with his fellow commissioners, who felt that the loyalty of the Jews was more international than national.[63]

The proposals of the Zionists alarmed the British Foreign Office. Weizmann, wishing to prevent local influences from impeding Jewish immigration, demanded Jewish representation in whatever government was set up for Palestine. Lloyd George, who in December 1918 had reached an understanding with Clemenceau that Palestine was to be a British sphere of influence and Syria a French dependency, thought that if the Jews expected to dominate the Holy Land under a British protectorate, they were putting their hopes too high.[64] Curzon, who was in charge of the Foreign

60. Polk to Ammission, December 24, 1918, January 1, 1919, N.A., R.G. 59, 763.72119/3204a and 3205. Tenzer, p. 309.

61. Bonsal, *Suitors and Suppliants*, p. 55.

62. House diary, January 6, 1919. Weizmann was commended to Wilson by C. P. Scott of the *Manchester Guardian* as a statesman of ability and "disinterested," Scott to Wilson, December 31, 1918, Wilson papers. See Manuel, *The Realities of American-Palestine Relations*, p. 220.

63. House diary, December 31, 1918, January 6, 1919. Minutes, ACTNP, January 3 and 4, 1919, Harrison papers, box 109, L.C.

64. Lloyd George to Kerr, February 15, 1919, enclosing a letter from Cardinal Bourne at Jerusalem, expressing the dismay of Christians and Arabs at the prospect of domination by a Jewish faction that, constituting less than a tenth of the population, was making itself disliked by "asserting themselves in every way . . . and generally interfering." On the opposition to Jewish colonization in Palestine, see

Office in Balfour's absence, sent more than that one warning.[65]

In the tradition of the Foreign Office, Balfour adhered to the Declaration that had been made under the stress of war. On February 7 the British delegation apprised the Crillon of its position. Actually, far less was conceded than had been claimed in a printed proposal that the Zionists had just circulated. Expressing a willingness to give the Jews wastelands "without driving the Arabs to the Wall," the British accepted the mission of training the two elements to work together. Nothing was said about a Jewish "commonwealth" or about any special status for Jews.[66]

When five Zionists pleaded before the Supreme Council on February 27, there was no American among them, for the Europeans mistrusted the liberal economic program of Brandeis for Palestine. Actually, the five pleaders were not of a single mind. Weizmann and Sokolow looked forward to the eventual emergence of an independent "commonwealth" that would take in not only Palestine, but all of southern Syria from Haifa to Akaba.[67]

As the American specialists studied the positions of the interested parties, differences of opinion developed among them. They were subject to persistent lobbying by American Zionists.[68] The Black Book stated: "It is right that Palestine should become a Jewish state, if the Jews, being given the full opportunity, make it such." The Inquiry proposed a British mandate, and Jews would be invited to settle and would be given all proper assistance that "may be consistent with the protection of the personal (especially the religious) and the property rights of the non-Jewish population."[69] Beer, however, thought the Zionist cause "impractical."[70] Wester-

A. W. Kiyyālī, *Palestine: A Modern History* (London, 1978), pp. 45 ff.

Westermann had been told by Ambassador Jusserand that French opinion was "on the whole not sympathetic" with the Zionists, diary, December 11, 1918. See Gelfand, *The Inquiry*, pp. 248–256, 327.

65. Curzon conveyed his misgivings to Balfour in a handwritten letter: "I entertain no doubt that he [Weizmann] is out for a Jewish government, if not at the moment, then in the near future. In the terms that he proposed to you . . . he deliberately inserted the underlined words: 'All necessary arrangements for the establishment in Palestine of a Jewish National Home *or Commonwealth.*' You meant the first, but he interpreted it as meaning the second. . . . Weizmann contemplates a Jewish State, a Jewish Nation, a subordinate population of Arabs, etc., ruled by Jews, the Jews in possession of the fat of the land, and directing the Administration. He is trying to effect this behind the screen and under the shelter of British trusteeship," Curzon to Balfour, January 26, 1919, Curzon papers, F / 112 / 208, box 65.

66. See Manuel, pp. 226–228.

67. *F.R., P.P.C.,* vol. 4, pp. 161–170. Bonsal, *Suitors and Suppliants,* pp. 52–53. Manuel, pp. 229–231. Requested on January 23 by Lansing to define his concept of a "Jewish National Home," Weizmann expressed a hope that "by Jewish immigration Palestine would ultimately become as Jewish as England is English," Chaim Weizmann, *Trial and Error* (New York, 1949), p. 305. Miller, *My Diary,* vol. 14, p. 115.

68. The Americans who signed a Zionist statement printed on February 3 were Judge Julian W. Mack, Rabbi Stephen Wise, Harry Friedenwald, Jacob deHaas, Mary Fels, Louis Robison, and Bernard Flexner. Frankfurter resigned from a position with the National Labor Relations Board and went to Paris to further the cause, acting under the remote control of Justice Brandeis. (He also gave advice on Labor aspects of the League of Nations.) He was regarded with some coolness by the older European leaders of the Zionist organization. He busied himself in talking with sympathetic American delegates and in guiding the drafting of a mandate for Palestine on which the Zionists of the world might agree, Manuel, pp. 227, 231–232. Frankfurter repeatedly urged Brandeis to act upon the plea of Weizmann that Brandeis come to Paris, Murphy, p. 61.

69. See Gelfand, pp. 248–256.

70. Beer diary, January 7, 1919. Professor Philip Marshall Brown, who had undertaken a mission to

mann inferred from talks with Zionist leaders that actually they did look forward to a Jewish state in Palestine.[71] He was concerned for the future of the native peoples there.

Unfortunately, at this time when good diplomacy called for a most precise weighing of words, it was discovered that the president of the United States had added to the confusion of tongues. At the beginning of March, while Frankfurter argued with American experts at Paris about a draft of a mandate for Palestine,[72] Wilson made an imprecise oral response to a petition that was presented to him by Zionists at Washington.[73] His remarks were published in the American press and raised hopes to an unwarranted height. Wilson went so far as to say, according to the press, that he was "persuaded that the allied nations, with the fullest concurrence of our own government and people, are agreed that in Palestine shall be laid the foundations of a Jewish commonwealth." Apparently the peacemakers at Paris did not take account of this startling commitment until April 11, when they discovered an allusion to it in a Cairo newspaper.[74] Apprised of the newspaper story, Lansing wrote to the president to ask whether he had been correctly quoted so that a denial might be issued if one was in order. This inquiry brought an immediate reply from Wilson, to the effect that though he "did not use any of the words" in the quotation, he "did in substance say" what was quoted. "The expression 'foundations of a Jewish commonwealth' goes a little further than my idea at that time," Wilson wrote. "All that I meant was to corroborate our expressed acquiescence in the position of the British government with regard to the future of Palestine."[75] The American peace commissioners concluded that "In view of the rather ambiguous phrasing of the president's reply . . . it would be safer not to make any official denial," as Westermann recommended.[76] A committee of American Zionists who had arrived at Paris on March 25 wished to hold the president literally to his words, but their claim to represent American Jewish opinion was challenged by a petition from 299 prominent Jews, among them Morgenthau, and by a declaration by thirty others that the Zionist project was "reactionary in its tendency, undemocratic in spirit, and totally

Palestine for the YMCA, had been reporting to Lansing for several months on the dangers that the Zionists posed both to the stability of Palestine and to the best interests of Jews, Manuel, pp. 224–225.

71. Westermann noted that all responsible American observers felt that Jewish purposes went far beyond what was implied in the phrase "national home," Westermann to Bullitt, January 16, February 28, March 15, April 11, 1919, Bullitt papers, Manuel, pp. 222–223. Westermann was indignant when, in one of his reports, a criticism of the "proposition of a Jewish State" was changed by Mezes to a recommendation, Gelfand, p. 327.

72. William Yale criticized a Frankfurter draft of a mandate for its socialistic provisions and for its presumption in asserting "the wish of the inhabitants of Palestine," and he cut it to pieces, Manuel, pp. 231–232.

73. The petition asked that the Peace Conference "recognize the aspirations and historic claims of the Jewish people in regard to Palestine" and vest its possession in the League of Nations with Great Britain its governor under a mandate. The establishment of a Jewish national home was recommended, and "ultimately . . . the creation of an autonomous Commonwealth," petition signed by Judge Mack, Stephen Wise, and Louis Marshall, March 1, 1919, Wilson papers.

74. "I called W. L. Westermann's attention to the statement in *The Egyptian Gazette*. He told me to draft a memorandum to Lansing," Yale to the author, September 10, 1968.

75. Memorandum, Westermann to Bullitt, April 11, 1919; memorandum, office of secretary general to the ACTNP, April 17, 1919, Yale papers, Y.H.C.

76. Minutes, ACTNP, April 18, 1919. Memorandum, Westermann to Bullitt, April 11, 1919.

contrary to the practices of free government."[77]

Frankfurter begged Wilson repeatedly for "a reassuring word, written or spoken," to the effect that the Balfour Declaration would be written into the peace treaty and put into effect before the president left Paris. Finally, Wilson replied that he "had never dreamed it was necessary" to give any further assurance of his "adhesion to the Balfour declaration." Though unwilling to make a public affirmation, he gave Frankfurter permission to show this statement to those interested, including Brandeis.[78]

Justice Brandeis came to Paris to advance the Zionist cause in June,[79] just as Wilson was informed by a telegram from an investigating commission that he had sent to Jerusalem that both Christians and Moslems showed "a most hostile attitude" toward Jewish immigration and would use force to oppose it.[80] Brandeis explained to Balfour that he had been led to espouse the cause of Zionism by the difficulties raised by the immigration into the United States of a vast number of Jews, many of them from Russia and subversive of civil order. It was his hope that in Palestine men such as these might find constructive channels for their energies and abilities. Considering the future of his people as a "world problem" rather than a matter to be settled on the basis of "self-determination" in Palestine, he put forward three conditions that he thought essential to the realization of the Zionist program;[81] and he expressed hope that while he made a brief visit to Palestine, nothing would be done at Paris that would obstruct the fulfillment of his three conditions.

In response, Balfour explained that Great Britain had to take account of Moslem restlessness and a new Arab imperialism as well as of relations with France. Nevertheless, he expressed agreement with the conditions of Brandeis, and gave his assurance that during the next month no decision would be taken on the matters involved.

77. Lilienthal, pp. 768–769.

78. Frankfurter to Wilson, May 8, 14, and 20, 1919; Wilson to Frankfurter, May 13 and 16, 1919; Close to Frankfurter, May 21, 1919, Frankfurter papers, box 6. "Frankfurter tried to elevate the exchange of letters to the level of a statement of official United States policy," Manuel, p. 244. Frankfurter kept closely in touch with Brandeis, to whom he wrote on May 25: "Weizmann . . . understands the British mentality and is able to deal with them, but very few of the eastern Jews have that understanding," Frankfurter papers, box 85, L.C.

79. Weizmann thought Brandeis was sometimes "hard to work with," observing that "like Wilson he was apt to evolve theories, based on the highest principles, from his inner consciousness, and then expect the facts to fit in with them," p. 248.

80. King to Wilson, June 20, 1919, quoted in Manuel, p. 248. Baker, vol. 2, pp. 213–216. On the King-Crane Commission, see below, p. 503.

Persistent efforts had been made by Frankfurter to have Palestine excluded from the purview of the investigating commission, which he deemed "a false façade in no way affecting the decision of the Council," Frankfurter to Brandeis, March 28, April 23, 1919; Frankfurter to Miller, March 28, May 29, 1919; Frankfurter to Croly, July 11, 1919, Frankfurter papers, boxes 6 and 85, L.C. Letters, Frankfurter to House, April 14, 16, and 30, 1919, Y.H.C.

81. According to a "strictly confidential" report of the interview by Frankfurter, who was present, the three conditions stated by Brandeis were, first, assurance that Palestine should be the Jewish homeland and not merely a Jewish homeland in Palestine; second, adequate boundaries (outlined by Brandeis in some detail) that would give self-sufficiency for a healthy social life insofar as this could be arranged by the British government with the French and the Arabs; third, control of the land and of natural resources that are at the heart of a sound economic life, typed copy of "memorandum of interview in Mr. Balfour's apartment, 23, rue Nitot, on Tuesday, June 24th at 4:45 P.M.," P.R.O., FO / 800 / 217.

Once in Palestine, Brandeis got the impression that British authorities were blocking the carrying out of the Balfour Declaration.[82]

After his return to Washington the president gave little attention to the urgent appeals of Zionists. On September 1 he thought them "a little too insistent upon a constant asseveration of our interest and sympathy" and explained that in this "delicate and dangerous situation" it would be imprudent for him to make any public expression of opinion.[83] Nevertheless, after his disabling illness he continued to regard the Balfour Declaration as "a solemn promise which we can in no circumstance afford to break or alter."[84]

The American Zionists derived comfort of a sort from a long paper that William Yale presented at Paris on July 26. This expert, who had been employed by the Standard Oil Company of New York in Jerusalem from 1915 to 1917 and so was well aware of American interest in deposits of oil in Palestine, envisioned the Zionist movement as one that would fall under the control of American Jews. "A Jewish Commonwealth in Palestine," he predicted, "will develop into an outpost in the Orient." In the course of the peacemaking, the Jewish pleaders had been remarkably successful in getting the two assurances that their people ardently desired. They were the beneficiaries of provisions that upheld the rights of minorities in the European nations in which half of them lived—Poland, Czechoslovakia, Romania, Yugoslavia, Greece, Austria, Hungary, Bulgaria, and Turkey—and they had a mandate for Palestine that opened an opportunity for the development of a national life there. In achieving these goals they had the support of Woodrow Wilson, and in consequence, Jewish leaders in America, both Zionist and non-Zionist, became active in Wilson's campaign for acceptance of the League of Nations by the United States. In the history of the century, however, the minority treaties were to prove to be without sanction, and the Jewish presence in Palestine, in becoming an American "outpost in the Orient," failed to prevent bloodshed among Semitic peoples.

The question of the future of Palestine, which at the time seemed to be of less consequence than it proved to be in the history of the century, could not be settled separately from the fate of neighboring peoples. Actually, it was but a part of the larger problem of the governance of all the lands that had been severed from Turkish rule by the Supreme Council on January 30, 1919. For a solution, the Peace Conference looked to the embryonic League of Nations and the system of mandates that was prescribed by its Covenant.

Wilson's devotion to self-determination as an "imperative principle of action" had led inevitably, in the cases of the Irish and Jewish activists, to complications that demonstrated the capacity of this doctrine to disrupt, as well as to adjust, political arrangements within modern nations. And, indeed, peace is still menaced by

82. Murphy, p. 92.
83. Wilson to Tumulty, September 1, 1919, Tumulty papers. Manuel, p. 255.
84. In a letter written in February 1920, Wilson asked Lansing to instruct Ambassador Wallace, at Paris, to do everything possible to impress upon the British and the French the importance of a plea that had come from Brandeis, Manuel, p. 256. On February 10 Wilson sent a message to the British and French governments in support of the Zionists, and Ambassador Davis delivered it at London with no enthusiasm. In May the British received a text of a mandate that Brandeis had helped to draft, Tenzer, p. 315.

violent appeals to self-determination—a principle that, as Elihu Root remarked in 1920, ''sounds too well''[85] and was actually a ''half-truth'' from which the world suffered.

85. Lamont, *Across World Frontiers*, p. 117.

25

The Mandates

When the Covenant of the League of Nations was approved by the Peace Conference and presented to the Germans as a part of the Treaty of Versailles, the precise terms of the several mandates had not been defined. However, in preparing the treaty given to the Germans on May 7 the Supreme Council, with Wilson acquiescent, made provision at the last moment for the allotment of "B" and "C" mandates for almost all of Germany's overseas possessions.[1] Despite the remoteness of the United States from some of the territories, appeals were made to Wilson by the European governments immediately involved. They continued to look to him as the symbol of "justice" to their several concerns. For example, Hymans of Belgium wrote to him, as well as to Clemenceau, in protest against the assignment to British trusteeship of a small but densely populated part of German East Africa that was occupied by Belgian forces.[2]

The restraint exerted on the president by the temper of his people and their Congress delayed decision as to mandatories for months. A week before the signing at Versailles, Wilson accepted a recommendation of House that, until the Senate ratified the treaty, Americans should not participate in the work of the League of Nations except as advisers.[3] Individuals, however, could play a part in developing mandates. George Louis Beer was asked to take charge of the mandates section of the League. Regretting that the negotiations at the Peace Conference were "a constant source of shirking responsibility," he perceived that certain of the smaller nations were more jingoistic than the large, and that mawkish concepts of freedom and independence, encouraged by the principle of self-determination, were leading to the formation of frontiers that could not be easily changed. Beer appreciated the quality of adjustability that made the British colonial system, at its best, a medium for liberty when liberty was due; and he put his faith in the application of the ideal of trusteeship. He would give to the League's permanent Mandates Commission the right of inspection, which would serve as a check upon the creation of native armies as well as upon the protection of Christian missionaries and of the civic rights of the inhabitants. If a trust was violated, the League would have power to revoke the

1. On the B and C Mandates and their assignment see above, pp. 76–77, 81, and Aaron M. Margolith, *The International Mandates*, pp. 28–34.

Hankey to Wilson, May 7, 1919, enclosing a copy of the agreement reached by the Council of Four, Wilson papers.

2. Hymans to Wilson, May 9, 1919, enclosing a letter to Clemenceau protesting against the award to a mandate for east Africa to Great Britain, Wilson papers. Wilson was advised by Beer that the fundamental question was whether to turn over 4 million natives in Ruanda and Urundi to a Belgian colonial administration that, though recently not impossible, had operated in the Congo on principles wholly unsound, Beer to Wilson, May 12, 1919, Wilson papers; Milner to Wilson, May 12, 1919, copy in Milner papers, New College, Oxford, box 152; Beer diary, May 15, 1919. See W. R. Louis, *Great Britain and Germany's Lost Colonies, 1914–1919*, p. 151.

3. House diary, June 20, 1919.

mandate and appoint another mandatory power.[4]

When Lloyd George commended a text that Lord Milner had prepared with representatives of the dominions, Wilson hesitated. He observed that neither the Milner draft nor one prepared by Lord Robert Cecil provided fully for the open door or for protection of native populations.[5] After Lloyd George defended Milner's paper as "very complete" though "going further than they had anticipated," it was agreed by the Supreme Council on June 27 that a committee of five deal with the question. Milner was to represent Great Britain, and House the United States with Beer as alternate.

The attitude of Lloyd George at the end of June was such that Wilson thought it well, after leaving Paris, to send a word of warning to House: "Milner . . . is inclined to go the full liberal length, I think, and will have to be supported as against his chief. . . . I believe that by devoting your most watchful attention to this business you can probably get it into shape that we will all be willing to support. The British chief is too much inclined to think that this is a business for the great powers and only in form for the League of Nations, and is apt to verify the impression that the Mandates are after all a means of distributing the spoils."[6]

The Mandates Commission met first during the summer in Paris and then several times in London with Milner in the chair and Cecil as adviser.[7] In its first session it undertook to provide controls of traffic in arms and in liquor and to revise sections of the General Act of Berlin of 1885 and of the Brussels Convention of 1890.[8] The commission found it difficult to cope with the concern that the British War Cabinet was showing about the delicate question of imperial preference in British mandatories and the possibility that the United States, if it accepted mandates, might discriminate against the trade of other nations as it had done in the Philippines.[9] House recognized the limitations under which his British colleagues worked. In so doing he provoked the criticism of Beer.[10]

House continued to keep the president in touch with the work of the commission.[11] Drafts for mandates of the "B" and "C" types were approved by Wilson[12] and were adopted ultimately by the League of Nations with only small modifications. House reported Lloyd George's approval[13] and French reservations that would per-

4. Shotwell, *George Louis Beer: A Tribute,* pp. 100–114; Shotwell, *At the Paris Peace Conference,* pp. 366–367.

5. Cecil to House, June 4, 1919, Y.H.C. Wilson asked House to compare Milner's draft with that of "Cecil and Beer" and to send advice promptly, Wilson to House, June 27, 1919. Beer diary, June 27, 1919.

6. Laurence Evans, *U.S. Policy and the Partition of Turkey,* pp. 206–209. Mantoux, *Délibérations,* vol. 2, pp. 527, 547–549. Wilson to House, June 28, July 1, 1919.

7. Milner diary, July 8, 9, 12, August 5, 1919, Milner papers. Miller papers, L.C., box 89, IV, 14, 15. N.A., R.G. 256, 185.1111. Beer diary, June 27, 1919, and *passim.*

8. A convention revising provisions of the pacts of Berlin and Brussels was signed on September 10, 1919, text in Y.H.C.

9. Minutes, B.W.C., July 8, 1919, P.R.O., Cab. / 23 / 11.

10. Beer diary, July 13–17, 1919.

11. Letters, House to Wilson, July 8, 10, 14, 17, and 30, 1919.

12. Wilson to House, July 18, 1919, N.A., R.G. 59, 763.72119 / 5619. See above, pp. 76–77, 81.

13. Ammission to the secretary of state for the president from House, August 6, 1919, N.A., R.G. 59, 763.72119 / 6024.

mit the use of native troops in defense of territory "tant colonial que métropolitain."[14] House, however, was not able to introduce a provision suggested by Wilson that would restrain a power exercising a mandate from vetoing the revocation of its trusteeship by the League's council.[15]

The most difficult problems with respect to the assignment of mandates arose in the case of those of Class A. These applied, according to the League Covenant, to "certain communities belonging to the Turkish Empire" that had "reached a stage of development where their existence as independent nations can be provisionally recognized subject to the rendering of advice by a mandatory until they are able to stand alone." Just before Wilson's departure from Paris in June, it was decided by the Council of Four that the distribution of mandates for Turkish lands would be deferred until it was known whether the United States would be willing to assume any responsibility. There was no assurance as to the role that the United States would play in filling the vacuum in western Asia. The Europeans could count on Washington for neither military force nor mandatory responsibility. They awaited a decision as to American policy; and Wilson warned the American peace commission in July that this might "involve a very considerable delay."[16] In September of 1919 the Near East, Milner wrote in his diary, was "all at sixes and sevens."[17]

Because his nation had not been at war with Turkey, Wilson had no well-established right to a voice in the settlement that was to be made in western Asia. Nevertheless, hopeful for American participation in the League of Nations, he insisted upon taking part in the development of its system of mandates. Although his people were not in a mood to enter into political commitments far beyond traditional bounds, some were involved in lands of the Turkish empire by commercial and charitable interests. Moreover, the United States was endowed with a surplus of wealth and power that might be directed toward a furthering of those interests.

14. Beer diary, July 7–13, 1919. A protracted controversy over this matter had begun in May, when Wilson was informed by Hankey that Clemenceau, with the assent of Lloyd George on January 30, had altered the text of Article 22 of the Covenant so that it failed to prohibit the arming of native troops for the defense of the mother country. The president ordered the American representative on the drafting committee to restore the original wording, which permitted military training of natives only for defense of their territory. In August the question was still open, and Wilson informed House that he hoped the difficulties raised by the French government would be overcome by patience and argument. Article III of the Class C mandates stated that "military training of the natives, otherwise than for purposes of internal police and the local defense of the Territory, shall be prohibited."

15. Wilson to House, August 15, 1919, House to Wilson, August 23, 1919, dispatch from the president for Colonel House, August 23, 1919.

16. Wilson to Ammission, July 15, 1919, Wilson papers. Polk to Clemenceau, August 13 and 25, 1919, Clemenceau to Polk, August 20, September 1, 1919, Y.H.C.

17. Letter, Lord Robert Cecil to Milner, July 11, 1919, Milner diary, September 9, 1919, Milner papers, New College Library, Oxford, box 152.

A memorandum written by Balfour on September 9 suggested that the "A" provisions would be hard to reconcile with "our quasiterritorial ambitions" and impossible to reconcile with the ambitions of France. "Neither of us wants much less than supreme economic and political control," he wrote. The general assumption that Mesopotamian oil would belong "to all intents and purposes to Britain" seemed to him quite inconsistent with the principle of the "open door." The foreign secretary suggested that these considerations be brought to the attention of Milner, memorandum signed "A. J. B.," Lloyd George papers, F / 89 / 4 / 19.

Secret agreements that were made during World War I had dealt with the disposition of the Ottoman Empire in the event of victory in the war.[18] However, the validity of these arrangements was brought in question when the revolutionary regime in Russia withdrew from the conflict.[19]

When Damascus fell at the end of September 1918 and four hundred years of Turkish rule came to an end, an opportunity was opened to seek an enduring solution of the "Eastern Question" that had long perplexed European diplomats. The British government, well aware of the existing tangle of national claims, jealousies, and suspicions, undertook immediately to apprise the American government of its policy with respect to Turkish lands.[20] On October 11, 1918, the British embassy at Washington notified the State Department that in the view of the Foreign Office the wartime treaties having to do with Turkish territory had no bearing at the present moment and that the whole situation had been explained to the president.[21]

Even before the United States entered the war, Wilson and House had agreed that the Turkish empire should cease to exist, and also that its lands should not be partitioned among the victors.[22] Point Twelve, assuring to nationalities under Turkish rule "an undoubted security of life and an absolutely unmolested opportunity of autonomous development," recommended an international guarantee of free transit of the Dardanelles. The interpretive commentary that House presented to the prearmistice meetings, attempting to elucidate the application of the word "autonomous," suggested that mandates provide for an open door to trade, the protection of minorities, and the internationalization of railroads. Responsibility should be given to France for Syria and to Great Britain for Palestine, Mesopotamia, and Arabia. The Armenians were to have a port on the Mediterranean and the protection of a great power and they were said to prefer Great Britain to France.

18. To two of these—the Anglo-Franco-Russian agreements of May 18, 1915, and March–April 1916—the government of the czar was a party. Later, in April 1917, diplomats of France, Great Britain, and Italy met at St. Jean de Maurienne and reached a tripartite agreement, subject to the consent of Russia. See above, p. 351. Still another understanding—the Sykes-Picot agreement—to which France and Great Britain were parties, was concluded in May 1916.

19. For discussions of the secret treaties that dealt with Turkish territory, see Evans, pp. 109–113; Stein, *The Balfour Declaration*, ch. 16; W. W. Gottlieb, *Studies in Secret Diplomacy during the First World War*, pp. 19–131; Nicolson, *Curzon*, pp. 83–87; Harry N. Howard, *The Partition of Turkey*, pp. 121–136, 181–187; Walworth, *Woodrow Wilson*, vol. 2, p. 307n.

20. The general tenor of British thinking after Russia's withdrawal had been revealed more than a year before in a paper entitled "Statement on Foreign Policy Made to the Imperial War Council." This document was sent to Secretary Lansing in May 1917 (*F.R., Lansing Papers*, vol. 2, p. 23) and also to President Wilson.

21. Minutes, B.W.C., October 14, 1918, P.R.O. Cab / 23 / 8. On November 7, 1918, His Majesty's government, at the direction of the Foreign Office and in conjunction with the French government, published an explanation of its purposes. These were "the complete and final emancipation of the peoples so long oppressed by the Turks and the establishment of governments and administrations deriving their authority from the initiative and the free choice of the native populations." The statement asserted that it was desired also to facilitate economic development by encouraging local initiative and to foster the spread of education. Lord Curzon told Ambassador Paul Cambon that this "Self-Determination Agreement" in effect largely canceled the Sykes-Picot arrangements, dispatch, Curzon to Derby, February 12, 1919, Curzon papers, mss. Euro. / F112 / 302.

22. House diary, January 3, 1917. On December 1, 1917, Wilson cabled to House: "Our people and Congress will not fight for any selfish aim on the part of any belligerent; . . . least of all for divisions of territory such as have been contemplated in Asia Minor."

In November, Wilson had opened his mind to the French ambassador at Washington, telling him that in accord with Point Twelve the subject peoples should be free to choose their destinies and that something should be done to help them to share in the benefits of Western civilization. Cautioning against discussion of "spheres of influence"—a phrase that to him suggested something rotten and had an imperialistic implication that might be misleading—he asked why a small country like Switzerland or Holland might not undertake the difficult task of tutelage.[23] Meanwhile, Near East Relief was dispensing vast quantities of food and clothing, and Americans were increasing the contributions in personnel and in funds that had flowed through missionary channels for decades past. At the beginning of the Peace Conference Dr. James L. Barton had proposed to go to Asia Minor and Syria and attempt to send up-to-the-minute intelligence to Paris. In mid-February he was authorized by the American commission to proceed with the present relief work.[24]

Barton joined with four of his countrymen at Constantinople in a message to Paris that alluded to the colleges and institutions of mercy to which thousands of Americans had devoted their lives and to which they had been loyal during the war regardless of the risk involved.[25] Traveling thousands of miles through western Asia, Barton sent brief dispatches to Paris that portrayed widespread destitution and political incompetence. He telegraphed to House from Beirut on April 9: "All classes, including Turks, urge early action in Paris removing suspense and guarantying safety. Large majority all populations prefer America as mandatory for entire country, while Armenians seem unanimous and Syrians more than three-quarters favorable."[26]

At the same time the American State Department was being reminded that American citizens held oil rights in the southern Ottoman lands; and studies by navy men explained "the utmost importance" to the American government of an open door to the oil fields of the Middle East. For some years Americans had been investing

23. Romée François de Villeneuve-Trans, *À l'ambassade de Washington*, p. 186.

24. Telegrams, Ammission to Barton, at Rome, February 2, 1919; Barton to Ammission, February 3, 1919; letter, Ammission to Barton, February 7, 1919, N.A., R.G. 256, 184.017 / 3a, 6, 8, 15, 103, 97 / 578 and 184.00101 / 19. Wilson to Barton, February 1, 1919; A. C. James to Wilson, February 3, 1919, Wilson papers. Dispatch, T. N. Page to Ammission for Lansing, February 3, 1919, Y.H.C. *F.R., P.P.C.*, vol. 11, pp. 8, 27.

Barton was a secretary of the American Board of Commissioners for Foreign Missions and an organizer of the work of the Near East Relief Organization, which was supported by contributors in the United States and aided by the American government.

Frederic C. Howe, who had been commissioner of immigration in the United States, was asked to accompany Barton. Howe traveled as far as Brindisi, where he fell ill. Returning to Paris, he left for the United States on February 27, informing House of his discouragement with power politics, Howe to House, February 25, 1919, Y.H.C. "It is a very dangerous thing," Howe had written to House on April 25, 1917, "to meddle with the age-long institutions of another people or to attempt to direct their institutions along the lines of Anglo-Saxon development." See James B. Gidney, *A Mandate for Armenia*, pp. 137–139, Howe observed that "Moslemism was the most cohesive force" in maintaining "some kind of unified rule for hundreds of years," Howe to H. White, February 19, 1919, Bliss papers, box 241. See Howe, *The Confessions of a Reformer* (New York, 1925), p. 291.

25. Dispatch, Barton and four others to Ammission, March 12, 1919, Wilson papers.

26. Dispatches and letters, December 1918–May 1919, in papers of the American Board of Commissioners for Foreign Missions, 16.5, vol. 6, Houghton Library, Harvard College. *F.R., P.P.C.*, vol. 11, pp. 8, 27. Dispatch, T. N. Page to Ammission for Lansing, February 3, 1919. Dispatches, Barton to House, February 28, March 27, April 9, 1919, Y.H.C., Gidney, pp. 138, 166–167.

in exploration for oil in Ottoman territory. The policy of their government in respect of the oil industry was the same as that applying to other businesses—namely, to insist the Americans should have the same commercial rights and opportunities in other lands as those granted to foreigners by the laws of the United States. It was thought that American interests should co-operate with those of other nations in producing oil, to the end that the risks be distributed and thus minimized, and also to prevent developments for the exclusive benefit of a single nation. However, reports came to the State Department from American oil companies that British officials were obstructing legitimate activities of American geologists in search of oil in Palestine and Mesopotamia.[27] American diplomats were not taken into the confidence of the British and French governments when a general understanding on the question of oil rights was concluded in May of 1919. In the correspondence that preceded the agreement there were expressions of a desire to keep American interests out of Mesopotamia.[28]

Another country in which the intrusion of American commercial interest seemed to be discouraged by Great Britain was Persia (later to be called Iran). The Anglo-Persian Oil Company, to which the British government contributed capital, had been operating under a concession granted to it by the Persian government in 1901, and it owned almost all of the country's productive wells.[29] Americans were resentful of British operations in oil-rich lands while they were being asked—as Polk asserted in July—to "nurse" two barren wastes in Anatolia and Armenia, which were "absolutely not self-supporting."[30]

The British delegates managed to keep questions relating to Persia out of the discussions at the Peace Conference, just as the Americans had excluded negotiations regarding Liberia.[31] Although Persia was not a belligerent, it sent a delegation to Paris to seek a seat in the Peace Conference on the grounds that the nation had suffered violations of its neutrality. They sought recognition and a strengthening of their country's national existence. They wanted foreign advisers and preferred Americans.[32] When they addressed a plea to Wilson, he brought it to the attention of Clemenceau and Lloyd George on April 23 and asked that it be answered. How-

27. John A. DeNovo, *American Interests and Policies in the Middle East, 1900–1939*, pp. 169–174.
    A report dated February 28, 1919, forward to Wilson by Harry A. Garfield, fuel administrator, said: "We are impressed with the seriousness of the efforts being made by the British and Dutch interests to dominate the petroleum supply of the world," Wilson papers. Also see a statement by H. M. Robinson, recorded in the minutes of the American economic group, April 2, 1919, N. H. Davis papers, box 46.
    28. When Lloyd George heard of the Berenger-Long understanding, he wrote immediately to Clemenceau to renounce at least a part of it, explaining that he did not wish to be under the thumb of any oil trust. The text of the understanding and British correspondence relating to it may be found in the Lloyd George papers, F / 92 / 1, 2, 3, 4.
    29. See A. C. Bedford, "The World Oil Situation," 106–107.
    30. Polk to Lansing, July 31, 1919, Y.H.C.
    31. See above, p. 66. Curzon explained to House in May that negotiations with the Persian government were "on the verge of a satisfactory conclusion" and might be seriously jeopardized if the Peace Conference intervened, telegram, Curzon to Balfour, May 22, 1919, Balfour papers, 48734; House diary, May 20, 1919. According to Louis H. Gray, the Inquiry's expert on Persia, Curzon intended that Wilson be fully informed about the secret negotiations, "Summary" of memorandum to Polk, Spetember 30, 1919, H. White papers, L.C., box 44.
    32. Report to the Inquiry from officials of an Anglo-Persian Relief Committee, Y.H.C.

ever, Lloyd George replied he would consider the question only in connection with the peace treaty to be made with Turkey, to which the United States would not be a party.[33] The Persians submitted three written statements of their claims, but their delegates were not heard.[34]

At the beginning of the Peace Conference the Supreme Council resolved that Arabia, Armenia, Mesopotamia, and Syria (including Palestine) be completely severed from the Turkish domain. Lloyd George spoke feelingly of the large and disproportionate burden that Great Britain was then bearing in the policing of these lands. On a motion by Wilson the military men were asked to make a decision as to the number of troops that it would be equitable for the several powers to contribute.[35] In many parts of Anatolia the Turks, hardly realizing the significance of their country's defeat, were still armed, militant, and beyond the control of the sultan. A dispatch from Constantinople had recommended to the American peacemakers that the Allies extend their occupation in order to pacify the country;[36] and this matter was the subject of discussion among the military advisers. Their report, to which General Bliss attached a reservation, pointing out that the consent of the American Congress could not be expected before the following winter, if at all, was considered in a heated and protracted debate in the Supreme Council at the beginning of February. This led Wilson to turn to Secretary of War Baker for advice. In a "very urgent" telegram to Washington he suggested that it was "only fair" to relieve Great Britain of a share of the burden of "occupations of which nobody but the whole group of nations is to get the ' ᵔnefit." "I would very much like your advice" the president wired to Baker, "first, as to the legality of sending American troops to those areas, presumably with the assent of Turkey because we have never been at war with her; second, as to [the] wisdom of such a step from the point of view of the probable attitude and temper of the people at home and the soldiers themselves; and third, as to the wisdom of such a course from the point of view of public policy. The interest of America in Robert College at Constantinople and in the pitiful fortunes of the Armenians is of such long standing and is so great and genuine that I am assuming that the occupation of Constantinople and Armenia would not strike our people as unreasonable or undesirable in view of the fact that it is already true that they would be more welcome and serviceable in those two places than any other troops would be and would be needed in smaller force. The latter statement is also true of the Syrian and Arabian countries, though I suppose

33. Mantoux, *Délibérations,* vol. 1, p. 342.

34. *Current History* 11, pt. 1, no. 2 (November 1919):346. Morgenthau recorded that when he "explained frankly" to the Persians that they would not be heard, "they were crestfallen and almost moaned over their fate," diary, May 1919.

The Inquiry recommended that the Anglo-Russian Convention of 1907, which had divided the country into spheres of influence, be terminated and that Persia should be treated "as an independent and sovereign state and recognized formally as such" if that was its desire, Gelfand, *The Inquiry,* p. 257.

Breckinridge Long of the State Department considered Persia to be "a Protectorate of England." "We have told England we do not sympathize and will not help her," he wrote, diary, August 24, 1919.

35. *F.R., P.P.C.,* vol. 3, pp. 805, 807, 816–817, 837–838.

36. Evans, pp. 170–171. Lewis Heck, the American trade commissioner, reported to Paris that the only hope for effective aid to relieve a shortage of food at Constantinople lay in an American relief expedition, dispatch, January 15, 1919, Wilson papers.

our public opinion would not be prepared in any degree for occupation there.''

Baker replied three days later. ''It seems certain,'' the secretary of war advised, ''that the dispatch of our troops to Turkey without some effort to prepare public opinion here in advance, would be unwise,'' and the congressional committees on foreign relations should be consulted.[37] Having failed in his efforts to get American troops out of Russia and out of the Adriatic region, the secretary of war now met with acceptance of his advice in general, although an American warship was stationed at the Turkish capital.[38]

The president, however, did not despair of meeting the desire of the Allies and that of the Turkish government[39] for American authority at Constantinople. ''The place where they all want us to accept a mandate most is at Constantinople,'' he said to influential Democrats in Washington on February 28. ''America is the only nation in the world that can undertake that mandate and have the rest of the world believe that it is undertaken in good faith and that we do not mean to stay there and set up our own sovereignty. So that it would be a very serious matter for the confidence of the world in this treaty if the United States did not accept a mandate for Constantinople.''[40]

After an intimation reached Washington that Turkey was very eager fully to renew diplomatic relations with the United States,[41] the State Department responded not by reopening its embassy at Constantinople but by appointing a trade commissioner, Lewis Heck, to observe conditions and report.[42] He found that American residents, some of whom took part in missions of education and relief, were the object of trust and good will at the Turkish capital.[43] Heck notified the American embassy at Paris that until the political destiny of the Ottoman realm was settled and its currency stabilized, little new business could be undertaken safely. Reporting that Italians were planning a new bank, that the operations of the American food administration were being financed by a British house, and that the other Allied countries were sending men to seize opportunities for financial service, he suggested that American bankers and exporters seek a share in the activity that he envisioned.[44]

The Allies, who before the Peace Conference opened sent warships to Constan-

37. Telegrams, for the secretary of war from the president, February 8, 1919; for the president from the secretary of war, February 11, 1919, N.A., R.G. 59, doc. 763.72 / 12770.

38. See below, p. 493.

39. *F.R., 1919,* vol. 1, pp. 359–360, 428.

40. Swem ms., Princeton University Library.

In advocating international control of Constantinople and the Straits, the Americans were undeterred by the possibility of setting a precedent for the internationalization of the Panama Canal, Harry N. Howard, ''The United States and the Problem of the Turkish Straits,'' *The Middle East Journal* 1, no. 1 (1947):63–64. This possibility had troubled House, House diary, April 30, 1917.

41. U.S. chargé in the Netherlands to the secretary of state, October 29, 1918, *F.R., 1918, I,* vol. 1, p. 416.

42. *F.R., 1919,* vol. 2, p. 810. On May 3 the State Department ordered Gabriel Ravndal to replace Heck and to open a consulate general but to refrain from undertaking full diplomatic relations, *ibid.,* pp. 811–812.

43. A petition to Clemenceau from the Wilson League at Constantinople sought his aid in persuading the American government to undertake to reorganize Turkey, copy in Klotz papers, B.D.I.C., Nanterre.

44. Dispatch, Heck (Pera) to American embassy (Paris), Wilson papers. In 1919 and earlier the volume of American shipping through the straits was very slight, Howard, ''The U. S. and the Problem of the Turkish Straits,'' 59.

tinople and set up military control in the city, consulted the American government regarding the execution of the provisions of their armistice with Turkey. When they appealed for American action in behalf of their special interests, the State Department escaped any commitment on the ground that its government was not a party to the armistice. However, Admiral Bristol, who was in command of the American warship stationed at Constantinople, requested permission to coordinate and supervise the work of all American agencies there. He immediately recommended that the blockade of Turkey be lifted and its trade regulated.[45]

On May 6 in the Supreme Council, Wilson, expressing doubt that his people would agree to the American administration of Asia Minor and Armenia, said that they would consent to the occupation of Constantinople if it were entrusted to them because that would liberate the city from the Turks, for whom the hatred of Americans ran deep because of Turkish persecution of Armenians.[46] In mid-May the president approved a directive to the effect that Americans assisting in discussions of questions affecting Turkey or Bulgaria, with which the United States had not been at war, should act only as advisers and not as interested parties.[47] Nevertheless, Wilson was aware that if the treaty with Turkey were to include the Covenant of the League of Nations, the United States as a member of the League would have to guarantee it. On May 13 in his living room he joined with his three colleagues of the Council of Four in kneeling to study maps of the Turkish territory to be partitioned. At this time Wilson was disposed to accept, subject to the Senate's consent, mandates over Armenia and over Constantinople, the Straits, the Sea of Marmara, and a small contiguous territory.

Lloyd George, however, almost immediately veered away from this understanding. He told Clemenceau and Wilson that Balfour thought mandatory rule imprac tical and that it would arouse the opposition of all Moslems, including those in India, whom he gratified by securing a hearing for them.[48]

Wilson, agreeing with Balfour's opinion that Anatolia should be independent, suggested on May 19 in the Council of Four that the sultan occupy a place at Constantinople similar to that of the pope at Rome. It occurred to him that France might be allowed to extend to matters of economics and policing the control that it already exerted in financial affairs, but only if its functions were clearly defined in the peace treaty rather than in a League mandate, which the Moslems had indicated

45. Dispatch, Sims to Benson, February 21, 1919, Bliss papers, box 227. "Bristol's papers indicate conclusively that, influenced by corporation executives, he acted on the assumption that . . . he should employ the Open Door principle aggressively to further American economic interests," Thomas A. Bryson, "Admiral Mark Bristol, an Open-Door Diplomat in Turkey," *International Journal of Middle East Studies* 5 (1974):450–467

46. Mantoux, *Délibérations,* vol. 1, p. 498.

47. Letter, Grew to the American secretaries, May 15, 1919.

48. Mantoux, *Délibérations,* vol. 2, pp. 56, 62, 88, 98–104. Lloyd George referred to a long paper that Balfour had circulated, which advocated rule by the sultan, with foreign advisers, over a homogeneous Turkish population in diminished territories. Balfour thought it best to try to satisfy the Italian ambition that haunted and hampered every step in their diplomacy by offering concessions now rather than let them be scrambled for by "the rival company-mongers of every country under heaven, supported no doubt by their ministers," paper by A. J. B., May 16, 1919, copy in Wilson papers; "Notes on Asia Minor Proposals," by A. J. B., May 15, 1919, Balfour papers, 49752.

would be offensive to their people.[49] Although he now appeared to be willing to take part in a diplomatic division of Turkey among the victors—always provided that it had the moral sanction of responsibility under the League of Nations—he was restrained by the uncertainty of his political position in the United States.[50] Thinking that his people would accept a mandate for Armenia for humanitarian reasons, he doubted that one for Anatolia would be acceptable; but he did not exclude the possibility of changing his mind.[51]

Nevertheless, Lloyd George, despite the aversion to "letting in" the Americans that he had expressed to the Imperial War Cabinet five months earlier, submitted a memorandum on May 21 that designated the United States as the only acceptable trustee for the foreign control that he thought essential in Anatolia. Only America, he said, could provide the resources needed to develop the country. But Wilson was not ready to come to a decision. "My mind is not yet made up," he said. "I shall examine the question. But it seems to me impossible that America would accept this mandate." He made it clear to Orlando that Italy must not expect to get, without the consent of the inhabitants, the lands in Asia Minor that were promised by the Treaty of London.[52]

Meanwhile, there came from Smyrna, where the Greeks had been permitted to land troops after the Italians had made secret landings at points farther south,[53] reports of rape, mutilation, and wholesale looting. American and British advisers hastened to devise schemes for enforcing civil order in Anatolia. Henry Morgenthau, who had been the American ambassador at Constantinople, proposed that the United States be given an exclusive mandate and a totally free hand in Turkish affairs, and that it alone supply capital to be used for the development of Turkey's resources, with advice from British and French financial experts. But a British adviser asked to what extent this scheme, which seemed not very closely reasoned, was prompted by American commercial imperialism.

There were indications already, however, that the future of Turkey would be settled not at Paris, but rather by the stirrings of an elemental spirit of nationalism. To be ruled by Greeks provoked in the Turks a resistance that sprang from the heart. The "sick man of Europe" undertook to cure himself and to assert his inalienable rights. The Turkish cabinet resigned on May 17 in protest against the Greek landing at Smyrna, and when a new one took office three days later there were new faces. In the interior of Anatolia armed peasants organized to defend the homeland. Three days after the landing at Smyrna, Mustafa Kemal Pasha, a brilliant military officer, arrived at Samsun and began to organize a crusade of national resistance.[54] On

49. Mantoux, *Délibérations*, vol. 2, pp. 111–112, 143. Wilson confessed to two advisers that he was not altogether satisfied with his suggestion of French aid to Turkey without responsibility to the League of Nations, "Interview of Magie and Westermann with Pres. Wilson on May 22, 1919," David Magie papers, box 1, Princeton University Library.

50. R. S. Baker's journal, May 28, 1919.

51. Mantoux, *Délibérations*, vol. 2, p. 142. *F.R., P.P.C.*, vol. 5, pp. 765–766.

52. Mantoux, *Délibérations*, vol. 2, pp. 134, 142, 211–213, 221–227.

53. See above, pp. 352–355. On the effect of the Smyrna landing upon the native Turks of Anatolia, see *What Really Happened at Paris*, ed. Seymour and House, pp. 192–195.

54. Evans, pp. 170–176. R. H. Davison, "Turkish Diplomacy from Mudros to Lausanne," in *The Diplomats*, ed. Craig and Gilbert, pp. 175–176. See Nicolson, *Curzon*, pp. 115–118.

September 12, Bristol reported that the nationalists were actually governing Turkey, except for Constantinople.[55]

Before the new regime became effective, however, prominent Turks sent appeals to Wilson; ministers of the cabinet asked that the American plenipotentiaries at Paris arrange for the protection of the Turkish population from Greek brutality; and the sultan's chief of staff sought an American mandate for all of Turkey and offered military support for such a regime. Admiral Bristol reported to the president that he had hundreds of messages of protest from foreigners and from Turks of all classes against the Greek occupation of Smyrna, which seemed as bad a move as he could imagine. Warning against the Balkanization of Turkey and stating that Greece was not able to rule any part of it, he expressed the opinion that if the United States were to assume responsibility, it should do so for the whole country. Admiral Benson, forwarding Bristol's letter to the president, suggested that Wilson had been "misinformed or deliberately deceived," and that the continuing presence of the battleship *Arizona* off Smyrna would tend to weaken or destroy American prestige.[56]

At the end of May the Supreme Council received an appeal from the grand vizier of the sultan for a hearing at Paris. When Wilson's two colleagues proposed on May 30 that Turkish spokesmen be given the privilege that had been denied to the Germans, the president agreed. He communicated the will of the council to the grand vizier.[57]

The Turkish delegation finally chosen represented a balance of British and French interests, which, according to Admiral Bristol, were "in desperate rivalry."[58] The emissaries presented a note that expressed respect for all religions, pledged reforms as soon as contact with the West was re-established, and asserted a desire "to continue the march toward progress." They asked that the empire be maintained.

In discussions of the note in the Council of Four on June 25 and 26, Wilson, calling its bearers "three ludicrous persons," said: "It is best to let them depart. They have given proof of a total lack of common sense and of complete misunderstanding of the West. They thought we didn't know any history and have given us monstrous untruths. ['That's Turkish diplomacy,' Lloyd George interjected.] We have given them attention enough and have treated them courteously."

"I have studied the Turkish question closely enough for a long time," Wilson remarked, "and I conclude that the only solution possible is to put the Turks out of Constantinople." It would be a mistake, psychologically, to create a mandate for Turkey, but it was necessary for one of the great powers to have a right, as an intermediary, to assist and supervise the administration of that country. This, and not a mandate, seemed to him the only possible solution. A month earlier he had

55. Dispatch, Turkey (Bristol) to State Department, September 12, 1919, N.A., R.G. 59, 763.72119 / 6973.
56. Benson to Wilson, May 31, 1919, enclosing letters from Bristol at Constantinople, and from Dr. Alexander Maclachlan, president of the American International College, Wilson papers.
57. *F.R., P.P.C.*, vol. 6, p. 115, Wilson to Benson, May 31, 1919.
58. Evans, pp. 192–193. Dispatches, Bristol to Benson, May 31, June 4, 5, 1919, Bristol papers, L.C., box 27. On the political situation of Constantinople and the Turkish mission to Paris, see Helmreich; *From Paris to Sèvres*, pp. 107–111.

suggested that they give France a mandate without calling it a mandate and without responsibility to the League. When asked now whether the United States would accept such a responsibility, Wilson replied: "I shall submit the proposition to the Senate." He thought now that it would be approved. "What will make this proposition acceptable in America," he explained, "is that it is not a business. . . . It would go there only to guard the Straits in the interest of all nations. That would not involve it in European politics—a thing of which America would be most afraid."

On June 27 the Supreme Council decided to suspend further consideration of a peace treaty with Turkey until the American government could state whether it would accept a mandate for a portion of Turkish territory. The next day, at the last meeting of the council at which Wilson was present, it approved a letter informing the Turks that nothing would be gained by their continuing presence at Paris. No terms were ready for them, and they had accomplished nothing.[59]

In the autumn the insurgent Turkish nationalists were bitterly opposed to any sort of European dominion in Asia Minor. According to a report of September 22 from Admiral Bristol, the congress that met at Sivas and formed a new government decided unanimously that they wanted the United States to take responsibility for the governance of Turkey as a whole, practically on America's own terms.[60] By this time, however, the relation between Washington and the Peace Conference was becoming tenuous. The settlement for Asia Minor was left in the hands of the European powers; and when a treaty with Turkey was finally signed at Sèvres in August of 1920, by Wilson's direction the United States was not represented.

In taking upon himself the responsibility of negotiating alone, firsthand, with Europeans who were accustomed to the ways of imperial dominion—a task that demanded the expertise of professional diplomats—Wilson had vacillated between idealism and *Realpolitik*. He had, to be sure, been consistent here, as in the conflict in respect of Fiume, in standing against Italian aggression; and he had constantly supported the dubious claim of his avowed disciple, Venizelos, to rule over the Smyrna region and its Turkish majority. In the latter case, however, he had put aside his commitment to self-determination; and he had departed from proclaimed principles also in his willingness to leave the sultan on his throne, to be advised by a foreign power in the nineteenth-century manner and without responsibility to the League of Nations. He did not respond to the genuine revolutionary voice that came from Sivas. He had found no diplomatic recourse to prevent open warfare between Greece and Turkey. In the very complex and secret negotiations with Lloyd George and Clemenceau, Wilson had often indulged in thinking aloud upon matters on

59. Mantoux, *Délibérations*, vol. 2, pp. 516–518, 520–521, 530–532, 549, 566. *F.R., P.P.C.,* vol. 6, pp. 675 ff. "Never has there been a more undignified proceeding," Lord Hardinge wrote, *The Old Diplomacy,* p. 239. See Evans, pp. 191–194.

60. Dispatch, Bristol to Ammission, September 22, 1919, Ravndal to the secretary of state, September 16, 1919, Ravndal to Ammission, September 23, 1919. On October 1 Bristol forwarded a report from the National Congress signed by Mustafa Kemal, requesting the U.S. Senate to send a commission to all parts of the Ottoman Empire before making any "arbitrary disposal of the peoples and territories," dispatch, Bristol to the secretary of state, October 1, 1919, N.A., R.G. 59, 763.72119/7533. Bristol advised that the nationalist movement was of greater importance than "selfish interests desire it to appear" to be.

which he was not adequately grounded by close communication with his advisers.[61] It became more difficult for idealists, already disillusioned by concessions made by Wilson in April, to concede him a place in history as an effective prophet. Bristol came to favor military occupation of Turkey and the establishment of an international commission to set up a government.[62] On October 16 he sent fundamental counsel to Heck, who had become head of the Near East division of the State Department: "I do hope that you will keep to the big idea all the time, i.e., that America believes in helping the whole of the Turkish Empire to obtain good government and the advantages of modern civilization. This is an unassailable position."[63] Endeavoring to bring about better coordination among the various United States agencies in Turkey, Bristol reported in mid-November: "Before this American interests were not much injured by the aggressiveness of the Allies and I have taken up the question simply on general principles of right and wrong. But now it is necessary to push American trade and interests. This is being done."[64]

With the president disabled and no one at Washington in a position to act authoritatively, Bristol's zeal evoked no response. Hostilities between Greeks and Turks escalated into a full-scale war after the Peace Conference rejected unanimous recommendations from a four-power Smyrna Commission on which Bristol served.[65]

Not the least sensitive of the Ottoman lands was Syria, where native Arabs resented both the aspirations of Zionists in Palestine and those of the French government in the regions of Damascus and Lebanon.

The Arabs did not lack a champion at Paris. During the war Husein, sharif of Mecca and king of the Hejaz, had led a general revolt of Arabs; and British agents abetted the uprising as a means of weakening the Turkish enemy. This encouraged the Arabs to expect indulgence at the Peace Conference. In order to win their military support, the British government had agreed, in the Husein-MacMahon correspondence of 1915–1916, that an Arab state, with boundaries not precisely defined, should be formed after the war. The British Foreign Office had confused matters when it so far departed from its tradition of precision as to become a party to

61. Cf. Helmreich, pp. 124–126.

62. Bristol to Polk, November 10, 1919. On November 10 Bristol thanked Polk for a reply indicating that Polk thought the admiral was "on the right track," dispatches in Bristol papers, box 36.

63. Bristol to Heck, October 16, 1919, Bristol papers, box 36.

64. "Report of Operations for Week Ending Nov. 23," Bristol papers, box 16. In this report Bristol likened the Near East to a mass of jelly. "If you touch any part," he wrote, ". . . the whole mass quivers."

65. Admiral Bristol was appointed to represent the United States in a four-power investigation of the Greek landing at Smyrna and its tragic aftermath. The Greeks were denied representation, Buckler to Mrs. Buckler, July 25, 1919, Y.H.C. Memorandum, Navy Department (F.D.R.) to State Department, August 19, 1919, N.A., R.G. 59, 763.72119/6068. The coommission's report concluded that the Greeks bore the burden of guilt for the violence at Smyrna and their troops should be withdrawn and replaced by Allied forces, Thomas A. Bryson, *American Diplomatic Relations with the Middle East—1784–1975: A Survey* (Metuchen, N.J., 1975), p. 69. Bristol reported that "where there was, comparatively speaking, peaceful conditions before the Greeks entered . . . , there is now more or less desolation and people living in misery and fighting. . . . This is what the Peace Conference did," dispatch, Bristol to Sims, January 17, 1920, Bristol papers.

commitments to France, to the Zionists, and to the Arabs that were not entirely consistent.[66]

Emir Faisul al Husein, the king's third son and the commander of the army of the Hejaz, expected that in 1919 the British pledge to the Arabs would be redeemed. Having joined with a British army in the occupation of Syria, he envisioned reigning in that land. The British government treated the prince as a protégé, bringing him to Paris in a warship and providing a counselor and interpreter in the person of Colonel T. E. Lawrence, who had fought with the army of the Hejaz. Faisul had instructions from his father the king to carry out all wishes of the British, his hosts, whether in the Peace Conference or elsewhere. Husein considered that he had an exclusive relationship[67] with His Majesty's government, and Clemenceau called Faisul "a soldier of England." At first French officials would not recognize him as an envoy. However, Lawrence persuaded the Foreign Office to exert pressure on the French government, and it was arranged that Faisul and another Arab delegate would be seated at the Peace Conference.[68]

Faisul had an uneradicable apprehension of Jewish rule in Palestine, despite the fact that under British persuasion he had signed an agreement in which he consented to accept Balfour's declaration in return for a promise from Weizmann to help the Arabs to develop their economy.[69] At the beginning of the Peace Conference, Lawrence said to House that a radical policy, carried out by Jews who seemed to show a very militant spirit, would result in ferment, chronic unrest, and sooner or later civil war in Palestine. Lawrence asserted that 120,000 Christian Arabs dwelling in Syria and Palestine were unfriendly to the Jews. To this House had no answer but a low whistle and a comment that "Balfour, with the best intentions in the world"

66. A memorandum written by Lord Grey on September 9, 1919, asserted that the engagements to King Husein were not incompatible with those to France and that the British government was entirely free to withdraw from Syria and let the French come in. In a minute on this paper Curzon wrote that though the assurances given to Husein were not incompatible with a French mandate for Syria, they did not quite square with the French concept of their mandate, documents in Lloyd George papers.

Under the Sykes-Picot agreement, Syria, with the exception of the southern region where an international administration was to govern Palestine, was to be a French sphere of influence, Zeine N. Zeine, *The Struggle for Arab Independence* (Beirut, 1960), pp. 8, 14, and Appendix A, p. 21. Grey had qualified his government's assent to the arrangments by writing to the French ambassador that they were contingent upon securing "the cooperation of the Arabs," Grey to Paul Cambon, May 16, 1916, F.R.O., Cab / 29 / 50.

67. Westermann, in Seymour and House, p. 190.

68. Villeneuve-Trans, p. 204. Westermann diary, January 20, 1919, Steed, *Through Thirty Years*, vol. 2, p. 300. Zeine, pp. 63–66, *q.v.* France had an interest in which sentiment played a strong part. Its spokesmen insisted on certain historic and contractual rights, which in their view derived from the aspirations and wishes of the native Syrians, who had long been "clients" of France. French scholars aspired to give intellectual leadership, Westermann diary, December 11, 1918, April 4, 1919, "La Syrie devant la Conférence," January 12, 1919, a pamphlet in the Klotz papers, B.D.I.C., Nanterre.

69. At the end of the Faisul-Weizmann agreement was a codicil requiring the fulfillment of conditions for Arab independence that Faisul had stated in a memorandum to the Foreign Office. The text of the agreement is in the Middle East Centre, St. Antony's College, Oxford. Evans, pp. 117–122, 137. M. Perlman, "Chapters of Arab-Jewish Diplomacy, 1918–1922," *Jewish Social Studies* 6, no. 2. Miller, *My Diary*, vol. 2, doc. 141. Manuel, *The Realities of American-Palestine Relations*, p. 221. A letter of March 31 from Faisul to Frankfurter professed the "deepest sympathy" with the "moderate and proper Zionist proposals," and extended to the Jews "a hearty welcome home," Joseph P. Lash, *From the Diaries of Felix Frankfurter*, p. 26. The publication of the letter in London and New York damaged Faisul's prestige among the Palestinian Arabs, Kedourie, *England and the Middle East*, pp. 152 ff.

had "rocked the boat that was already sailing on anything but an even keel."[70]

It was not long before the American delegates at Paris were sought out by the pleaders of the Arab cause. On the first day of 1919 Faisul issued a memorandum stating his father's purpose. Head of a great and ancient family, King Husein was custodian of the holy places of Islam. He felt that after six centuries of tenacious resistance to Turkish domination the Arabs had created a right to freedom. He recognized that the services of a great power were needed in Palestine to preserve a balance between Arabs and Jews, close though these peoples were in racial origin. What he sought was sufficient international protection to safeguard the Arab states against exploitation and to assure them of "open frontiers, common railways and telegraphs, and uniform systems of education." The Arabs asked that Westerners should not force their "whole civilization" upon them, but permit a selection of what served best. Having made sacrifices in the common effort against Turkey, they were determined not to allow Europeans to replace Turks as rulers though they recognized that a Western yoke would be less intolerable than that of Turkey.[71]

Faisul and Lawrence, who as the interpreter of the emir's remarks took opportunities to promote British interests, were very persuasive.[72] They dined with British and American advisers and found general approval of a system of mandates for parts of the Turkish empire.[73] The American experts, however, were not swept away by the glamorous emir. In their Black Book they had recommended the creation of native states in Mesopotamia, Syria, and Palestine. For Syria they favored a mandate, but named no power to exercise it. Setting down no definite provisions for the Arabian peninsula, they specified that in spite of the political prominence of King Husein of Hejaz, he be "not aided to establish an artificial and unwelcome dominion over tribes unwilling to accept his rule."

On January 29 Faisul requested of the Supreme Council that except for the independent Kingdom of the Hejaz and the British coaling station at Aden, the Arabic-speaking peoples "from the line Alexandretta-Diarbekr southward to the Indian Ocean" be recognized as sovereign under a guarantee of a league of nations. "I base my request," he said, "on the principles enunciated by President Wilson." It was his hope that the United States might serve as the guardian of an Arab Confederation.

70. Balfour later explained to House that his declaration insisted upon the protection of the religious and civil rights of non-Jewish citizens of Palestine, and grew out of war necessity and not from mere sentiment. The fact that his policy might prove a protection to the Suez Canal was mentioned by Balfour as "a happy coincidence," Bonsal, *Suitors and Suppliants,* pp. 55–57, 61. Bonsal recorded (p. 57) that Lawrence repeated time and again; "These new Jews are coming in a very militant spirit, natural enough, but still most regrettable."

71. Bonsal, pp. 32–39. Miller, vol. 4, doc. 250.

72. William Yale, who had worked for the Standard Oil Company in Palestine and became a special agent of the State Department in the Near East, wrote a series of realistic reports for the State Department, concluding with a statement that "in plain English, in spite of a widespread camouflage propaganda in regard to the liberation of oppressed races and the rights of small nations, the British and French are thinking and working only for their own interests in the Near East." See Manuel, pp. 179–204. Yale to the author, September 10, 1968.

73. After a dinner given for the American delegates by Faisul, George Louis Beer took his plea under consideration, Beer diary, January 7, 15, 1919. Westermann diary, January 20, 1919. Bonsal, pp. 39–40.

On the sixth of February, Faisul appeared before the Supreme Council in all the nobility of his dress and bearing. He spoke not as a suppliant but as a defender of rights conferred by solemn agreements. Wilson received him and was impressed by his noble bearing; but the president was so reserved that Lawrence, who interpreted, afterward described the meeting as merely a ceremonial contact.[74] When the prince attended a reception given by Mrs. Wilson, he wore a turban and a robe of gray silk edged with scarlet. She noted his fineness of feature, his pointed beard and long dark hair, and saw "a startling resemblance to . . . pictures of the Christ."[75] Wilson, though fearing that Faisul's was a stray voice from Asia, assured him of deep interest in the whole Arab question.

Five days later the Supreme Council was addressed by Dr. Howard S. Bliss, president of the American College at Beirut, who had come to Paris at the invitation of Wilson. He and his father, the founder of the college, were respected by Faisul, for the institution had trained many Arabs who had become statesmen and officials in various parts of the Turkish empire.[76] Dr. Bliss, whose college was in competition with French Jesuits, informed Wilson in February that the Syrians distrusted the French as exploiters and bad administrators, and he advised that no time should be lost in sending from Paris an inter-Allied or neutral commission in order to give the people an opportunity to make their will known.[77] He thought that the Syrians would prefer as a "protective power" first, the United States because of its "entire disinterestedness," and second, Great Britain because of its "capacity and justice." A French-inspired delegation followed Bliss in pleading before the council.[78]

On February 13 Faisul explained that, having received no encouragement from America, he hesitated to speak openly of his preference for an American mandate. He asked whether public instruction in the Arab region might be placed under American control. Stating that Syria was able to govern itself, he said he would accept a British mandate, which he preferred next to an American one, "as a drowning man grasps at anything at hand." He would fear absorption in the British Empire, he said, were it not for the new forces at work in Europe and the influence of France and the United States.[79]

While the president was away from Paris in March, the Arabs continued to seek the support of American delegates. Lawrence was very close to Faisul and seemed to have Arab diplomacy completely in his hands. He later admitted that, in order to save the mandate for Great Britain, he tried to frighten Americans by the size of the mandatory responsibility, hoping that they would withdraw in favor of Great Britain.[80]

74. Bonsal, pp. 322–34, 40.
75. Edith Bolling Wilson, *My Memoir*, p. 231. Raymond B. Fosdick's letter to his family, April 15, 1919. Wilson to Faisul, February 14, 1919, Wilson papers.
76. Shotwell, record in Columbia D.H.R.O., p. 103. "In my army," Faisul said to Bonsal, "those who had studied at the American College in Beirut were the most reliable and efficient," *Suitors and Suppliants*, p. 45.
77. H. S. Bliss to Wilson, February 7 and 11, 1919, Wilson papers.
78. *F.R., P.P.C.*, vol. 3, pp. 1016–1021. Evans, p. 125.
79. Notes by Yale on a talk with Faisul, Y.H.C.
80. Shotwell, *At the Paris Peace Conference*, pp. 130, 196–197. D. Garnett (ed.), *Letters of T. E. Lawrence* (London, 1921), p. 274.

When House discussed the subject with the European premiers on March 7, Lloyd George warned that if the French exerted force in Syria without reaching an agreement with Faisul there would be a long and bitter war.[81] Moreover, Cecil had expressed doubts about the establishment by a great power of an eastern empire athwart British interests in middle Asia.[82]

When Wilson returned to Paris, the Pandora's box was opened in a meeting of The Three on March 20. Although Lloyd George stoutly denied any British desire to rule Syria, Clemenceau remained fearful of action by Faisul that would counter French authority; and the two statesmen differed in their prescriptions for the disposal of Lebanon. As they argued the question heatedly during the president's absence, along with the questions of reparations and French security on the Rhine, each had appealed to House for support against what he thought the unreasonableness, and even the dishonesty, of the other. House, standing aside while the hassle continued, did not assert the American concept of justice under League mandates. Temporizing and soothing the tempers of the Europeans, he left to the strong voice of Wilson the task of challenging the bargaining premiers.

On March 20, after listening patiently while the Europeans wrangled, Wilson at length asserted his views. The principle of self-determination was being flouted, and American missionary and commercial interests in western Asia were involved.[83] Wilson and his advisers conceived that the essential element to be dealt with in that area was no longer any race or religion or social culture, but rather incipient nations. Putting aside the confusing claims and suspicions of the European powers, Wilson would seek the essential truth: the will of the peoples concerned. To this end he advocated the plan that Howard Bliss had proposed: that a commission of American, British, and French experts should visit the countries involved and bring back a report of public opinion.

This proposal was deplored by English and French experts on western Asia, who feared the awakening of false hopes and the sowing of seeds of civil disorder. The idea was taken up by Lloyd George with enthusiasm. But Clemenceau, fearing a weakening of the French position in Syria, raised questions: to elicit truth by probing Oriental minds was a delicate task, he said; and, moreover, there were historical claims to be considered. Unable to block the Anglo-American project, Clemenceau could but consent, while insisting that the investigation extend to lands in which the British were interested. Lloyd George acquiesced in including Mesopotamia and Palestine within the purview of the investigation. Wilson had won a moral victory.

Instructions for the commission were drafted on March 25, but the play of power politics prevented British and French participation in this project. Clemenceau would not appoint delegates until the British troops in Syria were replaced by a French

---

81. Evans, pp. 114–116.

82. "Everyone acquainted with Eastern administration," Cecil wrote, "knows that progress and tranquility in the East depend mainly upon depriving the oriental of his opportunity for intriguing between two protective and neighboring powers. For so long as opportunity for this pastime exists, he will spend his efforts in playing off one power against the other rather than in developing his own country. All experience proves this conclusively," comment in respect of a letter about Mesopotamia written by Hankey on August 12, 1918, Cecil papers, 51094.

83. DeNovo, esp. pp. 169, 332–337, 384–385.

garrison; and Lloyd George, advised by General Allenby that there would be Arab violence in Syria if French soldiers appeared there before a political settlement was reached, refused to withdraw the British troops. French spokesmen alleged that Faisul actually counted for nothing in the Arab world because he was known to be in the pay of English exploiters. But Faisul, who had told House that the Arabs in Syria would rather die than accept the supremacy of the French although it be sugar-coated as a mandate, thought the plan for an investigating commission the best thing he had ever heard of. He expressed the hope that the commission would report in favor of an American mandate. All parties in Syria were not united in wishing to be ruled by him; and he was probably counting on the commission to strengthen his claim to leadership. In any event, he showed his pleasure, according to Wester-mann's diary, by taking his first drink of champagne and from his automobile hurling pillows at the Crillon, the Majestic, and the Quai d'Orsay, explaining that since he had no bombs he could celebrate only in this way.[84] He left Paris on April 21, sending to Wilson a note of appreciation for the president's "beneficent endeavor in behalf of Syria." His parting word to House was that there would probably be war if the commission of inquiry did not go out at once; and House, reporting this to Wilson, endorsed Faisul's warning.[85]

The American specialists, however, observing that the French did not want the proposed commission of inquiry to go to Syria and the British feared that it would make trouble in neighboring Mesopotamia, concluded that it could do little good and might work much harm. It was thought that an inquiry would unsettle the countries it dealt with, create an impression that the Peace Conference was unable to make decisions, and open the door to intrigues and manifestations. All the information needed was at hand in Paris and delay would compound the difficulties. The battle for "the great loot of the war" in the Middle East must be fought at the Peace Conference, and the sooner the better.[86]

Wilson stood aside for weeks while Clemenceau and Lloyd George argued. At one point he reproached them for changing their minds "every day." On May 3 he remarked that the place where the arrangement of mandates seemed most difficult was Palestine, where the American and British governments had undertaken to establish "something that resembled an Israelite state." Wilson insisted that any mandate provide guarantees for the Jews and for the other peoples involved as well.[87] After listening patiently while the Europeans quarreled, he said at one point that they had been bad boys, and so it would be well for them to shake hands and make it up.[88] He remarked that he had never admitted the right of France and Great Britain to deliver peoples to anyone, that he agreed that the peoples of the region in question were not capable of government themselves, and that in their own interest they should be helped by a Western power of their own choosing. He explained that

84. Bonsal, pp. 48–49. Westermann diary, April 4, 1919.
85. House to Wilson, April 21, 1919, Wilson papers. House diary, April 21, 1919.
86. Two-page document "from the Division of Western Asia," n.d., filed under April 17, 1919, Wilson papers, 1919. Yale to the author. Yale's memo on Syria, March 26, 1919, Yale papers, Y.H.C.
87. Mantoux, *Délibérations,* vol. 1, pp. 378–379, 482–483. See Evans, pp. 148–150.
88. Grayson diary, May 21, 1919.

the Americans whom he had appointed to serve on a commission of investigation had been in Paris for some weeks, doing nothing, and now must start off on their mission or else return to the United States.[89]

On May 21 Lloyd George reported that, according to a telegram from General Allenby, the danger of an Arab uprising would be great if French troops entered Syria and if the commission of inquiry did not come from Paris. He would not participate without France, however, and Clemenceau was adamant and still unwilling to send commissioners until he knew that relief of the British troops by French had begun.[90] The American investigators appointed by Wilson—Richard Crane, a philanthropist, manufacturer, and loyal Democrat, and Henry C. King, president of Oberlin College[91]—set out early in June to sound political opinion not only in Syria but in other parts of the Ottoman lands that had been under Turkish rule. Lloyd George gave the American mission his blessing and promised that Britain would give "fullest weight" to its findings.[92]

Actually, although sponsorship of the King-Crane commission by the United States served to put American interest in this part of the world in an altruistic light and to demonstrate Wilson's concern for the preferences of the inhabitants of the region, the activities of the investigators had a negative effect on the prospect for agreement on practical arrangements for the future of the Ottoman lands.[93] After traveling through Syria and talking with Arab leaders, it reported to Paris on July 10 that most of the people were resolute against French control and also were opposed to Zionist plans. There was strong sentiment for the independence and unity of all Syria under Faisul and an American mandate. Great Britain was the second choice as mandatory. Impressed by Arab unrest and captivated by Faisul—"a real great lover of Christians" the report called him, a man longing to reconcile Christianity and Islam—it was thought that a large army would be required to protect a Jewish commonwealth. Foreseeing a bright future for Christian missions in the region, the commission recommended that Jewish immigration to Palestine be limited and that the idea of a commonwealth be given up, since it could not exist without the gravest trespass upon civil and religious rights of existing and non-Jewish communities.[94]

Copies of the King-Crane report did not circulate outside the American offices, though British officials were permitted to read it. The final version of August 28 was not delivered to the White House until September 27, too late for the president to see it before he was disabled. In view of the American withdrawal from the

---

89. Mantoux, *Délibérations*, vol. 2, pp. 142, 163.

90. *Ibid.*, pp. 263–264.

91. Putting a premium upon objectivity, Wilson had chosen two men who, he said, were very able and were particularly qualified to go to Syria because they knew nothing about it, minutes, ACTNP, March 27, 1919. House diary, May 20, 1919. Baker, vol. 1, pp. 77–78; *American Chronicle*, p. 394. Westermann refused to serve the commission as an expert, convinced that an investigation would add to the political turmoil. He designated two men from his office to serve. See Gelfand, pp. 251–253.

92. Tillman, *Anglo-American Relations at the Paris Peace Conference*, p. 152.

93. An Arab scholar has appraised the work of the commission: "The report . . . was as ill-informed as its influence was negligible. But their inquiry was the occasion of turbulence and unsettlement. It raised false hopes, and gave rise to intrigue and intimidation . . . and made a peaceful settlement immeasurably more difficult," Kedourie, p. 148.

94. Manuel, p. 249.

responsibilities of peacemaking in the autumn, and because of the offense that the conclusions of the commission would give to France and to the Zionists, its report was withheld from publication until 1922.[95]

The eventual fate of Syria was worked out along the time-honored lines of imperial diplomacy. On September 19 Lloyd George and Clemenceau came to an understanding for the evacuation of British troops in Syria and their replacement by French forces. Faisul protested bitterly and sought American intervention; but Polk, foreseeing that this might bring upon his nation reproaches from all three parties, explained that the United States could not interfere with the provisional military arrangements. He suggested an appeal to the League of Nations.[96] Faisul, bidden by the Foreign Office to negotiate with Clemenceau as best he could, reached an agreement that was rejected by the Arab leaders in Syria. After British troops withdrew, a French army broke the resistance of the Arabs.

A treaty of peace was presented to Turkey on May 11, 1920, and it was signed on August 10 at Sèvres. Under this, Great Britain was to take mandates for Mesopotamia and Palestine, and France, mandates for Syria and Lebanon. By Wilson's direction the United States was not officially represented at the signing.[97]

The efforts of the peacemakers to assign Class A mandates met with difficulties that had been foreseen by Secretary Lansing and General Bliss. Some Americans deemed it desirable that the mandatory powers should undertake to keep the door open not only to missionaries but to explorers for mineral wealth. In the summer and fall months of 1919, however, the behavior of British officials in Mesopotamia and Palestine led the Americans to fear that their businessmen might be excluded. Grave doubt arose as to Britain's use of the system of mandates. Would this new order serve as a cloak for imperial preference?[98]

The Allied governments did their utmost to induce the United States to take a mandate for Armenia, a barren land. During the war Armenian volunteers had fought with the Allies against the Turks, and at the end of hostilities the Armenians of Turkey had declared their independence. Their spokesmen joined a delegation of the Armenian Republic of Transcaucasia, which had declared its separation from Russia, in claiming a right to a hearing at the Peace Conference; and they pleaded there on February 28 for the creation of an independent state to include all of their people and to be governed under a mandate of the League of Nations. This plea found favor among the peace delegates. If the United States were to undertake any

95. See Harry N. Howard, *The King-Crane Commission.*

For discussions of the reasons for the withholding of the report of the commission, see Evans, pp. 133–135, DeNovo, p. 122, and Murphy, *The Brandeis-Frankfurter Connection* (New York, 1982), p. 91.

Clemenceau wrote to Polk that the King-Crane mission did "not appear to have contributed to calm the spirit of the people nor to have facilitated a solution," Clemenceau to Polk, August 23, 1919, Polk Papers, Y.H.C.

96. Buckler to Mrs Buckler, October 15, 17, November 8, 1919. Dispatches, J. W. Davis to the secretary of state, October 18, 1919, Polk to the secretary of state, October 19 and 24, 1919, Wilson papers. Dispatch in J. W. Davis papers, "undated."

97. State Department to Jusserand, March 24, 1920, N.A., R.G. 59, 763.72119 / 9608 and 9612b.

98. Lansing, *The Peace Negotiations,* pp. 151–153; private memoranda, June 9, 1919.

part in the governance of Ottoman lands, Armenia seemed the most likely place.[99] This was the desire of liberals everywhere, as well as of Armenian Christians, who hailed Wilson as a "liberator sent by God" and regarded his Fourteen Points as Holy Writ.[100]

Actually, the American people felt a sympathy for Armenia that was as profound as their ignorance of political conditions in that unhappy land. Americans had been generous in supporting ministrations by Protestant missionaries and relief workers to a population that suffered from extreme poverty and from civil violence that was chronic and peculiarly brutal. However, their president, devoted though he was to works of Christian charity, had responded with caution to appeals in behalf of the Armenians that came early in 1919 from organizations and individuals on both sides of the Atlantic. House, however, sympathizing with insistent Armenian pleaders at Paris, went so far as to foster an impression that the United States would accept a mandate.[101]

Early in May the pleading of Armenian spokesmen before the Supreme Council brought the question to the fore. On the fifth, in order to prevent an Italian occupation of Transcaucasia which the military advisers regarded as a preventive of chaos, Lloyd George asked for an American occupation. Great Britain already had too many responsibilities, he said, but the region in question had immense resources. Wilson was not tempted, however.[102]

In the middle of May, when "the Three" held sessions with no Italians present and took action on the allotment of A mandates, it was resolved that the United States, subject to the consent of its Senate, would be the mandatory for "the Province of Armenia." A week later the president remarked that the United States would take the Armenian mandate for humanitarian reasons.[103]

In June influential Americans who sympathized with Armenians were directing urgent appeals to Wilson.[104] Hoover, who was directing relief operations in Armenia as well as at Constantinople, learned from House that Wilson would appoint Hoover "governor" under the American mandate that the president had in mind. "I . . . knew from hard experience much about this part of the world," Hoover wrote later. "I was sure the president knew little of the conditions which had to be met. . . . I advised him [House] that Armenia could never protect herself from her fierce neighbors—Turkey and Azerbaijan—without a foreign garrison of at least 150,000 troops." If the United States took this responsibility, it would be at war with Turkey or Russia sooner or later, Hoover thought. Regarding Armenia as "the poor house of Europe," he proposed an American investigating mission.[105] At the beginning of

---

99. Lloyd George, *The Truth about the Peace Treaties,* p. 1260.

100. Bonsal, p. 187.

101. Gidney, pp. 78–86. House to Wilson, March 7, 1919. Memorandum, Kerr to Lloyd George, February 26, 1919, Lloyd George papers, F / 8 / 2 / 33. Westermann diary, March 27, 1919.

102. Mantoux, *Délibérations,* vol. 1, pp. 486–487.

103. *Ibid.,* vol. 2, pp. 58, 142. Charles T. Thompson, *The Peace Conference Day by Day,* p. 406.

104. For example, the American Committee for the Independence of Armenia, under the chairmanship of James W. Gerard, former ambassador to Germany, cabled on June 22 a request for immediate shipment of munitions and food to Armenia. Among the signers were Root, Lodge, and Hughes, Y.H.C.

105. Hoover, *The Ordeal of Woodrow Wilson,* p. 228; Hoover, *Memoirs,* vol. 1, pp. 455–456.

July he arranged for the appointment by the Supreme Council of an American high commissioner, Colonel Haskell, who was to attempt to direct all measures tending to aid Armenia. From him came grim reports of famine that led Hoover to inform Polk that there was danger of "a practical extermination of the Armenians."[106]

The question of an American mandate was wide open when Wilson left Paris. Indeed, even the possibility of military involvement was still alive in August. A disturbing report had come from American officials who met at Tiflis on July 23. It pointed out that lack of information in regard to the intentions and decisions of the Peace Conference was "intensifying disorders and undesirable political activities."[107]

When the British gave notice that they would like to withdraw their troops from Transcaucasia in mid-August, the question of protecting the Armenian Christians from Moslem violence became even more challenging. Wilson instructed Admiral Bristol to threaten the sultan's government with "absolute dissolution" of their empire unless they could and would prevent atrocities by Turks and Moslems. No excuses were to be accepted. As a result the grand vizier gave assurance that appropriate instructions had been sent to all provincial governors. He explained that the Turkish army had not been allowed enough troops to control popular passions, and the government at Constantinople could not take responsibility for events in the Caucasus.

Wilson's independent *démarche* did not escape the notice at the heads of delegations at the Peace Conference.[108] On August 25 Clemenceau protested, and it was agreed that no pressure should be brought upon the sultan by any power acting alone. As for saving the Armenians, he did not know what could be done. There were no American or British troops available; the Italians declined to replace the British in the Caucasus; the Turks were powerless even to control their own soldiers. When Balfour asked whether France might supply the peace-keeping force that was required, Clemenceau's response was noncommittal. Two days later, however, he told Polk that France would be willing to send 10,000 men to Armenia, but Polk construed this to be an attempt to get a foothold in Cilicia rather than a genuine proposal of aid to the Armenians.

The British government had just notified Ambassador Davis that it had begun to withdraw its troops from the Caucasus and that it hoped that the United States, as the probable mandatory for Armenia, would finance the British forces until they could be replaced by Americans. No funds were available at Washington, however, and to ask the Congress for a special appropriation would complicate the struggle for ratification of the Treaty of Versailles. However, at the request of Lansing, the British withdrawal was delayed.[109]

106. Hoover to Polk, July 30, 1919. Hoover, *The Ordeal of Woodrow Wilson*, p. 388.
107. Dispatch, N.A., R.G. 256, 867B.00 / 175.
108. Evans, p. 184.
109. Davis to Lansing, August 20, 1919; Lansing to Davis, August 23, 1919, *F.R., P.P.C.*, vol. 2, pp. 832–834.
"I am making every effort," Wilson wrote to Dodge on August 14, "to induce the British to change their military plans in that quarter," letter in Cleveland Dodge papers, Princeton University Library. In mid-September Wilson informed the State Department from the West that he was "heartily in favor" of

Reports from American investigating commissions that had gone from Paris to western Asia did not lead to any prompt determination of American policy. The King-Crane commission gave a hearing at Constantinople to Armenians of diverse Christian faiths and sundry political parties. Agreeing in seeking independence and political unity, the spokesmen differed as to the size and organization of the state that they envisioned.[110] The commission, denying the fitness of the Turks to rule even themselves, concluded that a strong mandatory power was required. They reported that the assumption of the responsibility by the United States was approved by the Armenians who were in contact with the West and was desired by the Allies, who had no wish to undertake so costly a humanitarian enterprise.

A second report came from a commission that Wilson sent to Armenia early in September and that was headed by Major-General James G. Harbord, Pershing's chief of staff, and advised by Stanley K. Hornbeck. It was instructed to "investigate and report on political, military, geographical, administrative, economic and other considerations involved in possible American interests and responsibilities in that region." The group went first to Sivas. There they were favorably impressed by the new government of Mustafa Kemal, from which permission was required to travel in the eastern regions. Going on to the Caucasus, they found that the relief work under Colonel Haskell had given luster to the repute of the United States among the turbulent peoples of the region. The massacres, it was concluded, seemed to have been instigated by orders from Constantinople. Fearful that any attempt to create a separate Armenia might give rise to further massacres, and noting that the successful exercise of a mandate would require control also of Anatolia and of Constantinople, the commission recommended that a single mandatory should govern all of European and Asiatic Turkey as well as Transcaucasia. The nation called upon would need the unanimous approval of the members of the League of Nations and must act with altruism and with devotion to an "international duty to the peace of the world." It was explained why the United States was better qualified to assume the hazards of the enterprise than any of the European powers. In conclusion, the commission's report balanced thirteen pros against thirteen cons, and ended with an unrefuted appeal that seemed to tip the balance toward acceptance of the mandate although no definite recommendation to this effect was made.[111]

Meanwhile, the American high commissioner at Constantinople was sending dispatches that gave a clear, independent view of the situation. Observing that Britain and France were inclining to continue the sultan's rule to some degree, Admiral Bristol expressed his personal abhorrence of such a solution.[112] Moreover, Bristol was annoyed by pressures that came from American relief workers, British leaders who wished to terminate an unprofitable use of their armed forces, and Armenians with special interests. He had no sympathy for Armenian aspirations for self-government and deplored their exaggeration of Turkish brutality. It seemed to him that

sending troops to Armenia if the Congress would authorize it, Wilson to William Phillips, September 16, 1919, Wilson papers. Evans, p. 218.

110. See Gidney, pp. 153–155. *F.R., P.P.C.,* vol. 12, pp. 804–829, and Howard, pp. 161–194.

111. Gidney, pp. 171–188.

112. Bristol to Polk, December 4, 1919, Y.H.C.

the Armenians were incapable of ruling themselves and were not without responsibility for the bloodshed, that their rebellion against Turkish rule was stimulated by neighboring Azerbaijan and that the Turks could not be blamed for reacting. He recommended to his government on August 17 that it "open the fight for one mandatory for the whole of Turkey."[113]

With Bristol's advice before him, confirming the preference of the Harbord commission for an American mandate for Turkey that would include Armenia, Polk was well briefed for discussion at the Peace Conference. But in this case, as in many others, his hands were tied by lack of guidance from Washington. On November 1 he commended the "remarkable" Harbord report to Lansing and urged him to make arrangements for the president to talk with General Harbord. The report, which dealt with the very controversial situation in Syria as well as with that in Armenia, had been kept from the public although it was shared with British officials. Months later, when the president partially recovered from the paralysis that afflicted him in October, his deep feeling for persecuted Christians drove him to a futile effort to persuade the Congress to consent to the acceptance of a mandate for Armenia. In 1920 he offered his personal services as mediator and asked for a plank in the Democratic platform that would assert "the Christian duty and privilege of our Government to assume the responsible guardianship of Armenia"; but the party's leaders would only express "deep and earnest sympathy for the unfortunate people of Armenia."[114] The American relief workers came home in mid-1920; and in the end Armenia, recognized in the Treaty of Sèvres as an independent state, was not able to resist the armies of its neighbors. It succumbed to a division between Russian and Turkish rule.

Despite the failure of the United States to take a responsible part in the new order that its president had so ardently advocated, there were farsighted individuals in Europe who had faith that, as Curzon wrote in March of 1920, American interest in western Asia had not abated and that at some future time the United States might be willing to assume a share of responsibility.[115] Many Europeans, however, were scornful of the mandates system; and at the end of 1919 officials of the Foreign Office were predicting that the League of Nations was doomed to failure without the degree of American participation in mandates that had been hoped for.[116] To some Europeans it seemed as unnecessary to supervise the colonial policies of their governments as it appeared to Americans to subject their nation's activities in such countries as Haiti and Liberia to international scrutiny. A feeling still persisted that

113. Evans, pp. 270–272. Warning that America's growing concern for Armenia was "tending to increase the tenseness amongst the Moslems" (copy of note to Harbord, Bristol papers, box 36), Bristol wrote to Polk on January 15, 1920: "I certainly hope that under no circumstances will our government recognize Armenia, even as a *de facto* government," Gidney, pp. 201–202.

114. Gidney, pp. 225–237, 245–246. Hoover, *Ordeal of Woodrow Wilson*, pp. 144–146.

115. Curzon memorandum, "The Turkish Situation and the American Government," March 6, 1920, Curzon papers, Mss. Eur. F / 112 / 278.

116. "America and the League of Nations," a brief dated November 14, 1919, Lothian papers, GD 40 / 17 / 51. According to this paper, American withdrawal from responsibility raised questions of a most far-reaching kind for the British Empire.

mandates were merely a cloak for annexation.[117]

All the while, keeping clear of responsibility for governing overseas regions under League mandates, the American peacemakers had managed, with the cooperation of the British Foreign Office, to keep the question of their position in Liberia out of the discussions at Paris and to exclude it from the purview of the League. The Treaty of Versailles had touched upon Liberia only so far as to require the renunciation of German overseas rights in general. It remained an American "sphere of influence."[118]

At the same time the British protectorate in Egypt and France's position in Morocco, which had been mutually recognized by the two powers, escaped international control by the Treaty of Versailles. Egyptian nationalists came to Paris to plead for self-determination, and the American minister at Cairo warned that the threat to civil order there was very grave.[119] The United States had never recognized the British protectorate; but in response to a request by Balfour to House, Wilson issued a statement of recognition in the hope that it might aid in the restoration of order and the prevention of bloodshed.[120]

Morocco had been under international restraints imposed by the Algeciras Act of 1906, which was regarded by many Americans as in keeping with the mandates principle. When, on February 25, France presented a plan for supervision in the future, it was challenged by George Louis Beer. The American specialists had warned in their Black Book against the erection of tariff barriers or the fortification of the north coast of Africa in disregard of the interests of Spain. Although White, who had taken part in the Algeciras Conference, fell in with the French plan, Beer advocated consideration of the question by a commission.[121] One was appointed, and he was included. The Treaty of Versailles went only so far as to require the renunciation of all German rights in Morocco.[122]

Although American assertion of those principles of colonial rule that had been upheld by British idealists exerted a benign influence at Paris, the hope of the British Round Table for American assumption of mandatory responsibility was not

117. Manley O. Hudson, "The Protection of Minorities," in Seymour and House, pp. 227–228.

118. Dispatches, Ammission to State Department, April 30, May 23, 1919, State Department to Ammission, May 26, 1919, N.A., R.G. 59, 763.72119 / 4815, 5074, 5445, 5449. See above, p. 67.

119. Minister Gary recommended that the exceedingly grave situation be met in a way agreeable to Zaghlul Pasha, the nationalist spokesman, H. Gary to embassy, Paris, April 15, 16, and 18, 1919, Wilson papers. The Egyptian National party had appealed to Wilson in a petition forwarded through Bern on December 10, 1918, and again in a statement sent to the president and to House on January 15, 1919, Y.H.C. The nationalist leaders were resentful when they were not so well received at Paris as the Arabs. They thought that the Americans had let them down, dispatch, Cairo to State Department, March 10, 1919, N.A., R.G. 59, 763.72119 / 4581. Westermann diary, June 28, 1919. DeNovo, p. 367.

120. Memorandum, Wiseman to House, April 17, 1919; letter, Wiseman to House, April 18, 1919, with related papers; House diary, April 8, 1919; House to Balfour, April 19, 1919, Y.H.C. Wilson to Lansing, April 21, 1919, Wilson papers. In the opinion of Gary, Wilson's statement in conjunction with General Allenby's strong hand "saved the situation," H. Gary to J. W. Davis, August 19, 1919, Davis papers.

121. Auchincloss diary, March 19, 1919; Polk diary, March 3, 1919.

122. *F.R., P.P.C.*, vol. 4, pp. 554–560. Beer diary, March 28, 31, April 4, 1919. Borden to Lloyd George, April 16 and 18, 1919. Lloyd George papers, F / 5 / 3 / 32. W. R. Louis, "The United States and the African Peace Settlement of 1919," 424–425.

realized. The tradition of isolation, and the reluctance of the governments of France and Great Britain to encourage the establishment of inexperienced American leadership in any regions of real economic promise, acted to retard for a quarter century the undertaking by the United States of commitments overseas that would be in keeping with its burgeoning power.

26

Disengagement: Economic and Military

The efforts of the Peace Conference to place Ottoman lands under League mandates evoked mixed feelings among Americans who sought an open door for educational and commercial enterprise. They were eager to teach and to trade under guarantees of equality of opportunity. In general, however, American businessmen were reluctant to accept regulation by any international body.

Americans found that in Europe they must deal with governments that during the war had assumed a large measure of control over economic life. Indeed, Europeans had become so accustomed to regulation that they were inclined to continue it and to persuade the Americans to join in; but the men of the New World, devoted to the creed of individual enterprise and the benefits of competition, would not be drawn in despite their president's commitment to international action for keeping the peace. The Americans were suspicious that the motives of the Europeans were those of monopolists and profiteers; and these suspicions were reciprocated in the European view of American business.

Unfortunately the Fourteen Points of the American president made but scanty provision for economic reconstruction and cooperation among the nations. Wilson had developed no program for an extension of his New Freedom to the rest of the world. He had offered in Point Three only the open door and "the removal as far as possible of all economic barriers and an equality of trade conditions among all nations." Article XXIII of the Covenant enjoined the League to "make provision to secure and maintain freedom of communications and of transit and equitable treatment for the commerce of all members." However, Wilson was disinclined to venture upon any specific economic commitment, either through the League or independent of it, that might exacerbate the political storm that was rising at Washington over ratification of the Treaty of Versailles.

At the same time, it was apparent that the interests of American traders might suffer if unprecedented action was not taken to restore Europe's economy. In April, when Wiseman put a fundamental proposal before House,[1] Lord Robert Cecil had approached the colonel about Europe's need of financial aid. They arranged for the appointment of a new committee of American, British, and French experts to study the questions raised by Cecil's searching analysis of Europe's economic dilemma. Clémentel agreed that France would cooperate.[2] However, when House turned this project over to Baruch, who would be one of two specialists to represent the United States, Baruch took an independent course. He wrote directly to Cecil to point out that he had already explained in discussions in the Supreme Economic Council that it would be inadvisable, for reasons given, to consider these questions at present;

1. See above, p. 289.
2. House diary, April 10, 1919.

and he then proceeded to scold the Allied governments for reluctance to rescind restrictions on German trade.[3]

To this Cecil, asserting his sincere sympathy for the American desire to relax restrictions upon the enemy, replied that he could not share Baruch's feeling that the financial question could be solved by the initiative of individuals unless arrangements were made for adequate credit. It was for that reason that he had asked for the summoning of the small expert committee to which House had agreed. He suggested that if the United States government intended to decline to aid on a large scale, it should make its attitude clear "quite openly and before the face of the world."[4] Thus the Americans were challenged to put in practice the devotion to international well-being that their president asserted and that John Foster Dulles proclaimed eloquently in addresses to the reparations commissions.[5]

Baruch was eager that private credit be used as far as possible to enable America to export its large surplus of cotton and to supply the other raw materials and the machinery and equipment that were needed to restore productivity in Europe. He wished to develop satisfactory arrangements for trade between the United States and Germany, which before the war had been largely based on agreements made with the German states before the empire came into being.[6] He contested efforts by commercial interests of the Allies to gain a head start over Germans in postwar trade[7] by making claim to priority in respect of certain raw materials.

Like other Americans solicitous for their nation's trade, Baruch dreaded any postwar commercial imperialism such as had been contemplated by the Allied governments when, meeting at Paris in 1916, they had approved eventual arrangement among themselves to control tariffs and supplies of raw materials. In his pursuit of "equality of trade opportunities" he appeared to be ready to challenge Britain's preferential tariffs for its empire.[8] He asserted in a letter to McAdoo that he had done all he could to keep the United States free from any promises that might result in financial guarantees in Europe. "Even an indirect promise of a great power like America," he warned, "becomes easily a fixed obligation."[9]

3. On Baruch's aggressive championing of Wilsonian idealism and American commercial interest, see Jordan A. Schwartz, *The Speculator,* pp. 130–139.
4. Letters in Baker, vol. 3, pp. 331–335.
5. See Keynes, "America at the Peace Conference," 93.
6. Minutes, ACTNP, March 5, 1919. Baruch recorded his work on industrial and commercial matters in *The Making of the Reparations and Economic Sections of the Treaty,* pp. 79–123.
7. See Baker, vol. 2, pp. 283–284.
8. C. V. Leith's notes, p. 9.
9. Baruch to McAdoo, May 2, 1919, McAdoo papers, L.C.
Baruch suggested a central United States agency to supervise trade, and his American colleagues proposed that their government collect statistics in Europe with a view to giving direct financial help to investors and exporters, Baruch to Eugene Meyer of the War Finance Corporations, April 7, May 3, 1919, Baruch to the secretary of state, May 12, 1919, Baruch papers. Baruch thought that the Treasury and War Finance Corporations should insist, when lending directly or indirectly to a foreign country, that no exclusive or preferential treatment be given to the citizens of that country over American citizens. Davis to the secretary of state for Rathbone, June 27, 1919, N. H. Davis papers, box 46. The activities of Baruch and his associates moved Willert to write to Northcliffe on June 13: "The Americans are out for world trade; they seem to be intriguing for it all over," letter, in Willert papers, Y.H.C. Lord Derby wrote on April 16 to Curzon that the controlling share of big business had been passing under American influence, letter in Curzon papers, 22: F / 6 / 2.

At the same time, Hoover was resisting British pressure for international control over food purchases that would drive down prices paid for the surpluses that he had encouraged in America. When Lloyd George complained to Wilson that the high cost of food would ruin Europe, the president was told by Hoover and the other advisers that no Allied combination could be binding enough to prevent the Americans from getting a free-market price and that indeed a lower price would result in decreased production and hence prices that would eventually go higher.[10]

Nevertheless, the resistance to interference with private enterprise that the Americans had shown in the early months of the Peace Conference weakened somewhat under the pressure of circumstances. Scores of questions involving the very existence of trade in Europe came to the desks of the American advisers. Some centralized machinery seemed essential, and they hoped that an economic commission might perform functions that were not to be found in the League of Nations. This was necessary, one of the men wrote, as "a step . . . in absolute self-defense."[11]

Wilson talked more than once with his advisers about assistance to Europe's economy, and he asked them to confer informally with the soundest of the European economic counselors and to get their views and proposals for maintaining the solvency of the European governments. He continued to remark to his European colleagues that it was not easy to establish systems of credit when no one knew just what the German liability for reparations was to be.[12] Nevertheless, although he insisted on American freedom of action and refused to give guarantees that seemed inconsistent with the laws of his government, the president reached out for some practical means for giving assistance to Europe, especially to governments newly constituted.[13] Davis and Lamont drafted at Wilson's request a proposal for new congressional legislation that would permit management of the international economy by efficient cooperation of experienced bankers with officials of governments.[14] Advocating that a campaign be organized to educate both senators and the people, and attributing opposition to political prejudice as well as to ignorance, Lamont wrote to Wilson: "Baruch thinks that when you once go back with the

10. Schwartz, p. 140.

11. C. K. Leith's notes, p. 9. American efforts toward equality in trade were being thwarted by special trade agreements that were being effected independently by the new states of Europe, Hoover and Gibson, *The Problems of a Lasting Peace*, p. 115.

12. Mantoux, *Délibérations*, vol. 2, p. 170.

13. Dispatch, Davis and Lamont to Leffingwell and Rathbone, April 28, 1919, Lamont papers, 164-14.

14. See above, pp. 300–301.

Davis and Lamont proposed "what became the quintessential themes in American reconstruction policy over the next decade. . . . As they saw it, this new version of dollar diplomacy conformed with the private character of the American political economy, avoided wasteful . . . state capitalism, and guaranteed a more efficient and peaceful management of world affairs," Michael J. Hogan, ch. 1, in *The U.S. Diplomats in Europe, 1919–1941*, ed. Kenneth Paul Jones, pp. 7–11.

It was the opinion of Lamont and Davis that after a period of six months or a year, after the stabilization of currency was well begun, exporters who were now inert would take risks again, and confidence would return. During the transition, however, government agencies should act. The English and the French were trying to devise "local machinery," and the United States might participate through the War Finance Corporation, cable from Davis and Lamont for Leffingwell, May 27, 1919, Davis papers, Ac.11,743, box II 29, N.2.

Treaty in your pocket our troubles will be over and the opposition fade away. . . . I am not at all confident of it."[15] Lamont forwarded to the president a message from his partner, Dwight Morrow, warning that opposition in the Senate would be "very formidable." Wilson replied appreciatively, invited practical suggestions, and wrote: "It is imperative that I myself should go home. The country is entitled to my services in helping it to think out the things in hand."[16] At this time, according to Cecil, Wilson was ready to recommend to the Congress on his return to Washington that the War Finance Corporation be authorized to advance funds at its own risk to finance trade in Europe, and moreover the president would urge that interest on the British debt to the United States be suspended for three years.[17]

In a session of the Council of Four on May 9 Wilson made a proposal, pressed by his advisers, for the creation of a new commission "to study and propose proper methods to assure countries that actually are in need of raw materials and foreign credits." To this Hoover added: "and victuals."[18] Such a commission was created, composed largely of men who had been sitting for two months on the original Supreme Economic Council.[19] It presented a report on June 4 in which both Americans and Europeans made significant but not major concessions. However, the Four, immersed at that time in considering protests of German delegates, did not take time to consider the document.[20]

At the end of June the Supreme Economic Council was still in being; but Hoover, with Wilson's support, gave notice that its continuance was undesirable[21] and that the question of international cooperation in economic matters "must rest for decision . . . with the permanent departments of government." However, Wilson recognized the practical difficulties that would be created by an abrupt breakup of the wartime arrangements among the victorious powers. At the same time, he feared that the world would regard them as an economic bloc and that the United States would appear to exploit the situation unfairly for its own advantage.[22] On his last day at Paris he joined with Cecil in sponsoring a resolution "that in some form international consultation in economic matters should be continued until the Council

15. According to Mrs. Lamont's record, Baruch embarrassed Lamont by telling Davis that the president weakened his political position by taking advice from Lamont, who was a partner of J. P. Morgan and Company, Mrs. Lamont's diary, Lamont papers, 164-20.

16. Dispatch, Lamont from Morrow through Polk, June 3, 1919, letter, Wilson to Lamont, June 7, 1919, Lamont papers, 165-30.

17. Cecil to the prime minister, May 31, 1919, Lothian papers, G.D. 40 / 17 / 1.

18. Mantoux, *Délibérations,* vol. 2, p. 13.

19. The American members of the Economic Commission that came into existence on March 1 were Baruch and Lamont, the latter being designated as an "alternate." They served also on the commission authorized on May 9. Keynes and Lord Robert Cecil represented Great Britain, Grew to Lamont, May 13, 1919, Lamont papers, 166-9.

20. Baker, vol. 3, pp. 363-372.

21. Schwartz has written that "the Americans unanimously favored scrapping . . . the Supreme Economic Council, . . . a theater for discord between delegations" that seemed to sharpen national differences instead of softening them. On June 22 the American economic advisers decided without a dissent to abolish the council, *The Speculator,* pp. 140-141.

22. Hoover, *Memoirs,* vol. 1, p. 423. Hoover likewise feared that the United States would become involved in trade rivalries, McCormick diary, June 11, 1919. For his proposals for economic reconstruction see Gelfand (ed.), *Herbert Hoover,* pp. 163-166.

of the League of Nations . . . had an opportunity of considering the present acute position of the economic situation.'' Wilson himself supplied the closing clause of the resolution: the Supreme Economic Council would be requested to suggest for the consideration of the several governments the methods of consultation which would be most serviceable. It was agreed that a committee on policy should meet and report as soon as possible as to the best method of giving effect to this resolution; and on July 10 such a committee recommended the formation of an International Economic Council to advise the various governments on economic matters pending the organization of the League.[23] However, the uncertainty at Washington as to the Senate's action on the treaty deterred Wilson from reaching a final decision as to the future of the Supreme Economic Council, which Cecil managed to keep alive at London for a while.[24]

In taking up the question of tariffs, which European governments had been accustomed to arrange by bargaining, the Americans, wishing to confer upon humanity some of the benefits they saw in the work of the regulatory commissions that functioned nationally at Washington, proposed the creation of an International Trade Commission[25] and the elimination of discriminatory tariffs save in regional customs unions and within the British Empire.[26] Asking whether it would not be more profitable to the world to trade with the Germans than to boycott their products, they opposed French and Belgian efforts to impose restrictions intended to strengthen the economies of their own peoples rather than that of Europe as a whole.[27]

When Europeans interpreted Wilson's Point Three as justification for "a new economic state" to be made up of the Allied powers, with free access by them to the raw materials of the world, the Americans perceived that this development was not unrelated to a desire for concessions as well as a determination to punish the enemy. Wilson wanted no part in a perpetuation of a regime of monopolies.[28]

Actually, however, the Americans had little success in lightening exactions upon the trade of Germany that were imposed by its neighbors for their own immediate advantage.[29] On June 16 the enemy was told that since its depredations had placed many of the Allies in a position of economic inferiority to Germany, whose territory

23. Mantoux, *Délibérations*, vol. 2, pp. 555, 560–561. Minutes, Supreme Economic Council, June 28, 1919.

24. Minutes, B.W.C., July 4, 1919, P.R.O. Cab / 23 / 11.

25. "Only an International Commerce Commission with very broad powers,'' Ray Stannard Baker wrote in 1922, "can really assure fair treatment for all . . . ; but whence is it to derive an authority equal to our Interstate Commerce Commission?'' Baker, vol. 2, p. 444.

26. Statement of policy in Lamont papers, 164-25. F. P. Garvan to Baruch, May 22, 1919, Baruch to Garvan, May 28, 1919, Baruch papers.

27. Baruch, *The Public Years*, pp. 100–101. Coit, *Mr. Baruch*, pp. 263–267. Memorandum, Davis, Baruch, McCormick, and Lamont to Wilson, June 6, 1919, Wilson papers.

28. Article by A. A. Young in Temperley (ed.), *A History of the Peace Conference at Paris*, vol. 5, pt. III, pp. 61–86. Baker, vol. 2, pp. 416–428. McCormick diary, June 23, 1919. Harrod, *Keynes*, p. 248.

29. Baruch, *The Making of the Reparations and Economic Sections of the Treaty*, pp. 81–123. The Americans did succeed in inserting in Articles 308 and 309 of the Treaty of Versailles a statement that the provisions therein, of which they did not approve, for the enforcement of patent and licensing rights would not apply as between the United States and Germany.

and factories were relatively undamaged, Germany would be deprived of the right that it claimed to be treated on a footing of complete equality with other nations, and that a "consideration of justice" impelled the powers to impose nonreciprocal conditions for commercial exchanges. These conditions were described as "measures of reparation." American influence contributed to their limitation to a period of five years after the treaty took effect. The council of the League of Nations was given authority to extend their life and to amend them; and it was understood that if and when Germany entered the League, the powers were to cooperate in arriving at a more permanent arrangement for regulating the commerce of all nations.[30] This was one of the several instances in which the Americans relied on the League to supplement provisions of the treaty that seemed to be inadequate. Their lively concern for trade with Germany was demonstrated as soon as the blockade was ended in July.[31]

The five-year control placed upon Germany's foreign commerce extended to transport on its waterways and railways. The regulation of river traffic in central Europe, for which the Congress of Vienna had made provision a century earlier, had become discriminatory. New landlocked states now required assurance of untrammeled access to the sea.[32] Moreover, French spokesmen were demanding that Germany's "virtual monopoly" of control of navigation on the Rhine be broken by an international regime that might serve also in respect of the Danube and of such waterways as the Dardanelles and the Kiel Canal.[33]

A Commission on Ports, Waterways and Railways had been set up by the Supreme Council on January 25 to provide for the free use of facilities that were essential to trade between nations. When this body made its report on March 20, it recommended international control of German arteries of transport. Authority over traffic on the large rivers was to be exercised by commissions. These bodies would be dominated by foreign members, to the regret of the Germans. The report was adopted by the Council of Four on April 26, and Wilson joined with the British in insisting that, with respect to the allocation of the Rhine's water power and its costs to France and Germany, the latter must be compensated for any loss sustained after a balancing of values.[34] When the British proposed that commissions be created to supervise important channels of international transit everywhere under the League's authority, Henry White, who with Miller spoke for the United States on this matter, drew back from so far-reaching a commitment.[35]

White did not lose sight of the effect that international regulation of transit would

30. Temperley, vol. 2, pp. 322–323. Luckau, *The German Delegation at the Paris Peace Conference*, p. 452.

31. Burton I. Kaufman, *Efficiency and Expansion: Foreign Trade Organization in the Wilson Administration, 1913–1921*, pp. 216–247.

32. Temperley, vol. 5, pp. 51–52

33. Statement of Captain Lorin, head of Clemenceau's Bureau of Economic Studies, to James Brown Scott, November 21, 1918, Scott papers, Georgetown University Library, ms. 105.

34. Mantoux, *Délibérations*, vol. 1, pp. 380–383.

35. Baker, vol. 2, pp. 435–436. White informed a friend that the work of the commission bristled with difficulties that made his experiences at four previous international conferences seem "the merest child's play," White to Dr. L. K. Rowe, February 17, 1919, White papers, Columbia University, notes and letters, box 2.

have on the United States.[36] He said that he could not advocate the demolition of the Kiel Canal fortifications in view of the fact that the United States had fortified the Panama Canal. Actually, he considered the German case to be even stronger than the American because the Kiel Canal was entirely in German territory. However, Balfour, remarking that the Suez Canal was unfortified and that the Kiel Canal doubled the naval power of Germany, stood with the French in favoring demilitarization; and Wilson, with reluctance, accepted a naval clause that the Allies advocated.[37]

When the Germans sent comments on the provisions in the draft of the treaty, White suggested modifications in their favor.[38] On July 1, however, deterred by uncertainty as to the Senate's action on the Treaty of Versailles, he made it clear that the United States would not take part in a general international convention that the British wished to summon. He notified the chairman of the commission that this matter had best be left in the hands of the League of Nations. Eventually, under Article 23e of the League Covenent, an International Transit Conference met at Barcelona in 1921 and drew up treaties. The United States did not participate.[39]

The whole question of future control of the transportation and communications of the world, not only on its surface but in the air and underseas as well, was raised at the Peace Conference. The magnitude of the prospects of commercial aviation were impressed upon the peacemakers in May, when the first Americans to fly across the Atlantic—a team of naval aviators—came to Paris and were received by the president. Here was a new opportunity for international regulation for the common good in a realm where rules had not yet been firmly fixed by national interests and prejudices. However, at the beginning of the Peace Conference the president and his military advisers had not been enthusiastic about a proposal of a general conference on aviation that might awaken the old American dread of "entangling alliances."[40]

The Americans found themselves aligned with Canadian delegates in opposing any world regulation of the air traffic of North America.[41] American officers, however, participated in the work of an Aviation Commission that was to advise the peacemakers on aeronautical provisions in the treaty with Germany and also was to

---

36. John P. Posey, "David Hunter Miller at the Paris Peace Conference," pp. 181–185. Baker, vol. 2, p. 330. H. White to Wilson, May 27, 1919, Wilson papers.

37. Mantoux, *Délibérations,* vol. 1, 263–264, 266, 268, 353, 372–374. *F.R., P.P.C.,* vol. 5, pp. 205–208, 235–238. Wilson to White, April 18, 1919, White to Wilson, April 21, 1919, Wilson papers. Article 195 of the Treaty of Versailles. Articles 380–386 of the treaty, to which Admiral Benson objected strenuously, forced Germany to open the Kiel Canal to vessels of all nations without discrimination, but provided for a German authority to deal with disputes and for a right of appeal to the League of Nations by "any interested power."

38. Changes that White proposed to the president were covered by six of the seven recommendations made by the Commission on Ports, Waterways, and Railways to the Council of Four, White to Wilson, June 5, 9, 1919, Wilson papers. White recommended a strengthening of the guarantee, in Article 89, of the right of free transit between Germany and East Prussia.

39. Baker, vol. 2, pp. 429–436.

40. Minutes, ACTNP, January 31, 1919.

41. General memorandum no. 17, April 19, 1919, Borden papers, OCA 198, 81688.

consider the drafting of a convention to prepare for the regulation of the aerial traffic of the world in time of peace. The Americans, willing to join in requiring the enemy to abolish its military air service, protested against long-term restrictions upon the manufacture and operation of commercial aircraft in Germany. Notifying the president of their dissent from recommendations made by the Aviation Commission, they argued that any measure that deprived Germany of the privilege of using air transport would be both unenforceable and irritating in the extreme, although they thought it feasible to exclude German aircraft from foreign commercial traffic.[42] Wilson supported their position, and the Americans brought about a shortening of the duration of prohibitions that the Allies proposed.

The Aviation Commission succeeded in writing a charter for an Aeronautical Convention that provided for a permanent commission, which was designated as "part of the organization of the League of Nations."[43] The United States, however, was not represented when delegates from fifteen nations met in the first formal gathering of this commission in 1922.

Still another aspect of twentieth-century communications calling for an international understanding was that of the control of the world's cables. At the request of Wilson, McCormick had talked with British delegates about removing wartime restrictions that were interfering with the transaction of business, and it was agreed that censorship would be abolished for cables connecting the United States with the major Allies and the countries of Central and South America.[44] Elaborate cooperative arrangements for the use of cables—a vital element in imperial expansion—had broken down under the impact of war. Americans, apprehensive that their nation's shipping and commerce would suffer under the domination that Great Britain had exercised over certain communications and had strengthened by taking over most of the German lines,[45] had a keen interest in the final disposition of the German rights as well as in the extension to all the world's cables of the sort of regulation that had long governed postal and telegraphic communications among the nations.

During Wilson's absence from Paris in February, Lansing, wishing to avoid a British monopoly, argued in the Supreme Council that cables could not properly be regarded as prizes of war and that the victors would not be justified in appropriating them, as his European colleagues wished.[46] In particular, the Americans argued that the island of Yap, a cable station of great value to American naval operations in the Pacific, should be put under an international regime.[47]

    42. Memorandum signed by Major General Mason M. Patrick, March 15, 1919, "Commercial Aerial Navigation in Germany after the Signature of the Treaty of Peace," Wilson papers.
    43. In the autumn of 1919 Polk declined to sign the Aeronautical Convention, believing it to be in the interest of British manufacturers, Polk diary, September 10, 1919. It was signed by the American ambassador at Paris with reservations but was not submitted to the Senate.
    44. Wilson to McCormick, March 28, 1919, McCormick to Wilson, April 17, 1919.
    45. It seemed to Robinson and Admiral Benson that Great Britain had its hand on "close to 90%" of the world's cables, J. J. Safford, *Wilsonian Maritime Diplomacy*, p. 196.
    46. At the suggestion of Admiral Benson, the matter was left to the decision of prize courts, which, he thought, would not seize the cables, memorandum for the president from Benson, February 7, 1919, N.A., R.G. 59, 763.72119 / 3824 1 / 2. *F.R., P.P.C.*, vol. 3, pp. 694–697, 705–714.
    47. On the question of Yap, see Sumitra Rattan, "The Yap Controversy and Its Significance," 124–136.

At the beginning of May, when the Council of Foreign Ministers had come to an impasse, Wilson tried to remove the whole question from national controversy.[48] He appealed to Clemenceau and Lloyd George, citing the common interest of all nations in the use of cables under conditions that would prevail universally. Objecting to the exclusive control of the German lines by the governments that had seized them, he proposed that they should be taken and held "jointly" by the great powers as trustees pending "common agreement as to the best system of administration and control." He advocated an "international congress to consider and report on all international aspects of telegraph, cable, and radio communication facilities on a fair, equitable basis."[49]

This proposal met with opposition from the Japanese, to whom the German cables at Tsingtao already had been awarded. Moreover, Lloyd George pointed out that some lines from Great Britain to the United States were owned privately by Americans and it would be difficult to establish an international control as long as these lines were not, like the British, state-owned. The prime minister agreed that there should be an international conference to consider the telegraphic communications of the whole world. Yet he insisted that the peace treaty should confirm the right of the governments that had restored the cut cables to operate them. This position was upheld by the Council of Four, and it was agreed that Wilson's proposal for international action should be the subject of a separate protocol among the Allied and Associate powers. Those who later explored the possibility of reaching an understanding like that of the International Postal Union continued to find formidable obstacles in imperial interests as well as in the private ownership of domestic lines of communication in the United States.[50]

A question of commercial advantage that touched sensitive nerves in London and Washington was that of the disposal of German ships that had been seized during the war by the United States and by Brazil. More than a year before America's entry into the war, the president had declared that it was intolerable that America's foreign commerce, and particularly that with Latin America, should have to depend upon the shipping of other nations.[51] Eager to have an adequate merchant marine, the United States and Brazil claimed all enemy ships that were seized in their ports when war was declared. The Americans took the position that, although under the Constitution their prize courts would have no jurisdiction after the conclusion of peace, present possession gave the United States title to the seized vessels. On April 23 Wilson made it clear that American opinion insisted on this interpretation. The retention of these ships was the one substantial item of reparation that the president demanded for his nation.[52] The British admiralty argued, however, that the Ameri-

---

48. Lansing to Wilson, May 1, 1919, Wilson papers.

49. *F.R., P.P.C.,* vol. 4, pp. 493–500. Mantoux, *Délibérations,* vol. 1, pp. 438–440, 464–467.

50. Miller, *My Diary,* vol. 15, pp. 194, 231–232, 484–497. *F.R., P.P.C.,* vol. 4, pp. 484–500, 645–654; vol. 5, pp. 437–438. Baker, vol. 2, pp. 466–487. The new medium of radio telephone was to be controlled under an international convention of 1912, subject to any revision approved by the Council of the League of Nations within five years.

51. Annual message to the Congress, December 7, 1915.

52. Safford, p. 187. *F.R., P.P.C.,* vol. 5, pp. 161–163.

The Americans had opposed the desire of the Allied governments to have German debts to Allied

can states, coming late into the conflict, had contributed little to the immobilization of the enemy's merchant marine and that the United States was claiming twice as many ships as it had lost. Lord Cunliffe asserted that the Americans were trying to override "international law," and British opinion resented American aggressiveness in this matter.[53]

The specialists of the two nations worked out a formula of agreement that was signed on May 3 by Wilson and Lloyd George. It provided that enemy ships captured or seized in ports should be kept by those who took them; that their value should be distributed on the basis of the total tonnage lost by the various states; and that countries like the United States, which captured more ships than it lost, should share the surplus value with the others. To this Wilson added a reservation, saying that he was confident that the Congress would authorize the payment to the general German reparation fund of the value of the ships seized in excess of American shipping losses, but he could not guarantee this. A similar agreement was concluded with Clemenceau. Actually, the United States had seized more than half of Germany's oil tankers and had been using them for two years. Its adviser on shipping, Robinson, feared that the British would renounce the agreement of May 3 because it was so unfavorable to them.[54]

The president, informed that there was a great deal of unrest at Washington about this matter, held the negotiations in deepest secrecy.[55] The State Department also

---

nationals paid immediately by the proceeds from the sale of German property located in the Allied countries; but they were forced to compromise on a settlement that required the immediate restoration of Allied property in Germany and, as compensation for what had been sold or damaged, the forefeit of German property within the countries of the owners, Luckau, pp. 263–266, 346–347. On entering the war the United States government had seized and sold the private property of Germans and held the funds against a final reckoning with the German government.

53. "Disposal of Enemy Merchant Shipping in Terms of Peace," memorandum by the First Sea Lord for the Prime Minister, April 7, 1919, Y.H.C. Wilson to H. M. Robinson, March 30, Apr. 7, 1919, Wilson papers. Borden to Lloyd George, April 18, May 2, 1919, Lloyd George papers, F/5/3/37. Mantoux, *Délibérations,* vol. 1, pp. 442 ff. The British and French argued that the "utility value" of the ships in question was greater than their value in money, Burnett, *Reparation at the Paris Peace Conference,* vol. 1, p. 124. Explaining this to The Four on June 10, Lloyd George said that those who could first establish themselves in foreign trade would gain enormously, Baker, vol. 2, p. 284. On the growth of the American merchant fleet during the war, see Demangeon, *Le Déclin de l'Europe,* pp. 72–100. Admiral Benson, fearing that Great Britain would outdo the United States in shipping, went so far as to warn the secretary of the navy that the American fleet should be "in every respect ready for action," Safford, pp. 196–197.

54. Safford, p. 203. Miller, vol. 1, p. 325, and docs. 900 and 979. It was to the advantage of France and Italy that the settlement be based not on their total losses during the war, but on their percentage of the total tonnage lost. Robinson, the American specialist, was able to work out an agreement with the new French minister of merchant marine that was similar to the general arrangement made on May 3, but it would apply only to the case of the United States. Clemenceau signed this on May 8. Brazil would have to negotiate as best it could with France, although Wilson assured the Brazilian delegate at this time that his government's position had not been overlooked, H. M. Robinson to Wilson, May 5, 6, and 7, 1919; Wilson to E. Pessoa, May 6, 1919; Wilson papers. Agreement signed by Clemenceau, May 8, 1919, Y.H.C.

55. Tumulty to Wilson, May 23, 1919, Wilson papers. Miller vol. 1, p. 325. House was advised by Miller that, because of the basing of the reckoning on actual tonnage lost, in accord with the American wishes, the plan was "grossly unjust to Italy" and "favored the British enormously." Robinson informed House that the British had "shown proper liberality"; and Polk thought that British interests had not been treated badly, Robinson to House, May 28, 1919, J. W. Davis papers. Polk diary, June 4, 1919. Polk wrote that it would be impolitic to question the agreement because this might provide an attack on it in the Senate.

held the shipping agreement in confidence. It was not until February 1920 that the text reached the Senate, with a message from the president saying that he had "intended to submit this to the Congress at the appropriate time," after the ratification of the treaty.

While Wilson was being forced to bow to the immediate necessity of writing a treaty of peace that all parties would sign, he lost much of his pristine enthusiasm for the gospel of internationalism. In the discussions of practical details into which he had been drawn, he found that he could not count on the allegiance that the peoples of Europe had seemed to give to his prophetic vision during the war.

Nationalism—whether encountered at Paris or at Washington—was the prevailing political force of the times. The peoples of the world, unwilling to place their lives and property unreservedly in the hands of an untried international organization, were reverting from wartime cooperation to economic autarchy. In undertaking to speak for all humanity Wilson was losing authority to speak for any nation, even his own. And without a national mandate he might become but a voice crying in the wilderness, a prophet scourging his people for their blindness to the way of salvation.

Nevertheless, American relief work went on, although Hoover recommended to the Supreme Economic Council that its food section be dissolved with the signing of the peace treaty.[56] The mammoth operation conducted by Hoover's organization, which distributed some 34 million tons of food and supplies to needy people in Europe, exerted a stabilizing political influence.[57] Hoover's men had extended their humanitarian program beyond mere succor. They used more than polite suggestions to discourage fighting among the factions of central Europe. When his men "suggested," Hoover wrote, "there was no mistake in somebody's mind as to what was what. I know the language they really used."[58] Hoover was as confident as his chief of the beneficence of his nation's mission. Like Wilson, he conceived of the United States as "the great moral reserve in the world," a potential "court of appeal" with strength that should be used independently to save Europe from "a sea of misery worse than the dark ages."[59]

The blockade was ended as the victors promised, as soon as the Treaty of Versailles was ratified by the German government.[60] The bars were lifted on July 12. Hoover, noting that the ideas of economic pools and joint action were "by no means dead," thought it extraordinary that the Europeans should make a concerted effort

56. *F.R., P.P.C.,* vol. 10, pp. 328, 342–343.

57. Food accounted for about 27 million tons. "In the total credits extended for supplies from all quarters, the United States carried over 96% and furnished 93% of the supplies," Hoover, vol. 1, p. 426.

58. *Ibid.,* p. 429. "Between September 1919 and July 1923 the allies and the United States were responsible for sending a further one and a half million tons of relief, mostly to Russia, but also to Poland, Austria, and Germany; and this was largely supplemented by charity," Arnold-Forster, *The Blockade, 1914–1919,* p. 38. On Hoover's relief work late in 1919 see Hoover, *An American Epic,* vol. 3, pp. 218 ff., Gelfand, pp. 12–13, 98 ff., 107, 165, 169.

59. Hoover to Wilson, April 11, 1919, in *Memoirs,* vol. 1, p. 457.

60. Clemenceau au Président de la délégation Allemande, June 7; von Lersner à Clemenceau, June 10, 1919, Archives du M.A.É., l'Europe 1918–29, Allemande, f. 209. Bane and Lutz, *The Blockade of Germany after the Armistice,* pp. 559 f.

to beat down American prices and at the same time ask the United States for financial assistance.[61] He was now criticizing the German and Austrian treaties with such virulence that he was about to join the many others who had overstepped the limit of Wilson's tolerance of dissent and become outcasts.[62]

On July 3 Hoover addressed to Wilson a long memorandum on the situation in Europe as to food, explaining the "demoralized productivity" of the Continent and the measures that should be taken. Hoover sent another paper on July 12, recommending that the United States form a committee to direct the American relationship to an international council and to issue an invitation to a general world conference that would settle questions of permanent organization. However, when an invitation to meet at Washington was extended and the European governments appeared unwilling to include cabinet ministers among their delegates, Hoover suggested to the president that the matter be dropped, at least until the Treaty of Versailles was ratified by the Senate.[63]

Balfour was advocating that the deficiency of Allied military power be made up by the use of economic weapons to bring unruly governments into line;[64] but Hoover, who went to London on July 31, would not accept such action as an avowed policy. He thought this would be contrary to "American idealism."[65] Nevertheless, his men had turned their economic power to political purposes more than once.

Hoover remained in Europe until mid-September, when the harvest mitigated the general shortage of food. The experience of his men in turbulent countries of Europe had convinced him that the peoples of the New World and the Old had "drifted farther and farther apart over 300 years" and were in fact now strangers. What was needed, he told Lloyd George, was an educational campaign that would encourage peoples to turn their armed men into workers in the factories and the fields, and to set them to producing goods for consumers with the same enthusiasm that they had shown in fighting and killing. He thought the only salvation of the impoverished

61. According to Lamont, the British were telling the small nations that they would care for them after Hoover's relief organization ended its ministration, but only on condition that these nations did all their business with Great Britain. "America came over here asking not a dollar and looking for no commercial value. . . . Great Britain . . . has been on the make from start to finish," Lamont to Mrs. Lamont, June 7, 1919, Lamont papers, 165-25.

62. Gelfand, p. 14. Hoover wrote: "He flashed angrily at these expressions as being personal accusations against him—which I, least of all persons, intended. But his nerves, like those of all of us, were taut," *Memoirs,* vol. 1, pp. 464–468. At luncheon with the Wilsons at St. Cloud, Baruch had encouraged a suspicion on the part of Wilson that Hoover wished to be president. Wilson had remarked that he did not consider Hoover a man able to carry the many questions that came before a president to a practical conclusion, Benham diary letter, Grayson diary, April 27, 1919. McCormick thought Hoover "a very exaggerated talker" and not always accurate in his premises, diary, June 14, 1919. Nevertheless, Hoover impressed House, to whom he sometimes took his troubles, as "one of the few big men of the conference," and was regarded by Auchincloss as "a perfect wonder . . . in spite of the fact that his methods are not always calculated to avoid friction," House diary, June 21, November 5, 1919; letter, Auchincloss to Polk, March 20, 1919, Y.H.C.

63. O'Brien, *Two Peacemakers in Paris,* pp. 191–193, 196–206, 211–212.

64. Memorandum by A.J.B., July 27, 1919, Balfour papers, 49750. Pointing out that the economic weapon had not been used on a large scale as an "engine of diplomatic persuasion" except in the crude form of a blockade, Balfour suggested a close study of its possiblities. Neither gratitude, in the case of small allies, nor fear, in that of small enemies, appeared to be strong enough to command obedience to the wishes of the great powers.

65. Hoover, *Memoirs,* vol. 1, p. 451.

countries lay in work, organization, and the establishment of sound exchanges. He accepted the fact that there was a real need for American credit, and regretted that the Congress was unresponsive to this.[66] He remained devoted to his policy of aiding Europe's economy to get on its feet.

The need for cooperation in matters of international finance became clearer as the currencies of European nations depreciated and their indebtedness increased. Constructive measures were suggested by bankers who were aware that financial instability in Europe not only might lead to social revolution but indeed might destroy the prosperous foreign trade of the United States.[67] Since it would be impossible to work through the League of Nations while the Treaty of Versailles was unratified, unofficial consultations among bankers and government officials were suggested.[68]

It seemed obvious to members of Wilson's cabinet that the treaty must be ratified so that the League might become effective in economic affairs. Indeed, Glass, expressing amazement that the Senate did not understand a situation "so critical in every respect" and "so patent to every businessman," asserted that it was a "political risk," rather than a "commercial or credit risk," that was standing in the way of private investment. "Definite action" by the reparation commission and ratification of the treaty were essential in order to prevent a stagnation of American commerce and a growth of "social disorder."[69]

The British Exchequer was concerned over the depreciation of its currency and foresaw difficulties in meeting its obligations in the United States. The situation was precisely set forth in a memorandum that Chancellor Austen Chamberlain gave to House on September 1. It was "of the greatest importance," this paper stated, that the Exchequer know to what extent the Treasury would allow British funds in America to be used for current transactions instead of being applied to reduction of indebtedness to the Treasury.[70] On the same day, Polk and Hoover, in Paris, agreed that the United States would have to make some financial concessions to Europe for the benefit of both the European and the American economy.[71]

On the last day of the month House, noting that the British and French had only makeshift plans for meeting a situation that could be evaded no longer, wrote a letter to Wilson that went to the root of the matter. The question of debts, he said, was the most urgent thing upon which he wanted to make suggestions when he

66. Memorandum, Kerr to Lloyd George, July 28, 1919, Lloyd George papers, p / 89 / 3 / 11. Kerr reported that Hoover said that his men found it easy to do business with the Germans, but "all the other nations in Eastern Europe were incompetent, untrustworthy, allowed politics to interfere with business and would invariably be forced to accept German leadership in trade and industry."

67. See Michael J. Hogan, *Informal Entente: The Private Structure of Cooperation in Anglo-American Economic Diplomacy, 1918–1928*, ch. 1.

68. Lamont had encouraged his partners in the House of Morgan to cooperate with European financiers and with American bankers for the extension of long-term credits to Europe, Stettinius to Davison, Stettinius to Loucheur, June 13, 1919, Lamont papers, 166-1.

69. Hogan, pp. 34–36.

70. Memorandum, n.d., identified by House's annotation, Y.H.C. Other statements of the British position may be found in communications from Grey to Curzon, September 29, and November 2 and 7, 1919, and Curzon to Grey, November 22, December 12, 1919, Curzon papers, f / 112 / 209.

71. Polk diary, September 1, 1919.

returned home. After tentative talks with Lloyd George, Law, Clemenceau, and Tardieu, and with the cooperation of a governor of the Federal Reserve Board, House had evolved a comprehensive plan that required concessions by the United States but also, in his opinion, offered certain benefits.[72] It would secure a large part of American foreign loans that otherwise would be worthless, and it would stabilize the finances of the world. Thus the foreign relations of the United States would be relieved of "their most dangerous and difficult elements." House believed that if the American people realized that England and France were charging a part of their foreign loans to war expenditures, they would be willing to do likewise. "If some such settlement as I have outlined is not made," House warned with great prescience, "it is certain that we will not be able to collect our debts in full, and it is also certain that we will incur the everlasting ill will of those to whom we have advanced loans."[73]

This proposal never was read by the president. It reached the White House at the time of his crippling illness. Apparently Mrs. Wilson, perhaps not uninfluenced by her personal distrust of House, deemed this communication to be one that might arouse the invalid in a way that Dr. Grayson warned might be fatal.[74] The letter of September 30, like one written by House on September 15,[75] was not opened until it came into the Library of Congress in 1952.[76]

Actually, the officials of the United States Treasury, lacking authority to extend further credits to foreign governments without the approval of the Congress, were not unresponsive to the needs of the world's economy. It seemed to Norman Davis that Europe could be stabilized for private investment if the League of Nations and the reparation commission were allowed to complete the work of the peace conference. "The whole prestige of the Treasury," he explained in a letter to a colleague on September 18, "is at stake in this matter . . . it gets my goat to have someone outside the Treasury to insist on appointing someone else outside the Treasury. . . . Baruch told me Rathbone couldn't do it."[77]

On the same day, Secretary Glass sent a telegram to the president that explained a change in his policy in respect of discussion of the war loans with the Allies. No

72. "The plan I have in mind . . . ," House wrote in his letter of September 30 to Wilson, "is: (1) The shifting of the burden of debt from one country to another and leaving the Central Powers to go bankrupt if any one indeed is to go. (2) The United States and Great Britain should fund the interest on the Allied debts for a period of from three to five years, and agree to defer capital payments for at least five years. (3) Great Britain to accept from France obligations of the Governments of Serbia, Rumania, Greece, etc., held by France; the United States to accept from Great Britain and France the obligations of nations indebted to them, and all in accordance with a well-worked-out formula which will make for an equitable adjustment. (4) The United States and possibly Great Britain to accept some portion of the Reparation bonds received from Germany in settlement of a certain percentage of the Allied debts remaining after the transfers have been made as suggested in paragraph 2. (5) When the reparations debts of the Central Powers are defined by the Reparations Commission for a practicable amount, then there should be a scaling of the German obligations between all the Allied and Associated nations. (6) The plan should contemplate some adjustment whereby foreign exchange should be stabilized," *I.P.*, vol. 4, pp. 501–503.
73. *Ibid.* House to Bonsal, August 1, 1931, Y.H.C.
74. See below, p. 542.
75. See above, pp. 411–412.
76. Wilson papers, reel 414.
77. Davis to Leffingwell, September 12, 1919, "Peace Mission" file, Treasury Department.

longer insistent upon confining talks on this subject to Washington, he now thought it important that Rathbone, the assistant secretary in charge of foreign loans, go abroad on a temporary basis and attempt to arrange an exchange of the demand obligations of foreign governments for time obligations. This would make it possible to postpone interest payments without further American legislation. In reply the president immediately wired from California, where he was campaigning for ratification of the peace treaty. He accepted the arrangement and expressed the hope that Rathbone would go "at once."[78] Accordingly, Rathbone went to Paris in mid-October and served as financial adviser of the American commission during its last weeks. Davis took his place at Washington.[79]

Rathbone worked with an organizing committee of the reparation commission, but this activity was limited when he was notified by the Treasury Department on December 19 that since the commission derived its authority from the Treaty of Versailles, which the Senate had rejected on November 19,[80] he could not officially take part in the deliberations of the commission. He was authorized, however, in order to safeguard the interests of the United States government, to attend the meetings and present its views in accordance with instructions from Washington.[81] The Treasury's opposition to any financial operations on the part of the League had been made clear to the president in August, and Wilson then indicated his approval. Doubtless he was convinced that any proposal for participation in an untraditional venture in finance would be futile, and even a deterrent to ratification of the Treaty of Versailles.[82] And so, while the Europeans were held strictly to their financial obligations, little help was offered in making it possible for them to meet them.

The disability of the president and the Senate's rejection of the Treaty of Versailles quenched the hopes that flickered in the autumn of 1919 for American participation in the restoration of Europe's economy. A quarter century was to pass and another world war to be waged before American officials were able to lead an awakened people into arrangements essential to the revival of war-shattered economies. Meanwhile Uncle Sam was to be taunted by the appelation "Uncle Shylock."

The Americans at the Peace Conference were as unsuccessful in implementing Wilson's Point Four as they were in respect of Point Three. Point Four called for a reduction of armaments to "the lowest point consistent with domestic safety." The prearmistice commentary had gone only so far as to advocate the adoption of the general principle and then the creation of "some kind of international commission to prepare detailed projects." The peacemakers found that in practice they could

78. Telegrams, Glass to Wilson, September 18, 1919, Wilson to Glass, September 19, 1919, "Peace Mission" file, Treasury Department.
79. Whiteman, "Norman H. Davis and the Search for International Peace and Security 1917–1944." Memorandum, Rathbone to Kelley, October 23, 1919, Treasury files, "Assistant Secretary Rathbone."
80. See below, p. 543.
81. Dispatch, Davis to Rathbone, December 19, 1919, Treasury Department, "Assistant Secretary Rathbone."
82. Rathbone to the secretary of state, November 11, 1919; Rathbone from Glass, November 13, 1919, N.A., R.G. 256, 185.111 / 387A and 391.

not prevent competition in arms even in those states that were their allies and protégés. However, Wilson and Lloyd George were forced by the will of their people
to reduce their governments' military commitments to a minimum; and the German
military establishment was cut to the size of a police force.

On May 14 Wilson made it clear to the Council of Four that he preferred to use
military means rather than a renewal of the blockade as a way of bringing Germany
to sign the treaty of peace, if further pressure became necessary.[83] However, the
president was obliged by public opinion, and the expiration of the wartime draft
law, to insist on continuing the withdrawal of American troops from the Rhineland.
In June, he agreed with Clemenceau, Foch, and Lloyd George that the American
force remaining in Germany should be no larger than one regiment, with auxili-
aries.[84]

The use of American troops in supervising plebiscites depended, as did so many
other matters, upon American ratification of the treaty of peace. Clemenceau asked
in August for the participation of 3,000 American soldiers in the four-power occupation of Upper Silesia.[85] This prospect, and also the landing of marines to restore
order in Dalmatia, aroused congressmen to demand the immediate recall of every
American soldier stationed on foreign soil.[86] Nevertheless, Bliss planned in October, contingent upon ratification of the treaty, to assign eight battalions to the supervision of plebiscites.[87]

A preamble in the Treaty of Versailles stated that it was "in order to render
possible the initiation of a general limitation of the armaments of all nations" that
Germany accepted the restrictions specified. It was obviously impractical, however,
to give effect to this limitation. The small nations were the less inclined to accept
restrictions when they saw the reluctance of the great powers to disarm. In the end
Wilson himself became an eloquent apologist for the position of the great powers,
saying to the small powers in a secret session on May 31: "The chief burden of the
war fell upon the greater powers, and if it had not been for their action, . . . we
would not be here to settle these questions. And . . . therefore . . . we must not
close our eyes to the fact that in the last analysis the military and naval strength of
the great powers will be the final guarantee of the peace of the world." To avoid
criticism from American liberals, Wilson forbade a verbatim release of this speech.[88]

83. Mantoux, *Délibérations,* vol. 2, p. 69.

84. Bliss to Wilson, June 25, 1919, memorandum of conference between Foch and Pershing, June
30, 1919, Pershing papers, box 373. Bliss to Wilson, May 19, June 6, 1919; Wilson to Bliss, May 20,
June 7, 1919, Wilson papers. Bliss to J. W. Davis, May 31, 1919, Y.H.C.

The American occupation force, under General Allen, consisted of 16,000 men in 1920 and was not
entirely removed until January 1923, Edward M. Coffman, *The War to End All Wars* (New York, 1968),
pp. 359–360.

85. Dispatch, Ammission to State Department, August 12, 1919, N.A., R.G. 59, 763.72119 / 6134.
See above, p. 423.

86. K. Nelson, *Victors Divided,* pp. 129–130.

87. Word came at this time from the State Department that six battalions of infantry that were due to
land at Brest on October 28 could be ordered to participate in the operation in Silesia if and when the
treaty was ratified by the United States. Bliss to General Weygand, Oct. 21, 1919; Bliss to General
Allen, Oct. 22, 1919, Bliss papers, box 233.

88. R. S. Baker's journal, May 31, 1919. General Bliss analyzed the reasons for failure to make
progress toward general disarmament in "The Problem of Disarmament," in *What Really Happened at*

Actually the great powers were no more prepared to disarm themselves than to enforce disarmament on the small nations. The president was once again caught in the conflict between principle and expediency, between one of his Points and the necessities of the moment. In supporting Bliss's recommendation for a larger army for the states that formed the *cordon sanitaire,* Wilson said that the most important consideration was that Poland and Romania be prepared to resist any menace from Bolshevist Russia. He counseled delay in reducing the armies of eastern Europe.[89] On June 5, after explaining to the leaders of the small powers the recommendations of the military advisers, Wilson responded with sympathy to a proposition that had the support of Vesmić, Venizelos, Bratianu, and Beneš to the effect that the limitations of armies be deferred until it could be undertaken universally by the League of Nations.[90]

Progress in both economic and military disarmament would have to await a growth of confidence in the new international system. The effectiveness of Wilson's Point Three and Point Four was to depend upon the development of a new, world-serving power through which national usages and requirements might be peacefully reconciled in a way that would win international acceptance. The outcome of the efforts made by the Americans at Paris to lift peacemaking to a new plane depended for their fulfillment largely on the efficacy of the League of Nations.

Paris, ed. Seymour and House, pp. 390 ff. See David F. Trask, "Woodrow Wilson and the Coordination of Force and Diplomacy."

89. Mantoux, *Délibérations,* vol. 2, pp. 181, 184–186.

90. *Ibid.,* pp. 313–318. For the provisions of the Covenant for disarmament see Article 8, Appendix A.

The deferment, in the opinion expressed by Hoover years later, was "one of the greatest of all mistakes" of the peacemakers of 1919, Hoover and Gibson, p. 119.

27

Paralysis at Washington

The peacemakers were handicapped in the last months of 1919, as we have seen, by uncertainty as to the acceptance by the United States of the commitments that had been made by its president. The American machinery for negotiation remained in the Crillon, but after Wilson and House left in June the mainspring was no longer at Paris. The complex settlement was incomplete in some respects. It would be ineffective in many of its provisions without a League of Nations in which the United States would play its part.[1]

When Wilson departed from Paris, the fortunes of the League were at hazard. Would it be in fact a Holy Alliance such as the European powers had formed a century earlier, a continuation of the collaboration that had won the war? Would it serve to extend to the whole world, with American participation, the mutual benefits that British statesmen saw in their empire? Was its function, in reality, merely to enforce the terms of the peace treaty and to collect debts? Of most immediate importance, what was the significance of the attitude of the United States Senate? It was suspected at Paris that criticism of the Covenant at Washington reflected a desire of American businessmen to make a separate peace for the advantage of their trade with Germany.[2]

Although Wilson had put on a bold front when he was directly challenged at Paris,[3] he had been anxious during the spring months about the fate of the treaties in the Senate. Indeed, one of the legal advisers had confessed that Senate acceptance of the League Covenant seemed unlikely. It had become more unlikely when Wilson took a defiant attitude toward the Senate's opposition.[4]

In the face of gathering hostility the president had been compelled by financial necessity to convoke the American Congress while the Peace Conference was still in session. His call to the Congress, written with great difficulty because of his ignorance of affairs at home,[5] appeared in the American press on May 8. The legislators convened on May 19 to hear the president's State of the Union message. At this time Miller advised House that Wilson had the situation "wholly in his own

---

1. On the importance of American membership in the League, see above, ch. 26, and James Barros, *Office without Power*, pp. 28–30.

2. Seymour, *Letters from the Paris Peace Conference*, p. 273.

3. When Ambassador Jusserand expressed at Paris a doubt as to the outcome of the conflict at Washington between the tradition of isolation and the doctrine of Wilson, the president responded with an assurance that was founded on the faith that he knew his country better than anyone, Jusserand to M.A.É., November 24, 1919, Archives du M.A.É., À paix, 1154.1, f. 156.

4. See above, p. 186. Nicolson recalled (orally to the author, October 25, 1959) that on an occasion at which he was present but could not date, Balfour asked very politely whether in view of all the concessions the Europeans were making the president could get the League Covenant accepted at Washington, and Wilson, rising from his chair and pacing up and down, turned pale but maintained he could so so.

5. Benham diary letter, May 14, 1919.

hands," that he, as well as the Senate, had certain "Constitutional rights," in particular that to decline to accept any reservation or annex and to insist on action upon the treaty as it stood.[6]

In the new Congress the Republicans had a majority of two in the Senate and thirty-nine in the House. The defenders of the faith, now a minority, were handicapped by the absence of their chief and by a lack of good publicity. Debate in the Senate soon made it clear that the changes that Wilson had brought about in the Covenant in order to satisfy American opinion—alterations that in the eyes of Europeans had given the United States a position of unwarranted privilege—had failed to mollify American critics.[7]

Elihu Root, of whose nine suggestions for revision of the Covenant only four had been accepted at Paris in April,[8] deplored the lack of arrangements for the development of international law. He noted a widespread feeling, shared even by some Democrats, that the president was moved more by his personal desire for re-election than by a wish to serve the interests of peace or those of his country. Almost constantly in correspondence with Lodge and other Republican senators, Root held to his conviction that the treaty should be ratified, but with amendments that he thought necessary.[9] The positive guarantee of Article X violated the belief that the United States—as Wilson had advocated during the period of neutrality—could best serve the world's peace by preserving its ideals untarnished by involvement in Europe's quarrels. It was regretted, as Lodge put it in a personal letter, that Wilson had "undertaken to be the final umpire in every European question, incurring hostility both for himself and his country, and meddling with things in which the United States had no interest whatever."[10] When Wilson asserted that the Covenant left the American Congress free to interpret it and when he called it a moral obligation, binding in conscience only and not in law, Root objected to the imprecision of the commitment. He wrote to Lodge of Wilson's "curious and childlike casuistry" and his "demoralizing and dishonest distinction."

Lodge, for his part, foresaw the possibility of an eventuality in which the Congress would not be able to exercise its constitutional rights without breaking a moral obligation. To prevent this embarrassment, he was to demand a reservation, among others, stating that the United States "assumes no obligation" under Article X "unless in any particular case the Congress" should "so provide."[11]

The president, receiving news of the opposition and convinced that he was the victim of implacable and malicious hostility, wrote to Lansing on May 24: "The attacks are all parts of the general plan to make as much mischief as possible. Article X is the kingpin of the whole structure . . . without it, the Covenant would mean nothing. If the Senate will not accept that, it will have to reject the whole

---

6. "Memo for Col. House," May 13, 1919, Y.H.C.
7. Debate in the Senate has been summarized by Rayford W. Logan in *The Senate and the Versailles Mandate System* (Washington, 1945), pp. 40–43.
8. See above, pp. 191–192, 306.
9. Philip C. Jessup, *Elihu Root*, vol. 2, pp. 397, 403.
10. Lodge to Lord Charnwood, July 2, 1919, quoted in Widenor, *Lodge*, pp. 326–327, *q.v.*
11. *Ibid.*, pp. 337–338, *q.v.*

treaty. Manifestly it is too late now to effect changes in the Covenant."[12] He made it clear to House that he would consider no more changes in the treaty. "Here I am," he said. "Here I have dug in."[13] Woodrow Wilson's mind had set in the way that ten years earlier had been fatal to the realization of his ideals for Princeton University.

Advisers at Paris who shared the president's faith in the League had been disappointed when in his visit to America in February he had failed to explain the significant features of the Covenant to the people.[14] Aware now of the seriousness of the dissent at Washington and of the necessity of educating the public, Wilson came to the Crillon in mid-May for a council of war with House in what Bonsal called "graveyard secrecy." Together they drew up a memorandum of arguments that he would use in an educational campaign in the United States.[15]

Wilson would emphasize the concern of the American government for small and weak nations and reaffirm his commitment to the principle of self-determination. He was ready to assert that, for the first time in history, the rights of those peoples who could not enforce them were to be safeguarded. Referring to the contention of those recently "redeemed" that they must have certain positions of military strength, he insisted that under the League of Nations this consideration would vanish. The new treaty had rectified some ancient wrongs, and those that persisted could be dealt with under his favorite article in the Covenant, the eleventh, which proclaimed that it was right of every nation, whether its own interest was involved or not, to bring before the League any issue that was likely to disturb the peace of the world. The president depended upon a rekindling of the fire that he had lighted in the hearts of his own people in time of war. He was already planning to speak directly to as many as he could reach in a tour of the United States;[16] and when he carried out his intention in the autumn, much of his argument was that of the memorandum that he and House drafted in May.

In June, as the president came to depend more and more on the League of Nations as an instrument for the execution and perfecting of the treaties of peace, opponents at Washington stepped up their attack on the Covenant. No sooner had Wilson's friends scotched a canard about the "leak" of the treaty through "special interests" on Wall Street[17] than Senators Knox and Fall introduced embarrassing resolutions.[18] The president was "greatly shocked," he confessed, and thought such res-

12. Cable, Polk for the secretary of state and House, May 17, 1919. Letter, Lansing to the president, May 19, 1919. Cable, Ammission (Lansing) to the secretary of state, May 26, 1919, including text of letter, Wilson to Lansing, May 24, 1919, N.A., R.G. 256, 185.111 / 298 and 307. Cf. above, p. 374.

13. Bonsal, *Suitors and Suppliants*, pp. 268, 272, 277–278. Secretary of state from Polk, May 31, 1919, Wilson to Lansing, June 3, 1919, N.A., R.G. 256, 185.111 / 325. On May 31, Wilson, appearing "quite well, . . . said that after the treaty was signed, he had to go home to lick those fellows in the Senate, after which he could sleep," J. W. Davis diary, May 31, 1919.

14. Lamont, *Across World Frontiers*, p. 185.

15. Half of the memorandum is reproduced in Bonsal, *Unfinished Business*, p. 275.

16. Cable, Wilson to Tumulty, May 2, 1919, Wilson papers.

17. See above, p. 396.

18. Knox's resolution, against accepting the Covenant as part of the treaty of peace, was introduced on June 6 and immediately reported out by the Foreign Relations Committee by a vote of 8 to 7. Senator Fall proposed that the war be brought to an end by a decree of Congress, and the president be required to withdraw American troops from Europe, Tumulty to Wilson, June 25, 1919, Wilson papers.

ervations as those proposed would be disastrous[19] and would require acceptance of them by the other signatories to the treaty. However, despite the concessions that he had won at great pains to the request of prominent Americans for special consideration of the United States in the Covenant,[20] Republican leaders continued to formulate changes.

The president then notified Tumulty that it was his "clear conviction" that the adoption of the treaty by the Senate with reservations would put the United States as clearly out of the concert of nations as a rejection, that "to stay out would be fatal to the influence and even to the commercial prospects of the United States, and to go in would give her a leading place in the affairs of the world," and that "reservations would postpone the conclusion of peace . . . until every other principal nation . . . had found out by negotiation what the reservations practically mean" and whether they could accept them. Tumulty was authorized to make this blunt declaration public, but he was dissuaded by Democratic senators.[21]

On July 10 Wilson went to Capitol Hill to present the Treaty of Versailles to the Senate. The tone of his address, boasting of the work of the Peace Conference, suggested contempt for his adversaries.[22] The treaty of guarantee with France, which was released to the press in Paris on the third, was withheld by the president until July 29, despite the stipulation in its text that it be presented to the Senate simultaneously with the Treaty of Versailles. On July 18 Wiseman, calling at the White House, was shocked to find Wilson obviously a sick man, his face drawn and gray and twitching. "I ask nothing better," the president said, "than to lay my case before the American people." He was prepared, however, to talk individually with senators and to accept some sort of interpretive reservations covering Articles II, X, and XXI of the Covenant.[23]

Near the end of the month Wilson acted in response to advice that he employ tact and gentleness to persuade wavering senators. He invited some of the more tractable Republicans to talk with him individually. He had daily conversations with Lan-

---

House was notified in mid-June by Miller that the battle to be fought with the Senate was "very serious" and extreme opponents were willing to defeat ratification of the treaty if that were necessary in order to reject the Covenant, Auchincloss from Miller, June 13, 1919, Auchincloss diary. It was the opinion of Miller that any separation of the Covenant from the Treaty of Versailles "would involve an entire re-writing of the Treaty," *My Diary*, vol. 20, p. 440.

19. Wilson to Lamont, letter of June 27, 1919, Lamont papers, 171-29. Wilson instructed Tumulty to take no notice of the Knox resolution and alleged that one of its objects was to stir him up, in which it had failed, Wilson to Tumulty, June 16, 1919, Wilson papers. Warned by Baker that by paying no attention to the resolution he would pique the Republican senators just as Theodore Roosevelt had been piqued, the president merely smiled, R. S. Baker journal, June 14, 1919. On June 20 Willert wrote to Northcliffe: "The president cannot be too much blamed for the arrogant way in which he has ignored and humiliated the dominant party," Steed papers.

20. See above, ch. 16.

21. Wilson to Tumulty, June 23 and 24, 1919, Tumulty to Wilson, June 25, 1919, Wilson papers, Tumulty papers, box 79. Before the end of June the Committee on Foreign Relations decided to let both the Knox and the Fall resolutions rest, Denna F. Fleming, *The United States and the League of Nations*, p. 228.

22. Arthur S. Link, *Woodrow Wilson, Revolution, War and Peace*, p. 107.

23. Wiseman to Murray, July 23, 1919, in Arthur C. Murray, *Master and Brother*, p. 157. *I.P.*, vol. 4, pp. 515–516.

sing, who continued to leak to Republican adversaries through his friend Chandler Anderson, as he had in indiscreet talks in Paris, his personal dissatisfaction with Wilson and the treaties. The president's image in the Congress suffered when he notified the Speaker of the House that instead of taking a contemplated August vacation they should remain in session and deal with pressing industrial and labor problems.[24]

In August what had been a political controversy became a personal feud between Wilson and Lodge. The president's leadership, a prerogative very dear to him, was being attacked by men who seemed to him determined to humiliate and destroy him. A learned and impassioned speech was delivered by Lodge on August 12, arguing that certain articles of the Covenant would induce war rather than peace. Wilson was harassed when the dissent of Lansing, Bliss, and White in the handling of the crisis over Shantung became known and when indignation rose among Americans sympathetic with China and antipathetic to Japan. And the Irish-Americans, who had been frustrated at Paris, continued their anti-British propaganda.

The president could not conceal certain acts of his that had offended his fellow delegates at Paris. When *The Nation* printed an account of Bullitt's aborted mission to Moscow that was close enough to the truth to be politically embarrassing, Wilson brushed it aside by writing to Tumulty: "I have an utter contempt for *The Nation* and its editor and do not want to get into a controversy with it."[25]

In mid-July Wilson was persuaded to write a courteous note to Lodge. The president was informed by Polk[26] that the senator had expressed a wish that he be consulted on the question of making an American appointment to the vital reparation commission at Paris.[27] A permanent commission was needed to replace the existing interim body—a "patchwork affair," according to Lamont—and it was apparent that an American representative would be valuable as an arbiter. But Lodge rebuffed Wilson's offer to confer about this matter.[28] This did not incline the president to accede to requests from the senator for documents recording deliberations at Paris on sensitive matters. Wilson at first returned an unsatisfactory reply to the effect that the very bulk of the documents made it impractical to bring them across the Atlantic. Sending only the formal report of the Commission on the League of Nations, Wilson explained to Lodge that it was agreed at Paris that records of intimate exchanges of opinion on delicate matters were confidential "on grounds of public policy" and for reasons that would be apparent to the senator. When Lodge persisted in asking for other papers Wilson sent some and withheld others.[29]

24. Lazo, "A Question of Loyalty," 44, 49–52. B. Long's diary, August 3, 1919.

25. Wilson to Tumulty, July 17, 1919, Wilson papers. Lansing's dissent on the question of Shantung was revealed by Bullitt in a hearing of the Foreign Relations Committee on September 12, Lazo, 46–49. Lansing's festering bitterness is revealed by Henry William Brands, Jr. in "Unpremeditated Lansing: His 'Scraps,' " *Diplomatic History* 9, no. 1 (Winter 1985):31–33.

26. Polk diary, July 16, 1919, Polk to Wilson, July 16, 1919, Y.H.C.

27. Lodge wrote of Polk: "He is a first-rate man in every way," Nevins, *White*, p. 465.

28. Wilson to Lodge, July 18, 1919, Lodge to Wilson, July 22, 1919, Wilson papers.

29. Lodge to Wilson, August 23, 1919, Wilson to Lodge, August 28, 1919, Lodge to Wilson, September 2, 1919, Wilson papers. The Rhineland agreement and the treaty with Poland protecting minorities were sent to the Senate, memorandum, Close to Forster, August 22, 1919, Lansing to Wilson, August 28, 1919, Wilson papers.

Quizzed by the Committee on Foreign Relations, the president, who had always found it difficult to give cool and clear answers to an inquisition, became confused and inaccurate and, in his desire to protect his position, positively deceitful.[30] On August 26 the committee adopted some fifty amendments that would prevent American participation in the work of the commissions that the Peace Conference was impatient to put in action. The Republican senators, refusing to accept reservations that would be merely interpretive in nature, held to the principle that they must be included in the act of ratification.[31]

Warned by members of his cabinet on the damaging effect of delay upon business and its menace to social stability,[32] Wilson looked upon the adversaries as villainous enemies of human society. His fighting blood aroused, he determined to give them a political thrashing. In September, while Lloyd George went to Paris with a view to expediting the settlement of difficult matters still before the Peace Conference, the American president, instead of following up his constructive work abroad by maintaining the close rapport with the Europeans that House had catalyzed, drained his remaining strength in a gallant but doomed crusade for votes in favor of the treaty and the League of Nations. Warning against future war and "a barbaric reversal of civilization," he pleaded fervently. When he broke down in Colorado and immediately after his return to Washington was completely paralyzed, any prospect of a continuance of official participation by Americans in the work at Paris vanished.

In his crippled condition the most unlovely traits of Woodrow Wilson prevailed. Unable to act himself, he was irritable, petulant, and jealous of anyone who tried to speak for him. He became completely dependent on Mrs. Wilson and Dr. Grayson, despite Tumulty's concern for the duties of the presidency. The government of the United States, like its president, was paralyzed. Grayson estimated that it would be weeks, and probably months, before his chief could resume his duties; and meanwhile the physician and Mrs. Wilson prevented effective action by any cabinet officer. Partial disablement was, for the cause of peace, the worst of all possible calamities. Having used the last ounce of his strength in castigating men whom he

---

Wilson followed Senator Hitchcock's advice against submission of the Treaty of St. Germain to the Senate because it would stimulate the opposition, Bonsal to House, April 10, 1920, Bonsal papers, box 2.

30. See Lawrence Evans, *U.S. Policy and the Partition of Turkey, 1914–1924*, p. 58n. Edwin A. Weinstein gives a psychological explanation of this much-debated occasion. *Woodrow Wilson*, p. 352.

31. For the reservations of Lodge and Wilson, see Thomas A. Bailey, *Wilson and the Peacemakers*, pp. 387–394.

Widenor observes that the so-called "mild reservationist" Republican senators, to whose views the Democratic leaders gave scant consideration, were wooed by Lodge and as a result the reservations that were presented were not so much Lodge's as they were the work of Root and the mild reservationists. Lodge, p. 330. Lodge's chief motive (if indeed one could be said to prime)—whether to secure ratifications with reservations that he sincerely believed necessary, or to bring about a defeat of the treaty by the obstruction that he foresaw would come from Wilson—has not been conclusively determined, *ibid.*, pp. 335–339. Cf. below, p. 342. Widenor, analyzing Lodge's "delicate balancing act," concluded that he became gradually more "irreconcilable," but "never became an isolationist," *ibid.*, pp. 335, 345–346.

32. "Europe is on the verge of catastrophe, political, economic and social. . . . Should the catastrophe occur, the blight of social disorder will spread to America," Glass to Wilson, letter and memorandum, August 13, 1919. Houston to Wilson, August 13, 1919, Wilson papers.

might better have worked to conciliate, Wilson had fallen into a condition in which he was to be an obstacle blocking anyone who might try to pick up the tangled reins that he had held all in his own failing hands.

With the president ill, and at sword's points with the most influential Republicans, the conciliatory ministration of House was needed more than in any other crisis in Wilson's career. Even before the League Covenant had been accepted by the Peace Conference at the end of April, House, uncertain though he was of the Senate's consent to American participation in the new world order, had taken initiative toward fulfillment of the vision of nations organized for peaceful co-existence under the leadership of a prosperous United States.

While Wilson was away from Paris in February, House had planned to continue the work of the commission that was drafting the League Covenant and to make it into a provisional executive council that would function immediately in matters referred to it by the Peace Conference. At that time, however, the president had cautioned him to move slowly in view of sentiment at Washington.[33] Early in April, even before the Covenant was accepted by the Peace Conference, House had obtained the approval of Lord Robert Cecil for the convoking of the League assembly at Washington in October, with Wilson in the chair. After a plenary session of the Peace Conference approved the creation of a committee to plan the organization, House welcomed it at its first meeting in the Crillon; and on May 5 he asked Pichon to take the chair. He had prepared a few simple resolutions for their approval.

In the organizing session there was no speechmaking, no argument; and in eight minutes the program had been adopted. The League was to hold its first meeting in Washington, with Wilson presiding. Marveling at the "sheepmindedness" of the other delegates, House told himself that the importance of the matter justified him in acting as if the whole thing were in his hands. He wished, above everything, to make it impossible for critics of the League to ruin it, and he laid plans for publicity that would make it perilous for any politician to oppose the new order publicly. He felt that "even reduced to bare poles" the League would help those who would have to clean up the confusion left by the Peace Conference, and would "give the world a chance to reflect before plunging into the abyss of war again."[34]

Under the restraint of the Treasury, House could do nothing to provide funds. Recording in his diary that none of the staff except the clerks was being paid and that while the American Senate debated, English and French friends of the League were scraping around for funds, he observed that the joint expenditure of all belligerents for one day during the war was more than the cost of the League of Nations would be for one hundred years.[35] In the organizing session he proposed a credit of £100,000 to be provided immediately on the guarantee of the states represented on the organizing committee, subject to any approval required by law. The Chancellor

---

33. See above, p. 187.

34. Bonsal, *Suitors and Suppliants*, p. 268. Miller, May 19, 1919. Memoranda on meetings concerning the organization of the League are in the Miller papers, box 89, "IV, Col. House's papers," 12, L.C. *I.P.*, vol. 4, pp. 460–462. House diary, April 4, 13, 14, May 2, 5, 15, 29, June 4, 1919.

35. House diary, July 28, 1919.

of the Exchequer, protesting that Wilson should not "leave his offspring on Britain's doorstep," remarked in a letter to Balfour that the British government, though bound by the same limitations that the Americans and French found "extremely convenient whenever they do not want to put down money," was accustomed to take the risk of spending funds in anticipation of parliamentary approval and would do what was absolutely necessary to support the League for a short time. Balfour agreed.[36] And Pichon promised to find a sum.

House, determined to keep the League free of domination by any power, reminded Sir Eric Drummond, who as secretary-general would be responsible for the organization and staffing of the body, that in his new office he was to be no longer in the service of the British government; and in choosing a French undersecretary-general there was insistence on Jean Monnet in preference to an official in the Quai d'Orsay.[37] Raymond B. Fosdick was offered a permanent appointment as American undersecretary, with the understanding that it came from Drummond and not from the United States government. His loyalty to the League brought him into conflict with the men of the State Department, and, lacking reassurance from Wilson after the president became incapacitated in October, Fosdick soon presented his resignation. He retained to his death a fervent devotion to the ideals of the League—and later those of the United Nations—never losing his belief that history would place Woodrow Wilson among its heroes and its prophets.[38]

The malfunctioning of American diplomacy at this critical time was due not entirely to Wilson's absence from the councils at Paris or to political opposition that he encountered when he returned to Washington. Actually, the failure of the American government to become a full partner in the works of reconstruction must be attributed in part to a widening of a rift that had appeared between the State Department and the ardent advocates of the League of Nations. The promoters of the League were as suspicious of the old diplomatic establishment as the professional diplomats were of the new and untried order.[39] Secretary Lansing, lacking any legal authorization to recognize the existence of the League, was at pains to dissociate the State Department entirely from the activities of Fosdick, refusing to see him, to answer letters written by him on stationery of the League, or to allow him to communicate with his chief at London, Drummond, through American diplomatic channels. Lansing held to his conviction that the affirmative guarantee in the Covenant was not practical and that the provisions for an international court were not adequate.[40]

36. Letters, A. Chamberlain to Balfour, May 16, Malcolm to Chamberlain, May 21, 1919, Balfour papers, 49751, p. 226.

37. Auchincloss diary, May 9 and 10, 1919. Several documents dated in May and dealing with the League's formation are in the Auchincloss papers, series III, box 10, Y.H.C. On the appointment of the League's officials and their policies, see Barros, ch. I.

38. Raymond B. Fosdick, *Letters on the League of Nations,* pp. 20–22 and *passim.*

39. "The Foreign Offices of all the chief powers are trying to get the control of diplomacy back into their own hands," Kerr wrote to Lloyd George on July 18, 1919, letter in Lloyd George papers, F / 89 / 3 / 6. Lansing desk diary, August 21, 1919.

40. Lansing, *The Peace Negotiations,* pp. 78–79. C. Anderson's diary, July 31, 1919, L.C. As early as April, Lansing had noted at Paris a "growing disposition . . . to ridicule and ignore the League of Nations," and by May 1 it had become in his view "a millstone about our necks" that made it difficult to oppose European purposes that violated Wilson's principles, desk diary, April 19, 1919, L.C., Lansing to Polk, May 1, 1919, Y.H.C.

The disaffection of the secretary of state made it seem to House the more important that he exert all the influence that he could command in behalf of the League. On its success, he perceived, Wilson's political solvency and his own place in history depended.[41] He advised the president that Americans should participate only "unofficially" in the work of the League until the Senate had ratified the Treaty of Versailles. The colonel thought that the League's judicial structure might be strengthened by the appointment of an American jurist that would please Republican opponents in the United States; and he reminded Wilson of the obligation, under Article XIV of the Covenant, to appoint a distinguished American man of law to sit at London on a committee to plan for an international court of justice. House's first choice was Elihu Root.[42]

Before Root was approached, however, he wrote on June 19 a public letter to Senator Lodge in which he denounced Article X and proposed further reservations in respect of the Monroe Doctrine and the right of member states to withdraw. He suggested that such qualifications could be included in the American instrument of ratification of the Treaty of Versailles without requiring a reopening of negotiations with the other signatories. "There is in the Covenant," he conceded, "a great deal of very high value which the world ought not to lose." Yet he thought the amendments already accepted at Paris were "very inadequate and unsatisfactory."[43] After expressing himself thus, Root felt constrained from accepting the appointment offered by the president, fearing that both his motive and that of Wilson might be misconstrued as tainted by political considerations. Yet he said that he was deeply interested in the project and would not be averse to considering the proposition later.[44]

House was no longer in a position to work effectively at Paris, where the meetings of the American commission, now held in Lansing's office,[45] seemed to him

---

41. House diary, June 4 and 20, 1919.

42. *I.P.*, vol. 4, pp. 479–481. House diary, June 10 and 11, 1919. House recorded that Wilson thought that Root was the best choice and that Taft could serve to greater effect as a proponent of the League in the United States.

43. Congressional Record, June 23, 1919, p. 1633.

44. Auchincloss diary, July 4, 1919. Root later accepted an invitation from the secretary general of the League to serve on an international commission to prepare plans for a world court, Polk to Root, March 9, 1920, Root to Polk, March 11, 1920, Bliss papers, box 25.

House sent a personal message that Miller forwarded to Root in a letter of July 7, 1919, saying that a formal invitation would be issued if there was assurance that Root would serve. House made it very clear that members of the proposed committee would not act as individuals representing their several countries, but as experts in international legal procedure who would advise the Council of the League, cables, Auchincloss to Miller, June 12, 24, 25, July 1, 1919, Miller to Root, July 7, 1919, Miller papers, box 89, III, 10. Miller to Auchincloss, June 23, 1919, Auchincloss diary. House to McAdoo, July 15, 1919, Y.H.C. Miller, vol. 20, pp. 346–347, 444, 453–465.

It was not likely that Root was impressed by any appeal from House, whom he regarded in retrospect as "a bright, clever little man" who had "some skill, some resource" but was "a . . . perfect child," like Wilson, "about the type of things with which he had to deal in Europe," Jessup conversation with Root, Jessup papers, box 243, L.C.

45. Three of House's able associates—Wiseman, Miller, and Bonsal—had gone to Washington, whence they were to keep him informed on American politics and to encourage ratification of the treaty. "I do not like the look of things," House wrote to Wiseman, deploring the lack of liaison between the American and British governments. "You can never know how much I have missed you here," House to Wiseman, July 4, 1919, Y.H.C. House diary, May 25, 26, 1919.

to have become almost "a talking fest by the president."[46] He wrote in his diary on June 10 that he aspired "to steer the League of Nations into safe waters, to become an advisor of peoples" and "accelerate, in a sane way, the cause of liberty and liberalism." After a program drafted by Cecil and Drummond failed to get approval in a meeting of the League's organizing committee on June 9, House deferred further action in order to avoid a recorded defeat. Proposing that the matter await the attention of the League's executive council, he then advised Cecil and Drummond to take more care in canvassing the committee before introducing measures in the future.[47] He was unwilling to believe that the United States would refuse to join the League. His reason had been telling him for some time that this outcome was not improbable, and yet he could not accept passively the ruin of the grand design that he still hoped would be saved by Wilson's prophetic power over the American people.[48] The colonel, although no longer intimate with the president, continued to play the game to which he was deeply committed and which he feared would be lost because of the president's capacity for making enemies and the failure of advisers who were now personally closer to Wilson to propose practical measures toward compromise and to persuade him of their necessity.

Going to England at the end of June he found himself isolated from news of affairs at both Paris and Washington; and when not meeting with the mandates commission, he spent much of his time in the countryside. Fearing that Wilson might think him a shirker, he wrote an explanation to his chief on July 14. "I thought the thing out carefully and came to the conclusion that it would be nearly impossible to continue there [at Paris] after you had gone and keep in cordial relations with the other commissioners. You may or may not know that there was considerable resentment that you did not consult them sufficiently and I came in for my share of this feeling. The members of the other delegations would almost surely have brought their difficulties to me and I would have been under the necessity of having to decline to take them up or to have created friction with my colleagues. I suppose you understand that it was really this that brought me over here [to England]." Still deploring the lack of "orderly executive action" in the peacemaking, he had given Wilson on June 28 a summary of the work of the Peace Conference and of the duties that would devolve upon the League of Nations. During July, realizing that the League could not operate until the Treaty of Versailles was ratified by at least three of the great powers, House remained convinced that he should act independently to cultivate the good relationship between the British and American governments that was essential to the success of the League. He was possessed by a fear that these governments might find themselves in economic and naval competition like that which had driven Great Britain and Germany toward war in 1914. Wilson shared this apprehension.

46. House diary, June 23, 1919.
47. *Ibid.*, June 9, 1919. Memorandum of discussions in May on the League's organization are in the Miller papers, box 89, IV, 12, L.C. House said good-bye to the American newsmen at Paris on June 23. "He has been a great help to us all," Baker wrote in his journal on that day. "He likes human beings—and so they like him. And he has shrewdness, too."
48. Bonsal, *Unfinished Business.* p. 63.

The departure of Lord Reading from Washington in May had left Great Britain without adequate representation there. The void was, in Wiseman's opinion, "nothing less than a scandal."[49] In view of the open and controversial issues of the moment—especially those of war debts, Irish independence, and naval and commercial rivalry—the appointment of an envoy was vitally important. During the summer, House, in England, perceived this. No one seemed to him so well suited to the delicate mission as Lord Grey, who regarded the League of Nations as "the pearl of great price." Grey had once warned House against the inclusion of a League constitution in a treaty that might be rejected by the Senate.[50] Now aging and growing blind, Grey would commit himself only to serving on a "special mission" for which he would write his own instructions. House persuaded him, Grey acknowledged, that this was his duty.[51] To House he seemed the best kind of idealist, a man who did not let his imagination run away with his judgment and who was not "consumed with ambition, with prejudice or self-importance."[52] Grey, for his part, liked and trusted House and proposed to rely on him as an intermediary in dealing with Wilson. The men spent a weekend together and they talked about the difficulties to be surmounted. It was agreed that Great Britain would be free to build up its navy for protection against any European power but would not attempt to outdo the United States. Reporting this and subsequent conferences with Grey, House assured Wilson that the proposed mission would put "vexatious subjects between the two countries . . . a fair way of settlement."[53]

Before Grey departed he expressed concern about the position of his government in Persia, as well as about that of the United States in Liberia. It seemed to him that each nation was active in its own interest without regard to the family of nations that was envisioned by proponents of the League. He wrote of his anxiety to Lord Curzon. This egocentric and aloof minister, who was in charge of Near Eastern affairs in the Foreign Office, was, in the opinion of Wiseman, "doing more harm to Anglo-American relations than any other man."[54]

Curzon had been secretive about an Anglo-Persian negotiation that he had mentioned to House when he asked that Persian delegates be kept away from the Peace Conference.[55] The British government had signed an agreement on August 9 that provided for the exploitation of Persia's oil; but Ambassador Davis was in the dark about this until he read about it in the newspapers.[56] Grey knew nothing about the agreement when he consented to go to Washington, and he was distressed when Davis gave him what he called "an unpleasant account" of a feeling on the part of

49. Wiseman to Murray, August 12, 1919, Y.H.C.
50. Grey to House, December 30, 1918, Y.H.C. See above, p. 41.
51. Memorandum, Grey to Curzon, August 5, 1918, Curzon papers, box 65, f.112 / 211. The dependence of British officials on House's advice is revealed by exchanges of letters between Curzon and Balfour in July 1919, Curzon papers, box 65, F / 112 / 208.
52. House to Seymour, September 23, 1922, Y.H.C.
53. *I.P.,* vol. 4. pp. 494–500.
54. Wiseman to Murray, August 12, 1919, Y.H.C. Nicolson, *Curzon,* pp. 32 ff.
55. See above, p. 490.
56. According to his daughter, Davis doubted Curzon's assertion that he had intended to inform Davis before the agreement became public, Julia Davis, *Legacy of Love* (New York, 1961), p. 181.

Americans that they might be excluded from developments in Persia. "I am quite prepared to push the point of the Liberian Treaty against America," Grey wrote to Curzon, "if not set a better example in the case of the Persian agreement. But if we ignore the League of Nations in the case of the Persian agreement and America does the same in the case of Liberia, it will be evident that neither country means to treat the League of Nations seriously and I shall return quickly from Washington." After reaching the United States, Grey sought assurance from his government that the United States might participate in Persia.[57]

Wilson assured House at the end of August that Grey would be "heartily welcome," although the fact that Great Britain continued to send special envoys instead of a permanent ambassador was causing a great deal of unfavorable comment in America. The president begged House to reconsider his own plans, and said the colonel "would make a grave mistake" by coming back before the ratification of the treaty, which Wilson then expected to occur early in October. Secretary Lansing and William Bullitt had just given testimony before the Foreign Relations Committee that appeared to discourage a favorable vote in the Senate, and the embattled president feared his adversaries would use the House in a similar way.[58] Grey made the voyage to America without House. Arriving just after Wilson was disabled, he was never received at the White House.

The reason for the estrangement was explained by Edith Benham, Mrs. Wilson's secretary, in a memorandum of February 18, 1920. Miss Benham wrote. "Mr. Lansing had wanted to arrange for Lord Grey to see the president; . . . he felt it was most important. . . . Mrs. Wilson sent for him to ask . . . if Lord Grey had sent [Major] Stuart home. (This man, who had served as Lord Reading's private secretary at Washington, allegedly had made scurrilous remarks about Mrs. Wilson at a dinner party.)[59] Mr. Lansing said they had not been able to get the affadivits, as all the women [witnesses] had refused when it came to the point to sign their names to any papers. Mr. Lansing told Mrs. Wilson also that Lord Grey in view of the lack of convincing evidence had refused to send Stuart home. Mrs. Wilson said that the president would not see Lord Grey if Stuart was still here and with Lord Grey."[60]

In the message asking House to reconsider his plan to come home, Wilson said it was "vitally important," in view of the situation at Washington, that House

---

57. Grey to Curzon, September 13, 15, October 17, 25, 1919, Curzon papers. In November the Anglo-Persian agreement was still disturbing Anglo-American relations, Buckler to Mrs. Buckler, November 12, 1919, Y.H.C.

58. House to Wilson, August 23, 1919. Dispatch from Lansing for Col. House's information, August 28, 1919, Y.H.C.

59. Sir Robert Hamilton Bruce Lockhart, *Giants Cast Long Shadows* (London, 1960), p. 77. According to Lockhart, Stuart remarked that Edith Galt had been so surprised when Woodrow Wilson proposed to her that she had fallen out of bed.

60. Memo by Edith Benham Helm, Helm papers, L.C., reproduced with editing by Joyce G. Williams in "The Resignation of Secretary Lansing," *Diplomatic History* 3, no. 3 (Summer 1979):342. It was the opinion of Mrs. Helm that the Stuart affair caused the failure of Grey's mission, Mrs. Helm to the author. See George W. Egerton, *Great Britain and the Creation of the League of Nations*, p. 191 and note, and Frances Stevenson, *Lloyd George*, p. 277. Grayson to R. S. Baker, January 22, 1920, Baker papers, I. B. Lansing desk diary, December 29, 1919.

cooperate with the peace commission at Paris in every way possible. The president had already told House that, because of the feeling in the Senate, it would be unwise at the moment to raise the question of American leadership in the commissions that were to function under the League in control of Danzig and the Saar. To an inquiry from House as to how news reports of a "break" between them should be treated, Wilson replied "with silent contempt."[61]

House went from England to Paris on September 13. By remaining aloof he had incurred the dislike of his fellows as one who appeared to be posing as a supercommissioner.[62] Renewing his close relationship with Clemenceau, he forwarded to Wilson a letter from the French premier that stressed the importance that European statesmen now attached to the early functioning of the League of Nations, both as a means of executing the Treaty of Versailles and as a repository for unsettled questions. Clemenceau endorsed House's plan for convening the first assembly of the League at Washington at the earliest data possible, with Wilson presiding.[63] House, advising the president that the meeting should be held promptly after the Senate ratified the treaty of peace, was resolved meanwhile to "hold down" the organizers of the League.[64]

In mid-September, after the Treaty of St. Germain with Austria had been signed and the British and Italian representation in the Supreme Council reduced to one man each, House, noting unpleasant comments about his lingering at Paris, felt that his work there was ended; and he realized that he could be criticized for interfering with the negotiations of the professional diplomats.[65] The American delegates were quick to perceive that House no longer was the president's spokesman.[66] He explained in a letter to Wilson that there would be much criticism if the delegation of the United States was not reduced like that of the other powers. Noting that if he tarried longer at Paris he would be thought to be reluctant to be questioned by the Foreign Relations Committee, he felt that he had nothing to conceal and could give testimony that would put the president, who had been "crucified by his friends," in a better light.

House's letter was not opened at the White House.[67] Receiving no reply, he concluded that Wilson acquiesced in his plan. When he left Paris on October 5, he found Clemenceau at the railway station to say farewell; but his fellow commission-

61. *I.P.*, vol. 4, pp. 514–515. Bell to Harrison, August 29, 1919, Harrison papers, L.C. Wilson's response to House was probably disingenuous. The president perhaps was fearful that political foes might exploit any evidence of personal disloyalty on his part.

62. B. Long's diary, November 14, December 23, 1919. A. W. Dulles to the author.

63. *I.P.*, vol. 4, pp. 491–493. Clemenceau said in the Chamber: "I would personally consider it a crime to identify myself with the slightest bit of the criticism that is being directed at him [Wilson]," Duroselle, in *Wilson's Diplomacy*, ed. Huthmacher and Susman, p. 37.

64. House diary, August 14, 1919.

65. House to Auchincloss, September 24, 1919.

66. Grew diary, October 3, 1919. Buckler observed that House took no part in the proceedings of the Peace Conference, had "scarcely any callers," was "frankly bored," and indeed was "quite useless," Buckler to Mrs. Buckler, September 24, 1919, Y.H.C. According to Polk, House favored dissolution of the Peace Conference, Polk diary, September 16, 1919.

67. House to Wilson, September 15, 1919. This letter, mailed in an envelope marked "important and strictly confidential," was not opened until it reached the Wilson Collection in the Library of Congress in 1952, Wilson papers, reel 414. Polk to Lansing, September 26, 1919, Y.H.C.

ers did not see him off. As he took ship, he was stricken by renal colic, and he was barely able to walk down the gangplank at New York. He was not invited to the White House, and a week after his landing word came from Mrs. Wilson that the president had not been told of his return or of his illness.[68]

House was beset with unfriendly influences not only at the White House. Officials of the Treasury and State Departments, fearful of encroachment by a new international authority upon their responsibilities, were unreceptive to his plan of convening the League of Nations in Washington. His isolation increased when Miller resigned from the State Department on October 11 after drafting a compromise resolution whereby the Senate might ratify the treaty with certain reservations that might be acceptable to European governments.[69] Nevertheless, proponents of the League were somewhat encouraged when the first International Labor Conference met at Washington on October 29 and the American secretary of labor delivered the opening address. There were no American funds available, and the British government advanced £3,000 to prevent a fiasco.[70] In the autumn of 1919 the country was beset by industrial unrest and by a general weariness with foreign affairs.

Any possibility of a restoration of the old Wilson-House relationship vanished when the president was stricken by paralysis at the beginning of October. While Wilson's wife and his physician faithfully discharged their responsibility for his physical survival, the overriding necessity for peace was not well served, despite House's continuing efforts.

At the end of October, House, convinced that ratification of the peace treaties was impossible without agreement with the Republican leadership on some sort of reservations, sent Bonsal to negotiate with Lodge and to repeat an offer to testify before the Foreign Relations Committee. This offer had been made by House in a letter to Lodge and had been declined. Bonsal reported on November 1 that Lodge was cordial and appreciative, but explained that formal hearings had ended and there was not one chance in a hundred that House would be summoned at this time, although his presence in Washington might prove to be helpful later on. Bidden by

68. House diary, October 2 and 21, 1919, Mrs. Wilson to Mrs. House, October 17, 1919, Y.H.C. When Wilson learned that House had left Paris before the other peace commissioners, he was displeased, R. S. Baker's journal, December 8, 1919. After Wilson was paralyzed, someone said something to him about writing to House, and he replied: "Don't mention House to me any more. The door is closed," Grayson, "The Colonel's Folly and the President's Distress," 101. He told his daughter Eleanor that House now seemed "to wear a different face" from that of his old friend, E. W. McAdoo to the author, October 1950.

69. Draft resolutions shown to Wiseman and Tyrell after lunch with Lord Grey and given to William Phillips of the State Department on that day and to Senator Hitchcock the next day, Miller papers, box 89, folder 16.

It seemed to Willert, the *Times* of London's correspondent at Washington, that the president was "surrounded by people keen to make trouble" between England and the United States, Willert to Steed, October 27, 1918, Steed papers.

70. James T. Shotwell, "Recollections on the Founding of the I.L.O."

The Congress stipulated that no American delegates could be appointed to the Labor Conference until the treaty was ratified. The United States did not join the ILO until 1934.

Secretary of Labor Wilson feared that the convening of the Labor Conference might turn the "invisible government" (the representatives of the manufacturers) against the League, W. B. Wilson to W. Wilson, August 4, 1919, Wilson papers. Fosdick reported to Drummond on November 30 that the conference ended "with complete success," *Docs. on British Foreign Policy, First Series*, vol. 5, 1050.

House to follow up a prospect of conciliation that Lodge seemed to suggest. Bonsal reported on two further interviews in which he and the senator went over the Covenant article by article. Lodge annotated a copy of it with about forty words of altered phrasing and about fifty inserts, effecting changes milder than those the senator officially proposed. He said that these alterations would make the treaty acceptable to him and, he felt sure but could not guarantee, to the Senate. Bonsal recorded that when House was told by telephone of this concession, he emitted ''a whoop of joy.'' When the colonel received the annotated document by mail, he forwarded it to the White House. It has never been found. Bonsal surmised that it was deposited in a wastebasket by the president's guardians.[71]

If Mrs. Wilson destroyed the document because of apprehension that it would excite her husband dangerously, her fear was perhaps not unjustified. Edward Bok, calling on the Wilsons just after they moved out of the White House in 1921, reported to House that Wilson, while dressing down Lloyd George and discussing the Senate in general and Lodge in particular in words ''not fit to print,'' suffered a spasm that lasted for fifty minutes. According to House's record, ''they thought he would surely die.''[72]

The explanation of the colonel's secrecy may be found in his statement, recorded by Viereck, to the effect that House's offer to testify before the Foreign Relations Committee (a possibility that Wilson dreaded) was used by the colonel's critics at the White House to create the impression in Wilson's mind that the colonel was an appeaser yielding to the enemy.[73] House wished, as he told Seymour in 1929, to spare Wilson the irritation he would feel if Lodge's proposal became generally known and the president were challenged to respond or else appear to obstruct ratification.[74] To have pursued further negotiation with Lodge without Wilson's consent, House said, he would have had to believe in Lodge's good faith, which actually he had questioned ''from the very beginning.'' He perceived that Lodge's

71. *I.P.*, vol. 4, pp. 505–506. Bonsal's diary, November 1919, Bonsal to Miss Fanny Denton, June 11, Bonsal to Seymour, June 11, 1928, Bonsal papers, box 3. Bonsal to Seymour, April 9, May 27, Bonsal to House, April 9, 1944, Y.H.C. Bonsal, *Unfinished Business*, pp. 274–278, 286–287. James B. Reynolds, the secretary of the Republican National Committee, who was grooming Lodge for the presidency in November 1919 and saw the senator almost every day and thought him peeved because Wilson seemed to be ignoring him, assured Seymour that Bonsal's story was ''perfectly correct,'' Seymour to Reynolds, June 5, Reynolds to Seymour, June 17, 1944. Quizzed by Seymour about the incident, House's confidential secretary testified that she had ''a not altogether reliable recollection'' of Lodge's annotated copy of the Covenant, Fanny Denton to Seymour, April 12, 1944. Bonsal wrote in a letter of April 9 to Seymour: ''This was the most hush-hush of the many 'graveyard' negotiations with House'' and House asked that nothing be said about it during his lifetime. Correspondence in Seymour papers, series 1, box 1, folder 102. See Seymour's review of Bonsal's *Unfinished Business* in the *American Foreign Service Journal* (May 1944).

72. House diary, April 3, 1921.

73. George S. Viereck, ''Behind the House-Wilson Break,'' p. 151. For a psychological explanation of Wilson's ''painful personal involvement'' in respect of his feelings toward Lodge, see George and George, *Woodrow Wilson and Colonel House*, pp. 46, 266. These scholars observe that without Lodge's document in hand, one cannot uncritically accept the conclusion of Bonsal, ''not an expert in international law,'' that the changes proposed by Lodge were ''less objectionable than those he was publicly sponsoring,'' *ibid.*, p. 352.

74. Seymour to Bonsal, April 6, 1944, Bonsal papers, box 3.

House explained to Bonsal that he had declined to make Wilson ''responsible for ignoring an opportunity which perhaps was never presented to him,'' Bonsal, *Unfinished Business*, p. 286.

self-interest would force him to conceal his concession made to Bonsal, for Lodge was aspiring to be the standard bearer of his party and would not wish to give any evidence of weakness. Moreover, Lodge appeared to be increasingly confident of the defeat of the treaty.[75]

Lodge, perhaps not surprised and indeed even pleased by the rebuff to his proposal, became more insistent on his reservations as the question of ratification approached a vote in the Senate.

After House had failed to break the deadlock and when Lansing despaired of any solution, the president regained enough strength in November so that he could advise Senator Hitchcock, the Democratic leader on the Foreign Relations Committee. The day for a vote in the Senate drew near. The parliaments of Great Britain and the dominions as well as the French and Italian chambers already had accepted the Treaty of Versailles; and the world awaited similar action at Washington so that ratifications could be exchanged with the Germans and the provisions of the treaty could be put into effect.

The Committee on Foreign Relations, which had presented fourteen reservations to the Senate on November 6, added one the next day that was particularly offensive to Wilson—a change in the preamble of the Covenant that would require acceptance of all reservations by at least three of the major co-signers of the treaty. Senator Hitchcock found his chief adamant at first. On November 17, however, Wilson gave some ground to meet the views of mild reservationists. At the same time, he told Hitchcock that he would give the treaty a veto if it were passed with the proposed reservation for Article Ten or the objectionable preamble. Rather than be forced to this action, however, and thus play out the role of obstructionist in which Lodge perhaps wished to cast him, Wilson supported a plan for Senate Democrats to vote against ratification with the Lodge reservations. When the Senate acted on November 19, therefore, Democratic senators joined Republican irreconcilables to block the two-thirds vote needed. Wilson's bitter foes had a day of rejoicing.[76]

After his disablement Wilson lost interest in the treaty of guarantee with France. This separate arrangement, upon which Clemenceau had depended heavily, and which upon America's rejection of the Covenant and its Article 10 became more than ever indispensable to the security of France, never came to a vote in the Senate, to whom Wilson had transmitted it on July 29.[77]

75. Bonsal, *Unfinished Business*, pp. 286–287.

76. "The intensity of the hatred of Wilson in and out of Congress . . . went to the extreme of vindictiveness," Lansing wrote. "It was irrational and cruel," "An Intimate and Frank Consideration of the Causes of Non-Ratification of the Treaty of Peace," November 22, 1919, Lansing's private memoranda.

House wrote in his diary on November 20: "It was not partisanship so much as bitter hatred of the president that prevented ratification of the treaty and this hatred is largely shared by Democratic senators."

77. Lodge, who agreed with Jusserand that the treaty of guarantee must be stripped of Article 3, which linked it with the League of Nations, consented to bring it to a vote in the Senate as soon as possible, dispatches, Jusserand to M.A.É., September 17, November 19, 24, 30, December 2, 8, 1919, Archives du M.A.É., À paix, 1154, f. 155, 156. See Louis A. R. Yates, *The U.S. and French Security*, pp. 122–138. According to Widenor, Lodge "was blocked by the same coalition of irreconcilables and loyal Wilson Democrats who refused to vote for the Covenant with the Lodge reservations attached," *Lodge*, p. 132.

House and the British and French diplomats were now confronted by the likelihood that the peace conceived at Paris would wither away. The nightmare of the political bankruptcy of Wilson, which had haunted the Europeans during the Peace Conference while their necessities constrained them to indulge America's chief executive, was becoming a reality.[78]

Ambassador Jusserand took the view that an amended treaty would be better than none.[79] Just before the Senate voted on the nineteenth, he complained bitterly to Lodge about both the form and the tenor of his proposals. He thought that the senator defended himself weakly and spoke like a man determined to kill the treaty. In another talk a little later Lodge gave the appearance of willingness to make some concessions, such as giving up his demand for the objectionable preamble.[80]

Grey also undertook to use the recourses of diplomacy. In a long talk with House on the day of the Senate's vote, the British envoy—an avid angler—said that he had "thrown a fly at Lodge, who did not rise to it." Four days later he reported to the Foreign Office that a compromise probably could be reached if only Wilson would consult with the Republican chiefs.[81] Grey was soon informed by Curzon, however, that the proposed reservation for Article 10, to the effect that the United States "assumes no responsibility," would make it impossible for Britain to commit itself to Article 10. Agreeing with House that he might be more useful in England than in Washington unless the president's condition improved significantly, and resolutely refusing to send home the young officer who had maligned Mrs. Wilson,[82] Grey reported to London on December 6 that there was no one in Washington with whom he could "discuss anything effectively" and therefore he had best end his mission. He maintained to the end his determination, which was fortified by advice from Lansing, to avoid exacerbating the situation by any appearance of interfering in American political processes.[83] Anyone who opposed the will of the Senate merely stiffened its stand; and any indication of willingness to accept reservations would infuriate the president.[84] With the withdrawal of Grey from the Washington

78. Nicolson, *Peacemaking, 1919,* p. 205.

79. Dispatches, Jusserand to M.A.É., November 30, 1919, *loc. cit.;* Grey to Curzon, December 11, 1919, *Docs. on British Foreign Policy, 1919–1939, First Series,* vol. 5, 1059.

80. Jusserand to M.A.É., November 19, December 3 and 8, 1919, *loc. cit.*

81. Tillman, *Anglo-American Relations at the Paris Peace Conference,* p. 396. In a talk with the French ambassador, Paul Cambon, who thought it might be as well to accept the Senate reservations inasmuch as the Senate actually would act anyway in particular situations to exert its power, Curzon said that the British view of the reservations was a more serious one, Curzon to Derby, November 25, 1919, Curzon papers, box 22, f 112 / 302.

82. "Grey's trouble with Stuart has become acute," House wrote in his diary on December 2. When Lloyd George heard of Grey's difficulty he said: "It need not have wrecked the man's career. Grey could have seen that he was promoted. That is what I always did in such emergencies," Stevenson, *Lloyd George,* p. 277.

83. Tillman, pp. 395–398. In Grey's view the Senate's preamble and the reservation preventing the British Empire from casting six votes in the League's assembly were the amendments most objectionable in England, Jusserand to M.A.É., dispatch of November 30, 1919, cited.

84. Once back in London—"for consultation," it was announced—Grey published in the *Times* a frank statement of the situation at Washington and pleaded with the Europeans to accept American reservations. This well-intentioned paper, which Lodge thought "splendid," fanned the wrath of the crippled president. See Leon Booth, "A Fettered Envoy: Lord Grey's Mission to the U.S. 1919–1920," *Review of Politics* (January 1971), and Egerton, pp. 199, 237.

scene, the last recourse of diplomacy was exhausted. The American ship of state, lacking a steady pilot, continued to career badly in a heavy sea of politics. In February of 1920 Secretary Lansing was dismissed.

Even after the defeat of November 19 in the Senate, however, House continued his efforts toward a compromise. Canvassing eleven prominent Democrats, he found all but Secretary of War Baker in sympathy with advice that he wished to give to the president.[85] Putting his counsel in two long letters, he mailed them to the White House on November 24 and 27. He had been convinced by Grey that the Allies would accept Lodge's reservations if only through them the United States could be brought into the League of Nations; and so he advised that Wilson let the Allied governments determine whether or not they would accept measures imposed by the Senate. He wrote that objectionable reservations could later be rectified and that the first essential was to have Wilson's great work at Paris live. In a note to Mrs. Wilson he said that her husband's place in history hung "in the balance."[86] But, again, there was no response. House was astonished that the president's wife, in her effort to shield her husband, should take the responsibility of suppressing advice from a man who had long been his most trusted counselor.[87] His standing at the White House did not improve when a friend[88] blurted out to Dr. Grayson, "House made Wilson!" This indiscreet assertion probably reached the ears of the Wilsons.

Sensing jealousy in the State Department, House tried to conceal his contacts with the British diplomats. Lansing gave some credence to the canard that "the mysterious Colonel House" was in reality a weak and vain little man. And yet the secretary of state was hoping that this little man would somehow rescue the United States government from a predicament that no one else seemed able to cope with.[89]

House deplored both the weakness of the Democratic leadership of the Senate and that of the stricken president, and he was contemptuous "beyond expression" of the intense desire of politicians to discredit Wilson. "I have been very ill," he wrote in his diary on December 12, "but I am doing day by day what I can to help with the Treaty and am pushing and advising in every direction where I think it may aid. My heart has seldom been so much in anything." He professed to be willing to give his life, if need be, to help the president, the country, and the world.[90] Before the year's end, despairing of victory in his Olympian game, he wrote: "We came near doing a great thing in a great way, but Fate ordained otherwise and while something may still be done, it will be done in a small way and in a way full of

85. House diary, November 27, December 2, 1919.

86. The letters of November 24 and 27 (in the Wilson papers, reel 105) were opened before they reached the Library of Congress archives. One of House's letters was delivered to Mrs. Wilson by Thomas W. Gregory, who told House that she showed resentment, Lansing, private memorandum, December 27, 1919.

87. House diary, November 20, 27, December 2, 1919.

88. Mrs. Borden Harriman, *ibid.,* December 20, 1919.

89. Lansing's private memoranda, November 22, 1919. Lansing to Polk, November 17, 1919, Y.H.C.

90. Wilson had written to Mrs. Galt in 1915 that House would gladly die for him, Edwin Tribble, *A President in Love* (Boston, 1981), p. 166. House diary, December 11, 12, 20, 1919.

"If Wilson had not begun to fail, physically and mentally," House wrote to Seymour on July 11, 1934, "they could never have separated us, for it was tried time and again when he was in vigorous health and failed," *I.P.,* vol. 4, pp. 514–517.

humiliation for those who wished to see the United States lead in a new world movement."[91] Four years later he was still looking to the future with unquenched optimism and patriotism. He wrote prophetically in *Foreign Affairs* in 1923: "The United States, after having risen to heights of courage and idealism in its entry and prosecution of the war, has gone to the other extreme in the making of peace. After 1917–18 Europe will scarcely make the mistake of thinking that we are as timid and selfish as our present attitude would indicate. Our people, native and foreign-born, cherish the belief that this Republic was created to become an instrument for the betterment of man, and not merely a pleasant and safe abiding place. They will not be content until the United States has again assumed the leadership and responsibilities in world affairs commensurate with her moral, economic and political position."

91. House diary, December 11, 12, 20, 1919.

28

The Retreat from Paris

As the great vision of a new world faded, the diplomats at Paris fell back upon the recourse that had furthered understanding among peoples for centuries past. Economic necessity and political stability demanded reliable arrangements among governments, and custom required the Foreign Offices of the nations to negotiate practical terms of understanding. To this responsibility the diplomats tried to respond, while idealists preached and politicians operated. In view of the political impasse at Washington, however, the Americans at the Peace Conference could not speak with authority for their government.

When House and Lansing lost interest in the talks at Paris.[1] Polk persisted in pursuing the duty of a diplomat after he became head of the American delegation on July 29. He was disappointed by a lack of attention on the part of British leaders to the situations that still required decisions. Balfour was ordered by his doctor to take a rest, and upon his departure Polk noted that British policy became less "straightforward" and more difficult to understand.[2]

Lloyd George came to Paris for three days in September and talked of dissolving the Peace Conference.[3] Polk, however, distressed by the British intention to keep no top-level spokesman at Paris after Lloyd George returned to London, protested against its dissolution and was assured that the British would keep the conference going.[4] Wilson, campaigning in the American West and told of developments at Paris, thought that Polk was "taking exactly the right position" and that "it would be nearly fatal to the whole state of mind of the world if the British were to withdraw."[5]

Conferring with House before the colonel's departure, Polk took an inventory of the principal questions that were still unsolved. They had to do with the settlements with five countries: Russia, Hungary, Romania, Turkey, and Italy. (Other difficulties appeared with respect to the boundaries of Poland and Greece.)[6] Russia appeared

1. "Lansing came to see Colonel House today, and agreed with him that the Paris Conference should be broken up as soon as possible," Auchincloss diary, October 18, 1919. See Kell Mitchell, Jr., "Frank L. Polk and Continued American Participation in the Paris Peace Conference, 1919."

2. Polk diary, September 11, 1919.

3. "They [the British] are all getting sick of it and I don't blame them," Polk wrote to Ambassador Davis on September 11, 1919, letter in Davis papers, Y.H.C.

The Heads of Delegations discussed a palpable breach of the terms of the armistice: the failure of Germany to remove its troops from the Baltic States. When Lloyd George proposed that Polish troops be used to drive the malingerers from Lithuania, Polk, who would at one time have agreed, now said that the United States could not concur. Polk to Clemenceau, September 16, 1919, Polk papers, Y.H.C.

4. Polk diary, September 16, 1919, Y.H.C. "He [Lloyd George] was a little irritated and I more so," Polk wrote. Telegram, Phillips to the president, September 16, 1919, quoting dispatches from Polk, September 9 and 16, 1919, Wilson papers.

5. Lines typed by Wilson "to Lansing," September 16, 1919, Wilson papers. Dispatch, September 19, 1919, N.A., R.G. 59, 763.72119 / 6823.

6. Paderewski told Allen Dulles on October 13 that his government would be overthrown if he returned from Paris without any satisfactory decision as to the future of eastern Galicia, which the Council of

to be in the hands of a revolutionary government with which negotiations were prevented by ideological propaganda. The conclusion of a treaty with Hungary depended upon the establishment of a stable government there, and that in turn was contingent upon the checking of Romanian aggression.

Final arrangements for the governance of Ottoman lands awaited definite advice from the United States as to its assumption of mandatory responsibility, either under mandates or independently.[7]

For Turkey, Admiral Bristol had come to favor military occupation and the establishment of an international commission to set up a government.[8] On October 16 he advised the State Department to "keep to the big idea all the time, i.e., that America believes in helping the whole of the Turkish Empire to obtain good government and the advantages of modern civilization . . . this is an unassailable position."[9] He likened the whole Near East to "a mass of jelly." "If you touch any part," he wrote, ". . . the whole mass quivers."[10]

The Standard Oil Company of New York, pleading the importance of its operations to the national interest, urged the State Department to protest to the British government against what was alleged to be interference with legitimate commercial

---

Foreign Ministers had authorized Polish troops to occupy in order to check bolshevism. The Polish premier was assured of Polk's "active support." Dulles memorandum on a talk with Paderewski, A. W. Dulles papers, "Polk" folder. Just after the Americans left the Peace Conference in December, the plan for a twenty-five-year mandate under Poland was given up, leaving the Polish government free to assert its rule in eastern Galicia without any international supervision. See above, p. 334. On the settlement for Thrace, see above, p. 467.

7. See above, ch. 25. Faisul continued to importune the American delegates to hasten negotiations that might save Syria from French control, but the British and French delegates were opposed to giving the United States any voice in this matter, White to Lansing, October 23, 1919. Polk, impressed by Faisul's pleading, told the French that they were not treating him as well as he deserved, Derby diary, October 29, 1919, Curzon papers, Mss. Eur. F. 112 / 196. On November 24 Lloyd George told Polk that he assumed, regretfully, that the United States would not accept mandates, which were "the only real solution," *F.R., P.P.C.*, vol. 11, pp. 675–676. On the uncertainty of American policy in respect of mandates, see Tillman, *Anglo-American Relations at the Paris Peace Conference*, pp. 367–371.

8. Bristol to Polk, November 10, 1919. Bristol thanked Polk for a reply indicating that Polk thought the admiral was "on the right track," dispatches in Bristol papers, box 36.

9. Bristol to Heck, October 16, 1919, Bristol papers, box 36. Endeavoring to bring about better coordination among the various U.S. agencies in Turkey, Bristol reported in mid-November: "Before this American interests were not much injured by the aggressiveness of the Allies and I have taken up the question simply on general principles of right and wrong. But now it is necessary to push American trade and interests. This is being done."

10. Bristol's "Report of Operations . . . ," November 23, 1919, Bristol papers, box 16. Bristol represented the United States on a four-power commission that had been appointed by the Supreme Council at Paris on July 18 to investigate the Greek landing at Smyrna and its tragic aftermath of atrocities. The Greeks were denied representation. Buckler to Mrs. Buckler, July 25, 1919, Y.H.C. Memorandum, Navy Department (FDR) to State Department, August 19, 1919, N.A.R., R.G. 59, 763.72119 / 6068. The commission reported unanimously to the council that the occupation was useless and unjustifiable, and that the Greeks were principally, though not alone, at fault. It proposed that until order was restored, the Greek army should be replaced by a much smaller number of Allied contingents in which Greeks might be permitted to serve, and that the Turkish civil government should be restored and the Turkish *gendarmerie* reorganized under Allied supervision. Peter M. Buzanski, "The Interallied Investigation of the Greek Invasion of Smyrna, 1919," 325–340. Venizelos pleaded in the council that Lloyd George had recognized Greece's right to Smyrna and Wilson had approved the Greek claim to the vilayet of Aidin; and he succeeded in having the censorious report suppressed, *ibid.*, 340–342. It appears in *F.R., P.P.C.*, vol. 9, pp. 44–73.

rights. The American Petroleum Institute exerted pressure, and the issue was raised in the Congress.[11]

To the call from Paris for decision and precision there was no response from the politics-ridden American government or from its incapacitated president. Lansing had already forwarded to the White House a summary of queries from the peace commission, which reported that the British government was asking whether the United States would permit the other powers to proceed with arrangements for Ottoman lands. On November 12 Mrs. Wilson replied: "The president says it is impossible for him to take up such matters until he is stronger and can study them. So if an answer must be made, the secretary of state can say he cannot act without the president's consent and that the president directs the matter be held in abeyance until he can act."[12]

Polk, consistently avoiding commitments, confessed to Ambassador Davis that he was "unwilling to take part in the disgraceful scramble for territory and oil wells." Loath either to block the ambitions of the Allies or "to leave the unfortunate natives in the lurch," he hoped that his government might "withdraw with dignity."[13] Nevertheless, in a memorandum addressed to Washington on November 26 the peace commission advocated active American intervention in the final peace settlement in western Asia, in the interest of both the general peace and of American "commercial opportunities" and the "open door." The government at Washington was called upon to decide to what extent it would adopt the report of King and Crane and that of Harbord;[14] whether the so-called "secret treaties" should be recognized; whether, in case of nonrecognition, the United States would provide funds and troops to prevent their implementation; and whether America was ready to cooperate in international arrangements of control. There was no satisfactory reply.

By February of 1920 the United States had retreated from Wilson's position of involvement to the traditional stance of noninterference in the politics of western Asia. The hostilities between Greeks and Turks soon escalated into a full-scale war.

With respect to Italy the Americans worked diligently to repair the damage that their president had done by his ill-considered grant of territory in the Tyrol, by his rigid opposition to Italian possession of Fiume, and by his offensive appeal to the Italian people over the heads of their leaders.[15] The Italian government felt the effect of the deadlock in diplomacy when it tried to carry on financial and economic negotiations with the United States. Tittoni, who had replaced Sonnino as foreign

11. DeNovo, *American Interests and Policies in the Middle East, 1900–1939*, pp. 169–174. Curzon met a protest from Ambassador Davis by explaining that the barring of American oilmen from inspecting their properties in Palestine was in keeping with a general policy of the British government pending the grant of a mandate; *viz.*, to veto any proceedings that "might compromise the ultimate mandatory" or cause trouble while the country remained under a military administration. Curzon to Grey, October 30, 1919, Curzon papers, mss. Eur. F / 112 / 278. See above p. 490.

12. Lansing to Wilson, November 12, 1919, Edith Wilson to Lansing, November 12, 1919, Wilson papers.

13. Polk to Davis, November 15, 1919, Y.H.C. DeNovo, pp. 126–127. Polk to the secretary of state, October 24, Wilson papers.

14. See above, pp. 507–508.

15. See above, pp. 345–347.

minister, earnestly desired friendly relations with America, without whose economic support he thought it impossible for Italy to exist.[16] When Lansing made it clear that Italian sovereignty over Fiume was entirely out of the question, Tittoni agreed, in confidence, not to insist on this if a face-saving formula could be worked out.[17] Negotiations went on into the autumn and more than once very nearly produced an agreement. An elaborate proposal sponsored by Clemenceau and Lloyd George, and modified by Polk, was accepted in general by a message from Wilson, who asked for neutralization of the eastern coast of Istria.[18]

However, on September 12, just as the prospect of settlement brightened, the poet Gabriele d'Annunzio dramatized and inflamed the Italian passion for Fiume by seizing control of the city with a band of volunteers.[19] This defiant act made it seem impossible for the Italian statesmen to accept any plan that might deprive Italy of eventual possession. Indeed, it appeared to the Americans at Paris that the Roman populace, as well as the army, were almost beyond the control of the new government.[20] With the approval of the president, two American warships were ordered to Spalato, an Adriatic port that seemed in danger of seizure by d'Annunzio; and Polk, with the consent of the Supreme Council, ordered their commander to intercept, by force if necessary, any Italian warships that might attempt to go to Spalato.[21] The Italian ambassador informed the State Department that Premier Nitti had proclaimed Italy's solidarity with its allies and would enforce the penal code against the mutineers at Fiume. This, however, the premier found himself powerless to do.[22] Tittoni, now rejecting modifications that Wilson sought in the plan that he had tentatively approved, demanded that Italy have "satisfaction of a purely moral character" through outright possession of the "corpus separatum" of Fiume—the city

16. Italy needed credits, coal, and food. "Beside the threat of economic disaster, Fiume mattered little," Christopher Seton-Watson, *Italy from Liberalism to Fascism*, pp. 537–538, *q.v.* Ammission to the secretary of state, July 29, 1919, N.A., R.G. 59, 763.72119 / 5883. Ambassador di Cellere was informed by Wilson that there would be ships available in September to take coal to Italy for commercial purposes, but not for the Italian government, Wilson to di Cellere, August 21, 1919, Wilson papers.

17. Dispatch, Lansing for the president, July 8, 1919, N.A., R.G. 59, 763.72119 / 5575.

18. This solution would give to Italy a mandate over all of Albania and sovereignty over Valona, and would set the boundary with Greece substantially on the line that the American experts had proposed in March. See above, pp. 60–62, and 351, and Petsalis-Diomidis, *Greece at the Paris Peace Conference,* pp. 300–301 and map.

Dispatch, Polk to the secretary of state for the president, August 29, 1919, N.A., R.G. 59, 763.72119 / 6448. Telegrams, Phillips for the president, September 6 and 11, 1919, quoting dispatch, the secretary of state from Polk, September 10, 1919, *ibid.,* / 6669. Wilson to Phillips, September 13, 1919, Wilson papers.

19. "It is a fairly open secret," a historian has written, "that d'Annunzio's escapade was largely financed from Trieste and Venice with no other purpose than to destroy Fiume commercially," C. A. Macartney, *Hungary and Her Neighbors, 1919–1937* (London, 1937), p. 442.

20. Telegram, State Department to the president, September 24, 1919, dispatches, Rome embassy to State Department, September 24, 1919, Ammission to the president, September 25, 1919, N.A., R.G. 59, 763.72119 / 6900, 6932, 6935. A royal decree dissolved the Chamber of Deputies at Rome and called for a general election, *ibid.,* / 7061. The crisis was so grave that the king made a personal appeal to Wilson, Jay to the secretary of state, September 12, 1919, N.A., R.G. 59, 763.72119 / 6709. Premier Nitti, fearing the outbreak of a Balkan war, also sent a personal message to the president, telegram, Phillips to Wilson, September 23, 1919, Wilson papers.

21. Telegram, Phillips to Wilson, September 26, 1919. The president, just before he was stricken, approved Polk's action as "entirely right," Wilson to Phillips, September 27, 1919, Wilson papers.

22. Ammission to the secretary of state, September 29 and 30, 1919, N.A., R.G. 59, 763.72119 /7027, 7029, 7074. Telegram, Phillips to Wilson, September 15, 1919, Wilson papers.

proper.[23] At this time Clemenceau addressed a message to Wilson that explained that d'Annunzio's coup left Tittoni no choice and his solution, which Lloyd George approved, would have the advantage of giving to the Yugoslavs immediately certain territory for which they would have had to wait five years under a plebiscite plan proposed by Wilson.[24]

At this critical juncture the president, having failed in his remoteness in the Far West to negotiate effectively in this very delicate matter and very near to physical collapse, was possessed by his recollection of his bitter conflict with Orlando and Sonnino. "I am amazed and deeply distressed," he said in a message to Polk, "that Lloyd George and Clemenceau should now talk of Fiume passing under the sovereignty of Italy. That is the one point upon which they were firm when I was in consultation with them. I can of course in no circumstances consent to Italian sovereignty over Fiume in any form whatever." He suggested that consent that he had given for an Italian mandate over Albania was a big price to pay. Yet he offered one concession: the determination of the future of the disputed territory by the League rather than by a plebiscite. A week later, however, the frustrated and failing prophet sent grim instructions to the American chargé at Rome: "Do not allow yourself to be, or even to seem to be, impressed by what is being said to you by members of the Italian Government with regard to the present crisis. It is all part of a desperate endeavor to get me to yield to claims which, if allowed, would destroy the peace of Europe. You cannot make the impression too definite and final that I cannot and will not yield; that they must work out their crisis for themselves. With a little decision and courage they could have stopped this agitation long ago, but they fomented it rather than checked it. The only course to be pursued is one of absolute firmness in which the whole responsibility is put upon the Italian Government."[25]

Before he was completely disabled, however, Wilson asked Isaiah Bowman to return to Paris to negotiate with the Italians. Recommending that all of the American arguments be recast in order to permit no logical escape, Bowman proposed that Wilson make five concessions.[26]

Early in October, Polk was advised that the Italian government could cope with d'Annunzio if Italy were given a strip of land around the coast of Istria. He agreed with Tittoni to work out a solution, thinking it unwise for the United States to take responsibility for setting all Europe on fire when no great principle was at stake. Washington, however, was intransigent.[27] At the end of the month Lloyd George

23. Telegrams, Phillips to the president, September 18 and 23, 1919, Wilson papers. Tittoni told Polk on September 16 that if Italy were assured of the city of Fiume, he would give "all kinds of guaranties" and put the railroad and harbor facilities under the League of Nations, Polk diary, September 16 and 24, 1919.

24. For the president and the secretary of state from Polk, September 18, 1919, N.A., R.G. 59, 763.72119 / 6814, forwarded to the president by Phillips, September 18, 1919, Wilson papers.

25. Wilson to State Department, September 21, 1919, letter, Wilson to Phillips, September 28, 1919, Wilson papers.

26. Bowman to Johnson, October 3, 1921, G. Martin papers.

27. Polk diary, October 1, 8, 25 and 26, 1919. Lansing to Ammission, October 29, 1919, White papers, box 45, L.C.

instructed Lord Grey to beg Wilson not to precipitate a serious crisis over points that were not "of real principle," since Nitti was doing his best to curb the spirit of "jingo" in Italy. However, the president was then paralyzed and estranged from Grey.[28]

In November, Tittoni, who had become ill, resigned. D'Annunzio defied Nitti and carried with him admirals and generals whom the premier had trusted.[29] Polk was finding the Italians difficult to handle because they were carrying on negotiations at both Paris and Washington and their memory seemed "extremely faulty." He gave them to understand that in no circumstances would the president yield further.

At the instigation of the American delegates, representatives of the three great powers joined in signing a note of December 9 to Italy.[30] Their project came to nothing, however, when Nitti wrote to Lloyd George on January 6 to demand fulfillment of the Treaty of London and when Wilson protested undiplomatically in February against an Anglo-French proposal to moderate the note.[31]

The Europeans concluded that it would be futile to try to make contact with the White House. A year later they consented to the signing of the Treaty of Rapallo by Italy and Yugoslavia, under which Italy received less in Dalmatia than had been promised under the Treaty of London. Fiume was included in an independent free state that was annexed by Italy in 1924.

From beginning to end the negotiations with respect to Fiume had been clouded by sentiment. A covenanter's devotion to a political creed and the jingoism of Italian patriots had made it difficult for experienced diplomats to find a way out of a situation that had grown from the exigencies of war and the secret treaties. Eco-

28. Lloyd George to Grey (Washington), telegram, October 31, 1919, Lloyd George papers, F/60/7/16. Imperiali to Lloyd George, October 28, 1919, Lloyd George papers, F/60/4/39.

29. Italy (embassy) to State Department, November 23, 1919, N.A., R.G. 59, 763.72119/7983. Chargé Jay to H. White, November 22, 1919, White papers, L.C., box 45.

30. Of this note Bowman wrote: "It gave way in many places and was a vast improvement over the president's earlier position," Bowman to Miller, April 27, 1921, G. Martin papers. The proposal of December 9 appeared in the *New York Times* on February 20 and 27, 1920. In the opinion of Seymour, it gave Italy its "full strategic necessities, provided for every demand of her commerce," and left hardly 30,000 Italians under Yugoslav sovereignty as compared with 400,000 Yugoslavs under Italy, letter from Seymour to the editor of the *New York Times,* January 18, 1920. Three of the five concessions recommended by Bowman were embodied in the proposal. See Miller, "The Adriatic Negotiations at Paris." "It was virtually the December agreement that she [Italy] incorporated into the Treaty of Rapallo," Bowman to Miller, letter cited.

31. Dispatch of February 7, 1920, secretary of state to the French Ministry of Foreign Affairs and the British embassy at Paris supplied also to the prime ministers of France and Great Britain, N.A., R.G. 59, 763.72119/0010½. Drafted by Johnson and approved by Wilson, this message went so far as to threaten to withdraw the Treaty of Versailles and the American guarantee of French security from further consideration by the Senate. Lloyd George thought it "a most pompous, dictatorial document." (Actually, according to his mistress, Lloyd George was "simply furious," Stevenson, *Lloyd George,* p. 201.)

"A half dozen times from July on," Bowman wrote, "the matter could have been settled but for Johnson's role of mentor to the president." He "submitted memo. after memo. to keep his mood in the narrow Johnsonian groove. This was a great mistake. Our signatures [those of the six experts on the memorandum of April 17] gave him a toehold with the President," letter to Miller cited.

The subsequent correspondence of the State Department with the embassies at Paris and London reveals the strain put upon diplomacy by the political uncertainty at Washington, State Department to France (embassy), February 20, 21, and 23, 1920, N.A., R.G. 59, 9163, 9206, 9208, 9224b, 9284; J. W. Davis to the secretary of state, February 20, 25, 26, and 27, 1920, *ibid.,* 9174, 9261, 9288, 9307.

nomic necessity had served to hold the Italian statesmen at Paris for a sharing of the spoils; but not even the financial constriction that Wilson exerted could make Italy abate its passion for Fiume. The moralizing Americans had failed in the delicate and difficult service to peace that English statesmen, embarrassed by the Treaty of London, had hoped the Americans would perform. The wound inflicted on the national ego of Italy by the maladroit interference of the American government in this essentially European controversy did not heal quickly. Twenty years later the next clash of martial power in Europe would find Italy in the opposing camp.

Of more immediate importance than the various territorial settlements that were at issue was the prompt establishment of some thirty-five commissions of control that were provided for in the Treaty of Versailles and in other agreements made at Paris. The most vital arrangements having to do with territorial matters were those to be constituted by the League of Nations for the disputed Saar basin and for Danzig. In the Saar there would be no authority after the deposit of ratifications of the treaty ended German rule. To avoid an interregnum and possible outbreaks of violence, the Council of Heads of Delegations decided on October 15[32] that members of the executive council of the League should be appointed immediately in order to consider what should be done when the treaty was brought into effect by the deposit of ratifications.

Agreement was reached among the chiefs that in addition to delineating the Saar entity and arranging for its government, measures should be considered that would be necessary in the matters of governments of Memel, Danzig, and German colonies; High Commission of occupied Rhine provinces; plebiscite commissions; state of Silesia, East Prussia (Allenstein and Marienwerder), Schleswig; delimitation commissions; Belgium, Czechoslovakia (Ratibor), Poland, Danzig (including high commissioner); commissions of control: military, naval, and air; commission for prisoners of war; commission for demolition in Heligoland; commission on reparations; waterways commissions: Rhine, Danube, Elbe, Oder; lists of persons accused of violation of laws and customs of war to be surrendered by Germany. Already operating at Paris under treaties signed were a committee on organization of the reparations commission, a committee on interpretation and coordination of the peace treaty (which practically superseded a committee on the execution of the peace treaty); a committee on political clauses of the peace treaty; and the Rhineland Commission appointed under the terms of the armistice.[33]

At the same time, it was acknowledged by the Heads of Delegations that the United States had a right to agree to the functioning of the commissions without being obliged to agree and without affecting the validity of their proceedings with or without American representatives. An immediate expression of opinion on this matter was requested of the State Department. Apparently it was still assumed that the treaty would be accepted by the Senate and that America could act, as European leaders wished, as an arbiter that would deploy its economic and political influence

32. J. B. Scott to Harrison, November 6, 1919, N.A., R.G. 256, 185.111 / 384.
33. Memo by D. H. Miller, September 19, 1919, Miller papers, box 89, III, 16 (12).

in such a way as to keep the peace and protect small nations against aggression.[34]

Three days later an unsatisfactory response came from Lansing. Expressing appreciation of the European willingness to permit participation of the United States on its own terms, he said his hands were tied by the attitude of the Senate and, at best, America might be represented by unofficial "observers" in cases in which "express authority" was given by the State Department. He was fearful that the Senate might be antagonized or the United States unwisely committed by acts of commissions in which the American government might take part. Lansing went so far as to state, however, that he "entirely approved" the immediate consideration of measures that should be taken when the treaty came into force.[35]

Although by the end of October all the great powers except the United States had ratified the Treaty of Versailles, the Allied governments procrastinated in arranging for the deposit of their ratifications at Paris with that of Germany. The French, apparently with British concurrence, were delaying the official ending of hostilities because of the difficulties that the commissions would have in operating without a definite understanding as to American participation. Henry White described the state of mind of the French government as "one of profound alarm." To White it seemed "really monstrous that they [the American president and Senate] were holding up . . . the peace of the world." He observed in a letter to his friend Lodge that "no doubt the greater the delay in putting the treaty into effect, the greater is the danger of one or more explosions somewhere."[36]

Finally, on November 21, the Council of Heads of Delegations fixed December 1 as the day for deposit of the ratifications of the Treaty of Versailles by Germany and by France, Great Britain, and Italy. A week later the voice of Wilson, for which the Europeans had been hopefully waiting while the State Department temporized, came through to Paris. The president sent instructions that, in view of the Senate's adverse vote two days before, all American representation be ended on all commissions that grew out of the Peace Conference. The next day he relented to the extent of sanctioning unofficial representation on the interim reparation commission.[37]

34. Dispatch, the secretary of state from Polk, October 19, 1919, N.A., R.G. 59, 763.72119 / 7338. For a review of the question of American participation in the work of the commission on reparations and other bodies at the Peace Conference, see Mitchell, 52–55. On Polk's efforts to assure continuing participation see *ibid.*, 58–60.

A resolution adopted by the Heads of Delegations provided: "All commissions to be constituted by the Allied and Associated Powers shall be duly imposed and shall function regularly with the representatives designated by the powers having ratified the treaty or who, without having ratified, have agreed to proceed with the designation of a representative to the commission. If all the powers whose representation is provided for in the treaty have not designated their representatives at the time of the entry into force of the treaty, the decisions taken by the commission shall be none the less valid."

Polk pointed out that actually this action gave effect to the intent of the American plenipotentiaries when they had proposed that the treaty should come into force when ratified by Germany and three of five principal powers.

35. Ammission from Lansing, October 22, 1919, N.A., R.G. 59, 763.72119 / 7338.

36. Nevins, *White,* p. 473.

37. Dispatches, State Department to Ammission, November 27 and 28, 1919, N.A., R.G. 59, 763.72119 /7808, 7948. Lansing, still suspicious of "intrigue" at Paris and resenting the "dominance" of French influence, informed Ambassador Davis that "from now on diplomatic channels will be the best for handling the questions which arise." "Our people are tired out with the bickering and petty quarrels," he wrote, Lansing to J. W. Davis, November 18, 1919, Lansing papers, Princeton University Library, box 3.

Despite the discouragement from Washington, Polk advocated repeatedly that his government be represented in subsequent negotiations at Paris, either by Ambassador Wallace or by General Bliss. He argued that, in addition to the obligations that the president had assumed in signing the Treaty of Versailles, the United States was committed under the armistice agreement, concluded a year ago, to assure the carrying-out of its terms. Fearful that American vacillation might tempt Germany to rebel against ratification of the treaty, he ventured to send a private warning to the Germans who had come to Paris for the deposit of ratifications. He told them that they would embitter American opinion if they depended on the state of affairs at Washington to justify any procrastination on their part. When an ambiguous answer came, suggesting that Germany would feel more secure if America joined in the ratification, Polk replied that a German default at this point would create a state of war. According to the British ambassador at Paris, Polk was "very angry with his government" and expected that he might be discharged for his independent action.[38]

Clemenceau was alarmed by the possibility that the Germans would not sign a new protocol accepting provisions of the armistice agreements that they had not fulfilled to the satisfaction of the Allies. Lacking confidence in any military fortification against German revenge in the coming age of air-power, the French premier had staked his country's security upon the treaties of guarantee that Wilson and Lloyd George had agreed to, even though Wilson had warned him that the American Senate might not give its consent.[39] This was the trump card that he waved before the French chamber when his adversaries attacked the peace settlement. Now that its validity was put in question by the paralysis of America's president and its government, the old Tiger, clinging precariously to his office, protested in a dispatch to Ambassador Jusserand. He could not conceive of American withdrawal before the treaty with Germany was ratified. The Yugoslavs and Romanians were about ready to sign declarations of adherence to the Treaty of St. Germain, with its clauses protecting minorities; the treaty with Hungary, for which the American delegates had shown concern, was ready with a prospect of being signed very soon; and a fortnight would suffice to settle ten or so other matters that were of secondary importance but should not be left in the air. The Germans, resisting the execution of the clauses of the armistice and delaying the exchange of ratifications that was scheduled for December 1, were making the most of the parliamentary difficulties in the United States. By leaving the conference now, Clemenceau asserted, "America would commit bankruptcy at the last moment, giving the impression that it was abandoning the cause that it has so nobly upheld. Never would France, which felt such deep gratitude and trust for the United States, be able to understand." The immediate departure of the American delegates "would be understood by no one, would cause prejudice, perhaps decisive, in Europe (very especially in France), and would risk putting in question the fruits of victory."[40]

Refusing to believe that such considerations would not weigh heavily in the opin-

---

38. Derby to Curzon, December 8, 9, 1919, Curzon papers, box 22, F / 6 / 2.
39. See above, p. 326.
40. Telegram, Clemenceau to Jusserand, November 27, 1919, Archives du M.A.É., À paix, vol. 156, pp. 41–44.
This dispatch is on microfilm in the Walworth papers, Y.H.C. Lloyd George later wrote that "the

ion of Wilson and his counselors, Clemenceau urged Jusserand to present them at Washington with all his eloquence and authority. A few days later he informed Polk of his anxiety. Only a feeling of imperative duty and certain peril, he wrote, justified him in appealing in a sense contrary to Polk's instructions from Washington. "I am emboldened," he wrote, "to defend the interests not only of France but of America itself and of the peace of the world."[41] He implored Polk to remain at Paris until the crisis was over and the ratifications were deposited.[42]

When the Germans failed to sign the protocol of ratification by December 1, Polk inquired of the State Department whether he might delay his departure, which he had set for the fifth. His inquiry elicited the response that the president had no objection but wanted all the American commissioners to leave Paris by the ninth.[43] When Polk was asked by Clemenceau who of the Americans was to remain at Paris the answer was "No one." The old man seemed very upset, but his sense of humor did not fail. He jocosely threatened to detain Polk by arresting him, promising that the charge would be for some crime that would be worthwhile. He said France was in a desperate plight and felt that it was being abandoned, and that the British were saying "You cannot depend upon the Americans." His bitterness against Wilson went so deep that he said to the British ambassador: "What on earth is the Lord Almighty doing that he does not take him to his bosom?"[44]

Polk, Bliss, and White set out from France on December 9, leaving Europeans who viewed their departure as a desertion. The secession of the United States undermined the moral sanction of the peace settlement as well as the ground for economic reconstruction.

A Council of Ambassadors, with which Ambassador Wallace sat as an observer,[45] proceeded to restore peace by occasional conferences and ad hoc arrangements. On January 10, 1920, it concluded the exchange of ratifications with Germany, and in that month the Council of the League of Nations held its first meeting without American participation. It was not until the summer of 1921 that the state of war of the United States with Germany and Austria was ended by a joint resolution of the Congress, signed by President Harding.

---

damage done to the careful structure of the Treaty was almost irreparable" and the League of Nations lost 50 percent of its power and influence, *The Truth about the Peace Treaties,* pp. 1411–1412.

41. Clemenceau to Polk, December 2, 1919, *Docs. on British Foreign Policy, First Series,* vol. 5, 1053.

42. Nevins, p. 477. Buckler to Mrs. Buckler, November 23, December 1, 1919, Y.H.C. Buckler wrote to House that Clemenceau was "almost passionately insistent." Bowman, in Seymour and House (eds.), *What Really Happened at Paris,* p. 165.

43. Phillips from Polk, December 4, 1919, N.A., R.G. 59, 763.72119 / 817. State Department to Polk, December 2, 1919, *ibid.,* / 8074.

44. Derby to Curzon, December 1919, Curzon papers, Mss. Eur. F112 / 196.

45. The youthful Allen Dulles, one of those who remained at Paris, found it difficult to sit with commissions without taking part in the proceedings. A. W. Dulles to Alexander Kirk, November 13, December 20, 1919, A. W. Dulles papers. The first session of the Council of Ambassadors was held on January 20 with Lloyd George and Clemenceau, who was voted out of office six days later. Wallace reported to Washington that it was agreed in the council that Americans should co-operate in the vital settlement of pressing European problems, France, embassy, to State Department, January 21, 1920, N.A., R.G. 59, 763.72119 / 8765.

Epilogue

When its president left Paris at the end of June, the United States was tentatively committed as never before to an active role in the affairs of the world. In addition to the vital questions raised at Paris by national interests, divers pleas for social and political causes had sought satisfaction at the Peace Conference. The American delegates were importuned by advocates of labor, the press, and organized womanhood. They were urged also to promote the creation of a Jewish homeland, Irish independence, and welfare of other peoples that had kin in the United States. Under these pressures and those exerted by commercial and humanitarian impulses, the Americans interceded in the making of arrangements for the Old World to an extent that could hardly be considered legitimate under the code of European diplomacy of the nineteenth century.

The American ship of state was tugging at its old isolationist moorings. The United States was engaged militarily in several remote areas. It was subsidizing equipment for White Russian armies. Its troops were still helping to police the eastern shore of the Adriatic. American regiments were occupying German territory on the Rhine, and others were ready to serve in patrolling plebiscites. Moreover, the vast program of relief that Hoover administered was providing essential supplies to the peoples of the lands of east central Europe, and the American government had supplied credits to make this possible. Furthermore, in response to pressure from aggressive minority groups in the United States, the Americans at Paris exerted their influence toward the conclusion of treaties that would protect minorities in the new states. The participation of American scholars in the peacemaking had contributed much to a judicious delineation of frontiers and to rational consideration of economic issues. Nevertheless, some among the Europeans, noting Hoover's desire to liquidate surpluses of food in America, Baruch's concern for American trade, and the provisos attached by the Treasury to some of its credits, were asking whether the American eagle in its unprecedented flights was not fixing its eye on legitimate prey that would nourish the economic life of the United States, perhaps to the disadvantage of European interests. The wonder of the Europeans grew when the eagle that had soared so high returned to its nest and behaved like an ostrich, leaving Europe to proceed to fulfill the prevailing expectation of prompt action to disarm Germany and to arrange for the functioning of the peace treaty and the League of Nations.

In his preoccupation with the power of ideals and in his faith in their appeal to the common man, Wilson had boldly challenged the actual powers of Europe. He learned, to his distress, that its statesmen had national mandates that were better respected than his spiritual revelations. Certain realities of power politics and of

557

economic necessity, and the limits imposed by the domestic politics of democracies, could not be escaped by a devotion to abstractions. As Holborn has written, the moral basis of the new treaties, which Wilson had been at such pains to establish, was in the end "weak and contradictory," and this "made people in later years unwilling to enforce them."[1]

The withdrawal of the United States left many of the expectations raised by its president unfulfilled. German Social Democrats, striving to operate a new government, were disappointed in their over-optimistic hopes. Contrary to the doctrine of self-determination, they found their population and that of Austria diminished by hundreds of thousands of people of their blood. Instead of sharing in the political reconstruction of the world's society that Wilson had advocated under economic arrangements that would make it possible to engage in productive industry and profitable trade, Germany could look forward only to inflation and bankruptcy. At the same time the American promises on which Clemenceau had staked the security of France were not to be redeemed. Moreover, Great Britain, for its part, was disappointed in its hope for some relief from the financial constriction that it suffered by virtue of its having acted as a banker of last resort of the victorious alliance. Moreover, the British Empire found that the United States would not work with the League that Wilson promoted in a way that would serve to strengthen the peacekeeping potential of the empire. Japan, though satisfied in its ambitions in the Pacific islands, had suffered deep wounds to its pride by the questioning of the honor of its intentions in China.

Only a few months after the signings at Paris, parts of Europe seemed to be reverting to international anarchy as lamentable as that of the Balkans in the nineteenth century. Certain disruptive forces that were well rooted in history were persisting. Mutual jealousies and suspicions were rife among the new nations. The Czechs, at swords' points with the Poles over the coal mines at Teschen, were failing to conciliate the German minority in Czechoslovakia and were alienating the Slovaks. Poland, whence messages from Minister Gibson told of "a very critical state of affairs," had to deal with recalcitrant Ukrainians in the territory that it was to "protect" in East Galicia. Romanians and Serbs, friends in the days of the revolt against the Hapsburg rule, were now at daggers drawn over a few square miles in the Banat of Temesvár. Bulgaria and Hungary had lost much of their native populations despite American concern. Yugoslavia, within which Croats and Serbs were in perpetual friction, was discontented with its borders on several sides. In the south Tyrol hundreds of thousands of German-Austrians were vowing to give all the trouble they could to the Italian government that annexed them.

The peacemakers of 1919, like those of 1815, had failed to satisfy the universal human longing for a new political order that would bring lasting peace. In the end, the national establishments, to which the peoples of the world had become accustomed to look for security, emerged from the peacemaking still the vital sources of political power. The advocates of collective security had been unable to cope conclusively with questions raised by considerations of sovereignty.[2] The essential con-

---

1. Holborn, "The Reasons for the Failure of the Paris Peace Conference," pp. 7–9.
2. The final collapse of the League of Nations as a keeper of the peace has been attributed to "trying to achieve a revolutionary change in international relations without any change in the distribution of

flict between national self-determination and supranational authority was still unresolved. Moreover, Europe had not been made "safe for democracy," and the states created or reorganized at the Peace Conference, with the exception of Czechoslovakia, would within a score of years be ruled dictatorially.[3] Man the political animal was to continue "to go on living in a twilight zone of fuzzy values, mixed and shifting emotions, wallowing in a sea of unsatisfactory and transitory compromises."[4]

Nevertheless, the great vision was to be kept alive in a League of Nations organization at Geneva, where devoted and enterprising individuals endeavored to further acceptance of the new order by the peoples and to get the co-operation of the national governments. Novelty in international usage was introduced principally in provisions for the protection of laborers from exploitation and for the prevention of white slavery and trade in opium. Even for the enforcement of these provisions, however, reliance was placed largely upon moral pressure. Although the League was to prove of some value as a keeper of the peace, international conflicts of interest and responsibility would still require accommodations negotiated by diplomats. At times it would seem that the League of Nations was little more than an enshrinement of the uneasy conscience that Wilson bequeathed to posterity.

Liberals in America and abroad were disappointed by the incompleteness of Wilson's achievement and by the failure to eliminate conditions such as those from which the catastrophe of 1914 had sprung. Many of the disillusioned were quick in immoderate criticism. To some, the mandate system seemed a hypocritical sanctification of imperial interests.[5] Indeed, one academic critic suggested that everyone who took part in the peacemaking would "henceforth have to hide it as a blot on the family scutcheon."[6]

Journalists and the "temporary gentlemen" of the Inquiry who had contributed essential and organized information to the deliberations, and in some cases had undertaken the work of diplomats,[7] returned to their bases in the United States; and in the press and in college classrooms they prepared the minds of Americans for the making of more intelligent provisions for the world's peace at the end of the next war.[8]

authority and power," Percy E. Corbett, *The Growth of World Law* (Princeton, 1971), p. 95. See Monnet, *Memoirs*, pp. 86–87.

3. Felix Gilbert, *The End of the European Era, 1890 to the Present*, 2d ed. (New York, 1970), pp. 177 ff.

4. Ferdinand Czernin, *Versailles, 1919*, p. 431.

5. *Ibid.*, p. 430. Of the books disparaging the work of the peacemakers, Keynes's *The Economic Consequences of the Peace* is the most prominent. Lord Bryce commended this volume to ex-President Eliot of Harvard and wrote: "Most people here who understand the European continent think there was never such a fiasco in diplomatic history as the Peace Conference has been," Bryce to Eliot, December 18 and 29, 1919, Bryce papers, vol. 2, pp. 204, 206, Bodleian Library. See Lawrence W. Martin, *Peace without Victory* (New Haven, 1958), pp. 204–206. For an analysis of Keynes's book, see Sontag, *A Broken World 1919–1939*, pp. 24–31.

6. A. C. Coolidge to J. R. Moulthrop, March 10, 1920, Coolidge papers, Widener Library, Harvard University. On the "disillusioned intelligentsia," see Mayer, *Politics and Diplomacy of Peacemaking*, epilogue.

7. For evaluations of the work of the Inquiry by two scholars whose conclusions are not entirely in agreement see Gelfand, *The Inquiry*, pp. 330–333, and Mayer, "Historical Thought and American Foreign Policy in the Era of the First World War," p. 8.

8. "Literally, the fundamental tone of American foreign policy during the second quarter of the

John Foster Dulles, coming back to his New York law firm well endowed with intimate knowledge of the ways of international finance, proceeded to advise both public and private agencies in the sort of co-operative ventures that had been envisioned by Lamont and his associates at Paris for the reconstruction of world trade.[9] Bernard M. Baruch, frequenting a park bench in New York, said one day to Frank I. Cobb: "I took no profit from my work for the government, but now I know where it is and I'm going to get it."[10]

Herbert Hoover converted the American Relief Administration into a private organization for distributing relief to the Old World.[11] Making speeches that appealed to American liberals and progressives, he addressed a letter to Wilson just before the Senate's vote on November 19, stressing the serious peril to the economic recovery of Europe and "the desperate necessity of early ratification." He ventured to say that on the whole the proposed reservations did not seem "to imperil the great principle of the League of Nations to prevent war."[12] Like House, he received no response. And after Hoover became the subject of a presidential boom in 1920,[13] Wilson, who at Paris had not considered the food administrator to be qualified for the office, wrote that Hoover was "no friend" of his.[14]

The president, shorn of his prophetic power by illness and shielded by a solicitous wife and doctor, behaved in a way that gave support to the allegations of his adversaries. He appeared indeed to be less the champion of a new world than a politician fighting for self-vindication and for re-election. And so, in the view of many Americans, the grand edifice that he had labored at Paris to build upon a solid Covenant took on the appearance of a structure set upon shifting sands.

The American peacemakers, by and large, had not overcome their distrust of Europe's diplomacy. Renouncing the traditional practice of negotiations among professionals without regard to immediate popular support—a practice obviously open to abuse and not without danger—they had given encouragement to open diplomacy by conference. This phenomenon of the twentieth century, as Nicolson observed, "entails much publicity, many rumors, and wide speculation," and, tempting politicians to achieve quick, spectacular, and often fictitious results, "tends to promote rather than allay suspicion, and to create those very states of uncertainty which it is the purpose of good diplomatic methods to prevent."[15]

The art of the diplomats had been corrupted by the poisons of politics in the democracies. Lloyd George, desiring to do the thing that he thought right, had to

---

twentieth century was altered by alumni of the American Commission," Lawrence E. Gelfand (ed.), *Herbert Hoover: The Great War and Its Aftermath*, p. 17, *q.v.*

9. See above, p. 513, and Pruessen, *John Foster Dulles*, chs. 4 and 5. On the continuing efforts of Lamont and others to bring about co-operation among public officials and private bankers and industrialists in America and abroad to generate needed credit, see Michael J. Hogan, "Thomas W. Lamont and European Recovery . . . ," in Jones (ed.), *U.S. Diplomats in Europe, 1919–1941*, pp. 9–11.

10. Margaret Cobb to the author.

11. O'Brien, *Two Peacemakers in Paris*, pp. 214, 232. Gelfand, *Herbert Hoover*, pp. 146, 156, 169.

12. Hoover, *The Ordeal of Woodrow Wilson*, pp. 282–283. See Robert F. Himmelberg, "Hoover's Public Image, 1919–1920," in Gelfand, *Herbert Hoover*, pp. 209–213.

13. O'Brien, pp. 214, 232.

14. Wilson to John W. Davis, December 9, 1920, Wilson papers. See above p. 522, n. 62.

15. Nicolson, *The Evolution of Diplomatic Method*, p. 89.

satisfy a majority of his parliament. Clemenceau was forced to think of the Chamber of Deputies. The Italian attitude at Paris reflected domestic politics. And so the peace that they made, although fashioned in secret deliberations at the summit, nevertheless coincided closely with prevailing opinion in the great democracies, deluded though that was in some instances. "When the statesmen departed from the popular mandate it was," according to Professor Young, "most often in the direction of moderation and tolerance."[16]

On his way to Europe in December of 1918 Wilson had told the scholars accompanying him that unless the Peace Conference was prepared to express the will of the people rather than that of their leaders at the conference, they would "soon be involved in another break-up of the world." Confessing before he left New York that he was "frightened" by the expectations of his people, and predicting that the peacemaking would be "the greatest success or the supremest tragedy in all history," he had looked to "a Divine Providence" to keep him sane.[17] At Paris he had made only occasional use of his diplomatic service or of the professional experience of the European foreign offices. He relied heavily upon his own political instinct and rhetorical brilliance in sanctifying the interests of his nation by appeals to Christian morality.

However, in depending on his own genius, which was impaired by illness, Wilson had misinterpreted the backsliding "common thought" of his own people; and so, as he himself had grimly predicted in September of 1918, he was in the end inevitably "broken." He handed down to the democracies that he was pledged to save the very doom that he had prophesied—"another break-up of the world." Yet he was not without faith in the future. Even after his body and spirit were warped, he persisted in proclaiming the ideals that were to rule the Western world of the twentieth century. "Perhaps the world charter which we finished will be redrawn in a happier form," he said to Bonsal three years later, "but as to its ultimate acceptance I have not the shadow of a doubt. The world will not commit suicide."[18]

Measuring up to the responsibility for leadership that had been thrust upon the United States by the inexorable forces of history, Wilson had extended the Monroe Doctrine's ban on aggression so that it would apply to the whole world. The Tiger of France, who had on occasion snarled at the American prophet, later testified to the grandeur of Wilson's role in history. By intervening in Europe in "the name of the historical solidarity of all civilized peoples," Clemenceau wrote in retrospect, Wilson "acted to the very best of his abilities in circumstances the origins of which escaped him and whose ulterior developments lay beyond his ken."[19]

Yet the prophet, in his departure from accepted ways, had thrown diplomats into confusion. In reporting his ill-advised manifesto to the Italian people, a London

16. Allyn A. Young to Baker, December 24, 1919, R. S. Baker papers.
17. See Walworth, *America's Moment: 1919*, p. 136.
18. Bonsal, *Unfinished Business*, p. 283.
19. Clemenceau, *Grandeur and Misery of Victory*, p. 167. H. G. Nicholas has written that in relation to "the central, crucial issue" of achieving orderly world government, Wilson "came nearer to transcending his personal and national limitations than any other statesman who had the responsibility of shaping the settlement of 1919," "Woodrow Wilson and Collective Security," in *Woodrow Wilson and a Revolutionary World 1913–1921*, ed. Link, p. 188.

newspaper used the phrase "wild-west diplomacy." The Europeans, who had been led by noble words to hope that America's isolation was ended, found themselves in a situation that David Hunter Miller had characterized early in the Peace Conference as "so unjust as to be difficult of characterization." The diplomats of Europe, baffled and frustrated, could not be sure which of America's voices spoke the first word and which the last, as they tried to cope with the two obvious menaces of the day: a prospect of a revived and vengeful Germany, and subversive propaganda from Moscow. The governments of the major European powers would have to try by concerted diplomacy, as they had after the peacemaking a century earlier, to meet threats to political stability as they arose.

For justification of their great-hearted and forward-looking venture into the politics of the whole world, the American pioneers at Paris had to look far into the future. They learned much that was to be of value to the men who, at the end of a second world war that Wilson foresaw, would lay the foundation for a *Pax Americana* that has survived the threat of world war longer than did the fragile truce that followed the unfinished business of 1919.

Appendix

The League of Nations Covenant Text in the Treaty of Versailles

[Paragraphs numbered pursuant to Assembly Resolution of September 21, 1926.]

THE COVENANT OF THE LEAGUE OF NATIONS.

The High Contracting Parties,
In order to promote international co-operation and to achieve international peace and security
by the acceptance of obligations not to resort to war,
by the prescription of open, just and honourable relations between nations,
by the firm establishment of the understandings of international law as the actual rule of conduct among Governments, and
by the maintenance of justice and a scrupulous respect for all treaty obligations in the dealings of organized peoples with one another,
Agree to this Covenant of the League of Nations.

ARTICLE 1.

1. The original Members of the League of Nations shall be those of the Signatories which are named in the Annex to this Covenant and also such of those other States named in the Annex as shall accede without reservation to this Covenant. Such accession shall be effected by a Declaration deposited with the Secretariat within two months of the coming into force of the Covenant. Notice thereof shall be sent to all other Members of the League.

2. Any fully self-governing State, Dominion or Colony not named in the Annex may become a Member of the League if its admission is agreed to by two-thirds of the Assembly, provided that it shall give effective guarantees of its sincere intention to observe its international obligations, and shall accept such regulations as may be prescribed by the League in regard to its military, naval and air forces and armaments.

3. Any Member of the League may, after two years' notice of its intention so to do, withdraw from the League, provided that all its international obligations and all its obligations under this Covenant shall have been fulfilled at the time of its withdrawal.

ARTICLE 2.

The action of the League under this Covenant shall be effected through the instrumentality of an Assembly and of a Council, with a permanent Secretariat.

ARTICLE 3.

1. The Assembly shall consist of Representatives of the Members of the League.

2. The Assembly shall meet at stated intervals and from time to time as occasion may require at the Seat of the League or at such other place as may be decided upon.

3. The Assembly may deal at its meetings with any matter within the sphere of action of the League or affecting the peace of the world.

4. At meetings of the Assembly each Member of the League shall have one vote, and may have not more than three Representatives.

ARTICLE 4.

1. The Council shall consist of Representatives of the Principal Allied and Associated Powers, together with Representatives of four other Members of the League. These four Members of the League shall be selected by the Assembly from time to time in its discretion. Until the appointment of the Representatives of the four Members of the League first selected by the Assembly, Representatives of Belgium, Brazil, Spain and Greece shall be members of the Council.

2. With the approval of the majority of the Assembly, the Council may name additional Members of the League whose Representatives shall always be members of the Council; the Council with like approval may increase the number of Members of the League to be selected by the Assembly for representation on the Council.

3. The Council shall meet from time to time as occasion may require, and at least once a year, at the Seat of the League, or at such other place as may be decided upon.

4. The Council may deal at its meetings with any matter within the sphere of action of the League or affecting the peace of the world.

5. Any Member of the League not represented on the Council shall be invited to send a Representative to sit as a member at any meeting of the Council during the consideration of matters specially affecting the interests of that Member of the League.

6. At meetings of the Council, each Member of the League represented on the Council shall have one vote, and may have not more than one Representative.

ARTICLE 5.

1. Except where otherwise expressly provided in this Covenant or by the terms of the present Treaty, decisions at any meeting of the Assembly or of the Council shall require the agreement of all the Members of the League represented at the meeting.

2. All matters of procedure at meetings of the Assembly or of the Council, including the appointment of Committees to investigate particular matters, shall be regulated by the Assembly or by the League represented at the meeting.

3. The first meeting of the Assembly and the first meeting of the Council shall be summoned by the President of the United States of America.

ARTICLE 6.

1. The permanent Secretariat shall be established at the Seat of the League. The Secretariat shall comprise a Secretary General and such secretaries and staff as may be required.

2. The first Secretary General shall be the person named in the Annex; thereafter the Secretary General shall be appointed by the Council with the approval of the majority of the Assembly.

3. The secretaries and staff of the Secretariat shall be appointed by the Secretary General with the approval of the Council.

4. The Secretary General shall act in that capacity at all meetings of the Assembly and of the Council.

5. The expenses of the Secretariat shall be borne by the Members of the League in accordance with the apportionment of the expenses of the International Bureau of the Universal Postal Union.

ARTICLE 7.

1. The Seat of the League is established at Geneva.

2. The Council may at any time decide that the Seat of the League shall be established elsewhere.

3. All positions under or in connection with the League, including the Secretariat, shall be open equally to men and women.

4. Representatives of the Members of the League and officials of the League when engaged on the business of the League shall enjoy diplomatic privileges and immunities.

5. The buildings and other property occupied by the League or its officials or by Representatives attending its meetings shall be inviolable.

ARTICLE 8.

1. The Members of the League recognize that the maintenance of peace requires the reduction of national armaments to the lowest point consistent with national safety and the enforcement by common action of international obligations.

2. The Council, taking account of the geographical situation and circumstances of each State, shall formulate plans for such reduction for the consideration and action of the several Governments.

3. Such plans shall be subject to reconsideration and revision at least every ten years.

4. After these plans shall have been adopted by the several Governments, the limits of armaments therein fixed shall not be exceeded without the concurrence of the Council.

5. The Members of the League agree that the manufacture by private enterprise of munitions and implements of war is open to grave objections. The Council shall advise how the evil effects attendant upon such manufacture can be prevented, due regard being had to the necessities of those Members of the League which are not able to manufacture the munitions and implements of war necessary for their safety.

6. The Members of the League undertake to interchange full and frank information as to the scale of their armaments, their military, naval and air programmes and the condition of such of their industries as are adaptable to war-like purposes.

ARTICLE 9

A permanent Commission shall be constituted to advise the Council on the execution of the provisions of Articles 1 and 8 and on military, naval and air questions generally

ARTICLE 10.

The Members of the League undertake to respect and preserve as against external aggression the territorial integrity and existing political independence of all Members of the League. In case of any such aggression or in case of any threat or danger of such aggression the Council shall advise upon the means by which this obligation shall be fulfilled.

ARTICLE 11.

1. Any war or threat of war, whether immediately affecting any of the Members of the League or not, is hereby declared a matter of concern to the whole League, and the League shall take any action that may be deemed wise and effectual to safeguard the peace of nations. In case any such emergency should arise the Secretary General shall on the request of any Member of the League forthwith summon a meeting of the Council.

2. It is also declared to be the friendly right of each Member of the League to bring to the attention of the Assembly or of the Council any circumstance whatever affecting international relations which threatens to disturb international peace or the good understanding between nations upon which peace depends.

ARTICLE 12.

1. The Members of the League agree that if there should arise between them any dispute likely to lead to a rupture, they will submit the matter either to arbitration or to inquiry by the Council, and they agree in no case to resort to war until three months after the award by the arbitrators or the report by the Council.

2. In any case under this Article the award of the arbitrators shall be made within a reasonable time, and the report of the Council shall be made within six months after the submission of the dispute.

ARTICLE 13.

1. The Members of the League agree that whenever any dispute shall arise between them which they recognise to be suitable for submission to arbitration and which cannot be satisfactorily settled by diplomacy, they will submit the whole subject-matter to arbitration.

2. Disputes as to the interpretation of a treaty, as to any question of international law, as to the existence of any fact which if established would constitute a breach of any international obligation, or as to the extent and nature of the reparation to be made for any such breach, are declared to be among those which are generally suitable for submission to arbitration.

3. For the consideration of any such dispute the court of arbitration to which the case is referred shall be the court agreed on by the parties to the dispute or stipulated in any convention existing between them.

4. The Members of the League agree that they will carry out in full good faith any award that may be rendered, and that they will not resort to war against a Member of the League which complies therewith. In the event of any failure to carry out such an award, the Council shall propose what steps should be taken to give effect thereto.

ARTICLE 14.

The Council shall formulate and submit to the Members of the League for adoption plans for the establishment of a Permanent Court of International Justice. The Court shall be competent to hear and determine any dispute of an international character which the parties thereto submit to it. The Court may also give an advisory opinion upon any dispute or question referred to it by the Council or by the Assembly.

ARTICLE 15.

1. If there should arise between Members of the League any dispute likely to lead to a rupture, which is not submitted to arbitration in accordance with Article 13, the Members of the League agree that they will submit the matter to the Council. Any party to the dispute may effect such submission by giving notice of the existence of the dispute to the Secretary General, who will make all necessary arrangements for a full investigation and consideration thereof.

2. For this purpose the parties to the dispute will communicate to the Secretary General, as promptly as possible, statements of their case with all the relevant facts and papers, and the Council may forthwith direct the publication thereof.

3. The Council shall endeavour to effect a settlement of the dispute, and if such efforts are successful, a statement shall be made public giving such facts and explanations regarding the dispute and the terms of settlement thereof as the Council may deem appropriate.

4. If the dispute is not thus settled, the Council either unanimously or by a majority vote shall make and publish a report containing a statement of the facts of the dispute and the recommendations which are deemed just and proper in regard thereto.

5. Any Member of the League represented on the Council may make public a statement of the facts of the dispute and of its conclusions regarding the same.

6. If a report by the Council is unanimously agreed to by the members thereof other than the Representatives of one or more of the parties to the dispute, the Members of the League agree that they will not go to war with any party to the dispute which complies with the recommendations of the report.

7. If the Council fails to reach a report which is unanimously agreed to by the members thereof, other than the Representatives of one or more of the parties to the dispute, the Members of the League reserve to themselves the right to take such action as they shall consider necessary for the maintenance of right and justice.

8. If the dispute between the parties is claimed by one of them, and is found by the Council, to arise out of a matter which by international law is solely within the domestic jurisdiction of that party, the Council shall so report, and shall make no recommendation as to its settlement.

9. The Council may in any case under this Article refer the dispute to the Assembly. The dispute shall be so referred at the request of either party to the dispute, provided that such request be made within fourteen days after the submission of the dispute to the Council.

10. In any case referred to the Assembly, all the provisions of this Article and of Article 12 relating to the action and powers of the Council shall apply to the action and powers of the Assembly, provided that a report made by the Assembly, if concurred in by the Representatives of those Members of the League represented on the Council and of a majority of the other Members of the League, exclusive in each case of the Representatives of the parties to the dispute, shall have the same force as a report by the Council concurred in by all the members thereof other than the Representatives of one or more of the parties to the dispute.

ARTICLE 16.

1. Should any Member of the League resort to war in disregard of its covenants under Articles 12, 13 or 15, it shall *ipso facto* be deemed to have committed an act of war against all other Members of the League, which hereby undertake immediately to subject it to the severance of all trade or financial relations, the prohibition of all intercourse between their nationals and the nationals of the covenant-breaking State, and the prevention of all financial, commercial or personal intercourse between the nations of the Covenant-breaking State and the nationals of any other State, whether a Member of the League or not.

2. It shall be the duty of the Council in such case to recommend to the several Governments concerned what effective military, naval or air force the Members of the League shall severally contribute to the armed forces to be used to protect the covenants of the League.

3. The Members of the League agree, further, that they will mutually support one another in the financial and economic measures which are taken under this Article, in order to minimise the loss and inconvenience resulting from the above measures, and that they will mutually support one another in resisting any special measures aimed at one of their number by the covenant-breaking State, and that they will take the necessary steps to afford passage through their territory to the forces of any of the Members of the League which are co-operating to protect the covenants of the League.

4. Any Member of the League which has violated any covenant of the League may be declared to be no longer a Member of the League by a vote of the Council concurred in by the Representatives of all the other Members of the League represented thereon.

ARTICLE 17.

1. In the event of a dispute between a Member of the League and a State which is not a Member of the League, or between States not Members of the League, the State or States not Members of the League shall be invited to accept the obligations of membership in the League for the purposes of such dispute, upon such conditions as the Council may deem just. If such invitation is accepted, the provisions of Articles 12 to 16 inclusive shall be applied with such modifications as may be deemed necessary by the Council.

2. Upon such invitation being given the Council shall immediately institute an inquiry into the circumstances of the dispute and recommend such action as may seem best and most effectual in the circumstances.

3. If a State so invited shall refuse to accept the obligations of membership in the League for the purposes of such dispute, and shall resort to war against a Member of the League, the provisions of Article 16 shall be applicable as against the State taking such action.

4. If both parties to the dispute when so invited refuse to accept the obligations of membership in the League for the purposes of such dispute, the Council may take such measures and make such recommendations as will prevent hostilities and will result in the settlement of the dispute.

Article 18.

Every treaty or international engagement entered into hereafter by any Member of the League shall be forthwith registered with the Secretariat and shall as soon as possible be published by it. No such treaty or international engagement shall be binding until so registered.

Article 19.

The Assembly may from time to time advise the reconsideration by Members of the League of treaties which have become inapplicable and the consideration of international conditions whose continuance might endanger the peace of the world.

Article 20.

1. The Members of the League severally agree that this Covenant is accepted as abrogating all obligations or understandings *inter se* which are inconsistent with the terms thereof, and solemnly undertake that they will not hereafter enter into any engagements inconsistent with the terms thereof.

2. In case any Member of the League shall, before becoming a Member of the League, have undertaken any obligations inconsistent with the terms of this Covenant, it shall be the duty of such Member to take immediate steps to procure its release from such obligations.

Article 21.

Nothing in this Covenant shall be deemed to affect the validity of international engagements, such as treaties of arbitration or regional understandings like the Monroe doctrine, for securing the maintenance of peace.

Article 22.

1. To those colonies and territories which as a consequence of the late war have ceased to be under the sovereignty of the States which formerly governed them and which are inhabited by peoples not yet able to stand by themselves under the strenuous conditions of the modern world, there should be applied the principle that the well-being and development of such peoples form a sacred trust of civilisation and that securities for the performance of this trust should be embodied in this Covenant.

2. The best method of giving practical effect to this principle is that the tutelage of such peoples should be entrusted to advanced nations who by reason of their resources, their experience or their geographical position can best undertake this responsibility, and who are willing to accept it, and that this tutelage should be exercised by them as Mandatories on behalf of the League.

3. The character of the mandate must differ according to the stage of the development of the people, the geographical situation of the territory, its economic conditions and other similar circumstances.

4. Certain communities formerly belonging to the Turkish Empire have reached a stage of development where their existence as independent nations can be provisionally recognised subject to the rendering of administrative advice and assistance by a Mandatory until such time as they are able to stand alone. The wishes of these communities must be a principal consideration in the selection of the Mandatory.

5. Other peoples, especially those of Central Africa, are at such a stage that the Mandatory must be responsible for the administration of the territory under conditions which will guarantee freedom of conscience and religion, subject only to the maintenance of public order and morals, and prohibition of abuses such as the slave trade, the arms traffic and the liquor traffic, and the prevention of the establishment of fortifications or military and naval bases and of military training of the natives for other than police purposes and the defense of

territory, and will also secure equal opportunities for the trade and commerce of other Members of the League.

6. There are territories, such as South-West Africa and certain of the South Pacific Islands, which, owing to the sparseness of their population, or their small size, or their remoteness from the centres of civilisation, or their geographical contiguity to the territory of the Mandatory, and other circumstances, can be best administered under the laws of the Mandatory as integral portions of its territory, subject to the safeguards above mentioned in the interests of the indigenous population.

7. In every case of mandate, the Mandatory shall render to the Council an annual report in reference to the territory committed to its charge.

8. The degree of authority, control, or administration to be exercised by the Mandatory shall, if not previously agreed upon by the Members of the League, be explicitly defined in each case by the Council.

9. A permanent Commission shall be constituted to receive and examine the annual reports of the Mandatories and to advise the Council on all matters relating to the observance of the mandates.

ARTICLE 23.

Subject to and in accordance with the provisions of international conventions existing or hereafter to be agreed upon, the Members of the League:

(a) will endeavour to secure and maintain fair and humane conditions of labour for men, women, and children, both in their own countries and in all countries to which their commercial and industrial relations extend, and for that purpose will establish and maintain the necessary international organisations;

(b) undertake to secure just treatment of the native inhabitants of territories under their control;

(c) will entrust the League with the general supervision over the execution of agreements with regard to the traffic in women and children, and the traffic in opium and other dangerous drugs;

(d) Will entrust the League with the general supervision of the trade in arms and ammunition with the countries in which the control of this traffic is necessary in the common interest;

(e) will make provision to secure and maintain freedom of communications and of transit and equitable treatment for the commerce of all Members of the League. In this connection the special necessities of the regions devastated during the war of 1914–1918 shall be borne in mind;

(f) will endeavour to take steps in matters of international concern for the prevention and control of disease.

ARTICLE 24.

1. There shall be placed under the direction of the League all international bureaux already established by general treaties if the parties to such treaties consent. All such international bureaux and all commissions for the regulation of matters of international interest hereafter constituted shall be placed under the direction of the League.

2. In all matters of international interest which are regulated by general conventions but which are not placed under the control of international bureaux or commissions, the Secretariat of the League shall, subject to the consent of the Council and if desired by the parties, collect and distribute all relevant information and shall render any other assistance which may be necessary or desirable.

3. The Council may include as part of the expenses of the Secretariat the expenses of any bureau or commission which is placed under the direction of the League.

ARTICLE 25.

The Members of the League agree to encourage and promote the establishment and co-operation of duly authorised voluntary national Red Cross organisations having as purposes the improvement of health, the prevention of disease and the mitigation of suffering throughout the world.

ARTICLE 26.

1. Amendments to this Covenant will take effect when ratified by the Members of the League whose Representatives compose the Council and by a majority of the Members of the League whose Representatives compose the Assembly.

2. No such amendment shall bind any Member of the League which signifies its dissent therefrom, but in that case it shall cease to be a Member of the League.

ANNEX.

ORIGINAL MEMBERS OF THE LEAGUE OF NATIONS
SIGNATORIES OF THE TREATY OF PEACE.

United States of America.
Belgium.
Bolivia.
Brazil.
British Empire.
  Canada.
  Australia.
  South Africa.
  New Zealand.
  India.
China.
Cuba.
Ecuador.
France.
Greece.
Guatemala.

Haiti.
Hedjaz.
Honduras.
Italy.
Japan.
Liberia.
Nicaragua.
Panama.
Peru.
Poland.
Portugal.
Roumania.
Serb-Croat-Slovene State.
Siam.
Czecho-Slovakia.
Uruguay.

STATES INVITED TO ACCEDE TO THE COVENANT.

Argentine Republic.
Chile.
Colombia.
Denmark.
Netherlands.
Norway.
Paraguay.

Persia.
Salvador.
Spain.
Sweden.
Switzerland.
Venezuela.

List of Abbreviations Used in Footnotes

ACTNP—American Commission to Negotiate Peace
A.E.F.—American Expeditionary Force
A.F.L.—American Federation of Labor
AMTC—Allied Maritime Transport Council
Baker—*Woodrow Wilson and World Settlement*
B.D.I.C.—Bibliothèque de Documentation Internationale Contemporaine
B.W.C.—British War Cabinet
f.—fascicule
F.C.—Fonds Clemenceau, Archives Historiques du Ministère de la Guerre
F.O.— British Foreign Office
F.R.—*Papers Relating to the Foreign Relations of the United States*
I.P.—*The Intimate Papers of Colonel House*
I.W.C.—Imperial War Cabinet
L.C.—Library of Congress
M.A.É.— Ministère des Affaires Étrangères
N.A.—National Archives of the United States
O.H.R.O.—Oral History Research Office, Columbia University
P.P.—*The Public Papers of Woodrow Wilson*
P.P.C.—The thirteen volumes in *F.R.* that pertain to the Paris Peace Conference
P.R.O.— Public Records Office, London
R.G.— Record Group
S.W.C.—Supreme War Council
Y.H.C.—Yale House Collection and related papers, Manuscripts and Archives Room, Yale University Library

Bibliography

The official American documents that bear upon the Paris Peace Conference of 1919 are of enormous volume and are located in several archives. Thousands have been printed in one or both of two basic collections: (1) *Papers Relating to the Foreign Relations of the United States,* 1918 and 1919 series, Paris Peace Conference series and Lansing Papers, vol. 2 (published by the State Department, Washington, D.C.); and (2) *My Diary,* by David Hunter Miller, consisting of twenty-one volumes (repr. Peter Smith, Gloucester, Mass.). Miller, in editing his twenty-one volumes, drew upon his papers in the Library of Congress.

I have searched the files from which the documents in the above compilations were taken and have made use of some papers not previously printed. Moreover, I have drawn upon relevant documents of the Treasury Department, both those in the National Archives and those in the "Peace Commission" file in the Bureau of Accounts. In many cases it has been possible to compare the written record with oral testimony from interviews granted to me by men who wrote the documents. Witnesses who have contributed information in an interview or by correspondence, other than those whose papers are listed below, are Philip Noel-Baker, Sir James R. M. Butler, François Charles-Roux, Robert H. George, Andrew Géraud ("Pertinax"), Ulysses S. Grant III, Lord Hankey, Mrs. J. Borden Harriman, Wunsz King, Arthur Krock, David Lawrence, Eleanor Wilson McAdoo, Francis C. MacDonald, René Massigli, George Bernard Noble, Bliss Perry, William Phillips, André Portier, René de St. Quentin, Sir Arthur Salter, Francis B. Sayre, Herbert Bayard Swope, Arnold Toynbee, and Mona House Tucker.

The following collections have been used; and in many cases I have talked with those who created them.

In the Library of Congress the papers of these people: Carl Ackerman, General Henry T. Allen, Newton D. Baker, Ray Stannard Baker, Admiral William S. Benson, General Tasker H. Bliss, Stephen Bonsal, Admiral Mark Bristol, Frank I. Cobb, George Creel, Josephus Daniels, Norman H. Davis, Raymond B. Fosdick, Felix Frankfurter, Huntington Gilchrist, Thomas W. Gregory, Charles S. Hamlin, Leland Harrison, Ralph Hayes, Edith Benham Helm, Gilbert Hitchcock, Irwin H. Hoover, Philip C. Jessup, Robert Lansing, Henry Cabot Lodge, Breckinridge Long, Charles O. Maas, William G. McAdoo, Theodore Marburg, David Hunter Miller, John Bassett Moore, Henry Morgenthau, Roland S. Morris, General John J. Pershing, Elihu Root, Arthur Sweetser, William Howard Taft, Joseph P. Tumulty, Henry White, William Allen White, Edith Bolling Wilson, Woodrow Wilson, Robert W. Woolley, and Lester H. Woolsey.

At Yale University in the Manuscripts and Archives division of the Sterling Memorial Library: the Edward M. House Collection, designated in this book as "Y.H.C." and including the diaries and papers of Edward M. House; also the papers of Gordon Auchincloss, William H. Buckler, William C. Bullitt, John W. Davis, Walter G. Davis, Clive Day, Arthur Hugh Frazier, Edward M. House, Walter Lippmann, Vance McCormick, Wallace Notestein, Frank L. Polk, Charles Seymour, Sir Arthur Willert, Sir William Wiseman, and William Yale; also at the Yale Library, certain documents of the Inquiry, microfilms of the papers of Sidney Sonnino, and papers of Willard Straight.

At Princeton University in the Firestone Library: the papers of Bernard M. Baruch, Ray Stannard Baker, Gilbert F. Close, John Foster Dulles, Dr. Albert Lamb, Robert Lansing, and Charles L. Swem; and in the Mudd Library, the papers of Allen W. Dulles and Charles H. Haskins.

At Harvard University in the Houghton Library: the papers of Ellis L. Dresel, Joseph C. Grew, Walter Hines Page, William Phillips, Leon Trotsky, and Oswald Garrison Villard; in the Widener Library archives, the papers of Archibald Cary Coolidge; in the Baker Library, the papers of Thomas W. Lamont.

At Columbia University: in the Butler Library: the papers of V. K. Wellington Koo, Sidney E. Mezes, James T. Shotwell, and Henry White, the diaries of George Louis Beer and William L. Westermann; and records of Boris A. Bakhmeteff, William Phillips, DeWitt Poole, James T. Shotwell, and others in the Oral History Research Office.

At Stanford University: in the Hoover Institution Archives: the papers of Edwin F. Gay, Hugh Gibson, Stanley K. Hornbeck, Vance C. McCormick, Ignace Jan Paderewski, and Brand Whitlock, and the Records of the American Relief Administration.

At the Duke University Library: the papers of Thomas Nelson Page.

At the Georgetown University Library: the papers of James Brown Scott.

At the Massachusetts Historical Society: the

papers of Henry Cabot Lodge and John T. Morse, Jr.

At the Johns Hopkins University in the Eisenhower Library: the papers of Isaiah Bowman. Additional papers of Bowman were read by the courtesy of Geoffrey J. Martin.

At the Franklin D. Roosevelt Library at Hyde Park: the papers of Adolph A. Berle and Henry Morgenthau.

At the University of Virginia: in the Alderman Library: the papers of Carter Glass.

At Cornell University: in the John M. Olin Library: the papers of Willard Straight.

At Cambridge University: in the University Library, the papers of Jan Christiaan Smuts; in the King's College Library, the papers of John Maynard Keynes.

At the London School of Political and Economic Science: in the British Library of Political and Economic Science, the papers of Sir Charles Webster.

At Oxford University: in the Bodleian Library, the papers of Vicount Bryce, Gilbert Murray, and Herbert Henry Asquith, Earl of Oxford and Asquith; in the Library of New College, the papers of Alfred Lord Milner.

At the Public Record Office, London: the minutes of the British War Cabinet and the Imperial War Cabinet and the papers of the Foreign Office and its officials pertaining to the ending of the war and the peacemaking.

At the House of Lords Record Office, London: the papers of Lord Beaverbrook, Frances Stevenson Lloyd George, David Lloyd George, Andrew Bonar Law, and St. Loe Strachey.

At the British Museum: the papers of Lord Robert Cecil, and of Arthur James Balfour, Earl of Balfour.

At the India House Library and Records: the papers of Lord Curzon.

In the Printing House Square Papers of *The Times* of London: the papers of Geoffrey Dawson, Wickham Steed, and Sir Arthur Willert.

At the Scottish Record Office, Edinburgh: the papers of Philip Henry Kerr, Marquess of Lothian.

In the National Archives of Canada, Ottawa: the papers of Sir Robert L. Borden and Sir G. E. Foster.

In the Archives Diplomatiques of the Ministère des Affaires Étrangères (M.A.É.), Paris: the series "À paix, 1918–1929" and "Europe 1918–29," "Grande Bretagne," and "L'Amérique."

In the Archives Historiques du Ministère de la Guerre, Château de Vincennes, Paris: "Fonds Clemenceau."

At the Bibliothèque de Documentation Internationale Contemporaine, University of Paris, Nanterre: the papers of Paul Mantoux, Louis Lucien Klotz, and André Chéradame.

At the Archives Nationales, Paris: the papers of the Ministry of Commerce and Industry, and the papers of André Tardieu.

I am deeply indebted to the many kindly custodians who have facilitated my study of these prime sources over a period of a quarter century.

A valuable bibliographical guide is Nina Almond's *An Introduction to a Bibliography of the Paris Peace Conference* (Stanford, Calif., 1935).

On the care and eventual disposition of the original records of the Peace Conference, see Carl L. Lokke, "A Sketch of the Interallied Organizations of the First World War Period and Their Records," *The American Archivist* (October 1944): 229–235.

Documents

Akten zur Deutschen Auswärtigen Politik, 1919–1945; Serie A, 1918–1925, band 1 and band 2. Göttingen, 1982, 1984.

Aldrovandi-Marescotti, Count Luigi. *Guerra Diplomatica.* Milan, 1937. Interpreter's notes on proceedings in sessions of the Supreme Council. Much of the notes for the period of April 17–27, 1919, is printed in English translation in Albrecht-Carrié, *Italy at the Paris Peace Conference* See under "Other Books."

————. *Nuovi Ricordi é Frammenti di Diario,* Milan, 1938. This covers the period of June 3–28, 1919. These notes and those in *Guerra Diplomatica* for April 17–27 have been published in French translation by F. Cravoisier in *Guerre Diplomatique* (Paris, [1939]).

Almond, Nina, and Lutz, Ralph H. (eds.). *The Blockade of Germany after the Armistice of 1918–1919: Selected Documents of the Supreme Economic Council, Superior Blockade Council,*

American Relief Administration, and Other Wartime Organizations. Stanford, 1942.

————. *The Treaty of St. Germain: A Documentary History of Its Territorial and Political Clauses.* Stanford, 1935.

Baker, Ray Stannard. *Woodrow Wilson and World Settlement.* 3 vols. Vol. 3. See below under "Other Books."

Baker, Ray Stannard, and Dodd, William E. (eds.). *Woodrow Wilson: War and Peace: Presidential Messages, Addresses, and Public Papers (1917–1924).* New York, 1927.

Bane, Suda L., and Lutz, Ralph H. *The Blockade of Germany after the Armistice, 1918–1919.* Stanford, 1942.

————. (eds.). *The Organization of American Relief in Europe, 1918–1919.* Stanford, 1943.

British and Foreign State Papers. Vol. 112. London, 1921–1922.

Cocks, F. Seymour (ed.). *The Secret Treaties*. 2d ed. London, 1918.

Conférence de la Paix. *Receuil des Actes de la Conférence*. 39 vols. Paris, 1922–1935. Vol. 1: *Actes du Conseil Supreme*. 4 vols. 1934.

Congressional Record. Vols. 57 and 58.

Documents on British Foreign Policy 1919–1939, eds. E. L. Woodward and Rohan Butler. First series. Vols. 1 and 2. London, 1947, 1949. Minutes of the Supreme Council, July 1919–January 1920.

Hancock, William Keith, and Van der Poel, Jean (eds.). *Selections from the Smuts Papers*. 7 vols. Vol. 4. Cambridge, Eng., 1966.

I documenti diplomatici italiani. 6th series (1918–1922). Vols. 1 and 2. Rome, 1955.

Lapradelle, A. Geouffre de (ed.). *La Paix de Versailles: La Conférence de la paix et la Société des Nations*. 11 vols. Paris, 1930–1939.

Mantoux, Paul. *Les Délibérations du Conseil du Quatre (24 Mars–27 Juin 1919): Notes de l'Officier Interprète*. 2 vols. Paris, 1955.

———. *The Proceedings of the Council of Four (March 24–April 18)*. A translation of Mantoux's notes by John Boardman Whitton. Geneva, 1964.

Marburg, Theodore, and Flack, H. E. (eds.). *Taft Papers on the League of Nations*. New York, 1920.

Miller, David Hunter. *The Drafting of the Covenant*. 2 vols. Vol. 2. New York, 1928.

———. *My Diary at the Conference of Paris*. 21 vols. and index. New York, 1924.

Scott, James Brown (ed.). *Official Statements of War Aims and Peace Proposals, Dec. 1916–Nov. 1918*. Washington, 1921.

Shotwell, James T. (ed.). *The Origins of the International Labor Organization*. 2 vols. Vol. 2: *Documents*. New York, 1934.

Temperley, Harold W. V. (ed.). *A History of the Peace Conference at Paris*. 6 vols. London, 1920–1924.

U.S. Dept. of State. *The Treaty of Versailles and After: Annotations of the Text of the Treaty*. Washington, 1947.

Diaries, Letters, Memoirs, Etc.

Adam, H. Pearl. *Paris Sees It Through*. London, 1919.

Baker, Ray Stannard. *American Chronicle*. New York, 1945.

Barnes, James Strachey. *Half a Life*. London, 1933.

Baruch, Bernard M. *The Public Years*. New York, 1960.

Berle, Beatrice B., and Jacobs, Travis B. (eds.). *Navigating the Rapids, 1918–1971: From the Papers of A. A. Berle*. New York, 1973.

Bonsal, Stephen. *Suitors and Suppliants*. New York, 1946.

———. *Unfinished Business*. New York, 1944.

Borden, Robert L. *Robert Land Borden, His Memoirs*. New York, 1938.

Bullitt, William C. *The Bullitt Mission to Russia*. New York, 1919.

Butler, Nicholas Murray. *Across the Busy Years*. 2 vols. Vol. 2. New York, 1940.

Callwell, Sir Charles E. *F. M. Sir Henry Wilson: His Life and Diaries*. 2 vols. Vol. 2. London, 1927.

Cambon, Paul. *Correspondance*. 3 vols. Vol. 3. Paris, 1946.

Cecil, Lord Robert. *A Great Experiment*. New York, 1941.

Charles-Roux, François. *Souvenirs diplomatiques: Rome-Quirinal*. Paris, 1958.

———. *Une Grande Ambassade à Rome*. Paris, 1961.

Clemenceau, Georges. *Grandeur and Misery of Victory*. New York, 1930.

Creel, George. *Rebel at Large, Recollections of Fifty Crowded Years*. New York, 1947.

Daniels, Josephus. *The Cabinet Diaries of Josephus Daniels*. Ed. E. David Cronon. Lincoln, Neb., 1963.

———. *The Wilson Era, 1917–1923*. 2 vols. Vol. 2. Chapel Hill, N.C., 1946.

Frankfurter, Felix. *The Diaries of Felix Frankfurter*. Ed. Joseph P. Lash, New York, 1975.

Gompers, Samuel. *Seventy Years of Life and Labor*. 2 vols. Vol. 2. New York, 1925.

Grayson, Cary T. *Woodrow Wilson: An Intimate Memoir*. New York, 1960.

Grew, Joseph C. *Turbulent Era*. Ed. Walter Johnson. 2 vols. Vol. 1. Boston, 1952.

Hankey, Maurice Pascal Alers, Baron. *The Supreme Control*. London, 1963.

Hardinge, Charles. *Baron Hardinge of Penshurst: The Old Diplomacy*. London, 1947.

Headlam-Morley, James W. *A Memoir of the Paris Peace Conference, 1919*. Ed. Agnes Headlam-Morley, Russell Bryant, and Anna Cienciala. London, 1972.

Helm, Edith Benham. *The Captains and the Kings*. New York, 1954.

Hoover, Herbert C. *An American Epic*. Vol 3. Chicago, 1961.

———. *The Memoirs of Herbert Hoover*. 3 vols. Vol. 1. New York, 1951.

———. *Years of Adventure, 1914–1920*. New York, 1951.

———. *The Ordeal of Woodrow Wilson*. New York, 1958.

Hoover, Irwin Hood. *Forty-two Years in the White House*. Boston, 1934.

Howard, Sir Esmé. *Theatre of Life.* 2 vols. Vol. 2. London, 1936.

Hughes, William M. *Policies and Potentates.* Sydney, 1950.

Hurley, Edward N. *The Bridge to France.* Philadelphia and London, 1927.

Jefferson, Mark. *Paris Peace Conference Diary.* Ed. Geoffrey J. Martin. Microfilm. Ann Arbor, 1966.

Jones, Thomas. *Whitehall Diary.* Ed. Keith Middlemas. 3 vols. Vol. 1. London, 1969.

Keynes, John Maynard. *The Collected Writings of John Maynard Keynes.* Vol. 16: *Activities 1914–1919: The Treasury and Versailles.* Ed. Elizabeth Johnson. London, 1971.

———. *Two Memoirs.* London, 1949.

Lamont, Thomas W. *Across World Frontiers.* New York, 1951.

Lane, Franklin K. *The Letters of Franklin K. Lane.* Ed. A. W. Lane and L. H. Wall. Boston, 1922.

Lansing, Robert. *The Peace Negotiations: A Personal Narrative.* Boston, 1921.

Laroche, Jules. *Au Quai d'Orsay avec Briand et Poincaré.* Paris, 1957.

Lloyd George, David. *The Truth about the Peace Treaties.* 2 vols. London, 1938.

Loucheur, Louis. *Carnets Secrets 1908–1932.* Brussels, 1962.

McAdoo, William G. *Crowded Years.* Boston, 1931.

Masaryk, Thomas G. *The Making of a State.* New York, 1957.

Monnet, Jean. *Memoirs.* London, 1978.

Morgenthau, Henry. *All in a Life-Time.* New York, 1922.

Mott, Thomas Bentley. *Twenty Years as Military Attaché.* New York, 1937.

Page, Thomas Nelson. *Italy and the World War.* New York, 1920.

Percy, Eustace. *Some Memories.* London, 1958.

Pershing, John J. *My Experiences in the World War.* 2 vols. Vol. 2. New York, 1931.

Phillips, William. *Adventures in Diplomacy.* Portland, Maine, 1952.

Poincaré, Raymond. *Au Service de la France.* 11 vols. Vol. 10: Paris, 1923; Vol. 11: Paris, 1974.

Recouly, Raymond. *Foch: My Conversations with the Marshal.* New York, 1929.

Riddell, George Allerdice. *Lord Riddell's Intimate Diary of the Peace Conference and After, 1918–1923.* New York, 1934.

Roosevelt, Nicholas. *A Front Row Seat.* Norman, Okla., 1953.

Salter, Sir James Arthur Lord. *Memoirs of a Public Servant.* London, 1961.

Sayre, Francis B. *Glad Adventure.* New York, 1957.

Scott, C. P. *The Political Diaries of C. P. Scott.* Ed. Trevor Wilson. Ithaca, N.Y., 1970.

Seymour, Charles. *The Intimate Papers of Colonel House.* Arranged as a narrative. 4 vols. Vol. 4. Boston, 1928. This work is designated in footnotes as *I.P.*

———. *Letters from the Paris Peace Conference.* New Haven, 1965.

Sharp, William G. *The War Memoirs of William Graves Sharp.* Ed. Warrington Dawson, London, 1931.

Shartle, Samuel G. *Spa, Versailles, Munich.* Philadelphia, 1941.

Shotwell, James T. *At the Paris Peace Conference.* New York, 1937.

———. *The Autobiography of James T. Shotwell.* Indianapolis and New York, 1961.

Smuts, Jan Christiaan. See above under "Documents": Hancock and Van der Poel.

Sonnino, Sidney. *Diario, 1916–1922.* Ed. Pietro Pastorelli. 3 vols. Vol. 3. Bari, 1972.

Speranza, Gino Charles. *Gino Speranza's Diary.* New York, 1941.

Steed, Henry Wickham. *Through Thirty Years, 1892–1922.* 2 vols. Vol. 2. London, 1924.

Steffens, Joseph Lincoln. *Autobiography.* 2 vols. Vol. 2. New York, 1931.

———. *Letters.* 2 vols. Vol. 1. New York, 1938.

Stevenson, Frances. *Lloyd George: A Diary by Frances Stevenson.* Ed. A. J. P. Taylor. London, 1971.

Straus, Oscar S. *Under Four Administrations.* Boston, 1922.

Tumulty, Joseph P. *Woodrow Wilson as I Know Him.* New York, 1921.

Vandervelde, Émile. *Souvenirs d'un militant socialiste.* Paris, 1939.

Villard, Oswald Garrison. *Fighting Years.* New York, 1939.

Wemyss, Victoria Lady Wester. *Life and Letters of Lord Wester Wemyss.* London, 1935.

Weygand, General Maxime. *Mémoires: Mirages et réalité.* 2 vols. Vol. 2. Paris, 1957.

White, William Allen. *The Autobiography of William Allen White.* New York, 1946.

———. *Selected Letters of William Allen White.* Ed. Walter Johnson. New York, 1947.

Willert, Sir Arthur. *Washington and Other Memories.* Boston, 1972.

Wilson, Edith Bolling. *My Memoir.* Indianapolis and New York, 1938.

Other Books

Albrecht-Carrié, René. *Italy at the Paris Peace Conference.* New York, 1938.

Angell, Norman. *The Peace Treaty and the Economic Chaos of Europe.* London, 1919.

Armstrong. Hamilton Fish. *Peace and Counterpeace*. New York, 1971.

Aubert, Louis. *Tardieu, haut-commissionaire en Amérique*. Paris, 1957.

Bailey, Thomas A. *Wilson and the Peacemakers*. New York, 1947. (Combines *Woodrow Wilson and the Lost Peace* and *Woodrow Wilson and the Great Betrayal*.)

Baker, Ray Stannard. *The Versailles Treaty and After*. New York, 1924.

———. *What Wilson Did at Paris*. New York, 1919.

———. *Woodrow Wilson and World Settlement*. 3 vols. New York, 1922. Designated in footnotes as "Baker."

Barnes, George Nicoll. *From Workshop to Cabinet*. London, 1924.

Barros, James. *Office without Power: Secretary-General Sir Eric Drummond, 1919–1923*. Oxford, 1979.

Barthou, Louis. *Le Traité de paix*. Paris, 1919.

Bartlett, Ruhl J. *The League to Enforce Peace*. Chapel Hill, N.C., 1944.

Bartlett, Vernon. *Behind the Scenes at the Peace Conference*. London, 1920.

Baruch, Bernard M. *The Making of the Reparations and Economic Sections of the Treaty*. New York, 1920.

———. *The Public Years*. New York, 1960.

Baumont, Maurice. *La Faillite de la paix (1918–1939)*. 3d ed. 2 vols. Vol. 1. Paris, 1951.

Beer, George Louis. *African Questions at the Paris Peace Conference*. Ed. Louis H. Gray. New York, 1933.

Beers, Burton F. *Vain Endeavor: Robert Lansing's Attempts to End the American-Japanese Rivalry*. Durham, N.C., 1962.

Bell, H. C. F. *Woodrow Wilson and the People*. Garden City, N.Y., 1945.

Berard, Victor. *La Paix française*. Paris, 1919.

Berdahl, Clarence A. *The Policy of the United States with Respect to the League of Nations*. Geneva, 1932.

Berger, Marcel, and Allard, Paul. *Les Dessous du Traité de Versailles*. Paris, 1933.

Bergmann, Karl, *The History of Reparations*. London, 1927.

Bethlen, Stephen Count. *The Treaty of Trianon*. New York, 1934.

Birdsall, Paul. *Versailles Twenty Years After*. New York, 1944.

Blake, Robert. *The Unknown Prime Minister: The Life and Times of Andrew Bonar Law, 1858–1923*. London, 1955.

Blum, John M. *Joe Tumulty and the Wilson Era*. Boston, 1951.

———. *The Progressive Presidents*. New York, 1980.

Bourgeois, Léon. *Le Traité de paix de Versailles*. Paris, 1919.

Bowman, Isaiah. *The New World*. 4th ed. New York, 1928.

Bradley, John. *Allied Intervention in Russia*. New York, 1968.

Brenier, Henry. *Le Traité de Versailles et la problème des réparations, le point de vue français, une réfutation par les faits du livre de M. Keynes*. Marseille, 1921.

Brooks, Sidney. *America and Germany 1918–1925*. 2d rev. ed. New York, 1927.

Bruun, Geoffrey. *Clemenceau*. Cambridge, Mass., 1943.

Buehrig, Edward H. *Woodrow Wilson and the Balance of Power*. Bloomington, Ind., 1955.

——— (ed.). *Woodrow Wilson's Foreign Policy in Today's Perspective*. Bloomington, Ind., 1957.

Bullitt, Orville H. (ed.). *For the President: Personal and Secret*. Boston, 1972.

Bullitt, William C. *The Bullitt Mission to Russia*. New York, 1919.

Bullitt, William C., and Freud, Sigmund. *Thomas Woodrow Wilson*. Boston, 1967.

Bunselmeyer, Robert E. *The Cost of the War, 1914–1919: British Economic War Aims and the Origins of Reparation*. Hamden, Conn., 1975.

Burner, David. *Herbert Hoover: A Public Life*. New York, 1979.

Burnett, Philip M. *Reparation at the Paris Peace Conference from the Standpoint of the American Delegation*. Foreword by John Foster Dulles. 2 vols. New York, 1940.

Butler, J. R. M. *Lord Lothian, 1882–1940*. London, 1960.

Caldis, Calliope G. *The Council of Four as a Joint Emergency Authority in the European Crisis at the Paris Peace Conference 1919*. Ambilly-Annemasse, 1953.

Carr, Edward H. *The Bolshevik Revolution, 1917–1921*. Vol. 3. London, 1953.

Centenaire Woodrow Wilson, 1856–1956. Geneva, 1956.

Cheever, D. S., and Haviland, H. F., Jr. *American Foreign Policy and the Separation of Powers*. Preface by Harvey H. Bundy. Cambridge, Mass., 1961.

Chicherin, George. *Two Years of Foreign Policy, 1917–1919*. New York, 1920.

Churchill, Winston S. *The Aftermath*. New York, 1929.

Clémentel, Étienne. *La France at la politique économique interallié*. Preface by James T. Shotwell. Paris, 1931.

Coit, Margaret L. *Mr. Baruch*. Boston, 1957.

Coolidge, Archibald. *Ten Years of War and Peace*. Cambridge, Mass., 1927.

Coolidge, Harold J., and Lord, Robert H. *Archibald Cary Coolidge, Life and Letters*. Cambridge, Mass., 1932.

Corwin, Edward S. *The Constitution and World Organization.* Princeton, 1944.

Craig, Gordon A. *Germany 1866–1945.* New York, 1978.

Craig, Gordon A., and Gilbert, Felix (eds.). *The Diplomats, 1919–1939.* Princeton, 1953.

Creel, George. *The World, the War, and Woodrow Wilson.* New York, 1920.

Curry, Roy Watson. *Woodrow Wilson and Far Eastern Policy, 1913–1921.* New York, 1957.

Czernin, Ferdinand. *Versailles, 1919.* New York, 1964.

Davis, George T. *A Navy Second to None.* New York, 1940.

Deák, Francis. *Hungary at the Paris Peace Conference.* New York, 1942.

Demangeon, Albert. *Le Déclin de l'Europe.* Paris, 1920. 2d ed. with preface by Aimé Perpillou: Paris, 1975.

DeNovo, John A. *American Interests and Policies in the Middle East, 1900–1939.* Minneapolis, 1963.

Diamond, William. *The Economic Thought of Woodrow Wilson.* Baltimore, 1943.

Dillon, E. J. *The Inside Story of the Peace Conference.* New York, 1920.

"Diplomate, Un," *Paul Cambon, ambassadeur de France (1843–1924).* Paris, 1937.

Dugdale, Blanche E. C. *Arthur James Balfour.* 2 vols. Vol. 2. London, 1936.

Duggan, Stephen P. H. (ed.). *The Collected Papers of John Bassett Moore.* 7 vols. Vol. 5. New Haven, 1944.

Duroselle, Jean-Baptiste. *Les Cours de Sorbonne: La Politique extérieure de la France de 1914 à 1945.* Vol. 1. Paris, n.d.

———. *France and the United States.* Chicago, 1978.

———. *From Wilson to Roosevelt.* Cambridge, Mass., 1963.

Egerton, George W. *Great Britain and the Creation of the League of Nations.* Chapel Hill, N.C., 1978.

Elcock, Howard J. *Portrait of a Decision.* London, 1972.

Evans, Laurence. *U.S. Policy and the Partition of Turkey, 1914–1924.* Baltimore, 1965.

Farnsworth, Beatrice. *William C. Bullitt and the Soviet Union.* Bloomington, Ind., 1967.

Feinburg, Nathan. *Le Question des minorités à la Conférence de la Paix de 1919–1920 et l'action juive en faveur de la protection internationale des minorités.* Paris, 1929.

Fifield, Russell H. *Woodrow Wilson and the Far East.* New York, 1952.

Fisher, H. H., and Brooks, Sidney. *America and the New Poland.* New York, 1928.

Fisher, Louis. *The Soviets in World Affairs.* 2d ed. Vol. 1. Princeton, 1951.

Fitzroy, Sir Almeric. *Memoirs.* 2 vols. Vol. 2. London, 1925.

Fleming, Denna F. *The United States and the League of Nations, 1918–1920.* New York, 1932.

Floto, Inga. *Colonel House in Paris.* Copenhagen, 1973.

Fosdick, Raymond B. *Letters on the League of Nations.* Princeton, 1966.

Fowler, Wilton B. *British-American Relations, 1917–1918: The Role of Sir William Wiseman.* Princeton, 1969.

Freud, Sigmund. See Bullitt, William C., and Freud, Sigmund.

Gardner, Lloyd C. *Wilson and Revolutions, 1913–1921.* Philadelphia, 1976.

Garraty, John A. *Henry Cabot Lodge.* New York, 1953.

Gelfand, Lawrence E. *The Inquiry: American Preparations for Peace, 1917–1919.* New Haven, 1963.

——— (ed.). *Herbert Hoover: The Great War and Its Aftermath: 1914–1923.* Iowa City, 1979.

George, Alexander L., and George, Juliette L. *Woodrow Wilson and Colonel House: A Personality Study.* New York, 1956.

Gerson, Louis L. *Woodrow Wilson and the Rebirth of Poland.* New Haven, 1953.

Gidney, James B. *A Mandate for Armenia.* Oberlin, Ohio, 1967.

Gilbert, Martin. *The European Powers 1900–1945.* London, 1965.

———. *Winston S. Churchill. Vol. 4 1911–1922.* London, 1975.

Glazebrook, G. P. de T. *Canada at the Paris Peace Conference.* London and New York, 1942.

Gollin, Alfred M. *Proconsul in Politics: A Study of Lord Milner in Opposition and in Power.* London, 1964.

Gottlieb, W. W. *Studies in Secret Diplomacy during the First World War.* London, 1957.

Graham, M. W., Jr., assisted by Binkley, Robert C. *New Governments of Central Europe.* New York, 1924.

Grant, James. *Bernard M. Baruch: The Adventures of a Wall Street Legend.* New York, 1983.

Griswold, A. Whitney. *Far Eastern Policy of the United States.* New York, 1938.

Hammond, J. L. *C. P. Scott of the Manchester Guardian.* London, 1934.

Hancock, W. K. *Smuts. The Sanguine Years, 1870–1919.* Cambridge, Eng., 1962.

Hankey, Maurice, Lord. *Diplomacy by Conference.* London, 1920.

Hanotaux, Gabriel. *Le Traité de Versailles du 28 Juin 1919.* Paris, 1919.

Harbaugh, William H. *Lawyer's Lawyer: The Life of John W. Davis.* New York, 1973.

Harbord, James G. *The American Army in France 1917–1919.* Boston, 1936.

Harris, H. Wilson. *The Peace in the Making.* New York, 1920.

Harrod, Sir Roy Forbes. *The Life of John Maynard Keynes.* New York, 1951.

Haskins, Charles H., and Lord, Robert H. *Some Problems of the Peace Conference.* Cambridge, Mass., 1920.

Hatch, Alden. *Edith Bolling Wilson.* New York, 1961.

Headlam-Morley, Sir James. *Studies in Diplomatic History.* London, 1930.

Heinrichs, Waldo H. *American Ambassador.* Boston, 1966.

Helmreich, Paul C. *From Paris to Sèvres.* Columbus, 1974.

Hitchcock, Edward B. *"I Built a Temple for Peace": The Life of Edward Beneš.* Introduction by Jan Masaryk. New York, 1940.

Hogan, Michael J. *Informal Entente: The Private Structure of Cooperation in Anglo-American Economic Diplomacy, 1918–1928.* Columbia, Mo., 1977.

Holborn, Hajo. *A History of Modern Germany.* 3 vols. Vol. 3. New York, 1969.

———. *The Political Collapse of Europe.* New York, 1958.

Holt, W. Stull. *Treaties Defeated by the Senate.* Baltimore, 1933.

Hoover, Herbert C., and Gibson, Hugh. *The Problems of a Lasting Peace.* New York, 1942.

House, Edward M. See Seymour, Charles, and House, Edward M. (eds.).

Howard, Harry N. *The King-Crane Commission.* Beirut, 1963.

———. *The Partition of Turkey.* Norman, Okla., 1931.

Howard-Ellis, C. *The Origin, Structure and Working of the League of Nations.* Boston and New York, 1928.

Hudson, W. J. *The Birth of Australian Diplomacy.* West Melbourne, 1978.

Huthmacher, J. Joseph, and Susman, Warren I. (eds.). *Wilson's Diplomacy: An International Symposium.* With contributions by Arthur S. Link, Jean-Baptiste Duroselle, Ernest Fraenkel, and H. G. Nicholas. Cambridge, Mass., 1973.

Hyde, H. Montgomery. *Lord Reading.* London, 1967.

Jessup, Philip C. *Elihu Root.* 2 vols. Vol. 2. New York, 1938.

Johnson, Walter (ed.). *William Allen White's America.* New York, 1947.

Jones, Kenneth Paul (ed.). *U.S. Diplomats in Europe, 1919–1941.* Santa Barbara, 1981.

Jordan, W. M. *Britain, France, and the German Problem, 1918–1939.* Preface by C. K. Webster. London, 1943.

Kahn, E. J., Jr. *The World of Swope.* New York, 1965.

Kaltenbach, Frederick W. *Self-Determination, 1919.* London, 1938.

Kaplan, Justin. *Lincoln Steffens.* New York, 1974.

Kaufman, Burton I. *Efficiency and Expansion: Foreign Trade Organization in the Wilson Administration, 1913–1921.* Westport, Conn., 1974.

Kedourie, Ellie. *England and the Middle East.* London, 1956.

Kennan, George F. *Russia and the West under Lenin and Stalin.* Boston, 1960.

Kennedy, Aubrey L. *Old Diplomacy and New, 1876–1922.* Introduction by V. Chirol. New York, 1933.

Kerner, Robert J. (ed.). *Czechoslovakia: Twenty Years of Independence.* Berkeley and Los Angeles, 1940.

———. *Yugoslavia.* Berkeley, 1949.

Kessler, Harry K. U. *Germany and Europe.* New Haven, 1923.

Keynes, John Maynard. *The Economic Consequences of the Peace.* New York, 1920.

———. *Essays in Biography.* New York, 1933.

Killen, Linda. *The Russian Bureau.* Lexington, Ky., 1983.

Kimmich, Christoph M. *Germany and the League of Nations.* Chicago, 1976.

King, Jere C. *Clemenceau vs. Foch: France and German Dismemberment, 1918–1919.* Harvard Historical Monograph No. 44. Cambridge, Mass., 1960.

Kitsikēs, Demētrēs. *Propagande et pressions en politique internationale, la Grèce et ses révendications à la Conférence de la Paix (1919–1920).* Paris, 1963.

———. *La Rôle des experts à la Conférence de la Paix de 1919.* Ottawa, 1972.

Komarnicki, Titus. *The Rebirth of the Polish Republic: A Study of the Diplomatic History of Europe, 1914–1919.* London, 1957.

Kuehl, Warren F. *Hamilton Holt.* Gainesville, Fla., 1960.

Lansing, Robert. *The Big Four and Others of the Peace Conference.* Boston, 1921.

Lasch, Christopher. *The American Liberals and the Russian Revolution.* New York, 1962.

Lash, Joseph P. *From the Diaries of Felix Frankfurter.* New York, 1975.

Lawrence, David. *The True Story of Woodrow Wilson.* New York, 1924.

Lederer, Ivo J. *Yugoslavia at the Paris Peace Conference.* New Haven, 1963.

Lentin, A. *Lloyd George, Woodrow Wilson and the Guilt of Germany.* Baton Rouge, 1985.

Lerski, George J. (comp.). *Herbert Hoover and Poland, a Documentary History of a Friendship.* Stanford, 1977.

Levin, Norman Gordon, Jr. *Woodrow Wilson and World Politics: America's Response to War and Revolution.* New York, 1968.

Lhôpital, René M. M. *Foch, l'armistice et la paix.* Paris, 1938.

Lilienthal, Alfred M. *The Zionist Connection.* New York, 1978.

Link, Arthur S. *Wilson the Diplomatist.* Baltimore, 1957.

———— (ed.). *Woodrow Wilson and a Revolutionary World, 1913–1921.* Chapel Hill, N.C., 1982.

————. *Woodrow Wilson: Revolution, War and Peace.* Arlington Heights, Ill., 1979.

Lochner, Louis P. *Herbert Hoover and Germany.* New York, 1960.

Lodge, Henry Cabot. *The Senate and the League of Nations.* New York, 1925.

Louis, William Roger. *Great Britain and Germany's Lost Colonies, 1914–1919.* Oxford, 1967.

Low, Alfred D. *The Anschluss Movement, 1918–1919.* Memoirs of the American Philosophical Society. Vol. 103, Philadelphia, 1974.

————. *The Soviet Hungarian Republic and the Paris Peace Conference.* Transactions of the American Philosophical Society. New Series, Vol. 53, pt. 10. Philadelphia, 1963.

Luckau, Alma Maria. *The German Delegation at the Paris Peace Conference.* New York, 1941.

Lundgreen-Nielsen, Kay. *The Polish Problem at the Paris Peace Conference: A Study of the Policies of the Great Powers and the Poles, 1918 1919.* Odense, Denmark, 1979.

McCallum, Ronald B. *Public Opinion and the Last Peace.* London, 1944.

McDougall, Walter A. *France's Rhineland Diplomacy, 1914–1924.* Princeton, 1978.

Mackinder, Sir Halford J. *Democratic Ideals and Reality.* London, 1919.

Mamatey, Victor S. *The U.S. and East Central Europe, 1914–1918: A Study in Wilsonian Diplomacy and Propaganda.* Princeton, 1957.

Mamatey, Victor S., and Radomir Luza (eds.). *A History of the Czechoslovak Republic, 1918–1948.* Princeton, 1973.

Mantoux, Étienne, *The Carthaginian Peace, or the Economic Consequences of Mr. Keynes.* New York, 1952.

Manuel, Frank E. *The Realities of American-Palestine Relations.* Washington, D.C., 1949.

Marburg, Theodore. *Development of the League of Nations Idea.* Ed. John H. Latané. 2 vols. Vol. 2. New York, 1932.

Margolith, Aaron M. *The International Mandates.* Baltimore, 1930.

Marin, Louis. *Le Traité de paix.* Paris, 1920.

Marks, Sally. *Innocent Abroad: Belgium at the Paris Peace Conference of 1919.* Chapel Hill, N.C., 1981.

Marston, F. S. *The Peace Conference of 1919: Organization and Procedure.* Foreword by Sir Charles Webster. London, 1944.

Martel, René. *The Eastern Frontiers of Germany.* London, 1930.

Martin, Geoffrey J. *The Life and Thought of Isaiah Bowman.* Hamden, Conn., 1981.

————. *Mark Jefferson: Cartographer.* Ypsilanti, 1968.

Martin, William. *Statesmen of the War in Retrospect, 1918–1928.* New York, 1928.

Martini, Alexis G., and Orgias, Maurice. *Le Traité de Versailles devant le Droit.* Paris, 1921.

Mason, John Brown. *The Danzig Dilemma.* Stanford, 1946.

Mayer, Arno J. *Political Origins of the New Diplomacy.* New Haven, 1959.

————. *Politics and Diplomacy of Peacemaking: Containment and Counterrevolution at Versailles, 1918–1919.* New York, 1967.

Meintjes, Johannes. *General Louis Botha.* London, 1970.

Mermeix (pseud. for G. Terrail). *Le Combat des trois.* Paris, 1922.

————. *Les Négociations secrétes et les quatres armistices.* 5th ed. Paris, 1921.

Miller, David Hunter. *The Drafting of the Covenant.* 2 vols. New York, 1928.

Miquel, Pierre. *La Paix de Versailles et l'opinion publique française.* Paris, 1972.

Monroe, Elizabeth. *Britain's Moment in the Middle East 1914–1956.* London, 1963.

Moodie, A. E. *The Italo-Yugoslav Boundary.* London, 1945.

Mordacq, General Jean J. H. *Le Ministère Clemenceau.* 4 vols. Vol. 4. Paris, 1931.

Morrow, Ian F. P. *The Peace Settlement in the German-Polish Borderlands.* London, 1936.

Mosky, Leonard. *Curzon, the End of an Epoch.* London, 1960.

Murray, Arthur C. *Master and Brother.* London, 1945.

Nelson, Harold I. *Land and Power: British and Allied Policy on Germany's Frontiers 1916–1919.* London and Toronto, 1963.

Nelson, Keith L. *Victors Divided.* Berkeley, Calif., 1975.

Nevins, Allan. *Henry White: Thirty Years of American Diplomacy.* New York, 1930.

Nicolson, Sir Harold. *Curzon, the Last Phase.* London, 1934.

————. *Diplomacy.* New York, 1939.

————. *The Evolution of Diplomatic Method.* London, 1954.

————. *Peacemaking: 1919.* Rev. ed. London, 1943.

Noble, George Bernard. *Policies and Opinions at Paris, 1919.* New York, 1935.

Notter, Harley. *The Origins of the Foreign Policy of Woodrow Wilson.* Baltimore, 1937.

O'Brien, Francis W. *Two Peacemakers in Paris: The Hoover-Wilson Post-Armistice Letters, 1918–1920.* College Station, Texas, 1972.

O'Grady, Joseph P. (ed.). *The Immigrants' Influence on Wilson's Peace Policies*. Louisville, 1967.

Osgood, Robert E. *Ideals and Self-Interest in America's Foreign Relations*. Chicago, 1953.

Owen, Frank. *Temptestuous Journey: Lloyd George, His Life and Times*. London, 1954.

Page, Stanley W. *The Formation of the Baltic States*. Cambridge, Mass., 1959.

Page, Thomas Nelson. *Italy and the World War*. New York, 1920.

Palmer, Frederick. *Bliss, Peacemaker: The Life and Letters of General Tasker Howard Bliss*. New York, 1934.

―――. *John J. Pershing*. Harrisburg, Pa., 1948.

Parrini, Carl P. *Heir to Empire: U.S. Economic Diplomacy, 1916–1923*. Pittsburgh, 1969.

Pastor, Peter. *Hungary between Wilson and Lenin: The Hungarian Revolution of 1918–1919 and the Big Three*. New York, 1976.

Perman, Dagmar. *The Shaping of the Czechoslovak State*. Leiden, 1962.

Petit, Lucien. *Le Règlement des dettes interalliés (1919–1929)*. Paris, 1932.

Petsalis-Diomidis, N. *Greece at the Paris Peace Conference*. Thessaloniki, 1978.

Pringle, Henry F. *The Life and Times of William Howard Taft*. 2 vols. Vol. 2. New York, 1939.

Pruessen Ronald W. *John Foster Dulles: The Road to Power*. New York, 1982.

Ratinaud, Jean. *Clemenceau, ou la colère et la gloire*. Paris, 1958.

Reading, Gerald Rufus Isaacs. *Rufus Isaacs, First Marquess of Reading*. 2 vols. Vol 2. London, 1945.

Renouvin, Pierre. *Les Crises du XXe siècle*. 2 vols. Vol. 1: *De 1914 à 1929*. Paris, 1957. English translation: *War and Aftermath*. New York, 1968.

―――. *Le Traité de Versailles*. Paris, 1969.

Roskill, Stephen, *Hankey, Man of Secrets*. 3 vols. Vols. 1 and 2. London, 1972.

―――. *Naval Policy between the Wars*. New York, 1968.

Rothwell, V. H. *British War Aims and Peace Diplomacy*. Oxford, 1971.

Rowland, Peter. *David Lloyd George*. London, 1975.

Roz, Firmin. *L'Amérique nouvelle: les États-Unis et la guerre, les États-Unis et la paix*. Paris, 1923.

Safford, Jeffrey J. *Wilsonian Maritime Diplomacy, 1913–1921*. New Brunswick, N.J., 1978.

Salter, Sir James Arthur Lord. *Allied Shipping Control: An Experiment in International Administration*. London, 1921.

―――. *Personality in Politics*. London, 1947.

Sanders, Ronald. *The High Walls of Jerusalem: A History of the Balfour Declaration and the Birth of the British Mandate for Palestine*. New York, 1984.

Savage, Carlton. *Policy of the U.S. toward Maritime Commerce in War 1776–1918*. 2 vols. Washington, 1934–1936.

Scelle, Georges, and Lange, Robert. *Les Origines et l'oeuvre de la Société des Nations*. 2 vols. Copenhagen, 1923.

Schiff, Victor. *The Germans at Versailles, 1919*. London, 1930.

Schulz, Gerhard. *Revolutions and Peace Treaties, 1917–1920*. London, 1972.

Schwabe, Klaus. *Woodrow Wilson, Revolutionary Germany, and Peacemaking, 1918–1919*. Chapel Hill, N.C., 1985.

―――. *Woodrow Wilson*. Göttingen, 1971.

Schwartz, Jordan A. *The Speculator: Bernard M. Baruch in Washington 1917–1965*. Chapel Hill, N.C., 1981.

Scott, Arthur P. *An Introduction to the Peace Treaties*. Chicago, 1920.

Seaman, L. C. B. *From Vienna to Versailles*. New York, 1956.

Seton-Watson, Christopher. *Italy from Liberalism to Fascism 1870–1925*. London, 1967.

Seymour, Charles. *Geography, Justice, and Politics at the Paris Peace Conference of 1919*. New York, 1951.

Seymour, Charles, and House, Edward M. (eds.). *What Really Happened at Paris*. New York, 1921.

Sforza, Count Carlo. *Makers of Modern Europe*. Indianapolis, 1928.

Shelton, Brenda K. *President Wilson and the Russian Revolution*. Monograph in History no. 7. The University of Buffalo Studies 23, no. 3 (March 1957).

Shotwell, James T. (ed.). *The Origins of the International Labor Organization*. 2 vols. New York, 1934.

Shotwell, James T., and Laserson, Max M. *Poland and Russia, 1919–1945*. New York, 1945.

Shotwell, James T., *et al. George Louis Beer: A Tribute*. New York, 1924.

Skidelsky, Robert. *John Maynard Keynes*. London, 1983.

Smuts, J. C. *Jan Christiaan Smuts*. New York, 1952.

Sontag, Raymond J. *A Broken World 1919–1939*. New York, 1971.

―――. *European Diplomatic History, 1871–1932*. New York, 1933.

Spector, Sherman D. *Rumania at the Paris Peace Conference*. New York, 1962.

Stein, Leonard J. *The Balfour Declaration*. London and New York, 1961.

Strakhovsky, Leonid I. *American Opinion about Russia, 1917–1920*. Toronto, 1961.

Suarez, Georges. *Soixante années d'histoire française: Clemenceau dans l'action*. Nouvelle ed. 2 vols. Vol. 2. Paris, 1932.

Surface, Frank M., and Bland, Raymond L.

American Food in the World War and Reconstruction Period. Stanford, 1931.

Sylvester, A. J. *The Real Lloyd George.* London, 1947.

Tabouis, Geneviève. *The Life of Jules Cambon.* London, 1938.

Tardieu, André. *France and America.* Boston, 1927.

———. *La Paix.* Paris, 1921.

———. *The Truth about the Treaty.* Indianapolis, 1921.

Taylor, Alan J. P. (ed.). *Lloyd George: Twelve Essays.* London, 1971.

———. *The Origins of the Second World War.* London, 1961.

Terrail, G. See Mermeix.

Thompson, Charles T. *The Peace Conference Day by Day.* New York, 1920.

Thompson, John M. *Russia, Bolshevism, and the Versailles Peace.* Princeton, 1966.

Tillman, Seth P. *Anglo-American Relations at the Paris Peace Conference.* Princeton, 1961.

The Times History of the War. 21 vols. Vol. 21. London, 1920.

Toynbee, Arnold J. *Acquaintances.* London, 1967.

Trachtenberg, Marc. *Reparation in World Politics: France and European Economic Diplomacy, 1916–1923.* New York, 1980.

Trask, David F. *General Tasker Howard Bliss and the "Sessions of the World," 1919.* Philadelphia, 1966.

———. *The U.S. in the Supreme War Council.* Middletown, Conn., 1961.

The Treaty of Versailles and After. Papers by Lord Riddell, Arnold J. Toynbee, C. K. Webster, et al. London, 1935.

Ullman, Richard H. *Intervention and the War.* Princeton, 1961.

———. *Britain and the Russian Civil War.* Princeton, 1968.

Unterberger, Betty Miller. *America's Siberian Expedition, 1918–1920.* Durham, N.C., 1956.

Valiani, Leo. *The End of Austria-Hungary.* London, 1973.

Van der Slice, Austin. *International Labor Diplomacy and Peace, 1914–1919.* Philadelphia, 1941.

Venizelos, Eleutherios. *Greece before the Peace Congress.* Rev. ed. Trans. from French. New York, 1919.

Viereck, George Sylvester. *The Strangest Friendship in History: Woodrow Wilson and Colonel House.* New York, 1932.

Villeneuve-Trans, Romée François de. *À l'Ambassade de Washington, Oct. 1917–Avril 1919.* Paris, 1921.

Walters, Frank P. *A History of the League of Nations,* 2 vols. Vol. 1: *The Making of the League.* London, 1952.

Walworth, Arthur. *America's Moment: 1918.* New York, 1977.

———. *Woodrow Wilson.* 3d ed. New York, 1978.

Wandycz, Piotr S. *France and Her Eastern Allies, 1919–1925.* Minneapolis, 1960.

———. *The United States and Poland.* Cambridge, Mass., 1980.

Watson, David R. *Georges Clemenceau.* New York, 1974.

Watt, Richard M. *The Kings Depart.* New York, 1968.

———. *Bitter Poland.* New York, 1979.

Webster, Charles K., with Herbert, Sidney, *The League of Nations in Theory and Practice.* Vol. 1: *The Founding of the League.* London, 1933.

Wehle, Louis B. *Hidden Threads of History.* New York, 1953.

Weill-Raynal, Étienne. *Les Réparations allemandes et la France.* 3 vols. Vol. 1: *Des Origines jusqu'à l'institution de l'état des payements (Novembre 1918–Mai 1921).* Paris, 1947.

Weinstein, Edwin A. *Woodrow Wilson: A Medical and Psychological Biography.* Princeton, 1981.

Widenor, William C. *Henry Cabot Lodge and the Search for an American Foreign Policy.* Berkeley, 1980.

Williams, William A. *American-Russian Relations, 1781–1947.* New York, 1952.

Wilson, Florence. *The Origins of the League Covenant: A Documentary History of Its Drafting.* Introduction by Philip J. Noel-Baker. London, 1928.

Wilson, Joan Hoff. *Herbert Hoover, Forgotten Progressive.* Boston, 1975.

Wormser, Georges Marcel. *La République de Clemenceau.* Paris, 1961.

Wright, Quincy. *Mandates under the League of Nations.* Chicago, 1930.

Yates, Louis A. R. *The U.S. and French Security.* New York, 1957.

Zebel, Sidney H. *Balfour: A Political Biography.* Cambridge, Eng., 1973.

Ziegler, Wilhelm. *Versailles, die Geschicte eines missglückten Friedens.* 4th ed. Hamburg, 1933.

Zimmern, Sir Alfred. *The American Road to World Peace.* New York, 1953.

———. *The League of Nations and the Rule of Law.* Rev. ed. New York, 1939.

Zinojinović, Dragan R. *America, Italy and the Birth of Yugoslavia.* Boulder, Col., 1972.

Articles and Pamphlets

Adler, Selig. "The Palestine Question in the Wilson Era." *Jewish Social Studies* 10, no. 4 (October 1948).

Ambrosius, Lloyd E. "Wilson's League of Nations." *Modern History Magazine* 65, no. 4 (Winter 1970).

———. "Wilson, the Republicans, and French Security." *Journal of American History* 59, no. 2 (September 1972).

Arnold-Forster, William. *The Blockade 1914–1919*. Oxford, 1939. Pamphlet no. 17 in Oxford Pamphlets on World Affairs.

Bedford, Alfred C. "The World Oil Situation." *Foreign Affairs* 1, no. 3 (March 1923).

Beer, George Louis. "America and World Responsibility." *The Round Table* no. 35 (March 1919).

Benedetti, Charles. "James F. Shotwell and American Internationalism." In *Makers of American Diplomacy*, ed. Frank J. Merli and Theodore A. Wilson. New York, 1974.

Binkley, Robert C. "New Light on the Paris Peace Conference." *Political Science Quarterly* 46, nos. 3 and 4 (1931).

———. "The 'Guilt' Clause in the Versailles Treaty." *Current History* (May 1929).

Birdsall, Paul. "The Second Decade of Peace Conference History." *Journal of Modern History* 11 (September 1939).

Bliss, Tasker H. "The Armistices." A review of Mermeix, *Les Négociations secrètes et les quatre armistices*, 5th ed., Paris, 1921, in *The American Journal of International Law* 16 (1922).

Bowman, Isaiah. "The Strategy of Territorial Decisions." *Foreign Affairs* 24, no. 2 (January 1946).

Brand, Carl F. "The Attitude of British Labour toward President Wilson during the Peace Conference." *American Historical Review* 42 (1937).

Buzansky, Peter M. "The Interallied Investigation of the Greek Invasion of Smyrna, 1919." *The Historian* 25, no. 3 (May 1963).

Cambon, Jules. "La paix (notes inédités, 1919)." *Revue de Paris* 44th yr., no. 6 (November 1937).

———. "The Permanent Bases of French Foreign Policy." *Foreign Affairs* 8, no. 2 (January 1930).

Campbell, F. Gregory. "The Struggle for Upper Silesia, 1919–1922." *Journal of Modern History* 42, no. 3 (September 1970).

Coggeshall, Reginald. "Was There Censorship at the Paris Peace Conference?" *Journalism Quarterly* 16 (1939).

Contee, Clarence G. "DuBois, the NAACP, and the Pan-African Congress of 1919." *Journal of Negro History* 57, no. 1 (January 1972).

Curry, George. "Woodrow Wilson, Jan Smuts, and the Versailles Settlement." *American Historical Review* 66, no. 4 (July 1961).

Duff, John B. "The Versailles Treaty and the Irish-Americans." *Journal of American History* 55, no. 3 (December 1966).

Fifield, Russell H. "Disposal of the Carolines, Marshalls, and Marianas at the Paris Peace Conference." *American Historical Review* 51 (April 1946).

Fitzhardinge, L. F. "W. M. Hughes and the Treaty of Versailles, 1919." *Journal of Commonwealth Political Studies* 5, no. 22 (July 1967).

Frear, Mary Reno. "Did President Wilson Contradict Himself on the Secret Treaties?" *Current History* (June 1929).

George, Robert H. "The Scheldt Dispute." *Foreign Affairs* 6, no. 1 (October 1927).

Géraud, André (Pertinax). "Diplomacy Old and New." *Foreign Affairs* 23 (1945).

Grayson, Cary T. "The Colonel's Folly and the President's Distress." *American Heritage* 15, nos. 4 and 7 (October 1964).

———. "Memories of Woodrow Wilson." *Atlantic Monthly* 11 (November 1959).

Gregory, Ross. "Woodrow Wilson and America's Mission." In *Makers of American Diplomacy*, ed. Frank J. Merli and Theodore A. Wilson. New York, 1974.

Halm, Erich J. C. "The German Foreign Ministry and the Question of War Guilt in 1918–1919." In *German Nationalism and the European Response, 1891–1945*, ed. Carole Fink, Isabelle V. Hull, and McGregor Knox. Norman, Okla., 1985.

Holborn, Hajo. "The Reasons for the Failure of the Paris Peace Settlement." In *Henry Wells Lawrence Memorial Lectures*. Vol. 3. New London, Conn., 1953.

Holt, Hamilton. "Republican Contributions to the Covenant." *The Independent* 97 (February 15, 1919).

House, Edward M. "The Freedom of the Seas." *The Contemporary Review* 133, no. 748 (April 1928).

Hudson, Manley O. "America's Relation to World Peace." A lecture at the Geneva Institute of International Relations. In *Problems of Peace*, 3d series, 1928.

Huston, James A. "The Allied Blockade of Germany, 1918–1919." *The Journal of Central European Affairs* 10, no. 2 (July 1950).

Johnson, Elizabeth. "John Maynard Keynes: Scientist or Politician?" *Journal of Political Economy* 82 (January–February 1974).

Jones, Paul V. B. "Italy and the Peace Conference." *University of Illinois Bulletin* 16, no. 16 (December 16, 1918).

Kennedy, A. L. "America's Part in the Treaty of Versailles." *Edinburgh Review* 237 (April 1923).

Kernek, Sterling J. "Woodrow Wilson and National

Self-Determination along Italy's Frontier: A Study of the Manipulation of Principles in the Pursuit of Political Interests." *Proceedings of the American Philosophical Society* 126, no. 4 (August 1982).

Kerner, Robert J. "Two Architects of New Europe: Masaryk and Beneš." *Journal of International Relations* 12, no. 1 (July 1921).

Keynes, John Maynard. "America at the Peace Conference," *Living Age* 8th series, no. 21 (January–May 1921).

Killen, Linda. "The Search for a Democratic Russia: Bakhmetev and the U.S." *Diplomatic History* 2, no. 3 (Summer 1978).

King, Wensz. "China at the Paris Peace Conference in 1919." *Asia in the Modern World.* Pamphlet no. 2. New York, 1961.

Kusielewicz, Eugene F. W. "Wilson and the Polish Cause at Paris." *The Polish Review* 1, no. 1 (Winter 1956).

Lansing, Robert. "Some Legal Questions of the Paris Peace Conference." *American Journal of International Law* 18 (1919).

Lauren, Paul G. "Human Rights in History: Diplomacy and Racial Equality at the Paris Peace Conference." *Diplomatic History* 2, no. 3 (Summer 1978).

Lazo, Dimitri D. "A Question of Loyalty: Robert Lansing and the Treaty of Versailles." *Diplomatic History* 9, no. 1 (Winter 1985).

Link, Arthur S. *President Wilson and His English Critics.* An inaugural lecture delivered before the University of Oxford, May 13, 1959. Pamphlet. Oxford, 1959.

Lippmann, Walter. "The Peace Conference." *Yale Review* 8, no. 4 (July 1919).

Louis, William Roger. "The United States and the African Peace Settlement of 1919: The Pilgrimage of George Louis Beer." *Journal of African History* 4, no. 3 (1963).

McDougall, Walter A. "Political Economy versus National Sovereignty: French Structures for German Economic Integration after Versailles." *Journal of Modern History* 51, no. 1 (March 1979).

Maier, Charles S. "The Truth about the Treaties?" *Journal of Modern History* 51, no. 1 (March 1979).

Marks, Sally. "Reparations Reconsidered: A Reminder." *Central European History* 2 (1969).

Mayer, Arno J. "Historical Thought and American Foreign Policy in the Era of the First World War." In *The Historian and the Diplomat,* ed. Francis L. Lowenheim. New York, 1967.

Miller, David Hunter. "The Adriatic Negotiations at Paris." *Atlantic Monthly* 128, no. 2 (August 1921).

———. "The Economic Consequences of the Peace." A review of Keynes's book in the *New York Evening Post* (February 6 and 10, 1920).

———. "Origins of the Mandates System." *Foreign Affairs* 6, no. 2 (January 1928).

———. "Some Legal Aspects of the visit of President Wilson to Paris." *Harvard Law Review* 36, no. 1, pt. 7 (1922).

Mitchell, Kell, Jr. "Frank L. Polk and Continued American Participation in the Paris Peace Conference, 1919." *North Dakota Quarterly* 41, no. 2 (Spring 1973).

———. "The United States and Greek Policy at the Paris Peace Conference, 1919." *North Dakota Quarterly* 47 (Summer 1979).

Orlando, Vittorio Emanuele. "Wilson and Lansing." *Saturday Evening Post* 201, no. 38 (March 23, 1929).

Raffo, Peter. "The League of Nations Philosophy of Lord Robert Cecil." *Australian Journal of Politics and History* 20, no. 2 (August 1974).

Rappaport, Armin. "Freedom of the Seas." In Alexander de Conde, *Encyclopedia of American Foreign Policy.* vol. 2, p. 395. New York, 1978.

Rattan, Sumitra. "The Yap Controversy and Its Significance." *Journal of Pacific History* 7 (1972).

Rudin, Harry R. "Diplomacy, Democracy, Security: Two Centuries in Contrast." *Political Science Quarterly* 71, no. 2 (June 1956).

Safford, Jeffrey J. "Edward Hurley and American Shipping Policy: An Elaboration on Wilsonian Diplomacy, 1918–1919." *The Historian* 35, no. 4 (August 1973).

Schmitt, Bernadotte E. "The Peace Conference of 1919." *Journal of Modern History* 16 (1944).

———. "The Peace Treaties of 1919–1920." *Proceedings of the American Philosophical Society* 104, no. 1 (February 1960).

Schwabe, Klaus. "Comment on Trachtenberg and McDougall." *Journal of Modern History* 51, no. 1 (March 1979).

Seymour, Charles. "Czechslovak Frontiers." *Yale Review* 28, no. 2 (December 1938).

———. "End of a Friendship." *American Heritage* 14, no. 5 (August 1963).

———. "The League of Nations." *Yale Review* 9, no. 1 (October 1919).

———. "The Paris Education of Woodrow Wilson." *Virginia Quarterly Review* 32, no. 4 (Autumn, 1956).

———. "Policy and Personality at the Paris Peace Conference." *Virginia Quarterly Review* 21, no. 4 (Autumn 1945).

———. "The Struggle for the Adriatic." *Yale Review* 9, no. 3 (April 1920).

———. "Wilson Analyzed." *Virginia Quarterly Review* 34, no. 4 (Spring 1958).

———. "Woodrow Wilson: A Political Balance Sheet." *Proceedings of the American Philosophical Society* 101, no. 2 (April 1957).

———. "Woodrow Wilson and Self-Determination in the Tyrol." *Virginia Quarterly Review* 38, no. 4 (Autumn 1962).

——. "Woodrow Wilson in Perspective." *Foreign Affairs* 34 (January 1956).

Shantung: Treaties and Agreements. Carnegie Endowment, Division of International Law. Pamphlet no. 42.

Shotwell, James T. "The Leadership of Woodrow Wilson." *Current History* (November 1951).

——. "Recollections on the Founding of the I.L.O." *Monthly Labor Review* 82, no. 6 (June 1959).

Smallwood, James. "Banquo's Ghost." *East European Quarterly* 12, no. 3 (Fall 1978).

Smuts, Jan Christiaan. *The League of Nations: A Practical Suggestion.* Pamphlet. London, 1918.

Snell, John L. "Wilson on Germany and the Fourteen Points." *Journal of Modern History* 26, no. 4 (December 1954).

Snelling, R. C. "Peacemaking, 1919: Australia, New Zealand and the British Empire Delegation at Versailles." *Journal of Imperial Commonwealth History* 4 (October 1975).

Strunsky, Simeon. "The Peace-Makers." *Atlantic Monthly* 123, no. 4 (April 1919).

——. "Woodrow Wilson and World Settlement." A review of Baker's book in *Foreign Affairs* 2, no. 1 (September 1923).

Tardieu, André. "The Policy of France." *Foreign Affairs* 1, no. 1 (September 1922).

Taylor, A. J. P. "The War Aims of the Allies in the First World War." In *Essays Presented to Sir Lewis Namier.* London, 1956.

Tawney, R. H. "The Abolition of Economic Controls, 1918–1921." *Economic Historical Review* 13, no. 1 (1943).

Thompson, John M. "Allied and American Intervention in Russia 1918–1921." In *Rewriting Russian History: Soviet Interpretations of Russia's Past,* ed. Cyril E. Black. 2d ed. New York, 1962.

Trachtenberg, Marc. "Reparations at the Paris Peace Conference." *Journal of Modern History* 51, no. 1 (July 1979).

Trask, David F. "Sino-Japanese-American Relations during the Paris Peace Conference of 1919," In *Aspects of Sino-American Relations since 1784,* ed. Thomas H. Etzold. New York, 1978.

——. "Woodrow Wilson and the Coordination of Force and Diplomacy." *SHAFR Newsletter* (September 1981).

Tuchman, Barbara. "Woodrow Wilson on Freud's Couch." *Atlantic Monthly* (February 1967).

Unterberger, Betty Miller. "National Self-Determination." In *Encyclopedia of American Foreign Policy,* ed. Alexander De Conde. New York, 1978.

Viereck, George S. "Behind the House-Wilson Break." In *The Inside Story,* ed. Robert S. Benjamin. New York, 1940.

Warrin, Frank Lord, Jr. *The Neutrality of Belgium.* Pamphlet. Washington, 1918.

Watson, David R. "The Making of the Treaty of Versailles." In *Troubled Neighbours: Franco-British Relations in the Twentieth Century,* ed. Neville Waites. London, 1971.

Webster, Charles K. "The Congress of Vienna, 1814–1815, and the Conference of Paris, 1919: A Comparison of Their Organization and Results." *The Historical Association,* leaflet no. 56. London, 1923.

Wells, Samuel F., Jr. "New Perspectives on Wilsonian Diplomacy: The Secular Evangelism of American Political Economy." *Perspectives in American History* 6 (1972).

Williams, Edward T. "Japan's Mandate in the Pacific." *The American Journal of International Law* 27, no. 3 (July 1933).

Willis, Edward R. "Herbert Hoover and the Blockade of Germany." In *Studies in Modern European History in Honor of Franklin Charles Palm,* ed. Frederick J. Cox, Richard M. Brace, Bernard C. Weber, and John F. Ramsey. New York, 1956.

Wright, Gordon. "Comment" on papers by McDougall, Trachtenberg, Maier, and Schwabe. *Journal of Modern History* 51, no. 1 (March 1979).

Dissertations

Ambrosius, Lloyd E. "The U.S. and the Weimar Republic, 1918–1923." University of Illinois, 1967.

Berbusse, Edward J. "Diplomatic Relations between the United States and Weimar Germany 1919–1929." Georgetown University, 1951.

Binkley, Robert C. "Reactions of European Public Opinion to Woodrow Wilson's Statesmanship from the Armistice to the Peace of Versailles." Stanford University, 1927.

Bourret, Mary-Louise. "The German-Polish Frontier of 1919 and Self-Determination." Stanford University, 1946.

Dumin, Frederick. "Background of the Austro-German Anschluss Movement, 1918–1919." Columbia University, 1963.

Foltz, David Albert. "The War Crimes Issue at the Paris Peace Conference 1919–1920." American University, 1978.

Gould, John Wells. "Italy and the U.S. 1914–1918: Background to Confrontation." Yale University, 1969.

Harvin, Harry L. Jr. "The Far East in the Peace Conference." Duke University, 1957.

Helde, Thomas T. "The Blockade of Germany, November 1918–July 1919." Yale University, 1949.

Hester, James McNaughton. "America and the Weimar Republic 1918–1925." Oxford, 1955.

Klachko, Mary. "Anglo-American Naval Competition, 1918–1922." Columbia University, 1962.

Knock, Thomas J. "Woodrow Wilson and the Origins of the League of Nations." Princeton University, 1982.

Kusielewicz, Eugene F. "The Teschen Question at the Paris Peace Conference." Fordham University, 1963.

Lever, Alfred W. "The British Empire and the German Colonies." University of Wisconsin, 1964.

Lowry, Francis B. "The Generals, the Armistice, and the Treaty of Versailles, 1919." Duke University, 1963.

Myers, Duane Paul. "Germany and the Question of the Austrian Anschluss, 1918–1922." Yale University, 1968.

Posey, John F. "David Hunter Miller at the Paris Peace Conference." University of Georgia, 1962.

Pyne, John Michael. "Woodrow Wilson's Abdication of Domestic and Party Leadership, Autumn 1918 to Autumn 1919." Notre Dame University 1979.

Rizopoulos Nicholas X. "Greece at the Paris Peace Conference, 1919." Yale University, 1963.

Roberts, J. Claude. "Austria at the Paris Peace Conference: A Diplomatic History of the Treaty of St. Germain." University of Texas, 1956.

Schaefer, Ludwig F. "German Peace Strategy in 1918–1919." Yale University, 1958.

Sieńkowski-Biskupski, M. B. "The United States and the Rebirth of Poland." Yale University, 1981.

Sonderman, Fred A. "The Wilson Administration's Image of Germany." Yale University, 1953.

Strickland, Roscoe Lee, Jr. "Czechoslovakia at the Paris Peace Conference, 1919." University of North Carolina, 1958.

Whiteman, Harold B., Jr. "Norman H. Davis and the Search for International Peace and Security 1917–1944." Yale University, 1958.

Woodall, Robert Larry. "The Albanian Problem during the Peacemaking." Memphis State University, 1978.

Index